The Science Fiction Century

Tor Books by David G. Hartwell

Age of Wonders

EDITOR

The Ascent of Wonder (with Kathryn Cramer)
Christmas Forever
Christmas Stars
The Dark Descent
Foundations of Fear
The Science Fiction Century
Visions of Wonder (with Milton T. Wolf)

Edited by **DAVID G. HARTWELL**

The Science Fiction Century

A Tom Doherty Associates Book

New York

THE SCIENCE FICTION CENTURY

This book is printed on acid-free paper.

A Tor Book
Published by Tom Doherty Associates, Inc.
175 Fifth Avenue
New York, NY 10010

Tor Books on the World Wide Web:
http://www.tor.com

Tor® is a registered trademark of Tom Doherty Associates, Inc.

Design by Fritz Metsch

Library of Congress Cataloging-in-Publication Data

The science fiction century / edited by David G. Hartwell. — 1st ed.
p. cm.
ISBN 0-312-86338-1 (hard cover: alk. paper)
1. Science fiction. 2. Fiction—20th century. I. Hartwell, David G.
PN6120.95.S33S355 1997
808.83'8762—dc21 96-54591
CIP

First Edition: November 1997

Printed in the United States of America

0 9 8 7 6 5 4 3 2 1

Copyright Acknowledgments

"Liquid Sunshine" translation copyright © 1982 by Leland Fetzer. Used by permission of the translator, Leland Fetzer.

"Great Work of Time" copyright © 1989 by John Crowley. Used by permission of the author's agent, Ralph M. Vicinanza, Ltd.

"Sundance" copyright © 1968 by Agberg, Ltd. Used by permission of the author.

"Greenslaves" copyright © 1965 by Frank Herbert. Used by permission of the author's Estate.

"Rumfuddle" copyright © 1973 by Jack Vance. Used by permission of the author.

"The Dimple in Draco" copyright © 1967 by Philip Latham. Used by permission of the Estate's agent, Scott Meredith.

"Consider Her Ways" copyright © 1956 by the John Wyndham Estate Trust. Used by permission of the author's Estate.

"Something Ending" original Dutch version "Het einde van iets" copyright © 1971 by Eddy C. Bertin. English translation © 1982 by Eddy C. Bertin. Used by permission.

"He Who Shapes" copyright © 1967 by Roger Zelazny. Used by permission of the author's agent, The Pimlico Agency.

"Swarm" copyright © 1982 by Mercury Press, Inc. Used by permission of the author.

"Beggars in Spain" copyright © 1991 by Nancy Kress. First published by Axolotl Press. Used by permission of the author.

"Johnny Mnemonic" copyright © 1981 by Omni Publications. Used by permission of the author.

"'Repent, Harlequin!' Said the Ticktockman" by Harlan Ellison. Copyright © 1965 by Harlan Ellison. Renewed, copyright © 1993 by Harlan Ellison. Reprinted by arrangement with, and permission of, the author and the author's agent, Richard Curtis Associates, Inc., New York, USA. All rights reserved.

"Blood's a Rover" copyright © 1952 by Chad Oliver. Used by permission of the author's Estate.

"Sail the Tide of Mourning" copyright © 1975 by Richard A. Lupoff. Used by permission of the author.

Acknowledgments

To Maron Waxman, Susan Ann Protter, Les Pockell, and Kathryn Cramer, without whom this book would never have been completed.

I would like to acknowledge the significant presence of John W. Campbell, Isaac Asimov, Robert A. Heinlein, and Arthur C. Clarke, and all the other science fiction writers who are not reprinted in this book. I used their work to support my argument for the consideration of science fiction as a worthwhile literature in *The World Treasury of Science Fiction*. I used many of them again to illuminate and uphold the value of the hard SF tradition in *The Ascent of Wonder*. In this book, I chose the work of other major writers, some of them less familiar, some of them equally famous, so as not to allow my argument to get lost in the particular aesthetic of SF that is so dominant in their work. But their presence is here anyway, anyhow, even in the absence of representative examples of their work.

Contents

The Science Fiction Century

Rooted as they are in the facts of contemporary life, the phantasies of even a second-rate writer of modern Science Fiction are incomparably richer, bolder, and stranger than the Utopian or Millennial imaginings of the past.

—ALDOUS HUXLEY

Science fiction is no more written for scientists than ghost stories are written for ghosts. Most frequently, the scientific dressing clothes fantasy. As fantasies are as meaningful as science, the phantasms of technology now fittingly embody our hopes and anxieties.

—BRIAN W. ALDISS

Introduction

David G. Hartwell

Science fiction is the characteristic literary genre of the century. It is the genre that stands in opposition to literary Modernism. It is the paraliterary shadow of Modernism.

The twentieth century is the science fiction century. By the middle of the 1990s, we are living in the world of the future described by genre science fiction of the 1930s and '40s and '50s, a world of technologies we love and fear, sciences so increasingly complex and steeped in specialized diction and jargon that fewer and fewer of us understand science on what used to be called a "high school level." These are the days, as Paul Simon sings, of miracles and wonders.

Science fiction is a literature for people who value knowledge and who desire to understand how things work in the world and in the universe. In science fiction, knowledge is power and power is technology and technology is good and useful in improving the human condition. It is, by extension, a literature of empowerment. The lesson of the genre megatext, that body of genre literature that in aggregate embodies the standard plots, tropes, images, specialized diction, and clichés, is that one can solve problems through the application of knowledge of science and technology. By further extension, the SF megatext is an allegory of faith in science. Everyone knows there are SF addicts—I am one—and this is why: it expresses, represents, and confirms faith in science and reason.

Life is never so neat that abstract patterns, such as centuries, are more than arbitrary dividers. In the case of science fiction, this century really began about 1895, with the first stories of H. G. Wells, the greatest writer in a vigorous literary tradition now superseded, called the Scientific Romance. Wells had many contemporaries writing Scientific Romances, such as George Griffith and M. P. Shiel; predecessors include Jules Verne and Sir Edward Bulwer-Lytton. But the tradition did end in Wells's lifetime, although Brian Stableford, in *Scientific Romance in Britain, 1890–1950* (1985), revives the term, which fell out of usage by World War II, to emphasize the differences between the evolution of American and British science fiction. Olaf Stapledon, S. Fowler Wright, Aldous Huxley, and George Orwell, for instance, might properly be considered as having written late examples of Scientific Romance.

But Wells, especially in his works between 1895 and 1911, was the primary model for a variety of other writers, in many languages, to explore the explosion of ideas and technologies that the advent of the new century promised. Not the only model, I hasten to add. I have included a fine story by J. H. Rosny *aîné*, from the French, in this anthology and examples from Rudyard Kipling and Jack London. And as the genre of science fiction began to coalesce in the teens and twenties of the new century, it became evident that a number of earlier writers, first of all Jules Verne but also many others from Mary Shelley and Edgar Allan Poe to Fitz-James O'Brien and Sir Edward Bulwer-Lytton might provide variant models for science fiction. Wells, however, was that spark that ignited the genre.

But the fires of science fiction did not blaze in the United States until April 1926, when editor and publisher Hugo Gernsback launched *Amazing Stories*, the first magazine devoted to the new genre and which provided, as it were, a fireplace. To give examples of the new literature he proposed to support and publish, Gernback filled parts of his issues with "classic reprints" of Wells and many of the others named above. And in his oft-quoted first editorial, in which he defined *scientifiction* (the term *science fiction* was not coined until 1929), he said it was in the manner of Poe, Verne, and Wells: "charming romance intermingled with scientific fact and prophetic vision."

In addition to this relative confusion, Gernsback, an eccentric immigrant and technological visionary, was tone-deaf to the English language, printing barely literate stories, often by enthusiastic teenagers, about new inventions and the promise of a wondrous technological future cheek by jowl with fiction by Wells, Poe, Edgar Rice Burroughs, and a growing number of professional pulp writers who simply wanted to break into the new market. Gernsback was the man who first saw science fiction as the ordinary pleasure reading of the new technological world. But his standards were not the standards of a literary man, of a modernist. They were the standards of a publisher of popular entertainment in pulp magazines, low-class, low-paying, low-priced popular entertainment serving the mass market.

So genre science fiction became, was founded to be, antimodernist. It rapidly developed a loyal readership, literary conventions, and a body of specialized writers who, converted by the evangelical pitch of Gernsback and the other early editors—chief among them John W. Campbell, Jr., who took over the helm of *Astounding* in the late 1930s and set higher stylistic standards for the genre (his was for decades the highest-paying market)—set about improving themselves.

Of all the pulp magazine genres, science fiction was the most socially unacceptable for decades, so it attracted the alienated of all stripes, some of them extremely talented writers. By the early 1940s the SF field had come into being. And it decided to rule the world. "Science fiction is the central literature of our time. It is not part of the mainstream. It is the mainstream," says Ray Bradbury, and such grandiose claims are part of the essence of the SF field. Bradbury was a teenager who published a fanzine in the late 1930s and became a writer in the 1940s under the tutelage of such established SF professionals as Leigh Brackett (who coauthored the script for *The Big Sleep* with William Faulkner, and later wrote the screenplay for *The Empire Strikes Back*). Science fiction did not aspire to take over literature, but reality.

The field (an aggregation of people) as opposed to the genre (a body of texts) was originally a closely knit international group of passionate readers and writers of science fiction in the 1930s and 1940s, people who knew each other for the most part only through correspondence and rarely met. They published fanzines and sent them to one another. They developed and evolved their own practical literary criticism and their own literary standards. Most of them were teenagers at the start—including the writers. Practically speaking, none of them had the benefit of a literary or humanist education. They read a lot. Some of them had technical training, some a scientific education—like Wells. But they were organized, and when the economy and publishing opportunities expanded after World War II, the SF field was ready to expand.

In its own view, science fiction had already grown up, in Campbell's *Astounding*: the 1940s were the Golden Age of SF. But by any sensible calculation, the SF field really began to grow up after the war and blossom with the first publications of genre science fiction in hardcover books; the founding of major new magazines, such as *Galaxy* and *Fantasy & Science Fiction* in 1949; and the growth of the mass market paperback publishing industry in the early 1950s, which discovered science fiction right away. Most of the stories in this book are post-WWII mainly because that was the time at which the idea of revision took hold in the SF writing community, with a concomitant improvement in the fiction; it was a time when the money improved, although not enough for any but five or six of the highest paid writers to make a living without "a day job"; and most of all it was a time of optimism in the West after the terrible war.

The international SF field grew with the sudden influx of American science fiction, and a dialogue began among literatures that grows and continues today. In Russia in the 1940s, one of the key texts is a story written in response to a Murray Leinster story in *Astounding*. In France, Boris Vian translated A. E. van Vogt's uneven English (*The World of Null-A*) into literate French and launched van Vogt as the most important SF writer of the period in France. American science fiction, in translation or in the original, dominated the discourse worldwide. It still does; even though there have been major writers in other languages who have made major contributions. American science fiction is still the dominant partner in all the dialogues. I have attempted, in this anthology, to provide some translations that give evidence of the growth of other traditions, but the overwhelming evidence is that American science fiction and the American marketplace drive the SF world.

It is a source of both amusement and frustration to SF people, writers and readers, that public consciousness of science fiction has almost never penetrated beyond the first decade of the field's development. Sure, *Star Wars* is wonderful, but in precisely the same way and at the same level of consciousness and sophistication that science fiction from the late twenties and early thirties was: fast, almost plotless stories of zipping through the ether in spaceships, meeting aliens, using futuristic devices, and fighting the bad guys (and winning). SF people generally call this sci-fi (affectionately, "skiffy"), to distinguish it from the real, grown-up pure quill.

Science fiction is read throughout the English language–reading world, and in many other languages for pleasure and entertainment. But it is not read with much comprehension or pleasure by the dominant literary culture, the writers and academics who, on the whole, define literary fashions and instruct us in the values and virtues of fashionable literatures. This is understandable given the literary history of the genre, which has now outlasted all the other counterculture or outsider literary movements of the century. Science fiction is read with ease and comprehension by the teenage children of educated adults who can derive little or no pleasure from it. I have written an entire book, *Age of Wonders* (1984, 1996), devoted to elucidating the nature of the field and the problems of understanding it, and the literature associated with it, for outsiders, but one particular point needs to be repeated each time the subject arises. Science fiction is read properly, as an experienced reader can, only if the givens of the story are granted as literal, so that if the story is set on Mars in the future, that is the literal time and place. It might secondarily be interpretable as "only" a metaphor for the human condition, or for some abnormal psychological state of the character or characters, but with rare exceptions in science fiction, the literal truth of the time and place and ideas is a necessary preconditon to making sense of the story. This is because only through this literality (the real world is pared away and reduced to an imaginable invented world, in which we can focus on things happening that could not happen in the mainstream world of everyday reality) can the emotional significance of totally imaginary times and places and events be felt.

Kingsley Amis, in *New Maps of Hell* (1960), quotes his friend Edmund Crispin as saying, "Where an ordinary novel or short story resembles portraiture or at widest the domestic interior, science fiction offers the less cosy satisfaction of a landscape with figures; to ask that these distant manikins be shown in as much detail as the subject of a portrait is evidently to ask the impossible"; he then goes on himself to say: "This is perhaps partisan in tone, but it does indicate a scale of priorities which operates throughout the medium and which, of course, is open to objection, though this is not often based on much more than an expectation that science fiction should treat the future as fiction of the main stream treats the present, an expectation bound to be defeated" (p. 128).

Tom Shippey, in his introduction to *The Oxford Book of Science Fiction Stories*, comments, "What, then, has science fiction had to offer its human readers? Whatever it is, it has been enough for the genre to make its way into a prominent, if not dominant place in popular literary culture despite every kind of literary misunderstanding or discouragement. A very basic answer must be, Truth. Not every science fiction story, of course, can 'come true,' indeed . . . probably none of them do, can, or ever will. Just the same, many of them (perhaps all of them, in some way or another) may be trying to solve a question for which many people this century have had no acceptable answer."

In the end this anthology is a collection of attempts to get at the truth of the human condition in this century, so contoured and conditioned by science and technology. Overall, perhaps, you can see the big picture, surely a bigger picture than any other. One might even get some intimations of the scope of the future—which of course leads us always back to the ground of the present. And perhaps we return illuminated.

—PLEASANTVILLE, N.Y.
1996

James Tiptree, Jr.

James Tiptree, Jr. was the pseudonym of Alice B. Sheldon (1915–87), an ex-employee of the CIA who became a psychologist and then, secretly, an SF writer. Unlike the pseudonymous Cordwainer Smith, a writer who remained silent and mysterious, Tiptree was vociferous, opinionated, passionate, and involved in the SF field. Thus it was a substantial shock to the social system of science fiction in the late 1970s when the Tiptree pseudonym was penetrated, when in the midst of a rising tide of feminist consciousness he was discovered to be a feminist she.

Tiptree made her essential impact with a continuing stream of powerful short stories. Many of her best stories appeared in her first four collections (*Ten Thousand Light Years from Home* [1973], *Warm Worlds and Otherwise* [1975], *Star Songs of an Old Primate* [1978], and *Out of the Everywhere and Other Extraordinary Visions* [1981]). Her two novels, *Up the Walls of the World* (1978) and *Brightness Falls from the Air* (1985), are underappreciated. Perhaps the shock of her suicide in 1987 has made it difficult for many readers to gain perspective on her later, darker stories.

The closest parallel to her work in impact, in attitude, in attention to craft and art, is Theodore Sturgeon's writing of the 1950s. Also like him, when she erred it was in the direction of too much sentiment. She was obsessed with the theme and the imagery of the alien biologically and emotionally. Yet at least one of her stories, "The Girl Who Was Plugged In" (1973, one of her several award-winners), is acknowledged by William Gibson as one of the sources of cyberpunk.

Tiptree continually challenged the idea of the coldness of the universe, portraying that coldness as a negative aspect of human character rather than an affect existing somehow in external reality—until her last stories. *Crown of Stars* (1988) gathers most of her final tales, suicide-filled and full of the idea of honorable death. She was a deeply moral writer, even when embracing death.

In the 1990s, friends and especially a younger generation of woman SF writers have created an award in her memory, the annual James Tiptree, Jr., Award "for gender-bending science fiction." A collection of her nonfiction pieces and a biography have been announced as forthcoming. This story, one of Tiptree's earliest, refers to the influence of a certain television show popular among the young in the 1960s, *Star Trek* (though the name is never mentioned in the text). Joanna Russ, the feminist critic and a correspondent of Tiptree's, sometimes tells this story aloud, and then weeps.

BEAM US HOME

Hobie's parents might have seen the first signs if they had been watching about eight-thirty on Friday nights. But Hobie was the youngest of five active bright-normal kids. Who was to notice one more uproar around the TV?

A couple of years later, Hobie's Friday-night battles shifted to 10 P.M. and then his sisters got their own set. Hobie was growing fast then. In public he featured chiefly as a tanned streak on the tennis courts and a ninety-ninth percentile series of math grades. To his parents, Hobie featured as the one without problems. This was hard to avoid in a family that included a diabetic, a girl with an IQ of 185 and another with controllable petit mal, and a would-be ski star who spent most of his time in a cast. Hobie's own IQ was in the fortunate 140s, the range where you're superior enough to lead, but not too superior to be followed. He seemed perfectly satisfied with his communications with his parents, but he didn't use them much.

Not that he was in any way neglected when the need arose. The time he got staph in a corneal scratch, for instance, his parents did a great job of supporting him through the pain bit and the hospital bit and so on. But they couldn't know all the little incidents. Like the night when Hobie called so fiercely for Dr. McCoy that a young intern named McCoy went in and joked for half an hour with the feverish boy in his dark room.

To the end, his parents probably never understood that there was anything to understand about Hobie. And what was to see? His tennis and his model rocket collection made him look almost too normal for the small honors school he went to first.

Then his family moved to an executive bedroom suburb where the school system had a bigger budget than Monaco and a soccer team loaded with National Merit Science finalists. Here Hobie blended right in with the scenery. One more healthy, friendly, polite kid with bright gray eyes under a blond bowl-cut and very fast with any sort of ball game.

The brightest eyes around him were reading *The Double Helix* to find out how to make it in research, or marking up the Dun & Bradstreet flyers. If Hobie stood out at all, it was only that he didn't seem to be worried about making it in research or any other way, particularly. But that fitted in, too. Those days a lot of boys were standing around looking as if they couldn't believe what went on, as if they were waiting for—who knows?—a better world, their glands, something. Hobie's faintly aghast expression was not unique. Events like the installation of an armed patrol around the school enclave were bound to have a disturbing effect on the more sensitive kids.

People got the idea that Hobie *was* sensitive in some indefinite way. His usual manner was open but quiet, tolerant of a put-on that didn't end.

His adviser did fret over his failure to settle on a major field in time for the oncoming threat of college. First his math interest seemed to evaporate after the special calculus course, although he never blew an exam. Then he switched to the precollege anthropology panel the school was trying. Here he made good grades and acted very motivated, until the semester when the visiting research team began pounding on sampling techniques and statistical significance. Hobie had no trouble with things like Chi square, of course. But after making his A in the final he gave them his sweet, unbelieving smile and faded. His adviser found him spending a lot of hours polishing a six-inch telescope lens in the school shop.

So Hobie was tagged as some kind of an underachiever, but nobody knew what kind because of those grades. And something about that smile bothered them; it seemed to stop sound.

The girls liked him, though, and he went through the usual phases rather fast. There was the week he and various birds went to thirty-five drive-in movies. And the month he went around humming "Mrs. Robinson" in a meaningful way. And the warm, comfortable summer when he and his then-girl and two other couples went up to Stratford, Ontario, with sleeping bags to see the Czech multimedia thing.

Girls regarded him as different, although he never knew why. "You look at me like it's always good bye," one of them told him. Actually, he treated girls with an odd detached gentleness, as though he knew a secret that might make them all disappear. Some of them hung around because of his quick brown hands or his really great looks, some because they hoped to share the secret. In this they were disappointed. Hobie talked and he listened carefully, but it wasn't the mutual talk-talk-talk of total catharsis that most couples went through. But how could Hobie know that?

Like most of his peer group, Hobie stayed away from heavies and agreed that pot was preferable to getting juiced. His friends never crowded him too much after the beach party where he spooked everybody by talking excitedly for hours to people who weren't there. They decided he might have a vulnerable ego-structure.

The official high school view was that Hobie had no real problems. In this they were supported by a test battery profile that could have qualified him as the ideal normal control. Certainly there was nothing to get hold of in his routine interviews with the high school psychologist.

Hobie came in after lunch, a time when Dr. Morehouse knew he was not at his most intuitive. They went through the usual openers, Hobie sitting easily, patient and interested, with an air of listening to some sound back of the acoustical ceiling tiles.

"I meet a number of young people involved in discovering who they really are. Searching for their own identities," Morehouse offered. He was idly trueing up a stack of typing headed *Sex Differences in the Adolescent Identity Crisis*.

"Do you?" Hobie asked politely.

Morehouse frowned at himself and belched disarmingly.

"Sometimes I wonder who *I* am," he smiled.

"Do you?" inquired Hobie.

"Don't you?"

"No," said Hobie.

Morehouse reached for the hostility that should have been there, found it wasn't. Not passive aggression. What? His intuition awoke briefly. He looked into Hobie's light hazel eyes and suddenly found himself slipping toward some very large uninhabited dimension. A real pubescent preschiz, he wondered hopefully? No again, he decided, and found himself thinking, What if a person is sure of his identity but it isn't his identity? He often wondered that; perhaps it could be worked up into a creative insight.

"Maybe it's the other way around," Hobie was saying before the pause grew awkward.

"How do you mean?"

"Well, maybe you're all wondering who you are," Hobie's lips quirked; it was clear he was just making conversation.

"I asked for that," Morehouse chuckled. They chatted about sibling rivalry and psychological statistics and wound up in plenty of time for Morehouse's next boy, who turned out to be a satisfying High Anx. Morehouse forgot about the empty place he had slid into. He often did that too.

It was a girl who got part of it out of Hobie, at three in the morning. "Dog" she was called then, although her name was Jane. A tender, bouncy little bird who cocked her head to listen up at him in a way Hobie liked. Dog would listen with the same soft intensity to the supermarket clerk and the pediatrician later on, but neither of them knew that.

They had been talking about the state of the world, which was then quite prosperous and peaceful. That is to say, about seventy million people were starving to death, a number of advanced nations were maintaining themselves on police terror tactics, four or five borders were being fought over, Hobie's family's maid had just been cut up by the suburban peacekeeper squad, and the school had added a charged wire and two dogs to its patrol. But none of the big nations were waving fissionables, and the U.S.-Sino-Soviet détente was a twenty-year reality.

Dog was holding Hobie's head over the side of her car because he had been the one who found the maid crawling on her handbones among the azaleas.

"If you feel like that, why don't you do something?" Dog asked him between spasms. "Do you want some Slurp? It's all we've got."

"Do what?" Hobie quavered.

"Politics?" guessed Dog. She really didn't know. The Protest Decade was long over, along with the New Politics and Ralph Nader. There was a school legend about a senior who had come back from Miami with a busted collarbone. Sometime after that the kids had discovered that flowers weren't really very powerful, and that movement organizers had their own bag. Why go on the street when you could really do more in one of the good jobs available Inside? So Dog could offer only a vague image of Hobie running for something, a sincere face on TV.

"You could join the Young Statesmen."

"Not to interfere," gasped Hobie. He wiped his mouth. Then he pulled himself together and tried some of the Slurp. In the dashlight his seventeen-year-old sideburns struck Dog as tremendously mature and beautiful.

"Oh, it's not so bad," said Hobie. "I mean, it's not *unusually* bad. It's just a stage. This world is going through a primitive stage. There's a lot of stages. It takes a long time. They're just very very backward, that's all."

"They," said Dog, listening to every word.

"I mean," he said.

"You're alienated," she told him. "Rinse your mouth out with that. You don't relate to people."

"I think you're people," he said, rinsing. He'd heard this before. "I relate to you," he said. He leaned out to spit. Then he twisted his head to look up at the sky and stayed that way a while, like an animal's head sticking out of a crate. Dog could feel him trembling the car.

"Are you going to barf again?" she asked.

"No."

But then suddenly he did, roaringly. She clutched at his shoulders while he heaved. After a while he sagged down, his head lolling limply out at one arm.

"It's such a mess," she heard him whispering. "It's such a s——ting miserable mess mess mess MESS MESS—"

He was pounding his hand on the car side.

"I'll hose it," said Dog, but then she saw he didn't mean the car.

"Why does it have to go on and on?" he croaked. "Why don't they just *stop* it? I can't bear it much longer, please, please, I can't—"

Dog was scared now.

"Honey, it's not that bad. Hobie honey, it's not that bad," she told him, patting at him, pressing her soft front against his back.

Suddenly he came back into the car on top of her, spent.

"It's unbearable," he muttered.

"What's unbearable?" she snapped, mad at him for scaring her. "What's unbearable for you and not for me? I mean, I know it's a mess, but why is it so bad for *you?* I have to live here too."

"It's your world," he told her absently, lost in some private desolation.

Dog yawned.

"I better drive you home now," she said.

He had nothing more to say and sat quietly. When Dog glanced at his profile, she decided he looked calm. Almost stupid, in fact; his mouth hung open a little. She didn't recognize the expression, because she had never seen people looking out of cattle cars.

Hobie's class graduated that June. His grades were well up, and everybody understood that he was acting a little unrelated because of the traumatic business with the maid. He got a lot of sympathy.

It was after the graduation exercises that Hobie surprised his parents for the first and last time. They had been congratulating themselves on having steered their fifth offspring safely through the college crisis and into a high-status Eastern. Hobie announced that he had applied for the United States Air Force Academy.

This was a bomb, because Hobie had never shown the slightest interest in things military. Just the opposite, really. Hobie's parents took it for granted that the educated classes viewed the military with tolerant distaste. Why did their son want this? Was it another of his unstable motivational orientations?

But Hobie persisted. He didn't have any reasons, he had just thought carefully and felt that this was for him. Finally they recalled that early model rocket collection; his father decided he was serious, and began sorting out the generals his research firm did business with. In September Hobie disappeared into Colorado Springs. He reappeared for Christmas in the form of an exotically hairless, erect and polite stranger in uniform.

During the next four years, Hobie the person became effectively invisible behind a growing pile of excellent evaluation reports. There seemed to be no doubt that he was working very hard, and his motivation gave no sign of flagging. Like any cadet, he bitched about many of the Academy's little ways and told some funny stories. But he never seemed discouraged. When he elected to spend his summers in special aviation skills training, his parents realized that Hobie had found himself.

Enlightenment—of a sort—came in his senior year when he told them he had applied for and been accepted into the new astronaut training program. The

U.S. space program was just then starting up again after the revulsion caused by the tragic loss of the manned satellite lab ten years before.

"I bet that's what he had in mind all along," Hobie's father chuckled. "He didn't want to say so before he made it." They were all relieved. A son in the space program was a lot easier to live with, statuswise.

When she heard the news, Dog, who was now married and called herself Jane, sent him a card with a picture of the Man in the Moon. Another girl, more percipient, sent him a card showing some stars.

But Hobie never made it to the space program.

It was the summer when several not-very-serious events happened all together. The British devalued their wobbly pound again, just when it was found that far too many dollars were going out of the States. North and South Korea moved a step closer to reunion, which generated a call for strengthening the U.S. contribution to the remains of SEATO. Next there was an expensive, though luckily nonlethal, fire at Kennedy, and the Egyptians announced a new Soviet aid pact. And in August it was discovered that the Guévarrista rebels in Venezuela were getting some very unpleasant-looking hardware from their Arab allies.

Contrary to the old saying that nations never learn from history, the U.S. showed that it had learned from its long agony in Vietnam. What it had learned was not to waste time messing around with popular elections and military advisory and training programs, but to ball right in. Hard.

When the dust cleared, the space program and astronaut training were dead on the pad and a third of Hobie's graduating class was staging through Caracas. Technically, he had volunteered.

He found this out from the task force medico.

"Look at it this way, lieutenant. By entering the Academy, you volunteered for the Air Force, right?"

"Yes. But I opted for the astronaut program. The Air Force is the only way you can get in. And I've been accepted."

"But the astronaut program has been suspended. Temporarily, of course. Meanwhile the Air Force—for which you volunteered—has an active requirement for your training. You can't expect them just to let you sit around until the program resumes, can you? Moreover you have been given the very best option available. Good God, man, the Volunteer Airpeace Corps is considered a superelite. You should see the fugal depressions we have to cope with among men who have been rejected for the VAC."

"Mercenaries," said Hobie. "Regressive."

"Try 'professional,' it's a better word. Now—about those headaches."

The headaches eased up some when Hobie was assigned to long-range sensor recon support. He enjoyed the work of flying, and the long, calm, lonely sensor missions were soothing. They were also quite safe. The Guévarristas had no air strength to waste on recon planes and the U.A.R. SAM sites were not yet operational. Hobie flew the pattern, and waited zombielike for the weather, and flew again. Mostly he waited, because the fighting was developing in a steamy jungle province where clear sensing was a sometimes thing. It was poorly mapped. The ground troops could never be sure about the little brown square men who gave them so much trouble; on one side of an unknown line they were Guévarristas who should be obliterated, and on the other side they were legitimate national troops warning the blancos away. Hobie's recon tapes were urgently needed, and for several weeks he was left alone.

Then he began to get pulled up to a forward strip for one-day chopper duty when their tactical duty roster was disrupted by gee-gee. But this was relatively peaceful too, being mostly defoliant spray missions. Hobie, in fact, put in several months without seeing, hearing, smelling, or feeling the war at all. He would have been grateful for this if he had realized it. As it was he seemed to be trying not to realize anything much. He spoke very little, did his work, and moved like a man whose head might fall off if he jostled anything.

Naturally he was one of the last to hear the rumors about gee-gee when they filtered back to the coastal base, where Hobie was quartered with the long-range stuff. Gee-gee's proper name was Guairas Grippe. It was developing into a severe problem in the combat zone. More and more replacements and relief crews were being called forward for temporary tactical duty. On Hobie's next trip in, he couldn't help but notice that people were acting pretty haggard, and the roster was all scrawled up with changes. When they were on course, he asked about it.

"Are you kidding?" his gunner grunted.

"No. What is it?"

"B.W."

"What?"

"Bacteriological weapon, skyhead. They keep promising us vaccines. Stuck in their zippers—look out, there's a ground burst."

They held Hobie up front for another mission, and another after that, and then they told him that a sector quarantine was now in force.

The official notice said that movement of personnel between sectors would be reduced to a minimum as a temporary measure to control the spread of respiratory ailments. Translation: you could go from the support zone to the front, but you couldn't go back.

Hobie was moved into a crowded billet and assigned to Casualty and Supply. Shortly he discovered that there was a translation for respiratory ailments too. Gee-gee turned out to be a multiform misery of groin rash, sore throat, fever, and unending trots. It didn't seem to become really acute; it just cycled along. Hobie was one of those who were only lightly affected, which was lucky because the hospital beds were full. So were the hospital aisles. Evacuation of all casualties had been temporarily suspended until a controlled corridor could be arranged.

The Gués did not, it seemed, get gee-gee. The ground troops were definitely sure of that. Nobody knew how it was spread. Rumor said it was bats one week, and then the next week they were putting stuff in the water. Poisoned arrows, roaches, women, disintegrating canisters, all had their advocates. However it was done, it was clear that the U.A.R. technological aid had included more than hardware. The official notice about a forthcoming vaccine yellowed on the board.

Ground fighting was veering closer to Hobie's strip. He heard mortars now and then, and one night the Gués ran in a rocket launcher and nearly got the fuel dump before they were chased back.

"All they got to do is wait," said the gunner. "We're dead."

"Geegee doesn't kill you," said C/S control. "You just wish it did."

"They say."

The strip was extended, and three attack bombers came in. Hobie looked them over. He had trained on AX92's all one summer; he could fly them in his sleep. It would be nice to be alone.

He was pushing the C/S chopper most of the daylight hours now. He had gotten used to being shot at and to being sick. Everybody was sick, except a couple of replacement crews who were sent in two weeks apart, looking startlingly healthy. They said they had been immunized with a new antitoxin. Their big news was that gee-gee could be cured outside the zone.

"We're getting reinfected," the gunner said. "That figures. They want us out of here."

That week there was a big drive on bats, but it didn't help. The next week the first batch of replacements were running fevers. Their shots hadn't worked and neither did the stuff they gave the second batch.

After that, no more men came in except a couple of volunteer medicos. The billets and the planes and the mess were beginning to stink. That dysentery couldn't be controlled after you got weak.

What they did get was supplies. Every day or so another ton of stuff would drift down. Most of it was dragged to one side and left to rot. They were swimming in food. The staggering cooks pushed steak and lobster at men who shivered and went out to retch. The hospital even had ample space now, because it turned out that gee-gee really did kill you in the end. By that time, you were glad to go. A cemetery developed at the far side of the strip, among the skeletons of the defoliated trees.

On the last morning Hobie was sent out to pick up a forward scout team. He was one of the few left with enough stamina for long missions. The three-man team was far into Gué territory, but Hobie didn't care. All he was thinking about was his bowels. So far he had not fouled himself or his plane. When he was down by their signal, he bolted out to squat under the chopper's tail. The grunts climbed in, yelling at him.

They had a prisoner with them. The Gué was naked and astonishingly broad. He walked springily; his arms were lashed with wire and a shirt was tied over his head. This was the first Gué Hobie had been close to. As he got in he saw how the Gué's firm brown flesh glistened and bulged around the wire. He wished he could see his face. The gunner said the Gué was a Sirionó, and this was important because the Sirionós were not known to be with the Gués. They were a very primitive nomadic tribe.

When Hobie began to fly home, he realized he was getting sicker. It became a fight to hold onto consciousness and keep on course. Luckily nobody shot at them. At one point he became aware of a lot of screaming going on behind him, but couldn't pay attention. Finally he came over the strip and horsed the chopper down. He let his head down on his arms.

"You okay?" asked the gunner.

"Yeah," said Hobie, hearing them getting out. They were moving something heavy. Finally he got up and followed them. The floor was wet. That wasn't unusual. He got down and stood staring in, the floor a foot under his nose. The wet stuff was blood. It was sprayed around, with one big puddle. In the puddle was something soft and fleshy-looking.

Hobie turned his head. The ladder was wet. He held up one hand and looked at the red. His other hand too. Holding them out stiffly, he turned and began to walk away across the strip.

Control, who still hoped to get an evening flight out of him, saw him fall and called the hospital. The two replacement parameds were still in pretty good shape. They came out and picked him up.

When Hobie came to, one of the parameds was tying his hands down to the bed so he couldn't tear the IV out again.

"We're going to die here," Hobie told him.

The paramed looked noncommittal. He was a thin dark boy with a big Adam's apple.

" 'But I shall dine at journey's end with Landor and with Donne,' " said Hobie. His voice was light and facile.

"Yeats," said the paramed. "Want some water?"

Hobie's eyes flickered. The paramed gave him some water.

"I really believed it, you know," Hobie said chattily. "I had it all figured out." He smiled, something he hadn't done for a long time.

"Landor and Donne?" asked the medic. He unhooked the empty IV bottle and hung up a new one.

"Oh, it was pathetic, I guess," Hobie said. "It started out . . . I believed they were real, you know? Kirk, Spock, McCoy, all of them. And the ship. To this day, I swear . . . one of them talked to me once; I mean, he really did . . . I had it all figured out; they had me left behind as an observer." Hobie giggled.

"They were coming back for me. It was secret. All I had to do was sort of fit in and observe. Like a report. One day they would come back and haul me up in that beam thing; maybe you know about that? And there I'd be back in real time where human beings were, where they were human. I wasn't really stuck here in the past. On a backward planet."

The paramed nodded.

"Oh, I mean, I didn't really *believe* it; I knew it was just a show. But I did believe it, too. It was like *there,* in the background, underneath, no matter what was going on. They were coming for me. All I had to do was observe. And not to interfere. You know? Prime directive . . . Of course after I grew up, I realized they weren't; I mean, I realized consciously. So I was going to go to them. Somehow, somewhere. Out there . . . Now I know. It really isn't so. None of it. Never. There's nothing . . . Now I know I'll die here."

"Oh now," said the paramed. He got up and started to take things away. His fingers were shaky.

"It's clean there," said Hobie in a petulant voice. "None of this shit. Clean and friendly. They don't torture people," he explained, thrashing his head. "They don't kill—" He slept. The paramed went away.

Somebody started to yell monotonously.

Hobie opened his eyes. He was burning up.

The yelling went on, became screaming. It was dusk. Footsteps went by, headed for the screaming. Hobie saw they had put him in a bed by the door.

Without his doing much about it, the screaming seemed to be lifting him out of the bed, propelling him through the door. Air. He kept getting close-ups of his hands clutching things. Bushes, shadows. Something scratched him.

After a while the screaming was a long way behind him. Maybe it was only in his ears. He shook his head, felt himself go down onto boards. He thought he was in the cemetery.

"No," he said. "Please. Please no." He got himself up, balanced, blundered on, seeking coolness.

The side of the plane felt cool. He plastered his hot body against it, patting it affectionately. It seemed to be quite dark now. Why was he inside with no lights? He tried the panel, the lights worked perfectly. Vaguely he noticed some yelling starting outside again. It ignited the screaming in his head. The screaming got very loud—loud—LOUD—and appeared to be moving him, which was good.

He came to above the overcast and climbing. The oxy-support tube was hitting him in the nose. He grabbed for the mask, but it wasn't there. Automatically, he had leveled off. Now he rolled and looked around.

Below him was a great lilac sea of cloud, with two mountains sticking through it, their western tips on fire. As he looked, they dimmed. He shivered, found he was wearing only sodden shorts. How had he got here? Somebody had screamed intolerably and he had run.

He flew along calmly, checking his board. No trouble except the fuel. Nobody serviced the AX92's any more. Without thinking about it, he began to climb again. His hands were a yard away and he was shivering but he felt clear. He reached up and found his headphones were in place; he must have put them on along with the rest of the drill. He clicked on. Voices rattled and roared at him. He switched off. Then he took off the headpiece and dropped it on the floor.

He looked around: 18,000, heading 88-05. He was over the Atlantic. In front of him the sky was darkening fast. A pinpoint glimmer ten o'clock high. Sirius, probably.

He thought about Sirius, trying to recall his charts. Then he thought about turning and going back down. Without paying much attention, he noticed he was crying with his mouth open.

Carefully he began feeding his torches and swinging the nose of his pod around and up. He brought it neatly to a point on Sirius. Up. Up. Behind him a great pale swing of contrail fell away above the lilac shadow, growing, towering to the tiny plane that climbed at its tip. Up. Up. The contrail cut off as the plane burst into the high cold dry.

As it did so, Hobie's ears skewered and he screamed wildly. The pain quit; his drums had burst. Up! Now he was gasping for air, strangling. The great torches drove him up, up, over the curve of the world. He was hanging on the star. Up! The fuel gauges were knocking. Any second they would quit and he and the bird would be a falling stone. "Beam us up, Scotty!" he howled at Sirius, laughing, coughing—coughing to death, as the torches faltered—

—And was still coughing as he sprawled on the shining resiliency under the arcing grids. He gagged, rolled, finally focused on a personage leaning toward him out of a complex chair. The personage had round eyes, a slitted nose, and the start of a quizzical smile.

Hobie's head swiveled slowly. It was not the bridge of the *Enterprise*. There were no viewscreens, only a View. And Lieutenant Uhura would have had trouble with the freeform flashing objects suspended in front of what appeared to be a girl wearing spots. The spots, Hobie made out, were fur.

Somebody who was not Bones McCoy was doing something to Hobie's stomach. Hobie got up a hand and touched the man's gleaming back. Under the mesh it was firm and warm. The man looked up, grinned; Hobie looked back at the captain.

"Do not have fear," a voice was saying. It seemed to be coming out of a globe by the captain's console. "We will tell you where you are."

"I know where I am," Hobie whispered. He drew a deep, sobbing breath.

"I'm HOME!" he yelled. Then he passed out.

C. S. Lewis

C. S. Lewis (1898–1963) is important both as a writer and as a critic of science fiction. He is indeed one of the significant literary men of the century, whose scholarship and criticism of medieval and Renaissance literature were unsurpassed. Such critical works as *The Allegory of Love* (1936) and his volume in the *Oxford History of English Literature* are rich and illuminating. Lewis's Christian fantasy fiction, including *The Screwtape Letters* (1942) and most especially his Narnia series of fantasy tales for children, is enormously influential. Nearly fifty books on Lewis and his works have been published, and a film has been made on his life.

He was a member, with Charles Williams, J. R. R. Tolkein, and Dorothy Sayers, of a casual literary society in Oxford called The Inklings, at whose meetings they read each other's works in progress. His science fiction novels, also Christian allegories, *Out of the Silent Planet* (1938), *Perelandra* (1943) and *That Hideous Strength* (1945), overshadow the few SF short stories he published in the 1950s and '60s. They were only collected after his death (*Of Other Worlds*, 1966), along with his critical pieces examining and providing an eloquent defense of genre science fiction—which are generally overshadowed by his more famous critical work in other areas. Those, together with his learned and sensible *An Experiment in Criticism,* which includes perhaps the single best argument ever constructed on the appeal of science fiction, did not appear until the 1960s and have not, in the main, been given much notice. Perhaps the SF and fantasy novels and stories of R. A. Lafferty from the 1960s to the 1980s are the body of work after Lewis most centrally in that Christian tradition.

This story originally appeared in *Fantasy and Science Fiction.* It shows how the ordinary tropes of genre SF can be applied with wit and humor to spiritual concerns. It is also uproariously politically incorrect.

MINISTERING ANGELS

The Monk, as they called him, settled himself on the camp-chair beside his bunk and stared through the window at the harsh sand and black-blue sky of Mars. He did not mean to begin his "work" for ten minutes yet. Not, of course, the work he had been brought there to do. He was the meteorologist of the party, and his work in that capacity was largely done; he had found out whatever could be found out. There was nothing more, within the limited radius he could investigate, to be observed for at least twenty-five days. And meteorology had not been his real motive. He had chosen three years on Mars as the nearest modern equivalent to a hermitage in the desert. He had come there to meditate: to continue the slow, perpetual rebuilding of that inner structure which, in his view, it was the main purpose of life to rebuild. And now his ten minutes' rest was over. He began with his well-used formula. "Gentle and patient Master, teach me to need men less and to love thee more." Then to it. There was no time to waste. There were barely six months of this lifeless, sinless, unsuffering wilderness ahead of him. Three years were short—but when the shout came he rose out of his chair with the practised alertness of a sailor.

The Botanist in the next cabin responded to the same shout with a curse. His eye had been at the microscope when it came. It was maddening. Constant interruption. A man might as well try to work in the middle of Piccadilly as in this infernal camp. And his work was already a race against time. Six months more—and he had hardly begun. The flora of Mars, these tiny, miraculously hardy organisms, the ingenuity of their contrivances to live under all but impossible conditions—it was a feast for a lifetime. He would ignore the shout. But then came the bell. All hands to the main room.

The only person who was doing, so to speak, nothing when the shout came was the Captain. To be more exact, he was (as usual) trying to stop thinking about Clare, and get on with his official journal. Clare kept on interrupting from forty million miles away. It was preposterous. "*Would have needed all hands*," he wrote. Hands . . . his own hands . . . his own hands, hands, he felt, with eyes in them, travelling over all the warm-cool, soft-firm, smooth, yielding, resisting aliveness of her. "Shut up, there's a dear," he said to the photo on his desk. And so back to the journal, until the fatal words "*had been causing me some anxiety.*" Anxiety—oh God, what might be happening to Clare now? How did he know there was a Clare by this time? Anything could happen. He'd been a fool ever to accept this job. What other newly married man in the world would have done it? But it had seemed so sensible. Three years of horrid separation but then . . . oh, they were made for life. He had been promised the post that, only a few months before, he would not have dared to dream of. He'd never need to go to Space again. And all the by-products; the lectures, the book, probably a title. Plenty of children. He knew she wanted that, and so in a queer way (as he began to find) did he. But damn it, the journal. Begin a new paragraph—and then the shout came.

It was one of the two youngsters, technicians both, who had given it. They had been together since dinner. At least Paterson had been standing at the open door of Dickson's cabin, shifting from foot to foot and swinging the door, and Dickson had been sitting on his berth and waiting for Paterson to go away.

"What are you talking about, Paterson?" he said. "Who ever said anything about a quarrel?"

"That's all very well, Bobby," said the other, "but we're not friends like we used to be. You know we're not. Oh, *I'm* not blind. I *did* ask you to call me Clifford. And you're always so stand-offish."

"Oh, get to hell out of this!" cried Dickson. "I'm perfectly ready to be good friends with you and everyone else in an ordinary way, but all this gas—like a pair of schoolgirls—I will not stand. Once and for all—"

"Oh look, look, look," said Paterson. And it was then that Dickson shouted and the Captain came and rang the bell and within twenty seconds they were all crowded behind the biggest of the windows. A spaceship had just made a beautiful landing about a hundred and fifty yards from camp.

"Oh boy!" exclaimed Dickson. "They're relieving us before our time."

"Damn their eyes. Just what they would do," said the Botanist.

Five figures were descending from the ship. Even in space-suits it was clear that one of them was enormously fat; they were in no other way remarkable.

"Man the air-lock," said the Captain.

Drinks from their limited store were going round. The Captain had recognized in the leader of the strangers an old acquaintance, Ferguson. Two were ordinary young men, not unpleasant. But the remaining two?

"I don't understand," said the Captain, "who exactly—I mean we're delighted to see you all of course—but what exactly . . . ?"

"Where are the rest of your party?" said Ferguson.

"We've had two casualties, I'm afraid," said the Captain. "Sackville and Dr. Burton. It was a most wretched business. Sackville tried eating the stuff we called Martian cress. It drove him fighting mad in a matter of minutes. He knocked Burton down and by sheer bad luck Burton fell in just the wrong position: across that table there. Broke his neck. We got Sackville tied down on a bunk but he was dead before the evening."

"Hadna he even the gumption to try it on the guinea-pig first?" said Ferguson.

"Yes," said the Botanist. "That was the whole trouble. The funny thing is that the guinea-pig lived. But its behaviour was remarkable. Sackville wrongly concluded that the stuff was alcoholic. Thought he'd invent a new drink. The nuisance is that once Burton was dead, none of us could do a reliable post-mortem on Sackville. Under analysis this vegetable shows—"

"A-a-a-h," interrupted one of those who had not yet spoken. "We must beware of oversimplifications. I doubt if the vegetable substance is the real explanation. There are stresses and strains. You are all, without knowing it, in a highly unstable condition, for reasons which are no mystery to a trained psychologist."

Some of those present had doubted the sex of this creature. Its hair was very short, its nose very long, its mouth very prim, its chin sharp, and its manner authoritative. The voice revealed it as, scientifically speaking, a woman. But no one had had any doubt about the sex of her nearest neighbour, the fat person.

"Oh dearie," she wheezed. "Not now. I tell you straight I'm that flustered and faint, I'll scream if you go on so. Suppose there ain't such a thing as a port and lemon handy? No? Well, a little drop more gin would settle me. It's me stomach reelly."

The speaker was infinitely female and perhaps in her seventies. Her hair had been not very successfully dyed to a colour not unlike that of mustard. The powder (scented strongly enough to throw a train off the rails) lay like snow drifts in the complex valleys of her creased, many-chinned face.

"Stop!" roared Ferguson. "Whatever ye do, dinna give her a drap mair to drink."

" 'E's no 'art, ye see," said the old woman with a whimper and an affectionate leer directed at Dickson.

"Excuse me," said the Captain. "Who are these—ah—ladies and what is this all about?"

"I have been waiting to explain," said the Thin Woman, and cleared her throat. "Anyone who has been following World-Opinion-Trends on the problems arising out of the psychological welfare aspect of interplanetary communication will be conscious of the growing agreement that such a remarkable advance inevitably demands of us far-reaching ideological adjustments. Psychologists are now well aware that a forcible inhibition of powerful biological urges over a protracted period is likely to have unforeseeable results. The pioneers of space-travel are exposed to this danger. It would be unenlightened if a supposed ethicality were allowed to stand in the way of their protection. We must therefore nerve ourselves to face the view that immorality, as it has hitherto been called, must no longer be regarded as unethical—"

"I don't understand that," said the Monk.

"She means," said the Captain, who was a good linguist, "that what you call fornication must no longer be regarded as immoral."

"That's right, dearie,' said the Fat Woman to Dickson, "she only means a poor boy needs a woman now and then. It's only natural."

"What was required, therefore," continued the Thin Woman, "was a band of devoted females who would take the first step. This would expose them, no doubt, to obloquy from many ignorant persons. They would be sustained by the consciousness that they were performing an indispensable function in the history of human progress."

"She means you're to have tarts, duckie," said the Fat Woman to Dickson.

"Now you're talking," said he with enthusiasm. "Bit late in the day, but better late than never. But you can't have brought many girls in that ship. And why didn't you bring them in? Or are they following?"

"We cannot indeed claim," continued the Thin Woman, who had apparently not noticed the interruption, "that the response to our appeal was such as we had hoped. The personnel of the first unit of the Woman's Higher Aphrodisio-Therapeutic Humane Organization (abbreviated WHAT-HO) is not perhaps . . . well. Many excellent women, university colleagues of my own, even senior colleagues, to whom I applied, showed themselves curiously conventional. But at least a start has been made. And here," she concluded brightly, "we are."

And there, for forty seconds of appalling silence, they were. Then Dickson's face, which had already undergone certain contortions, became very red; he applied his handkerchief and spluttered like a man trying to stifle a sneeze, rose abruptly, turned his back on the company, and hid his face. He stood slightly stooped and you could see his shoulders shaking.

Paterson jumped up and ran towards him; but the Fat Woman, though with infinite gruntings and upheavals, had risen too.

"Get art of it, Pansy," she snarled at Paterson. "Lot o' good your sort ever did." A moment later her vast arms were round Dickson; all the warm, wobbling maternalism of her engulfed him.

"There, sonny," she said, "it's goin' to be OK. Don't cry, honey. Don't cry. Poor boy, then. Poor boy. I'll give you a good time."

"I think," said the Captain, "the young man is laughing, not crying."

It was the Monk who at this point mildly suggested a meal.

Some hours later the party had temporarily broken up.

Dickson (despite all his efforts the Fat Woman had contrived to sit next to him; she had more than once mistaken his glass for hers) had hardly finished his last mouthful when he said to the newly arrived technicians:

"I'd love to see over your ship, if I could."

You might expect that two men who had been cooped up in that ship so long, and had only taken off their space-suits a few minutes ago, would have been reluctant to reassume the one and return to the other. That was certainly the Fat Woman's view. "Nar, nar," she said. "Don't you go fidgeting, sonny. They seen enough of that ruddy ship for a bit, same as me. 'Tain't good for you to go rushing about, not on a full stomach, like." But the two young men were marvellously obliging.

"Certainly. Just what I was going to suggest," said the first. "OK by me, chum," said the second. They were all three of them out of the air-lock in record time.

Across the sand, up the ladder, helmets off, and then:

"What in the name of thunder have you dumped those two bitches on us for?" said Dickson.

"Don't fancy 'em?" said the Cockney stranger. "The people at 'ome thought as 'ow you'd be a bit sharp set by now. Ungrateful of you, I call it."

"Very funny to be sure," said Dickson. "But it's no laughing matter for us."

"It hasn't been for us either, you know," said the Oxford stranger. "Cheek by jowl with them for eighty-five days. They palled a bit after the first month."

"You're telling me," said the Cockney.

There was a disgusted pause.

"Can anyone tell me," said Dickson at last, "who in the world, and why in the world, out of all possible women, selected those two horrors to send to Mars?"

"Can't expect a star London show at the back of beyond," said the Cockney.

"My dear fellow," said his colleague, "isn't the thing perfectly obvious? What kind of woman, without force, is going to come and live in this ghastly place—on rations—and play doxy to half a dozen men she's never seen? The Good Time Girls won't come because they know you can't have a good time on Mars. An ordinary professional prostitute won't come as long as she has the slightest chance of being picked up in the cheapest quarter of Liverpool or Los Angeles. And you've got one who hasn't. The only other who'd come would be a crank who believes all that blah about the new ethicality. And you've got one of that too."

"Simple, ain't it?" said the Cockney.

"Anyone," said the other, "except the Fools at the Top could of course have foreseen it from the word go."

"The only hope now is the Captain," said Dickson.

"Look, mate," said the Cockney, "if you think there's any question of our taking back returned goods, you've 'ad it. Nothing doing. Our Captain'll 'ave a mutiny to settle if he tries that. Also 'e won't. 'E's 'ad 'is turn. So've we. It's up to you now."

"Fair's fair, you know," said the other. "We've stood all we can."

"Well," said Dickson, "we must leave the two chiefs to fight it out. But discipline or not, there are some things a man can't stand. That bloody school-marm—"

"She's a lecturer at a redbrick university, actually."

"Well," said Dickson after a long pause, "you were going to show me over the ship. It might take my mind off it a bit."

The Fat Woman was talking to the Monk. ". . . and oh, Father dear, I know you'll think that's the worst of all. I didn't give it up when I could. After me brother's wife died . . . 'e'd 'ave 'ad me 'ome with 'im, and money wasn't that short. But I went on, Gawd 'elp me, I went on."

"Why did you do that, daughter?" said the Monk. "Did you *like* it?"

"Well not all that, Father. I was never partikler. But you see—oh, Father, I was the goods in those days, though you wouldn't think it now . . . and the poor gentlemen, they did so enjoy it."

"Daughter," he said, "you are not far from the Kingdom. But you were wrong. The desire to give is blessed. But you can't turn bad bank-notes into good ones just by giving them away."

The Captain had also left the table pretty quickly, asking Ferguson to accompany him to his cabin. The Botanist had leaped after them.

"One moment, sir, one moment," he said excitedly. "I am a scientist. I'm working at very high pressure already. I hope there is no complaint to be made about my discharge of all those other duties which so incessantly interrupt my work. But if I am going to be expected to waste any more time entertaining those abominable females—"

"When I give you any orders which can be considered *ultra vires*," said the Captain, "it will be time to make your protest."

Paterson stayed with the Thin Woman. The only part of any woman that interested him was her ears. He liked telling women about his troubles; especially about the unfairness and unkindness of other men. Unfortunately the lady's idea was that the interview should be devoted either to Aphrodisio-Therapy or to instruction in psychology. She saw, indeed, no reason why the two operations should not be carried out simultaneously; it is only untrained minds that cannot hold more than one idea. The difference between these two conceptions of the conversation was well on its way to impairing its success. Paterson was becoming ill-tempered; the lady remained bright and patient as an iceberg.

"But as I was saying," grumbled Paterson, "what I do think so rotten is a fellow being quite fairly decent one day and then—"

"Which just illustrates my point. These tensions and maladjustments are bound, under the unnatural conditions, to arise. And provided we disinfect the obvious remedy of all those sentimental or—which is quite as bad—prurient associations which the Victorian age attached to it—"

"But I haven't yet told you. Listen. Only two days ago—"

"One moment. This ought to be regarded like any other injection. If once we can persuade—"

"How any fellow can take a pleasure—"

"I agree. The association of it with pleasure (that is purely an adolescent fixation) may have done incalculable harm. Rationally viewed—"

"I say, you're getting off the point."

"One moment—"

The dialogue continued.

They had finished looking over the spaceship. It was certainly a beauty. No one afterwards remembered who had first said, "Anyone could manage a ship like this."

Ferguson sat quietly smoking while the Captain read the letter he had brought him. He didn't even look in the Captain's direction. When at last conversation began there was so much circumambient happiness in the cabin that they took a long time to get down to the difficult part of their business. The Captain seemed at first wholly occupied with its comic side.

"Still," he said at last, "it has its serious side too. The impertinence of it, for one thing! Do they think—"

"Ye maun recall," said Ferguson, "they're dealing with an absolutely new situation."

"Oh, *new* be damned! How does it differ from men on whalers, or even on windjammers in the old days? Or on the North-west Frontier? It's about as new as people being hungry when food was short."

"Eh mon, but ye're forgettin' the new light of modern psychology."

"I think those two ghastly women have already learned some newer psychology since they arrived. Do they really suppose every man in the world is so combustible that he'll jump into the arms of any woman whatever?"

"Aye, they do. They'll be sayin' you and your party are verra abnormal. I wadna put it past them to be sending you out wee packets of hormones next."

"Well, if it comes to that, do they suppose men would volunteer for a job like this unless they could, or thought they could, or wanted to try if they could, do without women?"

"Then there's the new ethics, forbye."

"Oh stow it, you old rascal. What is new there either? Who ever tried to live clean except a minority who had a religion or were in love? They'll try it still on Mars, as they did on Earth. As for the majority, did they ever hesitate to take their pleasures wherever they could get them? The ladies of the profession know better. Did you ever see a port or a garrison town without plenty of brothels? Who are the idiots on the Advisory Council who started all this nonsense?"

"Och, a pack o' daft auld women (in trousers for the maist part) who like onything sexy, and onything scientific, and onything that makes them feel important. And this gives them all three pleasures at once, ye ken."

"Well, there's only one thing for it, Ferguson. I'm not going to have either your Mistress Overdone or your extension lecturer here. You can just—"

"Now there's no manner of use talkin' that way. I did my job. Another voyage with sic a cargo o' livestock I will not face. And my two lads the same. There'd be mutiny and murder."

"But you must, I'm—"

At that moment a blinding flash came from without and the earth shook.

"Ma ship! Ma ship!" cried Ferguson. Both men peered out on empty sand. The spaceship had obviously made an excellent take-off.

"But what's happened?" said the Captain. "They haven't—"

"Mutiny, desertion, and theft of a government ship, that's what's happened," said Ferguson. "Ma twa lads and your Dickson are awa' hame."

"But good Lord, they'll get hell for this. They've ruined their careers. They'll be—"

"Aye. Nae dout. And they think it cheap at the price. Ye'll be seeing why, maybe, before ye are a fortnight older."

A gleam of hope came into the Captain's eyes. "They couldn't have taken the women with them?"

"Talk sense, mon, talk sense. Or if ye hanna ony sense, use your ears."

In the buzz of excited conversation which became every moment more audible from the main room, female voices could be intolerably distinguished.

As he composed himself for his evening meditation the Monk thought that perhaps he had been concentrating too much on "needing less" and that must be why he was going to have a course (advanced) in "loving more." Then his face twitched into a smile that was not all mirth. He was thinking of the Fat Woman. Four things made an exquisite chord. First, the horror of all she had done and suffered. Secondly, the pity—thirdly, the 'omicality—of her belief that she could still excite desire; fourthly, her bless'd ignorance of that utterly different loveliness which already existed within her and which, under grace, and with such poor direction as even he could supply, might one day set her, bright in the land of brightness, beside the Magdalene.

But wait! There was yet a fifth note in the chord. "Oh, Master," he murmured, "forgive—or can you enjoy?—my absurdity also. I had been supposing you sent me on a voyage of forty million miles merely for my own spiritual convenience."

Edgar Pangborn

Edgar Pangborn (1909–76) attended Harvard and The New England Conservatory of Music and then published his first novel, a mystery (*A-100*, under the pseudonym Bruce Harrison). Two decades later, he turned to writing science fiction and wrote several SF novels and a number of stories from the 1950s through the 1970s. Damon Knight, describing Pangborn's first story, "Angel's Egg," and his novels *West of the Sun* (1953) and *A Mirror for Observers* (1954), says, "The style is leisurely and reflective; the mood is one of blended sorrow and delight. . . . It is as if [Pangborn's] eye sees only certain moral and emotional colors . . . we can only assume that he has blinded himself in half the spectrum in order to see more radiantly in the rest. Certainly nothing is lacking in these stories for want of skill. It may well be that this is the only song Pangborn was made to sing; and a mournfully beautiful one it is—very like the thing that Stapledon was always talking about but never managed to convey: the regretful, ironic, sorrowful, deeply joyous—and purblind—love of the world and all in it."

Davy (1964) is generally considered his masterpiece. Critics generally find it hard to articulate the virtues of this novel that Robert A. Heinlein compared to *Huckleberry Finn.* Perhaps this is in part because there was little discourse about gay fiction until recently. *Dictionary of Literary Biography* (volume 8), for instance, says it "reads like a collaboration between Mark Twain, Dylan Thomas, and André Gide." There is more warmth than illumination in such statements. It is an intensely sensual book. His later works include two collections of stories, *Good Neighbors and Other Strangers* (1972) and *Still I Persist in Wondering* (1978).

This story is from his 1950s advent, the mournfully beautiful period that so impressed Knight and others.

THE MUSIC MASTER OF BABYLON

For twenty-five years no one came.

In the seventy-sixth year of his life Brian Van Anda was still trying not to remember a happy boyhood. To do so was irrelevant and dangerous, although every instinct of his old age tempted him to reject the present and live in the lost times. He would recall stubbornly that the present year, for example, was 2096 according to the Christian calendar, that he had been born in 2020, seven years after the close of the civil war, fifty years before the last war, twenty-five years before the departure of the First Interstellar. The First and Second Interstellar would be still on the move, he supposed. It had been understood, obvious, long ago, that after radio contact faded out the world would not hear of them again for many lifetimes, if ever. They would be on the move, farther and farther away from a planet no longer capable of understanding such matters.

Brian sometimes recalled his place of birth, New Boston, the fine planned city far inland from the old metropolis which a rising sea had reclaimed after the earthquake of 1994. Such things, places and dates, were factual props, useful when Brian wanted to impose an external order on the vagueness of his immediate existence. He tried to make sure they became no more than that, to shut away the colors, the poignant sounds, the parks and the playgrounds of New Boston, the known faces (many of them loved), and the later years when he had experienced a curious intoxication called fame.

It was not necessarily better or wiser to reject these memories, but it was safer, and nowadays Brian was often sufficiently tired, sufficiently conscious of his growing weakness and lonely unimportance, to crave safety as a meadow mouse craves a burrow.

He tied his canoe to the massive window which for many years had been a port and a doorway. Lounging there with a suspended sense of time, he hardly knew he was listening. In a way, all the twenty-five years had been a listening. He watched Earth's patient star sink toward the rim of the forest on the Palisades. At this hour it was sometimes possible, if the sun-crimsoned water lay still, to cease grieving at the greater stillness.

There must be scattered human life elsewhere, he knew—probably a great deal of it. After twenty-five years alone, that also often seemed irrelevant. At other times than mild evenings—on hushed noons or in the mornings always so empty of human commotion—Brian might lapse into anger, fight the calm by yelling, resent the swift dying of his own echoes. Such moods were brief. A kind of humor remained in him, not to be ruined by any sorrow.

He remembered how, ten months or possibly ten years ago, he had encountered a box turtle in a forest clearing, and had shouted at it: "They went thataway!" The turtle's rigidly comic face, fixed in a caricature of startled disapproval, had seemed to point up some truth or other. Brian had hunkered down on the moss and laughed uproariously until he observed that some of the laughter was weeping.

Today had been rather good. He had killed a deer on the Palisades, and with bow and arrow, not spending a bullet—irreplaceable toy of civilization.

Not that he needed to practice such economy. He could live, he supposed, another ten years at the outside. His rifles were in good condition, his hoarded ammunition would easily outlast him. So would the stock of canned and dried food stuffed away in his living quarters. But there was satisfaction in primitive effort, and no compulsion to analyze the why of it.

The stored food was more important than the ammunition; a time was coming soon enough when he would no longer have the strength for hunting. He would lose the inclination to depart from his fortress for trips to the mainland. He would yield to such timidity or laziness for days, then weeks. Sometime, after such an interlude, he might find himself too feeble to risk climbing the cliff wall into the forest. He would then have the good sense, he hoped, to destroy the canoe, thus making of his weakness a necessity.

There were books. There was the Hall of Music on the next floor above the water, probably safe from its lessening encroachment. To secure fresh water he need only keep track of the tides, for the Hudson had cleaned itself and now rolled down sweet from the lonely uncorrupted hills. His decline could be comfortable. He had provided for it and planned it.

Yet now, gazing across the sleepy water, seeing a broad-winged hawk circle in freedom above the forest, Brian was aware of the old thought moving in him: *If I could hear voices—just once, if I could hear human voices . . .*

The Museum of Human History, with the Hall of Music on what Brian thought of as the second floor, should also outlast his requirements. In the flooded lower floor and basement the work of slow destruction must be going on: Here and there the unhurried waters could find their way to steel and make rust of it; the waterproofing of the concrete was nearly a hundred years old. But it ought to be good for another century or two.

Nowadays the ocean was mild. There were moderate tides, winds no longer destructive. For the last six years there had been no more of the heavy storms out of the south; in the same period Brian had noted a rise in the water level of a mere nine inches. The windowsill, his port, stood six inches above high-tide mark this year. Perhaps Earth was settling into a new amiable mood. The climate had become delightful, about like what Brian remembered from a visit to southern Virginia in his childhood.

The last earthquake had come in 2082—a large one, Brian guessed, but its center could not have been close to the rock of Manhattan. The Museum had only shivered and shrugged—it had survived much worse than that, half a dozen times since 1994. Long after the tremor, a tall wave had thundered in from the south. Its force, like that of others, had mostly been dissipated against the barrier of tumbled rock and steel at the southern end of the submerged island—an undersea dam, man-made though not man-intended—and when it reached the Museum it did no more than smash the southern windows in the Hall of Music, which earlier waves had not been able to reach; then it passed on up the river enfeebled.

The windows of the lower floor had all been broken long before that. After the earthquake of '82 Brian had spent a month in boarding up all the openings on the south side of the Hall of Music—after all, it was home—with lumber painfully ferried over from mainland ruins. By that year he was sixty-two years old and not moving with the ease of youth. He deliberately left cracks and knotholes. Sunlight sifted through in narrow beams, like the bars of dusty gold Brian could remember in a hayloft at his uncle's farm in Vermont.

That hawk above the Palisades soared nearer over the river and receded. Caught in the evening light, he was himself a little sun, dying and returning.

The Museum had been finished in 2003. Manhattan, strangely enough, had never taken a bomb, although in the civil war two of the type called "small clean fission" had fallen on the Brooklyn and New Jersey sides—so Brian recalled from the jolly history books which had informed his adolescence that war was definitely a thing of the past. By the time of the next last war, in 2070, the sea, gorged on melting ice caps, had removed Manhattan Island from current history.

Everything left standing above the waters south of the Museum had been knocked flat by the tornadoes of 2057 and 2064. A few blobs of empty rock still demonstrated where Central Park and Mount Morris Park had been: not significant. Where Long Island once rose, there was a troubled area of shoals and small islands, probably a useful barrier of protection for the receding shore of Connecticut. Men had yielded their great city inch by inch, then foot by foot; a full mile in 2047, saying: "The flood years have passed their peak, and a return to normal is expected." Brian sometimes felt a twinge of sympathy for the Neanderthal experts who must have told each other to expect a return to normal at the very time when the Cro-Magnons were drifting in.

In 2057 the Island of Manhattan had to be yielded. New York City, half-new, half-ancient, sprawled stubborn and enormous upstream, on both sides of a river not done with its anger. Yet the Museum stood. Aided by sunken rubble of other buildings of its kind, aided also by men because they still had time to move it, the museum stood, and might for a long time yet—weather permitting.

The hawk floated out of sight above the Palisades into the field of the low sun.

The Museum of Human History covered an acre of ground north of 125th Street, rising a modest fifteen stories, its foundation secure in that layer of rock which mimics eternity. It deserved its name; here men had brought samples of everything man-made, literally everything known in the course of human creation since prehistory. Within human limits it was definitive.

No one had felt anything unnatural in the refusal of the Directors of the Museum to move the collection after the building weathered the storm of 2057. Instead, ordinary people donated money so that a mighty abutment could be built around the ground floor and a new entrance designed on the north side of the second. The abutment survived the greater tornado of 2064 without damage, although during those seven years the sea had risen another eight feet in its old ever-new game of making monkeys out of the wise. (It was left for Brian Van Anda, alone, in 2079, to see the waters slide quietly over the abutment, opening the lower regions for the use of fishes and the more secret water-dwellers who like shelter and privacy. In the '90s, Brian suspected the presence of an octopus or two in the vast vague territory that had once been parking lot, heating plant, storage space, air-raid shelter, etc. He couldn't prove it; it just seemed like a decent, comfortable place for an octopus.) In 2070 plans were under consideration for building a new causeway to the Museum from the still expanding city in the north. In 2070, also, the last war began and ended.

When Brian Van Anda came down the river late in 2071, a refugee from certain unfamiliar types of savagery, the Museum was empty of the living. He spent many days in exhaustive exploration of the building. He did this systematically, toiling at last up to the Directors' meeting room on the top floor. There he observed how they must have been holding a conference at the very time when a new gas was tried out over New York in a final effort to persuade the Western Federation that the end justifies the means. (Too bad, Brian sometimes thought, that he would never know exactly what had become of the Asian Empire. In the little splinter state called the Soviet of North America, from which Brian had fled in '71, the official doctrine was that the Asian Empire had won the war and the saviors of humanity would be flying in any day now. Brian had inadvertently doubted this out loud and then stolen a boat and gotten away safely under cover of night.)

Up in the meeting room, Brian had seen how that up-to-date neurotoxin had been no respecter of persons. An easy death, however, by the look of it. He observed also how some things endure. The Museum, for instance: virtually unharmed.

Brian often recalled those moments in the meeting room as a sort of island in time. They were like the first day of falling in love, the first hour of discovering that he could play Beethoven. And a little like the curiously cherished, more than life-size half-hour back there in Newburg, in that ghastly year 2071, when he had briefly met and spoken with an incredibly old man, Abraham Brown. Brown had been President of the Western Federation at the time of the civil war. Later, retired from the uproar of public affairs, he had devoted himself to philosophy, unofficial teaching. In 2071, with the world he had loved in almost total ruin around him, Brown had spoken pleasantly to Brian Van Anda of small things—of chrysanthemums that would soon be blooming in the front yard of the house where he lived with friends, of a piano recital by Van Anda back in 2067 which the old man still remembered with warm enthusiasm.

Only a month later more hell was loose and Brian himself in flight.

Yes, the Museum Directors had died easily. Brooding in the evening sunlight, Brian reflected that now, all these years later, the innocent bodies would be perfectly decent. No vermin in the Museum. The doorways and the floors were tight, the upper windows unbroken.

One of the white-haired men had had a Ming vase on his desk. He had not dropped out of his chair, but looked as if he had fallen asleep in front of the vase with his head on his arms. Brian had left the vase untouched, but had taken one other thing, moved by some stirring of his own never-certain philosophy and knowing that he would not return to this room, ever.

One of the Directors had been opening a wall cabinet when he fell; the key lay near his fingers. Their discussion had not been concerned only with war, perhaps not at all with war. After all, there were other topics. The Ming vase must have had a part in it. Brian wished he could know what the old man had meant to take from the cabinet. Sometimes he dreamed of conversations with that man, in which the Director told him the truth of this and other matters, but what was certainty in sleep was in the morning gone like childhood.

For himself Brian had taken a little image of rock-hard clay, blackened, two-faced, male and female. Prehistoric, or at any rate wholly savage, unsophisticated, meaningful like the blameless motion of an animal in sunlight. Brian had said: "With your permission, gentlemen." He had closed the cabinet and then, softly, the outer door.

"I'm old, too," Brian said to the red evening. He searched for the hawk and could no longer find it in the deepening sky. "Old, a little foolish—talk aloud to myself. I'll have some Mozart before supper."

He transferred the fresh venison from the canoe to a small raft hitched inside the window. He had selected only choice pieces, as much as he could cook and eat in the few days before it spoiled, leaving the rest for the wolves or any other forest scavengers which might need it. There was a rope strung from the window to the marble steps leading to the next floor of the Museum, which was home.

It had not been possible to save much from the submerged area, for its treasure was mostly heavy statuary. Through the still water, as he pulled the raft along the rope, the Moses of Michelangelo gazed up at him in tranquillity. Other faces watched him; most of them watched infinity. There were white hands that occasionally borrowed motion from ripples made by the raft. "I got a deer, Moses," said Brian Van Anda, smiling down in companionship, losing track of time. . . . "Good night, Moses." He carried his juicy burden up the stairway.

Brian's living quarters had once been a cloakroom for Museum attendants. Four close walls gave it a feel of security. A ventilating shaft now served as a chimney for the wood stove Brian had salvaged from a mainland farmhouse. The door could be tightly locked. There were no windows. You do not want windows in a cave.

Outside was the Hall of Music, a full acre, an entire floor of the Museum, containing an example of every musical instrument that was known or could be reconstructed in the twenty-first century. The library of scores and recordings lacked nothing—except electricity to make the recordings speak. A few might still be made to sound on a hand-cranked phonograph, but Brian had not bothered with that toy for years; the springs were probably rusted.

Brian sometimes took out orchestra and chamber music scores to read at random. Once, reading them, his mind had been able to furnish ensembles, orchestras, choirs of a sort, but lately the ability had weakened. He remembered a day, possibly a year ago, when his memory refused to give him the sound of oboe and clarinet in unison. He had wandered, peevish, distressed, unreasonably alarmed, among the racks and cases of woodwinds and brasses and violins. He tried to sound a clarinet; the reed was still good in the dust proof case, but he had no lip. He had never mastered any instrument except the pianoforte.

He recalled—it might have been that same day—opening a chest of double basses. There was a three-stringer in the group, old, probably from the early nineteenth century, a trifle fatter than its more modern companions. Brian touched its middle string in an idle caress, not intending to make it sound, but it had done so. When in use, it would have been tuned to D; time had slackened the heavy murmur to A or something near it. That had throbbed in the silent room with finality, a sound such as a programmatic composer, say Tchaikovsky, might have used as a tonal symbol for the breaking of a heart. It stayed in the air as other instruments whispered a dim response. "All right, gentlemen," Brian said, "that was your A. . . ."

Out in the main part of the hall, a place of honor was given to what may have been the oldest of the instruments, a seven-note marimba of phonolitic schist discovered in Indo-China in the twentieth century and thought to be at least 5,000 years of age. The xylophone-type rack was modern. Brian for twenty-five years had obeyed a compulsion to keep it free of cobwebs. Sometimes he touched the singing stones, not for amusement but because there was comfort in it. They answered to the light tap of a fingernail. Beside them on a little table of its own he had placed the Stone Age god of two faces.

On the west side of the Hall of Music, a rather long walk from Brian's cave, was a small auditorium. Lectures, recitals, chamber music concerts had been given there in the old days. The pleasant room held a twelve-foot concert grand, made in 2043, probably the finest of the many pianos in the Hall of Music, a summit of technical achievement. Brian had done his best to preserve this beautiful artifact, prayerfully tuning it three times a year, robbing other pianos in the Museum to provide a reserve supply of strings, oiled and sealed against rust. When not in use his great piano was covered by stitched-together sheets. To remove the cover was a somber ritual. Before touching the keys, Brian washed his hands with needless fanatical care.

Some years ago he had developed the habit of locking the auditorium doors before he played. Yet even then he preferred not to glance toward the vista of empty seats, not much caring whether this inhibition derived from a Stone Age fear of finding someone there or from a flat civilized understanding that no one could be. It never occurred to him to lock the one door he used, when he was absent from the auditorium. The key remained on the inside; if he went in merely to tune the piano or to inspect the place, he never turned it.

The habit of locking it when he played might have started (he could not remember) back in the year 2076, when so many bodies had floated down from the north on the ebb tides. Full horror had somehow been lacking in the sight of all that floating death. Perhaps it was because Brian had earlier had his fill of horrors, or perhaps in 2076 he already felt so divorced from his own kind that what happened to them was like the photograph of a war in a distant country. Some had bobbed and floated quite near the Museum. Most of them had the gaping obvious wounds of primitive warfare, but some were oddly discolored—a new pestilence? So there was (or had been) more trouble up there in what was (or had been) the short-lived Soviet of North America, a self-styled "nation" that took in east central New York and most of New England. So . . . Yes, that was probably the year when he had started locking the doors between his private concerts and an empty world.

He dumped the venison in his cave. He scrubbed his hands, showing high blue veins now, but still tough, still knowing. Mozart, he thought, and walked, not with much pleasure of anticipation but more like one externally driven, through the enormous hall that was so full and yet so empty and growing dim with evening, with dust, with age, with loneliness. Music should not be silent.

When the piano was uncovered, Brian delayed. He exercised his hands unnecessarily. He fussed with the candelabrum on the wall, lighting three candles, then blowing out two for economy. He admitted presently that he did not want the emotional clarity of Mozart at all, not now. The darkness of 2070 was too close, closer than he had felt it for a long time. It would never have occurred to Mozart, Brian thought, that a world could die. Beethoven could have entertained the idea soberly enough, and Chopin probably; even Brahms. Mozart, Haydn, Bach would surely have dismissed it as somebody's bad dream, in poor taste. Andrew Carr, who lived and died in the latter half of the twentieth century, had endured the idea deep in his bloodstream from the beginning of his childhood.

The date of Hiroshima was 1945; Carr was born in 1951. The wealth of his music was written between 1969, when he was eighteen, and 1984, when he died among the smells of an Egyptian jail from injuries received in a street brawl.

"If not Mozart," said Brian Van Anda to his idle hands, "there is always the Project."

To play Carr's last sonata as it should be played—as Carr was supposed to have said he couldn't play it himself: Brian had been thinking of that as the Project for many years. It had begun teasing his mind long before the war, at the time of his triumphs in a civilized world which had been warmly appreciative of the polished interpretive artist (once he got the breaks) although no more awake than in any other age to the creative sort. Back there in the undestroyed society, Brian had proposed to program that sonata in the company of works that were older but no greater, and to play it—well, beyond his best, so that even music critics would begin to see its importance in history.

He had never done it, had never felt the necessary assurance that he had entered into the sonata and learned the depth of it. Now, when there was none to hear or care, unless the harmless brown spiders in the corners of the auditorium had a taste for music, there was still the Project. *I* hear, Brian thought. *I* care, and with myself for audience I wish to hear it once as it ought to be, a final statement for a world that was (I think) too good to die.

Technically, of course, he had it. The athletic demands Carr made on the performer were tremendous, but, given technique, there was nothing impossible about them. Anyone capable of concert work could at least play the notes at the required tempi. And any reasonably shrewd pianist could keep track of the dynamics, saving strength for the shattering finale. Brian had heard the sonata played by others two or three times in the old days—competently. Competency was not enough.

For example, what about the third movement, the mad scherzo, and the five tiny interludes of quiet scattered through its plunging fury? They were not alike. Related, but each one demanded a new climate of heart and mind—tenderness, regret, simple relaxation. Flowers on a flood—no. Window lights in a storm—no. The innocence of a child in a bombed city—no, not really. Something of all those. Much more, too, defying words.

What of the second movement, the largo, where in a way the pattern was reversed, the midnight introspection interrupted by moments of anger, or longing, or despair like the despair of an angel beating his wings against a prison of glass?

It was a work in which something of Carr's life, Carr's temperament, had to come into you, whether you dared welcome it or not; otherwise your playing was no more than reproduction of notes on a page. Carr's life was not for the contemplation of the timid.

The details were superficially well-known; the biographies were like musical notation, meaningless without interpretation and insight. Carr was a drunken roarer, a young devil-god with such a consuming hunger for life that he choked to death on it. His friends hated him for the way he drained their lives, loving them to distraction and the next moment having no time for them because he loved his work more. His enemies must have had times of helplessly admiring him if only because of a translucent honesty that made him more and less than human. A rugged Australian, not tall but built like a hero, a face all forehead and jaw and glowing hyperthyroid eyes. He wept only when he was angry, the biographic storytellers said. In one minute of talk he might shift from gutter obscenity to some extreme of altruistic tenderness, and from that perhaps to a philosophic comment of cold intelligence. He passed his childhood on a sheep farm, ran away on a freighter at thirteen, was flung out of two respectable conservatories for drunkenness and "public lewdness," then studied like a slave in London with single-minded desperation, as if he knew the time was short. He was married twice and twice divorced. He killed a man in a silly brawl on the New Orleans docks, and wrote his First Symphony while he was in jail for that. He died of stab wounds from a broken bottle in a Cairo jail, and was recognized by the critics. It all had relevancy; relevant or not, if the sonata was in your mind, so was the life.

You had to remember also that Andrew Carr was the last of civilization's great composers. No one in the twenty-first century approached him—they ignored his explorations and carved cherrystones. He belonged to no school, unless you wanted to imagine a school of music beginning with Bach, taking in perhaps a dozen along the way, and ending with Carr himself. His work was a summary as well as an advance along the mainstream into the unknown; in the light of the year 2070, it was also a completion.

Brian was certain he could play the first movement of the sonata as he wished to. Technically it was not revolutionary, and remained rather close to the ancient sonata form. Carr had even written in a double bar for a repeat of the entire opening statement, something that had made his cerebral contemporaries sneer with great satisfaction; it never occurred to them that Carr was inviting the performer to use his head.

The bright-sorrowful second movement, unfashionably long, with its strange pauses, unforeseen recapitulations, outbursts of savage change—that was where Brian's troubles began. ("Reminiscent of Franck," said the hunters for comparisons whom we have always with us.) It did not help Brian to be old, remembering the inner storms of forty years ago and more.

His single candle fluttered. For once Brian had forgotten to lock the door into the Hall of Music. This troubled him, but he did not rise from the piano chair. He chided himself instead for the foolish neuroses of aloneness—what could it matter? Let it go. He shut his eyes. The sonata had long ago been memorized; printed copies were safe in the library. He played the opening of the first movement as far as the double bar, opened his eyes to the friendly black-and-white of clean keys, and played the repetition with new lights, new emphasis. Better than usual, he thought—

Yes. Good. . . . Now that naïve-appearing modulation into A major, which only Carr would have wanted just there in that sudden obvious way, like the opening of a door on shining fields. On toward the climax—*I am playing it, I think*—through the intricate revelations of development and recapitulation. And the conclusion, lingering, half-humorous, not unlike a Beethoven *I'm-not-gone-yet* ending, but with a questioning that was all Andrew Carr. After that—

"No more tonight," said Brian aloud. "Some night, though . . . Not competent right now, my friend." He replaced the cover of the piano and blew out the candle. He had brought no torch, long use having taught his feet every inch of the small journey. It was quite dark. The never-opened western windows of the auditorium were dirty, most of the dirt on the outside, crusted windblown salt.

In this partial darkness something was wrong.

At first Brian found no source for the faint light, dim orange with a hint of motion. He peered into the gloom of the auditorium, fixing his eyes on the oblong of blacker shadow that was the doorway into the Hall of Music. The windows, of course!—he had almost forgotten there were any. The light, hardly deserving the name of light, was coming through them. But sunset was surely past. He had been here a long time, delaying and brooding before he played. Sunset should not flicker.

So there was some kind of fire on the mainland. There had been no thunderstorm. How should fire start, over there where no one ever came?

He stumbled a few times, swearing petulantly, locating the doorway again and groping through it into the Hall of Music. The windows out here were just as dirty; no use trying to see through them. There must have been a time when he had looked through them, enjoyed looking through them. He stood shivering in the marble silence, trying to remember.

Time was a gradual, continual dying. Time was the growth of dirt and ocean salt, sealing in, covering over. He stumbled for his cloakroom cave, hurrying now, and lit two candles. He left one by the cold stove and used the other to light his way down the stairs to his raft; once down there, he blew it out, afraid. The room a candle makes in the darkness is a vulnerable room. Having no walls, it closes in a blindness. He pulled the raft by the guide-rope, gently, for fear of noise.

He found his canoe tied as he had left it. He poked his white head slowly beyond the sill, staring west.

Merely a bonfire gleaming, reddening the blackness of the cliff.

Brian knew the spot, a ledge almost at water level, at one end of it the troublesome path he usually followed in climbing to the forest at the top of the Palisades. Usable driftwood was often there, the supply renewed by the high tides.

"No," Brian said. "Oh, no! . . ."

Unable to accept or believe, or not believe, he drew his head in, resting his forehead on the coldness of the sill, waiting for dizziness to pass, reason to return.

It might have been a long time, a kind of blackout. Now he was again in command of his actions and even rather calm, once more leaning out over the sill. The fire still shone and was therefore not a disordered dream of old age. It was dying to a dull rose of embers.

He wondered about the time. Clocks and watches had stopped long ago; Brian had ceased to want them. A sliver of moon was hanging over the water to the east. He ought to be able to remember the phases, deduce the approximate time from that. But his mind was too tired or distraught to give him the data. Maybe it was somewhere around midnight.

He climbed on the sill and lifted the canoe over it to the motionless water inside. Useless, he decided, as soon as the grunting effort was finished. That fire had been lit before daylight passed; whoever lit it would have seen the canoe, might even have been watching Brian himself come home from his hunting. The canoe's disappearance in the night would only rouse further curiosity. But Brian was too exhausted to lift it back.

And why assume that the maker of the bonfire was necessarily hostile? Might be good company . . . He pulled his raft through the darkness, secured it at the stairway, and groped back to his cave.

He locked the door. The venison was waiting; the sight made him ravenous. He lit a small fire in the stove, one that he hoped would not still be sending smoke from the ventilator shaft when morning came. He cooked the meat crudely and wolfed it down, all enjoyment gone at the first mouthful. He was shocked to discover the dirtiness of his white beard. He hadn't given himself a real bath in—weeks, was it? He searched for scissors and spent an absentminded while in trimming the beard back to shortness. He ought to take some soap—valuable stuff—down to Moses' room, and wash.

Clothes, too. People probably still wore clothes. He had worn none for years, except for sandals. He used a carrying satchel for trips to the mainland. He had enjoyed the freedom at first, and especially the discovery that in his rugged fifties he did not need clothes even for the soft winters, except perhaps a light covering when he slept. Later, total nakedness had become so natural it required no thought at all. But the owner of that bonfire could have inherited or retained the pruderies of the lost culture.

He checked his rifles. The .22 automatic, an Army model from the 2040's, was the best—any amount of death in that. The tiny bullets carried a paralytic poison: graze a man's finger and he was almost painlessly dead in three minutes. Effective range, with telescopic sights, three kilometers; weight, a scant five pounds. Brian sat a long time cuddling that triumph of military science, listening for sounds that never came. Would it be two o'clock? He wished he could have seen the Time Satellite, renamed in his mind the Midnight Star, but when he was down there at his port, he had not once looked up at the night sky. Delicate and beautiful, bearing its everlasting freight of men who must have been dead now for twenty-five years and who would be dead a very long time—well, it was better than a clock, if you happened to look at the midnight sky at the right time of the month when the man-made star caught the moonlight. But he had missed it tonight. Three o'clock? . . .

At some time during the long dark he put the rifle away on the floor. With studied, self-conscious contempt for his own weakness, he unlocked the door and strode out noisily into the Hall of Music, with a fresh-lit candle. This same bravado, he knew, might dissolve at the first alien noise. While it lasted, it was invigorating.

The windows were still black with night. As if the candle flame had found its own way, Brian was standing by the ancient marimba in the main hall, the gleam slanting carelessly away from his gaunt hand. And nearby sat the Stone Age god.

It startled him. He remembered clearly how he himself had placed it there, obeying a half-humorous whim. The image and the singing stones were both magnificently older than history, so why shouldn't they live together? Whenever he dusted the marimba, he dusted the image respectfully, and its table. It would not have needed much urging from the impulses of a lonely mind to make him place offerings before it—winking first, of course, to indicate that rituals suitable to a pair of aging gentlemen did not have to be sensible in order to be good.

The clay face remembering eternity was not deformed by the episode of civilization. Chipped places were simple honorable scars. The two faces stared mildly from the single head, uncommunicative, serene.

A wooden hammer of modern make rested on the marimba. Softly Brian tapped a few of the stones. He struck the shrillest one harder, waking many slow-dying overtones, and laid the hammer down, listening until the last murmur perished and a drop of wax hurt his thumb. He returned to his cave and blew out the candle, never thinking of the door, or if he thought, not caring.

Face down, he rolled his head and clenched his fingers into his pallet, seeking in pain, finding at last the relief of stormy childish weeping in the dark.

Then he slept.

They looked timid. The evidence of it was in their tense squatting pose, not in what the feeble light allowed Brian to see of their faces, which were blank as rock. Hunkered down just inside the doorway of the dim cloakroom cave, a morning grayness from the Hall of Music behind them, they were ready for flight, and Brian's intelligence warned his body to stay motionless. Readiness for flight could also be readiness for attack. He studied them through slit eyelids, knowing he was in deep shadow.

They were very young, sixteen or seventeen, firm-muscled, the boy slim but heavy in the shoulders, the girl a fully developed woman. They were dressed alike: loincloths of some coarse dull fabric, and moccasins that were probably deerhide. Their hair grew nearly to the shoulders and was cut off carelessly, but they were evidently in the habit of combing it. They appeared to be clean. Their complexion, so far as Brian could guess it in the meager light, was brown, like a heavy tan. With no immediate awareness of emotion, he decided they were beautiful, and then within his own poised and perilous silence Brian reminded himself that the young are always beautiful.

The woman muttered softly: "He wake."

A twitch of the man's head was probably meant to warn her to be quiet. He clutched the shaft of a javelin with a metal blade which had once belonged to a breadknife. The blade was polished, shining, lashed to a peeled stick. The javelin trailed, ready for use at a flick of the young man's arm. Brian sighed deliberately. "Good morning."

The man, or boy, said: "Good morning, sa."

"Where do you come from?"

"Millstone." The man spoke automatically, but then his facial rigidity dissolved into astonishment and some kind of distress. He glanced at his companion, who giggled uneasily.

"The old man pretends to not know," she said, and smiled, and seemed to be waiting for the young man's permission to go on speaking. He did not give it, but she continued: "Sa, the old ones of Millstone are dead." She thrust her hand out and down, flat, a picture of finality, adding with nervous haste: "As the Old Man knows. He who told us to call him Jonas, she who told us to call her Abigail, dead. They are still-without-moving the full six days, then we do the burial as they told us. As the Old Man knows."

"But I don't know!" said Brian, and sat up on his pallet too quickly, startling them. But their motion was backward, a readying for flight. "Millstone? Where is Millstone?"

They looked wholly bewildered and dismayed. They stood up with animal grace, stepping backward out of the cave, the girl whispering in the man's ear. Brian caught two words: "—is angry."

He jumped up. "Don't go! Please don't go!" He followed them out of the cave, slowly now, aware that he might be an object of terror in the half-dark, aware of his gaunt, graceless age, and nakedness, and dirty hacked-off beard. Almost involuntarily he adopted something of the flat stilted quality of their speech. "I will not hurt you. Do not go."

They halted. The girl smiled dubiously. The man said: "We need old ones. They die. He who told us to call him Jonas said, many days in the boat, not with the sun-path, he said, across the sun-path, he said, keeping land on the left hand. We need old ones, to speak the—to speak . . . The Old Man is angry?"

"No. I am not angry. I am never angry." Brian's mind groped, certain of nothing. No one came, for twenty-five years.

Millstone?

There was red-gold on the dirty eastern windows of the Hall of Music, a light becoming softness as it slanted down, touching the long rows of cases, the warm brown of an antique spinet, the clean gold of a twentieth century harp, the gray of singing stones five thousand years old and a two-faced god much older than that. "Millstone." Brian pointed in inquiry, southwest.

The girl nodded, pleased and not at all surprised that he should know, watching him now with a squirrel's stiff curiosity. Hadn't there been a Millstone River in or near Princeton, once upon a time? Brian thought he remembered that it emptied into the Raritan Canal. There was some moderately high ground there. Islands now, no doubt. Perhaps they would tell him. "There were old people in Millstone," he said, trying for peaceful dignity, "and they died. So now you need old ones to take their place."

The girl nodded vigorously many times. Her glance at the young man was shy, possessive, maybe amused. "He who told us to call him Jonas said no marriage without the words of Abraham."

"Abr—" Brian checked himself. If this was religion, it would not do to speak the name Abraham with a rising inflection. "I have been for a long time—" He checked himself again: A man old, ugly, and strange enough to be sacred should never stoop to explain anything.

They were standing by the seven-stone marimba. His hand dropped, his thumbnail clicking against the deepest stone and waking a murmur. The children drew back, alarmed. Brian smiled. "Don't be afraid." He tapped the other stones lightly. "It is only music. It will not hurt you." They were patient and respectful, waiting for more light. He said carefully: "He who told you to call him Jonas—he taught you all the things you know?"

"All things," the boy said, and the girl nodded three or four times, so that the soft brownness of her hair tumbled about her face, and she pushed it back in a small human motion as old as the clay image.

"Do you know how old you are?"

They looked blank. Then the girl said: "Oh—summers!" She held up her two hands with spread fingers, then one hand. "Three fives." She chuckled, and sobered quickly. "As the Old Man knows."

"I am very old," said Brian. "I know many things, but sometimes I wish to forget, and sometimes I wish to hear what others know, even though I may know it myself."

They looked uncomprehending and greatly impressed. Brian felt a smile on his face and wondered why it should be there. They were nice children. Born ten years after the death of a world; twenty, perhaps. *I think I am seventy-six, but what if I dropped a decade somewhere and never noticed the damned thing . . . ?* "He who told you to call him Jonas—he taught you all you know of Abraham?"

At the sound of the name, both made swift circular motions, first at the forehead, then at the breast. "He taught us all things," the young man said. "He, and she who told us to call her Abigail. The hours to rise, to pray, to wash, to eat. The laws for hunting, and I know the Abraham-words for that: Sol-Amra, I take this for my need."

Brian felt lost again, and looked down to the clay faces of the image for counsel, and found none. "They who told you to call them Jonas and Abigail, they were the only ones who lived with you?—the only old ones?"

Again that look of bewilderment and disappointment. "The only ones, sa," the young man said. "As the Old Man knows."

I could never persuade them that, being old, I know very nearly nothing. . . .

Brian straightened to his full great height. The young people were not tall. Though stiff and worn with age, Brian knew he was still overpowering. Once, among men, he had gently enjoyed being more than life-size. As a shield for loneliness and fright within, he now adopted a phony sternness. "I wish to examine you for your own good, my children, about Millstone and your knowledge of Abraham. How many others live at Millstone, tell me."

"Two fives, sa," said the boy promptly, "and I the one who may be called Jonason and this girl who may be called Paula. Two fives and two. We are the biggest. The others are only children, but the one who may be called Jimi has killed his deer; he sees after them now while we go across the sun-path."

Under Brian's questioning, more of the story came, haltingly, obscured by the young man's conviction that the Old Man already knew everything. Sometime, probably in the middle 2080's, Jonas and Abigail (whoever they were) had come on a group of twelve wild children who were keeping alive somehow in a ruined town where their elders had all died. Jonas and Abigail had brought them all to an island they called Millstone. Jonas and Abigail came originally from "up across the sun-path"—the boy seemed to mean north—and they were very old, which might mean, Brian guessed, anything between thirty and ninety. In teaching the children primitive means of survival, Jonas and Abigail had brought off a brilliant success: Jonason and Paula were well-fed, shining with health and the strength of wildness, and clean. Their speech, limited and odd though it was, had not been learned from the ignorant. Its pronunciation faintly suggested New England, so far as it had any local accent. "Did they teach you reading and writing?" Brian asked, and made writing motions on the flat of his palm, which the two watched in vague alarm.

The boy asked: "What is that?"

"Never mind." *I could quarrel with some of your theories, Mister-whom-I-may-call-Jonas*. But maybe, he thought, there had been no books, no writing materials, no way to get them. What's the minimum of technology required to keep the human spirit alive? . . . "Well—well, tell me what they taught you of Abraham. I wish to hear how well you remember."

Both made again the circular motion at forehead and breast, and the young man said with the stiffness of recitation: "Abraham was the Son of Heaven who died that we might live." The girl, her obligation discharged with the religious gesture, tapped the marimba shyly, fascinated, and drew her finger back, smiling up at Brian in apology for naughtiness. "He taught the laws, the everlasting truth of all time," the boy gabbled, "and was slain on the wheel at Nuber by the infidels; therefore since he died for us, we look up across the sun-path when we pray to Abraham Brown who will come again." The boy Jonason sighed and relaxed.

Abraham—Brown? But—

But I knew him. I met him. Nuber? Newburg, temporary capital of the Soviet of—oh, damn that . . . Met him, 2071—the concert of mine he remembered . . . The wheel? The wheel? "And when did Abraham die, boy?"

"Oh—" Jonason moved fingers helplessly, embarrassed. Dates would be no part of the doctrine. "Long ago. A—a—" He glanced up hopefully. "A thousand years? I think—he who told us to call him Jonas did not teach us that."

"I see. Never mind. You speak well, boy." *Oh, my good Doctor, ex-President—after all! Artist, statesman, student of ethics, agnostic philosopher—all that long life you preached charity and skepticism, courage without the need of faith, the positive uses of the suspended judgment. All so clear, simple, obvious—needing only that little bit more of patience and courage which your human hearers were not ready to give. You must have known they were not, but did you know this would happen?*

Jonas and Abigail—some visionary pair, Brian supposed, full of this theory and that, maybe gone a bit foolish under the horrors of those years. Unthinking admirers of Brown, or perhaps not even that, perhaps just brewing their own syncretism because they thought a religion was needed, and using Brown's name—why? Because it was easy to remember? They probably felt some pride of creation in the job; possibly belief even grew in their own minds as they found the children accepting it and building a ritual life around it.

It was impossible, Brian thought, that Jonas and Abigail could have met the living Abraham Brown. Brown accepted mysteries because he faced the limitations of human intelligence; he had only contempt for the needless making of mysteries. He was without arrogance. No one could have talked five minutes with him without hearing a tranquil: "I don't know."

The *wheel* at Nuber?—but Brian realized he would never learn how Brown actually died. *I hope you suffered no more than most prophets. . . .*

He was pulled from the pit of abstraction by the girl's awed question: "What is that?"

She was pointing to the clay image in its dusty sunlight. Brian was almost deaf to his own words until they were past recovering: "Oh, that—that is very old. Very old and very sacred." She nodded, round-eyed, and stepped back a pace or two. "And that was all they taught you of Abraham Brown?"

Astonished, the boy asked: "Is it not enough?"

There is always the Project. "Why, perhaps—"

"We know all the prayers, Old Man."

"Yes, yes, I'm sure you do."

"The Old Man will come with us." It was not a question.

"Eh?" *There is always the Project . . .* "Come with you?"

"We look for old ones." There was a new note in the young man's fine firm voice, and it was impatience. "We traveled many days, up across the sun-path. We want you to speak the Abraham-words for marriage. The old ones said we must not mate as the animals do without the words. We want—"

"Marry, of course," Brian grumbled. *Poor old Jonas and Abigail, faithful to your century, such as it was*! Brian felt tired and confused, and rubbed a great long-fingered hand across his face so that the words might have come out blurred and dull. "Naturally, kids. Beget. Replenish the earth. I'm damned tired. I don't know any special hocus-pocus—I mean, any Abraham-words—for marriage. Just go ahead and breed. Try again—"

"But the Old Ones said—"

"Wait!" Brian cried. "Wait! Let me think . . . Did he—he who told you to call him Jonas—did he teach you anything about the world as it was in the old days, before you were born?"

"Before—the Old Man makes fun of us."

"No, no." Since he now had to fight down a certain physical fear as well as confusion, Brian spoke more harshly than he intended: "Answer my question! What do you know of the old days? I was a young man once, do you understand that?—as young as you. What do you know about the world I lived in?"

The young man laughed. There was new-born suspicion in him as well as anger, stiffening his shoulders, narrowing his innocent gray eyes. "There was always the world," he said, "ever since God made it a thousand years ago."

"Was there? . . . I was a musician. Do you know what a musician is?"

The young man shook his head lightly, watching Brian, too alertly, watching his hands, aware of him in a new way, no longer humble. Paula sensed the tension and did not like it. She said worriedly, politely: "We forget some of the things they taught us, sa. They were Old Ones. Most of the days they were away from us in places where we were not to go, praying. Old Ones are always praying."

"I will hear this Old Man pray," said Jonason. The butt of the javelin rested against Jonason's foot, the blade swaying from side to side, a waiting snake's head. A misstep, a wrong word—any trifle, Brian knew, could make them decide he was evil and not sacred. Their religion would inevitably require a devil.

He thought also: *It would merely be one of the ways of dying, not the worst.*

"You shall hear me make music," he said sternly, "and you shall be content with that. Come this way!" In fluctuating despair, he was wondering if any good might come of anger. "Come this way! You shall hear a world you never knew."

Naked and ugly, he stalked across the Hall of Music, not looking behind him, though he sensed every glint of light from that bread-knife javelin. "This way!" he shouted. "Come in here!" He flung open the door of the auditorium and strode up on the platform. "Sit down!" he roared at them. "Sit down over there and be quiet, be quiet!"

He thought they did—he could not look at them. He knew he was muttering between his noisy outbursts as he twitched the cover off the piano and raised the lid, muttering bits and fragments from the old times and the new: "They went thataway. . . . Oh, Mr. Van Anda, it just simply goes right through me—I can't express it. Madam, such was my intention, or as Brahms is supposed to have said on a slightly different subject, any ass knows that. . . . Brio, Rubato, and Schmalz went to sea in a—Jonason, Paula, this is a pianoforte; it will not hurt you. Sit there, be quiet, and I pray you listen. . . ."

He found calm. *Now, if ever, when there is living proof that human nature, some sort of human nature, is continuing—now if ever, the Project—*

With the sudden authority that was natural to Andrew Carr, Andrew Carr took over. In the stupendous opening chords of the introduction, Brian very nearly forgot his audience. Not quite. The children had sat down out there in the dusty region where none but ghosts had lingered for twenty-five years, but the piano's first sound brought them to their feet. Brian played through the first four bars, piling the chords like mountains, then held the last one with the pedal and waved his right hand at Jonason and Paula in a furious downward motion.

He thought they understood. He thought he saw them sit down again. But he could pay them no more attention, for the sonata was coming alive under his fingers, waking, growing, rejoicing.

He did not forget the children. They were important, too important, terrifying at the fringe of awareness. But he could not look toward them any more, and presently he shut his eyes.

He had never played like this in the flood of his prime, in the old days, before audiences that loved him. Never.

His eyes were still closed, holding him secure in a world that was not all darkness, when he ended the first movement, paused very briefly, and moved on with complete assurance to explore the depth and height of the second. This was true statement. This was Andrew Carr; he lived, even if after this late morning he might never live again.

And now the third, the storm and the wrath, the interludes of calm, the anger, denials, affirmations . . .

Without hesitation, without awareness of self, of age or pain or danger or loss, Brian was entering on the broad reaches of the last movement when he glanced out into the auditorium and understood the children were gone.

Too big. It had frightened them away. He could visualize them, stealing out with backward looks of panic, and remembering apparently to close the exit door. To them it was incomprehensible thunder. Children—savages—to see or hear or comprehend the beautiful, you must first desire it. he could not think much about them now, when Andrew Carr was still with him. He played on with the same assurance, the same sense of victory. Children and savages, so let them go, with leave and goodwill.

Some external sound troubled him, something that must have begun under cover of these rising, pealing octave passages—storm waves, each higher than the last, until even the superhuman swimmer must be exhausted. It was some indefinable alien noise, a humming. Wind perhaps. Brian shook his head in irritation, not interrupting the work of his hands. It couldn't matter—everything was here, in the labors his hands still had to perform. The waves were growing more quiet, subsiding, and he must play the curious arpeggios he had never quite understood—but for this interpretation he understood them. Rip them out of the piano like showers of sparks, like distant lightning moving farther and farther away across a world that could never be at rest.

The final section at last. Why, it was a variation—and why had he never quite recognized it?—on a theme of Brahms, from the German Requiem. Quite plain, simple—Brahms would have approved. *Blessed are the dead* . . . Something more remained to be said, and Brian searched for it through the mighty unfolding of the finale. No hurrying, no crashing impatience any more, but a moving through time without fear of time, through radiance and darkness with no fear of either. *That they may rest from their labors, and their works do follow after them.*

Brian stood up, swaying and out of breath. So the music was over, and the children were gone, but a jangling, humming confusion was filling the Hall of Music out there—hardly a wind—distant but entering with some violence even here, now that the piano was silent. He moved stiffly out of the small auditorium, more or less knowing what he would find.

The noise became immense, the unchecked overtones of the marimba fuming and quivering as the smooth, high ceiling of the Hall of Music caught them and flung them about against the answering strings of pianos and harps and violins, the sulky membranes of drums, the nervous brass of cymbals.

The girl was playing it. Brian laughed once, softly, in the shadows, and was not heard. She had hit on a primeval rhythm natural for children or savages and needed nothing else, banging it out on one stone and another, wanting no rest or variation.

The boy was dancing, slapping his feet and pounding his chest, thrusting out his javelin in time to the clamor, edging up to his companion, grimacing, drawing back in order to return. Neither one was laughing, or close to laughter. Their faces were savage-solemn, grim with the excitement and healthy lust. All as spontaneous as the drumming of partridges. It was a long time before they saw Brian in the shadows.

Reaction was swift. The girl dropped the hammer. The boy froze, his javelin raised, then jerked his head at Paula, who snatched at something—only moments later did Brian understand she had taken the clay image before she fled.

Jonason covered her retreat, stepping backward, his face blank and dangerous with fear. So swiftly, so easily, by grace of great civilized music and a few wrong words, had a sacred Old One become a Bad Old One.

They were gone, down the stairway, leaving the echo of Brian's voice crying: "Don't go! Please don't go!"

Brian followed them. Unwillingly. He was slow to reach the bottom of the stairway; there he looked across the shut-in water to his raft, which they had used and left at the windowsill port. Brian had never been a good swimmer, and would not attempt it now, but clutched the rope and hitched himself hand over hand to the windowsill, collapsing awhile until he found strength to scramble into his canoe and grope for the paddle.

The children's canoe was already far off. Heading up the river, the boy paddling with deep powerful strokes. Up the river, of course. They had to find the right kind of Old Ones. Up across the sun-path.

Brian dug his blade in the quiet water. For a time his rugged, ancient muscles were willing. There was sap in them yet. Perhaps he was gaining. He shouted hugely: "Bring back my two-faced god! And what about my music? You? Did you like it? Speak up!"

They must have heard his voice booming at them. At least the girl looked back, once. The boy, intent on his paddling, did not. Brian roared: "Bring back my little god!"

He was not gaining on them. After all they had a mission. They had to find an Old One with the right Abraham-words. Brian thought: *Damn it, hasn't MY world some rights? We'll see about this!*

He lifted his paddle like a spear, and flung it, knowing even as his shoulder winced with the backlash of the thrust that his action was at the outer limit of absurdity. The children were so far away that even an arrow from a bow might not have reached them. The paddle splashed in the water. Not far away. A small infinity.

It swung about, adjusting to the current, the heavy end pointing downstream, obeying the river and the ebb tide. It nuzzled companionably against a gray-faced chunk of driftwood, diverting it, so that presently the chunk floated into Brian's reach. He flung it back toward the paddle, hoping it might fall on the other side and send the paddle near him, but it fell short. In his unexpectedly painless extremity Brian was not surprised, but merely watched the gray face floating and bobbing along beside him out of reach, and his irritation became partly friendliness. The driftwood fragment suggested the face of a music critic he had once met—New Boston, was it? Denver? London?—no matter.

"Why," he said aloud, detachedly observing the passage of his canoe beyond the broad morning shadow of the Museum, "why, I seem to have killed myself."

"Mr. Van Anda has abundantly demonstrated a mastery of the instrument and of the"—*Oh, go play solfeggio on your linotype!*—"literature of both classic and contemporary repertory. While we cannot endorse the perhaps overemotional quality of his Bach, and there might easily be two views of his handling of the passage in double thirds which—"

"I can't swim it, you know," said Brian. "Not against the ebb, that's for sure."

"—so that on the whole one feels he has earned himself a not discreditable place among—" Gaining on the canoe, passing it, the gray-faced chip moved on benignly twittering toward the open sea, where the canoe must follow. With a final remnant of strength Brian inched forward to the bow and gathered the full force of his lungs to shout up the river to the children: "Go in peace!"

They could not have heard him. They were too far away, and a new morning wind was blowing, fresh and sweet, out of the northwest.

H. G. Wells

H. G. Wells (1866–1946) is the Shakespeare of science fiction: not the first SF writer but, thus far, the best. H. G. Wells is simply the most important writer to influence—both directly, through his works, and indirectly, through the other major writers in his tradition—the course of science fiction in its formative decades. His influence transformed, in the long run, all later science fiction, and his shadow grows longer as the century ends.

The implications of Darwinian evolution and social criticism are the major themes of his works and his principal novels, *The Time Machine* (1895), *The Island of Dr. Moreau* (1896), *The Invisible Man* (1897), *The War of the Worlds* (1898), *When the Sleeper Wakes* (1899), and *The First Men in the Moon* (1901), as well as five collections of short stories later combined as *The Short Stories of H. G. Wells* (1927). A popular and influential intellectual throughout the first half of the twentieth century, he was devoted to the idea of progress. He became arguably the most famous living writer in the English language, but at the cost of his literary reputation as a modernist artist, which he ceded to Henry James after years of argument, in favor of bestseller popularity.

Although Wells lived until 1946, he was never personally associated with genre science fiction; nonetheless, many of his stories were reprinted in the early years of *Amazing Stories* as paradigms of the new kind of fiction that editor Hugo Gernsback wished to bring forth. Wells called himself a Scientific Romancer early in his career, and his fiction was certainly the pinnacle of that genre that preceded science fiction and existed parallel to it into the 1940s in the works of Olaf Stapledon, Aldous Huxley, Evgeny Zamiatin, Karel Čapek, and George Orwell (to name only the five most important writers influenced by Wells's early works).

Kingsley Amis, in his literate, opinionated, and now somewhat neglected study of science fiction, *New Maps of Hell* (1960), comments on the (quite surprising) virtual exclusion of some of Wells's work from the SF canon, including "A Story of the Days to Come," which Amis calls "an early and lively piece . . . it forecasts the modern satirical utopia with fantastic exactness." He summarizes the many accurate prophecies of the story, concluding that "quite likely Wells will soon get all, instead of part, of the recognition as a pioneer he clearly deserves."

"A Story of the Days to Come" is actually a kind of compressed novel by Wells, and yields many unexpected pleasures. Zamiatin calls it "the sharpest, most ironic of Wells's grotesques." It is the story of two young lovers who reject the technological future for pastoral bliss, and learn better.

A STORY OF THE DAYS TO COME

I. THE CURE FOR LOVE

The excellent Mr. Morris was an Englishman, and he lived in the days of Queen Victoria the Good. He was a prosperous and very sensible man; he read *The Times* and went to church, and as he grew towards middle age an expression of quiet contented contempt for all who were not as himself settled on his face. He was one of those people who do everything that is right and proper and sensible with inevitable regularity. He always wore just the right and proper clothes, steering the narrow way between the smart and the shabby, always subscribed to the right charities, just the judicious compromise between ostentation and meanness, and never failed to have his hair cut to exactly the proper length.

Everything that it was right and proper for a man in his position to possess, he possessed; and everything that it was not right and proper for a man in his position to possess, he did not possess.

And among other right and proper possessions, this Mr. Morris had a wife and children. They were the right sort of wife, and the right sort and number of children, of course; nothing imaginative or highty-flighty about any of them, so far as Mr. Morris could see; they wore perfectly correct clothing, neither smart nor hygienic nor faddy in any way, but just sensible; and they lived in a nice sensible house in the later Victorian sham Queen Anne style of architecture, with sham half-timbering of chocolate-painted plaster in the gables, Lincrusta Walton sham carved oakpanels, a terrace of terra cotta to imitate stone, and cathedral glass in the front door. His boys went to good solid schools, and were put to respectable professions; his girls, in spite of a fantastic protest or so, were all married to suitable, steady, oldish young men with good prospects. And when it was a fit and proper thing for him to do so, Mr. Morris died. His tomb was of marble, and, without any art nonsense or laudatory inscription, quietly imposing—such being the fashion of his time.

He underwent various changes according to the accepted custom in these cases, and long before this story begins his bones even had become dust, and were scattered to the four quarters of heaven. And his sons and his grandsons and his great-grandsons and great-great-grandsons, they too were dust and ashes, and were scattered likewise. It was a thing he could not have imagined, that a day would come when even his great-great-grandsons would be scattered to the four winds of heaven. If any one had suggested it to him he would have resented it. He was one of those worthy people who take no interest in the future of mankind at all. He had grave doubts, indeed, if there was any future for mankind after he was dead.

It seemed quite impossible and quite uninteresting to imagine anything happening after he was dead. Yet the thing was so, and when even his great-great-grandson was dead and decayed and forgotten, when the sham half-timbered house had gone the way of all shams, and *The Times* was extinct, and the silk hat a ridiculous antiquity, and the modestly imposing stone that had been sacred to Mr. Morris had been burnt to make lime for mortar, and all that Mr. Morris had found real and important was sere and dead, the world was still going on, and people were still going about it, just as heedless and impatient of the Future, or, indeed, of anything but their own selves and property, as Mr. Morris had been.

And, strange to tell, and much as Mr. Morris would have been angered if any one had foreshadowed it to him, all over the world there were scattered a multitude of people, filled with the breath of life, in whose veins the blood of Mr. Morris flowed. Just as some day the life which is gathered now in the reader of this very story may also be scattered far and wide about this world, and mingled with a thousand alien strains, beyond all thought and tracing.

And among the descendants of this Mr. Morris was one almost as sensible and clear-headed as his ancestor. He had just the same stout, short frame as that ancient man of the nineteenth century, from whom his name of Morris—he spelt it Mwres—came; he had the same half-contemptuous expression of face. He was a prosperous person, too, as times went, and he disliked the "newfangled," and bothers about the future and the lower classes, just as much as the ancestral Morris had done. He did not read *The Times*: indeed, he did not know there ever had been a *Times*—that institution had foundered somewhere in the intervening gulf of years; but the phonograph machine, that talked to him as he made his toilet of a morning, might have been the voice of a reincarnated Blowitz when it dealt with the world's affairs. This phonographic machine was the size and shape of a Dutch clock, and down the front of it were electric barometric indicators, and an electric clock and calendar, and automatic engagement reminders, and where the clock would have been was the mouth of a trumpet. When it had news the trumpet gobbled like a turkey, "Galloop, galloop," and then brayed out its message as, let us say, a trumpet might bray. It would tell Mwres in full, rich, throaty tones about the overnight accidents to the omnibus flying-machines that plied around the world, the latest arrivals at the fashionable resorts in Tibet, and of all the great monopolist company meetings of the day before, while he was dressing. If Mwres did not like hearing what it said, he had only to touch a stud, and it would choke a little and talk about something else.

Of course his toilet differed very much from that of his ancestor. It is doubtful which would have been the more shocked and pained to find himself in the clothing of the other. Mwres would certainly have sooner gone forth to the world stark naked than in the silk hat, frock coat, grey trousers and watch-chain that had filled Mr. Morris with sombre self-respect in the past. For Mwres there was no shaving to do: a skilful operator had long ago removed every hair-root from his face. His legs he encased in pleasant pink and amber garments of an airtight material, which with the help of an ingenious little pump he distended so as to suggest enormous muscles. Above this he also wore pneumatic garments beneath an amber silk tunic, so that he was clothed in air and admirably protected against sudden extremes of heat or cold. Over this he flung a scarlet cloak with its edge fantastically curved. On his head, which had been skilfully deprived of every scrap of hair, he adjusted a pleasant little cap of bright scarlet, held on by suction and inflated with hydrogen, and curiously like the comb of a cock. So his toilet was complete; and, conscious of being soberly and becomingly attired, he was ready to face his fellow-beings with a tranquil eye.

This Mwres—the civility of "Mr." had vanished ages ago—was one of the officials under the Wind Vane and Waterfall Trust, the great company that owned every wind wheel and waterfall in the world, and which pumped all the water and supplied all the electric energy that people in these latter days required. He lived in a vast hotel near that part of London called Seventh Way, and had very large and comfortable apartments on the seventeenth floor. Households and family life had long since disappeared with the progressive refinement of manners; and indeed the steady rise in rents and land values, the disappearance of domestic servants, the elaboration of cookery, had rendered the separate domicile of Victorian times impossible, even had any one desired such a savage seclusion. When his toilet was completed he went towards one of the two doors of his apartment—there were doors at opposite ends, each marked with a huge arrow pointing one one way and one the other—touched a stud to open it, and emerged on a wide passage, the centre of which bore chairs and was moving at a steady pace to the left. On some of these chairs were seated gaily-dressed men and women. He nodded to an acquaintance—it was not in those days etiquette to talk before breakfast—and seated himself on one of these chairs, and in a few seconds he had been carried to the doors of a lift, by which he descended to the great and splendid hall in which his breakfast would be automatically served.

It was a very different meal from a Victorian breakfast. The rude masses of bread needing to be carved and smeared over with animal fat before they could be made palatable, the still recognisable fragments of recently killed animals, hideously charred and hacked, the eggs torn ruthlessly from beneath some protesting hen,—such things as these, though they constituted the ordinary fare of Victorian times, would have awakened only horror and disgust in the refined minds of the people of these latter days. Instead were pastes and cakes of agreeable and variegated design, without any suggestion in colour or form of the unfortunate animals from which their substance and juices were derived. They appeared on little dishes sliding out upon a rail from a little box at one side of the table. The surface of the table, to judge by touch and eye, would have appeared to a nineteenth-century person to be covered with fine white damask, but this was really an oxidised metallic surface, and could be cleaned instantly after a meal. There were hundreds of such little tables in the hall, and at most of them were other latter-day citizens singly or in groups. And as Mwres seated himself before his elegant repast, the invisible orchestra, which had been resting during an interval, resumed and filled the air with music.

But Mwres did not display any great interest either in his breakfast or the music; his eye wandered incessantly about the hall, as though he expected a belated guest. At last he rose eagerly and waved his hand, and simultaneously across the hall appeared a tall dark figure in a costume of yellow and olive green. As this person, walking amidst the tables with measured steps, drew near, the pallid earnestness of his face and the unusual intensity of his eyes became apparent. Mwres reseated himself and pointed to a chair beside him.

"I feared you would never come," he said. In spite of the intervening space of time, the English language was still almost exactly the same as it had been in England under Victoria the Good. The invention of the phonograph and such like means of recording sound, and the gradual replacement of books by such contrivances, had not only saved the human eyesight from decay, but had also by the establishment of a sure standard arrested the process of change in accent that had hitherto been so inevitable.

"I was delayed by an interesting case," said the man in green and yellow. "A prominent politician—ahem!—suffering from overwork." He glanced at the breakfast and seated himself. "I have been awake for forty hours."

"Eh dear!" said Mwres: "fancy that! You hypnotists have your work to do."

The hypnotist helped himself to some attractive amber-coloured jelly. "I happen to be a good deal in request," he said modestly.

"Heaven knows what we should do without you."

"Oh! we're not so indispensable as all that," said the hypnotist, ruminating the flavour of the jelly. "The world did very well without us for some thousands of years. Two hundred years ago even—not one! In practice, that is. Physicians by the thousand, of course—frightfully clumsy brutes for the most part, and following one another like sheep—but doctors of the mind except a few empirical flounderers there were none."

He concentrated his mind on the jelly.

"But were people so sane—?" began Mwres.

The hypnotist shook his head. "It didn't matter then if they were a bit silly or faddy. Life was so easy-going then. No competition worth speaking of—no pressure. A human being had to be very lopsided before anything happened. Then, you know, they clapped 'em away in what they called a lunatic asylum."

"I know," said Mwres. "In these confounded historical romances that every one is listening to, they always rescue a beautiful girl from an asylum or something of the sort. I don't know if you attend to that rubbish."

"I must confess I do," said the hypnotist. "It carries one out of oneself to hear of those quaint, adventurous, half-civilised days of the nineteenth century, when men were stout and women simple. I like a good swaggering story before all things. Curious times they were, with their smutty railways and puffing old iron trains, their rum little houses and their horse vehicles. I suppose you don't read books?"

"Dear, no!" said Mwres. "I went to a modern school and we had none of that old-fashioned nonsense. Phonographs are good enough for me."

"Of course," said the hypnotist, "of course"; and surveyed the table for his next choice. "You know," he said, helping himself to a dark blue confection that promised well, "in those days our business was scarcely thought of. I daresay if any one had told them that in two hundred years' time a class of men would be entirely occupied in impressing things upon the memory, effacing unpleasant ideas, controlling and overcoming instinctive but undesirable impulses, and so forth, by means of hypnotism, they would have refused to believe the thing possible. Few people knew that an order made during a mesmeric trance, even an order to forget or an order to desire, could be given so as to be obeyed after the trance was over. Yet there were men alive then who could have told them the thing was as absolutely certain to come about as—well, the transit of Venus."

"They knew of hypnotism, then?"

"Oh, dear, yes! They used it—for painless dentistry and things like that! This blue stuff is confoundedly good: what is it?"

"Haven't the faintest idea," said Mwres, "but I admit it's very good. Take some more."

The hypnotist repeated his praises, and there was an appreciative pause.

"Speaking of these historical romances," said Mwres, with an attempt at an easy, off-hand manner, "brings me—ah—to the matter I—ah—had in mind when I asked you—when I expressed a wish to see you." He paused and took a deep breath.

The hypnotist turned an attentive eye upon him, and continued eating.

"The fact is," said Mwres, "I have a—in fact a—daughter. Well, you know I have given her—ah—every educational advantage. Lectures—not a solitary lecturer of ability in the world but she has had a telephone direct, dancing, deportment, conversation, philosophy, art criticism. . . ." He indicated catholic culture by a gesture of his hand. "I had intended her to marry a very good friend of mine—Bindon of the Lighting Commission—plain little man, you know, and a bit unpleasant in some of his ways, but an excellent fellow really—an excellent fellow."

"Yes," said the hypnotist, "go on. How old is she?"

"Eighteen."

"A dangerous age. Well?"

"Well: it seems that she has been indulging in these historical romances—excessively. Excessively. Even to the neglect of her philosophy. Filled her mind with unutterable nonsense about soldiers who fight—what is it?—Etruscans?"

"Egyptians."

"Egyptians—very probably. Hack about with swords and revolvers and things—blood-shed galore—horrible!—and about young men on torpedo catchers who blow up—Spaniards, I fancy—and all sorts of irregular adventurers. And she has got it into her head that she must marry for Love, and that poor little Bindon—"

"I've met similar cases," said the hypnotist. "Who is the other young man?"

Mwres maintained an appearance of resigned calm. "You may well ask," he said. "He is"—and his voice sank with shame—"a mere attendant upon the stage on which the flying-machines from Paris alight. He has—as they say in the romances—good looks. He is quite young and very eccentric. Affects the antique—he can read and write! So can she. And instead of communicating by telephone, like sensible people, they write and deliver—what is it?"

"Notes?"

"No—not notes. . . . Ah—poems."

The hypnotist raised his eyebrows. "How did she meet him?"

"Tripped coming down from the flying-machine from Paris—and fell into his arms. The mischief was done in a moment!"

"Yes?"

"Well—that's all. Things must be stopped. That is what I want to consult you about. What must be done? What *can* be done? Of course I'm not a hypnotist; my knowledge is limited. But you—?"

"Hypnotism is not magic," said the man in green, putting both arms on the table.

"Oh, precisely! But still—!"

"People cannot be hypnotised without their consent. If she is able to stand out against marrying Bindon, she will probably stand out against being hypnotised. But if once she can be hypnotised—even by somebody else—the thing is done."

"You can—?"

"Oh, certainly! Once we get her amenable, then we can suggest that she *must* marry Bindon—that that is her fate; or that the young man is repulsive, and that when she sees him she will be giddy and faint, or any little thing of that sort. Or if we can get her into a sufficiently profound trance we can suggest that she should forget him altogether—"

"Precisely."

"But the problem is to get her hypnotised. Of course no sort of proposal or suggestion must come from you—because no doubt she already distrusts you in the matter."

The hypnotist leant his head upon his arm and thought.

"It's hard a man cannot dispose of his own daughter," said Mwres irrelevantly.

"You must give me the name and address of the young lady," said the hypnotist, "and any information bearing upon the matter. And, by the bye, is there any money in the affair?"

Mwres hesitated.

"There's a sum—in fact, a considerable sum—invested in the Patent Road Company. From her mother. That's what makes the thing so exasperating."

"Exactly," said the hypnotist. And he proceeded to cross-examine Mwres on the entire affair.

It was a lengthy interview.

And meanwhile "Elizebeθ Mwres," as she spelt her name or "Elizabeth Morris," as a nineteenth-century person would have put it, was sitting in a quiet waiting-place beneath the great stage upon which the flying-machine from Paris descended. And beside her sat her slender, handsome lover reading her the poem he had written that morning while on duty upon the stage. When he had finished they sat for a time in silence; and then, as if for their special entertainment, the great machine that had come flying through the air from America that morning rushed down out of the sky.

At first it was a little oblong, faint and blue amidst the distant fleecy clouds; and then it grew swiftly large and white, and larger and whiter, until they could see the separate tiers of sails, each hundreds of feet wide, and the lank body they supported, and at last even the swinging seats of the passengers in a dotted row. Although it was falling it seemed to them to be rushing up the sky, and over the roof-spaces of the city below its shadow leapt towards them. They heard the whistling rush of the air about it and its yelling siren, shrill and swelling, to warn those who were on its landing-stage of its arrival. And abruptly the note fell down a couple of octaves, and it had passed, and the sky was clear and void, and she could turn her sweet eyes again to Denton at her side.

Their silence ended; and Denton, speaking in a little language of broken English that was, they fancied, their private possession—though lovers have used such little languages since the world began—told her how they too would leap into the air one morning out of all the obstacles and difficulties about them, and fly to a sunlit city of delight he knew of in Japan, half-way about the world.

She loved the dream, but she feared the leap; and she put him off with "Some day, dearest one, some day," to all his pleading that it might be soon; and at last came a shrilling of whistles, and it was time for him to go back to his duties on the stage. They parted—as lovers have been wont to part for thousands of years. She walked down a passage to a lift, and so came to one of the streets of that latter-day London, all glazed in with glass from the weather, and with incessant moving platforms that went to all parts of the city. And by one of these she returned to her apartments in the Hotel for Women where she lived, the apartments that were in telephonic communication with all the best lecturers in the world. But the sunlight of the flying stage was in her heart, and the wisdom of all the best lecturers in the world seemed folly in that light.

She spent the middle part of the day in the gymnasium, and took her midday meal with two other girls and their common chaperone—for it was still the custom to have a chaperone in the case of motherless girls of the more prosperous classes. The chaperone had a visitor that day, a man in green and yellow, with a white face and vivid eyes, who talked amazingly. Among other things, he fell to praising a new historical romance that one of the great popular storytellers of the day had just put forth. It was, of course, about the spacious times of Queen Victoria; and the author, among other pleasing novelties, made a little argument before each section of the story, in imitation of the chapter headings of the old-fashioned books: as for example, "How the Cabmen of Pimlico stopped the Victoria Omnibuses, and of the Great Fight in Palace Yard," and "How the Piccadilly Policeman was slain in the midst of his Duty." The man in green and yellow praised this innovation. "These pithy sentences," he said, "are admirable. They show at a glance those headlong, tumultuous times, when men and animals jostled in the filthy streets, and death might wait for one at every corner. Life was life then! How great the world must have seemed then! How marvellous! There were still parts of the world absolutely unexplored. Nowadays we have almost abolished wonder, we lead lives so trim and orderly that courage, endurance, faith, all the noble virtues seem fading from mankind."

And so on, taking the girls' thoughts with him, until the life they led, life in the vast and intricate London of the twenty-second century, a life interspersed with soaring excursions to every part of the globe, seemed to them a monotonous misery compared with the dædal past.

At first Elizabeth did not join in the conversation, but after a time the subject became so interesting that she made a few shy interpolations. But he scarcely seemed to notice her as he talked. He went on to describe a new method of entertaining people. They were hypnotised, and then suggestions were made to them so skilfully that they seemed to be living in ancient times again. They played out a little romance in the past as vivid as reality, and when at last they awakened they remembered all they had been through as though it were a real thing.

"It is a thing we have sought to do for years and years," said the hypnotist. "It is practically an artificial dream. And we know the way at last. Think of all it opens out to us—the enrichment of our experience, the recovery of adventure, the refuge it offers from this sordid, competitive life in which we live! Think!"

"And you can do that!" said the chaperone eagerly.

"The thing is possible at last," the hypnotist said. "You may order a dream as you wish."

The chaperone was the first to be hypnotised, and the dream, she said, was wonderful, when she came to again.

The other two girls, encouraged by her enthusiasm, also placed themselves in the hands of the hypnotist and had plunges into the romantic past. No one suggested that Elizabeth should try this novel entertainment; it was at her own request at last that she was taken into that land of dreams where there is neither any freedom or choice nor will. . . .

And so the mischief was done.

One day, when Denton went down to that quiet seat beneath the flying stage, Elizabeth was not in her wonted place. He was disappointed, and a little angry. The next day she did not come, and the next also. He was afraid. To hide his fear from himself, he set to work to write sonnets for her when she should come again. . . .

For three days he fought against his dread by such distraction, and then the truth was before him clear and cold, and would not be denied. She might be ill, she might be dead; but he would not believe that he had been betrayed. There followed a week of misery. And then he knew she was the only thing on earth worth having, and that he must seek her, however hopeless the search, until she was found once more.

He had some small private means of his own, and so he threw over his appointment on the flying stage, and set himself to find this girl who had become at last all the world to him. He did not know where she lived, and little of her circumstances; for it had been part of the delight of her girlish romance that he should know nothing of her, nothing of the difference of their station. The ways of the city opened before him east and west, north and south. Even in Victorian days London was a maze, that little London with its poor four millions of people; but the London he explored, the London of the twenty-second century, was a London of thirty million souls. At first he was energetic and headlong, taking time neither to eat nor sleep. He sought for weeks and months, he went through every imaginable phase of fatigue and despair, over-excitement and anger. Long after hope was dead, by the sheer inertia of his desire he still went to and fro, peering into faces and looking this way and that, in the incessant ways and lifts and passages of that interminable hive of men.

At last chance was kind to him, and he saw her.

It was in a time of festivity. He was hungry; he had paid the inclusive fee and had gone into one of the gigantic dining places of the city; he was pushing his way among the tables and scrutinising by mere force of habit every group he passed.

He stood still, robbed of all power of motion, his eyes wide, his lips apart. Elizabeth sat scarcely twenty yards away from him, looking straight at him. Her eyes were as hard to him, as hard and expressionless and void of recognition, as the eyes of a statue.

She looked at him for a moment, and then her gaze passed beyond him.

Had he had only her eyes to judge by he might have doubted if it was indeed Elizabeth, but he knew her by the gesture of her hand, by the grace of a wanton little curl that floated over her ear as she moved her head. Something was said to her, and she turned smiling tolerantly to the man beside her, a little man in foolish raiment knobbed and spiked like some old reptile with pneumatic horns—the Bindon of her father's choice.

For a moment Denton stood white and wild-eyed; then came a terrible faintness, and he sat before one of the little tables. He sat down with his back to her, and for a time he did not dare to look at her again. When at last he did, she and Bindon and two other people were standing up to go. The others were her father and her chaperone.

He sat as if incapable of action until the four figures were remote and small, and then he rose up possessed with the one idea of pursuit. For a space he feared he had lost them, and then he came upon Elizabeth and her chaperone again in one of the streets of moving platforms that intersected the city. Bindon and Mwres had disappeared.

He could not control himself to patience. He felt he must speak to her forthwith, or die. He pushed forward to where they were seated, and sat down beside them. His white face was convulsed with half-hysterical excitement.

He laid his hand on her wrist. "Elizabeth?" he said.

She turned in unfeigned astonishment. Nothing but the fear of a strange man showed in her face.

"Elizabeth," he cried, and his voice was strange to him: "dearest—you *know* me?"

Elizabeth's face showed nothing but alarm and perplexity. She drew herself away from him. The chaperone, a little grey-headed woman with mobile features, leant forward to intervene. Her resolute bright eyes examined Denton. "*What* do you say?" she asked.

"This young lady," said Denton,—"she knows me."

"Do you know him, dear?"

"No," said Elizabeth in a strange voice, and with a hand to her forehead, speaking almost as one who repeats a lesson. "No, I do not know him. I *know*—I do not know him."

"But—but . . . Not know me! It is I—Denton. Denton! To whom you used to talk. Don't you remember the flying stages? The little seat in the open air? The verses—"

"No," cried Elizabeth,—"no. I do not know him. I do not know him. There is something . . . But I don't know. All I know is that I do not know him." Her face was a face of infinite distress.

The sharp eyes of the chaperone flitted to and fro from the girl to the man. "You see?" she said, with the faint shadow of a smile. "She does not know you."

"I do not know you," said Elizabeth. "Of that I am sure."

"But, dear—the songs—the little verses—"

"She does not know you," said the chaperone. "You must not . . . You have made a mistake. You must not go on talking to us after that. You must not annoy us on the public ways."

"But—" said Denton, and for a moment his miserably haggard face appealed against fate.

"You must not persist, young man," protested the chaperone.

"*Elizabeth!*" he cried.

Her face was the face of one who is tormented. "I do not know you," she cried, hand to brow. "Oh, I do not know you!"

For an instant Denton sat stunned. Then he stood up and groaned aloud.

He made a strange gesture of appeal towards the remote glass roof of the public way, then turned and went plunging recklessly from one moving platform to another, and vanished amidst the swarms of people going to and fro thereon. The chaperone's eyes followed him, and then she looked at the curious faces about her.

"Dear," asked Elizabeth, clasping her hand, and too deeply moved to heed observation, "who was that man? Who *was* that man?"

The chaperone raised her eyebrows. She spoke in a clear, audible voice. "Some half-witted creature. I have never set eyes on him before."

"Never?"

"Never, dear. Do not trouble your mind about a thing like this."

And soon after this the celebrated hypnotist who dressed in green and yellow had another client. The young man paced his consulting-room, pale and disordered. "I want to forget," he cried. "I *must* forget."

The hypnotist watched him with quiet eyes, studied his face and clothes and bearing. "To forget anything—pleasure or pain—is to be, by so much—*less*. However, you know your own concern. My fee is high."

"If only I can forget—"

"That's easy enough with you. You wish it. I've done much harder things. Quite recently. I hardly expected to do it: the thing was done against the will of the hypnotised person. A love affair too—like yours. A girl. So rest assured."

The young man came and sat beside the hypnotist. His manner was a forced calm. He looked into the hypnotist's eyes. "I will tell you. Of course you will want to know what it is. There was a girl. Her name was Elizabeth Mwres. Well . . ."

He stopped. He had seen the instant surprise on the hypnotist's face. In that instant he knew. He stood up. He seemed to dominate the seated figure by his side. He gripped the shoulder of green and gold. For a time he could not find words.

"Give her me back!" he said at last. "Give her me back!"

"What do you mean?" gasped the hypnotist.

"Give her me back."

"Give whom?"

"Elizabeth Mwres—the girl—"

The hypnotist tried to free himself; he rose to his feet. Denton's grip tightened.

"Let go!" cried the hypnotist, thrusting an arm against Denton's chest.

In a moment the two men were locked in a clumsy wrestle. Neither had the slightest training—for athleticism, except for exhibition and to afford opportunity for betting, had faded out of the earth—but Denton was not only the younger but the stronger of the two. They swayed across the room, and then the hypnotist had gone down under his antagonist. They fell together. . . .

Denton leaped to his feet, dismayed at his own fury; but the hypnotist lay still, and suddenly from a little white mark where his forehead had struck a stool shot a hurrying band of red. For a space Denton stood over him irresolute, trembling.

A fear of the consequences entered his gently nurtured mind. He turned towards the door. "No," he said aloud, and came back to the middle of the room. Overcoming the instinctive repugnance of one who had seen no act of violence in all his life before, he knelt down beside his antagonist and felt his heart. Then he peered at the wound. He rose quickly and looked about him. He began to see more of the situation.

When presently the hypnotist recovered his senses, his head ached severely, his back was against Denton's knees and Denton was sponging his face.

The hypnotist did not speak. But presently he indicated by a gesture that in his opinion he had been sponged enough. "Let me get up," he said.

"Not yet," said Denton.

"You have assaulted me, you scoundrel!"

"We are alone," said Denton, "and the door is secure."

There was an interval of thought.

"Unless I sponge," said Denton, "your forehead will develop a tremendous bruise."

"You can go on sponging," said the hypnotist sulkily.

There was another pause.

"We might be in the Stone Age," said the hypnotist. "Violence! Struggle!"

"In the Stone Age no man dared to come between man and woman," said Denton.

The hypnotist thought again.

"What are you going to do?" he asked.

"While you were insensible I found the girl's address on your tablets. I did not know it before. I telephoned. She will be here soon. Then—"

"She will bring her chaperone."

"That is all right."

"But what—? I don't see. What do you mean to do?"

"I looked about for a weapon also. It is an astonishing thing how few weapons there are nowadays. If you consider that in the Stone Age men owned scarcely anything *but* weapons. I hit at last upon this lamp. I have wrenched off the wires and things, and I hold it so." He extended it over the hypnotist's shoulders. "With that I can quite easily smash your skull. I *will*—unless you do as I tell you."

"Violence is no remedy," said the hypnotist, quoting from the "Modern Man's Book of Moral Maxims."

"It's an undesirable disease," said Denton.

"Well?"

"You will tell that chaperone you are going to order the girl to marry that knobby little brute with the red hair and ferrety eyes. I believe that's how things stand?"

"Yes—that's how things stand."

"And, pretending to do that, you will restore her memory of me."

"It's unprofessional."

"Look here! If I cannot have that girl I would rather die than not. I don't propose to respect your little fancies. If anything goes wrong you shall not live five minutes. This is a rude makeshift of a weapon, and it may quite conceivably be painful to kill you. But I will. It is unusual, I know, nowadays to do things like this—mainly because there is so little in life that is worth being violent about."

"The chaperone will see you directly she comes—"

"I shall stand in that recess. Behind you."

The hypnotist thought. "You are a determined young man," he said, "and only half civilised. I have tried to to my duty to my client, but in this affair you seem likely to get your own way. . . ."

"You mean to deal straightly."

"I'm not going to risk having my brains scattered in a petty affair like this."

"And afterwards?"

"There is nothing a hypnotist or doctor hates so much as a scandal. I at least am no savage. I am annoyed. . . . But in a day or so I shall bear no malice. . . ."

"Thank you. And now that we understand each other, there is no necessity to keep you sitting any longer on the floor."

II. THE VACANT COUNTRY

The world, they say, changed more between the year 1800 and the year 1900 than it had done in the previous five hundred years. That century, the nineteenth century, was the dawn of a new epoch in the history of mankind—the epoch of the great cities, the end of the old order of country life.

In the beginning of the nineteenth century the majority of mankind still lived upon the countryside, as their way of life had been for countless generations. All over the world they dwelt in little towns and villages then, and engaged either directly in agriculture, or in occupations that were of service to the agriculturist. They travelled rarely, and dwelt close to their work, because swift means of transit had not yet come. The few who travelled went either on foot, or in slow sailing-ships, or by means of jogging horses incapable of more than sixty miles a day. Think of it!—sixty miles a day. Here and there, in those sluggish times, a town grew a little larger than its neighbours, as a port or as a centre of government; but all the towns in the world with more than a hundred thousand inhabitants could be counted on a man's fingers. So it was in the beginning of the nineteenth century. By the end, the invention of railways, telegraphs, steamships, and complex agricultural machinery, had changed all these things: changed them beyond all hope of return. The vast shops, the varied pleasures, the countless conveniences of the larger towns were suddenly possible, and no sooner existed than they were brought into competition with the homely resources of the rural centres. Mankind were drawn to the cities by an overwhelming attraction. The demand for labour fell with the increase of machinery, the local markets were entirely superseded, and there was a rapid growth of the larger centres at the expense of the open country.

The flow of population townward was the constant preoccupation of Victorian writers. In Great Britain and New England, in India and China, the same thing was remarked: everywhere a few swollen towns were visibly replacing the ancient order. That this was an inevitable result of improved means of travel and transport—that, given swift means of transit, these things must be—was realised by few; and the most puerile schemes were devised to overcome the mysterious magnetism of the urban centres, and keep the people on the land.

Yet the developments of the nineteenth century were only the dawning of the new order. The first great cities of the new time were horribly inconvenient, darkened by smoky fogs, insanitary and noisy; but the discovery of new methods of building, new methods of heating, changed all this. Between 1900 and 2000 the march of change was still more rapid; and between 2000 and 2100 the continually accelerated progress of human invention made the reign of Victoria the Good seem at last an almost incredible vision of idyllic tranquil days.

The introduction of railways was only the first step in that development of those means of locomotion which finally revolutionised human life. By the year 2000 railways and roads had vanished together. The railways, robbed of their rails, had become weedy ridges and ditches upon the face of the world; the old roads, strange barbaric tracks of flint and soil, hammered by hand or rolled by rough iron rollers, strewn with miscellaneous filth, and cut by iron hoofs and wheels into ruts and puddles often many inches deep, had been replaced by patent tracks made of a substance called Eadhamite. This Eadhamite—it was named after its patentee—ranks with the invention of printing and steam as one of the epoch-making discoveries of the world's history.

When Eadham discovered the substance, he probably thought of it as a mere cheap substitute for india-rubber; it cost a few shillings a ton. But you can never tell all an invention will do. It was the genius of a man named Warming that pointed to the possibility of using it, not only for the tires of wheels, but as a road substance, and who organised the enormous network of public ways that speedily covered the world.

These public ways were made with longitudinal divisions. On the outer on either side went foot cyclists and conveyances travelling at a less speed than twenty-five miles an hour; in the middle, motors capable of speed up to a hundred; and the inner, Warming (in the face of enormous ridicule) reserved for vehicles travelling at speeds of a hundred miles an hour and upward.

For ten years his inner ways were vacant. Before he died they were the most crowded of all, and vast light frameworks with wheels of twenty and thirty feet in diameter, hurled along them at paces that year after year rose steadily towards two hundred miles an hour. And by the time this revolution was accomplished, a parallel revolution had transformed the ever-growing cities. Before the development of practical science the fogs and filth of Victorian times vanished. Electric heating replaced fires (in 2013 the lighting of a fire that did not absolutely consume its own smoke was made an indictable nuisance), and all the city ways, all public squares and places, were covered in with a recently invented glasslike substance. The roofing of London became practically continuous. Certain short-sighted and foolish legislation against tall buildings was abolished, and London, from a squat expanse of petty houses—feebly archaic in design—rose steadily towards the sky. To the municipal responsibility for water, light, and drainage, was added another, and that was ventilation.

But to tell of all the changes in human convenience that these two hundred years brought about, to tell of the long foreseen invention of flying, to describe how life in households was steadily supplanted by life in interminable hotels, how at last even those who were still concerned in agricultural work came to live in the towns and to go to and fro to their work every day, to describe how at last in all England only four towns remained, each with many millions of people, and how there were left no inhabited houses in all the countryside: to tell all this would take us far from our story of Denton and his Elizabeth. They had been separated and reunited, and still they could not marry. For Denton—it was his only fault—he had no money. Neither had Elizabeth until she was twenty-one, and as yet she was only eighteen. At twenty-one all the property of her mother would come to her, for that was the custom of the time. She did not know that it was possible to anticipate her fortune, and Denton was far too delicate a lover to suggest such a thing. So things stuck hopelessly between them. Elizabeth said that she was very unhappy, and that nobody understood her but Denton, and that when she was away from him she was wretched; and Denton said that his heart longed for her day and night. And they met as often as they could to enjoy the discussion of their sorrows.

They met one day at their little seat upon the flying stage. The precise site of this meeting was where in Victorian times the road from Wimbledon came out upon the common. They were, however, five hundred feet above that point. Their seat looked far over London. To convey the appearance of it all to a nineteenth-century reader would have been difficult. One would have had to tell him to think of the Crystal Palace, of the newly built "mammoth" hotels—as those little affairs were called—of the larger railway stations of his time, and to imagine such buildings enlarged to vast proportions and run together and continuous over the whole metropolitan area. If then he was told that this continuous roof-space bore a huge forest of rotating wind-wheels, he would have begun very dimly to appreciate what to these young people was the commonest sight in their lives.

To their eyes it had something of the quality of a prison, and they were talking, as they had talked a hundred times before, of how they might escape from it and be at last happy together: escape from it, that is, before the appointed three years were at an end. It was, they both agreed, not only impossible but almost wicked, to wait three years. "Before that," said Denton—and the notes of his voice told of a splendid chest—"*we might both be dead!*"

Their vigorous young hands had to grip at this, and then Elizabeth had a still more poignant thought that brought the tears from her wholesome eyes and down her healthy cheeks. "*One* of us," she said, "*one* of us might be—"

She choked; she could not say the word that is so terrible to the young and happy.

Yet to marry and be very poor in the cities of that time was—for any one who had lived pleasantly—a very dreadful thing. In the old agricultural days that had drawn to an end in the eighteenth century there had been a pretty proverb of love in a cottage; and indeed in those days diamond-windowed cottages of thatch and plaster, with the sweet air and earth about them, amidst tangled hedges and the song of birds, and with the ever-changing sky overhead. But all this had changed (the change was already beginning in the nineteenth century), and a new sort of life was opening for the poor—in the lower quarters of the city.

In the nineteenth century the lower quarters were still beneath the sky; they were areas of land on clay or other unsuitable soil, liable to floods or exposed to the smoke of more fortunate districts, insufficiently supplied with water, and as insanitary as the great fear of infectious diseases felt by the wealthier classes permitted. In the twenty-second century, however, the growth of the city storey above storey, and the coalescence of buildings, had led to a different arrangement. The prosperous people lived in a vast series of sumptuous hotels in the upper storeys and halls of the city fabric; the industrial population dwelt beneath in the tremendous ground-floor and basement, so to speak, of the place.

In the refinement of life and manners these lower classes differed little from their ancestors, the East-enders of Queen Victoria's time; but they had developed a distinct dialect of their own. In these underways they lived and died, rarely ascending to the surface except when work took them there. Since for most of them this was the sort of life to which they had been born, they found no great misery in such circumstances; but for people like Denton and Elizabeth, such a plunge would have seemed more terrible than death.

"And yet what else is there?" asked Elizabeth.

Denton professed not to know. Apart from his own feeling of delicacy, he was not sure how Elizabeth would like the idea of borrowing on the strength of her expectations.

The passage from London to Paris even, said Elizabeth, was beyond their means; and in Paris, as in any other city in the world, life would be just as costly and impossible as in London.

Well might Denton cry aloud: "If only we had lived in those days, dearest! If only we had lived in the past!" For to their eyes even nineteenth-century Whitechapel was seen through a mist of romance.

"Is there *nothing?*" cried Elizabeth, suddenly weeping. "Must we really wait for these three long years? Fancy *three* years—six-and-thirty months!" The human capacity for patience had not grown with the ages.

Then suddenly Denton was moved to speak of something that had already flickered across his mind. He had hit upon it at last. It seemed to him so wild a suggestion that he made it only half seriously. But to put a thing into words has ever a way of making it seem more real and possible than it seemed before. And so it was with him.

"Suppose," he said, "we went into the country?"

She looked at him to see if he was serious in proposing such an adventure.

"The country?"

"Yes—beyond there. Beyond the hills."

"How could we live?" she said. "*Where* could we live?"

"It is not impossible," he said. "People used to live in the country."

"But then there were houses."

"There are the ruins of villages and towns now. On the clay lands they are gone, of course. But they are still left on the grazing land, because it does not pay the Food Company to remove them. I know that—for certain. Besides, one sees them from the flying machines, you know. Well, we might shelter in some one of these, and repair it with our hands. Do you know, the thing is not so wild as it seems. Some of the men who go out every day to look after the crops and herds might be paid to bring us food. . . ."

She stood in front of him. "How strange it would be if one really could. . . ."

"Why not?"

"But no one dares."

"That is no reason."

"It would be—oh! it would be so romantic and strange. If only it were possible."

"Why not possible?"

"There are so many things. Think of all the things we have, things that we should miss."

"Should we miss them? After all, the life we lead is very unreal—very artificial." He began to expand his idea, and as he warmed to his exposition the fantastic quality of his first proposal faded away.

She thought. "But I have heard of prowlers—escaped criminals."

He nodded. He hesitated over his answer because he thought it sounded boyish. He blushed. "I could get some one I know to make me a sword."

She looked at him with enthusiasm growing in her eyes. She had heard of swords, had seen one in a museum; she thought of those ancient days when men wore them as a common thing. His suggestion seemed an impossible dream to her, and perhaps for that reason she was eager for more detail. And inventing for the most part as he went along, he told her how they might live in the country as the old-world people had done. With every detail her interest grew, for she was one of those girls for whom romance and adventure have a fascination.

His suggestion seemed, I say, an impossible dream to her on that day, but the next day they talked about it again, and it was strangely less impossible.

"At first we should take food," said Denton. "We could carry food for ten or twelve days." It was an age of compact artificial nourishment, and such a provision had none of the unwieldy suggestion it would have had in the nineteenth century.

"But—until our house," she asked—"until it was ready, where should we sleep?"

"It is summer."

"But . . . What do you mean?"

"There was a time when there were no houses in the world; when all mankind slept always in the open air."

"But for us! The emptiness! No walls—no ceiling!"

"Dear," he said, "in London you have many beautiful ceilings. Artists paint them and stud them with lights. But I have seen a ceiling more beautiful than any in London. . . ."

"But where?"

"It is the ceiling under which we two would be alone. . . ."

"You mean . . . ?"

"Dear," he said, "it is something the world has forgotten. It is Heaven and all the host of stars."

Each time they talked the thing seemed more possible and more desirable to them. In a week or so it was quite possible. Another week, and it was the inevitable thing they had to do. A great enthusiasm for the country seized hold of them and possessed them. The sordid tumult of the town, they said, overwhelmed them. They marvelled that this simple way out of their troubles had never come upon them before.

One morning near Midsummer-day, there was a new minor official upon the flying stage, and Denton's place was to know him no more.

Our two young people had secretly married, and were going forth manfully out of the city in which they and their ancestors before them had lived all their days. She wore a new dress of white cut in an old-fashioned pattern, and he had a bundle of provisions strapped athwart his back, and in his hand he carried—rather shamefacedly it is true, and under his purple cloak—an implement of archaic form, a cross-hilted thing of tempered steel.

Imagine that going forth! In their days the sprawling suburbs of Victorian times with their vile roads, petty houses, foolish little gardens of shrub and geranium, and all their futile, pretentious privacies, had disappeared: the towering buildings of the new age, the mechanical ways, the electric and water mains, all came to an end together, like a wall, like a cliff, near four hundred feet in height, abrupt and sheer. All about the city spread the carrot, swede, and turnip fields of the Food Company, vegetables that were the basis of a thousand varied foods, and weeds and hedgerow tangles had been utterly extirpated. The incessant expense of weeding that went on year after year in the petty, wasteful and barbaric farming of the ancient days, the Food Company had economised for ever more by a campaign of extermination. Here and there, however, neat rows of bramble standards and apple trees with white-washed stems, intersected the fields, and at places groups of gigantic teazles reared their favored spikes. Here and there huge agricultural machines hunched under waterproof covers. The mingled waters of the Wey and Mole and Wandle ran in rectangular channels; and wherever a gentle elevation of the ground permitted a fountain of deodorised sewage distributed its benefits athwart the land and made a rainbow of the sunlight.

By a great archway in that enormous city wall emerged the Eadhamite road to Portsmouth, swarming in the morning sunshine with an enormous traffic bearing the blue-clad servants of the Food Company to their toil. A rushing traffic, beside which they seemed two scarce-moving dots. Along the outer tracks hummed and rattled the tardy little old-fashioned motors of such as had duties within twenty miles or so of the city; the inner ways were filled with vaster mechanisms—swift monocycles bearing a score of men, lank multicycles, quadricycles sagging with heavy loads, empty gigantic produce carts that would come back again filled before the sun was setting, all with throbbing engines and noiseless wheels and a perpetual wild melody of horns and gongs.

Along the very verge of the outermost way our young people went in silence, newly wed and oddly shy of one another's company. Many were the things shouted to them as they tramped along, for in 2100 a foot-passenger on an English road was almost as strange a sight as a motor car would have been in 1800. But they went on with steadfast eyes into the country, paying no heed to such cries.

Before them in the south rose the Downs, blue at first, as they came nearer changing to green, surmounted by the row of gigantic wind-wheels that supplemented the wind-wheels upon the roof-spaces of the city, and broken and restless with the long morning shadows of those whirling vanes. By midday they had come so near that they could see here and there little patches of pallid dots—the sheep the Meat Department of the Food Company owned. In another hour they had passed the clay and the root crops and the single fence that hedged them in, and the prohibition against trespass no longer held: the levelled roadway plunged into a cutting with all its traffic, and they could leave it and walk over the greensward and up the open hillside.

Never had these children of the latter days been together in such a lonely place.

They were both very hungry and footsore—for walking was a rare exercise—and presently they sat down on the weedless, close-cropped grass, and looked back for the first time at the city from which they had come, shining wide and splendid in the blue haze of the valley of the Thames. Elizabeth was a little afraid of the unenclosed sheep away up the slope—she had never been near big unrestrained animals before—but Denton reassured her. And overhead a white-winged bird circled in the blue.

They talked but little until they had eaten, and then their tongues were loosened. He spoke of the happiness that was now certainly theirs, of the folly of not breaking sooner out of that magnificent prison of latter-day life, of the old romantic days that had passed from the world for ever. And then he became boastful. He took up the sword that lay on the ground beside him, and she took it from his hand and ran a tremulous finger along the blade.

"And you could," she said, "*you*—could raise this and strike a man?"

"Why not? If there were need."

"But," she said, "it seems so horrible. It would slash. . . . There would be"—her voice sank—"*blood.*"

"In the old romances you have read often enough . . ."

"Oh: I know in those—yes. But that is different. One knows it is not blood, but just a sort of red ink . . . And *you*—killing!"

She looked at him doubtfully, and then handed him back the sword.

After they had rested and eaten, they rose up and went on their way towards the hills. They passed quite close to a huge flock of sheep, who stared and bleated at their unaccustomed figures. She had never seen sheep before, and she shivered to think such gentle things must needs be slain for food. A sheep-dog barked from a distance, and then a shepherd appeared amidst the supports of the wind-wheels, and came down towards them.

When he drew near he called out asking whither they were going.

Denton hesitated, and told him briefly that they sought some ruined house among the Downs, in which they might live together. He tried to speak in an offhand manner, as though it was a usual thing to do. The man stared incredulously.

"Have you *done* anything?" he asked.

"Nothing," said Denton. "Only we don't want to live in a city any longer. Why should we live in cities?"

The shepherd stared more incredulously than ever. "You can't live here," he said.

"We mean to try."

The shepherd stared from one to the other. "You'll go back to-morrow," he said. "It looks pleasant enough in the sunlight. . . . Are you sure you've done nothing? We shepherds are not such *great* friends of the police."

Denton looked at him steadfastly. "No," he said. "But we are too poor to live in the city, and we can't bear the thought of wearing clothes of blue canvas and doing drudgery. We are going to live a simple life here, like the people of old."

The shepherd was a bearded man with a thoughtful face. He glanced at Elizabeth's fragile beauty.

"They had simple minds," he said.

"So have we," said Denton.

The shepherd smiled.

"If you go along here," he said, "along the crest beneath the wind-wheels, you will see a heap of mounds and ruins on your right-hand side. That was once a town called Epsom. There are no houses there, and the bricks have been used for a sheep pen. Go on, and another heap on the edge of the root-land is Leatherhead; and then the hill turns away along the border of a valley, and there are woods of beech. Keep along the crest. You will come to quite wild places. In some parts, in spite of all the weeding that is done, ferns and bluebells and other such useless plants are growing still. And through it all underneath the wind-wheels runs a straight lane paved with stones, a roadway of the Romans two thousand years old. Go to the right of that, down into the valley and follow it along by the banks of the river. You come presently to a street of houses, many with the roofs still sound upon them. There you may find shelter."

They thanked him.

"But it's a quiet place. There is no light after dark there, and I have heard tell of robbers. It is lonely. Nothing happens there. The phonographs of the story-tellers, the kinematograph entertainments, the news machines—none of them are to be found there. If you are hungry there is no food, if you are ill no doctor. . . ." He stopped.

"We shall try it," said Denton, moving to go on. Then a thought struck him, and he made an agreement with the shepherd, and learnt where they might find him, to buy and bring them anything of which they stood in need, out of the city.

And in the evening they came to the deserted village, with its houses that seemed so small and odd to them: they found it golden in the glory of the sunset, and desolate and still. They went from one deserted house to another, marvelling at their quaint simplicity, and debating which they should choose. And at last, in a sunlit corner of a room that had lost its outer wall, they came upon a wild flower, a little flower of blue that the weeders of the Food Company had overlooked.

That house they decided upon; but they did not remain in it long that night, because they were resolved to feast upon nature. And moreover the houses became very gaunt and shadowy after the sunlight had faded out of the sky. So after they had rested a little time they went to the crest of the hill again to see with their own eyes the silence of heaven set with stars, about which the old poets had had so many things to tell. It was a wonderful sight, and Denton talked like the stars, and when they went down the hill at last the sky was pale with dawn. They slept but little, and in the morning when they woke a thrush was singing in a tree.

So these young people of the twenty-second century began their exile. That morning they were very busy exploring the resources of this new home in which they were going to live the simple life. They did not explore very fast or very far, because they went everywhere hand-in-hand; but they found the beginnings of some furniture. Beyond the village was a store of winter fodder for the sheep of the Food Company, and Denton dragged great armfuls to the house to make a bed; and in several of the houses were old fungus-eaten chairs and tables—rough, barbaric, clumsy furniture, it seemed to them, and made of wood. They repeated many of the things they had said on the previous day, and towards evening they found another flower, a harebell. In the late afternoon some Company shepherds went down the river valley riding on a big multicycle; but they hid from them, because their presence, Elizabeth said, seemed to spoil the romance of this old-world place altogether.

In this fashion they lived a week. For all that week the days were cloudless, and the nights, nights of starry glory, that were invaded each a little more by a crescent moon.

Yet something of the first splendour of their coming faded—faded imperceptibly day after day; Denton's eloquence became fitful, and lacked fresh topics of inspiration; the fatigue of their long march from London told in a certain stiffness of the limbs, and each suffered from a slight unaccountable cold. Moreover, Denton became aware of unoccupied time. In one place among the carelessly heaped lumber of the old times he found a rust-eaten spade, and with this he made a fitful attack on the razed and grass-grown garden—though he had nothing to plant or sow. He returned to Elizabeth with a sweat-streaming face, after half an hour of such work.

"There were giants in those days," he said, not understanding what wont and training will do. And their walk that day led them along the hills until they could see the city shimmering far away in the valley. "I wonder how things are going on there," he said.

And then came a change in the weather. "Come out and see the clouds," she cried; and behold! they were a sombre purple in the north and east, streaming up to ragged edges at the zenith. And as they went up the hill these hurrying streamers blotted out the sunset. Suddenly the wind set the beech-trees swaying and whispering, and Elizabeth shivered. And then far away the lightning flashed, flashed like a sword that is drawn suddenly, and the distant thunder marched about the sky, and even as they stood astonished, pattering upon them came the first headlong raindrops of the storm. In an instant the last streak of sunset was hidden by a falling curtain of hail, and the lightning flashed again, and the voice of the thunder roared louder, and all about them the world scowled dark and strange.

Seizing hands, these children of the city ran down the hill to their home, in infinite astonishment. And ere they reached it, Elizabeth was weeping with dismay, and the darkling ground about them was white and brittle and active with the pelting hail.

Then began a strange and terrible night for them. For the first time in their civilised lives they were in absolute darkness; they were wet and cold and shivering; all about them hissed the hail, and through the long neglected ceilings of the derelict home came noisy spouts of water and formed pools and rivulets on the creaking floors. As the gusts of the storm struck the worn-out building, it groaned and shuddered, and now a mass of plaster from the wall would slide and smash, and now some loosened tile would rattle down the roof and crash into the empty greenhouse below. Elizabeth shuddered, and was still; Denton wrapped his gay and flimsy city cloak about her, and so they crouched in the darkness. And ever the thunder broke louder and nearer, and ever more lurid flashed the lightning, jerking into a momentary gaunt clearness the steaming, dripping room in which they sheltered.

Never before had they been in the open air save when the sun was shining.

All their time had been spent in the warm and airy ways and halls and rooms of the latter-day city. It was to them that night as if they were in some other world, some disordered chaos of stress and tumult, and almost beyond hoping that they should ever see the city ways again.

The storm seemed to last interminably, until at last they dozed between the thunderclaps, and then very swiftly it fell and ceased. And as the last patter of the rain died away they heard an unfamiliar sound.

"What is that?" cried Elizabeth.

It came again. It was the barking of dogs. It drove down the desert lane and passed; and through the window, whitening the wall before them and throwing upon it the shadow of the window-frame and of a tree in black silhouette, shone the light of the waxing moon.

Just as the pale dawn was drawing the things about them into sight, the fitful barking of dogs came near again, and stopped. They listened. After a pause they heard the quick pattering of feet seeking round the house, and short, half-smothered barks. Then again everything was still.

"Ssh!" whispered Elizabeth, and pointed to the door of their room.

Denton went half-way towards the door, and stood listening. He came back with a face of affected unconcern. "They must be the sheep-dogs of the Food Company," he said. "They will do us no harm."

He sat down again beside her. "What a night it has been!" he said, to hide how keenly he was listening.

"I don't like dogs," answered Elizabeth, after a long silence.

"Dogs never hurt any one," said Denton. "In the old days—in the nineteenth century—everybody had a dog."

"There was a romance I heard once. A dog killed a man."

"Not this sort of dog," said Denton confidently. "Some of those romances—are exaggerated."

Suddenly a half bark and a pattering up the staircase; the sound of panting. Denton sprang to his feet and drew the sword out of the damp straw upon which they had been lying. Then in the doorway appeared a gaunt sheep-dog, and halted there. Behind it stared another. For an instant man and brute faced each other, hesitating.

Then Denton, being ignorant of dogs, made a sharp step forward. "Go away," he said, with a clumsy motion of his sword.

The dog started and growled. Denton stopped sharply. "Good dog!" he said.

The growling jerked into a bark.

"Good dog!" said Denton. The second dog growled and barked. A third out of sight down the staircase took up the barking also. Outside others gave tongue—a large number it seemed to Denton.

"This is annoying," said Denton, without taking his eye off the brutes before him. "Of course the shepherds won't come out of the city for hours yet. Naturally these dogs don't quite make us out."

"I can't hear," shouted Elizabeth. She stood up and came to him.

Denton tried again, but the barking still drowned his voice. The sound had a curious effect upon his blood. Odd disused emotions began to stir, his face changed as he shouted. He tried again; the barking seemed to mock him, and one dog danced a pace forward, bristling. Suddenly he turned, and uttering certain words in the dialect of the underways, words incomprehensible to Elizabeth, he made for the dogs. There was a sudden cessation of the barking, a growl and a snapping. Elizabeth saw the snarling head of the foremost dog, its white teeth and retracted ears, and the flash of the thrust blade. The brute leapt into the air and was flung back.

Then Denton, with a shout, was driving the dogs before him. The sword flashed above his head with a sudden new freedom of gesture, and then he vanished down the staircase. She made six steps to follow him, and on the landing there was blood. She stopped, and hearing the tumult of dogs and Denton's shouts pass out of the house, ran to the window.

Nine wolfish sheep-dogs were scattering, one writhed before the porch; and Denton, tasting that strange delight of combat that slumbers still in the blood of even the most civilised man, was shouting and running across the garden space. And then she saw something that for a moment he did not see. The dogs circled round this way and that, and came again. They had him in the open.

In an instant she divined the situation. She would have called to him. For a moment she felt sick and helpless, and then, obeying a strange impulse, she gathered up her white skirt and ran downstairs. In the hall was the rusting spade. That was it! She seized it and ran out.

She came none too soon. One dog rolled before him, well-nigh slashed in half; but a second had him by the thigh, a third gripped his collar behind, and a fourth had the blade of the sword between his teeth, tasting its own blood. He parried the leap of a fifth with his left arm.

It might have been the first century instead of the twenty-second, so far as she was concerned. All the gentleness of her eighteen years of city life vanished before this primordial need. The spade smote hard and sure, and cleft a dog's skull. Another, crouching for a spring, yelped with dismay at this unexpected antagonist, and rushed aside. Two wasted precious moments on the binding of a feminine skirt.

The collar of Denton's cloak tore and parted as he staggered back; and that dog too felt the spade, and ceased to trouble him. He sheathed his sword in the brute at his thigh.

"To the wall!" cried Elizabeth; and in three seconds the fight was at an end, and our young people stood side by side, while a remnant of five dogs, with ears and tails of disaster, fled shamefully from the stricken field.

For a moment they stood panting and victorious, and then Elizabeth, dropping her spade, covered her face, and sank to the ground in a paroxysm of weeping. Denton looked about him, thrust the point of his sword into the ground so that it was at hand, and stooped to comfort her.

At last their more tumultuous emotions subsided, and they could talk again. She leant upon the wall, and he sat upon it so that he could keep an eye open for any returning dogs. Two, at any rate, were up on the hillside and keeping up a vexatious barking.

She was tear-stained, but not very wretched now, because for half an hour he had been repeating that she was brave and had saved his life. But a new fear was growing in her mind.

"They are the dogs of the Food Company," she said. "There will be trouble."

"I am afraid so. Very likely they will prosecute us for trespass."

A pause.

"In the old times," he said, "this sort of thing happened day after day."

"Last night!" she said. "I could not live through another such night."

He looked at her. Her face was pale for want of sleep, and drawn and haggard. He came to a sudden resolution. "We must go back," he said.

She looked at the dead dogs, and shivered. "We cannot stay here," she said.

"We must go back," he repeated, glancing over his shoulder to see if the enemy kept their distance. "We have been happy for a time. . . . But the world is too civilised. Ours is the age of cities. More of this will kill us."

"But what are we to do? How can we live there?"

Denton hesitated. His heel kicked against the wall on which he sat. "It's a thing I haven't mentioned before," he said, and coughed; "but . . ."

"Yes?"

"You could raise money on your expectations," he said.

"Could I?" she said eagerly.

"Of course you could. What a child you are!"

She stood up, and her face was bright. "Why did you not tell me before?" she asked. "And all this time we have been here!"

He looked at her for a moment, and smiled. Then the smile vanished. "I thought it ought to come from you," he said. "I didn't like to ask for your money. And besides—at first I thought this would be rather fine."

There was a pause.

"It *has* been fine," he said; and glanced once more over his shoulder. "Until all this began."

"Yes," she said, "those first days. The first three days."

They looked for a space into one another's faces, and then Denton slid down from the wall and took her hand.

"To each generation," he said, "the life of its time. I see it all plainly now. In the city—that is the life to which we were born. To live in any other fashion . . . Coming here was a dream, and this—is the awakening."

"It was a pleasant dream," she said,—"in the beginning."

For a long space neither spoke.

"If we would reach the city before the shepherds come here, we must start," said Denton. "We must get our food out of the house and eat as we go."

Denton glanced about him again, and, giving the dead dogs a wide berth, they walked across the garden space and into the house together. They found the wallet with their food, and descended the blood-stained stairs again. In the hall Elizabeth stopped. "One minute," she said. "There is something here."

She led the way into the room in which that one little blue flower was blooming. She stooped to it, she touched it with her hand.

"I want it," she said; and then, "I cannot take it. . . ."

Impulsively she stooped and kissed its petals.

Then silently, side by side, they went across the empty garden-space into the old high road, and set their faces resolutely towards the distant city—towards the complex mechanical city of those latter days, the city that had swallowed up mankind.

III. THE WAYS OF THE CITY

Prominent if not paramount among world-changing inventions in the history of man is that series of contrivances in locomotion that began with the railway and ended for a century or more with the motor and the patent road. That these contrivances, together with the device of limited liability joint stock companies and the supersession of agricultural labourers by skilled men with ingenious machinery, would necessarily concentrate mankind in cities of unparalleled magnitude and work an entire revolution in human life, became, after the event, a thing so obvious that it is a matter of astonishment it was not more clearly anticipated. Yet that any steps should be taken to anticipate the miseries such a revolution might entail does not appear even to have been suggested; and the idea that the moral prohibitions and sanctions, the privileges and concessions, the conception of property and responsibility, of comfort and beauty, that had rendered the mainly agricultural states of the past prosperous and happy, would fail in the rising torrent of novel opportunities and novel stimulations, never seems to have entered the nineteenth-century mind. That a citizen, kindly and fair in his ordinary life, could as a shareholder become almost murderously greedy; that commercial methods that were reasonable and honourable on the old-fashioned countryside, should on an enlarged scale be deadly and overwhelming; that ancient charity was modern pauperisation, and ancient employment modern sweating; that, in fact, a revision and enlargement of the duties and rights of man had become urgently necessary, were things it could not entertain, nourished as it was on an archaic system of education and profoundly retrospective and legal in all its habits of thought. It was known that the accumulation of men in cities involved unprecedented dangers of pestilence; there was an energetic development of sanitation; but that the diseases of gambling and usury, of luxury and tyranny should become endemic, and produce horrible consequences was beyond the scope of nineteenth-century thought. And so, as if it were some inorganic process, practically unhindered by the creative will of man, the growth of the swarming unhappy cities that mark the twenty-first century accomplished itself.

The new society was divided into three main classes. At the summit slumbered the property owner, enormously rich by accident rather than design, potent save for the will and aim, the last *avatar* of Hamlet in the world. Below was the enormous multitude of workers employed by the gigantic companies that monopolised control; and between these two the dwindling middle class, officials of innumerable sorts, foremen, managers, the medical, legal, artistic, and scholastic classes, and the minor rich, a middle class whose members led a life of insecure luxury and precarious speculation amidst the movements of the great managers.

Already the love story and the marrying of two persons of this middle class have been told: how they overcame the obstacles between them, and how they tried the simple old-fashioned way of living on the countryside and came back speedily enough into the city of London. Denton had no means, so Elizabeth borrowed money on the securities that her father Mwres held in trust for her until she was one-and-twenty.

The rate of interest she paid was of course high, because of the uncertainty of her security, and the arithmetic of lovers is often sketchy and optimistic. Yet they had very glorious times after that return. They determined they would not go to a Pleasure city nor waste their days rushing through the air from one part of the world to the other, for in spite of one disillusionment, their tastes were still old-fashioned. They furnished their little room with quaint old Victorian furniture, and found a shop on the forty-second floor in Seventh Way where printed books of the old sort were still to be bought. It was their pet affectation to read print instead of hearing phonographs. And when presently there came a sweet little girl, to unite them further if it were possible, Elizabeth would not send it to a *creche,* as the custom was, but insisted on nursing it at home. The rent of their apartments was raised on account of this singular proceeding, but they did not mind. It only meant borrowing a little more.

Presently Elizabeth was of age, and Denton had a business interview with her father that was not agreeable. An exceedingly disagreeable interview with their moneylender followed, from which he brought home a white face. On his return Elizabeth had to tell him of a new and marvellous intonation of "Goo" that their daughter had devised, but Denton was inattentive. In the midst, just as she was at the cream of her description, he interrupted. "How much money do you think we have left, now that everything is settled?"

She stared and stopped her appreciative swaying of the Goo genius that had accompanied her description.

"You don't mean . . . ?"

"Yes," he answered. "Ever so much. We have been wild. It's the interest. Or something. And the shares you had, slumped. Your father did not mind. Said it was not his business, after what had happened. He's going to marry again. . . . Well—we have scarcely a thousand left!"

"Only a thousand?"

"Only a thousand."

And Elizabeth sat down. For a moment she regarded him with a white face, then her eyes went about the quaint, old-fashioned room, with its middle Victorian furniture and genuine oleographs, and rested at last on the little lump of humanity within her arms.

Denton glanced at her and stood downcast. Then he swung round on his heel and walked up and down very rapidly.

"I must get something to do," he broke out presently. "I am an idle scoundrel. I ought to have thought of this before. I have been a selfish fool. I wanted to be with you all day . . ."

He stopped, looking at her white face. Suddenly he came and kissed her and the little face that nestled against her breast.

"It's all right, dear," he said, standing over her; "you won't be lonely now—now Dings is beginning to talk to you. And I can soon get something to do, you know. Soon . . . Easily . . . It's only a shock at first. But it will come all right. It's sure to come right. I will go out again as soon as I have rested, and find what can be done. For the present it's hard to think of anything . . ."

"It would be hard to leave these rooms," said Elizabeth; "but—"

"There won't be any need of that—trust me."

"They are expensive."

Denton waved that aside. He began talking of the work he could do. He was not very explicit what it would be; but he was quite sure that there was something to keep them comfortably in the happy middle class, whose way of life was the only one they knew.

"There are three-and-thirty million people in London," he said; "some of them *must* have need of me."

"Some *must.*"

"The trouble is . . . Well Bindon, that brown little old man your father wanted you to marry. He's an important person. . . . I can't go back to my flying-stage work, because he is now a Commissioner of the Flying Stage Clerks."

"I didn't know that," said Elizabeth.

"He was made that in the last few weeks . . . or things would be easy enough, for they liked me on the flying stage. But there's dozens of other things to be done—dozens. Don't you worry, dear. I'll rest a little while, and then we'll dine, and then I'll start on my rounds. I know lots of people—lots."

So they rested, and then they went to the public dining-room and dined, and then he started on his search for employment. But they soon realised that in the matter of one convenience the world was just as badly off as it had ever been, and that was a nice, secure, honourable, remunerative employment, leaving ample leisure for the private life, and demanding no special ability, no violent exertion nor risk, and no sacrifice of any sort for its attainment. He evolved a number of brilliant projects, and spent many days hurrying from one part of the enormous city to another in search of influential friends; and all his influential friends were glad to see him, and very sanguine until it came to definite proposals, and then they became guarded and vague. He would part with them coldly, and think over their behaviour, and get irritated on his way back, and stop at some telephone office and spend money on an animated but unprofitable quarrel. And as the days passed, he got so worried and irritated that even to seem kind and careless before Elizabeth cost him an effort—as she, being a loving woman, perceived very clearly.

After an extremely complex preface one day, she helped him out with a painful suggestion. He had expected her to weep and give way to despair when it came to selling all their joyfully bought early Victorian treasures, their quaint objects of art, their antimacassars, bead mats, repp curtains, veneered furniture, gold-framed steel engravings and pencil drawings, wax flowers under shades, stuffed birds, and all sorts of choice old things; but it was she who made the proposal. The sacrifice seemed to fill her with pleasure, and so did the idea of shifting to apartments ten or twelve floors lower in another hotel. "So long as Dings is with us, nothing matters," she said. "It's all experience." So he kissed her, said she was braver than when she fought the sheep-dogs, called her Boadicea, and abstained very carefully from reminding her that they would have to pay a considerably higher rent on account of the little voice with which Dings greeted the perpetual uproar of the city.

His idea had been to get Elizabeth out of the way when it came to selling the absurd furniture about which their affections were twined and tangled; but when it came to the sale it was Elizabeth who haggled with the dealer while Denton went about the running ways of the city, white and sick with sorrow and the fear of what was still to come. When they moved into their sparsely furnished pink-and-white apartments in a cheap hotel, there came an outbreak of furious energy on his part, and then nearly a week of lethargy during which he sulked at home. Though those days Elizabeth shone like a star, and at the end Denton's misery found a vent in tears. And then he went out into the city ways again, and—to his utter amazement—found some work to do.

His standard of employment had fallen steadily until at last it had reached the lowest level of independent workers. At first he had aspired to some high official position in the great Flying or Windvane or Water Companies, or to an appointment on one of the General Intelligence Organisations that had replaced newspapers, or to some professional partnership, but those were the dreams of the beginning. From that he had passed to speculation, and three hundred gold "lions" out of Elizabeth's thousand had vanished one evening in the share market. Now he was glad his good looks secured him a trial in the position of salesman to the Suzannah Hat Syndicate, a Syndicate dealing in ladies' caps, hair decorations, and hats—for though the city was completely covered in, ladies still wore extremely elaborate and beautiful hats at the theatres and places of public worship.

It would have been amusing if one could have confronted a Regent Street shopkeeper of the nineteenth century with the development of his establishment in which Denton's duties lay. Nineteenth Way was still sometimes called Regent Street, but it was now a street of moving platforms and nearly eight hundred feet wide. The middle space was immovable and gave access by staircases descending into subterranean ways to the houses on either side. Right and left were an ascending series of continuous platforms each of which travelled about five miles an hour faster than the one internal to it, so that one could step from platform to platform until one reached the swiftest outer way and so go about the city. The establishment of the Suzannah Hat Syndicate projected a vast *façade* upon the outer way, sending out overhead at either end an overlapping series of huge white glass screens, on which gigantic animated pictures of the faces of well-known beautiful living women wearing novelties in hats were thrown. A dense crowd was always collected in the stationary central way watching a vast kinematograph which displayed the changing fashion. The whole front of the building was in perpetual chromatic change, and all down the *façade*—four hundred feet it measured—and all across the street of moving ways, laced and winked and glittered in a thousand varieties of colour and lettering the inscription—

SUZANNA! 'ETS! SUZANNA! 'ETS!

A broadside of gigantic phonographs drowned all conversation in the moving way and roared "*hats*" at the passerby, while far down the street and up, other batteries counselled the public to "walk down for Suzannah," and queried, "Why *don't* you buy the girl a hat?"

For the benefit of those who chanced to be deaf—and deafness was not uncommon in the London of that age, inscriptions of all sizes were thrown from the roof above upon the moving platforms themselves, and on one's hand or on the bald head of the man before one, or on a lady's shoulders, or in a sudden jet of flame before one's feet, the moving finger wrote in unanticipated letters of fire " *'ets r chip t'de,*" or simply " *'ets.*" And spite of all these efforts so high was the pitch at which the city lived, so trained became one's eyes and ears to ignore all sorts of advertisement, that many a citizen had passed that place thousands of times and was still unaware of the existence of the Suzannah Hat Syndicate.

To enter the building one descended the staircase in the middle way and walked through a public passage in which pretty girls promenaded, girls who were willing to wear a ticketed hat for a small fee. The entrance chamber was a large hall in which wax heads fashionably adorned rotated gracefully upon pedestals, and from this one passed through a cash office to an interminable series of little rooms, each room with its salesman, its three or four hats and pins, its mirrors, its kinematographs, telephones and hat slides in communication with the central depôt, its comfortable lounge and tempting refreshments. A salesman in such an apartment did Denton now become. It was his business to attend to any of the incessant stream of ladies who chose to stop with him, to behave as winningly as possible, to offer refreshment, to converse on any topic the possible customer chose, and to guide the conversation dexterously but not insistently towards hats. He was to suggest trying on various types of hat and to show by his manner and bearing, but without any coarse flattery, the enhanced impression made by the hats he wished to sell. He had several mirrors, adapted by various subtleties of curvature and tint to different types of face and complexion, and much depended on the proper use of these.

Denton flung himself at these curious and not very congenial duties with a good will and energy that would have amazed him a year before; but all to no purpose. The Senior Manageress, who had selected him for appointment and conferred various small marks of favour upon him, suddenly changed in her manner, declared for no assignable cause that he was stupid, and dismissed him at the end of six weeks of salesmanship. So Denton had to resume his ineffectual search for employment.

This second search did not last very long. Their money was at the ebb. To eke it out a little longer they resolved to part with their darling Dings, and took that small person to one of the public *creches* that abounded in the city. That was the common use of the time. The industrial emancipation of women, the correlated disorganisation of the secluded "home," had rendered *creches* a necessity for all but very rich and exceptionally-minded people. Therein children encountered hygienic and educational advantages impossible without such organisation. *Creches* were of all classes and types of luxury, down to those of the Labour Company, where children were taken on credit, to be redeemed in labour as they grew up.

But both Denton and Elizabeth being, as I have explained, strange old-fashioned young people, full of nineteenth-century ideas, hated these convenient *creches* exceedingly and at last took their little daughter to one with extreme reluctance. They were received by a motherly person in a uniform who was very brisk and prompt in her manner until Elizabeth wept at the mention of parting from her child. The motherly person, after a brief astonishment at this unusual emotion, changed suddenly into a creature of hope and comfort, and so won Elizabeth's gratitude for life. They were conducted into a vast room presided over by several nurses and with hundreds of two-year-old girls grouped about the toy-covered floor. This was the Two-year-old Room. Two nurses came forward, and Elizabeth watched their bearing towards Dings with jealous eyes. They were kind—it was clear they felt kind, and yet . . .

Presently it was time to go. By that time Dings was happily established in a corner, sitting on the floor with her arms filled, and herself, indeed, for the most part hidden by an unaccustomed wealth of toys. She seemed careless of all human relationships as her parents receded.

They were forbidden to upset her by saying good-bye.

At the door Elizabeth glanced back for the last time, and behold! Dings had dropped her new wealth and was standing with a dubious face. Suddenly Elizabeth gasped, and the motherly nurse pushed her forward and closed the door.

"You can come again soon, dear," she said, with unexpected tenderness in her eyes. For a moment Elizabeth stared at her with a blank face. "You can come again soon," repeated the nurse. Then with a swift transition Elizabeth was weeping in the nurse's arms. So it was that Denton's heart was won also.

And three weeks after our young people were absolutely penniless, and only one way lay open. They must go to the Labour Company. So soon as the rent was a week overdue their few remaining possessions were seized, and with scant courtesy they were shown the way out of the hotel. Elizabeth walked along the passage towards the staircase that ascended to the motionless middle way, too dulled by misery to think. Denton stopped behind to finish a stinging and unsatisfactory argument with the hotel porter, and then came hurrying after her, flushed and hot. He slackened his pace as he overtook her, and together they ascended to the middle way in silence. There they found two seats vacant and sat down.

"We need not go there—*yet?*" said Elizabeth.

"No—not till we are hungry," said Denton.

They said no more.

Elizabeth's eyes sought a resting-place and found none. To the right roared the eastward ways, to the left the ways in the opposite direction, swarming with people. Backwards and forwards along a cable overhead rushed a string of gesticulating men, dressed like clowns, each marked on back and chest with one gigantic letter, so that altogether they spelt out:

PURKINJE'S DIGESTIVE PILLS.

An anæmic little woman in horrible coarse blue canvas pointed a little girl to one of this string of hurrying advertisements.

"Look!" said the anæmic woman: "there's yer father."

"Which?" said the little girl.

" 'Im wiv his nose coloured red," said the anæmic woman. The little girl began to cry, and Elizabeth could have cried too.

"Ain't 'e kickin' 'is legs!—*just!*" said the anæmic woman in blue, trying to make things bright again. "Looky—*now!*"

On the *façade* to the right a huge intensely bright disc of weird colour spun incessantly, and letters of fire that came and went spelt out—

DOES THIS MAKE YOU GIDDY?

Then a pause, followed by

TAKE A PURKINJE'S DIGESTIVE PILL.

A vast and desolating braying began. "If you love Swagger Literature, put your telephone on to Bruggles, the Greatest Author of all Time. The Greatest Thinker of all Time. Teaches you Morals up to your Scalp! The very image of Socrates, except the back of his head, which is like Shakespeare. He has six toes, dresses in red, and never cleans his teeth. Hear HIM!"

Denton's voice became audible in a gap in the uproar. "I never ought to have married you," he was saying. "I have wasted your money, ruined you, brought you to misery. I am a scoundrel . . . Oh, this accursed world!"

She tried to speak, and for some moments could not. She grasped his hand. "No," she said at last.

A half-formed desire suddenly became determination. She stood up. "Will you come?"

He rose also. "We need not go there yet."

"Not that. But I want you to come to the flying stages—where we met. You know? The little seat."

He hesitated. "*Can* you?" he said, doubtfully.

"Must," she answered.

He hesitated still for a moment, then moved to obey her will.

And so it was they spent their last half-day of freedom out under the open air in the little seat under the flying stages where they had been wont to meet five short years ago. There she told him, what she could not tell him in the tumultuous public ways, that she did not repent even now of their marriage—that whatever discomfort and misery life still had for them, she was content with the things that had been. The weather was kind to them, the seat was sunlit and warm, and overhead the shining aeroplanes went and came.

At last towards sunsetting their time was at an end, and they made their vows to one another and clasped hands, and then rose up and went back into the ways of the city, a shabby-looking, heavy-hearted pair, tired and hungry. Soon they came to one of the pale blue signs that marked a Labour Company Bureau. For a space they stood in the middle way regarding this and at last descended, and entered the waiting-room.

The Labour Company had originally been a charitable organisation; its aim was to supply food, shelter, and work to all comers. This it was bound to do by the conditions of its incorporation, and it was also bound to supply food and shelter and medical attendance to all incapable of work who chose to demand its aid. In exchange these incapables paid labour notes, which they had to redeem upon recovery. They signed these labour notes with thumb-marks, which were photographed and indexed in such a way that this world-wide Labour Company could identify any one of its two or three hundred million clients at the cost of an hour's inquiry. The day's labour was defined as two spells in a treadmill used in generating electrical force, or its equivalent, and its due performance could be enforced by law. In practice the Labour Company found it advisable to add to its statutory obligations of food and shelter a few pence a day as an inducement to effort; and its enterprise had not only abolished pauperisation altogether, but supplied practically all but the very highest and most responsible labour throughout the world. Nearly a third of the population of the world were its serfs and debtors from the cradle to the grave.

In this practical, unsentimental way the problem of the unemployed had been most satisfactorily met and overcome. No one starved in the public ways, and no rags, no costume less sanitary and sufficient than the Labour Company's hygienic but inelegant blue canvas, pained the eye throughout the whole world. It was the constant theme of the phonographic newspapers how much the world had progressed since nineteenth-century days, when the bodies of those killed by the vehicular traffic or dead of starvation, were, they alleged, a common feature in all the busier streets.

Denton and Elizabeth sat apart in the waiting-room until their turn came. Most of the others collected there seemed limp and taciturn, but three or four young people gaudily dressed made up for the quietude of their companions. They were life clients of the Company, born in the Company's *creche* and destined to die in its hospital, and they had been out for a spree with some shillings or so of extra pay. They talked vociferously in a later development of the Cockney dialect, manifestly very proud of themselves.

Elizabeth's eyes went from these to the less assertive figures. One seemed exceptionally pitiful to her. It was a woman of perhaps forty-five, with gold-stained hair and a painted face, down which abundant tears had trickled; she had a pinched nose, hungry eyes, lean hands and shoulders, and her dusty worn-out finery told the story of her life. Another was a grey-bearded old man in the costume of a bishop of one of the high episcopal sects—for religion was now also a business, and had its ups and downs. And beside him a sickly, dissipated-looking boy of perhaps two-and-twenty glared at Fate.

Presently Elizabeth and then Denton interviewed the manageress—for the Company preferred women in this capacity—and found she possessed an energetic face, a contemptuous manner, and a particularly unpleasant voice. They were given various cheques, including one to certify that they need not have their heads cropped; and when they had given their thumb-marks, learnt the number corresponding thereunto, and exchanged their shabby middleclass clothes for duly numbered blue canvas suits, they repaired to the huge plain dining-room for their first meal under these new conditions. Afterwards they were to return to her for instructions about their work.

When they had made the exchange of their clothing Elizabeth did not seem able to look at Denton at first; but he looked at her, and saw with astonishment that even in blue canvas she was still beautiful. And then their soup and bread came sliding on its little rail down the long table towards them and stopped with a jerk, and he forgot the matter. For they had had no proper meal for three days.

After they had dined they rested for a time. Neither talked—there was nothing to say; and presently they got up and went back to the manageress to learn what they had to do.

The manageress referred to a tablet. "Y'r rooms won't be here; it'll be in the Highbury Ward, Ninety-seventh way, number two thousand and seventeen. Better make a note of it on y'r card. *You*, nought nought nought, type seven, sixty-four, b.c.d., *gamma* forty-one, female; you 'ave to go to the Metal-beating Company, and try that for a day—fourpence bonus if ye're satisfactory; and *you*, nought seven one, type four, seven hundred and nine, g.f.b., *pi* five and ninety, male; you 'ave to go to the Photographic Company on Eighty-first way, and learn something or other—*I* don't know—thrippence. 'Ere's y'r cards. That's all. Next! *What?* Didn't catch it all? Lor! So suppose I must go over it all again. Why don't you listen? Keerless, unprovident people! One'd think these things didn't matter."

Their ways to their work lay together for a time. And now they found they could talk. Curiously enough, the worst of their depression seemed over now that they had actually donned the blue. Denton could talk with interest even of the work that lay before them. "Whatever it is," he said, "it can't be so hateful as that hat shop. And after we have paid for Dings, we shall still have a whole penny a day between us even now. Afterwards—we may improve,—get more money."

Elizabeth was less inclined to speech. "I wonder why work should seem so hateful," she said.

"It's odd," said Denton. "I suppose it wouldn't be if it were not the thought of being ordered about. . . . I hope we shall have decent managers."

Elizabeth did not answer. She was not thinking of that. She was tracing out some thoughts of her own.

"Of course," she said presently, "we have been using up work all our lives. It's only fair—"

She stopped. It was too intricate.

"We paid for it," said Denton, for at that time he had not troubled himself about these complicated things.

"We did nothing—and yet we paid for it. That's what I cannot understand."

"Perhaps we are paying," said Elizabeth presently—for her theology was old-fashioned and simple.

Presently it was time for them to part, and each went to the appointed work.

Denton's was to mind a complicated hydraulic press that seemed almost an intelligent thing. This press worked by the sea-water that was destined finally to flush the city drains—for the world had long since abandoned the folly of pouring drinkable water into its sewers. This water was brought close to the eastward edge of the city by a huge canal, and then raised by an enormous battery of pumps into reservoirs at a level of four hundred feet above the sea, from which it spread by a billion arterial branches over the city. Thence it poured down, cleansing, sluicing, working machinery of all sorts, through an infinite variety of capillary channels into the great drains, the *cloacae maximae*, and so carried the sewage out to the agricultural areas that surrounded London on every side.

The press was employed in one of the processes of the photographic manufacture, but the nature of the process it did not concern Denton to understand. The most salient fact to his mind was that it had to be conducted in ruby light, and as a consequence the room in which he worked was lit by one coloured globe that poured a lurid and painful illumination about the room. In the darkest corner stood the press whose servant Denton had now become; it was a huge, dim, glittering thing with a projecting hood that had a remote resemblance to a bowed head, and, squatting like some metal Buddha in this weird light that ministered to its needs, it seemed to Denton in certain moods almost as if this must needs be the obscure idol to which humanity in some strange aberration had offered up his life. His duties had a varied monotony. Such items as the following will convey an idea of the service of the press. The thing worked with a busy clicking so long as things went well; but if the paste that came pouring through a feeder from another room and which it was perpetually compressing into thin plates, changed in quality the rhythm of its click altered and Denton hastened to make certain adjustments. The slightest delay involved a waste of paste and the docking of one or more of his daily pence. If the supply of paste waned—there were hand processes of a peculiar sort involved in its preparation, and sometimes the workers had convulsions which deranged their output—Denton had to throw the press out of gear. In the painful vigilance a multitude of such trivial attentions entailed, painful because of the incessant effort its absence of natural interest required, Denton had now to pass one-third of his days. Save for an occasional visit from the manager, a kindly but singularly foul-mouthed man, Denton passed his working hours in solitude.

Elizabeth's work was of a more social sort. There was a fashion for covering the private apartments of the very wealthy with metal plates beautifully embossed with repeated patterns. The taste of the time demanded, however, that the repetition of the patterns should not be exact—not mechanical, but "natural"—and it was found that the most pleasing arrangement of pattern irregularity was obtained by employing women of refinement and natural taste to punch out the patterns with small dites. So many square feet of plates was exacted from Elizabeth as a minimum, and for whatever square feet she did in excess she received a small payment. The room, like most rooms of women workers, was under a manageress: men had been found by the Labour Company not only less exacting but extremely liable to excuse favoured ladies from a proper share of their duties. The manageress was a not unkindly, taciturn person, with the hardened remains of beauty of the brunette type; and the other women workers, who of course hated her, associated her name scandalously with one of the metal-work directors in order to explain her position.

Only two or three of Elizabeth's fellow-workers were born labour serfs; plain, morose girls, but most of them corresponded to what the nineteenth century would have called a "reduced" gentlewoman. But the ideal of what constituted a gentlewoman had altered: the faint, faded, negative virtue, the modulated voice and restrained gesture of the old-fashioned gentlewoman had vanished from the earth. Most of her companions showed in discoloured hair, ruined complexions, and the texture of their reminiscent conversations, the vanished glories of a conquering youth. All of these artistic workers were much older than Elizabeth, and two openly expressed their surprise that any one so young and pleasant should come to share their toil. But Elizabeth did not trouble them with her old-world moral conceptions.

They were permitted, and even encouraged to converse with each other, for the directors very properly judged that anything that conduced to variations of mood made for pleasing fluctuations in their patterning; and Elizabeth was almost forced to hear the stories of these lives with which her own interwove: garbled and distorted they were by vanity indeed and yet comprehensible enough. And soon she began to appreciate the small spites and cliques, the little misunderstandings and alliances that enmeshed about her. One woman was excessively garrulous and descriptive about a wonderful son of hers; another had cultivated a foolish coarseness of speech, that she seemed to regard as the wittiest expression of originality conceivable; a third mused for ever on dress, and whispered to Elizabeth how she saved her pence day after day, and would presently have a glorious day of freedom, wearing . . . and then followed hours of description; two others sat always together, and called one another pet names, until one day some little thing happened, and they sat apart, blind and deaf as it seemed to one another's being. And always from them all came an incessant tap, tap, tap, tap, and the manageress listened always to the rhythm to mark if one fell away. Tap, tap, tap, tap: so their days passed, so their lives must pass. Elizabeth sat among them, kindly and quiet, gray-hearted, marvelling at Fate: tap, tap, tap; tap, tap, tap; tap, tap, tap.

So there came to Denton and Elizabeth a long succession of laborious days, that hardened their hands, wove strange threads of some new and sterner substance into the soft prettiness of their lives, and drew grave lines and shadows on their faces. The bright, convenient ways of the former life had receded to an inaccessible distance; slowly they learnt the lesson of the under-world—sombre and laborious, vast and pregnant. There were many little things happened: things that would be tedious and miserable to tell, things that were bitter and grievous to bear—indignities, tyrannies, such as must ever season the bread of the poor in cities; and one thing that was not little, but seemed like the utter blackening of life to them, which was that the child they had given life to sickened and died. But that story, that ancient, perpetually recurring story, has been told so often, has been told so beautifully, that there is no need to tell it over again here. There was the same sharp fear, the same long anxiety, the deferred inevitable blow, and the black silence. It has always been the same; it will always be the same. It is one of the things that must be.

And it was Elizabeth who was the first to speak, after an aching, dull interspace of days: not, indeed, of the foolish little name that was a name no longer, but of the darkness that brooded over her soul. They had come through the shrieking, tumultuous ways of the city together; the clamour of trade, of yelling competitive religions, of political appeal, had beat upon deaf ears; the glare of focused lights, of dancing letters, and fiery advertisements, had fallen upon the set, miserable faces unheeded. They took their dinner in the dining-hall at a place apart. "I want," said Elizabeth clumsily, "to go out to the flying stages—to that seat. Here, one can say nothing. . . ."

Denton looked at her. "It will be night," he said.

"I have asked,—it is a fine night." She stopped.

He perceived she could find no words to explain herself. Suddenly he understood that she wished to see the stars once more, the stars they had watched together from the open downland in that wild honeymoon of theirs five years ago. Something caught at his throat. He looked away from her.

"There will be plenty of time to go," he said, in a matter-of-fact tone.

And at last they came out to their little seat on the flying stage, and sat there for a long time in silence. The little seat was in shadow, but the zenith was pale blue with the effulgence of the stage overhead, and all the city spread below them, squares and circles and patches of brilliance caught in a mesh-work of light. The little stars seemed very faint and small: near as they had been to the old-world watcher, they had become now infinitely remote. Yet one could see them in the darkened patches amidst the glare, and especially in the northward sky, the ancient constellations gliding steadfast and patient about the pole.

Long our two people sat in silence, and at last Elizabeth sighed.

"If I understood," she said, "if I could understand. When one is down there the city seems everything—the noise, the hurry, the voices—you must live, you must scramble. Here—it is nothing; a thing that passes. One can think in peace."

"Yes," said Denton. "How flimsy it all is! From here more than half of it is swallowed by the night. . . . It will pass."

"We shall pass first," said Elizabeth.

"I know," said Denton. "If life were not a moment, the whole of history would seem like the happening of a day. . . . Yes—we shall pass. And the city will pass, and all the things that are to come. Man and the Overman and wonders unspeakable. And yet . . ."

He paused, and then began afresh. "I know what you feel. At least I fancy. . . . Down there one thinks of one's work, one's little vexations and pleasures, one's eating and drinking and ease and pain. One lives, and one must die. Down there and everyday—our sorrow seemed the end of life. . . .

"Up here it is different. For instance, down there it would seem impossible almost to go on living if one were horribly disfigured, horribly crippled, disgraced. Up here—under these stars—none of those things would matter. They don't matter. . . . They are a part of something. One seems just to touch that something—under the stars. . . ."

He stopped. The vague, impalpable things in his mind, cloudy emotions half shaped towards ideas, vanished before the rough grasp of words. "It is hard to express," he said lamely.

They sat through a long stillness.

"It is well to come here," he said at last. "We stop—our minds are very finite. After all we are just poor animals rising out of the brute, each with a mind, the poor beginning of a mind. We are so stupid. So much hurts. And yet. . . .

"I know, I know—and some day we shall *see*.

"All this frightful stress, all this discord will resolve to harmony, and we shall know it. Nothing is but it makes for that. Nothing. All the failures—every little thing makes for that harmony. Everything is necessary to it, we shall find. We shall find. Nothing, not even the most dreadful thing, could be left out. Not even the most trivial. Every tap of your hammer on the brass, every moment of work, my idleness even. . . . Dear one! every movement of our poor little one. . . . All these things go on for ever. And the faint impalpable things. We, sitting here together.—Everything. . . .

"The passion that joined us, and what has come since. It is not passion now. More than anything else it is sorrow. *Dear. . . .*"

He could say no more, could follow his thoughts no further.

Elizabeth made no answer—she was very still; but presently her hand sought his and found it.

IV. UNDERNEATH

Under the stars one may reach upward and touch resignation, whatever the evil thing may be, but in the heat and stress of the day's work we lapse again, come disgust and anger and intolerable moods. How little is all our magnanimity—an accident! a phase! The very Saints of old had first to flee the world. And Denton and Elizabeth could not flee their world, no longer were there open roads to unclaimed lands where men might live freely—however hardly—and keep their souls in peace. The city had swallowed up mankind.

For a time these two Labour Serfs were kept at their original occupations, she sat at her brass stamping and Denton at his press; and then came a move for him that brought with it fresh and still bitterer experiences of life in the underways of the great city. He was transferred to the care of a rather more elaborate press in the central factory of the London Tile Trust.

In this new situation he had to work in a long vaulted room with a number of other men, for the most part born Labour Serfs. He came to this intercourse reluctantly. His upbringing had been refined, and, until his ill fortune had brought him to that costume, he had never spoken in his life, except by way of command or some immediate necessity, to the white-faced wearers of the blue canvas. Now at last came contact; he had to work beside them, share their tools, eat with them. To both Elizabeth and himself this seemed a further degradation.

His taste would have seemed extreme to a man of the nineteenth century. But slowly and inevitably in the intervening years a gulf had opened between the wearers of the blue canvas and the classes above, a difference not simply of circumstances and habits of life, but of habits of thought—even of language. The underways had developed a dialect of their own: above, too, had arisen a dialect, a code of thought, a language of "culture," which aimed by a sedulous search after fresh distinction to widen perpetually the space between itself and "vulgarity." The bond of a common faith, moreover, no longer held the race together. The last years of the nineteenth century were distinguished by the rapid development among the prosperous idle of esoteric perversions of the popular religion: glosses and interpretations that reduced the broad teachings of the carpenter of Nazareth to the exquisite narrowness of their lives. And, in spite of their inclination towards the ancient fashion of living, neither Elizabeth nor Denton had been sufficiently original to escape the suggestion of their surroundings. In matters of common behaviour they had followed the ways of their class, and so when they fell at last to be Labour Serfs it seemed to them almost as though they were falling among offensive inferior animals; they felt as a nineteenth-century duke and duchess might have felt who were forced to take rooms in the Jago.

Their natural impulse was to maintain a "distance." But Denton's first idea of a dignified isolation from his new surroundings was soon rudely dispelled. He had imagined that his fall to the position of a Labour Serf was the end of his lesson, that when their little daughter had died he had plumbed the deeps of life; but indeed these things were only the beginning. Life demands something more from us than acquiescence. And now in a roomful of machine minders he was to learn a wider lesson, to make the acquaintance of another factor in life, a factor as elemental as the loss of things dear to us, more elemental even than toil.

His quiet discouragement of conversation was an immediate cause of offence—was interpreted, rightly enough I fear, as disdain. His ignorance of the vulgar dialect, a thing upon which he had hitherto prided himself, suddenly took upon itself a new aspect. He failed to perceive at once that his reception of the coarse and stupid but genially intended remarks that greeted his appearance must have stung the makers of these advances like blows in their faces. "Don't understand," he said rather coldly, and at hazard, "No, thank you."

The man who had addressed him stared, scowled, and turned away.

A second, who also failed at Denton's unaccustomed ear, took the trouble to repeat his remark, and Denton discovered he was being offered the use of an oil can. He expressed polite thanks, and this second man embarked upon a penetrating conversation. Denton, he remarked, had been a swell, and he wanted to know how he had come to wear the blue. He clearly expected an interesting record of vice and extravagance. Had Denton ever been at a Pleasure City? Denton was speedily to discover how the existence of these wonderful places of delight permeated and defiled the thought and honour of these unwilling, hopeless workers of the underworld.

His aristocratic temperament resented these questions. He answered "No" curtly. The man persisted with a still more personal question, and this time it was Denton who turned away.

"Gorblimey!" said his interlocutor, much astonished.

It presently forced itself upon Denton's mind that this remarkable conversation was being repeated in indignant tones to more sympathetic hearers, and that it gave rise to astonishment and ironical laughter. They looked at Denton with manifestly enhanced interest. A curious perception of isolation dawned upon him. He tried to think of his press and its unfamiliar peculiarities. . . .

The machines kept everybody pretty busy during the first spell, and then came a recess. It was only an interval for refreshment, too brief for any one to go out to a Labour Company dining-room. Denton followed his fellow-workers into a short gallery, in which were a number of bins and refuse from the presses.

Each man produced a packet of food. Denton had no packet. The manager, a careless young man who held his position by influence, had omitted to warn Denton that it was necessary to apply for this provision. He stood apart, feeling hungry. The others drew together in a group and talked in undertones, glancing at him ever and again. He became uneasy. His appearance of disregard cost him an increasing effort. He tried to think of the levers of his new press.

Presently one, a man shorter but much broader and stouter than Denton, came forward to him. Denton turned to him as unconcernedly as possible. "Here!" said the delegate—as Denton judged him to be—extending a cube of bread in a not too clean hand. He had a swart, broad-nosed face, and his mouth hung down towards one corner.

Denton felt doubtful for the instant whether this was meant for civility or insult. His impulse was to decline. "No, thanks," he said; and, at the man's change of expression, "I'm not hungry."

There came a laugh from the group behind. "Told you so," said the man who had offered Denton the loan of an oil can. "He's top side, he is. You ain't good enough for 'im."

The swart face grew a shade darker.

"Here," said its owner, still extending the bread, and speaking in a lower tone; "you got to eat this. See?"

Denton looked into the threatening face before him, and odd little currents of energy seemed to be running through his limbs and body.

"I don't want it," he said, trying a pleasant smile that twitched and failed.

The thickset man advanced his face, and the bread became a physical threat in his hand. Denton's mind rushed together to the one problem of his antagonist's eyes.

"Eat it," said the swart man.

There came a pause, and then they both moved quickly. The cube of bread described a complicated path, a curve that would have ended in Denton's face; and then his fist hit the wrist of the hand that gripped it, and it flew upward, and out of the conflict—its part played.

He stepped back quickly, fists clenched and arms tense. The hot, dark countenance receded, became an alert hostility, watching its chance. Denton for one instant felt confident, and strangely buoyant and serene. His heart beat quickly. He felt his body alive, and glowing to the tips.

"Scrap, boys!" shouted some one, and then the dark figure had leapt forward, ducked back and sideways, and come in again. Denton struck out, and was hit. One of his eyes seemed to him to be demolished, and he felt a soft lip under his fist just before he was hit again—this time under the chin. A huge fan of fiery needles shot open. He had a momentary persuasion that his head was knocked to pieces, and then something hit his head and back from behind, and the fight became an uninteresting, an impersonal thing.

He was aware that time—seconds or minutes—had passed, abstract, uneventful time. He was lying with his head in a heap of ashes, and something wet and warm ran swiftly into his neck. The first shock broke up into discrete sensations. All his head throbbed; his eye and his chin throbbed exceedingly, and the taste of blood was in his mouth.

"He's all right," said a voice. "He's opening his eyes."

"Serve him—well right," said a second.

His mates were standing about him. He made an effort and sat up. He put his hand to the back of his head, and his hair was wet and full of cinders. A laugh greeted the gesture. His eye was partially closed. He perceived what had happened. His momentary anticipation of a final victory had vanished.

"Looks surprised," said some one.

" 'Ave any more?" said a wit; and then, imitating Denton's refined accent: "No, thank you."

Denton perceived the swart man with a blood-stained handkerchief before his face, and somewhat in the background.

"Where's that bit of bread he's got to eat?" said a little ferret-faced creature; and sought with his foot in the ashes of the adjacent bin.

Denton had a moment of internal debate. He knew the code of honour requires a man to pursue a fight he has begun to the bitter end; but this was his first taste of the bitterness. He was resolved to rise again, but he felt no passionate impulse. It occurred to him—and the thought was no very violent spur—that he was perhaps after all a coward. For a moment his will was heavy, a lump of lead.

" 'Ere it is," said the little ferret-faced man, and stooped to pick up a cindery cube. He looked at Denton, then at the others.

Slowly, unwillingly, Denton stood up.

A dirty-faced albino extended a hand to the ferret-faced man.

"Gimme that toke," he said. He advanced threateningly, bread in hand, to Denton. "So you ain't 'ad your bellyful yet," he said. "Eh?"

Now it was coming. "No, I haven't," said Denton, with a catching of the breath, and resolved to try this brute behind the ear before he himself got stunned again. He knew he would be stunned again. He was astonished how ill he had judged himself beforehand. A few ridiculous lunges, and down he would go again. He watched the albino's eyes. The albino was grinning confidently, like a man who plans an agreeable trick. A sudden perception of impending indignities stung Denton.

"You leave 'im alone, Jim," said the swart man suddenly over the bloodstained rag. "He ain't done nothing to you."

The albino's grin vanished. He stopped. He looked from one to the other. It seemed to Denton that the swart man demanded the privilege of his destruction. The albino would have been better.

"You leave 'im alone," said the swart man. "See? 'E's 'ad 'is licks."

A clattering bell lifted up its voice and solved the situation. The albino hesitated. "Lucky for you," he said, adding a foul metaphor, and turned with the others towards the press-room again. "Wait for the end of the spell, mate," said the albino over his shoulder—an afterthought. The swart man waited for the albino to precede him. Denton realised that he had a reprieve.

The men passed towards an open door. Denton became aware of his duties, and hurried to join the tail of the queue. At the doorway of the vaulted gallery of presses a yellow-uniformed labour policeman stood ticking a card. He had ignored the swart man's hæmorrhage.

"Hurry up there!" he said to Denton.

"Hello!" he said, at the sight of his facial disarray. "Who's been hitting *you?*"

"That's my affair," said Denton.

"Not if it spiles your work, it ain't," said the man in yellow. "You mind that."

Denton made no answer. He was a rough—a labourer. He wore the blue canvas. The laws of assault and battery, he knew, were not for the likes of him. He went to his press.

He could feel the skin of his brow and chin and head lifting themselves to noble bruises, felt the throb and pain of each aspiring contusion. His nervous system slid down to lethargy; at each movement in his press adjustment he felt he lifted a weight. And as for his honour—that too throbbed and puffed. How did he stand? What precisely had happened in the last ten minutes? What would happen next? He knew that there was enormous matter for thought, and he could not think save in disordered snatches.

His mood was a sort of stagnant astonishment. All his conceptions were overthrown. He had regarded his security from physical violence as inherent, as one of the conditions of life. So, indeed, it had been while he wore his middle-class costume, had his middle-class property to serve for his defence. But who would interfere among Labour roughs fighting together? And indeed in those days no man would. In the Underworld there was no law between man and man; the law and machinery of the state had become for them something that held men down, fended them off from much desirable property and pleasure, and that was all. Violence, that ocean in which the brutes live for ever, and from which a thousand dykes and contrivances have won our hazardous civilised life, had flowed in again upon the sinking underways and submerged them. The fist ruled. Denton had come right down at last to the elemental—fist and trick and the stubborn heart and fellowship—even as it was in the beginning.

The rhythm of his machine changed, and his thoughts were interrupted.

Presently he could think again. Strange how quickly things had happened! He bore these men who had thrashed him no very vivid ill-will. He was bruised and enlightened. He saw with absolute fairness now the reasonableness of his unpopularity. He had behaved like a fool. Disdain, seclusion, are the privilege of the strong. The fallen aristocrat still clinging to his pointless distinction is surely the most pitiful creature of pretence in all this clamant universe. Good heavens! what was there for him to despise in these men?

What a pity he had not appreciated all this better five hours ago!

What would happen at the end of the spell? He could not tell. He could not imagine. He could not imagine the thoughts of these men. He was sensible only of their hostility and utter want of sympathy. Vague possibilities of shame and violence chased one another across his mind. Could he devise some weapon? He recalled his assault upon the hypnotist, but there were no detachable lamps here. He could see nothing that he could catch up in his defence.

For a space he thought of a headlong bolt for the security of the public ways directly the spell was over. Apart from the trivial consideration of his self-respect, he perceived that this would be only a foolish postponement and aggravation of his trouble. He perceived the ferret-faced man and the albino talking together with their eyes towards him. Presently they were talking to the swart man, who stood with his broad back studiously towards Denton.

At last came the end of the second spell. The lender of oil cans stopped his press sharply and turned round, wiping his mouth with the back of his hand. His eyes had the quiet expectation of one who seats himself in a theatre.

Now was the crisis, and all the little nerves of Denton's being seemed leaping and dancing. He had decided to show fight if any fresh indignity was offered him. He stopped his press and turned. With an enormous affectation of ease he walked down the vault and entered the passage of the ash pits, only to discover he had left his jacket—which he had taken off because of the heat of the vault—beside his press. He walked back. He met the albino eye to eye.

He heard the ferret-faced man in expostulation. " 'E reely ought, eat it," said the ferret-faced man. " 'E did reely."

"No—you leave 'im alone," said the swart man.

Apparently nothing further was to happen to him that day. He passed out to the passage and staircase that led up to the moving platforms of the city.

He emerged on the livid brilliance and streaming movement of the public street. He became acutely aware of his disfigured face, and felt his swelling bruises with a limp, investigatory hand. He went up to the swiftest platform, and seated himself on a Labour Company bench.

He lapsed into a pensive torpor. The immediate dangers and stresses of his position he saw with a sort of static clearness. What would they do tomorrow?

He could not tell. What would Elizabeth think of his brutalisation? He could not tell. He was exhausted. He was aroused presently by a hand upon his arm.

He looked up, and saw the swart man seated beside him. He started. Surely he was safe from violence in the public way!

The swart man's face retained no traces of his share in the fight; his expression was free from hostility—seemed almost deferential. " 'Scuse me," he said, with a total absence of truculence. Denton realised that no assault was intended. He stared, awaiting the next development.

It was evident the next sentence was premeditated. "Whad—I—was—going—to say—was this," said the swart man, and sought through a silence for further words.

"Whad—I—was—going—to say—was this," he repeated.

Finally he abandoned that gambit. "*You're* aw right," he cried, laying a grimy hand on Denton's grimy sleeve. "*You're* aw right. You're a ge'man. Sorry—very sorry. Wanted to tell you that."

Denton realised that there must exist motives beyond a mere impulse to abominable proceedings in the man. He meditated, and swallowed an unworthy pride.

"I did not mean to be offensive to you," he said, "in refusing that bit of bread."

"Meant it friendly," said the swart man, recalling the scene; "but—in front of that blarsted Whitey and his snigger—well—I'*ad* to scrap."

"Yes," said Denton with sudden fervour: "I was a fool."

"Ah," said the swart man, with great satisfaction. "*That's* aw right. Shake!"

And Denton shook.

The moving platform was rushing by the establishment of a face moulder, and its lower front was a huge display of mirror, designed to stimulate the thirst for more symmetrical features. Denton caught the reflection of himself and his new friend, enormously twisted and broadened. His own face was puffed, one-sided, and blood-stained; a grin of idiotic and insincere amiability distorted its latitude. A wisp of hair occluded one eye. The trick of the mirror presented the swart man as a gross expansion of lip and nostril. They were linked by shaking hands. Then abruptly this vision passed—to return to memory in the anæmic meditations of a waking dawn.

As he shook, the swart man made some muddled remark, to the effect that he had always known he could get on with a gentleman if one came his way. He prolonged the shaking until Denton, under the influence of the mirror, withdrew his hand. The swart man became pensive, spat impressively on the platform, and resumed his theme.

"Whad I was going to say was this," he said; was gravelled, and shook his head at his foot.

Denton became curious. "Go on," he said, attentive.

The swart man took the plunge. He grasped Denton's arm, became intimate in his attitude. " 'Scuse me," he said. "Fact is, you done know *'ow* to scrap. Done know *'ow* to. Why—you done know 'ow to *begin*. You'll get killed if you don't mind. 'Ouldin' your 'ands—*There!*"

He reinforced his statement by objurgation, watching the effect of each oath with a wary eye.

"F'r instance. You're tall. Long arms. You got a longer reach than anyone in the brasted vault. Gobblimey, but I thought I'd got a tough on. 'Stead of which . . . 'Scuse me. I wouldn't have *'it* you if I'd known. It's like fighting sacks. 'Tisn't right. Y'r arms seemed 'ung on 'ooks. Reg'lar 'ung on 'ooks. There!"

Denton stared, and then surprised and hurt his battered chin by a sudden laugh. Bitter tears came into his eyes.

"Go on," he said.

The swart man reverted to his formula. He was good enough to say he liked the look of Denton, thought he had stood up "amazing plucky. On'y pluck ain't no good ain't no brasted good—if you don't 'old your 'ands.

"Whad I was going to say was this," he said. "Lemme show you 'ow to scrap. Just lemme. You're ig'nant, you ain't no class; but you might be a very decent scrapper—very decent. Shown. That's what I meant to say."

Denton hesitated. "But—" he said, "I can't give you anything—"

"That's the ge'man all over," said the swart man. "Who arst you to?"

"But your time?"

"If you don't get learnt scrapping you'll get killed,—don't you make no bones of that."

Denton thought. "I don't know," he said.

He looked at the face beside him, and all its native coarseness shouted at him. He felt a quick revulsion from his transient friendliness. It seemed to him incredible that it should be necessary for him to be indebted to such a creature.

"The chaps are always scrapping," said the swart man. "Always. And, of course—if one gets waxy and 'its you vital . . ."

"By God!" cried Denton; "I wish one would."

"Of course, if you feel like that—"

"You don't understand."

"P'raps I don't," said the swart man; and lapsed into a fuming silence.

When he spoke again his voice was less friendly, and he prodded Denton by way of address. "Look see!" he said: "are you going to let me show you 'ow to scrap?"

"It's tremendously kind of you," said Denton; "but—"

There was a pause. The swart man rose and bent over Denton.

"Too much ge'man," he said—"eh? I got a red face. . . . By gosh! you are—you *are* a brasted fool!"

He turned away, and instantly Denton realised the truth of this remark.

The swart man descended with dignity to a cross way, and Denton, after a momentary impulse to pursuit, remained on the platform. For a time the things that had happened filled his mind. In one day his graceful system of resignation had been shattered beyond hope. Brute force, the final, the fundamental, had thrust its face through all his explanations and glosses and consolations and grinned enigmatically. Though he was hungry and tired, he did not go on directly to the Labour Hotel, where he would meet Elizabeth. He found he was beginning to think, he wanted very greatly to think; and so, wrapped in a monstrous cloud of meditation, he went the circuit of the city on his moving platform twice. You figure him, tearing through the glaring, thunder-voiced city at a pace of fifty miles an hour, the city upon the planet that spins along its chartless path through space many thousands of miles an hour, funking most terribly, and trying to understand why the heart and will in him should suffer and keep alive.

When at last he came to Elizabeth, she was white and anxious. He might have noted she was in trouble, had it not been for his own preoccupation. He feared most that she would desire to know every detail of his indignities, that she would be sympathetic or indignant. He saw her eyebrows rise at the sight of him.

"I've had rough handling," he said, and gasped. "It's too fresh—too hot. I don't want to talk about it." He sat down with an unavoidable air of sullenness.

She stared at him in astonishment, and as she read something of the significant hieroglyphic of his battered face, her lips whitened. Her hand—it was thinner now than in the days of their prosperity, and her first finger was a little altered by the metal punching she did—clenched convulsively. "This horrible world!" she said, and said no more.

In these latter days they had become a very silent couple; they said scarcely a word to each other that night, but each followed a private train of thought. In the small hours, as Elizabeth lay awake, Denton started up beside her suddenly—he had been lying as still as a dead man.

"I cannot stand it!" cried Denton. "I *will* not stand it!"

She saw him dimly, sitting up; saw his arm lunge as if in a furious blow at the enshrouding night. Then for a space he was still.

"It is too much—it is more than one can bear!"

She could say nothing. To her, also, it seemed that this was as far as one could go. She waited through a long stillness. She could see that Denton sat with his arms about his knees, his chin almost touching them.

Then he laughed.

"No," he said at last, "I'm going to stand it. That's the peculiar thing. There isn't a grain of suicide in us—not a grain. I suppose all the people with a turn that way have gone. We're going through with it—to the end."

Elizabeth thought grayly, and realised that this also was true.

"We're going through with it. To think of all who have gone through with it: all the generations—endless—endless. Little beasts that snapped and snarled, snapping and snarling, snapping and snarling, generation after generation."

His monotone, ended abruptly, resumed after a vast interval.

"There were ninety thousand years of stone age. A Denton somewhere in all those years. Apostolic succession. The grace of going through. Let me see! Ninety—nine hundred—three nines, twenty-seven—*three thousand* generations of men!—men more or less. And each fought, and was bruised, and shamed, and somehow held his own—going through with it—passing it on. . . . And thousands more to come perhaps—thousands!

"Passing it on. I wonder if they will thank us."

His voice assumed an argumentative note. "If one could find something definite. . . . If one could say, 'This is why—this is why it goes on. . . .' "

He became still, and Elizabeth's eyes slowly separated him from the darkness until at last she could see how he sat with his head resting on his hand. A sense of the enormous remoteness of their minds came to her; that dim suggestion of another being seemed to her a figure of their mutual understanding. What could he be thinking now? What might he not say next? Another age seemed to elapse before he sighed and whispered: "No. I don't understand it. No!" Then a long interval, and he repeated this. But the second time it had the tone almost of a solution.

She became aware that he was preparing to lie down. She marked his movements, perceived with astonishment how he adjusted his pillow with a careful regard to comfort. He lay down with a sigh of contentment almost. His passion had passed. He lay still, and presently his breathing became regular and deep.

But Elizabeth remained with eyes wide open in the darkness, until the clamour of a bell and the sudden brilliance of the electric light warned them that the Labour Company had need of them for yet another day.

That day came a scuffle with the albino Whitey and the little ferret-faced man. Blunt, the swart artist in scrapping, having first let Denton grasp the bearing of his lesson, intervened, not without a certain quality of patronage. "Drop 'is 'air, Whitey, and let the man be," said his gross voice through a shower of indignities. "Can't you see 'e don't know *'ow* to scrap?" And Denton, lying shamefully in the dust, realised that he must accept that course of instruction after all.

He made his apology straight and clean. He scrambled up and walked to Blunt. "I was a fool, and you are right," he said. "If it isn't too late . . ."

That night, after the second spell, Denton went with Blunt to certain waste and slime-soaked vaults under the Port of London, to learn the first beginnings of the high art of scrapping as it had been perfected in the great world of the underways: how to hit or kick a man so as to hurt him excruciatingly or make him violently sick, how to hit or kick "vital," how to use glass in one's garments as a club and to spread red ruin with various domestic implements, how to anticipate and demolish your adversary's intentions in other directions; all the pleasant devices, in fact, that had grown up among the disinherited of the great cities of the twentieth and twenty-first centuries, were spread out by a gifted exponent for Denton's learning. Blunt's bashfulness fell from him as the instruction proceeded, and he developed a certain expert dignity, a quality of fatherly consideration. He treated Denton with the utmost consideration, only "flicking him up a bit" now and then, to keep the interest hot, and roaring with laughter at a happy fluke of Denton's that covered his mouth with blood.

"I'm always keerless of my mouth," said Blunt, admitting a weakness. "Always. It don't seem to matter, like just getting bashed in the mouth—not if your chin's all right. Tastin' blood does me good. Always. But I better not 'it you again."

Denton went home to fall asleep exhausted and wake in the small hours with aching limbs and all his bruises tingling. Was it worth while that he should go on living? He listened to Elizabeth's breathing, and remembering that he must have awaked her the previous night, he lay very still. He was sick with infinite disgust at the new conditions of his life. He hated it all, hated even the genial savage who had protected him so generously. The monstrous fraud of civilisation glared stark before his eyes; he saw it as a vast lunatic growth, producing a deepening torrent of savagery below, and above ever more flimsy gentility and silly wastefulness. He could see no redeeming reason, no touch of honour, either in the life he had led or in this life to which he had fallen. Civilisation presented itself as some castastrophic product as little concerned with men—save as victims—as a cyclone or a planetary collision. He, and therefore all mankind, seemed living utterly in vain. His mind sought some strange expedients of escape, if not for himself then at least for Elizabeth. But he meant them for himself. What if he hunted up Mwres and told him of their disaster? It came to him as an astonishing thing how utterly Mwres and Bindon had passed out of his range. Where were they? What were they doing? From that he passed to thoughts of utter dishonour. And finally, not arising in any way out of this mental tumult, but ending it as dawn ends the night, came the clear and obvious conclusion of the night before: the conviction that he had to go through with things; that, apart from any remoter view and quite sufficient for all his thought and energy, he had to stand up and fight among his fellows and quit himself like a man.

The second night's instruction was perhaps less dreadful than the first; and the third was even endurable, for Blunt dealt out some praise. The fourth day Denton chanced upon the fact that the ferret-faced man was a coward. There passed a fortnight of smouldering days and feverish instruction at night; Blunt, with many blasphemies, testified that never had he met so apt a pupil; and all night long Denton dreamt of kicks and counters and gouges and cunning tricks. For all that time no further outrages were attempted, for fear of Blunt; and then came the second crisis. Blunt did not come one day—afterwards he admitted his deliberate intention—and through the tedious morning Whitey awaited the interval between the spells with an ostentatious impatience. He knew nothing of the scrapping lessons, and he spent the time in telling Denton and the vault generally of certain disagreeable proceedings he had in mind.

Whitey was not popular, and the vault disgorged to see him haze the new man with only a languid interest. But matters changed when Whitey's attempt to open the proceedings by kicking Denton in the face was met by an excellently executed duck, catch and throw, and completed the flight of Whitey's foot in its orbit and brought Whitey's head into the ash-heap that had once received Denton's. Whitey arose a shade whiter, and now blasphemously bent upon vital injuries. There were indecisive passages, foiled enterprises that deepened Whitey's evidently growing perplexity; and then things developed into a grouping of Denton uppermost with Whitey's throat in his hand, his knee on Whitey's chest, and a tearful Whitey with a black face, protruding tongue and broken finger endeavouring to explain the misunderstanding by means of hoarse sounds. Moreover, it was evident that among the bystanders there had never been a more popular person than Denton.

Denton, with proper precaution, released his antagonist and stood up. His blood seemed changed to some sort of fluid fire, his limbs felt light and supernaturally strong. The idea that he was a martyr in the civilisation machine had vanished from his mind. He was a man in a world of men.

The little ferret-faced man was the first in the competition to pat him on the back. The lender of oil cans was a radiant sun of genial congratulation. . . . It seemed incredible to Denton that he had ever thought of despair.

Denton was convinced that not only had he to go through with things, but that he could. He sat on the canvas pallet expounding this new aspect to Elizabeth. One side of his face was bruised. She had not recently fought, she had not been patted on the back, there were no hot bruises upon her face, only a pallor and a new line or so about the mouth. She was taking the woman's share. She looked steadfastly at Denton in his new mood of prophecy. "I feel that there is something," he was saying, "something that goes on, a Being of Life in which we live and move and have our being, something that began fifty—a hundred million years ago, perhaps, that goes on—on: growing, spreading, to things beyond us—things that will justify us all. . . . That will explain and justify my fighting—these bruises, and all the pain of it. It's the chisel—yes, the chisel of the Maker. If only I could make you feel as I feel, if I could make you! You *will*, dear, I know you will."

"No," she said in a low voice. "No, I shall not."

"So I might have thought—"

She shook her head. "No," she said, "I have thought as well. What you say—doesn't convince me."

She looked at his face resolutely. "I hate it," she said, and caught at her breath. "You do not understand, you do not think. There was a time when you said things and I believed them. I am growing wiser. You are a man, you can fight, force your way. You do not mind bruises. You can be coarse and ugly, and still a man. Yes—it makes you. It makes you. You are right. Only a woman is not like that. We are different. We have let ourselves get civilised too soon. This underworld is not for us."

She paused and began again.

"I hate it! I hate this horrible canvas! I hate it more than—more than the worst that can happen. It hurts my fingers to touch it. It is horrible to the skin. And the women I work with day after day! I lie awake at nights and think how I may be growing like them. . . ."

She stopped. "I *am* growing like them," she cried passionately.

Denton stared at her distress. "But—" he said and stopped.

"You don't understand. What have I? What have I to save me? *You* can fight. Fighting is man's work. But women—women are different. . . . I have thought it all out, I have done nothing but think night and day. Look at the colour of my face! I cannot go on. I cannot endure this life. . . . I cannot endure it."

She stopped. She hesitated.

"You do not know all," she said abruptly, and for an instant her lips had a bitter smile. "I have been asked to leave you."

"Leave me!"

She made no answer save an affirmative movement of the head.

Denton stood up sharply. They stared at one another through a long silence.

Suddenly she turned herself about, and flung face downward upon their canvas bed. She did not sob, she made no sound. She lay still upon her face. After a vast, distressful void her shoulders heaved and she began to weep silently.

"Elizabeth!" he whispered—"Elizabeth!"

Very softly he sat down beside her, bent down, put his arm across her in a doubtful caress, seeking vainly for some clue to this intolerable situation.

"Elizabeth," he whispered in her ear.

She thrust him from her with her hand. "I cannot bear a child to be a slave!" and broke out into loud and bitter weeping.

Denton's face changed—became blank dismay. Presently he slipped from the bed and stood on his feet. All the complacency had vanished from his face, had given place to impotent rage. He began to rave and curse at the intolerable forces which pressed upon him, at all the accidents and hot desires and heedlessness that mock the life of man. His little voice rose in that little room, and he shook his fist, this animalcule of the earth, at all that environed him about, at the millions about him, at his past and future and all the insensate vastness of the overwhelming city.

V. BINDON INTERVENES

In Bindon's younger days he had dabbled in speculation and made three brilliant flukes. For the rest of his life he had the wisdom to let gambling alone, and the conceit to believe himself a very clever man. A certain desire for influence and reputation interested him in the business intrigues of the giant city in which his flukes were made. He became at last one of the most influential shareholders in the company that owned the London flying-stages to which the aeroplanes came from all parts of the world. This much for his public activities. In his private life he was a man of pleasure. And this is the story of his heart.

But before proceeding to such depths, one must devote a little time to the exterior of this person. Its physical basis was slender, and short, and dark; and the face, which was fine-featured and assisted by pigments, varied from an insecure self-complacency to an intelligent uneasiness. His face and head had been depilated, according to the cleanly and hygienic fashion of the time, so that the colour and contour of his hair varied with his costume. This he was constantly changing.

At times he would distend himself with pneumatic vestments in the rococo vein. From among the billowy developments of this style, and beneath a translucent and illuminated head-dress, his eye watched jealously for the respect of the less fashionable world. At other times he emphasied his elegant slenderness in close-fitting garments of black satin. For effects of dignity he would assume broad pneumatic shoulders, from which hung a robe of carefully arranged folds of China silk, and a classical Bindon in pink tights was also a transient phenomenon in the eternal pageant of Destiny. In the days when he hoped to marry Elizabeth, he sought to impress and charm her, and at the same time to take off something of his burthen of forty years, by wearing the last fancy of the contemporary buck, a costume of elastic material with distensible warts and horns, changing in colour as he walked, by an ingenious arrangement of versatile chromatophores. And no doubt, if Elizabeth's affection had not been already engaged by the worthless Denton, and if her tastes had not had that odd bias for old-fashioned ways, this extremely *chic* conception would have ravished her. Bindon had consulted Elizabeth's father before presenting himself in this garb—he was one of those men who always invite criticism of their costume—and Mwres had pronounced him all that the heart of woman could desire. But the affair of the hypnotist proved that his knowledge of the heart of woman was incomplete.

Bindon's idea of marrying had been formed some little time before Mwres threw Elizabeth's budding womanhood in his way. It was one of Bindon's most cherished secrets that he had a considerable capacity for a pure and simple life of a grossly sentimental type. The thought imparted a sort of pathetic seriousness to the offensive and quite inconsequent and unmeaning excesses, which he was pleased to regard as dashing wickedness, and which a number of good people also were so unwise as to treat in that desirable manner. As a consequence of these excesses, and perhaps by reason also of an inherited tendency to early decay, his liver became seriously affected, and he suffered increasing inconvenience when travelling by aeroplane. It was during his convalescence from a protracted bilious attack that it occurred to him that in spite of all the terrible fascinations of Vice, if he found a beautiful, gentle, good young woman of a not too violently intellectual type to devote her life to him, he might yet be saved to Goodness, and even rear a spirited family in his likeness to solace his declining years. But like so many experienced men of the world, he doubted if there were any good women. Of such as he had heard tell he was outwardly sceptical and privately much afraid.

When the aspiring Mwres affected his introduction to Elizabeth, it seemed to him that his good fortune was complete. He fell in love with her at once. Of course, he had always been falling in love since he was sixteen, in accordance with the extremely varied recipes to be found in the accumulated literature of many centuries. But this was different. This was real love. It seemed to him to call forth all the lurking goodness in his nature. He felt that for her sake he could give up a way of life that had already produced the gravest lesions on his liver and nervous system. His imagination presented him with idyllic pictures of the life of the reformed rake. He would never be sentimental with her, or silly; but always a little cynical and bitter, as became the past. Yet he was sure she would have an intuition of his real greatness and goodness. And in due course he would confess things to her, pour his version of what he regarded as his wickedness—showing what a complex of Goethe, and Benvenuto Cellini, and Shelley, and all those other chaps he really was—into her shocked, very beautiful, and no doubt sympathetic ear. And preparatory to these things he wooed her with infinite subtlety and respect. And the reserve with which Elizabeth treated him seemed nothing more nor less than an exquisite modesty touched and enhanced by an equally exquisite lack of ideas.

Bindon knew nothing of her wandering affections, nor of the attempt made by Mwres to utilise hypnotism as a corrective to this digression of her heart; he conceived he was on the best of terms with Elizabeth, and had made her quite successfully various significant presents of jewellery and the more virtuous cosmetics, when her elopement with Denton threw the world out of gear for him. His first aspect of the matter was rage begotten of wounded vanity, and as Mwres was the most convenient person, he vented the first brunt of it upon him.

He went immediately and insulted the desolate father grossly, and then spent an active and determined day going to and fro about the city and interviewing people in a consistent and partly-successful attempt to ruin that matrimonial speculator. The effectual nature of these activities gave him a temporary exhilaration, and he went to the dining-place he had frequented in his wicked days in a devil-may-care frame of mind, and dined altogether too amply and cheerfully with two other golden youths in the early forties. He threw up the game; no woman was worth being good for, and he astonished even himself by the strain of witty cynicism he developed. One of the other desperate blades, warmed with wine, made a facetious allusion to his disappointment, but at the time this did not seem unpleasant.

The next morning found his liver and temper inflamed. He kicked his phonographic-news machine to pieces, dismissed his valet, and resolved that he would perpetrate a terrible revenge upon Elizabeth. Or Denton. Or somebody. But anyhow, it was to be a terrible revenge; and the friend who had made fun at him should no longer see him in the light of a foolish girl's victim. He knew something of the little property that was due to her, and that this would be the only support of the young couple until Mwres should relent. If Mwres did not relent, and if unpropitious things should happen to the affair in which Elizabeth's expectations lay, they would come upon evil times and be sufficiently amenable to temptation of a sinister sort. Bindon's imagination, abandoning its beautiful idealism altogether, expanded the idea of temptation of a sinister sort. He figured himself as the implacable, the intricate and powerful man of wealth pursuing this maiden who had scorned him. And suddenly her image came upon his mind vivid and dominant, and for the first time in his life Bindon realised something of the real power of passion.

His imagination stood aside like a respectful footman who has done his work in ushering in the emotion.

"My God!" cried Bindon: "I will have her! If I have to kill myself to get her! And that other fellow—!"

After an interview with his medical man and a penance for his overnight excesses in the form of bitter drugs, a mitigated but absolutely resolute Bindon sought out Mwres. Mwres he found properly smashed, and impoverished and humble, in a mood of frantic self-preservation, ready to sell himself body and soul, much more any interest in a disobedient daughter, to recover his lost position in the world. In the reasonable discussion that followed, it was agreed that these misguided young people should be left to sink into distress, or possibly even assisted towards that improving discipline by Bindon's financial influence.

"And then?" said Mwres.

"They will come to the Labour Company," said Bindon. "They will wear the blue canvas."

"And then?"

"She will divorce him," he said, and sat for a moment intent upon that prospect. For in those days the austere limitations of divorce of Victorian times were extraordinarily relaxed, and a couple might separate on a hundred different scores.

Then suddenly Bindon astonished himself and Mwres by jumping to his feet. "She *shall* divorce him!" he cried. "I will have it so—I will work it so. By God! it shall be so. He shall be disgraced, so that she must. He shall be smashed and pulverised."

The idea of smashing and pulverising inflamed him further. He began a Jovian pacing up and down the little office. "I will have her," he cried. "I *will* have her! Heaven and Hell shall not save her from me!" His passion evaporated in its expression, and left him at the end simply histrionic. He struck an attitude and ignored with heroic determination a sharp twinge of pain about the diaphragm. And Mwres sat with his pneumatic cap deflated and himself very visibly impressed.

And so, with a fair persistence, Bindon set himself to the work of being Elizabeth's malignant providence, using with ingenious dexterity every particle of advantage wealth in those days gave a man over his fellow-creatures. A resort to the consolation of religion hindered these operations not at all. He would go and talk with an interesting, experienced and sympathetic Father of the Huysmanite sect of the Isis cult, about all the irrational little proceedings he was pleased to regard as his Heaven-dismaying wickedness, and the interesting, experienced and sympathetic Father representing Heaven dismayed, would with a pleasing affection of horror, suggest simple and easy penances, and recommend a monastic foundation that was airy, cool, hygienic, and not vulgarised, for viscerally disordered penitent sinners of the refined and wealthy type. And after these excursions, Bindon would come back to London quite active and passionate again. He would machinate with really considerable energy, and repair to a certain gallery high above the street of moving ways, from which he could view the entrance to the barrack of the Labour Company in the ward which sheltered Denton and Elizabeth. And at last one day he saw Elizabeth go in, and thereby his passion was renewed.

So in the fullness of the time the complicated devices of Bindon ripened, and he could go to Mwres and tell him that the young people were near despair.

"It's time for you," he said, "to let your parental affections have play. She's been in blue canvas some months, and they've been cooped together in one of those Labour dens, and the little girl is dead. She knows now what his manhood is worth to her, by way of protection, poor girl. She'll see things now in a clearer light. You go to her—I don't want to appear in this affair yet—and point out to her how necessary it is that she should get a divorce from him. . . ."

"She's obstinate," said Mwres doubtfully.

"Spirit!" said Bindon. "She's a wonderful girl—a wonderful girl!"

"She'll refuse."

"Of course she will. But leave it open to her. Leave it open to her. And some day—in that stuffy den, in that irksome, toilsome life they can't help it—*they'll have a quarrel. And then—*"

Mwres meditated over the matter, and did as he was told.

Then Bindon, as he had arranged with his spiritual adviser, went into retreat. The retreat of the Huysmanite sect was a beautiful place, with the sweetest air in London, lit by natural sunlight, and with restful quadrangles of real grass open to the sky, where at the same time the penitent man of pleasure might enjoy all the pleasures of loafing and all the satisfaction of distinguished austerity. And, save for participation in the simple and wholesome dietary of the place and in certain magnificent chants, Bindon spent all his time in meditation upon the theme of Elizabeth, and the extreme purification his soul had undergone since he first saw her, and whether he would be able to get a dispensation to marry her from the experienced and sympathetic Father in spite of the approaching "sin" of her divorce; and then . . . Bindon would lean against a pillar of the quadrangle and lapse into reveries on the superiority of virtuous love to any other form of indulgence. A curious feeling in his back and chest that was trying to attract his attention, a disposition to be hot or shiver, a general sense of ill-health and cutaneous discomfort he did his best to ignore. All that of course belonged to the old life that he was shaking off.

When he came out of retreat he went at once to Mwres to ask for news of Elizabeth. Mwres was clearly under the impression that he was an exemplary father, profoundly touched about the heart by his child's unhappiness. "She was pale," he said, greatly moved; "She was pale. When I asked her to come away and leave him—and be happy—she put her head down upon the table"—Mwres sniffed—"and cried."

His agitation was so great that he could say no more.

"Ah!" said Bindon, respecting this manly grief. "Oh!" said Bindon quite suddenly, with his hand to his side.

Mwres looked up sharply out of the pit of his sorrows, startled. "What's the matter?" he asked, visibly concerned.

"A most violent pain. Excuse me! You were telling me about Elizabeth."

And Mwres, after a decent solicitude for Bindon's pain, proceeded with his report. It was even unexpectedly hopeful. Elizabeth, in her first emotion at discovering that her father had not absolutely deserted her, had been frank with him about her sorrows and disgusts.

"Yes," said Bindon, magnificently, "I shall have her yet." And then that novel pain twiched him for the second time.

For these lower pains the priest was comparatively ineffectual, inclining rather to regard the body and them as mental illusions amenable to contemplation; so Bindon took it to a man of a class he loathed, a medical man of extraordinary repute and incivility. "We must go all over you," said the medical man, and did so with the most disgusting frankness. "Did you ever bring any children into the world?" asked this gross materialist among other impertinent questions.

"Not that I know of," said Bindon, too amazed to stand upon his dignity.

"Ah!" said the medical man, and proceeded with his punching and sounding. Medical science in those days was just reaching the beginnings of precision. "You'd better go right away," said the medical man, "and make the Euthanasia. The sooner the better."

Bindon gasped. He had been trying not to understand the technical explanations and anticipations in which the medical man had indulged.

"I say!" he said. "But do you mean to say . . . Your science . . ."

"Nothing," said the medical man. "A few opiates. The thing is your own doing, you know, to a certain extent."

"I was sorely tempted in my youth."

"It's not that so much. But you come of a bad stock. Even if you'd have taken precautions you'd have had bad times to wind up with. The mistake was getting born. The indiscretions of the parents. And you've shirked exercise, and so forth."

"I had no one to advise me."

"Medical men are always willing."

"I was a spirited young fellow."

"We won't argue; the mischief's done now. You've lived. We can't start you again. You ought never to have started at all. Frankly—the Euthanasia!"

Bindon hated him in silence for a space. Every word of this brutal expert jarred upon his refinements. He was so gross, so impermeable to all the subtler issues of being. But it is no good picking a quarrel with a doctor. "My religious beliefs," he said. "I don't approve of suicide."

"You've been doing it all your life."

"Well, anyhow, I've come to take a serious view of life now."

"You're bound to, if you go on living. You'll hurt. But for practical purposes it's late. However, if you mean to do that—perhaps I'd better mix you a little something. You'll hurt a great deal. These little twinges . . ."

"Twinges!"

"Mere preliminary notices."

"How long can I go on? I mean, before I hurt—really."

"You'll get it hot soon. Perhaps three days."

Bindon tried to argue for an extension of time, and in the midst of his pleading gasped, put his hand to his side. Suddenly the extraordinary pathos of his life came to him clear and vivid. "It's hard," he said. "It's infernally hard! I've been no man's enemy but my own. I've always treated everybody quite fairly."

The medical man stared at him without any sympathy for some seconds. He was reflecting how excellent it was that there were no more Bindons to carry on that line of pathos. He felt quite optimistic. Then he turned to his telephone and ordered up a prescription from the Central Pharmacy.

He was interrupted by a voice behind him. "By God!" cried Bindon; "I'll have her yet."

The physician stared over his shoulder at Bindon's expression, and then altered the prescription.

So soon as this painful interview was over, Bindon gave way to rage. He settled that the medical man was not only an unsympathetic brute and wanting in the first beginnings of a gentleman, but also highly incompetent; and he went off to four other practitioners in succession, with a view to the establishment of this intuition. But to guard against surprises he kept that little prescription in his pocket. With each he began by expressing his grave doubts of the first doctor's intelligence, honesty and professional knowledge, and then stated his symptoms, suppressing only a few more material facts in each case. These were always subsequently elicited by the doctor. In spite of the welcome depreciation of another practitioner, none of these eminent specialists would give Bindon any hope of eluding the anguish and helplessness that loomed now close upon him. To the last of them he unburthened his mind of an accumulated disgust with medical science. "After centuries and centuries," he exclaimed hotly; "and you can do nothing—except admit your helplessness. I say, 'Save me'—and what do you do?"

"No doubt it's hard on you," said the doctor. "But you should have taken precautions."

"How was I to know?"

"It wasn't our place to run after you," said the medical man, picking a thread of cotton from his purple sleeve. "Why should we save *you* in particular? You see—from one point of view—people with imaginations and passions like yours have to go—they have to go."

"Go?"

"Die out. It's an eddy."

He was a young man with a serene face. He smiled at Bindon. "We get on with research, you know; we give advice when people have the sense to ask for it. And we bide our time."

"Bide your time?"

"We hardly know enough yet to take over the management, you know."

"The management?"

"You needn't be anxious. Science is young yet. It's got to keep on growing for a few generations. We know enough now to know we don't know enough yet. . . . But the time is coming, all the same. *You* won't see the time. But, between ourselves, you rich men and party bosses, with your natural play of the passions and patriotism and religion and so forth, have made rather a mess of things; haven't you? These underways! And all that sort of thing. Some of us have a sort of fancy that in time we may know enough to take over a little more than the ventilation and drains. Knowledge keeps on piling up, you know. It keeps on growing. And there's not the slightest hurry for a generation or so. Some day—some day, men will live in a different way." He looked at Bindon and meditated. "There'll be a lot of dying out before that day can come."

Bindon attempted to point out to this young man how silly and irrelevant such talk was to a sick man like himself, how impertinent and uncivil it was to him, an older man occupying a position in the official world of extraordinary power and influence. He insisted that a doctor was paid to cure people—he laid great stress on "*paid*"—and had no business to glance even for a moment at "those other questions." "But we do," said the young man, insisting upon facts, and Bindon lost his temper.

His indignation carried him home. That these incompetent imposters, who were unable to save the life of a really influential man like himself, should dream of some day robbing the legitimate property owners of social control, of inflicting one knew not what tyranny upon the world. Curse science! He fumed over the intolerable prospect for some time, and then the pain returned, and he recalled the made-up prescription of the first doctor, still happily in his pocket. He took a dose forthwith.

It calmed and soothed him greatly, and he could sit down in his most comfortable chair beside his library (of phonographic records), and think over the altered aspect of affairs. His indignation passed, his anger and his passion crumbled under the subtle attack of that prescription, pathos became his sole ruler. He stared about him, at his magnificent and voluptuously appointed apartment, at his statuary and discreetly veiled pictures, and all the evidences of a cultivated and elegant wickedness; he touched a stud and the sad pipings of Tristan's shepherd filled the air. His eye wandered from one object to another. They were costly and gross and florid—but they were his. They presented in concrete form his ideals, his conceptions of beauty and desire, his idea of all that is precious in life. And now—he must leave it all like a common man. He was, he felt, a slender and delicate flame, burning out. So must all life flame up and pass, he thought. His eyes filled with tears.

Then it came into his head that he was alone. Nobody cared for him, nobody needed him! At any moment he might begin to hurt vividly. He might even howl. Nobody would mind. According to all the doctors he would have excellent reason for howling in a day or so. It recalled what his spiritual adviser had said of the decline of faith and fidelity, the degeneration of the age. He beheld himself as a pathetic proof of this; he, the subtle, able, important, voluptuous, cynical, complex Bindon, possibly howling, and not one faithful simple creature in all the world to howl in sympathy. Not one faithful simple soul was there—no shepherd to pipe to him! Had all such faithful simple creatures vanished from this harsh and urgent earth? He wondered whether the horrid vulgar crowd that perpetually went about the city could possibly know what he thought of them. If they did he felt sure *some* would try to earn a better opinion. Surely the world went from bad to worse. It was becoming impossible for Bindons. Perhaps some day . . . He was quite sure that the one thing he had needed in life was sympathy. For a time he regretted that he left no sonnets—no enigmatical pictures or something of that sort behind him to carry on his being until at last the sympathetic mind should come. . . .

It seemed incredible to him that this that came was extinction. Yet his sympathetic spiritual guide was in this matter annoyingly figurative and vague. Curse science! It had undermined all faith—all hope. To go out, to vanish from theatre and street, from office and dining-place, from the dear eyes of womankind. And not to be missed! On the whole to leave the world happier!

He reflected that he had never worn his heart upon his sleeve. Had he after all been *too* unsympathetic? Few people could suspect how subtly profound he really was beneath the mask of that cynical gaiety of his. They would not understand the loss they had suffered. Elizabeth, for example, had not suspected. . . .

He had reserved that. His thoughts having come to Elizabeth gravitated about her for some time. How *little* Elizabeth understood him!

That thought became intolerable. Before all other things he must set that right. He realised that there was still something for him to do in life, his struggle against Elizabeth was even yet not over. He could never overcome her now, as he had hoped and prayed. But he might still impress her!

From that idea he expanded. He might impress her profoundly—he might impress her so that she should for evermore regret her treatment of him. The thing that she must realise before everything else was his magnanimity. His magnanimity! Yes! he had loved her with amazing greatness of heart. He had not seen it so clearly before—but of course he was going to leave her all his property. He saw it instantly, as a thing determined and inevitable. She would think how good he was, how spaciously generous; surrounded by all that makes life tolerable from his hand, she would recall with infinite regret her scorn and coldness. And when she sought expression for that regret, she would find that occasion gone forever, she should be met by a locked door, by a disdainful stillness, by a white dead face. He closed his eyes and remained for a space imagining himself that white dead face.

From that he passed to other aspects of the matter, but his determination was assured. He meditated elaborately before he took action, for the drug he had taken inclined him to a lethargic and dignified melancholy. In certain respects he modified details. If he left all his property to Elizabeth it would include the voluptuously appointed room he occupied, and for many reasons he did not care to leave that to her. On the other hand, it had to be left to some one. In his clogged condition this worried him extremely.

In the end he decided to leave it to the sympathetic exponent of the fashionable religious cult whose conversation had been so pleasing in the past. "*He* will understand," said Bindon with a sentimental sigh. "He knows what Evil means—he understands something of the Stupendous Fascination of the Sphinx of Sin. Yes—he will understand." By that phrase it was that Bindon was pleased to dignify certain unhealthy and undignified departures from sane conduct to which a misguided vanity and an ill-controlled curiosity had led him. He sat for a space thinking how very Hellenic and Italian and Neronic, and all those things, he had been. Even now—might one not try a sonnet? A penetrating voice to echo down the ages, sensuous, sinister, and sad. For a space he forgot Elizabeth. In the course of half an hour he spoilt three phonographic coils, got a headache, took a second dose to calm himself, and reverted to magnanimity and his former design.

At last he faced the unpalatable problem of Denton. It needed all his newborn magnanimity before he could swallow the thought of Denton; but at last this greatly misunderstood man, assisted by his sedative and the near approach of death, effected even that. If he was at all exclusive about Denton, if he should display the slightest distrust, if he attempted any specific exclusion of that young man, she might—*misunderstand*. Yes—she should have her Denton still. His magnanimity must go even to that. He tried to think only of Elizabeth in the matter.

He rose with a sigh, and limped across to the telephonic apparatus that communicated with his solicitor. In ten minutes a will duly attested and with its proper thumb-mark signature lay in the solicitor's office three miles away. And then for a space Bindon sat very still.

Suddenly he started out of a vague reverie and pressed an investigatory hand to his side.

Then he jumped eagerly to his feet and rushed to the telephone. The Euthanasia Company had rarely been called by a client in a greater hurry.

So it came at last that Denton and his Elizabeth, against all hope, returned unseparated from the labour servitude to which they had fallen. Elizabeth came out from her cramped subterranean den of metal-beaters and all the sordid circumstances of blue canvas, as one comes out of a nightmare. Back towards the sunlight their fortune took them; once the bequest was known to them, the bare thought of another day's hammering became intolerable. They went up long lifts and stairs to levels that they had not seen since the days of their disaster. At first she was full of this sensation of escape; even to think of the underways was intolerable; only after many months could she begin to recall with sympathy the faded women who were still below there, murmuring scandals and reminiscences and folly, and tapping away their lives.

Her choice of the apartments they presently took expressed the vehemence of her release. They were rooms upon the very verge of the city; they had a roof space and a balcony upon the city wall, wide open to the sun and wind, the country and the sky.

And in that balcony comes the last scene in this story. It was a summer sunsetting, and the hills of Surrey were very blue and clear. Denton leant upon the balcony regarding them, and Elizabeth sat by his side. Very wide and spacious was the view, for their balcony hung five hundred feet above the ancient level of the ground. The oblongs of the Food Company, broken here and there by the ruins—grotesque little holes and sheds—of the ancient suburbs, and intersected by shining streams of sewage, passed at last into a remote diapering at the foot of the distant hills. There once had been the squatting-place of the children of Uya. On those further slopes gaunt machines of unknown import worked slackly at the end of their spell, and the hill crest was set with stagnant wind vanes. Along the great south road the Labour Company's field workers in huge wheeled mechanical vehicles, were hurrying back to their meals, their last spell finished. And through the air a dozen little private aëropiles sailed down towards the city. Familiar scene as it was to the eyes of Denton and Elizabeth, it would have filled the minds of their ancestors with incredulous amazement. Denton's thoughts fluttered towards the future in a vain attempt at what that scene might be in another two hundred years, and, recoiling, turned towards the past.

He shared something of the growing knowledge of the time; he could picture the quaint smoke-grimed Victorian city with its narrow little roads of beaten earth, its wide common-land, ill-organised, ill-built suburbs, and irregular enclosures; the old countryside of the Stuart times, with its little villages and its petty London; the England of the monasteries, the far older England of the Roman dominion, and then before that a wild country with here and there the huts of some warring tribe. These huts must have come and gone and come again through a space of years that made the Roman camp and villa seem but yesterday; and before those years, before even the huts, there had been men in the valley. Even then—so recent had it all been when one judged it by the standards of geological time—this valley had been here; and those hills yonder, higher, perhaps, and snow-tipped, had still been yonder hills, and the Thames had flowed down from the Cotswolds to the sea. But the men had been but the shapes of men, creatures of darkness and ignorance, victims of beasts and floods, storms and pestilence and incessant hunger. They had held a precarious foothold amidst bears and lions and all the monstrous violence of the past. Already some at least of these enemies were overcome. . . .

For a time Denton pursued the thoughts of this spacious vision, trying in obedience to his instinct to find his place and proportion in the scheme.

"It has been chance," he said, "it has been luck. We have come through. It happens we have come through. Not by any strength of our own. . . .

"And yet . . . No. I don't know."

He was silent for a long time before he spoke again.

"After all—there is a long time yet. There have scarcely been men for twenty thousand years—and there has been life for twenty millions. And what are generations? What are generations? It is enormous, and we are so little. Yet we know—we feel. We are not dumb atoms, we are part of it—part of it—to the limits of our strength and will. Even to die is part of it. Whether we die or live, we are in the making. . . .

"As time goes on—*perhaps*—men will be wiser. . . . Wiser. . . .

"Will they ever understand?"

He became silent again. Elizabeth said nothing to these things, but she regarded his dreaming face with infinite affection. Her mind was not very active that evening. A great contentment possessed her. After a time she laid a gentle hand on his beside her. He fondled it softly, still looking out upon the spacious gold-woven view. So they sat as the sun went down. Until presently Elizabeth shivered.

Denton recalled himself abruptly from these spacious issues of his leisure, and went in to fetch her a shawl.

Hal Clement

Hal Clement (the pen name of Harry Clement Stubbs [1922–]) is a retired science teacher who has published science fiction since 1942, and whose work has become a paradigm for that branch of science fiction that delights in careful extrapolation from a scientific principle or idea. *Science Fiction Writers* (1996) says, "Clement and his classic fiction are mentioned whenever the discussion of science in the genre comes up . . . their distinguishing characteristic is that a problematic condition in physical reality, or simply a condition of difference such as an increase or decrease in heat or gravity, must be elaborated upon, explained, and taken through certain plot changes so that the reader can simply understand the problem or the difference. This is a literature of total mimesis, in which the facts of the universe are mimed." It is commonly referred to as hard science fiction (think of hard rock or the hard sciences—physics, chemistry, astronomy).

Clement's mastery of the astronomy, physics, and chemistry in stories set in space and on other worlds became famous with the publication of the *Astounding* serial, "Heavy Planet" (later published as *Mission of Gravity*, 1954), but especially with the immediately subsequent publication of a nonfiction article in the same magazine, detailing the process by which he had figured out the physics, astronomy, and biochemistry of the world of Mesklin. With the publication of *Mission of Gravity*, Clement in effect redefined the game of hard SF as an exercise in interrelating the sciences to achieve a created world that would plausibly withstand rigorous examination from many angles. Of such conceptual breakthroughs are scientific revolutions accomplished, and this was a revolution in science fiction, a slow and subtle one that took more than a decade to take hold. Gradually Clement gained a worldwide reputation as a quintessential hard SF writer whose works in later years more or less defined the term.

"Hot Planet" builds a consistent and detailed world for its alien characters to operate in, a world radically distanced from our own by its physical nature but also clearly, through our knowledge of science, connected to it: it is plausible. The story has the beauty of science at its heart, the awe-inspiring vistas of universal truth made manifest. Clement's work is presently the most influential model for hard science fiction writers.

HOT PLANET

The wind which had nearly turned the *Albireo*'s landing into a disaster instead of a mathematical exercise was still playing tunes about the fins and landing legs as Schlossberg made his way down to Deck Five.

The noise didn't bother him particularly, though the endless seismic tremors made him dislike the ladders. But just now he was able to ignore both. He was curious—though not hopeful.

"Is there anything at all obvious on the last sets of tapes, Joe?"

Mardikian, the geophysicist, shrugged. "Just what you'd expect . . . on a planet which has at least one quake in each fifty-mile-square area every five minutes. You know yourself we had a nice seismic program set up, but when we touched down we found we couldn't carry it out. We've done our best with the natural tremors—incidentally stealing most of the record tapes the other projects would have used. We have a lot of nice information for the computers back home; but it will take all of them to make any sense out of it."

Schlossberg nodded; the words had not been necessary. His astronomical program had been one of those sabotaged by the transfer of tapes to the seismic survey.

"I just hoped," he said. "We each have an idea why Mercury developed an atmosphere during the last few decades, but I guess the high school kids on Earth will know whether it's right before we do. I'm resigned to living in a chess-type universe—few and simple rules, but infinite combinations of them. But it would be nice to know an answer sometime."

"So it would. As a matter of fact, I need to know a couple right now. From you. How close to finished are the other programs—or what's left of them?"

"I'm all set," replied Schlossberg. "I have a couple of instruments still monitoring the sun just in case, but everything in the revised program is on tape."

"Good. Tom, any use asking you?"

The biologist grimaced. "I've been shown two hundred and sixteen different samples of rock and dust. I have examined in detail twelve crystal growths which looked vaguely like vegetation. Nothing was alive or contained living things by any standards I could conscientiously set."

Mardikian's gesture might have meant sympathy.

"Camille?"

"I may as well stop now as any time. I'll never be through. Tape didn't make much difference to me, but I wish I knew what weight of specimens I could take home."

"Eileen?" Mardikian's glance at the stratigrapher took the place of the actual question.

"Cam speaks for me, except that I could have used any more tape you could have spared. What I have is gone."

"All right, that leaves me, the tape-thief. The last spools are in the seismographs now, and will start running out in seventeen hours. The tractors will start out on their last rounds in sixteen, and should be back in roughly a week. Will, does that give you enough to figure the weights we rockhounds can have on the return trip?"

The *Albireo*'s captain nodded. "Close enough. There really hasn't been much question since it became evident we'd find nothing for the mass tanks here. I'll have a really precise check in an hour, but I can tell right now that you have about one and a half metric tons to split up among the three of you.

"Ideal departure time is three hundred ten hours away, as you all know. We can stay here until then, or go into a parking-and-survey orbit at almost any time before then. You have all the survey you need, I should think, from the other time. But suit yourselves."

"I'd just as soon be space-sick as seasick," remarked Camille Burkett. "I still hate to think that the entire planet is as shivery as the spot we picked."

Willard Rowson smiled. "You researchers told me where to land after ten days in orbit mapping this rockball. I set you just where you asked. If you'd found even five tons of juice we could use in the reaction tanks I could still take you to another one—if you could agree which one. I hate to say, 'Don't blame me,' but I can't think of anything else that fits."

"So we sit until the last of the tractors is back with the precious seismo tapes, playing battleship while our back teeth are being shaken out by earthquakes—excuse the word. What a thrill! Glorious adventure!" Zaino, the communications specialist who had been out of a job almost constantly since the landing, spoke sourly. The captain was the only one who saw fit to answer.

"If you want adventure, you made a mistake exploring space. The only space adventures I've heard of are secondhand stories built on guesswork; the people who really had them weren't around to tell about it. Unless Dr. Marini discovers a set of Mercurian monsters at the last minute and they invade the ship or cut off one of the tractors, I'm afraid you'll have to do without adventures." Zaino grimaced.

"That sounds funny coming from a spaceman, Captain. I didn't really mean adventure, though; all I want is something to do besides betting whether the next quake will come in one minute or five. I haven't even had to fix a suit-radio since we touched down. How about my going out with one of the tractors on this last trip, at least?"

"It's all right with me," replied Rowson, "but Dr. Mardikian runs the professional part of this operation. I require that Spurr, Trackman, Hargedon and Aiello go as drivers, since without them even a minor mechanical problem would be more than an adventure. As I recall it, Dr. Harmon, Dr. Schlossberg, Dr. Marini and Dr. Mardikian are scheduled to go; but if any one of them is willing to let you take his or her place, I certainly don't mind."

The radioman looked around hopefully. The geologists and the biologist shook their heads negatively, firmly and unanimously; but the astronomer pondered for a moment. Zaino watched tensely.

"It may be all right," Schlossberg said at last. "What I want to get is a set of wind, gas pressure, gas temperature and gas composition measures around the route. I didn't expect to be more meteorologist than astronomer when we left Earth, and didn't have exactly the right equipment. Hargedon and Aiello helped me improvise some, and this is the first chance to use it on Darkside. If you can learn what has to be done with it before starting time, though, you are welcome to my place."

The communicator got to his feet fast enough to leave the deck in Mercury's feeble gravity.

"Lead me to it, Doc. I guess I can learn to read a homemade weathervane!"

"Is that merely bragging, or a challenge?" drawled a voice which had not previously joined the discussion. Zaino flushed a bit.

"Sorry, Luigi," he said hastily. "I didn't mean it just that way. But I still think I can run the stuff."

"Likely enough," Aiello replied. "Remember though, it wasn't made just for talking into." Schlossberg, now on his feet, cut in quickly.

"Come on, Arnie. We'll have to suit up to see the equipment; it's outside."

He shepherded the radioman to the hatch at one side of the deck and shooed him down toward the engine and air lock levels. Both were silent for some moments; but safely out of earshot of Deck Five the younger man looked up and spoke.

"You needn't push, Doc. I wasn't going to make anything of it. Luigi was right, and I asked for it." The astronomer slowed a bit in his descent.

"I wasn't really worried," he replied, "but we have several months yet before we can get away from each other, and I don't like talk that could set up grudges. Matter of fact, I'm even a little uneasy about having the girls along, though I'm no misogynist."

"Girls? They're not—"

"There goes your foot again. Even Harmon is about ten years older than you, I suppose. But they're girls to me. What's more important, they no doubt think of themselves as girls."

"Even Dr. Burkett? That is—I mean—"

"Even Dr. Burkett. Here, get into your suit. And maybe you'd better take out the mike. It'll be enough if you can listen for the next hour or two." Zaino made no answer, suspecting with some justice that anything he said would be wrong.

Each made final checks on the other's suit; then they descended one more level to the airlock. This occupied part of the same deck as the fusion plants, below the wings and reaction mass tanks but above the main engine. Its outer door was just barely big enough to admit a space-suited person. Even with the low air pressure carried by spaceships, a large door area meant large total force on jamb, hinges and locks. It opened onto a small balcony from which a ladder led to the ground. The two men paused on the balcony to look over the landscape.

This hadn't changed noticeably since the last time either had been out, though there might have been some small difference in the volcanic cones a couple of miles away to the northeast. The furrows down the sides of these, which looked as though they had been cut by water but were actually bone-dry ash slides, were always undergoing alteration as gas from below kept blowing fresh scoria fragments out of the craters.

The spines—steep, jagged fragments of rock which thrust upward from the plain beyond and to both sides of the cones—seemed dead as ever.

The level surface between the *Albireo* and the cones was more interesting. Mardikian and Schlossberg believed it to be a lava sheet dating from early in Mercury's history, when more volatile substances still existed in the surface rocks to cut down their viscosity when molten. They supposed that much—perhaps most—of the surface around the "twilight" belt had been flooded by this very liquid lava, which had cooled to a smoother surface than most Earthly lava flows.

How long it had stayed cool they didn't guess. But both men felt sure that Mercury must have periodic upheavals as heat accumulated inside it—heat coming not from radioactivity but from tidal energy. Mercury's orbit is highly eccentric. At perihelion, tidal force tries to pull it apart along the planet-to-sun line, while at aphelion the tidal force is less and the little world's own gravity tries to bring it back to a spherical shape. The real change in form is not great, but a large force working through even a small amount of distance can mean a good deal of energy.

If the energy can't leak out—and Mercury's rocks conduct heat no better than those of Earth—the temperature must rise.

Sooner or later, the men argued, deeply buried rock must fuse to magma. Its liquefaction would let the bulk of the planet give farther under tidal stress, so heat would be generated even faster. Eventually a girdle of magma would have to form far below the crust all around the twilight strip, where the tidal strain would be greatest. Sooner or later this would melt its way to the surface, giving the zone a period of intense volcanic activity and, incidentally, giving the planet a temporary atmosphere.

The idea was reasonable. It had, the astronomer admitted, been suggested long before to account for supposed vulcanism on the moon. It justified the careful examination that Schlossberg and Zaino gave the plain before they descended the ladder; for it made reasonable the occasional changes which were observed to occur in the pattern of cracks weaving over its surface.

No one was certain just how permanent the local surface was—though no one could really justify feeling safer on board the *Albireo* than outside on the lava. If anything really drastic happened, the ship would be no protection.

The sun, hanging just above the horizon slightly to the watcher's right, cast long shadows which made the cracks stand out clearly; as far as either man could see, nothing had changed recently. They descended the ladder carefully—even the best designed space suits are somewhat vulnerable—and made their way to the spot where the tractors were parked.

A sheet-metal fence a dozen feet high and four times as long provided shade, which was more than a luxury this close to the sun. The tractors were parked in this shadow, and beside and between them were piles of equipment and specimens. The apparatus Schlossberg had devised was beside the tractor at the north end of the line, just inside the shaded area.

It was still just inside the shade when they finished, four hours later. Hargedon had joined them during the final hour and helped pack the equipment in the tractor he was to drive. Zaino had had no trouble in learning to make the observations Schlossberg wanted, and the youngster was almost unbearably cocky. Schlossberg hoped, as they returned to the *Albireo*, that no one would murder the communications expert in the next twelve hours. There would be nothing to worry about after the trip started; Hargedon was quite able to keep anyone in his place without being nasty about it. If Zaino had been going with Aiello or Harmon—but he wasn't, and it was pointless to dream up trouble.

And no trouble developed all by itself.

Zaino was not only still alive but still reasonably popular when the first of the tractors set out, carrying Eileen Harmon and Eric Trackman, the *Albireo*'s nuclear engineer.

It started more than an hour before the others, since the stratigrapher's drilling program, "done" or not, took extra time. The tractor hummed off to the south, since both Darkside routes required a long detour to pass the chasm to the west. Routes had been worked out from the stereo-photos taken during the orbital survey. Even Darkside had been covered fairly well with Uniquantum film under Venus light.

The Harmon-Trackman vehicle was well out of sight when Mardikian and Aiello started out on one of the Brightside routes, and a few minutes later Marini set out on the other with the space-suit technician, Mary Spurr, driving.

Both vehicles disappeared quickly into a valley to the northeast, between the ash cones and a thousand-foot spine which rose just south of them. All the tractors were in good radio contact; Zaino made sure of that before he abandoned the radio watch to Rowson, suited up and joined Hargedon at the remaining one. They climbed in, and Hargedon set it in motion.

At about the same time, the first tractor came into view again, now traveling north on the farther side of the chasm. Hargedon took this as evidence that the route thus far was unchanged, and kicked in highest speed.

The cabin was pretty cramped, even though some of the equipment had been attached outside. The men could not expect much comfort for the next week.

Hargedon was used to the trips, however. He disapproved on principle of people who complained about minor inconveniences such as having to sleep in space suits; fortunately, Zaino's interest and excitement overrode any thought he might have had about discomfort.

This lasted through the time they spent doubling the vast crack in Mercury's crust, driving on a little to the north of the ship on the other side and then turning west toward the dark hemisphere. The route was identical to that of Harmon's machine for some time, though no trace of its passage showed on the hard surface. Then Hargedon angled off toward the southwest. He had driven this run often enough to know it well even without the markers which had been set out with the seismographs. The photographic maps were also aboard. With them, even Zaino had no trouble keeping track of their progress while they remained in sunlight.

However, the sun sank as they traveled west. In two hours its lower rim would have been on the horizon, had they been able to see the horizon; as it was, more of the "sea level" lava plain was in shadow than not even near the ship, and their route now lay in semidarkness.

The light came from peaks projecting into the sunlight, from scattered skylight which was growing rapidly fainter and from the brighter celestial objects such as Earth. Even with the tractor's lights it was getting harder to spot crevasses and seismometer markers. Zaino quickly found the fun wearing off . . . though his pride made him cover this fact as best he could.

If Hargedon saw this, he said nothing. He set Zaino to picking up every other instrument, as any partner would have, making no allowance for the work the youngster was doing for Schlossberg. This might, of course, have had the purpose of keeping the radioman too busy to think about discomfort. Or it might merely have been Hargedon's idea of normal procedure.

Whatever the cause, Zaino got little chance to use the radio once they had driven into the darkness. He managed only one or two brief talks with those left at the ship.

The talks might have helped his morale, since they certainly must have given the impression that nothing was going on in the ship while at least he had something to do in the tractor. However, this state of affairs did not last. Before the vehicle was four hours out of sight of the *Albireo*, a broadcast by Camille Burkett reached them.

The mineralogist's voice contained at least as much professional enthusiasm as alarm, but everyone listening must have thought promptly of the dubious stability of Mercury's crust. The call was intended for her fellow geologists Mardikian and Harmon. But it interested Zaino at least as much.

"Joe! Eileen! There's a column of what looks like black smoke rising over Northeast Spur. It can't be a real fire, of course; I can't see its point of origin, but if it's the convection current it seems to me the source must be pretty hot. It's the closest thing to a genuine volcano I've seen since we arrived; it's certainly not another of those ash mounds. I should think you'd still be close enough to make it out, Joe. Can you see anything?"

The reply from Mardikian's tractor was inaudible to Zaino and Hargedon, but Burkett's answer made its general tenor plain.

"I hadn't thought of that. Yes, I'd say it was pretty close to the Brightside route. It wouldn't be practical for you to stop your run now to come back to see. You couldn't do much about it anyway. I could go out to have a look and then report to you. If the way back is blocked there'll be plenty of time to work out another." Hargedon and Zaino passed questioning glances at each other during the shorter pause that followed.

"I know there aren't," the voice then went on, responding to the words they could not hear, "but it's only two or three miles, I'd say. Two to the spur and not much farther to where I could see the other side. Enough of the way is in shade so I could make it in a suit easily enough. I can't see calling back either of the Darkside tractors. Their work is just as important as the rest—anyway, Eileen is probably out of range. She hasn't answered yet."

Another pause.

"That's true. Still, it would mean sacrificing that set of seismic records—no, wait. We could go out later for those. And Mel could take his own weather measures on the later trip. There's plenty of time!"

Pause, longer this time.

"You're right, of course. I just wanted to get an early look at this volcano, if it is one. We'll let the others finish their runs, and when you get back you can check the thing from the other side yourself. If it is blocking your way there's time to find an alternate route. We could be doing that from the maps in the meantime, just in case."

Zaino looked again at his companion.

"Isn't that just my luck!" he exclaimed. "I jump at the first chance to get away from being bored to death. The minute I'm safely away, the only interesting thing of the whole operation happens—back at the ship!"

"Who asked to come on this trip?"

"Oh, I'm not blaming anyone but myself. If I'd stayed back there the volcano would have popped out here somewhere, or else waited until we were gone."

"If it is a volcano. Dr. Burkett didn't seem quite sure."

"No, and I'll bet a nickel she's suiting up right now to go out and see. I hope she comes back with something while we're still near enough to hear about it."

Hargedon shrugged. "I suppose it was also just your luck that sent you on a Darkside trip? You know the radio stuff. You knew we couldn't reach as far this way with the radios. Didn't you think of that in advance?"

"I didn't think of it, any more than you would have. It was bad luck, but I'm not grousing about it. Let's get on with this job." Hargedon nodded with approval, and possibly with some surprise, and the tractor hummed on its way.

The darkness deepened around the patches of lava shown by the driving lights; the sky darkened toward a midnight hue, with stars showing ever brighter through it; and radio reception from the *Albireo* began to get spotty. Gas density at the ion layer was high enough so that recombination of molecules with their radiation-freed electrons was rapid. Only occasional streamers of ionized gas reached far over Darkside. As these thinned out, so did radio reception. Camille Burkett's next broadcast came through very poorly.

There was enough in it, however, to seize the attention of the two men in the tractor.

She was saying:"—real all right, and dangerous. It's the . . . thing I ever saw . . . kinds of lava from what looks like . . . same vent. There's high viscosity stuff building a spatter cone to end all spatter cones, and some very thin fluid from somewhere at the bottom. The flow has already blocked the valley used by the Brightside routes and is coming along it. A new return route will have to be found for the tractors that . . . was spreading fast when I saw it. I can't tell how much will come. But unless it stops there's nothing at all to keep the flow away from the ship. It isn't coming fast, but it's coming. I'd advise all tractors to turn back. Captain Rowson reminds me that only one takeoff is possible. If we leave this site, we're committed to leaving Mercury. Arnie and Ren, do you hear me?"

Zaino responded at once. "We got most of it, Doctor. Do you really think the ship is in danger?"

"I don't know. I can only say that *if* this flow continues the ship will have to leave, because this area will sooner or later be covered. I can't guess how likely . . . check further to get some sort of estimate. It's different from any Earthly lava source—maybe you heard—should try to get Eileen and Eric back, too. I can't raise them. I suppose they're well out from under the ion layer by now. Maybe you're close enough to them to catch them with diffracted waves. Try, anyway. Whether you can raise them or not you'd better start back yourself."

Hargedon cut in at this point. "What does Dr. Mardikian say about that? We still have most of the seismometers on this route to visit."

"I think Captain Rowson has the deciding word here, but if it helps your decision Dr. Mardikian has already started back. He hasn't finished his route, either. So hop back here, Ren. And Arnie, put that technical skill you haven't had to use yet to work raising Eileen and Eric."

"What I can do, I will," replied Zaino, "but you'd better tape a recall message and keep it going out on—let's see—band F."

"All right. I'll be ready to check the volcano as soon as you get back. How long?"

"Seven hours—maybe six and a half," replied Hargedon. "We have to be careful."

"Very well. Stay outside when you arrive; I'll want to go right out in the tractor to get a closer look." She cut off.

"And *that* came through clearly enough!" remarked Hargedon as he swung the tractor around. "I've been awake for fourteen hours, driving off and on for ten of them; I'm about to drive for another six; and then I'm to stand by for more."

"Would you like me to do some of the driving?" asked Zaino.

"I guess you'll have to, whether I like it or not," was the rather lukewarm reply. "I'll keep on for a while, though—until we're back in better light. You get at your radio job."

Zaino tried. Hour after hour he juggled from one band to another. Once he had Hargedon stop while he went out to attach a makeshift antenna which, he hoped, would change his output from broadcast to some sort of beam; after this he kept probing the sky with the "beam," first listening to the *Albireo*'s broadcast in an effort to find projecting wisps of ionosphere and then, whenever he thought he had one, switching on his transmitter and driving his own message at it.

Not once did he complain about lack of equipment or remark how much better he could do once he was back at the ship.

Hargedon's silence began to carry an undercurrent of approval not usual in people who spent much time with Zaino. The technician made no further reference to the suggestion of switching drivers. They came in sight of the *Albireo* and doubled the chasm with Hargedon still at the wheel, Zaino still at his radio and both of them still uncertain whether any of the calls had gotten through.

Both had to admit, even before they could see the ship, that Burkett had had a right to be impressed.

The smoke column showed starkly against the sky, blowing back over the tractor and blocking the sunlight which would otherwise have glared into the driver's eyes. Fine particles fell from it in a steady shower; looking back, the men could see tracks left by their vehicle in the deposit which had already fallen.

As they approached the ship the dark pillar grew denser and narrower, while the particles raining from it became coarser. In some places the ash was drifting into fairly deep piles, giving Hargedon some anxiety about possible concealed cracks. The last part of the trip, along the edge of the great chasm and around its end, was really dangerous; cracks running from its sides were definitely spreading. The two men reached the *Albireo* later than Hargedon had promised, and found Burkett waiting impatiently with a pile of apparatus beside her.

She didn't wait for them to get out before starting to organize.

"There isn't much here. We'll take off just enough of what you're carrying to make room for this. No—wait. I'll have to check some of your equipment; I'm going to need one of Milt Schlossberg's gadgets, I think, so leave that on. We'll take—"

"Excuse me, Doctor," cut in Hargedon. "Our suits need servicing, or at least mine will if you want me to drive you. Perhaps Arnie can help you load for a while, if you don't think it's too important for him to get at the radio—"

"Of course. Excuse me. I should have had someone out here to help me with this. You two go on in. Ren, please get back as soon as you can. I can do the work here; none of this stuff is very heavy."

Zaino hesitated as he swung out of the cab. True, there wasn't too much to be moved, and it wasn't very heavy in Mercury's gravity, and he really should be at the radio; but the thirty-nine-year-old mineralogist was a middle-aged lady by his standards, and shouldn't be allowed to carry heavy packages . . .

"Get along, Arnie!" the middle-aged lady interrupted this train of thought. "Eric and Eileen are getting farther away and harder to reach every second you dawdle!"

He got, though he couldn't help looking northeast as he went rather than where he was going.

The towering menace in that direction would have claimed anyone's attention. The pillar of sable ash was rising straighter, as though the wind were having less effect on it. An equally black cone had risen into sight beyond Northeast Spur—a cone that must have grown to some two thousand feet in roughly ten hours. It had far steeper sides than the cinder mounds near it; it couldn't be made of the same loose ash. Perhaps it consisted of half-melted particles which were fusing together as they fell—that might be what Burkett had meant by "spatter-cone." Still, if that were the case, the material fountaining from the cone's top should be lighting the plain with its incandescence rather than casting an inky shadow for its entire height.

Well, that was a problem for the geologists; Zaino climbed aboard and settled to his task.

The trouble was that he could do very little more here than he could in the tractor. He could have improvised longer-wave transmitting coils whose radiations would have diffracted a little more effectively beyond the horizon, but the receiver on the missing vehicle would not have detected them. He had more power at his disposal, but could only beam it into empty space with his better antennae. He had better equipment for locating any projecting wisps of charged gas which might reflect his waves, but he was already located under a solid roof of the stuff—the *Albireo* was technically on Brightside. Bouncing his beam from this layer still didn't give him the range he needed, as he had found both by calculation and trial.

What he really needed was a relay satellite. The target was simply too far around Mercury's sharp curve by now for anything less.

Zaino's final gesture was to set his transmission beam on the lowest frequency the tractor would pick up, aim it as close to the vehicle's direction as he could calculate from map and itinerary and set the recorded return message going. He told Rowson as much.

"Can't think of anything else?" the captain asked. "Well, neither can I, but of course it's not my field. I'd give a year's pay if I could. How long before they should be back in range?"

"About four days. A hundred hours, give or take a few. They'll be heading back anyway by that time."

"Of course. Well, keep trying."

"I am—or rather, the equipment is. I don't see what else I can do unless a really bright idea should suddenly sprout. Is there anywhere else I could be useful? I'm as likely to have ideas working as just sitting."

"We can keep you busy, all right. But how about taking a transmitter up one of those mountains? That would get your wave farther."

"Not as far as it's going already. I'm bouncing it off the ion layer, which is higher than any mountain we've seen on Mercury even if it's nowhere near as high as Earth's."

"Hmph. All right."

"I could help Ren and Dr. Burkett. I could hang on outside the tractor—"

"They've already gone. You'd better call them, though, and keep a log of what they do."

"All right." Zaino turned back to his board and with no trouble raised the tractor carrying Hargedon and the mineralogist. The latter had been trying to call the *Albireo* and had some acid comments about radio operators who slept on the job.

"There's only one of me, and I've been trying to get the Darkside team," he pointed out. "Have you found anything new about this lava flood?"

"Flow, not flood," corrected the professional automatically. "We're not in sight of it yet. We've just rounded the corner that takes us out of your sight. It's over a mile yet, and a couple of more corners, before we get to the spot where I left it. Of course, it will be closer than that by now. It was spreading at perhaps a hundred yards an hour then. That's one figure we must refine. . . . Of course, I'll try to get samples, too. I wish there were some way to get samples of the central cone. The whole thing is the queerest volcano I've ever heard of. Have you gotten Eileen started back?"

"Not as far as I can tell. As with your cone samples, there are practical difficulties," replied Zaino. "I haven't quit yet, though."

"I should think not. If some of us were paid by the idea we'd be pretty poor, but the perspiration part of genius is open to all of us."

"You mean I should charge a bonus for getting this call through?" retorted the operator.

Whatever Burkett's reply to this might have been was never learned; her attention was diverted at that point.

"We've just come in sight of the flow. It's about five hundred yards ahead. We'll get as close as seems safe, and I'll try to make sure whether it's really lava or just mud."

"Mud? Is that possible? I thought there wasn't—couldn't be—any water on this planet!"

"It is, and there probably isn't. The liquid phase of mud doesn't have to be water, even though it usually is on Earth. Here, for example, it might conceivably be sulfur."

"But if it's just mud, it wouldn't hurt the ship, would it?"

"Probably not."

"Then why all this fuss about getting the tractors back in a hurry?"

The voice which answered reminded him of another lady in his past, who had kept him after school for drawing pictures in math class.

"Because in my judgment the flow is far more likely to be lava than mud, and if I must be wrong I'd rather my error were one that left us alive. I have no time at the moment to explain the basis of my judgment. I will be reporting our activities quite steadily from now on, and would prefer that you not interrupt unless a serious emergency demands it, or you get a call from Eileen.

"We are about three hundred yards away now. The front is moving about as fast as before, which suggests that the flow is coming only along this valley. It's only three or four feet high, so viscosity is very low or density very high. Probably the former, considering where we are. It's as black as the smoke column."

"Not glowing?" cut in Zaino thoughtlessly.

"*Black,* I said. Temperature will be easier to measure when we get closer. The front is nearly straight across the valley, with just a few lobes projecting ten or twelve yards and one notch where a small spine is being surrounded. By the way, I trust you're taping all this?" Again Zaino was reminded of the afternoon after school.

"Yes, Ma'am," he replied. "On my one and only monitor tape."

"Very well. We're stopping near the middle of the valley one hundred yards from the front. I am getting out, and will walk as close as I can with a sampler and a radiometer. I assume that the radio equipment will continue to relay my suit broadcast back to you." Zaino cringed a little, certain as he was that the tractor's electronic apparatus was in perfect order.

It struck him that Dr. Burkett was being more snappish than usual. It never crossed his mind that the woman might be afraid.

"Ren, don't get any closer with the tractor unless I call. I'll get a set of temperature readings as soon as I'm close enough. Then I'll try to get a sample. Then I'll come back with that to the tractor, leave it and the radiometer and get the markers to set out."

"Couldn't I be putting out the markers while you get the sample, Doctor?"

"You could, but I'd rather you stayed at the wheel." Hargedon made no answer, and Burkett resumed her description for the record.

"I'm walking toward the front, a good deal faster than it's flowing toward me. I am now about twenty yards away, and am going to take a set of radiation-temperature measures." A brief pause. "Readings coming. Nine sixty. Nine eighty. Nine ninety—that's from the bottom edge near the spine that's being surrounded. Nine eighty-five—" The voice droned on until about two dozen readings had been taped. Then, "I'm going closer now. The sampler is just a ladle on a twelve-foot handle we improvised, so I'll have to get that close. The stuff is moving slowly; there should be no trouble. I'm in reach now. The lava is very liquid; there's no trouble getting the sampler in—or out again—it's not very dense, either. I'm heading back toward the tractor now. No, Ren, don't come to meet me."

There was a minute of silence, while Zaino pictured the space-suited figure with its awkwardly long burden, walking away from the creeping menace to the relative safety of the tractor. "It's frozen solid already; we needn't worry about spilling. The temperature is about—five eighty. Give me the markers, please."

Another pause, shorter this time. Zaino wondered how much of that could be laid to a faster walk without the ladle and how much to the lessening distance between flow and tractor. "I'm tossing the first marker close to the edge—it's landed less than a foot from the lava. They're all on a light cord at ten-foot intervals; I'm paying out the cord as I go back to the tractor. Now we'll stand by and time the arrival at each marker as well as we can."

"How close are you to the main cone?" asked Zaino.

"Not close enough to see its base, I'm afraid. Or to get a sample of it, which is worse. We—goodness, what was that?"

Zaino had just time to ask, "What was what?" when he found out.

For a moment, he thought that the *Albireo* had been flung bodily into the air. Then he decided that the great metal pillar had merely fallen over. Finally he realized that the ship was still erect, but the ground under it had just tried to leave.

Everyone in the group had become so used to the almost perpetual ground tremors that they had ceased to notice them; but this one demanded attention. Rowson, using language which suggested that his career might not have been completely free of adventure after all, flashed through the communication level on his way down to the power section. Schlossberg and Babineau followed, the medic pausing to ask Zaino if he were all right. The radioman merely nodded affirmatively; his attention was already back at his job. Burkett was speaking a good deal faster than before.

"Never mind if the sample isn't lashed tight yet—if it falls off there'll be plenty more. There isn't time! Arnie, get in touch with Dr. Mardikian and Dr. Marini. Tell them that this volcano is explosive, that all estimates of what the flow may do are off until we can make more measures, and in any case the whole situation is unpredictable. Everyone should get back as soon as possible. Remember, we decided that those big craters Eileen checked were not meteor pits. I don't know whether this thing will let go in the next hour, the next year, or at all. Maybe what's happening now will act as a safety valve—but let's get out. Ren, that flow is speeding up and getting higher, and the ash rain is getting a lot worse. Can you see to drive?"

She fell silent. Zaino, in spite of her orders, left his set long enough to leap to the nearest port for a look at the volcano.

He never regretted it.

Across the riven plain, whose cracks were now nearly hidden under the new ash, the black cone towered above the nearer elevations. It was visibly taller than it had been only a few hours before. The fountain from its top was thicker, now jetting straight up as though wind no longer meant a thing to the fiercely driven column of gas and dust. The darkness was not so complete; patches of red and yellow incandescence showed briefly in the pillar, and glowing sparks rather than black cinders rained back on the steep slopes. Far above, a ring of smoke rolled and spread about the column, forming an ever-broadening blanket of opaque cloud above a landscape which had never before been shaded from the sun. Streamers of lightning leaped between cloud and pillar, pillar and mountain, even cloud and ground. Any thunder there might have been was drowned in the howl of the escaping gas, a roar which seemed to combine every possible note from the shrillest possible whistle to a bass felt by the chest rather than heard by the ears. Rowson's language had become inaudible almost before he had disappeared down the hatch.

For long moments the radioman watched the spreading cloud, and wondered whether the *Albireo* could escape being struck by the flickering, ceaseless lightning. Far above the widening ring of cloud the smoke fountain drove, spreading slowly in the thinning atmosphere and beyond it. Zaino had had enough space experience to tell at a glance whether a smoke or dust cloud was in air or not. This wasn't, at least at the upper extremity . . .

And then, quite calmly, he turned back to his desk, aimed the antenna straight up, and called Eileen Harmon. She answered promptly.

The stratigrapher listened without interruption to his report and the order to return. She conferred briefly with her companion, replied, "We'll be back in twelve hours," and signed off. And that was that.

Zaino settled back with a sigh, and wondered whether it would be tactful to remind Rowson of his offer of a year's pay.

All four vehicles were now homeward bound; all one had to worry about was whether any of them would make it. Hargedon and Burkett were fighting their way through an ever-increasing ash rain a scant two miles away—ash which not only cut visibility but threatened to block the way with drifts too deep to negotiate. The wind, now blowing fiercely toward the volcano, blasted the gritty stuff against their front window as though it would erode through; and the lava flow, moving far faster than the gentle ooze they had never quite measured, surged—and glowed—grimly behind.

A hundred miles or more to the east, the tractors containing Mardikian, Marini and their drivers headed southwest along the alternate route their maps had suggested; but Mardikian, some three hours in the lead, reported that he could see four other smoke columns in that general direction.

Mercury seemed to be entering a new phase. The maps might well be out of date.

Harmon and Trackman were having no trouble at the moment, but they would have to pass the great chasm. This had been shooting out daughter cracks when Zaino and Hargedon passed it hours before. No one could say what it might be like now, and no one was going out to make sure.

"We can see you!" Burkett's voice came through suddenly. "Half a mile to go, and we're way ahead of the flow."

"But it's coming?" Rawson asked tensely. He had returned from the power level at Zaino's phoned report of success.

"It's coming."

"How fast? When will it get here? Do you know whether the ship can stand contact with it?"

"I don't know the speed exactly. There may be two hours, maybe five or six. The ship can't take it. Even the temperature measures I got were above the softening point of the alloys, and it's hotter and much deeper now. Anyway, if the others aren't back before the flow reaches the ship they won't get through. The tractor wheels would char away, and I doubt that the bodies would float. You certainly can't wade through the stuff in a space suit, either."

"And you think there can't be more than five or six hours before the flow arrives?"

"I'd say that was a very optimistic guess. I'll stop and get a better speed estimate if you want, but won't swear to it."

Rowson thought for a moment.

"No," he said finally, "don't bother. Get back here as soon as you can. We need the tractor and human muscles more than we need even expert guesses." He turned to the operator.

"Zaino, tell all the tractors there'll be no answer from the ship for a while, because no one will be aboard. Then suit up and come outside." He was gone.

Ten minutes later, six human beings and a tractor were assembled in the flame-lit near-darkness outside the ship. The cloud had spread to the horizon, and the sun was gone. Burkett and Hargedon had arrived, but Rowson wasted no time on congratulations.

"We have work to do. It will be easy enough to keep the lava from the ship, since there seems to be a foot or more of ash on the ground and a touch of main drive would push it into a ringwall around us; but that's not the main problem. We have to keep it from reaching the chasm anywhere south of us, since that's the way the others will be coming. If they're cut off, they're dead. It will be brute work. We'll use the tractor any way we can think of. Unfortunately it has no plow atttachment, and I can't think of anything aboard which could be turned into one. You have shovels, such as they are. The ash is light, especially here, but there's a mile and a half of dam to be built. I don't see how it can possibly be done . . . but it's going to be."

"Come on, Arnie! You're young and strong," came the voice of the mineralogist. "You should be able to lift as much of this stuff as I can. I understand you were lucky enough to get hold of Eileen—have you asked for the bonus yet?—but your work isn't done."

"It wasn't luck," Zaino retorted. Burkett, in spite of her voice, seemed much less of a schoolmistress when encased in a space suit and carrying a shovel, so he was able to talk back to her. "I was simply alert enough to make use of existing conditions, which I had to observe for myself in spite of all the scientists around. I'm charging the achievement to my regular salary. I saw—"

He stopped suddenly, both with tongue and shovel. Then, "Captain!"

"What is it?"

"The only reason we're starting this wall here is to keep well ahead of the flow so we can work as long as possible, isn't it?"

"Yes, I suppose so. I never thought of trying anywhere else. The valley would mean a much shorter dam, but if the flow isn't through it by now it would be before we could get there—oh! Wait a minute!"

"Yes, sir. You can put the main switch anywhere in a D.C. circuit. Where are the seismology stores we never had to use?"

Four minutes later the tractor set out from the *Albireo*, carrying Rowson and Zaino. Six minutes after that it stopped at the base of the ash cone which formed the north side of the valley from which the lava was coming. They parked a quarter of the way around the cone's base from the emerging flood and started to climb on foot, both carrying burdens.

Forty-seven minutes later they returned empty-handed to the vehicle, to find that it had been engulfed by the spreading liquid.

With noticeable haste they floundered through the loose ash a few yards above the base until they had outdistanced the glowing menace, descended and started back across the plain to where they knew the ship to be, though she was invisible through the falling detritus. Once they had to detour around a crack. Once they encountered one which widened toward the chasm on their right, and they knew a detour would be impossible. Leaping it seemed impossible, too, but they did it. Thirty seconds after this, forty minutes after finding the tractor destroyed, the landscape was bathed in a magnesium-white glare as the two one-and-a-half kiloton charges planted just inside the crater rim let go.

"Should we go back and see if it worked?" asked Zaino.

"What's the use? The only other charges we had were in the tractor. Thank goodness they were nuclear instead of H.E. If it didn't work we'd have more trouble to get back than we're having now."

"If it didn't work, is there any point in going back?"

"Stop quibbling and keep walking. Dr. Burkett, are you listening?"

"Yes, Captain."

"We're fresh out of tractors, but if you want to try it on foot you might start a set of flow measures on the lava. Arnie wants to know whether our landslide slid properly."

However, the two were able to tell for themselves before getting back to the *Albireo*.

The flow didn't stop all at once, of course; but with the valley feeding it blocked off by a pile of volcanic ash four hundred feet high on one side, nearly fifty on the other and more than a quarter of a mile long, its enthusiasm quickly subsided. It was thin, fluid stuff, as Burkett had noted; but as it spread it cooled, and as it cooled it thickened.

Six hours after the blast it had stopped with its nearest lobe almost a mile from the ship, less than two feet thick at the edge.

When Mardikian's tractor arrived, Burkett was happily trying to analyze samples of the flow, and less happily speculating on how long it would be before the entire area would be blown off the planet. When Marini's and Harmon's vehicles arrived, almost together, the specimens had been loaded and everything stowed for acceleration. Sixty seconds after the last person was aboard, the *Albireo* left Mercury's surface at two gravities.

The haste, it turned out, wasn't really necessary. She had been in parking orbit nearly forty-five hours before the first of the giant volcanoes reached its climax, and the one beside their former site was not the first. It was the fourth.

"And that seems to be that," said Camille Burkett rather tritely as they drifted a hundred miles above the little world's surface. "Just a belt of white-hot calderas all around the planet. Pretty, if you like symmetry."

"I like being able to see it from this distance," replied Zaino, floating weightless beside her. "By the way, how much bonus should I ask for getting that idea of putting the seismic charges to use after all?"

"I wouldn't mention it. Any one of us might have thought of that. We all knew about them."

"Anyone *might* have. Let's speculate on how long it would have been before anyone *did*."

"It's still not like the other idea, which involved your own specialty. I still don't see what made you suppose that the gas pillar from the volcano would be heavily charged enough to reflect your radio beam. How did that idea strike you?"

Zaino thought back, and smiled a little as the picture of lightning blazing around pillar, cloud and mountain rose before his eyes.

"You're not quite right," he said. "I was worried about it for a while, but it didn't actually strike me."

It fell rather flat; Camille Burkett, Ph.D., had to have it explained to her.

James Blish

James Blish (1921–75) was perhaps the most sophisticated of the literary critics grown inside the SF field. Though self-educated, he was respected as a James Joyce scholar and was a music critic as well. Of all SF writers at mid-century, Blish most worshipped the Modernists and most aspired to "high" art.

Blish moved permanently to England in the 1960s, where his writing was taken more seriously as contemporary literature than in the U.S. His major achievements in science fiction are generally regarded as the four-volume *Cities in Flight* (1970) and *A Case of Conscience* (1958), a classic theological SF novel. His short fiction, collected in *The Seedling Stars* (1957), *The Best of James Blish* (1979), and several other volumes, is also a major body of work in the modern field. He also edited the first SF anthology about the arts of the future, *New Dreams This Morning* (1966).

Perhaps his most ambitious project began with *A Case of Conscience*, about the discovery of Christian aliens without original sin, which is linked to an even larger literary construct (Blish called it *After Such Knowledge*—essentially an ongoing theological argument) involving an additional non-genre novel about Francis Bacon, *Doctor Mirabilis* (1964), and two fantasy novels about the end of the world, *Black Easter* (1968) and *The Day After Judgement* (1971).

At a time in the 1950s when science fiction as a whole had ignored the arts and artists as subjects for most of its history, Blish published this story. Blish said: "Ostensibly this is a story about the future of serious music." It is of course more broadly about art. Such writers as Brian Aldiss, Samuel R. Delany, Michael Moorcock, and Bruce Sterling carry on the intellectual tradition of Blish today.

A WORK OF ART

Instantly, he remembered dying. He remembered it, however, as if at two removes—as though he were remembering a memory, rather than an actual event; as though he himself had not really been there when he died.

Yet the memory was all from his own point of view, not that of some detached and disembodied observer which might have been his soul. He had been most conscious of the rasping, unevenly drawn movements of the air in his chest. Blurring rapidly, the doctor's face had bent over him, loomed, come closer, and then had vanished as the doctor's head passed below his cone of vision, turned sideways to listen to his lungs.

It had become rapidly darker, and then, only then, had he realized that these were to be his last minutes. He had tried dutifully to say Pauline's name, but his memory contained no record of the sound—only of the rattling breath and of the film of sootiness thickening in the air, blotting out everything for an instant.

Only an instant, and then the memory was over. The room was bright again, and the ceiling, he noticed with wonder, had turned a soft green. The doctor's head lifted again and looked down at him.

It was a different doctor. This one was a far younger man, with an ascetic face and gleaming, almost fey eyes. There was no doubt about it. One of the last conscious thoughts he had had was that of gratitude that the attending physician, there at the end, had not been the one who secretly hated him for his one-time associations with the Nazi hierarchy. The attending doctor, instead, had worn an expression amusingly proper for that of a Swiss expert called to the deathbed of an eminent man: a mixture of worry at the prospect of losing so eminent a patient, and complacency at the thought that, at the old man's age, nobody could blame this doctor if he died. At eighty-five, pneumonia is a serious matter, with or without penicillin.

"You're all right now," the new doctor said, freeing his patient's head of a whole series of little silver rods which had been clinging to it by a sort of network cap. "Rest a minute and try to be calm. Do you know your name?"

He drew a cautious breath. There seemed to be nothing at all the matter with his lungs now; indeed, he felt positively healthy. "Certainly," he said, a little nettled. "Do you know yours?"

The doctor smiled crookedly. "You're in character, it appears," he said. "My name is Barkun Kris; I am a mind sculptor. Yours?"

"Richard Strauss."

"Very good," Dr. Kris said, and turned away. Strauss, however, had already been diverted by a new singularity. *Strauss* is a word as well as a name in German; it has many meanings—an ostrich, a bouquet; von Wolzogen had had a high old time working all the possible puns into the libretto of *Feuersnot.* And it happened to be the first German word to be spoken either by himself or by Dr. Kris since that twice-removed moment of death. The language was not French or Italian, either. It was most like English, but not the English Strauss knew; nevertheless, he was having no trouble speaking it and even thinking in it.

Well, he thought, *I'll be able to conduct* The Love of Danae, *after all. It isn't every composer who can premier his own opera posthumously.* Still, there was something queer about all this—the queerest part of all being that conviction, which would not go away, that he had actually been dead for just a short time. Of course, medicine was making great strides, but . . .

"Explain all this," he said, lifting himself to one elbow. The bed was different, too, and not nearly as comfortable as the one in which he had died. As for the room, it looked more like a dynamo shed than a sickroom. Had modern medicine taken to reviving its corpses on the floor of the Siemanns-Schukert plant?

"In a moment," Dr. Kris said. He finished rolling some machine back into what Strauss impatiently supposed to be its place, and crossed to the pallet. "Now. There are many things you'll have to take for granted without attempting to understand then, Dr. Strauss. Not everything in the world today is explicable in terms of your assumptions. Please bear that in mind."

"Very well. Proceed."

"The date," Dr. Kris said, "is 2161 by your calendar—or, in other words, it is now two hundred and twelve years after your death. Naturally, you'll realize that by this time nothing remains of your body but the bones. The body you have now was volunteered for your use. Before you look into a mirror to see what it's like, remember that its physical difference from the one you were used to is all in your favor. It's in perfect health, not unpleasant for other people to look at, and its physiological age is about fifty."

A miracle? No, not in this new age, surely. It is simply a work of science. But what a science! This was Nietzsche's eternal recurrence and the immortality of the superman combined into one.

"And where is this?" the composer said.

"In Port York, part of the State of Manhattan, in the United States. You will find the country less changed in some respects than I imagine you anticipate. Other changes, of course, will seem radical to you, but it's hard for me to predict which ones will strike you that way. A certain resilience on your part will bear cultivating."

"I understand," Strauss said, sitting up. "One question, please; is it still possible for a composer to make a living in this century?"

"Indeed it is," Dr. Kris said, smiling. "As we expect you to do. It is one of the purposes for which we've—brought you back."

"I gather, then," Strauss said somewhat dryly, "that there is still a demand for my music. The critics in the old days—"

"That's not quite how it is," Dr. Kris said. "I understand some of your work is still played, but frankly I know very little about your current status. My interest is rather—"

A door opened somewhere, and another man came in. He was older and more ponderous than Kris and had a certain air of academicism, but he, too, was wearing the oddly tailored surgeon's gown and looked upon Kris' patient with the glowing eyes of an artist.

"A success, Kris?" he said. "Congratulations."

"They're not in order yet," Dr. Kris said. "The final proof is what counts. Dr. Strauss, if you feel strong enough, Dr. Seirds and I would like to ask you some questions. We'd like to make sure your memory is clear."

"Certainly. Go ahead."

"According to our records," Kris said, "you once knew a man whose initials were R. K. L.; this was while you were conducting at the Vienna *Staatsoper*." He made the double "a" at least twice too long, as though German were a dead language he was striving to pronounce in some "classical" accent. "What was his name, and who was he?"

"That would be Kurt List—his first name was Richard, but he didn't use it. He was assistant stage manager."

The two doctors looked at each other. "Why did you offer to write a new overture to *The Woman Without a Shadow* and give the manuscript to the city of Vienna?"

"So I wouldn't have to pay the garbage removal tax on the Maria Theresa villa they had given me."

"In the backyard of your house at Garmisch-Partenkirchen there was a tombstone. What was written on it?"

Strauss frowned. That was a question he would be happy to be unable to answer. If one is to play childish jokes upon oneself, it's best not to carve them in stone and put the carving where you can't help seeing it every time you go out to tinker with the Mercedes. "It says," he replied wearily, " 'Sacred to the memory of Guntram, Minnesinger, slain in a horrible way by his father's own symphony orchestra.' "

"When was *Guntram* premiered?"

"In—let me see—1894, I believe."

"Where?"

"In Weimar."

"Who was the leading lady?"

"Pauline de Ahna."

"What happened to her afterwards?"

"I married her. Is she . . . ," Strauss began anxiously.

"No," Dr. Kris said. "I'm sorry, but we lack the data to reconstruct more or less ordinary people."

The composer sighed. He did not know whether to be worried or not. He had loved Pauline, to be sure; on the other hand, it would be pleasant to be able to live the new life without being forced to take off one's shoes every time one entered the house, so as not to scratch the polished hardwood floors. And also pleasant, perhaps, to have two o'clock in the afternoon come by without hearing Pauline's everlasting, "Richard—*jetzt komponiert!*"

"Next question," he said.

For reasons which Strauss did not understand, but was content to take for granted, he was separated from Drs. Kris and Seirds as soon as both were satisfied that the composer's memory was reliable and his health stable. His estate, he was given to understand, had long since been broken up—a sorry end for what had been one of the principal fortunes of Europe—but he was given sufficient money to set up lodgings and resume an active life. He was provided, too, with introductions which proved valuable.

It took longer than he had expected to adjust to the changes that had taken place in music alone. Music was, he quickly began to suspect, a dying art, which would soon have a status not much above that held by flower arranging back in what he thought of as his own century. Certainly it couldn't be denied that the trend toward fragmentation, already visible back in his own time, had proceeded almost to completion in 2161.

He paid no more attention to American popular tunes than he had bothered to pay in his previous life. Yet it was evident that their assembly-line production methods—all the ballad composers openly used a slide-rule-like device called a Hit Machine—now had their counterparts almost throughout serious music.

The conservatives these days, for instance, were the twelve-tone composers—always, in Strauss's opinion, dryly mechanical but never more so than now. Their gods—Berg, Schoenberg, Webern—were looked upon by the concert-going public as great masters, on the abstruse side perhaps, but as worthy of reverence as any of the Three B's.

There was one wing of the conservatives however, that had gone the twelve-tone procedure one better. These men composed what was called "stochastic music," put together by choosing each individual note by consultation with tables of random numbers. Their bible, their basic text, was a volume called *Operational Aesthetics*, which in turn derived from a discipline called information theory, and not one word of it seemed to touch upon any of the techniques and customs of composition which Strauss knew. The ideal of this group was to produce music which would be "universal"—that is, wholly devoid of any trace of the composer's individuality, wholly a musical expression of the universal Laws of Chance. The Laws of Chance seemed to have a style of their own, all right, but to Strauss it seemed the style of an idiot child being taught to hammer a flat piano, to keep him from getting into trouble.

By far the largest body of work being produced, however, fell into a category misleadingly called science-music. The term reflected nothing but the titles of the works, which dealt with space flight, time travel, and other subjects of a romantic or an unlikely nature. There was nothing in the least scientific about the music, which consisted of a mélange of clichés and imitations of natural sounds, in which Strauss was horrified to see his own time-distorted and diluted image.

The most popular form of science-music was a nine-minute composition called a concerto, though it bore no resemblance at all to the classical concerto form; it was instead a sort of free rhapsody after Rachmaninoff—long after. A typical one—"Song of Deep Space," it was called, by somebody named H. Valerion Krafft—began with a loud assault on the tam-tam, after which all the strings rushed up the scale in unison, followed at a respectful distance by the harp and one clarinet in parallel 6/4's. At the top of the scale cymbals were bashed together, *forte possible*, and the whole orchestra launched itself into a major-minor wailing sort of melody; the whole orchestra, that is, except for the French horns, which were plodding back down the scale again in what was evidently supposed to be a countermelody. The second phrase of the theme was picked up by a solo trumpet with a suggestion of tremolo, the orchestra died back to its roots to await the next cloudburst, and at this point—as any four-year-old could have predicted—the piano entered with the second theme.

Behind the orchestra stood a group of thirty women, ready to come in with a wordless chorus intended to suggest the eeriness of Deep Space—but at this point, too, Strauss had already learned to get up and leave. After a few such experiences he could also count upon meeting in the lobby Sindi Noniss, the agent to whom Dr. Kris had introduced him and who was handling the reborn composer's output—what there was of it thus far. Sindi had come to expect these walkouts on the part of his client and patiently awaited them, standing beneath a bust of Gian-Carlo Menotti, but he liked them less and less, and lately had been greeting them by turning alternately red and white, like a totipotent barber pole.

"You shouldn't have done it," he burst out after the Krafft incident. "You can't just walk out on a new Krafft composition. The man's the president of the Interplanetary Society for Contemporary Music. How am I ever going to persuade them that you're a contemporary if you keep snubbing them?"

"What does it matter?" Strauss said. "They don't know me by sight."

"You're wrong; they know you very well, and they're watching every move you make. You're the first major composer the mind sculptors ever tackled, and the ISCM would be glad to turn you back with a rejection slip."

"Why?"

"Oh," said Sindi, "there are lots of reasons. The sculptors are snobs; so are the ISCM boys. Each of them wanted to prove to the other that their own art is the king of them all. And then there's the competition; it would be easier to flunk you than to let you into the market. I really think you'd better go back in. I could make up some excuse—"

"No," Strauss said shortly. "I have work to do."

"But that's just the point. Richard. How are we going to get an opera produced without the ISCM? It isn't as though you wrote theremin solos, or something that didn't cost so—"

"I have work to do," he said, and left.

And he did, work which absorbed him as had no other project during the last thirty years of his former life. He had scarcely touched pen to music paper—both had been astonishingly hard to find—when he realized that nothing in his long career had provided him with touchstones by which to judge what music he should write *now*.

The old tricks came swarming back by the thousands, to be sure: the sudden, unexpected key changes at the crest of a melody, the interval stretching, the piling of divided strings, playing in the high harmonics, upon the already tottering top of a climax, the scurry and bustle as phrases were passed like lightning from one choir of the orchestra to another, the flashing runs in the brass, the chuckling in the clarinets, the snarling mixtures of colors to emphasize dramatic tension—all of them.

But none of them satisfied him now. He had been content with them for most of a lifetime and had made them do an astonishing amount of work. But now it was time to strike out afresh. Some of the tricks, indeed, actively repelled him: Where had he gotten the notion, clung to for decades, that violins screaming out in unison somewhere in the stratosphere were a sound interesting enough to be worth repeating inside a single composition, let alone in all of them?

And nobody, he reflected contentedly, ever approached such a new beginning better equipped. In addition to the past lying available in his memory, he had always had a technical armamentarium second to none; even the hostile critics had granted him that. Now that he was, in a sense, composing his first opera—his first after fifteen of them!—he had every opportunity to make it a masterpiece.

And every such intention.

There were of course, many minor distractions. One of them was that search for old-fashioned score paper, and a pen and ink with which to write on it. Very few of the modern composers, it developed, wrote their music at all. A large bloc of them used tape, patching together snippets of tone and sound snipped from other tapes, superimposing one tape on another, and varying the results by twirling an elaborate array of knobs this way or that. Almost all the composers of 3-V scores, on the other hand, wrote on the sound track itself, rapidly scribbling jagged wiggly lines which, when passed through a photocell-audio circuit, produced a noise reasonably like an orchestra playing music, overtones and all.

The last-ditch conservatives who still wrote notes on paper did so with the aid of a musical typewriter. The device, Strauss had to admit, seemed perfected at last; it had manuals and stops like an organ, but it was not much more than twice as large as a standard letter-writing typewriter and produced a neat page. But he was satisfied with his own spidery, highly legible manuscript and refused to abandon it, badly though the one pen nib he had been able to buy coarsened it. It helped to tie him to his past.

Joining the ISCM had also caused him some bad moments, even after Sindi had worked him around the political roadblocks. The Society man who examined his qualifications as a member had run through the questions with no more interest than might have been shown by a veterinarian examining his four-thousandth sick calf.

"Had anything published?"

"Yes, nine tone poems, about three hundred songs, an—"

"Not when you were alive," the examiner said, somewhat disquietingly. "I mean since the sculptors turned you out again."

"Since the sculptors—ah, I understand. Yes, a string quartet, two song cycles, a—"

"Good. Alfie, write down, 'Songs.' Play an instrument?"

"Piano."

"Hmmm." The examiner studied his fingernails. "Oh well. Do you read music? Or do you use a Scriber, or tape clips? Or a Machine?"

"I read."

"Here." The examiner sat Strauss down in front of a viewing lectern, over the lit surface of which an endless belt of translucent paper was traveling. On the paper was an immensely magnified sound track. "Whistle me the tune of that, and name the instruments it sounds like."

"I don't read that *Musiksticheln*," Strauss said frostily, "or write it, either. I use standard notation, on music paper."

"Alfie, write down, 'Reads notes only.' " He laid a sheet of grayly printed music on the lectern above the ground glass. "Whistle me that."

"That" proved to be a popular tune called "Vangs, Snifters, and Store-Credit Snooky," which had been written on a Hit Machine in 2159 by a guitar-faking politician who sang it at campaign rallies. (In some respects, Strauss reflected, the United States had indeed not changed very much.) It had become so popular that anybody could have whistled it from the title alone, whether he could read the music or not. Strauss whistled it and, to prove his bona fides, added, "It's in the key of B flat."

The examiner went over to the green-painted upright piano and hit one greasy black key. The instrument was horribly out of tune—the note was much nearer to the standard 440/cps A than it was to B flat—but the examiner said, "So it is. Alfie, write down, 'Also reads flats.' All right, son, you're a member. Nice to have you with us; not many people can read that old-style notation anymore. A lot of them think they're too good for it."

"Thank you," Strauss said.

"My feeling is, if it was good enough for the old masters, it's good enough for us. We don't have people like them with us these days, it seems to me. Except for Dr. Krafft, of course. They were *great* back in the old days—men like Shilkrit, Steiner, Tiomkin, and Pearl . . . and Wilder and Jannsen. Real goffin."

"*Doch gewiss*," Strauss said politely.

But the work went forward. He was making a little income now, from small works. People seemed to feel a special interest in a composer who had come out of the mind sculptors' laboratories, and in addition the material itself, Strauss was quite certain, had merits of its own to help sell it.

It was the opera that counted, however. That grew and grew under his pen, as fresh and new as his new life, as founded in knowledge and ripeness as his long, full memory. Finding a libretto had been troublesome at first. While it was possible that something existed that might have served among the current scripts for 3-V—though he doubted it—he found himself unable to tell the good from the bad through the fog cast over both by incomprehensibly technical production directions. Eventually, and for only the third time in his whole career, he had fallen back upon a play written in a language other than his own, and—for the first time—decided to set it in that language.

The play was Christopher Fry's *Venus Observed*, in all ways a perfect Strauss opera libretto, as he came gradually to realize. Though nominally a comedy, with a complex farcical plot, it was a verse play with considerable depth to it, and a number of characters who cried out to be brought by music into three dimensions, plus a strong undercurrent of autumnal tragedy, of leaf-fall and apple-fall—precisely the kind of contradictory dramatic mixture which von Hofmannsthal had supplied him with in *The Knight of the Rose*, in *Ariadne at Naxos*, and in *Arabella*.

Alas for von Hofmannsthal, but here was another long-dead playwright who seemed nearly as gifted, and the musical opportunities were immense. There was, for instance, the fire which ended Act II; what a gift for a composer to whom orchestration and counterpoint were as important as air and water! Or take the moment where Perpetua shoots the apple from the Duke's hand; in that one moment a single passing reference could add Rossini's marmoreal *William Tell* to the musical texture as nothing but an ironic footnote! And the Duke's great curtain speech, beginning:

Shall I be sorry for myself? In Mortality's name
I'll be sorry for myself. Branches and boughs,
Brown hills, the valleys faint with brume,
A burnish on the lake. . . .

There was a speech for a great tragic comedian in the spirit of Falstaff: the final union of laughter and tears, punctuated by the sleepy comments of Reedbeck, to whose sonorous snore (trombones, no less than five of them, *con sordini?*) the opera would gently end. . . .

What could be better? And yet he had come upon the play only by the unlikeliest series of accidents. At first he had planned to do a straight knockabout farce, in the idiom of *The Silent Woman*, just to warm himself up. Remembering that Zweig had adapted that libretto for him, in the old days, from a play by Ben Jonson, Strauss had begun to search out English plays of the period just after Jonson's, and had promptly run aground on an awful specimen in heroic couplets called *Venice Preserv'd*, by one Thomas Otway. The Fry play had directly followed the Otway in the card catalogue, and he had looked at it out of curiosity; why should a twentieth-century playwright be punning on a title from the eighteenth?

After two pages of the Fry play, the minor puzzle of the pun disappeared entirely from his concern. His luck was running again; he had an opera.

Sindi worked miracles in arranging for the performance. The date of the premiere was set even before the score was finished, reminding Strauss pleasantly of those heady days when Fuestner had been snatching the conclusion of *Elektra* off his worktable a page at a time, before the ink was even dry, to rush it to the engraver before publication deadline. The situation now, however, was even more complicated, for some of the score had to be scribed, some of it taped, some of it engraved in the old way, to meet the new techniques of performance; there were moments when Sindi seemed to be turning quite gray.

But *Venus Observed* was, as usual, forthcoming complete from Strauss's pen in plenty of time. Writing the music in first draft had been hellishly hard work, much more like being reborn than had been that confused awakening in Barkun Kris' laboratory, with its overtones of being dead instead, but Strauss found that he still retained all of his old ability to score from the draft almost effortlessly, as undisturbed by Sindi's half-audible worrying in the room with him as he was by the terrifying supersonic bangs of the rockets that bulleted invisibly over the city.

When he was finished, he had two days still to spare before the beginning of rehearsals. With those, furthermore, he would have nothing to do. The techniques of performance in this age were so completely bound up with the electronic arts as to reduce his own experience—he, the master *Kapellmeister* of them all—to the hopelessly primitive.

He did not mind. The music, as written, would speak for itself. In the meantime he found it grateful to forget the months-long preoccupation with the stage for a while. He went back to the library and browsed lazily through old poems, vaguely seeking texts for a song or two. He knew better than to bother with recent poets; they could not speak to him, and he knew it. The Americans of his own age, he thought, might give him a clue to understanding this America of 2161, and if some such poem gave birth to a song, so much the better.

The search was relaxing, and he gave himself up to enjoying it. Finally he struck a tape that he liked; a tape read in a cracked old voice that twanged of Idaho as that voice had twanged in 1910, in Strauss' own ancient youth. The poet's name was Pound; he said, on the tape:

"*. . . the souls of all men great*
At times pass through us,
And we are melted into them, and are not
Save reflexions of their souls.
Thus I am Dante for a space and am
One François Villon, a ballad-lord and thief,
Or am such holy ones I may not write,
Lest Blasphemy be writ against my name;
This for an instant and the flame is gone.
'Tis as in midmost us there glows a sphere
Translucent, molten gold, that is the 'I'
And into this some form projects itself:
Christus, or John, or eke the Florentine;
And as the clear space is not if a form's
Imposed thereon,
So cease we from all being for the time,
And these, the masters of the Soul, live on."

He smiled. That lesson had been written again and again from Plato onward. Yet the poem was a history of his own case, a sort of theory for the metempsychosis he had undergone, and in its formal way it was moving. It would be fitting to make a little hymn of it, in honor of his own rebirth, and of the poet's insight.

A series of solemn, breathless chords framed themselves in his inner ear, against which the words might be intoned in a high, gently bending hush at the beginning . . . and then a dramatic passage in which the great names of Dante and Villon would enter ringing like challenges to Time. . . . He wrote for a while in his notebook before he returned the spool to its shelf.

These, he thought, are good auspices.

And so the night of the premiere arrived, the audience pouring into the hall, the 3-V cameras riding on no visible supports through the air, and Sindi calculating his share of his client's earnings by a complicated game he played on his fingers, the basic law of which seemed to be that one plus one equals ten. The hall filled to the roof with people from every class, as though what was to come would be a circus rather than an opera.

There were, surprisingly, nearly fifty of the aloof and aristocratic mind sculptors, clad in formal clothes which were exaggerated black versions of their surgeons' gowns. They had bought a block of seats near the front of the auditorium, where the gigantic 3-V figures which would shortly fill the "stage" before them (the real singers would perform on a small stage in the basement) could not but seem monstrously out of proportion, but Strauss supposed that they had taken this into account and dismissed it.

There was a tide of whispering in the audience as the sculptors began to trickle in, and with it an undercurrent of excitement, the meaning of which was unknown to Strauss. He did not attempt to fathom it, however; he was coping with his own mounting tide of opening-night tension, which, despite all the years, he had never quite been able to shake.

The sourceless, gentle light in the auditorium dimmed, and Strauss mounted the podium. There was a score before him, but he doubted that he would need it. Directly before him, poking up from among the musicians, were the inevitable 3-V snouts, waiting to carry his image to the singers in the basement.

The audience was quiet now. This was the moment. His baton swept up and then decisively down, and the prelude came surging up out of the pit.

For a little while he was deeply immersed in the always tricky business of keeping the enormous orchestra together and sensitive to the flexing of the musical web beneath his hand. As his control firmed and became secure, however, the task became slightly less demanding, and he was able to pay more attention to what the whole sounded like.

There was something decidedly wrong with it. Of course there were the occasional surprises as some bit of orchestral color emerged with a different *Klang* than he had expected; that happened to every composer, even after a lifetime of experience. And there were moments when the singers, entering upon a phrase more difficult to handle than he had calculated, sounded like someone about to fall off a tightrope (although none of them actually fluffed once; they were as fine as troupe of voices as he had ever had to work with).

But these were details. It was the overall impression that was wrong. He was losing not only the excitement of the premiere—after all, that couldn't last at the same pitch all evening—but also his very interest in what was coming from the stage and the pit. He was gradually tiring, his baton arm becoming heavier; as the second act mounted to what should have been an impassioned outpouring of shining tone, he was so bored as to wish he could go back to his desk to work on that song.

Then the act was over; only one more to go. He scarcely heard the applause. The twenty minutes' rest in his dressing room was just barely enough to give him the necessary strength.

And suddenly, in the middle of the last act, he understood.

There was nothing new about the music. It was the old Strauss all over again—but weaker, more dilute than ever. Compared with the output of composers like Krafft, it doubtless sounded like a masterpiece to this audience. But he knew.

The resolutions, the determination to abandon the old clichés and mannerisms, the decision to say something new—they had all come to nothing against the force of habit. Being brought to life again meant bringing to life as well all those deeply graven reflexes of his style. He had only to pick up his pen and they overpowered him with easy automatism, no more under his control than the jerk of a finger away from a flame.

His eyes filled; his body was young, but he was an old man, an old man. Another thirty-five years of this? Never. He had said all this before, centuries before. Nearly a half century condemned to saying it all over again, in a weaker and still weaker voice, aware that even this debased century would come to recognize in him only the burnt husk of greatness?—no, never, never.

He was aware, dully, that the opera was over. The audience was screaming its joy. He knew the sound. They had screamed that way when *Day of Peace* had been premiered, but they had been cheering the man he had been, not the man that *Day of Peace* showed with cruel clarity he had become. Here the sound was even more meaningless: cheers of ignorance, and that was all.

He turned slowly. With surprise, and with a surprising sense of relief, he saw that the cheers were not, after all, for him.

They were for Dr. Barkun Kris.

Kris was standing in the middle of the bloc of mind sculptors, bowing to the audience. The sculptors nearest him were shaking his hand one after the other. More grasped at it as he made his way to the aisle and walked forward to the podium. When he mounted the rostrum and took the composer's limp hand, the cheering became delirious.

Kris lifted his arm. The cheering died instantly to an intent hush.

"Thank you," he said clearly. "Ladies and gentlemen, before we take leave of Dr. Strauss, let us again tell him what a privilege it has been for us to hear this fresh example of his mastery. I am sure no farewell could be more fitting."

The ovation lasted five minutes and would have gone another five if Kris had not cut it off.

"Dr. Strauss," he said, "in a moment, when I speak a certain formulation to you, you will realize that your name is Jerom Bosch, born in our century and with a life in it all your own. The superimposed memories which have made you assume the mask, the *persona*, of a great composer will be gone. I tell you this so that you may understand why these people here share your applause with me."

A wave of asserting sound.

"The art of mind sculpture—the creation of artificial personalities for aesthetic enjoyment—may never reach such a pinnacle again. For you should understand that as Jerom Bosch you had no talent for music at all; indeed, we searched a long time to find a man who was utterly unable to carry even the simplest tune. Yet we were able to impose upon such unpromising material not only the personality, but the genius, of a great composer. That genius belongs entirely to you—to the *persona* that thinks of itself as Richard Strauss. None of the credit goes to the man who volunteered for the sculpture. That is your triumph, and we salute you for it."

Now the ovation could no longer be contained. Strauss, with a crooked smile, watched Dr. Kris bow. This mind sculpturing was a suitably sophisticated kind of cruelty for this age, but the impulse, of course, had always existed. It was the same impulse that had made Rembrandt and Leonardo turn cadavers into art works.

It deserved a suitably sophisticated payment under the *lex talionis:* an eye for an eye, a tooth for a tooth—and a failure for a failure.

No, he need not tell Dr. Kris that the "Strauss" he had created was as empty of genius as a hollow gourd. The joke would always be on the sculptor, who was incapable of hearing the hollowness of the music now preserved on the 3-V tapes.

But for an instant a surge of revolt poured through his bloodstream. *I am I,* he thought. *I am Richard Strauss until I die, and will never be Jerom Bosch, who was utterly unable to carry even the simplest tune.* His hand, still holding the baton, came sharply up, through whether to deliver or to ward off a blow he could not tell.

He let it fall again, and instead, at last, bowed—not to the audience, but to Dr. Kris. He was sorry for nothing, as Kris turned to him to say the word that would plunge him back into oblivion, except that he would now have no chance to set that poem to music.

E. M. Forster

E. M. Forster (1879–1970) was one of the great novelists (*Howard's End* [1910]; *A Passage to India* [1924]) of the century and one of the great literary critics (*Aspects of the Novel* [1927]). Leslie A. Fiedler, in the introduction to his excellent anthology of SF, *In Dreams Awake* (1975), summarizes how the personal and aesthetic rupture between Henry James and H. G. Wells after about 1900 became metaphorically institutionalized in the Jamesian separation of literature into "high" and "low." Forster, like James, felt that Wells was a pernicious literary and cultural influence and wrote this story as an anti-Wellsian piece, in reaction to *A Modern Utopia* (1905), in 1908—though it was not collected until 1928. It stands as an eloquent criticism of the urban and technological strain that pervades science fiction by a high Modernist.

Modernism was certainly opposed to science fiction from early in the century, and more so when science fiction became in the 1920s a low-class genre. C. S. Lewis was one of the few respectable academics who could see any value in the genre. Forster, who had no use for worship of the machine, portrays his future hive-world as reducing humans to insects, fungus, cripples. And Forster's story is a dystopia, or anti-utopia, one of the crucial texts that gave the anti-utopian story the odor of "high" art and respectability in this century—and the utopia the aura of "low."

THE MACHINE STOPS

PART I
The Airship

Imagine, if you can, a small room, hexagonal in shape like the cell of a bee. It is lighted neither by window nor by lamp, yet it is filled with a soft radiance. There are no apertures for ventilation, yet the air is fresh. There are no musical instruments, and yet, at the moment that my meditation opens, this room is throbbing with melodious sounds. An armchair is in the center, by its side a reading desk—that is all the furniture. And in the armchair there sits a swaddled lump of flesh—a woman, about five feet high, with a face as white as a fungus. It is to her that the little room belongs.

An electric bell rang.

The woman touched a switch and the music was silent.

"I suppose I must see who it is," she thought, and set her chair in motion. The chair, like the music, was worked by machinery, and it rolled her to the other side of the room, where the bell still rang importunately.

"Who it is?" she called. Her voice was irritable, for she had been interrupted often since the music began. She knew several thousand people; in certain directions human intercourse had advanced enormously.

But when she listened into the receiver, her white face wrinkled into smiles, and she said:

"Very well. Let us talk, I will isolate myself. I do not expect anything important will happen for the next five minutes—for I can give you fully five minutes, Kuno. Then I must deliver my lecture on 'Music during the Australian Period.' "

She touched the isolation knob, so that no one else could speak to her. Then she touched the lighting apparatus, and the little room was plunged into darkness.

"Be quick!" she called, her irritation returning. "Be quick, Kuno; here I am in the dark wasting my time."

But it was fully fifteen seconds before the round plate that she held in her hands began to glow. A faint blue light shot across it, darkening to purple, and presently she could see the image of her son, who lived on the other side of the earth, and he could see her.

"Kuno, how slow you are."

He smiled gravely.

"I really believe you enjoy dawdling."

"I have called you before, Mother, but you were always busy or isolated. I have something particular to say."

"What is it, dearest boy? Be quick. Why could you not send it by pneumatic post?"

"Because I prefer saying such a thing. I want—"

"Well?"

"I want you to come and see me."

Vashti watched his face in the blue plate.

"But I can see you!" she exclaimed. "What more do you want?"

"I want to see you not through the Machine," said Kuno. "I want to speak to you not through the wearisome Machine."

"Oh, hush!" said his mother, vaguely shocked. "You mustn't say anything against the Machine."

"Why not?"

"One mustn't."

"You talk as if a god had made the Machine," cried the other. "I believe that you pray to it when you are unhappy. Men made it, do not forget that. Great men, but men. The Machine is much, but it is not everything. I see something like you in this plate, but I do not see you. I hear something like you through this telephone, but I do not hear you. That is why I want you to come. Come and stop with me. Pay me a visit, so that we can meet face to face, and talk about the hopes that are in my mind."

She replied that she could scarcely spare the time for a visit.

"The airship barely takes two days to fly between me and you."

"I dislike airships."

"Why?"

"I dislike seeing the horrible brown earth, and the sea, and the stars when it is dark. I get no ideas in an airship."

"I do not get them anywhere else."

"What kind of ideas can the air give you?"

He paused for an instant.

"Do you not know four big stars that form an oblong, and three stars close together in the middle of the oblong, and hanging from these stars, three other stars?"

"No, I do not. I dislike the stars. But did they give you an idea? How interesting; tell me."

"I had an idea that they were like a man."

"I do not understand."

"The four big stars are the man's shoulders and his knees. The three stars in the middle are like the belts that men wore once, and the three stars hanging are like a sword."

"A sword?"

"Men carried swords about with them, to kill animals and other men."

"It does not strike me as a very good idea, but it is certainly original. When did it come to you first?"

"In the airship—" He broke off, and she fancied that he looked sad. She could not be sure, for the Machine did not transmit *nuances* of expression. It gave only a general idea of people—an idea that was good enough for all practical purposes, Vashti thought. The imponderable bloom, declared by a discredited philosophy to be the actual essence of intercourse, was rightly ignored by the Machine, just as the imponderable bloom of the grape was ignored by the manufacturers of artificial fruit. Something "good enough" had long since been accepted by our race.

"The truth is," he continued, "that I want to see these stars again. They are curious stars. I want to see them not from the airship, but from the surface of the earth, as our ancestors did, thousands of years ago. I want to visit the surface of the earth."

She was shocked again.

"Mother, you must come, if only to explain to me what is the harm of visiting the surface of the earth."

"No harm," she replied, controlling herself. "But no advantage. The surface of the earth is only dust and mud; no life remains on it, and you would need a respirator, or the cold of the outer air would kill you. One dies immediately in the outer air."

"I know; of course I shall take all precautions."

"And besides—"

"Well?"

She considered, and chose her words with care. Her son had a queer temper, and she wished to dissuade him from the expedition.

"It is contrary to the spirit of the age," she asserted.

"Do you mean by that, contrary to the Machine?"

"In a sense, but—"

His image in the blue plate faded.

"Kuno!"

He had isolated himself.

For a moment Vashti felt lonely.

Then she generated the light, and the sight of her room, flooded with radiance and studded with electric buttons, revived her. There were buttons and switches everywhere—buttons to call for food, for music, for clothing. There was the hot-bath button, by pressure of which a basin of (imitation) marble rose out of the floor, filled to the brim with a warm deodorized liquid. There was the cold-bath button. There was the button that produced literature. And there were of course the buttons by which she communicated with her friends. The room, though it contained nothing, was in touch with all that she cared for in the world.

Vashti's next move was to turn off the isolation switch, and all the accumulations of the last three minutes burst upon her. The room was filled with the noise of bells, and speaking tubes. What was the new food like? Could she recommend it? Had she had any ideas lately? Might one tell her one's own ideas? Would she make an engagement to visit the public nurseries at an early date?—say this day month.

To most of these questions she replied with irritation—a growing quality in that accelerated age. She said that the new food was horrible. That she could not visit the public nurseries through press of engagements. That she had no ideas of her own but had just been told one—that four stars and three in the middle were like a man: she doubted there was much in it. Then she switched off her correspondents, for it was time to deliver her lecture on Australian music.

The clumsy system of public gatherings had been long since abandoned; neither Vashti nor her audience stirred from their rooms. Seated in her armchair she spoke, while they in their armchairs heard her, fairly well, and saw her, fairly well. She opened with a humorous account of music in the pre-Mongolian epoch, and went on to describe the great outburst of song that followed the Chinese conquest. Remote and primeval as were the methods of I-San-So and the Brisbane school, she yet felt (she said) that study of them might repay the musician of today: they had freshness; they had, above all, ideas.

Her lecture, which lasted ten minutes, was well received, and at its conclusion she and many of her audience listened to a lecture on the sea; there were ideas to be got from the sea; the speaker had donned a respirator and visited it lately. Then she fed, talked to many friends, had a bath, talked again, and summoned her bed.

The bed was not to her liking. It was too large, and she had a feeling for a small bed. Complaint was useless, for beds were of the same dimension all over the world, and to have had an alternative size would have involved vast alterations in the Machine. Vashti isolated herself—it was necessary, for neither day nor night existed under the ground—and reviewed all that had happened since she had summoned the bed last. Ideas? Scarcely any. Events—was Kuno's invitation an event?

By her side, on the little reading desk, was a survival from the ages of litter—one book. This was the Book of the Machine. In it were instructions against every possible contingency. If she was hot or cold or dyspeptic or at a loss for a word, she went to the book, and it told her which button to press. The Central Committee published it. In accordance with a growing habit, it was richly bound.

Sitting up in the bed, she took it reverently in her hands. She glanced round the glowing room as if someone might be watching her. Then, half ashamed, half joyful, she murmured, "O Machine! O Machine!" and raised the volume to her lips. Thrice she kissed it, thrice inclined her head, thrice she felt the delirium of acquiescence. Her ritual performed, she turned to page 1367, which gave the times of the departure of the airships from the island in the Southern Hemisphere, under whose soil she lived, to the island in the Northern Hemisphere, whereunder lived her son.

She thought, "I have not the time."

She made the room dark and slept; she awoke and made the room light; she ate and exchanged ideas with her friends, and listened to music and attended lectures; she made the room dark and slept. Above her, beneath her, and around her, the Machine hummed eternally; she did not notice the noise, for she had been born with it in her ears. The earth, carrying her, hummed as it sped through silence, turning her now to the invisible sun, now to the invisible stars. She awoke and made the room light.

"Kuno!"

"I will not talk to you," he answered, "until you come."

"Have you been on the surface of the earth since we spoke last?"

His image faded.

Again she consulted the book. She became very nervous and lay back in her chair palpitating. Think of her as without teeth or hair. Presently she directed the chair to the wall, and pressed an unfamiliar button. The wall swung apart slowly. Through the opening she saw a tunnel that curved slightly, so that its goal was not visible. Should she go to see her son, here was the beginning of the journey.

Of course, she knew all about the communication system. There was nothing mysterious in it. She would summon a car and it would fly with her down the tunnel until it reached the lift that communicated with the airship station: the system had been in use for many, many years, long before the universal establishment of the Machine. And of course she had studied the civilization that had immediately preceded her own—the civilization that had mistaken the functions of the system, and had used it for bringing people to things, instead of for bringing things to people. Those funny old days, when men went for change of air instead of changing the air in their rooms! And yet—she was frightened of the tunnel: she had not seen it since her last child was born. It curved—but not quite as she remembered; it was brilliant—but not quite as brilliant as a lecturer had suggested. Vashti was seized with the terrors of direct experience. She shrank back into the room, and the wall closed up again.

"Kuno," she said, "I cannot come to see you. I am not well."

Immediately an enormous apparatus fell onto her out of the ceiling, a thermometer was automatically inserted between her lips, a stethoscope was automatically laid upon her heart. She lay powerless. Cool pads soothed her forehead. Kuno had telegraphed to her doctor.

So the human passions still blundered up and down in the Machine. Vashti drank the medicine that the doctor projected into her mouth, and the machinery retired into the ceiling. The voice of Kuno was heard asking how she felt.

"Better." Then, with irritation: "But why do you not come to me instead?"

"Because I cannot leave this place."

"Why?"

"Because, any moment, something tremendous may happen."

"Have you been on the surface of the earth yet?"

"Not yet."

"Then what is it?"

"I will not tell you through the machine."

She resumed her life.

But she thought of Kuno as a baby, his birth, his removal to the public nurseries, her one visit to him there, his visits to her—visits which stopped when the Machine had assigned him a room on the other side of the earth. "Parents, duties of," said the book of the Machine, "cease at the moment of birth. P. 422327483." True, but there was something special about Kuno—indeed there had been something special about all her children—and, after all, she must brave the journey if he desired it. And "something tremendous might happen." What did that mean? The nonsense of a youthful man, no doubt, but she must go. Again she pressed the unfamiliar button, again the wall swung back, and she saw the tunnel that curved out of sight. Clasping the Book, she rose, tottered onto the platform, and summoned the car. Her room closed behind her: the journey to the Northern Hemisphere had begun.

Of course, it was perfectly easy. The car approached and in it she found armchairs exactly like her own. When she signaled, it stopped, and she tottered into the lift. One other passenger was in the lift, the first fellow creature she had seen face to face for months. Few traveled in these days, for, thanks to the advance of science, the earth was exactly alike all over. Rapid intercourse, from which the previous civilization had hoped so much, had ended by defeating itself. What was the good of going to Peking when it was just like Shrewsbury? Why return to Shrewsbury when it would be just like Peking? Men seldom moved their bodies; all unrest was concentrated in the soul.

The airship service was a relic from the former age. It was kept up because it was easier to keep it up than to stop it or to diminish it, but it now far exceeded the wants of the population. Vessel after vessel would rise from the vomitories of Rye or of Christchurch (I use the antique names), would sail into the crowded sky, and would draw up at the wharves of the south—empty. So nicely adjusted was the system, so independent of meteorology, that the sky, whether calm or cloudy, resembled a vast kaleidoscope whereon the same patterns periodically recurred. The ship on which Vashti sailed started now at sunset, now at dawn. But always, as it passed above Rheims, it would neighbor the ship that served between Helsingfors and the Brazils, and, every third time it surmounted the Alps, the fleet of Palermo would cross its track behind. Night and day, wind and storm, tide and earthquake impeded man no longer. He had harnessed Leviathan. All the old literature, with its praise of Nature and its fear of Nature, rang false as the prattle of a child.

Yet as Vashti saw the vast flank of the ship, stained with exposure to the outer air, her horror of direct experience returned. It was not quite like the airship in the cinematophote. For one thing it smelled—not strongly or unpleasantly, but it did smell, and with her eyes shut she should have known that a new thing was close to her. Then she had to walk to it from the lift, had to submit to glances from the other passengers. The man in front dropped his Book—no great matter, but it disquieted them all. In the rooms, if the Book was dropped, the floor raised it mechanically, but the gangway to the airship was not so prepared, and the sacred volume lay motionless. They stopped—the thing was unforeseen—and the man, instead of picking up his property, felt the muscles of his arm to see how they had failed him. Then someone actually said with direct utterance: "We shall be late"—and they trooped on board, Vashti treading on the pages as she did so.

Inside, her anxiety increased. The arrangements were old-fashioned and rough. There was even a female attendant, to whom she would have to announce her wants during the voyage. Of course, a revolving platform ran the length of the boat, but she was expected to walk from it to her cabin. Some cabins were better than others, and she did not get the best. She thought the attendant had been unfair, and spasms of rage shook her. The glass valves had closed; she could not go back. She saw, at the end of the vestibule, the lift in which she had ascended going quietly up and down, empty. Beneath those corridors of shining tiles were rooms, tier below tier, reaching far into the earth, and in each room there sat a human being, eating, or sleeping, or producing ideas. And buried deep in the hive was her own room. Vashti was afraid.

"O Machine! O Machine!" she murmured, and caressed her Book, and was comforted.

Then the sides of the vestibule seemed to melt together, as do the passages that we see in dreams; the lift vanished, the Book that had been dropped slid to the left and vanished, polished tiles rushed by like a stream of water, there was a slight jar, and the airship, issuing from its tunnel, soared above the waters of a tropical ocean.

It was night. For a moment she saw the coast of Sumatra edged by the phosphorescence of waves, and crowned by lighthouses, still sending forth their disregarded beams. These also vanished, and only the stars distracted her. They were not motionless, but swayed to and fro above her head, thronging out of one skylight into another, as if the universe and not the airship was careening. And, as often happens on clear nights, they seemed now to be in perspective, now on a plane; now piled tier beyond tier into the infinite heavens, now concealing infinity, a roof limiting for ever the visions of men. In either case they seemed intolerable. "Are we to travel in the dark?" called the passengers angrily, and the attendant, who had been careless, generated the light and pulled down the blinds of pliable metal. When the airships had been built, the desire to look direct at things still lingered in the world. Hence the extraordinary number of skylights and windows, and the proportionate discomfort to those who were civilized and refined. Even in Vashti's cabin one star peeped through a flaw in the blind, and after a few hours' uneasy slumber, she was disturbed by an unfamiliar glow, which was the dawn.

Quick as the ship had sped westward, the earth had rolled eastward quicker still, and had dragged back Vashti and her companions toward the sun. Science could prolong the night, but only for a little, and those high hopes of neutralizing the earth's diurnal revolution had passed, together with hopes that were possibly higher. To "keep pace with the sun," or even to outstrip it, had been the aim of the civilization preceding this. Racing airplanes had been built for the purpose, capable of enormous speed, and steered by the greatest intellects of the epoch. Round the globe they went, round and round, westward, westward, round and round, amidst humanity's applause. In vain. The globe went eastward quicker still, horrible accidents occurred, and the Committee of the Machine, at the time rising into prominence, declared the pursuit illegal, unmechanical, and punishable by Homelessness.

Of Homelessness more will be said later.

Doubtless the Committee was right. Yet the attempt to "defeat the sun" aroused the last common interest that our race experienced about the heavenly bodies, or indeed about anything. It was the last time that men were compacted by thinking of a power outside the world. The sun had conquered, yet it was the end of his spiritual dominion. Dawn, midday, twilight, the zodiacal path, touched neither men's lives nor their hearts, and science retreated into the ground, to concentrate herself upon problems that she was certain of solving.

So when Vashti found her cabin invaded by a rosy finger of light, she was annoyed and tried to adjust the blind. But the blind flew up altogether, and she saw through the skylight small pink clouds, swaying against a background of blue, and as the sun crept higher, its radiance entered direct, brimming down the wall, like a golden sea. It rose and fell with the airship's motion, just as waves rise and fall, but it advanced steadily, as the tide advances. Unless she was careful, it would strike her face. A spasm of horror shook her, and she rang for the attendant. The attendant too was horrified, but she could do nothing; it was not her place to mend the blind. She could only suggest that the lady should change her cabin, which she accordingly prepared to do.

People were almost exactly alike all over the world, but the attendant of the airship, perhaps owing to her exceptional duties, had grown a little out of the common. She had often to address passengers with direct speech, and this had given her a certain roughness and originality of manner. When Vashti swerved away from the sunbeams with a cry, she behaved barbarically—she put out her hand to steady her.

"How dare you!" exclaimed the passenger. "You forget yourself!"

The woman was confused, and apologized for not having let her fall. People never touched one another. The custom had become obsolete, owing to the Machine.

"Where are we now?" asked Vashti haughtily.

"We are over Asia," said the attendant, anxious to be polite.

"Asia?"

"You must excuse my common way of speaking. I have got into the habit of calling places over which I pass by their unmechanical names."

"Oh, I remember Asia. The Mongols came from it."

"Beneath us, in the open air, stood a city that was once called Simla."

"Have you ever heard of the Mongols and of the Brisbane school?"

"No."

"Brisbane also stood in the open air."

"Those mountains to the right—let me show you them." She pushed back a metal blind. The main chain of the Himalayas was revealed. "They were once called the Roof of the World, those mountains."

"What a foolish name!"

"You must remember that, before the dawn of civilization, they seemed to be an impenetrable wall that touched the stars. It was supposed that no one but the gods could exist above their summits. How we have advanced, thanks to the Machine!"

"How we have advanced, thanks to the Machine!" said Vashti.

"How we have advanced, thanks to the Machine!" echoed the passenger who had dropped his Book the night before and who was standing in the passage.

"And that white stuff in the cracks?—what is it?"

"I have forgotten its name."

"Cover the window, please. These mountains give me no ideas."

The northern aspect of the Himalayas was in deep shadow: on the Indian slope the sun had just prevailed. The forests had been destroyed during the literature epoch for the purpose of making newspaper pulp, but the snows were awakening to their morning glory, and clouds still hung on the breasts of Kinchinjunga. In the plain were seen the ruins of cities, with diminished rivers creeping by their walls, and by the sides of these were sometimes the signs of vomitories, marking the cities of today. Over the whole prospect airships rushed, crossing and intercrossing with incredible aplomb, and rising nonchalantly when they desired to escape the perturbations of the lower atmosphere and to traverse the Roof of the World.

"We have indeed advanced, thanks to the Machine," repeated the attendant, and hid the Himalayas behind a metal blind.

The day dragged wearily forward. The passengers sat each in his cabin, avoiding one another with an almost physical repulsion and longing to be once more under the surface of the earth. There were eight or ten of them, mostly young males, sent out from the public nurseries to inhabit the rooms of those who had died in various parts of the earth. The man who had dropped his Book was on the homeward journey. He had been sent to Sumatra for the purpose of propagating the race. Vashti alone was traveling by her private will.

At midday she took a second glance at the earth. The airship was crossing another range of mountains, but she could see little, owing to clouds. Masses of black rock hovered below her and merged indistinctly into gray. Their shapes were fantastic; one of them resembled a prostrate man.

"No ideas here," murmured Vashti, and hid the Caucasus behind a metal blind.

In the evening she looked again. They were crossing a golden sea, in which lay many small islands and one peninsula.

She repeated, "No ideas here," and hid Greece behind a metal blind.

PART II
The Mending Apparatus

By a vestibule, by a lift, by a tubular railway, by a platform, by a sliding door—by reversing all the steps of her departure did Vashti arrive at her son's room, which exactly resembled her own. She might well declare that the visit was superfluous. The buttons, the knobs, the reading desk with the Book, the temperature, the atmosphere, the illumination—all were exactly the same. And if Kuno himself, flesh of her flesh, stood close beside her at last, what profit was there in that? She was too well bred to shake him by the hand.

Averting her eyes, she spoke as follows:

"Here I am. I have had the most terrible journey and greatly retarded the development of my soul. It is not worth it, Kuno; it is not worth it. My time is too precious. The sunlight almost touched me, and I have met with the rudest people. I can stop only a few minutes. Say what you want to say, and then I must return."

"I have been threatened with Homelessness," said Kuno.

She looked at him now.

"I have been threatened with Homelessness, and I could not tell you such a thing through the Machine."

Homelessness means death. The victim is exposed to the air, which kills him.

"I have been outside since I spoke to you last. The tremendous thing has happened, and they have discovered me."

"But why shouldn't you go outside?" she exclaimed. "It is perfectly legal, perfectly mechanical, to visit the surface of the earth. I have lately been to a lecture on the sea; there is no objection to that; one simply summons a respirator and gets an Egression permit. It is not the kind of thing that spiritually minded people do, and I begged you not to do it, but there is no legal objection to it."

"I did not get an Egression permit."

"Then how did you get out?"

"I found out a way of my own."

The phrase conveyed no meaning to her, and he had to repeat it.

"A way of your own?" she whispered. "But that would be wrong."

"Why?"

The question shocked her beyond measure.

"You are beginning to worship the Machine," he said coldly. "You think it irreligious of me to have found out a way of my own. It was just what the Committee thought, when they threatened me with Homelessness."

At this she grew angry. "I worship nothing!" she cried. "I am most advanced. I don't think you irreligious, for there is no such thing as religion left. All the fear and the superstition that existed once have been destroyed by the Machine. I meant only that to find out a way of your own was—Besides there is no new way out."

"So it is always supposed."

"Except through the vomitories, for which one must have an Egression permit, it is impossible to get out. The Book says so."

"Well, the Book's wrong, for I have been out on my feet."

For Kuno was possessed of a certain physical strength.

By these days it was a demerit to be muscular. Each infant was examined at birth, and all who promised undue strength were destroyed. Humanitarians may protest, but it would have been no true kindness to let an athlete live; he would never have been happy in that state of life to which the Machine had called him; he would have yearned for trees to climb, rivers to bathe in, meadows and hills against which he might measure his body. Man must be adapted to his surroundings, must he not? In the dawn of the world our weakly must be exposed on Mount Taygetus; in its twilight our strong will suffer euthanasia, that the Machine may progress, that the Machine may progress, that the Machine may progress eternally.

"You know that we have lost the sense of space. We say space is 'annihilated,' but we have annihilated not space but the sense thereof. We have lost a part of ourselves. I determined to recover it, and I began by walking up and down the platform of the railway outside my room. Up and down, until I was tired, and so did recapture the meaning of 'Near' and 'Far.' 'Near' is a place to which I can get quickly *on my feet*, not a place to which the train or the airship will take me quickly. 'Far' is a place to which I cannot get quickly on my feet; the vomitory is 'far,' though I could be there in thirty-eight seconds by summoning the train. Man is the measure. That was my first lesson. Man's feet are the measure for distance, his hands are the measure for ownership, his body is the measure for all that is lovable and desirable and strong. Then I went further: it was then that I called to you for the first time, and you would not come.

"This city, as you know, is built deep beneath the surface of the earth, with only the vomitories protruding. Having paced the platform outside my own room, I took the lift to the next platform and paced that also, and so with each in turn, until I came to the topmost, above which begins the earth. All the platforms were exactly alike, and all that I gained by visiting them was to develop my sense of space and my muscles. I think I should have been content with this—it is not a little thing—but as I walked and brooded, it occurred to me that our cities had been built in the days when men still breathed the outer air, and that there had been ventilation shafts for the workmen. I could think of nothing but these ventilation shafts. Had they been destroyed by all the food-tubes and medicine tubes and music tubes that the Machine has evolved lately? Or did traces of them remain? One thing was certain. If I came upon them anywhere, it would be in the railway tunnels of the topmost story. Everywhere else, all space was accounted for.

"I am telling my story quickly, but don't think that I was not a coward or that your answers never depressed me. It is not the proper thing, it is not mechanical, it is not decent to walk along a railway tunnel. I did not fear that I might tread upon a live rail and be killed. I feared something far more intangible—doing what was not contemplated by the Machine. Then I said to myself, 'Man is the measure,' and I went, and after many visits I found an opening.

"The tunnels, of course, were lighted. Everything is light, artificial light; darkness is the exception. So when I saw a black gap in the tiles, I knew that it was an exception, and rejoiced. I put in my arm—I could put in no more at first—and waved it round and round in ecstasy. I loosened another tile, and put in my head, and shouted into the darkness: 'I am coming, I shall do it yet,' and my voice reverberated down endless passages. I seemed to hear the spirits of those dead workmen who had returned each evening to the starlight and to their wives, and all the generations who had lived in the open air called back to me, 'You will do it yet, you are coming.' "

He paused, and, absurd as he was, his last words moved her. For Kuno had lately asked to be a father, and his request had been refused by the Committee. His was not a type that the Machine desired to hand on.

"Then a train passed. It brushed by me, but I thrust my head and arms into the hole. I had done enough for one day, so I crawled back to the platform, went down in the lift, and summoned my bed. Ah, what dreams! And again I called you, and again you refused."

She shook her head and said:

"Don't. Don't talk of these terrible things. You make me miserable. You are throwing civilization away."

"But I had got back the sense of space, and a man cannot rest then. I determined to get in at the hole and climb the shaft. And so I exercised my arms. Day after day I went through ridiculous movements, until my flesh ached, and I could hang by my hands and hold the pillow of my bed outstretched for many minutes. Then I summoned a respirator, and started.

"It was easy at first. The mortar had somehow rotted, and I soon pushed some more tiles in, and clambered after them into the darkness, and the spirits of the dead comforted me. I don't know what I mean by that. I just say what I felt. I felt, for the first time, that a protest had been lodged against corruption, and that even as the dead were comforting me, so I was comforting the unborn. I felt that humanity existed, and that it existed without clothes. How can I possibly explain this? It was naked, humanity seemed naked, and all these tubes and buttons and machineries neither came into the world with us, nor will they follow us out, nor do they matter supremely while we are here. Had I been strong, I would have torn off every garment I had, and gone out into the outer air unswaddled. But this is not for me, nor perhaps for my generation. I climbed with my respirator and my hygienic clothes and my dietetic tabloids! Better thus than not at all.

"There was a ladder, made of some primeval metal. The light from the railway fell upon its lowest rungs, and I saw that it led straight upward out of the rubble at the bottom of the shaft. Perhaps our ancestors ran up and down it a dozen times daily, in their building. As I climbed, the rough edges cut through my gloves so that my hands bled. The light helped me for a little, and then came darkness and, worse still, silence which pierced my ears like a sword. The Machine hums! Did you know that? Its hum penetrates our blood, and may even guide our thoughts. Who knows! I was getting beyond its power. Then I thought: 'This silence means that I am doing wrong.' But I heard voices in the silence, and again they strengthened me." He laughed. "I had need of them. The next moment I cracked my head against something."

She sighed.

"I had reached one of those pneumatic stoppers that defend us from the outer air. You may have noticed them on the airship. Pitch dark, my feet on the rungs of an invisible ladder, my hands cut; I cannot explain how I lived through this part, but the voices still comforted me, and I felt for fastenings. The stopper, I suppose, was about eight feet across. I passed my hand over it as far as I could reach. It was perfectly smooth. I felt it almost to the center. Not quite to the center, for my arm was too short. Then the voice said: 'Jump. It is worth it. There may be a handle in the center, and you may catch hold of it and so come to us your own way. And if there is no handle, so that you may fall and are dashed to pieces—it is still worth it: you will still come to us your own way.' So I jumped. There was a handle, and—"

He paused. Tears gathered in his mother's eyes. She knew that he was fated. If he did not die today he would die tomorrow. There was not room for such a person in the world. And with her pity disgust mingled. She was ashamed at having borne such a son, she who had always been so respectable and so full of ideas. Was he really the little boy to whom she had taught the use of his stops and buttons, and to whom she had given his first lessons in the Book? The very hair that disfigured his lip showed that he was reverting to some savage type. On atavism the Machine can have no mercy.

"There was a handle, and I did catch it. I hung tranced over the darkness and heard the hum of these workings as the last whisper in a dying dream. All the things I had cared about and all the people I had spoken to through tubes appeared infinitely little. Meanwhile the handle revolved. My weight had set something in motion and I spun slowly, and then—

"I cannot describe it. I was lying with my face to the sunshine. Blood poured from my nose and ears and I heard a tremendous roaring. The stopper, with me clinging to it, had simply been blown out of the earth, and the air that we make down here was escaping through the vent into the air above. It burst up like a fountain. I crawled back to it—for the upper air hurts—and, as it were, I took great sips from the edge. My respirator had flown goodness knows where, my clothes were torn. I just lay with my lips close to the hole, and I sipped until the bleeding stopped. You can imagine nothing so curious. This hollow in the grass—I will speak of it in a minute—the sun shining into it, not brilliantly but through marbled clouds—the peace, the nonchalance, the sense of space, and, brushing my cheek, the roaring fountain of our artificial air! Soon I spied my respirator, bobbing up and down in the current high above my head, and higher still were many airships. But no one ever looks out of airships, and in any case they could not have picked me up. There I was, stranded. The sun shone a little way down the shaft, and revealed the topmost rung of the ladder, but it was hopeless trying to reach it. I should either have been tossed up again by the escape, or else have fallen in, and died. I could only lie on the grass, sipping and sipping, and from time to time glancing around me.

"I knew that I was in Wessex, for I had taken care to go to a lecture on the subject before starting. Wessex lies above the room in which we are talking now. It was once an important state. Its kings held all the southern coast from the Andredswald to Cornwall, while the Wansdyke protected them on the north, running over the high ground. The lecturer was concerned only with the rise of Wessex, so I do not know how long it remained an international power, nor would the knowledge have assisted me. To tell the truth, I could do nothing but laugh during this part. There was I, with a pneumatic stopper by my side and a respirator bobbing over my head, imprisoned, all three of us, in a grass-grown hollow that was edged with fern."

Then he grew grave again.

"Lucky for me that it was a hollow. For the air began to fall back into it and to fill it as water fills a bowl. I could crawl about. Presently I stood. I breathed a mixture, in which the air that hurts predominated whenever I tried to climb the sides. This was not so bad. I had not lost my tabloids and remained ridiculously cheerful, and as for the Machine, I forgot about it altogether. My one aim now was to get to the top, where the ferns were, and to view whatever objects lay beyond.

"I rushed the slope. The new air was still too bitter for me and I came rolling back, after a momentary vision of something gray. The sun grew very feeble, and I remembered that he was in Scorpio—I had been to a lecture on that too. If the sun is in Scorpio and you are in Wessex, it means that you must be as quick as you can or it will get too dark. (This is the first bit of useful information I have ever got from a lecture, and I expect it will be the last.) It made me try frantically to breathe the new air, and to advance as far as I dared out of my pond. The hollow filled so slowly. At times I thought that the fountain played with less vigor. My respirator semed to dance nearer the earth; the roar was decreasing."

He broke off.

"I don't think this is interesting you. The rest will interest you even less. There are no ideas in it, and I wish that I had not troubled you to come. We are too different, Mother."

She told him to continue.

"It was evening before I climbed the bank. The sun had very nearly slipped out of the sky by this time, and I could not get a good view. You, who have just crossed the Roof of the World, will not want to hear an account of the little hills that I saw—low colorless hills. But to me they were living and the turf that covered them was a skin, under which their muscles rippled, and I felt that those hills had called with incalculable force to men in the past, and that men had loved them. Now they sleep—perhaps for ever. They commune with humanity in dreams. Happy the man, happy the woman, who awakes the hills of Wessex. For though they sleep, they will never die."

His voice rose passionately.

"Cannot you see, cannot all you lecturers see, that it is we that are dying, and that down here the only thing that really lives is the Machine? We created the Machine, to do our will, but we cannot make it do our will now. It has robbed us of the sense of space and of the sense of touch; it has blurred every human relation and narrowed down love to a carnal act, it has paralyzed our bodies and our wills, and now it compels us to worship it. The Machine develops—but not on our lines. The Machine proceeds—but not to our goal. We exist only as the blood corpuscles that course through its arteries, and if it could work without us, it would let us die. Oh, I have no remedy—or, at least, only one—to tell men again and again that I have seen the hills of Wessex as Aelfrid saw them when he overthrew the Danes.

"So the sun set. I forgot to mention that a belt of mist lay between my hill and other hills, and that it was the color of pearl."

He broke off for the second time.

"Go on," said his mother wearily.

He shook his head.

"Go on. Nothing that you say can distress me now. I am hardened."

"I had meant to tell you the rest, but I cannot: I know that I cannot: goodbye."

Vashti stood irresolute. All her nerves were tingling with his blasphemies. But she was also inquisitive.

"This is unfair," she complained. "You have called me across the world to hear your story, and hear it I will. Tell me—as briefly as possible, for this is a disastrous waste of time—tell me how you returned to civilization."

"Oh—that!" he said, starting. "You would like to hear about civilization. Certainly. Had I got to where my respirator fell down?"

"No—but I understand everything now. You put on your respirator, and managed to walk along the surface of the earth to a vomitory, and there your conduct was reported to the Central Committee."

"By no means."

He passed his hand over his forehead, as if dispelling some strong impression. Then, resuming his narrative, he warmed to it again.

"My respirator fell about sunset. I had mentioned that the fountain seemed feebler, had I not?"

"Yes."

"About sunset, it let the respirator fall. As I said, I had entirely forgotten about the Machine, and I paid no great attention at the time, being occupied with other things. I had my pool of air, into which I could dip when the outer keenness became intolerable, and which would possibly remain for days, provided that no wind sprang up to disperse it. Not until it was too late did I realize what the stoppage of the escape implied. You see—the gap in the tunnel had been mended; the Mending Apparatus; the Mending Apparatus, was after me.

"One other warning I had, but I neglected it. The sky at night was clearer than it had been in the day, and the moon, which was about half the sky behind the sun, shone into the dell at moments quite brightly. I was in my usual place—on the boundary between the two atmospheres—when I thought I saw something dark move across the bottom of the dell, and vanish into the shaft. In my folly, I ran down. I bent over and listened, and I thought I heard a faint scraping noise in the depths.

"At this—but it was too late—I took alarm. I determined to put on my respirator and to walk right out of the dell. But my respirator had gone. I knew exactly where it had fallen—between the stopper and the aperture—and I could even feel the mark that it had made in the turf. It had gone, and I realized that something evil was at work, and I had better escape to the other air, and, if I must die, die running toward the cloud that had been the color of a pearl. I never started. Out of the shaft—it is too horrible. A worm, a long white worm, had crawled out of the shaft and was gliding over the moonlit grass.

"I screamed. I did everything that I should not have done; I stamped upon the creature instead of flying from it, and it at once curled round the ankle.

Then we fought. The worm let me run all over the dell, but edged up my leg as I ran. 'Help!' I cried. (That part is too awful. It belongs to the part that you will never know.) 'Help!' I cried. (Why cannot we suffer in silence?) 'Help!' I cried. Then my feet were wound together. I fell, I was dragged away from the dear ferns and the living hills, and past the great metal stopper (I can tell you this part), and I thought it might save me again if I caught hold of the handle. It also was enwrapped, it also. Oh, the whole dell was full of the things. They were searching it in all directions; they were denuding it, and the white snouts of others peeped out of the hole, ready if needed. Everything that could be moved they brought—brushwood, bundles of fern, everything, and down we all went intertwined into hell. The last things that I saw, ere the stopper closed after us, were certain stars, and I felt that a man of my sort lived in the sky. For I did fight, I fought till the very end, and it was only my head hitting against the ladder that quieted me. I woke up in this room. The worms had vanished; I was surrounded by artificial air, artificial light, artificial peace, and my friends were calling to me down speaking-tubes to know whether I had come across any new ideas lately."

Here his story ended. Discussion of it was impossible, and Vashti turned to go.

"It will end in Homelessness," she said quietly.

"I wish it would," retorted Kuno.

"The Machine has been most merciful."

"I prefer the mercy of God."

"By that superstitious phrase, do you mean that you could live in the outer air?"

"Yes."

"Have you ever seen, round the vomitories, the bones of those who were extruded after the Great Rebellion?"

"Yes."

"They were left where they perished for our edification. A few crawled away, but they perished, too—who can doubt it? And so with the Homeless of our own day. The surface of the earth supports life no longer."

"Indeed."

"Ferns and a little grass may survive, but all higher forms have perished. Has any airship detected them?"

"No."

"Has any lecturer dealt with them?"

"No."

"Then why this obstinacy?"

"Because I have seen them," he exploded.

"Seen *what?*"

"Because I have seen her in the twilight—because she came to my help when I called—because she, too, was entangled by the worms, and, luckier than I, was killed by one of them piercing her throat."

He was mad. Vashti departed, nor, in the troubles that followed, did she ever see his face again.

PART III
The Homeless

During the years that followed Kuno's escapade, two important developments took place in the Machine. On the surface they were revolutionary, but in either case men's minds had been prepared beforehand, and they did but express tendencies that were latent already.

The first of these was the abolition of respirators.

Advanced thinkers, like Vashti, had always held it foolish to visit the surface of the earth. Airships might be necessary, but what was the good of going out for mere curiosity and crawling along for a mile or two in a terrestrial motor? The habit was vulgar and perhaps faintly improper: it was unproductive of ideas, and had no connection with the habits that really mattered. So respirators were abolished, and with them, of course, the terrestrial motors, and except for a few lecturers, who complained that they were debarred access to their subject matter, the development was accepted quietly. Those who still wanted to know what the earth was like had after all only to listen to some gramophone or to look into some cinematophote. And even the lecturers acquiesced when they found that a lecture on the sea was none the less stimulating when compiled out of other lectures that had already been delivered on the same subject. "Beware of firsthand ideas!" exclaimed one of the most advanced of them. "Firsthand ideas do not really exist. They are but the physical impressions produced by love and fear, and on this gross foundation who could erect a philosophy? Let your ideas be secondhand, and if possible tenthhand, for then they will be far removed from that disturbing element—direct observation. Do not learn anything about this subject of mine—the French Revolution. Learn instead what I think that Enicharmon thought Urizen thought Gutch thought Ho-Yung thought Chi-Bo-Sing thought Lafcadio Hearn thought Carlyle thought Mirabeau said about the French Revolution. Through the medium of these ten great minds the blood that was shed at Paris and the windows that were broken at Versailles will be clarified to an idea which you may employ most profitably in your daily lives. But be sure that the intermediates are many and varied, for in history one authority exists to counteract another. Urizen must counteract the skepticism of Ho-Young and Enicharmon, I must myself counteract the impetuosity of Gutch. You who listen to me are in a better position to judge about the French Revolution than I am. Your descendants will be even in a better position than you, for they will learn what you think. I think, and yet another intermediate will be added to the chain. And in time"—his voice rose—"there will come a generation that has got beyond facts, beyond impressions, a generation absolutely colorless, a generation

> "*seraphically free*
> *From taint of personality,*

"which will see the French Revolution not as it happened, nor as they would like it to have happened, but as it would have happened had it taken place in the days of the Machine."

Tremendous applause greeted this lecture, which did but voice a feeling already latent in the minds of men—a feeling that terrestrial facts must be ignored, and that the abolition of respirators was a positive gain. It was even suggested that airships should be abolished too. This was not done, because airships had somehow worked themselves into the Machine's system. But year by year they were used less, and mentioned less by thoughtful men.

The second great development was the reestablishment of religion.

This, too, had been voiced in the celebrated lecture. No one could mistake the reverent tone in which the peroration had concluded, and it awakened a responsive echo in the heart of each. Those who had long worshiped silently now began to talk. They described the strange feeling of peace that came over them when they handled the Book of the Machine, the pleasure that it was to repeat certain numerals out of it, however little meaning those numerals conveyed to the outward ear, the ecstasy of touching a button however unimportant, or of ringing an electric bell however superfluously.

"The Machine," they exclaimed, "feeds us and clothes us and houses us; through it we speak to one another, through it we see one another, in it we have our being. The Machine is the friend of ideas and the enemy of superstition: the Machine is omnipotent, eternal; blessed is the Machine." And before long this allocution was printed on the first page of the Book, and in subsequent editions the ritual swelled into a complicated system of praise and prayer. The word "religion" was sedulously avoided, and in theory the Machine was still the creation and the implement of man. But in practice all, save a few retrogrades, worshiped it as divine. Nor was it worshiped in unity. One believer would be chiefly impressed by the blue optic plates, through which he saw other believers; another by the Mending Apparatus, which sinful Kuno had compared to worms; another by the lifts, another by the Book. And each would pray to this or to that, and ask it to intercede for him with the Machine as a whole. Persecution—that also was present. It did not break out, for reasons that will be set forward shortly. But it was latent, and all who did not accept the minimum known as "undenominational Mechanism" lived in danger of Homelessness, which means death, as we know.

To attribute these two great developments to the Central Committee is to take a very narrow view of civilization. The Central Committee announced the developments, it is true, but they were no more the cause of them than were the kings of the imperialistic period the cause of war. Rather did they yield to some invincible pressure, which came no one knew whither, and which, when gratified, was succeeded by some new pressure equally invincible. To such a state of affairs it is convenient to give the name of progress. No one confessed the Machine was out of hand. Year by year it was served with increased efficiency and decreased intelligence. The better a man knew his own duties upon it, the less he understood the duties of his neighbor, and in all the world there was not one who understood the monster as a whole. Those master brains had perished. They had left full directions, it is true, and their successors had each of them mastered a portion of those directions. But Humanity, in its desire for comfort, had overreached itself. It had exploited the riches of nature too far. Quietly and complacently, it was sinking into decadence, and progress had come to mean the progress of the Machine.

As for Vashti, her life went peacefully forward until the final disaster. She made her room dark and slept; she awoke and made the room light. She lectured and attended lectures. She exchanged ideas with her innumerable friends and believed she was growing more spiritual. At times a friend was granted Euthanasia, and left his or her room for the homelessness that is beyond all human conception. Vashti did not much mind. After an unsuccessful lecture, she would sometimes ask for Euthanasia herself. But the death rate was not permitted to exceed the birth rate, and the Machine had hitherto refused it to her.

The troubles began quietly, long before she was conscious of them.

One day she was astonished at receiving a message from her son. They never communicated, having nothing in common, and she had only heard indirectly that he was still alive, and had been transferred from the Northern Hemisphere, where he had behaved so mischievously, to the Southern—indeed, to a room not far from her own.

"Does he want me to visit him?" she thought. "Never again, never. And I have not the time."

No, it was madness of another kind.

He refused to visualize his face upon the blue plate, and speaking out of the darkness with solemnity said:

"The Machine stops."

"What do you say?"

"The Machine is stopping, I know it; I know the signs."

She burst into a peal of laughter. He heard her and was angry, and they spoke no more.

"Can you imagine anything more absurd?" she cried to a friend. "A man who was my son believes that the Machine is stopping. It would be impious if it was not mad."

"The Machine is stopping?" her friend replied. "What does that mean? The phrase conveys nothing to me."

"Nor to me."

"He does not refer, I suppose, to the trouble there has been lately with the music?"

"Oh, no, of course not. Let us talk about music."

"Have you complained to the authorities?"

"Yes, and they say it wants mending, and referred me to the Committee of the Mending Apparatus. I complained of those curious gasping sighs that disfigure the symphonies of the Brisbane school. They sound like someone in pain. The Committee of the Mending Apparatus say that it shall be remedied shortly."

Obscurely worried, she resumed her life. For one thing, the defect in the music irritated her. For another thing, she could not forget Kuno's speech. If he had known that the music was out of repair—he could not know it, for he detested music—if he had known that it was wrong, "the Machine stops" was exactly the venomous sort of remark he would have made. Of course, he had made it at a venture, but the coincidence annoyed her, and she spoke with some petulance to the Committee of the Mending Apparatus.

They replied, as before, that the defect would be set right shortly.

"Shortly! At once!" she retorted. "Why should I be worried by imperfect music? Things are always put right at once. If you do not mend it at once, I shall complain to the Central Committee."

"No personal complaints are received by the Central Committee," the Committee of the Mending Apparatus replied.

"Through whom am I to make my complaint, then?"

"Through us."

"I complain then."

"Your complaint shall be forwarded in its turn."

"Have others complained?"

This question was unmechanical, and the Committee of the Mending Apparatus refused to answer it.

"It is too bad!" she exclaimed to another of her friends. "There never was such an unfortunate woman as myself. I can never be sure of my music now. It gets worse and worse each time I summon it."

"I too have my troubles," the friend replied. "Sometimes my ideas are interrupted by a slight jarring noise."

"What is it?"

"I do not know whether it is inside my head or inside the wall."

"Complain in either case."

"I have complained, and my complaint will be forwarded in its turn to the Central Committee."

Time passed, and they resented the defects no longer. The defects had not been remedied, but the human tissues in that latter day had become so subservient that they readily adapted themselves to every caprice of the Machine. The sigh at the crisis of the Brisbane symphony no longer irritated Vashti; she accepted it as part of the melody. The jarring noise, whether in the head or in the wall, was no longer resented by her friend. And so with the moldy artificial fruit, so with the bath water that began to stink, so with the defective rhymes that the poetry machine had taken to emitting. All were bitterly complained of at first, and then acquiesced in and forgotten. Things went from bad to worse unchallenged.

It was otherwise with the failure of the sleeping apparatus. That was a more serious stoppage. There came a day when over the whole world—in Sumatra, in Wessex, in the innumerable cities of Courland and Brazil—the beds, when summoned by their tired owners, failed to appear. It may seem a ludicrous matter, but from it we may date the collapse of humanity. The Committee responsible for the failure was assailed by complaints, whom it referred, as usual, to the Committee of the Mending Apparatus, who in its turn assured them that their complaints would be forwarded to the Central Committee. But the discontent grew, for mankind was not yet sufficiently adaptable to do without sleeping.

"Someone is meddling with the Machine—" they began.

"Someone is trying to make himself king, to reintroduce the personal element."

"Punish that man with Homelessness."

"To the rescue! Avenge the Machine! Avenge the Machine!"

"War! Kill the man!"

But the Committee of the Mending Apparatus now came forward, and allayed the panic with well-chosen words. It confessed that the Mending Apparatus was itself in need of repair.

The effect of this frank confession was admirable.

"Of course," said a famous lecturer—he of the French Revolution, who gilded each new decay with splendor—"of course we shall not press our complaints now. The Mending Apparatus has treated us so well in the past that we all sympathize with it, and will wait patiently for its recovery. In its own good time it will resume its duties. Meanwhile let us do without our beds, our tabloids, our other little wants. Such, I feel sure, would be the wish of the Machine."

Thousands of miles away his audience applauded. The Machine still linked them. Under the seas, beneath the roots of the mountains, ran the wires through which they saw and heard, the enormous eyes and ears that were their heritage, and the hum of many workings clothed their thoughts in one garment of subserviency. Only the old and sick remained ungrateful, for it was rumored that Euthanasia, too, was out of order, and that pain had reappeared among men.

It became difficult to read. A blight entered the atmosphere and dulled its luminosity. At times Vashti could scarcely see across her room. The air, too, was foul. Loud were the complaints, impotent the remedies, heroic the tone of the lecturer as he cried: "Courage! courage! What matter so long as the Machine goes on? To it the darkness and the light are one." And though things improved again after a time, the old brilliancy was never recaptured, and humanity never recovered from its entrance into twilight. There was hysterical talk of "measures," of "provisional dictatorship," and the inhabitants of Sumatra were asked to familiarize themselves with the workings of the central power station, the said power station being situated in France. But for the most part panic reigned, and men spent their strength praying to their Books, tangible proofs of the Machine's omnipotence. There were gradations of terror—at times came rumors of hope—the Mending Apparatus was almost mended—the enemies of the Machine had been got under—new "nerve centers" were evolving which would do the work even more magnificently than before. But there came a day when, without the slightest warning, without any previous hint of feebleness, the entire communication system broke down, all over the world, and the world, as they understood it, ended.

Vashti was lecturing at the time, and her earlier remarks had been punctuated with applause. As she proceeded the audience became silent, and at the conclusion there was no sound. Somewhat displeased, she called to a friend who was a specialist in sympathy. No sound: doubtless the friend was sleeping. And so with the next friend whom she tried to summon, and so with the next, until she remembered Kuno's cryptic remark, "The Machine stops."

The phrase still conveyed nothing. If Eternity was stopping it would of course be set going shortly.

For example, there were still a little light and air—the atmosphere had improved a few hours previously. There was still the Book, and while there was the Book there was security.

Then she broke down, for with the cessation of activity came an unexpected terror—silence.

She had never known silence, and the coming of it nearly killed her—it did kill many thousands of people outright. Ever since her birth she had been surrounded by the steady hum. It was to the ear what artificial air was to the lungs, and agonizing pains shot across her head. And scarcely knowing what she did, she stumbled forward and pressed the unfamiliar button, the one that opened the door of her cell.

Now the door of the cell worked on a simple hinge of its own. It was not connected with the central power station, dying far away in France. It opened, rousing immoderate hopes in Vashti, for she thought that the Machine had been mended. It opened, and she saw the dim tunnel that curved far away toward freedom. One look, and then she shrank back. For the tunnel was full of people—she was almost the last in that city to have taken alarm.

People at any time repelled her, and these were nightmares from her worst dreams. People were crawling about, people were screaming, whimpering, gasping for breath, touching each other, vanishing in the dark, and ever and anon being pushed off the platform on to the live rail. Some were fighting round the electric bells, trying to summon trains which could not be summoned. Others were yelling for Euthanasia or for respirators, or blaspheming the Machine. Others stood at the doors of their cells fearing, like herself, either to stop in them or to leave them, and behind all the uproar was silence—the silence which is the voice of the earth and of the generations who have gone.

No—it was worse than solitude. She closed the door again and sat down to wait for the end. The disintegration went on, accompanied by horrible cracks and rumbling. The valves that restrained the Medical Apparatus must have been weakened, for it ruptured and hung hideously from the ceiling. The floor heaved and fell and flung her from her chair. A tube oozed toward her serpent fashion. And at last the final horror approached—light began to ebb, and she knew that civilization's long day was closing.

She whirled round, praying to be saved from this, at any rate, kissing the Book, pressing button after button. The uproar outside was increasing, and even penetrated the wall. Slowly the brilliancy of her cell was dimmed, the reflections faded from her metal switches. Now she could not see the reading stand, now not the Book, though she held it in her hand. Light followed the flight of sound, air was following light, and the original void returned to the cavern from which it had been so long excluded. Vashti continued to whirl, like the devotees of an earlier religion, screaming, praying, striking at the buttons with bleeding hands.

It was thus that she opened her prison and escaped—escaped in the spirit: at least so it seems to me, ere my meditation closes. That she escapes in the body—I cannot perceive that. She struck, by chance, the switch that released the door, and the rush of foul air on her skin, the loud throbbing whispers in her ears, told her that she was facing the tunnel again, and that tremendous platform on which she had seen men fighting. They were not fighting now. Only the whispers remained, and the little whimpering groans. They were dying by hundreds out in the dark.

She burst into tears.

Tears answered her.

They wept for humanity, those two, not for themselves. They could not bear that this should be the end. Ere silence was completed their hearts were opened, and they knew what had been important on the earth. Man, the flower of all flesh, the noblest of all creatures visible, man who had once made god in his image, and had mirrored his strength on the constellations, beautiful naked man was dying, strangled in the garments that he had woven. Century after century had he toiled, and here was his reward. Truly the garment had seemed heavenly at first, shot with the colors of culture, sewn with the threads of self-denial. And heavenly it had been so long as it was a garment and no more, so long as man could shed it at will and live by the essence that is his soul, and the essence, equally divine, that is his body. The sin against the body—it was for that they wept in chief; the centuries of wrong against the muscles and the nerves, and those five portals by which we can alone apprehend—glozing it over with talk of evolution, until the body was white pap, the home of ideas as colorless, last sloshy stirrings of a spirit that had grasped the stars.

"Where are you?" she sobbed.

His voice in the darkness said, "Here."

"Is there any hope, Kuno?"

"None for us."

"Where are you?"

She crawled toward him over the bodies of the dead. His blood spurted over her hands.

"Quicker," he gasped, "I am dying—but we touch, we talk, not through the Machine."

He kissed her.

"We have come back to our own. We die, but we have recaptured life, as it was in Wessex, when Aelfrid overthrew the Danes. We know what they know outside, they who dwelt in the cloud that is the color of a pearl."

"But, Kuno, is it true? Are there still men on the surface of the earth? Is this—this tunnel, this poisoned darkness—really not the end?"

He replied:

"I have seen them, spoken to them, loved them. They are hiding in the mist and the ferns until our civilization stops. Today they are the Homeless—tomorrow—"

"Oh, tomorrow—some fool will start the Machine again, tomorrow."

"Never," said Kuno, "never. Humanity has learned its lesson."

As he spoke the whole city was broken like a honeycomb. An airship had sailed in through the vomitory into a ruined wharf. It crashed downward, exploding as it went, rending gallery after gallery with its wings of steel. For a moment they saw the nations of the dead, and, before they joined them, scraps of the untainted sky.

Margaret St. Clair

Margaret St. Clair (1911–96) was a prolific and popular writer who published more than 130 stories and eight SF novels from 1945 to the 1980s. Some of her stories have been collected in *Three Worlds of Futurity* (1964), *Change the Sky and Other Stories* (1974) and *The Best of Margaret St. Clair* (1985). *The Dolphins of Altair* (1967) is probably the most ambitious of the novels.

The majority of the novels were written after 1960 but nearly all of the stories in the 1950s, when she also published under the pseudonym Idris Seabright, under which she was for a time more highly regarded. (It was a common practice that allowed a writer to sell more stories to a single magazine . . . two could appear in a single issue without the feeling of overexposure. In the 1940s, Henry Kuttner's pseudonym, Lewis Padgett, was arguably more respected than his own name. In fact a few writers, including Randall Garrett and Robert Silverberg at one point in the 1950s, wrote the entire contents of magazine issues under a variety of pseudonyms.) St. Clair's short stories represent her at her best. She is two of the significant woman writers operating in science fiction at a time when it was overwhelmingly written and read by men.

"The historic task of science fiction is to develop a global consciousness," she said in an essay introducing her collection, *The Best of Margaret St. Clair,* in 1985. This affecting story is certainly an example. It is about beauty, death, and colonialism.

BRIGHTNESS FALLS FROM THE AIR

Kerr used to go into the tepidarium of the identification bureau to practice singing. The tepidarium was a big room, filled almost from wall to wall by the pool of glittering preservative, and he liked its acoustics. The bodies of the bird people would drift a little back and forth in the pellucid fluid as he sang, and he liked to look at them. If the tepidarium was a little morbid as a place to practice singing, it was (Kerr used to think) no more morbid than the rest of the world in which he was living. When he had sung for as long as he thought good for his voice—he had no teacher—he would go to one of the windows and watch the luminous trails that meant the bird people were fighting again. The trails would float down slowly against the night sky as if they were made of star dust. But after Kerr met Rhysha, he stopped all that.

Rhysha came to the bureau one evening just as he was going on duty. She had come to claim a body. The bodies of the bird people often stayed in the bureau for a considerable time. Ordinary means of transportation were forbidden to the bird people because of their extra-terrestrial origin, and it was hard for them to get to the bureau to identify their dead. Rhysha made the identification—it was her brother—paid the bureau's fee from a worn purse, and indicated on the proper form the disposal she wanted made of the body. She was quiet and controlled in her grief. Kerr had watched the televised battles of the bird people once or twice, but this was the first time he had ever seen one of them alive and face to face. He looked at her with interest and curiosity, and then with wonder and delight.

The most striking thing about Rhysha was her glowing, deep turquoise plumage. It covered her from head to heels in what appeared to be a clinging velvet cloak. The coloring was so much more intense than that of the bodies in the tepidarium that Kerr would have thought she belonged to a different species than they.

Her face, under the golden top-knot, was quite human, and so were her slender, leaf-shaped hands; but there was a fantastic, light-boned grace in her movements such as no human being ever had. Her voice was low, with a 'cello's fullness of tone. Everything about her, Kerr thought, was rare and delightful and curious. But there was a shadow in her face, as if a natural gaiety had been repressed by the overwhelming harshness of circumstance.

"Where shall I have the ashes sent?" Kerr asked as he took the form.

She plucked indecisively at her pink lower lip. "I am not sure. The manager where we are staying has told us we must leave tonight, and I do not know where we will go. Could I come back again to the bureau when the ashes are ready?"

It was against regulations, but Kerr nodded. He would keep the capsule of ashes in his locker until she came. It would be nice to see her again.

She came, weeks later, for the ashes. There had been several battles of the bird people in the interval, and the pool in the tepidarium was full. As Kerr looked at her, he wondered how long it would be before she too was dead.

He asked her new address. It was a fantastic distance away, in the worst part of the city, and after a little hesitation he told her that if she could wait until his shift was over he would be glad to walk back with her.

She looked at him doubtfully. "It is most kind of you, but—but an Earthman was kind to us once. The children used to stone him."

Kerr had never thought much about the position of the non-human races in his world. If it was unjust, if they were badly treated, he had thought it no more than a particular instance of the general cruelty and stupidity. Now anger flared up in him.

"That's all right," he said harshly. "If you don't mind waiting."

Rhysha smiled faintly. "No, I don't mind," she said.

Since there were still some hours to go on his shift, he took her into a small reception room where there was a chaise longue. "Try to sleep," he said.

A little before three he came to rouse her, and found her lying quiet but awake. They left the bureau by a side door.

The city was as quiet at this hour as it ever was. All the sign projectors, and most of the street lights, had been turned off to save power, and even the vast, disembodied voices that boomed out of the air all day long and half the night were almost silent. The darkness and quiescence of the city made it seem easy for them to talk as they went through the streets.

Kerr realised afterwards how confident he must have been of Rhysha's sympathy to have spoken to her as freely as he did. And she must have felt an equal confidence in him, for after a little while she was telling him fragments of her history and her people's past without reserve.

"After the Earthmen took our planet," she said, "we had nothing left they wanted. But we had to have food. Then we discovered that they liked to watch us fight."

"You fought before the Earthmen came?" Kerr asked.

"Yes. But not as we fight now. It was a ritual then, very formal, with much politeness and courtesy. We did not fight to get things from each other, but to find out who was brave and could give us leadership. The Earth people were impatient with our ritual—they wanted to see us hurting and being hurt. So we learned to fight as we fight now, hoping to be killed.

"There was a time, when we first left our planet and went to the other worlds where people liked to watch us, when there were many of us. But there have been many battles since then. Now there are only a few left."

At the cross street a beggar slouched up to them. Kerr gave him a coin. The man was turning away with thanks when he caught sight of Rhysha's golden top-knot. "God-damned Extey!" he said in sudden rage. "Filth! And you, a man, going around with it! Here!" He threw the coin at Kerr.

"Even the beggars!" Rhysha said. "Why is it, Kerr, you hate us so?"

"Because we have wronged you," he answered, and knew it was the truth. "Are we always so unkind, though?"

"As the beggar was? Often . . . it is worse."

"Rhysha, you've got to get away from here."

"Where?" she answered simply. "Our people have discussed it so many times! There is no planet on which there are not already billions of people from Earth. You increase so fast!

"And besides, it doesn't matter. You don't need us, there isn't any place for us. We cared about that once, but not any more. We're so tired—all of us, even the young ones like me—we're so tired of trying to live."

"You mustn't talk like that," Kerr said harshly. "I won't let you talk like that. You've got to go on. If we don't need you now, Rhysha, we will."

From the block ahead of them there came the wan glow of a municipal telescreen. Late as the hour was, it was surrounded by a dense knot of spectators. Their eyes were fixed greedily on the combat that whirled dizzily over the screen.

Rhysha tugged gently at Kerr's sleeve. "We had better go around," she said in a whisper. Kerr realized with a pang that there would be trouble if the viewers saw a "man" and an Extey together. Obediently he turned.

They had gone a block further when Kerr (for he had been thinking) said: "My people took the wrong road, Rhysha, about two hundred years ago. That was when the council refused to accept, even in principle, any form of population control. By now we're stifling under the pressure of our own numbers, we're crushed shapeless under it. Everything has had to give way to our one basic problem, how to feed an ever-increasing number of hungry mouths. Morality has dwindled into feeding ourselves. And we have the battle sports over the telecast to keep us occupied.

"But I think—I believe—that we'll get into the right road again sometime. I've read books of history, Rhysha. This isn't the first time we've chosen the wrong road. Some day there'll be room for your people, Rhysha, if only—" he hesitated—"if only because you're so beautiful."

He looked at her earnestly. Her face was remote and bleak. An idea came to him. "Have you ever heard anyone sing, Rhysha?"

"Sing? No, I don't know the word."

"Listen, then." He fumbled over his repertory and decided, though the music was not really suited to his voice, on Tamino's song to Pamina's portrait. He sang it for her as they walked along.

Little by little Rhysha's face relaxed. "I like that," she said when the song was over. "Sing more, Kerr."

"Do you see what I was trying to tell you?" he said at last, after many songs. "If we could make songs like that, Rhysha, isn't there hope for us?"

"For you, perhaps. Not us," Rhysha answered. There was anger in her voice. "Stop it, Kerr. I do not want to be waked."

But when they parted she clasped hands with him and told him where they could meet again. "You are really our friend," she said without coquetry.

When he next met Rhysha, Kerr said: "I brought you a present. Here." He handed her a parcel. "And I've some news, too."

Rhysha opened the little package. An exclamation of pleasure broke from her lips. "Oh, lovely! What a lovely thing! Where did you get it, Kerr?"

"In a shop that sells old things, in the back." He did not tell her he had given ten days' pay for the little turquoise locket. "But the stones are lighter than I realized. I wanted something that would be the color of your plumage."

Rhysha shook her head. "No, this is the color it should be. This is right." She clasped the locket around her neck and looked down at it with pleasure. "And now, what is the news you have for me?"

"A friend of mine is a clerk in the city records. He tells me a new planet, near gamma Cassiopeiae, is being opened for colonization.

"I've filed the papers, and everything is in order. The hearing will be held on Friday. I'm going to appear on behalf of the Ngayir, your people, and ask that they be allotted space on the new world."

Rhysha turned white. He started toward her, but she waved him away. One hand was still clasping her locket, that was nearly the color of her plumage.

The hearing was held in a small auditorium in the basement of the Colonization building. Representatives of a dozen groups spoke before Kerr's turn came.

"Appearing on behalf of the Ngayir," the arbitrator read from a form in his hand, "S 3687 Kerr. And who are the Ngayir, S-Kerr? Some Indian group?"

"No, sir," Kerr said. "They are commonly known as the bird people."

"Oh, a conservationist!" The arbitrator looked at Kerr not unkindly. "I'm sorry, but your petition is quite out of order. It should never have been filed. Immigration is restricted by executive order to terrestials . . ."

Kerr dreaded telling Rhysha of his failure, but she took it with perfect calm.

"After you left I realised it was impossible," she said.

"Rhysha, I want you to promise me something. I can't tell you how sure I am that humanity is going to need your people sometime. It's true, Rhysha. I'm going to keep trying. I'm not going to give up.

"Promise me this, Rhysha: promise me that neither you nor the members of your group will take part in the battles until you hear from me again."

Rhysha smiled. "All right, Kerr."

Preserving the bodies of people who have died from a variety of diseases is not without its dangers. Kerr did not go to work that night or the next or for many nights. His dormitory chief, after listening to him shout in delirium for some hours, called a doctor, who filled out a hospital requisition slip.

He was gravely ill, and his recovery was slow. It was nearly five weeks before he was released.

He wanted above all things to find Rhysha. He went to the place where she had been living and found that she had gone, no one knew where. In the end, he went to the identification bureau and begged for his old job there. Rhysha would, he was sure, think of coming to the bureau to get in touch with him.

He was still shaky and weak when he reported for work the next night. He went into the tepidarium about nine o'clock, during a routine inspection. And there Rhysha was.

He did not know her for an instant. The lovely turquoise of her plumage had faded to a dirty drab. But the little locket he had given her was still around her neck.

He got the big jointed tongs they used for moving bodies out of the pool, and put them in position. He lifted her out very gently and put her down on the edge of the pool. He opened the locket. There was a note inside.

"Dear Kerr," he read in Rhysha's clear, handsome script, "you must forgive me for breaking my promise to you. They would not let me see you when you were sick, and we were all so hungry. Besides, you were wrong to think your people would ever need us. There is no place for us in your world.

"I wish I could have heard you sing again. I liked to hear you sing. Rhysha."

Kerr looked from the note to Rhysha's face, and back at the note. It hurt too much. He did not want to realize that she was dead.

Outside, one of the vast voices that boomed portentously down from the sky half the night long began to speak: "Don't miss the newest, fastest battle sport. View the Durga battles, the bloodiest combats ever televised. Funnier than the bird people's battles, more thrilling than an Anda war, you'll . . ."

Kerr gave a cry. He ran to the window and closed it. He could still hear the voice. But it was all that he could do.

Michael Shaara

Michael Shaara (1929–88) was one of the bright young SF writers of the early 1950s, who left the genre in 1957 after producing a number of fine short stories, and later wrote a boxing novel and the Pulitzer Prize-winning American Civil War novel, *The Killer Angels* (1974). Most of his short stories are collected in *Soldier Boy* (1982), along with an afterword reminiscing about his early days in science fiction, the excitement of selling to John W. Campbell's *Astounding*, the frustrations of dealing with genre markets. Algis Budrys remembers that Robert Sheckley, Michael Shaara and he were the hot new writers of 1952–53.

After the generally positive editorial reaction to *Soldier Boy*, Shaara completed an SF novel, *The Herald* (1981—actually published before the collection, which was delayed, but not published as a genre novel, since Shaara had won the Pulitzer and his publisher was certain that a genre label would compromise his, and their, reputation). *The Encyclopedia of Science Fiction* praises his writing for its "quick, revelatory ironies about the human condition." I recall joking with him in 1982 that this, of all his stories, was predictive and that it had already come true. It is still coming true.

2066: ELECTION DAY

Early that afternoon Professor Larkin crossed the river into Washington, a thing he always did on Election Day, and sat for a long while in the Polls. It was still called the Polls, in this year A.D. 2066, although what went on inside bore no relation at all to the elections of primitive American history. The Polls was now a single enormous building which rose out of the green fields where the ancient Pentagon had once stood. There was only one of its kind in Washington, only one Polling Place in each of the forty-eight states, but since few visited the Polls nowadays, no more were needed.

In the lobby of the building, a great hall was reserved for visitors. Here you could sit and watch the many-colored lights dancing and flickering on the huge panels above, listen to the weird but strangely soothing hum and click of the vast central machine. Professor Larkin chose a deep soft chair near the long line of booths and sat down. He sat for a long while smoking his pipe, watching the people go in and out of the booths with strained, anxious looks on their faces.

Professor Larkin was a lean, boyish-faced man in his late forties. With the pipe in his hand he looked much more serious and sedate than he normally felt, and it often bothered him that people were able to guess his profession almost instantly. He had a vague idea that it was not becoming to look like a college professor, and he often tried to change his appearance—a loud tie here, a sport coat there—but it never seemed to make any difference. He remained what he was, easily identifiable, Professor Harry L. (Lloyd) Larkin, Ph.D., Dean of the Political Science Department at a small but competent college just outside of Washington.

It was his interest in Political Science which drew him regularly to the Polls at every election. Here he could sit and feel the flow of American history in the making, and recognize, as he did now, perennial candidates for the presidency. Smiling, he watched a little old lady dressed in pink, very tiny and very fussy, flit doggedly from booth to booth. Evidently her test marks had not been very good. She was clutching her papers tightly in a black-gloved hand, and there was a look of prim irritation on her face. But *she* knew how to run this country, by George, and one of these days *she* would be President. Harry Larkin chuckled.

But it did prove one thing. The great American dream was still intact. The tests were open to all. And anyone could still grow up to be President of the United States.

Sitting back in his chair, Harry Larkin remembered his own childhood, how the great battle had started. There were examinations for everything in those days—you could not get a job streetcleaning without taking a civil-service examination—but public office needed no qualification at all. And first the psychologists, then the newspapers, had begun calling it a national disgrace. And, considering the caliber of some of the men who went into public office, it *was* a national disgrace. But then psychological testing came of age, really became an exact science, so that it was possible to test a man thoroughly—his knowledge, his potential, his personality. And from there it was a short but bitterly fought step to—SAM.

SAM. UNCLE SAM, as he had been called originally, the last and greatest of all electronic brains. Harry Larkin peered up in unabashed awe at the vast battery of lights which flickered above him. He knew that there was more to SAM than just this building, more than all the other forty-eight buildings put together, that SAM was actually an incredibly enormous network of electronic cells which had its heart in no one place, but its arms in all. It was an unbelievably complex analytical computer which judged a candidate far more harshly and thoroughly than the American public could ever have judged him. And crammed in its miles of memory banks lay almost every bit of knowledge mankind had yet discovered. It was frightening, many thought of it as a monster, but Harry Larkin was unworried.

The thirty years since the introduction of SAM had been thirty of America's happiest years. In a world torn by continual war and unrest, by dictators, puppet governments, the entire world had come to know and respect the American President for what he was: the best possible man for the job. And there was no doubt that he was the best. He had competed for the job in fair examination against the cream of the country. He had to be a truly remarkable man to come out on top.

The day was long since past when just any man could handle the presidency. A full century before men had begun dying in office, cut down in their prime by the enormous pressures of the job. And that was a hundred years ago. Now the job had become infinitely more complex, and even now President Creighton lay on his bed in the White House, recovering from a stroke, an old, old man after one term of office.

Harry Larkin shuddered to think what might have happened had America not adopted the system of "the best qualified man." All over the world this afternoon men waited for word from America, the calm and trustworthy words of the new President, for there had been no leader in America since President Creighton's stroke. His words would mean more to the people, embroiled as they were in another great crisis, than the words of their own leaders. The leaders of other countries fought for power, bought it, stole it, only rarely earned it. But the American President was known the world over for his honesty, his intelligence, his desire for peace. Had he not those qualities, "old UNCLE SAM" would never have elected him.

Eventually, the afternoon nearly over, Harry Larkin rose to leave. By this time the President was probably already elected. Tomorrow the world would return to peace. Harry Larkin paused in the door once before he left, listened to the reassuring hum from the great machine. Then he went quietly home, walking quickly and briskly toward the most enormous fate on Earth.

"My name is Reddington. You know me?"

Harry Larkin smiled uncertainly into the phone.

"Why . . . yes, I believe so. You are, if I'm not mistaken, general director of the Bureau of Elections."

"Correct," the voice went on quickly, crackling in the receiver, "and you are supposed to be an authority on Political Science, right?"

"Supposed to be?" Larkin bridled. "Well, it's distinctly possible that I—"

"All right, all right," Reddington blurted. "No time for politeness. Listen, Larkin, this is a matter of urgent national security. There will be a car at your door—probably be there when you put this phone down. I want you to get into it and hop on over here. I can't explain further. I know your devotion to the country, and if it wasn't for that I would not have called you. But don't ask questions. Just come. No time. Good-bye."

There was a click. Harry Larkin stood holding the phone for a long shocked moment, then he heard a pounding at the door. The housekeeper was out, but he waited automatically before going to answer it. He didn't like to be rushed, and he was confused. Urgent national security? Now what in blazes—

The man at the door was an Army major. He was accompanied by two young but very large sergeants. They identified Larkin, then escorted him politely but firmly down the steps into a staff car. Larkin could not help feeling abducted, and a completely characteristic rage began to rise in him. But he remembered what Reddington had said about national security and so sat back quietly with nothing more than an occasional grumble.

He was driven back into Washington. They took him downtown to a small but expensive apartment house he could neither identify nor remember, and escorted him briskly into an elevator. When they reached the suite upstairs they opened the door and let him in, but did not follow him. They turned and went quickly away.

Somewhat ruffled, Larkin stood for a long moment in the hall by the hat table, regarding a large rubber plant. There was a long sliding door before him, closed, but he could hear an argument going on behind it. He heard the word "SAM" mentioned many times, and once he heard a clear sentence: ". . . Government by machine. I will not tolerate it!" Before he had time to hear any more, the doors slid back. A small, square man with graying hair came out to meet him. He recognized the man instantly as Reddington.

"Larkin," the small man said, "glad you're here." The tension on his face showed also in his voice. "That makes all of us. Come in and sit down." He turned back into the large living room. Larkin followed.

"Sorry to be so abrupt," Reddington said, "but it was necessary. You will see. Here, let me introduce you around."

Larkin stopped in involuntary awe. He was used to the sight of important men, but not so many at one time, and never so close. There was Secretary Kell, of Agriculture; Wachsmuth, of Commerce; General Vines, Chief of Staff; and a battery of others so imposing that Larkin found his mouth hanging embarrassingly open. He closed it immediately.

Reddington introduced him. The men nodded one by one, but they were all deathly serious, their faces drawn, and there was now no conversation. Reddington waved him to a chair. Most of the others were standing, but Larkin sat.

Reddington sat directly facing him. There was a long moment of silence during which Larkin realized that he was being searchingly examined. He flushed, but sat calmly with his hands folded in his lap. After a while Reddington took a deep breath.

"Dr. Larkin," he said slowly, "what I am about to say to you will die with you. There must be no question of that. We cannot afford to have any word of this meeting, any word at all, reach anyone not in this room. This includes your immediate relatives, your friends, anyone—anyone at all. Before we continue, let me impress you with that fact. This is a matter of the gravest national security. Will you keep what is said here in confidence?"

"If the national interests—" Larkin began, then he said abruptly, "of course."

Reddington smiled slightly.

"Good. I believe you. I might add that just the fact of your being here, Doctor, means that you have already passed the point of no return . . . well, no matter. There is no time. I'll get to the point."

He stopped, looking around the room. Some of the other men were standing and now began to move in closer. Larkin felt increasingly nervous, but the magnitude of the event was too great for him to feel any worry. He gazed intently at Reddington.

"The Polls close tonight at eight o'clock." Reddington glanced at his watch. "It is now six-eighteen. I must be brief. Doctor, do you remember the prime directive that we gave to SAM when he was first built?"

"I think so," said Larkin slowly.

"Good. You remember then that there was one main order. SAM was directed to elect, quote, *the best qualified man.* Unquote. Regardless of any and all circumstances, religion, race, so on. The orders were clear—the best qualified man. The phrase has become world famous. But unfortunately"—he glanced up briefly at the men surrounding him—"the order was a mistake. Just whose mistake does not matter. I think perhaps the fault lies with all of us, but—it doesn't matter. What matters is this: SAM will not elect a president."

Larkin struggled to understand. Reddington leaned forward in his chair.

"Now follow me closely. We learned this only late this afternoon. We are always aware, as you no doubt know, of the relatively few people in this country who have a chance for the presidency. We know not only because they are studying for it, but because such men as these are marked from their childhood to be outstanding. We keep close watch on them, even to assigning the Secret Service to protect them from possible harm. There are only a very few. During this last election we could not find more than fifty. All of those people took the tests this morning. None of them passed."

He paused, waiting for Larkin's reaction. Larkin made no move.

"You begin to see what I'm getting at? *There is no qualified man.*"

Larkin's eyes widened. He sat bolt upright.

"Now it hits you. If none of those people this morning passed, there is no chance at all for any of the others tonight. What is left now is simply crackpots and malcontents. They are privileged to take the tests, but it means nothing. SAM is not going to select anybody. Because sometime during the last four years the presidency passed the final limit, the ultimate end of man's capabilities, and with scientific certainty we know that there is probably no man alive who is, according to SAM's directive, qualified."

"But," Larkin interrupted, "I'm not quite sure I follow. Doesn't the phrase 'elect the best qualified man' mean that we can at least take the best we've got?"

Reddington smiled wanly and shook his head.

"No. And that was our mistake. It was quite probably a psychological block, but none of us ever considered the possibility of the job surpassing human ability. Not then, thirty years ago. And we also never seemed to remember that SAM is, after all, only a machine. He takes the words to mean exactly what they say: Elect the best, comma, *qualified*, comma, man. But do you see, if there is *no* qualified man, SAM cannot possibly elect the best. So SAM will elect no one at all. Tomorrow this country will be without a president. And the result of that, more than likely, will mean a general war."

Larkin understood. He sat frozen in his chair.

"So you see our position," Reddington went on wearily. "There's nothing we can do. Reelecting President Creighton is out of the question. His stroke was permanent, he may not last the week. And there is no possibility of tampering with SAM, to change the directive. Because, as you know, SAM is foolproof, had to be. The circuits extend through all forty-eight states. To alter the machine at all requires clearing through all forty-eight entrances. We can't do that. For one thing, we haven't time. For another, we can't risk letting the world know there is no qualified man.

"For a while this afternoon, you can understand, we were stumped. What could we do? There was only one answer, we may come back to it yet. Give the presidency itself to SAM—"

A man from across the room, whom Larkin did not recognize, broke in angrily.

"Now Reddington, I told you, that is government by machine! And I will not stand—"

"What else can you *do!*" Reddington whirled, his eyes flashing, his tension exploding now into rage. "Who else knows all the answers? Who else can compute in two seconds the tax rate for Mississippi, the parity levels for wheat, the probable odds on a military engagement? Who else but SAM! And why didn't we do it long ago, just feed the problems to *him*, SAM, and not go on killing man after man, great men, *decent* men like poor Jim Creighton, who's on his back now and dying because people like you—" He broke off suddenly and bowed his head. The room was still. No one looked at Reddington. After a moment he shook his head. His voice, when he spoke, was husky.

"Gentlemen, I'm sorry. This leads nowhere." He turned back to Larkin.

Larkin had begun to feel the pressure. But the presence of these men, of Reddington's obvious profound sincerity, reassured him. Creighton had been a great president; he had surrounded himself with some of the finest men in the country. Larkin felt a surge of hope that such men as these were available for one of the most critical hours in American history. For critical it was, and Larkin knew as clearly as anyone there what the absence of a president in the morning—no deep reassurance, no words of hope—would mean. He sat waiting for Reddington to continue.

"Well, we have a plan. It may work, it may not. We may all be shot. But this is where you come in. I hope for all our sakes you're up to it."

Larkin waited.

"The plan," Reddington went on, slowly, carefully, "is this. SAM has one defect. We can't tamper with it. But we *can* fool it. Because when the brain tests a man, it does not at the same time identify him. We do the identifying ourselves. So if a man named Joe Smith takes the personality tests and another man also named Joe Smith takes the Political Science tests, the machine has no way of telling them apart. Unless our guards supply the difference, SAM will mark up the results of both tests to one Joe Smith. We can clear the guards, no problem there. The first problem was to find the eight men to take the eight tests."

Larkin understood. He nodded.

"Exactly. Eight specialists," Reddington said. "General Vines will take the Military; Burden, Psychology; Wachsmuth, Economics; and so on. You, of course, will take the Political Science. We can only hope that each man will come out with a high enough score in his own field so that the combined scores of our mythical 'candidate' will be enough to qualify him. Do you follow me?"

Larkin nodded dazedly. "I think so. But—"

"It should work. It has to work."

"Yes," Larkin murmured, "I can see that. But who, who will actually wind up—"

"As president?" Reddington smiled very slightly and stood up.

"That was the most difficult question of all. At first we thought there was no solution. Because a president must be so many things—consider. A president blossoms instantaneously, from nonentity, into the most important job on earth. Every magazine, every newspaper in the country immediately goes to work on his background, digs out his life story, anecdotes, sayings, and so on. Even a very strong fraud would never survive it. So the first problem was believability. The new president must be absolutely believable. He must be a man of obvious character, of obvious intelligence, but more than that, his former life must fit the facts: he must have had both the time and the personality to prepare himself for the office.

"And you see immediately what all that means. Most businessmen are out. Their lives have been too social, they wouldn't have had the time. For the same reason all government and military personnel are also out, and we need hardly say that anyone from the Bureau of Elections would be immediately suspect. No. You see the problem. For a while we thought that the time was too short, the risk too great. But then the only solution, the only possible chance, finally occurred to us.

"The only believable person would be—a professor. Someone whose life has been serious but unhurried, devoted to learning but at the same time isolated. The only really believable person. And not a scientist, you understand, for a man like that would be much too overbalanced in one direction for our purpose. No, simply a professor, preferably in a field like Political Science, a man whose sole job for many years has been teaching, who can claim to have studied in his spare time, his summers—never really expected to pass the tests and all that, a humble man, you see—"

"Political Science," Larkin said.

Reddington watched him. The other men began to close in on him.

"Yes," Reddington said gently. "Now do you see? It is our only hope. Your name was suggested by several sources, you are young enough, your reputation is well known. We think that you would be believable. And now that I've seen you"—he looked around slowly—"I for one am willing to risk it. Gentlemen, what do you say?"

Larkin, speechless, sat listening in mounting shock while the men agreed solemnly, one by one. In the enormity of the moment he could not think at all. Dimly, he heard Reddington.

"I know. But, Doctor, there is no time. The Polls close at eight. It is now almost seven."

Larkin closed his eyes and rested his head on his hands. Above him, Reddington went on inevitably.

"All right. You are thinking of what happens after. Even if we pull this off and you are accepted without question, what then? Well, it will simply be the old system all over again. You will be at least no worse off than presidents before SAM. Better even, because if worse comes to worst, there is always SAM. You can feed all the bad ones to him. You will have the advice of the cabinet, of the military staff. We will help you in every way we can, some of us will sit with you on all conferences. And you know more about this than most of us, you have studied government all your life.

"But all this, what comes later, is not important. Not now. If we can get through tomorrow, the next few days, all the rest will work itself out. Eventually we can get around to altering SAM. But we must have a president in the morning. You are our only hope. You can do it. We all know you can do it. At any rate there is no other way, no time. Doctor," he reached out and laid his hand on Larkin's shoulder, "shall we go to the Polls?"

It passed, as most great moments in a man's life do, with Larkin not fully understanding what was happening to him. Later he would look back to this night and realize the enormity of the decision he had made, the doubts, the sleeplessness, the responsibility and agony toward which he moved. But in that moment he thought nothing at all. Except that it was Larkin's country, Larkin's America. And Reddington was right. There was nothing else to do. He stood up.

They went to the Polls.

At 9:30 that evening, sitting alone with Reddington back at the apartment, Larkin looked at the face of the announcer on the television screen, and heard himself pronounced President-elect of the United States.

Reddington wilted in front of the screen. For a while neither man moved. They had come home alone, just as they had gone into the Polls one by one in the hope of arousing no comment. Now they sat in silence until Reddington turned off the set. He stood up and straightened his shoulders before turning to Larkin. He stretched out his hand.

"Well, may God help us," he breathed, "we did it."

Larkin took his hand. He felt suddenly weak. He sat down again, but already he could hear the phone ringing in the outer hall. Reddington smiled.

"Only a few of my closest friends are supposed to know about that phone. But every time anything big comes up—" He shrugged. "Well," he said, still smiling, "let's see how it works."

He picked up the phone and with it an entirely different manner. He became amazingly light and cheerful, as if he was feeling nothing more than the normal political goodwill.

"Know him? Of course I know him. Had my eye on the guy for months. Really nice guy, wait'll you meet him . . . yup, college professor, Political Science, written a couple of books . . . must know a hell of a lot more than Poli Sci, though. Probably been knocking himself out in his spare time. But those teachers, you know how it is, they don't get any pay, but all the spare time in the world. . . . Married? No, not that I know of—"

Larkin noticed with wry admiration how carefully Reddington had slipped in that bit about spare time, without seeming to be making an explanation. He thought wearily to himself, I hope that I don't have to do any talking myself. I'll have to do a lot of listening before I can chance any talking.

In a few moments Reddington put down the phone and came back. He had on his hat and coat.

"Had to answer a few," he said briefly, "make it seem natural. But you better get dressed."

"Dressed? Why?"

"Have you forgotten?" Reddington smiled patiently. "You're due at the White House. The Secret Service is already tearing the town apart looking for you. We were supposed to alert them. Oh, by the saints, I hope that wasn't too bad a slip."

He pursed his mouth worriedly while Larkin, still dazed, got into his coat. It was beginning now. It had already begun. He was tired but it did not matter. That he was tired would probably never matter again. He took a deep breath. Like Reddington, he straightened his shoulders.

The Secret Service picked them up halfway across town. That they knew where he was, who he was, amazed him and worried Reddington. They went through the gates of the White House and drove up before the door. It was opened for him as he put out his hand, he stepped back in a reflex action, from the sudden blinding flares of the photographer's flashbulbs. Reddington behind him took him firmly by the arm. Larkin went with him gratefully, unable to see, unable to hear anything but the roar of the crowd from behind the gates and the shouted questions of the reporters.

Inside the great front doors it was suddenly peaceful again, very quiet and pleasantly dark. He took off his hat instinctively. Luckily he had been here before, he recognized the lovely hall and felt not awed but at home. He was introduced quickly to several people whose names made no impression on him. A woman smiled. He made an effort to smile back. Reddington took him by the arm again and led him away. There were people all around him, but they were quiet and hung back. He saw the respect on their faces. It sobered him, quickened his mind.

"The President's in the Lincoln Room," Reddington whispered. "He wants to see you. How do you feel?"

"All right."

"Listen."

"Yes."

"You'll be fine. You're doing beautifully. Keep just that look on your face."

"I'm not trying to keep it there."

"You aren't?" Reddington looked at him. "Good. Very good." He paused and looked again at Larkin. Then he smiled.

"It's done it. I thought it would but I wasn't sure. But it does it every time.

A man comes in here, no matter what he was before, no matter what he is when he goes out, but he feels it. Don't you feel it?"

"Yes. It's like—"

"What?"

"It's like . . . when you're in here . . . you're *responsible.*"

Reddington said nothing. But Larkin felt a warm pressure on his arm.

They paused at the door of the Lincoln Room. Two Secret Service men, standing by the door, opened it respectfully. They went on in, leaving the others outside.

Larkin looked across the room to the great, immortal bed. He felt suddenly very small, very tender. He crossed the soft carpet and looked down at the old man.

"Hi," the old man said. Larkin was startled, but he looked down at the broad weakly smiling face, saw the famous white hair and the still-twinkling eyes, and found himself smiling in return.

"Mr. President," Larkin said.

"I hear your name is Larkin." The old man's voice was surprisingly strong, but as he spoke now Larkin could see that the left side of his face was paralyzed. "Good name for a president. Indicates a certain sense of humor. Need a sense of humor. Reddington, how'd it go?"

"Good as can be expected, sir." He glanced briefly at Larkin. "The President knows. Wouldn't have done it without his okay. Now that I think of it, it was probably he who put the Secret Service on us."

"You're doggone right," the old man said. "They may bother the by-jingo out of you, but those boys are necessary. And also, if I hadn't let them know we knew Larkin was material—" He stopped abruptly and closed his eyes, took a deep breath. After a moment he said: "Mr. Larkin?"

"Yes, sir."

"I have one or two comments. You mind?"

"Of course not, sir."

"I couldn't solve it. I just . . . didn't have time. There were so many other things to do." He stopped and again closed his eyes. "But it will be up to you, son. The presidency . . . must be preserved. What they'll start telling you now is that there's only one way out, let SAM handle it. Reddington, too," the old man opened his eyes and gazed sadly at Reddington, "he'll tell you the same thing, but don't you believe it.

"Sure, SAM knows all the answers. Ask him a question on anything, on levels of parity tax rates, on anything. And right quick SAM will compute you out an answer. So that's what they'll try to do, they'll tell you to take it easy and let SAM do it.

"Well, all right, up to a certain point. But, Mr. Larkin, understand this. SAM is like a book. Like a book, he knows the answers. *But only those answers we've already found out.* We gave SAM those answers. A machine is not creative, neither is a book. Both are only the product of creative minds. Sure, SAM could hold the country together. But growth, man, there'd be no more growth! No new ideas, new solutions, change, progress, development! And America *must* grow, must progress—"

He stopped, exhausted. Reddington bowed his head. Larkin remained idly calm. He felt a remarkable clarity in his head.

"But, Mr. President," he said slowly, "if the office is too much for one man, then all we can do is cut down on his powers—"

"Ah," the old man said faintly, "there's the rub. Cut down on what? If I sign a tax bill, I must know enough about taxes to be certain that the bill is the right one. If I endorse a police action, I must be certain that the strategy involved is militarily sound. If I consider farm prices . . . you see, you see, what will you cut? The office is responsible for its acts. It must remain responsible. You cannot take just someone else's word for things like that, you must make your own decisions. Already we sign things we know nothing about, bills for this, bills for that, on somebody's word."

"What do you suggest?"

The old man cocked an eye toward Larkin, smiled once more with half his mouth, anciently worn, only hours from death, an old, old man with his work not done, never to be done.

"Son, come here. Take my hand. Can't lift it myself."

Larkin came forward, knelt by the side of the bed. He took the cold hand, now gaunt and almost translucent, and held it gently.

"Mr. Larkin," the President said. "God be with you, boy. Do what you can. Delegate authority. Maybe cut the term in half. But keep us human, please, keep us growing, keep us alive." His voice faltered, his eyes closed. "I'm very tired. God be with you."

Larkin laid the hand gently on the bed cover. He stood for a long moment looking down. Then he turned with Reddington and left the room.

Outside, he waited until they were past the Secret Service men and then turned to Reddington.

"Your plans for SAM. What do you think now?"

Reddington winced.

"I couldn't see any way out."

"But what about now? I have to know."

"I don't know. I really don't know. But . . . let me tell you something."

"Yes."

"Whatever I say to you from now on is only advice. You don't have to take it. Because understand this: however you came in here tonight, you're going out the president. You were elected. Not by the people maybe, not even by SAM. But you're President by the grace of God and that's enough for me. From this moment on you'll be President to everybody in the world. We've all agreed. Never think that you're only a fraud, because you aren't. You heard what the President said. You take it from here."

Larkin looked at him for a long while. Then he nodded once, briefly.

"All right," he said.

"One more thing."

"Yes?"

"I've got to say this, Tonight, this afternoon, I didn't really know what I was doing to you. I thought . . . well . . . the crisis came. But you had no time to think. That wasn't right. A man shouldn't be pushed into a thing like this without time to think. The old man just taught me something about making your own decisions. I should have let you make yours."

"It's all right."

"No, it isn't. You remember him in there. Well. That's you four years from tonight. If you live that long."

Now it was Larkin who reached out and patted Reddington on the shoulder.

"That's all right, too," he said.

Reddington said nothing. When he spoke again, Larkin realized he was moved.

"We have the greatest luck, this country," he said tightly. "At all the worst times we always seem to find all the best people."

"Well," Larkin said hurriedly, "we'd better get to work. There's a speech due in the morning. And the problem of SAM. And . . . oh, I've got to be sworn in."

He turned and went off down the hall. Reddington paused a moment before following him. He was thinking that he could be watching the last human President the United States would ever have. But—once more he straightened his shoulders.

"Yes, sir," he said softly, "Mr. President."

Charles Harness

Charles Harness (1915–) wrote one highly regarded SF novel in the 1950s, *Flight into Yesterday* (*The Paradox Men*, 1953). Damon Knight, in a famous review essay, said, "Harness told me in 1950 that he had spent two years writing the story, and had put into it every fictional idea that occurred to him during the time. He must have studied his model [van Vogt] with painstaking care." But Knight's point is that Harness surpasses van Vogt in SF: "All this, packed even more tightly than the original, symmetrically arranged, the loose ends tucked in, and every outrageous twist of the plot fully justified both in science and in logic." Brian W. Aldiss is also partisan to it: "This novel may be considered as the climax to the billion year spree . . . I call it Wide Screen Baroque . . . Harness's novel has a zing of its own, like whiskey and champagne, the drink of the Nepalese sultans."

After such praise, it is difficult to understand why Harness has suffered such comparative neglect, except that his career as a patent attorney allowed him only occasional time to write. His second novel, *The Ring of Ritornel*, was not published until 1968, and this third, *Wolfhead*, in 1978. Seven more novels followed between 1980 and 1991, altogether a significant body of genre work. Most of his short fiction has never been collected.

His only collection, *The Rose* (1966), was an obscure paperback original, containing the title novella and two other fine stories. Michael Moorcock, though, in an essay about "The Rose," calls it Harness's "greatest novel," and says, "although most of Harness's work is written in the magazine style of the time and at first glance appears to have only the appeal of colorful escapism, reminiscent of A. E. van Vogt or James Blish of the same period, it contains nuances and "throw away" ideas that show a serious (never earnest) mind operating at a much deeper and broader level than its contemporaries."

Moorcock goes on to say, " 'The Rose' [is] crammed with delightful notions—what some SF readers call 'ideas'—but these are essentially icing on the cake of Harness's fiction. [His] stories are what too little science fiction is—true stories of ideas, coming to grips with the big abstract problems of human existence and attempting to throw fresh, philosophical light on them."

"The Rose" was first published in a British SF magazine in 1953, at a time when not a hundred copies of such a publication were seen in the U.S., and not reprinted in America until 1966, long after the dust had settled from *Flight into Yesterday.* Except for the few new readers caught by the sixties paperbacks, the story, which deserves a place on the shelf next to the works of Cordwainer Smith, fell into obscurity. Here it is again, at last, one of the finest examples of "Grand Opera" science fiction.

THE ROSE

CHAPTER ONE

Her ballet slippers made a soft slapping sound, moody, mournful, as Anna van Tuyl stepped into the annex of her psychiatrical consulting room and walked toward the tall mirror.

Within seconds she would know whether she was ugly.

As she had done half a thousand times in the past two years, the young woman faced the great glass squarely, brought her arms up gracefully and rose upon her tip-toes. And there resemblance to past hours ceased. She did not proceed to an uneasy study of her face and figure. She could not. For her eyes, as though acting with a wisdom and volition of their own, had closed tightly.

Anna van Tuyl was too much the professional psychiatrist not to recognize that her subconscious mind had shrieked its warning. Eyes still shut, and breathing in great gasps, she dropped from her toes as if to turn and leap away. Then gradually she straightened. She must force herself to go through with it. She might not be able to bring herself here, in this mood of candid receptiveness, twice in one lifetime. It must be now.

She trembled in brief, silent premonition, then quietly raised her eyelids.

Sombre eyes looked out at her, a little darker than yesterday: pools ploughed around by furrows that today gouged a little deeper—the result of months of squinting up from the position into which her spinal deformity had thrust her neck and shoulders. The pale lips were pressed together just a little tighter in their defence against unpredictable pain. The cheeks seemed bloodless having been bleached finally and completely by the Unfinished Dream that haunted her sleep, wherein a nightingale fluttered about a white rose.

As if in brooding confirmation, she brought up simultaneously the pearl-translucent fingers of both hands to the upper borders of her forehead, and there pushed back the incongruous masses of newly-grey hair from two tumorous bulges—like incipient horns. As she did this she made a quarter turn, exposing to the mirror the humped grotesquerie of her back.

Then by degrees, like some netherworld Narcissus, she began to sink under the bizarre enchantment of that misshapen image. She could retain no real awareness that this creature was she. That profile, as if seen through witch-opened eyes, might have been that of some enormous toad, and this flickering metaphor paralyzed her first and only forlorn attempt at identification.

In a vague way, she realized that she had discovered what she had set out to discover. She was ugly. She was even very ugly.

The change must have been gradual, too slow to say of any one day: Yesterday I was not ugly. But even eyes that hungered for deception could no longer deny the cumulative evidence.

So slow—and yet so fast. It seemed only yesterday that had found her face down on Matthew Bell's examination table, biting savagely at a little pillow as his gnarled fingertips probed grimly at her upper thoracic vertebrae.

Well, then, she was ugly. But she'd not give in to self-pity. To hell with what she looked like! To hell with mirrors!

On sudden impulse she seized her balancing tripod with both hands, closed her eyes, and swung.

The tinkling of falling mirror glass had hardly ceased when a harsh and gravelly voice hailed her from her office. "Bravo!"

She dropped the practice tripod and whirled, aghast. "Matt!"

"Just thought it was time to come in. But if you want to bawl a little, I'll go back out and wait. No?" Without looking directly at her face or pausing for a reply, he tossed a packet on the table. "There it is. Honey, if I could write a ballet score like your *Nightingale and the Rose,* I wouldn't care if my spine was knotted in a figure eight."

"You're crazy," she muttered stonily, unwilling to admit that she was both pleased and curious. "You don't know what it means to have once been able to pirouette, to balance *en arabesque.* And anyway"—she looked at him from the corner of her eye—"how could anyone tell whether the score's good? There's no Finale as yet. It isn't finished."

"Neither is the Mona Lisa, *Kublai Khan,* or a certain symphony by Schubert."

"But this is different. A plotted ballet requires an integrated sequence of events leading up to a climax—to a Finale. I haven't figured out the ending. Did you notice I left a thirty-eight-beat hiatus just before The Nightingale dies? I still need a death song for her. She's entitled to die with a flourish." She couldn't tell him about The Dream—that she always awoke just before that death song began.

"No matter. You'll get it eventually. The story's straight out of Oscar Wilde, isn't it? As I recall, The Student needs a Red Rose as admission to the dance, but his garden contains only white roses. A foolish, if sympathetic Nightingale thrusts her heart against a thorn on a white rose stem, and the resultant ill-advised transfusion produces a Red Rose . . . and a dead Nightingale. Isn't that about all there is to it?"

"Almost. But I still need The Nightingale's death song. That's the whole point of the ballet. In a plotted ballet, every chord has to be fitted to the immediate action, blended with it, so that it supplements it, explains it, unifies it, and carries the action toward the climax. That death song will make the difference between a good score and a superior one. Don't smile. I think some of my individual scores are rather good, though of course I've never heard them except on my own piano. But without a proper climax, they'll remain unintegrated. They're all variants of some elusive dominating leitmotiv—some really marvellous theme I haven't the greatness of soul to grasp. I know it's something profound and poignant, like the *liebestod* theme in *Tristan.* It probably states a fundamental musical truth, but I don't think I'll ever find it. The Nightingale dies with her secret."

She paused, opened her lips as though to continue, and then fell moodily silent again. She wanted to go on talking, to lose herself in volubility. But now the reaction of her struggle with the mirror was setting in, and she was suddenly very tired. Had she ever wanted to cry? Now she thought only of sleep. But a furtive glance at her wristwatch told her it was barely ten o'clock.

The man's craggy eyebrows dropped in an imperceptible frown, faint, yet craftily alert. "Anna, the man who read your *Rose* score wants to talk to you about staging it for the Rose Festival—you know, the annual affair in the Via Rosa."

"I—an unknown—write a Festival ballet?" She added with dry incredulity: "The Ballet Committee is in complete agreement with your friend, of course?"

"He *is* the Committee."

"What did you say his name was?"

"I didn't."

She peered up at him suspiciously. "I can play games, too. If he's so anxious to use my music, why doesn't *he* come to see *me?*"

"He isn't that anxious."

"Oh, a big shot, eh?"

"Not exactly. It's just that he's fundamentally indifferent toward the things that fundamentally interest him. Anyway, he's got a complex about the Via Rosa—loves the district and hates to leave it, even for a few hours."

She rubbed her chin thoughtfully. "Will you believe it, I've never been there. That's the rose-walled district where the ars-gratia-artis professionals live, isn't it? Sort of a plutocratic Rive Gauche?"

The man exhaled in expansive affection. "That's the Via, all right. A six-hundred pound chunk of Carrara marble in every garret, resting most likely on the grand piano. Poppa chips furiously away with an occasional glance at his model, who is momma, posed *au naturel.*"

Anna watched his eyes grow dreamy as he continued. "Momma is a little restless, having suddenly recalled that the baby's bottle and that can of caviar should have come out of the atomic warmer at some nebulous period in the past. Daughter sits before the piano keyboard, surreptitiously switching from Czerny to a torrid little number she's going to try on the trap-drummer in Dorran's Via orchestra. Beneath the piano are the baby and mongrel pup. Despite their tender age, this thing is already in their blood. Or at least, their stomachs, for they have just finished an *hors d'oeuvre* of marble chips and now amiably share the *pièce de résistance*, a battered but rewarding tube of Van Dyke brown."

Anna listened to this with widening eyes. Finally she gave a short amazed laugh. "Matt Bell, you really love that life, don't you?"

He smiled. "In some ways the creative life is pretty carefree. I'm just a psychiatrist specializing in psychogenetics. I don't know an arpeggio from a drypoint etching, but I like to be around people that do." He bent forward earnestly. "These artists—these golden people—they're the coming force in society. And you're one of them, Anna, whether you know it or like it. You and your kind are going to inherit the earth—only you'd better hurry if you don't want Martha Jacques and her National Security scientists to get it first. So the battle lines converge in Renaissance II. Art versus Science. Who dies? Who lives?" He looked thoughtful, lonely. He might have been pursuing an introspective monologue in the solitude of his own chambers.

"This Mrs. Jacques," said Anna. "What's she like? You asked me to see her tomorrow about her husband, you know."

"Darn good looking woman. The most valuable mind in history, some say. And if she really works out something concrete from her Sciomnia equation, I guess there won't be any doubt about it. And that's what makes her potentially the most dangerous human being alive: National Security is fully aware of her value, and they'll coddle her tiniest whim—at least until she pulls something tangible out of Sciomnia. Her main whim for the past few years has been her errant husband, Mr. Ruy Jacques."

"Do you think she really loves him?"

"Just between me and you she hates his guts. So naturally she doesn't want any other woman to get him. She has him watched, of course. The Security Bureau cooperate with alacrity, because they don't want foreign agents to approach *her* through *him*. There have been ugly rumors of assassinated models . . . But I'm digressing." He cocked a quizzical eye at her. "Permit me to repeat the invitation of your unknown admirer. Like you, he's another true child of the new Renaissance. The two of you should find much in common—more than you can now guess. I'm very serious about this, Anna. Seek him out immediately—tonight—now. There aren't any mirrors in the Via."

"Please, Matt."

"Honey," he growled, "to a man my age you aren't ugly. And this man's the same. If a woman is pretty, he paints her and forgets her. But if she's some kind of an artist, he talks to her, and he can get rather endless sometimes. If it's any help to your self-assurance, he's about the homeliest creature on the face of the earth. You'll look like De Milo alongside him."

The woman laughed shortly. "I can't get mad at you, can I? Is he married?"

"Sort of." His eyes twinkled. "But don't let that concern you. He's a perfect scoundrel."

"Suppose I decide to look him up. Do I simply run up and down the Via paging all homely friends of Dr. Matthew Bell?"

"Not quite. If I were you I'd start at the entrance—where they have all those queer side-shows and one-man exhibitions. Go on past the vendress of love philters and work down the street until you find a man in a white suit with polka dots."

"How perfectly odd! And then what? How can I introduce myself to a man whose name I don't know? Oh, Matt, this is so silly, so *childish* . . ."

He shook his head in slow denial. "You aren't going to think about names when you see him. And your name won't mean a thing to him, anyway. You'll be lucky if you aren't 'hey you' by midnight. But it isn't going to matter."

"It isn't too clear why you don't offer to escort me." She studied him calculatingly. "And I think you're withholding his name because you know I wouldn't go if you revealed it."

He merely chuckled.

She lashed out: "Damn you, get me a cab."

"I've had one waiting half an hour."

CHAPTER TWO

"Tell ya what the professor's gonna do, ladies and gentlemen. He's gonna defend not just one paradox. Not just two. Not just a dozen. No, ladies and gentlemen, the professor's gonna defend *seventeen*, and all in the space of one short hour, without repeating himself, and including a brand-new one he has just thought up today: 'Music owes its meaning to its ambiguity.' Remember, folks, an axiom is just a paradox the professor's already got hold of. The cost of this dazzling display . . . don't crowd there, mister . . ."

Anna felt a relaxing warmth flowing over her mind, washing at the encrusted strain of the past hour. She smiled and elbowed her way through the throng and on down the street, where a garishly lighted sign, bat-wing doors, and a forlorn cluster of waiting women announced the next attraction:

"FOR MEN ONLY. Daring blindfold exhibitions and variety entertainments continuously."

Inside, a loudspeaker was blaring: "Thus we have seen how to compose the ideal end-game problem in chess. And now, gentlemen, for the small consideration of an additional quarter . . ."

But Anna's attention was now occupied by a harsh cawing from across the street.

"Love philters! Works on male or female! Any age! Never fails!"

She laughed aloud. Good old Matt! He had foreseen what these glaring multifaceted nonsensical stimuli would do for her. Love philters! Just what she needed!

The vendress of love philters was of ancent vintage, perhaps seventy-five years old. Above cheeks of wrinkled leather her eyes glittered speculatively. And how weirdly she was clothed! Her bedraggled dress was a shrieking purple. And under that dress was another of the same hue, though perhaps a little faded. And under *that,* still another.

"That's why they call me Violet," cackled the old woman, catching Anna's stare. "Better come over and let me mix you one."

But Anna shook her head and passed on, eyes shining. Fifteen minutes later, as she neared the central Via area, her receptive reverie was interrupted by the outburst of music ahead.

Good! Watching the street dancers for half an hour would provide a highly pleasant climax to her escapade. Apparently there wasn't going to be any man in a polka dot suit. Matt was going to be disappointed but it certainly wasn't her fault she hadn't found him.

There was something oddly familiar about that music.

She quickened her pace, and then, as recognition came, she began to run as fast as her crouching back would permit. This was *her* music—the prelude to Act III of her ballet!

She burst through the mass of spectators lining the dance square. The music stopped. She stared out into the scattered dancers, and what she saw staggered the twisted frame of her slight body. She fought to get air through her vacuously wide mouth.

In one unearthly instant, a rift had threaded its way through the dancer-packed square, and a pasty white face, altogether spectral, had looked down that open rift into hers. A face over a body that was enveloped in a strange glowing gown of shimmering white. She thought he had also been wearing a white academic mortar board, but the swarming dancers closed in again before she could be sure.

She fought an unreasoning impulse to run.

Then, as quickly as it had come, logic reasserted itself; the shock was over. Odd costumes were no rarity on the Via. There was no cause for alarm.

She was breathing almost normally when the music died away and someone began a harsh harangue over the public address system. "Ladies and gentlemen, it is our rare good fortune to have with us tonight the genius who composed the music you have been enjoying."

A sudden burst of laughter greeted this, seeming to originate in the direction of the orchestra, and was counterpointed by an uncomplimentary blare from one of the horns.

"Your mockery is misplaced, my friends. It just so happens that this genius is not I, but another. And since she has thus far had no opportunity to join in the revelry, your inimitable friend, as The Student, will take her hand, as The Nightingale, in the final *pas de deux* from Act III. That should delight her, yes?"

The address system clicked off amid clapping and a buzz of excited voices, punctuated by occasional shouts.

She must escape! She must get away!

Anna pressed back into the crowd. There was no longer any question about finding a man in a polka dot suit. *That* creature in white certainly wasn't he. Though how could he have recognized her?

She hesitated. Perhaps he had a message from the other one, if there really was one with polka dots.

No, she'd better go. This was turning out to be more of a nightmare than a lark.

Still—

She peeked back from behind the safety of a woman's sleeve, and after a moment located the man in white.

His pasty-white face with its searching eyes was much closer. But what had happened to his *white* cap and gown? *Now,* they weren't white at all! What optical fantasy was this? She rubbed her eyes and looked again.

The cap and gown seemed to be made up of green and purple polka dots on a white background! So he was her man!

She could see him now as the couples spread out before him, exchanging words she couldn't hear, but which seemed to carry an irresistible laugh response.

Very well, she'd wait.

Now that everything was cleared up and she was safe again behind her armor of objectivity, she studied him with growing curiosity. Since that first time she had never again got a good look at him. Someone always seemed to get in the way. It was almost, she thought, as though he was working his way out toward her, taking every advantage of human cover, like a hunter closing in on wary quarry, until it was too late . . .

He stood before her.

There were harsh clanging sounds as his eyes locked with hers. Under that feral scrutiny the woman maintained her mental balance by the narrowest margin.

The Student.

The Nightingale, for love of The Student, makes a Red Rose. An odious liquid was burning in her throat, but she couldn't swallow.

Gradually she forced herself into awareness of a twisted, sardonic mouth framed between aquiline nose and jutting chin. The face, plastered as it was by white powder, had revealed no distinguishing features beyond its unusual size. Much of the brow was obscured by the many tassels dangling over the front of his travestied mortarboard cap. Perhaps the most striking thing about the man was not his face, but his body. It was evident that he had some physical deformity, to outward appearances not unlike her own. She knew intuitively that he was not a true hunchback. His chest and shoulders were excessively broad, and he seemed, like her, to carry a mass of superfluous tissue on his upper thoracic vertebrae. She surmised that the scapulae would be completely obscured.

His mouth twisted in subtle mockery. "Bell said you'd come." He bowed and held out his right hand.

"It is very difficult for me to dance," she pleaded in a low hurried voice. "I'd humiliate us both."

"I'm no better at this than you, and probably worse. But I'd never give up dancing merely because someone might think I look awkward. Come, we'll use the simplest steps."

There was something harsh and resonant in his voice that reminded her of Matt Bell. Only . . . Bell's voice had never set her stomach churning.

He held out his other hand.

Behind him the dancers had retreated to the edge of the square, leaving the centre empty, and the first beats of her music from the orchestra pavilion floated to her with ecstatic clarity.

Just the two of them, out there . . . before a thousand eyes. . . .

Subconsciously she followed the music. There was her cue—the signal for The Nightingale to fly to her fatal assignation with the white rose.

She must reach out both perspiring hands to this stranger, must blend her deformed body into his equally misshapen one. She must, because he was The Student, and she was The Nightingale.

She moved toward him silently and took his hands.

As she danced, the harsh-lit street and faces seemed gradually to vanish. Even The Student faded into the barely perceptible distance, and she gave herself up to The Unfinished Dream.

CHAPTER THREE

She dreamed that she danced alone in the moonlight, that she fluttered in solitary circles in the moonlight, fastened and appalled by the thing she must do to create a Red Rose. She dreamed that she sang a strange and magic song, a wondrous series of chords, the song she had so long sought. Pain buoyed her on excruciating wings, then flung her heavily to earth. The Red Rose was made, and she was dead.

She groaned and struggled to sit up.

Eyes glinted at her out of pasty whiteness. "That was quite a *pas*—only more *de seul* than *de deux*," said The Student.

She looked about in uneasy wonder.

They were sitting together on a marble bench before a fountain. Behind them was a curved walk bounded by a high wall covered with climbing green, dotted here and there with white.

She put her hand to her forehead. "Where are we?"

"This is White Rose Park."

"How did I get here?"

"You danced in on your own two feet through the archway yonder."

"I don't remember . . ."

"I thought perhaps you were trying to lend a bit of realism to the part. But you're early."

"What do you mean?"

"There are only white roses growing in here, and even *they* won't be in full bloom for another month. In late June they'll be a real spectacle. You mean you didn't know about this little park?"

"No. I've never ever been in the Via before. And yet . . ."

"And yet what?"

She hadn't been able to tell anyone—not even Matt Bell—what she was now going to tell this man, an utter stranger, her companion of an hour. He had to be told because, somehow, he too was caught up in the dream ballet.

She began haltingly. "Perhaps I *do* know about this place. Perhaps someone told me about it, and the information got buried in my subconscious mind until I wanted a white rose. There's really something behind my ballet that Dr. Bell didn't tell you. He couldn't, because I'm the only one who knows. The *Rose* comes from my dreams. Only, a better word is nightmares. Every night the score starts from the beginning. In The Dream, I dance. Every night, for months and months, there was a little more music, a little more dancing. I tried to get it out of my head, but I couldn't. I started writing it down, the music and the choreography."

The man's unsmiling eyes were fixed on her face in deep absorption.

Thus encouraged, she continued. "For the past several nights I have dreamed almost the complete ballet, right up to the death of The Nightingale. I suppose I identify myself so completely with The Nightingale that I subconsciously censor her song as she presses her breast against the thorn on the white rose. That's where I always awakened, or at least, always did before tonight. But I think I heard the music tonight. It's a series of chords . . . thirty-eight chords, I believe. The first nineteen were frightful, but the second nineteen were marvellous. Everything was too real to wake up. The Student, The Nightingale, the white roses."

But now the man threw back his head and laughed raucously. "You ought to see a psychiatrist!"

Anna bowed her head humbly.

"Oh, don't take it too hard," he said. "My wife's even after *me* to see a psychiatrist."

"Really?" Anna was suddenly alert. "What seems to be wrong with you? I mean, what does she object to?"

"In general, my laziness. In particular, it seems I've forgotten how to read and write." He gave her widening eyes a sidelong look. "I'm a perfect parasite, too. Haven't done any real work in months. What would *you* call it if you couldn't work until you had the final measures of the *Rose*, and you kept waiting, and nothing happened?"

"Hell."

He was glumly silent.

Anna asked, hesitantly, yet with a growing certainty. "This thing you're waiting for . . . might it have anything to do with the ballet? Or to phrase it from your point of view, do you think the completion of my ballet may help answer your problem?"

"Might. Couldn't say."

She continued quietly. "You're going to have to face it eventually, you know. Your psychiatrist is going to ask you. How will you answer?"

"I won't. I'll tell him to go to the devil."

"How can you be so sure he's a *he*?"

"Oh? Well, if he's a *she*, she might be willing to pose *al fresco* an hour or so. The model shortage is quite grave you know, with all of the little dears trying to be painters."

"But if she doesn't have a good figure?"

"Well, maybe her face has some interesting possibilities. It's a rare woman who's a total physical loss."

Anna's voice was very low. "But what if *all* of her were very ugly? What if your proposed psychiatrist were me, *Mr. Ruy Jacques?*"

His great dark eyes blinked, then his lips pursed and exploded into insane laughter. He stood up suddenly. "Come, my dear, whatever your name is, and let the blind lead the blind."

"Anna van Tuyl," she told him, smiling.

She took his arm. Together they strolled around the arc of the walk toward the entrance arch.

She was filled with a strange contentment.

Over the green-crested wall at her left, day was about to break, and from the Via came the sound of groups of die-hard revellers, breaking up and drifting away, like spectres at cock-crow. The cheerful clatter of milk bottles got mixed up in it somehow.

They paused at the archway while the man kicked at the seat of the pants of a spectre whom dawn had returned to slumber beneath the arch. The sleeper cursed and stumbled to his feet in bleary indignation.

"Excuse us, Willie," said Anna's companion, motioning for her to step through.

She did, and the creature of the night at once dropped into his former sprawl.

Anna cleared her throat. "Where now?"

"At this point I must cease to be a gentleman, *I'm* returning to the studio for some sleep, and *you* can't come. For, if your physical energy is inexhaustible, mine is not." He raised a hand as her startled mouth dropped open. "Please, dear Anna, don't insist. Some other night, perhaps."

"Why, you—"

"Tut tut." He turned a little and kicked again at the sleeping man. "I'm not an utter cad, you know. I would never abandon a weak, frail, unprotected woman in the Via."

She was too amazed now even to splutter.

Ruy Jacques reached down and pulled the drunk up against the wall of the arch, where he held him firmly. "Dr. Anna van Tuyl, may I present Willie the Cork."

The Cork grinned at her in unfocused somnolence.

"Most people call him the Cork because, that's what seals in the bottle's contents," said Jacques. "*I* call him the Cork because he's always bobbing up. He looks like a bum, but that's just because he's a good actor. He's really a Security man tailing me at my wife's request, and he'd only be too delighted for a little further conversation with you. A cheery good morning to you both!"

A milk truck wheeled around the corner. Jacques leaped for its running board, and he was gone before the psychiatrist could voice the protest boiling up in her.

A gurgling sigh at her feet drew her eyes down momentarily. The Cork was apparently bobbing once more on his own private alcoholic ocean.

Anna snorted in mingled disgust and amusement, then hailed a cab. As she slammed the door, she took one last look at Willie. Not until the cab rounded the corner and cut off his muffled snores did she realize that people usually don't snore with their eyes half-opened and looking at you, especially with eyes no longer blurred with sleep, but hard and glinting.

CHAPTER FOUR

Twelve hours later, in another cab and in a different part of the city, Anna peered absently out at the stream of traffic. Her mind was on the coming conference with Martha Jacques. Only twelve hours ago Mrs. Jacques had been just a bit of necessary case history. Twelve hours ago Anna hadn't really cared whether Mrs. Jacques followed Bell's recommendation and gave her the case. Now it was all different. She wanted the case, and she was going to get it.

Ruy Jacques—how many hours awaited her with this amazing scoundrel, this virtuoso of liberal—nay, loose—arts, who held locked within his remarkable mind the missing pieces of their joint jigsaw puzzle of The Rose?

That jeering, mocking face—what would it look like without makeup? Very ugly, she hoped. Beside his, her own face wasn't too bad.

Only—he was married, and she was en route at this moment to discuss preliminary matters with his wife, who, even if she no longer loved him, at least had prior rights to him. There were considerations of professional ethics even in thinking about him. Not that she could ever fall in love with him or any other patient. Particularly with one who had treated her so cavalierly. Willie the Cork, indeed!

As she waited in the cold silence of the great antechamber adjoining the office of Martha Jacques, Anna sensed that she was being watched. She was quite certain that by now she'd been photographed, x-rayed for hidden weapons, and her fingerprints taken from her professional card. In colossal central police files a thousand miles away, a bored clerk would be leafing through her dossier for the benefit of Colonel Grade's visigraph in the office beyond.

In a moment—

"Dr. van Tuyl to see Mrs. Jacques. Please enter door B-3," said the tinny voice of the intercom.

She followed a guard to the door, which he opened for her.

This room was smaller. At the far end a woman, a very lovely woman, whom she took to be Martha Jacques, sat peering in deep abstraction at something on the desk before her. Beside the desk, and slightly to the rear, a moustached man in plain clothes stood, reconnoitring Anna with hawklike eyes. The description fitted what Anna had heard of Colonel Grade, Chief of the National Security Bureau.

Grade stepped forward and introduced himself curtly, then presented Anna to Mrs. Jacques.

And then the psychiatrist found her eyes fastened to a sheet of paper on Mrs. Jacques' desk. And as she stared, she felt a sharp dagger of ice sinking into her spine, and she grew slowly aware of a background of brooding whispers in her mind, heart-constricting in their suggestions of mental disintegration.

For the thing drawn on the paper, in red ink, was—although warped, incomplete, and misshapen—unmistakably a rose.

"Mrs. Jacques!" cried Grade.

Martha Jacques must have divined simultaneously Anna's great interest in the paper. With an apologetic murmur she turned it face down. "Security regulations, you know. I'm really supposed to keep it locked up in the presence of visitors." Even a murmur could not hide the harsh metallic quality of her voice.

So *that* was why the famous Sciomnia formula was sometimes called the "Jacques Rosette": when traced in an everexpanding wavering red spiral in polar coordinates, it was . . . a Red Rose.

The explanation brought at once a feeling of relief and a sinister deepening of the sense of doom that had overshadowed her for months. So you, too, she thought wonderingly, seek The Rose. Your artist-husband is wretched for want of it, and now you. But do you seek the same rose? Is the rose of the scientist the true rose, and Ruy Jacques' the false? What *is* The Rose? Will I ever know?

Grade broke in. "Your brilliant reputation is deceptive, Dr. van Tuyl. From Dr. Bell's description, we had pictured you as an older woman."

"Yes," said Martha Jacques, studying her curiously. "We really had in mind an older woman, one less likely to . . . to—"

"To involve your husband emotionally?"

"Exactly," said Grade. "Mrs. Jacques must have her mind completely free from distractions. However"—he turned to the woman scientist—"it is my studied opinion that we need not anticipate difficulty from Dr. van Tuyl on that account."

Anna felt her throat and cheeks going hot as Mrs. Jacques nodded in damning agreement: "I think you're right, Colonel."

"Of course," said Grade, "*Mr.* Jacques may not accept her."

"That remains to be seen," said Martha Jacques. "He might tolerate a fellow artist." To Anna: "Dr. Bell tells us that you compose music, or something like that?"

"Something like that," nodded Anna. She wasn't worried. It was a question of waiting. This woman's murderous jealousy, though it might some day destroy her, at the moment concerned her not a whit.

Colonel Grade said: "Mrs. Jacques has probably warned you that her husband is somewhat eccentric; he may be somewhat difficult to deal with at times. On this account, the Security Bureau is prepared to triple your fee, if we find you acceptable."

Anna nodded gravely. Ruy Jacques and money, too!

"For most of your consultations you'll have to track him down," said Martha Jacques. "He'll never come to you. But considering what we're prepared to pay, this inconvenience should be immaterial."

Anna thought briefly of that fantastic creature who had singled her out of a thousand faces. "That will be satisfactory. And now, Mrs. Jacques, for my preliminary orientation, suppose you describe some of the more striking behaviorisms that you've noted in your husband."

"Certainly. Dr. Bell, I presume, has already told you that Ruy has lost the ability to read and write. Ordinarily that's indicative of advanced dementia praecox, isn't it? However, I think Mr. Jacques' case presents a more complicated picture, and my own guess is schizophrenia rather than dementia. The dominant and most frequently observed psyche is a megalomanic phase, during which he tends to harangue his listeners on various odd subjects. We've picked up some of these speeches on a hidden recorder and made a Zipf analysis of the word-frequencies."

Anna's brows creased dubiously. "A Zipf count is pretty mechanical."

"But scientific, undeniably scientific. I have made a careful study of the method, and can speak authoritatively. Back in the forties Zipf of Harvard proved that in a representative sample of English, the interval separating the repetition of the same word was inversely proportional to its frequency. He provided a mathematical formula for something previously known only qualitatively: that a too-soon repetition of the same or similar sound is distracting and grating to the cultured mind. If we must say the same thing in the next paragraph, we avoid repetition with an appropriate synonym. But not the schizophrenic. His disease disrupts his higher centres of association, and certain discriminating neural networks are no longer available for his writing and speech. He has no compunction against immediate and continuous tonal repetition."

"A rose is a rose is a rose . . ." murmured Anna.

"Eh? How did you know what this transcription was about? Oh, you were just quoting Gertrude Stein? Well, I've read about her, and she proves my point. She admitted that she wrote under autohypnosis, which we'd call a light case of schizo. But she could be normal, too. My husband never is. He goes on like this all the time. This was transcribed from one of his monologues. Just listen:

" 'Behold, Willie, through yonder window the symbol of your mistress' defeat: the rose! The rose, my dear Willie, grows not in murky air. The smoky metropolis of yester-year drove it to the country. But now, with the unsullied skyline of your atomic age, the red rose returns. How mysterious, Willie, that the rose continues to offer herself to us dull, plodding humans. We see nothing in her but a pretty flower. Her regretful thorns forever declare our inept clumsiness, and her lack of honey chides our gross sensuality. Ah, Willie, let us become as birds! For only the winged can eat the fruit of the rose and spread her pollen . . .' "

Mrs. Jacques looked up at Anna. "Did you keep count? He used the word 'rose' no less than five times, when once or twice was sufficient. He certainly had no lack of mellifluous synonyms at his disposal, such as 'red flower,' 'thorned plant,' and so on. And instead of saying 'the red rose returns' he should have said something like 'it comes back'."

"And lose the triple alliteration?" smiled Anna. "No, Mrs. Jacques, I'd reexamine that diagnosis very critically. Everyone who talks like a poet isn't necessarily insane."

A tiny bell began to jangle on a massive metal door in the right-hand wall.

"A message for me," growled Grade. "Let it wait."

"We don't mind," said Anna, "if you want to have it sent in."

"It isn't *that*. That's my private door, and I'm the only one who knows the combination. But I told them not to interrupt us, unless it dealt with this specific interview."

Anna thought of the eyes of Willie the Cork, hard and glistening. Suddenly she knew that Ruy Jacques had not been joking about the identity of the man. Was The Cork's report just now getting on her dossier? Mrs. Jacques wasn't going to like it. Suppose they turned her down. Would she dare seek out Ruy Jacques under the noses of Grade's trigger men?

"Damn that fool," muttered Grade. "I left strict orders about being disturbed. Excuse me."

He strode angrily toward the door. After a few seconds of dial manipulation, he turned the handle and pulled it inward. A hand thrust something metallic at him. Anna caught whispers. She fought down a feeling of suffocation as Grade opened the cassette and read the message.

The Security officer walked leisurely back toward them. He stroked his moustache coolly, handed the bit of paper to Martha Jacques, then clasped his hands behind his back. For a moment he looked like a glowering bronze statue. "Dr. van Tuyl, you didn't tell us that you were already acquainted with Mr. Jacques. Why?"

"You didn't ask me."

Martha Jacques said harshly: "That answer is hardly satisfactory. How long have you known Mr. Jacques? I want to get to the bottom of this."

"I met him last night for the first time in the Via Rosa. We danced. That's all. The whole thing was purest coincidence."

"You are his lover," accused Martha Jacques.

Anna colored. "You flatter me, Mrs. Jacques."

Grade coughed. "She's right. Mrs. Jacques. I see no sex-based espionage."

"Then maybe it's even subtler," said Martha Jacques. "These platonic females are still worse, because they sail under false colors. She's after Ruy, I tell you."

"I assure you," said Anna, "that your reaction comes as a complete surprise to me. Naturally, I shall withdraw from the case at once."

"But it doesn't end with that," said Grade curtly. "The national safety may depend on Mrs. Jacques' peace of mind during the coming weeks. I *must* ascertain your relation with Mr. Jacques. And I must warn you that if a compromising situation exists, the consequences will be most unpleasant." He picked up the telephone. "Grade. Get me the O.D."

Anna's palms were uncomfortably wet and sticky. She wanted to wipe them on the sides of her dress, but then decided it would be better to conceal all signs of nervousness.

Grade barked into the mouthpiece. "Hello! That you, Packard? Send me—"

Suddenly the room vibrated with the shattering impact of massive metal on metal.

The three whirled toward the sound.

A stooped, loudly dressed figure was walking away from the great and inviolate door of Colonel Grade, drinking in with sardonic amusement the stuporous faces turned to him. It was evident he had just slammed the door behind him with all his strength.

Insistent squeakings from the teleset stirred Grade into a feeble response. "Never mind . . . it's Mr. Jacques . . ."

CHAPTER FIVE

The swart ugliness of that face verged on the sublime. Anna observed for the first time the two horn-like protuberances on his forehead, which the man made no effort to conceal. His black woollen beret was cocked jauntily over one horn; the other, the visible one, bulged even more than Anna's horns, and to her fascinated eyes he appeared as some Greek satyr; Silenus with an eternal hangover, or Pan wearying of fruitless pursuit of fleeting nymphs. It was the face of a cynical post-gaol Wilde, of a Rimbaud, of a Goya turning his brush in saturnine glee from Spanish grandees to the horror-world of Ensayos.

Like a phantom voice Matthew Bell's cryptic prediction seemed to float into her ears again: ". . . much in common . . . more than you guess . . ."

There was so little time to think. Ruy Jacques must have recognized her frontal deformities even while that tasselated mortar-board of his Student costume had prevented her from seeing his. He must have identified her as a less advanced case of his own disease. Had he foreseen the turn of events here? Was he here to protect the only person on earth who might help him? That wasn't like him. He just wasn't the sensible type. She got the uneasy impression that he was here solely for his own amusement—simply to make fools of the three of them.

Grade began to sputter. "Now see here, Mr. Jacques. It's impossible to get in through that door. It's my private entrance. I changed the combination myself only this morning." The moustache bristled indignantly. "I must ask the meaning of this."

"Pray do, Colonel, pray do."

"Well, then, what is the meaning of this?"

"None, Colonel. Have you no faith in your own syllogisms? No one can open your private door but you. Q.E.D. No one did. I'm not really here. No smiles? Tsk tsk! Paragraph 6, p. 80 of the Manual of Permissible Military Humor officially recognizes the paradox."

"There's no such publication—" stormed Grade.

But Jacques brushed him aside. He seemed now to notice Anna for the first time, and bowed with exaggerated punctilio. "My profound apologies, madame. You were standing so still, so quiet, that I mistook you for a rose bush." He beamed at each in turn. "Now isn't this delightful? I feel like a literary lion. It's the first time in my life that my admirers ever met for the express purpose of discussing my work."

How could he know that we were discussing his "composition," wondered Anna. *And how did he open the door?*

"If you'd eavesdropped long enough," said Martha Jacques, "you'd have learned we weren't admiring your 'prose poem'. In fact, I think it's pure nonsense."

No, thought Anna, he couldn't have eavesdropped, because we didn't talk about his speech after Grade opened the door. There's something here—in this room—that *tells* him.

"You don't even think it's poetry?" repeated Jacques, wide-eyed. "Martha, coming from one with your scientifically developed poetical sense, this is utterly damning."

"There *are* certain well recognized approaches to the appreciation of poetry," said Martha Jacques doggedly. "You ought to have the autoscanner read you some books on the aesthetic laws of language. It's all there."

The artist blinked in great innocence. "*What's* all there?"

"Scientific rules for analyzing poetry. Take the mood of a poem. You can very easily learn whether it's gay or sombre just by comparing the proportion of low-pitched vowels—*u* and *o*, that is—to the high-pitched vowels—*a*, *e* and *i*."

"Well, what do you know about that!" He turned a wondering face to Anna. "And she's right! Come to think of it, in Milton's *L'Allegro*, most of the vowels are high-pitched, while in his *Il Penseroso*, they're mostly low-pitched. Folks, I believe we've finally found a yardstick for genuine poetry. No longer must we flounder in poetastical soup. Now let's see." He rubbed his chin in blank-faced thoughtfulness. "Do you know, for years I've considered Swinburne's lines mourning Charles Baudelaire to be the distillate of sadness. But that, of course, was before I had heard of Martha's scientific approach, and had to rely solely on my unsophisticated, untrained, uninformed feelings. How stupid I was! For the thing is crammed with high-pitched vowels, and long *e* dominates: 'thee,' 'sea,' 'weave,' 'eve,' 'heat,' 'sweet,' 'feet' . . ." He struck his brow as if in sudden comprehension. "Why, it's gay! I must set it to a snappy polka!"

"Drivel," sniffed Martha Jacques. "Science—"

"—is simply a parasitical, adjectival, and useless occupation devoted to the quantitative restatement of Art," finished the smiling Jacques. "Science is functionally sterile; it creates nothing; it says nothing new. The scientist can never be more than a humble camp-follower of the artist. There exists no scientific truism that hasn't been anticipated by creative art. The examples are endless. Uccello worked out mathematically the laws of perspective in the fifteenth century; but Kallicrates applied the same laws two thousand years before in designing the columns of the Parthenon. The Curies thought they invented the idea of 'half-life'—of a thing vanishing in proportion to its residue. The Egyptians tuned their lyre-strings to dampen according to the same formula. Napier thought he invented logarithms—entirely overlooking the fact that the Roman brass workers flared their trumpets to follow a logarithmic curve."

"You're deliberately selecting isolated examples," retorted Martha Jacques.

"Then suppose you name a few so-called scientific discoveries," replied the man. "I'll prove they were scooped by an artist, every time."

"I certainly shall. How about Boyle's gas law? I suppose you'll say Praxiteles knew all along that gas pressure runs inversely proportional to its volume at a given temperature?"

"I expected something more sophisticated. That one's too easy. Boyle's gas law, Hooke's law of springs, Galileo's law of pendulums, and a host of similar hogwash simply state that compression, kinetic energy, or whatever name you give it, is inversely proportional to its reduced dimensions, and is proportional to the amount of its displacement in the total system. Or, as the artist says, impact results from, and is proportional to, displacement of an object within its milieu. Could the final couplet of a Shakespearean sonnet enthral us if our minds hadn't been conditioned, held in check, and compressed in suspense by the preceding fourteen lines? Note how cleverly Donne's famous poem builds up to its crash line, 'It tolls for thee!' By blood, sweat, and genius, the Elizabethans lowered the entrophy of their creations in precisely the same manner and with precisely the same result as when Boyle compressed his gases. And the method was long old when *they* were young. It was old when the Ming artists were painting the barest suggestions of landscapes on the disproportionate backgrounds of their vases. The Shah Jahan was aware of it when he designed the long eye-restraining reflecting pool before the Taj Mahal. The Greek tragedians knew it. Sophocles' *Oedipus* is still unparalleled in its suspensive pacing toward climax. Solomon's imported Chaldean arthitects knew the effect to be gained by spacing the Holy of Holies at a distance from the temple pylae, and the Cro-Magnard magicians with malice aforethought painted their marvellous animal scenes only in the most inaccessible crannies of their limestone caves."

Martha Jacques smiled coldly. "Drivel, drivel, drivel. But never mind. One of these days soon I'll produce evidence you'll be *forced* to admit art can't touch."

"If you're talking about Sciomnia, there's *real* nonsense for you," countered Jacques amiably. "Really, Martha, it's a frightful waste of time to reconcile biological theory with the unified field theory of Einstein, which itself merely reconciles the relativity and quantum theories, a futile gesture in the first place. Before Einstein announced *his* unified theory in 1949, the professors handled the problem very neatly. They taught the quantum theory on Mondays, Wednesdays and Fridays and the relativity theory on Tuesdays, Thursdays and Saturdays. On the Sabbath they rested in front of their television sets. What's the good of Sciomnia, anyway?"

"It's the final summation of all physical and biological knowledge," retorted Martha Jacques. "And as such, Sciomnia represents the highest possible aim of human endeavor. Man's goal in life is to understand his environment, to analyze it to the last iota—to know what he controls. The first person to understand Sciomnia may well rule not only this planet, but the whole galaxy—not that he'd want to, but he could. That person may not be me—but will certainly be a scientist, and not an irresponsible artist."

"But Martha," protested Jacques. "Where did you pick up such a weird philosophy? The highest aim of man is *not* to analyze, but to synthesize—to *create*. If you ever solve all of the nineteen sub-equations of Sciomnia, you'll be at a dead end. There'll be nothing left to analyze. As Dr. Bell the psychogeneticist says, overspecialization, be it mental, as in the human scientist, or dental, as in the sabre-tooth tiger, is just a synonym for extinction. But if we continue to create, we shall eventually discover how to transcend—"

Grade coughed, and Martha Jacques cut in tersely: "Never mind what Dr. Bell says. Ruy, have you ever seen this woman before?"

"The rose bush? Hmm." He stepped over to Anna and looked squarely down at her face. She flushed and looked away. He circled her in slow, critical appraisal, like a prospective buyer in a slave market of ancient Baghdad. "Hmm," he repeated doubtfully.

Anna breathed faster; her cheeks were the hue of beets. But she couldn't work up any sense of indignity. On the contrary, there was something illogically delicious about being visually pawed and handled by this strange leering creature.

Then she jerked visibly. What hypnotic insanity was this? This man held her life in the palm of his hand. If he acknowledged her, the vindictive creature who passed as his wife would crush her professionally. If he denied her, they'd know he was lying to save her—and the consequences might prove even less pleasant. And what difference would her ruin make to *him?* She had sensed at once his monumental selfishness. And even if that conceit, that gorgeous self-love, urged him to preserve her for her hypothetical value in finishing up the *Rose* score, she didn't see how he was going to manage it.

"Do you recognize her, Mr. Jacques," demanded Grade.

"I do," came the solemn reply.

Anna stiffened.

Martha Jacques smiled thinly. "Who is she?"

"Miss Ethel Twinkham, my old spelling teacher. How are you, Miss Twinkham? What brings you out of retirement?"

"I'm not Miss Twinkham," said Anna dryly. "My name is Anna van Tuyl. For your information, we met last night in the Via Rosa."

"Oh! Of course!" He laughed happily. "I seem to remember now, quite indistinctly. And I want to apologize, Miss Twinkham. My behavior was execrable, I suppose. Anyway, if you will just leave the bill for damages with Mrs. Jacques, her lawyer will take care of everything. You can even throw in ten per cent, for mental anguish."

Anna felt like clapping her hands in glee. The whole Security office was no match for this fiend.

"You're getting last night mixed up with the night before," snapped Martha Jacques. "You met Miss van Tuyl last night. You were with her several hours. Don't lie about it."

Again Ruy Jacques peered earnestly into Anna's face. He finally shook his head. "Last night? Well, I can't deny it. Guess you'll have to pay up, Martha. Her face *is* familiar, but I just can't remember what I did to make her mad. The bucket of paint and the slumming dowager was *last* week, wasn't it?"

Anna smiled. "You didn't injure me. We simply danced together on the square, that's all. I'm here at Mrs. Jacques' request." From the corner of her eye she watched Martha Jacques and the colonel exchange questioning glances, as if to say, "Perhaps there is really nothing between them."

But the scientist was not completely satisfied. She turned her eyes on her husband. "It's a strange coincidence that you should come just at this time. Exactly why *are* you here, if not to becloud the issue of this woman and your future psychiatrical treatment? Why don't you answer? What is the matter with you?"

For Ruy Jacques stood there, swaying like a stricken satyr, his eyes coals of pain in a face of anguished flames. He contorted backward once, as though attempting to placate furious fangs tearing at the hump on his back.

Anna leaped to catch him as he collapsed.

He lay cupped in her lap moaning voicelessly. Something in his hump, which lay against her left breast, seethed and raged like a genie locked in a bottle.

"Colonel Grade," said the psychiatrist quietly, "you will order an ambulance. I must analyze this pain syndrome at the clinic immediately."

Ruy Jacques was hers.

CHAPTER SIX

"Thanks awfully for coming, Matt," said Anna warmly.

"Glad to, honey." He looked down at the prone figure on the clinic cot. "How's our friend?"

"Still unconscious, and under general analgesic. I called you in because I want to air some ideas about this man that scare me when I think about them alone."

The psychogeneticist adjusted his spectacles with elaborate casualness. "Really? Then you think you've found what's wrong with him? Why he can't read or write?"

"Does it have to be something *wrong?*"

"What else would you call it? A . . . *gift?*"

She studied him narrowly. "I might—and you might—if he got something in return for his loss. That would depend on whether there was a net gain, wouldn't it? And don't pretend you don't know what I'm talking about. Let's get out in the open. You've known the Jacques—both of them—for years. You had me put on his case because you think he and I might find in the mind and body of the other a mutual solution to our identical aberrations. Well?"

Bell tapped imperturbably at his cigar. "As you say, the question is, whether he got enough in return—enough to compensate for his lost skills."

She gave him a baffled look. "All right, then, I'll do the talking. Ruy Jacques opened Grade's private door, when Grade alone knew the combination. And when he got in the room with us, he knew what we had been talking about. It was just as though it had all been written out for him, somehow. You'd have thought the lock combination had been pasted on the door, and that he'd looked over a transcript of our conversation."

"Only, he can't read," observed Bell.

"You mean, he can't read . . . *writing?*"

"What else is there?"

"Possibly some sort of thought residuum . . . in *things*. Perhaps some message in the metal of Grade's door, and in certain objects in the room." She watched him closely. "I see you aren't surprised. You've known this all along."

"I admit nothing. You, on the other hand, must admit that your theory of thought-reading is superficially fantastic."

"So would writing be—to a Neanderthal cave dweller. But tell me, Matt, where do our thoughts go after we think them? What is the extra-cranial fate of those feeble, intricate electric oscillations we pick up on the encephalograph? We know they can and do penetrate the skull, that they can pass through bone, like radio waves. Do they go on out into the universe forever? Or do dense substances like Grade's door eventually absorb them all? Do they set up their wispy patterns in metals, which then begin to vibrate in sympathy, like piano wires responding to a noise?"

Bell drew heavily on his cigar. "Seriously, I don't know. But I will say this: your theory is not inconsistent with certain psychogenetic predictions."

"Such as?"

"Eventual telemusical communication of all thought. The encephalograph, you know, looks oddly like a musical sound track. Oh, we can't expect to convert overnight to communication of pure thought by pure music. Naturally, crude transitional forms will intervene. But *any* type of direct idea transmission that involves the sending and receiving of rhythm and modulation as such is a cut higher than communication in a verbal medium, and may be a rudimentary step upward toward true musical communion, just as dawn man presaged true words with allusive, onomatapoeic monosyllables."

"There's your answer, then," said Anna. "Why should Ruy Jacques trouble to read, when every bit of metal around him is an open book?" She continued speculatively. "You might look at it this way. Our ancestors forgot how to swing through the trees when they learned how to walk erect. Their history is recapitulated in our very young. Almost immediately after birth, a human infant can hang by his hands, apelike. And then, after a week or so, he forgets what no human infant ever really needed to know. So now Ruy forgets how to read. A great pity. Perhaps. But if the world were peopled with Ruys, they wouldn't need to know how, for after the first few years of infancy, they'd learn to use their metal-empathic sense. They might even say, 'It's all very nice to be able to read and write and swing about in trees when you're *quite* young, but after all, one matures.' "

She pressed a button on the desk slide viewer that sat on a table by the artist's bed. "This is a radiographic slide of Ruy's cerebral hemispheres as viewed from above, probably old stuff to you. It shows that the 'horns' are not mere localized growths in the prefrontal area, but extend as slender tracts around the respective hemispheric peripheries to the visuo-sensory area of the occipital lobes, where they turn and enter the cerebral interior, there to merge in an enlarged ball-like juncture at a point over the cerebellum where the pineal 'eye' is ordinarily found."

"But the pineal is completely missing in the slide," demurred Bell.

"That's the question," countered Anna. "*Is* the pineal absent—or, are the 'horns' actually the pineal, enormously enlarged and bifurcated? I'm convinced that the latter is the fact. For reasons presently unknown to me, this heretofore small, obscure lobe has grown, bifurcated, and forced its destructive dual limbs not only through the soft cerebral tissue concerned with the ability to read, but also has gone on to skirt half the cerebral circumference to the forehead, where even the hard frontal bone of the skull has softened under its pressure." She looked at Bell closely. "I infer that it's just a question of time before I, too, forget how to read and write."

Bell's eyes drifted evasively to the immobile face of the unconscious artist. "But the number of neurons in a given mammalian brain remains constant after birth," he said. "These cells can throw out numerous dendrites and create increasingly complex neural patterns as the subject grows older, but he can't grow any more of the primary neurons."

"I know. That's the trouble. Ruy can't grow more brain, but he has." She touched her own "horns" wonderingly. "And I guess I have, too. *What—?*"

Following Bell's glance, she bent over to inspect the artist's face, and started as from a physical blow.

Eyes like anguished talons were clutching hers.

His lips moved, and a harsh whisper swirled about her ears like a desolate wind: ". . . The Nightingale . . . in death . . . greater beauty unbearable . . . *but watch . . . THE ROSE!*"

White-faced, Anna staggered backwards through the door.

CHAPTER SEVEN

Bell's hurried footsteps were just behind her as she burst into her office and collapsed on the consultation couch. Her eyes were shut tight, but over her labored breathing she heard the psychogeneticist sit down and leisurely light another cigar.

Finally she opened her eyes. "Even *you* found out something that time. There's no use asking me what he meant."

"Isn't there? Who will dance the part of The Student on opening night?"

"Ruy. Only, he will really do little beyond provide support to the prima ballerina, The Nightingale, that is, at the beginning and end of the ballet."

"And who plays The Nightingale?"

"Ruy hired a professional—La Tanid."

Bell blew a careless cloud of smoke toward the ceiling. "Are you sure *you* aren't going to take the part?"

"The role is strenuous in the extreme. For me, it would be a physical impossibility."

"Now."

"What do you mean—*now?*"

He looked at her sharply. "You know very well what I mean. You know it so well your whole body is quivering. Your ballet première is four weeks off—but you know and I know that Ruy has already seen it. Interesting." He tapped coolly at his cigar. "*Almost as interesting as your belief he saw you playing the part of The Nightingale.*"

Anna clenched her fists. This must be faced rationally. She inhaled deeply, and slowly let her breath out. "How can even *he* see things that haven't happened yet?"

"I don't know for sure. But I can guess, and so could you if you'd calm down a bit. We do know that the pineal is a residuum of the single eye that our very remote seagoing ancestors had in the centre of their fishy foreheads. Suppose this fossil eye, now buried deep in the normal brain, were reactivated. What would we be able to see with it? Nothing spatial, nothing dependent on light stimuli. But let us approach the problem inductively. I shut one eye. The other can fix Anna van Tuyl in a depthless visual plane. But with two eyes I can follow you stereoscopically, as you move about in space. Thus, adding an eye adds a dimension. With the pineal as a third eye I should be able to follow you through time. So Ruy's awakened pineal should permit him at least a hazy glimpse of the future."

"What a marvellous—and terrible gift."

"But not without precedent," said Bell. "I suspect that a more or less reactivated pineal lies behind every case of clairvoyance collected in the annals of para-psychology. And I can think of at least one historical instance in which the pineal has actually tried to penetrate the forehead, though evidently only in monolobate form. All Buddhist statues carry a mark on the forehead symbolic of an 'inner eye'. From what we know now, Budda's 'inner eye' was something more than symbolic."

"Granted. But a time-sensitive pineal still doesn't explain the pain in Ruy's hump. Nor the hump itself, for that matter."

"What," said Bell, "makes you think the hump is anything more than what it seems—a spinal disease characterized by a growth of laminated tissue?"

"It's not that simple, and you know it. You're familiar with 'phantom limb' cases, such as where the amputee retains an illusion of sensation or pain in the amputated hand or foot?"

He nodded.

She continued: "But you know, of course, that amputation isn't an absolute prerequisite to a 'phantom'. A child born armless may experience phantom limb sensations for years. Suppose such a child were thrust into some improbable armless society, and their psychiatrists tried to cast his sensory pattern into their own mould. How could the child explain to them the miracle of arms, hands, fingers—things of which he had occasional sensory intimations, but had never seen, and could hardly imagine? Ruy's case is analogous. He is four-limbed and presumably springs from normal stock. Hence the phantom sensations in his hump point toward a *potential* organ—a foreshadowing of the future, rather than toward memories of a limb once possessed. To use a brutish example, Ruy is like the tadpole rather than the snake. The snake had his legs briefly, during the evolutionary recapitulation of his embryo. The tadpole has yet to shed his tail and develop legs. But one might assume that each has some faint phantom sensoria of legs."

Bell appeared to consider this. "That still doesn't account for Ruy's pain. I wouldn't think the process of growing a tail would be painful for a tadpole, nor a phantom limb for Ruy—if it's inherent in his physical structure. But be that as it may, from all indications he is still going to be in considerable pain when that narcotic wears off. What are you going to do for him *then?* Section the ganglia leading to his hump?"

"Certainly not. Then he would *never* be able to grow that extra organ. Anyhow, even in normal phantom limb cases, cutting nerve tissue doesn't help. Excision of neuromas from limb stumps brings only temporary relief—and may actually aggravate a case of hyperaesthesia. No, phantom pain sensations are central rather then peripheral. However, as a temporary analgesic I shall try a two per cent solution of novocaine near the proper thoracic ganglia." She looked at her watch. "We'd better be getting back to him."

CHAPTER EIGHT

Anna withdrew the syringe needle from the man's side and rubbed the last puncture with an alcoholic swab.

"How do you feel, Ruy?" asked Bell.

The woman stooped beside the sterile linens and looked at the face of the prone man. "He doesn't," she said uneasily. "He's out cold again."

"Really?" Bell bent over beside her and reached for the man's pulse. "But it was only two per cent novocaine. Most remarkable."

"I'll order a counter-stimulant," said Anna nervously. "I don't like this."

"Oh, come, girl. Relax. Pulse and respiration normal. In fact, I think you're nearer collapse than he. This is very interesting . . ." His voice trailed off in musing surmise. "Look, Anna, there's nothing to keep both of us here. He's in no danger whatever. I've got to run along. I'm sure you can attend to him."

I know, she thought. You want me to be alone with him.

She acknowledged his suggestion with a reluctant nod of her head, and the door closed behind his chuckle.

For some moments thereafter she studied in deep abstraction the regular rise and fall of the man's chest.

So Ruy Jacques had set another medical precedent. He'd received a local anaesthetic that should have done nothing more than desensitise the deformed growth in his back for an hour or two. But here he lay, in apparent coma, just as though under a general cerebral anaesthetic.

Her frown deepened.

X-ray plates had showed his dorsal growth simply as a compacted mass of cartilaginous laminated tissue (the same as hers) penetrated here and there by neural ganglia. In deadening those ganglia she should have accomplished nothing more than local anaesthetization of that tissue mass, in the same manner that one anaesthetizes an arm or leg by deadening the appropriate spinal ganglion. But the actual result was not local, but general. It was as though one had administered a mild local to the radial nerve of the forearm to deaden pain in the hand, but had instead anaesthetized the cerebrum.

And *that,* of course, was utterly senseless, completely incredible, because anaesthesia works from the higher neural centres down, not vice versa. Deadening a certain area of the parietal lobe could kill sensation in the radial nerve and the hand, but a hypo in the radial nerve wouldn't knock out the parietal lobe of the cerebrum, because the parietal organization was neurally superior. Analogously, anaesthetizing Ruy Jacques' hump shouldn't have deadened his entire cerebrum, because certainly his cerebrum was to be presumed neurally superior to that dorsal malformation.

To be presumed . . .

But with Ruy Jacques, presumptions were—invalid.

So *that* was what Bell had wanted her to discover. Like some sinister reptile of the Mesozoic, Ruy Jacques had *two* neural organizations, one in his skull and one on his back, the latter being superior to, and in some degree controlling, the one in his skull, just as the cerebral cortex in human beings and other higher animals assists and screens the work of the less intricate cerebellum, and just as the cerebellum governs the still more primitive medulla oblongata in the lower vertebrata, such as in frogs and fishes. In anaesthetizing his bump, she had disrupted communications in his highest centres of consciousness, and in anaesthetizing the higher, dorsal centre, she had apparently simultaneously deactivated his "normal" brain.

As full realization came, she grew aware of a curious numbness in her thighs, and of faint overtones of mingled terror and awe in the giddy throbbing in her forehead. Slowly, she sank into the bedside chair.

For as this man was, so must she become. The day lay ahead when *her* pineal growths must stretch to the point of disrupting the grey matter in her occipital lobes, and destroy her ability to read. And the time must come, too, when *her* dorsal growth would inflame her whole body with its anguished writhing, as it had done his, and try with probable equal futility to burst its bonds.

And all of this must come—soon; before her ballet première, certainly. The enigmatic skein of the future would be unravelled to her evolving intellect even as it now was to Ruy Jacques'. She could find all the answers she sought . . . Dream's end . . . The Nightingale's death song . . . The Rose. And she would find them whether she wanted to or not.

She groaned uneasily.

At the sound, the man's eyelids seemed to tremble; his breathing slowed momentarily, then became faster.

She considered this in perplexity. He was unconscious, certainly; yet he made definite responses to aural stimuli. Possibly she had anaesthetized neither member of the hypothetical brain-pair, but had merely cut, temporarily, their lines of intercommunication, just as one might temporarily disorganize the brain of a laboratory animal by anaesthetizing the pons Varolii linking the two cranial hemispheres.

Of one thing she was sure: Ruy Jacques, unconscious, and temporarily mentally disintegrate, was not going to conform to the behavior long standardized for other unconscious and disintegrate mammals. Always one step beyond what she ever expected. Beyond man. Beyond genius.

She arose quietly and tiptoed the short distance to the bed.

When her lips were a few inches from the artist's right ear, she said softly: "What is your name?"

The prone figure stirred uneasily. His eyelids fluttered, but did not open. His wine-colored lips parted, then shut, then opened again. His reply was a harsh, barely intelligible whisper: "Zhak."

"What are you doing?"

"Searching . . ."

"For what?"

"A red rose."

"There are many red roses."

Again his somnolent, metallic whisper: "No, there is but one."

She suddenly realized that her own voice was becoming tense, shrill. She forced it back into a lower pitch. "Think of that rose. Can you see it?"

"Yes . . . yes!"

She cried: "*What is the rose?*"

It seemed that the narrow walls of the room would clamour forever their outraged metallic modesty, if something hadn't frightened away their pain. Ruy Jacques opened his eyes and struggled to rise on one elbow.

On his sweating forehead was a deep frown. But his eyes were apparently focused on nothing in particular, and despite his seemingly purposive motor reaction, she knew that actually her question had but thrown him deeper into his strange spell.

Swaying a little on the dubious support of his right elbow, he muttered: "*You* are not the rose . . . not yet . . . not yet . . ."

She gazed at him in shocked stupor as his eyes closed slowly and he slumped back on the sheet. For a long moment there was no sound in the room but his deep and rhythmic breathing.

CHAPTER NINE

Without turning form her glum perusal of the clinic grounds framed in her window, Anna threw the statement over her shoulder as Bell entered the office. "Your friend Jacques refuses to return for a check-up. I haven't seen him since he walked out a week ago."

"Is that fatal?"

She turned blood-shot eyes on him. "Not to Ruy."

The man's expression twinkled. "He's your patient, isn't he? It's your duty to make a house call."

"I certainly shall. I was going to call him on the visor to make an appointment."

"He doesn't have a visor. Everybody just walks in. There's something doing in his studio nearly every night. If you're bashful, I'll be glad to take you."

"No thanks. I'll go alone—early."

Bell chuckled. "I'll see you tonight."

CHAPTER TEN

Number 98 was a sad, ramshackled, four-storey, plaster-front affair, evidently thrown up during the materials shortage of the late forties.

Anna took a deep breath, ignored the unsteadiness of her knees, and climbed the half dozen steps of the front stoop.

There seemed to be no exterior bell. Perhaps it was inside. She pushed the door in and the waning evening light followed her into the hall. From somewhere came a frantic barking, which was immediately silenced.

Anna peered uneasily up the rickety stairs, then whirled as a door opened behind her.

A fuzzy canine muzzle thrust itself out of the crack in the doorway and growled cautiously. And in the same crack, farther up, a dark wrinkled face looked out at her suspiciously. "Whaddaya want?"

Anna retreated half a step. "Does he bite?"

"Who, Mozart? Nah, he couldn't dent a banana." The creature added with anile irrelevance, "Ruy gave him to me because Mozart's dog followed him to the grave."

"Then this is where Mr. Jacques lives?"

"Sure, fourth floor, but you're early." The door opened wider. "Say, haven't I seen you somewhere before?"

Recognition was simultaneous. It was that animated stack of purple dresses, the ancient vendress of love philters.

"Come in, dearie," purred the old one, "and I'll mix you up something special."

"Never mind," said Anna hurriedly. "I've got to see Mr. Jacques." She turned and ran toward the stairway.

A horrid floating cackle whipped and goaded her flight, until she stumbled out on the final landing and set up an insensate skirling on the first door she came to.

From within an irritated voice called: "Aren't you getting a little tired of that? Why don't you come in and rest your knuckles?"

"Oh." She felt faintly foolish. "It's me—Anna van Tuyl."

"Shall I take the door off its hinges, doctor?"

Anna turned the knob and stepped inside.

Ruy Jacques stood with his back to her, palette in hand, facing an easel bathed in the slanting shafts of the setting sun. He was apparently blocking in a caricature of a nude model lying, face averted, on a couch beyond the easel.

Anna felt a sharp pang of disappointment. She'd wanted him to herself a little while. Her glance flicked about the studio.

Framed canvases obscured by dust were stacked willy-nilly about the walls of the big room. Here and there were bits of statuary. Behind a nearby screen the disarray of a cot peeped out at her. Beyond the screen was a wire-phono. In the opposite wall was a door that evidently opened into the model's dressing alcove. In the opposite corner stood a battered electronic piano which she recognized as the Fourier audiosynthesizer type.

She gave an involuntary gasp as the figure of a man suddenly separated from the piano and bowed to her.

Colonel Grade.

So the lovely model with the invisible face must be—Martha Jacques.

There was no possibility of mistake, for now the model had turned her face a little, and acknowledged Anna's faltering stare with complacent mockery.

Of all evenings, why did Martha Jacques have to pick *this* one?

The artist faced the easel again. His harsh jeer floated back to the psychiatrist: "Behold the perfect female body!"

Perhaps it was the way he said this that saved her. She had a fleeting suspicion that he had recognized her disappointment, had anticipated the depths of her gathering despair, and had deliberately shaken her back into reality.

In a few words he had borne upon her the idea that his enormously complex mind contained neither love nor hate, even for his wife, and that while he found in her a physical perfection suitable for transference to canvas or marble, nevertheless he writhed in a secret torment over this very perfection, as though in essence the woman's physical beauty simply stated a lack he could not name, and might never know.

With a wary, futile motion he lay aside his brushes and palette. "Yes, Martha is perfect, physically and mentally, and knows it." He laughed brutally. "What she doesn't know, is that frozen beauty admits of no plastic play of meaning. There's nothing behind perfection, because it has no meaning but itself."

There was a clamour on the stairs. "Hah!" cried Jacques. "*More* early-comers. The word must have got around that Martha brought the liquor. School's out, Mart. Better hop into the alcove and get dressed."

Matthew Bell was among the early arrivals. His face lighted up when he saw Anna, then clouded when he picked out Grade and Martha Jacques.

Anna noticed that his mouth was twitching worriedly as he motioned to her.

"What's wrong?" she asked.

"Nothing—yet. But I wouldn't have let you come if I'd known *they'd* be here. Has Martha given you any trouble?"

"No. Why should she? I'm here ostensibly to observe Ruy in my professional capacity."

"You don't believe that, and if you get careless, *she* won't either. So watch your step with Ruy while Martha's around. And even when she's not around. Too many eyes here—Security men—Grade's crew. Just don't let Ruy involve you in anything that might attract attention. So much for that. Been here long?"

"I was the first guest—except for *her* and Grade."

"Hmm. I should have escorted you. Even though you're his psychiatrist, this sort of thing sets her to thinking."

"I can't see the harm of coming alone. It isn't as though Ruy were going to try to make love to me in front of all these people."

"That's exactly what it is as though!" He shook his head and looked about him. "Believe me, I know him better than you. The man is insane . . . unpredictable."

Anna felt a tingle of anticipation . . . or was it of apprehension? "I'll be careful," she said.

"Then come on. If I can get Martha and Ruy into one of their eternal Science-versus-Art arguments, I believe they'll forget about you."

CHAPTER ELEVEN

"I repeat," said Bell, "we are watching the germination of another Renaissance. The signs are unmistakable, and should be of great interest to practicing sociologists and policemen." He turned from the little group beginning to gather about him and beamed artlessly at the passing fate of Colonel Grade.

Grade paused. "And just what are the signs of a renaissance?" he demanded.

"Mainly climatic change and enormously increased leisure, Colonel. Either alone can make a big difference, combined, the result is multiplicative rather than additive."

Anna watched Bell's eyes rove the room and join with those of Martha Jacques, as he continued: "Take temperature. In seven thousand B.C. *homo sapiens*, even in the Mediterranean area, was a shivering nomad; fifteen or twenty centuries later a climatic upheaval had turned Mesopotamia, Egypt and the Yangste valley into garden spots, and the first civilizations were born. Another warm period extending over several centuries and ending about twelve hundred A.D. launched the Italian Renaissance and the great Ottoman culture, before the temperature started falling again. Since the middle of the seventeenth century the mean temperature of New York City has been increasing at the rate of about one-tenth of a degree per year. In another century palm trees will be commonplace on Fifth Avenue." He broke off and bowed benignantly. "Hello, Mrs. Jacques. I was just mentioning that in past renaissances, mild climates and bounteous crops gave man leisure to think, and to create."

When the woman shrugged her shoulders and made a gesture as though to walk on, Bell continued hurriedly: "Yes, *those* renaissances gave us the Parthenon, *The Last Supper*, the Taj Mahal. *Then*, the *artist* was supreme. But this time it might not happen that way, because we face a simultaneous technologic and climatic optimum. Atomic energy has virtually abolished labor as such, but without the international leavening of common art that united the first Egyptian, Sumerian, Chinese and Greek cities. Without pausing to consolidate his gains, the scientist rushes on to greater things, to Sciomnia, and to a Sciomnic power source"—he exchanged a sidelong look with the woman scientist—"a machine which, we are informed, may overnight fling man toward the nearer stars. When that day comes, the artist is through . . . unless . . ."

"Unless what?" asked Martha Jacques coldly.

"Unless this Renaissance, sharpened and intensified as it has been by its double maxima of climate and science, is able to force a response comparable to that of the Aurignacean Renaissance of twenty-five thousand B.C., to wit, the flowering of the Cro-Magnon, the first of the modern men. Wouldn't it be ironic if our greatest scientist solved Sciomnia, only to come a cropper at the hands of what may prove to be one of the first primitive specimens of *homo superior*—her husband?"

Anna watched with interest as the psychogeneticist smiled engagingly at Martha Jacques' frowning face, while at the same time he looked beyond her to catch the eye of Ruy Jacques, who was plinking in apparent aimlessness at the keyboard of the Fourier piano.

Martha Jacques said curtly: "I'm afraid, Dr. Bell, that I can't get too excited about your Renaissance. When you come right down to it, local humanity, whether dominated by art or science, is nothing but a temporary surface scum on a primitive backwoods planet."

Bell nodded blandly. "To most scientists Earth is admittedly commonplace. Psychogeneticists, on the other hand, consider this planet and its people one of the wonders of the universe."

"Really?" asked Grade. "And just what have we got here that they don't have on Betelgeuse?"

"Three things," replied Bell. "One—Earth's atmosphere has enough carbon dioxide to grow the forest-spawning grounds of man's primate ancestors, thereby ensuring an unspecialized, quasi-erect, manually-activated species capable of indefinite psychophysical development. It might take the saurian life of a desert planet another billion years to evolve an equal physical and mental structure. Two—that same atmosphere had a surface pressure of 760 mm. of mercury and a mean temperature of about 25 degrees Centigrade—excellent conditions for the transmission of sound, speech, and song; and those early men took to it like a duck to water. Compare the difficulty of communication by direct touching of antennae, as the arthropodic pseudo-homindal citizens of certain airless worlds must do. Three—the solar spectrum within its very short frequency range of 760 to 390 millimicrons offers seven colors of remarkable variety and contrast, which our ancestors quickly made their own. From the beginning, they could see that they moved in multichrome beauty. Consider the ultra-sophisticate dwelling in a dying sun system—and pity him for he can see only red and a little infra red."

"If that's the only difference," snorted Grade, "I'd say you psychogeneticists were getting worked up over nothing."

Bell smiled past him at the approaching figure of Ruy Jacques. "You may be right, of course, Colonel, but I think you're missing the point. To the psychogeneticist it appears that terrestrial environment is promoting the evolution of a most extraordinary being—a type of *homo* whose energies beyond the barest necessities are devoted to strange, unproductive activities. And to what end? We don't know—yet. But we can guess. Give a psychogeneticist Eohippus and the grassy plains, and he'd predict the modern horse. Give him archeopteryx and a dense atmosphere, and he could imagine the swan. Give him *h. sapiens* and a two-day work week, or better yet, Ruy Jacques and a no-day work week, and what will he predict?"

"The poorhouse?" asked Jacques, sorrowfully.

Bell laughed. "Not quite. An evolutionary spurt, rather. As *sapiens* turns more and more into his abstract world of the arts, music in particular, the psychogeneticist foresees increased communication in terms of music. This might require certain cerebral realignments in *sapiens*, and perhaps the development of special membranous neural organs—which in turn might lead to completely new mental and physical abilities, and the conquest of new dimensions—just as the human tongue eventually developed from a tasting organ into a means of long distance vocal communication."

"Not even in Ruy's Science/Art diatribes," said Mrs. Jacques, "have I heard greater nonsense. If this planet is to have any future worthy of the name, you can be sure it will be through the leadership of her scientists."

"I wouldn't be too sure," countered Bell. "The artist's place in society has advanced tremendously in the past half-century. And I mean the minor artist—who is identified simply by his profession and not by any exceptional reputation. In our own time we have seen the financier forced to extend social equality to the scientist. And today the palette and musical sketch pad are gradually toppling the test tube and the cyclotron from their pedestals. In the first Renaissance the merchant and soldier inherited the ruins of church and feudal empire; in this one we peer through the crumbling walls of capitalism and nationalism and see the artist . . . or the scientist . . . ready to emerge as the cream of society. The question is, *which one?*"

"For the sake of law and order," declared Colonel Grade, "it must be the scientist, working in the defence of his country. Think of the military insecurity of an art-dominated society. If—"

Ruy Jacques broke in: "There is only one point on which I must disagree with you." He turned a disarming smile on his wife. "I really don't see how the scientist fits into the picture at all. Do you, Martha? For the artist is *already* supreme. He dominates the scientist, and if he likes, he is perfectly able to draw upon his more sensitive intuition for those various restatements of artistic principles that the scientists are forever trying to fob off on a decreasingly gullible public under the guise of novel scientific laws. I say that the artist is aware of those 'new' laws long before the scientist, and has the option of presenting them to the public in a pleasing art form or as a dry, abstruse equation. He may, like da Vinci, express his discovery of a beautiful curve in the form of a breathtaking spiral staircase in a *château* at Blois, or, like Dürer, he may analyze the curve mathematically and announce its logarithmic formula. In either event he anticipates Descartes, who was the first mathematician to rediscover the logarithmic spiral."

The woman laughed grimly. "All right. *You're* an artist. Just what scientific law have *you* discovered?"

"I have discovered," answered the artist with calm pride, "what will go down in history as 'Jacques' Law of Stellar Radiation'."

Anna and Bell exchanged glances. The older man's look of relief said plainly: "The battle is joined; they'll forget you."

Martha Jacques peered at the artist suspiciously. Anna could see that the woman was genuinely curious but caught between her desire to crush, to damn any such amateurish "discovery" and her fear that she was being led into a trap. Anna herself, after studying the exaggerated innocence of the man's wide, unblinking eyes knew immediately that he was subtly enticing the woman out on the rotten limb of her own dry perfection.

In near-hypnosis Anna watched the man draw a sheet of paper from his pocket. She marvelled at the superb blend of diffidence and braggadocio with which he unfolded it and handed it to the woman scientist.

"Since I can't write, I had one of the fellows write it down for me, but I think he got it right," he explained. "As you see, it boils down to seven prime equations."

Anna watched a puzzled frown steal over the woman's brow. "But each of these equations expands into hundreds more, especially the seventh, which is the longest of them all." The frown deepened. "Very interesting. Already I see hints of the Russell diagram . . ."

The man started. "What! H. N. Russell, who classified stars into spectral classes? You mean he scooped me?"

"Only if your work is accurate, which I doubt."

The artist stammered: "But—"

"And here," she continued in crisp condemnation, "is nothing more than a restatement of the law of light-pencil wavering, which explains why stars twinkle and planets don't, and which has been known for two hundred years."

Ruy Jacques' face lengthened lugubriously.

The woman smiled grimly and pointed. "These parameters are just a poor approximation of the Bethe law of nuclear fission in stars—old since the thirties."

The man stared at the scathing finger. "Old . . . ?"

"I fear so. But still not bad for an amateur. If you kept at this sort of thing all your life, you might eventually develop something novel. But this is a mere hodge-podge, a rehash of material any real scientist learned in his teens."

"But Martha," pleaded the artist, "surely it isn't *all* old?"

"I can't say with certainty, of course," returned the woman with malice-edged pleasure, "until I examine every sub-equation. I can only say that, fundamentally, scientists long ago anticipated the artist, represented by the great Ruy Jacques. In the aggregate, your amazing Law of Stellar Radiation has been known for two hundred years or more."

Even as the man stood there, as though momentarily stunned by the enormity of his defeat, Anna began to pity his wife.

The artist shrugged his shoulders wistfully. "Science versus Art. So the artist has given his all, and lost. Jacques' Law must sing its swan song, then be forever forgotten." He lifted a resigned face toward the scientist. "Would you, my dear, administer the *coup de grâce* by setting up the proper co-ordinates in the Fourier audiosynthesizer?"

Anna wanted to lift a warning hand, cry out to the man that he was going too far, that the humiliation he was preparing for his wife was unnecessary, unjust, and would but thicken the wall of hatred that cemented their antipodal souls together.

But it was too late. Martha Jacques was already walking toward the Fourier piano, and within seconds had set up the polar-defined data and had flipped the toggle switch. The psychiatrist found her mind and tongue to be literally paralyzed by the swift movement of this unwitting drama, which was now toppling over the brink of its tragicomic climax.

A deep silence fell over the room.

Anna caught an impression of avid faces, most of whom—Jacques' most intimate friends—would understand the nature of his little playlet and would rub salt into the abraded wound he was delivering his wife.

Then in the space of three seconds, it was over.

The Fourier piano had synthesized the seven equations, six short, one long, into their tonal equivalents, and it was over.

Dorran, the orchestra leader, broke the uneasy stillness that followed. "I say, Ruy old chap," he blurted, "just what is the difference in 'Jacques' Law of Stellar Radiation' and 'Twinkle, twinkle, little star'?"

Anna, in mingled amusement and sympathy, watched the face of Martha Jacques slowly turn crimson.

The artist replied in amazement. "Why, now that you mention it, there does seem to be a little resemblance."

"It's a dead ringer!" cried a voice.

" 'Twinkle, twinkle' is an old continental folk tune," volunteered another. "I once traced it from Haydn's 'Surprise Symphony' back to the fourteenth century."

"Oh, but that's quite impossible," protested Jacques. "Martha has just stated that science discovered it first, only two hundred years ago."

The woman's voice dripped *aqua regia.* "You planned this deliberately, just to humiliate me in front of these . . . these clowns."

"Martha, I assure you . . . !"

"I'm warning you for the last time, Ruy. If you ever again humiliate me, I'll probably kill you!"

Jacques backed away in mock alarm until he was swallowed up in a swirl of laughter.

The group broke up, leaving the two women alone. Suddenly aware of Martha Jacques' bitter scrutiny. Anna flushed and turned toward her.

Martha Jacques said: "Why can't you make him come to his senses? I'm paying you enough."

Anna gave her a slow wry smile. "Then I'll need your help. And you aren't helping when you deprecate his sense of values—odd though they may seem to you."

"But Art is really so *foolish!* Science—"

Anna laughed shortly. "You see? Do you wonder he avoids you?"

"What would *you* do?"

"*I?*" Anna swallowed dryly.

Martha Jacques was watching her with narrowed eyes. "Yes, you. *If you wanted him?*"

Anna hesitated, breathing uneasily. Then gradually her eyes widened, became dreamy and full, like moons rising over the edge of some unknown, exotic land. Her lips opened with a nerveless fatalism. She didn't care what she said:

"I'd forget that I want, above all things, to be beautiful. I would think only of him. I'd wonder what he's thinking, and I'd forsake my mental integrity and try to think as he thinks. I'd learn to see through his eyes, and to hear through his ears. I'd sing over his successes, and hold my tongue when he failed. When he's moody and depressed, I wouldn't probe or insist that-I-could-help-you-if-you'd-only-let-me. Then—"

Martha Jacques snorted. "In short, you'd be nothing but a selfless shadow, devoid of personality or any mind or individuality of your own. That might be all right for one of your type. But for a scientist, the very thought is ridiculous!"

The psychiatrist lifted her shoulders delicately. "I agree. It *is* ridiculous. What *sane* woman at the peak of her profession would suddenly toss up her career to merge—you'd say 'submerge'—her identity, her very existence, with that of an utterly alien male mentality?"

"What woman, indeed?"

Anna mused to herself, and did not answer. Finally she said: "And yet, that's the price; take it or leave it, they say. What's a girl to do?"

"Stick up for her rights!" declared Martha Jacques spiritedly.

"All hail to unrewarding perseverance!" Ruy Jacques was back, swaying slightly. He pointed his half-filled glass toward the ceiling and shouted: "Friends! A toast! Let us drink to the two charter members of the Knights of the Crimson Grail." He bowed in saturnine mockery to his glowering wife. "To Martha! May she soon solve the Jacques Rosette and blast humanity into the heavens!"

Simultaneously he drank and held up a hand to silence the sudden spate of jeers and laughter. Then, turning toward the now apprehensive psychiatrist, he essayed a second bow of such sweeping grandiosity that his glass was upset. As he straightened, however, he calmly traded glasses with her. "To my old schoolteacher, Dr. van Tuyl. A nightingale whose secret ambition is to become as beautiful as a red red red rose. May Allah grant her prayers." He blinked at her beatifically in a sudden silence. "What was that comment, doctor?"

"I said you were a drunken idiot," replied Anna. "But let it pass." She was panting, her head whirling. She raised her voice to the growing cluster of faces. "Ladies and gentlemen, I offer you the third seeker of the grail! A truly great artist. Ruy Jacques, a child of the coming epoch, whose sole aim is not aimlessness, as he would like you to think, but a certain marvellous rose. Her curling petals shall be of subtle texture, yet firm withal, and brilliant red. It is this rose that he must find, to save his mind and body, and to put a soul in him."

"She's right!" cried the artist in dark glee. "To Ruy Jacques, then! Join in, everybody. The party's on Martha!"

He downed his glass, then turned a suddenly grave face to his audience. "But it's really such a pity in Anna's case, isn't it? Because her cure is so simple."

The psychiatrist listened; her head was throbbing dizzily.

"As any *competent* psychiatrist could tell her," continued the artist mercilessly, "she has identified herself with the nightingale in her ballet. The nightingale isn't much to look at. On top it's a dirty brown; at bottom, you might say it's a drab grey. But ah! The soul of this plain little bird! Look into my soul, she pleads. Hold me in your strong arms, look into my soul, and think me as lovely as a red rose."

Even before he put his wineglass down on the table, Anna knew what was coming. She didn't need to watch the stiffening cheeks and flaring nostrils of Martha Jacques, nor the sudden flash of fear in Bell's eyes, to know what was going to happen next.

He held out his arms to her, his swart satyr-face nearly impassive save for its eternal suggestion of sardonic mockery.

"You're right," she whispered, half to him, half to some other part of her, listening, watching. "I *do* want you to hold me in your arms and think me beautiful. But you can't, because you don't love me. It won't work. Not yet. Here, I'll prove it.

As from miles and centuries away, she heard Grade's horrified gurgle.

But her trance held. She entered the embrace of Ruy Jacques, and held her face up to his as much as her spine would permit, and closed her eyes.

He kissed her quickly on the forehead and released her. "There! Cured!"

She stood back and surveyed him thoughtfully. "I wanted you to see for yourself, that nothing can be beautiful to you—at least not until you learn to regard someone else as highly as you do Ruy Jacques."

Bell had drawn close. His face was wet, grey. He whispered: "Are you two insane? Couldn't you save this sort of thing for a less crowded occasion?"

But Anna was rolling rudderless in a fatalistic calm. "I had to show him something. Here. Now. He might never have tried it if he hadn't had an audience. Can you take me home now?"

"Worst thing possible," replied Bell agitatedly. "That'd just confirm Martha's suspicions." He looked around nervously. "She's gone. Don't know whether that's good or bad. But Grade's watching us. Ruy, if you've got the faintest intimations of decency, you'll wander over to that group of ladies and kiss a few of them. May throw Martha off the scent. Anna, you stay here. Keep talking. Try to toss it off as an amusing incident." He gave a short strained laugh. "Otherwise you're going to wind up as the First Martyr in the Cause of Art."

"I beg your pardon, Dr. van Tuyl."

It was Grade. His voice was brutally cold, and the syllables were clipped from his lips with a spine-tingling finality.

"Yes, Colonel?" said Anna nervously.

"The Security Bureau would like to ask you a few questions."

"Yes?"

Grade turned and stared icily at Bell. "It is preferred that the interrogation be conducted in private. It should not take long. If the lady would kindly step into the model's dressing room, my assistant will take over from there."

"Dr. van Tuyl was just leaving," said Bell huskily. "Did you have a coat, Anna?"

With a smooth unobtrusive motion Grade unsnapped the guard on his hip holster. "If Dr. van Tuyl leaves the dressing room within ten minutes, alone, she may depart from the studio in any manner she pleases."

Anna watched her friend's face become even paler. He wet his lips, then whispered, "I think you'd better go, Anna. Be careful."

CHAPTER TWELVE

The room was small and nearly bare. Its sole furnishings were an ancient calendar, a clothes tree, a few stacks of dusty books, a table (bare save for a roll of canvas patching tape) and three chairs.

In one of the chairs, across the table, sat Martha Jacques.

She seemed almost to smile at Anna; but the amused curl of her beautiful lips was totally belied by her eyes, which pulsed hate with the paralyzing force of physical blows.

In the other chair sat Willie the Cork, almost unrecognizable in his groomed neatness.

The psychiatrist brought her hand to her throat as though to restore her voice, and at the movement, she saw from the corner of her eye that Willie, in a lightning motion, had simultaneously thrust his hand into his coat pocket, invisible below the table. She slowly understood that he held a gun on her.

The man was the first to speak, and his voice was so crisp and incisive that she doubted her first intuitive recognition. "Obviously, I shall kill you if you attempt any unwise action. So please sit down, Dr. van Tuyl. Let us put our cards on the table."

It was too incredible, too unreal, to arouse any immediate sense of fear. In numb amazement she pulled out the chair and sat down.

"As you may have suspected for some time," continued the man curtly, "I am a Security agent."

Anna found her voice. "I know only that I am being forcibly detained. What do you want?"

"Information, doctor. What government do you represent?"

"None."

The man fairly purred. "Don't you realize, doctor, that as soon as you cease to answer responsively, I shall kill you?"

Anna van Tuyl looked from the man to the woman. She thought of circling hawks, and felt the intimations of terror. What could she have done to attract such wrathful attention? She didn't know. But then, *they* couldn't be sure about *her*, either. This man didn't want to kill her until he found out more. And by that time surely he'd see that it was all a mistake.

She said: "Either I am a psychiatrist attending a special case, or I am not. I am in no position to prove the positive. Yet, by syllogistic law, you must accept it as a possibility until you prove the negative. Therefore, until you have given me an opportunity to explain or disprove any evidence to the contrary, you can never be certain in your own mind that I am other than what I claim to be."

The man smiled, almost genially. "Well put, doctor. I hope they've been paying you what you are worth." He bent forward suddenly. "Why are you trying to make Ruy Jacques fall in love with you?"

She stared back with widening eyes. "What did you say?"

"Why are you trying to make Ruy Jacques fall in love with you?"

She could meet his eyes squarely enough, but her voice was now very faint: "I didn't understand you at first. You said . . . that I'm trying to make him fall in love with me." She pondered this for a long wondering moment, as though the idea were utterly new. "And I guess . . . it's true."

The man looked blank, then smiled with sudden appreciation. "You *are* clever. Certainly, you're the first to try *that* line. Though I don't know what you expect to gain with your false candour."

"False? Didn't you mean it yourself? No, I see you didn't. But Mrs. Jacques does. And she hates me for it. But I'm just part of the bigger hate she keeps for *him*. Even her Sciomnia equation is just part of that hate. She isn't working on a biophysical weapon just because she's a patriot, but more to spite him, to show him that her science is superior to—"

Martha Jacques' hand lashed viciously across the little table and struck Anna in the mouth.

The man merely murmured: "Please control yourself a bit longer, Mrs. Jacques. Interruptions from outside would be most inconvenient at this point." His humorless eyes returned to Anna. "One evening a week ago, when Mr. Jacques was under your care at the clinic, you left stylus and paper with him."

Anna nodded. "I wanted him to attempt automatic writing."

"What is 'automatic writing'?"

"Simply writing done while the conscious mind is absorbed in a completely extraneous activity, such as music. Mr. Jacques was to focus his attention on certain music composed by me while holding stylus and paper in his lap. If his recent inability to read and write was caused by some psychic block, it was quite possible that his subconscious mind might bypass the block, and he would write—just as one 'doodles' unconsciously when talking over the visor."

He thrust a sheet of paper at her. "Can you identify this?"

What was he driving at? She examined the sheet hesitantly. "It's just a blank sheet from my private monogrammed stationery. Where did you get it?"

"From the pad you left with Mr. Jacques."

"So?"

"We also found another sheet from the same pad under Mr. Jacques' bed. It had some interesting writing on it."

"But Mr. Jacques personally reported nil results."

"He was probably right."

"But you said he wrote something?" she insisted; momentarily her personal danger faded before her professional interest.

"I didn't say *he* wrote anything."

"Wasn't it written with that same stylus?"

"It was. But I don't think he wrote it. It wasn't in his handwriting."

"That's often the case in automatic writing. The script is modified according to the personality of the dissociated subconscious unit. The alteration is sometimes so great as to be unrecognizable as the handwriting of the subject."

He peered at her keenly. "This script was perfectly recognizable, Dr. van Tuyl. I'm afraid you've made a grave blunder. Now, shall I tell you in *whose* handwriting?"

She listened to her own whisper: "Mine?"

"Yes."

"What does it say?"

"You know very well."

"But I don't." Her underclothing was sticking to her body with a damp clammy feeling. "At least you ought to give me a chance to explain it. May I see it?"

He regarded her thoughtfully for a moment, then reached into his pocket sheaf. "Here's an electrostat. The paper, texture, ink, everything, is a perfect copy of your original."

She studied the sheet with a puzzled frown. There were a few lines of scribblings in purple. But it *wasn't* in her handwriting. In fact, it wasn't even handwriting—just a mass of illegible scrawls!

Anna felt a thrill of fear. She stammered: "What are you trying to do?"

"You don't deny you wrote it?"

"Of course I deny it." She could no longer control the quaver in her voice. Her lips were leaden masses, her tongue a stone slab. "It's—unrecognizable . . ."

The Cork floated with sinister patience. "In the upper left hand corner is your monogram: 'A. vT.', the same as on the first sheet. You will admit that, at least?"

For the first time, Anna really examined the presumed trio of initials enclosed in the familiar ellipse. The ellipse was there. But the print within it was—gibberish. She seized again at the first sheet—the blank one. The feel of the paper, even the smell, stamped it as genuine. It had been hers. But the monogram! "Oh no!" she whispered.

Her panic-stricken eyes flailed about the room. The calendar . . . same picture of the same cow . . . *but the rest . . . !* A stack of books in the corner . . . titled in gold leaf . . . gathering dust for months . . . the label on the roll of patching tape on the table . . . even the watch on her wrist.

Gibberish. She could no longer read. She had forgotten how. Her ironic gods had chosen this critical moment to blind her with their brilliant bounty.

Then take it! And play for time!

She wet trembling lips. "I'm unable to read. My reading glasses are in my bag, outside." She returned the script. "If *you'd* read it, I might recognize the contents."

The man said: "I thought you might try this, just to get my eyes off you. If you don't mind, I'll quote from memory:

" '—what a queer climax for The Dream! Yet, inevitable. Art versus Science decrees that one of us must destroy the Sciomniac weapon; but that could wait until we become more numerous. So, what I do is for him alone, and his future depends on appreciating it. Thus, Science bows to Art, but even Art isn't all. The Student must know the one greater thing when he sees The Nightingale dead, for only then will he recognize . . .' "

He paused.

"Is that all?" asked Anna.

"That's all."

"Nothing about a . . . rose?"

"No. What is 'rose' a code word for?"

Death? mused Anna. Was the rose a cryptolalic synonym for the grave? She closed her eyes and shivered. Were those really *her* thoughts, impressed into the mind and wrist of Ruy Jacques from some grandstand seat at her own ballet three weeks hence? But after all, why was it so impossible? Coleridge claimed *Kublai Khan* had been dictated to him through automatic writing. And that English mystic, William Blake, freely acknowledged being the frequent amanuensis for an unseen personality. And there were numerous other cases. So, from some unseen time and place, the mind of Anna van Tuyl had been attuned to that of Ruy Jacques, and his mind had momentarily forgotten that both of them could no longer write, and had recorded a strange reverie.

It was then that she noticed the—whispers.

No—not whispers—not exactly. More like rippling vibrations, mingling, rising, falling. Her heart beats quickened when she realized that their eerie pattern was soundless. It was as though something in her mind was suddenly vibrating *en rapport* with a subetheric world. Messages were beating at her for which she had no tongue or ear; they were beyond sound—beyond knowledge, and they swarmed dizzily around her from all directions. From the ring she wore. From the bronze buttons of her jacket. From the vertical steam piping in the corner. From the metal reflector of the ceiling light.

And the strongest and most meaningful of all showered steadily from the invisible weapon. The Cork grasped in his coat pocket. Just as surely as though she had seen it done, she knew that the weapon had killed in the past. And not just once. She found herself attempting to unravel those thought residues of death—once—twice—three times . . . beyond which they faded away into steady, indecipherable time-muted violence.

And now that gun began to scream: "Kill! Kill! Kill!"

She passed her palm over her forehead. Her whole face was cold and wet. She swallowed noisily.

CHAPTER THIRTEEN

Ruy Jacques sat before the metal illuminator near his easel, apparently absorbed in the profound contemplation of his goatish features, and oblivious to the mounting gaiety about him. In reality he was almost completely lost in a soundless, sardonic glee over the triangular death-struggle that was nearing its climax beyond the inner wall of his studio, and which was magnified in his remarkable mind to an incredible degree by the paraboloid mirror of the illuminator.

Bell's low urgent voice began hacking at him again. "Her blood will be on your head. All you need to do is to go in there. Your wife wouldn't permit any shooting with you around."

The artist twitched his misshapen shoulders irritably. "*Maybe.* But why should I risk my skin for a silly little nightingale?"

"Can it be that your growth beyond *sapiens* has served simply to sharpen your objectivity, to accentuate your inherent egregious want to identity with even the best of your fellow creatures? Is the indifference that has driven Martha nearly insane in a bare decade now too ingrained to respond to the first known female of your own unique breed?" Bell sighed heavily. "You don't have to answer. The very senselessness of her impending murder amuses you. Your nightingale is about to be impaled on her thorn—for nothing—as always. Your sole regret at the moment is that you can't twit her with the assurance that you will study her corpse diligently to find there the rose you seek."

"Such unfeeling heartlessness," said Jacques in regretful agreement, "is only to be expected in one of Martha's blunderings. I mean The Cork, of course. Doesn't he realize that Anna hasn't finished the score of her ballet? Evidently has no musical sense at all. I'll bet he was even turned down for the policemen's charity quarter. You're right, as usual, doc. We must punish such philistinism." He tugged at his chin, then rose from the folding stool.

"What are you going to do?" demanded the other sharply.

The artist weaved toward the phono cabinet. "Play a certain selection from Tchaikovsky's *Sixth.* If Anna's half the girl you think, she and Peter Ilyitch will soon have Mart eating out of their hands."

Bell watching him in anxious, yet half-trusting frustration as the other selected a spool from his library of electronic recordings and inserted it into the playback sprocket. In mounting mystification, he saw Jacques turn up the volume control as far as it would go.

CHAPTER FOURTEEN

Murder, a one-act play directed by Mrs. Jacques, thought Anna. With sound effects by Mr. Jacques. But the facts didn't fit. It was unthinkable that Ruy would do anything to accommodate his wife. If anything, he would try to thwart Martha. But what was his purpose in starting off in the finale of the first movement of the *Sixth?* Was there some message there that he was trying to get across to her?

There was. She had it. She was going to live. If—

"In a moment," she told The Cork in a tight voice, "you are going to snap off the safety catch of your pistol, revise slightly your estimated line of fire, and squeeze the trigger. Ordinarily you could accomplish all three acts in almost instantaneous sequence. At the present moment, if I tried to turn the table over on you, you could put a bullet in my head before I could get well started. But in another sixty seconds you will no longer have that advantage, because your motor nervous system will be laboring under the superimposed pattern of the extraordinary Second Movement of the symphony that we now hear from the studio."

The Cork started to smile, then he frowned faintly. "What do you mean?"

"All motor acts are carried out in simple rhythmic patterns. We walk in the two-four time of the march. We waltz, use a pickaxe, and manually grasp or replace objects in three-four rhythm."

"This nonsense is purely a play for time," interjected Martha Jacques. "Kill her."

"It is a fact," continued Anna hurriedly. (Would that Second Movement never begin?) "A decade ago, when there were still a few factories using hand-assembly methods, the workmen speeded their work by breaking down the task into these same elemental rhythms, aided by appropriate music." (There! It was beginning! The immortal genius of that suicidal Russian was reaching across a century to save her!) "It so happens that the music you are hearing *now* is the Second Movement that I mentioned, and it's neither two-four nor three-four but *five*-four, an oriental rhythm that gives difficulty even to skilled occidental musicians and dancers. Subconsciously you are going to try to break it down into the only rhythms to which your motor nervous system is attuned. But you can't. Nor can *any* occidental, even a professional dancer, unless he has had special training"—her voice wobbled slightly—"in Delcrozian eurhythmics."

She crashed into the table.

Even though she had known that this must happen, her success was so complete, so overwhelming, that it momentarily appalled her.

Martha Jacques and The Cork had moved with anxious, rapid jerks, like puppets in a nightmare. But their rhythm was all wrong. With their ingrained four-time motor responses strangely modulated by a five-time pattern, the result was inevitably the arithmetical composite of the two: a neural beat, which could activate muscle tissue only when the two rhythms were in phase.

The Cork had hardly begun his frantic, spasmodic squeeze of the trigger when the careening table knocked him backward to the floor, stunned, beside Martha Jacques. It required but an instant for Anna to scurry around and extract the pistol from his numbed fist.

Then she pointed the trembling gun in the general direction of the carnage she had wrought and fought an urge to collapse against the wall.

She waited for the room to stop spinning, for the white, glass-eyed face of Martha Jacques to come into focus against the fuzzy background of the cheap paint-daubed rug. And then the eyes of the woman scientists flickered and closed.

With a wary glance at the weapon muzzle, The Cork gingerly pulled a leg from beneath the table edge: "You have the gun," he said softly. "You can't object if I assist Mrs. Jacques?"

"I *do* object," said Anna faintly. "She's merely unconscious . . . feels nothing. I want her to stay that way for a few minutes. If you approach her or make any unnecessary noise, I will probably kill you. So—both of you must stay here until Grade investigates. I know you have a pair of handcuffs. I'll give you ten seconds to lock yourself to that steam pipe in the corner—hands *behind* you, please."

She retrieved the roll of adhesive patching tape from the floor and fixed several strips across the agent's lips, following with a few swift loops around the ankles to prevent him stamping his feet.

A moment later, her face a damp mask, she closed the door leisurely behind her and stood there, breathing deeply and searching the room for Grade.

He was standing by the studio entrance, staring at her fixedly. When she favored him with a glassy smile, he simply shrugged his shoulders and began walking slowly toward her.

In growing panic her eyes darted about the room. Bell and Ruy Jacques were leaning over the phono, apparently deeply absorbed in the racing clangor of the music. She saw Bell nod a covert signal in her direction, but without looking directly at her. She tried not to seem hurried as she strolled over to join them. She knew that Grade was now walking toward them and was but a few steps away when Bell lifted his head and smiled.

"Everything all right?" said the psychogeneticist loudly.

She replied clearly: "Fine. Mrs. Jacques and a Security man just wanted to ask some questions." She drew in closer. Her lips framed a question to Bell: "Can Grade hear?"

Bell's lips formed a soft, nervous guttural: "No. He's moving off toward the dressing room door. If what I suspect happened behind that door is true, you have about ten seconds to get out of here. And then you've got to hide." He turned abruptly to the artist. "Ruy, you've got to take her down into the Via. Right now—*immediately*. Watch your opportunity and lose her when no one is looking. It shouldn't be too hard in that mob."

Jacques shook his head doubtfully. "Martha isn't going to like this. You know how strict she is on etiquette. I think there's a very firm statement in Emily Post that the host should never, never, *never* walk out on his guests before locking up the liquor and silverware. Oh, well, if you insist."

CHAPTER FIFTEEN

"Tell ya what the professor's gonna do, ladies and gentlemen. He's gonna defend not just one paradox. Not just two. But seventeen! In the space of one short hour, and without repeating himself, and including one he just thought up five minutes ago: 'Security is dangerous.' "

Ruy frowned, then whispered to Anna: "That was for us. He means Security men are circulating. Let's move on. Next door. They won't look for a woman there."

Already he was pulling her away toward the chess parlor. They both ducked under the For Men Only sign (which she could no longer read), pushed through the bat-wing doors, and walked unobtrusively down between the wall and a row of players. One man looked up briefly out of the corner of his eyes as they passed.

The woman paused uneasily. She had sensed the nervousness of the barker even before Ruy, and now still fainter impressions were beginning to ripple over the straining surface of her mind. They were coming from that chess player: from the coins in his pocket; from the lead weights of his chess pieces; and especially from the weapon concealed somewhere on him. The resonant histories of the chess pieces and coins she ignored. They held the encephalographic residua of too many minds. The invisible gun was clearer. There was something abrupt and violent, alternating with a more subtle, restrained rhythm. She put her hand to her throat as she considered one interpretation: *Kill—but wait.* Obviously, he'd dare not fire with Ruy so close.

"Rather warm here, too," murmured the artist. "Out we go."

As they stepped out into the street again, she looked behind her and saw that the man's chair was empty.

She held the artist's hand and pushed and jabbed after him, deeper into the revelling sea of humanity.

She ought to be thinking of ways to hide, of ways to use her new sensory gift. But another, more imperative train of thought continually clamored at her, until finally she yielded to a gloomy brooding.

Well, it was true. She wanted to be loved, and she wanted Ruy to love her. And he knew it. Every bit of metal on her shrieked her need for his love.

But—was she ready to love him? No! How could she love a man who lived only to paint that mysterious unpaintable scene of the nightingale's death, and who loved only himself? He was fascinating, but what sensible woman would wreck her career for such unilateral fascination? Perhaps Martha Jacques was right, after all.

"So you got him, after all!"

Anna whirled toward the crazy crackle, nearly jerking her hand from Ruy's grasp.

The vendress of love-philters stood leaning against the front centre pole of her tent, grinning toothily at Anna.

While the young woman stared dazedly at her, Jacques spoke up crisply: "Any strange men been around, Violet?"

"Why, Ruy," she replied archly, "I think you're jealous. What kind of men?"

"Not the kind that haul you off to the alcoholic ward on Saturday nights. Not city dicks. Security men—quiet—seem slow, but really fast—see everybody—everything."

"Oh, *them.* Three went down the street two minutes ahead of you."

He rubbed his chin. "That's not so good. They'll start at that end of the Via and work up toward us until they meet the patrol behind us."

"Like grains of wheat between the millstones," cackled the crone. "*I knew* you'd turn to crime, sooner or later, Ruy. You were the only tenant I had who paid the rent regular."

"Mart's lawyer did that."

"Just the same, it looked mighty suspicious. You want to try the alley behind the tent?"

"Where does it lead?"

"Cuts back into the Via, at White Rose Park."

Anna started. "White rose?"

"We were there that first night," said Jacques. "You remember it—big rose-walled cul-de-sac. Fountain. Pretty, but not for us, not now. Has only one entrance. We'll have to try something else."

The psychiatrist said hesitantly: "No, wait."

For some moments she had been struck by the sinister contrast in this second descent into the Via and the irresponsible gaiety of that first night. The street, the booths, the laughter seemed the same, but really weren't. It was like a familiar musical score, subtly altered by some demoniac hand, raised into some harsh and fatalistic minor key. It was like the second movement of Tchaikovsky's *Romeo and Juliet:* all the bright promises of the first movement were here, but repetition had transfigured them into frightful premonitions.

She shivered. That second movement, that echo of destiny, was sweeping through her in ever faster tempo, as though impatient to consummate its assignation with her. Come safety, come death, she must yield to the pattern of repetition.

Her voice had a dream-like quality: "Take me again to the White Rose Park."

"What! Talk sense! Out here in the open you may have a chance."

"But I *must* go there. Please, Ruy. I think it's something about a white rose. Don't look at me as though I were crazy. Of course I'm crazy. If you don't want to take me, I'll go alone. But I'm going."

His hard eyes studied her in speculative silence, then he looked away. As the stillness grew, his face mirrored his deepening introspection. "At that, the possibilities are intriguing. Martha's stooges are sure to look in on you. But will they be able to see you? Is the hand that wields the pistol equally skilled with the brush and palette? Unlikely. Art and Science again. Pointillist school versus police school. A good one on Martha—if it works. Anna's dress is green. Complement of green is purple. Violet's dress should do it."

"My dress?" cried the old woman. "What are you up to, Ruy?"

"Nothing. Luscious. I just want you to take off one of your dresses. The outer one will do."

"Sir!" Violet began to sputter in barely audible gasps.

Anna had watched all this in vague detachment, accepting it as one of the man's daily insanities. She had no idea what he wanted with a dirty old purple dress, but she thought she knew how she could get it for him, while simultaneously introducing another repetitive theme into this second movement of her hypothetical symphony.

She said: "He's willing to make you a fair trade, Violet."

The spluttering stopped. The old woman eyed them both suspiciously. "Meaning what?"

"He'll drink one of your love potions."

The leathery lips parted in amazement. "*I'm* agreeable, if *he* is, but I know he isn't. Why, that scamp doesn't love any creature in the whole world, except maybe himself."

"And yet he's ready to make a pledge to his beloved," said Anna.

The artist squirmed. "I like you, Anna, but I won't be trapped. Anyway, it's all nonsense. What's a glass of acidified water between friends?"

"The pledge isn't to me, Ruy. It's to a Red Rose." He peered at her curiously. "Oh? Well, if it will please you . . . All right, Violet, but off with that dress before you pour up."

Why, wondered Anna, do I keep thinking his declaration of love to a red rose is my death sentence? It's moving too fast. Who, what—is The Red Rose? The Nightingale dies in making the white rose red. So *she*—or I—can't be The Red Rose. Anyway, The Nightingale is ugly, and The Rose is beautiful. And why must The Student have a Red Rose? How will it admit him to his mysterious dance?

"Ah, Madame De Medici is back." Jacques took the glass and purple bundle the old woman put on the table. "What are the proper words?" he asked Anna.

"Whatever you want to say."

His eyes, suddenly grave, looked into hers. He said quietly: "If ever The Red Rose presents herself to me, I shall love her forever."

Anna trembled as he upended the glass.

CHAPTER SIXTEEN

A little later they slipped into the Park of the White Roses. The buds were just beginning to open, and thousands of white floreate eyes blinked at them in the harsh artificial light. As before, the enclosure was empty, and silent, save for the chattering splashing of its single fountain.

Anna abandoned a disconnected attempt to analyze the urge that had brought her here a second time. It's all too fatalistic, she thought, too involved. If I've entrapped myself, I can't feel bitter about it. "Just think," she murmured aloud, "in less than ten minutes it will all be over, one way or the other."

"Really? But where's my red rose?"

How could she even *consider* loving this jeering beast? She said coldly: "I think you'd better go. It may be rather messy in here soon." She thought of how her body would look, sprawling, misshapen, uglier than ever. She couldn't let him see her that way.

"Oh, we've plenty of time. No red rose, eh? Hmm. It seems to me, Anna, that you're composing yourself for death prematurely. There really is that little matter of the rose to be taken care of first, you know. As The Student, I must insist on my rights."

What made him be this way? "Ruy, please . . ." Her voice was trembling, and she was suddenly very near to tears.

"There, dear, don't apologize. Even the best of us are thoughtless at times. Though I must admit, I never expected such lack of consideration, such poor manners, in *you*. But then, at heart, you aren't really an artist. You've no appreciation of form." He began to untie the bundled purple dress, and his voice took on the argumentative dogmatism of a platform lecturer. "The perfection of form, of technique, is the highest achievement possible to the artist. When he subordinates form to subject matter, he degenerates eventually into a boot-lick, a scientist, or, worst of all, a Man with a Message. Here, catch!" He tossed the gaudy garment at Anna, who accepted it in rebellious wonder.

Critically, the artist eyed the nauseating contrast of the purple and green dresses, glanced momentarily toward the semi-circle of white-budded wall beyond, and then continued: "There's nothing like a school-within-a-school to squeeze dry the dregs of form. And whatever their faults, the pointillists of the impressionist movement could depict color with magnificent depth of chroma. Their palettes held only the spectral colors, and they never mixed them. Do you know why the Seines of Seurat are so brilliant and luminous? It's because the water is made of dots of pure green, blue, red and yellow, alternating with white in the proper proportion." He motioned with his hand, and she followed as he walked slowly on around the semi-circular gravel path. "What a pity Martha isn't here to observe our little experiment in tricolor stimulus. Yes, the scientific psychologists finally gave arithmetical vent to what the pointillists knew long before them—that a mass of points of any three spectral colors—or of one color and its complementary color—can be made to give any imaginable hue simply by varying their relative proportion."

Anna thought back to that first night of the street dancers. So *that* was why his green and purple polka dot academic gown had first seemed white!

At his gesture, she stopped and stood with her humped back barely touching the mass of scented buds. The arched entrance was a scant hundred yards to her right. Out in the Via an ominous silence seemed to be gathering. The Security men were probably roping off the area, certain of their quarry. In a minute or two, perhaps sooner, they would be at the archway, guns drawn.

She inhaled deeply and wet her lips.

The man smiled. "You hope I know what I'm doing, don't you? So do I."

"I think I understand your theory," said Anna, "but I don't think it has much chance of working."

"Tush, child." He studied the vigorous play of the fountain speculatively. "The pigment should never harangue the artist. You're forgetting that there isn't really such a color as white. The pointillists knew how to simulate white with alternating dots of primary colors long before the scientists learned to spin the same colors on a disc. And those old masters could even make white from just two colors: a primary and its complementary color. Your green dress is our primary; Violet's purple dress is its complementary. Funny, mix 'em as pigments into a homogeneous mass, and you get brown. But daub 'em on the canvas side by side, stand back the right distance, and they blend into white. All you have to do is hold Vi's dress at arm's length, at your side, with a strip of rosebuds and green leaves looking out between, and you'll have that white rose you came here in search of."

She demurred: "But the angle of visual interruption won't be small enough to blend the colors into white, even if the police don't come any nearer than the archway. The eye sees two objects as one only when the visual angle between the two is less than sixty seconds of arc."

"That old canard doesn't apply too strictly to colors. The artist relies more on the suggestibility of the mind rather than on the mechanical limitations of the retina. Admittedly, if our lean-jawed friends stared in your direction for more than a fraction of a second, they'd see you not as a whitish blur, but as a woman in green holding out a mass of something purple. But they aren't going to give your section of the park more than a passing glance." He pointed past the fountain toward the opposite horn of the semi-circular path. "I'm going to stand over *there,* and the instant someone sticks his head in through the archway, I'm going to start walking. Now, as every artist knows, normal people in western cultures absorb pictures from left to right, because they're laevo-dextro readers. So our agent's first glance will be toward you, and then his attention will be momentarily distracted by the fountain in the centre. And before he can get back to you, I'll start walking, and his eyes will have to come on to me. His attentive transition, of course, must be sweeping and imperative, yet so smooth, so subtle, that he will suspect no control. Something like Alexander's painting, *Lady on a Couch,* where the converging stripes of the lady's robe carry the eye forcibly from the lower left margin to her face at the upper right."

Anna glanced nervously toward the garden entrance, then whispered entreatingly, "Then you'd better go. You've got to be beyond the fountain when they look in."

He sniffed. "All right, I know when I'm not wanted. That's the gratitude I get for making you into a rose."

"I don't care a tinker's damn for a *white* rose. Scat!"

He laughed, then turned and started on around the path.

As Anna followed the graceful stride of his long legs, her face began to writhe in alternate bitterness and admiration. She groaned softly. "You—*fiend!* You gorgeous, egotistical, insufferable, unattainable *FIEND!* You aren't elated because you're saving my life; *I* am just a blotch of pigment in your latest masterpiece. *I hate you!*"

He was past the fountain now, and nearing the position he had earlier indicated.

She could see that he was looking toward the archway. She was afraid to look there.

Now he must stop and wait for his audience.

Only he didn't. His steps actually hastened.

That meant . . .

The woman trembled, closed her eyes, and froze into a paralytic stupor through which the crunch of the man's sandals filtered as from a great distance, muffled, mocking.

And then, from the direction of the archway, came the quiet scraping of more footsteps.

In the next split second she would know life or death.

But even now, even as she was sounding the iciest depths of her terror, her lips were moving with the clear insight of imminent death. "No, I don't hate you. I love you, Ruy. I have loved you from the first."

At that instant a blue-hot ball of pain began crawling slowly up within her body, along her spine, and then outward between her shoulder blades, into her spinal hump. The intensity of that pain forced her slowly to her knees and pulled her head back in an invitation to scream.

But no sound came from her convulsing throat.

It was unendurable, and she was fainting.

The sound of footsteps died away down the Via. At least Ruy's ruse had worked.

And as the mounting anguish spread over her back, she understood that all sound had vanished with those retreating footsteps, forever, because she could no longer hear, nor use, her vocal chords. She had forgotten how, but she didn't care.

For her hump had split open, and something had flopped clumsily out of it, and she was drifting gently outward into blackness.

CHAPTER SEVENTEEN

The glum face of Ruy Jacques peered out through the studio window into the night-awakening Via.

Before I met you, he brooded, loneliness was a magic, ecstatic blade drawn across my heart strings; it healed the severed strands with every beat, and I had all that I wanted save what I had to have—the Red Rose. My search for that Rose alone matters! I must believe this. I must not swerve, even for the memory of you, Anna, the first of my own kind I have ever met. I must not wonder if they killed you, nor even care. They must have killed you . . . It's been three weeks.

Now I can seek The Rose again. Onward into loneliness.

He sensed the nearness of familiar metal behind him. "Hello, Martha," he said, without turning. "Just get here?"

"Yes. How's the party going?" Her voice seemed carefully expressionless.

"Fair. You'll know more when you get the liquor bill."

"Your ballet opens tonight, doesn't it?" Still that studied tonelessness.

"You know damn well it doesn't." His voice held no rancour. "La Tanid took your bribe and left for Mexico. It's just as well. I can't abide a prima ballerina who'd rather eat than dance." He frowned slightly. Every bit of metal on the woman was singing in secret elation. She was thinking of a great triumph—something far beyond her petty victory in wrecking his opening night. His searching mind caught hints of something intricate, but integrated, completed—and deadly. Nineteen equations. The Jacques Rosette. Sciomnia.

"So you've finished your toy," he murmured. "You've got what you wanted, and you think you've destroyed what I wanted."

Her reply was harsh, suspicious. "How did you know, when not even Grade is sure? Yes, my weapon is finished. I can hold in one hand a thing that can obliterate your whole Via in an instant. A city, even a continent would take but a little longer. Science versus Art! Bah! This concrete embodiment of biophysics is the answer to your puerile Renaissance—your precious feather-bed world of music and painting! You and your kind are helpless when I and my kind choose to act. In the final analysis Science means *force*—the ability to control the minds and bodies of men."

The shimmering surface of his mind was now catching the faintest wisps of strange, extraneous impressions, vague and disturbing, and which did not seem to originate from metal within the room. In fact, he could not be sure they originated from metal at all.

He turned to face her. "How can Science control all men when it can't even control individuals—Anna van Tuyl, for example?"

She shrugged her shoulders. "You're only partly right. They failed to find her, but her escape was pure accident. In any event, she no longer represents any danger to me or to the political group that I control. Security has actually dropped her from their shoot-on-sight docket."

He cocked his head slightly and seemed to listen. "*You* haven't, I gather."

"You flatter her. She was never more than a pawn in our little game of Science versus Art. Now that she's off the board, and I've announced checkmate against you, I can't see that she matters."

"So Science announces checkmate? Isn't that a bit premature? Suppose Anna shows up again, with or without the conclusion of her ballet score? Suppose we find another prima? What's to keep us from holding *The Nightingale and the Rose* tonight, as scheduled?"

"Nothing," replied Martha Jacques coolly. "Nothing at all, except that Anna van Tuyl has probably joined your former prima at the South Pole by this time, and anyway, a new ballerina couldn't learn the score in the space of two hours, even if you found one. If this wishful thinking comforts you, why, pile it on!"

Very slowly Jacques put his wine glass on the nearby table. He washed his mind clear with a shake of his satyrish head, and strained every sense into receptivity. Something was being etched against that slurred background of laughter and clinking glassware. Then he sensed—or heard—something that brought tiny beads of sweat to his forehead and made him tremble.

"What's the matter with you?" demanded the woman.

As quickly as it had come, the chill was gone.

Without replying, he strode quickly into the centre of the studio.

"Fellow revellers!" he cried. "Let us prepare to double, nay, *re*-double our merriment!" With sardonic satisfaction he watched the troubled silence spread away from him, faster and faster, like ripples around a plague spot.

When the stillness was complete, he lowered his head, stretched out his hand as if in horrible warning, and spoke in the tense spectral whisper of Poe's Roderick Usher:

"*Madmen! I tell you that she now stands without the door!*"

Heads turned; eyes bulged toward the entrance.

There, the door knob was turning slowly.

The door swung in, and left a cloaked figure framed in the doorway.

The artist started. He had been certain that this must be Anna.

It *must* be Anna, yet it could not be. The once frail, cruelly bent body now stood superbly erect beneath the shelter of the cloak. There was no hint of spinal deformity in this woman, and there were no marring lines of pain about her faintly smiling mouth and eyes, which were fixed on his. In one graceful motion her hands reached up beneath the cloak and set it back on her shoulders. Then, after an almost instantaneous *demi-plie*, she floated twice, like some fragile flower dancing in a summer breeze, and stood before him *sur les pointes*, with her cape billowing and fluttering behind her in mute encore.

Jacques looked down into eyes that were dark fires. But her continued silence was beginning to disturb and irritate him. He responded to it almost by reflex, refusing to admit to himself his sudden enormous happiness: "A woman without a tongue! By the gods! Her sting is drawn!" He shook her by the shoulders, roughly, as though to punish this fault in her that had drawn the familiar acid to his mouth.

Her arms moved up, cross-fashioned, and her hands covered his. She smiled, and a harp-arpeggio seemed to wing across his mind, and the tones rearranged themselves into words, like images on water suddenly smooth:

"Hello again, darling. Thanks for being glad to see me."

Something in him collapsed. His arms dropped and he turned his head away. "It's no good, Anna. Why'd you come back? Everything's falling apart. Even our ballet. Martha bought out our prima."

Again that lilting cascade of tones in his brain: "I know, dear, but it doesn't matter. I'll sub beautifully for La Tanid. I know the part perfectly. And I know The Nightingale's death song, too."

"Hah!" he laughed harshly, annoyed at his exhibition of discouragement and her ready sympathy. He stretched his right leg into a mocking *pointe tendue*. "Marvellous! You have the exact amount of drab clumsiness that we need in a Nightingale. And as for the death song, why of course you and you alone know how that ugly little bird feels when"—his eyes were fixed on her mouth in sudden, startled suspicion, and he finished the rest of the sentence inattentively, with no real awareness of its meaning—"when she dies on the thorn."

As he waited, the melody formed, vanished, and reformed and resolved into the strangest thing he had ever known: "What you are thinking is true. My lips do not move. I cannot talk. I've forgotten how, just as we both forgot how to read and write. But even the plainest nightingale can sing, and make the white rose red."

This was Anna transfigured. Three weeks ago he had turned his back and left a diffident disciple to an uncertain fate. Confronting him now was this dark angel bearing on her face the luminous stamp of death. In some manner that he might never learn, the gods had touched her heart and body, and she had borne them straightway to him.

He stood, musing in alternate wonder and scorn. The old urge to jeer at her suddenly rose in his gorge. His lips contorted, then gradually relaxed, as an indescribable elation began to grow within him.

He could thwart Martha yet!

He leaped to the table and shouted: "Your attention, friends! In case you didn't get all this, we've found a ballerina! The curtain rises tonight on our première performance, as scheduled!"

Over the clapping and cheering, Dorran, the orchestra conductor, shouted: "Did I understand that Dr. van Tuyl has finished The Nightingale's death song? We'll have to omit that tonight, won't we? No chance to rehearse . . ."

Jacques looked down at Anna for a moment. His eyes were very thoughtful when he replied: "She says it won't be omitted. What I mean is, keep that thirty-eight rest sequence in the death scene. Yes, do that, and we shall see . . . what we shall see . . ."

"Thirty-eight rests as presently scored, then?"

"Yes. All right, boys and girls. Let's be on our way. Anna and I will follow shortly."

CHAPTER EIGHTEEN

Now it was a mild evening in late June, in the time of the full blooming of the roses, and the Via floated in a heady, irresistible tide of attar. It got into the tongues of the children and lifted their laughter and shouts an octave. It stained the palettes of the artists along the sidewalks, so that, despite the bluish glare of the artificial lights, they could paint only in delicate crimsons, pinks, yellows and whites. The petalled current swirled through the side-shows and eternally new exhibits and gave them a veneer of perfection; it eddied through the canvas flap of the vendress of love philters and erased twenty years from her face. It brushed a scented message across the responsive mouths of innumerable pairs of lovers, blinding them to the appreciative gaze of those who stopped to watch them.

And the lovely dead petals kept fluttering through the introspective mind of Ruy Jacques, clutching and whispering. He brushed their skittering dance aside and considered the situation with growing apprehension. In her recurrent Dreams he thought, Anna had always awakened just as the Nightingale began her death song. But now she knew the death song. So she knew the Dream's end. Well, it must not be so bad, or she wouldn't have returned. Nothing was going to happen, not really. He shot the question at her: There was no danger any more, was there? Surely the ballet would be a superb success? She'd be enrolled with the immortals.

Her reply was grave, yet it seemed to amuse her. It gave him a little trouble; there were no words for its exact meaning. It was something like "Immortality begins with death."

He glanced at her face uneasily. "Are you looking for trouble?"

"Everything will go smoothly."

After all, he thought, she believes she has looked into the future and has seen what will happen.

"The Nightingale will not fail The Student," she added with a queer smile. "You'll get your Red Rose."

"You can be plainer than that," he muttered. "Secrets . . . secrets . . . why all this you're-too-young-to-know business?"

But she laughed in his mind, and the enchantment of that laughter took his breath away. Finally he said: "I admit I don't know what you're talking about. But if you're about to get involved in anything on my account, forget it. I won't have it."

"Each does the thing that makes him happy. The Student will never be happy until he finds The Rose that will admit him to his Dance. The Nightingale will never be happy until The Student holds her in his arms and thinks her as lovely as a Red Rose. I think we may both get what we want."

He growled: "You haven't the faintest idea what you're talking about."

"Yes I have, especially right now. For ten years I've urged people not to inhibit their healthy inclinations. At the moment I don't have any inhibitions at all. It's a wonderful feeling. I've never been so happy, I think. For the first and last time in my life, I'm going to kiss you."

Her hand tugged at his sleeve. As he looked down into that enchanted face, he knew that this night was hers, that she was privileged in all things, and that whatever she willed must yield to her.

They had stopped at the temporarily-erected stage-door. She rose *sur les pointes*, took his face in her palms, and like a hummingbird drinking her first nectar, kissed him on the mouth.

A moment later she led him into the dressing-room corridor.

He stifled a confused impulse to wipe the back of his hand across his lips. "Well . . . well, just remember to take it easy. Don't try to be spectacular. The artificial wings won't take it. Canvas stretched on duralite and piano wire calls for adagio. A fast pirouette, and they're ripped off. Besides, you're out of practice. Control your enthusiasm in Act I or you'll collapse in Act II. Now, run on to your dressing room. Cue in five minutes!"

CHAPTER NINETEEN

There is a faint, yet distinct anatomical difference in the foot of the man and that of the woman, which keeps him earthbound, while permitting her, after long and arduous training, to soar *sur les pointes*. Owing to the great and varied beauty of the arabesques open to the ballerina poised on her extended toes, the male danseur at one time existed solely as a shadowy *porteur*, and was needed only to supply unobtrusive support and assistance in the exquisite *enchainements* of the ballerina. Iron muscles in leg and torso are vital in the danseur, who must help maintain the illusion that his whirling partner is made of fairy gossamer, seeking to wing skyward from his restraining arms.

All this flashed through the incredulous mind of Ruy Jacques as he whirled in a double *fouetté* and followed from the corner of his eye the grey figure of Anna van Tuyl, as, wings and arms aflutter, she pirouetted in the second *enchainement* of Act I, away from him and toward the *maître de ballet*.

It was all well enough to give the illusion of flying, of alighting apparently weightless, in his arms—that was what the audience loved. But that it could ever *really* happen—*that* was simply impossible. Stage wings—things of grey canvas and duralite frames—couldn't subtract a hundred pounds from one hundred and twenty.

And yet . . . it had seemed to him that she had actually flown.

He tried to pierce her mind—to extract the truth from the bits of metal about her. In a gust of fury he dug at the metal outline of those remarkable wings.

In the space of seconds his forehead was drenched in cold sweat, and his hands were trembling. Only the fall of the curtain on the first act saved him as he stumbled through his exit *entrechat*.

What had Matt Bell said? "To communicate in his new language of music, one may expect our man of the future to develop specialized membranous organs, which, of course, like the tongue, will have dual functional uses, possibly leading to the conquest of time as the tongue has conquered space."

Those wings were not wire and metal, but flesh and blood.

He was so absorbed in his ratiocination that he failed to become aware of an acutely unpleasant metal radiation behind him until it was almost upon him. It was an intricate conglomeration of matter, mostly metal, resting perhaps a dozen feet behind his back, showering the lethal presence of his wife.

He turned with nonchalant grace to face the first tangible spawn of the Sciomnia formula.

It was simply a black metal box with a few dials and buttons. The scientist held it lightly in her lap as she sat at the side of the table.

His eyes passed slowly from it to her face, and he knew that in a matter of minutes Anna van Tuyl—and all Via Rosa beyond her—would be soot floating in the night wind.

Martha Jacques' face was sublime with hate. "Sit down," she said quietly.

He felt the blood leaving his cheeks. Yet he grinned with a fair show of geniality as he dropped into the chair. "Certainly. I've got to kill time somehow until the end of Act I."

She pressed a button on the box surface.

His volition vanished. His muscles were locked, immobile. He could not breathe.

Just as he was convinced that she planned to suffocate him, her finger made another swift motion toward the box, and he sucked in a great gulp of air. His eyes could move a little, but his larnyx was still paralyzed.

Then the moments began to pass, endlessly, it seemed to him.

The table at which they sat was on the right wing of the stage. The woman sat facing into the stage, while his back was to it. She followed the preparations of the troupe for Act II with moody, silent eyes, he with straining ears and metal-empathic sense.

Only when he heard the curtain sweeping across the street-stage to open the second act did the woman speak.

"She *is* beautiful. And so graceful with those piano-wire wings, just as if they were part of her. I don't wonder she's the first woman who ever really interested you. Not that you really *love* her. You'll never love anyone."

From the depths of his paralysis he studied the etched bitterness of the face across the table. His lips were parched, and his throat a desert.

She thrust a sheet of paper at him, and her lip curled. "Are you still looking for that rose? Search no further, my ignorant friend. There it is—Sciomnia, complete, with its nineteen sub-equations."

The lines of unreadable symbols dug like nineteen relentless harpoons ever deeper into his twisting, racing mind.

The woman's face grimaced in fleeting despair. "Your own wife solves Sciomnia and you condescend to keep her company until you go on again at the end of Act III. I wish I had a sense of humor. All I knew was to paralyze your spinal column. Oh, don't worry. It's purely temporary. I just didn't want you to warn her. And I know what torture it is for you not to be able to talk." She bent over and turned a knurled knob on the side of the black steel box. "There, at least you can whisper. You'll be completely free after the weapon fires."

His lips moved in a rapid slur. "Let us bargain, Martha. Don't kill her. I swear never to see her again."

She laughed, almost gaily.

He pressed on. "But you have all you really want. Total fame, total power, total knowledge, the body perfect. What can her death and the destruction of the Via give you?"

"Everything."

"Martha, for the sake of all humanity to come, don't do this thing! I know something about Anna van Tuyl that perhaps even Bell doesn't—something she has concealed very adroitly. That girl is the most precious creature on earth!"

"It's precisely because of that opinion—which I do not necessarily share—that I shall include her in my general destruction of the Via." Her mouth slashed at him: "Oh, but it's wonderful to see you squirm. For the first time in your miserable thirty years of life you really want something. You've got to crawl down from that ivory tower of indifference and actually plead with me, whom you've never even taken the trouble to despise. You and your damned art. Let's see it save her now!"

The man closed his eyes and breathed deeply. In one rapid, complex surmise, he visualized an *enchainement* of postures, a *pas de deux* to be played with his wife as an unwitting partner. Like a skilled chess player, he had analyzed various variations of her probable responses to his gambit, and he had every expectation of a successful climax. And therein lay his hesitation, for success meant his own death.

Yes, he could not eradicate the idea from his mind. Even at this moment he believed himself intrigued more by the novel, if macabre, possibilities inherent in the theme rather than its superficial altruism. While seeming to lead Martha through an artistic approach to the murder of Anna and the Via, he could, in a startling, off key climax, force her to kill him instead. It amused him enormously to think that afterward, she would try to reduce the little comedy to charts and graph paper in an effort to discover how she had been hypnotized.

It was the first time in his life that he had courted physical injury. The emotional sequence was new, a little heady. He could do it; he need only be careful about his timing.

After hurling her challenge at him, the woman had again turned morose eyes downstage, and was apparently absorbed in a grudging admiration of the second act. But that couldn't last long. The curtain on Act II would be her signal.

And there it was, followed by a muffled roar of applause. He must stall her through most of Act III, and then . . .

He said quickly: "We still have a couple of minutes before the last act begins, where The Nightingale dies on the thorn. There's no hurry. You ought to take time to do this thing properly. Even the best assassinations are not purely a matter of science. I'll wager you never read De Quincey's little essay on murder as a fine art. No? You see, you're a neophyte, and could do with a few tips from an old hand. You must keep in mind your objects: to destroy both the Via and Anna. But mere killing won't be enough. You've got to make *me* suffer too. Suppose you shoot Anna when she comes on at the beginning of Act III. Only fair. The difficulty is that Anna and the others will never know what hit them. You don't give them the opportunity to bow to you as their conqueror."

He regarded her animatedly. "You see, can't you, my dear, that some extraordinarily difficult problems in composition are involved?"

She glared at him, and seemed about to speak.

He continued hastily: "Not that I'm trying to dissuade you. You have the basic concept, and despite your lack of experience, I don't think you'll find the problem of technique insuperable. Your prelude was rather well done: freezing me *in situ*, as it were, to state your theme simply and without adornment, followed immediately by variations of dynamic and suggestive portent. The finale is already implicit; yet it is kept at a disciplined arm's length while the necessary structure is formed to support it and develop its stern message."

She listened intently to him, and her eyes were narrow. The expression on her face said: "Talk all you like. This time, you won't win."

Somewhere beyond the flimsy building-board stage wing he heard Dorran's musicians tuning up for Act III.

His dark features seemed to grow even more earnest, but his voice contained a perceptible burble. "So you've blocked in the introduction and the climax. A beginning and an end. The *real* problem comes now: how much, and what kind—of a middle? Most beginning murderesses would simply give up in frustrated bafflement. A few would shoot the moment Anna floats into the white rose garden. In my opinion, however, considering the wealth of material inherent in your composition, such abbreviation would be inexcusably primitive and garish—if not actually vulgar."

Martha Jacques blinked, as though trying to break through some indescribable spell that was being woven about her. Then she laughed shortly. "Go on. I wouldn't miss this for anything. Just when *should* I destroy the Via?"

The artist sighed. "You see? Your only concern is the *result*. You completely ignore the *manner* of its accomplishment. Really, Mart, I should think you'd show more insight into your first attempt at serious art. Now please don't misunderstand me, dear. I have the warmest regard for your spontaneity and enthusiasm: to be sure, they're quite indispensable when dealing with hackneyed themes, but headlong eagerness is not a substitute for method, or for art. We must search out and exploit subsidiary themes, intertwine them in subtle counterpoint with the major motifs. The most obvious minor theme is the ballet itself. That ballet is the loveliest thing I've ever seen or heard. Nevertheless, *you* can give it a power, a dimension, that even Anna wouldn't suspect possible, simply by blending it contrapuntally into your own work. It's all a matter of firing at the proper instant." He smiled engagingly. "I see that you're beginning to appreciate the potentialities of such unwitting collaboration."

The woman studied him through heavy-lidded eyes. She said slowly: "You *are* a great artist—and a loathesome beast."

He smiled still more amiably. "Kindly restrict your appraisals to your fields of competence. You haven't, as yet, sufficient background to evaluate me as an artist. But let us return to your composition. Thematically, it's rather pleasing. The form, pacing, and orchestration are irreproachable. It is adequate. And its very adequacy condemns it. One detects a certain amount of diffident imitation and over-attention to technique common to artists working in a new medium. The overcautious sparks of genius aren't setting us aflame. The artist isn't getting enough of his own personality into the work. And the remedy is as simple as the diagnosis: the artist must penetrate his work, wrap it around him, give it the distilled, unique essence of his heart and mind, so that it will blaze up and reveal his soul even through the veil of unidiomatic technique."

He listened a moment to the music outside. "As Anna wrote her musical score, a hiatus of thirty-eight rests precedes the moment The Nightingale drops dying from the thorn. At the start of that silence, you could start to run off your nineteen sub-equations in your little tin box, audio-Fourier style. You might even route the equations into the loudspeaker system, if our gadget is capable of remote control."

For a long time she appraised him calculatingly. "I finally think I understand you. You hoped to unnerve me with your savage, over-accentuated satire, and make me change my mind. So you aren't a beast, and even though I see through you, you're even a greater artist than I at first imagined."

He watched as the woman made a number of adjustments on the control panel of the black box. When she looked up again, her lips were drawn into hard purple ridges.

She said: "But it would be too great a pity to let such art go to waste, especially when supplied by the author of 'Twinkle, twinkle, little star'. And you will indulge an amateur musician's vanity if I play *my* first Fourier composition *fortissimo*."

He answered her smile with a fleeting one of his own. "An artist should never apologize for self-admiration. But watch your cueing. Anna should be clasping the white rose thorn to her breast in thirty seconds, and that will be your signal to fill in the first half of the thirty-eight rest hiatus. Can you see her?"

The woman did not answer, but he knew that her eyes were following the ballet on the invisible stage and Dorran's baton, beyond, with fevered intensity.

The music glided to a halt.

"Now!" hissed Jacques.

She flicked a switch on the box.

They listened, frozen, as the multi-throated public address system blared into life up and down the two miles of the Via Rosa.

The sound of Sciomnia was chill, metallic, like the cruel crackle of ice heard suddenly in the intimate warmth of an enchanted garden, and it seemed to chatter derisively, well aware of the magic that it shattered.

As it clattered and skirled up its harsh tonal staircase, it seemed to shriek: "Fools! Leave this childish nonsense and follow me! I am Science! I AM ALL!"

And, Ruy Jacques, watching the face of the prophetess of the God of Knowledge, was for the first time in his life aware of the possibility of utter defeat.

As he stared in mounting horror, her eyes rolled slightly upward, as though buoyed by some irresistible inner flame, which the pale translucent cheeks let through.

But as suddenly as they had come, the nineteen chords were over, and then, as though to accentuate the finality of that mocking manifesto, a ghastly aural afterimage of silence began building up around his world.

For a near eternity it seemed to him that he and this woman were alone in the world, that, like some wicked witch, she had, through her cacophonic creation, immutably frozen the thousands of invisible watchers beyond the thin walls of the stage wings.

It was a strange, yet simple thing that broke the appalling silence and restored sanity, confidence, and the will to resist to the man: from somewhere far away, a child whimpered.

Breathing as deeply as his near paralysis would permit, the artist murmured: "Now, Martha, in a moment I think you will hear why I suggested your Fourier broadcast. I fear Science has been had once mo—"

He never finished, and her eyes, which were crystallising into question marks, never fired their barbs.

A towering tidal wave of tone was engulfing the Via, apparently of no human source and from no human instrument.

Even he, who had suspected in some small degree what was coming, now found his paralysis once more complete. Like the woman scientist opposite him, he could only sit in motionless awe, with eyes glazing, jaw dropping, and tongue cleaving to the roof of his mouth.

He knew that the heart strings of Anna van Tuyl were one with this mighty sea of song, and that it took its ecstatic timbre from the reverberating volutes of that godlike mind.

And as the magnificent chords poured out in exquisite consonantal sequence, now with a sudden reedy delicacy, now with the radiant gladness of cymbals, he knew that his plan must succeed.

For, chord for chord, tone for tone, and measure for measure, The Nightingale was repeating in her death song the nineteen chords of Martha Jacques' Sciomnia equations.

Only now those chords were transfigured, as though some Parnassian composer were compassionately correcting and magically transmuting the work of a dull pupil.

The melody spiralled heavenward on wings. It demanded no allegiance; it hurled no pronunciamento. It held a message, but one almost too glorious to be grasped. It was steeped in boundless aspiration, but it was at peace with man and his universe. It sparkled humility, and in its abnegation there was grandeur. Its very incompleteness served to hint at its boundlessness.

And then it, too, was over. The death song was done.

Yes, thought Ruy Jacques, it is the Sciomnia, rewritten, recast, and breathed through the blazing soul of a goddess. And when Martha realizes this, when she sees how I tricked her into broadcasting her trifling, inconsequential effort, she is going to fire her weapon—at *me*.

He watched the woman's face go livid, her mouth work in speechless hate.

"You *knew!*" she screamed. "You did it to humiliate me!"

Jacques began to laugh. It was a nearly silent laughter, rhythmic with mounting ridicule, pitiless in its mockery.

"Stop that!"

But his abdomen was convulsing in rigid helplessness, and tears began to stream down his cheeks.

"I warned you once before!" yelled the woman. Her hand darted toward the black box and turned its long axis toward the man.

Like a period punctuating the rambling, aimless sentence of his life, a ball of blue light burst from a cylindrical hole in the side of the box.

His laughter stopped suddenly. He looked from the box to the woman with growing amazement. He could bend his neck. His paralysis was gone.

She stared back, equally startled. She gasped: "Something went wrong! *You should be dead!*"

The artist didn't linger to argue.

In his mind was the increasingly urgent call of Anna van Tuyl.

CHAPTER TWENTY

Dorran waved back the awed mass of spectators as Jacques knelt and transferred the faerie body from Bell's arms into his own.

"I'll carry you to your dressing room," he whispered. "I might have known you'd over-exert yourself."

Her eyes opened in the general direction of his face; in his mind came the tinkling of bells: "No . . . don't move me."

He looked up at Bell. "I think she's hurt! Take a look here!" He ran his hands over the seething surface of the wing folded along her side and breast: It was fevered fire.

"I can do nothing," replied the latter in a low voice. "She will tell you that I can do nothing."

"Anna!" cried Jacques. "What's wrong? What happened?"

Her musical reply formed in his mind. "Happened? Sciomnia was quite a thorn. Too much energy for one mind to disperse. Need two . . . three. Three could dematerialize weapon itself. Use wave formula of matter. Tell the others."

"*Others?* What are you talking about?" His thoughts whirled incoherently.

"Others like us. Coming soon. Bakine, dancing in streets of Leningrad. In Mexico City . . . the poetess Orteza. Many . . . this generation. *The Golden People*. Matt Bell guessed. Look!"

An image took fleeting form in his mind. First it was music, and then it was pure thought, and then it was a crisp strange air in his throat and the twang of something marvellous in his mouth. Then it was gone. "What was that?" he gasped.

"The Zhak symposium, seated at wine one April evening in the year 2437. Probability world. May . . . not occur. Did you recognize yourself?"

"Twenty-four thirty-seven?" His mind was fumbling.

"Yes. Couldn't you differentiate your individual mental contour from the whole? I thought you might. The group was still somewhat immature in the twenty-hundreds. By the fourteenth millennium . . ."

His head reeled under the impact of something titanic.

". . . your associated mental mass . . . creating a star of the M spectral class . . . galaxy now two-thirds terrestrialized . . ."

In his arms her wings stirred uneasily; all unconsciously he stroked the hot membranous surface and rubbed the marvellous bony framework with his fingers. "But Anna," he stammered, "I do not understand how this can be."

Her mind murmured in his. "Listen carefully, Ruy. Your pain . . . when your wings tried to open and couldn't . . . you needed certain psychoglandular stimulus. When you learn how to"—here a phrase he could not translate—"afterwards, they open . . ."

"When I learn—*what?*" he demanded. "What did you say I had to know, to open my wings?"

"One thing. The one thing . . . must have . . . to see the Rose."

"Rose—rose—*rose!*" he cried in near exasperation. "All right, then, my dutiful Nightingale, how long must I wait for you to make this remarkable Red Rose? I ask you, where is it?"

"Please . . . not just yet . . . in your arms just a little longer . . . while we finish ballet. Forget yourself, Ruy. Unless . . . leave prison . . . own heart . . . never find The Rose. Wings never unfold . . . remain a mortal. Science . . . isn't all. Art isn't . . . one thing greater . . . Ruy! I can't prolong . . ."

He looked up wildly at Bell.

The psychogeneticist turned his eyes away heavily. "Don't you understand? She has been dying ever since she absorbed that Sciomniac blast."

A faint murmur reached the artist's mind. "So you couldn't learn . . . poor Ruy . . . poor Nightingale . . ."

As he stared stuporously, her dun-colored wings began to shudder like leaves in an October wind.

From the depths of his shock he watched the fluttering of the wings give way to a sudden convulsive straining of her legs and thighs. It surged upward through her blanching body, through her abdomen and chest, pushing her blood before it and out into her wings, which now appeared more purple than grey.

To the old woman standing at his side, Bell observed quietly: "Even *homo superior* has his death struggle . . ."

The vendress of love philters nodded with anile sadness. "And she knew the answer . . . lost . . . lost . . ."

And still the blood came, making the wing membranes thick and taut.

"Anna!" shrieked Ruy Jacques. "You *can't* die. I won't let you! I love you! *I love you!*"

He had no expectation that she could still sense the images in his mind, nor even that she was still alive.

But suddenly, like stars shining their brief brilliance through a rift in storm clouds, her lips parted in a gay smile. Her eyes opened and seemed to bathe him in an intimate flow of light. It was during this momentary illumination, just before the lips solidified into their final enigmatic mask, that he thought he heard, as from a great distance, the opening measures of Weber's *Invitation to the Dance*.

At this moment the conviction formed in his numbed understanding that her loveliness was now supernal, that greater beauty could not be conceived or endured.

But even as he gazed in stricken wonder, the blood-gorged wings curled slowly up and out, enfolding the ivory breast and shoulders in blinding scarlet, like the petals of some magnificent rose.

Frank Belknap Long

Frank Belknap Long (1903–92) as a young man was the closest friend and associate of H. P. Lovecraft. Long was a poet and fiction writer who became adept at the new SF genre in the 1920s and continued to publish widely for decades. His first book (of poetry) appeared in 1924, and he remained actively writing through the 1980s.

Weird science fiction, which borders on the supernatural, was characteristic of the Lovecraft "Circle" that included Long, Donald and Howard Wandrei, Clark Ashton Smith, Robert E. Howard, Robert Bloch, Fritz Leiber, and others, and centered around the pulp magazine *Weird Tales* in the 1920s and '30s. Lovecraft was a rationalist, but the affect of the fiction was fear and wonder.

Long's reputation in later years, after the 1960s, was dominated by the impact of his early horror fiction, and he suffered as well as benefitted from the adulation of the followers of Lovecraft, who cared little for his non-Lovecraftian writings. He wrote a number of women's gothic romances under his wife's name when he found it difficult to sell his own books.

His early stories are clearly influenced by Lovecraft, and of them the most famous is this one, which decades later would be one of the models for Stephen King's "The Mist." It is a paradigm of the alien creatures from another dimension story in genre science fiction.

THE HOUNDS OF TINDALOS

1

I'm glad you came," said Chalmers. He was sitting by the window and his face was very pale. Two tall candles guttered at his elbow and cast a sickly amber light over his long nose and slightly receding chin. Chalmers would have nothing modern about his apartment. He had the soul of a mediaeval ascetic, and he preferred illuminated manuscripts to automobiles, and leering stone gargoyles to radios and adding-machines.

As I crossed the room to the settee he had cleared for me I glanced at his desk and was surprised to discover that he had been studying the mathematical formulae of a celebrated contemporary physicist, and that he had covered many sheets of thin yellow paper with curious geometric designs.

"Einstein and John Dee are strange bedfellows," I said as my gaze wandered from his mathematical charts to the sixty or seventy quaint books that comprised his strange little library. Plotinus and Emanuel Moscopulus, St. Thomas Aquinas and Frenicle de Bessy stood elbow to elbow in the somber ebony bookcase, and chairs, table and desk were littered with pamphlets about mediaeval sorcery and witchcraft and black magic, and all of the valiant glamorous things that the modern world has repudiated.

Chalmers smiled engagingly, and passed me a Russian cigarette on a curiously carved tray. "We are just discovering now," he said, "that the old alchemists and sorcerers were two-thirds *right*, and that your modern biologist and materialist is nine-tenths *wrong*."

"You have always scoffed at modern science," I said, a little impatiently.

"Only at scientific dogmatism," he replied. "I have always been a rebel, a champion of originality and lost causes; that is why I have chosen to repudiate the conclusions of contemporary biologists."

"And Einstein?" I asked.

"A priest of transcendental mathematics!" he murmured reverently. "A profound mystic and explorer of the great *suspected*."

"Then you do not entirely despise science."

"Of course not," he affirmed. "I merely distrust the scientific positivism of the past fifty years, the positivism of Haeckel and Darwin and of Mr. Bertrand Russell. I believe that biology has failed pitifully to explain the mystery of man's origin and destiny."

"Give them time," I retorted.

Chalmers' eyes glowed. "My friend," he murmured, "your pun is sublime. Give them *time*. That is precisely what I would do. But your modern biologist scoffs at time. He has the key but he refuses to use it. What do we know of time, really? Einstein believes that it is relative, that it can be interpreted in terms of space, of *curved* space. But must we stop there? When mathematics fails us can we not advance by—insight?"

"You are treading on dangerous ground," I replied. "That is a pitfall that your true investigator avoids. That is why modern science has advanced so slowly. It accepts nothing that it cannot demonstrate. But you—"

"I would take hashish, opium, all manner of drugs. I would emulate the sages of the East. And then perhaps I would apprehend—"

"What?"

"The fourth dimension."

"Theosophical rubbish!"

"Perhaps. But I believe that drugs expand human consciousness. William James agreed with me. And I have discovered a new one."

"A new drug?"

"It was used centuries ago by Chinese alchemists, but it is virtually unknown in the West. Its occult properties are amazing. With its aid and the aid of my mathematical knowledge I believe that I can *go back through time*."

"I do not understand."

"Time is merely our imperfect perception of a new dimension of space. Time and motion are both illusions. Everything that has existed from the beginning of the world *exists now*. Events that occurred centuries ago on this planet continue to exist in another dimension of space. Events that will occur centuries from now *exist already*. We cannot perceive their existence because we cannot enter the dimension of space that contains them. Human beings as we know them are merely fractions, infinitesimally small fractions of one enormous whole. Every human being is linked with *all* the life that has preceded him on this planet. All of his ancestors are parts of him. Only time separates him from his forebears, and time is an illusion and does not exist."

"I think I understand," I murmured.

"It will be sufficient for my purpose if you can form a vague idea of what I wish to achieve. I wish to strip from my eyes the veils of illusion that time has thrown over them, and see the *beginning and the end.*"

"And you think this new drug will help you?"

"I am sure that it will. And I want you to help me. I intend to take the drug immediately. I cannot wait. I must *see.*" His eyes glittered strangely. "I am going back, back through time."

He rose and strode to the mantel. When he faced me again he was holding a small square box in the palm of his hand. "I have here five pellets of the drug Liao. It was used by the Chinese philosopher Lao Tze, and while under its influence he visioned Tao. Tao is the most mysterious force in the world; it surrounds and pervades all things; it contains the visible universe and everything that we call reality. He who apprehends the mysteries of Tao sees clearly all that was and will be."

"Rubbish!" I retorted.

"Tao resembles a great animal, recumbent, motionless, containing in its enormous body all the worlds of our universe, the past, the present and the future. We see portions of this great monster through a slit, which we call time. With the aid of this drug I shall enlarge the slit. I shall behold the great figure of life, the great recumbent beast in its entirety."

"And what do you wish me to do?"

"Watch, my friend. Watch and take notes. And if I go back too far you must recall me to reality. You can recall me by shaking me violently. If I appear to be suffering acute physical pain you must recall me at once."

"Chalmers," I said, "I wish you wouldn't make this experiment. You are taking dreadful risks. I don't believe that there is any fourth dimension and I emphatically do not believe in Tao. And I don't approve of your experimenting with unknown drugs."

"I know the properties of this drug," he replied. "I know precisely how it affects the human animal and I know its dangers. The risk does not reside in the drug itself. My only fear is that I may become lost in time. You see, I shall assist the drug. Before I swallow this pellet I shall give my undivided attention to the geometric and algebraic symbols that I have traced on this paper." He raised the mathematical chart that rested on his knee. "I shall prepare my mind for an excursion into time. I shall approach the fourth dimension with my conscious mind before I take the drug which will enable me to exercise occult powers of perception. Before I enter the dream world of the Eastern mystics I shall acquire all of the mathematical help that modern science can offer. This mathematical knowledge, this conscious approach to an actual apprehension of the fourth dimension of time, will supplement the work of the drug. The drug will open up stupendous new vistas—the mathematical preparation will enable me to grasp them intellectually. I have often grasped the fourth dimension in dreams, emotionally, intuitively, but I have never been able to recall, in waking life, the occult splendors that were momentarily revealed to me.

"But with your aid, I believe that I can recall them. You will take down everything that I say while I am under the influence of the drug. No matter how strange or incoherent my speech may become you will omit nothing. When I awake I may be able to supply the key to whatever is mysterious or incredible. I am not sure that I shall succeed, but if I *do* succeed"—his eyes were strangely luminous—"*time will exist for me no longer!*"

He sat down abruptly. "I shall make the experiment at once. Please stand over there by the window and watch. Have you a fountain pen?"

I nodded gloomily and removed a pale green Waterman from my upper vest pocket.

"And a pad, Frank?"

I groaned and produced a memorandum book. "I emphatically disapprove of this experiment," I muttered. "You're taking a frightful risk."

"Don't be an asinine old woman!" he admonished. "Nothing that you can say will induce me to stop now. I entreat you to remain silent while I study these charts."

He raised the charts and studied them intently. I watched the clock on the mantel as it ticked out the seconds, and a curious dread clutched at my heart so that I choked.

Suddenly the clock stopped ticking, and exactly at that moment Chalmers swallowed the drug.

I rose quickly and moved toward him, but his eyes implored me not to interfere. "The clock has stopped," he murmured. "The forces that control it approve of my experiment. *Time* stopped, and I swallowed the drug. I pray God that I shall not lose my way."

He closed his eyes and leaned back on the sofa. All of the blood had left his face and he was breathing heavily. It was clear that the drug was acting with extraordinary rapidity.

"It is beginning to get dark," he murmured. "Write that. It is beginning to get dark and the familiar objects in the room are fading out. I can discern them vaguely through my eyelids, but they are fading swiftly."

I shook my pen to make the ink come and wrote rapidly in shorthand as he continued to dictate.

"I am leaving the room. The walls are vanishing and I can no longer see any of the familiar objects. Your face, though, is still visible to me. I hope that you are writing. I think that I am about to make a great leap—a leap through space. Or perhaps it is through time that I shall make the leap. I cannot tell. Everything is dark, indistinct."

He sat for a while silent, with his head sunk upon his breast. Then suddenly he stiffened and his eyelids fluttered open. "God in heaven!" he cried. "I *see!*"

He was straining forward in his chair, staring at the opposite wall. But I knew that he was looking beyond the wall and that the objects in the room no longer existed for him. "Chalmers," I cried, "Chalmers, shall I wake you?"

"Do not!" he shrieked. "I see *everything.* All of the billions of lives that preceded me on this planet are before me at this moment. I see men of all ages, all races, all colors. They are fighting, killing, building, dancing, singing. They are sitting about rude fires on lonely gray deserts, and flying through the air in monoplanes. They are riding the seas in bark canoes and enormous steamships; they are painting bison and mammoths on the walls of dismal caves and covering huge canvases with queer futuristic designs. I watch the migrations from Atlantis. I watch the migrations from Lemuria. I see the elder races—a strange horde of black dwarfs overwhelming Asia, and the Neandertalers with lowered heads and bent knees ranging obscenely across Europe. I watch the Achaeans streaming into the Greek islands, and the crude beginnings of Hellenic culture. I am in Athens and Pericles is young. I am standing on the soil of Italy. I assist in the rape of the Sabines; I march with the Imperial Legions. I tremble with awe and wonder as the enormous standards go by and the ground shakes with the tread of the victorious *bastati.* A thousand naked slaves grovel before me as I pass in a litter of gold and ivory drawn by night-black oxen from Thebes, and the flower-girls scream *'Ave Caesar'* as I nod and smile. I am myself a slave on a Moorish galley. I watch the erection of a great cathedral. Stone by stone it rises, and through months and years I stand and watch each stone as it falls into place. I am burned on a cross head downward in the thyme-scented gardens of Nero, and I watch with amusement and scorn the torturers at work in the chambers of the Inquisition.

"I walk in the holiest sanctuaries; I enter the temples of Venus. I kneel in adoration before the Magna Mater, and I throw coins on the bare knees of the sacred courtesans who sit with veiled faces in the groves of Babylon. I creep into an Elizabethan theater and with the stinking rabble about me I applaud *The Merchant of Venice.* I walk with Dante through the narrow streets of Florence. I meet the young Beatrice, and the hem of her garment brushes my sandals as I stare enraptured. I am a priest of Isis, and my magic astounds the nations. Simon Magus kneels before me, imploring my assistance, and Pharaoh trembles when I approach. In India I talk with the Masters and run screaming from their presence, for their revelations are as salt on wounds that bleed.

"I perceive everything *simultaneously.* I perceive everything from all sides; I am a part of all the teeming billions about me. I exist in all men and all men exist in me. I perceive the whole of human history in a single instant, the past and the present.

"By simply *straining* I can see farther and farther back. Now I am going back through strange curves and angles. Angles and curves multiply about me. I perceive great segments of time through *curves.* There is *curved time,* and *angular time.* The beings that exist in angular time cannot enter curved time. It is very strange.

"I am going back and back. Man has disappeared from the earth. Gigantic reptiles crouch beneath enormous palms and swim through the loathly black waters of dismal lakes. Now the reptiles have disappeared. No animals remain upon the land, but beneath the waters, plainly visible to me, dark forms move slowly over the rotting vegetation.

"The forms are becoming simpler and simpler. Now they are single cells. All about me there are angles—strange angles that have no counterparts on the earth. I am desperately afraid.

"There is an abyss of being which man has never fathomed."

I stared. Chalmers had risen to his feet and he was gesticulating helplessly with his arms. "I am passing through unearthly angles; I am approaching—oh, the burning horror of it."

"Chalmers!" I cried. "Do you wish me to interfere?"

He brought his right hand quickly before his face, as though to shut out a vision unspeakable. "Not yet!" he cried; "I will go on. I will see—what—lies—beyond—"

A cold sweat streamed from his forehead and his shoulders jerked spasmodically. "Beyond life there are"—his face grew ashen with terror—"*things* that I cannot distinguish. They move slowly through angles. They have no bodies, and they move slowly through outrageous angles."

It was then that I became aware of the odor in the room. It was a pungent, indescribable odor, so nauseous that I could scarcely endure it. I stepped quickly to the window and threw it open. When I returned to Chalmers and looked into his eyes I nearly fainted.

"I think they have scented me!" he shrieked. "They are slowly turning toward me."

He was trembling horribly. For a moment he clawed at the air with his hands. Then his legs gave way beneath him and he fell forward on his face, slobbering and moaning.

I watched him in silence as he dragged himself across the floor. He was no longer a man. His teeth were bared and saliva dripped from the corners of his mouth.

"Chalmers," I cried. "Chalmers, stop it! Stop it, do you hear?"

As if in reply to my appeal he commenced to utter hoarse convulsive sounds which resembled nothing so much as the barking of a dog, and began a sort of hideous writhing in a circle about the room. I bent and seized him by the shoulders. Violently, desperately, I shook him. He turned his head and snapped at my wrist. I was sick with horror, but I dared not release him for fear that he would destroy himself in a paroxysm of rage.

"Chalmers," I muttered, "you must stop that. There is nothing in this room that can harm you. Do you understand?"

I continued to shake and admonish him, and gradually the madness died out of his face. Shivering convulsively, he crumpled into a grotesque heap on the Chinese rug.

I carried him to the sofa and deposited him upon it. His features were twisted in pain, and I knew that he was still struggling dumbly to escape from abominable memories.

"Whisky," he muttered. "You'll find a flask in the cabinet by the window—upper left-hand drawer."

When I handed him the flask his fingers tightened about it until the knuckles showed blue. "They nearly got me," he gasped. He drained the stimulant in immoderate gulps, and gradually the color crept back into his face.

"That drug was the very devil!" I murmured.

"It wasn't the drug," he moaned.

His eyes no longer glared insanely, but he still wore the look of a lost soul.

"They scented me in time," he moaned. "I went too far."

"What were *they* like?" I said, to humor him.

He leaned forward and gripped my arm. He was shivering horribly. "No words in our language can describe them!" He spoke in a hoarse whisper. "They are symbolized vaguely in the myth of the Fall, and in an obscene form which is occasionally found engraved on ancient tablets. The Greeks had a name for them, which veiled their essential foulness. The tree, the snake and the apple—these are the vague symbols of a most awful mystery.

His voice had risen to a scream. "Frank, Frank, a terrible and unspeakable *deed* was done in the beginning. Before time, the *deed*, and from the deed—"

He had risen and was hysterically pacing the room. "The seeds of the deed move through angles in dim recesses of time. They are hungry and athirst!"

"Chalmers," I pleaded to quiet him. "We are living in the third decade of the Twentieth Century."

"They are lean and athirst!" he shrieked. "*The Hounds of Tindalos!*"

"Chalmers, shall I phone for a physician?"

"A physician cannot help me now. They are horrors of the soul, and yet"—

he hid his face in his hands and groaned—"they are real, Frank. I saw them for a ghastly moment. For a moment I stood on the *other side.* I stood on the pale gray shores beyond time and space. In an awful light that was not light, in a silence that shrieked, I saw *them.*

"All the evil in the universe was concentrated in their lean, hungry bodies. Or had they bodies? I saw them only for a moment; I cannot be certain. *But I heard them breathe.* Indescribably for a moment I felt their breath upon my face. They turned toward me and I fled screaming. In a single moment I fled screaming through time. I fled down quintillions of years.

"But they scented me. Men awake in them cosmic hungers. We have escaped, momentarily, from the foulness that rings them round. They thirst for that in us which is clean, which emerged from the deed without stain. There is a part of us which did not partake in the deed, and that they hate. But do not imagine that they are literally, prosaically evil. They are beyond good and evil as we know it. They are that which in the beginning fell away from cleanliness. Through the deed they became bodies of death, receptacles of all foulness. But they are not evil in *our* sense because in the spheres through which they move there is no thought, no morals, no right or wrong as we understand it. There is merely the pure and the foul. The foul expresses itself through angles; the pure through curves. Man, the pure part of him, is descended from a curve. Do not laugh. I mean that literally."

I rose and searched for my hat. "I'm dreadfully sorry for you, Chalmers," I said, as I walked toward the door. "But I don't intend to stay and listen to such gibberish. I'll send my physician to see you. He's an elderly, kindly chap and he won't be offended if you tell him to go to the devil. But I hope you'll respect his advice. A week's rest in a good sanitarium should benefit you immeasurably."

I heard him laughing as I descended the stairs, but his laughter was so utterly mirthless that it moved me to tears.

2

When Chalmers phoned the following morning my first impulse was to hang up the receiver immediately. His request was so unusual and his voice was so wildly hysterical that I feared any further association with him would result in the impairment of my own sanity. But I could not doubt the genuineness of his misery, and when he broke down completely and I heard him sobbing over the wire I decided to comply with his request.

"Very well," I said. "I will come over immediately and bring the plaster."

En route to Chalmers' home I stopped at a hardware store and purchased twenty pounds of plaster of Paris. When I entered my friend's room he was crouching by the window watching the opposite wall out of eyes that were feverish with fright. When he saw me he rose and seized the parcel containing the plaster with an avidity that amazed and horrified me. He had extruded all of the furniture and the room presented a desolate appearance.

"It is just conceivable that we can thwart them!" he exclaimed, "But we must work rapidly. Frank, there is a stepladder in the hall. Bring it here immediately. And then fetch a pail of water."

"What for?" I murmured.

He turned sharply and there was a flush on his face. "To mix the plaster, you fool!" he cried. "To mix the plaster that will save our bodies and souls from a contamination unmentionable. To mix the plaster that will save the world from—Frank, *they must be kept out!*"

"Who?" I murmured.

"The Hounds of Tindalos!" he muttered. "They can only reach us through angles. We must eliminate all angles from this room. I shall plaster up all of the corners, all of the crevices. We must make this room resemble the interior of a sphere."

I knew that it would have been useless to argue with him. I fetched the stepladder, Chalmers mixed the plaster, and for three hours we labored. We filled in the four corners of the wall and the intersections of the floor and wall and the wall and ceiling, and we rounded the sharp angles of the window-seat.

"I shall remain in this room until they return in time," he affirmed when our task was completed. "When they discover that the scent leads through curves they will return. They will return ravenous and snarling and unsatisfied to the foulness that was in the beginning, before time, beyond space."

He nodded graciously and lit a cigarette. "It was good of you to help," he said.

"Will you not see a physician, Chalmers?" I pleaded.

"Perhaps—tomorrow," he murmured. "But now I must watch and wait."

"Wait for what?" I urged.

Chalmers smiled wanly. "I know that you think me insane," he said. "You have a shrewd but prosaic mind, and you cannot conceive of an entity that does not depend for its existence on force and matter. But did it ever occur to you, my friend, that force and matter are merely the barriers to perception imposed by time and space? When one knows, as I do, that time and space are identical and that they are both deceptive because they are merely imperfect manifestations of a higher reality, one no longer seeks in the visible world for an explanation of the mystery and terror of being."

I rose and walked toward the door.

"Forgive me," he cried. "I did not mean to offend you. You have a superlative intellect, but I—I have a *superhuman* one. It is only natural that I should be aware of your limitations."

"Phone if you need me," I said, and descended the stairs two steps at a time. "I'll send my physician over at once," I muttered, to myself. "He's a hopeless maniac, and heaven knows what will happen if someone doesn't take charge of him immediately."

3

The following is a condensation of two announcements which appeared in the Partridgeville Gazette *for July 3, 1928:*

Earthquake Shakes Financial District

At 2 o'clock this morning an earth tremor of unusual severity broke several plate-glass windows in Central Square and completely disorganized the electric and street railway systems. The tremor was felt in the outlying districts and the steeple of the First Baptist

Church on Angell Hill (designed by Christopher Wren in 1717) was entirely demolished. Firemen are now attempting to put out a blaze which threatens to destroy the Partridgeville Glue Works. An investigation is promised by the mayor and an immediate attempt will be made to fix responsibility for this disastrous occurrence.

OCCULT WRITER MURDERED BY UNKNOWN GUEST

Horrible Crime in Central Square

Mystery Surrounds Death of Halpin Chalmers

At 9 A.M. today the body of Halpin Chalmers, author and journalist, was found in an empty room above the jewelry store of Smithwick and Isaacs, 24 Central Square. The coroner's investigation revealed that the room had been rented furnished to Mr. Chalmers on May 1, and that he had himself disposed of the furniture a fortnight ago. Chalmers was the author of several recondite books on occult themes, and a member of the Bibliographic Guild. He formerly resided in Brooklyn, New York.

At 7 A.M. Mr. L. E. Hancock, who occupies the apartment opposite Chalmers' room in the Smithwick and Isaacs establishment, smelt a peculiar odor when he opened his door to take in his cat and the morning edition of the *Partridgeville Gazette.* The odor he describes as extremely acrid and nauseous, and he affirms that it was so strong in the vicinity of Chalmers' room that he was obliged to hold his nose when he approached that section of the hall.

He was about to return to his own apartment when it occurred to him that Chalmers might have accidentally forgotten to turn off the gas in his kitchenette. Becoming considerably alarmed at the thought, he decided to investigate, and when repeated tappings on Chalmers' door brought no response he notified the superintendent. The latter opened the door by means of a pass key, and the two men quickly made their way into Chalmers' room. The room was utterly destitute of furniture, and Hancock asserts that when he first glanced at the floor his heart went cold within him, and that the superintendent, without saying a word, walked to the open window and stared at the building opposite for fully five minutes.

Chalmers lay stretched upon his back in the center of the room. He was starkly nude, and his chest and arms were covered with a peculiar bluish pus or ichor. His head lay grotesquely upon his chest. It had been completely severed from his body, and the features were twisted and torn and horribly mangled. Nowhere was there a trace of blood.

The room presented a most astonishing appearance. The intersections of the walls, ceiling and floor had been thickly smeared with plaster of Paris, but at intervals fragments had cracked and fallen off, and someone had grouped these upon the floor about the murdered man so as to form a perfect triangle.

Beside the body were several sheets of charred yellow paper. These bore fantastic geometric designs and symbols and several hastily scrawled sentences. The sentences were almost illegible and so absurd in content that they furnished no possible clue to the perpetrator of the crime. "I am waiting and watching," Chalmers wrote. "I sit by the window and watch walls and ceiling. I do not believe they can reach me, but I must beware of the Doels. Perhaps *they* can help them break through. The satyrs will help, and they can advance through the scarlet circles. The Greeks knew a way of preventing that. It is a great pity that we have forgotten so much."

On another sheet of paper, the most badly charred of the seven or eight fragments found by Detective Sergeant Douglas (of the Partridgeville Reserve), was scrawled the following:

"Good God, the plaster is falling! A terrific shock has loosened the plaster and it is falling. An earthquake perhaps! I never could have anticipated this. It is growing dark in the room. I must phone Frank. But can he get here in time? I will try. I will recite the Einstein formula. I will—God, they are breaking through! They are breaking through! Smoke is pouring from the corners of the wall. Their tongues—ahhhhh—"

In the opinion of Detective Sergeant Douglas, Chalmers was poisoned by some obscure chemical. He has sent specimens of the strange blue slime found on Chalmers' body to the Partridgeville Chemical Laboratories; and he expects the report will shed new light on one of the most mysterious crimes of recent years. That Chalmers entertained a guest on the evening preceding the earthquake is certain, for his neighbor distinctly heard a low murmur of conversation in the former's room as he passed it on his way to the stairs. Suspicion points strongly to this unknown visitor and the police are diligently endeavoring to discover his identity.

4

Report of James Morton, chemist and bacteriologist:

My dear Mr. Douglas:

The fluid sent to me for analysis is the most peculiar that I have ever examined. It resembles living protoplasm, but it lacks the peculiar substances known as enzymes. Enzymes catalyze the chemical reactions occurring in living cells, and when the cell dies they cause it to disintegrate by hydrolyzation. Without enzymes protoplasm should possess enduring vitality, i.e., immortality. Enzymes are the negative components, so to speak, of unicellular organism, which is the basis of all life. That living matter can exist without enzymes biologists emphatically deny. And yet the substance that you have sent me is alive and it lacks these "indispensable" bodies. Good God, sir, do you realize what astounding new vistas this opens up?

5

Excerpt from The Secret Watchers *by the late Halpin Chalmers:*

What if, parallel to the life we know, there is another life that does not die, which lacks the elements that destroy *our* life? Perhaps in another dimension there is a *different* force from that which generates our life. Perhaps this force emits energy, or something similar to energy, which passes from the unknown dimension where *it* is and creates a new form of cell life in our dimension. No one knows that such new cell life does exist in our dimension. Ah, but I have seen *its* manifestations. I have *talked* with them. In my room at night I have talked with the Doels. And in dreams I have seen their maker. I have stood on the dim shore beyond time and matter and seen *it*. *It* moves through strange curves and outrageous angles. Some day I shall travel in time and meet *it* face to face.

Adam Wiśniewski-Snerg
Translated by Tomasz Mirkowicz

Adam Snerg (1937–95) lived in Warsaw, Poland. He published his first story in 1968 and his first novel, *Robot* in 1973. *Robot* takes place inside a bomb shelter below a large city torn out of the Earth by an alien spaceship and carried through space to an unknown destination as a scientists' sample collected for later study. It is an ambitious investigation into the nature of time, evolution, free will, and the theory of relativity. Polish SF fans voted in the best Polish SF book published since World War Two, quite an honor in Stanislaw Lem's native country.

He published three later novels that were fantastic but not science fiction, and then in 1990 published an original and highly controversial non-fiction work presenting his own theory of the space-time continuum. At the time of his death by his own hand in August, 1995, he had been working on another non-fiction book, a more accessible version of his theory.

"The Angel of Violence" is one of his six uncollected short stories and the first of his works to be translated into English, in a translation commissioned for this book.

THE ANGEL OF VIOLENCE

On the thirteenth floor of the Cybernetics Institute Lucy interrupted the guide's patter to tell her that several of the tourists were missing. They had lagged behind the group and probably lost their way in the maze of corridors and rooms of the vast building, the chief attraction of the tour around the recently excavated ancient city. The guide did not seem in the least put out. Instead of worrying about her missing charges or explaining the exhibits on display to the remaining tourists, she continued to praise the sound and light show her agency organized every night in the ruins of a nearby nuclear power plant.

Lucy got lost on the sixteenth floor. She had lingered a moment too long by the main computer, staring dumbly at the old cabinets housing the giant electronic brain. The guide had said that it makers, medieval craftsmen once known as "programmers," were assured a permanent place in the annals of history. And yet "the moving beauty of this priceless treasure"—the guide's exact words—did not move Lucy in the least. She decided to ask the woman for some pointers on appreciating ancient artifacts. But when she went out into the corridor, it was empty.

She couldn't hear the other tourists and had no idea which way they had gone. She started looking for them, wandering in and out of ancient labs filled with primitive, twenty-first-century equipment.

Time had not been kind to the priceless exhibits. Their plastic parts were full of holes made by second-generation borers, and their metal parts, the paint removed long ago by colonies of industrious, once unknown microorganisms, were corroded and covered with rust peeling away in large flakes.

The group was nowhere in sight. After another fifteen minutes Lucy gave up her search and, feeling oppressed by the somber atmosphere of the ancient building, decided to forgo the rest of the tour. She resolved to take the elevator to the ground floor and find her way to the antique bus waiting in front of the Institute.

She had her first misadventure in the elevator: it stopped between floors. Lucy pressed the alarm button. After a brief silence a male voice spoke to her from a speaker set above the buttons.

"Do you want to be the queen?" it asked.

"Do I want to be *what?*"

"The king's wife, the first lady of the realm."

"The king's wife?"

"Yes."

"You must be joking!"

"No, I'm not. You can become the queen."

"How?"

"No problem. It so happens we are looking for the right candidate. The former queen had to go. The tourists are already downstairs, waiting for you."

"Where?"

"Press the sixth floor button. Then go to room 628."

The unusual offer had taken her by surprise, but Lucy quickly guessed what it was all about: some kind of show put on by the tourist agency in the ruins of the freshly excavated city. It sounded intriguing. She liked surprises. Why shouldn't she play a part in some medieval drama? She had heard of picturesque castles built on the forbidden peaks of nuclear power plants by tyrants armed with tridents who forced their subjects to watch television. Maybe she wasn't confusing different historical periods, but she was overjoyed at the prospect of participating in the show, the more so since she'd be viewing everything from the queen's throne.

Although she pressed the right button, the elevator passed the sixth floor and continued to descend; it passed the ground floor and finally stopped on the sixth underground level. Lucy hadn't even known there were any underground levels in the building.

She walked down a wide, clean corridor until she reached room 628. She opened the door and walked in.

The first things she saw were the bare legs of a woman standing behind a metal screen suspended from the ceiling.

"Excuse me," Lucy said, "I was told some kind of show is being staged here."

The woman hidden by the screen gave a jump and moved a little closer. But the screen, hanging in front of an open doorway leading to the next room, continued to cover her, so all Lucy saw were the woman's legs.

"Do you know where the tourists are waiting?"

The legs were very shapely. But when they walked out from behind the screen and with one bare foot kicked the door shut, Lucy stopped admiring their proportions. She could hardly believe her eyes.

The legs weren't attached to a body! Lucy screamed with horror and ran into the next room. Inside, she saw many more pairs of moving legs. Although no people were present, the whole room was filled with animated motion.

A sign on the wall said: "PROSTHETIC WORKS—LOWER LIMBS." A slowly moving conveyor belt passed along a row of machines. Each machine was operated by a pair of synthetic hands steered efficiently by invisible plastic tendons. Imitating human hands to perfection, they were assembling artificial legs. At the end of the assembly line the legs jumped off the conveyor belt. The last machine joined them into matching pairs and sent them off to an obstacle course. After completing it, the legs marched obediently to the next section, where a mechanical fitter equipped them with arms.

Each hasp joining the legs together, its ends inserted into their thighs, had the shape of an inverted U. The fitter attached the arms to the top of the hasp. A dozen of such limbomats were already working on the assembly line or molding parts from which the limbs were made; others were repairing defective machines or building new ones.

Lucy noticed one limbomat standing by a high-tension console and suddenly felt the muscles of her legs and arms tense as if she were a weightlifter readying to set a world record. When she caught sight of the video cameras and antennas attached to the walls, she began to understand what had happened.

She knew that the twenty-first century scientists who had abandoned the building during an earthquake had left all the machinery running, supplied with energy from a local source. The room she was in was an old workshop that had originally produced prototypes of artificial limbs for the handicapped. Cut off for centuries from the rest of the world, the Institute's main computer had carried on production, resourcefully modifying and improving the artificial limbs. It was a case of perfect symbiosis: the computer created more and more advanced limbomats, steering their artificial nervous systems by remote control, while they—replacing the human technicians—maintained and expanded his electronic brain.

When Lucy had walked into the view of the computer's video cameras, she had immediately caught its attention. After years of controlling artificial limbs the computer wanted to test its power over real ones. A live human being was just what it needed.

Lucy wanted to flee, but as soon as the computer registered her presence, her muscles turned rigid as if numbed by electric shock. For several minutes her whole body jerked convulsively, until finally, after a violent battle over its control between two command centers—her own brain and the electronic brain of the computer—her body began to carry out the machine's orders.

Propelled by regular impulses, she passed the conveyor belt and came to a large door which opened by itself, revealing an unusual sight.

All the tourists who had strayed from the group were standing in the middle of an enormous chamber. They smiled at the terrified girl. After her initial shock she smiled back at them. She wondered whether the computer had really forced her to walk in here; maybe she had just imagined it. Anyway, now she was back among people she knew; she was so relieved, she could have hugged them.

She took a few steps in their direction, then once again looked at them, and froze.

The very moment she had sighed with relief, happy her misadventures were over, one of the men raised the heavy ax he was holding and with one blow split in two the skull of the tourist standing next to him. As the man toppled to the floor, a stiff cable with a sharp hook at the end shot out from the side of the chamber. It embedded itself in the body and began pulling it toward the wall, to a pile of similarly massacred corpses, leaving an ugly red stain on the shiny marble floor.

Lucy screamed with horror, but her scream was cut short by a painful constriction of her throat. The strange power was again taking control of her body. Plastic limbs ripped off her clothes. She stumbled toward the exit. She would have fallen, but her leg muscles held her up, artificially tensed by the computer's will.

Naked, her back toward the silent group, she waited for a deadly blow. The brutal murder she had witnessed kept replaying itself in her mind. She was overcome by a sense of unreality, just like a few minutes ago, when she walked into the workshop and saw the moving legs.

Instead of an ax blow, she felt the touch of another of the limbed monsters. It was pulling over her head a long dress richly decorated with golden lace. Although her heart was pounding with fear, outwardly she seemed as calm as if she were getting ready for a party. She could move her head freely. All of a sudden she realized there was something odd about the tourists and, in spite of her fear, looked at them more closely.

They were all smiling and standing as still as statues, not saying a word. And they were all dressed in costumes from early antiquity and armed with equally ancient weapons: axes, tridents, swords, spears, even clubs studded with iron nails.

A minute later another incident made her blood curdle. As she watched, a woman lifted her spear and threw it with incredible strength. It pierced the chest of a young man, its tip coming out his back. When he fell the woman walked over to him, surefooted, and pulled her weapon out of his bloodied chest. The dying man continued to smile even when the hook embedded itself in his side and started dragging him off toward the wall.

What happened over the next twenty minutes in the huge silent chamber was as mysterious as the computer's method of controlling the nervous systems of living organisms. Tensing the tourists' muscles, it forced them to participate in what seemed like a cross between an exotic ritual dance and the drill of ancient recruits.

During this macabre extravaganza the hook pulled away two more corpses. The limbomats left the chamber, closing the door behind them. Before leaving, they attached something heavy to Lucy's back. Forced by a series of impulses, she began walking toward the group of tourists. Suddenly she was made to stop and turn around. Looking at the wall, she saw a large white computer set in a deep recess.

Then she saw a second computer, a black one, set in a recess in the opposite wall.

Just as she began to grasp what was happening, a thin wisp of smoke shot out from the black computer. There was a crackle of short-circuiting cables and the overhead lights went out. The stench of burning insulation filled the air. Both computer screens were still alight in the dark, and so was every other square of the marble floor: it became clear to the terror-stricken tourists that they were standing on a huge chessboard and were the unwilling participants in a game of chess played by two computers.

A limbomat with a burning torch in one hand rushed into the chamber. Two others opened a fuse box and began repairing the damage. The tourists remained in their spots on the chessboard. One of the pieces, a man dressed in white, made a move. The white computer clearly didn't need the overhead lights and, having summoned the repair crew, continued the game.

Each side of the huge chessboard measured eight yards. In the light of the torch the white squares became somewhat dimmer but remained visible. The insulation must have caught fire when the cable was overloaded by the sudden surge in electricity needed by one of the players to solve an exceptionally difficult problem. Now Lucy knew why the limbomats had dressed some tourists in white and some in black costumes. She noted that she herself was wearing a white dress and was standing outside the chessboard, though near its edge, on the side of the black computer. At first this seemed a good sign: she was beyond the battlefield and hadn't yet participated in the game that obviously had been going on for some time.

Did this mean that she was in no danger?

There were twenty people on the chessboard. The corpses of twelve more, eliminated from the game, were piled by the wall. The tourists wore hats and helmets in the shapes of the pieces they represented in the game. Miserable, they twisted their necks looking around. So far they had been convinced that they'd either be killed by a sudden blow or have to deal one themselves at a random moment picked by the main computer; now they realized their fate depended on the situation on the chessboard. If the two computers involved in the game decided on a draw or if one checkmated the other, this would save the lives of the remaining tourists; otherwise only the two kings were certain to survive.

The white computer had foreseen many of the moves a long time ago. That's why, when Lucy entered the elevator, it invited her to be the queen. As soon as she thought of this, the man in front of her walked off the chessboard, while she, obeying the impulses in her legs, quickly took his place.

The man, a white pawn, had reached the eighth line and so could be replaced by any figure of the white computer's choice. The pawn's promotion, when Lucy took his place, seemed as innocent as a change of guards.

As soon as she stepped on the chessboard, she lifted her hands to the mysterious weight on her back; with one hand she detached a crossbow and a quiver of bolts and with the other a golden crown, which she placed on her head. The crossbow's string was drawn. Lucy notched a bolt and aimed it at the black king.

In response to the white computer's "check" the black player shielded his king with a knight. Lucy turned to the middle of the chessboard. A sudden impulse made her release the bolt. She heard the twang of the bowstring but, having quickly closed her eyes, did not see the bolt hit its target. She opened them at the sound of a deadweight dropping to the floor. A black bishop's helmet rolled toward her feet. The bolt had pierced the heart of the felled figure. Lucy recognized the woman who had earlier thrown her spear at the young man. After the shot, Lucy's muscles forced her to leave her square. She walked, surefooted, to the spot where her victim had stood.

The black computer wasted no time in responding to its opponent's move: one of its pawns decapitated with his sword a white knight. The role of knight was played by an old boxing coach armed with a trident; the pawn was his pupil, a young, superbly built heavyweight. The blow was delivered with such force that the old man's weapon flew out of his hand and with a loud *clunk!* hit the white computer.

Several crooked lines appeared on its screen; the image wavered and split. As this was happening, Lucy was forced to walk to a new spot. The next moment the screen returned to normal and Lucy felt her legs tense again; she marched back to her former position.

She knew she was the white queen. At an earlier stage of the game the white player had lost or, more likely, sacrificed this piece to improve his overall position. Now, after the foreseen promotion of the pawn and the exchange of several pieces, neither player had a visible lead or more pieces than his opponent—a situation typical of most games played by champions. Even if she had known chess well enough to tell whether the white computer had a positional advantage, she would have been unable to do so at this macabre moment when, in the glow of the burning torch, the hook pulled two more bodies toward the wall.

A red light began blinking on top of the black computer, and it pointed its video camera's snout at Lucy. The white computer rewound a few feet of its videotape and played the last segment to show the accident it had suffered. It even made Lucy stomp her foot, but the black computer—as if refusing to accept the white player's arguments—repeated its angry signals.

It was clear that the black chess player, citing the accepted rules, was protesting his opponent's decision to take back the move he had made with his queen, while the white player was trying to explain he had been temporarily indisposed.

A limbomat controlled by the judge—the main computer—rushed up to the white computer and, brandishing a heavy hammer, forced the machine to obey the rules. Lucy received a command to return to the spot in question. She did so. Walking to it, she saw a man who, when they were sightseeing the city, had always lagged behind, lost in thought, until finally one of the other tourists, as a joke, had discreetly pinned to his back a scrap of paper with the words: TOUR'S END. Lucy had talked with this man, a composer, the day before and had enjoyed their conversation.

Now he marched past her, a black rook shaped helmet on his head, and stopped three squares away, ready to defend the black queen, played by Lucy's friend.

The black queen had not yet removed her weapon from her back. She was waiting for the white computer's move. Lucy could see her imploring gaze. She herself felt she was going to faint, but she rested her crossbow against the floor and began turning its handle to draw the bowstring. Her heart was pounding; she realized the white computer had decided on an exchange of queens in order to force the black rook—by making it kill Lucy—to move to a less advantageous spot.

She felt as if she were shooting at her own mirror image when her bolt hit the other queen in the belly.

She didn't look at the composer's face when the hook started to pull away her friend's body. She didn't want to see the smile the machine forced him to wear. Wishing to shorten her own agony, she stretched her neck toward the black rook's descending ax. It dropped past her head and chopped off her arm and then rose once more, glinting in the light of the torch—and fell again.

She heard waves beating softly against the shore and, instead of pain in her arm, felt a gentle breeze caress her naked skin. Only the golden crown was still exerting pressure on her temples, so she lifted her hand to push it back. She could move her limbs freely. When she opened her eyes, she was sure she was dreaming.

First she saw the sky. There were a few small clouds, but otherwise it was clear blue, stretching to the horizon. When she raised herself a little, she saw the sea. She was lying under a red umbrella, dressed in a swimming suit. The sparse clouds were hanging low over the beach. The gentle breeze rippled the water. A number of people were sunbathing on the sand.

For a moment she stared into the distance, and then she noticed cables running from her forehead to the plastic box standing by her bag. Suddenly she regained her awareness of time and place. She took the heavy ring off her head, wound the cable around it, and placed it on the blanket. She knew now who she was and where she was. Although this wasn't the first cassette she had seen, she still had trouble believing that what had happened to her a moment ago was just a nightmarish illusion. The magnetic dream produced by the local videofate company had seemed incredibly real.

She walked out from under the umbrella into the sun. She was still thinking of what she'd been through when she heard her husband's voice:

"Why don't we go swimming before lunch?"

"Where were you?"

"Talking to the engineer of this beach. In exchange for the Martian's ear I gave him, he told me about the secret report he just received. The news is really alarming."

"What's happening?"

"The seventh squadron of shuffling dishes is swimming our way. They are expected to invade this shore tomorrow." He laughed. "The locals are preparing nets, clubs, impregnating agents, and glow paints for painting their tentacles. Maybe here, in Borneo, where everybody's already got a flying saucer, an attack by tentacled sea monsters is exactly what is needed to alleviate the boredom. And it should create a boom in the souvenir trade. How did you like *The Angel of Violence?*"

"What?"

He bent over the machine, took out the cassette, and showed her the colorful label with the words THE ANGEL OF VIOLENCE printed across the drawing of a white computer.

"It was a nightmare!" she cried. "How could you get me something so awful?"

"You wanted to see a horror videofate."

"You should have warned me what it was about!"

"That wouldn't have done you any good. The moment you turn on the machine you lose all consciousness of your real past. It becomes replaced by a fictitious one, created to fit the plot on tape."

"Do all horror videofates end with the viewer's simulated death?"

"Yes, with no exception. If the viewing is interrupted, he or she dies in a sudden accident. Time flies with incredible speed in a videofate; in one day you go through a whole life."

A child left alone under the next umbrella suddenly began crying and jumping around on one foot. From the radio tack stuck to the heel of its other foot emerged an announcer's voice:

"We have just received news from Singapore concerning the anthropoid apes living in a nature preserve on one of the islands off the coast of Borneo. The leader of the gorillas, who have reached a very high level of intelligence, called a press conference and proudly announced that scientists from his pack will soon construct their first atom bomb. The gorillas, of course, do not intend to use this medieval weapon against the chimpanzees inhabiting the neighboring preserve, although the gorilla leader did say its detonation would be a definite solution to their differences. He also said the gorillas feel their security among all of the island's inhabitants."

Lucy pulled the talking tack out of the child's foot, still thinking of the videofate. She could not get used to the sudden change of environment, the more so since she was now twenty years older than in the film.

"Where is that island?" she asked her husband.

"There." He pointed toward the horizon.

For several minutes they stared in silence.

"Time for lunch," Lucy's husband finally said. "I want to go for a last swim before we leave the beach. You coming?"

The water was clear and warm. On the way back to their spot on the sand they passed a group of people playing volleyball. Suddenly Lucy screamed and covered her face with her hands. A move made by one of the players who jumped to hit the ball had terrified her. The strangers stopped playing and stood there, waiting.

They smiled at her, but this was no help; she felt she was back on the chessboard and a deadly blow would split her skull any moment.

"Why did these machines force people to kill their friends?" she asked her husband when they reached their blanket.

"You mean in *The Angel of Violence?*"

"Yes."

"Simple. They were programmed by two chess players and were checking the merits of their respective game plans."

"On people?"

He looked at her serious face. "Is that what's bothering you? Look, it was just a story, some improbable rubbish made up by the scriptwriters of horror videofates."

"Wait. . . . Didn't multimillion medieval armies murder each other freely? they weren't made-up criminals, were they?"

He laughed loudly. "Of course not! You silly thing, you really don't know? Soldiers killed willingly and died gladly. And they weren't criminals because in those days all bad people locked away in prisons. Just think! If things were otherwise, if good people did not kill of their own free will, then in order to explain the mechanism of war we'd have to accept as fact a version of history very much like the plot of *The Angel of Violence.* And because the idea of two invisible players hunched over the chessboard of the world is too fanciful to contemplate, we would be forced to assume that medieval kings had at their disposal fantastic machines allowing them to control remotely the muscles of millions and that they used these machines to make peace loving people kill each other."

"But it does sound fantastic, doesn't it? Bad people locked away in prisons, and good people—" She didn't finish. As she spoke the beach became dissected by long black shadows cast by standing tourists. It seemed as if a blindingly brilliant sun had torn asunder the darkness of night. The glow of the most nightmarish dawn imaginable illuminated the sky behind Lucy's back.

In the blink of an eye the whole shore was drenched with heat. A crimson flash, ten times brighter than the sun, scorched the lush vegetation, engulfing it in flames and reducing to ash; human bodies were transformed into pillars of fire.

A fraction of a second earlier Lucy had turned toward the source of light. The cloud of an atomic explosion, gigantic in size, mushroomed over the island of the apes. Its top reached high into the atmosphere. She knew that in a few seconds the coast would be hit by a thundering shock wave and everything, including her, would be swept off the surface of the earth.

But she wasn't there to see this.

She discovered that she was lying inside a glass cubicle. Her naked body was submerged in a transparent liquid. In the sudden silence a pleasant female voice spoke into her ear:

"We apologize for interrupting your videofate. Is your number nine hundred forty billion five million seventy-one?"

On a small console at the end of the glass container she saw the silver number 940,005,000,071.

"Yes," she said.

"How old are you?"

The age indicator had golden numerals. "Nineteen."

"Then everything's in order," the pleasant voice said. "After waiting your turn for a hundred and twenty years you have obtained the right to twenty-four hours of authentic life. Your place will be free in an hour's time; that's why we had to wake you. Get ready! In fifteen minutes an express elevator will take your cabin two and a half miles up, to the roof of Europe. You will see the real sun, water, and trees. Once again we apologize for turning off your videofate. Enjoy yourself!"

All around, behind the glass walls of their cubicles, narrow as coffins, rested the sleeping forms of human beings. Only Lucy lay with her eyes open. For a dozen minutes or so she stared at the millions of naked bodies arranged symmetrically in lighted glass rows, converging in infinity.

The indicators on the console were behind a pane of glass. Lucy broke it with her elbow. She closed her eyes and yanked out all the cables, but when she opened her eyes and saw the world around her unchanged, she placed her wrist on the broken glass—to turn the picture off forever.

Algis Budrys

Algis Budrys (1931–) is the author of a number of SF novels including the highly regarded *Rogue Moon* (1960) and *Michelmas* (1977), the latest of which is *Hard Landing* (1993). Some of his short fiction, predominantly from the 1950s, is collected in *The Unexpected Dimension* (1960), *Budrys's Inferno* (1963), and *Blood and Burning* (1978).

James Blish in a laudatory essay on Budrys in his famous critical work, *More Issues at Hand* (1970), says, "His gifts go far beyond craftsmanship into that instinctual realm where dwell the genuine ear for the melos and the polyphony of the English language, and the fundamental insight into the human heart." Gene Wolfe, in *Science Fiction Writers*, says "Every age and every genre produce a few writers too good for them . . . Budrys is one of these. He is, in the best sense, too serious a writer for science fiction." And like Blish, Budrys is one of the best critics of science fiction, probably the best in the generation after Blish, Damon Knight, and Theodore Sturgeon, from the mid-'60s to the mid-'80s. A collection of his reviews and essays from *Galaxy* in the 1960s is *Benchmarks: Galaxy Bookshelf* (1985). Presently he is publishing and editing his own magazine of SF, *Tomorrow*.

Most SF writers sooner or later address the theme of human evolution and many attempt to portray what a superior human might be like. Budrys imagines he might be like Gus.

NOBODY BOTHERS GUS

Two years earlier, Gus Kusevic had been driving slowly down the narrow back road into Boonesboro.

It was good country for slow driving, particularly in the late spring. There was nobody else on the road. The woods were just blooming into a deep, rich green as yet unburned by summer, and the afternoons were still cool and fresh. And, just before he reached the Boonesboro town line, he saw the locked and weathered cottage standing for sale on its quarter acre lot.

He had pulled his roadcar up to a gentle stop, swung sideways in his seat, and looked at it.

It needed paint; the siding had gone from white to gray, and the trim was faded. There were shingles missing here and there from the roof, leaving squares of darkness on the sun-bleached rows of cedar, and inevitably, some of the windowpanes had cracked. But the frame hadn't slouched out of square, and the roof hadn't sagged. The chimney stood up straight.

He looked at the straggled clumps and windrowed hay that were all that remained of the shrubbery and the lawn. His broad, homely face bunched itself into a quiet smile along its well-worn seams. His hands itched for the feel of a spade.

He got out of the roadcar, walked across the road and up to the cottage door, and copied down the name of the real estate dealer listed on the card tacked to the door frame.

Now it was almost two years later, early in April, and Gus was top-dressing his lawn.

Earlier in the day he'd set up a screen beside the pile of topsoil behind his house, shoveled the soil through the screen, mixed it with broken peat moss, and carted it out to the lawn, where he left it in small piles. Now he was carefully raking it out over the young grass in a thin layer that covered only the roots, and let the blades peep through. He intended to be finished by the time the second half of the Giants-Kodiaks doubleheader came on. He particularly wanted to see it because Halsey was pitching for the Kodiaks, and he had something of an avuncular interest in Halsey.

He worked without waste motion or excess expenditure of energy. Once or twice he stopped and had a beer in the shade of the rose arbor he'd put up around the front door. Nevertheless, the sun was hot; by early afternoon, he had his shirt off.

Just before he would have been finished, a battered flivver settled down in front of the house. It parked with a flurry of its rotors, and a gangling man in a worn serge suit, with thin hair plastered across his tight scalp, climbed out and looked at Gus uncertainly.

Gus had glanced up briefly while the flivver was on its silent way down. He'd made out the barely-legible "Falmouth County Clerk's Office" lettered over the faded paint on its door, shrugged, and gone on with what he was doing.

Gus was a big man. His shoulders were heavy and broad; his chest was deep, grizzled with thick, iron-gray hair. His stomach had gotten a little heavier with the years, but the muscles were still there under the layer of flesh. His upper arms were thicker than a good many thighs, and his forearms were enormous.

His face was seamed by a network of folds and creases. His flat cheeks were marked out by two deep furrows that ran from the sides of his bent nose, merged with the creases bracketing his wide lips, and converged toward the blunt point of his jaw. His pale blue eyes twinkled above high cheekbones which were covered with wrinkles. His close-cropped hair was as white as cotton.

Only repeated and annoying exposure would give his body a tan, but his face was permanently browned. The pink of his body sunburn was broken in several places by white scar tissue. The thin line of a knife cut emerged from the tops of his pants and faded out across the right side of his stomach. The other significant area of scarring lay across the uneven knuckles of his heavy-fingered hands.

The clerk looked at the mailbox to make sure of the name, checking it against an envelope he was holding in one hand. He stopped and looked at Gus again, mysteriously nervous.

Gus abruptly realized that he probably didn't present a reassuring appearance. With all the screening and raking he'd been doing, there'd been a lot of dust in the air. Mixed with perspiration, it was all over his face, chest, arms, and back. Gus knew he didn't look very gentle even at his cleanest and best-dressed. At the moment, he couldn't blame the clerk for being skittish.

He tried to smile disarmingly.

The clerk ran his tongue over his lips, cleared his throat with a slight cough, and jerked his head toward the mail box. "Is that right? You Mr. Kusevic?"

Gus nodded. "That's right. What can I do for you?"

The clerk held up the envelope. "Got a notice here from the County Council," he muttered, but he was obviously much more taken up by his effort to equate Gus with the rose arbor, the neatly edged and carefully tended flower beds, the hedges, the flagstoned walk, the small goldfish pond under the willow tree, the white-painted cottage with its window boxes and bright shutters, and the curtains showing inside the sparkling windows.

Gus waited until the man was through with his obvious thoughts, but something deep inside him sighed quietly. He had gone through this moment of bewilderment with so many other people that he was quite accustomed to it, but that is not the same thing as being oblivious.

"Well, come on inside," he said after a decent interval. "It's pretty hot out here, and I've got some beer in the cooler."

The clerk hesitated again. "Well, all I've got to do it deliver this notice—" he said, still looking around. "Got the place fixed up real nice, don't you?"

Gus smiled. "It's my home. A man likes to live in a nice place. In a hurry?"

The clerk seemed to be troubled by something in what Gus had said. Then he looked up suddenly, obviously just realizing he'd been asked a direct question. "Huh?"

"You're not in any hurry, are you? Come on in; have a beer. Nobody's expected to be a ball of fire on a spring afternoon."

The clerk grinned uneasily. "No . . . nope, guess not." He brightened. "O.K.! Don't mind if I do."

Gus ushered him into the house, grinning with pleasure. Nobody's seen the inside of the place since he'd fixed it up; the clerk was the first visitor he'd had since moving in. There weren't even any delivery men; Boonesboro was so small you had to drive in for your own shopping. There wasn't any mail carrier service, of course—not that Gus ever received any mail.

He showed the clerk into the living room. "Have a seat. I'll be right back." He went quickly out to the kitchen, took some beer out of the cooler, loaded a tray with glasses, a bowl of chips and pretzels, and the beer, and carried it out.

The clerk was up, looking around the library that covered two of the living room walls.

Looking at his expression, Gus realized with genuine regret that the man wasn't the kind to doubt whether an obvious clod like Kusevic had read any of this stuff. A man like that could still be talked to, once the original misconceptions were knocked down. No, the clerk was too plainly mystified that a grown man would fool with books. Particularly a man like Gus; now, one of these kids that messed with college politics, that was something else. But a grown man oughtn't to act like that.

Gus saw it had been a mistake to expect anything of the clerk. He should have known better, whether he was hungry for company or not. He'd *always* been hungry for company, and it was time he realized, once and for all, that he just plain wasn't going to find any.

He set the tray down on the table, uncapped a beer quickly, and handed it to the man.

"Thanks," the clerk mumbled. He took a swallow, sighed loudly, and wiped his mouth with the back of his hand. He looked around the room again. "Cost you a lot to have all this put in?"

Gus shrugged. "Did most of it myself. Built the shelves and furniture; stuff like that. Some of the paintings I had to buy, and the books and records."

The clerk grunted. He seemed to be considerably ill at ease, probably because of the notice he'd brought, whatever it was. Gus found himself wondering what it could possibly be, but, now that he'd made the mistake of giving the man a beer, he had to wait politely until it was finished before he could ask.

He went over to the TV set. "Baseball fan?" he asked the clerk.

"Sure!"

"Giants-Kodiaks ought to be on." He switched the set on and pulled up a hassock, sitting on it so as not to get one of the chairs dirty. The clerk wandered over and stood looking at the screen, taking slow swallows of his beer.

The second game had started, and Halsey's familiar figure appeared on the screen as the set warmed up. The lithe young lefthander was throwing with his usual boneless motion, apparently not working hard at all, but the ball was whipping past the batters with a sizzle that the home plate microphone was picking up clearly.

Gus nodded toward Halsey. "He's quite a pitcher, isn't he?"

The clerk shrugged. "Guess so. Walker's their best man, though."

Gus sighed as he realized he'd forgotten himself again. The clerk wouldn't pay much attention to Halsey, naturally.

But he was getting a little irritated at the man, with his typical preconceptions of what was proper and what wasn't, of who had a right to grow roses and who didn't.

"Offhand," Gus said to the clerk, "could you tell me what Halsey's record was, last year?"

The clerk shrugged. "Couldn't tell you. Wasn't bad—I remember that much. 13-7, something like that."

Gus nodded to himself. "Uh-huh. How'd Walker do?"

"Walker! Why, man, Walker just won something like twenty-five games, that's all. And three no-hitters. How'd Walker do? Huh!"

Gus shook his head. "Walker's a good pitcher, all right—but he didn't pitch any no-hitters. And he only won eighteen games."

The clerk wrinkled his forehead. He opened his mouth to argue and then stopped. He looked like a sure-thing better who'd just realized that his memory had played him a trick.

"Say—I think you're right! Huh! Now what the Sam Hill made me think Walker was the guy? And you know something—I've been talking about him all winter, and nobody once called me wrong?" The clerk scratched his head. "Now, *somebody* pitched them games! Who the dickens was it?" He scowled in concentration.

Gus silently watched Halsey strike out his third batter in a row, and his face wrinkled into a slow smile. Halsey was still young; just hitting his stride. He threw himself into the game with all the energy and enjoyment a man felt when he realized he was at his peak, and that, out there on the mound in the sun, he was as good as any man who ever had gone before him in this profession.

Gus wondered how soon Halsey would see the trap he'd set for himself.

Because it wasn't a contest. Not for Halsey. For Christy Mathewson, it had been a contest. For Lefty Grove and Dizzy Dean, for Bob Feller and Slats Gould, it had been a contest. But for Halsey it was just a complicated form of solitaire that always came out right.

Pretty soon, Halsey'd realize that you can't handicap yourself at solitaire. If you knew where all the cards are; if you knew that unless you deliberately cheated against yourself, you couldn't help but win—what good was it? One of these days, Halsey'd realize there wasn't a game on Earth he couldn't beat; whether it was a physical contest, organized and formally recognized as a game, or whether it was the billion-triggered pinball machine called Society.

What then, Halsey? What then? And if you find out, please, in the name of whatever kind of brotherhood we share, let me know.

The clerk grunted. "Well, it don't matter, I guess. I can always look it up in the record book at home."

Yes, you can, Gus commented silently. But you won't notice what it says, and, if you do, you'll forget it and never realize you've forgotten.

The clerk finished his beer, set it down on the tray, and was free to remember what he'd come here for. He looked around the room again, as though the memory were a cue of some kind.

"Lots of books," he commented.

Gus nodded, watching Halsey walk out to the pitcher's mound again.

"Uh . . . you read 'em all?"

Gus shook his head.

"How about that one by the Miller fellow? I hear that's a pretty good one."

So. The clerk had a certain narrow interest in certain aspects of certain kinds of literature.

"I suppose it is," Gus answered truthfully. "I read the first three pages, once." And, having done so, he'd known how the rest of it was going to go, who would do what when, and he'd lost interest. The library had been a mistake, just one of a dozen similar experiments. If he'd wanted an academic familiarity with human literature, he could just as easily have picked it up by browsing through bookstores, rather than buying the books and doing substantially the same thing at home. He couldn't hope to extract any emotional empathies, no matter what he did.

Face it, though; rows of even useless books were better than bare wall. The trappings of culture were a bulwark of sorts, even though it was a learned culture and not a *felt* one, and meant no more to him than the culture of the Incas. Try as he might, he could never be an Inca. Nor even a Maya or an Aztec, or any kind of kin, except by the most tenuous of extensions.

But he had no culture of his own. There was the thing; the emptiness that nevertheless ached; the rootlessness, the complete absence of a place to stand and say: "This is my own."

Halsey struck out the first batter in the inning with three pitches. Then he put a slow floater precisely where the next man could get the best part of his bat on it, and did not even look up as the ball screamed out of the park. He struck out the next two men with a total of eight pitches.

Gus shook his head slowly. That was the first symptom; when you didn't bother to be subtle about your handicapping any more.

The clerk held out the envelope. "Here," he said brusquely, having finally shilly-shallied his resolution up to the point of doing it despite his obvious nervousness at Gus' probable reaction.

Gus opened the envelope and read the notice. Then, just as the clerk had been doing, he looked around the room. A dark expression must have flickered over his face, because the clerk became even more hesitant. "I . . . I want you to know I regret this. I guess all of us do."

Gus nodded hastily. "Sure, sure." He stood up and looked out the front window. He smiled crookedly, looking at the top-dressing spread carefully over the painstakingly rolled lawn, which was slowly taking form on the plot where he had plowed last year and picked out pebbles, seeded and watered, shoveled topsoil, laid out flower beds . . . ah, there was no use going into that now. The whole plot, cottage and all, was condemned, and that was that.

"They're . . . they're turnin' the road into a twelve-lane freight highway," the clerk explained.

Gus nodded absently.

The clerk moved closer and dropped his voice. "Look—I was told to tell you this. Not in writin'." He sidled even closer, and actually looked around before he spoke. He laid his hand confidentially on Gus' bare forearm.

"Any price you ask for," he muttered, "is gonna be O.K., as long as you don't get too greedy. The county isn't paying this bill. Not even the state, if you get what I mean."

Gus got what he meant. Twelve-lane highways aren't built by anything but national governments.

He got more than that. National governments don't work this way unless there's a good reason.

"Highway between Hollister and Farnham?" he asked.

The clerk paled. "Don't know for sure," he muttered.

Gus smiled thinly. Let the clerk wonder how he'd guessed. It couldn't be much of a secret, anyway—not after the grade was laid out and the purpose became self-evident. Besides, the clerk wouldn't wonder very long.

A streak of complete perversity shot through Gus. He recognized its source in his anger at losing the cottage, but there was no reason why he shouldn't allow himself to cut loose.

"What's your name?" he asked the clerk abruptly.

"Uh . . . Harry Danvers."

"Well, Harry, suppose I told you I could stop that highway, if I wanted to? Suppose I told you that no bulldozer could get near this place without breaking down, that no shovel could dig this ground, that sticks of dynamite just plain wouldn't explode if they tried to blast? Suppose I told you that if they put in the highway, it would turn soft as ice cream if I wanted it to, and run away like a river?"

"Huh?"

"Hand me your pen."

Danvers reached out mechanically and handed it to him. Gus put it between his palms and rolled it into a ball. He dropped it and caught it as it bounced up sharply from the soft, thick rug. He pulled it out between his fingers, and it returned to its cylindrical shape. He unscrewed the cap, flattened it out into a sheet between two fingers, scribbled on it, rolled it back into a cap, and, using his fingernail to draw out the ink which was now part of it, permanently inscribed Danvers' name just below the surface of the metal. Then he screwed the cap on again and handed the pen back to the country clerk. "Souvenir," he said.

The clerk looked down at it.

"Well?" Gus asked. "Aren't you curious about how I did it and what I am?"

The clerk shook his head. "Good trick. I guess you magician fellows must spend a lot of time practicing, huh? Can't say I could see myself spendin' that much working time on a hobby."

Gus nodded. "That's a good, sound, practical point of view," he said. Particularly when all of us automatically put out a field that damps curiosity, he thought. What point of view *could* you have?

He looked over the clerk's shoulder at the lawn, and one side of his mouth twisted sadly.

Only God can make a tree, he thought, looking at the shrubs and flower beds. Should we all, then, look for our challenge in landscape gardening? Should we become the gardeners of the rich humans in the expensive houses, driving up in our old, rusty trucks, oiling our lawnmowers, kneeling on the humans' lawns with our clipping shears, coming to the kitchen door to ask for a drink of water on a hot summer day?

The highway. Yes, he could stop the highway. Or make it go around him. There was no way of stopping the curiosity damper, no more than there was a way of willing his heart to stop, but it could be stepped up. He could force his mind to labor near overload, and no one would ever even *see* the cottage, the lawn, the rose arbor, or the battered old man, drinking his beer. Or rather, seeing them, would pay them absolutely no attention.

But the first time he went into town, or when he died, the field would be off, and then what? The curiosity, then investigation, then, perhaps a fragment of theory here or there to be fitted to another somewhere else. And then what? Pogrom?

He shook his head. The humans couldn't win, and would lose monstrously. *That* was why he couldn't leave the humans a clue. He had no taste for slaughtering sheep, and he doubted if his fellows did.

His fellows. Gus stretched his mouth. The only one he could be sure of was Halsey. There had to be others, but there was no way of finding them. They provoked no reaction from the humans; they left no trail to follow. It was only if they showed themselves, like Halsey, that they could be seen. There was, unfortunately, no private telepathic party line among them.

He wondered if Halsey hoped someone would notice him and get in touch. He wondered if Halsey even suspected there were others like himself. He wondered if anyone had noticed *him*, when Gus Kusevic's name had been in the papers occasionally.

It's the dawn of my race, he thought. The first generation—or is it, and does it matter—and I wonder where the females are.

He turned back to the clerk. "I want what I paid for the place," he said. "No more."

The clerk's eyes widened slightly, then relaxed, and he shrugged. "Suit yourself. But if it was me, I'd soak the government good."

Yes, Gus thought, you doubtless would. But I don't want to, because you simply don't take candy from babies.

So the superman packed his bags and got out of the human's way. Gus choked a silent laugh. The damping field. The damping-field. The thrice-cursed, ever-benevolent, foolproof, autonomic, protective damping field.

Evolution had, unfortunately, not yet realized that there was such a thing as human society. It produced a being with a certain modification from the human stock, thereby arriving at practical psi. In order to protect this feeble new species, whose members were so terribly sparse, it gave them the perfect camouflage.

Result: When young Augustin Kusevic was enrolled in school, it was discovered that he had no birth certificate. No hospital recalled his birth. As a matter of brutal fact, his human parents sometimes forgot his existence for days at a time.

Result: When young Gussie Kusevic tried to enter high school, it was discovered that he had never entered grammar school. No matter that he could quote teachers' names, textbooks, or classroom numbers. No matter if he could produce report cards. They were misfiled, and the anguished interviews forgotten. No one doubted his existence—people remembered the fact of his being, and the fact of his having acted and being acted upon. But only as though they had read it in some infinitely boring book.

He had no friends, no girl, no past, no present, no love. He had no place to stand. Had there been such things as ghosts, he would have found his fellowship there.

By the time of his adolescence, he had discovered an absolute lack of involvement with the human race. He studied it, because it was the salient feature of his environment. He did not live with it. It said nothing to him that was of personal value; its motivations, morals, manners and morale did not find responsive reactions in him. And his, of course, made absolutely no impression on it.

The life of the peasant of ancient Babylon is of interest to only a few historical anthropologists, none of whom actually want to *be* Babylonian peasants.

Having solved the human social equation from his dispassionate viewpoint, and caring no more than the naturalist who finds that deer are extremely fond of green aspen leaves, he plunged into physical release. He discovered the thrill of picking fights and winning them; of *making* somebody pay attention to him by smashing his nose.

He might have become a permanent fixture on the Manhattan docks, if another longshoreman hadn't slashed him with a carton knife. The cultural demand on him had been plain. He'd had to kill the man.

That had been the end of unregulated personal combat. He discovered, not to his horror but to his disgust, that he could get away with murder. No investigation had been made; no search was attempted.

So that had been the end of that, but it had led him to the only possible evasion of the trap to which he had been born. Intellectual competition being meaningless, organized sports became the only answer. Simultaneously regulating his efforts and annotating them under a mound of journalistic record-keeping, they furnished the first official continuity his life had ever known. People still forgot his accomplishments, but when they turned to the records, his name was undeniably there. A dossier can be misfiled. School records can disappear. But something more than a damping field was required to shunt aside the mountain of news copy and statistics that drags, ball-like, at the ankle of even the mediocre athlete.

It seemed to Gus—and he thought of it a great deal—that this chain of progression was inevitable for any male of his kind. When, three years ago, he had discovered Halsey, his hypothesis was bolstered. But what good was Halsey to another male? To hold mutual consolation sessions with? He had no intention of ever contacting the man.

The clerk cleared his throat. Gus jerked his head around to look at him, startled. He'd forgotten him.

"Well, guess I'll be going. Remember, you've only got two months."

Gus gestured noncommittally. The man had delivered his message. Why didn't he acknowledge he'd served his purpose, and go?

Gus smiled ruefully. What purpose did *homo nondescriptus* serve, and where was he going? Halsey was already walking downhill along the well-marked trail. *Were* there others? If so, then they were in another rut, somewhere, and not even the tops of their heads showed. He and his kind could recognize each other only by an elaborate process of elimination; they had to watch for the people no one noticed.

He opened the door for the clerk, saw the road, and found his thoughts back with the highway.

The highway would run from Hollister, which was a railroad junction, to the Air Force Base at Farnham, where his calculations in sociomathematics had long ago predicted the first starship would be constructed and launched. The trucks would rumble up the highway, feeding the open maw with men and material.

He cleaned his lips. Up there in space, somewhere; somewhere outside the Solar System, was another race. The imprint of their visits here was plain. The humans would encounter them, and again he could predict the result; the humans would win.

Gus Kusevic could not go along to investigate the challenges that he doubted lay among the stars. Even with scrapbooks full of notices and clippings, he had barely made his career penetrate the public consciousness. Halsey, who had exuberantly broken every baseball record in the books, was known as a "pretty fair country pitcher."

What credentials could he present with his application to the Air Force? Who would remember them the next day if he had any? What would become of the records of his inoculations, his physical check-ups, his training courses? Who would remember to reserve a bunk for him, or stow supplies for him, or add his consumption to the total when the time came to allow for oxygen?

Stow away? Nothing easier. But, again; who would die so he could live within the tight lattice of shipboard economy? Which sheep would he slaughter, and to what useful purpose, in the last analysis?

"Well, so long," the clerk said.

"Good-bye," Gus said.

The clerk walked down the flagstones and out to his flivver.

I think, Gus said to himself, it would have been much better for us if Evolution had been a little less protective and a little more thoughtful. An occasional pogrom wouldn't have done us any harm. A ghetto at least keeps the courtship problem solved.

Our seed has been split on the ground.

Suddenly, Gus ran forward, pushed by something he didn't care to name. He looked up through the flivver's open door, and the clerk looked down apprehensively.

"Danvers, you're a sports fan," Gus said hastily, realizing his voice was too urgent; that he was startling the clerk with his intensity.

"That's right," the clerk answered, pushing himself nervously back along the seat.

"Who's heavyweight champion of the world?"

"Mike Frazier. Why?"

"Who'd he beat for the title? Who used to be champion?"

The clerk pursed his lips. "Huh! It's been years—gee, I don't know. I don't remember. I could look it up, I guess."

Gus exhaled slowly. He half-turned and looked back toward the cottage, the lawn, the flower beds, the walk, the arbor, and the fish pond under the willow tree. "Never mind," he said, and walked back into the house while the clerk wobbled his flivver into the air.

The TV set was blaring with sound. He checked the status of the game.

It had gone quickly. Halsey had pitched a one-hitter so far, and the Giants' pitcher had done almost as well. The score was tied at 1–1, the Giants were at bat, and it was the last out in the ninth inning. The camera boomed in on Halsey's face.

Halsey looked at the batter with complete disinterest in his eyes, wound up, and threw the home-run ball.

Dino Buzzati

Dino Buzzati (1906–72) was one of the important Italian writers to emerge after the second world war. His principal modes were the absurd and the fantastic. He first came to international attention with his contemporary novel *The Tartar Steppe* (1945). His only SF novel, *Larger Than Life* (1960), a big computer story (a mainframe computer is programmed with the personality of a woman), is undistinguished. Critics agree, however, that his major work was in his short stories.

"The effectiveness of a fantastic story will depend on its being told in the most simple and practical terms . . . fantasy should be as close as possible to journalism," Buzzati said. He wrote a number of SF stories but has never been published or recognized as a writer of the genre in English. A collection of his fantasy and SF is, it seems to me, overdue. This story is a small, graceful piece on a classic SF idea.

THE TIME MACHINE

The first great installation to slow down time was built near Grosseto, in Mariscano. In fact, the inventor, the famous Aldo Cristofari, was a native of Grosseto. This Cristofari, a professor at the University of Pisa, had been interested in the problem for at least twenty years and had conducted marvelous experiments in his laboratory, especially on the germination of legumes. In the academic world, however, he was thought a visionary. Until, under the aegis of his supporter, the financier Alfredo Lopez, the society for the construction of Diacosia was created. From then on Aldo Cristofari was regarded as a genius, a benefactor to humanity.

His invention consisted of a special electrostatic field called "Field C," within which natural phenomena required an abnormally longer period of time to complete their life cycles. In the first decisive experiments, this delay did not exceed five or six units per thousand; in practice, that is to say, it was almost unnoticeable. Yet once Cristofari had discovered the principle, he made very rapid progress. With the installation at Mariscano the rate of retardation was increased to nearly half. This meant that an organism with an average life span of ten years could be inserted in Field C and reach an age of twenty years.

The installation was built in a hilly zone, and it was not effective beyond a range of 800 meters. In a circle with a diameter of one and a half kilometers, animals and plants would grow and age half as quickly as those on the rest of the earth. Man could now hope to live for two centuries. And so—from the Greek for two hundred—the name Diacosia was chosen.

The zone was practically uninhabited. The few peasants who lived there were given the choice of staying or relocating elsewhere with a sizeable settlement.

They preferred to clear out. The area was entirely enclosed within an insurmountable fence. There was only one entrance, and it was carefully guarded. In a short time there rose immense skyscrapers, a gigantic nursing home (for terminally ill patients who desired to prolong the little life they had left), movie houses, and theaters, all amid a forest of villas. And in the middle, at a height of forty meters, stood a circular antenna similar to those used for radar; this constituted the center of Field C. The power plant was completely underground.

Once the installation was finished, the entire world was informed that within three months the city would open its doors. To gain admission, and above all to reside there, cost an enormous sum. All the same, thousands of people from every corner of the globe were tempted. The subscriptions quickly exhausted the available housing. But then the fear began, and the flow of applicants was slower than anticipated.

What was there to fear? First of all, anyone who had settled in the city for any appreciable length of time could not leave without injury. Imagine an organism accustomed to the new, slower pace of physical existence. Suddenly transplant it from Field C to an area where life moves twice as fast; the function of every organ would have to accelerate immediately. And if it is easy for a runner to slow down, it is not so easy for someone moving slowly to bolt into a mad dash. The violent disequilibrium could have harmful or simply fatal consequences.

As a result, anyone who was born in the city was strictly forbidden to leave it. It was only logical to expect that an organism created in that slower speed could not be shifted to an environment that ran, we might say, in double time without risking destruction. In anticipation of this problem, special booths for acceleration and retardation were to be constructed on the perimeter of Field C so that anyone who left or entered it might gradually acclimate himself to the new pace and avoid the trauma of an abrupt change (they were similar to decompression chambers for deep-sea divers). But these booths were delicate devices, still in the planning stage. They would not be in service for many years.

In short, the citizens of Diacosia would live much longer than other men and women, but in exile. They were forced to give up their country, old friends, travel. They could no longer have a variety of lovers and acquaintances. It was as if they had been sentenced to life imprisonment, although they enjoyed every imaginable luxury and convenience.

But there was more. The danger posed by an escape could also be caused by any damage to the installation. It is true that there were two generators in the power plant, and that if one stopped, the other began to operate automatically. But what if both malfunctioned? What if there was a blackout? What if a cyclone or lightning struck the antenna? What if there was a war, or some outrage?

Diacosia was inaugurated at a celebration for its first group of citizens, who numbered 11,365. For the most part, they were people over fifty. Cristofari, who did not intend to settle in the city, was absent. He was represented by one Stoermer, a Swiss who was the director of the installation. There was a simple ceremony.

At the foot of the transmitting antenna that rose in the public garden, precisely at noon, Stoermer announced that from that moment on in Diacosia men and women would age exactly one-half as slowly as before. The antenna emitted a very soft hum, which was, moreover, pleasing to the ear. In the beginning, no one noticed the altered conditions. Only toward evening did some people feel a kind of lethargy, as if they were being held back. Very soon they started to talk, walk, chew with their usual composure. The tension of life subsided. Everything required greater effort.

About one month later, in *Technical Monthly*, a magazine based in Buffalo, the Nobel laureate Edwin Mediner published an article that proved to be the death knell for Diacosia. Mediner maintained that Cristofari's installation carried a grave threat. Time—we here present a synthesis of his argument in plain words—tends to rush headlong, and if it does not encounter the resistance of any matter, it will assume a progressively accelerated pace, with a tendency to increase to infinity. Thus any retardation of the flow of time requires immense effort, while it is nothing at all to augment its speed—just as in a river it is difficult to go against the current, but easy to follow it. From this observation Mediner formulated the following law: If one wishes to slow down natural phenomena, the necessary energy is directly proportional to the square of the retardation to be obtained; if one wishes to speed them up, on the other hand, the acceleration is directly proportional to the cube of the necessary energy. For example, ten units of energy are enough to achieve an acceleration of one thousand units; but the same ten units of energy applied to achieve the opposite purpose hardly produce a retardation of three units. In the first case, in fact, the human intervention operates in the same direction as time, which expects as much, so to speak. Mediner argued that Field C was such that it could operate in both directions; and an error in maintenance or a breakdown of some minor mechanism was sufficient to reverse the effect of the emission. In this case, instead of extending life to twice its average length, the machine would devour it precipitously. In the space of a few minutes, the citizens of Diacosia would age decades. And there followed the mathematical proof.

After Edwin Mediner's revelation, a wave of panic swept through the city of longevity. A few people, overlooking the risk of abruptly reentering an "accelerated environment," took flight. But Cristofari's assurances about the efficiency of the installation and the very fact that nothing had happened placated the anxieties. Life in Diacosia continued its monotonous succession of identical, placid, colorless days. Pleasures were weak and insipid, the throbbing delirium of love lacked the overpowering force it once had, news, voices, even the music that came from the outside world were now unpleasant because of their great speed. In a word, life was less interesting, despite the constant distractions. And yet this boredom was slight when compared to the thought that tomorrow, when one by one their contemporaries would pass away, the citizens of Diacosia would still be young and strong; and then their contemporaries' children would gradually die off, but the Diacosians would be full of vigor; and even their contemporaries' grandchildren and great-grandchildren would leave the world, and they who were still alive, with decades of good years ahead of them, would read the obituary notices. This was the thought that dominated the community, that calmed restless spirits, that resolved jealousies and quarrels; this was why they were not agonized as before by the passage of time and the future presented itself as a vast landscape and when confronted by disappointment men and women told themselves: Why worry about it? I'll think about it tomorrow, there isn't any hurry.

After two years, the population had climbed to 52,000, and already the first generation of Diacosians had been born. They would reach full maturity at forty. After ten years, more than 120,000 creatures swarmed over that square kilometer, and slowly, much more slowly than in other cities where time galloped, the skyline rose to dizzying heights. Diacosia had now become the greatest wonder of the world. Caravans of tourists lined the periphery, observing through the gates those people who were so different, who moved with the slowness of MS victims succumbing to paralysis.

The phenomenon lasted twenty years. And a few seconds were enough to destroy it. How did the tragedy occur? Was it caused by a man's will? Or was it chance? Perhaps one of the technicians, anguished by love or illness, wanted to abbreviate his torment and set the catastrophe in motion. Or was he maddened simply from exasperation with that empty, egocentric life, concerned only with self-preservation? And so he purposely reversed the effect of the machine, freeing the vandal forces of time.

It was May 17th, a warm, sunny day. In the fields, along the fence that ran around the perimeter, hundreds of curious observers were stationed, their eyes riveted to people just like them, whose life passed twice as slowly. From within the city came the thin, harmonious voice of the antenna. It had a bell-like resonance. The present writer was there that day and he observed a group of four children playing with a ball. "How old are you?" I asked the oldest one. "Last month I was twenty," she answered politely, but with exaggerated slowness. And their way of running was strange: all soft, viscous movements, like a film shot in slow motion. Even the ball had less bounce for them.

Beyond the fence were the lawns and paths of a garden; the barrier surrounding the buildings began at about fifty meters. A breeze moved the leaves in the trees, yet languidly, it seemed, as if they were leaden. Suddenly, about three in the afternoon, the remote hum of antenna grew more intense and rose like a siren, an unbearable piercing whistle. I will never forget what happened. Even today, at a distance of years, I awake in the dead of night with a start, confronting that horrible vision.

Before my eyes the four children stretched monstrously. I saw them grow, fatten, become adults. Beards sprouted from male chins. Transformed this way and half naked, their childhood clothes having split under the pressure of the lightning growth, they were seized with terror. They opened their mouths to speak, but what came out was a strange noise I had never heard before. In the vortex of unleashed time, the syllables all ran together, like a record played at a higher, mad speed. That gurgling quickly turned into a wheeze, then a desperate shout.

The four children looked around for help, saw us and rushed toward the railing. But life burned inside them; at the railing, a matter of seven or eight seconds, four old people arrived, with white hair and beards, flaccid and bony. One managed to seize the fence with his skeletal hands. He collapsed at once, together with his companions. They were dead. And the decrepit bodies of those poor children immediately gave off a foul odor. They were decomposing, flesh fell away, bones appeared, even the bones—before my very eyes—dissolved into a whitish dust.

Only then did the fatal scream of the machine subside and finally fall silent. Mediner's prophecy came true. For reasons that will forever remain unknown, the time machine had reversed its operation, and a few seconds were enough to swallow three or four centuries of life.

Now a gloomy, sepulchral silence has frozen the city. The shadow of abject old age has fallen over the skyscrapers, which had just been resplendent with glory and hope. The walls are wrinkled; ominous lines and creases have appeared, oozing black liquids amid a fringe of rotting spider webs. And there is dust everywhere. Dust, stillness, silence. Of the two hundred thousand wealthy, fortunate people who had wanted to live for centuries there remained nothing but white dust, collecting here and there, as on millennial tombs.

Philip José Farmer

Philip José Farmer (1918–   ) is a powerful and energetic writer of fantasy and SF who has published over fifty novels and hundreds of short stories. His most famous novels and stories are the Riverworld series, beginning with *To Your Scattered Bodies Go* (1971), which feature such historical personages as Richard Francis Burton, Mark Twain, and Jack London as central characters. He entered the genre with a powerful short story, "The Lovers" (1952), a mixture of alien biology and sex that earned him a not-undeserved reputation as a taboo-breaker and a somewhat shocking writer, if not downright disgusting. He has written most often about psychology, sex, and race, often all three at once.

Leslie A. Fiedler called him the best living science fiction writer. *The Encyclopedia of Science Fiction* says, "Farmer is governed by an instinct for extremity. Of all science fiction writers of the first or second rank, he is perhaps the most threateningly impish, and the most anarchic."

Farmer was so underpaid and underappreciated for so long in his career that when Kurt Vonnegut wrote of a fictional hack SF writer Kilgore Trout, who was psychologically and philosophically profound while writing of absurd things, Farmer identified with Trout and ultimately obtained Vonnegut's permission to write an SF novel under that name—even though Vonnegut had really been thinking of himself.

Farmer's chief mode is a startling confrontation with psychological states and symbols made literal and manifest. This story certainly does that. It is Freudian science fiction.

MOTHER

I

"Look, Mother. The clock is running backward."

Eddie Fetts pointed to the hands on the pilot room dial.

Dr. Paula Fetts said, "The crash must have reversed it."

"How could it do that?"

"I can't tell you. I don't know everything, Son."

"Oh!"

"Well, don't look at me so disappointedly. I'm a pathologist, not an electronician."

"Don't be so cross, Mother. I can't stand it. Not now."

He walked out of the pilot room. Anxiously, she followed him. The burial of the crew and her fellow scientists had been very trying for him. Spilled blood had always made him dizzy and sick; he could scarcely control his hands enough to help her sack the scattered bones and entrails.

He had wanted to put the corpses in the nuclear furnace, but she had forbidden that. The Geigers amidships were ticking loudly, warning that there was invisible death in the stern.

The meteor that struck the moment the ship came out of Translation into normal space had probably wrecked the engine room. So she had understood from the incoherent high-pitched phrases of a colleague before he fled to the pilot room. She had hurried to find Eddie. She feared his cabin door would still be locked, as he had been making a tape of the aria "Heavy Hangs the Albatross" from Gianelli's *Ancient Mariner.*

Fortunately, the emergency system had automatically thrown out the locking circuits. Entering, she had called out his name in fear he'd been hurt. He was lying half unconscious on the floor, but it was not the accident that had thrown him there. The reason lay in the corner, released from his lax hand; a quart free-fall Thermos, rubber-nippled. From Eddie's open mouth charged a breath of rye that not even Nodor pills had been able to conceal.

Sharply she had commanded him to get up and onto the bed. Her voice, the first he had ever heard, pierced through the phalanx of Old Red Star. He struggled up, and she, though smaller, had thrown every ounce of her weight into getting him up and onto the bed.

There she had lain down with him and strapped them both in. She understood that the lifeboat had been wrecked also, and that it was up to the captain to bring the yacht down safely to the surface of this charted but unexplored planet, Baudelaire. Everybody else had gone to sit behind the captain, strapped in crash-chairs, unable to help except with their silent backing.

Moral support had not been enough. The ship had come in on a shallow slant. Too fast. The wounded motors had not been able to hold her up. The prow had taken the brunt of the punishment. So had those seated in the nose.

Dr. Fetts had held her son's head on her bosom and prayed out loud to her God. Eddie had snored and muttered. Then there was a sound like the clashing of the gates of doom—a tremendous bong as if the ship were a clapper in a gargantuan bell tolling the most frightening message human ears may hear—a blinding blast of light—and darkness and silence.

A few moments later Eddie began crying out in a childish voice, "Don't leave me to die, Mother! Come back! Come back!"

Mother was unconscious by his side, but he did not know that. He wept for a while, then he lapsed back into his rye-fogged stupor—if he had ever been out of it—and slept. Again, darkness and silence.

It was the second day since the crash, if "day" could describe that twilight state on Baudelaire. Dr. Fetts followed her son wherever he went. She knew he was very sensitive and easily upset. All his life she had known it and had tried to get between him and anything that would cause trouble. She had succeeded, she thought, fairly well until three months ago when Eddie had eloped.

The girl was Polina Fameux, the ash-blond long-legged actress whose tridi image, taped, had been shipped to frontier stars where a small acting talent meant little and a large and shapely bosom much. Since Eddie was a well-known Metro tenor, the marriage made a big splash whose ripples ran around the civilized Galaxy.

Dr. Fetts had felt very bad about the elopement, but she had, she hoped, hidden her grief very well beneath a smiling mask. She didn't regret having to give him up; after all, he was a full-grown man, no longer her little boy. But, really, aside from the seasons at the Met and his tours, he had not been parted from her since he was eight.

That was when she went on a honeymoon with her second husband. And then she and Eddie had not been separated long, for Eddie had gotten very sick, and she'd had to hurry back and take care of him, as he had insisted she was the only one who could make him well.

Moreover, you couldn't count his days at the opera as a total loss, for he vised her every noon and they had a long talk—no matter how high the vise bills ran.

The ripples caused by her son's marriage were scarcely a week old before they were followed by even bigger ones. They bore the news of the separation of Eddie and his wife. A fortnight later, Polina applied for divorce on grounds of incompatibility. Eddie was handed the papers in his mother's apartment. He had come back to her the day he and Polina had agreed they "couldn't make a go of it," or, as he phrased it to his mother, "couldn't get together."

Dr. Fetts was, of course, very curious about the reason for their parting, but, as she explained to her friends, she "respected" his silence. What she didn't say was that she had told herself the time would come when he would tell her all.

Eddie's "nervous breakdown" started shortly afterward. He had been very irritable, moody, and depressed, but he got worse the day a so-called friend told Eddie that whenever Polina heard his name mentioned, she laughed loud and long. The friend added that Polina had promised to tell some day the true story of their brief merger.

That night his mother had to call in a doctor.

In the days that followed, she thought of giving up her position as research pathologist at De Kruif and taking all her time to help him "get back on his feet." It was a sign of the struggle going on in her mind that she had not been able to decide within a week's time. Ordinarily given to swift consideration and resolution of a problem, she could not agree to surrender her beloved quest into tissue regeneration.

Just as she was on the verge of doing what was for her the incredible and the shameful, tossing a coin, she had been vised by her superior. He told her she had been chosen to go with a group of biologists on a research cruise to ten preselected planetary systems.

Joyfully, she had thrown away the papers that would turn Eddie over to a sanatorium. And, since he was quite famous, she had used her influence to get the government to allow him to go along. Ostensibly, he was to make a survey of the development of opera on planets colonized by Terrans. That the yacht was not visiting any colonized globes seemed to have been missed by the bureaus concerned. But it was not the first time in the history of a government that its left hand knew not what its right was doing.

Actually, he was to be "rebuilt" by his mother, who thought herself much more capable of curing him than any of the prevalent A, F, J, R, S, K, or H therapies. True, some of her friends reported amazing results with some of the symbol-chasing techniques. On the other hand, two of her close companions had tried them all and had gotten no benefits from any of them. She was his mother; she could do more for him than any of those "alphabatties"; he was flesh of her flesh, blood of her blood. Besides, he wasn't so sick. He just got awfully blue sometimes and made theatrical but insincere threats of suicide or else just sat and stared into space. But she could handle him.

II

So now it was that she followed him from the backward-running clock to his room. And saw him step inside, look for a second, and then turn to her with a twisted face.

"Neddie is ruined, Mother. Absolutely ruined."

She glanced at the piano. It had torn from the wall-racks at the moment of impact and smashed itself against the opposite wall. To Eddie it wasn't just a piano; it was Neddie. He had a pet name for everything he contacted for more than a brief time. It was as if he hopped from one appellation to the next, like an ancient sailor who felt lost unless he was close to the familiar and designated points of the shoreline. Otherwise, Eddie seemed to be drifting helplessly in a chaotic ocean, one that was anonymous and amorphous.

Or, analogy more typical of him, he was like the nightclubber who feels submerged, drowning, unless he hops from table to table, going from one well-known group of faces to the next, avoiding the featureless and unnamed dummies at the strangers' tables.

He did not cry over Neddie. She wished he would. He had been so apathetic during the voyage. Nothing, not even the unparalleled splendor of the naked stars nor the inexpressible alienness of strange planets, had seemed to lift him very long. If he would only weep or laugh loudly or display some sign that he was reacting violently to what was happening. She would even have welcomed his striking her in anger or calling her "bad" names.

But no, not even during the gathering of the mangled corpses, when he looked for a while as if he were going to vomit, would he give way to his body's demand for expression. She understood that if he were to throw up, he would be much better for it, would have gotten rid of much of the psychic disturbance along with the physical.

He would not. He had kept on raking flesh and bones into the large plastic bags and kept a fixed look of resentment and sullenness.

She hoped now that the loss of his piano would bring tears and shaking shoulders. Then she could take him in her arms and give him sympathy. He would be her little boy again, afraid of the dark, afraid of the dog killed by a car, seeking her arms for the sure safety, the sure love.

"Never mind, Baby," she said. "When we're rescued, we'll get you a new one."

"When—!"

He lifted his eyebrows and sat down on the bed's edge.

"What do we do now?"

She became very brisk and efficient.

"The ultrad automatically started working the moment the meteor struck. If it's survived the crash, it's still sending SOS's. If not, then there's nothing we can do about it. Neither of us knows how to repair it.

"However, it's possible that in the last five years since this planet was located, other expeditions may have landed here. Not from Earth but from some of the colonies. Or from nonhuman globes. Who knows? It's worth taking a chance. Let's see."

A single glance was enough to wreck their hopes. The ultrad had been twisted and broken until it was no longer recognizable as the machine that sent swifter-than-light waves through the no-ether.

Dr. Fetts said with false cheeriness, "Well, that's that! So what? It makes things too easy. Let's go into the storeroom and see what we can see."

Eddie shrugged and followed her. There she insisted that each take a panrad. If they had to separate for any reason, they could always communicate and also, using the DF's—the built-in direction finders—locate each other. Having used them before, they knew the instruments' capabilities and how essential they were on scouting or camping trips.

The panrads were lightweight cylinders about two feet high and eight inches in diameter. Crampacked, they held the mechanisms of two dozen different utilities. Their batteries lasted a year without recharging, they were practically indestructible and worked under almost any conditions.

Keeping away from the side of the ship that had the huge hole in it, they took the panrads outside. The long wave bands were searched by Eddie while his mother moved the dial that ranged up and down the shortwaves. Neither really expected to hear anything, but to search was better than doing nothing.

Finding the modulated wave-frequencies empty of any significant noises, he switched to the continuous waves. He was startled by a dot-dashing.

"Hey, Mom! Something in the 1000 kilocycles! Unmodulated!"

"Naturally, Son," she said with some exasperation in the midst of her elation. "What would you expect from a radio-telegraphic signal?"

She found the band on her own cylinder. He looked blankly at her. "I know nothing about radio, but that's not Morse."

"What? You must be mistaken!"

"I—I don't think so."

"Is it or isn't it? Good God, Son, can't you be certain of *anything!*"

She turned the amplifier up. As both of them had learned Galacto-Morse through sleeplearn techniques, she checked him at once.

"You're right. What do you make of it?"

His quick ear sorted out the pulses.

"No simple dot and dash. Four different time-lengths."

He listened some more.

"They've got a certain rhythm, all right. I can make out definite groupings. Ah! That's the sixth time I've caught that particular one. And there's another. And another."

Dr. Fetts shook her ash-blond head. She could make out nothing but a series of zzt-zzt-zzt's.

Eddie glanced at the DF needle.

"Coming from NE by E. Should we try to locate?"

"Naturally," she replied. "But we'd better eat first. We don't know how far away it is, or what we'll find there. While I fix a hot meal, you get our field trip stuff ready."

"O.K.," he said with more enthusiasm than he had shown for a long time.

When he came back he ate everything in the large dish his mother had prepared on the unwrecked galley stove.

"You always did make the best stew," he said.

"Thank you. I'm glad you're eating again, Son. I am surprised. I thought you'd be sick about all this."

He waved vaguely but energetically.

"The challenge of the unknown. I have a sort of feeling this is going to turn out much better than we thought. Much better."

She came close and sniffed his breath. It was clean, innocent even of stew. That meant he'd taken Nodor, which probably meant he'd been sampling some hidden rye. Otherwise, how explain his reckless disregard of the possible dangers? It wasn't like him.

She said nothing, for she knew that if he tried to hide a bottle in his clothes or field sack while they were tracking down the radio signals, she would soon find it. And take it away. He wouldn't even protest, merely let her lift it from his limp hand while his lips swelled with resentment.

III

They set out. Both wore knapsacks and carried the panrads. He carried a gun over his shoulder, and she had snapped onto her sack her small black bag of medical and lab supplies.

High noon of late autumn was topped by a weak red sun that barely managed to make itself seen through the eternal double layer of clouds. Its companion, an even smaller blob of lilac, was setting on the northwestern horizon. They walked in a sort of bright twilight, the best that Baudelaire ever achieved. Yet, despite the lack of light, the air was warm. It was a phenomenon common to certain planets behind the Horsehead Nebula, one being investigated but as yet unexplained.

The country was hilly, with many deep ravines. Here and there were prominences high enough and steep-sided enough to be called embryo mountains. Considering the roughness of the land however, there was a surprising amount of vegetation. Pale green, red, and yellow bushes, vines, and little trees clung to every bit of ground, horizontal or vertical. All had comparatively broad leaves that turned with the sun to catch the light.

From time to time, as the two Terrans strode noisily through the forest, small multicolored insect-like and mammal-like creatures scuttled from hiding place to hiding place. Eddie decided to carry his gun in the crook of his arm. Then, after they were forced to scramble up and down ravines and hills and fight their way through thickets that became unexpectedly tangled, he put it back over his shoulder, where it hung from a strap.

Despite their exertions, they did not tire quickly. They weighed about twenty pounds less than they would have on Earth and, though the air was thinner, it was richer in oxygen.

Dr. Fetts kept up with Eddie. Thirty years the senior of the twenty-three-year-old, she passed even at close inspection for his older sister. Longevity pills took care of that. However, he treated her with all the courtesy and chivalry that one gave one's mother and helped her up the steep inclines, even though the climbs did not appreciably cause her deep chest to demand more air.

They paused once by a creek bank to get their bearings.

"The signals have stopped," he said.

"Obviously," she replied.

At that moment the radar-detector built into the panrad began to ping. Both of them automatically looked upward.

"There's no ship in the air."

"It can't be coming from either of those hills," she pointed out. "There's nothing but a boulder on top of each one. Tremendous rocks."

"Nevertheless, it's coming from there, I think. Oh! Oh! Did you see what I saw? Looked like a tall stalk of some kind being pulled down behind that big rock."

She peered through the dim light. "I think you were imagining things, Son. I saw nothing."

Then, even as the pinging kept up, the zzting started again. But after a burst of noise, both stopped.

"Let's go up and see what we shall see," she said.

"Something screwy," he commented. She did not answer.

They forded the creek and began the ascent. Halfway up, they stopped to sniff in puzzlement at a gust of some heavy odor coming downwind.

"Smells like a cageful of monkeys," he said.

"In heat," she added. If his was the keener ear, hers was the sharper nose.

They went on up. The RD began sounding its tiny hysterical gonging. Nonplused, Eddie stopped. The DF indicated the radar pulses were not coming from the top of the hill they were climbing, as formerly, but from the other hill across the valley. Abruptly, the panrad fell silent.

"What do we do now?"

"Finish what we started. This hill. Then we go to the other one."

He shrugged and then hastened after her tall slim body in its long-legged coveralls. She was hot on the scent, literally, and nothing could stop her. Just before she reached the bungalow-sized boulder topping the hill, he caught up with her. She had stopped to gaze intently at the DF needle, which swung wildly before it stopped at neutral. The monkey-cage odor was very strong.

"Do you suppose it could be some sort of radio-generating mineral?" she asked, disappointedly.

"No. Those groupings were semantic. And that smell . . ."

"Then what—?"

He didn't know whether to feel pleased or not that she had so obviously and suddenly thrust the burden of responsibility and action on him. Both pride and a curious shrinking affected him. But he did feel exhilarated. Almost, he thought, he felt as if he were on the verge of discovering what he had been looking for for a long time. What the object of his search had been, he could not say. But he was excited and not very much afraid.

He unslung his weapon, a two-barreled combination shotgun and rifle. The panrad was still quiet.

"Maybe the boulder is camouflage for a spy outfit," he said. He sounded silly, even to himself.

Behind him, his mother gasped and screamed. He whirled and raised his gun, but there was nothing to shoot. She was pointing at the hilltop across the valley, shaking, and saying something incoherent.

He could make out a long slim antenna seemingly projecting from the monstrous boulder crouched there. At the same time, two thoughts struggled for first place in his mind: one, that it was more than a coincidence that both hills had almost identical stone structures on their brows, and, two, that the antenna must have been recently stuck out, for he was sure he had not seen it the last time he looked.

He never got to tell her his conclusions, for something thin and flexible and irresistible seized him from behind. Lifted into the air, he was borne backward. He dropped the gun and tried to grab the bands or tentacles around him and tear them off with his bare hands. No use.

He caught one last glimpse of his mother running off down the hillside. Then a curtain snapped down, and he was in total darkness.

IV

Eddie sensed himself, still suspended, twirled around. He could not know for sure, of course, but he thought he was facing in exactly the opposite direction. Simultaneously, the tentacles binding his legs and arms were released. Only his waist was still gripped. It was pressed so tightly that he cried out with pain.

Then, boot-toes bumping on some resilient substance, he was carried forward. Halted, facing he knew not what horrible monster, he was suddenly assailed—not by a sharp beak or tooth or knife or some other cutting or mangling instrument—but by a dense cloud of that same monkey perfume.

In other circumstances, he might have vomited. Now his stomach was not given the time to consider whether it should clean house or not. The tentacle lifted him higher and thrust him against something soft and yielding—something fleshlike and womanly—almost breastlike in texture and smoothness and warmth and in its hint of gentle curving.

He put his hands and feet out to brace himself, for he thought for a moment he was going to sink in and be covered up—enfolded—ingested. The idea of a gargantuan amoeba-thing hiding within a hollow rock—or a rocklike shell—made him writhe and yell and shove at the protoplasmic substance.

But nothing of the kind happened. He was not plunged into a smothering and slimy jelly that would strip him of his skin and then his flesh and then dissolve his bones. He was merely shoved repeatedly against the soft swelling. Each time, he pushed or kicked or struck at it. After a dozen of these seemingly purposeless acts, he was held away, as if whatever was doing it was puzzled by his behavior.

He had quit screaming. The only sounds were his harsh breathing and the zzts and pings from the panrad. Even as he became aware of them, the zzts changed tempo and settled into a recognizable pattern of bursts—three units that crackled out again and again.

"Who are you? Who are you?"

Of course, it could just as easily had been, "What are you?" or "What the hell!" or "Nov smoz ka pop?"

Or nothing—semantically speaking.

But he didn't think the latter. And when he was gently lowered to the floor, and the tentacle went off to only-God-knew-where in the dark, he was sure that the creature was communicating—or trying to—with him.

It was this thought that kept him from screaming and running around in the lightless and fetid chamber, brainlessly seeking an outlet. He mastered his panic and snapped open a little shutter in the panrad's side and thrust in his right-hand index finger. There he poised it above the key and in a moment, when the thing paused in transmitting, he sent back, as best he could, the pulses he had received. It was not necessary for him to turn on the light and spin the dial that would put him on the 1000 kc band. The instrument would automatically key that frequency in with the one he had just received.

The oddest part of the whole procedure was that his whole body was trembling almost uncontrollably—one part excepted. That was his index finger, his one unit that seemed to him to have a definite function in this otherwise meaningless situation. It was the section of him that was helping him to survive—the only part that knew how—at that moment. Even his brain seemed to have no connection with his finger. That digit was himself, and the rest just happened to be linked to it.

When he paused, the transmitter began again. This time the units were unrecognizable. There was a certain rhythm to them, but he could not know what they meant. Meanwhile, the RD was pinging. Something somewhere in the dark hole had a beam held tightly on him.

He pressed a button on the panrad's top, and the built-in flashlight illuminated the area just in front of him. He saw a wall of reddish-gray rubbery substance. On the wall was a roughly circular, light gray swelling about four feet in diameter. Around it, giving it a Medusa appearance, were coiled twelve very long, very thin tentacles.

Though he was afraid that if he turned his back to them the tentacles would seize him once more, his curiosity forced him to wheel about and examine his surroundings with the bright beam. He was in an egg-shaped chamber about thirty feet long, twelve wide, and eight to ten high in the middle. It was formed of a reddish-gray material, smooth except for irregular intervals of blue or red pipes. Veins and arteries?

A door-sized portion of the wall had a vertical slit running down it. Tentacles fringed it. He guessed it was a sort of iris and that it had opened to drag him inside. Starfish-shaped groupings of tentacles were scattered on the walls or hung from the ceiling. On the wall opposite the iris was a long and flexible stalk with a cartilaginous ruff around its free end. When Eddie moved, it moved, its blind point following him as a radar antenna tracks the thing it is locating. That was what it was. And unless he was wrong, the stalk was also a C.W. transmitter-receiver.

He shot the light round. When it reached the end farthest from him, he gasped. Ten creatures were huddled together facing him! About the size of half-grown pigs, they looked like nothing so much as unshelled snails; they were eyeless, and the stalk growing from the forehead of each was a tiny duplicate of that on the wall. They didn't look dangerous. Their open mouths were little and toothless, and their rate of locomotion must be slow, for they moved like snails, on a large pedestal of flesh—a foot-muscle.

Nevertheless, if he were to fall asleep they could overcome him by force of numbers, and those mouths might drip an acid to digest him, or they might carry a concealed poisonous sting.

His speculations were interrupted violently. He was seized, lifted, and passed on to another group of tentacles. He was carried beyond the antenna-stalk and toward the snail-beings. Just before he reached them, he was halted, facing the wall. An iris, hitherto invisible, opened. His light shone into it, but he could see nothing but convolutions of flesh.

His panrad gave off a new pattern of dit-dot-deet-dats. The iris widened until it was large enough to admit his body, if he were shoved in head first. Or feet first. It didn't matter. The convolutions straightened out and became a tunnel. Or a throat. From thousands of little pits emerged thousands of tiny, razor sharp teeth. They flashed out and sank back in, and before they had disappeared thousands of other wicked little spears darted out and past the receding fangs.

Meat-grinder.

Beyond the murderous array, at the end of the throat, was a huge pouch of water. Steam came from it, and with it an odor like that of his mother's stew. Dark bits, presumably meat, and pieces of vegetables floated on the seething surface.

Then the iris closed, and he was turned around to face the slugs. Gently, but unmistakably, a tentacle spanked his buttocks. And the panrad zzzted a warning.

Eddie was not stupid. He knew now that the ten creatures were not dangerous unless he molested them. In which case he had just seen where he would go if he did not behave.

Again he was lifted and carried along the wall until he was shoved against the light gray spot. The monkey-cage odor, which had died out, became strong again. Eddie identified its source with a very small hole which appeared in the wall.

When he did not respond—he had no idea yet how he was supposed to act—the tentacles dropped him so unexpectedly that he fell on his back. Unhurt by the yielding flesh, he rose.

What was the next step? Exploration of his resources. Itemization: The panrad. A sleeping-bag, which he wouldn't need as long as the present too-warm temperature kept up. A bottle of Old Red Star capsules. A free-fall Thermos with attached nipple. A box of A-2-Z rations. A Foldstove. Cartridges for his double-barrel, now lying outside the creature's boulderish shell. A roll of toilet paper. Toothbrush. Paste. Soap. Towel. Pills: Nodor, hormone, vitamin, longevity, reflex, and sleeping. And a thread-thin wire, a hundred feet long when uncoiled, that held prisoner in its molecular structure a hundred symphonies, eighty operas, a thousand different types of musical pieces, and two thousand great books ranging from Sophocles and Dostoyevsky to the latest bestseller. It could be played inside the panrad.

He inserted it, pushed a button, and spoke, "Eddie Fetts's recording of Puccini's '*Che gelida manina,*' please."

And while he listened approvingly to his own magnificent voice, he zipped open a can he had found in the bottom of the sack. His mother had put into it the stew left over from their last meal in the ship.

Not knowing what was happening, yet for some reason sure he was for the present safe, he munched meat and vegetables with a contented jaw. Transition from abhorrence to appetite sometimes came easily for Eddie.

He cleaned out the can and finished with some crackers and a chocolate bar. Rationing was out. As long as the food lasted, he would eat well. Then, if nothing turned up, he would . . . But then, he reassured himself as he licked his fingers, his mother, who was free, would find some way to get him out of his trouble.

She always had.

V

The panrad, silent for a while, began signaling. Eddie spotlighted the antenna and saw it was pointing at the snail-beings, which he had, in accordance with his custom, dubbed familiarly. Sluggos he called them.

The Sluggos crept toward the wall and stopped close to it. Their mouths, placed on the tops of their heads, gaped like so many hungry young birds. The iris opened, and two lips formed into a spout. Out of it streamed steaming-hot water and chunks of meat and vegetables. Stew! Stew that fell exactly into each waiting mouth.

That was how Eddie learned the second phrase of Mother Polyphema's language. The first message had been, "What are you?" This was, "Come and get it!"

He experimented. He tapped out a repetition of what he'd last heard. As one, the Sluggos—except the one then being fed—turned to him and crept a few feet before halting, puzzled.

Inasmuch as Eddie was broadcasting, the Sluggos must have had some sort of built-in DF. Otherwise they wouldn't have been able to distinguish between his pulses and their Mother's.

Immediately after, a tentacle smote Eddie across the shoulders and knocked him down. The panrad zzzted its third intelligible message: "Don't ever do that!"

And then a fourth, to which the ten young obeyed by wheeling and resuming their former positions.

"This way, children."

Yes, they were the offspring, living, eating, sleeping, playing, and learning to communicate in the womb of their mother—the Mother. They were the mobile brood of this vast immobile entity that had scooped up Eddie as a frog scoops up a fly. This Mother. She who had once been just such a Sluggo until she had grown hog-sized and had been pushed out of her Mother's womb. And who, rolled into a tight ball, had free-wheeled down her natal hill, straightened out at the bottom, inched her way up the next hill, rolled down, and so on. Until she found the empty shell of an adult who had died. Or, if she wanted to be a first class citizen in her society and not a prestigeless *occupée*, she found the bare top of a tall hill—or any eminence that commanded a big sweep of territory—and there squatted.

And there she put out many thread-thin tendrils into the soil and into the cracks in the rocks, tendrils that drew sustenance from the fat of her body and grew and extended downward and ramified into other tendrils. Deep underground the rootlets worked their instinctive chemistry; searched for and found the water, the calcium, the iron, the copper, the nitrogen, the carbons, fondled earthworms and grubs and larvae, teasing them for the secrets of their fats and proteins; broke down the wanted substance into shadowy colloidal particles; sucked them up the thready pipes of the tendrils and back to the pale and slimming body crouching on a flat space atop a ridge, a hill, a peak.

There, using the blueprints stored in the molecules of the cerebellum, her body took the building blocks of elements and fashioned them into a very thin shell of the most available material, a shield large enough so she could expand to fit it while her natural enemies—the keen and hungry predators that prowled twilighted Baudelaire—nosed and clawed it in vain.

Then, her evergrowing bulk cramped, she would resorb the hard covering. And if no sharp tooth found her during that process of a few days, she would cast another and a larger. And so on through a dozen or more.

Until she had become the monstrous and much reformed body of an adult and virgin female. Outside would be the stuff that so much resembled a boulder, that was, actually, rock: either granite, diorite, marble, basalt, or maybe just plain limestone. Or sometimes iron, glass, or cellulose.

Within was the centrally located brain, probably as large as a man's. Surrounding it, the tons of organs: the nervous system, the mighty heart, or hearts, the four stomachs, the microwave and longwave generators, the kidneys, bowels, tracheae, scent and taste organs, the perfume factory which made odors to attract animals and birds close enough to be seized, and the huge womb. And the antennae—the small one inside for teaching and scanning the young, and a long and powerful stalk on the outside, projecting from the shelltop, retractable if danger came.

The next step was from virgin to Mother, lower-case to upper-case as designated in her pulse-language by a longer pause before a word. Not until she was deflowered could she take a high place in her society. Immodest, unblushing, she herself made the advances, the proposals, and the surrender.

After which, she ate her mate.

The clock in the panrad told Eddie he was in his thirtieth day of imprisonment when he found out that little bit of information. He was shocked, not because it offended his ethics, but because he himself had been intended to be the mate. And the dinner.

His finger tapped, "Tell me, Mother, what you mean."

He had not wondered before how a species that lacked males could reproduce. Now he found that, to the Mothers, all creatures except themselves were male. Mothers were immobile and female. Mobiles were male. Eddie had been mobile. He was, therefore, a male.

He had approached this particular Mother during the mating season, that is, midway through raising a litter of young. She had scanned him as he came along the creekbanks at the valley bottom. When he was at the foot of the hill, she had detected his odor. It was new to her. The closest she could come to it in her memorybanks was that of a beast similar to him. From her description, he guessed it to be an ape. So she had released from her repertoire its rut stench. When he seemingly fell into the trap, she had caught him.

He was supposed to attack the conception-spot, that light gray swelling on the wall. After he had ripped and torn it enough to begin the mysterious workings of pregnancy, he would have been popped into her stomach-iris.

Fortunately, he had lacked the sharp beak, the fang, the claw. And she had received her own signals back from the panrad.

Eddie did not understand why it was necessary to use a mobile for mating. A Mother was intelligent enough to pick up a sharp stone and mangle the spot herself.

He was given to understand that conception would not start unless it was accompanied by a certain titillation of the nerves—a frenzy and its satisfaction. Why this emotional state was needed, Mother did not know.

Eddie tried to explain about such things as genes and chromosomes and why they had to be present in highly developed species.

Mother did not understand.

Eddie wondered if the number of slashes and rips in the spot corresponded to the number of young. Or if there were a large number of potentialities in the heredity-ribbons spread out under the conception-skin. And if the haphazard irritation and consequent stimulation of the genes paralleled the chance combining of genes in human male-female mating. Thus resulting in offspring with traits that were combinations of their parents.

Or did the inevitable devouring of the mobile after the act indicate more than an emotional and nutritional reflex? Did it hint that the mobile caught up scattered gene-nodes, like hard seeds, along with the torn skin, in its claws and tusks, that these genes survived the boiling in the stew-stomach, and were later passed out in the feces? Where animals and birds picked them up in beak, tooth, or foot, and then, seized by other Mothers in this oblique rape, transmitted the heredity-carrying agents to the conception-spots while attacking them, the nodules being scraped off and implanted in the skin and blood of the swelling even as others were harvested? Later, the mobiles were eaten, digested, and ejected in the obscure but ingenious and never-ending cycle? Thus ensuring the continual, if haphazard, recombining of genes, chances for variations in offspring, opportunities for mutations, and so on?

Mother pulsed that she was nonplused.

Eddie gave up. He'd never know. After all, did it matter?

He decided not, and rose from his prone position to request water. She pursed up her iris and spouted a tepid quartful into his Thermos. He dropped in a pill, swished it around till it dissolved, and drank a reasonable facsimile of Old Red Star. He preferred the harsh and powerful rye, though he could have afforded the smoothest. Quick results were what he wanted. Taste didn't matter, as he disliked all liquor tastes. Thus he drank what the Skid Row bums drank and shuddered even as they did, renaming it Old Rotten Tar and cursing the fate that had brought them so low they had to gag such stuff down.

The rye glowed in his belly and spread quickly through his limbs and up to his head, chilled only by the increasing scarcity of the capsules. When he ran out—then what? It was at times like this that he most missed his mother.

Thinking about her brought a few large tears. He snuffled and drank some more and when the biggest of the Sluggos nudged him for a back-scratching, he gave it instead a shot of Old Red Star. A slug for Sluggo. Idly, he wondered what effect a taste for rye would have on the future of the race when these virgins became Mothers.

At that moment he was shaken by what seemed a lifesaving idea. These creatures could suck up the required elements from the earth and with them duplicate quite complex molecular structures. Provided, of course, they had a sample of the desired substance to brood over in some cryptic organ.

Well, what easier to do than give her one of the cherished capsules? One could become any number. Those, plus the abundance of water pumped up through hollow underground tendrils from the nearby creek, would give enough to make a master-distiller green!

He smacked his lips and was about to key her his request when what she was transmitting penetrated his mind.

Rather cattily, she remarked that her neighbor across the valley was putting on airs because she, too, held prisoner a communicating mobile.

VI

The Mothers had a society as hierarchical as table-protocol in Washington or peck-order in a barnyard. Prestige was what counted, and prestige was determined by the broadcasting power, the height of the eminence on which the Mother sat, which governed the extent of her radar-territory, and the abundance and novelty and wittiness of her gossip. The creature that had snapped Eddie up was a queen. She had precedence over thirty-odd of her kind; they all had to let her broadcast first, and none dared start pulsing until she quit. Then, the next in order began, and so on down the line. Any of them could be interrupted at any time by Number One, and if any of the lower echelon had something interesting to transmit, she could break in on the one then speaking and get permission from the queen to tell her tale.

Eddie knew this, but he could not listen in directly to the hilltop-gabble. The thick pseudo-granite shell barred him from that and made him dependent upon her womb-stalk for relayed information.

Now and then Mother opened the door and allowed her young to crawl out. There they practiced beaming and broadcasting at the Sluggos of the Mother across the valley. Occasionally that Mother deigned herself to pulse the young, and Eddie's keeper reciprocated to her offspring.

Turnabout.

The first time the children had inched through the exit-iris, Eddie had tried, Ulysses-like, to pass himself off as one of them and crawl out in the midst of the flock. Eyeless, but no Polyphemus, Mother had picked him out with her tentacles and hauled him back in.

It was following that incident that he had named her Polyphema.

He knew she had increased her own already powerful prestige tremendously by possession of that unique thing—a transmitting mobile. So much had her importance grown that the Mothers on the fringes of her area passed on the news to others. Before he had learned her language, the entire continent was hooked up. Polyphema had become a veritable gossip columnist; tens of thousands of hillcrouchers listened in eagerly to her accounts of her dealings with the walking paradox: a semantic male.

That had been fine. Then, very recently, the Mother across the valley had captured a similar creature. And in one bound she had become Number Two in the area and would, at the slightest weakness on Polyphema's part, wrest the top position away.

Eddie became wildly excited at the news. He had often daydreamed about his mother and wondered what she was doing. Curiously enough, he ended many of his fantasies with lip-mutterings, reproaching her almost audibly for having left him and for making no try to rescue him. When he became aware of his attitude, he was ashamed. Nevertheless, the sense of desertion colored his thoughts.

Now that he knew she was alive and had been caught, probably while trying to get him out, he rose from the lethargy that had lately been making him doze the clock around. He asked Polyphema if she would open the entrance so he could talk directly with the other captive. She said yes. Eager to listen in on a conversation between two mobiles, she was very cooperative. There would be a mountain of gossip in what they would have to say. The only thing that dented her joy was that the other Mother would also have access.

Then, remembering she was still Number One and would broadcast the details first, she trembled so with pride and ecstasy that Eddie felt the floor shaking.

Iris open, he walked through it and looked across the valley. The hillsides were still green, red, and yellow, as the plants on Baudelaire did not lose their leaves during winter. But a few white patches showed that winter had begun. Eddie shivered from the bite of cold air on his naked skin. Long ago he had taken off his clothes. The womb-warmth had made garments too uncomfortable; moreover, Eddie, being human, had had to get rid of waste products. And Polyphema, being a Mother, had had periodically to flush out the dirt with warm water from one of her stomachs. Every time the tracheae-vents exploded streams that swept the undesirable elements out through her door-iris, Eddie had become soaked. When he abandoned dress, his clothes had gone floating out. Only by sitting on his pack did he keep it from a like fate.

Afterward, he and the Sluggos had been dried off by warm air pumped through the same vents and originating from the mighty battery of lungs. Eddie was comfortable enough—he'd always liked showers—but the loss of his garments had been one more thing that kept him from escaping. He would soon freeze to death outside unless he found the yacht quickly. And he wasn't sure he remembered the path back.

So now, when he stepped outside, he retreated a pace or two and let the warm air from Polyphema flow like a cloak from his shoulders.

Then he peered across the half-mile that separated him from his mother, but he could not see her. The twilight state and the dark of the unlit interior of her captor hid her.

He tapped in Morse, "Switch to the talkie, same frequency." Paula Fetts did so. She began asking him frantically if he were all right.

He replied he was fine.

"Have you missed me terribly, Son?"

"Oh, very much."

Even as he said this he wondered vaguely why his voice sounded so hollow. Despair at never again being able to see her, probably.

"I've almost gone crazy, Eddie. When you were caught I ran away as fast as I could. I had no idea what horrible monster it was that was attacking us. And then, halfway down the hill, I fell and broke my leg . . ."

"Oh, no, Mother!"

"Yes. But I managed to crawl back to the ship. And there, after I'd set it myself, I gave myself B.K. shots. Only, my system didn't react like it's supposed to. There are people that way, you know, and the healing took twice as long.

"But when I was able to walk, I got a gun and a box of dynamite. I was going to blow up what I thought was a kind of rock-fortress, an outpost for some kind of extee. I'd no idea of the true nature of these beasts. First, though, I decided to reconnoiter. I was going to spy on the boulder from across the valley. But I was trapped by this thing.

"Listen, Son. Before I'm cut off, let me tell you not to give up hope. I'll be out of here before long and over to rescue you."

"How?"

"If you remember, my lab kit holds a number of carcinogens for field work. Well, you know that sometimes a Mother's conception-spot when it is torn up during mating, instead of begetting young, goes into cancer—the opposite of pregnancy. I've injected a carcinogen into the spot and a beautiful carcinoma has developed. She'll be dead in a few days."

"Mom! You'll be buried in that rotting mass!"

"No. This creature has told me that when one of her species dies, a reflex opens the labia. That's to permit their young—if any—to escape. Listen, I'll—"

A tentacle coiled about him and pulled him back through the iris, which shut.

When he switched back to C.W., he heard, "Why didn't you communicate? What were you doing? Tell me! Tell me!"

Eddie told her. There was a silence that could only be interpreted as astonishment. After Mother had recovered her wits, she said, "From now on, you will talk to the other male through me."

Obviously, she envied and hated his ability to change wave-bands and, perhaps, had a struggle to accept the idea.

"Please," he persisted, not knowing how dangerous were the waters he was wading in, "please let me talk to my mother di—"

For the first time, he heard her stutter.

"Wha-wha-what? Your Mo-Mo-Mother?"

"Yes. Of course."

The floor heaved violently beneath his feet. He cried out and braced himself to keep from falling and then flashed on the light. The walls were pulsating like shaken jelly, and the vascular columns had turned from red and blue to gray. The entrance-iris sagged open, like a lax mouth, and the air cooled. He could feel the drop in temperature in her flesh with the soles of his feet.

It was some time before he caught on.

Polyphema was in a state of shock.

What might have happened had she stayed in it, he never knew. She might have died and thus forced him out into the winter before his mother could escape. If so, and he couldn't find the ship, he would die. Huddled in the warmest corner of the egg-shaped chamber, Eddie contemplated that idea and shivered to a degree for which the outside air couldn't account.

VII

However, Polyphema had her own method of recovery. It consisted of spewing out the contents of her stew-stomach, which had doubtless become filled with poisons draining out of her system from the blow. Her ejection of the stuff was the physical manifestation of the psychical catharsis. So furious was the flood that her foster son was almost swept out in the hot tide, but she, reacting instinctively, had coiled tentacles about him and the Sluggos. Then she followed the first upchucking by emptying her other three water-pouches, the second hot and the third lukewarm and the fourth, just filled, cold.

Eddie yelped as the icy water doused him.

Polyphema's irises closed again. The floor and walls gradually quit quaking; the temperature rose; and her veins and arteries regained their red and blue. She was well again. Or so she seemed.

But when, after waiting twenty-four hours, he cautiously approached the subject, he found she not only would not talk about it, she refused to acknowledge the existence of the other mobile.

Eddie, giving up hope of conversation, thought for quite a while. The only conclusion he could come to, and he was sure he'd grasped enough of her psychology to make it valid, was that the concept of a mobile female was utterly unacceptable.

Her world was split into two: mobile and her kind, the immobile. Mobile meant food and mating. Mobile meant—male. The Mothers were—female.

How the mobiles reproduced had probably never entered the hillcrouchers' minds. Their science and philosophy were on the instinctive body-level. Whether they had some notion of spontaneous generation or amoeba-like fission being responsible for the continued population of mobiles, or they'd just taken for granted they "growed," like Topsy, Eddie never found out. To them, they were female and the rest of the protoplasmic cosmos was male.

That was that. Any other idea was more than foul and obscene and blasphemous. It was—unthinkable.

Polyphema had received a deep trauma from his words. And though she seemed to have recovered, somewhere in those tons of unimaginably complicated flesh a bruise was buried. Like a hidden flower, dark purple, it bloomed, and the shadow it cast was one that cut off a certain memory, a certain tract, from the light of consciousness. That bruise-stained shadow covered that time and event which the Mother, for reasons unfathomable to the human being, found necessary to mark KEEP OFF.

Thus, though Eddie did not word it, he understood in the cells of his body, he felt and knew, as if his bones were prophesying and his brain did not hear, what came to pass.

Sixty-six hours later by the panrad clock, Polyphema's entrance-lips opened. Her tentacles darted out. They came back in, carrying his helpless and struggling mother.

Eddie, roused out of a doze, horrified, paralyzed, saw her toss her lab kit at him and heard an inarticulate cry from her. And saw her plunged, headforemost, into the stomach-iris.

Polyphema had taken the one sure way of burying the evidence.

Eddie lay face down, nose mashed against the warm and faintly throbbing flesh of the floor. Now and then his hands clutched spasmodically as if he were reaching for something that someone kept putting just within his reach and then moving away.

How long he was there he didn't know, for he never again looked at the clock.

Finally, in the darkness, he sat up and giggled inanely, "Mother always did make good stew."

That set him off. He leaned back on his hands and threw his head back and howled like a wolf under a full moon.

Polyphema, of course, was dead-deaf, but she could radar his posture, and her keen nostrils deduced from his body-scent that he was in terrible fear and anguish.

A tentacle glided out and gently enfolded him.

"What is the matter?" zzted the panrad.

He stuck his finger in the keyhole.

"I have lost my mother!"

"?"

"She's gone away, and she'll never come back."

"I don't understand. *Here I am.*"

Eddie quit weeping and cocked his head as if he were listening to some inner voice. He snuffled a few times and wiped away the tears, slowly disengaged the tentacle, patted it, walked over to his pack in a corner, and took out the bottle of Old Red Star capsules. One he popped into the Thermos; the other he gave to her with the request she duplicate it, if possible. Then he stretched out on his side, propped on one elbow like a Roman in his sensualities, sucked the rye through the nipple, and listened to a medley of Beethoven, Mussorgsky, Verdi, Strauss, Porter, Feinstein, and Waxworth.

So the time—if there were such a thing there—flowed around Eddie. When he was tired of music or plays or books, he listened in on the area hookup. Hungry, he rose and walked—or often just crawled—to the stew-iris. Cans of rations lay in his pack; he had planned to eat those until he was sure that—what was it he was forbidden to eat? Poison? Something had been devoured by Polyphema and the Sluggos. But sometime during the music-rye orgy, he had forgotten. He now ate quite hungrily and with thought for nothing but the satisfaction of his wants.

Sometimes the door-iris opened, and Billy Greengrocer hopped in. Billy looked like a cross between a cricket and a kangaroo. He was the size of a collie, and he bore in a marsupialian pouch vegetables and fruit and nuts. These he extracted with shiny green, chitinous claws and gave to Mother in return for meals of stew. Happy symbiote, he chirruped merrily while his many-faceted eyes, revolving independently of each other, looked one at the Sluggos and the other at Eddie.

Eddie, on impulse, abandoned the 1000 kc band and roved the frequencies until he found that both Polyphema and Billy were emitting a 108 wave. That, apparently, was their natural signal. When Billy had his groceries to deliver, he broadcast. Polyphema, in turn, when she needed them, sent back to him. There was nothing intelligent on Billy's part; it was just his instinct to transmit. And the Mother was, aside from the "semantic" frequency, limited to that one band. But it worked out fine.

VIII

Everything was fine. What more could a man want? Free food, unlimited liquor, soft bed, air-conditioning, shower-baths, music, intellectual works (on the tape), interesting conversation (much of it was about him), privacy, and security.

If he had not already named her, he would have called her Mother Gratis.

Nor were creature comforts all. She had given him the answers to all his questions, all . . .

Except one.

That was never expressed vocally by him. Indeed, he would have been incapable of doing so. He was probably unaware that he had such a question.

But Polyphema voiced it one day when she asked him to do her a favor.

Eddie reacted as if outraged.

"One does not—! One does not—!"

He choked, and then he thought, How ridiculous! She is not—

And looked puzzled, and said, "But she is."

He rose and opened the lab kit. While he was looking for a scalpel, he came across the carcinogens. He threw them through the half-opened labia far out and down the hillside.

Then he turned and, scalpel in hand, leaped at the light gray swelling on the wall. And stopped, staring at it, while the instrument fell from his hand. And picked it up and stabbed feebly and did not even scratch the skin. And again let it drop.

"What is it? What is it?" crackled the panrad hanging from his wrist.

Suddenly, a heavy cloud of human odor—mansweat—was puffed in his face from a nearby vent.

"????"

And he stood, bent in a half-crouch, seemingly paralyzed. Until tentacles seized him in fury and dragged him toward the stomach-iris, yawning man-sized.

Eddie screamed and writhed and plunged his finger in the panrad and tapped, "All right! All right!"

And once back before the spot, he lunged with a sudden and wild joy; he slashed savagely; he yelled. "Take that! And that, P . . ." and the rest was lost in a mindless shout.

He did not stop cutting, and he might have gone on and on until he had quite excised the spot had not Polyphema interfered by dragging him toward her stomach-iris again. For ten seconds he hung there, helpless and sobbing with a mixture of fear and glory.

Polyphema's reflexes had almost overcome her brain. Fortunately, a cold spark of reason lit up a corner of the vast, dark, and hot chapel of her frenzy.

The convolutions leading to the steaming, meat-laden pouch closed and the foldings of flesh rearranged themselves. Eddie was suddenly hosed with warm water from what he called the "sanitation" stomach. The iris closed. He was put down. The scalpel was put back in the bag.

For a long time Mother seemed to be shaken by the thought of what she might have done to Eddie. She did not trust herself to transmit until her nerves were settled. When they were, she did not refer to his narrow escape. Nor did he.

He was happy. He felt as if a spring, tight-coiled against his bowels since he and his wife had parted, was now, for some reason, released. The dull vague pain of loss and discontent, the slight fever and cramp in his entrails, and the apathy that sometimes afflicted him, were gone. He felt fine.

Meanwhile, something akin to deep affection had been lighted, like a tiny candle under the drafty and overtowering roof of a cathedral. Mother's shell housed more than Eddie; it now curved over an emotion new to her kind. This was evident by the next event that filled him with terror.

For the wounds in the spot healed and the swelling increased into a large bag. Then the bag burst and ten mouse-sized Sluggos struck the floor. The impact had the same effect as a doctor spanking a newborn baby's bottom; they drew in their first breath with shock and pain; their uncontrolled and feeble pulses filled the ether with shapeless SOS's.

When Eddie was not talking with Polyphema or listening in or drinking or sleeping or eating or bathing or running off the tape, he played with the Sluggos. He was, in a sense, their father. Indeed, as they grew to hog-size, it was hard for their female parent to distinguish him from her young. As he seldom walked any more, and was often to be found on hands and knees in their midst, she could not scan him too well. Moreover, something in the heavywet air or in the diet had caused every hair on his body to drop off. He grew very fat. Generally speaking, he was one with the pale, soft, round, and bald offspring. A family likeness.

There was one difference. When the time came for the virgins to be expelled, Eddie crept to one end, whimpering, and stayed there until he was sure Mother was not going to thrust him out into the cold, dark, and hungry world.

The final crisis over, he came back to the center of the floor. The panic in his breast had died out, but his nerves were still quivering. He filled his Thermos and then listened for a while to his own tenor singing the "Sea Things" aria from his favorite opera, Gianelli's *Ancient Mariner*. Suddenly, he burst out and accompanied himself, finding himself thrilled as never before by the concluding words.

And from my neck so free
The Albatross fell off, and sank
Like lead into the sea.

Afterward, voice silent but heart singing, he switched off the wire and cut in on Polyphema's broadcast.

Mother was having trouble. She could not precisely describe to the continent-wide hookup this new and almost inexpressible emotion she felt about the mobile. It was a concept her language was not prepared for. Nor was she helped any by the gallons of Old Red Star in her bloodstream.

Eddie sucked at the plastic nipple and nodded sympathetically and drowsily at her search for words. Presently, the Thermos rolled out of his hand.

He slept on his side, curled in a ball, knees on his chest and arms crossed, neck bent forward. Like the pilot room chronometer whose hands reversed after the crash, the clock of his body was ticking backward, ticking backward . . .

In the darkness, in the moistness, safe and warm, well fed, much loved.

Rudyard Kipling

Rudyard Kipling (1865–1936) is one of the major literary figures influencing the flowering of science fiction in the twentieth century. Kipling wrote two great SF stories, "With the Night Mail" and this one, a sequel set in the same imagined future. With them he became one of the progenitors of the genre. H. G. Wells was the great imaginative force behind Scientific Romance from 1895 to at least the 1920s, but Rudyard Kipling was the most popular English language writer of his day, and it was not Wellsian but Kiplingesque storytelling and attitudes—and politics—that dominated American science fiction in the 1940s and '50s. While Robert A. Heinlein certainly borrowed techniques liberally from the fiction of H. G. Wells, the effect of his classic stories is markedly Kiplingesque. Poul Anderson and Gordon R. Dickson, to name only two others among many, also acknowledge a debt to Kipling.

Even though he wrote very little actual science fiction, fantastic elements abound in Kipling's fiction. The recent (1992) publication of a volume of *The Science Fiction of Rudyard Kipling*, laden with encomiums from such diverse SF writers as Jerry Pournelle, Gene Wolfe, and John Brunner, only confirms his enduring appeal and influence.

In his introduction to that volume John Brunner points out that Kipling uses the historic present tense, in his day an unusual usage in English, which became part of the arsenal of SF writers. He also points out, in his introduction to "As Easy as ABC," the crucial fact that Kipling was, politically, the ancestor of what we today call Libertarians. Brunner quotes Kipling's 1923 speech at St. Andrews to this effect: "At any price I can pay, let me own myself. And the price is worth paying if you keep what you have bought."

"As Easy as ABC" is if anything a companion piece to Forster's "The Machine Stops," a criticism of the Wellsian urban utopia, but with an attitude that leads toward, not away from, genre science fiction.

AS EASY AS ABC

The ABC, that semi-elected, semi-nominated body of a few score persons, controls the Planet. Transportation is Civilization, our motto runs. Theoretically we do what we please, so long as we do not interfere with the traffic and all it implies. Practically, the ABC confirms or annuals all international arrangements, and, to judge from its last report, finds our tolerant, humorous, lazy little Planet only too ready to shift the whole burden of public administration on its shoulders.

"With the Night Mail," *Actions and Reactions*

Isn't it almost time that our Planet took some interest in the proceedings of the Aerial Board of Control? One knows that easy communications nowadays, and lack of privacy in the past, have killed all curiosity among mankind, but as the Board's Official Reporter I am bound to tell my tale.

At 9:30 A.M., 26 August, A.D. 2065, the Board, sitting in London, was informed by De Forest that the District of Northern Illinois had riotously cut itself out of all systems and would remain disconnected till the Board should take over and administer it direct.

Every Northern Illinois freight and passenger tower was, he reported, out of action; all District main, local, and guiding lights had been extinguished; all General Communications were dumb, and through traffic had been diverted. No reason had been given, but he gathered unofficially from the Mayor of Chicago that the District complained of "crowd-making and invasion of privacy."

As a matter of fact, it is of no importance whether Northern Illinois stay in or out of planetary circuit; as a matter of policy, any complaint of invasion of privacy needs immediate investigation, lest worse follow.

By 9:45 A.M. De Forest, Dragomiroff (Russia), Takahira (Japan), and Pirolo (Italy) were empowered to visit Illinois and "to take such steps as might be necessary for the resumption of traffic and *all that that implies.*" By 10 A.M. the Hall was empty, and the four Members and I were aboard what Pirolo insisted on calling "my leetle godchild"—that is to say, the new *Victor Pirolo*. Our Planet prefers to know Victor Pirolo as a gentle, grey-haired enthusiast who spends his time near Foggia, inventing or creating new breeds of Spanish-Italian olive-trees; but there is another side to his nature—the manufacture of quaint inventions, of which the *Victor Pirolo* is, perhaps, not the least surprising. She and a few score sister-craft of the same type embody his latest ideas. But she is not comfortable. An ABC boat does not take the air with the level-keeled lift of a liner, but shoots up rocket-fashion like the "aeroplane" of our ancestors, and makes her height at top-speed from the first. That is why I found myself sitting suddenly on the large lap of Eustace Arnott, who commands the ABC Fleet. One knows vaguely that there is such a thing as a Fleet somewhere on the planet, and that, theoretically, it exists for the purposes of what used to be known as "war." Only a week before, while visiting a glacier sanatorium behind Gothaven, I had seen some squadrons making false auroras far to the north while they maneuvered round the Pole; but, naturally, it had never occurred to me that the things could be used in earnest.

Said Arnott to De Forest as I staggered to a seat on the chart-room divan: "We're tremendously grateful to 'em in Illinois. We've never had a chance of exercising all the Fleet together. I've turned in a General Call, and I expect we'll have at least two hundred keels aloft this evening."

"Well aloft?" De Forest asked.

"Of course, sir. Out of sight till they're called for."

Arnott laughed as he lolled over the transparent chart-table where the map of the summer-blue Atlantic slid along, degree by degree, in exact answer to our progress. Our dial already showed 320 m.p.h. and we were two thousand feet above the uppermost traffic lines.

"Now, where is this Illinois District of yours?" said Dragomiroff. "One travels so much, one sees so little. Oh, I remember! It is in North America."

De Forest, whose business it is to know the out districts, told us that it lay at the foot of Lake Michigan, on a road to nowhere in particular, was about half an hour's run from end to end, and, except in one corner, as flat as the sea. Like most flat countries nowadays, it was heavily guarded against invasion of privacy by forced timber—fifty-foot spruce and tamarack, grown in five years. The population was close on two millions, largely migratory between Florida and California, with a backbone of small farms (they call a thousand acres a farm in Illinois) whose owners come into Chicago for amusements and society during the winter. They were, he said, noticeably kind, quiet folk, but a little exacting, as all flat countries must be, in their notions of privacy. There had, for instance, been no printed news-sheet in Illinois for twenty-seven years. Chicago argued that engines for printed news sooner or later developed into engines for invasion of privacy, which in turn might bring the old terror of Crowds and blackmail back to the Planet. So news-sheets were not.

"And that's Illinois," De Forest concluded. "You see, in the Old Days, she was in the forefront of what they used to call 'progress,' and Chicago—"

"Chicago?" said Takahira. "That's the little place where there is Salati's Statue of the Negro in Flames? A fine bit of old work."

"When did you see it?" asked De Forest quickly. "They only unveil it once a year."

"I know. At Thanksgiving. It was then," said Takahira, with a shudder. "And they sang MacDonough's Song, too."

"Whew!" De Forest whistled. "I did not know that! I wish you'd told me before. MacDonough's Song may have had its uses when it was composed, but it was an infernal legacy for any man to leave behind."

"It's protective instinct, my dear fellows," said Pirolo, rolling a cigarette. "The Planet, she has had her dose of popular government. She suffers from inherited agoraphobia. She has no—ah—use for crowds."

Dragomiroff leaned forward to give him a light. "Certainly," said the white-bearded Russian, "the Planet has taken all precautions against crowds for the past hundred years. What is our total population today? Six hundred million, we hope; five hundred, we think; but—but if next year's census shows more than four hundred and fifty, I myself will eat all the extra little babies. We have cut the birth-rate out—right out! For a long time we have said to Almighty God, 'Thank You, Sir, but we do not much like Your game of life, so we will not play.' "

"Anyhow," said Arnott defiantly, "men live a century apiece on the average now."

"Oh, that is quite well! I am rich—you are rich—we are all rich and happy because we are so few and we live so long. Only *I* think Almighty God He will remember what the Planet was like in the time of Crowds and the Plague. Perhaps He will send us nerves. Eh, Pirolo?"

The Italian blinked into space. "Perhaps," he said, "He has sent them already. Anyhow, you cannot argue with the Planet. She does not forget the Old Days, and—what can you do?"

"For sure we can't remake the world." De Forest glanced at the map flowing smoothly across the table from west to east. "We ought to be over our ground by nine tonight. There won't be much sleep afterwards."

On which hint we dispersed, and I slept till Takahira waked me for dinner. Our ancestors thought nine hours' sleep ample for their little lives. We, living thirty years longer, feel ourselves defrauded with less than eleven out of the twenty-four.

By ten o'clock we were over Lake Michigan. The west shore was lightless, except for a dull ground-glare at Chicago, and a single traffic-directing light—its leading beam pointing north—at Waukegan on our starboard bow. None of the Lake villages gave any sign of life; and inland, westward, so far as we could see, blackness lay unbroken on the level earth. We swooped down and skimmed low across the dark, throwing calls county by county. Now and again we picked up the faint glimmer of a house-light, or heard the rasp and rend of a cultivator being played across the fields, but Northern Illinois as a whole was one inky, apparently uninhabited, waste of high, forced woods. Only our illuminated map, with its little pointer switching from county to county, as we wheeled and twisted, gave us any idea of our position. Our calls, urgent, pleading, coaxing or commanding, through the General Communicator brought no answer. Illinois strictly maintained her own privacy in the timber which she grew for that purpose.

"Oh, this is absurd!" said De Forest. "We're like an owl trying to work a wheat-field. Is this Bureau Creek? Let's land, Arnott, and get hold of some one."

We brushed over a belt of forced woodland—fifteen-year-old maple sixty feet high—grounded on a private meadow-dock, none too big, where we moored to our own grapnels, and hurried out through the warm dark night towards a light in a verandah. As we neared the garden gate I could have sworn we had stepped knee-deep in quicksand, for we could scarcely drag our feet against the prickling currents that clogged them. After five paces we stopped, wiping our foreheads, as hopelessly stuck on dry smooth turf as so many cows in a bog.

"Pest!" cried Pirolo angrily. "We are ground-circuited. And it is my own system of ground-circuits too! I know the pull."

"Good evening," said a girl's voice from the verandah. "Oh, I'm sorry! We've locked up. Wait a minute."

We heard the click of a switch, and almost fell forward as the currents round our knees were withdrawn.

The girl laughed, and laid aside her knitting. An old-fashioned Controller stood at her elbow, which she reversed from time to time, and we could hear the snort and clank of the obedient cultivator half a mile away, behind the guardian woods.

"Come in and sit down," she said. "I'm only playing a plough. Dad's gone to Chicago to—Ah! Then it was *your* call I heard just now!"

She had caught sight of Arnott's Board uniform, leaped to the switch, and turned it full on.

We were checked, gasping, waist-deep in current this time, three yards from the verandah.

"We only want to know what's the matter with Illinois," said De Forest placidly.

"Then hadn't you better go to Chicago and find out?" she answered. "There's nothing wrong here. We own ourselves."

"How can we go anywhere if you won't loose us?" De Forest went on, while Arnott scowled. Admirals of Fleets are still quite human when their dignity is touched.

"Stop a minute—you don't know how funny you look!" She put her hands on her hips and laughed mercilessly.

"Don't worry about that," said Arnott, and whistled. A voice answered from the *Victor Pirolo* in the meadow.

"Only a single-fuse ground-circuit!" Arnott called. "Sort it out gently, please."

We heard the ping of a breaking lamp; a fuse blew out somewhere in the verandah roof, frightening a nest full of birds. The ground-circuit was open. We stooped and rubbed our tingling ankles.

"How rude—how very rude of you!" the maiden cried.

"Sorry, but we haven't time to look funny," said Arnott. "We've got to go to Chicago; and if I were you, young lady, I'd go into the cellars for the next two hours, and take mother with me."

Off he strode, with us at his heels, muttering indignantly, till the humour of the thing struck and doubled him up with laughter at the foot of the gangway ladder.

"The Board hasn't shown what you might call a fat spark on this occasion," said De Forest, wiping his eyes. "I hope I didn't look as big a fool as you did, Arnott! Hullo! What on earth is that? Dad coming home from Chicago?"

There was a rattle and a rush, and a five-plough cultivator, blades in air like so many teeth, trundled itself at us round the edge of the timber, fuming and sparking furiously.

"Jump!" said Arnott, as we bundled ourselves through the none-too-wide door. "Never mind about shutting it. Up!"

The *Victor Pirolo* lifted like a bubble, and the vicious machine shot just underneath us, clawing high as it passed.

"There's a nice little spit-kitten for you!" said Arnott, dusting his knees. "We ask her a civil question. First she circuits us and then she plays a cultivator at us!"

"And then we fly," said Dragomiroff. "If I were forty years more young, I would go back and kiss her. Ho! Ho!"

"I," said Pirolo, "would smack her! My pet ship has been chased by a dirty plough; a—how do you say?—agricultural implement."

"Oh, that is Illinois all over," said De Forest. "They don't content themselves with talking about privacy. They arrange to have it. And now, where's your alleged fleet, Arnott? We must assert ourselves against this wench."

Arnott pointed to the black heavens.

"Waiting on—up there," said he. "Shall I give them the whole installation, sir?"

"Oh, I don't think the young lady is quite worth that," said De Forest. "Get over Chicago, and perhaps we'll see something."

In a few minutes we were hanging at two thousand feet over an oblong block of incandescence in the centre of the little town.

"That looks like the old City Hall. Yes, there's Salati's Statue in front of it," said Takahira. "But what on earth are they doing to the place? I thought they used it for a market nowadays! Drop a little, please."

We could hear the sputter and crackle of road-surfacing machines—the cheap Western type which fuse stone and rubbish into lava-like ribbed glass for their rough country roads. Three or four surfacers worked on each side of a square of ruins. The brick and stone wreckage crumbled, slid forward, and presently spread out into white-hot pools of sticky slag, which the levelling-rods smoothed more or less flat. Already a third of the big block had been so treated, and was cooling to dull red before our astonished eyes.

"It is the Old Market," said De Forest. "Well, there's nothing to prevent Illinois from making a road through a market. It doesn't interfere with traffic, that I can see."

"Hsh!" said Arnott, gripping me by the shoulder. "Listen! They're singing. Why on the earth are they singing?"

We dropped again till we could see the black fringe of people at the edge of that glowing square.

At first they only roared against the roar of the surfacers and levellers. Then the words came up clearly—the words of the Forbidden Song that all men knew, and none let pass their lips—poor Pat MacDonough's Song, made in the days of the Crowds and the Plague—every silly word of it loaded to sparking-point with the Planet's inherited memories of horror, panic, fear, and cruelty. And Chicago—innocent, contented little Chicago—was singing it aloud to the infernal tune that carried riot, pestilence and lunacy round our Planet a few generations ago!

Once there was The People—Terror gave it birth;
Once there was The People, and it made a hell of earth!

(Then the stamp and pause):

Earth arose and crushed it. Listen, oh, ye slain!
Once there was The People—it shall never be again!

The levellers thrust in savagely against the ruins as the song renewed itself again, again and again, louder than the crash of the melting walls.

De Forest frowned.

"I don't like that," he said. "They've broken back to the Old Days! They'll be killing somebody soon. I think we'd better divert 'em, Arnott."

"Ay, ay, sir." Arnott's hand went to his cap, and we heard the hull of the *Victor Pirolo* ring to the command: "Lamps! Both watches stand by! Lamps! Lamps! Lamps!"

"Keep still!" Takahira whispered to me. "Blinkers, please, quartermaster."

"It's all right—all right!" said Pirolo from behind, and to my horror slipped over my head some sort of rubber helmet that locked with a snap. I could feel thick colloid bosses before my eyes, but I stood in absolute darkness.

"To save the sight," he explained, and pushed me on to the chart-room divan. "You will see in a minute."

As he spoke I became aware of a thin thread of almost intolerable light, let down from heaven at an immense distance—one vertical hairsbreadth of frozen lightning.

"Those are our flanking ships," said Arnott at my elbow. "That one is over Galena. Look south—that other one's over Keithburg. Vincennes is behind us, and north yonder is Winthrop Woods. The Fleet's in position, sir"—this to De Forest. "As soon as you give the word."

"Ah no! No!" cried Dragomiroff at my side. I could feel the old man tremble. "I do not know all that you can do, but be kind! I ask you to be a little kind to them below! This is horrible—horrible!"

When a Woman kills a Chicken,
Dynasties and Empires sicken,

Takahira quoted. "It is too late to be gentle now."

"Then take off my helmet! Take off my helmet!" Dragomiroff began hysterically.

Pirolo must have put his arm round him.

"Hush," he said, "I am here. It is all right, Ivan, my dear fellow."

"I'll just send our little girl in Bureau County a warning," said Arnott. "She don't deserve it, but we'll allow her a minute or two to take mamma to the cellar."

In the utter hush that followed the growling spark after Arnott had linked up his Service Communicator with the invisible Fleet, we heard MacDonough's Song from the city beneath us grow fainter as we rose to position. Then I clapped my hand before my mask lenses for it was as though the floor of Heaven had been riddled and all the inconceivable blaze of suns in the making was poured through the manholes.

"You needn't count," said Arnott. I had had no thought of such a thing. "There are two hundred and fifty keels up there, five miles apart. Full power, please, for another twelve seconds."

The firmament, as far as eye could reach, stood on pillars of white fire. One fell on the glowing square at Chicago, and turned it black.

"Oh! Oh! Oh! Can men be allowed to do such things?" Dragomiroff cried, and fell across our knees.

"Glass of water, please," said Takahira to a helmeted shape that leaped forward. "He is a little faint."

The lights switched off, and the darkness stunned like an avalanche. We could hear Dragomiroff's teeth on the glass edge.

Pirolo was comforting him.

"All right, allra-ight," he repeated. "Come and lie down. Come below and take off your mask. I give you my word, old friend, it is all right. They are my siege-lights. Little Victor Pirolo's leetle lights. You know *me!* I do not hurt people."

"Pardon!" Dragomiroff moaned. "I have never seen Death. I have never seen the Board take action. Shall we go down and burn them alive, or is that already done?"

"Oh, hush," said Pirolo, and I think he rocked him in his arms.

"Do we repeat, sir?" Arnott asked De Forest.

"Give 'em a minute's break," De Forest replied. "They may need it."

We waited a minute, and then MacDonough's Song, broken but defiant, rose from undefeated Chicago.

"They seem fond of that tune," said De Forest. "I should let 'em have it, Arnott."

"Very good, sir," said Arnott, and felt his way to the Communicator keys.

No lights broke forth, but the hollow of the skies made herself the mouth for one note that touched the raw fibre of the brain. Men hear such sounds in delirium, advancing like tides from horizons beyond the ruled foreshores of space.

"That's our pitch-pipe," said Arnott. "We may be a bit ragged. I've never conducted two hundred and fifty performers before." He pulled out the couplers, and struck a full chord on the Service Communicators.

The beams of light leaped down again, and danced, solemnly and awfully, a stilt-dance, sweeping thirty or forty miles left and right at each stiff-legged kick, while the darkness delivered itself—there is no scale to measure against that utterance—of the tune to which they kept time. Certain notes—one learnt to expect them with terror—cut through one's marrow, but, after three minutes, thought and emotion passed in indescribable agony.

We saw, we heard, but I think we were in some sort swooning. The two hundred and fifty beams shifted, re-formed, straddled and split, narrowed, widened, rippled in ribbons, broke into a thousand white-hot parallel lines, melted and revolved in interwoven rings like old-fashioned engine-turning, flung up to the zenith, made as if to descend and renew the torment, halted at the last instant, twizzled insanely round the horizon, and vanished, to bring back for the hundredth time darkness more shattering than their instantly renewed light over all Illinois. Then the tune and lights ceased together, and we heard one single devastating wail that shook all the horizon as a rubbed wet finger shakes the rim of a bowl.

"Ah, that is my new siren," said Pirolo. "You can break an iceberg in half, if you find the proper pitch. They will whistle by squadrons now. It is the wind through pierced shutters in the bows."

I had collapsed beside Dragomiroff, broken and snivelling feebly, because I had been delivered before my time to all the terrors of Judgement Day, and the Archangels of the Resurrection were hailing me naked across the Universe to the sound of the music of the spheres.

Then I saw De Forest smacking Arnott's helmet with his open hand. The wailing died down in a long shriek as a black shadow swooped past us, and returned to her place above the lower clouds.

"I hate to interrupt a specialist when he's enjoying himself," said De Forest. "But, as a matter of fact, all Illinois has been asking us to stop for these last fifteen seconds."

"What a pity." Arnott slipped off his mask. "I wanted you to hear us really hum. Our lower C can lift street-paving."

"It is Hell—Hell!" cried Dragomiroff, and sobbed aloud.

Arnott looked away as he answered:

"It's a few thousand volts ahead of the old shoot-'em-and-sink-'em game, but I should scarcely call it *that*. What shall I tell the Fleet, sir?"

"Tell 'em we're very pleased and impressed. I don't think they need wait on any longer. There isn't a spark left down there." De Forest pointed. "They'll be deaf and blind."

"Oh, I think not, sir. The demonstration lasted less than ten minutes."

"Marvellous!" Takahira sighed. "I should have said it was half a night. Now, shall we go down and pick up the pieces?"

"But first a small drink," said Pirolo. "The Board must not arrive weeping at its own works."

"I am an old fool—an old fool!" Dragomiroff began piteously. "I did not know what would happen. It is all new to me. We reason with them in Little Russia."

Chicago North landing-tower was unlighted, and Arnott worked his ship into the clips by her own lights. As soon as these broke out we heard groanings of horror and appeal from many people below.

"All right," shouted Arnott into the darkness. "We aren't beginning again!" We descended by the stairs, to find ourselves knee-deep in a grovelling crowd, some crying that they were blind, others beseeching us not to make anymore noises, but the greater part writhing face downward, their hands or their caps before their eyes.

It was Pirolo who came to our rescue. He climbed the side of a surfacing-machine, and there, gesticulating as though they could see, made oration to those afflicted people of Illinois.

"You stchewpids!" he began. "There is nothing to fuss for. Of course, your eyes will smart and be red tomorrow. You will look as if you and your wives had drunk too much, but in a little while you will see again as well as before. I tell you this, and I—*I* am Pirolo. Victor Pirolo!"

The crowd with one accord shuddered, for many legends attach to Victor Pirolo of Foggia, deep in the secrets of God.

"Pirolo?" An unsteady voice lifted itself. "Then tell us was there anything except light in those lights of yours just now?"

The question was repeated from every corner of the darkness.

Pirolo laughed.

"No!" he thundered. (Why have small men such large voices?) "I give you my word and the Board's word that there was nothing except light—just light! You stchewpids! Your birth rate is too low already as it is. Some day I must invent something to send it up, but send it down—never!"

"Is that true?—We thought—somebody said—"

One could feel the tension relax all round.

"You *too* big fools," Pirolo cried. "You could have sent us a call and we would have told you."

"Send you a call!" a deep voice shouted. "I wish you had been at our end of the wire."

"I'm glad I wasn't," said De Forest. "It was bad enough from behind the lamps. Never mind! It's over now. Is there any one here I can talk business with? I'm De Forest—for the Board."

"You might begin with me, for one—I'm Mayor," the bass voice replied.

A big man rose unsteadily from the street, and staggered towards us where we sat on the broad turf-edging, in front of the garden fences.

"I ought to be the first on my feet. Am I?" said he.

"Yes," said De Forest, and steadied him as he dropped down beside us.

"Hello, Andy. Is that you?" a voice called.

"Excuse me," said the Mayor; "that sounds like my Chief of Police, Bluthner!"

"Bluthner it is; and here's Mulligan and Keefe—on their feet."

"Bring 'em up please, Blut. We're supposed to be the Four in charge of this hamlet. What we says, goes. And, De Forest, what do you say?"

"Nothing—yet," De Forest answered, as we made room for the panting, reeling men. "*You*'ve cut out of system. Well?"

"Tell the steward to send down drinks, please," Arnott whispered to an orderly at his side.

"Good!" said the Mayor, smacking his dry lips. "Now I suppose we can take it, De Forest, that henceforward the Board will administer us direct?"

"Not if the Board can avoid it," De Forest laughed. "The ABC is responsible for the planetary traffic only."

"*And all that that implies.*" The big Four who ran Chicago chanted their Magna Charta like children at school.

"Well, get on," said De Forest wearily. "What is your silly trouble anyway?"

"Too much dam' Democracy," said the Mayor, laying his hand on De Forest's knee.

"So? I thought Illinois had had her dose of that."

"She has. That's why. Blut, what did you do with our prisoners last night?"

"Locked 'em in the water-tower to prevent the women killing 'em," the Chief of Police replied. "I'm too blind to move just yet, but—"

"Arnott, send some of your people, please, and fetch 'em along," said De Forest.

"They're triple-circuited," the Mayor called. "You'll have to blow out three fuses." He turned to De Forest, his large outline just visible in the paling darkness. "I hate to throw any more work on the Board. I'm an administrator myself, but we've had a little fuss with our Serviles. What? In a big city there's bound to be a few men and women who can't live without listening to themselves, and who prefer drinking out of pipes they don't own both ends of. They inhabit flats and hotels all the year round. They say it saves 'em trouble. Anyway, it gives 'em more time to make trouble for their neighbours. We call 'em Serviles locally. And they are apt to be tuberculous."

"Just so!" said the man called Mulligan. "Transportation is Civilization. Democracy is Disease. I've proved it by the blood-test, every time."

"Mulligan's our Health Officer, and a one-idea man," said the Mayor, laughing. "But it's true that most Serviles haven't much control. They *will* talk; and when people take to talking as a business, anything may arrive—mayn't it, De Forest?"

"Anything—except the facts of the case," said De Forest, laughing.

"I'll give you those in a minute," said the Mayor. "Our Serviles got to talking—first in their houses and then on the streets, telling men and women how to manage their own affairs. (You can't teach a Servile not to finger his neighbour's soul.) That's invasion of privacy, of course, but in Chicago we'll suffer anything sooner than make crowds. Nobody took much notice, and so I let 'em alone. My fault! I was warned there would be trouble, but there hasn't been a crowd or murder in Illinois for nineteen years."

"Twenty-two," said his Chief of Police.

"Likely. Anyway, we'd forgot such things. So, from talking in the houses and on the streets, our Serviles go to calling a meeting at the Old Market yonder." He nodded across the square where the wrecked buildings heaved up grey in the dawn-glimmer behind the square-cased statue of The Negro in Flames. "There's nothing to prevent any one calling meetings except that it's against human nature to stand in a crowd, besides being bad for the health. I ought to have known by the way our men and women attended that first meeting that trouble was brewing. There were as many as a thousand in the market-place, touching each other. Touching! Then the Serviles turned in all tongue-switches and talked, and we—"

"What did they talk about?" said Takahira.

"First, how badly things were managed in the city. That pleased us Four—we were on the platform—because we hoped to catch one or two good men for City work. You know how rare executive capacity is. Even if we didn't it's—it's refreshing to find any one interested enough in our job to damn our eyes. You don't know what it means to work, year in, year out, without a spark of difference with a living soul."

"Oh, don't we!" said De Forest. "There are times on the Board when we'd give our positions if any one would kick us out and take hold of things themselves."

"But they won't," said the Mayor ruefully. "I assure you, sir, we Four have done things in Chicago, in the hope of rousing people, that would have discredited Nero. But what do they say? 'Very good, Andy. Have it your own way. Anything's better than a crowd. I'll go back to my land.' You *can't* do anything with folk who can go where they please, and don't want anything on God's earth except their own way. There isn't a kick or a kicker left on the Planet."

"Then I suppose that little shed yonder fell down by itself?" said De Forest. We could see the bare and still smoking ruins, and hear the slag-pools crackle as they hardened and set.

"Oh, that's only amusement. Tell you later. As I was saying, our Serviles held the meeting, and pretty soon we had to ground-circuit the platform to save 'em from being killed. And that didn't make our people any more pacific."

"How d'you mean?" I ventured to ask.

"If you've ever been ground-circuited," said the Mayor, "you'll know it don't improve any man's temper to be held up straining against nothing. No, sir! Eight or nine hundred folk kept pawing and buzzing like flies in treacle for two hours, while a pack of perfectly safe Serviles invades their mental and spiritual privacy, may be amusing to watch, but they are not pleasant to handle afterwards."

Pirolo chuckled.

"Our folk own themselves. They were of opinion things were going too far and too fiery. I warned the Serviles; but they're born house-dwellers. Unless a fact hits 'em on the head, they cannot see it. Would you believe me, they went on to talk of what they called 'popular government'? They did! They wanted us to go back to the old Voodoo-business of voting with papers and wooden boxes, and word-drunk people and printed formulas, and news-sheets! They said they practised it among themselves about what they'd have to eat in their flats and hotels. Yes, sir! They stood up behind Bluthner's doubled ground-circuits, and they said that, in this present year of grace, *to* self-owning men and women, *on* that very spot! Then they finished"—he lowered his voice cautiously—"by talking about 'The People.' And then Bluthner he had to sit up all night in charge of the circuits because he couldn't trust his men to keep 'em shut."

"It was trying 'em too high," the Chief of Police broke in. "But we couldn't hold the crowd ground-circuited for ever. I gathered in all the Serviles on charge of crowd-making, and put 'em in the water-tower, and then I let things cut loose. I had to! The District lit like a sparked gas-tank!"

"The news was out over seven degrees of country," the Mayor continued; "and when once it's a question of invasion of privacy, goodbye to right and reason in Illinois! They began turning out traffic lights and locking up landing-towers on Thursday night. Friday, they stopped all traffic and asked for the Board to take over. Then they wanted to clean Chicago off the side of the Lake and rebuild elsewhere—just for a souvenir of 'The People' that the Serviles talked about. I suggested that they should slag the Old Market where the meeting was held, while I turned in a call to you all on the Board. That kept 'em quiet till you came along. And—and now *you* can take hold of the situation."

"Any chance of their quieting down?" De Forest asked.

"You can try," said the Mayor.

De Forest raised his voice in the face of the reviving crowd that had edged in towards us. Day was come.

"Don't you think this business can be arranged?" he began. But there was a roar of angry voices:

"We've finished with Crowds! We aren't going back to the Old Days! Take us over! Take the Serviles away! Administer direct or we'll kill 'em! Down with The People!"

An attempt was made to begin MacDonough's Song. It got no further than the first line, for the *Victor Pirolo* sent down a warning drone on one stopped horn. A wrecked side-wall of the Old Market tottered and fell inwards on the slag-pools. None spoke or moved till the last of the dust had settled down again, turning the steel case of Salati's Statue ashy grey.

"You see you'll just *have* to take us over," the Mayor whispered.

De Forest shrugged his shoulders.

"You talk as if executive capacity could be snatched out of the air like so much horse-power. Can't you manage yourselves on any terms?" he said.

"We can, if you say so. It will only cost those few lives to begin with."

The Mayor pointed across the square, where Arnott's men guided a stumbling group of ten or twelve men and women to the lake front and halted them under the Statue.

"Now I think," said Takahira under his breath, "there will be trouble."

The mass in front of us growled like beasts.

At that moment the sun rose clear, and revealed the blinking assembly to itself. As soon as it realized that it was a crowd we saw the shiver of horror and mutual repulsion shoot across it precisely as the steely flaws shot across the lake outside. Nothing was said, and, being half blind, of course it moved slowly. Yet in less than fifteen minutes most of that vast multitude—three thousand at the lowest count—melted away like frost on south eaves. The remnant stretched themselves on the grass, where a crowd feels and looks less like a crowd.

"These mean business," the Mayor whispered to Takahira. "There are a goodish few women there who've borne children. I don't like it."

The morning draught off the lake stirred the trees round us with promise of a hot day; the sun reflected itself dazzlingly on the canister-shaped covering of Salati's Statue; cocks crew in the gardens, and we could hear gate-latches clicking in the distance as people stumblingly resought their homes.

"I'm afraid there won't be any morning deliveries," said De Forest. "We rather upset things in the country last night."

"That makes no odds," the Mayor returned. "We're all provisioned for six months. *We* take no chances."

Nor, when you come to think of it, does any one else. It must be three-quarters of a generation since any house or city faced a food shortage. Yet is there house or city on the Planet today that has not half a year's provisions laid in? We are like the shipwrecked seamen in the old books, who, having once nearly starved to death, ever afterwards hide away bits of food and biscuit. Truly we trust no Crowds, nor system based on Crowds!

De Forest waited till the last footstep had died away. Meantime the prisoners at the base of the Statue shuffled, posed, and fidgeted, with the shamelessness of quite little children. None of them were more than six feet high, and many of them were as grey-haired as the ravaged, harassed heads of old pictures. They huddled together in actual touch, while the crowd, spaced at large intervals, looked at them with congested eyes.

Suddenly a man among them began to talk. The Mayor had not in the least exaggerated. It appeared that our Planet lay sunk in slavery beneath the heel of the Aerial Board of Control. The orator urged us to arise in our might, burst our prison doors and break our fetters (all his metaphors, by the way, were of the most medieval). Next he demanded that every matter of daily life, including most of the physical functions, should be submitted for decision at any time of the week, month, or year to, I gathered, anybody who happened to be passing by or residing within a certain radius, and that everybody should forthwith abandon his concerns to settle the matter, first by crowd-making, next by talking to the crowds made, and lastly by describing crosses on pieces of paper, which rubbish should later be counted with certain mystic ceremonies and oaths. Out of this amazing play, he assured us, would automatically arise a higher, nobler, and kinder world, based—he demonstrated this with the awful lucidity of the insane—based on the sanctity of the Crowd and the villainy of the single person. In conclusion, he called loudly upon God to testify to his personal merits and integrity. When the flow ceased, I turned bewildered to Takahira, who was nodding solemnly.

"Quite correct," said he. "It is all in the old books. He has left nothing out, not even the war-talk."

"But I don't see how this stuff can upset a child, much less a district," I replied.

"Ah, you are too young," said Dragomiroff. "For another thing, you are not a mamma. Please look at the mammas."

Ten or fifteen women who remained had separated themselves from the silent men, and were drawing in towards the prisoners. It reminded one of the stealthy encircling, before the rush in at the quarry, of wolves round musk-oxen in the North. The prisoners saw, and drew together more closely. The Mayor covered his face with his hands for an instant. De Forest, bareheaded, stepped forward between the prisoners and the slowly, stiffly moving line.

"That's all very interesting," he said to the dry-lipped orator. "But the point seems to be that you've been making crowds and invading privacy."

A woman stepped forward, and would have spoken, but there was a quick assenting murmur from the men, who realized that De Forest was trying to pull the situation down to ground-line.

"Yes! Yes!" they cried. "We cut out because they made crowds and invaded privacy! Stick to that! Keep on that switch! Lift the Serviles out of this! The Board's in charge! Hsh!"

"Yes, the Board's in charge," said De Forest. "I'll take formal evidence of crowd-making if you like, but the Members of the Board can testify to it. Will that do?"

The women had closed in another pace, with hands that clenched and unclenched at their sides.

"Good! Good enough!" the men cried. "We're content. Only take them away quickly."

"Come along up!" said De Forest to the captives. "Breakfast is quite ready."

It appeared, however, that they did not wish to go. They intended to remain in Chicago and make crowds. They pointed out that De Forest's proposal was gross invasion of privacy.

"My dear fellow," said Pirolo to the most voluble of the leaders, "you hurry, or your crowd that can't be wrong will kill you!"

"But that would be murder," answered the believer in crowds; and there was a roar of laughter from all sides that seemed to show the crisis had broken.

A woman stepped forward from the line of women, laughing, I protest, as merrily as any of the company. One hand, of course, shaded her eyes, the other was at her throat.

"Oh, they needn't be afraid of being killed!" she called.

"Not in the least," said De Forest. "But don't you think that, now the Board's in charge, you might go home while we get these people away?"

"I shall be home long before that. It—it has been rather a trying day."

She stood up to her full height, dwarfing even De Forest's six-foot-eight, and smiled, with eyes closed against the fierce light.

"Yes, rather," said De Forest. "I'm afraid you feel the glare a little. We'll have the ship down."

He motioned to the *Pirolo* to drop between us and the sun, and at the same time to loop-circuit the prisoners, who were a trifle unsteady. We saw them stiffen to the current where they stood. The woman's voice went on, sweet and deep and unshaken:

"I don't suppose you men realize how much this—this sort of thing means to a woman. I've borne three. We women don't want our children given to Crowds. It must be an inherited instinct. Crowds make trouble. They bring back the Old Days. Hate, fear, blackmail, publicity, 'The People'—*That! That! That!*" She pointed to the Statue, and the crowd growled once more.

"Yes, if they are allowed to go on," said De Forest. "But this little affair—"

"It means so much to us women that this—this little affair should never happen again. Of course, never's a big word, but one feels so strongly that it is important to stop crowds at the very beginning. Those creatures"—she pointed with her left hand at the prisoners swaying like seaweed in a tideway as the circuit pulled them—"those people have friends and wives and children in the city and elsewhere. One doesn't want anything done to *them,* you know. It's terrible to force a human being out of fifty or sixty years of good life. I'm only forty myself. *I* know. But, at the same time, one feels that an example should be made, because no price is too heavy to pay if—if these people and *all that they imply* can be put an end to. Do you quite understand, or would you be kind enough to tell your men to take the casing off the Statue? It's worth looking at."

"I understand perfectly. But I don't think anybody here wants to see the Statue on an empty stomach. Excuse me one moment." De Forest called up to the ship, "A flying loop ready on the port side, if you please." Then to the woman he said with some crispness, "You might leave us a little discretion in the matter."

"Oh, of course. Thank you for being so patient. I know my arguments are silly, but—" She half turned away and went on in a changed voice, "Perhaps this will help you to decide."

She threw out her right arm with a knife in it. Before the blade could be returned to her throat or her bosom it was twitched from her grip, sparked as it flew out of the shadow of the ship above, and fell flashing in the sunshine at the foot of the Statue fifty yards away. The outflung arm was arrested, rigid as a bar for an instant, till the releasing circuit permitted her to bring it slowly to her side. The other women shrank back silent among the men.

Pirolo rubbed his hands, and Takahira nodded.

"That was clever of you, De Forest," said he.

"What a glorious pose!" Dragomiroff murmured, for the frightened woman was on the edge of tears.

"Why did you stop me? I would have done it!" she cried.

"I have no doubt you would," said De Forest. "But we can't waste a life like yours on these people. I hope the arrest didn't sprain your wrist; it's so hard to regulate a flying loop. But I think you are quite right about those persons' women and children. We'll take them all away with us if you promise not to do anything stupid to yourself."

"I promise—I promise." She controlled herself with an effort. "But it is so important to us women. We know what it means; and I thought if you saw I was in earnest—"

"I saw you were, and you've gained your point. I shall take all your Serviles away with me at once. The Mayor will make lists of their friends and families in the city and the district, and he'll ship them after us this afternoon."

"Sure," said the Mayor, rising to his feet. "Keefe, if you can see, hadn't you better finish levelling off the Old Market? It don't look sightly the way it is now, and we shan't use it for crowds anymore."

"I think you had better wipe out that Statue as well, Mr Mayor," said De Forest. "I don't question its merits as a work of art, but I believe it's a shade morbid."

"Certainly, sir. Oh, Keefe! Slag the Negro before you go on to fuse the Market. I'll get to the Communicators and tell the District that the Board is in charge. Are you making any special appointments, sir?"

"None. We haven't men to waste on these backwoods. Carry on as before, but under the Board. Arnott, run your Serviles aboard, please. Ground ship and pass them through the bilge-doors. We'll wait till we've finished with this work of art."

The prisoners trailed past him, talking fluently, but unable to gesticulate in the drag of the current. Then the surfacers rolled up, two on each side of the Statue. With one accord the spectators looked elsewhere, but there was no need. Keefe turned on full power, and the thing simply melted within its case. All I saw was a surge of white-hot metal pouring over the plinth, a glimpse of Salati's inscription, "To the Eternal Memory of the Justice of the People," ere the stone base itself cracked and powdered into finest lime. The crowd cheered.

"Thank you," said De Forest; "but we want our breakfasts, and I expect you do too. Goodbye, Mr Mayor! Delighted to see you at any time, but I hope I shan't have to, officially, for the next thirty years. Goodbye, madam. Yes. We're all given to nerves nowadays. I suffer from them myself. Goodbye, gentlemen all! You're under the tyrannous heel of the Board from this moment, but if ever you feel like breaking your fetters you've only to let us know. This is no treat to us. Good luck!"

We embarked amid shouts, and did not check our lift till they had dwindled into whispers. Then De Forest flung himself on the chartroom divan and mopped his forehead.

"I don't mind men," he panted, "but women are the devil!"

"Still the devil," said Pirolo cheerfully. "That one would have suicided."

"I know it. That was why I signalled for the flying loop to be clapped on her. I owe you an apology for that, Arnott. I hadn't time to catch your eye, and you were busy with our caitiffs. By the way, who actually answered my signal? It was a smart piece of work."

"Ilroy," said Arnott; "but he overloaded the wave. It may be pretty gallery-work to knock a knife out of a lady's hand, but didn't you notice how she rubbed 'em? He scorched her fingers. Slovenly, I call it."

"Far be it from me to interfere with Fleet discipline, but don't be too hard on the boy. If that woman had killed herself they would have killed every Servile and everything related to a Servile throughout the district by nightfall."

"That was what she was playing for," Takahira said. "And with our Fleet gone we could have done nothing to hold them."

"I may be ass enough to walk into a ground-circuit," said Arnott, "but I don't dismiss my Fleet till I'm reasonably sure that trouble is over. They're in position still, and I intend to keep 'em there till the Serviles are shipped out of the district. That last little crowd meant murder, my friends."

"Nerves! All nerves!" said Pirolo. "You cannot argue with agoraphobia."

"And it is not as if they had seen much dead—or *is* it?" said Takahira.

"In all my ninety years I have never seen death." Dragomiroff spoke as one who would excuse himself. "Perhaps that was why—last night—"

Then it came out as we sat over breakfast, that, with the exception of Arnott and Pirolo, none of us had ever seen a corpse, or knew in what manner the spirit passes.

"We're a nice lot to flap about governing the Planet," De Forest laughed. "I confess, now it's all over, that my main fear was I mightn't be able to pull it off without losing a life."

"I thought of that too," said Arnott; "but there's no death reported, and I've enquired everywhere. What are we supposed to do with our passengers? I've fed 'em."

"We're between two switches," De Forest drawled. "If we drop them in any place that isn't under the Board, the natives will make their presence an excuse for cutting out, same as Illinois did, and forcing the Board to take over. If we drop them in any place under the Board's control they'll be killed as soon as our backs are turned."

"If you say so," said Pirolo thoughtfully, "I can guarantee that they will become extinct in process of time, quite happily. What is their birth-rate now?"

"Go down and ask 'em," said De Forest.

"I think they might become nervous and tear me to bits," the philosopher of Foggia replied.

"Not really? Well?"

"Open the bilge-doors," said Takahira with a downward jerk of the thumb.

"Scarcely—after all the trouble we've taken to save 'em," said De Forest.

"Try London," Arnott suggested. "You could turn Satan himself loose there, and they'd only ask him to dinner."

"Good man! You've given me an idea. Vincent! Oh, Vincent!" He threw the General Communicator open so that we could all hear, and in a few minutes the chartroom filled with the rich, fruity voice of Leopold Vincent, who has purveyed all London her choicest amusements for the last thirty years. We answered with expectant grins, as though we were actually in the stalls of, say, the Combination on a first night.

"We've picked up something in your line," De Forest began.

"That's good, dear man. If it's old enough. There's nothing to beat the old things for business purposes. Have you seen *London, Chatham, and Dover* at Earl's Court? No? I thought I missed you there. Im-mense! I've had the real steam locomotive engines built from the old designs and the iron rails cast specially by hand. Cloth cushions in the carriages, too! Im-mense! And paper railway tickets. And Polly Milton."

"Polly Milton back again!" said Arnott rapturously. "Book me two stalls for tomorrow night. What's she singing now, bless her?"

"The old songs. Nothing comes up to the old touch. Listen to this, dear men." Vincent carolled with flourishes:

Oh, cruel lamps of London,
If tears your light could drown,
Your victims' eyes would weep them,
Oh, lights of London Town!

"Then they weep."

"You see?" Pirolo waved his hands at us. "The old world always weeped when it saw crowds together. It did not know why, but it weeped. We know why, but we do not weep, except when we pay to be made to by fat, wicked old Vincent."

"Old, yourself!" Vincent laughed. "I'm a public benefactor, I keep the world soft and united."

"And I'm De Forest of the Board," said De Forest acidly, "trying to get a little business done. As I was saying, I've picked up a few people in Chicago."

"I cut out. Chicago is—"

"Do listen! They're perfectly unique."

"Do they build houses of baked mudblocks while you wait—eh? That's an old contact."

"They're an untouched primitive community, with all the old ideas."

"Sewing-machines and maypole-dances? Cooking on coal-gas stoves, lighting pipes with matches, and driving horses? Gerolstein tried that last year. An absolute blow-out!"

De Forest plugged him wrathfully, and poured out the story of our doings for the last twenty-four hours on the top-note.

"And they do it *all* in public," he concluded. "You can't stop 'em. The more public, the better they are pleased. They'll talk for hours—like you! Now you can come in again!"

"Do you really mean they know how to vote?" said Vincent. "Can they act it?"

"Act? It's their life to 'em! And you never saw such faces! Scarred like volcanoes. Envy, hatred, and malice in plain sight. Wonderfully flexible voices. They weep, too."

"Aloud? In public?"

"I guarantee. Not a spark of shame or reticence in the entire installation. It's the chance of your career."

"D'you say you've brought their voting props along—those papers and ballot-box things?"

"No, confound you! I'm not a luggage-lifter. Apply direct to the Mayor of Chicago. He'll forward you everything. Well?"

"Wait a minute. Did Chicago want to kill 'em? That 'ud look well on the Communicators."

"Yes! They were only rescued with difficulty from a howling mob—if you know what that is."

"But I don't," answered the Great Vincent simply.

"Well then, they'll tell you themselves. They can make speeches hours long."

"How many are there?"

"By the time we ship 'em all over they'll be perhaps a hundred, counting children. An old world in miniature. Can't you see it?"

"M-yes; but I've got to pay for it if it's a blow-out, dear man."

"They can sing the old war songs in the streets. They can get word-drunk, and make crowds, and invade privacy in the genuine old-fashioned way; and they'll do the voting trick as often as you ask 'em a question."

"Too good!" said Vincent.

"You unbelieving Jew! I've got a dozen head aboard here. I'll put you through direct. Sample 'em yourself."

He lifted the switch and we listened. Our passengers on the lower deck at once, but not less than five at a time, explained themselves to Vincent. They had been taken from the bosom of their families, stripped of their possessions, given food without finger-bowls, and cast into captivity in a noisome dungeon.

"But look here," said Arnott aghast; "they're saying what isn't true. My lower deck isn't noisome, and I saw to the finger-bowls myself."

"My people talk like that sometimes in Little Russia," said Dragomiroff. "We reason with them. We never kill. No!"

"But it's not true," Arnott insisted. "What can you do with people who don't tell facts? They're mad!"

"Hsh!" said Pirolo, his hand to his ear. "It is such a little time since all the Planet told lies."

We heard Vincent silkily sympathetic. Would they, he asked, repeat their assertions in public—before a vast public? only let Vincent give them a chance, and the Planet, they vowed, should ring with their wrongs. Their aim in life—two women and a man explained it together—was to reform the world. Oddly enough, this also had been Vincent's life-dream. He offered them an arena in which to explain, and by their living example to raise the Planet to loftier levels. He was eloquent on the moral uplift of a simple, old-world life presented in its entirety to a deboshed civilization.

Could they—would they—for three months certain, devote themselves under his auspices, as missionaries, to the elevation of mankind at a place called Earl's Court, which he said, with some truth, was one of the intellectual centres of the Planet? They thanked him, and demanded (we could hear his chuckle of delight) time to discuss and to vote on the matter. The vote, solemnly managed by counting heads—one head, one vote—was favourable. His offer, therefore, was accepted, and they moved a vote of thanks to him in two speeches—one by what they called the "proposer" and the other by the "seconder."

Vincent threw over to us, his voice shaking with gratitude:

"I've got 'em! Did you hear those speeches? That's Nature, dear men. Art can't teach *that*. And they voted as easily as lying. I've never had a troupe of natural liars before. Bless you, dear men! Remember, you're on my free lists for ever, anywhere—all of you. Oh, Gerolstein will be sick—sick!"

"Then you think they'll do?" said De Forest.

"Do? The Little Village'll go crazy! I'll knock up a series of old-world plays for 'em. Their voices will make you laugh and cry. My God, dear men, where *do* you suppose they picked up all their misery from, on this sweet earth? I'll have a pageant of the world's beginnings, and Mosenthal shall do the music. I'll—"

"Go and knock up a village for 'em by tonight. We'll meet you at No. 15 West Landing Tower," said De Forest. "Remember the rest will be coming along tomorrow."

"Let 'em all come!" said Vincent. "You don't know how hard it is nowadays even for me, to find something that really gets under the public's damned iridium-plated hide. But I've got it at last. Goodbye!"

"Well," said De Forest when we had finished laughing, "if any one understood corruption in London I might have played off Vincent against Gerolstein, and sold my captives at enormous prices. As it is, I shall have to be their legal adviser tonight when the contracts are signed. And they won't exactly press any commission on me, either."

"Meantime," said Takahira, "we cannot, of course, confine members of Leopold Vincent's last-engaged company. Chairs for the ladies, please, Arnott."

"Then I go to bed," said De Forest. "I can't face any more women!" And he vanished.

When our passengers were released and given another meal (finger-bowls came first this time) they told us what they thought of us and the Board; and, like Vincent, we all marvelled how they had contrived to extract and secrete so much bitter poison and unrest out of the good life God gives us. They raged, they stormed, they palpitated, flushed and exhausted their poor, torn nerves, panted themselves into silence, and renewed the senseless, shameless attacks.

"But can't you understand," said Pirolo pathetically to a shrieking woman, "that if we'd left you in Chicago you'd have been killed?"

"No, we shouldn't. You were bound to save us from being murdered."

"Then we should have had to kill a lot of other people."

"That doesn't matter. We were preaching the Truth. You can't stop us. We shall go on preaching in London; and *then* you'll see!"

"You can see now," said Pirolo, and opened a lower shutter.

We were closing on the Little Village, with her three million people spread out at ease inside her ring of girdling Main-Traffic lights—those eight fixed beams at Chatham, Tonbridge, Redhill, Dorking, Woking, St Albans, Chipping Ongar, and Southend.

Leopold Vincent's new company looked, with small pale faces, at the silence, the size, and the separated houses.

Then some began to weep aloud, shamelessly—always without shame.

Michael Swanwick

Michael Swanwick (1950–) distinguished himself with a group of notable short stories in the early and mid-'80s. He has written both science fiction and fantasy, and, after reaching the height of his powers as a SF novelist in *Stations of the Tide* (1991), has turned increasingly toward fantasy in his two most recent novels, *The Iron Dragon's Daughter* (1993) and *Jack Faust* (1997).

"My father was an engineer . . . but I was lured away from engineering by science, and then lured away from science by literature," he says. *Science Fiction Writers* calls him "an author who produces thoughtful, speculative work in a complex, literary style without a strong, action-oriented plot." His early short fiction is collected in *Gravity's Angels* (1991).

Swanwick is also the author of two influential critical essays, one on science fiction, "User's Guide to the Postmoderns" (1985), and one on fantasy, "In The Tradition . . ." (1994). He remains one of the most significant genre writers of the '90s. "Ginungagap" was his first published story. It appeared in a special SF issue of the distinguished literary magazine *Triquarterly*. The title refers to the primordial chaos out of which the universe was born in Norse mythology.

GINUNGAGAP

Abigail checked out of Mother of Mercy and rode the translator web to Toledo Cylinder in Juno Industrial Park. Stars bloomed, dwindled, disappeared five times. It was a long trek, halfway around the sun.

Toledo was one of the older commercial cylinders, now given over almost entirely to bureaucrats, paper pushers, and free-lance professionals. It was not Abigail's favorite place to visit, but she needed work and 3M had already bought out of her contract.

The job broker had dyed his chest hairs blond and his leg hairs red. They clashed wildly with his green *cache-sexe* and turquoise jewelry. His fingers played on a keyout, bringing up an endless flow of career trivia. "Cute trick you played," he said.

Abigail flexed her new arm negligently. It was a good job, but pinker than the rest of her. And weak, of course, but exercise would correct that. "Thanks," she said. She laid the arm underneath one breast and compared the colors. It matched the nipple perfectly. Definitely too pink. "Work outlook any good?"

"Naw," the broker said. A hummingbird flew past his ear, a nearly undetectable parting of the air. "I see here that you applied for the Proxima colony."

"They were full up," Abigail said. "No openings for a gravity bum, hey?"

"I didn't say that," the broker grumbled. "I'll find—Hello! What's this?" Abigail craned her neck, couldn't get a clear look at the screen. "There's a tag on your employment record."

"What's that mean?"

"Let me read." A honeysuckle flower fell on Abigail's hair and she brushed it off impatiently. The broker had an open-air office, framed by hedges and roofed over with a trellis. Sometimes Abigail found the older Belt cylinders a little too lavish for her taste.

"Mmp." The broker looked up. "Bell-Sandia wants to hire you. Indefinite term one-shot contract." He swung the keyout around so she could see. "*Very* nice terms, but that's normal for a high risk contract."

"High risk? From B-S, the Friendly Communications People? What kind of risk?"

The broker scrolled up new material. "There." He tapped the screen with a finger. "The language is involved, but what it boils down to is they're looking for a test passenger for a device they've got that uses black holes for interstellar travel."

"Couldn't work," Abigail said. "The tidal forces—"

"Spare me. Presumably they've found a way around that problem. The question is, are you interested or not?"

Abigail stared up through the trellis at a stream meandering across the curved land overhead. Children were wading in it. She counted to a hundred very slowly, trying to look as if she needed to think it over.

Abigail strapped herself into the translation harness and nodded to the technician outside the chamber. The tech touched her console and a light stasis field immobilized Abigail and the air about her while the chamber wall irised open. In a fluid bit of technological sleight of hand, the translator rechanneled her inertia and gifted her with a velocity almost, but not quite, that of the speed of light.

Stars bloomed about her and the sun dwindled. She breathed in deeply and—was in the receiver device. Relativity had cheated her of all but a fraction of the transit time. She shrugged out of harness and frog-kicked her way to the lip station's tug dock.

The tug pilot grinned at her as she entered, then turned his attention to his controls. He was young and wore streaks of brown makeup across his chest and thighs—only slightly darker than his skin. His mesh vest was almost in bad taste, but he wore it well and looked roguish rather than overdressed. Abigail found herself wishing she had more than a *cache-sexe* and nail polish on—some jewelry or makeup, perhaps. She felt drab in comparison.

The star-field wraparound held two inserts routed in by synchronous cameras. Alphanumerics flickered beneath them. One showed her immediate destination, the Bell-Sandia base *Arthur C. Clarke*. It consisted of five wheels, each set inside the other and rotating at slightly differing speeds. The base was done up in red-and-orange supergraphics. Considering its distance from the Belt factories, it was respectably sized.

Abigail latched herself into the passenger seat as the engines cut in. The second insert—

Ginungagap, the only known black hole in the sun's gravity field, was discovered in 2023, a small voice murmured. *Its presence explained the long-puzzling variations in the orbits of the outer planets. The* Arthur C. Clarke *was . . .*

"Is this necessary?" Abigail asked.

"Absolutely," the pilot said. "We abandoned the tourist program a year or so ago, but somehow the rules never caught up. They're very strict about the regs here." He winked at Abigail's dismayed expression. "Hold tight a minute while—" His voice faded as he tinkered with the controls.

. . . established forty years later and communications with the Proxima colony began shortly thereafter. Ginungagap . . .

The voice cut off. She grinned thanks. "Abigail Vanderhoek."

"Cheyney," the pilot said. "You're the gravity bum, right?"

"Yeah."

"I used to be a vacuum bum myself. But I got tired of it, and grabbed the first semipermanent contract that came along."

"I kind of went the other way."

"Probably what I should have done," Cheyney said amiably. "Still, it's a rough road. I picked up three scars along the way." He pointed them out: a thick slash across his abdomen, a red splotch beside one nipple, and a white crescent half obscured by his scalp. "I could've had them cleaned up, but the way I figure, life is just a process of picking up scars and experience. So I kept 'em."

If she had thought he was trying to impress her, Abigail would have slapped him down. But it was clearly just part of an ongoing self-dramatization, possibly justified, probably not. Abigail suspected that, tour trips to Earth excepted, the *Clarke* was as far down a gravity well as Cheyney had ever been. Still he did have an irresponsible, boyish appeal. "Take me past the net?" she asked.

Cheyney looped the tug around the communications net trailing the *Clarke.* Kilometers of steel lace passed beneath them. He pointed out a small dish antenna on the edge and a cluster of antennae on the back. "The loner on the edge transmits into Ginungagap," he said. "The others relay information to and from Mother."

"Mother?"

"That's the traditional name for the *Arthur C. Clarke.*" He swung the tug about with a careless sweep of one arm, and launched into a long and scurrilous story about the origin of the nickname. Abigail laughed, and Cheyney pointed a finger. "There's Ginungagap."

Abigail peered intently. "Where? I don't see a thing." She glanced at the second wraparound insert, which displayed a magnified view of the black hole. It wasn't at all impressive: a red smear against black nothingness. In the starfield it was all but invisible.

"Disappointing, hey? But still dangerous. Even this far out, there's a lot of ionization from the accretion disk."

"Is that why there's a lip station?"

"Yeah. Particle concentration varies, but if the translator was right at the *Clarke*, we'd probably lose about a third of the passengers."

Cheyney dropped Abigail off at Mother's crew lock and looped the tug off and away. Abigail wondered where to go, what to do now.

"You're the gravity bum we're dumping down Ginungagap." The short, solid man was upon her before she saw him. His eyes were intense. His *cache-sexe* was a conservative orange. "I liked the stunt with the arm. It takes a lot of guts to do something like that." He pumped her arm. "I'm Paul Girard. Head of external security. In charge of your training. You play verbal Ping-Pong?"

"Why do you ask?" she countered automatically.

"Don't you know?"

"Should I?"

"Do you mean now or later?"

"Will the answer be different later?"

A smile creased Paul's solid face. "You'll do." He took her arm, led her along a sloping corridor. "There isn't much prep time. The dry run is scheduled in two weeks. Things will move pretty quickly after that. You want to start your training now?"

"Do I have a choice?" Abigail asked, amused.

Paul came to a dead stop. "Listen," he said. "Rule number one: don't play games with *me*. You understand? Because I always win. Not sometimes, not usually—always."

Abigail yanked her arm free. "You maneuvered me into that," she said angrily.

"Consider it part of your training." He stared directly into her eyes. "No matter how many gravity wells you've climbed down, you're still the product of a near-space culture—protected, trusting, willing to take things at face value. This is a dangerous attitude, and I want you to realize it. I want you to learn to look behind the mask of events. I want you to grow up. And you will."

Don't be so sure. A small smile quirked Paul's face as if he could read her thoughts. Aloud, Abigail said, "That sounds a little excessive for a trip to Proxima."

"Lesson number two," Paul said: "don't make easy assumptions. You're not going to Proxima." He led her outward-down the ramp to the next wheel, pausing briefly at the juncture to acclimatize to the slower rate of revolution. "You're going to visit spiders." He gestured. "The crew room is this way."

The crew room was vast and cavernous, twilight gloomy. Keyouts were set up along winding paths that wandered aimlessly through the work space. Puddles of light fell on each board and operator. Dark-loving foliage was set between the keyouts.

"This is the heart of the beast," Paul said. "The green keyouts handle all Proxima communications—pretty routine by now. But the blue . . ." His eyes glinting oddly, he pointed. Over the keyouts hung silvery screens with harsh, grainy images floating on their surfaces, black-and-white blobs that Abigail could not resolve into recognizable forms.

"Those," Paul said, "are the spiders. We're talking to them in real-time. Response delay is almost all due to machine translation."

In a sudden shift of perception, the blobs became arachnid forms. That mass of black fluttering across the screen was a spider leg and *that* was its thorax. Abigail felt an immediate, primal aversion, and then it was swept away by an all-encompassing wonder.

"Aliens?" she breathed.

"Aliens."

They actually looked no more like spiders than humans looked like apes. The eight legs had an extra joint each, and the mandible configuration was all wrong. But to an untrained eye they would do.

"But this is—How long have you—? Why in God's name are you keeping this a secret?" An indefinable joy arose in Abigail. This opened a universe of possibilities, as if after a lifetime of being confined in a box someone had removed the lid.

"Industrial security," Paul said. "The gadget that'll send you through Ginungagap to *their* black hole is a spider invention. We're trading optical data for it, but the law won't protect our rights until we've demonstrated its use. We don't want the other corporations cutting in." He nodded toward the nearest black-and-white screen. "As you can see, they're weak on optics."

"I'd love to talk . . ." Abigail's voice trailed off as she realized how little-girl hopeful she sounded.

"I'll arrange an introduction."

There was a rustling to Abigail's side. She turned and saw a large black tomcat with white boots and belly emerge from the bushes. "This is the esteemed head of Alien Communications," Paul said sourly.

Abigail started to laugh, then choked in embarrassment as she realized that he was not speaking of the cat. "Julio Dominguez, section chief for translation," Paul said. "Abigail Vanderhoek, gravity specialist."

The wizened old man smiled professorially. "I assume our resident gadfly has explained how the communications net works, has he not?"

"Well—" Abigail began.

Dominguez clucked his tongue. He wore a yellow *cache-sexe* and matching bow tie, just a little too garish for a man his age. "Quite simple, actually. Escape velocity from a black hole is greater than the speed of light. Therefore, within Ginungagap the speed of light is no longer the limit to the speed of communications."

He paused just long enough for Abigail to look baffled. "Which is just a stuffy way of saying that when we aim a stream of electrons into the boundary of the stationary limit, they emerge elsewhere—out of another black hole. And if we aim them *just so*"—his voice rose whimsically—"they'll emerge from the black hole of our choosing. The physics is simple. The finesse is in aiming the electrons."

The cat stalked up to Abigail, pushed its forehead against her leg, and mewed insistently. She bent over and picked it up. "But nothing can emerge from a black hole," she objected.

Dominguez chuckled. "Ah, but anything can fall in, hey? A positron can fall in. But a positron falling into Ginungagap in positive time is only an electron falling out in negative time. Which means that a positron falling into a black hole in negative time is actually an electron falling out in positive time—exactly the effect we want. Think of Ginungagap as being the physical manifestation of an equivalence sign in mathematics."

"Oh," Abigail said, feeling very firmly put in her place. White moths flittered along the path. The cat watched, fascinated, while she stroked its head.

"At any rate, the electrons do emerge, and once the data are in, the theory has to follow along meekly."

"Tell me about the spiders," Abigail said before he could continue. The moths were darting up, sideward, down, a chance ballet in three dimensions.

"The *aliens*," Dominguez said, frowning at Paul, "are still a mystery to us. We exchange facts, descriptions, recipes for tools, but the important questions do not lend themselves to our clumsy mathematical codes. Do they know of love? Do they appreciate beauty? Do they believe in God, hey?"

"Do they want to eat us?" Paul threw in.

"Don't be ridiculous," Dominguez snapped. "Of course they don't."

The moths parted when they came to Abigail. Two went to either side; one flew over her shoulder. The cat batted at it with one paw. "The cat's name is Garble," Paul said. "The kids in Bio cloned him up."

Dominguez opened his mouth, closed it again.

Abigail scratched Garble under the chin. He arched his neck and purred all but noiselessly. "With your permission," Paul said. He stepped over to a keyout and waved its operator aside.

"Technically you're supposed to speak a convenience language, but if you keep it simple and non-idiomatic, there shouldn't be any difficulty." He touched the keyout. "Ritual greetings, spider." There was a blank pause. Then the spider moved, a hairy leg flickering across the screen.

"Hello, human."

"Introductions: Abigail Vanderhoek. She is our representative. She will ride the spinner." Another pause. More leg waving.

"Hello, Abigail Vanderhoek. Transition of vacuum garble resting garble commercial benefits garble still point in space."

"Tricky translation," Paul said. He signed to Abigail to take over.

Abigail hesitated, then said, "Will you come to visit us? The way we will visit you?"

"No, you see—" Dominguez began, but Paul waved him to silence.

"No, Abigail Vanderhoek. We are sulfur-based life."

"I do not understand."

"You can garble black hole through garble spinner because you are carbon-based life. Carbon forms chains easily but sulfur combines in lattices or rosettes. Our garble simple form garble. Sometimes sulfur forms short chains."

"We'll explain later," Paul said. "Go on, you're doing fine."

Abigail hesitated again. What do you say to a spider, anyway? Finally, she asked, "Do you want to eat us?"

"Oh, Christ, get her off that thing," Dominguez said, reaching for the keyout.

Paul blocked his arm. "No," he said. "I want to hear this."

Several of the spider legs wove intricate patterns. "The question is false. Sulfur based life derives no benefit from eating carbon-based life."

"You see," Dominguez said.

"But if it were possible," Abigail persisted. "If you *could* eat us and derive benefit. Would you?"

"Yes, Abigail Vanderhoek. With great pleasure."

Dominguez pushed her aside. "We're terribly sorry," he said to the alien. "This is a horrible, horrible misunderstanding. You!" he shouted to the operator. "Get back on and clear this mess up."

Paul was grinning wickedly. "Come," he said to Abigail. "We've accomplished enough here for one day."

As they started to walk away, Garble twisted in Abigail's arms and leaped free. He hit the floor on all fours and disappeared into the greenery. "Would they really eat us?" Abigail asked. Then amended it to, "Does that mean they're hostile?"

Paul shrugged. "Maybe they thought we'd be insulted if they *didn't* offer to eat us." He led her to her quarters. "Tomorrow we start training for real. In the meantime, you might make up a list of all the ways the spiders could hurt us if we set up transportation and they *are* hostile. Then another list of all the reasons we shouldn't trust them." He paused. "I've done it myself. You'll find that the lists get rather extensive."

Abigail's quarters weren't flashy, but they fit her well. A full star field was routed to the walls, floor, and ceiling, only partially obscured by a trellis inner frame that supported fox-grape vines. Somebody had done research into her tastes.

"Hi." The cheery greeting startled her. She whirled, saw that her hammock was occupied.

Cheyney sat up, swung his legs over the edge of the hammock, causing it to rock lightly. "Come on in." He touched an invisible control and the star field blue-shifted down to a deep, erotic purple.

"Just what do you think you're doing here?" Abigail asked.

"I had a few hours free," Cheyney said, "so I thought I'd drop by and seduce you."

"Well, Cheyney, I appreciate your honesty," Abigail said. "So I won't say no."

"Thank you."

"I'll say maybe some other time. Now get lost. I'm tired."

"Okay." Cheyney hopped down, walked jauntily to the door. He paused. "You said, 'Later,' right?"

"I said *maybe* later."

"Later. Gotcha." He winked and was gone.

Abigail threw herself into the hammock, red-shifted the star field until the universe was a sparse smattering of dying embers.

Annoying creature! There was no hope for anything more than the most superficial of relationships with him. She closed her eyes, smiled. Fortunately, she wasn't currently in the market for a serious relationship.

She slept.

She was falling . . .

Abigail had landed the ship an easy walk from 3M's robot laboratory. The lab's geodesic dome echoed white clouds to the north, where Nix Olympus peeked over the horizon. Otherwise all—land, sky, rocks—was standard issue Martian orange. She had clambered to the ground and shrugged on the supply backpack.

Resupplying 3M-RL stations was a gut contract, easy but dull. So perhaps she was less cautious than usual going down the steep, rock-strewn hillside, or perhaps the rock would have turned under her no matter how carefully she placed her feet. Her ankle twisted and she lurched sideways, but the backpack had shifted her center of gravity too much for her to be able to recover.

Arms windmilling, she fell.

The rock slide carried her downhill in a panicky flurry of dust and motion, tearing her flesh and splintering her bones. But before she could feel pain, her suit shot her full of a nerve synthetic, translating sensation into colors—reds, russets, and browns, with staccato yellow spikes when a rock smashed into her ribs. So that she fell in a whirling rainbow of glorious light.

She came to rest in a burst of orange. The rocks were settling about her. A spume of dust drifted away, out toward the distant red horizon. A large, jagged slab of stone slid by, gently shearing off her backpack. Tools, supplies, airpacks flew up and softly rained down.

A spanner as long as her arm slammed down inches from Abigail's helmet. She flinched, and suddenly events became real. She kicked her legs and sand and dust fountained up. Drawing her feet under her body—the one ankle bright gold—she started to stand.

And was jerked to the ground by a sudden tug on one arm. Even as she turned her head, she became aware of a deep purple sensation in her left hand. It was pinioned to a rock not quite large enough to stake a claim to. There was no color in the fingers.

"Cute," she muttered. She tugged at the arm, pushed at the rock. Nothing budged.

Abigail nudged the radio switch with her chin. "Grounder to Lip Station," she said. She hesitated, feeling foolish, then said, "Mayday. Repeat, Mayday. Could you guys send a rescue party down for me?"

There was no reply. With a sick green feeling in the pit of her stomach, Abigail reached a gloved hand around the back of her helmet. She touched something jagged, a sensation of mottled rust, the broken remains of her radio.

"I think I'm in trouble." She said it aloud and listened to the sound of it. Flat, unemotional—probably true. But nothing to get panicky about.

She took quick stock of what she had to work with. One intact suit and helmet. One spanner. A worldful of rocks, many close at hand. Enough air for—she checked the helmet readout—almost an hour. Assuming the lip station ran its checks on schedule and was fast on the uptake, she had almost half the air she needed.

Most of the backpack's contents were scattered too far away to reach. One rectangular gaspack, however, had landed nearby. She reached for it but could not touch it, squinted but could not read the label on its nozzle. It was almost certainly liquid gas—either nitrogen or oxygen—for the robot lab. There was a slim chance it was the spare airpack. If it was, she might live to be rescued.

Abigail studied the landscape carefully, but there was nothing more. "Okay, then, it's an airpack." She reached as far as her tethered arm would allow. The gaspack remained a tantalizing centimeter out of reach.

For an instant she was stymied. Then, feeling like an idiot, she grabbed the spanner. She hooked it over the gaspack. Felt the gaspack move grudgingly. Slowly nudged it toward herself.

By the time Abigail could drop the spanner and draw in the gaspack, her good arm was blue with fatigue. Sweat running down her face, she juggled the gaspack to read its nozzle markings.

It was liquid oxygen—useless. She could hook it to her suit and feed in the contents, but the first breath would freeze her lungs. She released the gaspack and lay back, staring vacantly at the sky.

Up there was civilization: tens of thousands of human stations strung together by webs of communication and transportation. Messages flowed endlessly on laser cables. Translators borrowed and lent momentum, moving streams of travelers and cargo at almost (but not quite) the speed of light. A starship was being readied to carry a third load of colonists to Proxima. Up there, free from gravity's relentless clutch, people lived in luxury and ease. Here, however . . .

"I'm going to die." She said it softly and was filled with wondering awe. Because it was true. She was going to die.

Death was a black wall. It lay before her, extending to infinity in all directions, smooth and featureless and mysterious. She could almost reach out an arm and touch it. Soon she would come up against it and, if anything lay beyond, pass through. Soon, very soon, she would *know*.

She touched the seal to her helmet. It felt gray—smooth and inviting. Her fingers moved absently, tracing the seal about her neck. With sudden horror, Abigail realized that she was thinking about undoing it, releasing her air, throwing away the little time she had left. . . .

She shuddered. With sudden resolve, she reached out and unsealed the shoulder seam of her captive arm.

The seal clamped down, automatically cutting off air loss. The flesh of her damaged arm was exposed to the raw Martian atmosphere. Abigail took up the gaspack and cradled it in the pit of her good arm. Awkwardly, she opened the nozzle with the spanner.

She sprayed the exposed arm with liquid oxygen for over a minute before she was certain it had frozen solid. Then she dropped the gaspack, picked up the spanner, and swung.

Her arm shattered into a thousand fragments.

She stood up.

Abigail awoke, tense and sweaty. She blue-shifted the walls up to normal light, and sat up. After a few minutes of clearing her head, she set the walls to cycle from red to blue in a rhythm matching her normal pulse. Eventually the womb-cycle lulled her back to sleep.

"Not even close," Paul said. He ran the tape backward, froze it on a still shot of the spider twisting two legs about each other. "That's the morpheme for 'extreme disgust,' remember. It's easy to pick out, and the language kids say that any statement with this gesture should be reversed in meaning. Irony, see? So when the spider says that the strong should protect the weak, it means—"

"How long have we been doing this?"

"Practically forever," Paul said cheerfully. "You want to call it a day?"

"Only if it won't hurt my standing."

"Hah! Very good." He switched off the keyout. "Nicely thought out. You're absolutely right; it would have. However, as reward for realizing this, you can take off early *without* it being noted on your record."

"Thank you," Abigail said sourly.

Like most large installations, the *Clarke* had a dozen or so smaller structures tagging along after it in minimum maintenance orbits. When Abigail discovered that these included a small wheel gymnasium, she had taken to putting in an hour's exercise after each training shift. Today she put in two.

The first hour she spent shadowboxing and practicing *savate* in heavy-gee to work up a sweat. The second hour she spent in the axis room, performing free-fall gymnastics. After the first workout, it made her feel light and nimble and good about her body.

She returned from the wheel gym sweaty and cheerful to find Cheyney in her hammock again. "Cheyney," she said, "this is not the first time I've had to kick you out of there. Or even the third, for that matter."

Cheyney held his palms up in mock protest. "Hey, no," he said. "Nothing like that today. I just came by to watch the raft debate with you."

Abigail felt pleasantly weary, decidedly uncerebral. "Paul said something about it, but . . ."

"Turn it on, then. You don't want to miss it." Cheyney touched her wall, and a cluster of images sprang to life at the far end of the room.

"Just what is a raft debate anyway?" Abigail asked, giving in gracefully. She hoisted herself onto the hammock, sat beside him. They rocked gently for a moment.

"There's this raft, see? It's adrift and powerless and there's only enough oxygen on board to keep one person alive until rescue. Only there are three on board—two humans and a spider."

"Do spiders breathe oxygen?"

"It doesn't matter. This is a hypothetical situation." Two thirds of the image area were taken up by Dominguez and Paul, quietly waiting for the debate to begin. The remainder showed a flat spider image.

"Okay, what then?"

"They argue over who gets to survive. Dominguez argues that he should, since he's human and human culture is superior to spider culture. The spider argues for itself and its culture." He put an arm around her waist. "You smell nice."

"Thank you." She ignored the arm. "What does Paul argue?"

"He's the devil's advocate. He argues that no one deserves to live and they should dump the oxygen."

"Paul would enjoy that role," Abigail said. Then, "What's the point to this debate?"

"It's an entertainment. There isn't supposed to be a point."

Abigail doubted it was that simple. The debate could reveal a good deal about the spiders and how they thought, once the language types were done with it. Conversely, the spiders would doubtless be studying the human responses. *This could be interesting,* she thought. Cheyney was stroking her side now, lightly but with great authority. She postponed reaction, not sure whether she liked it or not.

Louise Chang, a vaguely high-placed administrator, blossomed in the center of the image cluster. "Welcome," she said, and explained the rules of the debate. "The winner will be decided by acclaim," she said, "with half the vote being human and half alien. Please remember not to base your vote on racial chauvinism, but on the strengths of the arguments and how well they are presented." Cheyney's hand brushed casually across her nipples; they stiffened. The hand lingered. "The debate will begin with the gentleman representing the aliens presenting his thesis."

The image flickered as the spider waved several legs. "Thank you, Ms. Chairman. I argue that I should survive. My culture is superior because of our technological advancement. Three examples. Humans have used translation travel only briefly, yet we have used it for sixteens of garble. Our black hole technology is superior. And our garble has garble for the duration of our society."

"Thank you. The gentleman representing humanity?"

"Thank you, Ms. Chairman." Dominguez adjusted an armlet. Cheyney leaned back and let Abigail rest against him. Her head fit comfortably against his shoulder. "My argument is that technology is neither the sole nor the most important measure of a culture. By these standards dolphins would be considered brute animals. The aesthetic considerations—the arts, theology, and the tradition of philosophy—are of greater import. As I shall endeavor to prove."

"He's chosen the wrong tactic," Cheyney whispered in Abigail's ear. "That must have come across as pure garble to the spiders."

"Thank you. Mr. Girard?"

Paul's image expanded. He theatrically swigged from a small flask and hoisted it high in the air. "Alcohol! There's the greatest achievement of the human race!" Abigail snorted. Cheyney laughed out loud. "But I hold that neither Mr. Dominguez nor the distinguished spider deserves to live, because of the disregard both cultures have for sentient life." Abigail looked at Cheyney, who shrugged. "As I shall endeavor to prove." His image dwindled.

Chang said, "The arguments will now proceed, beginning with the distinguished alien."

The spider and then Dominguez ran through their arguments, and to Abigail they seemed markedly lackluster. She didn't give them her full attention, because Cheyney's hands were moving most interestingly across unexpected parts of her body. He might not be too bright, but he was certainly good at some things. She nuzzled her face into his neck, gave him a small peck, returned her attention to the debate.

Paul blossomed again. He juggled something in his palm, held his hand open to reveal three ball bearings. "When I was a kid I used to short out the school module and sneak up to the axis room to play marbles." Abigail smiled, remembering similar stunts she had played. "For the sake of those of us who are spiders, I'll explain that marbles is a game played in free-fall for the purpose of developing coordination and spatial perception. You make a six-armed star of marbles in the center . . ."

One of the bearings fell from his hand, bounced noisily, and disappeared as it rolled out of camera range. "Well, obviously it can't be played here. But the point is that when you shoot the marble just right, it hits the end of one arm and its kinetic energy is transferred from marble to marble along that arm. So that the shooter stops and the marble at the far end of the arm flies away." Cheyney was stroking her absently now, engrossed in the argument.

"Now, we plan to send a courier into Ginungagap and out the spiders' black hole. At least, that's what we say we're going to do.

"But what exits from a black hole is not necessarily the same as what went into its partner hole. We throw an electron into Ginungagap and another one pops out elsewhere. It's identical. It's a direct causal relationship. But it's like the marbles—they're identical to each other and have the same kinetic force. It's simply not the same electron."

Cheyney's hand was still, motionless. Abigail prodded him gently, touching his inner thigh. "Anyone who's interested can see the equations. Now, when we send messages, this doesn't matter. The message is important, not the medium. However, when we send a human being in . . . what emerges from the other hole will be cell for cell, gene for gene, atom for atom identical. *But it will not be the same person.*" He paused a beat, smiled.

"I submit, then, that this is murder. And further, that by conspiring to commit murder, both the spider and human races display absolute disregard for intelligent life. In short, no one on the raft deserves to live. And I rest my case."

"Mr. Girard!" Dominguez objected, even before his image was restored to full size. "The simplest mathematical proof is an identity: that A equals A. Are you trying to deny this?"

Paul held up the two ball bearings he had left. "These marbles are identical too. But they are not the same marble."

"We know the phenomenon you speak of," the spider said. "It is as if garble the black hole bulges out simultaneously. There is no violation of continuity. The two entities are the same. There is no death."

Abigail pulled Cheyney down, so that they were both lying on their sides, still able to watch the images. "So long as you happen to be the second marble and not the first," Paul said. Abigail tentatively licked Cheyney's ear.

"He's right," Cheyney murmured.

"No he's not," Abigail retorted. She bit his earlobe.

"You mean that?"

"Of course I mean that. He's confusing semantics with reality." She engrossed herself in a study of the back of his neck.

"Okay."

Abigail suddenly sensed that she was missing something. "Why do you ask?" She struggled into a sitting position. Cheyney followed.

"No particular reason." Cheyney's hands began touching her again. But Abigail was sure something had been slipped past her.

They caressed each other lightly while the debate dragged to an end. Not paying much attention, Abigail voted for Dominguez, and Cheyney voted for Paul. As a result of a nearly undivided spider vote, the spider won. "I told you Dominguez was taking the wrong approach," Cheyney said. He hopped off the hammock. "Look, I've got to see somebody about something. I'll be right back."

"You're not leaving *now?*" Abigail protested, dumbfounded. The door irised shut.

Angry and hurt, she leaped down, determined to follow him. She couldn't remember ever feeling so insulted.

Cheyney didn't try to be evasive; it apparently did not occur to him that she might follow. Abigail stalked him down a corridor, up an in-ramp, and to a door that irised open for him. She recognized that door.

Thoughtfully she squatted on her heels behind an untrimmed boxwood and waited. A minute later, Garble wandered by, saw her, and demanded attention. "Scat!" she hissed. He butted his head against her knee. "Then be quiet, at least." She scooped him up. His expression was smug.

The door irised open and Cheyney exited, whistling. Abigail waited until he was gone, stood, went to the door, and entered. Fish darted between long fronds under a transparent floor. It was an austere room, almost featureless. Abigail looked, but did not see a hammock.

"So Cheyney's working for you now," she said coldly. Paul looked up from a corner keyout.

"As a matter of fact, I've just signed him to permanent contract in the crew room. He's bright enough. A bit green. Ought to do well."

"Then you admit that you put him up to grilling me about your puerile argument in the debate?" Garble struggled in her arms. She juggled him into a more comfortable position. "And that you staged the argument for my benefit in the first place?"

"Ah," Paul said. "I knew the training was going somewhere. You've become very wary in an extremely short time."

"Don't evade the question."

"I needed your honest reaction," Paul said. "Not the answer you would have given me, knowing your chances of crossing Ginungagap rode on it."

Garble made an angry noise. "You tell him, Garble!" she said. "That goes double for me." She stepped out the door. "You lost the debate," she snapped.

Long after the door had irised shut, she could feel Paul's amused smile burning into her back.

Two days after she returned to kick Cheyney out of her hammock for the final time, Abigail was called to the crew room. "Dry run," Paul said. "Attendance is mandatory." And cut off.

The crew room was crowded with technicians, triple the number of keyouts. Small knots of them clustered before the screens, watching. Paul waved her to him.

"There," he motioned to one screen. "That's Clotho—the platform we built for the transmission device. It's a hundred kilometers off. I wanted more, but

Dominguez overruled me. The device that'll unravel you and dump you down Ginungagap is that doohickey in the center." He tapped a keyout and the platform zoomed up to fill the screen. It was covered by a clear, transparent bubble. Inside, a space-suited figure was placing something into a machine that looked like nothing so much as a giant armor-clad clamshell. Abigail looked, blinked, looked again.

"That's Garble," she said indignantly.

"Complain to Dominguez. I wanted a baboon."

The clamshell device closed. The space-suited tech left in his tug, and alphanumerics flickered, indicating the device was in operation. As they watched, the spider-designed machinery immobilized Garble, transformed his molecules into one long continuous polymer chain, and spun it out an invisible opening at near light speed. The water in his body was separated out, piped away, and preserved. The electrolyte balances were recorded and simultaneously transmitted in a parallel stream of electrons. It would reach the spider receiver along with the lead end of the cat-polymer, to be used in the reconstruction.

Thirty seconds passed. Now Garble was only partially in Clotho. The polymer chain, invisible and incredibly long, was passing into Ginungagap. On the far side the spiders were beginning to knit it up.

If all was going well . . .

Ninety-two seconds after they flashed on, the alphanumerics stopped twinkling on the screen. Garble was gone from Clotho. The clamshell opened and the remote cameras showed it to be empty. A cheer arose.

Somebody boosted Dominguez atop a keyout. Intercom cameras swiveled to follow. He wavered fractionally, said "My friends," and launched into a speech. Abigail didn't listen.

Paul's hand fell on her shoulder. It was the first time he had touched her since their initial meeting. "He's only a scientist," he said. "He had no idea how close you are to that cat."

"Look, I *asked* to go. I knew the risks. But Garble's just an animal; he wasn't given the choice."

Paul groped for words. "In a way, this is what your training has been about—the reason you're going across instead of someone like Dominguez. He projects his own reactions onto other people. If—"

Then, seeing that she wasn't listening, he said, "Anyway, you'll have a cat to play with in a few hours. They're only keeping him long enough to test out the life support systems."

There was a festive air to the second gathering. The spiders reported that Garble had translated flawlessly. A brief visual display showed him stalking about Clotho's sister platform, irritable but apparently unharmed.

"There," somebody said. The screen indicated that the receiver net had taken in the running end of the cat's polymer chain. They waited a minute and a half and the operation was over.

It was like a conjuring trick: the clamshell closed on emptiness. Water was piped in. Then it opened and Garble floated over its center, quietly licking one paw.

Abigail smiled at the homeliness of it. "Welcome back, Garble," she said quietly. "I'll get the guys in Bio to brew up some cream for you."

Paul's eyes flicked in her direction. They lingered for no time at all, long enough to file away another datum for future use, and then his attention was elsewhere. She waited until his back was turned and stuck out her tongue at him.

The tub docked with Clotho and a technician floated in. She removed her helmet self-consciously, aware of her audience. One hand extended, she bobbed toward the cat, calling softly.

"Get that jerk on the line," Paul snapped. "I want her helmet back on. That's sloppy. That's real—"

And in that instant Garble sprang.

Garble was a black-and-white streak that flashed past the astonished tech, through the air lock, and into the open tug. The cat pounced on the pilot panel. Its forelegs hit the controls. The hatch slammed shut, and the tug's motors burst into life.

Crew room techs grabbed wildly at their keyouts. The tech on Clotho frantically tried to fit her helmet back on. And the tug took off, blasting away half the protective dome and all the platform's air.

The screens showed a dozen different scenes, lenses shifting from close to distant and back. "Cheyney," Paul said quietly. Dominguez was frozen, looking bewildered. "Take it out."

"It's coming right at us!" somebody shouted.

Cheyney's fingers flicked: rap-tap-rap.

A bright nuclear flower blossomed.

There was silence, dead and complete, in the crew room. *I'm missing something,* Abigail thought. *We just blew up 5 percent of our tug fleet to kill a cat.*

"*Pull* that transmitter!" Paul strode through the crew room, scattering orders. "Nothing goes out! You, you, and you"—he yanked techs away from their keyouts—"*off* those things. I want the whole goddamned net shut *down.*"

"Paul . . . ," an operator said.

"Keep on receiving." He didn't bother to look. "Whatever they want to send. Dump it all in storage and don't merge any of it with our data until we've gone over it."

Alone and useless in the center of the room, Dominguez stuttered, "What—what happened?"

"You blind idiot!" Paul turned on him viciously. "Your precious aliens have just made their first hostile move. The cat that came back was nothing like the one we sent. They made changes. They retransmitted it with instructions wet-wired into its brain."

"But why would they want to steal a tug?"

"*We don't know!*" Paul roared. "Get that through your head. We don't know their motives and we don't know how they think. But we would have known a lot more about their intentions than we wanted if I hadn't rigged that tug with an abort device."

"You didn't—" Dominguez began. He thought better of the statement.

"—have the authority to rig that device," Paul finished for him. "That's right. I didn't." His voice was heavy with sarcasm.

Dominguez seemed to shrivel. He stared bleakly, blankly, about him, then turned and left, slightly hunched over. Thoroughly discredited in front of the people who worked for him.

That was cold, Abigail thought. She marveled at Paul's cruelty. Not for an instant did she believe that the anger in his voice was real, that he was capable of losing control.

Which meant that in the midst of confusion and stress, Paul had found time to make a swift play for more power. To Abigail's newly suspicious eye, it looked like a successful one, too.

For five days Paul held the net shut by sheer willpower and force of personality. Information came in but did not go out. Bell-Sandia administration was not behind him; too much time and money had been sunk into Clotho to abandon the project. But Paul had the support of the tech crew, and he knew how to use it.

"Nothing as big as Bell-Sandia runs on popularity," Paul explained. "But I've got enough sympathy from above, and enough hesitation and official cowardice to keep this place shut down long enough to get a message across."

The incoming information flow fluctuated wildly, shifting from subject to subject. Data sequences were dropped halfway through and incomplete. Nonsense came in. The spiders were shifting through strategies in search of the key that would reopen the net.

"When they start repeating themselves," Paul said, "we can assume they understand the threat."

"But we *wouldn't* shut the net down permanently," Abigail pointed out.

Paul shrugged. "So it's a bluff."

They were sharing an after-shift drink in a fifth-level bar. Small red lizards scuttled about the rock wall behind the bartender. "And if your bluff doesn't work?" Abigail asked. "If it's all for nothing—what then?"

Paul's shoulders sagged, a minute shifting of tensions. "Then we trust in the goodwill of the spiders," he said. "We let them call the shots. And they will treat us benevolently or not, depending. In either case," his voice became dark, "I'll have played a lot of games and manipulated a lot of people for no reason at all." He took her hand. "If that happens, I'd like to apologize." His grip was tight, his knuckles pale.

That night Abigail dreamed she was falling.

Light rainbowed all about her, in a violent splintering of bone and tearing of flesh. She flung out an arm and it bounced on something warm and yielding.

"Abigail."

She twisted and tumbled and something smashed into her ribs. Bright spikes of yellow darted up.

"Abigail!" Someone was shaking her, speaking loudly into her face. The rocks and sky went gray, were overlaid by unresolved images. Her eyelids struggled apart, fell together, opened.

"Oh," she said.

Paul rocked back on his heels. Fish darted about in the water beneath him. "There now," he said. Blue-green lights shifted gently underwater, moving in long, slow arcs. "Dream over?"

Abigail shivered, clutched his arm, let go of it almost immediately. She nodded.

"Good. Tell me about it."

"I—" Abigail began. "Are you asking me as a human being or in your official capacity?"

"I don't make that distinction."

She stretched out a leg and scratched her big toe, to gain time to think. She really didn't have any appropriate thoughts. "Okay," she said, and told him the entire dream.

Paul listened intently, rubbed a thumb across his chin thoughtfully when she was done. "We hired you on the basis of that incident, you know," he said. "Coolness under stress. Weak body image. There were a lot of gravity bums to choose from. But I figured you were just a hair tougher, a little bit grittier."

"What are you trying to tell me? That I'm replaceable?"

Paul shrugged. "Everybody's replaceable. I just wanted to be sure you knew that you could back out if you want. It wouldn't wreck our project."

"I don't want to back out." Abigail chose her words carefully, spoke them slowly, to avoid giving vent to the anger she felt building up inside. "Look, I've been on the gravity circuit for ten years. I've been everywhere in the system there is to go. Did you know that there are less than two thousand people alive who've set foot on Mercury *and* Pluto? We've got a little club; we get together once a year." Seaweed shifted about her; reflections of the floor lights formed nebulous swimming shapes on the walls. "I've spent my entire life going around and around and around the sun, and never really getting anywhere. I want to travel, and there's nowhere left for me to go. So you offer me a way out and then ask if I want to back down. Like hell I do!"

"Why don't you believe that going through Ginungagap is death?" Paul asked quietly. She looked into his eyes, saw cool calculations going on behind them. It frightened her, almost. He was measuring her, passing judgment, warping events into long logical chains that did not take human factors into account. He was an alien presence.

"It's—common sense, is all. I'll be the same when I exit as when I go in. There'll be no difference, not an atom's worth, not a scintilla."

"The *substance* will be different. Every atom will be different. Not a single electron in your body will be the same one you have now."

"Well, how does that differ so much from normal life?" Abigail demanded. "All our bodies are in constant flux. Molecules come and go. Bit by bit, we're replaced. Does that make us different people from moment to moment? 'All that is body is as coursing vapors,' right?"

Paul's eyes narrowed. "Marcus Aurelius. Your quotation isn't complete, though. It goes on: 'All that is of the soul is dreams and vapors.' "

"What's that supposed to mean?"

"It means that the quotation doesn't say what you claimed it did. If you care to read it literally, it argues the opposite of what you're saying."

"Still, you can't have it both ways. Either the me that comes out of the spider black hole is the same as the one who went in, or I'm not the same person as I was an instant ago."

"I'd argue differently," Paul said. "But no matter. Let's go back to sleep."

He held out a hand, but Abigail felt no inclination to accept it. "Does this mean I've passed your test?"

Paul closed his eyes, stretched a little. "You're still reasonably afraid of dying, and you don't believe that you will," he said. "Yeah. You pass."

"Thanks a heap," Abigail said. They slept, not touching, for the rest of the night.

Three days later Abigail woke up, and Paul was gone. She touched the wall and spoke his name. A recording appeared. "Dominguez has been called up to Administration," it said. Paul appeared slightly distracted; he had not looked directly into the recorder and his image avoided Abigail's eyes. "I'm going to re-open the net before he returns. It's best we beat him to the punch." The recording clicked off.

Abigail routed an intercom call through to the crew room. A small chime notified him of her call, and he waved a hand in combined greeting and direction to remain silent. He was hunched over a keyout. The screen above it came to life.

"Ritual greetings, spider," he said.

"Hello, human. We wish to pursue our previous inquiry: the meaning of the term 'art' which was used by the human Dominguez six-sixteenths of the way through his major presentation."

"This is a difficult question. To understand a definition of art, you must first know the philosophy of aesthetics. This is a comprehensive field of knowledge comparable to the study of perception. In many ways it is related."

"What is the trade value of this field of knowledge?"

Dominguez appeared, looking upset. He opened his mouth, and Paul touched a finger to his own lips, nodding his head toward the screen.

"Significant. Our society considers art and science as being of roughly equal value."

"We will consider what to offer in exchange."

"Good. We also have a question for you. Please wait while we select the phrasing." He cut the translation lines, turned to Dominguez. "Looks like your raft gambit paid off. Though I'm surprised they bit at that particular piece of bait."

Dominguez looked weary. "Did they mention the incident with the cat?"

"No, nor the communications blackout."

The old man sighed. "I always felt close to the aliens," he said. "Now they seem—cold, inhuman." He attempted a chuckle. "That was almost a pun, wasn't it?"

"In a human, we'd call it a professional attitude. Don't let it spoil your accomplishment," Paul said. "This could be as big as optics." He opened the communications line again. "Our question is now phrased." Abigail noted he had not told Dominguez of her presence.

"Please go ahead."

"Why did you alter our test animal?"

Much leg waving. "We improved the ratios garble centers of perception garble wetware garble making the animal twelve-sixteenths as intelligent as a human. We thought you would be pleased."

"We were not. Why did the test animal behave in a hostile manner toward us?"

The spider's legs jerked quickly and it disappeared from the screen. Like an echo, the machine said, "Please wait."

Abigail watched Dominguez throw Paul a puzzled look. In the background, a man with a leather sack looped over one shoulder was walking slowly along the twisty access path. His hand dipped into the sack, came out, sprinkled fireflies among the greenery. Dipped in, came out again. Even in the midst of crisis the trivia of day-to-day existence went on.

The spider reappeared, accompanied by two of its own kind. Their legs interlaced and retreated rapidly, a visual pantomime of an excited conversation. Finally one of their number addressed the screen.

"We have discussed the matter."

"So I see."

"It is our conclusion that the experience of translation through Ginungagap had a negative effect on the test animal. This was not anticipated. It is new knowledge. We know little of the psychology of carbon-based life."

"You're saying the test animal was driven mad?"

"Key word did not translate. We assume understanding. Steps must be taken to prevent a recurrence of this damage. Can you do this?"

Paul said nothing.

"Is this the reason why communications were interrupted?"

No reply.

"There is a cultural gap. Can you clarify?"

"Thank you for your cooperation," Paul said, and switched the screen off. "You can set your people to work," he told Dominguez. "No reason why they should answer the last few questions, though."

"Were they telling the truth?" Dominguez asked wonderingly.

"Probably not. But at least now they'll think twice before trying to jerk us around again." He winked at Abigail, and she switched off the intercom.

They re-ran the test using a baboon shipped out from the Belt Zoological Gardens. Abigail watched it arrive from the lip station, crated and snarling.

"They're a lot stronger than we are," Paul said. "Very agile. If the spiders want to try any more tricks, we couldn't offer them better bait."

The test went smooth as silk. The baboon was shot through Ginungagap, held by the spiders for several hours, and returned. Exhaustive testing showed no tampering with the animal.

Abigail asked how accurate the tests were. Paul hooked his hands behind his back. "We're returning the baboon to the Belt. We wouldn't do that if we had any doubts. But—" He raised an eyebrow, asking Abigail to finish the thought.

"But if they're really hostile, they won't underestimate us twice. They'll wait for a human to tamper with."

Paul nodded.

The night before Abigail's send-off they made love. It was a frenzied and desperate act, performed wordlessly and without tenderness. Afterward they lay together, Abigail idly playing with Paul's curls.

"Gail . . ." His head was hidden in her shoulder; she couldn't see his face. His voice was muffled.

"Mmmm?"

"Don't go."

She wanted to cry. Because as soon as he said it, she knew it was another test, the final one. And she also knew that Paul wanted her to fail it. That he honestly believed transversing Ginungagap would kill her, and that the woman who emerged from the spiders' black hole would not be herself.

His eyes were shut; she could tell by the creases in his forehead. He knew what her answer was. There was no way he could avoid knowing.

Abigail sensed that this was as close to a declaration of emotion as Paul was capable of. She felt how he despised himself for using his real emotions as yet another test, and how he could not even pretend to himself that there were circumstances under which he would *not* so test her. *This must be how it feels to think as he does,* she thought. *To constantly scrabble after every last implication, like eternally picking at a scab.*

"Oh, Paul," she said.

He wrenched about, turning his back to her. "Sometimes I wish"—his hands rose in front of his face like claws; they moved toward his eyes, closed into fists—"that for just ten goddamned minutes I could turn my mind off." His voice was bitter.

Abigail huddled against him, looped a hand over his side and onto his chest. "Hush," she said.

The tug backed away from Clotho, dwindling until it was one of a ring of bright sparks pacing the platform. Mother was a point source lost in the star field. Abigail shivered, pulled off her arm bands and shoved them into a storage sack. She reached for her *cache-sexe*, hesitated.

The hell with it, she thought. *It's nothing they haven't seen before*. She shucked it off, stood naked. Gooseflesh rose on the backs of her legs. She swam to the transmittal device, feeling awkward under the distant watching eyes.

Abigail groped into the clamshell. "Go," she said.

The metal closed about her seamlessly, encasing her in darkness. She floated in a lotus position, bobbing slightly.

A light, gripping field touched her, stilling her motion. On cue, hypnotic commands took hold in her brain. Her breathing became shallow; her heart slowed. She felt her body ease into stasis. The final command took hold.

Abigail weighed 50 keys. Even though the water in her body would not be transmitted, the polymer chain she was to be transformed into would be 275 kilometers long. It would take 15 minutes and 17 seconds to unravel at light speed, negligibly longer at translation speed. She would still be sitting in Clotho when the spiders began knitting her up.

It was possible that Garble had gone mad from a relatively swift transit. Paul doubted it, but he wasn't taking any chances. To protect Abigail's sanity, the meds had wet-wired a travel fantasy into her brain. It would blind her to external reality while she traveled.

She was an eagle. Great feathered wings extended out from her shoulders. Clotho was gone, leaving her alone in space. Her skin was red and leathery, her breasts hard and unyielding. Feathers covered her thighs, giving way at the knees to talons.

She moved her wings, bouncing lightly against the thin solar wind swirling down into Ginungagap. The vacuum felt like absolute freedom. She screamed a predator's exultant shrill. Nothing enclosed her; she was free of restrictions forever.

Below her lay Ginungagap, the primal chasm, an invisible challenge marked by a red smudge of glowing gases. It was inchoate madness, a gibbering, impersonal force that wanted to draw her in, to crush her in its embrace. Its hunger was fierce and insatiable.

Abigail held her place briefly, effortlessly. Then she folded her wings and dove.

A rain of X rays stung through her, the scattering of Ginungagap's accretion disk. They were molten iron passing through a ghost. Shrieking defiance, she attacked, scattering sparks in her wake.

Ginungagap grew, swelled until it swallowed up her vision. It was purest black, unseeable, unknowable, a thing of madness. It was Enemy.

A distant objective part of her knew that she was still in Clotho, the polymer chain being unraveled from her body, accelerated by a translator, passing through two black holes, and simultaneously being knit up by the spiders. It didn't matter.

She plunged into Ginungagap as effortlessly as if it were the film of a soap bubble.

In—

—And out.

It was like being reversed in a mirror, or watching an entertainment run backward. She was instantly flying out the way she came. The sky was a mottled mass of violet light.

The stars before her brightened from violet to blue. She craned her neck, looked back at Ginungagap, saw its disk-shaped nothingness recede, and screamed in frustration because it had escaped her. She spread her wings to slow her flight and—

—was sitting in a dark place. Her hand reached out, touched metal, recognized the inside of a clamshell device.

A hairline crack of light looped over her, widened. The clamshell opened.

Oceans of color bathed her face. Abigail straightened, and the act of doing so lifted her up gently. She stared through the transparent bubble at a phosphorescent foreverness of light.

My God, she thought. *The stars.*

The stars were thicker, more numerous than she was used to seeing them—large and bright and glittery rich. She was probably someplace significant, in a star cluster or the center of the galaxy; she couldn't guess. She felt irrationally happy to simply *be;* she took a deep breath, then laughed.

"Abigail Vanderhoek."

She turned to face the voice, and found that it came from a machine. Spiders crouched beside it, legs moving silently. Outside, in the hard vacuum, were more spiders.

"We regret any pain this may cause," the machine said.

Then the spiders rushed forward. She had no time to react. Sharp mandibles loomed before her, then dipped to her neck. Impossibly swift, they sliced through her throat, severed her spine. A sudden jerk and her head was separated from her body.

It happened in an instant. She felt brief pain, and the dissociation of actually *seeing* her decapitated body just beginning to react. And then she died.

A spark. A light. *I'm alive,* she thought. Consciousness returned like an ancient cathode tube warming up. Abigail stretched slowly, bobbing gently in the air, collecting her thoughts. She was in the sister-Clotho again—not in pain, her head and neck firmly on her shoulders. There were spiders in the platform, and a few floating outside.

"Abigail Vanderhoek," the machine said. "We are ready to begin negotiations."

Abigail said nothing.

After a moment, the machine said, "Are you damaged? Are your thoughts impaired?" A pause, then, "Was your mind not protected during transit?"

"Is that you waving the legs there? Outside the platform?"

"Yes. It is important that you talk with the other humans. You must convey our questions. They will not communicate with us."

"I have a few questions of my own," Abigail said. "I won't cooperate until you answer them."

"We will answer any questions provided you neither garble nor garble."

"What do you take me for?" Abigail asked. "Of course I won't."

Long hours later she spoke to Paul and Dominguez. At her request the spiders had withdrawn, leaving her alone. Dominguez looked drawn and haggard. "I swear we had no idea the spiders would attack you," Dominguez said. "We saw it on the screens. I was certain you'd been killed. . . ." His voice trailed off.

"Well, I'm alive, no thanks to you guys. Just what *is* this crap about an explosive substance in my bones, anyway?"

"An explosive—I swear we know nothing of anything of the kind."

"A close relative to plastique," Paul said. "I had a small editing device attached to Clotho's translator. It altered roughly half the bone marrow in your sternum, pelvis, and femurs in transmission. I'd hoped the spiders wouldn't pick up on it so quickly."

"You actually did," Abigail marveled. "The spiders weren't lying; they decapitated me in self-defense. What the holy hell did you think you were *doing?*"

"Just a precaution," Paul said. "We wet-wired you to trigger the stuff on command. That way, we could have taken out the spider installation if they'd tried something funny."

"Um," Dominguez said, "this *is* being recorded. What I'd like to know, Ms. Vanderhoek, is how you escaped being destroyed."

"I didn't," Abigail said. "The spiders killed me. Fortunately, they anticipated the situation, and recorded the transmission. It was easy for them to recreate me—after they edited out the plastique."

Dominguez gave her an odd look. "You don't—feel anything particular about this?"

"Like what?"

"Well—" He turned to Paul helplessly.

"Like the real Abigail Vanderhoek died and you're simply a very realistic copy," Paul said.

"Look, we've been through this garbage before," Abigail began angrily.

Paul smiled formally at Dominguez. It was hard to adjust to seeing the two in flat black-and-white. "She doesn't believe a word of it."

"If you guys can pull yourselves up out of your navels for a minute," Abigail said, "I've got a line on something the spiders have that you want. They claim they've sent probes through their black hole."

"Probes?" Paul stiffened. Abigail could sense the thoughts coursing through his skull, of defenses and military applications.

"Carbon-hydrogen chain probes. Organic probes. Self-constructing transmitters. They've got a carbon-based secondary technology."

"Nonsense," Dominguez said. "How could they convert back to coherent matter without a receiver?"

Abigail shrugged. "They claim to have found a loophole."

"How does it work?" Paul snapped.

"They wouldn't say. They seemed to think you'd pay well for it."

"That's very true," Paul said slowly. "Oh, yes."

The conference took almost as long as her session with the spiders had. Abigail was bone weary when Dominguez finally said, "That ties up the official minutes. We now stop recording." A line tracked across the screen, was gone. "If you want to speak to anyone off the record, now's your chance. Perhaps there is someone close to you . . ."

"Close? No." Abigail almost laughed. "I'll speak to Paul alone, though."

A spider floated by outside Clotho II. It was a golden, crablike being, its body slightly opalescent. It skittered along unseen threads strung between the open platforms of the spider star-city. "I'm listening," Paul said.

"You turned me into a *bomb*, you freak."

"So?"

"I could have been killed."

"Am I supposed to care?"

"You damn well ought to, considering the liberties you've taken with my fair white body."

"Let's get one thing understood," Paul said. "The woman I slept with, the woman I cared for, is dead. I have no feelings toward or obligations to you whatsoever."

"Paul," Abigail said. "*I'm not dead.* Believe me, I'd know if I were."

"How could I possibly trust what you think or feel? It could all be attitudes the spiders wet-wired into you. We know they have the technology."

"How do you know that *your* attitudes aren't wet-wired in? For that matter, how do you know anything is real? I mean, these are the most sophomoric philosophic ideas there are. But I'm the same woman I was a few hours ago. My memories, opinions, feelings—they're all the same as they were. There's absolutely no difference between me and the woman you slept with on the *Clarke*."

"I know." Paul's eyes were cold. "That's the horror of it." He snapped off the screen.

Abigail found herself staring at the lifeless machinery. *God, that hurt*, she thought. *It shouldn't, but it hurt*. She went to her quarters.

The spiders had done a respectable job of preparing for her. There were no green plants, but otherwise the room was the same as the one she'd had on the *Clarke*. They'd even been able to spin the platform, giving her an adequate down-orientation. She sat in her hammock, determined to think pleasanter thoughts. About the offer the spiders had made, for example. The one she hadn't told Paul and Dominguez about.

Banned by their chemistry from using black holes to travel, the spiders needed a representative to see to their interests among the stars. They had offered her the job.

Or perhaps the plural would be more appropriate—they had offered her the jobs. Because there were too many places to go for one woman to handle them all. They needed a dozen—in time, perhaps, a hundred—Abigail Vanderhoeks.

In exchange for licensing rights to her personality, the right to make as many duplicates of her as were needed, they were willing to give her the rights to the self-reconstructing black hole platforms.

It would make her a rich woman—a hundred rich women—back in human space. And it would open the universe. She hadn't committed herself yet, but there was no way she was going to turn down the offer. The chance to see a thousand stars? No, she would not pass it by.

When she got old, too, they could create another Abigail from their recording, burn her new memories into it, and destroy her old body.

I'm going to see the stars, she thought. *I'm going to live forever*. She couldn't understand why she didn't feel elated, wondered at the sudden rush of melancholy that ran through her like the precursor of tears.

Garble jumped into her lap, offered his belly to be scratched. The spiders had recorded him, too. They had been glad to restore him to his unaltered state when she made the request. She stroked his stomach and buried her face in his fur.

"Pretty little cat," she told him. "I thought you were dead."

Mildred Clingerman

Mildred Clingerman (1918–   ) wrote only a dozen or so SF and fantasy stories, but her works were a memorable feature of *The Magazine of Fantasy & Science Fiction* in the 1950s, and often reprinted. Her only book, *A Cupful of Space* (1961), collects all the stories. She was one of a notable group of women writers, including Judith Merril, Margaret St. Clair, and Shirley Jackson, who helped give *F & SF* a special aspect in that decade and beyond. I would describe that flavor, with the benefit of four decades of hindsight, as a *Twilight Zone* flavor.

In addition to genre science fiction and horror, *F & SF* published stories focused on an ordinary character (and this was unusual because genre science fiction had developed into a literature of extraordinary characters, usually exclusively men), often a woman, experiencing something extraordinary, something fantastic. The emotional point was often sentimental, as well as ironic.

This is the kind of plot Rod Serling appropriated, marketed, and made his own brand name, making television history in the process. Clingerman—along with Richard Matheson, Charles Beaumont and a few other men from *Fantasy & Science Fiction* who generally get almost all the credit—was one of the true originals.

This story, published in 1952, was her first. The central character is, to say the least, unusual in science fiction. She seems to have stepped out of a mid-century tale in *The Saturday Evening Post* into an SF story, and then to belong there.

MINISTER WITHOUT PORTFOLIO

Mrs. Chriswell's little roadster came to a shuddering halt. Here was the perfect spot. Only one sagging wire fence to step over and not a cow in sight. Mrs. Chriswell was terrified of cows, and if the truth were told, only a little less afraid of her daughter-in-law, Clara. It was all Clara's idea that her mother-in-law should now be lurking in meadows peering at birds. Clara had been delighted with the birdwatching idea, but frankly, Mrs. Chriswell was bored with birds. They *flew* so much. And as for their colours, it was useless for her to speculate. Mrs. Chriswell was one of those rare women who are quite, quite colour-blind.

"But, Clara," Mrs. Chriswell had pleaded, "what's the point if I can't tell what colour they are?"

"Well, but, darling," Clara had said crisply, "how much cleverer if you get to know them just from the distinctive markings!"

Mrs. Chriswell, sighing a little as she recalled the firm look of Clara's chin, manoeuvred herself and her burdens over the sagging wire fence. She successfully juggled the binoculars, the heavy bird book, and her purse, and thought how ghastly it was at sixty to be considered so useless that she must be provided with harmless occupations to keep her out of the way.

Since Mr. Chriswell's death she had moved in with her son and his wife to face a life of enforced idleness. The servants resented her presence in the kitchen, so cooking was out. Clara and the snooty nursemaid would brook no interference with the nursery routine, so Mrs. Chriswell had virtually nothing to do. Even her crocheted doilies disappeared magically soon after their presentation to Clara and the modern furniture.

Mrs. Chriswell shifted the heavy bird book and considered rebelling. The sun was hot and her load was heavy. As she toiled on across the field she thought she saw the glint of sun on water. She would sit and crochet in the shade nearby and remove the big straw cartwheel hat Clara termed "just the thing."

Arrived at the trees, Mrs. Chriswell dropped her burdens and flung the hat willy-nilly. Ugly, ridiculous thing. She glanced around for the water she thought she'd seen, but there was no sign of it. She leaned back against a tree trunk and sighed blissfully. A little breeze had sprung up and was cooling the damp tendrils on her forehead. She opened her big purse and scrambled through the muddle of contents for her crochet hook and the ball of thread attached to a half-finished doily. In her search she came across the snapshots of her granddaughters—in colour, they were, but unfortunately Mrs. Chriswell saw them only in various shades of grey. The breeze was getting stronger now, very pleasant, but the dratted old cartwheel monstrosity was rolling merrily down the slight grade to the tangle of berry bushes a few yards away. Well, it would catch on the brambles. But it didn't. The wind flirted it right around the bushes, and the hat disappeared.

"Fiddle!" Mrs. Chriswell dared not face Clara without the hat. Still hanging on to the bulky purse, she got up to give chase. Rounding the tangle of bushes, she ran smack into a tall young man in uniform.

"Oh!" Mrs. Chriswell said. "Have you seen my hat?"

The young man smiled and pointed on down the hill. Mrs. Chriswell was surprised to see her hat being passed from hand to hand among three other tall young men in uniform. They were laughing at it, and she didn't much blame them. They were standing beside a low, silvery aircraft of some unusual design. Mrs. Chriswell studied it a moment, but, really, she knew nothing about such things. . . . The sun glinted off it, and she realized this was what she had thought was water. The young man beside her touched her arm. She turned towards him and saw that he had put a rather lovely little metal hat on his head. He offered her one with grave courtesy. Mrs. Chriswell smiled up at him and nodded. The young man fitted the hat carefully, adjusting various little ornamental knobs on the top of it.

"Now we can talk," he said. "Do you hear well?"

"My dear boy," Mrs. Chriswell said, "of course I do. I'm not so old as all that." She found a smooth stone and sat down to chat. This was much nicer than birdwatching, or even crochet.

The tall young man grinned and signalled excitedly to his companions. They too put on little metal hats and came bounding up the hill. Still laughing, they deposited the cartwheel in Mrs. Chriswell's lap. She patted the stone by way of invitation, and the youngest looking one of the four dropped down beside her.

"What is your name, Mother?" he asked.

"Ida Chriswell," she said. "What's yours?"

"My name is Jord," the boy said.

Mrs. Chriswell patted his hand. "That's a nice, unusual name." The boy grabbed Mrs. Chriswell's hand and rubbed it against the smoothness of his cheek.

"You are like my Mother's Mother," the boy explained, "whom I have not seen in too long." The other young men laughed, and the boy looked abashed and stealthily wiped with his hands at a tear that slid down his nose.

Mrs. Chriswell frowned warningly at the laughter and handed him her clean pocket handkerchief, scented with lavender. Jord turned it over and over in his hands, and then tentatively sniffed at it.

"It's all right," Mrs. Chriswell said. "Use it. I have another." But Jord only breathed more deeply of the faint perfume in its folds.

"This is only the thinnest thread of melody," he said, "but, Mother Ida, it is very like one note from the Harmony Hills of home!" He passed the handkerchief all around the circle, and the young men sniffed at it and smiled.

Mrs. Chriswell tried to remember if she had ever read of the Harmony Hills, but Mr. Chriswell had always told her she was lamentably weak in geography, and she supposed that this was one of her blank spots, like where on earth was Timbuktu? Or the Hellandgone people were always talking about? But it was rude not to make some comment. Wars shifted people about such a lot, and these boys must be homesick and weary of being strangers, longing to talk of home. She was proud of herself for realizing that they were strangers. But there was something. . . . Hard to say, really. The way they had bounded up the hill? Mountain people, perhaps, to whom hills were mere springboards to heights beyond.

"Tell me about your hills," she said.

"Wait," Jord said. "I will show you." He glanced at his leader as if for approval. The young man who had fitted her hat nodded. Jord drew a fingernail across the breast of his uniform. Mrs. Chriswell was surprised to see a pocket opening where no pocket had been before. Really, the Air Force did amazing things with its uniforms, though, frankly, Mrs. Chriswell thought the cut of these a bit extreme.

Carefully, Jord was lifting out a packet of gossamer material. He gently pressed the centre of the packet and it blossomed out into voluminous clouds of featherweight threads, held loosely together in a wave like a giant spider web. To Mrs. Chriswell's eyes the mesh of threads was the colour of fog, and almost as insubstantial.

"Do not be afraid," Jord said softly, stepping closer to her. "Bend your head, close your eyes, and you shall hear the lovely Harmony Hills of home."

There was one quick-drawn breath of almost-fear, but before she shut her eyes Mrs. Chriswell saw the love in Jord's, and in that moment she knew how rarely she had seen this look, anywhere . . . anytime. If Jord had asked it of her, it was all right. She closed her eyes and bowed her head, and in that attitude of prayer she felt a soft weightlessness descend upon her. It was as if twilight had come down to drape itself on her shoulders. And then the music began. Behind the darkness of her eyes it rose in majesty and power, in colours she had never seen, never guessed. It blossomed like flowers—giant forests of them. Their scents were intoxicating and filled her with joy. She could not tell if the blending perfumes made the music, or if the music itself created the flowers and the perfumes that poured forth from them. She did not care. She wanted only to go on forever listening to all this colour. It seemed odd to be listening to colour, perhaps, but after all, she told herself, it would seem just as odd to me to *see* it.

She sat blinking at the circle of young men. The music was finished. Jord was putting away the gossamer threads in the secret pocket, and laughing aloud at her astonishment.

"Did you like it, Mother Ida?" He dropped down beside her again and patted her wrinkled face, still pink with excitement.

"Oh, Jord," she said, "how lovely . . . Tell me . . ."

But the leader was calling them all to order. "I'm sorry, Mother Ida, we must hurry about our business. Will you answer some questions? It is very important."

"Of course," Mrs. Chriswell said. She was still feeling a bit dazed.

"If I can . . . If it's like the quizzes on the TV, though, I'm not very good at it."

The young man shook his head. "We," he said, "have been instructed to investigate and report on the true conditions of this . . . of the world." He pointed at the aircraft glittering in the sunlight. "We have travelled all around in that slow machine, and our observations have been accurate. . . ." He hesitated, drew a deep breath and continued. ". . . and perhaps we shall be forced to give an unfavourable report, but this depends a great deal on the outcome of our talk with you. We are glad you stumbled upon us. We were about to set out on a foray to secure some individual for questioning. It is our last task." He smiled. "And Jord, here, will not be sorry. He is sick for home and loved ones." He sighed, and all the other young men echoed the sigh.

"Every night," Mrs. Chriswell said, "I pray for peace on earth. I cannot bear to think of boys like you fighting and dying, and the folks at home waiting and waiting . . ." She glanced all around at their listening faces. "And I'll tell you something else," she said, "I find I can't really hate anybody, even the enemy." Around the circle the young men nodded at each other. "Now ask me your questions." She fumbled in her purse for her crochet work and found it.

Beside her Jord exclaimed with pleasure at the sight of the half-finished doily. Mrs. Chriswell warmed to him even more.

The tall young man began his grave questioning. They were very simple questions, and Mrs. Chriswell answered them without hesitation. Did she believe in God? Did she believe in the dignity of man? Did she truly abhor war? Did she believe that man was capable of love for his neighbour? The questions went on and on, and Mrs. Chriswell crocheted while she gave her answers.

At last, when the young man had quite run out of questions, and Mrs. Chriswell had finished the doily, Jord broke the sun-lazy silence that had fallen upon them.

"May I have it, Mother?" He pointed to the doily. Mrs. Chriswell bestowed it upon him with great pleasure, and Jord, like a very small boy, stuffed it greedily into another secret pocket. He pointed at her stuffed purse.

"May I look, Mother?"

Mrs. Chriswell indulgently passed him her purse. He opened it and poured the litter of contents on the ground between them. The snapshots of Mrs. Chriswell's grandchildren stared up at him. Jord smiled at the pretty little-girl faces. He groped in the chest pocket and drew out snapshots of his own. "These," he told Mrs. Chriswell proudly, "are my little sisters. Are they not like these little girls of yours? Let us exchange, because soon I will be at home with them, and there will be no need for pictures. I would like to have yours."

Mrs. Chriswell would have given Jord the entire contents of the purse if he had asked for them. She took the snapshots he offered and looked with pleasure at the sweet-faced children. Jord still stirred at the pile of possessions from Mrs. Chriswell's purse. By the time she was ready to leave he had talked her out of three illustrated recipes torn from magazines, some swatches of material, and two pieces of peppermint candy.

The young man who was the leader helped her to remove the pretty little hat when Mrs. Chriswell indicated he should. She would have liked to keep it, but she didn't believe Clara would approve. She clapped the straw monstrosity on her head, kissed Jord's cheek, waved goodbye to the rest, and groped her way around the berry bushes. She had to grope because her eyes were tear-filled. They had saluted her so grandly as she left.

Clara's usually sedate household was in an uproar when Mrs. Chriswell returned. All the radios in the house were blaring. Even Clara sat huddled over the one in the library. Mrs. Chriswell heard a boy in the street crying "EXTRA! EXTRA!" and the upstairs maid almost knocked her down getting out the front door to buy one. Mrs. Chriswell, sleepy and somewhat sunburned, supposed it was something about the awful war.

She was just turning up the stairs to her room when the snooty nursemaid came rushing down to disappear kitchenwards with another newspaper in her hand. Good, the children were alone. She'd stop in to see them. Suddenly she heard the raised voices from the back of the house. The cook was yelling at somebody. "I tell you, I saw it! I took out some garbage and there it was, right over me!" Mrs. Chriswell lingered at the foot of the stairway puzzled by all the confusion. The housemaid came rushing in with the extra edition. Mrs. Chriswell quietly reached out and took it. "Thank you, Nadine," she said. The nursemaid was still staring at her as she climbed the stairs.

Edna and Evelyn were sitting on the nursery floor, a candy box between them, and shrieking at each other when their grandmother opened the door. They were cramming chocolates into their mouths between shrieks. Their faces and pinafores were smeared with the candy. Edna suddenly yanked Evelyn's hair, hard. "Pig!" she shouted. "You got three more than I did!"

"Children! Children! Not fighting?" Mrs. Chriswell was delighted. Here was something she could cope with. She led them firmly to the bathroom and washed their faces. "Change your frocks," she said, "and I'll tell you my adventure."

There were only hissing accusals and whispered countercharges behind her as she turned her back on the children to scan the newspaper. The headlines leapt up at her.

Mysterious broadcast interrupts programmes on all wave lengths
Unknown woman saves world, say men from space
One sane human found on earth
Cooking, needlework, home, religious interests sway space judges

Every column of the paper was crowded with the same unintelligible nonsense. Mrs. Chriswell folded it neatly, deposited it on the table, and turned to tie her granddaughters' sashes and tell her adventure.

". . . And then he gave me some lovely photographs. In colour, he said . . . Good little girls, just like Edna and Evelyn. Would you like to see them?"

Edna made a rude noise with her mouth pursed. Evelyn's face grew saintlike in retaliation. "Yes, show us," she said.

Mrs. Chriswell passed them the snapshots, and the children drew close together for the moment before Evelyn dropped the pictures as if they were blazing. She stared hard at her grandmother while Edna made a gagging noise.

"Green!" Edna gurgled. "Gaaa . . . green skins!"

"Grandmother!" Evelyn was tearful. "Those children are frog-coloured!"

Mrs. Chriswell bent over to pick up the pictures. "Now, now, children," she murmured absently. "We don't worry about the colour of people's skins. Red . . . yellow . . . black . . . we're all God's children. Asia or Africa, makes no difference . . ." But before she could finish her thought, the nursemaid loomed disapprovingly in the doorway. Mrs. Chriswell hurried out to her own room, while some tiny worry nagged at her mind. "Red, yellow, black, white," she murmured over and over, "and brown . . . but green . . . ?" Geography had always been her weak point. Green . . . Now where on earth . . . ?

William Tenn

William Tenn is the pseudonym of Philip Klass (1920–), most of whose major SF work was published in the 1950s. He is legendary in the SF field as a wit and a satirist—and for his writing block, which has prevented him from finishing nearly any fiction from the early 1960s to the mid-'90s. His one novel, *Of Men and Monsters* (1968), was published along with five volumes of his short fiction containing most of his earlier work in that year, but he has had no books since.

In an essay introducing his first collection, *Of All Possible Worlds* (1955), he offered an eloquent defense of the genre and revealed a "passionate belief in science fiction as a means of literary expression that has particular validity and significance in this age." He recently retired from a long and distinguished career as a teacher of writing at Pennsylvania State University, where he was the mentor of, among others, David Morrell. *The Encyclopedia of Science Fiction* calls Tenn "one of the genre's very few genuinely comic, genuinely incisive writers of short fiction."

Dictionary of Literary Biography (volume 8) singles out "Time in Advance" as "one of Tenn's most thoughtful satires . . . its protagonist is one of Tenn's best-developed characters." It is a complex moral and psychological investigation. What if it were possible to serve your punishment before committing your crime? It seems to me one of the best stories from one of the best writers in the history of genre science fiction.

TIME IN ADVANCE

Twenty minutes after the convict ship landed at the New York Spaceport, reporters were allowed aboard. They came boiling up the main corridor, pushing against the heavily armed guards who were conducting them, the feature-story men and by-line columnists in the lead, the TV people with their portable but still-heavy equipment cursing along behind.

As they went, they passed little groups of spacemen in the black-and-red uniform of the Interstellar Prison Service walking rapidly in the opposite direction, on their way to enjoy five days of planetside leave before the ship roared away once more with a new cargo of convicts.

The impatient journalists barely glanced at these drab personalities who were spending their lives in a continuous shuttle from one end of the Galaxy to the other. After all, the life and adventures of an IPS man had been done thousands of times, done to death. The big story lay ahead.

In the very belly of the ship, the guards slid apart two enormous sliding doors—and quickly stepped aside to avoid being trampled. The reporters almost flung themselves against the iron bars that ran from floor to ceiling and completely shut off the great prison chamber. Their eager, darting stares were met with at most a few curious glances from the men in coarse gray suits who lay or sat in the tiers of bunks that rose in row after sternly functional row all the way down the cargo hold. Each man clutched—and some caressed—small package neatly wrapped in plain brown paper.

The chief guard ambled up on the other side of the bars, picking the morning's breakfast out of his front teeth. "Hi, boys," he said. "Who're you looking for—as if I didn't know?"

One of the older, more famous columnists held the palm of his hand up warningly. "Look, Anderson: no games. The ship's been almost a half-hour late in landing and we were stalled for fifteen minutes at the gangplank. Now where the hell are they?"

Anderson watched the TV crews shoulder a place for themselves and their equipment right up to the barrier. He tugged a last bit of food out of one of his molars.

"Ghouls," he muttered. "A bunch of grave-happy, funeral-hungry ghouls." Then he hefted his club experimentally a couple of times and clattered it back and forth against the bars. "Crandall!" he bellowed. "Henck! Front and center!"

The cry was picked up by the guards strolling about, steadily, measuredly, club-twirlingly, inside the prison pen. "Crandall! Henck! Front and center!" It went ricocheting authoritatively up and down the tremendous curved walls. "Crandall! Henck! Front and center!"

Nicholas Crandall sat up cross-legged in his bunk on the fifth tier and grimaced. He had been dozing and now he rubbed a hand across his eyes to erase the sleep. There were three parallel scars across the back of his hand, old and brown and straight scars such as an animal's claws might rake out. There was also a curious zigzag scar just above his eyes that had a more reddish novelty. And there was a tiny, perfectly round hole in the middle of his left ear which, after coming fully awake, he scratched in annoyance.

"Reception committee," he grumbled. "Might have known. Same old goddam Earth as ever."

He flipped over on his stomach and reached down to pat the face of the little man snoring on the bunk immediately under him. "Otto," he called. "Blotto Otto—up and at 'em! They want us."

Henck immediately sat up in the same cross-legged fashion, even before his eyes had opened. His right hand went to his throat where there was a little network of zigzag scars of the same color and size as the one Crandall had on his forehead. The hand was missing an index and forefinger.

"Henck here, sir," he said thickly, then shook his head and stared up at Crandall. "Oh—Nick. What's up?"

"We've arrived, Blotto Otto," the taller man said from the bunk above. "We're on Earth and they're getting our discharges ready. In about half an hour, you'll be able to wrap that tongue of yours around as much brandy, beer, vodka and rotgut whiskey as you can pay for. No more prison-brew, no more raisin-jack from a tin can under the bed, Blotto Otto."

Henck grunted and flopped down on his back again. "In half an hour, but not now, so why did you have to go and wake me up? What do you take me for, some dewy, post-crime, petty-larceny kid, sweating out my discharge with my eyes open and my gut wriggling? Hey, Nick, I was dreaming of a new way to get Elsa, a brand-new, really ugly way."

"The screws are in an uproar," Crandall told him, still in a low, patient voice. "Hear them? They want us, you and me."

Henck sat up again, listened a moment, and nodded. "Why is it," he asked, "that only space-screws have voices like that?"

"It's a requirement of the service," Crandall assured him. "You've got to be at least a minimum height, have a minimum education and with a minimum nasty voice of just the right ear-splitting quality before you can get to be a space-screw. Otherwise, no matter how vicious a personality you have, you are just plain out of luck and have to stay behind on Earth and go on getting your kicks by running down slowpoke 'copters driven by old ladies."

A guard stopped below, banged angrily at one of the metal posts that supported their tier of bunks. "Crandall! Henck! You're still convicts, don't you forget that! If you don't front-and-center in a double-time hurry, I'll climb up there and work you over once more for old-time's sake!"

"Yes, *sir!* Coming, *sir!*" they said in immediate, mumbling unison and began climbing down from bunk to bunk, each still clutching the brown-paper package that contained the clothes they had once worn as free men and would shortly be allowed to wear again.

"Listen, Otto." Crandall leaned down as they climbed and brought his lips close to the little man's ear in the rapid-fire, extremely low-pitched prison whisper. "They're taking us to meet the television and news boys. We're going to be asked a lot of questions. One thing you want to be sure to keep your lip buttoned about—"

"Television and news? Why us? What do they want with us?"

"Because we're celebrities, knockhead! We've seen it through for the big rap and come out on the other side. How many men do you think have made it? But *listen,* will you? If they ask you who it is you're after, you just shut up and smile. You don't answer that question. Got that? You don't tell them whose murder you were sentenced for, no matter what they say. They can't make you. That's the law."

Henck paused a moment, one and a half bunks from the floor. "But, Nick, *Elsa* knows! I told her that day, just before I turned myself in. She knows I wouldn't take a murder rap for anyone but her!"

"She knows, she knows, of *course* she knows!" Crandall swore briefly and almost inaudibly. "But she can't *prove* it, you goddam human blotter! Once you say so in public, though, she's entitled to arm herself and shoot you down on sight—pleading self-defense. And till you say so, she can't; she's still your poor wife whom you've promised to love, honor and cherish. As far as the world is concerned—"

The guard reached up with his club and jolted them both angrily across the back. They dropped to the floor and cringed as he snarled over them: "Did I say you could have a talk-party? *Did I?* If we have any time left before you get your discharge, I'm taking you cuties into the guard-room for one last big going-over. Now pick them up and put them down!"

They scuttled in front of him obediently, like a pair of chickens before a snapping collie. At the barred gate near the end of the prison hold, he saluted and said: "Pre-criminals Nicholas Crandall and Otto Henck, sir."

Chief Guard Anderson wiped the salute back at him carelessly. "These gentlemen want to ask you fellas a couple of questions. Won't hurt you to answer. That's all, O'Brien."

His voice was very jovial. He was wearing a big, gentle, half-moon smile. As the subordinate guard saluted and moved away, Crandall let his mind regurgitate memories of Anderson all through this month-long trip from Proxima Centaurus.

Anderson nodding thoughtfully as that poor Minelli—Steve Minelli, hadn't that been his name?—was made to run through a gauntlet of club-swinging guards for going to the toilet without permission. Anderson chuckling just a moment before he'd kicked a gray-headed convict in the groin for talking on the chow-line. Anderson—

Well, the guy had guts, anyway, knowing that his ship carried two pre-criminals who had served out a murder sentence. But he probably also knew that they wouldn't waste the murder on him, however viciously he acted. A man doesn't volunteer for a hitch in hell just so he can knock off one of the devils.

"Do we have to answer these questions, sir?" Crandall asked cautiously, tentatively.

The chief guard's smile lost the tiniest bit of its curvature. "I said it wouldn't hurt you, didn't I? But other things might. They *still* might, Crandall. I'd like to do these gentlemen from the press a favor, so you be nice and cooperative, eh?" He gestured with his chin, ever so slightly, in the direction of the guard-room and hefted his club a bit.

"Yes, sir," Crandall said, while Henck nodded violently. "We'll be cooperative, sir."

Dammit, he thought, *if only I didn't have such a use for that murder! Let's keep remembering Stephanson, boy, no one but Stephanson! Not Anderson, not O'Brien, not anybody else: the name under discussion is Frederick Stoddard Stephanson!*

While the television men on the other side of the bars were fussing their equipment into position, the two convicts answered the preliminary, inevitable questions of the feature writers:

"How does it feel to be back?"

"Fine, just fine."

"What's the first thing you're going to do when you get your discharge?"

"Eat a good meal." (From Crandall.)

"Get roaring drunk." (From Henck.)

"Careful you don't wind up right behind bars again as a post-criminal." (From one of the feature writers.) A good-natured laugh in which all of them, the newsmen, Chief Guard Anderson, and Crandall and Henck, participated.

"How were you treated while you were prisoners?"

"Oh, pretty good." (From both of them, concurrent with a thoughtful glance at Anderson's club.)

"Either of you care to tell us who you're going to murder?"

(Silence.)

"Either of you changed your mind and decided not to commit the murder?"

(Crandall looked thoughtfully up, while Henck looked thoughtfully down.) Another general laugh, a bit more uneasy this time, Crandall and Henck not participating.

"All right, we're set. Look this way, please," the television announcer broke in. "And smile, men—let's have a really *big* smile."

Crandall and Henck dutifully emitted big smiles, which made three smiles, for Anderson had moved into the cheerful little group.

The two cameras shot out of the grasp of their technicians, one hovering over them, one moving restlessly before their faces, both controlled, at a distance, by the little box of switches in the cameramen's hands. A red bulb in the nose of one of the cameras lit up.

"Here we are, ladies and gentlemen of the television audience," the announcer exuded in a lavish voice. "We are on board the convict ship *Jean Valjean,* which has just landed at the New York Spaceport. We are here to meet two men—two of the rare men who have managed to serve all of a voluntary sentence for murder and thus are legally entitled to commit one murder apiece.

"In just a few moments, they will be discharged after having served out seven full years on the convict planets—and they will be free to kill any man or woman in the Solar System with absolutely no fear of any kind of retribution. Take a good look at them, ladies and gentlemen of the television audience—it might be you they are after!"

After this cheering thought, the announcer let a moment or two elapse while the cameras let their lenses stare at the two men in prison gray. Then he stepped into range himself and addressed the smaller man.

"What is your name, sir?" he asked.

"Pre-criminal Otto Henck, 525514," Blotto Otto responded automatically, though not able to repress a bit of a start at the *sir.*

"How does it feel to be back?"

"Fine, just fine."

"What's the first thing you're going to do when you get your discharge?"

Henck hesitated, then said, "Eat a good meal," after a shy look at Crandall.

"How were you treated while you were a prisoner?"

"Oh, pretty good. As good as you could expect."

"As good as a criminal could expect, eh? Although you're not really a criminal yet, are you? You're a pre-criminal."

Henck smiled as if this were the first time he was hearing the term. "That's right, sir. I'm a pre-criminal."

"Want to tell the audience who the person is you're going to become a criminal for?"

Henck looked reproachfully at the announcer, who chuckled throatily—and alone.

"Or if you've changed your mind about him or her?" There was a pause. Then the announcer said a little nervously: "You've served seven years on danger-filled, alien planets, preparing them for human colonization. That's the maximum sentence the law allows, isn't it?"

"That's right, sir. With the pre-criminal discount for serving the sentence in advance, seven years is the most you can get for murder."

"Bet you're glad we're not back in the days of capital punishment, eh? That would make the whole thing impractical, wouldn't it? Now, Mr. Henck—or pre-criminal Henck, I guess I should still call you—suppose you tell the ladies and gentlemen of our television audience: What was the most horrifying experience you had while you were serving your sentence?"

"Well," Otto Henck considered carefully. "About the worst of the lot, I guess, was the time on Antares VIII, the second prison camp I was in, when the big wasps started to spawn. They got a wasp on Antares VIII, see, that's about a hundred times the size of—"

"Is that how you lost two fingers on your right hand?"

Henck brought his hand up and studied it for a moment. "No. The forefinger—I lost the forefinger on Rigel XII. We were building the first prison camp on the planet and I dug up a funny kind of red rock that had all sorts of little bumps on it. I poked it, kind of—you know, just to see how hard it was or something—and the tip of my finger disappeared. *Pow*—just like that. Later on, the whole finger got infected and the medics had to cut it off.

"It turned out I was lucky, though; some of the men—the convicts, I mean—ran into bigger rocks than the one I found. Those guys lost arms, legs—one guy even got swallowed whole. They weren't really rocks, see. They were alive—they were alive and hungry! Rigel XII was lousy with them. The middle finger—I lost the middle finger in a dumb kind of accident on board ship while we were being moved to—"

The announcer nodded intelligently, cleared his throat and said: "But those wasps, those giant wasps on Antares VIII—they were the worst?"

Blotto Otto blinked at him for a moment before he found the conversation again.

"Oh. They sure were! They were used to laying their eggs in a kind of monkey they have on Antares VIII, see? It was real rough on the monkey, but that's how the baby wasps got their food while they were growing up. Well, we get out there and it turns out that the wasps can't see any difference between those Antares monkeys and human beings. First thing you know, guys start collapsing all over the place and when they're taken to the dispensary for an X-ray, the medics see that they're completely crammed—"

"Thank you very much, Mr. Henck, but Herkimer's Wasp has already been seen by and described to our audience at least three times in the past on the Interstellar Travelogue, which is carried by this network, as you ladies and gentlemen no doubt remember, on Wednesday evening from seven to seven-thirty P.M. terrestrial standard time. And now, Mr. Crandall, let me ask you, sir: How does it feel to be back?"

Crandall stepped up and was put through almost exactly the same verbal paces as his fellow prisoner.

There was one major difference. The announcer asked him if he expected to find Earth much changed. Crandall started to shrug, then abruptly relaxed and grinned. He was careful to make the grin an extremely wide one, exposing a maximum of tooth and a minimum of mirth.

"There's one big change I can see already," he said. "The way those cameras float around and are controlled from a little switch-box in the cameraman's hand. That gimmick wasn't around the day I left. Whoever invented it must have been pretty clever."

"Oh, yes?" The announcer glanced briefly backward. "You mean the Stephanson Remote Control Switch? It was invented by Frederick Stoddard Stephanson about five years ago—Was it five years, Don?"

"Six years," said the cameraman. "Went on the market five years ago."

"It was *invented* six years ago," the announcer translated. "It went on the market *five* years ago."

Crandall nodded. "Well, this Frederick Stoddard Stephanson must be a clever man, a very clever man." And he grinned again into the cameras. *Look at my teeth,* he thought to himself. *I know you're watching, Freddy. Look at my teeth and shiver.*

The announcer seemed a bit disconcerted. "Yes," he said. "Exactly. Now, Mr. Crandall, what would you describe as the most horrifying experience in your entire . . ."

After the TV men had rolled up their equipment and departed, the two precriminals were subjected to a final barrage of questions from the feature writers and columnists in search of odd shreds of color.

"What about the women in your life?" "What books, what hobbies, what amusements filled your time?" "Did you find out that there are no atheists on convict planets?" "If you had the whole thing to do over again—"

As he answered, drably, courteously, Nicholas Crandall was thinking about Frederick Stoddard Stephanson seated in front of his luxurious wall-size television set.

Would Stephanson have clicked it off by now? Would he be sitting there, staring at the blank screen, pondering the plans of the man who had outlived odds estimated at ten thousand to one and returned after seven full, unbelievable years in the prison camps of four insane planets?

Would Stephanson be examining his blaster with sucked-in lips—the blaster that he might use only in an open-and-shut situation of self-defense? Otherwise, he would incur the full post-criminal sentence for murder, which, without the fifty per cent discount for punishment voluntarily undergone in advance of the crime, was as much as fourteen years in the many-pronged hell from which Crandall had just returned?

Or would Stephanson be sitting, slumped in an expensive bubblechair, glumly watching a still-active screen, frightened out of his wits but still unable to tear himself away from the well-organized program the network had no doubt built around the return of two—count 'em: *two!*—homicidal pre-criminals?

At the moment, in all probability, the screen was showing an interview with some Earthside official of the Interstellar Prison Service, an expansive public relations character who had learned to talk in sociology.

"Tell me, Mr. Public Relations," the announcer would ask (a different announcer, more serious, more intellectual), "how often do pre-criminals serve out a sentence for murder and return?"

"According to statistics—" a rustle of papers at this point and a penetrating glance downward—"according to statistics, we may expect a man who has served a full sentence for murder, with the 50 per cent pre-criminal discount, to return only once in 11.7 years on the average."

"You would say, then, wouldn't you, Mr. Public Relations, that the return of two such men on the same day is a rather unusual situation?"

"*Highly* unusual or you television fellas wouldn't be in such a fuss over it." A thick chuckle here, which the announcer dutifully echoes.

"And what, Mr. Public Relations, happens to the others who don't return?"

A large, well-fed hand gestures urbanely. "They get killed. Or they give up. Those are the only two alternatives. Seven years is a long time to spend on those convict planets. The work schedule isn't for sissies and neither are the life-forms they encounter—the big man-eating ones as well as the small virus-sized types.

"That's why prison guards get such high salaries and such long leaves. In a sense, you know, we haven't really abolished capital punishment; we've substituted a socially useful form of Russian Roulette for it. Any man who commits or pre-commits one of a group of particularly reprehensible crimes is sent off to a planet where his services will benefit humanity and where he's forced to take his chances on coming back in one piece, if at all. The more serious the crime, the longer the sentence and, therefore, the more remote the chances."

"I see. Now, Mr. Public Relations, you say they either get killed or they give up. Would you explain to the audience, if you please, just how they give up and what happens if they do?"

Here a sitting back in the chair, a locking of pudgy fingers over paunch. "You see, any pre-criminal may apply to his warden for immediate abrogation of sentence. It's just a matter of filling out the necessary forms. He's pulled off work detail right then and there and is sent home on the very next ship out of the place. The catch is this: Every bit of time he's served up to that point is canceled—he gets nothing for it.

"If he commits an actual crime after being freed, he has to serve the full sentence. If he wants to be committed as a pre-criminal again, he has to start serving the sentence, with the discount, from the beginning. Three out of every four pre-criminals apply for abrogation of sentence in their very first year. You get a bellyful fast in those places."

"I guess you certainly do," agrees the announcer. "What about the discount, Mr. Public Relations? Aren't there people who feel that's offering the pre-criminal too much inducement?"

The barest grimace of anger flows across the sleek face, to be succeeded by a warm, contemptuous smile. "Those are people, I'm afraid, who, however well-intentioned, are not well versed in the facts of modern criminology and penology. We don't want to discourage pre-criminals; we want to *encourage* them to turn themselves in.

"Remember what I said about three out of four applying for abrogation of sentence in their very first year? Now these are individuals who were sensible enough to try to get a discount on their sentence. Are they likely to be foolish enough to risk twice as much when they have found out conclusively they can't stand a bare twelve months of it? Not to mention what they have discovered about the value of human life, the necessity for social cooperation and the general desirability of civilized processes on those worlds where simple survival is practically a matter of a sweepstakes ticket.

"The man who doesn't apply for abrogation of sentence? Well, he has that much more time to let the desire to commit the crime go cold—and that much greater likelihood of getting killed with nothing to show for it. Therefore, so few pre-criminals in *any* of the categories return to tell the tale and do the deed that the social profit is absolutely enormous! Let me give you a few figures.

"Using the Lazarus Scale, it has been estimated that the decline in premeditated homicides alone, since the institution of the pre-criminal discount, has been forty-one per cent on Earth, thirty-three and a third per cent on Venus, twenty-seven per cent—"

Cold comfort, chillingly cold comfort, that would be to Stephanson, Nicholas Crandall reflected pleasurably, those forty-one per cents and thirty-three and a third per cents. Crandall's was the balancing statistic: the man who wanted to murder, and for good and sufficient cause, one Frederick Stoddard Stephanson. He was a leftover fraction on a page of reductions and cancellations—he had returned, astonishingly, unbelievably, after seven years to collect the merchandise for which he had paid in advance.

He and Henck. Two ridiculously long long-shots. Henck's wife Elsa—was she, too, sitting in a kind of bird-hypnotized-by-a-snake fashion before her television set, hoping dimly and desperately that some comment of the Interstellar Prison Service official would show her how to evade her fate, how to get out from under the ridiculously rare disaster that was about to happen to her?

Well, Elsa was Blotto Otto's affair. Let him enjoy it in his own way; he'd paid enough for the privilege. But Stephanson was Crandall's.

Oh, let the arrogant bean-pole sweat, he prayed. *Let me take my time and let him sweat!*

The newsman kept squeezing them for story angles until a loudspeaker in the overhead suddenly cleared its diaphragm and announced:

"Prisoners, prepare for discharge! You will proceed to the ship warden's office in groups of ten, as your name is called. Convict ship discipline will be maintained throughout. Arthur, Augluk, Crandall, Ferrara, Fu-Yen, Garfinkel, Gomez, Graham, Henck—"

A half hour later, they were walking down the main corridor of the ship in their civilian clothes. They showed their discharges to the guard at the gangplank, smiled still cringingly back at Anderson, who called from a porthole, "Hey, fellas, come back soon!" and trotted down the incline to the surface of a planet they had not seen for seven agonizing and horror-crowded years.

There were a few reporters and photographers still waiting for them, and one TV crew which had been left behind to let the world see how they looked at the moment of freedom.

Questions, more questions to answer, which they could afford to be brusque about, although brusqueness to any but fellow prisoners still came hard.

Fortunately, the newsmen got interested in another pre-criminal who was with them. Fu-Yen had completed the discounted sentence of two years for aggravated assault and battery. He had also lost both arms and one leg to a corrosive moss on Procyon III just before the end of his term and came limping down the gangplank on one real and one artificial leg, unable to grasp the hand-rails.

As he was being asked, with a good deal of interest, just how he intended to commit simple assault and battery, let alone the serious kind, with his present limited resources, Crandall nudged Henck and they climbed quickly into one of the many hovering gyrocabs. They told the driver to take them to a bar—any quiet bar—in the city.

Blotto Otto almost went to pieces under the impact of actual free choice. "I can't do it," he whispered. "Nick, there's just too damn much to drink!"

Crandall settled it by ordering for him. "Two double scotches," he told the waitress. "Nothing else."

When the scotch came, Blotto Otto stared at it with the kind of affectionate and wistful astonishment a man might show toward an adolescent son whom he saw last as a babe in arms. He put out a gingerly, trembling hand.

"Here's death to our enemies," Crandall said, and tossed his down. He watched Otto sip slowly and carefully, tasting each individual drop.

"You'd better take it easy," he warned. "Elsa might have no more trouble from you than bringing flowers every visiting day to the alcoholic ward."

"No fear," Blotto Otto growled into his empty glass. "I was weaned on this stuff. And, anyway, it's the last drink I have until I dump her. That's the way I've been figuring it, Nick: one drink to celebrate, then Elsa. I didn't go through those seven years to mess myself up at the payoff."

He set the glass down. "Seven years in one steaming hell after another. And before that, twelve years with Elsa. Twelve years with her pulling every dirty trick in the book on me, laughing in my face, telling me she was my wife and had me legally where she wanted me, that I was gonna support her the way she wanted to be supported and I was gonna like it. And if I dared to get off my knees and stand on my hind legs, *pow*, she found a way to get me arrested.

"The weeks I spent in the cooler, in the workhouse, until Elsa would tell the judge maybe I'd learned my lesson, she was willing to give me one more chance! And me begging for a divorce on my knees—hell, on my belly!—no children, she's able-bodied, she's young, and her laughing in my face. When she wanted me in the cooler, see, then she's crying in front of the judge; but when we're alone, she's always laughing her head off to see me squirm.

"I supported her, Nick. Honest, I gave her almost every cent I made, but that wasn't enough. She liked to see me squirm; she *told* me she did. Well, who's squirming now?" He grunted deep in his throat. "Marriage—it's for chumps!"

Crandall looked out of the open window he was sitting against, down through the dizzy, busy levels of Metropolitan New York.

"Maybe it is," he said thoughtfully. "I wouldn't know. My marriage was good while it lasted, five years of it. Then, all of a sudden, it wasn't good any more, just so much rancid butter."

"At least she gave you a divorce," said Henck. "She didn't take you."

"Oh, Polly wasn't the kind of girl to take anyone. A little mixed up, but maybe no more than I was. Pretty Polly, I called her; Big Nick, she called me. The starlight faded and so did I, I guess. I was still knocking myself out then trying to make a go out of the wholesale electronics business with Irv. Anyone could tell I wasn't cut out to be a millionaire. Maybe that was it. Anyway, Polly wanted out and I gave it to her. We parted friends. I wonder, every once in a while, what she's—"

There was a slight splashy noise, like a seal's flipper making a gesture in the water. Crandall's eyes came back to the table a moment after the green, melon-like ball had hit it. And, at the same instant, Henck's hand had swept the ball up and hurled it through the window. The long, green threads streamed out of the ball, but by then it was falling down the side of the enormous building and the threads found no living flesh to take root in.

From the corner of his eye, Crandall had seen a man bolt out of the bar. By the way people kept looking back and forth fearfully from their table to the open doorway, he deduced that the man had thrown it. Evidently Stephanson had thought it worthwhile to have Crandall followed and neutralized.

Blotto Otto saw no point in preening over his reflexes. The two of them had learned to move fast a long time ago—over a lot of dead bodies. "A Venusian dandelion bomb," he observed. "Well, at least the guy doesn't want to kill you, Nick. He just wants to cripple you."

"That would be Stephanson's style," Crandall agreed, as they paid their check and walked past the faces which were just now beginning to turn white. "He'd never do it himself. He'd hire a bully-boy. And he'd do the hiring through an intermediary just in case the bully-boy ever got caught and blabbed. But that still wouldn't be safe enough: he wouldn't want to risk a post-criminal murder charge.

"A dose of Venusian dandelion, he'd figure, and he wouldn't have to worry about me for the rest of my life. He might even come to visit me in the home for incurables—like the way he sent me a card every Christmas of my sentence. Always the same message: 'Still mad? Love, Freddy.' "

"Quite a guy, this Stephanson," Blotto Otto said, peering around the entrance carefully before stepping out of the bar and onto the fifteenth level walkway.

"Yeah, quite a guy. He's got the world by the tail and every once in a while, just for fun, he twists the tail. I learned how he operated when we were room-mates way back in college, but do you think that did me any good? I ran into him just when that wholesale electronics business with Irv was really falling apart, about two years after I broke up with Polly.

"I was feeling blue and I wanted to talk to someone, so I told him all about how my partner was a penny-watcher and I was a big dreamer, and how between us we were turning a possible nice small business into a definite big bankruptcy. And then I got onto this remote-control switch I'd been fooling around with and how I wished I had time to develop it."

Blotto Otto kept glancing around uneasily, not from dread of another assassin, but out of the unexpected sensation of doing so much walking of his own free will. Several passersby turned around to have another stare at their out-of-fashion knee-length tunics.

"So there I was," Crandall went on. "I was a fool, I know, but take my word, Otto, you have no idea how persuasive and friendly a guy like Freddy Stephanson can be. He tells me he has this house in the country he isn't using right now and there's a complete electronics lab in the basement. It's all mine, if I want it, as long as I want it, starting next week; all I have to worry about is feeding myself. And he doesn't want any rent or anything—it's for old time's sake and because he wants to see me do something really big in the world.

"How smart could I be with a con-artist like that? It wasn't till two years later that I realized he must have had the electronics lab installed the same week I was asking Irv to buy me out of the business for a couple of hundred credits. After all, what would Stephanson, the owner of a brokerage firm, be doing with an electronics lab of his own? But who figures such things when an old roommate's so warm and friendly and interested in you?"

Otto sighed. "So he comes up to see you every few weeks. And then, about a month after you've got it all finished and working, he locks you out of the place and moves all your papers and stuff to another joint. And he tells you he'll have it patented long before you can get it all down on paper again, and anyhow it was his place—he can always claim he was subsidizing you. Then he laughs in your face, just like Elsa. Huh, Nick?"

Crandall bit his lip as he realized how thoroughly Otto Henck must have memorized the material. How many times had they gone over each other's planned revenge and the situations which had motivated it? How many times had they told and retold the same bitter stories to each other, elicited the same responses from each other, the same questions, the same agreements and even the very same disagreements?

Suddenly, he wanted to get away from the little man and enjoy the luxury of loneliness. He saw the sparkling roof of a hotel two levels down.

"Think I'll move into that. Ought to be thinking about a place to sleep tonight."

Otto nodded at his mood rather than at his statement. "Sure. I know just how you feel. But that's pretty plush, Nick: The Capricorn-Ritz. At least twelve credits a day."

"So what? I can live high for a week, if I want to. And with my background, I can always pick up a fast job as soon as I get low. I want something plush for tonight, Blotto Otto."

"Okay, okay. You got my address, huh, Nick? I'll be at my cousin's place."

"I have it, all right. Luck with Elsa, Otto."

"Thanks, Luck with Freddy. Uh—so long." The little man turned abruptly and entered a main street elevator. When the doors slid shut, Crandall found that he was feeling very uncomfortable. Henck had meant more to him than his own brother. Well, after all, he'd been with Henck day and night for a long time now. And he hadn't seen Dan for—how long was it?—almost nine years.

He reflected on how little he was attached to the world, if you excluded the rather negative desire of removing Stephanson from it. One thing he should get soon was a girl—almost any girl.

But, come to think of it, there was something he needed even more.

He walked swiftly to the nearest drugstore. It was a large one, part of a chain. And there, featured prominently in the window, was exactly what he wanted.

At the cigar counter, he said to the clerk: "It's pretty cheap. Do they work all right?"

The clerk drew himself up. "Before we put an item on sale, sir, it is tested thoroughly. We are the largest retail outlet in the Solar System—*that's* why it's so cheap."

"All right. Give me the medium-sized one. And two boxes of cartridges."

With the blaster in his possession, he felt much more secure. He had a good deal of confidence—based on years of escaping creatures with hair-trigger nervous systems—in his ability to duck and wriggle and jump to one side. But it would be nice to be able to fight back. And how did he know how soon Stephanson would try again?

He registered under a false name, a ruse he thought of at the last moment. That it wasn't worth much, as ruses went, he found out when the bellhop, after being tipped, said: "Thank you, Mr. Crandall. I hope you get your victim, sir."

So he was a celebrity. Probably everyone in the world knew exactly what he looked like. All of which might make it a bit more difficult to get at Stephanson.

While he was taking a bath, he asked the television set to check through Information's file on the man. Stephanson had been rich and moderately important seven years ago; with the Stephanson Switch—how do you like that, the *Stephanson* Switch!—he must be even richer now and much more important.

He was. The television set informed Crandall that in the last calendar month, there were sixteen news items relating to Frederick Stoddard Stephanson. Crandall considered, then asked for the most recent.

That was datelined today. "Frederick Stephanson, the president of the Stephanson Investment Trust and Stephanson Electronics Corporation, left early this morning for his hunting lodge in Central Tibet. He expects to remain there for at least—"

"That's enough!" Crandall called through the bathroom door.

Stephanson was scared! The arrogant bean-pole was frightened silly! That was something; in fact, it was a large part of the return on those seven years. Let him seethe in his own sweat for a while, until he found the actual killing, when it did come at last, almost welcome.

Crandall asked the set for the fresh news and was immediately treated to a bulletin about himself and how he had registered at the Capricorn-Ritz under the name of Alexander Smathers. "But neither is the correct name, ladies and gentlemen," the playback rolled out unctuously. "Neither Nicholas Crandall nor Alexander Smathers is the right name for this man. There is only one name for that man—and that name is death! Yes, the grim reaper has taken up residence at the Ritz-Capricorn Hotel tonight, and only he knows which one of us will not see another sunrise. That man, that grim reaper, that deputy of death, is the only one among us who knows—"

"Shut up!" Crandall yelled, exasperated. He had almost forgotten the kind of punishment a free man was forced to endure.

The private phone circuit on the television screen lit up. He dried himself, hurried into clothes and asked, "Who's calling?"

"Mrs. Nicholas Crandall," said the operator's voice.

He stared at the blank screen for a moment, absolutely thunderstruck. Polly! Where in the world had she come from? And how did she know where he was? No, the last part was easy—he was a celebrity.

"Put her on," he said at last.

Polly's face filled the screen. Crandall studied her quizzically. She'd aged a bit, but possibly it wasn't obvious at anything but this magnification.

As if she realized it herself, Polly adjusted the controls of her set and her face dwindled to life-size, the rest of her body as well as her surroundings coming into the picture. She was evidently in the living room of her home; it looked like a low-to-middle-income-range furnished apartment. But she looked good—awfully good. There were such warm memories . . .

"Hi, Polly. What's this all about? You're the last person I expected to call me."

"Hello, Nick." She lifted her hand to her mouth and stared over its knuckles for some time at him. Then: "Nick. Please. Please don't play games with me."

He dropped into a chair. "Huh?"

She began to cry. "Oh, Nick! *Don't!* Don't be that cruel! I know why you served that sentence—those seven years. The moment I heard your name today, I knew why you did it. But, Nick, it was only one man—just one man, Nick!"

"Just one man *what?*"

"It was just that one man I was unfaithful with. And I thought he loved me, Nick. I wouldn't have divorced you if I'd known what he was really like. But you know, Nick, don't you? You know how much he made me suffer. I've been punished enough. Don't kill me, Nick! Please don't kill me!"

"Listen, Polly," he began, completely confused. "Polly girl, for heaven's sake—"

"Nick!" she gulped hysterically. "Nick, it was over eleven years ago—ten, at least. Don't kill me for that, please, Nick, Nick, truly, I wasn't unfaithful to you for more than a year, two years at the most. Truly, Nick! And, Nick, it was only that one affair—the others didn't count. They were just, just casual things. They didn't matter at all, Nick! But don't kill me! Don't kill me!" She held both hands to her face and began rocking back and forth, moaning uncontrollably.

Crandall stared at her for a moment and moistened his lips. Then he said, "Whew!" and turned the set off. He leaned back in his chair. Again he said, "Whew!" and this time it hissed through his teeth.

Polly! Polly had been unfaithful during their marriage. For a year—no, two years! And—what had she said?—the others, the *others* had just been casual things!

The woman he had loved, the woman he suspected he had always loved, the woman he had given up with infinite regret and a deep sense of guilt when she had come to him and said that the business had taken the best part of him away from her, but that since it wasn't fair to ask him to give up something that obviously meant so much to him—

Pretty Polly. Polly girl. He'd never thought of another woman in all their time together. And if anyone, anyone at all, had ever suggested—had so much as *hinted*—he'd have used a monkey wrench on the meddler's face. He'd given her the divorce only because she'd asked for it, but he'd hoped that when the business got on its feet and Irv's bookkeeping end covered a wider stretch of it, they might get back together again. Then, of course, business grew worse, Irv's wife got sick and he put even less time in at the office and—

"I feel," he said to himself numbly, "as if I've just found out for certain that there is no Santa Claus. Not Polly, not all those good years! One affair! And the others were just casual things!"

The telephone circuit went off again. "Who is it?" he snarled.

"Mr. Edward Ballaskia."

"What's he want?" Not *Polly, not Pretty Polly!*

An extremely fat man came on the screen. He looked to right and left cautiously. "I must ask you, Mr. Crandall, if you are positive that this line isn't tapped."

"What the hell do you want?" Crandall found himself wishing that the fat man were here in person. He'd love to sail into sombody right now.

Mr. Edward Ballaskia shook his head disapprovingly, his jowls jiggling slowly behind the rest of his face. "Well, then, sir, if you won't give me your assurances, I am forced to take a chance. I am calling, Mr. Crandall, to ask you to forgive your enemies, to turn the other cheek. I am asking you to remember faith, hope and charity—and that the greatest of these is charity. In other words, sir, open your heart to him or her you intended to kill, understand the weaknesses which caused them to give offenses—and forgive them."

"Why should I?" Crandall demanded.

"Because it is to your profit to do so, sir. Not merely morally profitable—although let us not overlook the life of the spirit—but financially profitable. *Financially* profitable Mr. Crandall."

"Would you kindly tell me what you are talking about?"

The fat man leaned forward and smiled confidentially. "If you can forgive the person who caused you to go off and suffer seven long, seven *miserable* years of acute discomfort Mr. Crandall, I am prepared to make you a most attractive offer. You are entitled to commit one murder. I desire to have one murder committed. I am very wealthy. You, I judge—and please take no umbrage, sir—are very poor.

"I can make you comfortable for the rest of your life, extremely comfortable, Mr. Crandall, if only you will put aside your thoughts, your unworthy thoughts, of anger and personal vengeance. I have a business competitor, you see, who has been—"

Crandall turned him off. "Go serve your own seven years," he venomously told the blank screen. Then, suddenly, it was funny. He lay back in the chair and laughed his head off.

That butter-faced old slob! Quoting religious texts at him!

But the call had served a purpose. Somehow it put the scene with Polly in the perspective of ridicule. To think of the woman sitting in her frowsy little apartment, trembling over her dingy affairs of more than ten years ago! To think she was afraid he had bled and battled for seven years because of that!

He thought about it for a moment, then shrugged. "Well, anyway, I bet it did her good."

And now he was hungry.

He thought of having a meal sent up, just to avoid a possible rendezvous with another of Stephanson's ball-throwers but decided against it. If Stephanson was really hunting him seriously, it would not be much of a job to have something put into the food he was sent. He'd be much safer eating in a restaurant chosen at random.

Besides, a few bright lights, a little gaiety, would be really welcome. This was his first night of freedom—and he had to wash that Polly taste out of his mouth.

He checked the corridor carefully before going out. There was nothing, but the action reminded him of a tiny planet near Vega where you made exactly the same precautionary gesture every time you emerged from one of the tunnels formed by the long, parallel lines of moist, carboniferous ferns.

Because if you didn't—well, there was an enormous leech like mollusc that might be waiting there, a creature which could flip chunks of shell with prodigious force. The shell merely stunned its prey, but stunned it long enough for the leech to get in close.

And that leech could empty a man in ten minutes flat.

Once he'd been hit by a fragment of shell, and while he'd been lying there, Henck—Good old Blotto Otto! Crandall smiled. Was it possible that the two of them would look back on those hideous adventures, one day, with actual nostalgia, the kind of beery, pleasant memories that soldiers develop after even the ugliest of wars? Well, and if they did, they hadn't gone through them for the sake of fat cats like Mr. Edward Ballaskia and his sanctified dreams of evil.

Nor, when you came right down to it, for dismal little frightened trollops like Polly.

Frederick Stoddard Stephanson. Frederick Stoddard—

Somebody put an arm on his shoulder and he came to, realizing that he was halfway through the lobby.

"Nick," said a rather familiar voice.

Crandall squinted at the face at the end of the arm. That slight, pointed beard—he didn't know anyone with a beard like that, but the eyes looked so terribly familiar. . . .

"Nick," said the man with the beard. "I couldn't do it."

Those eyes—of course, it was his younger brother!

"Dan!" he shouted.

"It's me all right. Here." Something clattered to the floor. Crandall looked down and saw a blaster lying on the rug, a larger and much more expensive blaster than the one he was carrying. *Why was Dan toting a blaster? Who was after Dan?*

With the thought, there came half-understanding. And there was fear—fear of the words that might come pouring out of the mouth of a brother whom he had not seen for all these years . . .

"I could have killed you from the moment you walked into the lobby," Dan was saying. "You weren't out of the sights for a second. But I want you to know, Nick, that the post-criminal sentence wasn't the reason I froze on the firing button."

"No?" Crandall asked in a breath that was exhaled slowly through a retroactive lifetime.

"I just couldn't stand adding any more guilt about you. Ever since that business with Polly—"

"With Polly. Yes, of course, with Polly." Something seemed to hang like a weight from the point of his jaw; it pulled his head down and his mouth open. "With Polly. That business with Polly."

Dan punched his fist into an open palm twice. "I knew you'd come looking for me sooner or later. I almost went crazy waiting—and I did go nearly crazy with guilt. But I never figured you'd do it this way, Nick. Seven years to wait for you to come back!"

"That's why you never wrote to me, Dan?"

"What did I have to say? What *is* there to say? I thought I loved her, but I found out what I meant to her as soon as she was divorced. I guess I always wanted what was yours because you were my older brother, Nick. That's the only excuse I can offer and I know exactly what it's worth. Because I know what you and Polly had together, what I broke up as a kind of big practical joke. But one thing, Nick: I won't kill you and I won't defend myself. I'm too tired. I'm too guilty. You know where to find me. Anytime, Nick."

He turned and strode rapidly through the lobby, the metal spangles that were this year's high masculine fashion glittering on his calves. He didn't look back, even when he was walking past the other side of the clear plastic that enclosed the lobby.

Crandall watched him go, then said "Hm" to himself in a lonely kind of way. He reached down, retrieved the other blaster and went out to find a restaurant.

As he sat, poking around in the spiced Venusian food that wasn't one-tenth as good as he had remembered it, he kept thinking about Polly and Dan. The incidents—he could remember incidents galore, now that he had a couple of pegs on which to hang them. To think he'd never suspected—but who could suspect Polly, who could suspect Dan?

He pulled the prison discharge out of his pocket and studied it. *Having duly served a maximum penal sentence of seven years, discounted from fourteen years, Nicholas Crandall is herewith discharged in a pre-criminal status—*

—to murder his ex-wife, Polly Crandall?

—to murder his younger brother, Daniel Crandall?

Ridiculous!

But they hadn't found it so ridiculous. Both of them, so blissfully secure in their guilt, so egotistically certain that they and they alone were the objects of a hatred intense enough to endure the worst that the Galaxy had to offer in order to attain vengeance—why, they had both been so positive that their normal and already demonstrated cunning had deserted them and they had completely misread the warmth in his eyes! Either one could have switched confessions in mid-explanation. If they had only not been so preoccupied with self and had noted his astonishment in time, either or both of them could still be deceiving him!

Out of the corner of his eye, he saw that a woman was standing near his table. She had been reading his discharge over his shoulder. He leaned back and took her in while she stood and smiled at him.

She was fantastically beautiful. That is, she had everything a woman needs for great beauty—figure, facial structure, complexion, carriage, eyes, hair, all these to perfection—but she had those other final touches that, as in all kinds of art, make the difference between a merely great work and an all-time masterpiece. Those final touches included such things as sufficient wealth to create the ultimate setting in coiffure and gown, as well as the single Saturnian *paeaea* stone glowing in priceless black splendor between her breasts. Those final touches included the substantial feminine intelligence that beat in her steady eyes; and the somewhat overbred, overindulged, overspoiled quality mixed in with it was the very last piquant fillip of a positively brilliant composition in the human medium.

"May I sit with you, Mr. Crandall?" she asked in a voice of which no more could be said than that it fitted the rest of her.

Rather amused, but more exhilarated than amused, he slid over on the restaurant couch. She sat down like an empress taking her throne before the eyes of a hundred tributary kings.

Crandall knew, within approximate limits, who she was and what she wanted. She was either a reigning post-debutante from the highest social circles in the System, or a theatrical star newly arrived and still in a state of nova.

And he, as a just-discharged convict, with the power of life and death in his hands, represented a taste she had not yet been able to indulge but was determined to enjoy.

Well, in a sense it wasn't flattering, but a woman like this could only fall to the lot of an ordinary man in very exceptional circumstances; he might as well take advantage of his status. He would satisfy her whim, while she, on his first night of freedom—

"That's your discharge, isn't it?" she asked and looked at it again. There was a moistness about her upper lip as she studied it—what a strange, sense-weary patina for one so splendidly young!

"Tell me, Mr. Crandall," she asked at last, turning to him with the wet pinpoints on her lip more brilliant than ever. "You've served a pre-criminal sentence for murder. It is true, is it not, that the punishment for murder and the most brutal, degraded rape imaginable are exactly the same?"

After a long silence, Crandall called for his check and walked out of the restaurant.

He had subsided enough when he reached the hotel to stroll with care around the transparent lobby housing. No one who looked like a Stephanson trigger man was in sight, although Stephanson was a cautious gambler. One attempt having failed, he'd be unlikely to try another for some time.

But that girl! And Edward Ballaskia!

There was a message in his box. Someone had called, leaving only a number to be called back.

Now what? he wondered as he went back up to his room. Stephanson making overtures? Or some unhappy mother wanting him to murder her incurable child?

He gave the number to the set and sat down to watch the screen with a good deal of curiosity.

It flickered—a face took shape on it. Crandall barely restrained a cry of delight. He did have a friend in this city from pre-convict days. Good old dependable, plodding, realistic Irv. His old partner.

And then, just as he was about to shout an enthusiastic greeting, he locked it inside his mouth. Too many things had happened today. And there was something about the expression on Irv's face . . .

"Listen, Nick," Irv said heavily at last. "I just want to ask you one question."

"What's that, Irv?" Crandall kept himself rock-steady.

"How long have you known? When did you find out?"

Crandall ran through several possible answers in his mind, finally selecting one. "A long time now, Irv. I just wasn't in a position to do anything about it."

Irv nodded. "That's what I thought. Well, listen, I'm not going to plead with you. I know that after seven years of what you've gone through, pleading isn't going to do me any good. But, believe me or not, I didn't start dipping into the till very much until my wife got sick. My personal funds were exhausted. I couldn't borrow any more, and you were too busy with your own domestic troubles to be bothered. Then, when business started to get better, I wanted to prevent a sudden large discrepancy on the books.

"So I continued milking the business, not for hospital expenses any more and not to deceive you, Nick—really!—but just so you wouldn't find out how much I'd taken from it before. When you came to me and said you were completely discouraged and wanted out—well, there I'll admit I was a louse. I should have told you. But after all, we hadn't been doing too well as partners and I saw a chance to get the whole business in my name and on its feet, so I—I—"

"So you bought me out for three hundred and twenty credits," Crandall finished for him. "How much is the firm worth now, Irv?"

The other man averted his eyes. "Close to a million. But listen, Nick, business has been terrific this past year in the wholesale line. I didn't cheat you out of all that! Listen, Nick—"

Crandall blew a snort of grim amusement through his nostrils. "What is it, Irv?"

Irv drew out a clean tissue and wiped his forehead. "Nick," he said, leaning forward and trying hard to smile winningly. "Listen to me, Nick! You forget about it, you stop hunting me down, and I've got a proposition for you. I need a man with your technical know-how in top management. I'll give you a twenty per cent interest in the business, Nick—no, make it twenty-five per cent. Look, I'll go as high as thirty per cent—thirty-*five* per cent—"

"Do you think that would make up for those seven years?"

Irv waved trembling, conciliatory hands. "No, of course not, Nick. Nothing would. But listen, Nick. I'll make it forty-five per—"

Crandall shut him off. He sat for a while, then got up and walked around the room. He stopped and examined his blasters, the one he'd purchased earlier and the one he'd gotten from Dan. He took out his prison discharge and read it through carefully. Then he shoved it back into the tunic pocket.

He notified the switchboard that he wanted a long-distance Earthside call put through.

"Yes, sir. But there's a gentleman to see you, sir. A Mr. Otto Henck."

"Send him up. And put the call in on my screen as soon as it goes through, please, Miss."

A few moments later, Blotto Otto entered his room. He was drunk, but carried it, as he always did, remarkably well.

"What do you think, Nick? What the hell do you—"

"Sh-h-h," Crandall warned him. "My call's coming in."

The Tibetan operator said, "Go ahead, New York," and Frederick Stoddard Stephanson appeared on the screen. The man had aged more than any of the others Crandall had seen tonight. Although you never could tell with Stephanson: he always looked older when he was working out a complex deal.

Stephanson didn't say anything; he merely pursed his lips at Crandall and waited. Behind him and around him was a TV Spectacular's idea of a hunting lodge.

"All right, Freddy," Crandall said. "What I have to say won't take long. You might as well call off your dogs and stop taking chances trying to kill and/or injure me. As of this moment, I don't even have a grudge against you."

"You don't even have a grudge—" Stephanson regained his rigid self-control. "Why not?"

"Because—oh, because a lot of things. Because killing you just wouldn't be seven hellish years of satisfaction, now that I'm face to face with it. And because you didn't do any more to me than practically everybody else has done—from the cradle, for all I know. Because I've decided I'm a natural born sucker: that's just the way I'm constructed. All you did was take your kind of advantage of my kind of construction."

Stephanson leaned forward, peered intently, then relaxed and crossed his arms. "You're actually telling the truth!"

"Of course I'm telling the truth! You see these?" He held up the two blasters. "I'm getting rid of these tonight. From now on, I'll be unarmed. I don't want to have the least thing to do with weighing human life in the balance."

The other man ran an index nail under a thumb nail thoughtfully a couple of times. "I'll tell you what," he said. "If you mean what you say—and I think you do—maybe we can work out something. An arrangement, say, to pay you a bit—We'll see."

"When you don't have to?" Crandall was astonished. "But why didn't you make me an offer before this?"

"Because I don't like to be forced to do anything. Up to now, I was fighting force with more force."

Crandall considered the point. "I don't get it. But maybe that's the way you're constructed. Well, we'll see, as you said."

When he rose to face Henck, the little man was still shaking his head slowly, dazedly, intent only on his own problem. "What do you think, Nick? Elsa went on a sightseeing jaunt to the Moon last month. The line to her oxygen helmet got clogged, see, and she died of suffocation before they could do anything about it. Isn't that a *hell* of thing, Nick? One month before I finish my sentence—she couldn't wait one lousy little month! I bet she died laughing at me!"

Crandall put his arm around him. "Let's go out for a walk, Blotto Otto. We both need the exercise."

Funny how the capacity for murder affected people, he thought. There was Polly's way—and Dan's. There was old Irv bargaining frantically but still shrewdly for his life. Mr. Edward Ballaskia—and that girl in the restaurant. And there was Freddy Stephanson, the only intended victim—and the only one who wouldn't beg.

He wouldn't beg, but he might be willing to hand out largesse. Could Crandall accept what amounted to charity from Stephanson? He shrugged. Who knew what he or anyone else could or could not do?

"What do we do now, Nick?" Blotto Otto was demanding petulantly once they got outside the hotel. "That's what I want to know—what do we do?"

"Well, I'm going to do this," Crandall told him, taking a blaster in each hand. "Just this." He threw the gleaming weapons, right hand, left hand, at the transparent window walls that ran around the luxurious lobby of the Ritz-Capricorn. They struck *thunk* and then *thunk* again. The windows crashed down in long, pointed daggers. The people in the lobby swung around with their mouths open.

A policeman ran up, his badge jingling against his metallic uniform. He seized Crandall.

"I saw you! I saw you do that! You'll get thirty days for it!"

"Hm," said Crandall. "Thirty days?" He pulled his prison discharge out of his pocket and handed it to the policeman. "I tell you what we'll do, officer—Just punch the proper number of holes in this document or tear off what seems to you a proportionately sized coupon. Either or both. Handle it any way you like."

Lino Aldani

Translated by L. K. Conrad

Lino Aldani (1926–) is an Italian writer who is principally known for his science fiction. He is the author of a pioneering study on science fiction, *La fantascienza* (1962), the first of its kind to appear in Italy.

He began publishing SF stories in the magazine *Oltre il Cielo* in 1960, under the pseudonym of N. L. Janda. In 1963 he founded and edited, with Massimo Lo Jacono and Giulio Raiola, the magazine *Futuro*, featuring exclusively science fiction written by Italian authors. In 1964 he published his first collection, *Quarta dimensione*, and continued to sell stories to various magazines and anthologies, developing an individual style mixing traditional SF tropes and striking extrapolations with literate prose and a distinctive feel for realism. For this reason, his fiction can often be compared to that of better known Italian literary fantasists writing outside the SF genre. His situation, writing in the land of Italo Calvino and Dino Buzzati, has been analogous to the situation of, say, John Wyndham or Brian W. Aldiss publishing science fiction in the land of Aldous Huxley and George Orwell. Literary fashion seems to dictate that it matters more how and where you publish it, what class signals it gives off, than what it actually is.

Lino Aldani lived in Rome until 1968, when he decided to return to his native town. He had a variety of occupations, ranging from office worker to bartender, and later taught philosophy and mathematics in high school. He also served as mayor of his native town.

Aldani has never been a prolific writer, and only in 1977 published his first novel, *Quando le radici*. Two years later it was followed by the novella *Eclissi 2000* (included in a collection with the same title). In 1985 he published *Nel segno della luna bianca*, written in collaboration with Daniela Piegai, a skilled and enjoyable fantasy novel where his distinctive voice displays new overtones. A new collection of his short fiction appeared in 1987, *Parabole per domani*. His story "Quo Vadis Francisco?" was included in *The Penguin World Omnibus of Science Fiction* (1986), edited by Brian W. Aldiss and Sam J. Lundwall. He later developed it into his most recent novel, *La croce di ghiaccio*, published in 1989. His works have been translated worldwide and are well known in France, Germany, Russia, Japan, Spain, The Netherlands, and nearly all of Eastern Europe. He is surely the Italian SF genre writer who is best known abroad.

GOOD NIGHT, SOPHIE

Grey and blue overalls were running along the street. Grey and blue, no other colors. There were no stores, no agencies, there wasn't a single soda-fountain, or a window full of toys, or even a perfume store. Once in a while, on the fronts covered with soot, incrusted with rubbish and moss, the revolving door of a shop opened. Inside was dreamland: Oneirofilm, happiness within everybody's reach, to fit everybody's pocketbook; inside was Sophie Barlow, nude, for anyone who wanted to buy her.

There were seven of them and they were closing in from all sides. He swung violently, hitting one of them in the jaw, which sent him tumbling down the green marble staircase. Another, tall and brawny, appeared below, brandishing a bludgeon. He dodged the blow by hunching quickly, then grabbed the slave by the waist, hurling him against a column of the temple. Then, while he was trying to corner a third one, a vise of iron seized his neck. He tried to free himself, but another slave tackled his legs, and still another immobilized his left arm.

He was dragged away bodily. From the depths of the enormous cavern came the rhythmical notes of the sitars and tablas, an enervating, obsessive music, full of long quavers.

They tied him naked in front of the altar. Then the slaves fled into the galleries that opened like eye-sockets of skulls in the walls of the cavern. The air was filled with the smell of resin, a strong odor of musk and nard, and aphrodisiac atmosphere emitted by the burning torches, tripods and braziers.

When the dancing virgins appeared, the music stopped for a moment, then took up again, more intensely, accompanied by a distant choir of feminine voices.

It was an orgiastic, inebriating dance. The virgins passed by him one by one, they grazed his stomach, face and chest with their light veils and the long, soft feathers of their headdresses. Diadems and necklaces flashed in the half-light.

At the end the veils fell, slowly, one at a time. He saw the swelling of their breasts, almost felt the softness of all those limbs that were moving in front of him in a tangle of unsated desire.

Then, the long, freezing sound of a gong interrupted the dance. The music ceased. The dancers, like guilt-ridden phantoms, disappeared in the depths of the cave, and in the profound silence the priestess appeared, exceedingly beautiful, wrapped in a leopard cape. She had small bare pink feet, and between her hands clasped a long bluish knife. Her eyes, black, deep, constantly shifting, seemed to search his soul.

How long did the intolerable wait last? The knife cut his bonds with devastating slowness, her great black eyes, moist and desirous, continued to stare at him, while a jumble of words, whispering, murmuring, came to his ears in a persuasive, enticing rhythm.

She dragged him to the foot of the altar. The leopard cape slid to earth, she stretched out languidly and drew him to herself with a gesture at once sweet and imperious.

In the cavern, a conch shell of sounds and shadows, the world came and went in an ebb and flow of sighs.

Bradley turned off the machine and removed the plastic helmet. He came out of the booth, his hands and forehead damp with sweat, his breathing heavy, his pulse accelerated.

Twenty technicians, the director and the principal actress rushed to the supervisor, impatiently surrounding him. Bradley's eyes moved around, looking for an armchair.

"I want a glass of water," he said.

He stretched out gingerly on an air cushion with a long, sloping back, drying the beads of perspiration, and breathing deeply. A technician made his way through the group and handed Bradley a glass, which he emptied in one gulp.

"Well? What do you think of it?" the director asked anxiously.

Bradley waved impatiently, then shook his head.

"We're not there yet, Gustafson."

Sophie Barlow lowered her eyes. Bradley touched her hand.

"It has nothing to do with you, Sophie. You were terrific. I . . . only a great actress could have created that last embrace. But the Oneirofilm itself is artificial, unharmonious, unbalanced . . ."

"What's wrong with it?" the director asked.

"Gustafson! I said the film is *unharmonious*, don't you understand?"

"I heard you. You say it's 'unharmonious,' unbalanced. Okay, the music is Indian, four hundred years old, and the costumes are from central Africa. But the consumer isn't going to notice such subtleties, what interests him is—"

"Gustafson! The customer is always right, never forget that. Anyway, this has nothing to do with music or costumes. The problem is something else: this Oneirofilm would rattle even a bull's nerves!"

Gustafson frowned.

"Give me the script," said Bradley, "and call the aesthetic technician."

He rifled back and forth through the pages, muttering unintelligibly, as if to reconnect the ideas.

"All right," he said at last, closing the bundle of pages suddenly. "The film starts with a long canoe trip, the protagonist is alone in a hostile, strange world, there's a struggle with the river's crocodiles, and the canoe capsizes. Then we have a trek through the jungle, rather tiring, a hand-to-hand fight with the natives. The protagonist is shut up in a hut, but during the night the chieftain's daughter Aloa comes in, and provides him with directions to the temple. Then there's the embrace with Aloa in the moonlight. Speaking of which, where's Moa Mohagry?"

The technician and the director moved apart, and Moa Mohagry, a very tall Somalian woman with sculpturesque curves, stepped forward.

"You were great, Moa, but we're going to have to do the scene over again."

"Again?" Moa exclaimed. "I could do the scene over a hundred times, but I doubt it would get any better. I really gave it all I had, Bradley . . ."

"That's exactly what Gustafson's mistake was. In this Oneirofilm the major scene is the last one, when the priestess seduces the protagonist. All the other scenes are going to have to be toned down—they sould serve as atmosphere and preparation. You can't make an Oneirofilm composed of nothing but major scenes."

He turned to the aesthetic technician.

"What's the sensitivity index in the median sampling?"

"In Aloa's scene?"

"Yes, in Aloa's scene."

"84.5."

"And in the scene of the last embrace?"

"Just under 97."

Bradley shook his head.

"Theoretically it would be okay, but in practice it's all wrong. This morning I screened the scenes in the first part, one at a time. They're perfect. But the film doesn't end on the riverbank when Aloa gives herself to the protagonist. There are other, rather tiring episodes: the ones I just screened, then another trek through the jungle, and the fight with the slaves in the temple. By the time the consumer gets to this point in the film, he's exhausted, his sensory receptivity is down to a minimum. The virgins' erotic dance only partly solves the problem. I saw the film in two takes, and so I was able to appreciate the last embrace with Sophie in all its stylistic perfection. But, please, let's not mix up absolute index with relative index. The crucial thing is relative index. I'm positive that if we distributed the film the way it's put together now, the total receptivity index would fall by at least forty points, in spite of Sophie's performance."

"Bradley!" the director implored. "Now you're exaggerating."

"I'm not exaggerating," the supervisor insisted in a polemical tone. "I repeat, the last scene is a masterpiece, but the consumer gets there tired and already satisfied, in such a condition that even the most luscious fruit would taste insipid to him. Gustafson, you can't expect Sophie to accomplish miracles. The human nervous system has limits and laws."

"Then what should we do?"

"Listen to me, Gustafson. I was a director for twenty-five years, and for six years I've been a supervisor. I think I've had enough experience to give you some advice. If you leave this Oneirofilm the way it is, I won't pass it. I can't. Beyond not pleasing the public, I would risk undermining the career of an actress like Sophie Barlow. Pay attention to me, dilute all the scenes except the last, cut the embrace with Aloa, reduce it to a mere scuffle."

Moa Mohagry started angrily. Bradley took her wrist and forced her to sit on the arm of his chair.

"Listen to me, Moa. Don't think that I want to take away the right moment for you to make a big hit. You have talent, I know it. The riverbank episode shows true zeal and temperament, there's an innocent primitive passion there that would not fail to fascinate the consumer. You were fantastic, Moa. But I can't ruin a film that's cost millions, you understand, don't you? I'm going to suggest to the production committee a couple of films that will star you, Moa. There are millions and millions of consumers who go mad for Oneirofilms in a primitive setting. You'll make a big hit, too, I promise you. But not right now, it's not the right moment . . ."

Bradley got up. He felt faint, his legs weak and tired.

"Please, Gustafson. Also tone down the slaves' fight episode. Too much movement, too much violence. The waste of energy is enormous . . ."

He went tottering off, surrounded by technicians.

"Where's Sophie?" he asked as he got to the back of the room.

Sophie Barlow smiled at him.

"Come in my office," he said. "I have to talk to you."

"All right, I'm not saying anything new, they're old words, stale, you must have heard them a hundred times at school and during your training course. But it would benefit you to give them some thought."

Bradley was walking back and fourth in the room, slowly, his fingers laced together behind his back. Sophie Barlow was slouched in an armchair. From time to time she stretched out a leg and stared at the toe of her shoe.

Bradley stopped for a moment in front of her.

"What's the matter with you, Sophie? Are you having a crisis?"

The woman made a nervous, awkward gesture. "Having a crisis? Me?"

"Yes. That's why I called you into the office. You know, I don't want to read you the riot act. I simply want to remind you of the fundamental precepts of our system. I'm not young any more, Sophie. There are things I can spot right off, at the first sign. Sophie! you're running after a chimera!"

Sophie Barlow squinted and then opened her eyes wide as a cat's.

"A chimera? What's a chimera, Bradley?"

"I told you, I can spot some things right off. You're having a crisis, Sophie. I wouldn't be surprised if it had something to do with the propaganda that those pigs at the Anti-Dream League put out by the truckload to undermine our social order."

Sophie seemed not to pick up the insinuation. She said:

"Was Moa's performance really that good?"

Bradley passed a hand behind his neck. "Absolutely. Mohagry will make it big, I'm convinced of it . . ."

"Better than mine?"

Bradley snorted. "That's a meaningless question."

"I made myself clear. I want to know which of us you liked better, me or Moa."

"And I repeat, your question is idiotic, lacks common sense, and just goes to confirm my suspicion—in fact, my conviction—that you're going through a crisis. You'll get over it, Sophie. All actresses go through this phase sooner or later. It seems to be a necessary stage . . ."

"I would like to know just one thing, Bradley. Something that's never said in the schools, something nobody ever talks about. *Before.* What was there before? Was everybody really unhappy?"

Bradley took up pacing around the armchair.

"Before, there was chaos."

"Bradley! I want to know if they were really unhappy."

The man stretched out his arms disconsolately.

"I don't know, Sophie. I didn't exist at the time, I wasn't born yet. One thing is sure: if the system has asserted itself, it means that objective conditions have allowed it to do so. I would like you to be aware of one very simple fact: technology has permitted the realization of all our desires, even the most secret ones. Technology, progress, the perfection of instruments and the exact knowledge of our own minds, of our own egos . . . all of that is real, tangible. Hence even our dreams are real. Sophie, don't forget that only in very rare cases is the Oneirofilm an instrument of comfort or compensation. Almost always it is an end in itself, and when just now I had you, I enjoyed your body, your words, and your odors amid a play of exotic emotions."

"Yes, but it's always artificial . . ."

"Okay, but I wasn't aware of it. And then, even the meaning of words evolves. You use the word *artificial* in the pejorative sense it had two centuries ago. But not today, today an artificial product is no longer a surrogate, Sophie. A fluorescent lamp, correctly adjusted, gives better light than the sun. This is true of the Oneirofilm as well."

Sophie Barlow looked at her fingernails.

"When did it begin, Bradley?"

"What?"

"The system."

"Eighty-five years it's been now, as you should know."

"I do, but I mean the *dreams.* When did men begin to prefer them to reality?"

Bradley squeezed his nose, as if to collect his thoughts.

"Cinematography began to develop at the beginning of the twentieth century.

At first it was a question of two-dimensional images moving on a white screen. Then, sound, the panoramic screen, color photography were introduced. The consumers gathered by the hundreds in special projection halls to watch and listen, but they never *felt* the film, at most they experienced a latent participation through an effort of fantasy. Obviously the film was a surrogate, a real and proper artifice for titillating the erotic and adventurous taste of the public. However, movie-making then represented a very powerful instrument of psycho-social transformation. Women of that period felt the need of imitating actresses in their gestures, vocal inflections, dress. This was no less true of men. Life was lived according to the movies. First the economy was conditioned by it: the enormous demand for consumer goods—clothes, cars, comfortable housing—was of course due to real exigencies of nature, but also and above all to the ruthless, indefatigable advertising that harassed and seduced the consumer every minute of the day. Even then, men longed for the dream, were obsessed by it, day and night, but they were far from achieving it."

"They were unhappy, right?"

"I repeat, I don't know. I'm only trying to illustrate for you the stages of the process. Toward the middle of the twentieth century the standard woman, the standard situation was already in existence. It's true that there were directors and producers in those days that tried to produce cultural films, ideological movies, to communicate ideas and elevate the masses. But the phenomenon lasted only a short time. In 1956 scientists discovered the pleasure centers in the brain, and through experimentation revealed that electric stimulation of a certain part of the cortex produces an intense, voluptuous reaction in the subject. It was twenty years before the benefits of this discovery were made available to the public. The projection of the first three-dimensional movie with partial spectator participation signalled the death of the intellectual film. Now the public could experience odors and emotions; they could already partly identify with what was happening on the screen. The entire economy underwent an unprecedented transformation. The human race was starved for pleasure, luxury and power, and only asked to be satisfied at the cost of a few pennies."

"And the Oneirofilm?"

"The Oneirofilm came out, fully perfected, only a few years later. There's no reality that surpasses dreams, and the public became convinced of this very quickly. When participation is total, any competition from nature is ridiculous, any rebellion useless. If the product is perfect, the consumer is happy and the society is stable. That's the system, Sophie. And certainly your temporary crises are not likely to change it, not even the melodramatic chatter of the Naturists, unscrupulous people who go around collecting funds for the triumph of an idea that is unbalanced to start with, but for their own personal profit. If you want a good laugh—last week Herman Wolfried, one of the leaders of the Anti-Dream League, appeared in the offices of the Norfolk Company. And do you want to know why? He wanted a private Oneirofilm, five famous actresses in a mind-blowing orgy. Norfolk has accepted the commission and Wolfried is paying for it through the nose, so much the worse for him."

Sophie Barlow jumped up.

"You're lying, Bradley! You're lying on purpose, shamelessly."

"I have proof, Sophie. The Anti-Dream League is an organization out to dupe simpletons, incurable hypochondriacs and passéists. Perhaps there is some remnant of religious sentiment behind it, but at the center of it is only greed."

Sophie was on the verge of tears. Bradley moved toward her solicitously and put his hands on her shoulders in a tender, protective gesture.

"Don't think about it any more, Sophie."

He guided her over to the desk, opened the safe, and got out a small, flat, rectangular box.

"Here," said Bradley.

"What is it?"

"A present."

"For me?"

"Yes, actually it was to give you this that I called you into the office. You've made twenty Oneirofilms for our production company, an inspiring goal, as it were. The firm is honoring you with a small recognition of your worth . . ."

Sophie started to unwrap the present.

"Leave it," Bradley said. "You can open it at home. Run along now, I have a lot to do."

There was a line of helitaxis just outside the building. Sophie got into the first one, took a magazine from the side pocket of the vehicle, lit a cigarette and, flattered, contemplated her own face on the front cover. The helitaxi rose softly, steering for the center of the city.

Her lips were half-open in an attitude of offering, the color, the contrast between light and shadow, the expression ambiguous . . . Each detail seemed knowingly graded.

Sophie looked at herself as if in a mirror. At one time the job of acting had presented various negative aspects. When she made a love scene, there was a flesh and blood "partner," and she had to embrace him, tolerate the physical contact, kisses, words breathed straight into her face. The camera photographed the scene which the spectators then later saw on the screen. Now it was different. There was "Adam," the mannequin packed with electronic devices having two minute cameras conveniently placed in his eyes. "Adam" was a wonder of receptivity: if the actress caressed him, the receptivity valve registered the sensation of the caress and fixed it, together with the visual image, on the reel of Oneirofilm. Thus the consumer who would later use that reel would perceive the caress in all its sensory fidelity. The spectator was no longer passive but the protagonist.

Naturally, there were Oneirofilms for men and Oneirofilms for women. And they were not interchangeable: if a male consumer, plagued by morbid curiosity, inserted in his reception helmet a reel meant for female consumption, he would get an atrocious headache, and also risk short-circuiting the delicate wiring of the apparatus.

Sophie told the pilot to stop. The helitaxi had gone barely a dozen blocks, but Sophie decided to proceed on foot.

Grey and blue overalls were running along the street. Grey and blue, no other colors. There were no stores, no agencies, there wasn't a single soda-fountain, or a window full of toys, or even a perfume store. Once in a while, on the fronts covered with soot, incrusted with rubbish and moss, the revolving door of a shop opened. Inside, on the smooth glass counters, there was the *dream*, happiness for everybody, for all pocketbooks, and it was Sophie herself, nude, for anybody who wanted to have her.

They marched on. And Sophie Barlow marched along with them, an army of hallucinated people, people who worked three hours a day, prey to the spasms that the silence of their own shells yearned for: a room, an Amplex and a helmet. And reel after reel of Oneirofilms, millions of dreams of love, power and fame.

In the middle of the square, on a large platform draped in green, the fat man was gesticulating emphatically.

"Citizens!"

His voice raised itself as loud and clear as a dream speech, when the dreamer has the whole world singing hosannas at his feet.

"Citizens! An ancient philosopher once said that virtue is a habit. I am not here to ask the impossible of you. I would be a fool if I expected to renounce it immediately and completely. For years we have been slaves and succubuses, prisoners in the labyrinth of dreams, for years we have been groping in the dense darkness of uncommunicativeness and isolation. Citizens, I invite you to be free. Freedom is virtue, and virtue is a habit. We have cheated nature too long, we must rush to make amends, before we arrive at a total and definite death of the soul . . ."

How many times had she listened to speeches like that? The propaganda of the Anti-Dream League was sickening, it had always produced in her a profound sense of irritation. Lately, however, she had surprised and bewildered herself. Perhaps because she was an actress, when the orators in the squares spoke of sin, perdition, when they incited the crowds of consumers to abandon the "dream," she took the accusation as if it had been personally aimed at her; she felt a responsibility for the whole system. Perhaps behind the orators' emphatic tone there actually was some truth. Perhaps they hadn't told her everything at school. Maybe Bradley was wrong.

On the platform the fat man ranted and raved, pounding his fist on the wood of the lectern, red in the face, congested. Not a soul was listening to him.

When the veiled girl came out of a small side door, there were some in the crowd who stopped for a second. From the loudspeakers issued the sound of ancient oriental music. The girl began to take off her veils, dancing. She was pretty, very young, and made syncopated, light, eurhythmic gestures.

"An amateur," Sophie said to herself. "A would-be actress . . ."

When she was standing naked in the center of the platform, even the few men who had stopped to wait moved on. One or two of them laughed, and shook their heads, disappointed.

The Anti-Dream League girls stopped the passers-by, they approached the men, thrusting out their breasts in an absurd, pathetic offer.

Sophie lengthened her stride. But someone stopped her, grabbing her arm. It was a tall, dark young man, who stared at her with steady black eyes.

"What do you want?"

"To make you a proposition."

"Speak up."

"Come with me, tonight."

Sophie burst out laughing.

"With you! What for? What would I get out of it?"

The young man smiled faintly, patiently, a smile tinged with security and superiority. Clearly he was accustomed to this sort of refusal.

"Nothing," he admitted unperturbed. "But our duty is to—"

"Cut it out. We'd spend the night insulting each other, in a pitiful attempt to achieve 'natural harmony' . . . Dear boy, your friend up there on the platform is spewing forth a pile of nonsense."

"It's not nonsense," the young man retorted. "Virtue is a habit. I could—"

"No, you couldn't. You couldn't because you don't want me, and you don't want me because I'm real, true, living, human, because I would be a surrogate, a substitute for a reel of Oneirofilm which you could buy for a few pennies. And you? What could you offer me? Silly presumptuous young ass!"

"Wait! Listen to me, I beg of you—"

"Goodbye," Sophie cut him short. And continued her walk.

The words she aimed at the young man had been too harsh. It had been a uselessly hostile reaction; she might have rejected his proposition neither more nor less vehemently than the other passers-by did, with some grace, or better, with a self-sufficient smile. In the last analysis, what right did she have to insult him, perhaps to hurt his feelings? He was acting in good faith. But what about the leaders? Bradley had assured her a number of times that the directors of the Anti-Dream League were a band of swine. What if Bradley had been lying to her all along?

The suspicion had now been plaguing her for several weeks. All those speeches in the squares, the manifestos on the walks, the propagandistic pamphlets, the public proposition to experiment in natural relations with the League's activists . . . Was it possible that the whole thing was a lie? Perhaps there was some truth in what the orators and lecturers maintained, maybe the world was rotten to the core, and only a few enlightened men had eyes to see the horror and to assess such decadence.

Man as an island: they had all been reduced to this. On one side the producing class, a class that kept power and to which she herself belonged in her capacity of actress; on the other, the prostrate, blind army of consumers, men and women avid for solitude and darkness, silkworms coiled up in the silken filaments of their own dreams, pale bloodless larvae poisoned by inaction.

Sophie had been born in the glass. So had everybody else, for that matter. She did not know her mother. Millions of women, once a month, went to the Bank of Life; millions of men achieved orgasm by means of the Dream and donated semen to the Bank, which sorted it carefully and used it according to rigorous criteria. Marriage was an archaic institution. Sophie had been the child of a dream, of an unknown, anonymous man who in a dream had possessed an actress. Every man over forty could be her father, every woman between the age of forty and eighty her mother.

When she was younger, this thought had disturbed her greatly, then bit by bit she had got used to it. But lately all the doubts and anxieties of her adolescence had reared up again, vultures that patiently circled above, waiting for one of her moments of weakness. Who was that young man who had stopped her on the street? A champion of superior humanity, or a fool?

Certainly, if he had said to her, "I recognize you, Sophie Barlow. I recognize you in spite of your standard suit and your dark glasses." Or if he had said, "You're my favorite star, you're the obsession of all my days . . ." Or even if he'd said, "I want to get to know you, whoever you are, just as you really are . . ."

Instead, that lout had talked about duty. He had asked her to spend the night with him, but only to pay obeisance to the presumptuous new morality: Virtue is a habit. A habit, a routine of natural relations. Love one another, ladies and gentlemen, come together in self-denial! Each of your acts of love will contribute to the defeat and destruction of an unjust system. Unite yourselves, come together in reality, the sublime joy of the senses will not delay in manifesting itself! An exultation of sounds and lights will fill your souls, will glorify your bodies! And our children will once again be formed in the warmth of the womb, not in the cold glass of a test tube.—Wasn't this what the fat man on the platform had been preaching?

She went into a crowded store and made her way over to the sales counter, where hundreds and hundreds of Oneirofilms were neatly displayed, packed in elegant plastic boxes. She loved to read the descriptions printed on the covers, to listen to the conversations that the shoppers sometimes had with each other, or the zealous advice that the salesmen whispered in the ears of undecided customers.

She read a few titles.

Singapore: Eurasian singer (Milena Chung Lin) flees with the Spectator. Adventure in the underworld of this eastern port. Period, mid twentieth century. Night of love on a sampan.
The Battle: In the role of a heroic officer, the Spectator infiltrates an enemy encampment and sabotages its munitions dump. A last battle, bloody, victorious.
Ecstasy: The private jet of a Persian princess (masterful performance by Sophie Barlow) crashes in the Grand Canyon. Princess and Pilot (the Spectator) spend the night in a cave.

Descriptions in greater detail were to be found inside the boxes. There was no danger that an exact knowledge of the contents on the part of the consumer would lower its desirability index. Mental projection inside the Amplex was accompanied by catatonic stupor in which the memory of each independent episode never connected with the next to form a whole. One could not know, experiencing the first episode, what would happen in the second and following episodes. Even if plot descriptions were learned by heart, even if one saw the same film twenty times, the conscious ego, the everyday ego was sacrificed to the urges provoked by the reel: one ceased to be oneself in order to assume the personality, the mannerisms, the voice, the impulses suggested by the film.

A salesman sidled up to her solicitously.

"May I help you to choose a gift?"

Sophie suddenly noticed that among the mob of buyers there were no other women. This was the men's department. She moved off toward the opposite counter, mingling with women of all ages, lingering before the enormous photographs of the most popular actors.

Outer Space Belongs to Us: Commander of a spaceship (Alex Morrison) falls in love with the lady doctor on board (the Spectator), the rocket changes course to discharge the crew on one of Jupiter's moons, and the Commander heads off with his lover. Trans-galactic crossing.
Tortuga: Period, mid seventeenth century. Gallant pirate (Manuel Alvarez) abducts noblewoman (the Spectator). Jealousy and duels. Love and sea voyages under a fiery sky.

"What's it like?" asked a tall girl, her buxom body suffocating in a pair of overalls too small for her.

"Fascinating," her companion asserted. "I bought four more copies of it right away."

The other girl looked skeptical. She stretched her neck over the counter, stood on the tips of her toes to read the descriptions on the farthestmost boxes. She said something in a low voice, and her companion answered in a whisper. Sophie moved off. She spent a few minutes in the "classics" section, giving a fleeting glance to the back of the shop where men and women crowded together to buy the so-called "convenience" Oneirofilms.

When she had been younger, at school, they had told her that in former times men considered taboo anything that had to do with sex. It was highly improper to write or talk about the many aspects of love life. No woman would ever have described her desires and her sexual fantasies to a stranger. There were pornographic publications and photographs, many of which were illegal. People who bought them did it on the sly and always with a feeling of guilt or embarrassment, even when they had been passed by the Censor. But with the advent of the "system" the primitive custom of sexual modesty had become obsolete. Modesty existed, if at all, in some kinds of dreams, in "convenience" films made for the over-fifty set, where the consumer seduced or raped a teary, red-faced, trembling young girl. But in real life it had disappeared, or at least verbal modesty had. Without a shadow of embarrassment or discomfort, anybody could ask for an erotic film, the same as any other film about war or adventure.

But what about real and proper modesty? Among the many who crowded round the counters to buy the luxury in a box, who would have had the courage to disrobe in the middle of the mob? Only those activists of the Anti-Dream League, who were completely unselfconscious when they propositioned people, but perhaps not quite so unselfconscious when faced with performing what they themselves considered a weighty duty. The truth was, for nearly a century men and women had lived in a state of almost complete chastity. Solitude, the measured penumbra inside the narrow walls of their habitations, the armchairs with built-in Amplex: humanity had no desire for anything else. Faced with the greater attractions of dreams, the ambition to own a comfortable house, elegant clothes, a helicar, and other amenities had simply gone by the boards. Why beat one's brains out collecting real objects when, with an Oneirofilm that cost but a few pennies, one could live like a nabob for an hour, near stupendous women, admired, respected, served hand and foot?

Eight billion human beings vegetated inside squalid beehives, isolated in mean little holes, nourished by vitamin concentrates and soybean meal. And they felt no desire to consume anything real. After the bottom fell out of the market, the industries producing consumer goods had been abandoned all at once by financiers, who transferred their funds to companies producing Oneirofilms, the only merchandise for which there was any real demand.

She looked up toward the shining chart, and was disgusted at herself. The numbers spoke clearly. The sales chart was most eloquent. Her own Oneirofilms were the ones most in demand, more than everybody else's put together.

Sophie left the store. She walked homeward, her head bent, her step slow and listless. She didn't know how to judge that crowd of men who moved all around her, without recognizing her. Were they her slaves, or was she theirs?

The videophone rang: a streak of light in an abyss of black velvet, a peal from lofty cathedral spires in a sleepy, gray dawn.

Sophie stretched out a hand toward the pulsator-button.

A red snake zig-zagged onto the screen, lingered, seemed to explode; finally it resolved itself into Bradley's image.

"What do you want?" Sophie whined, her voice slurred with sleep. "For God's sake, what time is it?"

"It's noon. Wake up, my girl. You have to go to San Francisco."

"To San Francisco? What for? Are you out of your mind?"

"We have a co-production contract with Norfolk, Sophie. It was set for next Monday, but time presses. They need you now."

"But I'm still in bed, I'm deathly tired. I'll leave tomorrow, Bradley."

"Get dressed," the supervisor barked. "A Norfolk jet will be waiting for you at the West airport. Don't waste time."

Sophie was fuming. This extra work wasn't scheduled. What she wanted to do was spend the rest of the day in bed, resting.

She struggled out from under the covers, her eyes still shut, and sluggishly, halfheartedly undressed in the bathroom. The metallic jet of the cold shower made her shiver. She dried herself, dressed hurriedly, and left the house on the run.

She knew the methods of those types at Norfolk. They were worse than Bradley, real nitpickers. Always ready to find fault even with the scenes that had come off well.

In eight minutes, the helitaxi deposited her at the entrance to the airport. She entered by the door that led to the runway for private aircraft, and looked round for the Norfolk jet.

The pilot emerged from an outbuilding and walked over to meet her with a bouncy step.

"Sophie Barlow?"

He was tall, with light blond hair and a bronze complexion, a face that looked as if it had been baked in an oven.

"I'm Mirko Glikorich, from the Norfolk Company."

Sophie said nothing. The pilot did not think her worth a glance, and spoke staring at an indefinite point somewhere out in the airfield, two cold, aggressive eyes of a fine gray color like anthracite. He took Sophie's suitcase and marched off toward the main runway, where the Norfolk jet was being prepared for takeoff. Sophie had a hard time keeping up with him.

"Hey!" she exclaimed, balking like a thoroughbred. "I'm not a runner. Couldn't you walk a little slower?"

The pilot kept moving, without so much as turning around.

"We're late," he said curtly. "We have to be in San Francisco in three hours."

She was breathless by the time they reached the aircraft.

"Do you mind if I sit in front with you?" asked Sophie.

The pilot shrugged his shoulders. He helped her up, settled himself into the cockpit, and waited for the signal from the control tower.

Sophie looked around, full of curiosity, a bit intimidated by all the dials and switches on the instrument panel. The pilot whistled softly, impatient. Sophie groped around in the pocket of her seat and pulled out a dozen magazines. They were all at least several weeks old, some from the year before, dog-eared. Her face was on the cover of each of them. There was also an Oneirofilm catalogue folded open to the page that listed the films starring Sophie.

"Are these your things?"

The pilot didn't answer, but looked stiffly ahead. The takeoff had been gentle as a feather, and Sophie hadn't felt it at all. She glanced out the window and barely stifled an "Oh!" of surprise. A sea of houses extended itself beneath them; like a downy eyelid, the gray shell of the countryside opened up before them.

"Are these yours?" Sophie insisted.

The pilot turned his head slightly, an imperceptible movement, a lightning glance. Then he stiffened again.

"Yes," he said through his teeth.

She tried to hide the intimate gratification that always pervaded her when she met one of her ardent fans.

"What did you say your name was?"

"Glikorich," the pilot growled. "Mirko Glikorich."

"That's a Russian name, isn't it?"

"Yugoslav."

She watched him for a while. His lips were narrow and taut, his profile straight and sharp . . . Mirko looked as if he had been chiseled in rock, mute, motionless. Sophie grew impatient.

"Can I ask you a question?"

"Speak."

"Before—at the airport. You came to meet me and asked me if I was Sophie Barlow. Why? You know me, don't you? These magazines and the catalogue. I'll bet you're a fan of mine. Why did you pretend not to recognize me?"

"I didn't pretend. It's different, seeing you in person. In the end I recognized you because I knew you were supposed to turn up at that entrance at the airport. But in the middle of the crowd, no; you could have passed me without my noticing."

Sophie lit a cigarette. Maybe the pilot was right: in the crowd nobody would notice her, even without her dark glasses. She felt a kind of dull anger toward the man beside her. But she kept making an effort to talk to him. Mirko proved to be dense as a jungle, impenetrable, diffident.

"Why don't you turn on the automatic pilot?" Sophie asked. "I'm bored, Mirko. Say something to me."

The pilot remained impassive. He blinked once or twice, and stuck out his chin.

Sophie caught his arm. "Mirko! Pay attention to me! Turn on the automatic pilot and have a cigarette with me."

"I prefer to leave it on manual."

Sophie lit another cigarette, then another, using the butt of the second. She leafed through a magazine, worrying the pages in a fit of uncontrollable nervousness. She started to sing to herself, tapping her foot against the rubber lining of the cockpit. She snorted, fidgeting, and finally pretended to feel nauseated.

Mirko felt around inside the pocket of his flying suit and handed her a tablet.

Sophie was furious.

"Idiot!" she cried. "I won't stay here a moment longer. I'm going back in the cabin."

The little living room behind the cockpit was attractive. There was a couch, a stowable berth, a little table and a bar.

She poured herself a drink, a tall glass of brandy, which she gulped down at once. She poured herself another immediately, and the edges of objects began to vibrate in a bluish, inviting fog. She lowered herself to the couch, thinking of Mirko, a consumer like all the rest, an imbecile. She couldn't wait to get to San Francisco, make the film, and fly back to New York.

Now she sipped the brandy with less gusto. As she set the glass on the table, she began to feel groggy.

Suddenly, the arm of the couch was shoved against her, and an abyss seemed to open beneath, as when an elevator begins to move. She watched the glass start to slide along the tabletop, spill on the rug . . . Then, a pain in her shoulder, her forehead knocked against something . . . Fog. Red and blue globes. Roaring of motors gone wild.

"Mirko!" she cried, raising herself. The door to the cockpit seemed bolted shut. She squeezed the hostile handle and, lurching, tried to pull the door open. An emptiness inside her chest, a moment of balance, then the absurd feeling of weightlessness. She saw Mirko's back, his hands tense on the throttle, the clouds racing towards them like dream vapors.

Now Mirko was talking. In fact, he was shouting, but she wasn't aware of it. She pressed herself against the back of her seat, clenched her teeth and braced herself for the crash.

The aircraft plummeted like a corkscrew.

When she opened her eyes next, she saw a white cloud in the middle of the sky. A vulture circled far up. She was lying stretched out on her back, and something moist and fresh was pressed against her brow. She raised an arm, touched her face, temples, and removed the handkerchief soaked with water. Then she rolled over on her side.

Mirko was on his feet, over by the wrecked fuselage. Behind him, a cyclopean wall of red rock rose over the landscape.

"What happened?" she asked weakly.

The pilot stretched out his arms. "I don't know," he said, shaking his head. "I can't understand it. All of a sudden the controls weren't responding, the craft lost altitude, and then we were in a tailspin. I managed to regain control by a miracle, but it was too late. Look at the skid we took before we banged up against this rock!"

Sophie pulled herself up, rubbing her bruised shoulder.

"Do you have any idea where we are?"

Mirko lowered his eyes.

"This is the Grand Canyon," he said. "We're in one of the side chasms. This is one of the most inaccessible areas, but the Bright Angel Trail shouldn't be too far away . . ."

Sophie's eyes widened. "The Grand Canyon?"

For a moment she was speechless. Then she burst out laughing.

"The Grand Canyon!" she repeated. "That's very funny! In fact it's unbelievable."

"What's unbelievable?"

"Don't play dumb, Mirko. The engine failure, the forced landing, here, right in the middle of the Grand Canyon . . . Just like the film I made last year, *Ecstasy*. You do remember it, don't you?"

Suddenly a suspicion crossed her mind.

"Tell me something," she said, frowning. "You didn't by any chance do it on purpose, did you? I mean, there are an awful lot of coincidences here. You're a real pilot, and I may not be a Persian princess but on the other hand I am Sophie Barlow. You wanted to get marooned out here with me, didn't you? You planned it to happen just like the film."

Mirko puffed up indignantly. He turned his back on her and went over to the aircraft. Shifting aside the twisted pieces of fuselage, he managed to crawl into the cabin. He tossed out a pile of equipment, two blankets, two back-packs, a plastic canteen, a tin of synthetic food, a flashlight. He emerged from the wreck with the bottle of brandy in one hand and a heavy piece of equipment in the other.

"Let's go," he said. "Carry as much of this as you can."

"Go where?"

"Surely you don't want to rot out here among the rocks. We have to get to the main canyon. Phantom Ranch must be more than fifty miles east of here, but there's always some stupid sentimental tourist who will come west to take a picture of the pretty view."

"Did you try radioing?"

"The radio's broken. Get a move on. Take what you need and let's get out of here."

He moved fast, his stride long and springy. He had tucked the brandy bottle into his hip pocket, and he marched along stooping slightly under the burden of his pack, in which he had placed a battery and the heavy electronic device.

Sophie stumbled along behind him, carrying the food and water containers.

Half an hour later, they came to a halt. Sophie was out of breath, her eyes were pleading. Mirko stared straight ahead. It was clear that the woman was a hindrance to him, the classical ball and chain which he could not get rid of.

"Walk slower, Mirko."

The man looked at the sky, which was filling up with menacing clouds.

"Let's go," he said. "In a couple of hours it's going to be pitch black."

When they reached the main canyon, they could hardly see anything. Mirko pointed up at a place in the rocky wall, red and brown as a piece of burning paper.

"The cave," he said reverently.

"The cave," Sophie repeated. "Just like in the film. Everything is just like in the film, Mirko."

He helped her up the cliff, and lowered his pack to the floor of the black hole that opened into the rock.

She watched him as he clambered down the sandstone and granite crags, rooting out the dried-up shrubs, making big bundles of them and dragging them up to the cave entrance. "It'll be cold in a while," he said. "We'll have to start a fire."

He lit the flashlight and inspected the cave. It was about fifteen yards deep, and bent at right angles in the middle. He set the bundle of kindling right in the elbow of the cave, and lit the fire with savage delight.

They ate in silence, in the dark and glowing cave, under an enormous fluttering bat's wing.

"I opened your pack," Sophie said. "While you were down gathering kindling. I saw what you have inside there. An Amplex! What did you need to bring that along for?"

"It's worth 120 coupons," Mirko said. "For an actress like you, that's a pittance. But it takes me three months to earn that much, you see?"

He picked up the metal box and the reel case.

"Well?" Sophie asked, curious. "What are you up to now?"

"I'm going to the rear of the cave. I have a right to my privacy, don't I?"

"Yes, but what do you need the Amplex for? What are you up to, Mirko?"

The man snorted. When Sophie grabbed the reel case, he didn't put up a fight. Passive, he let the woman go through his reels at her leisure, let her read the descriptions printed on the plastic boxes.

"But these are all my films, Mirko! My heavens, you have every single one of them! *Blue Skies*, *Seduction*, *Adventure in Ceylon*. There's even a matrix, the matrix for *Ecstasy*. Is that your favorite Oneirofilm, Mirko?"

Mirko lowered his eyes without answering. Sophie closed the reel box. A matrix was a luxury relatively few people could permit themselves. The ordinary Oneirofilm, once viewed, was useless, because the Amplex demagnetized the tape as it ran through. But a matrix lasted forever, it was practically indestructible. For that reason, it cost a small fortune.

"When did you buy it?" Sophie asked.

The man shrugged, annoyed. "Oh, quit it," he snapped. "You're too curious. What do you want me to say? Your films sell millions of copies to millions and millions of consumers. I'm just one of them. I bought a matrix of *Ecstasy*. So what? What's so strange about that? There was something about it that I liked. I—"

"Go on," Sophie urged, squeezing his arm.

"A day doesn't pass that I don't watch it," the pilot said tartly. "So now why don't you leave me alone, go to sleep, because in a little while it will be daylight and we have to cover quite a few miles. I'm going to the back of the cave."

"With the Amplex?"

"Yes, for God's sake. What's it to you? I want to enjoy my film in peace."

Sophie gulped. A sudden feeling of frustration passed through her, as if all desire to live had left her. This is impossible, she thought. This can't be happening to me. What do I want, anyway, from this man who has a thousand reasons not to care a hoot about me?

She felt a desire to hurt him, to heap abuse on his head, to slap his face. But the image of Mirko embracing her broke through her inhibitions and spread through her mind.

"I'm here," she was surprised to hear herself say in a seductive tone.

Mirko wheeled round.

"What did you say?"

"I said, I'm here, Mirko. Tonight you don't need that reel."

"I don't need it?"

"No. You can have me, just like in the dream. Even better than in the dream . . ."

Mirko started to snicker. "It's not the same thing," he said. "And don't be ridiculous with this Anti-Dream League propaganda of yours. Who are you trying to kid, anyway?"

"I'll say it again: Mirko, you can have *me*."

"And I still say it's not the same thing."

"Mirko!" the woman pleaded, beside herself. "You need me, every day you run through that matrix, and you dream, dream, you keep on dreaming of this cave, the firelight, my kisses, this body of mine which I've just offered you. This is exactly like the film, you stupid fool. What are you waiting for? I can do everything that's in that film, even more, and it will be for real . . ."

For a moment Mirko wavered, then he shook his head. He turned and moved off toward the back of the cave.

"Mirko!" she cried, exasperated. "I am Sophie Barlow! Sophie Barlow, don't you understand?"

She pulled down the zipper of her overalls. Her shoulders shrugged out of the cloth shell, and she quickly pulled off the suit and threw it on the ground.

"Look at me!" she shouted. And as he turned around, she uncovered her breasts.

The fire burned brightly, red and green tongues lapping upward, emitting a penetrating odor of the primeval jungle. She watched the man's hands clench into fists, his lips trembling, as if in a long, wearisome struggle.

Mirko hesitated a moment longer, then threw the matrix in the fire and ran toward her.

First the blue light came and then the red. Then blue again. When the reel came to an end, the set turned off automatically.

Sophie lifted off the Amplex helmet. Her temples were perspiring, her heart pounding in spasms. All her extremities were trembling, particularly her hands. She couldn't keep them still. Never in her life had she lived a "dream" with such intensity, an Oneirofilm that forced her to be herself. She must thank Bradley right way.

She rang him up on the videophone. But faced with the image of the supervisor, the words stuck in her throat; she stammered, truly moved. Finally she started to cry.

Bradley waited patiently.

"A little present, Sophie. Just a trinket. When an actress reaches the peak of her career she deserves far greater rewards. And you will have them, Sophie. You will have all the recognition that's due you. Because the system is perfect. There's no going back."

"Yes, Bradley. I—"

"It will go away, Sophie. It happens to all actresses sooner or later. The last obstacle to overcome is always vanity. Even you felt that a man ought to prefer you to a dream. You fell into the most dangerous of all heresies, but we caught it in time and rushed to correct it. With a little gift. That matrix will help you to get over this crisis."

"Yes, Bradley. Please thank everybody for me, the machinist, the technicians, the director, everybody who was involved in making this Oneirofilm. Above all, thank the actor who played the pilot."

"He's a new fellow. A real live wire, no?"

"Well, thank him for me. I had some beautiful moments. And thank you too, Bradley. I can imagine how much time and money this film cost you. It's perfect. I'll keep it in the slot of honor in my Oneirofilm collection."

"Nonsense, Sophie. You belong to the ruling class. You can allow yourself a personal Oneirofilm from time to time. We have always helped each other out, haven't we?—But there's one thing I want you to bear in mind."

"What's that, Bradley?"

"That matrix. That's more than a gift. It's meant to be a warning."

"Okay, Bradley. I get your point."

"Don't forget it. Nothing is better than dreaming. And only in dreams can you deceive yourself to the contrary. I'm sure that after five or six viewings you will get the point and toss that matrix in the wastebasket."

She nodded, in tears.

"I'll see you tomorrow at nine in the screening room."

"Yes, Bradley, tomorrow at nine in the screening room. Good night, Bradley."

"Good night, Sophie."

James Morrow

James Morrow (1947–) is one of the leading literary satirists today, who chooses to work in the science fiction and fantasy mode. He is particularly notable for his willingness to take on large intellectual and metaphysical challenges, and for his accomplished prose style. He has often, and with some justice, been compared to Kurt Vonnegut, Jr. He is a moralist and an allegorist. He has never been comfortable with the conventions and literary habits of the SF field, and occasionally breaks them, sometimes to good effect. *The Encyclopedia of Science Fiction* says Morrow "has great difficulty giving credence to the artifices of fiction. This may be the price paid for passion and clarity of mind; and it may be a price worth paying." His major novels include *Only Begotten Daughter* (1990), in which God's daughter is born in New Jersey in the closing years of this century. *Towing Jehovah* (1994), in which God is dead and his corpse, about the size of a small city, is found floating in the Atlantic Ocean and must be towed to the Antarctic to be preserved; and its sequel, *Blameless in Abaddon* (1996), in which the corpse is sold.

"Veritas" is a satirical utopia. Kathryn Cramer, in "Sincerity and Doom," her long essay on Morrow and science fiction, says, "Beyond defrocking utopia, the story hits you in the face with the uncomfortable relationship between Art (particularly fiction) and the Lie." She also suggests that this story may be in opposition to Orson Scott Card's popular Ender series of SF novels, which aspire to a utopia in which everyone tells the truth. Morrow address the question: Will the truth set you free?

VERITAS

Pigs have wings. . . .

Rats chase cats. . . .

Snow is hot. . . .

Even now the old lies ring through the charred interior of my skull. I cannot speak them. I shall never be able to speak them—not without being dropped from here to hell in a bucket of pain. But they still inhabit me, just as they did on that momentous day when the city began to fall.

Grass is purple. . . .

Two and two make five. . . .

I awoke aggressively that morning, tearing the blankets away as if they were all that stood between myself and total alertness. Yawning vigorously, I charged into the shower, where warm water poured forth the instant the sensors detected me. I'd been with Overt Intelligence for over five years, and this was the first time I'd drawn an assignment that might be termed a plum. Spread your nostrils, Orville. Sniff her out. Sherry Urquist: some name! It sounded more like a mixed drink than like what she allegedly was, a purveyor of falsehoods, an enemy of the city, a member of the Dissemblage. The day could not begin soon enough.

The Dissemblage was like a deity. Not much tangible evidence, but people still had faith in it. Veritas, they reasoned, must harbor its normal share of those who believe the status quo is ipso facto wrong. Paradise will have its dissidents. The real question was not, Do subversives live in our city? The real question was, How do they tell lies without going mad?

My in-shower cablevision receiver winked on. Grimacing under the studio lights, our Assistant Secretary of Imperialism discussed Veritas's growing involvement in the Lethean civil war. "So far, over four thousand of our soldiers have died," the interviewer noted. "A senseless loss," the secretary conceded. "Our policy is impossible to justify on logical grounds, which is why we've started invoking national security and other shibboleths."

Have no illusions. The Sherry Urquist assignment did not fall into my lap because somebody at Overt Intelligence liked me. It was simply this: I am a roué. If any agent had a prayer of planting this particular Dissembler, that agent was me. It's the eyebrows that do it, great bushy extrusions suggesting a predatory mammal of unusual prowess, though I must admit they draw copious support from my straight nose and full, pillowlike lips. Am I handsome as a god? Metaphorically speaking, yes.

The picture tube had fogged over, so I activated the wiper. On the screen, a seedy-looking terrier scratched its fleas. "We seriously hope you'll consider By-product Brand Dog Food," said the voice-over. "Yes, we do tie up an enormous amount of protein that might conceivably be used in relieving worldwide starvation. However, if you'll consider the supposed benefits of dogs, we believe you may wish to patronize us."

On the surface, Ms. Urquist looked innocent enough. The dossier pegged her a writer, a former newspaper reporter with several popular self-help books under her belt. She had some other commodities under her belt, too, mainly fat, unless the accompanying OIA photos exaggerated. The case against her consisted primarily of rumor. Last week a neighbor, or possibly a sanitation engineer—the dossier contradicted itself on this point—had gone through her garbage. The yield was largely what you'd expect from someone in Ms. Urquist's profession: vodka bottles, outdated caffeine tablets, computer disk boxes, an early draft of her last bestseller, *How to Find a Certain Amount of Inner Peace Some of the Time If You Are Lucky.* Then came the kicker. The figurative smoking gun. The nonliteral forbidden fruit. At the bottom of the heap, the report asserted, lay "a torn and crumpled page" from what was "almost certainly a work of fiction."

Two hundred and thirty-nine words of it, to be precise. A story, a yarn, a legend. Something made up.

ART IS A LIE, the electric posters in Washington Park reminded us. Truth was beauty, but it simply didn't work the other way around.

I left the shower, which instantly shut itself down, and padded naked into my bedroom. Clothes per se were deceitful, of course, but this was the middle of winter, so I threw on some underwear and a gray suit with the lapels cut off—no integrity in freezing to death. My apartment was peeled to a core of rectitude. Most of my friends had curtains, wall hangings, and rugs, but not I. Why take chances with one's own sanity?

The odor of stale urine hit me as I rushed down the hall toward the lobby. How unfortunate that some people translated the ban on sexually segregated restrooms—PRIVACY IS A LIE, the posters reminded us—into a general fear of toilets. Hadn't they heard of public health? Public health was guileless.

Wrapped in dew, my Plymouth Adequate glistened on the far side of Probity Street. In the old days, I'd heard, you never knew for sure that your car would be unmolested, or even there, when you left it overnight. Twenty-eight degrees Fahrenheit, yet the thing started smoothly. I took off, zooming past the wonderfully functional cinderblocks that constituted city hall and heading toward the shopping district. My interview with Sherry Urquist was scheduled for ten, so I still had time to buy a gift for my nephew's brainburn party, which would happen around two-thirty that afternoon, right after he recovered. "Yes, I did take quite a few bribes during the Wheatstone Tariff affair," a thin-voiced senatorial candidate squeaked from out of my radio, "but you have to understand. . . ." His voice faded, pushed aside by the pressure of my thoughts. Today my nephew would learn to hate a lie. Today we would rescue him from deceit's boundless sea, tossing out our lifelines and hauling him aboard the ark called Veritas. So to speak.

Money grows on trees. . . .

Horses have six legs. . . .

And suddenly you're a citizen.

What could life have been like before the cure? How did the mind tolerate a world where politicians misled, advertisers overstated, women wore makeup, and people professed love for each other at the nonliteral drop of a hat? I shivered. Did the Dissemblers know what they were playing with? How I relished the thought of advancing their doom, how badly I wanted Sherry Urquist's bulky ass hanging figuratively over the mantel of my fireplace.

I was armed for the fight. Two days earlier, the clever doctors down at the agency's Medical Division had done a bit of minor surgery, and now one of my seminal vesicles contained not only its usual cargo but also a microscopic radio transmitter. My imagination showed it to me, poised in the duct like the Greek infantry waiting for the wooden horse to arrive inside Troy.

What will they think of next?

The problem was the itch. Not a literal itch—the transmitter was one thousandth the size of a pinhead. My discomfort was philosophical. Did the beeper lie or didn't it, that was the question. It purported to be only itself, a thing, a microtransmitter, and yet some variation of duplicity seemed afoot here.

I didn't like it.

MOLLY'S RATHER EXPENSIVE TOY STORE, the sign said. Expensive: that was okay. Christmas came every year, but a kid got cured only once.

"My, aren't *you* a pretty fellow?" a female citizen sang out as I strode through the door. Marionettes dangled from the ceiling like victims of a mass lynching. Stuffed animals stampeded gently toward me from all directions.

"Your body is desirable enough," I said, casting a candid eye up and down the sales clerk. A tattered wool sweater molded itself around her emphatic breasts. Grimy white slacks encased her tight thighs. "But that nose," I added forlornly. A demanding business, citizenship.

"What brings you here?" She had one of those rare brands in which every digit is the same. 9999W, her forehead said. "You playboys are never responsible enough for parenthood."

"A fair assessment. You have kids?"

"I'm not married."

"It figures. My nephew's getting burned today."

"And you're waiting till the last minute to buy him a gift?"

"Right."

"Electric trains are popular. We sold eleven sets last week. Two were returned as defective."

She led me to a raised platform overrun by a kind of Veritas in miniature and kicked up the juice on the power-pack. A streamlined locomotive whisked a string of gleaming coaches past a factory belching an impressive facsimile of smoke.

"I wonder—is this thing a lie?" I opened the throttle, and the locomotive nearly jumped the track.

"What do you mean?"

"It claims to be a train. But it's not."

"It claims to be a *model* of a train, which it is."

I eased the locomotive into the station. "Is your price as good as anybody else's?"

"You can get the same thing for six dollars less at Marquand's."

"Don't have the time. Can you gift-wrap it?"

"Not skillfully."

"Anything will do. I'm in a hurry."

The downtown traffic was light, the lull before lunch hour, so I arrived early at Sherry Urquist's Washington Park apartment, a crumbling glass-and-steel ziggurat surmounted by a billboard that said, ASSUMING THAT GOD EXISTS, JESUS MAY HAVE BEEN HIS SON. I rode the elevator to the twentieth floor, exiting into a foyer where a handsome display of old military recruitment posters covered the fissured plaster. It was nice when somebody took the trouble to decorate a place. One could never use paint, of course. Paint was a lie. But with a little imagination. . . .

I rang the bell. Nothing. Had I gotten the time wrong? CHANNEL YOUR VIOLENT IMPULSES IN A SALUTARY DIRECTION, the nearest poster said. BECOME A MARINE.

The door swung open, and there stood our presumed subversive, a figurative cloud of confusion hovering about her heavy face, darkening her soft-boiled eyes and pulpy lips, features somewhat more attractive than the agency's photos suggested. "Did I wake you?" I asked. Her thermal pajamas barely managed to hold their contents in check, and I gave her an honest ogle. "I'm two minutes early."

"You woke me," she said. Frankness. A truth-teller, then? No, if there was one thing a Dissembler could do, it was deceive.

"Sorry," I said. I remembered the old documentary films of the oil paintings being burned. Rubens, that was the kind of sensual plumpness Sherry had going for her. Good old Peter Paul Rubens. Sneaking the Greek army inside Troy might be more entertaining than I'd thought.

She frowned, stretching her forehead brand into El Greco numerals. No one down at headquarters doubted its authenticity. Ditto her cerebroscan, voicegram, fingerprints. . . .

A citizen, and yet she had written fiction.

Maybe.

"Who are you?" Her voice was wet and deep.

"Orville Prawn," I said. A permanent truth. "I work for *Tolerable Distortions*." A more transient one; the agency had arranged for the magazine to hire me—

payroll, medical plan, pension fund, the works—for the next forty-eight hours. "Our interview. . . ." I took out a pad and pencil.

Her pained expression seemed like the real thing. "Oh, damn, I'm *sorry.*" She snapped her fingers. "It's on my calendar, but I've been up against a dozen deadlines, and I—"

"Forgot?"

"Yeah." She patted my forearm and guided me into her sparsely appointed living room. "Excuse me. These pajamas are probably driving you crazy."

"Not the pajamas per se."

She disappeared, returning shortly in a dingy yellow blouse and a red skirt circumscribed by a cracked and blistered leather belt.

The interview went well, which is to say she never asked whether I worked for Overt Intelligence, whereupon the whole show would have abruptly ended. She did not wish to discuss her old books, only her current project, a popular explanation of psychoanalytic theory to be called *From Misery to Unhappiness.* My shame was like a fever, threading my body with sharp, chilled wires. A toy train was not a lie, that clerk believed. Then maybe my little transmitter wasn't one either. . . .

And maybe wishes were horses.

And maybe pigs had wings.

There was also this: Sherry Urquist was charming me. No doubt about it. A manufacturer of bestsellers is naturally stuffed with vapid thoughts and ready-made opinions, right? But instead I found myself sitting next to a first-rate mind (oh, the premier eroticism of intellect intersecting Rubens), one that could be severe with Freud for his lapses of integrity while still grasping his essential genius.

"You seem to love your work, Ms. Urquist."

"Writing is my life."

"Tell me, honestly—do you ever get any ideas for . . . fiction?"

"Fiction?"

"Short stories. Novels."

"That would be suicidal, wouldn't it?"

A blind alley, but I expected as much.

The diciest moment occurred when Sherry asked in which issue the interview would be published, and I replied that I didn't know. True enough, I told myself. Since the thing would never see print at all, it was accurate to profess ignorance of the corresponding date. Still, there came a sudden, mercifully brief surge of unease, the tides of an ancient nausea. . . .

"All this sexual tension," I said, returning the pad and pencil to my suit jacket. "Alone with a sensually plump woman in her apartment, and your face is appealing too, now that I see the logic of it. You probably even have a bedroom. I can hardly stand it."

"Sensually plump, Mr. Prawn? I'm fat."

"Eye of the beholder."

"You'd have to go through a lot of beholders in my case."

"I find you very attractive." I did.

She raised her eyebrows, corrugating her brand. "It's only fair to give warning—you try anything funny, I'll knock you flat."

I cupped her left breast, full employment for any hand, and asked, "Is this funny?"

"On one level, your action offends me deeply." She brushed my knee. "I find it presumptuous, adolescent, and symptomatic of the worst kind of male arrogance." If faking her candor, she was certainly doing a good job. "On another level . . . well, you *are* quite handsome."

"An Adonis analogue."

We kissed. She went for my belt buckle. Reaching under her blouse, I sent her bra on a well-deserved sabbatical.

"Any sexually-transmittable diseases?" she asked.

"None." I stroked her dry, stringy hair. The Trojan horse was poised to change history. "You?"

"No," she said.

The truth? I couldn't know.

To bed, then. Time to plant her and, concomitantly, the transmitter. Nice work if you can get it. I slowed myself down with irrelevant thoughts—dogs can talk, rain is red—and left her a satisfied woman.

Full of Greeks.

I had promised Gloria that I wouldn't just come to the party, I would attend the burn as well. Normally both parents were present, but Dixon's tropological scum-bucket of a father couldn't be bothered. It will only take an hour, Gloria had told me. I'd rather not, I replied. He's your nephew, for Christ's sake, she pointed out. All right, I said.

Burn hospitals were in practically every neighborhood, but Gloria insisted on the best, Veteran's Shock Institute. Taking Dixon's badly wrapped gift from the back seat, I started toward the building, a smoke-stained pile of bricks overlooking the Thomas More Bridge. I paused. Business first. In theory the transmitter was part of Sherry now, forever fixed to her uterine wall. Snug as a bug in a . . . I went back to my Adequate and slid the sensorchart out of the dash. Yes, there she was, my fine Dissembler, a flashing red dot floating near Washington Park. I wished for greater detail, so I could know exactly when she was in her kitchen, her bathroom, her bedroom. Peeping Tom goes high tech. No matter. The thing worked. We could stalk her from here to Satan's backyard. As it were.

Inside the hospital, the day's collection of burn patients was everywhere, hugging dads, clinging tearfully to moms' skirts. I'd never understood this child-worship nonsense our culture wallows in, but, even so, the whole thing started getting to me. Every eight-year-old had to do it, of course, and the disease was certainly worse than the cure. Still. . . .

I punished myself by biting my inner cheeks. Sympathy was fine, but sentimentality was wasteful. If I wanted to pity somebody, I should go up to Ward Six. Cystic fibrosis. Cancer. Am I going to die, Mommy?

Yes, dear.

Soon?

Yes, dear.

Will I see you in heaven?

Nobody knows.

I went to the front desk, where I learned that Dixon had been admitted half an hour earlier. "Room one-forty-five," said the nurse, a rotund man with a warty face. "The party will be in one-seventeen."

My nephew was already in the glass cubicle, dressed in a green smock and bound to the chair via leather thongs, one electrode strapped to his left arm, another to his right leg. Black wires trailed from the copper terminals like threads spun by a carnivorous spider. He welcomed me with a brave smile, and I held up his gift, hefting it to show that it had substance, it wasn't clothes. A nice enough kid—what I knew of him. Cute freckles, a wide, apple face. I remembered that for somebody his age, Dixon understood a great deal of symbolic logic.

A young, willowy, female nurse entered the cubicle and began snugging the helmet over his cranium. I gave Dixon a thumbs-up signal. (Soon it will be over, kid. Pigs have wings, rats chase cats, all of it.)

"Thanks for coming." Drifting out of her chair, Gloria took my arm. She was an attractive woman—same genes as me—but today she looked lousy: the anticipation, the fear. Sweat collected in her forehead brand. I had stopped proposing incest years ago. Not her game. "You're his favorite uncle, you know."

Uncle Orville. God help me. I was actually present when Gloria's marriage collapsed. The three of us were sitting in a Reconstituted Burgers when suddenly she said, I sometimes worry that you're having an affair—are you? And Tom said, yes, he was. And Gloria said, you fucker. And Tom said, right. And Gloria asked how many. And Tom said lots. And Gloria asked why. Did he do it to strengthen the marriage? And Tom said no, he just liked to screw other women.

Clipboard in hand, a small, homely doctor with MERRICK affixed to his tunic waddled into the room. "Good afternoon, folks," he said, his cheer a precarious mix of the genuine and the forced. "Bitter cold day out, huh? How are we doing here?"

"Do you care?" my sister asked.

"Hard to say." Dr. Merrick fanned me with his clipboard. "Friend of the family?"

"My brother," Gloria explained.

"He has halitosis. Glad there are two of you." Merrick smiled at the boy in the cubicle. "With just one, the kid'll sometimes go into clinical depression on us." He pressed the clipboard toward Gloria. "Informed consent, right?"

"They told me all the possibilities." She studied the clipboard. "Cardiac—"

"Cardiac arrest, cerebral hemorrhage, respiratory failure, kidney damage," Merrick recited.

"When was the last time anything like that happened?"

"They killed a little girl down at Mount Sinai on Tuesday. A freak thing, but now and then we really screw up."

After patting Dixon on his straw-colored bangs, the nurse left the cubicle and told Dr. Merrick that she was going to get some coffee.

"Be back in ten minutes," he ordered.

"Oh, but of course." Such sarcasm from one so young. "We mustn't have a *doctor* cleaning up, not when we can get some underpaid nurse to do it."

Gloria scrawled her signature.

The nurse edged out of the room.

Dr. Merrick went to the control panel.

And then it began. This bar mitzvah of the human conscience, this electroconvulsive rite of passage. A hallowed tradition. An unvarying text. Today I am a man. . . . We believe in one Lord, Jesus Christ. . . . I pledge allegiance to the flag. . . . Why is this night different from all other nights. . . . Dogs can talk. . . . Pigs have wings. To tell you the truth, I was not really thinking about Dixon's cure just then. My mind was abloom with Sherry Urquist.

Merrick pushed a button, and PIGS HAVE WINGS appeared before my nephew on a lucite tachistoscope screen. "Can you hear me, lad?" the doctor called into the microphone.

Dixon opened his mouth, and a feeble "Yes" dribbled out of the loudspeaker.

"You see those words?" Merrick asked. The lurid red characters hovered in the air like lethargic butterflies.

"Y-yes."

"When I give the order, read them aloud. Okay?"

"Is it going to hurt?" my nephew quavered.

"It's going to hurt a lot. Will you read the words when I say so?"

"I'm scared. Do I have to?"

"You have to." Merrick rested a pudgy finger on the switch. "Now!"

"P-pigs have wings." The volts ripped through Dixon. He yelped and burst into tears. "But they don't," he moaned. "Pigs don't. . . ."

My own burn flooded back. The pain. The anger.

"You're right, lad—they don't." Merrick gave the voltage regulator a subtle twist, and Gloria flinched. "You did reasonably well, boy," the doctor continued. "We're not yet disappointed in you." He handed the mike to Gloria.

"Oh, yes, Dixon," she said. "Keep up the awfully good work."

"It's not fair." Sweat speckled Dixon's forehead. "I want to go home."

As Gloria surrendered the mike, TWO AND TWO MAKE FIVE materialized.

"Now, lad! Read it!"

"T-t-two and two make . . . f-five." Lightning struck. The boy shuddered, howled. Blood rolled over his lower lip. During my own burn, I had practically bitten my tongue off. "I don't want this any more," he wailed.

"It's not a choice, lad."

"Two and two make *four*." Tears threaded Dixon's freckles together. "Please stop hurting me."

"Four. Right. Smart lad." Merrick cranked up the voltage. "Ready, Dixon? Here it comes."

HORSES HAVE SIX LEGS.

"Why do I have to do this? *Why?*"

"Everybody does it. All your friends."

"H-h-horses have . . . have . . . They have *four* legs, Dr. Merrick."

"Read the words, Dixon!"

"I hate you! I hate all of you!"

"Dixon!"

He raced through it. Zap. Two hundred volts. The boy began to cough and retch, and a string of white mucus shot from his mouth like a lizard's tongue. Nothing followed: burn patients fasted for sixteen hours prior to therapy.

"Too much!" cried Gloria. "Isn't that too much?"

"The goal is five hundred," said Merrick. "It's all been worked out. You want the treatment to take, don't you?"

"Mommy! Where's my Mommy?"

Gloria tore the mike away. "Right here, dear!"

"Mommy, make them stop!"

"I can't, dear. You must try to be brave."

The fourth lie appeared. Merrick upped the voltage. "Read it, lad!"

"No!"

"Read it!"

"Uncle Orville! I want Uncle Orville!"

My throat constricted, my stomach went sour. Uncle: such a strange sound. I really was one, wasn't I? "You're doing pretty swell, Dixon," I said, taking the mike. "I think you'll like your present."

"Uncle Orville, I want to go home!"

"I got you a fine toy."

"What is it?"

"Here's a hint. It has—"

"Dixon!" Merrick grabbed the mike. "Dixon, if you don't do this, you'll never get well. They'll take you away from your mother." A threat, but wholly accurate. "Understand? They'll take you away."

Dixon balled his face into a mass of wrinkles. "Grass!" he screamed, spitting blood. "Is!" he persisted. "Purple!" He jerked like a gaffed flounder, spasm after spasm. A broad urine stain blossomed on his crotch, and despite the obligatory enema a brown fluid dripped from the hem of his smock.

"Excellent!" Merrick increased the punishment to four hundred volts. "Your cure's in sight, lad!"

"No! Please! Please! Enough!" Sweat encased Dixon's face. Foam leaked from his mouth.

"You're almost halfway there!"

"Please!"

The war continued, five more pain-tipped rockets shooting through Dixon's nerves and veins, detonating inside his mind. He asserted that rats chase cats. He lied about money, saying that it grew on trees. Worms taste like honey, he said. Snow is hot. Rain is red.

He fainted just as the final lie arrived. Even before Gloria could scream, Merrick was inside the cubicle, checking the boy's heartbeat. A begrudging admiration seeped through me. The doctor had a job, and he did it.

A single dose of smelling salts brought Dixon around.

Guiding the boy's face toward the screen, Merrick turned to me. "Ready with the switch?"

"Huh? You want me—" Ridiculous.

"Let's just get it over with. Hit the switch when I tell you."

"I'd rather not." But already my finger rested on the damn thing. Doctor's orders.

"Read, Dixon," muttered Merrick.

"I c-can't."

"One more, Dixon. Just one more and you'll be a citizen."

Blood and spittle mingled on Dixon's chin. "You all hate me! Mommy hates me!"

"I love you as much as myself," said Gloria, leaning over my shoulder. "You're going to have a wonderful party. Almost certainly."

"Really?"

"Highly likely."

"Presumably wonderful," I said. The switch burned my finger. "I love you too."

"Dogs can talk," said Dixon.

And it truly was a wonderful party. All four of Dixon's grandparents showed up, along with his teacher and twelve of his friends, half of whom had been cured in recent months, one on the previous day. Dixon marched around Room

117 displaying the evidence of his burn like war medals. The brand, of course—performed under local anesthesia immediately after his cure—plus copies of his initial cerebroscan, voicegram, and fingerprint set.

Brand, scan, gram, prints: Sherry Urquist's had all been in perfect order. She had definitely been burned. And yet there was fiction in her garbage.

The gift-opening ceremony contained one bleak moment. Pulling the train from its wrapping, Dixon blanched, garroted by panic, and Gloria had to rush him into the bathroom, where he spent several minutes throwing up. I felt like a fool. To a boy who's just been through a brainburn, an electric train has gruesome connotations.

"Thanks for coming," said Gloria. She meant it.

"I *do* like my present," Dixon averred. "A freight train would have been nicer," he added. A citizen now.

I apologized for leaving early. A big case, I explained. Very hot, very political.

"Good-bye, Uncle Orville."

Uncle. Great stuff.

I spent the rest of the day tracking my adorable Dissembler, never letting her get more than a mile from me or closer than two blocks. What agonizing hopes that dot on the map inspired, what rampant expectations. With each flash my longing intensified. Oh, Sherry, Sherry, you pulsing red angel, you stroboscope of my desire. No mere adolescent infatuation this. I dared to speak its name. "Neurotic obsession," I gushed, kissing the dot as it crossed Aquinas Avenue. "Mixed with bald romantic fantasy and lust," I added. The radio shouted at me: a hot-blooded evangelist no less enraptured than I. "Does faith tempt you, my friends? Fear not! Look into your metaphoric hearts, and you will discover how subconscious human needs project themselves onto putative revelations!"

For someone facing a wide variety of deadlines, my quarry didn't push herself particularly hard. Sherry spent the hour from four to five at the Museum of Secondary Fossil Finds. From five to six she did the Imprisoned Animals Garden. From six to seven she treated herself to dinner at Danny's Digestibles, after which she went down to the waterfront.

I cruised along Third Street, twenty yards from the Pathogen River. This was the city's frankest district, a gray mass of warehouses and abandoned stores jammed together like dead cells waiting to be sloughed off. Sherry walked slowly, aimlessly, as if . . . could it be? Yes, damn, as if arm-in-arm with another person, as if meshing her movements with those of a second, intertwined body. Probably she had met the guy at Danny's, a conceited pile of muscles named Guido or something, and now they were having a cozy stroll along the Pathogen. I pressed the dot, as if to draw Sherry away. What if she spent the night in another apartment? That would pretty much cinch it. I wondered how their passion would register. I pictured the dot going wild, love's red fibrillation.

After pausing for several seconds on the bank, the dot suddenly began prancing across the river. Odd. I fixed on the map. The Saint Joan Tunnel was half a mile away, the Thomas More Bridge even farther. I doubted that she was swimming—not in this weather, and not in the Pathogen, where the diseases of the future were born. Flying, then? The dot moved too slowly to signify an airplane. A hot-air balloon? Probably she was in a boat. Sherry and Guido, off on a romantic cruise.

I hung a left on Beach Street and sped down to the docks. Moonlight coated the Pathogen, settling into the waves, figuratively bronzing a lone, swiftly moving tugboat. I checked the map. The dot placed Sherry at least ten yards from the tug, in the exact middle of the river and heading for the opposite shore. I studied her presumed location. Nothing. Submerged, then? I knew she hadn't committed suicide; the dot's progress was too resolute. Was she in scuba gear?

I abandoned the car and attempted to find where she had entered the water, a quest that took me down concrete steps to a pier hemmed by pylons smeared with gull dung. Jagged odors shot from the dead and rotting river; water lapped over the landing with a harsh sucking sound, as if a pride of invisible lions was drinking here. My gaze settled on a metal grate, barred like the ribcage of some promethean robot. It seemed slightly askew. . . . Oh, great, Orville, let's go traipsing through the sewers, with rats nipping at our heels and slugs the size of bagels falling on our shoulders. Terrific idea.

The grate yielded readily to my reluctant hands. Had she truly gone down there? Should I follow? A demented notion, but duty called, using its shrillest voice, and, besides, this was Sherry Urquist, this was irrational need. I secured a flashlight from the car and proceeded down the ladder. It was like entering a lung. Steamy, warm. The flashlight blazed through the blackness. A weapon, I decided. Look out, all you rats and slugs. Make way. Here comes Orville Prawn, the fastest flashlight in Veritas.

I moved through a multilayered maze of soggy holes and dripping catacombs. So many ways to descend: ladders, sloping tunnels, crooked little stairways—I used them all, soon moving beyond the riverbed into other territories, places not on the OIA map.

All around me Veritas's guts were spread: its concrete intestines, gushing lead veins, buzzing nerves of steel and gutta-percha. Much to my surprise, the city even had its parasites—shacks of corrugated tin leaned against the wet brick walls, sucking secretly on the power cables and water mains. This would not do. No, to live below Veritas like this, appropriating its juices, was little more than piracy. Overt Intelligence would hear of it.

My astonishment deepened as I advanced. I could understand a few hobos setting up a shantytown down here, but how might I explain these odd chunks of civilization? These blazing streetlamps, these freshly painted picket fences, these tidy grids of rose bushes, these fountains with their stone dolphins spewing water? Paint, flowers, sculpture: so many lies in one place! Peel back the streets of any city and do you find its warped reflection, its doppelgänger mirrored in distorting glass? Or did Veritas alone harbor such anarchy, this tumor spreading beneath her unsuspecting flesh?

A sleek white cat shot out of the rose bushes and disappeared down an open manhole. At first I thought that its pursuer was a dog, but no. Wrong shape. And that tail.

The shudder began in my lower spine and expanded.

A rat.

A rat the size of an armadillo.

Chasing a cat.

I moved on. Vegetable gardens now. Two bright yellow privies. Cottages defaced with gardenia plots and strings of clematis scurrying up trellises. A building that looked suspiciously like a chapel. A park of some kind, with flagstone paths and a duck pond. Ruddy puffs of vapor bumped against the treetops.

Rain is red. . . .

I entered the park.

A pig glided over my head like a miniature dirigible, wheeling across the sky on cherub wings. At first I assumed it was a machine, but its squeal was disconcertingly organic.

"You!"

A low, liquid voice. I dropped my gaze.

Sherry shared the bench with an enormous dog, some grotesque variation on the malamute, his chin snugged into her lap. "You!" she said again, erecting the word like a barrier, a spiked vocable stopping my approach. The dog lifted his head and growled.

"Correct," I said, stock still.

"You followed me?"

"I cannot tell a lie." I examined the nearest tree. No fruit, of course, only worms and paper money.

"Dirty spy."

"Half true. I am not dirty."

She wore a buttercup dress, decorated with lace. Her thick braid lay on her shoulder like a loaf of challah. Her eyes had become cartoons of themselves, starkly outlined and richly shaded. "If you try to return"—she patted the malamute—"Max will eat you alive."

"You bet your sweet ass," said the dog.

She massaged Max's head, as if searching for the trigger that would release his attack. "I expected better of you, Mr. Prawn."

We were in a contest. Who could act the more betrayed, the more disgusted? "I'd always assumed the Dissemblage was just a group." Spit dripped off my words. "I didn't know it was . . . all this."

"Two cities," muttered Sherry, launching her index finger upward. "Truth above, dignity below." The finger descended. Her nails, I noticed, were a fluorescent green.

"Her father built it," explained the dog.

"His life's work," added Sherry.

"Are there many of you?" I asked.

"I'm the first to reach adulthood," said Sherry.

"The prototype liar?"

Her sneer evolved into a grin. "Others are hatching."

"How can you betray your city like this?" I drilled her with my stare. "Veritas, who nurtured you, suckled you?"

"Shall I kill him now?" asked the dog.

Sherry chucked Max under the chin, told him to be patient. "Veritas did not suckle me." Her gesture encompassed the entire park and, by extension, the whole of Veritas's twisted double. "*This* was my cradle—my nursery." She took a lipstick from her purse. "It's not hard to make a lie. The money trees are props. The rats and pigs trace to avant-garde microbiology."

"All I needed were vocal cords," said the dog.

She began touching up her lips. "Thanks to my father, I reached my eighth birthday knowing that pigs had wings, that snow was hot, that two and two equaled five, that worms tasted like honey . . . all of it. So when my burn came—"

"You were incurable," I said. "You walked away from the hospital ready to swindle and cheat and—"

"Write fiction. Four novels so far. Maybe you'd like to read them. You might be a bureaucratic drudge, but I'm fond of you, Orville."

"How do I know you're telling the truth?"

"You don't. And when my cadre takes over and the burn ends—it won't be hard, we'll lie our way to the top—when that happens, you won't know when *anybody's* telling the truth."

"Right," said the dog, leaping off the bench.

"Truth is beauty," I said.

Sherry winced. "My father did not mind telling the truth." Here she became an actress, that consummate species of liar, dragging out her lines. "But he hated his inability to do otherwise. Honesty without choice, he said, is slavery with a smile."

A glorious adolescent girl rode through the park astride a six-legged horse, her skin dark despite her troglodytic upbringing, her eyes alive with deceit. The *gift* of deceit, as Sherry would have it. I wondered whether Dixon was playing with his electric train just then. Probably not. Past his bedtime. I kept envisioning his cerebrum, brocaded with necessary scars.

Sherry patted the spot where the dog had been, and I sat down cautiously. "Care for one?" she asked, plucking a worm off a money tree.

"No."

"Go ahead. Try it."

"Well. . . ."

"Open your mouth and close your eyes."

The creature wriggled on my tongue, and I bit down. Pure honey. Sweet, smooth, but I did not enjoy it.

Truth above, dignity below. My index finger throbbed, prickly with that irrevocable little tug of the switch in Room 145. Five hundred volts was a lot, but what was the alternative? To restore the age of thievery and fraud?

History has it I joined Sherry's city that very night. A lie, but what do you expect—all the books are written by Dissemblers. True, sometime before dawn I did push my car into the river, the better to elude Overt Intelligence. But fully a week went by before I told Sherry about her internal transmitter. She was furious. She vowed to have the thing cut out. Go ahead, I told her, do it—but don't expect my blessing. That's another thing the historians got wrong. They say I paid for the surgery.

Call me a traitor. Call me a coward. Call me love's captive. I have called myself all these things. But—really—I did not join Sherry's city that night. That night I merely sat on a park bench staring into her exotically adorned eyes, fixing on her bright lips, holding her fluorescent fingertips.

"I want to believe whatever you tell me," I said.

"Then you'll need to have faith in me," she said.

"It's raining," noted the dog, and then he launched into a talking-dog joke.

"My cottage is over there." Sherry replaced her lipstick in her purse. She tossed her wondrous braid over her shoulder.

We rose and started across the park, hand in hand, lost in the sweet uncertainty of the moment, oblivious to the chattering dog and the lashing wind and bright red rain dancing on the purple grass.

A. E. van Vogt

A. E. van Vogt (1912–) is one of the giants of the Golden Age of science fiction, specifically, the flowering of modern science fiction in John W. Campbell, Jr.'s magazine, *Astounding*, between 1939 and 1949. A Canadian writer, he moved to the U.S. after World War II and spent the 1950s deeply involved in his friend L. Ron Hubbard's Dianetics (later Scientology). He is one of the most influential SF writers of that period, in some ways the dominant SF writer of the 1940s. His novel, *Slan* (1946, appearing first as a serial in *Astounding* in 1940) metaphorically represented the previously unarticulated attitude in the SF field that SF readers and writers were somehow the next stage in human evolution. "Fans are Slans" became a motto of 1940s science fiction, and van Vogt was a hero of the evolution and his influence on the next generation of SF writers, including Philip José Farmer, Philip K. Dick, and Charles Harness, was profound. *The World of Null-A* (1948) was the first work of modern science fiction to be published by a respectable hardcover house and it was a worldwide success. His fiction is filled with powerful imagery and strange ideas, often presented in dreamlike sequence, not a rational flow. His critical reputation was demolished in the U.S. in the the 1950s by Damon Knight's essay, "Cosmic Jerrybuilder: A. E. van Vogt." But van Vogt's popularity did not decrease for decades. In the 1980s Leslie A. Fiedler (in his essay "The Criticism of Science Fiction," 1983) put it succinctly: "Any bright high school sophomore can identify all the things that are wrong about van Vogt. . . . But the challenge to criticism which pretends to do justice to science fiction is to say what is right about him: to identify his mythopoeic power, his ability to evoke primordial images, his gift for redeeming the marvelous in a world in which technology has preempted the province of magic and God is dead."

This story is one of his most memorable. Ray Bradbury's later stories of the desert planet Mars, with its hidden survivals of a once-great technological civilization, are strikingly similar in atmosphere. This is van Vogt's "Martian chronicle." In this case it is easy to understand van Vogt's appeal.

ENCHANTED VILLAGE

"Explorers of a new frontier" they had been called before they left for Mars.

For a while, after the ship crashed into a Martian desert, killing all on board except—miraculously—this one man, Bill Jenner spat the words occasionally into the constant, sand-laden wind. He despised himself for the pride he had felt when he first heard them.

His fury faded with each mile that he walked, and his black grief for his friends became a gray ache. Slowly he realized that he had made a ruinous misjudgment.

He had underestimated the speed at which the rocketship had been traveling.

He'd guessed that he would have to walk three hundred miles to reach the shallow, polar sea he and the others had observed as they glided in from outer space. Actually, the ship must have flashed an immensely greater distance before it hurtled down out of control.

The days stretched behind him, seemingly as numberless as the hot, red, alien sand that scorched through his tattered clothes. A huge scarecrow of a man, he kept moving across the endless, arid waste—he would not give up.

By the time he came to the mountain, his food had long been gone. Of his four water bags, only one remained, and that was so close to being empty that he merely wet his cracked lips and swollen tongue whenever his thirst became unbearable.

Jenner climbed high before he realized that it was not just another dune that had barred his way. He paused, and as he gazed up at the mountain that towered above him, he cringed a little. For an instant he felt the hopelessness of this mad race he was making to nowhere—but he reached the top. He saw that below him was a depression surrounded by hills as high as, or higher than, the one on which he stood. Nestled in the valley they made was a village.

He could see trees and the marble floor of a courtyard. A score of buildings was clustered around what seemed to be a central square. They were mostly low-constructed, but there were four towers pointing gracefully into the sky. They shone in the sunlight with a marble luster.

Faintly, there came to Jenner's ears a thin, high-pitched whistling sound. It rose, fell, faded completely, then came up again clearly and unpleasantly. Even as Jenner ran toward it, the noise grated on his ears, eerie and unnatural.

He kept slipping on smooth rock, and bruised himself when he fell. He rolled halfway down into the valley. The buildings remained new and bright when seen from nearby. Their walls flashed with reflections. On every side was vegetation—reddish-green shrubbery, yellow-green trees laden with purple and red fruit.

With ravenous intent, Jenner headed for the nearest fruit tree. Close up, the tree looked dry and brittle. The large red fruit he tore from the lowest branch, however, was plump and juicy.

As he lifted it to his mouth, he remembered that he had been warned during his training period to taste nothing on Mars until it had been chemically examined. But that was meaningless advice to a man whose only chemical equipment was in his own body.

Nevertheless, the possibility of danger made him cautious. He took his first bite gingerly. It was bitter to his tongue, and he spat it out hastily. Some of the juice which remained in his mouth seared his gums. He felt the fire on it, and he reeled from nausea. His muscles began to jerk, and he lay down on the marble to keep himself from falling. After what seemed like hours to Jenner, the awful trembling finally went out of his body and he could see again. He looked up despisingly at the tree.

The pain finally left him, and slowly he relaxed. A soft breeze rustled the dry leaves. Nearby trees took up that gentle clamor, and it struck Jenner that the wind here in the valley was only a whisper of what it had been on the flat desert beyond the mountain.

There was no other sound now. Jenner abruptly remembered the high-pitched, ever-changing whistle he had heard. He lay very still, listening intently, but there was only the rustling of the leaves. The noisy shrilling had stopped. He wondered if it had been an alarm, to warn the villagers of his approach.

Anxiously he climbed to his feet and fumbled for his gun. A sense of disaster shocked through him. It wasn't there. His mind was a blank, and then he vaguely recalled that he had first missed the weapon more than a week before. He looked around him uneasily, but there was not a sign of creature life. He braced himself. He couldn't leave, as there was nowhere to go. If necessary, he would fight to the death to remain in the village.

Carefully Jenner took a sip from his water bag, moistening his cracked lips and his swollen tongue. Then he replaced the cap and started through a double line of trees toward the nearest building. He made a wide circle to observe it from several vantage points. On one side a low, broad archway opened into the interior. Through it, he could dimly make out the polished gleam of a marble floor.

Jenner explored the buildings from the outside, always keeping a respectful distance between him and any of the entrances. He saw no sign of animal life. He reached the far side of the marble platform on which the village was built, and turned back decisively. It was time to explore interiors.

He chose one of the four tower buildings. As he came within a dozen feet of it, he saw that he would have to stoop low to get inside.

Momentarily, the implications of that stopped him. These buildings had been constructed for a life form that must be very different from human beings.

He went forward again, bent down, and entered reluctantly, every muscle tensed.

He found himself in a room without furniture. However, there were several low marble fences projecting from one marble wall. They formed what looked like a group of four wide, low stalls. Each stall had an open trough carved out of the floor.

The second chamber was fitted with four inclined planes of marble, each of which slanted up to a dais. Altogether there were four rooms on the lower floor. From one of them a circular ramp mounted up, apparently to a tower room.

Jenner didn't investigate the upstairs. The earlier fear that he would find alien life was yielding to the deadly conviction that he wouldn't. No life meant no food or chance of getting any. In frantic haste he hurried from building to building, peering into the silent rooms, pausing now and then to shout hoarsely.

Finally there was no doubt. He was alone in a deserted village on a lifeless planet, without food, without water—except for the pitiful supply in his bag—and without hope.

He was in the fourth and smallest room of one of the tower buildings when he realized that he had come to the end of his search. The room had a single stall jutting out from one wall. Jenner lay down wearily in it. He must have fallen asleep instantly.

When he awoke he became aware of two things, one right after the other. The first realization occurred before he opened his eyes—the whistling sound was back; high and shrill, it wavered at the threshold of audibility.

The other was that a fine spray of liquid was being directed down at him from the ceiling. It had an odor, of which technician Jenner took a single whiff. Quickly he scrambled out of the room, coughing, tears in his eyes, his face already burning from chemical reaction.

He snatched his handkerchief and hastily wiped the exposed parts of his body and face.

He reached the outside and there paused, striving to understand what had happened.

The village seemed unchanged.

Leaves trembled in a gentle breeze. The sun was poised on a mountain peak. Jenner guessed from its position that it was morning again and that he had slept at least a dozen hours. The glaring white light suffused the valley. Half hidden by trees and shrubbery, the buildings flashed and shimmered.

He seemed to be in an oasis in a vast desert. It was an oasis, all right, Jenner reflected grimly, but not for a human being. For him, with its poisonous fruit, it was more like a tantalizing mirage.

He went back inside the building and cautiously peered into the room where he had slept. The spray of gas had stopped, not a bit of odor lingered, and the air was fresh and clean.

He edged over the threshold, half inclined to make a test. He had a picture in his mind of a long-dead Martian creature lazing on the floor in the stall while a soothing chemical sprayed down on its body. The fact that the chemical was deadly to human beings merely emphasized how alien to man was the life that had spawned on Mars. But there seemed little doubt of the reason for the gas. The creature was accustomed to taking a morning shower.

Inside the "bathroom," Jenner eased himself feet first into the stall. As his hips came level with the stall entrance, the solid ceiling sprayed a jet of yellowish gas straight down upon his legs. Hastily Jenner pulled himself clear of the stall. The gas stopped as suddenly as it had started.

He tried it again, to make sure it was merely an automatic process. It turned on, then shut off.

Jenner's thirst-puffed lips parted with excitement. He thought, "If there can be one automatic process, there may be others."

Breathing heavily, he raced into the outer room. Carefully he shoved his legs into one of the two stalls. The moment his hips were in, a steaming gruel filled the trough beside the wall.

He stared at the greasy-looking stuff with a horrified fascination—food—and drink. He remembered the poison fruit and felt repelled, but he forced himself to bend down and put his finger into the hot, wet substance. He brought it up, dripping, to his mouth.

It tasted flat and pulpy, like boiled wood fiber. It trickled viscously into his throat. His eyes began to water and his lips drew back convulsively. He realized he was going to be sick, and ran for the outer door—but didn't quite make it.

When he finally got outside, he felt limp and unutterably listless. In that depressed state of mind, he grew aware again of the shrill sound.

He felt amazed that he could have ignored its rasping even for a few minutes. Sharply he glanced about, trying to determine its source, but it seemed to have none. Whenever he approached a point where it appeared to be loudest, then it would fade or shift, perhaps to the far side of the village.

He tried to imagine what an alien culture would want with a mind-shattering noise—although, of course, it would not necessarily have been unpleasant to them.

He stopped and snapped his fingers as a wild but nevertheless plausible notion entered his mind. Could this be music?

He toyed with the idea, trying to visualize the village as it had been long ago. Here a music-loving people had possibly gone about their daily tasks to the accompaniment of what was to them beautiful strains of melody.

The hideous whistling went on and on, waxing and waning. Jenner tried to put buildings between himself and the sound. He sought refuge in various rooms, hoping that at least one would be soundproof. None were. The whistle followed him wherever he went.

He retreated into the desert, and had to climb halfway up one of the slopes before the noise was low enough not to disturb him. Finally, breathless but immeasurably relieved, he sank down on the sand and thought blankly:

What now?

The scene that spread before him had in it qualities of both heaven and hell. It was all too familiar now—the red sands, the stony dunes, the small, alien village promising so much and fulfilling so little.

Jenner looked down at it with his feverish eyes and ran his parched tongue over his cracked, dry lips. He knew that he was a dead man unless he could alter the automatic food-making machines that must be hidden somewhere in the walls and under the floors of the buildings.

In ancient days, a remnant of Martian civilization had survived here in this village. The inhabitants had died off, but the village lived on, keeping itself clean of sand, able to provide refuge for any Martian who might come along. But there were no Martians. There was only Bill Jenner, pilot of the first rocketship ever to land on Mars.

He had to make the village turn out food and drink that he could take. Without tools, except his hands, with scarcely any knowledge of chemistry, he must force it to change its habits.

Tensely he hefted his water bag. He took another sip and fought the same grim fight to prevent himself from guzzling it down to the last drop. And, when he had won the battle once more, he stood up and started down the slope.

He could last, he estimated, not more than three days. In that time he must conquer the village.

He was already among the trees when it suddenly struck him that the "music" had stopped. Relieved, he bent over a small shrub, took a good firm hold of it—and pulled.

It came up easily, and there was a slab of marble attached to it. Jenner stared at it, noting with surprise that he had been mistaken in thinking the stalk came up through a hole in the marble. It was merely stuck to the surface. Then he noticed something else—the shrub had no roots. Almost instinctively, Jenner looked down at the spot from which he had torn the slab of marble along with the plant. There was sand there.

He dropped the shrub, slipped to his knees, and plunged his fingers into the sand. Loose sand trickled through them. He reached deep, using all his strength to force his arm and hand down; sand—nothing but sand.

He stood up and frantically tore up another shrub. It also came up easily, bringing with it a slab of marble. It had no roots, and where it had been was sand.

With a kind of mindless disbelief, Jenner rushed over to a fruit tree and shoved at it. There was a momentary resistance, and then the marble on which it stood split and lifted slowly into the air. The tree fell over with a swish and a crackle as its dry branches and leaves broke and crumbled into a thousand pieces. Underneath where it had been was sand.

Sand everywhere. A city built on sand. Mars, planet of sand. That was not completely true, of course. Seasonal vegetation had been observed near the polar ice caps. All but the hardiest of it died with the coming of summer. It had been intended that the rocketship land near one of those shallow, tideless seas.

By coming down out of control, the ship had wrecked more than itself. It had wrecked the chances for life of the only survivor of the voyage.

Jenner came slowly out of his daze. He had a thought then. He picked up one of the shrubs he had already torn loose, braced his foot against the marble to which it was attached, and tugged, gently at first, then with increasing strength.

It came loose finally, but there was no doubt that the two were part of a whole. The shrub was growing out of the marble.

Marble? Jenner knelt beside one of the holes from which he had torn a slab, and bent over an adjoining section. It was quite porous—calciferous rock, most likely, but not true marble at all. As he reached toward it, intending to break off a piece, it changed color. Astounded, Jenner drew back. Around the break, the stone was turning a bright orange-yellow. He studied it uncertainly, then tentatively he touched it.

It was as if he had dipped his fingers into searing acid. There was a sharp, biting, burning pain. With a gasp, Jenner jerked his hand clear.

The continuing anguish made him feel faint. He swayed and moaned, clutching the bruised members to his body. When the agony finally faded and he could look at the injury, he saw that the skin had peeled and that blood blisters had formed already. Grimly Jenner looked down at the break in the stone. The edges remained bright orange-yellow.

The village was alert, ready to defend itself from further attacks.

Suddenly weary, he crawled into the shade of a tree. There was only one possible conclusion to draw from what had happened, and it almost defied common sense. This lonely village was alive.

As he lay there, Jenner tried to imagine a great mass of living substance growing into the shape of buildings, adjusting itself to suit another life form, accepting the role of servant in the widest meaning of the term.

If it would serve one race, why not another? If it could adjust to Martians, why not to human beings?

There would be difficulties, of course. He guessed wearily that essential elements would not be available. The oxygen for water could come from the air . . . thousands of compounds could be made from sand. . . . Though it meant death if he failed to find a solution, he fell asleep even as he started to think about what they might be.

When he awoke it was quite dark.

Jenner climbed heavily to his feet. There was a drag to his muscles that alarmed him. He wet his mouth from his water bag and staggered toward the entrance of the nearest building. Except for the scraping of his shoes on the "marble," the silence was intense.

He stopped short, listened, and looked. The wind had died away. He couldn't see the mountains that rimmed the valley, but the buildings were still dimly visible, black shadows in a shadow world.

For the first time, it seemed to him that, in spite of his new hope, it might be better if he died. Even if he survived, what had he to look forward to? Only too well he recalled how hard it had been to rouse interest in the trip and to raise the large amount of money required. He remembered the colossal problems that had had to be solved in building the ship, and some of the men who had solved them were buried somewhere in the Martian desert.

It might be twenty years before another ship from Earth would try to reach the only other planet in the Solar System that had shown signs of being able to support life.

During those uncountable days and nights, those years, he would be here alone. That was the most he could hope for—if he lived. As he fumbled his way to a dais in one of the rooms, Jenner considered another problem: How did one let a living village know that it must alter its processes? In a way, it must already have grasped that it had a new tenant. How could he make it realize he needed food in a different chemical combination than that which it had served in the past; that he liked music, but on a different scale system; and that he could use a shower each morning—of water, not of poison gas?

He dozed fitfully, like a man who is sick rather than sleepy. Twice he wakened, his lips on fire, his eyes burning, his body bathed in perspiration. Several times he was startled into consciousness by the sound of his own harsh voice crying out in anger and fear at the night.

He guessed, then, that he was dying.

He spent the long hours of darkness tossing, turning, twisting, befuddled by waves of heat. As the light of morning came, he was vaguely surprised to realize that he was still alive. Restlessly he climbed off the dais and went to the door.

A bitingly cold wind blew, but it felt good to his hot face. He wondered if there were enough pneumococci in his blood for him to catch pneumonia. He decided not.

In a few moments he was shivering. He retreated back into the house, and for the first time noticed that, despite the doorless doorway, the wind did not come into the building at all. The rooms were cold but not draughty.

That started an association: Where had his terrible body heat come from? He teetered over to the dais where he spent the night. Within seconds he was sweltering in a temperature of about one hundred and thirty.

He climbed off the dais, shaken by his own stupidity. He estimated that he had sweated at least two quarts of moisture out of his dried-up body on that furnace of a bed.

This village was not for human beings. Here even the beds were heated for creatures who needed temperatures far beyond the heat comfortable for men.

Jenner spent most of the day in the shade of a large tree. He felt exhausted, and only occasionally did he even remember that he had a problem. When the whistling started, it bothered him at first, but he was too tired to move away from it. There were long periods when he hardly heard it, so dulled were his senses.

Late in the afternoon he remembered the shrubs and the trees he had torn up the day before and wondered what had happened to them. He wet his swollen tongue with the last few drops of water in his bag, climbed lackadaisically to his feet, and went to look for the dried-up remains.

There weren't any. He couldn't even find the holes where he had torn them out. The living village had absorbed the dead tissue into itself and had repaired the breaks in its "body."

That galvanized Jenner. He began to think again . . . about mutations, genetic readjustments, life forms adapting to new environments. There'd been lectures on that before the ship left Earth, rather generalized talks designed to acquaint the explorers with the problems men might face on an alien planet. The important principle was quite simple: adjust or die.

The village had to adjust to him. He doubted if he could seriously damage it, but he could try. His own need to survive must be placed on as sharp and hostile a basis as that.

Frantically Jenner began to search his pockets. Before leaving the rocket he had loaded himself with odds and ends of small equipment. A jackknife, a folding metal cup, a printed radio, a tiny superbattery that could be charged by spinning an attached wheel—and for which he had brought along, among other things, a powerful electric fire lighter.

Jenner plugged the lighter into the battery and deliberately scraped the red-hot end along the surface of the "marble." The reaction was swift. The substance turned an angry purple this time. When an entire section of the floor had changed color, Jenner headed for the nearest stall trough, entering far enough to activate it.

There was a noticeable delay. When the food finally flowed into the trough, it was clear that the living village had realized the reason for what he had done. The food was a pale, creamy color, where earlier it had been a murky gray.

Jenner put his finger into it but withdrew it with a yell and wiped his finger. It continued to sting for several moments. The vital question was: Had it deliberately offered him food that would damage him, or was it trying to appease him without knowing what he could eat?

He decided to give it another chance, and entered the adjoining stall. The gritty stuff that flooded up this time was yellower. It didn't burn his finger, but Jenner took one taste and spat it out. He had the feeling that he had been offered a soup made of a greasy mixture of clay and gasoline.

He was thirsty now with a need heightened by the unpleasant taste in his mouth. Desperately he rushed outside and tore open the water bag, seeking the wetness inside. In his fumbling eagerness, he spilled a few precious drops onto the courtyard. Down he went on his face and licked them up.

Half a minute later, he was still licking, and there was still water.

The fact penetrated suddenly. He raised himself and gazed wonderingly at the droplets of water that sparkled on the smooth stone. As he watched, another one squeezed up from the apparently solid surface and shimmered in the light of the sinking sun.

He bent, and with the tip of his tongue sponged up each visible drop. For a long time he lay with his mouth pressed to the "marble," sucking up the tiny bits of water that the village doled out to him.

The glowing white sun disappeared behind a hill. Night fell, like the dropping of a black screen. The air turned cold, then icy. He shivered as the wind keened through his ragged clothes. But what finally stopped him was the collapse of the surface from which he had been drinking

Jenner lifted himself in surprise, and in the darkness gingerly felt over the stone. It had genuinely crumbled. Evidently the substance had yielded up its available water and had disintegrated in the process. Jenner estimated that he had drunk altogether an ounce of water.

It was a convincing demonstration of the willingness of the village to please him, but there was another, less satisfying, implication. If the village had to destroy a part of itself every time it gave him a drink, then clearly the supply was not unlimited.

Jenner hurried inside the nearest building, climbed onto a dais—and climbed off again hastily, as the heat blazed up at him. He waited, to give the Intelligence a chance to realize he wanted a change, then lay down once more. The heat was as great as ever.

He gave that up because he was too tired to persist and too sleepy to think of a method that might let the village know he needed a different bedroom temperature. He slept on the floor with an uneasy conviction that it could *not* sustain him for long. He woke up many times during the night and thought, "Not enough water. No matter how hard it tries—" Then he would sleep again, only to wake once more, tense and unhappy.

Nevertheless, morning found him briefly alert; and all his steely determination was back—that iron will power that had brought him at least five hundred miles across an unknown desert.

He headed for the nearest trough. This time, after he had activated it, there was a pause of more than a minute; and then about a thimbleful of water made a wet splotch at the bottom.

Jenner licked it dry, then waited hopefully for more. When none came he reflected gloomily that somewhere in the village an entire group of cells had broken down and released their water for him.

Then and there he decided that it was up to the human being, who could move around, to find a new source of water for the village, which could not move.

In the interim, of course, the village would have to keep him alive, until he had investigated the possibilities. That meant, above everything else, he must have some food to sustain him while he looked around.

He began to search his pockets. Toward the end of his food supply, he had carried scraps and pieces wrapped in small bits of cloth. Crumbs had broken off into the pocket, and he had searched for them often during those long days in the desert. Now, by actually ripping the seams, he discovered tiny particles of meat and bread, little bits of grease and other unidentifiable substances.

Carefully he leaned over the adjoining stall and placed the scrapings in the trough there. The village would not be able to offer him more than a reasonable facsimile. If the spilling of a few drops on the courtyard could make it aware of his need for water, then a similar offering might give it the clue it needed as to the chemical nature of the food he could eat.

Jenner waited, then entered the second stall and activated it. About a pint of thick, creamy substance trickled into the bottom of the trough. The smallness of the quantity seemed evidence that perhaps it contained water.

He tasted it. It had a sharp, musty flavor and a stale odor. It was almost as dry as flour—but his stomach did not reject it.

Jenner ate slowly, acutely aware that at such moments as this the village had him at its mercy. He could never be sure that one of the food ingredients was not a slow-acting poison.

When he had finished the meal he went to a food trough in another building. He refused to eat the food that came up, but activated still another trough. This time he received a few drops of water.

He had come purposefully to one of the tower buildings. Now he started up the ramp that led to the upper floor. He paused only briefly in the room he came to, as he had already discovered that they seemed to be additional bedrooms. The familiar dais was there in a group of three.

What interested him was that the circular ramp continued to wind on upward. First to another, smaller room that seemed to have no particular reason for being. Then it wound on up to the top of the tower, some seventy feet above the ground. It was high enough for him to see beyond the rim of all the surrounding hilltops. He had thought it might be, but he had been too weak to make the climb before. Now he looked out to every horizon. Almost immediately the hope that had brought him up faded.

The view was immeasurably desolate. As far as he could see was an arid waste, and every horizon was hidden in a mist of wind-blown sand.

Jenner gazed with a sense of despair. If there were a Martian sea out there somewhere, it was beyond his reach.

Abruptly he clenched his hands in anger against his fate, which seemed inevitable now. At the very worst, he had hoped he would find himself in a mountainous region. Seas and mountains were generally the two main sources of water. He should have known, of course, that there were very few mountains on Mars. It would have been a wild coincidence if he had actually run into a mountain range.

His fury faded because he lacked the strength to sustain any emotion. Numbly he went down the ramp.

His vague plan to help the village ended as swiftly and finally as that.

The days drifted by, but as to how many he had no idea. Each time he went to eat, a smaller amount of water was doled out to him. Jenner kept telling himself that each meal would have to be his last. It was unreasonable for him to expect the village to destroy itself when his fate was certain now.

What was worse, it became increasingly clear that the food was not good for him. He had misled the village as to his needs by giving it stale, perhaps even tainted, samples, and prolonged the agony for himself. At times after he had eaten, Jenner felt dizzy for hours. All too frequently his head ached and his body shivered with fever.

The village was doing what it could. The rest was up to him, and he couldn't even adjust to an approximation of Earth food.

For two days he was too sick to drag himself to one of the troughs. Hour after hour he lay on the floor. Some time during the second night the pain in his body grew so terrible that he finally made up his mind

"If I can get to a dais," he told himself, "the heat alone will kill me; and in absorbing my body, the village will get back some of its lost water."

He spent at least an hour crawling laboriously up the ramp of the nearest dais, and when he finally made it, he lay as one already dead. His last waking thought was: "Beloved friends, I'm coming."

The hallucination was so complete that momentarily he seemed to be back in the control room of the rocketship, and all around him were his former companions.

With a sigh of relief Jenner sank into a dreamless sleep.

He woke to the sound of a violin. It was a sad-sweet music that told of the rise and fall of a race long dead.

Jenner listened for a while and then, with abrupt excitement, realized the truth. This was a substitute for the whistling—the village had adjusted its music to him!

Other sensory phenomena stole in upon him. The dais felt comfortably warm, not hot at all. He had a feeling of wonderful physical well-being.

Eagerly he scrambled down the ramp to the nearest food stall. As he crawled forward, his nose close to the floor, the trough filled with a steamy mixture. The odor was so rich and pleasant that he plunged his face into it and slopped it up greedily. It had the flavor of thick, meaty soup and was warm and soothing to his lips and mouth. When he had eaten it all, for the first time he did not need a drink of water.

"I've won!" thought Jenner. "The village has found a way!"

After a while he remembered something and crawled to the bathroom. Cautiously, watching the ceiling, he eased himself backward into the shower stall. The yellowish spray came down, cool and delightful.

Ecstatically Jenner wriggled his four-foot-tail and lifted his long snout to let the thin streams of liquid wash away the food impurities that clung to his sharp teeth.

Then he waddled out to bask in the sun and listen to the timeless music.

Wolfgang Jeschke

Wolfgang Jeschke (1936–) is one of the central figures in contemporary German science fiction. He began to write science fiction in 1959, but became more involved by becoming an editor in 1969. He has edited more than 100 SF anthologies since 1970, bringing much of the best science fiction in the world into print in German in the last three decades. Since 1972 he has been the editor of the largest and most successful SF publishing line on the continent, for Heyne Verlag. Most especially, he has been a crucial force in upholding literary standards in German science fiction and for maintaining links with the SF movement in other cultures. He is a commanding presence in international science fiction.

Although he has only published two novels, both have appeared in English: *The Last Day of Creation* (1981; 1984 U.S.) and *Midas* (1987; 1990 UK). He has written a number of stories, of which this one, the centerpiece of his collection, *Der Zeiter*, may be his best. Franz Rottensteiner, in *Science Fiction Writers*, calls it "a virtuoso performance, so complex and well constructed that it can stand beside the best time travel stories, a tour-de-force that turns artifice into high art." Two forces play a complex and perhaps deadly game of domination in the past and future. It is an interesting comparison to John Crowley's "Great Work of Time," and contrast to Connie Willis's "Fire Watch."

THE KING AND THE DOLLMAKER

Stay where you are, Collins! Every move now could mean a fracture."

"Yes, Your Majesty," said Collins, and stayed where he was.

"Keep your eyes upon us!" commanded the king.

"Yes, Your Majesty," said Collins, and kept his eyes on His Majesty.

Time was slipping by. There was a deadly silence in the hall. The king was perched nervously on the edge of his throne and stared anxiously at the flickering mirror on the wall. Every time a patrol officer stepped out of the mirror, the king gave a start and leveled his gun at the man. Collins could see that the barrel trembled and that beads of sweat had formed on His Majesty's brow. The intervals grew shorter, and the guards could hardly avoid stumbling over one another. The patrol now had the room under constant control. The mirror twitched every time a man was discharged from or reabsorbed into its field. One guard stepped out into the room, looked attentively about him, and returned with a backward step into the mirror. But there was nothing special to observe. The room was empty. The walls still showed the light spots where the valuable paintings had once hung. Generations of sovereigns who had once peered morosely, critically, or solemnly from the walls upon the most recent offspring of their lineage now peered morosely, critically, or solemnly into some dark corner of the palace cellar which they had never seen during their lifetime. Even the nails had been taken out of the walls, the tapestries removed, the curtains, the furniture, everything. There was only the throne, His Majesty, the patrol's time mirror, which occasionally disgorged and reswallowed a guard, and a man standing at the triply barred and shielded window—Collins, His Majesty's Minister of Personal Security and Futurology.

The throne room was hermetically sealed, doors and windows safeguarded by energy screens. Not an insect, not even a dust particle, could have penetrated the shield, not to mention a minibattleship or a remote-controlled needle grenade.

"Tell us how long this is to continue, Collins. We cannot bear it much longer!" The king gave his minister a beseeching look. He was trembling.

Collins tossed back his cape, unclasped the purse on his belt, and drew from it a temporal strip. He held it at arm's length, as he was a bit farsighted, and examined it scrupulously. He was calm and composed; only the corners of his mouth curled ever so slightly in scorn. He had seen through more ticklish situations than this. "By Your Majesty's leave," he said, "Your Majesty's alarm is really groundless. The patrol knows that it will all turn out for the best. We have twenty-seven more minutes, during which Your Majesty is constantly supervised, before the arrival of this impenetrable ten-second time seal. From the very second that we regain access to the mirror from the timeline, this room will once again be under control."

Collins's finger ran down the temporal strip, tracing the dots indicating the guards' positions, and compared them with the date and time printed continuously along the margin. He had even jotted down the guards' names on the strip. They were his best men. One could not do more. With the exception of one short interruption, the dots lay so close to one another that they formed a solid line. Collins looked at his watch. Everything was running according to schedule.

"What is the latest report?" demanded the king. His voice was horse, fear gripped his throat.

"Nothing precise, I'm afraid, in spite of all our efforts. Your Majesty is aware of the fact that WHITE has undertaken transformations which reach far into the future. The seals are fluid, and the impenetrable time block is constantly shifting position. Our investigations are valid for but a few hours, then the temporal strips are worth no more than the paper they are printed on. Yesterday we could still supervise four days into the future; at present, this period is reduced to a scant two hours, and the block continues to grow toward us. But according to our calculations it will soon come to a standstill, so that we will eventually have thirty minutes left to supervise. But all this can of course change, should WHITE undertake a fracture."

"That's just it. That is the problem," whimpered the king. "Do something! How can you loiter about idly when I am in danger?"

"Your Majesty is not in danger," sighed Collins. "That is practically the only thing about which we are certain. After the critical moment is past, Your Majesty will be sitting upon the throne just as Your Majesty does now. Of course . . ."

"Of course what?"

"Now, Your Majesty, we have discussed it often enough. By Your Majesty's leave, should we really bring this up again now, when the moment is nearing?"

The king slouched in his seat and chewed his fingernails.

"Are you certain that I am the one who will be sitting here after the critical moment?" he asked suspiciously.

"But, Your Majesty, who else?"

"Yes, who else," muttered the king, and looked at Collins.

The minister inspected his temporal strip. The stream of dots discontinued, reappeared, only eventually to disappear altogether. Here was the seal, there the block began. What took place at these inaccessible points? Why had WHITE placed them there? Was this some kind of a trap or ruse? He had spent a great deal of time on the problem, had assigned his best men to it, but he had found no solution in spite of the innumerable facts that had been compiled. He was tired. A holiday would do him good. He looked around him at the dreary room, examined its bare walls. Got to get out of here, he thought. Choose any other time. How about dinosaur hunting in the Mesozoic era? He had grown out of that age. And he detested hunting expeditions. Too loud, too much excitement, too much drinking, and for the last few decades terribly overcrowded. They went and killed off the beasts in less than no time with their laser guns. And what if they did? Ugly creatures they were anyway. A minimal fracture. A couple of bone-collecting scientists of some later age would probably be astonished that the animals had disappeared so quickly. They would certainly find an explanation, that was what they were scientists for. The Tertiary period—yes, that would be better. It had been nice and warm then in this region. A couple of weeks of Tertiary. The patrol had a holiday center there. Plenty of rest, excellent food, saber-toothed-tiger steaks. Once, though, he had chosen a year when he himself had been there. Not that it made much difference to him if he was constantly crossing his own path—that had happened to him before, one got used to it. One had a few drinks with oneself, talked about old times, complimented oneself on how good one had still looked then and how on the other hand one had hardly aged at all since; one bored oneself to tears, felt a certain envy appear which could grow to hatred when one saw the bad habits that one had already had then and had long since wanted to get rid of but still had years later. Youth and experience stood face to face, and in between were all those years that one circled about and avoided mentioning but still could not ignore. Everyone knew that this could bring on disastrous time fractures if one were not careful, irreparable damage, intervention by the Committee, at best deportation to an ice age or to one of the first three millennia, at worst eradication from the timeline, condemnation to nonexistence, unless amnesty were granted by means of a special dispensation from the Supreme Council on the Future.

"You just stand about and say nothing!" The king's voice snapped him out of thoughts. "We asked you a question."

"I beg Your Majesty's pardon."

"What exactly is going to happen?" demanded the king peevishly. "Explain it again, step by step."

"Certainly, Your Majesty. Our guards are in control of all of the timeline which is accessible to us and are closely observing the particular area around the palace. There is absolutely no action. That is, as Your Majesty already knows, apart from the doll. . . ."

"Nonsense! Always this damned doll! How often do I have to hear that ridiculous story? What am I paying you for? Always repeating the same foolishness!"

"A small mechanical figure appears," continued Collins, unmoved, "a sort of miniature robot, with which Your Majesty deigns to play."

"Rubbish! How often must I repeat it? What on earth would I be doing with a doll? Have you ever seen me play with dolls? This is utterly absurd!"

"But by Your Majesty's leave, according to the reports of the guards, Your Majesty seems to be quite taken with this small mechanical object."

"But that is just what I don't understand! What am I to do with a doll? Am I a child? Once and for all, enough of this doll! It is beginning to get on my nerves."

The minister shrugged his shoulders and looked at his watch. "I am reporting nothing but the facts when I say that Your Majesty takes pleasure in playing with this figure, actually lays his weapon aside and gives the impression of being relieved of a burden and in extreme good humor, not to say . . ."

"Not to say what?"

"Not to say, well—like a new man."

The king leaned back with a sigh, then shook his head in annoyance and slid nervously forward again to the edge of the throne. "Doll, doll, what the devil does this doll mean?" he brooded. Then, turning and launching into Collins, "For weeks now we have heard nothing from you but reports about dolls and other such nonsense. Collins, you have failed. As Minister for the Personal Security of Our Person you have failed miserably. That can cost you your head; you are well aware of that?"

"By Your Majesty's leave, we have done everything within our means to get hold of the producer of this doll and to find and destroy the doll itself. The research has cost hundreds of years of work by our best specialists in ancient history, time manipulation, and causal coordination. Let me assure Your Majesty without exaggeration that we have done everything, absolutely everything within our power."

"You had orders to cause a fracture in order to avoid this dreadful moment, and what did you do? Nothing! You had orders to find this man in the seventeenth century and to have him disposed of, and was this corrective measure taken? No! And you babble on about your specialists and their hundreds of years of work! It does not interest us in the slightest. Did you hear? Not in the slightest! You have failed!" The king trembled with anger; his fingers tightened around the handle of his weapon. It was aimed at Collins.

"I—I most humbly beg Your Majesty's forgiveness, but as I said, we have done everything within our power."

"Did you have the doll destroyed? Yes or no! If you did, why does it keep reappearing?"

"We did destroy it—at least we destroyed one doll, but an infinite number of such dolls could exist."

"Don't talk nonsense! This simple craftsman can't have made an infinite number of dolls."

"Of course not, Your Majesty, but perhaps two or three of this type."

"And why haven't they been destroyed? Because you failed!"

"As Your Majesty already knows, and as I have allowed myself to emphasize repeatedly, this is in all probability—and in my own humble opinion—not at all where the basic problem lies. This question of the doll is certainly peculiar, but it is clearly just as unimportant as is the craftsman in the seventeenth century. We are dealing with an intervention by WHITE in which this man in the distant past plays either no part or a very subordinate one, in which his function is to lure us onto the wrong track. Your Majesty knows that I have never considered this a very promising lead. How much of a chance could a man in the pretechnical age have had? I personally am convinced that at that time man did not even have electrical energy; they were still experimenting with frogs' legs."

"One can build mechanical automats, Collins, which if they are preserved in museums or private collections can survive several thousand years. But we have other grounds to find this man dangerous. You should have had him eliminated. You had explicit instructions to do so."

"WHITE prevented it," answered Collins with a shrug of his shoulders.

"WHITE, WHITE, WHITE! Let WHITE be damned!"

They were silent. Time was slipping by.

The guards came and went. They now registered every second.

"How long is this to continue, Collins?"

"Exactly eleven minutes and thirty seconds, Your Majesty," answered the minister. He now held his watch in the palm of his hand. After this period the time mirror would blank out and be impenetrable to the patrol for a span of ten seconds.

"What is the purpose of this seal, Collins? Can you explain why WHITE had the seal placed here? What is hidden behind it? Something is happening behind it, but what?"

The king's voice trembled. The tension in the room grew.

"We don't know, Your Majesty," said the minister. "Perhaps it is just a ruse—we will know soon. But Your Majesty need have no fears, there will be no change."

"That is what your guards say. They are dolts," said the king. He coughed and gasped for breath and tugged at the collar of his black cape as if it was too tight. The handkerchief with which he wiped his brow was soaked with perspiration.

"Have you given all the orders? Is everything sealed off?"

"Exactly as Your Majesty commanded. The entire palace has been thoroughly inspected several times, the throne room especially carefully of course. There is not a single square inch that hasn't been meticulously checked. All dolls, toys, and similar objects which we were able to seize in the vicinity of this time-space point have been destroyed. The palace is locked and bolted inside and out. Nothing can penetrate this room unnoticed. Any particle, even a speck of dust, would immediately disintegrate in the energy fields. The doll must either come through the mirror or materialize in a manner unknown us; it is not in the palace now, unless it has taken on a form of energy of which we have no knowledge."

The king looked about suspiciously, as if he could discover some clue that had escaped the attention of the minister's guards, but his weapon found no target. The room was bare, there were only His Majesty upon the throne, the minister, the mirror, and the stream of guards who formed the observation chain.

"I cannot bear to see these faces any longer, Collins."

"Your Majesty has given explicit orders . . ."

"Yes, yes, I know. Are these men absolutely reliable?"

"Absolutely."

"What do you know about this dollmaker?"

"It is an odd story, Your Majesty. A relatively large part of his life seems to contain important historical facts which WHITE does not wish to have changed. As Your Majesty knows, he appears in the year 1623 in a small city in what was then Europe—now our Operations Base 7—buys a house and apparently earns a living as a simple craftsman, makes few demands on others, mingles little with the townspeople but is respected by all. On August 17, 1629, the period suddenly becomes inaccessible, closed off by a seal which severely handicaps our operations. This seal extends as far as February 2, 1655, covering almost three decades. Nevertheless, we set several of our best specialists to the task of living through the time behind the seal. Your Majesty can hardly conceive of what this meant for those men. But in spite of all our efforts the venture failed; the men were never heard of again. We could find them in neither the fifth nor the sixth decade of that century. Times then were particularly hard, wars were raging, and morale was very low. In short, by the time we could operate again we discovered that our craftsman was dead. We questioned people who knew him. Naturally we cannot examine the validity of the information they gave us, as there are no written records, but this is what we were told: One night he went into a fit of raving madness, and from that moment on he was like a different person. Formerly he had been a respected man whose advice was sought by all, but after this attack he let himself go, fell into the habit of swearing, jabbered incoherently, neglected his work, took to drink, picked quarrels, and proved himself to be generally arrogant and overbearing. For instance, he demanded that his neighbors address him as His Majesty, for which the fellows soundly thrashed him. He had apparently gone mad. He went from bad to worse, living on alms and on what he could occasionally beg or steal. One day he was found hanging by a rope in a barn, where he had apparently been for several weeks. He himself had put an end to his miserable existence. He must have been hastily buried somewhere, for we could not find his grave. We were told that this is commonly done to victims of suicide. We can fix the date of his death with relative certainly to the autumn of the year 1650. As Your Majesty can see, it is all in all nothing remarkable, perhaps not a daily occurrence in those centuries, but by no means an unusual one."

"But this doll, Collins. What about the doll?"

"We succeeded in destroying one doll. Our men blasted it and it exploded. We were not able to reconstruct it completely, but the parts that we were able to gather up in our haste in the dark give evidence of an extremely simple spring-driven mechanism, such as one finds in the clocks and music boxes of that time. There doesn't seem to be anything special about the doll either."

"Did you find anything in the following centuries?"

"We have inspected innumerable mechanical toys, only sporadically, to be sure, from the mid-twentieth century on, as there are such vast quantities of them, but we never came across anything unusual. Occasionally we found in literature evidences of more highly developed mechanisms such as we were searching for, but all our attempts to test the validity of these allusions failed. The mechanical doll was a well-loved fiction at that time, a sort of fairy-tale figure, the forerunner of the robot, I surmise. But the technical basis necessary to develop it is lacking."

"Nothing! Absolutely nothing!"

The minister shrugged his shoulders regretfully.

"How many minutes, Collins?"

"Five, Your Majesty."

"It is enough to drive one mad! Can't a stop be put to this running about?"

"I am sorry, Your Majesty, but it is Your Majesty's own command that the room be under constant supervision. This supervision cannot be countermanded without causing delicate fractures which might have dire consequences for Your Majesty's safety."

The minister kept his eye on his watch and compared the time with the temporal strips in his hand. In four minutes and thirty seconds the stream of dots indicating the guards' positions would cease for a brief period.

"Collins, have you absolutely no idea what is going to happen in the next four minutes?"

"I am afraid we know nothing for certain, Your Majesty, but . . ."

"But what?"

"But, by Your Majesty's leave, I have my suspicions."

"It is your damned duty to give thought to the situation and to express your thoughts. So go on and express them!"

"Let us assume that Your Majesty himself, on the basis of experience which Your Majesty will have gained in the future and on the basis of further development of time-travel technique, makes certain points and periods of the time-line which seem important to Your Majesty inaccessible by means of this seal."

"We see. Collins, why did you not mention such an important aspect earlier? That is a very plausible possibility; one can hardly consider it seriously enough." The king smiled in relief. He clung to this thought as to a straw. The idea that he himself could be WHITE clearly flattered him. He snapped his fingers energetically and feverishly concentrated upon the thought. Then his face clouded over again.

"But we would at least have transmitted some kind of explanatory message to ourselves in order to make this horrid situation more bearable."

"Perhaps that is impossible for reasons of security," interjected Collins.

The king shook his head. "But this doll. Where does this confounded doll fit into the picture?"

"Perhaps it is supposed to bring Your Majesty some important piece of information."

"And the dollmaker? No, no, it doesn't fit in."

"Perhaps he has nothing to do with the whole affair, perhaps he is just a secondary figure; but, on the other hand, perhaps he is the source of information."

"Perhaps, perhaps! Is that all you have to say? What do you think you are here for—to reel off vague suspicions? We can do that ourselves. You are responsible for our security. Is that clear? Such nonsense! A primitive tinsmith from twelve thousand years ago has information for us, the ruler of four planet systems and all their moons—how ridiculous! Just empty speculation and foolish twaddle!"

The king was provoked. The barrel of his weapon roamed back and forth, and Collins tried to keep out of firing range.

"Then it was a blind alley, by Your Majesty's leave, which our best forces have wasted centuries in exploring."

The king stamped his foot. "Time doesn't interest us! We want information. We want absolute security for our person, even if your people need thousands of years to guarantee it. If you go down blind alleys, it's your problem, Collins, not ours! You are a miserable failure! We are holding you responsible for the consequences. You understand what that means."

"At Your Majesty's command."

"Our command was: bring information and more information about the present sphere of time and everything connected with it; and you dare to enter this room with your suspicions! You can go to the devil with your crazy notions! We want facts and nothing but facts."

"Very well, Your Majesty, but don't forget the seal on Operations Base 7, an intervention by WHITE which made our work extremely difficult and thwarted our action in the decisive years."

"That may very well be. Perhaps there was at that moment a historical event of great importance. As you said, there was a war at the time. Perhaps our intervention would have endangered a politician or scientist of top-ranking future valence, or the great-grandfather of a politician or scientist, or heaven knows who. But that is all irrelevant. What is going to happen here and now in a few seconds? That is the only thing that matters."

Time was slipping by.

The guards came and went, came and went, dots on the temporal strip.

The king leaned back, breathing heavily. He was as white as chalk and dripped with sweat.

"Thirty more seconds, Your Majesty."

"Collins!" The king's eyes were fixed upon him beseechingly; they were filled with tears. "Collins! Keep your eyes on me! Do you hear? Don't lose sight of me for a single moment! Take note of everything, everything!"

He was leaning far forward, and his eyes swept panic-stricken across the room. He began to see dolls everywhere. They crept out from beneath his throne, came out of the walls, slipped down from the ceiling on threads. Everywhere he saw dangling limbs, expressionless plastic faces, beady glass eyes that glared maliciously at him, tiny fists that brandished daggers as big as needles or aimed minute laser pistols at him.

The king trembled and gnawed incessantly at his lower lip. Fear had complete mastery over him now. It was suffocating him. He felt as if he must either crawl off into a hole somewhere or else scream and shoot about him in blind rage.

The minister gave him a worried look.

"I can't bear this any longer, Collins!" shrieked His Majesty. "Don't just stand idly about—do something!"

His shrill voice burst into thousands of tiny splinter-sharp fragments.

Collins followed the second hand of his watch as it ticked nearer and nearer to the critical moment.

"Now."

The mirror went blank.

The minister looked carefully about the room, then fixed his gaze upon the king. The king suddenly leaned back, crossed his legs, and put aside his pistol so that both hands were free to straighten out the clothing of a small plain doll which he was holding.

The minister blinked and shook his head to dispel the optical illusion, but the doll was still there. It hadn't been there before and now it was there. He tried without success to cope with this new situation. The brain refused to accept what the eyes clearly saw. His Majesty was sitting comfortably on the throne, smoothing out the dress of this small mechanical figure, and smiling delightedly.

"Come, Collins, why are you staring so aghast at us? Have you never seen a doll before? A pretty little toy, don't you think? A dollmaker's masterpiece."

The ten seconds were over. The mirror glowed once again and the first guard stepped out into the room.

"Hello, how are you? Have a nice trip?" the king asked him in good humor.

"He-hello," stammered the bewildered man, and fled back into the mirror.

"Good morning," the king greeted the next guard who appeared.

"G-good morning, Your Majesty," he managed to stutter, and stumbled over his feet in his haste to find the mirror and disappear into it.

"This is quite an amazing doll, Collins. Go ahead and take a closer look at it."

The minister approached hesitantly.

"Would Your Majesty deign . . . an explanation . . . the rapid transformation . . . I mean, I beg Your Majesty's pardon, but I find it incomprehensible that all of a sudden Your Majesty is . . ."

". . . Like a new man, you wanted to say?"

"Yes, Your Majesty."

"You will get your explanation soon enough, in a half hour or so, when this spying finally stops." He pointed to the mirror.

"But, Your Majesty, time is running out. Your Majesty's only chance is to explain the whole situation to me immediately, so that we can undertake a fracture and take all other necessary measures, so that all may still turn out for the best. I beseech Your Majesty, this is possible for only a few minutes longer."

The king let out a peal of laughter.

"What for, Collins? Everything *is* turning out for the best. Why are you so nervous? Fetch a chair and sit down! Aren't there any chairs here?"

"But certainly Your Majesty will explain . . ."

"All in good time, Collins, all in good time. Not now. Let us first take a look at this doll. It seems to be an old piece, doesn't it, perhaps thousands of years old, but still in quite good shape. I believe it even can dance. It has probably made a long trip, we should say a very long trip, but it is still fully intact. Hard to believe what can fit into this little head, if one only knows how to go about filling it properly!" He held the small metal head of the doll between thumb and forefinger and smiled pensively.

"But, Your Majesty, I don't understand. What does this all mean?"

"Be patient, Collins, be patient. You will find out. There are just twenty minutes left. In the meantime, let us watch the review of your troops. Then we will tell you a story, a very ordinary story, but we think it will interest you nevertheless. We would wager on it."

"I am breathless with anticipation, Your Majesty."

Meanwhile, the king continued to greet with a gracious wave of the hand the guards who appeared and disappeared, as if he were holding an audience. The men gave the minister a questioning look, which he answered with a regretful shrug of his shoulders and a resigned sigh. His Majesty continued to play with the doll and seemed to be in unusually high spirits, as if all this was great fun.

Now it was Collins's turn to become nervous. He found that he had torn the temporal strip in his hand to shreds. The king said to his minister, as if he too had noticed this, "That doesn't matter, Collins. We don't need it anymore. In a quarter of an hour the stream of dots will stop anyway."

"Well, that's that, Collins. Your guards can't penetrate the mirror anymore."

The mirror was not blank. It continued to flicker, but no one stepped out from it. The minister stared in astonishment first at the instrument, then at His Majesty.

"Surprises you, doesn't it?" laughed the king.

"Indeed it does," admitted Collins. "But how is it possible?"

"Let us not anticipate."

"As Your Majesty wishes. But it has always been my task to anticipate."

"You are right. Very well, then let us begin." The king settled comfortably into his throne and cleared his throat. "Collins, you are a clever man."

"Your Majesty honors me."

"But you have made several mistakes."

"I beg Your Majesty's pardon, but what mistakes?"

"First of all, you shouldn't have taken your eyes off the mirror for one single instant, for then you would have noticed that it wasn't blank for the entire ten seconds. Not that there was anything you could have done, but you might have gained some information which would have led you to make certain further considerations. And at times you were damned close to having the answer. You almost beat us in our little game."

"Perhaps, Your Majesty. It is not clear to me—what could I have done?"

"You should have thought out the problem more carefully. Fortunately for us, you didn't. You could for instance have given more consideration to the meaning of this seal and the intervention of WHITE."

"I considered the seal a protection of important timeline intersections, where a fracture could have devastating consequences."

"All of which is true, Collins. And WHITE has to intervene, because sometimes time fissures spread underneath the seals, as a result of imprudent operations, and make repairs necessary, in order to guarantee the safety of the future, our universe, and thereby the very existence of WHITE itself."

"I understand, but why didn't WHITE seal off the entire timeline and cut off all operations of the patrol?"

"A good question. Why not? Think hard, Collins. You have a good head on your shoulders."

"Of course. Your Majesty is right. That would mean cutting off all time travel, which would in turn mean no invention of time travel, as there could be no experiments, and then the existence of WHITE would be impossible."

"Very good! Therefore, WHITE interferes only when its existence is at stake."

"But what about my mistakes, Your Majesty?"

"Without this future power, which we call WHITE, the course of our planet would speedily deteriorate into a state of hopeless confusion. WHITE was actually your opponent, Collins, but you were always looking for an opponent elsewhere. And you didn't know where to look."

"At times I suspected it, but I thought it more probable that certain political-interest groups in the empire, perhaps operating from a base in the future, were giving us trouble. But Your Majesty spoke of several mistakes."

"That is all part of the story which we are about to tell you. You must pay especially close attention to it for reasons which will also be made clear. But we want to anticipate a bit. You were hunting down this dollmaker—"

"Indeed."

"—And at times you made life difficult for him."

"As Your Majesty commanded."

"Hmm," smiled the king.

"Although without much success, I must admit, because WHITE intervened with a seal."

"Why didn't you study the past history of this person more closely, at the very time and place in which it occurred?"

"We didn't think it necessary. We already knew something of the man, though it was second- and third-hand information. The question didn't seem to be worth going into more thoroughly. It was my opinion that we had already spent too much time on him. What we had found out about him didn't seem to be helpful enough. . . ."

"Then you know that this man was born in 1594, first learned the blacksmith's trade, then became apprenticed to a watchmaker, and afterward traveled about for five years as a journeyman. During this time war broke out and he was captured by recruiting officers and forced to serve in the army; he spent the next two years with a band of men who had joined Tilly's troops. . . ."

"Yes, Your Majesty, and settled down in the town which is now our Operations Base 7; he acquired money somehow, bought himself a cottage, set up a workshop, and devoted himself entirely to his hobby of making watches and mechanical toys. He became a respected citizen of the town but refused all public offices which were offered to him; he escaped the snares of all the spinsters in the neighborhood, having decided upon a bachelor life in order to have his evenings free to pore over blueprints and tinker with mechanical instruments. He engaged a housekeeper who cooked and cleaned the house but was not allowed into the workshop. The watchmaker became more and more withdrawn, hardly leaving his house. Finally he became mentally deranged and in 1650 hung himself. As Your Majesty can see, we know quite a bit about him, but nothing which appears noteworthy to me."

"Nothing noteworthy. You are quite right, Collins. But do you also know that this man was killed in action, near Heidelberg in the year 1621? Tilly's crowd murdered and plundered its way through the countryside. He was killed either by farmers or by one of his fellow cutthroats, who probably fought with him over his booty or some woman."

"I beg Your Majesty's pardon."

"You heard correctly, Collins. The man whom you supposedly investigated so carefully was no longer alive at the time Operations Base 7 was established."

"That would have been an inexcusable error. But how does Your Majesty know this?"

"More about that later. And your third error was that you failed to have photographs taken of this man in order to examine him more closely. You would perhaps have had quite a surprise. But you and your people had eyes only for the mechanical toys. Fortunately."

There was a crafty smile on the king's face.

"I considered his appearance fully irrelevant in this case, especially as I could never rid myself of the feeling that we were on the wrong track and had wasted much too much time on the man."

"So you yourself have never seen this Weisslinger."

"No, Your Majesty. Why should I have seen him?"

The king shook his head in disapproval. Collins felt more and more uncertain.

"What a pity. Weisslinger is an extremely interesting man. You should have become acquainted with him; you would certainly have learned a great deal from him. He had much to tell, for he had been through much in his life. Perhaps you would have noticed that he wore an ingenious mask, though it was no more ingenious than masks could be in that age. You know us well, Collins, and you have a good head on your shoulders."

"I am beginning to doubt that seriously, Your Majesty."

"Now, now, Collins. It is never too late. Perhaps you will yet meet him."

"How is that possible, Your Majesty? I don't understand. . . ."

"Patience, patience! Wait until you have heard our story. Then you will have to admit that you let yourself be checkmated too easily."

"By Your Majesty's leave, I am burning with eagerness to hear the story, for I see more and more clearly that I accomplished my task much more poorly than I had originally thought."

"Indeed you did, Collins. You played miserably and recklessly."

"I most humbly beg Your Majesty's pardon."

"On the other hand, you were pitted against no mean opponent. But everything in its turn. BLACK had the victory as good as in its pocket—the situation was grim. Then it was WHITE's turn, WHITE would have to be damned tricky. . . . But where shall we begin? Ah yes, on the day when . . . Now pay strict attention! One evening . . ."

It was evening. The night watchman had just sung out the eleventh hour and had gone down the street, when a carriage drawn by two magnificent horses rounded the corner, rumbled over the cobblestones of the market square, and pulled up in front of the Red Ox Inn, directly across from the house of the dollmaker Weisslinger. The dollmaker went to his window and opened the shutters a tiny crack. He peered out in order to inspect the travelers who were arriving so late at night. He saw two men alight from the vehicle and converse with the proprietor of the Red Ox, who had come out to greet the distinguished guests and escort them into the house. The strangers apparently did not intend to enter and partake of his board and lodging, as they involved him in a conversation on the doorstep. They had a number of questions and seemed to be looking for someone in the town, for the innkeeper nodded his head several times and pointed to Weisslinger's house across the street. The strangers' eyes followed the innkeeper's finger; they carefully surveyed the market square and the neighborhood. Then they took leave of the innkeeper, pressing a gold coin into his hand, and strode toward Weisslinger's house.

"Aha," said the dollmaker knowingly to himself, and cautiously closed the shutters. "The time has come."

He quickly cleared away his mechanical instruments, drew forth several large drawings, and spread them out upon table and workbench. Then he sat down and waited. As he heard the knock on his door he hesitated, then went to the window and spoke quietly out into the darkness: "Who is there?"

"We beg your forgiveness, Master, for disturbing you at this late hour. The roads are bad and we have made very slow progress. On our travels we heard of a famous watchmaker in this area by the name of Weisslinger. Are you this man?"

"I am Weisslinger, but you honor me, I am certainly not famous. Come in."

Their thick accents indicated that they were foreigners. Weisslinger unbolted the door.

"Please forgive us for disturbing you. But we have little time and must speak with you."

"Come in, gentlemen. You aren't disturbing me at all, I was still up and working. Please excuse the disorderly room. I seldom clean it up and my housekeeper isn't allowed to come in here, she is too careless and always breaks something. Please take a seat. What brings you to this town?"

"We heard of your fame as a maker of highly ingenious dolls."

"That is not my main occupation. By trade I am actually a smith, and I have learned the watchmaker's arts as well. It is true that I have spent much of my—well—spare time making small mechanical toys such as music boxes and dancing dolls—although, I must admit, with little success, due to my insufficient craftsmanship. Please forgive me, gentlemen, I am neglecting my duties as host. But I never expect visitors and have nothing in the house to offer you. I can recommend the Red Ox across the road. You will certainly be pleased with the service there. I often have my meals there myself. The food is good and the wine cellar even better."

"That is not necessary. We have already had our evening meal."

Weisslinger took a closer look at the strangers. Their clothing was simple but elegant: black capes of fine material, close-fitting, well-cut trousers, and low boots fashioned of supple leather. They were examining the room which served both as living room and workshop. They seemed to be particularly interested in his machines, tools, and measuring instruments, which hung on the wall or lay on the workbench; it was not difficult to read from the disappointment on their faces that they had expected more.

"Would you be so kind as to demonstrate one of your models for us?" asked one of the men, trying without success to hide his discontent.

"Of course," answered Weisslinger. He carefully put away his drawings and cleared the workbench, then placed upon it one of his carved music boxes. He wound it up and let it play, then wound up a second and a third music box; the tinny tones of their simple melodies made an odd jingle-jangle. He then took up a small dancing doll with movable limbs, wound it up, and placed it on the bench with the music boxes. The springs whirred, and the doll made stiff, jerky pirouettes on the tabletop.

The gentlemen did not seem to take great interest in the demonstration; they continued to look about the room, glanced at each other and shrugged their shoulders, but pretended to be extremely interested whenever Weisslinger gave them a questioning look. Then one gentleman's eyes fell upon a grandfather clock which was standing in a corner of the room. It was an extraordinary piece with painted face, beautiful case carved out of valuable dark wood, decorated porcelain weights suspended from delicate chains, and a finely chased pendulum on which the astronomic tables and the allegorical figures of the horoscope were engraved.

"Is this clock also a work of yours?"

"Yes, sir. Does it please you?"

"It is a beautiful piece, but it doesn't keep accurate time."

"This is a curious point. You may find it hard to believe, but the clock is not supposed to keep accurate time."

"How can that be?"

"It is a long story, which I am afraid would bore you."

"Not at all!"

"Very well, if you really want to hear it. Please be seated. One day a man came to see me, a Polish count who had spent a good part of his life in Seville and Zaragoza. He was returning to his home in Poland; on his travels he had heard of me and sought me out. He inspected my clocks and toys, my tools and measuring instruments as well, and seemed to know quite a bit about the craft, as I could judge from his questions. But he denied having any extensive knowledge about such things. In any case, he was apparently satisfied with what he saw and commissioned me to build a clock for him. Nothing simpler, I thought to myself, but I was soon to change my mind. In fact, this man showed me very detailed drawings according to which the clock was to be constructed; these he had bought for a high price from a Jew in Seville. At first everything seemed simple, but I soon ran into difficulties. The more closely I investigated the drawings, the more complicated the works appeared, and I began to doubt seriously that this instrument which I was to build would function at all. The drawings were accompanied by instructions written in Arabic. The count, who could not read Arabic, had had the text translated into Spanish; this he had translated into his mother tongue and had scrawled along the margins of the old parchment documents. We spent several days trying to translate this text into German, but neither of us was capable of making enough sense out of these descriptions so that they might serve me as instructions, which they were obviously intended to be. They were more confusing than the drawings themselves, especially as they were worded in a figurative language which spoke of flowers, fragrant perfumes, and unknown spices, of strange oceans and distant lands, angels and demons, when there should have been nothing but metals and weights, screws and springs, coils and tractive forces, balances and swings of the pendulum. I was utterly bewildered and wanted to refuse the commission, but the count promised me a princely sum for my efforts, even if they should fail. In addition, he placed at my disposal a considerable percentage of this sum in cash, with which I was to procure the necessary materials and tools. I still hesitated, then he raised the sum, imploring me to at least try it. Finally I gave in and set to work. It took me weeks in these troubled times to gather the materials, as only the best would do. I had the face of the clock drawn up according to specifications; it was to be divided into sixteen hours, as if it were to measure some foreign time. I canvassed the countryside to find a cabinetmaker who could build and ornament the case according to the instructions; then we both traveled about selecting and buying the different types of wood out of which he was to construct the case—all of this in wartime, when we never knew at night if we were to see the sun the next morning. But God, all praise be His, held His shielding hand over me and my work, and in spite of all the difficulties the clock eventually took its present form, as it stands before you. It cost me three years' work. When it was finally finished, the clock actually ran, which was the last thing I expected. But the way it ran! According to the drawings, the clock was to have five hands, each of which was to trace its circle with varying speed and direction. The clock could tell the most improbable intervals and constellations of the heavenly bodies, but not the hours of the day. This must have been the invention of some insane infidel who wanted to measure the ages his damned soul would have to spend in Purgatory. It is the unchristian work of the devil which measures the eternity of Hell. Every chime of the evening bell sends its hands spinning in a different direction. . . . But I see that my story bores you, gentlemen. Please pardon my prattling on so. I don't have visitors often."

"Who gave you this commission?" inquired one of the strangers.

"A Polish count, as I already mentioned. I never did know his name. He came back once to see me, when the clock was almost finished. He spent hours studying the drawings, measured the positions of the hands, listened to the ticking of the works, made notes in a small book, sighed and shook his head, seemed at times to be discontented with the clock, then again pleasantly surprised, then once again dissatisfied; his eyes followed the pendulum as it swung back and forth, his ears noticed every change in rhythm of the buzzing and whirring mechanism, which sometimes ticked as slowly as drops of water falling from the ceiling of a cave, then again as rapidly as the hoofbeats of a herd of galloping horses—but the man never uttered a word. When I questioned him he cut me off with a wave of the hand, put his finger to his lips, and listened with such concentration to the ticking and whirring of the clock that—I hope you will pardon this severe judgment—I slowly began to question his sanity. As he departed he left me a sack of gold coins. I thanked him profusely, for this was a much greater sum than he had promised me. He smiled and promised to return soon to pick up the clock, but I never saw him again. Heaven knows why he didn't come back; perhaps he was not satisfied with my work, perhaps he had been expecting too much. Who knows? He never spoke a word of praise, which I must admit I would have been glad to hear after all the effort I put into the making of the clock; after all, I did my very best to carry out the order to his satisfaction. But perhaps he perished in that terrible war, God save his poor straying soul. These are frightful times. But you know as well as I, gentlemen, what it is to live in these times. God be merciful to us and let there at last be peace. Please blame it on my advancing age if I have gone prattling on again."

"Do you still have the drawings?"

"No, the Pole took them with him when he left this workshop for the last time. The clock was finished, I didn't need the drawings anymore. And I didn't want to keep them any longer, as they were quite valuable."

"So you know nothing more of the background or the whereabouts of your client?" inquired the strangers.

"I'm afraid not; otherwise I would have tried to find him myself. The clock has been standing in that corner now for two years. It takes up too much space in my workshop, but I can neither sell it nor give it away, much less take it apart or destroy it, because it doesn't belong to me. I am beginning to develop a passionate dislike for it; I usually cover it with a cloth and let it run down, but the silence that then fills the room is even more unbearable than the crazy ticking, so I wind it up again. But I removed three of the hands and replaced the face with a normal one; it was the only way I could bear the situation. . . ."

"Tell us if that isn't a good story, Collins!"

"It certainly is, Your Majesty. But I know it all too well. I fell for it from beginning to end."

"Why didn't you follow up that business about the clock?"

"I held this insane instrument to be the product of a sick mind, not worth our time and attention."

"We assure you, you would have had a surprise. You and your people have been standing a whisker away from the secret of the time seal. If you had only held out a little longer . . . but we expect Weisslinger would have had something to say about that."

"Your Majesty, I am an idiot."

"Dear Collins!" laughed the king. "We judged you right! You have no use for metaphysics and unsound logic, for secrets and mysterious strangers. By the way, that Polish count was an invention of ours, but he was rather good, wasn't he?"

"Yes, indeed, Your Majesty."

"And something else, Collins. Do you know that the pendulum clock was not invented before 1657 by Huygens and was patented in the same year in the States General?"

"My God." Collins was embarrassed.

"Your idiots have missed the anachronism—but not Weiss, who thereupon traced down the dollmaker and let him have some part to assemble a machine, in order to move the time seals."

"I am deeply ashamed, Your Majesty."

"Very good. Now let us continue. We haven't finished yet."

"I am curious to hear how these events untangle themselves."

"Perhaps you will be disappointed. Don't set your hopes too high. It is all very simple. Now, these two gentlemen, who had come to see Weisslinger so late at night and had listened with more and more evident boredom to his story, finally purchased one of the mechanical dolls and two other toys, paid the dollmaker well, and took their leave politely but without concealing their disappointment, exhaustion, and ill humor. After refreshing themselves at the Red Ox, they traveled on, although it was well past midnight. Weisslinger watched the coach as it rounded the corner and rumbled out of the city. He closed the shutters again and rubbed his hands with delight, as if he had just made an excellent bargain. Then he blew out the light and went to bed.

"Do you still have the doll, Collins?"

"Of course, Your Majesty, but if I may say so, it is of little value to us. We have examined it carefully. By means of a simple spring mechanism the figure rotates about a fixed point."

"Collins, you are judging things only by their source of power and mobility potential. In a way you are right; the doll isn't worth much, but it is a nice toy, one that would make many a little girl happy, even nowadays. And it is all handmade, every screw is hand-threaded."

"It is no doubt interesting, Your Majesty, but by far not as interesting as the doll Your Majesty is holding now."

"There you are right, Collins. Technique has a way of improving on the product."

"Is this doll also one of Weisslinger's creations?"

The king gave no answer, but leaning down from his throne he carefully set the doll on the floor. It took a few cautious steps to test the smoothness of the surface, then made two or three elaborate pirouettes, sprang nimbly into the air, turned a somersault, landed lightly on its feet, and ended its performance with a courteous bow. The minister applauded in admiration; the king was sunk deep in thought, but suddenly he turned to Collins.

"Where did we leave off?"

"The dollmaker, Your Majesty."

"Oh yes, we remember. Now then, listen carefully!"

It was evening. The night watchman had just sung out the eleventh hour and had gone down the street, when a carriage drawn by two magnificent horses rounded the corner, rumbled over the cobblestones of the market square, and pulled up in front of the Red Ox Inn, directly across from the house of the dollmaker Weisslinger. The dollmaker went to his window and opened the shutters a tiny crack. He peered out in order to inspect the travelers who were arriving so late at night. The innkeeper came to the door to greet the distinguished guests and escort them into the house. Much to his astonishment, nobody descended from the carriage. The coachman made no move to climb down from his box. Upon being questioned by the innkeeper, he explained by means of gestures that he was mute. The innkeeper looked about him uncertainly, then turned with a shrug of the shoulders and went back into the house, closing the door behind him. But Weisslinger remained at his post and continued to gaze in fascination at the carriage. The carriage curtains were closed, but as his eyes became more and more accustomed to the darkness, he noticed that someone had pulled one of the curtains aside and was examining his house with great interest. Time passed by, and neither observer gave up his station. At last the stranger in the carriage lit a cigarette.

"Bungler," muttered Weisslinger contemptuously, and closed the shutters. He did not bother to look again as the carriage rumbled out of the city an hour later. He was already sound asleep.

"What do you think of this version, Collins?"

"Inexcusable, Your Majesty. A cigarette in the seventeenth century! Such a mistake should never have been made by a patrolman. I give up."

"Not so fast, not so fast, Collins! Let us think. Where did we leave off?"

"The dollmaker, Your Majesty, had that evening . . ."

"Oh yes, we remember. Now pay attention!"

It was evening. The night watchman had just sung out the eleventh hour and had gone down the street, when a carriage drawn by two magnificent horses rounded the corner, rumbled over the cobblestones of the market square, and pulled up in front of the Red Ox Inn, directly across from the house of the dollmaker Weisslinger. The dollmaker went to his window and opened the shutters a tiny crack. He peered out in order to inspect the travelers who were arriving so late at night. He saw two men alight from the vehicle and converse with the innkeeper, who had come out to greet the distinguished guests and escort them into the house. The two strangers apparently did not intend to enter and partake of his board and lodging, as they involved him in a conversation on the doorstep. They had a number of questions and seemed to be looking for someone in the town, for the innkeeper nodded his head and pointed repeatedly to Weisslinger's house across the street. The strangers' eyes followed the innkeeper's finger; they carefully surveyed the market square and the neighborhood. Then they took leave of the innkeeper, pressing a gold coin into his hand, and strode toward Weisslinger's house.

At this very moment the dollmaker wound up one of his dolls and set it on the windowsill. The doll hopped nimbly to the ground and began to run. One of the men noticed it and called out to the other. They searched the square, trying to pierce the darkness with their eyes. Suddenly one of them took a leap and threw himself at the running figure, but it escaped him. The second man drew a small pistol and, aiming it, sent a spitting stream of fire whizzing toward the doll. But the tiny doll zigzagged agilely across the square and disappeared unscathed.

The long blue tongues of flame that came whipping out of the weapon licked up over the housetops, leaving glowing streaks behind them. Flashes of ghostly light lit up the market place, and the spitting, hissing, and roaring resounded so that the nearby streets fairly rattled with the echoes.

Weisslinger watched all the commotion in front of his house with amusement. In fact, he had to laugh so hard that his ribs ached.

"You miserable farmers!" he roared. "You louts! Idiots! You heroes of the laser pistols! Just take a look at that! Isn't this a marvelous joke?"

The disturbance outside had developed into a regular street fight. Fearful cries were heard as the people in the houses on the market square were awakened by the uproar. Shutters were thrown open on all sides and slammed shut again in panic as the shooting grew wilder. The townsmen suspected bold thieves or even enemy troops of causing the tumult, but in the general excitement and by the dim light they could not make out the target of the shooting.

In the meantime, something very odd had happened. Out of the carriage, which was built for four and could hold six at the very most, had swarmed fifteen or twenty shadow forms, which set about madly chasing the doll. Their chase gave off a fireworks display of constantly flickering pale streaks of flame, and in their robes they fluttered about the square and the fountain like an eerie swarm of giant moths. This frightful sight caused the inhabitants of the town who had been disturbed by the commotion to bar their doors and windows and to hide their valuables hastily in every niche and cranny they could find.

Master Weisslinger, however, remained at his window and watched the scuffle with growing amusement. He even goaded on the scufflers, but his laughing, jeering cries were drowned in the general uproar. At last one of the armed figures succeeded in hitting the fleeing doll. It exploded with a dull boom and the parts of its mechanism were scattered in the street. The dark-clad, shadowy forms feverishly searched for these fragments. They threw themselves upon the pavement, lights flared up and died out again, and the men crawled about in the street until they had convinced themselves that not a single screw or spring had escaped them. They were like a pack of hounds fighting over a few bones thrown into their midst.

At last every inch of pavement had been inspected and the men began to climb back into the carriage. There was a great rush and pushing; the carriage swayed on its wheels until at last all twenty men had managed to squeeze into it. It had taken four men to hold the horses, which had been frightened by the shooting and would not stop rearing and kicking. Held no longer, they set off at a gallop, and sparks flew from the wheels as the carriage, skidding and rocking, sped around the corner and out of the town.

As soon as the air had cleared and all was quiet outside, a few stout-hearted citizens dared to peek out of their doors and windows to see if body and soul were still in danger. Some courageously left their houses—carrying weapons—and after taking a rapid look about the square began to strut about fearlessly. Loud debates were carried on about the nocturnal raid, who the bold raiders could have been, whom the attack was intended for, what damage had been done, and what kind of an odd burning smell was still in the air. It turned out that nobody had suffered any harm, and nobody's property or possessions had been damaged or stolen. For the time being, no other conclusion could be reached than that at least one hundred heavily armed men had caused the tumult. They had appeared out of nowhere and disappeared again like lightning into thin air, because the appearance and intervention of so many valiant citizens had put dread fear into their hearts.

The night watchman reported that he had intended to throw himself resolutely before the galloping horses, but then thought better of it and decided to avoid meaningless sacrifice—not to mention the town's loss of his valuable services. Therefore, he had moved out of the path of the madly careening beasts and had contented himself with a loud and distinct "Stop!" which the coachman, however, who brutally whipped the horses and looked like the Old Nick himself, had insolently disregarded.

The discussions were carried on by torchlight long into the night and were not given up until the dawn appeared and the innkeeper was too tired to continue filling beermugs and carrying them across the square to sell to those thirsty citizens who stood about the fountain celebrating their victory.

After several days and many all-night debates in the inns, the townsmen came to the agreement, after having consulted the priest, who had shown a great interest in the speculations, that it must have been a devilish apparition which had come to haunt the town. Some surmised that it was an evil omen, others went so far as to interpret it as a warning to the innkeeper of the Red Ox, who had developed the bad habit of filling his mugs less and less full, and whose beer and wine tasted more and more watered down. The rumor spread about town and came in time to the innkeeper's hearing. The evil omen before his very house gave him grounds for reflection, and soon it could be noticed, to the satisfaction of all, that he had taken his lesson to heart and no longer gave his customers any reason to complain in this respect, at least for a time.

The dollmaker meanwhile had nothing to report about the nocturnal incident. He claimed to have slept so soundly that he hadn't heard the uproar at all, although it had taken place directly outside his window. The innkeeper, who wanted to hush the nasty rumors which were damaging his business, declared that the strangers had actually wanted to talk to Weisslinger. The dollmaker laughed and replied that the innkeeper was just looking for someone else to put the blame on and that he himself had and would have nothing to do with any of these brawlers, be it the Devil Himself. After all, the rowdies had given the innkeeper and not himself the first honors of a visit, which everybody well knew and which the innkeeper had already admitted. Everybody laughed along with Weisslinger, because he knew how to use his cleverness and wit to drive his opponent into a corner. The innkeeper said no more about the matter from that time on.

"What do you say to this version, Collins?"

"Bad work, Your Majesty. Very bad work."

"Like a whole herd of bulls in a china shop. Why this large-scale action? You sent a whole regiment in there! You were lucky that the people of this period are rather superstitious. Imagine that taking place in the twentieth or twenty-first century. Interventions of such dimensions could easily start a war, if you have bad luck. Did it at least help you?"

"Not much, Your Majesty. The doll was much more complex than the ones we had bought from Weisslinger, one could say unbelievably complex by the technical standards of that time, which of course increased our suspicion. But on the other hand, there was nothing mysterious about its mechanism. We couldn't completely reconstruct it from the pieces we had collected, but there was no indication of any electronic instruments—it was certainly a purely mechanical construction. But it seems to me now almost as if the dollmaker wanted to play a trick on us, and we promptly fell for it. He probably already knew that we came from a different age. But by Your Majesty's leave, how can such an idea occur to a man in the seventeenth century?"

The king laughed.

"Don't underestimate the human imagination! The concept that man can travel in time is much older than you think."

"That may be so. We'd have to look into it," said the minister.

"Now look at that! A simple seventeenth-century mechanic has played a trick on our Collins. Shall we give you an early pension?"

"I most humbly beg Your Majesty's forgiveness. We wanted to eliminate this fracture, but it was not possible."

The minister stared at the floor in shame.

The doll now tried to walk on its hands. It succeeded on the first try.

The king smirked.

"It didn't work? Well, well. Think of that! It didn't work!"

"No, Your Majesty. It was our last chance to intervene successfully, WHITE had made everything else impossible. The seal started suddenly to move. We even had to leave important instruments at Operations Base 7. . . ."

"Time mirrors too?"

"Time mirrors too. We had to evacuate the station in a great hurry. The seal grew with threatening speed in our direction, as members of the patrol reported."

"Hmm. Does that surprise you? That could have caused a nasty fracture. Imagine the results if in this wild shooting someone had been seriously wounded or even killed. It would have put our entire history in a complete muddle. WHITE was forced to intervene, or else your people would have made more irreparable blunders."

"I beg Your Majesty's pardon, but it was an extremely important matter. For the first time one of these mysterious dolls appeared, time was pressing, and I had strictest orders. . . ."

"But you are in charge of security and must certainly be aware of the consequences of intervening along the timeline. That's what you had special training for."

Collins stared contritely at the toes of his shoes.

"Your Majesty is right. It was careless of me."

"Now then, don't make such a face about it. Nothing really serious happened," laughed the king.

"Your Majesty deigns to laugh?"

"Yes, we were just imagining the twenty men squeezing into the coach. We assume that you had an instrument installed in the coach."

"Yes, Your Majesty, one of the time mirrors from Operations Base 7."

The conversation ceased, and both men silently watched the doll. It was dancing now on its hands, now on its feet. One somersault followed another.

"Where were we?"

"The dollmaker, Your Majesty, had on that evening . . ."

"Oh yes, we remember. Now, listen carefully!"

It was evening. The night watchman had just sung out the eleventh hour and had gone down the street, when a carriage drawn by two magnificent horses rounded the corner, rumbled over the cobblestones of the market square, and pulled up in front of the Red Ox Inn, directly across from the house of the dollmaker Weisslinger. The dollmaker went to his window and opened the shutters a tiny crack. He peered out in order to inspect the travelers who were arriving so late at night. The innkeeper had come out to greet the distinguished guests and escort them into the house. To his astonishment, no one got out of the carriage. The coachman made no preparation to climb down from his box. In answer to a question from the innkeeper, he indicated by gestures that he did not understand the language. But the innkeeper did not give up so easily. In sign language he asked again if the coachman was hungry or thirsty. After a moment's hesitation the coachman nodded, pulled the brake, knotted the reins, and climbed down from the box. The innkeeper wanted to lead him into the house, but the coachman preferred first to walk up and down a bit to stretch his legs, then to see to the horses and take another look at the carriage. He then took off his dark cape and shook it out, as if to leave the dust of long journeys on bad roads behind him, hung it about his shoulders with the pale lining to the outside, and at last was ready to follow the innkeeper into the house. Master Weisslinger, at first alarmed and then pleased, had watched the whole scene with breathless interest. The coachman had not taken a deep breath inside the inn before Weisslinger was hard at work. He did something rather odd. Using special tools, he opened the enormous grandfather clock, removed the hands, loosened and pried off the face, replaced some of the works with other pieces, and tightened wires and made new connections. He then put in a new face, fastened on five hands and set them according to the new face, measured the angles they formed, reset them, measured again, wound up the clock, tightened a screw here and loosened one there, listened carefully to the irregular ticking of the clock, checked the movement of the hands, and made new adjustments until a high chirping could be heard above the ticking. Weisslinger cautiously touched some of the wire connections, and they were warm and began to glow—the wires were live then; he had tapped the timeline. The air began to crackle, and sparks flitted along the wires and bathed the room in an eerie light. The chirping had now become so loud that it drowned out the ticking of the works. Weisslinger put down his tools, wiped the sweat from his forehead, and leaned back with a sigh of relief.

"I've done it," he said. "At least it looks like it."

Then he blew out the light and went to the window again. He had to wait over an hour before the stranger finally left the inn. The latter seemed to have refreshed himself liberally, for he swayed slightly as he walked and the innkeeper escorted him to the door.

"Hallooooo there!" he called out, and waved in the direction of Weisslinger's house.

The dollmaker shook his head and said, "Just you wait!"

The innkeeper was helping the coachman to store away the horses' feedbags and to climb up onto the box again.

"Hallooo!" called the stranger again. Receiving no reply, he grunted and gave his whip a jerk, but so clumsily that it nearly hit the innkeeper. The carriage started up and rumbled at a leisurely pace out of the town, although it was well past midnight.

Weisslinger watched it disappear. Then he took a small, delicate doll out of its hiding place, took one last careful look at it, and wound it up. The doll woke up and stretched its legs. He held its little smooth head between thumb and forefinger and murmured, "You can do it. You will penetrate thousands of years and will bring me a sign. I know it now."

He put the doll on the windowsill. The little creature cautiously examined the market square.

"Run!" said the dollmaker, and gave the figure a push. With one spring the doll was on the street, whisked over the square like a shadow, and was gone. Weisslinger closed and barred the shutters and retired to bed.

"What do you think of this version, Collins?"

"I hadn't heard that one before, Your Majesty."

"We believe that, Collins, but you will get to know it well."

"How is that, Your Majesty?"

"Just wait. We are not finished yet. We are going to have to act it out together in order to round off the story."

"Your Majesty said 'together'?"

"Yes, Collins, you heard quite rightly. We are going to have to act it out together, the two of us."

"How am I to understand this?"

"It is very simple, and you will understand it clearly, as clearly as we are sitting here."

"Does Your Majesty permit me to ask a question?"

"Naturally."

"Was this doll that Weisslinger sent off that evening the same one with which Your Majesty is now playing?"

"The very same one, Collins. A few thousand years old and still fully intact. Go ahead and take a good look at it."

As if it had understood the conversation, the doll hopped upon the minister's arm, held on to his shoulder, and looked him in the eye.

"By Your Majesty's leave, it is really a marvel."

"Yes, isn't it! But where had we left off, Collins?"

"The dollmaker, Your Majesty, had on that evening . . ."

"Oh yes, now we remember. Now listen carefully!"

It was evening. The night watchman had just sung out the eleventh hour and had gone down the street, when a carriage drawn by two magnificent horses rounded the corner, rumbled over the cobblestones of the market square, and pulled up in front of the Red Ox Inn, directly across from the house of the dollmaker Weisslinger. The dollmaker went to his window and opened the shutters a tiny crack. He peered out in order to inspect the travelers who were arriving so late at night. The innkeeper had come out to greet the distinguished guests and escort them into the house. To his astonishment, no one got out of the carriage. The coachman made no move to climb down from his box, and, in answer to a question from the innkeeper, explained by means of gestures that he did not understand the language. The innkeeper looked uncertainly about him for a while, then shrugging his shoulders returned into the house and closed the door. But Weisslinger continued to stare in fascination at the carriage. The curtains of the carriage windows were drawn, but now that his eyes had become accustomed to the darkness he could see that the interior of the coach was illuminated by a pale and flickering light. Weisslinger gave a small sigh of relief, but for a while absolutely nothing happened. The coachman sat motionless and lost in thought upon his box; the reins were tied up and the brakes drawn. The horses snorted, chafed against the shaft of the carriage, and shook their harnesses. Time slipped by. At last the man climbed down, walked up and down to stretch his legs, saw to the horses, then took off his dark cape and shook it out, as if to leave the dust of long journeys on bad roads behind him, and hung it about his shoulders with the pale lining to the outside. He stepped up to the carriage and opened the door a crack. A small figure hopped out, flitted like a shadow across the square directly to the dollmaker's house, with a single spring bound to the windowsill, raised its little metallic face to Weisslinger, and made a courteous bow.

The master closed the window and unbolted the door. He cautiously peered about the market square, listened to hear if anyone might be passing by at so late an hour or if the night watchman might be approaching on his rounds, but there was no one in sight. Muffled noises drifted across from the Red Ox, where a few townsmen were drinking beer and whiling away the time with politics and card games. For the rest, all was quiet. The fountain in the market square splashed, and the horses snorted and pawed the paving stones. There was not a soul in sight. The stillness of the night lay peacefully over the town. The war was far away.

Weisslinger gave the coachman a sign.

The coachman immediately ripped open the carriage door, leaned far in and hauled out a long and obviously heavy bundle, got it with difficulty onto his shoulder, and staggered over to the dollmaker's house. The dollmaker hurried to help him carry the burden.

"Who are you, stranger?" asked the master in a whisper.

"WHITE," answered the man just as quietly. "Thank you for helping me carry him. He is damned heavy."

The bundle was a body. They carried it into the house and laid it carefully on the bed.

"Is he dead?" asked Weisslinger anxiously.

"No, he's only unconscious. He'll wake up soon."

The stranger breathed heavily.

"Damned heavy, that—uh . . . I beg your pardon . . . that fellow. Got me worked up into a good sweat. I'm getting old."

"Did everything go off all right?" Weisslinger wanted to know.

"You can see that it did."

"How did it go?"

"More about that later."

The stranger did not want to waste time. Weisslinger turned to the person on the bed and took a good look at his face.

"He has gotten fat," he laughed. Then he began to transform himself. He took off his wig, removed the clipped gray beard, and with a few clever strokes completely transformed his face, so that he looked like the mirror image of the unconscious man on the bed.

"Finished?" asked the coachman.

"Just one more minute," said Weisslinger. He rolled up the plans which hung on the walls and lay on the table, ripped them up, and threw the scraps into the fire. Then he took a hammer from the workbench and approached the grandfather clock.

"But—" interrupted the stranger, and added hesitantly, "Excuse my meddling, but shouldn't he have a chance?"

"How big were my chances?" replied Weisslinger, and gave the stranger a searching look. He swung the heavy hammer and let it smash into the clock. Glass flew, the valuable case splintered. With the second blow there was a crunching of metal, the pendulum began to clatter, and the hands whirred with increasing speed. The third blow brought the works to a standstill. He took another swing but did not finish it.

"You are right. It is a pity to destroy the clock. It cost me hours of work. With luck and skill it could be repaired. We'll leave him the tools. He can sell them, if he can find somebody to buy them. The materials alone that went into that clock are worth a pretty penny. But if he sells it all he'll be sorry. In any case, he'll get less for it than it is worth. If he can get it back into salable condition at all."

"If," said the stranger.

"I am ready," said Weisslinger.

"Take my cape." And the coachman removed his cape from his shoulders. The dollmaker drew it about himself.

"Not like that—the pale side to the inside."

Weisslinger turned it inside out. The other side was dark.

"Come quickly! He is waking up," urged the coachman.

The figure on the bed rolled over and groaned. Weisslinger took one last look around the room which had been his home for years and in which he had spent many an anxious hour between hope and desperation, many a night, half awake, half dreaming, pondering over and developing fantastic projects. Bent over his workbench, working all night through, summer and winter, he had drawn up plans, with primitive tools had turned and filed and fashioned mechanisms the precision of which his colleagues could not begin to copy. All the while he was on the lookout, constantly stepping to the window and peering out in fear, whenever strangers came to the town and stopped at the Red Ox Inn, that they were already on his trail and wanted to kidnap him or kill him or at least destroy his work.

Weisslinger turned away. He motioned to the doll, which sprang onto his shoulder, and followed the stranger, who was already impatiently waiting at the carriage and holding open the door.

"I'll climb up on the box next to you. I am curious to hear how it all went."

"All right," said the coachman, and helped him up to his perch. The carriage started up, and rumbled at a leisurely pace over the market square and out of the town.

"Now listen carefully," said the coachman. "You must put yourself into the situation and play the exact part which I am now going to describe to you. Pay very close attention, every detail is of the utmost importance."

The stranger then proceeded to give Weisslinger specific instructions on how he was to behave, what he had to say, what gestures he should make. The dollmaker had many questions, and to all of them the coachman had exact answers. He concluded all the descriptions and explanations as the carriage drew up to a dark, secluded farm, which lay deep in a vast forest through which the carriage had been driving for over an hour along narrow and overgrown tracks. They stopped. The moon had risen high in the sky and poured its cold light over the collapsing roofs of barn and sheds, over the muddy barnyard whose deep ruts were filled with water that glittered in the light, over the gardens that had run to seed, in which the weeds had grown high above the crooked fences. Everything looked dirty and dilapidated.

"Is this Operations Base 7?" asked Weisslinger.

"Yes," answered the coachman.

"It is a pigsty."

"That is the best camouflage for it. If anyone wanders into this deserted area, he should not have the impression that there is anything here worth stealing. We are fairly certain that nobody has been snuffling around here. But of course now it doesn't make any difference anymore."

The coachman took the bridle and reins off the horses, let them loose, and chased them out of the farmyard with cries and cracks of the whip.

"It's a pity. They were beautiful beasts," said Weisslinger.

"They'll find another master. First they should enjoy their freedom for a while."

They ransacked the house and sheds, destroyed all the instruments, and set fire to the farmstead. The dry wood of the old building burned like tinder; the flame shot up and in no time had reached the rooftree. The thatched roofs of the sheds blazed like torches in the night and scattered a shower of dark red sparks into the forest.

"A devilishly dangerous business we're doing," commented Weisslinger.

"But it's fun," laughed the coachman, and threw more fuel onto the fire. The heat was tremendous, and the two men withdrew into the carriage. The built-in mirror flickered and quivered in a milky light. The dollmaker smiled.

"Ready?" asked the stranger.

"Ready," said Weisslinger, and picked up the doll. Then they stepped, one after the other, through the mirror.

They had just disappeared when the rooftree of the farmhouse fell in with a great crash and a splash of sparks. The farmyard was strewn with burning shingles and splinters of wood. The fire now blazed several hundred feet into the sky and gave an eerie light far into the night. A few minutes later, a violent explosion demolished the carriage.

"What do you think of this version of the story, Collins?"

"It too is completely new to me, Your Majesty. Not only that, it is inexplicable. But still, the picture seems complete. All the pieces of the puzzle fit together. There seem to be a few pieces still missing however. Am I right, Your Majesty?"

"Quite right, Collins. But those pieces will turn up. Just have a little patience. We haven't finished the story yet."

"So WHITE intervened . . ."

The king smirked.

"We couldn't do anything about that."

"Not anymore, Collins. Not anymore."

"Right, Your Majesty, not anymore. I have to admit defeat."

"Nothing doing, Collins! There will be no giving up now. The story isn't complete. You have to keep playing. We insist on it, even if we have to order you to play. Don't disappoint us. Maybe you can make one more important move."

"I wouldn't know where to . . ."

"We have to fit all the pieces of the puzzle together to get the complete picture. Something is missing."

"Yes—for instance, why this substitution and with whom? . . . and what information did this Weisslinger receive from WHITE? That is, if—and I am not so sure of this—the coachman is in fact WHITE. What did Weisslinger find out from this stranger?"

"He was told the very same story that you just heard. But the dollmaker also heard the end of the story, which you will find out in a moment too. Then you will understand the substitution."

"I already have an idea, Your Majesty. Please carry on with the story."

"Patience, Collins. We have time, plenty of time. Limitless time is at our disposal. You will hear everything."

"I am very eager to hear it all, Your Majesty."

"Very well then. This part of the story is quite different. It takes place much earlier than all the rest that we have already told you."

The king reflected a moment before continuing.

In the meantime, the doll had begun to include double flips in its dance and whirled across the room.

"As you perhaps know, Collins, we once had a brother."

"Your Majesty has strictly forbidden any mention or even knowledge of this fact. I believe he met with a fatal accident many years ago while making some rash experiment in physics."

"That is quite right. He was killed in a time-travel experiment. How that came about, you are now about to hear. Once upon a time . . ."

Once upon a time there was a king, who was very rich and whose power extended over four solar systems and all celestial bodies within a radius of twenty light-years. This king had two sons who were very close to each other in age. When the sons were still children there lived in the palace an eccentric old man, of whom nobody at the court took any real notice. He was a mathematician and physicist and it was his responsibility to look after the electronic systems and computer center of the palace. His entire life was devoted solely to his profession, and he never participated in the social life of the court. His wife had died at an early age and since then he had lived like a recluse, eating and sleeping amid his scientific apparatus and computers and seeing and being seen by nobody for weeks on end, unless he was needed to repair a defective stereo tele-wall or one of the transmitters. He had been born on one of the most godforsaken planets of the kingdom, on which his ancestors, of ancient colonial settler stock, had settled. They had adapted themselves to the climate of the planet and could even exist out of doors in the open air. We believe his father was even a farmer.

He was sent to school, proved to be very bright, studied electronic sciences, and made quite a name for himself in his field. One day his young wife was killed in a transfer ship accident. He must have taken that very hard. He gave up physics and lived like a hermit. His resources were soon exhausted and he suffered bitter want. So he started writing stories, fairy tales full of profound and hidden meaning. He was very gifted at this but good fortune evaded him. His colleagues laughed at him because they did not understand his stories, and many people said that his great misfortune had driven him out of his senses. He was soon forgotten—no one read his works—and he led a wretched and lonely existence in a poor hut outside the city. One day the king heard of his tragic fate and commanded him to come to the palace. After much hesitation he finally accepted a position at the court. He was kept busy with occasional repairs and with the supervision of the automatic central control station and the computer installations, an occupation which did not demand much time or effort. He continued to write his fairy tales and to be derided for doing so. No one took him very seriously. But that did not seem to bother him very much. He only smiled enigmatically whenever he was asked to tell one of his stories, and his listeners turned away shaking their heads. And so he came to be known at the court as an eccentric old man whose thoughts were bewildering and whose logic was peculiar, but he seemed to be harmless, so people left him alone. Only the two princes were genuinely fond of him and considered him to be their good friend. He in turn loved them dearly, but not because he expected to gain anything by it—he had never thought of such a thing. He loved them because they were his most patient listeners and would listen for hours on end and still beg for more, delighted with his stories and never tired of hearing them. He would tell of the past and the future, of distant unknown kingdoms and their strange inhabitants; he could describe in detail the cities, the streets and squares, the palaces and markets, he could give such a clear picture of the clothing and language and the customs and habits of their inhabitants, that it seemed as if he had been to all these marvelous places and had seen them all with his own eyes. And yet he seldom left the windowless rooms of the royal computer control station, passing his days amid computers and field generators, matter transmitters and receiving sets.

Although the princes did not always understand everything he told them, it was always exciting. They liked him because he could tell fascinating stories without constantly putting in flattering phrases or wagging a moralizing finger, as the others always did.

More and more often they found the old man in his laboratory bent over technical drawings or bustling about complicated instruments. He seemed to have rediscovered his profession, but he always rolled up his drawings or wiped his hands and had time for them when they came to see him. Sometimes they watched him at work. The computers were at work day and night, figuring out integral equations which he fed into them. He fitted together tiny parts and wired electrical connections, ordered raw materials and new parts which often had to be sent in from great distances. The princes enjoyed the tingling feeling when he opened one of the small packages which had traveled through half the galaxy and now lay on his workbench, and tiny glittering instruments appeared which specialists in another part of the inhabited universe several thousand light-years away had carefully put together and packed.

One day the two boys noticed that their friend had aged visibly. He had always been in excellent health but was now suddenly declining rapidly. From one week to the next, from one day to the next, he seemed to age several years. His hair turned gray, his face became wrinkled, his eyes grew tired and red-rimmed. He became forgetful and absentminded and often had difficulty remembering the events and conversations of the previous day. His mind and body disintegrated with terrifying rapidity.

It wasn't until much later that the two boys found out the reason for this startling transformation. The old man had developed an instrument by means of which he could travel in time, and he had been spending months and years at other points on the timeline. In order not to awaken any suspicion, he always returned to the point in time from which he had departed, so that nobody noticed that he was gone and started unpleasant investigations. He had succeeded masterfully in avoiding this. No one had had the slightest notion of his excursions.

And so the years passed. The princes grew into young men and had to study a great deal, but whenever they had time they went to see their friend. One day they found him ill. His hair had turned snow-white and his cheeks were hollow and sunken. He knew that he would not live much longer but he seemed happy, as if he could look back with satisfaction on a fulfilled life. He motioned the two princes to his bedside and in a faint voice initiated them into his secret. He had used his last ounce of strength to destroy his wonderful machine, for some unknown reason, but he left behind drawings, plans, and descriptions, which would enable someone with a clever mind to reconstruct the instrument.

A few days later he died and his body was blasted after a short ceremony which few people attended. Nobody missed him at court; only the two young princes mourned their old friend.

Then they went through his legacy, rummaged through the drawers, drained all the information from the data banks, and set about puzzling out the complicated plans and drawings. The remains of the instrument were painstakingly examined and classified. The princes applied themselves with the greatest zeal to the problem, but it proved to be extraordinarily difficult. The old man's descriptions were as strange and paradoxical as his stories had been. But now the fact that they had so carefully listened to his tales proved to be a great advantage, for they had little trouble in fathoming his odd and apparently illogical way of thinking. Still, the work progressed very slowly, although they spent days and months in the laboratory of the computer control station, brooding over sketches. The king gave them complete freedom to pursue their own interests, in order that their abilities might develop more fully, and no one else paid any attention to how they spent their time.

Soon the princes quarreled, because each one had developed his own theory as to how the problem was best to be approached. Nevertheless, they managed to cooperate to such an extent that one day the mirror of the instrument began to flicker, as the descriptions indicated that it should. But what a disappointment! Its surface proved to be impenetrable. Something was missing.

Despondency seized them. Could it be that their friend had really just played a trick on them, fooled them as he had so often done with his stories? He was entirely capable of having done just that, although in this case much spoke against it. However, after more intensive study of the plans they found that the person who wished to step through the mirror had to take with him a particular instrument which would allow him to penetrate the energy field behind the mirror. This energy field would then transport him along the timeline until the poles of the instrument were reversed, at which point the person would be ejected from the energy field onto a given point on the timeline. Here he would materialize and move with normal speed in time. This mechanism had the form of an attractive brooch the size of a ten Solar piece and consisted of tiny silver leaves and innumerable microscopic crystals in which very fine copper wires were fixed; these were interconnected according to an extremely intricate circuit diagram. The reconstruction of this diagram turned out to be the knottiest problem of all.

The elder of the two princes, who was especially talented in handling tiny mechanical parts, succeeded one day in assembling this extremely complex mechanism. His brother watched as he disappeared and reappeared, only to slip off and return again through the mirror, but he could report little more than that behind the mirror he was swept away by an indefinable current, had a slight feeling of giddiness, and after a few moments was ejected from the instrument again. One could see nothing. The space behind the mirror was immersed in an impermeable milky WHITE, which surrounded one like a heavy fog through which one couldn't see one's hand before one's face. It was impossible to land in another time or even take a peek into another period; one was always thrown out of the field at the same point at which one had entered. The puzzle was still to be solved. Much later the prince discovered that this part of the timeline had been sealed off and that the seal had made travel there impossible. The inventor himself had placed this seal and many others along the timeline, in order to protect its network from careless, unintentional, or even malicious interference.

As soon as the seal was behind them, the brooch functioned perfectly, and the brothers traveled up and down and back and forth along the timeline. They got into extremely confusing situations, since they had absolutely no experience and did not know how to handle the brooch properly. They could set themselves in motion in the machine's time field but had no influence over the time and place at which they were ejected again. Fortunately, this always occurred after a very few minutes. They cautiously increased the field energy and found that they could manage stretches of a day or two, but they still could neither predict nor influence the point at which they were forced out of the field. One of the two disappeared once for six days, and his brother had trouble concealing his absence at court, but the great similarity in their appearance came to his aid.

Then came—this was all many, many years ago—the problem of the succession to the throne, which the king wanted to have settled before his death. He wanted his kingdom to remain undivided, and, according to the ancient right of the firstborn, granted the older son the crown. The second son was to be so well provided for that he could devote himself for the rest of his life to his interests, be they of an artistic or a scientific nature.

Now misfortune had it that the younger son was filled with ambition to rule the kingdom, whereas the designated heir apparent was much more inclined to the sciences than to power. It was he who had contributed the most to the construction of the instrument.

Ill-will and dissension grew and estranged the two brothers, who had once been inseparable. The heir apparent would have preferred to give up his claim to the throne in order to put an end to the wretched and disgraceful quarrel, but the king stubbornly clung to his decision, to conform to tradition and to satisfy the strong conservative elements in the kingdom. He wanted to avoid outbreaks of violence, which would only have shaken the country and awakened the avidity of greedy and jealous neighbors.

The younger brother felt slighted and sank deeper and deeper into malevolent envy. Evil courtiers encouraged him, giving him dubious advice and finally bringing him to the conclusion that he in some way or other had to have his brother eliminated. He succeeded magnificently in doing so, in a cunning manner of which no one would have thought him capable. He used the time-travel machine. The older brother could not rest until he had figured out how to materialize in times where there was no mirror and how to place and remove the seals. As he once again stepped through the mirror, his brother crept up and turned the energy of the time field up to full strength. He himself was horrified as some of the mechanisms suddenly broke down, wired connections burned out, and finally the mirror exploded. The field collapsed and the older brother, who had been carried by the ultra-high-powered transporter to some remote part of the timeline, was thrown out and landed in that distant age. What age it was nobody knew, least of all he himself, but it had to be in the past, since that was the direction in which he had set out to travel.

The court was in an uproar as the terrible accident was discovered. It was feared that the frightful event could have political consequences. Now everyone found out what the two princes had been up to for years and they cursed the dangerous games and fateful legacy of the crazy old physicist—and waited. The days turned into weeks, the weeks lengthened into months, finally an entire year had passed, but there was no sign or trace of the heir to the throne. The king ordered court mourning, for no one could imagine how or where the young man could reappear. Except his brother, of course, who from then on had an exceedingly bad conscience and lived in the constant fear that the victim of his malicious deed could reappear someday and call him to account. He could sleep only when the room was brightly lighted, awoke bathed in sweat out of a sleep troubled by uneasy dreams, started convulsively at every unaccustomed sound, grew more and more nervous and impatient, was convinced he was being pursued, treated his inferiors unjustly, and trusted no one.

• • •

"Didn't you have that impression, Collins?"

"Indeed, Your Majesty."

"As the old king died and the younger son acceded to the throne, he could not rest until he had rebuilt the time instrument, to ensure himself against all eventualities. He built up a police corps, which had to travel about in time, searching for suspicious signs along the timeline. The guards had to follow up and report on every trace which could possibly be construed as endangering His Majesty. Their supreme duty was to guarantee the security of the king under all conditions and at all times. Carelessness on the part of the patrol caused innumerable fractures, especially in the first period, and an army of scientists and mechanics was required to repair them. No great damage was done to past history, thanks to the seals, which the patrol came across in many places and which they called WHITE because the area behind the mirror within the sealed time spaces was white and permitted neither takeoff nor landing. But it was no future power which had made these points inaccessible; it was the old man, who in his wise foresight—or perhaps I should say in his better judgment—had placed the seals there. He had accomplished an enormous amount of work, both in the future and in the past; that must have cost him decades, by the way. But back to the patrol. They put in much time and effort learning ancient languages, they studied the customs of bygone civilizations, practiced using primitive weapons and instruments, learned how to handle animals, sleep in the open atmosphere and tolerate vermin and poisoned air, and accustomed their stomachs to barbaric foods, but their success was only moderate. They hunted phantoms and waylaid mechanical dolls. That is the funniest part of the whole story. They hunted a doll which they could not catch and in fact never even saw until it was too late. But why are we telling this to you? You know this part best, don't you, Collins? After all, you directed the operation."

"Quite right, Your Majesty."

"But we must tell you the rest of the story too—it is the ugliest and most distressing part. Let us tell you the fate of the prince whose bitter lot it was to be banned to a distant and obscure century, and how he fared there."

The prince had stepped through the mirror and had directed his path toward the past, in order to examine the seal which had given him trouble at the beginning of his experiments. He let himself be carried through the glimmering darkness by a slight current, then noticed suddenly that his speed was accelerating rapidly. He felt himself being whirled about, as if he were being drawn into a vortex, and nearly lost consciousness. All at once the motion ceased, the field ejected him, and it was light.

Until then he had had no idea how one could materialize without a mirror, what field energy was necessary to accomplish this, and what precautionary measures had to be taken. Now he learned it through personal experience. He materialized at about fifteen feet in the air and fell heavily to the ground. There was a stabbing pain in his right hip and he rolled over onto his face. At the same time, he realized that his hair was singed and his clothing had caught fire. He wallowed in the damp soil and smothered the flames. Exhausted, filthy, and tormented by pains, he lay immobile and tried to overcome the shock. He had to fight back tears, but after a few minutes he was able to pull himself together and attempt to sort out what had happened to him. He had not the slightest notion in which era he was stranded. His first impression was that he must be in an extremely remote area of the past, for there was still agriculture, as he could clearly see by the furrows in the ground, with which he had so painfully become acquainted. Cautiously he looked about him. He lay in the middle of an open field. There was no human settlement in the vicinity. The area was hilly, with a few isolated clumps of trees here and there. A row of scraggly bushes lined a brook which meandered down a wide valley. The countryside seemed ugly and unkempt. There was wild undergrowth everywhere, the plants were neither symmetrical nor genetically refined, and the trees appeared to be authentic and natural. Someone must have recently watered the land absurdly heavily, as the ground was damp and there were great puddles in the overgrown fields and meadows. The sky was so hazy that he could hardly tell where the sun was, but he figured that it must be near midday.

In all his misfortune he had still had the good luck not to materialize amid a thickly populated area. The pressure wave that he must have caused would certainly have torn to pieces the lungs of all living beings within a radius of a hundred yards. And if he had materialized within a solid body, the effect would have been like that of a medium-sized atom bomb, and there would have been nothing left of him. He looked about for a hiding place. He was as clearly visible to air reconnaissance here in the middle of the field as if he were lying on a silver platter. He could not stay here. His clothing, strange and in addition singed, his sudden appearance literally out of the nowhere, and his ignorance of the native language would all make him a suspicious character, and if he were picked up he would certainly be in for severe cross-examination. But nobody would believe him if he told the truth. He searched the sky but there was, fortunately, no helicopter in the area. The best thing would be to seek cover in a wood and wait there until dark. Then he would keep a lookout for lights and try to find a house or small village where he could perhaps get native clothing, food, and a minimum of equipment. After that he would see.

He got up. At once a sharp pang ran through his right hip. He must have injured himself in the unexpected fall. I hope nothing is broken, he thought, that would be a catastrophe. He limped across the fields to the nearest clump of trees, making slow and painful progress. He cursed the meteorologists who had watered the area too heavily. They must not have gotten far in developing their climate regulators. The damp earth clung in heavy clods to his soles and he often had to retrieve his shoes from the sodden field, where they stuck in the mud. He was very inadequately equipped and too lightly clothed, but it could have been worse—he could have landed in an icy winter. The trees that he was heading for stood on the far side of the narrow brook. He would have to wade the brook; jumping over it was out of the question. Every step was torture to him. As he finally reached the bank he suddenly stopped short. In the bed of the stream, washed by the shallow water, lay the mutilated corpses of two men. They were only half clothed, obviously plundered, and must have lain there for many days, for the bodies were bloated and deformed and gave off a nauseating smell. Both of them had ghastly wounds on the head and throat. They had been barbarously murdered and thrown into the brook. He had never seen anything so abhorrent before, and turned away revolted. Was this a crime? That was all he needed! There was nothing worse than getting involved in such business. He must leave the area as quickly as possible. He walked on faster, following the stream down the valley. Three hundred yards farther he came upon a caved-in bridge of rotting wood, over which a narrow road had crossed the stream. He could see that it had been destroyed by force. Here he found a third body, this time of a woman. It lay near an overturned vehicle which had been plundered and destroyed. Apparently the culprits had intended to steal the belongings of the woman, for baskets and crates that had been broken open lay trampled in the fields on either side of the road and in the stream; articles of clothing and pieces of cloth, shoes of various sizes, and objects whose function he could not make out were strewn about. The vehicle appeared to have been a sort of supply wagon. The woman must have defended herself to the very last, for even in death she still clutched some of her belongings. She had apparently been shot through the head with a large-caliber weapon; the shot had ripped away part of her skull. He turned away, nauseated, and gathered up a few pieces of cloth, with which he covered the body. Then he collected everything that could be of use to him. He found an odd piece of clothing whose two tubelike appendages were apparently intended to encase legs, and a jacket of heavy material, torn and wet but still quite serviceable. He tried on this and that until he had outfitted himself like a native. He had more trouble with footwear but finally found two different foot containers made of animal skin which did not fit too badly. He overcame his disgust at wearing the skin of a dead being next to his skin and put them on.

He had reached his first goal, and although he did not fancy himself a looter of corpses, at least he was not so conspicuous in his new clothing. He was aware of the danger of his undertaking, for if he was found near the scene of the crime, he would not have to worry much about his future. As far as he could see, a man's life was not worth much here, and short work was made of it. He had to be on his guard, but fortunately there was not a human being in sight. The region must be very thinly populated and seemed to be completely inaccessible by any means of transport—otherwise, the dead would have been found long ago.

He took a closer look at the destroyed vehicle. It was made entirely of genuine wood held together by bolts and strips and rings of iron, and had the most primitive steering system imaginable. It had no means of propulsion but seemed to have been pulled by some mechanism or even animals, which had been detached and removed from the wagon. This disconcerted him greatly. This sort of vehicle had not been in existence for many thousand years. In which age had he landed? He searched his mind for historical dates. How long had there been automobiles? Their development lay just before the discovery of atomic energy and electronics. That was the end of the second and the beginning of the third millennium. All the horror stories and gruesome reports of those barbaric centuries which he had heard as a child now came to mind again. Had he landed in the twentieth century or even earlier? The transport field couldn't have carried him that far; its energy was too low. Unless . . . That couldn't be! Just keep calm, he told himself. No hasty conclusions. First think it all over. It was surely possible that in an electronic civilization there were people who delighted in imitating the ancients and even had vehicles drawn by animals. Still, the dead woman hadn't looked as if she had been traveling about on a pleasure outing. He examined the articles of clothing—no synthetics, all were made of organic substances. All observations led to the same conclusion. He must be in a pretechnical age. If that were the case, his position was hopeless. Without great sources of electrical energy, without electronics, precision instruments, and high-quality raw materials, he could not help himself out of the situation. He could only wait until help came from the future. They would search for him; his brother would do everything in his power to find him and get him out. But how would he find him, if he had no idea where he was? Keep calm, he repeated to himself. There are several possibilities. He would have to find a way to send information into the future, so that they would take notice of him. He could for instance paint cryptic paintings or write enigmatic books whose anachronisms and precognition would be striking and could be interpreted as a message. But was he a painter or a writer? Would his works survive thousands of years of changing intellectual tendencies, wars and barbarianism, fire and anarchy, vandalism and the condemnation of purist sects—would they even survive him? And if so, would they be understood at the right moment as a message from him? Would anyone consider them worthy of keeping in a library or museum? Would they even be discovered among the thousands of testimonies of the art of clairvoyance and astrology, alchemy and obscure speculative philosophy, black and white magic, science fiction and fairy tales of the distant past? And after all, did his brother—the terrible suspicion which he had been constantly pushing out of his mind took clear form—did his brother have any interest at all in finding him again?

No useless speculations, he warned himself. He would find out. There was plenty of time. Perhaps he could build mechanisms which if well protected could survive several civilizations, ticking like time bombs through the ages, and at a given point attract attention to themselves and to him. If time travel were possible, then they would certainly look into his case again, whether they received a message or not. The important point was for him to establish contact, then perhaps they would find a way to him. He had to be on the alert not to overlook any signs or signals. If they really wanted to help him out of this mess, there would be no problem. It was just better for him to be a bit wary, because if it were in their interest to leave him here, then it would be up to him to make the decisive move. He must be very careful not to cause any contradictions or anachronisms; no camouflage was perfect. But this meant that he would have to know the age perfectly, would have to study it thoroughly and adapt himself completely as a contemporary, no matter how difficult this might be. He would have to gain a firm footing in this involuntary exile, and circumstances dictated that he must do so immediately. At first he was concerned only with pure survival: food, weapons, money, a relatively safe place to live, and information. All the rest he would take care of later. He was perhaps inferior to the natives in physical resistance and hardiness, but his scientific and technical knowledge would stand him in good stead. He just had to make the best use he could of the primitive resources.

He left the scene of horror behind him and scrambled over the remains of the bridge across the stream, turned off from the road, and sought a relatively dry place among the trees and bushes where he would be hidden from the eyes of any natives who might come along. It was warm and he spread out the captured clothing to dry, then examined his injured leg. The injury was painful but there was apparently no break, only a bone bruise. A few hours of rest would do him good. He let himself down upon the ground and had a more leisurely look at his surroundings. The native plants which grew on all sides of him were indescribably ugly. Birds twittered in the branches above him, but he did not have the impression that they were the diverting artificial mechanisms that he was accustomed to, for they behaved in a shy and strange manner. They must be organic beings, but he had to admit that they sang just as nicely as the artificial ones he knew. Every place he set his eyes on was swarming with life. On the ground, in the grass, on the leaves, in the bark of the trees, everywhere tiny animals were creeping and crawling, chirping and rustling. He was somewhat nauseated by so much organic life. He had been brought up in the sterile world of the plastic region, into which every few weeks a stray animal found its way, an odd insect like a fly or moth, which—if it had in some inexplicable manner penetrated the energy screen without being burned—was immediately traced by infrared searchers and chased out of the airspace or killed. I will have to get used to it, he thought. Overcoming his aversion, he let one of the quick, black, six-footed animals run across the back of his hand. It did not hurt and the animal seemed not to be poisonous.

He looked at the sky. It was empty; there were no condensation trails of departing or landing transfer ships to be seen, no observation platforms on invisible gravitation anchors, no programmed control floater in the complex network of directive beams of a ground station for surface inspection, no reflex of an energy halo which surrounded the planet and protected it from extraterrestrial attacks. The sun broke through the thin cloud layer and scattered the clouds. Its warmth and beams of energy pierced the atmosphere and gave the skin a prickling sensation.

He listened. Something had been irritating him all this time, and now he knew what it was. The environment was so quiet. Although there were birds twittering and leaves rustling, it was so unbelievably quiet that he could hear his own pulse. His ears were accustomed to a great jumble of constant sounds caused by the innumerable transport craft, the control and service mechanisms, and other useful apparatus in the palace which he had never really noticed before, as he had heard them all since birth. Now this stillness seemed like a constant dull sound to him, one that lies just under the threshold of hearing and is perceived rather than heard. The sun dried his clothing and lay with calming warmth on his face, and afternoon dozed peacefully over the countryside. The prince felt that he was tired and before he knew it he was fast asleep.

When he awoke, night had come and he saw the stars. He had never seen the inhabited universe with such clarity from the surface of the earth. With his bare eyes he could recognize two of the solar systems which belonged to his father's kingdom. Nonsense, he told himself, in this era not all of that space was settled. It gave him an odd feeling to see that the remote suns formed almost the same constellations that he knew. He shivered. In the distance he heard a strange noise. It sounded like the rumbling of thunder, and flashes of lightning blazed on the horizon, but the sky was completely clear. It looked like a bombardment with explosive chemical weapons. Could it be . . . ? Of course! That was the explanation for the signs of destruction and the bodies that he had found. It was wartime! What he saw on the horizon was the reflection of discharged explosive weapons. There must be a battle raging there. The sky grew red, probably from great fires.

That was all he had needed, to land in the middle of a period of war. Still, he thought, there might be advantages to this situation. In the general confusion it would be easier for him to mingle with the natives, to get money and weapons somehow, and to settle down somewhere. At times like this no one was going to ask many questions about his identity and background. That simplified many matters, but at the same time his situation was much more dangerous, as he might easily land between the two fronts. If he was found he might be put to the sword. He would have to trust to his good fortune.

He got up. His hip ached but he could walk. He dressed himself, tied his possessions together in a bundle, and headed off in the direction of the shooting. There must be a larger settlement there. He would cautiously approach and at first remain withdrawn but observe and gather information. After that he would decide on the further steps to be taken.

Walking across the fields and meadows turned out to be harder than he had thought. The footwork of animal skin was stiff and rubbed him so that his feet were soon in great pain. After an hour he was completely exhausted and had to rest. In addition, hunger began to gnaw at his insides. He pulled himself together and set out again, making a great detour around a forest that frightened him because he did not know how wild plants and animals reacted at night. He plodded through swamps, waded streams, and made very slow progress, because he had to stop more and more often to rest.

Emerging from a large wooded area, he heard loud cries and explosions and saw the glare of a fire. There was a farmstead in front of him. A barn was blazing in flames. He heard more explosions, laughter and piercing screams, and saw figures running and falling to the ground. He limped faster, thinking that he could perhaps help, but as he came closer he saw that even with the best intentions there was nothing he could do. He was witness to an atrocity of war. Hidden behind a hedge, he watched the actions of these people at first with astonishment and then with growing horror. They had built up a great fire, onto which they threw household utensils and furniture. The rain of sparks had set the thatched roof of the barn on fire, and the fire threatened to spread to the other buildings, but this did not seem to disturb anyone. In the flickering firelight he was presented with a grotesque and macabre scene. Several men, who were strangely clothed and who wore on their heads gigantic headgear onto which they had fixed bushes of some fluffy material, staggered about with some sort of container in their hands, from which they occasionally drank. They all appeared to be under the influence of a drug, as they could hardly stay on their feet, vomited, slipped, fell down, and tried in vain to regain their footing. Some of them lay motionless on the ground, either dead or sleeping where they had fallen. They had killed a large animal, lopped off its head, ripped out its intestines, driven a spit in barbaric manner from the hind quarters through to the neck, and hung it over the fire. Others were occupied with forcing open boxes and barrels and rummaging through their contents, over which they fought in the wildest manner, striking one another with fists and weapons and screaming curses at one another. Yet others had captured several women and girls. They formed a ring about them and, roaring with laughter, ripped their clothes from their bodies. Then they threw the poor creatures to the ground and mounted them so brutally that his breath caught in his throat. The women, also partly under the influence of the drug which they had been forced to drink, half numbed from blows on the head, weakly let themselves be mishandled and whimpered with fear, pain, and terror, while the rest of the men followed the doings of their companions and egged them on with loud cries until it was their turn. Horrified and trembling with loathing, the prince felt a great powerless rage surge up in him. If he had only had his laser gun at hand he would have blasted that rabble into the dirt until the water exploded out of their miserable skins. He shook with anger and realized with alarm that he was tending toward more aggression than he had ever thought himself capable of feeling. Had this world already drawn him into its ways, was he beginning to act like a wild man? In what frightful age had he landed?

He fled into the forest and squatted all night long under a tree, his teeth chattering, shivering with cold and horror, watching the glare of the fire and hearing the loathsome cries of the wild men in the distance.

The temperature sank lower and lower. That must be due to the missing energy halo; at night the surface of the earth gave off unhampered into space all the warmth which it had stored up during the day, causing these variations in temperature. He looked into the starlit sky. Even the distant suns looked cold and uninviting; they were still wild and uncolonized systems.

He crouched tightly, in order to gather his own body heat, but his legs grew stiff and he had to stand up and walk up and down. He was grateful to see the gray of dawn and then the sun slowly rising, and the temperature of the atmosphere soon began also to rise to a tolerable warmth. In the course of the morning the disorderly band of debauched soldiers who had afflicted the whole region with their looting and murdering finally moved on, but not until they had set fire to all that was left of the farm. They took a number of animals with them, on the backs of which they had fixed seats. Some of the men had climbed onto these seats and let themselves be carried by the patient beasts. An ingenious arrangement of cords and chains fixed about the mouth of the animal enabled the rider seated on its back to direct the organic vehicle. The prince found it most astonishing that the big strong animals submitted to such treatment.

When the band had disappeared, the prince dared to come out from his hiding place and examine the scene of devastation once again. Perhaps someone had been left behind who needed help, but basically it was hunger that drove him forward. Perhaps he could capture something edible, perhaps he could even find more information on this age, some papers or a calendar.

A gruesome sight met his eye. The charred corpses of men and women who had been shot or beaten to death lay strewn about among the smashed and smoldering remains of buildings and household goods. The women and girls had been massacred in the most grisly manner and left lying in their own blood. They were hardly distinguishable from the ravaged ground onto which they had been thrown and trampled.

The buildings of the farmstead had long since fallen in, and the flames had destroyed what remained of them. Broken vessels and smashed furniture lay in the flattened grass and in food which had been trampled into the dirt. Driven by hunger, he searched about and finally found two or three pieces of some vegetable substance which had been roasted in the fire and which seemed edible. With aversion he bit into one. It was almost tasteless but after much chewing the saliva rendered it rather sweet. He choked it down, and every bite seemed tastier than the last. Searching for something to drink, he came across the dregs of a sour, spicy liquid in the drinking vessels. He smelled it. This must be the drug. Perhaps it is alcohol, he thought, but was not quite certain. He continued the search and found a hole in the ground that was lined with stones and equipped with an instrument by means of which a container could be let down and drawn up again. He tried it out and drew up a bucket of water. Examining it carefully, he found it to be rather clean and drank in great greedy gulps. I am already a regular wild man, he told himself. I drink water out of the ground, which must be teeming with pathogenic agents, and eat dirty food in the company of corpses and surrounded by the stench of half-burnt animals and people. I may already have poisoned myself, but what can I do. I have the alternative of either dying of hunger and thirst or of being killed by the poisons and bacteria of this barbaric food. The problem was purely academic. He had no choice but to take the risk.

He examined the clothing of the corpses, which were stiff with indescribable filth, and discovered two letters in the pocket of a dead soldier. He couldn't read the handwriting, but the numbers were Arabic. They were obviously dated; both bore the figures 1619.

According to this, he was approximately twelve thousand years in the past, or, more precisely, in the first half of the seventeenth century (old calendar), if the dates were accurate. At any rate, the papers appeared not to be very old. The energy of the time field had been far from high enough at the time of his departure to transport him this far. Could the machine have had a breakdown? But then it would have been impossible for the field energy to increase. Someone must have had his hand in the matter, and who could it have been but his brother? He wouldn't have thought it possible, but he had to get used to the idea.

He put both letters in his pocket. They were addressed to a certain Weisslinger, as he found out later when he had learned to decipher the handwriting, and were written by the priest of a small town, who begged the man to return home immediately, as his wife was dangerously ill, the household going to ruin, and his children suffering bitter want. In the second letter the priest informed him that in the meantime his wife had died and had been buried at the costs of the community, his workshop had been demolished, and his five children were being seen after by various families, where they had to work for bed and board. They were cared for well enough but the stern hand of a father was obviously lacking, as they had been occasionally caught thieving. Their father was an unscrupulous vagabond whom God would one day punish for his sins and his disgraceful life by allotting him a base and unworthy death. The man had met his fate; he had died of a slit throat.

The prince also found near the dead man one of those primitive firearms which function on the basis of the rapid expansion of gases which develop from the ignition of certain chemical substances, whereby a small piece of metal is set into rapid motion and is aimed at its target through a pipe in which the explosion takes place. He also found a stock of the burning substance and of the little pieces of metal, which fit exactly into the pipe of the weapon. Outfitted with these, he was no longer defenseless and faced the future more calmly.

Then he dragged all the bodies to one spot and piled wood over them. He set the wood on fire and quickly left the site of horror. He hoped to find a larger settlement. But he was to find even more gruesome scenes of devastation.

"Yes, Collins, and so his life went on. That was the beginning of a period of the most varied adventures and dangers. He struggled along, a prey to good and bad fortune, and learned how to use the cut-and-thrust weapon as well as pistols, muskets, and heavier explosive weapons. He learned many different languages. From the first he attracted no attention to himself, because soldiers from all corners of the earth served in the armies. He learned their coarse and savage customs, learned how to fight and how to kill. It is amazing and frightening, Collins, how quickly one can learn such things. He had soon become so well adapted that he could behave like a man of the seventeenth century in all situations without being the least bit conspicuous. He traveled through many lands in which the war was raging—and God knows there were plenty of them. He was witness to nameless misery and himself bore unspeakable adversity; he was often desperate and sometimes happy, but above all he survived. And he had learned. He had learned how to plunder, how to prepare trick-playing dice, how to protect his property with cunning and spite, force and coldbloodedness. At last he had amassed enough money to insure himself of a carefree existence, and he withdrew from the tradings of war, much to the dismay of his generals, for his knowledge of mechanics and ballistics had made him one of the most sought-after artillerymen and he could have easily earned military distinctions as cannoneer or pyrotechnician, cannonsmith or rocket launcher. But this was not his goal; he had in the true sense of the word more far-reaching plans. One thing had always sustained him and helped him overcome all dangers—his brooch. He often slipped his hand into his pocket to reassure himself that he wasn't simply dreaming of returning, but then he felt the crystal screen vibrate and come alive in the time stream, and as long as there was life in this mechanism there was activity on the timeline in the section where he was helplessly floating along, there were time travelers and there was hope for him. He was cut off, for without a mirror he could not construct a time field. Help must come from outside, even if unwillingly or unwittingly; he was clever enough to know that there was at least one man who considered the present solution to be the better one—his opponent in the little game that he wanted to chance. First he needed a permanent location which could satisfy all the requirements of offering relative safety, raw materials, and tools. Then he would have to wait until someone appeared from the future with a mirror.

"After months and years of restless wandering he found a small town in the south which was fortified and pleased him and was far from all battlefronts. Here he decided to settle down. With his gold he bought a small house on the market square and installed a workshop in it. He took advantage of his technical knowledge and established a modest mechanic's shop. At first he made hinges and handles and repaired locks; later he constructed all manner of clever toys, which he sold or gave away to travelers or citizens of the town. He was friendly and open to everyone, always considerate and ready to help, and he soon came to enjoy the reputation of being the most upright member of the community. Nevertheless, he led a secluded life and was seldom seen in the Red Ox Inn, although it stood directly across from his house.

"He waited. No traveler who entered the town and stopped at the Red Ox escaped his eye. Every evening he put out the lamp and peered for hours through the crack in the shutters at the market place, in case anything suspicious should happen. He spent every free moment which his numerous contracts left him pondering over sketches and plans for solving his problem with only the most primitive means which were available to him and with no source of electrical energy. There were two possibilities which seemed feasible. He could build a mechanism that would survive the twelve thousand years and would bring help by means of some clever trick. This would cause a fracture, but it would be a small one. He would be taking no chances, as this solution worked, if at all, only with complete success. When the mechanism gave him a sign, that would mean at the same time that he had won the move, for that was the prerequisite of the help; he would have to return sooner or later to the future. The second possibility was to build an apparatus which would allow him directly to tap the energy of the time field. With its help he could set up a primitive electronic system which would localize activities on the timeline. He could then establish the position of the seal and perhaps even shift it, for on this subject his research was far more advanced than his brother imagined. He decided to try both possibilities and set to work. Then there was nothing to do but wait. He soon had proof that his work would bring results. The first spies soon showed up, and he could quickly tell by their behavior that they were the wrong ones and had no intention of helping Weisslinger out of his predicament. Are we right, Collins?"

"To be sure, Your Majesty, that was not our intention."

"Now, Weisslinger had expected that and had long since taken it into account. He had even made some preparations. His appearance had changed no small amount during his life in this time period. He had grown older, his features were harder and his body stronger. And he had contributed to the effect somewhat too; he looked older than he actually was, his hair was streaked with gray and reached to his shoulders. He wanted to take no risks, for this move was far too important to him.

"Soon the guests from the future were arriving by the dozen. He registered one fracture and anachronism after another. Obviously they had found him. The visitors gave Weisslinger many an evening's entertainment. But we already told you about that. Then the master started his counterattack. Now it was his move. Who the better player was would soon be seen.

"What do you say now, Collins?"

"I almost know it, Your Majesty. It is not difficult to infer, from Your Majesty's manner of choosing his words and reporting out of the distant past, that it was Your Majesty who outwitted me. Your Majesty must have spent much time in that age, otherwise Your Majesty would not have gained such deep knowledge of it. To think that I didn't realize it earlier!" The minister struck his forehead with the flat of his hand. "Many things are becoming clear to me now, Your Majesty. But there is still something missing in the story."

"You are right there, Collins, something is still missing. The last piece of the puzzle, the decisive move."

"By Your Majesty's leave, who is WHITE in reality?"

"That is unfair, Collins. That means giving up the game. Just try and think back! We have told you everything. You have a good head on your shoulders."

Collins pondered and stared in absorption at the doll, which was making a whirlwind chain of pirouettes.

"It could be the inventor, Your Majesty, the old man who devised the time machine and who appeared as the Polish count—"

"He was a pure figment of the imagination, as we already mentioned," interjected the king.

"—to whom Your Majesty or I tell the story," continued the minister without interruption. "He brings the information to Weisslinger. And Weisslinger in turn, by Your Majesty's leave, exchanges . . ."

"Just wait a minute, Collins! What are you trying to do? Your imagination is running away with you. Take things in their turn! Why try to bring another figure into our game? The old man left all questions unanswered. So let us leave him out of the game. He played neither for WHITE nor for BLACK. He was, let us say, GRAY. Perhaps he knows the whole game, has seen all the moves, but is keeping out of it himself. Perhaps he is playing an entirely different game, which requires all his attention. Anything is possible. The future is vast. Perhaps thousands have watched our moves, in order to learn from them for their own games. We don't need any additional figures. Try it from another angle. How would it be if we finished the story together, gave it a happy end, so to speak?"

"Does Your Majesty mean that . . . that *I* am to play WHITE?"

"What else did you expect, Collins? You've been on our side for a long time, otherwise you would long ago have put an end to Weisslinger and we wouldn't be sitting here. After all, you are our best man. Now, pay close attention! You will take our cloak here and at the appropriate time turn it so that the pale lining is on the outside. The contrast of BLACK and WHITE will be noticed. But you will also give Weisslinger another sign. Upon receiving it he will set the seal in motion and put to rout the crew of Operations Base 7. Later you will get Weisslinger out of the affair. Off with you now! Do exactly what we told you to do. And have a good time!"

"A good time or a good age, Your Majesty?"

"However you prefer to take it, Collins."

"With pleasure, Your Majesty. I am honored to be allowed to finish the game together with Your Majesty."

The minister stepped through the mirror and returned again. He swayed slightly.

"Finished?" asked the king.

"Finished," answered Collins, and rubbed his eyes.

"You took advantage of the occasion to stop in at the Red Ox, we see," laughed the king. "That is our fault, we suppose. We made your mouth water long enough, and you had to stand here over two hours and listen to our stories. We could stand a cool drink too, but first we'll finish the game. The decisive move is still ahead of us. Will you manage, Collins?"

"No question about it, Your Majesty. The long ride through the forest and the cool night air have sobered me up again."

"Very well," said the king. "Now we're going to checkmate you, brother of ours! Collins! Get going now and appear at the critical moment in the throne room, exactly under the seal that is ten seconds long. You will have to make very careful adjustments to accomplish this. You won't be able to see yourself, as you will be working in Zerotime, that is, in complete darkness. This is something which only the seals permit. Here is the equipment you need to get through the mirror. This is an improved model of the brooch. You will cautiously feel your way over to the throne and hoist our brother onto your shoulders. That won't be easy, because he is heavy and of course during Zerotime as stiff as a board. If you were to drop him, you would break all his bones. He won't feel a thing and will think he is still sitting on his little throne. Then you will calmly carry him through the mirror into the carriage and let him smell this excellent essence, which will send him into a deep and beneficial sleep." He handed the minister a small vial. "All the rest you know as well as we do. You did pay extremely close attention to our story, didn't you? A silly question, we see."

"Yes indeed, Your Majesty—that is—I meant, not the question but about the story."

"Then tell it exactly like that to Weisslinger. Teach him how to sit on the throne properly, how to behave—and he had better not make any mistakes! That goes for you too, Collins!"

"Just as Your Majesty commands. But what would happen if I did make a mistake, if I forgot a part of the story or told it incorrectly?"

"We are sure you won't make any mistakes, otherwise we couldn't retell the story to you. How do you think we know it if not from you?"

"But what if I—by Your Majesty's leave, it is just a thought—what if I intentionally twisted the story or told Weisslinger something completely different, which would cause a fracture at the last moment?"

"That, dear Collins, would be damned unfair of you. That would mean changing the rules of the game. That would mean starting all over again from the beginning, and an entirely different story would develop. Neither we two nor anyone else would ever know our story. It would all have been invented in vain. The situation would look like this: you would return to find our brother here and would have no explanation for your absence. The whole game would start again from scratch but you would have a trick card up your sleeve. That could easily cost you your head. But we will take the risk. We trust you. Now, let's get on to the last move! Checkmate the king!"

His Majesty smiled in delight. The doll stopped dancing, sprang into Collins's arms, and clung fast to his cape.

"Checkmate the king!" said the minister, who disappeared into the mirror and stepped out from it again. He was a bit out of breath.

"It all went off as planned, we see."

"At Your Majesty's command. Together we put on pretty fireworks at Operations Base 7, as Your Majesty remembers. Not a stick remained."

"Yes, we remember. And now, how did you like the whole story, Collins?"

"One can imagine it all very well, Your Majesty."

"Quite right, especially as we never did have a brother." The king winked at his minister.

"Especially as Your Majesty never had a brother, as Your Majesty expressly decreed," returned Collins with a smile.

The king stood up and gave his minister a friendly slap on the shoulder.

"We have made a good job of it, the two of us. We have taken many points into consideration, discarded this one, improved that one, added yet another one. Now the picture is complete. The last piece of the puzzle has been fitted in. We think it is rather good. What do you say, Collins?"

"Oh yes, good, Your Majesty, very good. When I think of Weisslinger—he was killed plundering a farmhouse, turns into a dollmaker, and becomes a respected citizen of the town . . ."

"We can afford that fracture. It is insignificant. He had no children, as far as he knew."

". . . One day, that is, one night he awakes with a splitting headache and from that time on is like a different person. He can't put together the simplest clock, is prey to fits of delirium, becomes addicted to the bottle, gets a thrashing at the Red Ox by the young men of the town because of his sudden overbearing behavior, becomes more and more depraved, and all of this, mind you, he can foresee, including the bitter end: one day he will have his fill of it, will put a noose around his neck and will make an end to it all."

"Rather cruel, don't you think?" put in the king doubtfully.

"Hmm," said Collins and nodded. "Hideous."

"But we insist on the sound thrashing at the Red Ox!"

"That he richly deserved, Your Majesty!" smirked the minister.

"We can still grant the poor devil a better fate. But let's let him struggle for a while before we intervene. Do you see, Collins, that is the best part of our story; we can still change any piece of it, if something better occurs to us. But now it is BLACK's move. We shouldn't underestimate him. After all, he went through the same apprenticeship we did. Let us wait and see. It would be a pity if the game were already over. At our leisure we will think through all of the possibilities he has in his position. Agreed, Collins?"

"Agreed, Your Majesty."

They both fell silent and watched the doll as it started an elaborate new dance and tried out the first steps.

"Does Your Majesty permit one last question?"

"But of course, Collins. And we know what is going to come. You are going to say, there is one piece left over."

"Yes, Your Majesty. The picture is complete, but where does the doll fit in? It is useless; I mean, it has absolutely no purpose in our story as it now stands. It was entirely unnecessary."

The king gave a resigned sigh.

"Yes, Collins. You have a good head on your shoulders, but why can't you see that not everything must have a purpose?"

"But, Your Majesty, the question is justified. Why did Weisslinger go to the trouble of making a doll, if he knew from the start that it would have no—"

"Good God, Collins! You and your frightful utilitarian reasoning! You still haven't understood. Do you think we are setting our minds together to solve the problems of the universe when we make up these stories of ours? All day long we have to grapple with this problem. At least a few hours should remain for us to paint our fantasies in the air and do cerebral gymnastics. And we often get a good idea out of it, for free, so to speak, if you are so intent on utility!"

The king glared at him and the minister hastened to appease him: "Certainly, Your Majesty."

"For instance, why do you suppose we made up this story?"

"Out of boredom, perhaps, if I may allow myself to say so, and because Your Majesty delights in the play of thoughts," suggested the minister doubtfully.

"One could put it that way. Isn't it wonderful that in our world, which is so entirely oriented to purpose and utility, profit and efficiency, there are still things which seem to have no purpose or usefulness, because their meaning lies only in the fact that they exist, like the doll in our story? And yet this little doll is delightful—or perhaps it is so for that very reason."

Collins nodded.

"I find it quite nice," he ventured, and pointed to the doll.

"One ought to be able to invent better ones," answered the king disparagingly. "Let us think of something new, Collins."

The king brooded and stared at the empty walls as if he were lost in the contemplation of a picture.

The minister looked pensively at the delicate mechanical figure as it accomplished its last spin and then with a courteous bow announced the end of the performance.

Connie Willis

Connie Willis (1945–) began publishing SF stories in the 1970s and became a leading writer in the genre in the late 1980s and early 1990s, following several short fiction awards and the publication of her first collection (*Fire Watch*, 1985) and novel (*Lincoln's Dreams*, 1987). Her humorous science fiction is clever and sophisticated, the work of a frantic garrulous monologuist (she is popular as a humorous speaker at SF events), but her most significant work to date appears to be in the mode of "Fire Watch," concerned with history. Her most ambitious novel to date, *Doomsday Book* (1992), a winner of the Hugo Award for best novel, is a sequel to this story.

Time travel is one of her characteristic literary devices, but her stories cover a broad range of moods and subjects. *The Encyclopedia of Science Fiction* says, "In the best of her stories, and in her novels, a steel felicity of mind and style appears effortlessly married to a copious empathy."

This story uses a standard SF idea, the use of time travel to preserve or retrieve the treasures of the past, in a new way. Willis writes science fiction in the tradition of the 1950s, of Mildred Clingerman, Judith Merril, and Margaret St. Clair, with character foregrounded and technology and the standard tropes of science fiction in the background.

FIRE WATCH

History hath triumphed over time, which besides
it nothing but eternity hath triumphed over.
—Sir Walter Raleigh

S*eptember 20*—Of course the first thing I looked for was the fire watch stone. And of course it wasn't there yet. It wasn't dedicated until 1951, accompanying speech by the Very Reverend Dean Walter Matthews, and this is only 1940. I knew that. I went to see the fire watch stone only yesterday, with some kind of misplaced notion that seeing the scene of the crime would somehow help. It didn't.

The only things that would have helped were a crash course in London during the Blitz and a little more time. I had not gotten either.

"Traveling in time is not like taking the tube, Mr. Bartholomew," the esteemed Dunworthy had said, blinking at me through those antique spectacles of his. "Either you report on the twentieth or you don't go at all."

"But I'm not ready," I'd said. "Look, it took me four years to get ready to travel with St. Paul. *St. Paul.* Not St. Paul's. You can't expect me to get ready for London in the Blitz in two days."

"Yes," Dunworthy had said. "We can." End of conversation.

"Two days!" I had shouted at my roommate Kivrin. "All because some computer adds an 's. And the esteemed Dunworthy doesn't even bat an eye when I tell him. 'Time travel is not like taking the tube, young man,' he says. 'I'd suggest you get ready. You're leaving day after tomorrow.' The man's a total incompetent."

"No," she said. "He isn't. He's the best there is. He wrote the book on St. Paul's. Maybe you should listen to what he says."

I had expected Kivrin to be at least a little sympathetic. She had been practically hysterical when she got her practicum changed from fifteenth- to fourteenth-century England, and how did either century qualify as a practicum? Even counting infectious diseases they couldn't have been more than a five. The Blitz is an eight, and St. Paul's itself is, with my luck, a ten.

"You think I should go see Dunworthy again?" I said.

"Yes."

"And then what? I've got two days. I don't know the money, the language, the history. Nothing."

"He's a good man," Kivrin said. "I think you'd better listen to him while you can." Good old Kivrin. Always the sympathetic ear.

The good man was responsible for my standing just inside the propped-open west doors, gawking like the country boy I was supposed to be, looking for a stone that wasn't there. Thanks to the good man, I was about as unprepared for my practicum as it was possible for him to make me.

I couldn't see more than a few feet into the church. I could see a candle gleaming feebly a long way off and a closer blur of white moving toward me. A verger, or possibly the Very Reverend Dean himself. I pulled out the letter from my clergyman uncle in Wales that was supposed to gain me access to the dean, and patted my back pocket to make sure I hadn't lost the microfiche *Oxford English Dictionary, Revised, with Historical Supplements*, I'd smuggled out of the Bodleian. I couldn't pull it out in the middle of the conversation, but with luck I could muddle through the first encounter by context and look up the words I didn't know later.

"Are you from the ayarpee?" he said. He was no older than I am, a head shorter and much thinner. Almost ascetic looking. He reminded me of Kivrin. He was not wearing white, but clutching it to his chest. In other circumstances I would have thought it was a pillow. In other circumstances I would know what was being said to me, but there had been no time to unlearn sub-Mediterranean Latin and Jewish law and learn Cockney and air raid procedures. Two days, and the esteemed Dunworthy, who wanted to talk about the sacred burdens of the historian instead of telling me what the ayarpee was.

"Are you?" he demanded again.

I considered whipping out the *OED* after all on the grounds that Wales was a foreign country, but I didn't think they had microfilm in 1940. Ayarpee. It could be anything, including a nickname for the fire watch, in which case the impulse to say no was not safe at all. "No." I said.

He lunged suddenly toward and past me and peered out the open doors. "Damn," he said, coming back to me. "Where are they then? Bunch of lazy bourgeois tarts!" And so much for getting by on context.

He looked at me closely, suspiciously, as if he thought I was only pretending not to be with the ayarpee. "The church is closed," he said finally.

I held up the envelope and said, "My name's Bartholomew. Is Dean Matthews in?"

He looked out the door a moment longer as if he expected the lazy bourgeois tarts at any moment and intended to attack them with the white bundle; then he turned and said, as if he were guiding a tour, "This way, please," and took off into the gloom.

He led me to the right and down the south aisle of the nave. Thank God I had memorized the floor plan or at that moment, heading into total darkness, led by a raving verger, the whole bizarre metaphor of my situation would have been enough to send me out the west doors and back to St. John's Wood. It helped a little to know where I was. We should have been passing number twenty-six: Hunt's painting of "The Light of the World"—Jesus with his lantern—but it was too dark to see it. We could have used the lantern ourselves.

He stopped abruptly ahead of me, still raving. "We weren't asking for the bloody savoy, just a few cots. Nelson's better off than we are—at least he's got a pillow provided." He brandished the white bundle like a torch in the darkness. It was a pillow after all. "We asked for them over a fortnight ago, and here we still are, sleeping on the bleeding generals from Trafalgar because those bitches want to play tea and crumpets with the tommies at victoria and the hell with us!"

He didn't seem to expect me to answer his outburst, which was good, because I had understood perhaps one key word in three. He stomped on ahead, moving out of sight of the one pathetic altar candle and stopping again at a black hole. Number twenty-five: stairs to the Whispering Gallery, the Dome, the library (not open to the public). Up the stairs, down a hall, stop again at a medieval door and knock. "I've got to go wait for them," he said. "If I'm not there they'll likely take them over to the Abbey. Tell the Dean to ring them up again, will you?" and he took off down the stone steps, still holding his pillow like a shield against him.

He had knocked, but the door was at least a foot of solid oak, and it was obvious the Very Reverend Dean had not heard. I was going to have to knock again. Yes, well, and the man holding the pinpoint had to let go of it, too, but even knowing it will all be over in a moment and you won't feel a thing doesn't make it any easier to say, "Now!" So I stood in front of the door, cursing the history department and the esteemed Dunworthy and the computer that had made the mistake and brought me here to this dark door with only a letter from a fictitious uncle that I trusted no more than I trusted the rest of them.

Even the old reliable Bodleian had let me down. The batch of research stuff I cross-ordered through Balliol and the main terminal is probably sitting in my room right now, a century out of reach. And Kivrin, who had already done her practicum and should have been bursting with advice, walked around as silent as a saint until I begged her to help me.

"Did you go to see Dunworthy?" she said.

"Yes. You want to know what priceless bit of information he had for me? 'Silence and humility are the sacred burdens of the historian.' He also told me I would love St. Paul's. Golden gems from the Master. Unfortunately, what I need to know are the times and places of the bombs so one doesn't fall on me." I flopped down on the bed. "Any suggestions?"

"How good are you at memory retrieval?" she said.

I sat up. "I'm pretty good. You think I should assimilate?"

"There isn't time for that," she said. "I think you should put everything you can directly into long-term."

"You mean endorphins?" I said.

The biggest problem with using memory-assistance drugs to put information into your long-term memory is that it never sits, even for a microsecond, in your short-term memory, and that makes retrieval complicated, not to mention unnerving. It gives you the most unsettling sense of déjà vu to suddenly know something you're positive you've never seen or heard before.

The main problem, though, is not eerie sensations but retrieval. Nobody knows exactly how the brain gets what it wants out of storage, but short-term is definitely involved. That brief, sometimes microscopic, time information spends in short-term is apparently used for something besides tip-of-the-tongue availability. The whole complex sort-and-file process of retrieval is apparently centered in short-term, and without it, and without the help of the drugs that put it there or artificial substitutes, information can be impossible to retrieve. I'd used endorphins for examinations and never had any difficulty with retrieval, and it looked like it was the only way to store all the information I needed in anything approaching the time I had left, but it also meant that I would *never* have known any of the things I needed to know, even for long enough to have forgotten them. If and when I could retrieve the information, I would know it. Till then I was as ignorant of it as if it were not stored in some cobwebbed corner of my mind at all.

"You can retrieve without artificials, can't you?" Kivrin said, looking skeptical.

"I guess I'll have to."

"Under stress? Without sleep? Low body endorphin levels?" What exactly had her practicum been? She had never said a word about it, and undergraduates are not supposed to ask. Stress factors in the Middle Ages? I thought everybody slept through them.

"I hope so," I said. "Anyway, I'm willing to try this idea if you think it will help."

She looked at me with that martyred expression and said, "Nothing will help." Thank you, St. Kivrin of Balliol.

But I tried it anyway. It was better than sitting in Dunworthy's rooms having him blink at me through his historically accurate eyeglasses and tell me I was going to love St. Paul's. When my Bodleian requests didn't come, I overloaded my credit and bought out Blackwell's. Tapes on World War II, Celtic literature, history of mass transit, tourist guidebooks, everything I could think of. Then I rented a high-speed recorder and shot up. When I came out of it, I was so panicked by the feeling of not knowing any more than I had when I started that I took the tube to London and raced up Ludgate Hill to see if the fire watch stone would trigger any memories. It didn't.

"Your endorphin levels aren't back to normal yet," I told myself and tried to relax, but that was impossible with the prospect of the practicum looming up before me. And those are real bullets, kid. Just because you're a history major doing his practicum doesn't mean you can't get killed. I read history books all the way home on the tube and right up until Dunworthy's flunkies came to take me to St. John's Wood this morning.

Then I jammed the microfiche *OED* in my back pocket and went off feeling as if I would have to survive by my native wit and hoping I could get hold of artificials in 1940. Surely I could get through the first day without mishap, I thought, and now here I was, stopped cold by almost the first word that was spoken to me.

Well, not quite. In spite of Kivrin's advice that I not put anything in short-term, I'd memorized the British money, a map of the tube system, a map of my own Oxford. It had gotten me this far. Surely I would be able to deal with the Dean.

Just as I had almost gotten up the courage to knock, he opened the door, and as with the pinpoint, it really was over quickly and without pain. I handed him my letter and he shook my hand and said something understandable like, "Glad to have another man, Bartholomew." He looked strained and tired and as if he might collapse if I told him the Blitz had just started. I know, I know: Keep your mouth shut. The sacred silence, etc.

He said, "We'll get Langby to show you round, shall we?" I assumed that was my Verger of the Pillow, and I was right. He met us at the foot of the stairs, puffing a little but jubilant.

"The cots came," he said to Dean Matthews. "You'd have thought they were doing us a favor. All high heels and hoity-toity. 'You made us miss our tea, luv,' one of them said to me. 'Yes, well, and a good thing, too,' I said. 'You look as if you could stand to lose a stone or two.' "

Even Dean Matthews looked as though he did not completely understand him. He said, "Did you set them up in the crypt?" and then introduced us. "Mr. Bartholomew's just got in from Wales," he said. "He's come to join our volunteers." Volunteers, not fire watch.

Langby showed me round, pointing out various dimnesses in the general gloom and then dragged me down to see the ten folding canvas cots set up among the tombs in the crypt, also in passing, Lord Nelson's black marble sarcophagus. He told me I don't have to stand a watch the first night and suggested I go to bed, since sleep is the most precious commodity in the raids. I could well believe it. He was clutching that silly pillow to his breast like his beloved.

"Do you hear the sirens down here?" I asked, wondering if he buried his head in it.

He looked round at the low stone ceilings. "Some do, some don't. Brinton has to have his Horlich's. Bence-Jones would sleep if the roof fell in on him. I have to have a pillow. The important thing is to get your eight in no matter what. If you don't, you turn into one of the walking dead. And then you get killed."

On that cheering note he went off to post the watches for tonight, leaving his pillow on one of the cots with orders for me to let nobody touch it. So here I sit, waiting for my first air raid siren and trying to get all this down before I turn into one of the walking or non-walking dead.

I've used the stolen *OED* to decipher a little Langby. Middling success. A tart is either a pastry or a prostitute. (I assume the latter, although I was wrong about the pillow.) Bourgeois is a catchall term for all the faults of the middle class. A Tommy's a soldier. Ayarpee I could not find under any spelling and I had nearly given up when something in long-term about the use of acronyms and abbreviations in wartime popped forward (bless you, St. Kivrin) and I realized it must be an abbreviation. ARP. Air Raid Precautions. Of course. Where else would you get the bleeding cots from?

September 21—Now that I'm past the first shock of being here, I realize that the history department neglected to tell me what I'm supposed to do in the three-odd months of this practicum. They handed me this journal, the letter from my uncle, and ten pounds in pre-war money and sent me packing into the past. The ten pounds (already depleted by train and tube fares) is supposed to last me until the end of December and get me back to St. John's Wood for pickup when the second letter calling me back to Wales to sick uncle's bedside comes. Till then I live here in the crypt with Nelson, who, Langby tells me, is pickled in alcohol inside his coffin. If we take a direct hit, will he burn like a torch or simply trickle out in a decaying stream onto the crypt floor, I wonder. Board is provided by a gas ring, over which are cooked wretched tea and indescribable kippers. To pay for all this luxury I am to stand on the roofs of St. Paul's and put out incendiaries.

I must also accomplish the purpose of this practicum, whatever it may be. Right now the only purpose I care about is staying alive until the second letter from uncle arrives and I can go home.

I am doing make-work until Langby has time to "show me the ropes." I've cleaned the skillet they cook the foul little fishes in, stacked wooden folding chairs at the altar end of the crypt (flat instead of standing because they tend to collapse like bombs in the middle of the night), and tried to sleep.

I am apparently not one of the lucky ones who can sleep through the raids. I spent most of the night wondering what St. Paul's risk rating is. Practica have to be at least a six. Last night I was convinced this was a ten, with the crypt as ground zero, and that I might as well have applied for Denver.

The most interesting thing that's happened so far is that I've seen a cat. I am fascinated, but trying not to appear so, since they seem commonplace here.

September 22—Still in the crypt. Langby comes dashing through periodically cursing various government agencies (all abbreviated) and promising to take me up on the roofs. In the meantime I've run out of make-work and taught myself to work a stirrup pump. Kivrin was overly concerned about my memory retrieval abilities. I have not had any trouble so far. Quite the opposite. I called up firefighting information and got the whole manual with pictures, including instructions on the use of the stirrup pump. If the kippers set Lord Nelson on fire, I shall be a hero.

Excitement last night. The sirens went early and some of the chars who clean offices in the City sheltered in the crypt with us. One of them woke me out of a sound sleep, going like an air raid siren. Seems she'd seen a mouse. We had to go whacking at tombs and under the cots with a rubber boot to persuade her it was gone. Obviously what the history department had in mind: murdering mice.

September 24—Langby took me on rounds. Into the choir, where I had to learn the stirrup pump all over again, assigned rubber boots and a tin helmet. Langby says Commander Allen is getting us asbestos firemen's coats, but hasn't yet, so it's my own wool coat and muffler and very cold on the roofs even in September. It feels like November and looks it, too, bleak and cheerless with no sun. Up to the dome and onto the roofs, which should be flat but in fact are littered with towers, pinnacles, gutters, statues, all designed expressly to catch and hold incendiaries out of reach. Shown how to smother an incendiary with sand before it burns through the roof and sets the church on fire. Shown the ropes (literally) lying in a heap at the base of the dome in case somebody has to go up one of the west towers or over the top of the dome. Back inside and down to the Whispering Gallery.

Langby kept up a running commentary through the whole tour, part practical instruction, part church history. Before we went up into the Gallery he dragged me over to the south door to tell me how Christopher Wren stood in the smoking rubble of Old St. Paul's and asked a workman to bring him a stone from the graveyard to mark the cornerstone. On the stone was written in Latin, "I shall rise again," and Wren was so impressed by the irony that he had the word inscribed above the door. Langby looked as smug as if he had not told me a story every first-year history student knows, but I suppose without the impact of the fire watch stone, the other is just a nice story.

Langby raced me up the steps and onto the narrow balcony circling the Whispering Gallery. He was already halfway round to the other side, shouting dimensions and acoustics at me. He stopped facing the wall opposite and said softly, "You can hear me whispering because of the shape of the dome. The sound waves are reinforced around the perimeter of the dome. It sounds like the very crack of doom up here during a raid. The dome is one hundred and seven feet across. It is eighty feet above the nave."

I looked down. The railing went out from under me and the black-and-white marble floor came up with dizzying speed. I hung onto something in front of me and dropped to my knees, staggered and sick at heart. The sun had come out, and all of St. Paul's seemed drenched in gold. Even the carved wood of the choir, the white stone pillars, the leaden pipes of the organ, all of it golden, golden.

Langby was beside me, trying to pull me free. "Bartholomew," he shouted, "what's wrong? For God's sake, man."

I knew I must tell him that if I let go, St. Paul's and all the past would fall in on me, and that I must not let that happen because I was an historian. I said something, but it was not what I intended because Langby merely tightened his grip. He hauled me violently free of the railing and back onto the stairway, then let me collapse limply on the steps and stood back from me, not speaking.

"I don't know what happened in there," I said. "I've never been afraid of heights before."

"You're shaking," he said sharply. "You'd better lie down." He led me back to the crypt.

September 25—Memory retrieval: ARP manual. Symptoms of bombing victims. Stage one—shock; stupefaction; unawareness of injuries; words may not make sense except to victim. Stage two—shivering; nausea; injuries, losses felt; return to reality. Stage three—talkativeness that cannot be controlled; desire to explain shock behavior to rescuers.

Langby must surely recognize the symptoms, but how does he account for the fact there was no bomb? I can hardly explain my shock behavior to him, and it isn't just the sacred silence of the historian that stops me.

He has not said anything, in fact assigned me my first watches for tomorrow night as if nothing had happened, and he seems no more preoccupied than anyone else. Everyone I've met so far is jittery (one thing I had in short-term was how calm everyone was during the raids) and the raids have not come near us since I got here. They've been mostly over the East End and the docks.

There was a reference tonight to a UXB, and I have been thinking about the Dean's manner and the church being closed when I'm almost sure I remember reading it was open through the entire Blitz. As soon as I get a chance, I'll try to retrieve the events of September. As to retrieving anything else, I don't see how I can hope to remember the right information until I know what it is I am supposed to do here, if anything.

There are no guidelines for historians, and no restrictions either. I could tell everyone I'm from the future if I thought they would believe me. I could murder Hitler if I could get to Germany. Or could I? Time paradox talk abounds in the history department, and the graduate students back from their practica don't say a word one way or the other. Is there a tough, immutable past? Or is there a new past every day and do we, the historians, make it? And what are the consequences of what we do, if there are consequences? And how do we dare do anything without knowing them? Must we interfere boldly, hoping we do not bring about all our downfalls? Or must we do nothing at all, not interfere, stand by and watch St. Paul's burn to the ground if need be so that we don't change the future?

All those are fine questions for a late-night study session. They do not matter here. I could no more let St. Paul's burn down than I could kill Hitler. No, that is not true. I found that out yesterday in the Whispering Gallery. I could kill Hitler if I caught him setting fire to St. Paul's.

September 26—I met a young woman today. Dean Matthews has opened the church, so the watch have been doing duties as chars and people have started coming in again. The young woman reminded me of Kivrin, though Kivrin is a good deal taller and would never frizz her hair like that. She looked as if she had been crying. Kivrin has looked like that since she got back from her practicum. The Middle Ages were too much for her. I wonder how she would have coped with this. By pouring out her fears to the local priest, no doubt, as I sincerely hoped her look-alike was not going to do.

"May I help you?" I said, not wanting in the least to help. "I'm a volunteer."

She looked distressed. "You're not paid?" she said, and wiped at her reddened nose with a handkerchief. "I read about St. Paul's and the fire watch and all, and I thought perhaps there's a position there for me. In the canteen, like, or something. A paying position." There were tears in her red-rimmed eyes.

"I'm afraid we don't have a canteen," I said as kindly as I could, considering how impatient Kivrin always makes me, "and it's not actually a real shelter. Some of the watch sleep in the crypt. I'm afraid we're all volunteers, though."

"That won't do, then," she said. She dabbed at her eyes with the handkerchief. "I love St. Paul's, but I can't take on volunteer work, not with my little brother Tom back from the country." I was not reading this situation properly. For all the outward signs of distress she sounded quite cheerful and no closer to tears than when she had come in. "I've got to get us a proper place to stay. With Tom back, we can't go on sleeping in the tubes."

A sudden feeling of dread, the kind of sharp pain you get sometimes from involuntary retrieval, went over me. "The tubes?" I said, trying to get at the memory.

"March Arch, usually," she went on. "My brother Tom saves us a place early and I go . . ." She stopped, held the handkerchief close to her nose, and exploded into it. "I'm sorry," she said, "this awful cold!"

Red nose, watering eyes, sneezing. Respiratory infection. It was a wonder I hadn't told her not to cry. It's only by luck that I haven't made some unforgivable mistake so far, and this is not because I can't get at the long-term memory. I don't have half the information I need even stored: cats and colds and the way St. Paul's looks in full sun. It's only a matter of time before I am stopped cold by something I do not know. Nevertheless, I am going to try for retrieval tonight after I come off watch. At least I can find out whether and when something is going to fall on me.

I have seen the cat once or twice. He is coal-black with a white patch on his throat that looks as if it were painted on for the blackout.

September 27—I have just come down from the roofs. I am still shaking.

Early in the raid the bombing was mostly over the East End. The view was incredible. Searchlights everywhere, the sky pink from the fires and reflecting in the Thames, the exploding shells sparkling like fireworks. There was a constant, deafening thunder broken by the occasional droning of the planes high overhead, then the repeating stutter of the ack-ack guns.

About midnight the bombs began falling quite near with a horrible sound like a train running over me. It took every bit of will I had to keep from flinging myself flat on the roof, but Langby was watching. I didn't want to give him the satisfaction of watching a repeat performance of my behavior in the dome. I kept my head up and my sand bucket firmly in hand and felt quite proud of myself.

The bombs stopped roaring past about three, and there was a lull of about half an hour, and then a clatter like hail on the roofs. Everybody except Langby dived for shovels and stirrup pumps. He was watching me. And I was watching the incendiary.

It had fallen only a few meters from me, behind the clock tower. It was much smaller than I had imagined, only about thirty centimeters long. It was sputtering violently, throwing greenish-white fire almost to where I was standing. In a minute it would simmer down into a molten mass and begin to burn through the roof. Flames and the frantic shouts of firemen, and then the white rubble stretching for miles, and nothing, nothing left, not even the fire watch stone.

It was the Whispering Gallery all over again. I felt that I had said something, and when I looked at Langby's face he was smiling crookedly.

"St. Paul's will burn down," I said. "There won't be anything left."

"Yes," Langby said. "That's the idea, isn't it? Burn St. Paul's to the ground? Isn't that the plan?"

"Whose plan?" I said stupidly.

"Hitler's, of course," Langby said. "Who did you think I meant?" and, almost casually, picked up his stirrup pump.

The page of the ARP manual flashed suddenly before me. I poured the bucket of sand around the still sputtering bomb, snatched up another bucket and dumped that on top of it. Black smoke billowed up in such a cloud that I could hardly find my shovel. I felt for the smothered bomb with the tip of it and scooped it into the empty bucket, then shoveled the sand in on top of it. Tears were streaming down my face from the acrid smoke. I turned to wipe them on my sleeve and saw Langby.

He had not made a move to help me. He smiled. "It's not a bad plan, actually. But of course we won't let it happen. That's what the fire watch is here for. To see that it doesn't happen. Right, Bartholomew?"

I know now what the purpose of my practicum is. I must stop Langby from burning down St. Paul's.

September 28—I try to tell myself I was mistaken about Langby last night, that I misunderstood what he said. Why would he want to burn down St. Paul's unless he is a Nazi spy? How can a Nazi spy have gotten on the fire watch? I think about my faked letter of introduction and shudder.

How can I find out? If I set him some test, some fatal thing that only a loyal Englishman in 1940 would know, I fear I am the one who would be caught out. I *must* get my retrieval working properly.

Until then, I shall watch Langby. For the time being at least that should be easy. Langby has just posted the watches for the next two weeks. We stand every one together.

September 30—I know what happened in September. Langby told me.

Last night in the choir, putting on our coats and boots, he said, "They've already tried once, you know."

I had no idea what he meant. I felt as helpless as that first day when he asked me if I was from the ayarpee.

"The plan to destroy St. Paul's They've already tried once. The tenth of September. A high explosive bomb. But of course you didn't know about that. You were in Wales."

I was not even listening. The minute he had said "high explosive bomb," I had remembered it all. It had burrowed in under the road and lodged on the foundations. The bomb squad had tried to defuse it, but there was a leaking gas main. They decided to evacuate St. Paul's, but Dean Matthews refused to leave, and they got it out after all and exploded it in Barking Marshes. Instant and complete retrieval.

"The bomb squad saved her that time," Langby was saying. "It seems there's always somebody about."

"Yes," I said, "there is," and walked away from him.

October 1—I thought last night's retrieval of the events of September tenth meant some sort of breakthrough, but I have been lying here on my cot most of the night trying for Nazi spies in St. Paul's and getting nothing. Do I have to know exactly what I'm looking for before I can remember it? What good does that do me?

Maybe Langby is not a Nazi spy. Then what is he? An arsonist? A madman? The crypt is hardly conducive to thought, being not at all as silent as a tomb. The chars talk most of the night and the sound of the bombs is muffled, which somehow makes it worse. I find myself straining to hear them. When I did get to sleep this morning, I dreamed about one of the tube shelters being hit, broken mains, drowning people.

October 4—I tried to catch the cat today. I had some idea of persuading it to dispatch the mouse that has been terrifying the chars. I also wanted to see one up close. I took the water bucket I had used with the stirrup pump last night to put out some burning shrapnel from one of the antiaircraft guns. It still had a bit of water in it, but not enough to drown the cat, and my plan was to clamp the bucket over him, reach under, and pick him up, then carry him down to the crypt and point him at the mouse. I did not even come close to him.

I swung the bucket, and as I did so, perhaps an inch of water splashed out. I thought I remembered that the cat was a domesticated animal, but I must have been wrong about that. The cat's wide complacent face pulled back into a skull-like mask that was absolutely terrifying, vicious claws extended from what I had thought were harmless paws, and the cat let out a sound to top the chars.

In my surprise I dropped the bucket and it rolled against one of the pillars. The cat disappeared. Behind me, Langby said, "That's no way to catch a cat."

"Obviously," I said, and bent to retrieve the bucket.

"Cats hate water," he said, still in that expressionless voice.

"Oh," I said, and started in front of him to take the bucket back to the choir. "I didn't know that."

"Everybody knows it. Even the stupid Welsh."

October 8—We have been standing double watches for a week—bomber's moon. Langby didn't show up on the roofs, so I went looking for him in the church. I found him standing by the west doors talking to an old man. The man had a newspaper tucked under his arm and he handed it to Langby, but Langby gave it back to him. When the man saw me, he ducked out. Langby said, "Tourist. Wanted to know where the Windmill Theater is. Read in the paper the girls are starkers."

I know I looked as if I didn't believe him because he said, "You look rotten, old man. Not getting enough sleep, are you? I'll get somebody to take the first watch for you tonight."

"No," I said coldly. "I'll stand my own watch. I like being on the roofs," and added silently, where I can watch you.

He shrugged and said, "I suppose it's better than being down in the crypt. At least on the roofs you can hear the one that gets you."

October 10—I thought the double watches might be good for me, take my mind off my inability to retrieve. The watched-pot idea. Actually, it sometimes works. A few hours of thinking about something else, or a good night's sleep, and the fact pops forward without any prompting, without any artificials.

The good night's sleep is out of the question. Not only do the chars talk constantly, but the cat has moved into the crypt and sidles up to everyone, making siren noises and begging for kippers. I am moving my cot out of the transept and over by Nelson before I go on watch. He may be pickled, but he keeps his mouth shut.

October 11—I dreamed Trafalgar, ships' guns and smoke and falling plaster and Langby shouting my name. My first waking thought was that the folding chairs had gone off. I could not see for all the smoke.

"I'm coming," I said, limping toward Langby and pulling on my boots. There was a heap of plaster and tangled folding chairs in the transept. Langby was digging in it. "Bartholomew!" he shouted, flinging a chunk of plaster aside. "Bartholomew!"

I still had the idea it was smoke. I ran back for the stirrup pump and then knelt beside him and began pulling on a splintered chair back. It resisted, and it came to me suddenly, There is a body under here. I will reach for a piece of the ceiling and find it is a hand. I leaned back on my heels, determined not to be sick, then went at the pile again.

Langby was going far too fast, jabbing with a chair leg. I grabbed his hand to stop him, and he struggled against me as if I were a piece of rubble to be thrown aside. He picked up a large flat square of plaster, and under it was the floor. I turned and looked behind me. Both chars huddled in the recess by the altar. "Who are you looking for?" I said, keeping hold of Langby's arm.

"Bartholomew," he said, and swept the rubble aside, his hands bleeding through the coating of smoky dust.

"I'm here," I said. "I'm all right." I choked on the white dust. "I moved my cot out of the transept."

He turned sharply to the chars and then said quite calmly, "What's under here?"

"Only the gas ring," one of them said timidly from the shadowed recess, "and Mrs. Galbraith's pocketbook." He dug through the mess until he had found them both. The gas ring was leaking at a merry rate, though the flame had gone out.

"You've saved St. Paul's and me after all," I said, standing there in my underwear and boots, holding the useless stirrup pump. "We might all have been asphyxiated."

He stood up. "I shouldn't have saved you," he said.

Stage one: shock, stupefaction, unawareness of injuries, words may not make sense except to victim. He would not know his hand was bleeding yet. He would not remember what he had said. He had said he shouldn't have saved my life.

"I shouldn't have saved you," he repeated. "I have my duty to think of."

"You're bleeding," I said sharply. "You'd better lie down." I sounded just like Langby in the gallery.

October 13—It was a high explosive bomb. It blew a hole in the Choir, and some of the marble statuary is broken, but the ceiling of the crypt did not collapse, which is what I thought at first. It only jarred some plaster loose.

I do not think Langby has any idea what he said. That should give me some sort of advantage, now that I am sure where the danger lies, now that I am sure it will not come crashing down from some other direction. But what good is all this knowing, when I do not know what he will do? Or when?

Surely I have the facts of yesterday's bomb in long-term, but even falling plaster did not jar them loose this time. I am not even trying for retrieval, now. I lie in the darkness waiting for the roof to fall in on me. And remembering how Langby saved my life.

October 15—The girl came in again today. She still has the cold, but she has gotten her paying position. It was a joy to see her. She was wearing a smart uniform and open-toed shoes, and her hair was in an elaborate frizz around her face. We are still cleaning up the mess from the bomb, and Langby was out with Allen getting wood to board up the Choir, so I let the girl chatter at me while I swept. The dust made her sneeze, but at least this time I knew what she was doing.

She told me her name is Enola and that she's working for the WVS, running one of the mobile canteens that are sent to the fires. She came, of all things, to thank me for the job. She said that after she told the WVS that there was no proper shelter with a canteen for St. Paul's, they gave her a run in the City. "So I'll just pop in when I'm close and let you know how I'm making out, won't I just?"

She and her brother Tom are still sleeping in the tubes. I asked her if that was safe and she said probably not, but at least down there you couldn't hear the one that got you and that was a blessing.

October 18—I am so tired I can hardly write this. Nine incendiaries tonight and a land mine that looked as though it was going to catch on the dome till the wind drifted its parachute away from the church. I put out two of the incendiaries. I have done that at least twenty times since I got here and helped with dozens of others, and still it is not enough. One incendiary, one moment of not watching Langby, could undo it all.

I know that is partly why I feel so tired. I wear myself out every night trying to do my job and watch Langby, making sure none of the incendiaries falls without my seeing it. Then I go back to the crypt and wear myself out trying to retrieve something, anything, about spies, fires, St. Paul's in the fall of 1940, anything. It haunts me that I am not doing enough, but I do not know what else to do. Without the retrieval, I am as helpless as these poor people here, with no idea what will happen tomorrow.

If I have to, I will go on doing this till I am called home. He cannot burn down St. Paul's so long as I am here to put out the incendiaries. "I have my duty," Langby said in the crypt.

And I have mine.

October 21—It's been nearly two weeks since the blast and I just now realized we haven't seen the cat since. He wasn't in the mess in the crypt. Even after Langby and I were sure there was no one in there, we sifted through the stuff twice more. He could have been in the Choir, though.

Old Bence-Jones says not to worry. "He's all right," he said. "The jerries could bomb London right down to the ground and the cats would waltz out to greet them. You know why? They don't love anybody. That's what gets half of us killed. Old lady out in Stepney got killed the other night trying to save her cat. Bloody cat was in the Anderson."

"Then where is he?"

"Someplace safe, you can bet on that. If he's not around St. Paul's, it means we're for it. That old saw about the rats deserting a sinking ship, that's a mistake, that is. It's cats, not rats."

October 25—Langby's tourist showed up again. He cannot still be looking for the Windmill Theatre. He had a newspaper under his arm again today, and he asked for Langby, but Langby was across town with Allen, trying to get the asbestos firemen's coats. I saw the name of the paper. It was *The Worker*. A Nazi newspaper?

November 2—I've been up on the roofs for a week straight, helping some incompetent workmen patch the hole the bomb made. They're doing a terrible job. There's still a great gap on one side a man could fall into, but they insist it'll be all right because, after all, you wouldn't fall clear through but only as far as the ceiling, and "the fall can't kill you." They don't seem to understand it's a perfect hiding place for an incendiary.

And that is all Langby needs. He does not even have to set a fire to destroy St. Paul's. All he needs to do is let one burn uncaught until it is too late.

I could not get anywhere with the workmen. I went down into the church to complain to Matthews, and saw Langby and his tourist behind a pillar, close to one of the windows. Langby was holding a newspaper and talking to the man. When I came down from the library an hour later, they were still there. So is the gap. Matthews says we'll put planks across it and hope for the best.

November 5—I have given up trying to retrieve. I am so far behind on my sleep I can't even retrieve information on a newspaper whose name I already know. Double watches the permanent thing now. Our chars have abandoned us altogether (like the cat), so the crypt is quiet, but I cannot sleep.

If I do manage to doze off, I dream. Yesterday I dreamed Kivrin was on the roofs, dressed like a saint. "What was the secret of your practicum?" I said. "What were you supposed to find out?"

She wiped her nose with a handkerchief and said, "Two things. One, that silence and humility are the sacred burdens of the historian. Two"—she stopped and sneezed into the handkerchief—"don't sleep in the tubes."

My only hope is to get hold of an artificial and induce a trance. That's a problem. I'm positive it's too early for chemical endorphins and probably hallucinogens. Alcohol is definitely available, but I need something more concentrated than ale, the only alcohol I know by name. I do not dare ask the watch. Langby is suspicious enough of me already. It's back to the *OED*, to look up a word I don't know.

November 11—The cat's back. Langby was out with Allen again, still trying for the asbestos coats, so I thought it was safe to leave St. Paul's. I went to the grocer's for supplies, and hopefully an artificial. It was late, and the sirens sounded before I had even gotten to Cheapside, but the raids do not usually start until after dark. It took awhile to get all the groceries and to get up my courage to ask whether he had any alcohol—he told me to go to a pub—and when I came out of the shop, it was as if I had pitched suddenly into a hole.

I had no idea where St. Paul's lay, or the street, or the shop I had just come from. I stood on what was no longer the sidewalk, clutching my brown-paper parcel of kippers and bread with a hand I could not have seen if I held it up before my face. I reached up to wrap my muffler closer about my neck and prayed for my eyes to adjust, but there was no reduced light to adjust to. I would have been glad of the moon, for all St. Paul's watch cursed it and called it a fifth columnist. Or a bus, with its shuttered headlights giving just enough light to orient myself by. Or a searchlight. Or the kickback flare of an ack-ack gun. Anything.

Just then I did see a bus, two narrow yellow slits a long way off. I started toward it and nearly pitched off the curb. Which meant the bus was sideways in the street, which meant it was not a bus. A cat meowed, quite near, and rubbed against my leg. I looked down into the yellow lights I had thought belonged to the bus. His eyes were picking up light from somewhere, though I would have sworn there was not a light for miles, and reflecting it flatly up at me.

"A warden'll get you for those lights, old tom," I said, and then as a plane droned overhead, "Or a jerry."

The world exploded suddenly into light, the searchlights and a glow along the Thames seeming to happen almost simultaneously, lighting my way home.

"Come to fetch me, did you, old tom?" I said gaily. "Where've you been? Knew we were out of kippers, didn't you? I call that loyalty." I talked to him all the way home and gave him half a tin of the kippers for saving my life. Bence-Jones said he smelled the milk at the grocer's.

November 13—I dreamed I was lost in the blackout. I could not see my hands in front of my face, and Dunworthy came and shone a pocket torch at me, but I could only see where I had come from and not where I was going.

"What good is that to them?" I said. "They need a light to show them where they're going."

"Even the light from the Thames? Even the light from the fires and the ack-ack guns?" Dunworthy said.

"Yes. Anything is better than this awful darkness." So he came closer to give me the pocket torch. It was not a pocket torch, after all, but Christ's lantern from the Hunt picture in the south nave. I shone it on the curb before me so I could find my way home, but it shone instead on the fire watch stone and I hastily put the light out.

November 20—I tried to talk to Langby today. "I've seen you talking to the old gentleman," I said. It sounded like an accusation. I meant it to. I wanted him to think it was and stop whatever he was planning.

"Reading," he said. "Not talking." He was putting things in order in the choir, piling up sandbags.

"I've seen you reading then," I said belligerently, and he dropped a sandbag and straightened.

"What of it?" he said. "It's a free country. I can read to an old man if I want, same as you can talk to that little WVS tart."

"What do you read?" I said.

"Whatever he wants. He's an old man. He used to come home from his job, have a bit of brandy and listen to his wife read the papers to him. She got killed in one of the raids. Now I read to him. I don't see what business it is of yours."

It sounded true. It didn't have the careful casualness of a lie, and I almost believed him, except that I had heard the tone of truth from him before. In the crypt. After the bomb.

"I thought he was a tourist looking for the Windmill," I said.

He looked blank only a second, and then he said, "Oh, yes, that. He came in with the paper and asked me to tell him where it was. I looked it up to find the address. Clever, that. I didn't guess he couldn't read it for himself." But it was enough. I knew that he was lying.

He heaved a sandbag almost at my feet. "Of course you wouldn't understand a thing like that, would you? A simple act of human kindness?"

"No," I said coldly. "I wouldn't."

None of this proves anything. He gave away nothing, except perhaps the name of an artificial, and I can hardly go to Dean Matthews and accuse Langby of reading aloud.

I waited till he had finished in the choir and gone down to the crypt. Then I lugged one of the sandbags up to the roof and over to the chasm. The planking has held so far, but everyone walks gingerly around it, as if it were a grave. I cut the sandbag open and spilled the loose sand into the bottom. If it has occurred to Langby that this is the perfect spot for an incendiary, perhaps the sand will smother it.

November 21—I gave Enola some of "uncle's" money today and asked her to get me the brandy. She was more reluctant than I thought she'd be, so there must be societal complications I am not aware of, but she agreed.

I don't know what she came for. She started to tell me about her brother and some prank he'd pulled in the tubes that got him in trouble with the guard, but after I asked her about the brandy, she left without finishing the story.

November 25—Enola came today, but without bringing the brandy. She is going to Bath for the holidays to see her aunt. At least she will be away from the raids for a while. I will not have to worry about her. She finished the story of her brother and told me she hopes to persuade this aunt to take Tom for the duration of the Blitz but is not at all sure the aunt will be willing.

Young Tom is apparently not so much an engaging scapegrace as a near criminal. He has been caught twice picking pockets in the Bank tube shelter, and they have had to go back to Marble Arch. I comforted her as best I could, told her all boys were bad at one time or another. What I really wanted to say was that she needn't worry at all, that young Tom strikes me as a true survivor type, like my own tom, like Langby, totally unconcerned with anybody but himself, well-equipped to survive the Blitz and rise to prominence in the future.

Then I asked her whether she had gotten the brandy.

She looked down at her open-toed shoes and muttered unhappily, "I thought you'd forgotten all about that."

I made up some story about the watch taking turns buying a bottle, and she seemed less unhappy, but I am not convinced she will not use this trip to Bath as an excuse to do nothing. I will have to leave St. Paul's and buy it myself, and I don't dare leave Langby alone in the church. I made her promise to bring the brandy today before she leaves. But she is still not back, and the sirens have already gone.

November 26—No Enola, and she said their train left at noon. I suppose I should be grateful that at least she is safely out of London. Maybe in Bath she will be able to get over her cold.

Tonight one of the ARP girls breezed in to borrow half our cots and tell us about a mess over in the East End where a surface shelter was hit. Four dead, twelve wounded. "At least it wasn't one of the tube shelters!" she said. "Then you'd see a real mess, wouldn't you?"

November 30—I dreamed I took the cat to St. John's Wood.

"Is this a rescue mission?" Dunworthy said.

"No, sir," I said proudly. "I know what I was supposed to find in my practicum. The perfect survivor. Tough and resourceful and selfish. This is the only one I could find. I had to kill Langby, you know, to keep him from burning down St. Paul's. Enola's brother has gone to Bath, and the others will never make it. Enola wears open-toed shoes in the winter and sleeps in the tubes and puts her hair up on metal pins so it will curl. She cannot possibly survive the Blitz."

Dunworthy said, "Perhaps you should have rescued her instead. What did you say her name was?"

"Kivrin," I said, and woke up cold and shivering.

December 5—I dreamed Langby had the pinpoint bomb. He carried it under his arm like a brown-paper parcel, coming out of St. Paul's Station and around Ludgate Hill to the west doors.

"This is not fair," I said, barring his way with my arm. "There is no fire watch on duty."

He clutched the bomb to his chest like a pillow. "That is your fault," he said, and before I could get to my stirrup pump and bucket, he tossed it in the door.

The pinpoint was not even invented until the end of the twentieth century, and it was another ten years before the dispossessed communists got hold of it and turned it into something that could be carried under your arm. A parcel that could blow a quarter mile of the City into oblivion. Thank God that is one dream that cannot come true.

It was a sunlit morning in the dream, and this morning when I came off watch the sun was shining for the first time in weeks. I went down to the crypt and then came up again, making the rounds of the roofs twice more, then the steps and the grounds and all the treacherous alleyways between where an incendiary could be missed. I felt better after that, but when I got to sleep I dreamed again, this time of fire and Langby watching it, smiling.

December 15—I found the cat this morning. Heavy raids last night, but most of them over toward Canning Town and nothing on the roofs to speak of. Nevertheless the cat was quite dead. I found him lying on the steps this morning when I made my own, private rounds. Concussion. There was not a mark on him anywhere except the white blackout patch on his throat, but when I picked him up, he was all jelly under the skin.

I could not think what to do with him. I thought for one mad moment of asking Matthews if I could bury him in the crypt. Honorable death in war or something. Trafalgar, Waterloo, London, died in battle. I ended by wrapping him in my muffler and taking him down Ludgate Hill to a building that had been bombed out and burying him in the rubble. It will do no good. The rubble will be no protection from dogs or rats, and I shall never get another muffler. I have gone through nearly all of uncle's money.

I should not be sitting here. I haven't checked the alleyways or the rest of the steps, and there might be a dud or a delayed incendiary or something that I missed.

When I came here, I thought of myself as the noble rescuer, the savior of the past. I am not doing very well at the job. At least Enola is out of it. I wish there were some way I could send St. Paul's to Bath for safekeeping. There were hardly any raids last night. Bence-Jones said cats can survive anything. What if he was coming to get me, to show me the way home? All the bombs were over Canning Town.

December 16—Enola has been back a week. Seeing her, standing on the west steps where I found the cat, sleeping in Marble Arch and not safe at all, was more than I could absorb. "I thought you were in Bath," I said stupidly.

"My aunt said she'd take Tom but not me as well. She's got a houseful of evacuation children, and what a noisy lot. Where is your muffler?" she said. "It's dreadful cold up here on the hill."

"I . . ." I said, unable to answer, "I lost it."

"You'll never get another one," she said. "They're going to start rationing clothes. And wool, too. You'll never get another one like that."

"I know," I said, blinking at her.

"Good things just thrown away," she said. "It's absolutely criminal, that's what it is."

I don't think I said anything to that, just turned and walked away with my head down, looking for bombs and dead animals.

December 20—Langby isn't a Nazi. He's a communist. I can hardly write this. A communist.

One of the chars found *The Worker* wedged behind a pillar and brought it down to the crypt as we were coming off the first watch.

"Bloody communists," Bence-Jones said. "Helping Hitler, they are. Talking against the king, stirring up trouble in the shelters. Traitors, that's what they are."

"They love England same as you," the char said.

"They don't love nobody but themselves, bloody selfish lot. I wouldn't be surprised to hear they were ringing Hitler up on the telephone," Bence-Jones said. " 'Ello, Adolf, here's where to drop the bombs."

The kettle on the gas ring whistled. The char stood up and poured the hot water into a chipped teapot, then sat back down. "Just because they speak their minds don't mean they'd burn down old St. Paul's, does it now?"

"Of course not," Langby said, coming down the stairs. He sat down and pulled off his boots, stretching his feet in their wool socks. "Who wouldn't burn down St. Paul's?"

"The communists," Bence-Jones said, looking straight at him, and I wondered if he suspected Langby too.

Langby never batted an eye. "I wouldn't worry about them if I were you," he said. "It's the jerries that are doing their bloody best to burn her down tonight. Six incendiaries so far, and one almost went into that great hole over the choir." He held out his cup to the char, and she poured him a cup of tea.

I wanted to kill him, smashing him to dust and rubble on the floor of the crypt while Bence-Jones and the char looked on in helpless surprise, shouting warnings to them and the rest of the watch. "Do you know what the communists did?" I wanted to shout. "Do you? We have to stop him." I even stood up and started toward him as he sat with his feet stretched out before him and his asbestos coat still over his shoulders.

And then the thought of the Gallery drenched in gold, the communist coming out of the tube station with the package so casually under his arm, made me sick with the same staggering vertigo of guilt and helplessness, and I sat back down on the edge of my cot and tried to think what to do.

They do not realize the danger. Even Bence-Jones, for all his talk of traitors, thinks they are capable only of talking against the king. They do not know, cannot know, what the communists will become. Stalin is an ally. Communists mean Russia. They have never heard of Karinsky or the New Russia or any of the things that will make "communist" into a synonym for "monster." They will never know it. By the time the communists become what they became, there will be no fire watch. Only I know what it means to hear the name "communist" uttered here, so carelessly, in St. Paul's.

A communist. I should have known. I should have known.

December 22—Double watches again. I have not had any sleep and I am getting very unsteady on my feet. I nearly pitched into the chasm this morning, only saved myself by dropping to my knees. My endorphin levels are fluctuating wildly, and I know I must get some sleep soon or I will become one of Langby's walking dead, but I am afraid to leave him alone on the roofs, alone in the church with his communist party leader, alone anywhere. I have taken to watching him when he sleeps.

If I could just get hold of an artificial, I think I could induce a trance, in spite of my poor condition. But I cannot even go out to a pub. Langby is on the roofs constantly, waiting for his chance. When Enola comes again I must convince her to get the brandy for me. There are only a few days left.

December 28—Enola came this morning while I was on the west porch, picking up the Christmas tree. It has been knocked over three nights running by concussion. I righted the tree and was bending down to pick up the scattered tinsel when Enola appeared suddenly out of the fog like some cheerful saint. She stooped quickly and kissed me on the cheek. Then she straightened up, her nose red from her perennial cold, and handed me a box wrapped in colored paper.

"Merry Christmas," she said. "Go on then, open it. It's a gift."

My reflexes are almost totally gone. I knew the box was far too shallow for a bottle of brandy. Nevertheless, I believed she had remembered, had brought me my salvation. "You darling," I said, and tore it open.

It was a muffler. Gray wool. I stared at it for fully half a minute without realizing what it was. "Where's the brandy?" I said.

She looked shocked. Her nose got redder and her eyes started to blur. "You need this more. You haven't any clothing coupons and you have to be outside all the time. It's been so dreadful cold."

"I *needed* the brandy," I said angrily.

"I was only trying to be kind," she started, and I cut her off.

"Kind?" I said. "I asked you for brandy. I don't recall ever saying I needed a muffler." I shoved it back at her and began untangling a string of colored lights that had shattered when the tree fell.

She got that same holy martyr look Kivrin is so wonderful at. "I worry about you all the time up here," she said in a rush. "They're *trying* for St. Paul's, you know. And it's so close to the river. I didn't think you should be drinking. I—it's a crime when they're trying so hard to kill us all that you won't take care of yourself. It's like you're in it with them. I worry someday I'll come up to St. Paul's and you won't be here."

"Well, and what exactly am I supposed to do with a muffler? Hold it over my head when they drop the bombs?"

She turned and ran, disappearing into the gray fog before she had gone down two steps. I started after her, still holding the string of broken lights, tripped over it, and fell almost all the way to the bottom of the steps.

Langby picked me up. "You're off watches," he said grimly.

"You can't do that," I said.

"Oh, yes, I can. I don't want any walking dead on the roofs with me."

I let him lead me down here to the crypt, make me a cup of tea, put me to bed, all very solicitous. No indication that this is what he has been waiting for. I will lie here till the sirens go. Once I am on the roofs he will not be able to send me back without seeming suspicious. Do you know what he said before he left, asbestos coat and rubber boots, the dedicated fire watcher? "I want you to get some sleep." As if I could sleep with Langby on the roofs. I would be burned alive.

December 30—The sirens woke me, and old Bence-Jones said, "That should have done you some good. You've slept the clock round."

"What day is it?" I said, going for my boots.

"The twenty-ninth," he said, and as I dived for the door, "No need to hurry. They're late tonight. Maybe they won't come at all. That'd be a blessing, that would. The tide's out."

I stopped by the door to the stairs, holding on to the cool stone. "Is St. Paul's all right?"

"She's still standing," he said. "Have a bad dream?"

"Yes," I said, remembering the bad dreams of all the past weeks—the dead cat in my arms in St. John's Wood, Langby with his parcel and his *Worker* under his arm, the fire watch stone garishly lit by Christ's lantern. Then I remembered I had not dreamed at all. I had slept the kind of sleep I had prayed for, the kind of sleep that would help me remember.

Then I remembered. Not St. Paul's, burned to the ground by the communists. A headline from the dailies. "Marble Arch hit. Eighteen killed by blast." The date was not clear except for the year. 1940. There were exactly two more days left in 1940. I grabbed my coat and muffler and ran up the stairs and across the marble floor.

"Where the hell do you think you're going?" Langby shouted to me. I couldn't see him.

"I have to save Enola," I said, and my voice echoed in the dark sanctuary. "They're going to bomb Marble Arch."

"You can't leave now," he shouted after me, standing where the fire watch stone would be. "The tide's out. You dirty—"

I didn't hear the rest of it. I had already flung myself down the steps and into a taxi. It took almost all the money I had, the money I had so carefully hoarded for the trip back to St. John's Wood. Shelling started while we were still in Oxford Street, and the driver refused to go any farther. He let me out into pitch blackness, and I saw I would never make it in time.

Blast. Enola crumpled on the stairway down to the tube, her open-toed shoes still on her feet, not a mark on her. And when I try to lift her, jelly under the skin. I would have to wrap her in the muffler she gave me, because I was too late. I had gone back a hundred years to be too late to save her.

I ran the last blocks, guided by the gun emplacement that had to be in Hyde Park, and skidded down the steps into Marble Arch. The woman in the ticket booth took my last shilling for a ticket to St. Paul's Station. I stuck it in my pocket and raced toward the stairs.

"No running," she said placidly. "To your left, please." The door to the right was blocked off by wooden barricades, the metal gates beyond pulled to and chained. The board with names on it for the stations was x-ed with tape, and a new sign that read ALL TRAINS was nailed to the barricade, pointing left.

Enola was not on the stopped escalators or sitting against the wall in the hallway. I came to the first stairway and could not get through. A family had set out, just where I wanted to step, a communal tea of bread and butter, a little pot of jam sealed with waxed paper, and a kettle on a ring like the one Langby and I had rescued out of the rubble, all of it spread on a cloth embroidered at the corners with flowers. I stood staring down at the layered tea, spread like a waterfall down the steps.

"I—Marble Arch—" I said. Another twenty killed by flying tiles. "You shouldn't be here."

"We've as much right as anyone," the man said belligerently, "and who are you to tell us to move on?"

A woman lifting saucers out of a cardboard box looked up at me, frightened. The kettle began to whistle.

"It's you that should move on," the man said. "Go on then." He stood off to one side so I could pass. I edged past the embroidered cloth apologetically.

"I'm sorry," I said. "I'm looking for someone. On the platform."

"You'll never find her in there, mate," the man said, thumbing in that direction. I hurried past him, nearly stepping on the tea cloth, and rounded the corner into hell.

It was not hell. Shopgirls folded coats and leaned back against them, cheerful or sullen or disagreeable, but certainly not damned. Two boys scuffled for a shilling and lost it on the tracks. They bent over the edge, debating whether to go after it, and the station guard yelled to them to back away. A train rumbled through, full of people. A mosquito landed on the guard's hand and he reached out to slap it and missed. The boys laughed. And behind and before them, stretching in all directions down the deadly tile curves of the tunnel like casualties, backed into the entranceways and onto the stairs, were people. Hundreds and hundreds of people.

I stumbled back onto the stairs, knocking over a teacup. It spilled like a flood across the cloth.

"I told you, mate," the man said cheerfully. "It's hell in there, ain't it? And worse below."

"Hell," I said. "Yes." I would never find her. I would never save her. I looked at the woman mopping up the tea, and it came to me that I could not save her either. Enola or the cat or any of them, lost here in the endless stairways and cul-de-sacs of time. They were already dead a hundred years, past saving. The past is beyond saving. Surely that was the lesson the history department sent me all this way to learn. Well, fine, I've learned it. Can I go home now?

Of course not, dear boy. You have foolishly spent all your money on taxicabs and brandy, and tonight is the night the Germans burn the City. (Now it is too late, I remember it all. Twenty-eight incendiaries on the roofs.) Langby must have his chance, and you must learn the hardest lesson of all and the one you should have known from the beginning. You cannot save St. Paul's.

I went back out onto the platform and stood behind the yellow line until a train pulled up. I took my ticket out and held it in my hand all the way to St. Paul's Station. When I got there, smoke billowed toward me like an easy spray of water. I could not see St. Paul's.

"The tide's out," a woman said in a voice devoid of hope, and I went down in a snake pit of limp cloth hoses. My hands came up covered with rank-smelling mud, and I understood finally (and too late) the significance of the tide. There was no water to fight the fires.

A policeman barred my way and I stood helplessly before him with no idea what to say. "No civilians allowed here," he said. "St. Paul's is for it." The smoke billowed like a thundercloud, alive with sparks, and the dome rose golden above it.

"I'm fire watch," I said, and his arm fell away, and then I was on the roofs.

My endorphin levels must have been going up and down like an air raid siren. I do not have any short-term from then on, just moments that do not fit together: the people in the church when we brought Langby down, huddled in a corner playing cards, the whirlwind of burning scraps of wood in the dome, the ambulance driver who wore open-toed shoes like Enola and smeared salve on my burned hands. And in the center, the one clear moment when I went after Langby on a rope and saved his life.

I stood by the dome, blinking against the smoke. The City was on fire and it seemed as if St. Paul's would ignite from the heat, would crumble from the noise alone. Bence-Jones was by the northwest tower, hitting at an incendiary with a spade. Langby was too close to the patched place where the bomb had gone through, looking toward me. An incendiary clattered behind him. I turned to grab a shovel, and when I turned back, he was gone.

"Langby!" I shouted, and could not hear my own voice. He had fallen into the chasm and nobody saw him or the incendiary. Except me. I do not remember how I got across the roof. I think I called for a rope. I got a rope. I tied it around my waist, gave the ends of it into the hands of the fire watch, and went over the side. The fires lit the walls of the hole almost all the way to the bottom. Below me I could see a pile of whitish rubble. He's under there, I thought, and jumped free of the wall. The space was so narrow there was nowhere to throw the rubble. I was afraid I would inadvertently stone him, and I tried to toss the pieces of planking and plaster over my shoulder, but there was barely room to turn. For one awful moment I thought he might not be there at all, that the pieces of splintered wood would brush away to reveal empty pavement, as they had in the crypt.

I was numbed by the indignity of crawling over him. If he was dead I did not think I could bear the shame of stepping on his helpless body. Then his hand came up like a ghost's and grabbed my ankle, and within seconds I had whirled and had his head free.

He was the ghastly white that no longer frightens me. "I put the bomb out," he said. I stared at him, so overwhelmed with relief I could not speak. For one hysterical moment I thought I would even laugh, I was so glad to see him. I finally realized what it was I was supposed to say.

"Are you all right?" I said.

"Yes," he said, and tried to raise himself on one elbow. "So much the worse for you."

He could not get up. He grunted with pain when he tried to shift his weight to his right side and lay back, the uneven rubble crunching sickeningly under him. I tried to lift him gently so I could see where he was hurt. He must have fallen on something.

"It's no use," he said, breathing hard. "I put it out."

I spared him a startled glance, afraid that he was delirious and went back to rolling him onto his side.

"I know you were counting on this one," he went on, not resisting me at all. "It was bound to happen sooner or later with all these roofs. Only I went after it. What'll you tell your friends?"

His asbestos coat was torn down the back in a long gash. Under it his back was charred and smoking. He had fallen on the incendiary. "Oh, my God," I said, trying frantically to see how badly he was burned without touching him. I had no way of knowing how deep the burns went, but they seemed to extend only in the narrow space where the coat had torn. I tried to pull the bomb out from under him, but the casing was as hot as a stove. It was not melting, though. My sand and Langby's body had smothered it. I had no idea if it would start up again when it was exposed to the air. I looked around, a little wildly, for the bucket and stirrup pump Langby must have dropped when he fell.

"Looking for a weapon?" Langby said, so clearly it was hard to believe he was hurt at all. "Why not just leave me here? A bit of overexposure and I'd be done for by morning. Or would you rather do your dirty work in private?"

I stood up and yelled to the men on the roof above us. One of them shone a pocket torch down at us, but its light didn't reach.

"Is he dead?" somebody shouted down to me.

"Send for an ambulance," I said. "He's been burned."

I helped Langby up, trying to support his back without touching the burn. He staggered a little and then leaned against the wall, watching me as I tried to bury the incendiary, using a piece of the planking as a scoop. The rope came down and I tied Langby to it. He had not spoken since I helped him up. He let me tie the rope around his waist, still looking steadily at me. "I should have let you smother in the crypt," he said.

He stood leaning easily, almost relaxed against the wooden supports, his hands holding him up. I put his hands on the slack rope and wrapped it once around them for the grip I knew he didn't have. "I've been onto you since that day in the Gallery. I knew you weren't afraid of heights. You came down here without any fear of heights when you thought I'd ruined your precious plans. What was it? An attack of conscience? Kneeling there like a baby, whining, 'What have we done? What have we done?' You made me sick. But you know what gave you away first? The cat. Everybody knows cats hate water. Everybody but a dirty Nazi spy."

There was a tug on the rope. "Come ahead," I said, and the rope tautened.

"That WVS tart? Was she a spy, too? Supposed to meet you in Marble Arch? Telling me it was going to be bombed. You're a rotten spy, Bartholomew. Your friends already blew it up in September. It's open again."

The rope jerked suddenly and began to lift Langby. He twisted his hands to get a better grip. His right shoulder scraped the wall. I put up my hands and pushed him gently so that his left side was to the wall. "You're making a big mistake, you know," he said. "You should have killed me. I'll tell."

I stood in the darkness, waiting for the rope. Langby was unconscious when he reached the roof. I walked past the fire watch to the dome and down to the crypt.

This morning the letter from my uncle came and with it a five-pound note.

December 31—Two of Dunworthy's flunkies met me in St. John's Wood to tell me I was late for my exams. I did not even protest. I shuffled obediently after them without even considering how unfair it was to give an exam to one of the walking dead. I had not slept in—how long? Since yesterday when I went to find Enola. I had not slept in a hundred years.

Dunworthy was in the Examination Buildings, blinking at me. One of the flunkies handed me a test paper and the other one called time. I turned the paper over and left an oily smudge from the ointment on my burns. I stared uncomprehendingly at them. I had grabbed at the incendiary when I turned Langby over, but these burns were on the backs of my hands. The answer came to me suddenly in Langby's unyielding voice. "They're rope burns, you fool. Don't they teach you Nazi spies the proper way to come up a rope?"

I looked down at the test. It read, "Number of incendiaries that fell on St. Paul's———Number of land mines———Number of high explosive bombs——— Method most commonly used for extinguishing incendiaries———land mines———high explosive bombs———Number of volunteers on first watch ———second watch———Casualties———Fatalities———" The questions made no sense. There was only a short space, long enough for the writing of a number, after any of the questions. Method most commonly used for extinguishing incendiaries. How would I ever fit what I knew into that narrow space? Where were the questions about Enola and Langby and the cat?

I went up to Dunworthy's desk. "St. Paul's almost burned down last night," I said. "What kind of questions are these?"

"You should be answering questions, Mr. Bartholomew, not asking them."

"There aren't any questions about the people," I said. The outer casing of my anger began to melt.

"Of course there are," Dunworthy said, flipping to the second page of the test. "Number of casualties, 1940. Blast, shrapnel, other."

"Other?" I said. At any moment the roof would collapse on me in a shower of plaster dust and fury. "Other? Langby put out a fire with his own body. Enola has a cold that keeps getting worse. The cat . . ." I snatched the paper back from him and scrawled "one cat" in the narrow space next to "blast." "Don't you care about them at all?"

"They're important from a statistical point of view," he said, "but as individuals they are hardly relevant to the course of history."

My reflexes were shot. It was amazing to me that Dunworthy's were almost as slow. I grazed the side of his jaw and knocked his glasses off. "Of course they're relevant!" I shouted. "They *are* the history, not all these bloody numbers!"

The reflexes of the flunkies were very fast. They did not let me start another swing at him before they had me by both arms and were hauling me out of the room.

"They're back there in the past with nobody to save them. They can't see their hands in front of their faces and there are bombs falling down on them and you tell me they aren't important? You call that being an historian?"

The flunkies dragged me out the door and down the hall. "Langby saved St. Paul's. How much more important can a person get? You're no historian! You're nothing but a—" I wanted to call him a terrible name, but the only curses I could summon up were Langby's. "You're nothing but a dirty Nazi spy!" I bellowed. "You're nothing but a lazy bourgeois tart!"

They dumped me on my hands and knees outside the door and slammed it in my face. "I wouldn't be an historian if you paid me!" I shouted, and went to see the fire watch stone.

December 31—I am having to write this in bits and pieces. My hands are in pretty bad shape, and Dunworthy's boys didn't help matters much. Kivrin comes in periodically, wearing her St. Joan look, and smears so much salve on my hands that I can't hold a pencil.

St. Paul's Station is not there, of course, so I got out at Holborn and walked, thinking about my last meeting with Dean Matthews on the morning after the burning of the city. This morning.

"I understand you saved Langby's life," he said. "I also understand that between you, you saved St. Paul's last night."

I showed him the letter from my uncle and he stared at it as if he could not think what it was. "Nothing stays saved forever," he said, and for a terrible moment I thought he was going to tell me Langby had died. "We shall have to keep on saving St. Paul's until Hitler decides to bomb something else."

The raids on London are almost over, I wanted to tell him. He'll start bombing the countryside in a matter of weeks. Canterbury, Bath, aiming always at the cathedrals. You and St. Paul's will both outlast the war and live to dedicate the fire watch stone.

"I am hopeful, though," he said. "I think the worst is over."

"Yes, sir." I thought of the stone, its letters still readable after all this time. No, sir, the worst is not over.

I managed to keep my bearings almost to the top of Ludgate Hill. Then I lost my way completely, wandering about like a man in a graveyard. I had not remembered that the rubble looked so much like the white plaster dust Langby had tried to dig me out of. I could not find the stone anywhere. In the end I nearly fell over it, jumping back as if I had stepped on a body.

It is all that's left. Hiroshima is supposed to have had a handful of untouched trees at ground zero. Denver the capitol steps. Neither of them says, "Remember men and women of St. Paul's Watch who by the grace of God saved this cathedral." The grace of God.

Part of the stone is sheared off. Historians argue there was another line that said, "for all time," but I do not believe that, not if Dean Matthews had anything to do with it. And none of the watch it was dedicated to would have believed it for a minute. We saved St. Paul's every time we put out an incendiary, and only until the next one fell. Keeping watch on the danger spots, putting out the little fires with sand and stirrup pumps, the big ones with our bodies, in order to keep the whole vast complex structure from burning down. Which sounds to me like a course description for History Practicum 401. What a fine time to discover what historians are for when I have tossed my chance for being one out the windows as easily as they tossed the pinpoint bomb in! No, sir, the worst is not over.

There are flash burns on the stone, where legend says the Dean of St. Paul's was kneeling when the bomb went off. Totally apocryphal, of course, since the front door is hardly an appropriate place for prayers. It is more likely the shadow of a tourist who wandered in to ask the whereabouts of the Windmill Theatre, or the imprint of a girl bringing a volunteer his muffler. Or a cat.

Nothing is saved forever, Dean Matthews, and I knew that when I walked in the west doors that first day, blinking into the gloom, but it is pretty bad nevertheless. Standing here knee-deep in rubble out of which I will not be able to dig any folding chairs or friends, knowing that Langby died thinking I was a Nazi spy, knowing that Enola came one day and I wasn't there. It's pretty bad.

But it is not as bad as it could be. They are both dead, and Dean Matthews too, but they died without knowing what I knew all along, what sent me to my knees in the Whispering Gallery, sick with grief and guilt: that in the end none of us saved St. Paul's. And Langby cannot turn to me, stunned and sick at heart, and say, "Who did this? Your friends the Nazis?" And I would have to say, "No, the communists." That would be the worst.

I have come back to the room and let Kivrin smear more salve on my hands. She wants me to get some sleep. I know I should pack and get gone. It will be humiliating to have them come and throw me out, but I do not have the strength to fight her. She looks so much like Enola.

January 1—I have apparently slept not only through the night, but through the morning mail drop as well. When I woke up just now, I found Kivrin sitting on the end of the bed holding an envelope. "Your grades came," she said.

I put my arm over my eyes. "They can be marvelously efficient when they want to, can't they?"

"Yes," Kivrin said.

"Well, let's see it," I said, sitting up. "How long do I have before they come and throw me out?"

She handed the flimsy computer envelope to me. I tore it along the perforation. "Wait," she said. "Before you open it, I want to say something." She put her hand gently on my burns. "You're wrong about the history department. They're very good."

It was not exactly what I expected her to say. "Good is not the word I'd use to describe Dunworthy," I said and yanked the inside slip free.

Kivrin's look did not change, not even when I sat there with the printout on my knees where she could surely see it.

"Well," I said.

The slip was hand-signed by the esteemed Dunworthy. I have taken a first. With honors.

January 2—Two things came in the mail today. One was Kivrin's assignment. The history department thinks of everything—even to keeping her here long enough to nursemaid me, even to coming up with a prefabricated trial by fire to send their history majors through.

I think I wanted to believe that was what they had done, Enola and Langby only hired actors, the cat a clever android with its clockwork innards taken out for the final effect, not so much because I wanted to believe Dunworthy was not good at all, but because then I would not have this nagging pain at not knowing what had happened to them.

"You said your practicum was England in 1400?" I said, watching her as suspiciously as I had watched Langby.

"1349," she said, and her face went slack with memory. "The plague year."

"My God," I said. "How could they do that? The plague's a ten."

"I have a natural immunity," she said, and looked at her hands.

Because I could not think of anything to say, I opened the other piece of mail. It was a report on Enola. Computer-printed, facts and dates and statistics, all the numbers the history department so dearly loves, but it told me what I thought I would have to go without knowing: that she had gotten over her cold and survived the Blitz. Young Tom had been killed in the Baedaker raids on Bath, but Enola had lived until 2006, the year before they blew up St. Paul's.

I don't know whether I believe the report or not, but it does not matter. It is, like Langby's reading aloud to the old man, a simple act of human kindness. They think of everything.

Not quite. They did not tell me what happened to Langby. But I find as I write this that I already know: I saved his life. It does not seem to matter that he might have died in hospital next day, and I find, in spite of all the hard lessons the history department has tried to teach me, I do not quite believe this one: that nothing is saved forever. It seems to me that perhaps Langby is.

January 3—I went to see Dunworthy today. I don't know what I intended to say—some pompous drivel about my willingness to serve in the fire watch of history, standing guard against the falling incendiaries of the human heart, silent and saintly.

But he blinked at me nearsightedly across his desk, and it seemed to me that he was blinking at that last bright image of St. Paul's in sunlight before it was gone forever and that he knew better than anyone that the past cannot be saved, and I said instead, "I'm sorry that I broke your glasses, sir."

"How did you like St. Paul's?" he said, and like my first meeting with Enola,

I felt I must be somehow reading the signals all wrong, that he was not feeling loss, but something quite different.

"I loved it, sir," I said.

"Yes," he said. "So do I."

Dean Matthews is wrong. I have fought with memory my whole practicum only to find that it is not the enemy at all, and being an historian is not some saintly burden after all. Because Dunworthy is not blinking against the fatal sunlight of the last morning, but into the gloom of that first afternoon, looking in the great west doors of St. Paul's at what is, like Langby, like all of it, every moment, in us, saved forever.

Poul Anderson

Poul Anderson (1926–   ) has written over sixty novels and published over forty collections of short stories in his long and influential career in science fiction. James Blish called Anderson "the enduring explosion" because of the high quality of his continuing literary production. Distinguished as a fantasy writer (*The Broken Sword* [1954] was his first adult novel) and a mystery writer (his first mystery, *Perish By the Sword* [1959], won the Cock Robin prize), he is nevertheless principally one of the heroic figures of hard science fiction. While a devotee of the hard science approach of Hal Clement, he is given to making his stories vehicles for philosophical and social commentary, in the manner of Heinlein.

Anderson has always defended the traditions of military honor in his fiction, and devoted much of his effort to adventure plots. But he has also turned out a number of colorful, powerful SF stories and novels, from *Brain Wave* (1954) to *The Boat of a Million Years* (1989), that are generally perceived as his major works—the most famous is probably *Tau Zero* (1970). These are marked by astronomical and physical speculation and large-scale Stapledonian vistas of time and space. Even in his swashbuckling adventure stories, Anderson is famous for beginning with calculations of the elements of the orbit of the world to be his setting, and allowing the physics, chemistry, and biology to follow logically, thus generating the parameters in which human beings would have to live and survive.

He is also interested in mythology and often uses myth in his fiction, as in this story. "Goat Song," from the 1970s, is one of his many Hugo Award-winning stories, hard science fiction with an overlay of mythic fantasy.

GOAT SONG

Three women: one is dead; one is alive; One is both and neither, and will never live and never die, being immortal in SUM.

On a hill above that valley through which runs the highroad, I await Her passage. Frost came early this year, and the grasses have paled. Otherwise the slope is begrown with blackberry bushes that have been harvested by men and birds, leaving only briars, and with certain apple trees. They are very old, those trees, survivors of an orchard raised by generations which none but SUM now remembers (I can see a few fragments of wall thrusting above the brambles)—scattered crazily over the hillside and as crazily gnarled. A little fruit remains on them. Chill across my skin, a gust shakes loose an apple. I hear it knock on the earth, another stroke of some eternal clock. The shrubs whisper to the wind.

Elsewhere the ridges around me are wooded, afire with scarlets and brasses and bronzes. The sky is huge, the westering sun wanbright. The valley is filling with a deeper blue, a haze whose slight smokiness touches my nostrils. This is Indian summer, the funeral pyre of the year.

There have been other seasons. There have been other lifetimes, before mine and hers; and in those days they had words to sing with. We still allow ourselves music, though, and I have spent much time planting melodies around my rediscovered words. *"In the greenest growth of the May-time—"* I unsling the harp on my back, and tune it afresh, and sing it to her, straight into autumn and the waning day.

> *"—You came, and the sun came after,*
> *And the green grew golden above:*
> *And the flag-flowers lightened with laughter,*
> *And the meadowsweet shook with love."*

A footfall stirs the grasses, quite gently, and the woman says, trying to chuckle, "Why, thank you."

Once, so soon after my one's death that I was still dazed by it, I stood in the home that had been ours. This was on the hundred and first floor of a most desirable building. After dark the city flamed for us, blinked, glittered, flung immense sheets of radiance forth like banners. Nothing but SUM could have controlled the firefly dance of a million aircars among the towers: or, for that matter, have maintained the entire city, from nuclear powerplants through automated factories, physical and economic distribution networks, sanitation, repair, services, education, culture, order, everything as one immune immortal organism. We had gloried in belonging to this as well as to each other.

But that night I told the kitchen to throw the dinner it had made for me down the waste chute, and ground under my heel the chemical consolations which the medicine cabinet extended to me, and kicked the cleaner as it picked up the mess, and ordered the lights not to go on, anywhere in our suite. I stood by the vieWall, looking out across megalopolis, and it was tawdry. In my hands I had a little clay figure she had fashioned herself. I turned it over and over and over.

But I had forgotten to forbid the door to admit visitors. It recognized this woman and opened for her. She had come with the kindly intention of teasing me out of a mood that seemed to her unnatural. I heard her enter, and looked around through the gloom. She had almost the same height as my girl did, and her hair chanced to be bound in a way that my girl often favored, and the figurine dropped from my grasp and shattered, because for an instant I thought she was my girl. Since then I have been hard put not to hate Thrakia.

This evening, even without so much sundown light, I would not make that mistake. Nothing but the silvery bracelet about her left wrist bespeaks the past we share. She is in wildcountry garb: boots, kilt of true fur and belt of true leather, knife at hip and rifle slung on shoulder. Her locks are matted and snarled, her skin brown from weeks of weather; scratches and smudges show beneath the fantastic zigzags she has painted in many colors on herself. She wears a necklace of bird skulls.

Now that one who is dead was, in her own way, more a child of trees and horizons than Thrakia's followers. She was so much at home in the open that she had no need to put off clothes or cleanliness, reason or gentleness, when we sickened of the cities and went forth beyond them. From this trait I got many of the names I bestowed on her, such as Wood's Colt or Fallow Hind or, from my prowlings among ancient books, Dryad and Elven. (She liked me to choose her names, and this pleasure had no end, because she was inexhaustible.)

I let my harpstring ring into silence. Turning about, I say to Thrakia, "I wasn't singing for you. Not for anyone. Leave me alone."

She draws a breath. The wind ruffles her hair and brings me an odor of her: not female sweetness, but fear. She clenches her fists and says, "You're crazy."

"Wherever did you find a meaningful word like that?" I gibe; for my own pain and—to be truthful—my own fear must strike out at something, and here she stands. "Aren't you content any longer with 'untranquil' or 'disequilibrated'?"

"I got it from you," she says defiantly, "you and your damned archaic songs. There's another word, 'damned.' And how it suits you! When are you going to stop this morbidity?"

"And commit myself to a clinic and have my brain laundered nice and sanitary? Not soon, darling." I use *that* last word aforethought, but she cannot know what scorn and sadness are in it for me, who know that once it could also have been a name for my girl. The official grammar and pronunciation of language is as frozen as every other aspect of our civilization, thanks to electronic recording and neuronic teaching; but meanings shift and glide about like subtle serpents. (O adder that stung my Foalfoot!)

I shrug and say in my driest, most city-technological voice, "Actually, I'm the practical, nonmorbid one. Instead of running away from my emotions—via drugs, or neuroadjustment, or playing at savagery like you, for that matter—I'm about to implement a concrete plan for getting back the person who made me happy."

"By disturbing Her on Her way home?"

"Anyone has the right to petition the dark Queen while she's abroad on earth."

"But this is past the proper time—"

"No law's involved, just custom. People are afraid to meet Her outside a crowd, a town, bright flat lights. They won't admit it, but they are. So I came here precisely not to be part of a queue. I don't want to speak into a recorder for subsequent computer analysis of my words. How could I be sure She was listening? I want to meet Her as myself, a unique being, and look in Her eyes while I make my prayer."

Thrakia chokes a little. "She'll be angry."

"Is She able to be angry, anymore?"

"I . . . I don't know. What you mean to ask for is so impossible, though. So absurd. That SUM should give you back your girl. You know It never makes exceptions."

"Isn't She Herself an exception?"

"That's different. You're being silly. SUM has to have a, well, a direct human liaison. Emotional and cultural feedback, as well as statistics. How else can It govern rationally? And She must have been chosen out of the whole world. Your girl, what was she? Nobody!"

"To me, she was everybody."

"You—" Thrakia catches her lip in her teeth. One hand reaches out and closes on my bare forearm, a hard hot touch, the grimy fingernails biting. When I make no response, she lets go and stares at the ground. A V of outbound geese passes overhead. Their cries come shrill through the wind, which is loudening in the forest.

"Well," she says, "you are special. You always were. You went to space and came back, with the Great Captain. You're maybe the only man alive who understands about the ancients. And your singing, yes, you don't really entertain, your songs trouble people and can't be forgotten. So maybe She will listen to you. But SUM won't. It can't give special resurrections. Once that was done, a single time, wouldn't it have to be done for everybody? The dead would overrun the living."

"Not necessarily," I say. "In any event, I mean to try."

"Why can't you wait for the promised time? Surely, then, SUM will re-create you two in the same generation."

"I'd have to live out this life, at least, without her," I say, looking away also, down to the highroad which shines through shadow like death's snake, the length of the valley. "Besides, how do you know there ever will be any resurrections? We have only a promise. No, less than that. An announced policy."

She gasps, steps back, raises her hands as if to fend me off. Her soul bracelet casts light into my eyes. I recognize an embryo exorcism. She lacks ritual; every "superstition" was patiently scrubbed out of our metal-and-energy world, long ago. But if she has no word for it, no concept, nevertheless she recoils from blasphemy.

So I say, wearily, not wanting an argument, wanting only to wait here alone: "Never mind. There could be some natural catastrophe, like a giant asteroid striking, that wiped out the system before conditions had become right for resurrections to commence."

"That's impossible," she says, almost frantic. "The homeostats, the repair functions—"

"All right, call it a vanishingly unlikely theoretical contingency. Let's declare that I'm so selfish I want Swallow Wing back now, in this life of mine, and don't give a curse whether that'll be fair to the rest of you."

You won't care either, anyway, I think. None of you. You don't grieve. It is your own precious private consciousnesses that you wish to preserve; no one else is close enough to you to matter very much. Would you believe me if I told you I am quite prepared to offer SUM my own death in exchange for It releasing Blossom-in-the-Sun?

I don't speak that thought, which would be cruel, nor repeat what is crueller: my fear that SUM lies, that the dead never will be disgorged. For (I am not the All-Controller, I think not with vacuum and negative energy levels but with ordinary begotten molecules; yet I can reason somewhat dispassionately, being disillusioned) consider—

The object of the game is to maintain a society stable, just, and sane. This requires satisfaction not only of somatic, but of symbolic and instinctual needs. Thus children must be allowed to come into being. The minimum number per generation is equal to the maximum: that number which will maintain a constant population.

It is also desirable to remove the fear of death from men. Hence the promise: At such time as it is socially feasible, SUM will begin to refashion us, with our complete memories but in the pride of our youth. This can be done over and over, life after life across the millennia. So death is, indeed, a sleep.

—*in that sleep of death, what dreams may come*— No. I myself dare not dwell on this. I ask merely, privately: Just when and how does SUM expect conditions (in a stabilized society, mind you) to have become so different from today's that the reborn can, in their millions, safely be welcomed back?

I see no reason why SUM should not lie to us. We, too, are objects in the world that It manipulates.

"We've quarreled about this before, Thrakia," I sigh. "Often. Why do you bother?"

"I wish I knew," she answers low. Half to herself, she goes on: "Of course I want to copulate with you. You must be good, the way that girl used to follow you about with her eyes, and smile when she touched your hand, and— But you can't be better than everyone else. That's unreasonable. There are only so many possible ways. So why do I care if you wrap yourself up in silence and go off alone? Is it that that makes you a challenge?"

"You think too much," I say. "Even here. You're a pretend primitive. You visit wildcountry to 'slake inborn atavistic impulses' . . . but you can't dismantle that computer inside yourself and simply feel, simply be."

She bristles. I touched a nerve there. Looking past her, along the ridge of fiery maple and sumac, brassy elm and great dun oak, I see others emerge from beneath the trees. Women exclusively, her followers, as unkempt as she; one has a brace of ducks lashed to her waist, and their blood has trickled down her thigh and dried black. For this movement, this unadmitted mystique has become Thrakia's by now: that not only men should forsake the easy routine and the easy pleasure of the cities, and become again, for a few weeks each year, the carnivores who begot our species; women too should seek out starkness, the better to appreciate civilization when they return.

I feel a moment's unease. We are in no park, with laid-out trails and campground services. We are in wildcountry. Not many men come here, ever, and still fewer women; for the region is, literally, beyond the law. No deed done here is punishable. We are told that this helps consolidate society, as the most violent among us may thus vent their passions. But I have spent much time in wildcountry since my Morning Star went out—myself in quest of nothing but solitude—and I have watched what happens through eyes that have also read anthropology and history. Institutions are developing; ceremonies, tribalisms, acts of blood and cruelty and acts elsewhere called unnatural are becoming more elaborate and more expected every year. Then the practitioners go home to their cities and honestly believe they have been enjoying fresh air, exercise, and good tension-releasing fun.

Let her get angry enough and Thrakia can call knives to her aid.

Wherefore I make myself lay both hands on her shoulders, and meet the tormented gaze, and say most gently, "I'm sorry. I know you mean well. You're afraid She will be annoyed and bring misfortune on your people."

Thrakia gulps. "No," she whispers. "That wouldn't be logical. But I'm afraid of what might happen to you. And then—" Suddenly she throws herself against me. I feel arms, breasts, belly press through my tunic, and smell meadows in her hair and musk in her mouth. "You'd be gone!" she wails. "Then who'd sing to us?"

"Why, the planet's crawling with entertainers," I stammer.

"You're more than that," she says. "So much more. I don't like what you sing, not really—and what you've sung since that stupid girl died, oh, meaningless, horrible!—but, I don't know why, I *want* you to trouble me."

Awkward, I pat her back. The sun now stands very little above the treetops. Its rays slant interminably through the booming, frosting air. I shiver in my tunic and buskins and wonder what to do.

A sound rescues me. It comes from one end of the valley below us, where further view is blocked off by two cliffs; it thunders deep in our ears and rolls through the earth into our bones. We have heard that sound in the cities, and been glad to have walls and lights and multitudes around us. Now we are alone with it, the noise of Her chariot.

The women shriek, I hear them faintly across wind and rumble and my own pulse, and they vanish into the woods. They will seek their camp, dress warmly, build enormous fires; presently they will eat their ecstatics, and rumors are uneasy about what they do after that.

Thrakia seizes my left wrist, above the soul bracelet, and hauls. "Harper, come with me!" she pleads. I break loose from her and stride down the hill toward the road. A scream follows me for a moment.

Light still dwells in the sky and on the ridges, but as I descend into that narrow valley I enter dusk, and it thickens. Indistinct bramblebushes whicker where I brush them, and claw back at me. I feel the occasional scratch on my legs, the tug as my garment is snagged, the chill that I breathe, but dimly. My perceived-outer-reality is overpowered by the rushing of Her chariot and my blood. My inner-universe is fear, yes, but exaltation too, a drunkenness which sharpens instead of dulling the senses, a psychedelia which opens the reasoning mind as well as the emotions; I have gone beyond myself, I am embodied purpose. Not out of need for comfort, but to voice what Is, I return to words whose speaker rests centuries dust, and lend them my own music. I sing:

"—Gold is my heart, and the world's golden,
And one peak tipped with light;
And the air lies still about the hill
With the first fear of night;

"Till mystery down the soundless valley
Thunders, and dark is here;
And the wind blows, and the light goes,
And the night is full of fear.

"And I know one night, on some far height,
In a tongue I never knew,
I yet shall hear the tidings clear
From them that were friends of you.

"They'll call the news from hill to hill,
Dark and uncomforted,
Earth and sky and the winds; and I
Shall know that you are dead.—"

But I have reached the valley floor, and She has come in sight.

Her chariot is unlit, for radar eyes and inertial guides need no lamps, nor sun nor stars. Wheel-less, the steel tear rides on its own roar and thrust of air. The pace is not great, far less than any of our mortals' vehicles are wont to take. Men say the Dark Queen rides thus slowly in order that She may perceive with Her own senses and so be the better prepared to counsel SUM. But now Her annual round is finished; She is homeward bound; until spring She will dwell with It Which is our lord. Why does She not hasten tonight?

Because Death has never a need of haste? I wonder. And as I step into the middle of the road, certain lines from the yet more ancient past rise tremendous within me, and I strike my harp and chant them louder than the approaching car:

> "*I that in heill was and gladnèss*
> *Am trublit now with great sickness*
> *And feblit with infirmitie:—*
> Timor mortis conturbat me."

The car detects me and howls a warning. I hold my ground. The car could swing around, the road is wide and in any event a smooth surface is not absolutely necessary. But I hope, I believe that She will be aware of an obstacle in Her path, and tune in Her various amplifiers, and find me abnormal enough to stop for. Who, in SUM's world—who, even among the explorers that It has sent beyond in Its unappeasable hunger for data—would stand in a cold wildcountry dusk and shout while his harp snarls

> "*Our pleasance here is all vain glory,*
> *This fals world is but transitory,*
> *The flesh is bruckle, the Feynd is slee:—*
> Timor mortis conturbat me.
>
> "*The state of man does change and vary,*
> *Now sound, now sick, now blyth, now sary,*
> *No dansand mirry, now like to die:—*
> Timor mortis conturbat me.
>
> "*No state in Erd here standis sicker;*
> *As with the wynd wavis the wicker*
> *So wannis this world's vanitie:—*
> Timor mortis conturbat me.—?"

The car draws alongside and sinks to the ground. I let my strings die away into the wind. The sky overhead and in the west is gray-purple; eastward it is quite dark and a few early stars peer forth. Here, down in the valley, shadows are heavy and I cannot see very well.

The canopy slides back. She stands erect in the chariot, thus looming over me. Her robe and cloak are black, fluttering like restless wings; beneath the cowl Her face is a white blur. I have seen it before, under full light, and in how many thousands of pictures; but at this hour I cannot call it back to my mind, not entirely. I list sharp-sculptured profile and pale lips, sable hair and long green eyes, but these are nothing more than words.

"What are you doing?" She has a lovely low voice; but is it, as oh, how rarely since SUM took Her to Itself, is it the least shaken? "What is that you were singing?"

My answer comes so strong that my skull resonates; for I am borne higher and higher on my tide. "Lady of Ours, I have a petition."

"Why did you not bring it before Me when I walked among men? Tonight I am homebound. You must wait till I ride forth with the new year."

"Lady of Ours, neither You nor I would wish living ears to hear what I have to say."

She regards me for a long while. Do I indeed sense fear also in Her? (Surely not of me. Her chariot is armed and armored, and would react with machine speed to protect Her should I offer violence. And should I somehow, incredibly, kill Her, or wound Her beyond chemosurgical repair, She of all beings has no need to doubt death. The ordinary bracelet cries with quite sufficient radio loudness to be heard by more than one thanatic station, when we die; and in that shielding the soul can scarcely be damaged before the Winged Heels arrive to bear it off to SUM. Surely the Dark Queen's circlet can call still further, and is still better insulated, than any mortal's. And She will most absolutely be re-created. She has been, again and again; death and rebirth every seven years keep Her eternally young in the service of SUM. I have never been able to find out when She was first born.)

Fear, perhaps, of what I have sung and what I might speak?

At last She says—I can scarcely hear through the gusts and creakings in the trees—"Give me the Ring, then."

The dwarf robot which stands by Her throne when She sits among men appears beside Her and extends the massive dull-silver circle to me. I place my left arm within, so that my soul is enclosed. The tablet on the upper surface of the Ring, which looks so much like a jewel, slants away from me; I cannot read what flashes onto the bezel. But the faint glow picks Her features out of murk as She bends to look.

Of course, I tell myself, the actual soul is not scanned. That would take too long. Probably the bracelet which contains the soul has an identification code built in. The Ring sends this to an appropriate part of SUM, Which instantly sends back what is recorded under that code. I hope there is nothing more to it. SUM has not seen fit to tell us.

"What do you call yourself at the moment?" She asks.

A current of bitterness crosses my tide. "Lady of Ours, why should You care? Is not my real name the number I got when I was allowed to be born?"

Calm descends once more upon Her. "If I am to evaluate properly what you say, I must know more about you than these few official data. Name indicates mood."

I too feel unshaken again, my tide running so strong and smooth that I might not know I was moving did I not see time recede behind me. "Lady of Ours, I cannot give You a fair answer. In this past year I have not troubled with names, or with much of anything else. But some people who knew me from earlier days call me Harper."

"What do you do besides make that sinister music?"

"These days, nothing, Lady of Ours. I've money to live out my life, if I eat sparingly and keep no home. Often I am fed and housed for the sake of my songs."

"What you sang is unlike anything I have heard since—" Anew, briefly, that robot serenity is shaken. "Since before the world was stabilized. You should not wake dead symbols, Harper. They walk through men's dreams."

"Is that bad?"

"Yes. The dreams become nightmares. Remember: Mankind, every man who ever lived, was insane before SUM brought order, reason, and peace."

"Well, then," I say, "I will cease and desist if I may have my own dead wakened for me."

She stiffens. The tablet goes out. I withdraw my arm and the Ring is stored away by Her servant. So again She is faceless, beneath flickering stars, here at the bottom of this shadowed valley. Her voice falls cold as the air: "No one can be brought back to life before Resurrection Time is ripe."

I do not say, "What about You?" for that would be vicious. What did She think, how did She weep, when SUM chose Her of all the young on earth? What does She endure in Her centuries? I dare not imagine.

Instead, I smite my harp and sing, quietly this time:

"Strew on her roses, roses,
And never a spray of yew.
In quiet she reposes:
Ah! Would that I did too."

The Dark Queen cries, "What are you doing? Are you really insane?" I go straight to the last stanza.

"Her cabin'd, ample Spirit
It flutter'd and fail'd for breath.
To-night it doth inherit
The vasty hall of Death."

I know why my songs strike so hard: because they bear dreads and passions that no one is used to—that most of us hardly know could exist—in SUM's ordered universe. But I had not the courage to hope She would be as torn by them as I see. Has She not lived with more darkness and terror than the ancients themselves could conceive? She calls, "Who has died?"

"She had many names, Lady of Ours," I say. "None was beautiful enough. I can tell You her number, though."

"Your daughter? I . . . sometimes I am asked if a dead child cannot be brought back. Not often, anymore, when they go so soon to the crèche. But sometimes. I tell the mother she may have a new one; but if ever We started re-creating dead infants, at what age level could We stop?"

"No, this was my woman."

"Impossible!" Her tone seeks to be not unkindly but is, instead, well-nigh frantic. "You will have no trouble finding others. You are handsome, and your psyche is, is, is extraordinary. It burns like Lucifer."

"Do You remember the name Lucifer, Lady of Ours?" I pounce. "Then You are old indeed. So old that You must also remember how a man might desire only one woman, but her above the whole world and heaven."

She tries to defend Herself with a jeer: "Was that mutual, Harper? I know more of mankind than you do, and surely I am the last chaste woman in existence."

"Now that she is gone, Lady, yes, perhaps You are. But we— Do you know how she died? We had gone to a wildcountry area. A man saw her, alone, while I was off hunting gem rocks to make her a necklace. He approached her. She refused him. He threatened force. She fled. This was desert land, viper land, and she was barefoot. One of them bit her. I did not find her till hours later. By then the poison and the unshaded sun— She died quite soon after she told me what had happened and that she loved me. I could not get her body to chemosurgery in time for normal revival procedures. I had to let them cremate her and take her soul away to SUM."

"What right have you to demand her back, when no one else can be given their own?"

"The right that I love her, and she loves me. We are more necessary to each other than sun or moon. I do not think You could find another two people of whom this is so, Lady. And is not everyone entitled to claim what is necessary to his life? How else can society be kept whole?"

"You are being fantastic," She says thinly. "Let me go."

"No, Lady, I am speaking sober truth. But poor plain words won't serve me. I sing to You because then maybe You will understand." And I strike my harp anew; but it is more to her than Her that I sing.

"If I had thought thou couldst have died,
I might not weep for thee:
But I forgot, when by thy side,
That thou couldst mortal be:

"It never through my mind had past
The time would e'er be o'er,
And I on thee should look my last,
And though shouldst smile no more!"

"I cannot—" She falters. "I do not know—any such feelings—so strong—existed any longer."

"Now You do, Lady of Ours. And is that not an important datum for SUM?"

"Yes. If true." Abruptly She leans toward me. I see Her shudder in the murk, under the flapping cloak, and hear Her jaws clatter with cold. "I cannot linger here. But ride with Me. Sing to Me. I think I can bear it."

So much have I scarcely expected. But my destiny is upon me. I mount into the chariot. The canopy slides shut and we proceed.

The main cabin encloses us. Behind its rear door must be facilities for Her living on earth; this is a big vehicle. But here is little except curved panels. They are true wood of different comely grains: so She also needs periodic escape from our machine existence, does She? Furnishing is scant and austere. The only sound is our passage, muffled to a murmur for us; and, because their photomultipliers are not activated, the scanners show nothing outside but night. We huddle close to a glower, hands extended toward its fieriness. Our shoulders brush, our bare arms, Her skin is soft and Her hair falls loose over the thrown-back cowl, smelling of the summer which is dead. What, is She still human?

After a timeless time, She says, not yet looking at me: "The thing you sang, there on the highroad as I came near—I do not remember it. Not even from the years before I became what I am."

"It is older than SUM," I answer, "and its truth will outlive It."

"Truth?" I see Her tense Herself. "Sing Me the rest."

My fingers are no longer too numb to call forth chords.

"*—Unto the Death gois all Estatis,*
Princis, Prelattis, and Potestatis,
Baith rich and poor of all degree:—
Timor mortis conturbat me.

"He takis the knichtis in to the field
Enarmit under helm and scheild;
Victor he is at all mellie:—
Timor mortis conturbat me.

"That strong unmerciful tyrand
Takis, on the motheris breast
sowkand,
The babe full of benignitie:—
Timor mortis conturbat me.

"He takis the campion in the stour,
The captain closit in the tour,
The ladie in bour full of bewtie:—"

(There I must stop a moment.)

"Timor mortis conturbat me.

"He sparis no lord for his piscence,
Na clerk for his intelligence;
His awful straik may no man flee:—
Timor mortis conturbat me."

She breaks me off; clapping hands to ears and half shrieking, "No!"

I, grown unmerciful, pursue Her: "You understand now, do You not? You are not eternal either. SUM isn't. Not Earth, not sun, not stars. We hid from the truth. Every one of us. I too, until I lost the one thing which made everything make sense. Then I had nothing left to lose, and could look with clear eyes. And what I saw was Death."

"Get out! Let Me alone!"

"I will not let the whole world alone, Queen, until I get her back. Give me her again, and I'll believe in SUM again. I'll praise It till men dance for joy to hear Its name."

She challenges me with wildcat eyes. "Do you think such matters to It?"

"Well," I shrug, "songs could be useful. They could help achieve the great objective sooner. Whatever that is. 'Optimization of total human activity'—wasn't that the program? I don't know if it still is. SUM has been adding to Itself so long. I doubt if You Yourself understand Its purpose, Lady of Ours."

"Don't speak as if It were alive," She says harshly. "It is a computer-effector complex. Nothing more."

"Are You certain?"

"I—yes. It thinks, more widely and deeply than any human ever did or could; but It is not alive, not aware, It has no consciousness. That is one reason why It decided It needed Me."

"Be that as it may, Lady," I tell Her, "the ultimate result, whatever It finally does with us, lies far in the future. At present I care about that; I worry; I resent our loss of self-determination. But that's because only such abstractions are left to me. Give me back my Lightfoot, and she, not the distant future, will be my concern. I'll be grateful, honestly grateful, and You Two will know it from the songs I then choose to sing. Which, as I said, might be helpful to It."

"You are unbelievably insolent," She says without force.

"No, Lady, just desperate," I say.

The ghost of a smile touches Her lips. She leans back, eyes hooded, and murmurs, "Well, I'll take you there. What happens then, you realize, lies outside My power. My observations, My recommendations, are nothing but a few items to take into account, among billions. However . . . we have a long way to travel this night. Give me what data you think will help you, Harper."

I do not finish the Lament. Nor do I dwell in any other fashion on grief. Instead, as the hours pass, I call upon those who dealt with the joy (not the fun, not the short delirium, but the joy) that man and woman might once have of each other.

Knowing where we are bound, I too need such comfort.

And the night deepens, and the leagues fall behind us, and finally we are beyond habitation, beyond wildcountry, in the land where life never comes. By crooked moon and waning starlight I see the plain of concrete and iron, the missiles and energy projectors crouched like beasts, the robot aircraft wheeling aloft: and the lines, the relay towers, the scuttling beetle-shaped carriers, that whole transcendent nerve-blood-sinew by which SUM knows and orders the world. For all the flitting about, for all the forces which seethe, here is altogether still. The wind itself seems to have frozen to death. Hoarfrost is gray on the steel shapes. Ahead of us, tiered and mountainous, begins to appear the castle of SUM.

She Who rides with me does not give sign of noticing that my songs have died in my throat. What humanness She showed is departing; Her face is cold and shut, Her voice bears a ring of metal. She looks straight ahead. But She does speak to me for a little while yet:

"Do you understand what is going to happen? For the next half year I will be linked with SUM, integral, another component of It. I suppose you will see Me, but that will merely be My flesh. What speaks to you will be SUM."

"I know." The words must be forced forth. My coming this far is more triumph than any man in creation before me has won; and I am here to do battle for my Dancer-on-Moonglades; but nonetheless my heart shakes me, and is loud in my skull, and my sweat stinks.

I manage, though, to add: "You *will* be a part of It, Lady of Ours. That gives me hope."

For an instant She turns to me, and lays Her hand across mine, and something makes Her again so young and untaken that I almost forget the girl who died; and she whispers, "If you knew how I hope!"

The instant is gone, and I am alone among machines.

We must stop before the castle gate. The wall looms sheer above, so high and high that it seems to be toppling upon me against the westward march of the stars, so black and black that it does not only drink down every light, it radiates blindness. Challenge and response quiver on electronic bands I cannot sense. The outer-guardian parts of It have perceived a mortal aboard this craft. A missile launcher swings about to aim its three serpents at me. But the Dark Queen answers— She does not trouble to be peremptory—and the castle opens its jaws for us.

We descend. Once, I think, we cross a river. I hear a rushing and hollow echoing and see droplets glitter where they are cast onto the viewports and outlined against dark. They vanish at once: liquid hydrogen, perhaps, to keep certain parts near absolute zero?

Much later we stop and the canopy slides back. I rise with Her. We are in a room, or cavern, of which I can see nothing, for there is no light except a dull bluish phosphorescence which streams from every solid object, also from Her flesh and mine. But I judge the chamber is enormous, for a sound of great machines at work comes very remotely, as if heard through dream, while our own voices are swallowed up by distance. Air is pumped through, neither warm nor cold, totally without odor, a dead wind.

We descend to the floor. She stands before me, hands crossed on breast, eyes half shut beneath the cowl and not looking at me nor away from me. "Do what you are told, Harper," She says in a voice that has never an overtone, "precisely as you are told." She turns and departs at an even pace. I watch Her go until I can no longer tell Her luminosity from the formless swirlings within my own eyeballs.

A claw plucks my tunic. I look down and am surprised to see that the dwarf robot has been waiting for me this whole time. How long a time that was, I cannot tell.

Its squat form leads me in another direction. Weariness crawls upward through me, my feet stumble, my lips tingle, lids are weighted and muscles have each their separate aches. Now and then I feel a jag of fear, but dully. When the robot indicates *Lie down here*, I am grateful.

The box fits me well. I let various wires be attached to me, various needles be injected which lead into tubes. I pay little attention to the machines which cluster and murmur around me. The robot goes away. I sink into blessed darkness.

I wake renewed in body. A kind of shell seems to have grown between my forebrain and the old animal parts. Far away I can feel the horror and hear the screaming and thrashing of my instincts; but awareness is chill, calm, logical. I have also a feeling that I slept for weeks, months, while leaves blew loose and snow fell on the upper world. But this may be wrong, and in no case does it matter. I am about to be judged by SUM.

The little faceless robot leads me off, through murmurous black corridors where the dead wind blows. I unsling my harp and clutch it to me, my sole friend and weapon. So the tranquility of the reasoning mind which has been decreed for me cannot be absolute. I decide that It simply does not want to be bothered by anguish. (No; wrong; nothing so humanlike; It has no desires; beneath that power to reason is nullity.)

At length a wall opens for us and we enter a room where She sits enthroned. The self-radiation of metal and flesh is not apparent here, for light is provided, a featureless white radiance with no apparent source. White, too, is the muted sound of the machines which encompass Her throne. White are Her robe and face. I look away from the multitudinous unwinking scanner eyes, into Hers, but She does not appear to recognize me. Does She even see me? SUM has reached out with invisible fingers of electromagnetic induction and taken Her back into Itself. I do not tremble or sweat—I cannot—but I square my shoulders, strike one plangent chord, and wait for It to speak.

It does, from some invisible place. I recognize the voice It has chosen to use: my own. The overtones, the inflections are true, normal, what I myself would use in talking as one reasonable man to another. Why not? In computing what to do about me, and in programming Itself accordingly, SUM must have used so many billion bits of information that adequate accent is a negligible subproblem.

No . . . there I am mistaken again . . . SUM does not do things on the basis that It might as well do them as not. This talk with myself is intended to have some effect on me. I do not know what.

"Well," It says pleasantly, "you made quite a journey, didn't you? I'm glad. Welcome."

My instincts bare teeth to hear those words of humanity used by the unfeeling unalive. My logical mind considers replying with an ironic "Thank you," decides against it, and holds me silent.

"You see," SUM continues after a moment that whirrs, "you are unique. Pardon Me if I speak a little bluntly. Your sexual monomania is just one aspect of a generally atavistic, superstition-oriented personality. And yet, unlike the ordinary misfit, you're both strong and realistic enough to cope with the world. This chance to meet you, to analyze you while you rested, has opened new insights for Me on human psychophysiology. Which may lead to improved techniques for governing it and its evolution."

"That being so," I reply, "give me my reward."

"Now look here," SUM says in a mild tone, "you if anyone should know I'm not omnipotent. I was built originally to help govern a civilization grown too complex. Gradually, as My program of self-expansion progressed, I took over more and more decision-making functions. They were *given* to Me. People were happy to be relieved of responsibility, and they could see for themselves how much better I was running things than any mortal could. But to this day, My authority depends on a substantial consensus. If I started playing favorites, as by re-creating your girl, well, I'd have troubles."

"The consensus depends more on awe than on reason," I say. "You haven't abolished the gods, You've simply absorbed them into Yourself. If You choose to pass a miracle for me, your prophet singer—and I will be Your prophet if You do this—why, that strengthens the faith of the rest."

"So you think. But your opinions aren't based on any exact data. The historical and anthropological records from the past before Me are unquantitative. I've already phased them out of the curriculum. Eventually, when the culture's ready for such a move, I'll order them destroyed. They're too misleading. Look what they've done to you."

I grin into the scanner eyes. "Instead," I say, "people will be encouraged to think that before the world was, was SUM. All right. I don't care, as long as I get my girl back. Pass me a miracle, SUM, and I'll guarantee You a good payment."

"But I have no miracles. Not in your sense. You know how the soul works. The metal bracelet encloses a pseudovirus, a set of giant protein molecules with taps directly to the bloodstream and nervous system. They record the chromosome pattern, the synapse flash, the permanent changes, everything. At the owner's death, the bracelet is dissected out. The Winged Heels bring it here, and the information contained is transferred to one of My memory banks. I can use such a record to guide the growing of a new body in the vats: a young body, on which the former habits and recollections are imprinted. But you don't understand the complexity of the process, Harper. It takes Me weeks, every seven years, and every available biochemical facility, to re-create My human liaison. And the process isn't perfect, either. The pattern is affected by storage. You might say that this body and brain you see before you remembers each death. And those are short deaths. A longer one—man, use your sense. Imagine."

I can; and the shield between reason and feeling begins to crack. I had sung, of my darling dead,

> *"No motion has she now, no force;*
> *She neither hears nor sees;*
> *Roll'd round in earth's diurnal course,*
> *With rocks, and stones, and trees."*

Peace, at least. But if the memory-storage is not permanent but circulating; if, within those gloomy caverns of tubes and wire and outerspace cold, some remnant of her psyche must flit and flicker, alone, unremembering, aware of nothing but having lost life—No!

I smite the harp and shout so the room rings: "Give her back! Or I'll kill you!"

SUM finds it expedient to chuckle; and, horribly, the smile is reflected for a moment on the Dark Queen's lips, though otherwise She never stirs. "And how do you propose to do that?" It asks me.

It knows, I know, what I have in mind, so I counter: "How do You propose to stop me?"

"No need. You'll be considered a nuisance. Finally someone will decide you ought to have psychiatric treatment. They'll query My diagnostic outlet. I'll recommend certain excisions."

"On the other hand, since You've sifted my mind by now, and since You know how I've affected people with my songs—even the Lady yonder, even Her—wouldn't you rather have me working for You? With words like, '*O taste, and see, how gracious the Lord is; blessed is the man that trusteth in him. O fear the Lord, ye that are his saints; for they that fear him lack nothing.*' I can make You into God."

"In a sense, I already am God."

"And in another sense not. Not yet." I can endure no more. "Why are we arguing? You made Your decision before I woke. Tell me and let me go!"

With an odd carefulness, SUM responds: "I'm still studying you. No harm in admitting to you, My knowledge of the human psyche is as yet imperfect. Certain areas won't yield to computation. I don't know precisely what you'd do, Harper. If to that uncertainty I added a potentially dangerous precedent—"

"Kill me, then." Let my ghost wander forever with hers, down in Your cryogenic dreams.

"No, that's also inexpedient. You've made yourself too conspicuous and controversial. Too many people know by now that you went off with the Lady." Is it possible that, behind steel and energy, a nonexistent hand brushes across a shadow face in puzzlement? My heartbeat is thick in the silence.

Suddenly It shakes me with decision: "The calculated probabilities do favor your keeping your promises and making yourself useful. Therefore I shall grant your request. However—"

I am on my knees. My forehead knocks on the floor until blood runs into my eyes. I hear through storm winds:

"—testing must continue. Your faith in Me is not absolute; in fact, you're very skeptical of what you call My goodness. Without additional proof of your willingness to trust Me, I can't let you have the kind of importance which your getting your dead back from Me would give you. Do you understand?"

The question does not sound rhetorical. "Yes," I sob.

"Well, then," says my civilized, almost amiable voice, "I computed that you'd react much as you have done, and prepared for the likelihood. Your woman's body was re-created while you lay under study. The data which make personality are now being fed back into her neurones. She'll be ready to leave this place by the time you do.

"I repeat, though, there has to be a testing. The procedure is also necessary for its effect on you. If you're to be My prophet, you'll have to work pretty closely with Me; you'll have to undergo a great deal of reconditioning; this night we begin the process. Are you willing?"

"Yes, yes, yes, what must I do?"

"Only this: Follow the robot out. At some point, she, your woman, will join you. She'll be conditioned to walk so quietly you can't hear her. Don't look back. Not once, until you're in the upper world. A single glance behind you will be an act of rebellion against Me, and a datum indicating you can't really be trusted . . . and that ends everything. Do you understand?"

"Is that all?" I cry. "Nothing more?"

"It will prove more difficult than you think," SUM tells me. My voice fades, as if into illimitable distances: "Farewell, worshipper."

The robot raises me to my feet, I stretch out my arms to the Dark Queen. Half blinded with tears, I nonetheless see that She does not see me. "Good-bye," I mumble, and let the robot lead me away.

Our walking is long through those mirk miles. At first I am in too much of a turmoil, and later too stunned, to know where or how we are bound. But later still, slowly, I become aware of my flesh and clothes and the robot's alloy, glimmering blue in blackness. Sounds and smells are muffled; rarely does another machine pass by, unheeding of us. (What work does SUM have for them?) I am so careful not to look behind me that my neck grows stiff.

Though it is not prohibited, is it, to lift my harp past my shoulder, in the course of strumming a few melodies to keep up my courage, and see if perchance a following illumination is reflected in this polished wood?

Nothing. Well, her second birth must take time—O SUM, be careful of her!—and then she must be led through many tunnels, no doubt, before she makes rendezvous with my back. Be patient, Harper.

Sing. Welcome her home. No, these hollow spaces swallow all music; and she is as yet in that trance of death from which only the sun and my kiss can wake her; if, indeed, she has joined me yet. I listen for other footfalls than my own.

Surely we haven't much farther to go. I ask the robot, but of course I get no reply. Make an estimate. I know about how fast the chariot traveled coming down. . . . The trouble is, time does not exist here. I have no day, no stars, no clock but my heartbeat, and I have lost the count of that. Nevertheless, we must come to the end soon. What purpose would be served by walking me through this labyrinth till I die?

Well, if I am totally exhausted at the outer gate, I won't make undue trouble when I find no Rose-in-Hand behind me.

No, now that's ridiculous. If SUM didn't want to heed my plea, It need merely say so. I have no power to inflict physical damage on Its parts.

Of course, It might have plans for me. It did speak of reconditioning. A series of shocks, culminating in that last one, could make me ready for whatever kind of gelding It intends to do.

Or It might have changed Its mind. Why now? It was quite frank about an uncertainty factor in the human psyche. It may have reevaluated the probabilities and decided: better not to serve my desire.

Or It may have tried, and failed. It admitted the recording process is imperfect. I must not expect quite the Gladness I knew; she will always be a little haunted. At best. But suppose the tank spawned a body with no awareness behind the eyes? Or a monster? Suppose, at this instant, I am being followed by a half-rotten corpse?

No! Stop that! SUM would know, and take corrective measures.

Would It? *Can It?*

I comprehend how this passage through night, where I never look to see what follows me, how this is an act of submission and confession. I am saying, with my whole existent being, that SUM is all-powerful, all-wise, all-good. To SUM I offer the love I came to win back. Oh, It looked more deeply into me than ever I did myself.

But I shall not fail.

Will SUM, though? If there has indeed been some grisly error . . . let me not find it out under the sky. Let her, my only, not. For what then shall we do? Could I lead her here again, knock on the iron gate, and cry, "Master, You have given me a thing unfit to exist. Destroy it and start over."—? For what might the wrongness be? Something so subtle, so pervasive, that it does not show in any way save my slow, resisted discovery that I embrace a zombie? Doesn't it make better sense to look—make certain while she is yet drowsy with death—use the whole power of SUM to correct what may be awry?

No, SUM wants me to believe that It makes no mistakes. I agreed to that price. And to much else . . . I don't know how much else, I am daunted to imagine, but that word "recondition" is ugly. . . . Does not my woman have some rights in the matter too? Shall we not at least ask her if she wants to be the wife of a prophet; shall we not, hand in hand, ask SUM what the price of her life is to her?

Was that a footfall? Almost, I whirl about. I check myself and stand shaking; names of hers break from my lips. The robot urges me on.

Imagination. It wasn't her step. I am alone. I will always be alone.

The halls wind upward. Or so I think; I have grown too weary for much kinesthetic sense. We cross the sounding river and I am bitten to the bone by the cold which blows upward around the bridge, and I may not turn about to offer the naked newborn woman my garment. I lurch through endless chambers where machines do meaningless things. She hasn't seen them before. Into what nightmare has she risen; and why don't I, who wept into her dying sense that I loved her, why don't I look at her, why don't I speak?

Well, I could talk to her. I could assure the puzzled mute dead that I have come to lead her back into sunlight. Could I not? I ask the robot. It does not reply. I cannot remember if I may speak to her. If indeed I was ever told. I stumble forward.

I crash into a wall and fall bruised. The robot's claw closes on my shoulder. Another arm gestures. I see a passageway, very long and narrow, through the stone. I will have to crawl through. At the end, at the end, the door is swinging wide. The dear real dusk of Earth pours through into this darkness. I am blinded and deafened.

Do I hear her cry out? Was that the final testing; or was my own sick, shaken mind betraying me; is there a destiny which, like SUM with us, makes tools of suns and SUM? I don't know. I know only that I turned, and there she stood. Her hair flowed long, loose, past the remembered face from which the trance was just departing, on which the knowing and the love of me had just awakened—flowed down over the body that reached forth arms, that took one step to meet me and was halted.

The great grim robot at her own back takes her to it. I think it sends lightning through her brain. She falls. It bears her away.

My guide ignores my screaming. Irresistible, it thrusts me out through the tunnel. The door clangs in my face. I stand before the wall which is like a mountain. Dry snow hisses across concrete. The sky is bloody with dawn; stars still gleam in the west, and arc lights are scattered over the twilit plain of the machines.

Presently I go dumb. I become almost calm. What is there left to have feelings about? The door is iron, the wall is stone fused into one basaltic mass. I walk some distance off into the wind, turn around, lower my head, and charge. Let my brains be smeared across Its gate; the pattern will be my hieroglyphic for hatred.

I am seized from behind. The force that stops me must needs be bruisingly great. Released, I crumple to the ground before a machine with talons and wings. My voice from it says, "Not here. I'll carry you to a safe place."

"What more can You do to me?" I croak.

"Release you. You won't be restrained or molested on any orders of Mine."

"Why not?"

"Obviously you're going to appoint yourself My enemy forever. This is an unprecedented situation, a valuable chance to collect data."

"You tell me this, You warn me, deliberately?"

"Of course. My computation is that these words will have the effect of provoking your utmost effort."

"You won't give her again? You don't want my love?"

"Not under the circumstances. Too uncontrollable. But your hatred should, as I say, be a useful experimental tool."

"I'll destroy You," I say.

It does not deign to speak further. Its machine picks me up and flies off with me. I am left on the fringes of a small town farther south. Then I go insane.

I do not much know what happens during that winter, nor care. The blizzards are too loud in my head. I walk the ways of Earth, among lordly towers, under neatly groomed trees, into careful gardens, over bland, bland campuses. I am unwashed, uncombed, unbarbered; my tatters flap about me and my bones are near thrusting through the skin; folk do not like to meet these eyes sunken so far into this skull, and perhaps for that reason they give me to eat. I sing to them.

"From the hag and hungry goblin
That into rags would rend ye
And the spirit that stan' by the naked man
In the Book of Moons defend ye!
That of your five sound senses
You never be forsaken
Nor travel from yourselves with Tom
Abroad to beg your bacon."

Such things perturb them, do not belong in their chrome-edged universe. So I am often driven away with curses, and sometimes I must flee those who would arrest me and scrub my brain smooth. An alley is a good hiding place, if I can find one in the oldest part of a city; I crouch there and yowl with the cats. A forest is also good. My pursuers dislike to enter any place where any wildness lingers.

But some feel otherwise. They have visited parklands, preserves, actual wild-country. Their purpose was overconscious—measured, planned savagery, and a clock to tell them when they must go home—but at least they are not afraid of silences and unlighted nights. As spring returns, certain among them begin to follow me. They are merely curious, at first. But slowly, month by month, especially among the younger ones, my madness begins to call to something in them.

"With an host of furious fancies
Whereof I am commander
With a burning spear, and a horse of air,
To the wilderness I wander.
By a knight of ghosts and shadows
I summoned am to tourney
Ten leagues beyond the wild world's edge.
Me thinks it is no journey."

They sit at my feet and listen to me sing. They dance, crazily, to my harp. The girls bend close, tell me how I fascinate them, invite me to copulate. This I refuse, and when I tell them why they are puzzled, a little frightened maybe, but often they strive to understand.

For my rationality is renewed with the hawthorn blossoms. I bathe, have my hair and beard shorn, find clean raiment, and take care to eat what my body needs. Less and less do I rave before anyone who will listen; more and more do I seek solitude, quietness, under the vast wheel of the stars, and think.

What is man? Why is man? We have buried such questions; we have sworn they are dead—that they never really existed, being devoid of empirical meaning—and we have dreaded that they might raise the stones we heaped on them, rise and walk the world again of nights. Alone, I summon them to me. They cannot hurt their fellow dead, among whom I now number myself.

I sing to her who is gone. The young people hear and wonder. Sometimes they weep.

"Fear no more the heat o' the sun,
Nor the furious winter's rages;
Thou thy worldly task hast done,
Home art gone, and ta'en thy wages:
Golden lads and girls all must
As chimney-sweepers, come to dust."

"But this is not so!" they protest. "We will die and sleep a while, and then we will live forever in SUM."

I answer as gently as may be: "No. Remember I went there. So I know you are wrong. And even if you were right, it would not be right that you should be right."

"What?"

"Don't you see, it is not right that a thing should be the lord of man. It is not right that we should huddle through our whole lives in fear of finally losing them. You are not parts in a machine, and you have better ends than helping the machine run smoothly."

I dismiss them and stride off, solitary again, into a canyon where a river clangs, or onto some gaunt mountain peak. No revelation is given me. I climb and creep toward the truth.

Which is that SUM must be destroyed, not in revenge, not in hate, not in fear, simply because the human spirit cannot exist in the same reality as It.

But what, then, is our proper reality? And how shall we attain it?

I return with my songs to the lowlands. Word about me has gone widely. They are a large crowd who follow me down the highroad until it has changed into a street.

"The Dark Queen will soon come to these parts," they tell me. "Abide till She does. Let Her answer those questions you put to us, which make us sleep so badly."

"Let me retire to prepare myself," I say. I go up a long flight of steps. The people watch from below, dumb with awe, till I vanish. Such few as were in the building depart. I walk down vaulted halls, through hushed high-ceilinged rooms full of tables, among shelves made massive by books. Sunlight slants dusty through the windows.

The half memory has plagued me of late: once before, I know not when, this year of mine also took place. Perhaps in this library I can find the tale that—casually, I suppose, in my abnormal childhood—I read. For man is older than SUM: wiser, I swear; his myths hold more truth than Its mathematics. I spend three days and most of three nights in my search. There is scant sound but the rustling of leaves between my hands. Folk place offerings of food and drink at the door. They tell themselves they do so out of pity, or curiosity, or to avoid the nuisance of having me die in an unconventional fashion. But I know better.

At the end of the three days I am little further along. I have too much material; I keep going off on sidetracks of beauty and fascination. (Which SUM means to eliminate.) My Education was like everyone else's, science, rationality, good sane adjustment. (SUM writes our curricula, and the teaching machines have direct connections to It.) Well, I can make some of my lopsided training work for me. My reading has given me sufficient clues to prepare a search program. I sit down before an information retrieval console and run my fingers across its keys. They make a clattery music.

Electron beams are swift hounds. Within seconds the screen lights up with words, and I read who I am.

It is fortunate that I am a fast reader. Before I can press the Clear button, the unreeling words are wiped out. For an instant the screen quivers with formlessness, then appears

I HAD NOT CORRELATED THESE DATA WITH THE FACTS CONCERNING YOU. THIS INTRODUCES A NEW AND INDETERMINATE QUANTITY INTO THE COMPUTATIONS.

The nirvana which has come upon me (yes, I found that word among the old books, and how portentous it is) is not passiveness, it is a tide more full and strong than that which bore me down to the Dark Queen those ages apast in wildcountry. I say, as coolly as may be, "An interesting coincidence. If it is a coincidence." Surely sonic receptors are emplaced hereabouts.

EITHER THAT, OR A CERTAIN NECESSARY CONSEQUENCE OF THE LOGIC OF EVENTS.

The vision dawning within me is so blinding bright that I cannot refrain from answering, "Or a destiny, SUM?"

MEANINGLESS. MEANINGLESS. MEANINGLESS.

"Now why did You repeat Yourself in that way? Once would have sufficed. Thrice, though, makes an incantation. Are You by any chance hoping Your words will make me stop existing?"

I DO NOT HOPE. YOU ARE AN EXPERIMENT. IF I COMPUTE A SIGNIFICANT PROBABILITY OF YOUR CAUSING SERIOUS DISTURBANCE, I WILL HAVE YOU TERMINATED.

I smile. "SUM," I say, "I am going to terminate You." I lean over and switch off the screen. I walk out into the evening.

Not everything is clear to me yet, that I must say and do. But enough is that I can start preaching at once to those who have been waiting for me. As I talk, others come down the street, and hear, and stay to listen. Soon they number in the hundreds.

I have no immense new truth to offer them: nothing that I have not said before, although piecemeal and unsystematically; nothing they have not felt themselves, in the innermost darkness of their beings. Today, however, knowing who I am and therefore why I am, I can put these things in words. Speaking quietly, now and then drawing on some forgotten song to show my meaning, I tell them how sick and starved their lives are; how they have made themselves slaves; how the enslavement is not even to a conscious mind, but to an insensate inanimate thing which their own ancestors began; how that thing is not the centrum of existence, but a few scraps of metal and bleats of energy, a few sad stupid patterns, adrift in unbounded space-time. Put not your faith in SUM, I tell them. SUM is doomed, even as you and I. Seek out mystery; what else is the whole cosmos but mystery? Live bravely, die and be done, and you will be more than any machine. You may perhaps be God.

They grow tumultuous. They shout replies, some of which are animal howls. A few are for me, most are opposed. That doesn't matter. I have reached into them, my music is being played on their nervestrings, and this is my entire purpose.

The sun goes down behind the buildings. Dusk gathers. The city remains unilluminated. I soon realize why. She is coming, the Dark Queen Whom they wanted me to debate with. From afar we hear Her chariot thunder. Folk wail in terror. They are not wont to do that either. They used to disguise their feelings from Her and themselves by receiving Her with grave sparse ceremony. Now they would flee if they dared. I have lifted the masks.

The chariot halts in the street. She dismounts, tall and shadowy cowled. The people make way before Her like water before a shark. She climbs the stairs to face me. I see for the least instant that Her lips are not quite firm and Her eyes abrim with tears. She whispers, too low for anyone else to hear, "Oh, Harper, I'm sorry."

"Come join me," I invite. "Help me set the world free."

"No. I cannot. I have been too long with It." She straightens. Imperium descends upon Her. Her voice rises for everyone to hear. The little television robots flit close, bat shapes in the twilight, that the whole planet may witness my defeat. "What is this freedom you rant about?" She demands.

"To feel," I say. "To venture. To wonder. To become men again."

"To become beasts, you mean. Would you demolish the machines that keep us alive?"

"Yes. We must. Once they were good and useful, but we let them grow upon us like a cancer, and now nothing but destruction and a new beginning can save us."

"Have you considered the chaos?"

"Yes. It too is necessary. We will not be men without the freedom to know suffering. In it is also enlightenment. Through it we travel beyond ourselves, beyond earth and stars, space and time, to Mystery."

"So you maintain that there is some undefined ultimate vagueness behind the measurable universe?" She smiles into the bat eyes. We have each been taught, as children, to laugh on hearing sarcasms of this kind. "Please offer me a little proof."

"No," I say. "Prove to me instead, beyond any doubt, that there is *not* something we cannot understand with words and equations. Prove to me likewise that I have no right to seek for it.

"The burden of proof is on You Two, so often have You lied to us. In the name of rationality, You resurrected myth. The better to control us! In the name of liberation, You chained our inner lives and castrated our souls. In the name of service, You bound and blinkered us. In the name of achievement, You held us to a narrower round than any swine in its pen. In the name of beneficence, You created pain, and horror, and darkness beyond darkness." I turn to the people. "I went there. I descended into the cellars. I know!"

"He found that SUM would not pander to his special wishes, at the expense of everyone else," cries the Dark Queen. Do I hear shrillness in Her voice? "Therefore he claims SUM is cruel."

"I saw my dead," I tell them. "She will not rise again. Nor yours, nor you. Not ever. SUM will not, cannot raise us. In Its house is death indeed. We must seek life and rebirth elsewhere, among the mysteries."

She laughs aloud and points to my soul bracelet, glimmering faintly in the gray-blue thickening twilight. Need She say anything?

"Will someone give me a knife and an ax?" I ask.

The crowd stirs and mumbles. I smell their fear. Streetlamps go on, as if they could scatter more than this corner of the night which is rolling upon us. I fold my arms and wait. The Dark Queen says something to me. I ignore Her.

The tools pass from hand to hand. He who brings them up the stairs comes like a flame. He kneels at my feet and lifts what I have desired. The tools are good ones, a broad-bladed hunting knife and a long double-bitted ax.

Before the world, I take the knife in my right hand and slash beneath the bracelet on my left wrist. The connections to my inner body are cut. Blood flows, impossibly brilliant under the lamps. It does not hurt; I am too exalted.

The Dark Queen shrieks. "You meant it! Harper, Harper!"

"There is no life in SUM," I say. I pull my hand through the circle and cast the bracelet down so it rings.

A voice of brass: "*Arrest that maniac for correction. He is deadly dangerous.*"

The monitors who have stood on the fringes of the crowd try to push through. They are resisted. Those who seek to help them encounter fists and fingernails.

I take the ax and smash downward. The bracelet crumples. The organic material within, starved of my secretions, exposed to the night air, withers.

I raise the tools, ax in right hand, knife in bleeding left. "I seek eternity where it is to be found," I call. "Who goes with me?"

A score or better break loose from the riot, which is already calling forth weapons and claiming lives. They surround me with their bodies. Their eyes are the eyes of prophets. We make haste to seek a hiding place, for one military robot has appeared and others will not be long in coming. The tall engine strides to stand guard over Our Lady, and this is my last glimpse of Her.

My followers do not reproach me for having cost them all they were. They are mine. In me is the godhead which can do no wrong.

And the war is open, between me and SUM. My friends are few, my enemies many and mighty. I go about the world as a fugitive. But always I sing. And always I find someone who will listen, will join us, embracing pain and death like a lover.

With the Knife and the Ax I take their souls. Afterward we hold for them the ritual of rebirth. Some go thence to become outlaw missionaries; most put on facsimile bracelets and return home, to whisper my word. It makes little difference to me. I have no haste, who own eternity.

For my word is of what lies beyond time. My enemies say I call forth ancient bestialities and lunacies; that I would bring civilization down in ruin; that it matters not a madman's giggle to me whether war, famine, and pestilence will again scour the earth. With these accusations I am satisfied. The language of them shows me that here, too, I have reawakened anger. And that emotion belongs to us as much as any other. More than the others, maybe, in this autumn of mankind. We need a gale, to strike down SUM and everything It stands for. Afterward will come the winter of barbarism.

And after that the springtime of a new and (perhaps) more human civilization. My friends seem to believe this will come in their very lifetimes: peace, brotherhood, enlightenment, sanctity. I know otherwise. I have been in the depths. The wholeness of mankind, which I am bringing back, has its horrors.

When one day

the Eater of the Gods returns
the Wolf breaks his chain
the Horsemen ride forth
the Age ends
the Beast is reborn

then SUM will be destroyed; and you, strong and fair, may go back to earth and rain.

I shall await you.

My aloneness is nearly ended, Daybright. Just one task remains. The god must die, that his followers may believe he is raised from the dead and lives forever. Then they will go on to conquer the world.

There are those who say I have spurned and offended them. They too, borne on the tide which I raised, have torn out their machine souls and seek in music and ecstasy to find a meaning for existence. But their creed is a savage one, which has taken them into wildcountry, where they ambush the monitors sent against them and practice cruel rites. They believe that the final reality is female. Nevertheless, messengers of theirs have approached me with the suggestion of a mystic marriage. This I refused; my wedding was long ago, and will be celebrated again when this cycle of the world has closed.

Therefore they hate me. But I have said I will come and talk to them.

I leave the road at the bottom of the valley and walk singing up the hill. Those few I let come this far with me have been told to abide my return. They shiver in the sunset; the vernal equinox is three days away. I feel no cold myself. I stride exultant among briars and twisted ancient apple trees. If my bare feet leave a little blood in the snow, that is good. The ridges around are dark with forest, which waits like the skeleton dead for leaves to be breathed across it again. The eastern sky is purple, where stands the evening star. Overhead, against blue, cruises an early flight of homebound geese. Their calls drift faintly down to me. Westward, above me and before me, smolders redness. Etched black against it are the women.

Jack London

Jack London (1876–1916) wrote enough science fiction to fill a substantial collection. This story is one of his best (his other high point is "The Red One") and certainly his most influential. It is in the tradition of the last man on Earth story, a subgenre that extends in fiction from Cousin de Grainville's *Le Dernier Homme* (1805), through Mary Shelley's *The Last Man* (1826) and M. P. Shiel's *The Purple Cloud* (1900), to George R. Stewart's *Earth Abides* (1950) and the many British SF disaster novels of the 1950s and '60s by John Wyndham, John Christopher, J. G. Ballard, and others.

London's story introduces a notable alteration in this tradition. Earlier stories show a Romantic resurgence of nature, crumbling buildings and beautiful natural vistas. London portrays the scientifically possible descent, perhaps devolution, of civilized humans into barbarism. It is an interesting contrast to Forster's "The Machine Stops." It is also one of the ancestors of the large-scale disaster novel, so much a feature of this century.

"There was a hidden side to primitivism," says Richard Gid Powers in his introduction to London's collected science fiction, *The Science Fiction of Jack London* (1975), "and that was a hatred of civilization, an almost pathological longing for a catastrophe that would sweep away civilization and restore the pre-Adamite ceremony of innocence—a will to believe that the future would be a restoration of a past that would eclipse the obscenities of the present." London's twin themes in his science fiction are Social Darwinism and revolutionary socialism. It seems possible that London's character of the Chauffeur (the dark side of J. M. Barrie's admirable Crichton) is a partial inspiration for the Boss in H. G. Wells's *Things to Come*.

THE SCARLET PLAGUE

I

The way led along upon what had once been the embankment of a railroad. But no train had run upon it for many years. The forest on either side swelled up the slopes of the embankment and crested across it in a green wave of trees and bushes. The trail was as narrow as a man's body, and was no more than a wild-animal runway. Occasionally, a piece of rusty iron, showing through the forest-mould, advertised that the rail and the ties still remained. In one place, a ten-inch tree, bursting through at a connection, had lifted the end of a rail clearly into view. The tie had evidently followed the rail, held to it by the spike long enough for its bed to be filled with gravel and rotten leaves, so that now the crumbling, rotten timber thrust itself up at a curious slant. Old as the road was, it was manifest that it had been of the mono-rail type.

An old man and a boy travelled along this runway. They moved slowly, for the old man was very old, a touch of palsy made his movements tremulous, and he leaned heavily upon his staff. A rude skull-cap of goat-skin protected his head from the sun. From beneath this fell a scant fringe of stained and dirty-white hair. A visor, ingeniously made from a large leaf, shielded his eyes, and from under this he peered at the way of his feet on the trail. His beard, which should have been snow-white but which showed the same weather-wear and camp-stain as his hair, fell nearly to his waist in a great tangled mass. About his chest and shoulders hung a single, mangy garment of goat-skin. His arms and legs, withered and skinny, betokened extreme age, as well as did their sunburn and scars and scratches betoken long years of exposure to the elements.

The boy, who led the way, checking the eagerness of his muscles to the slow progress of the elder, likewise wore a single garment—a ragged-edged piece of bear-skin, with a hole in the middle through which he had thrust his head. He could not have been more than twelve years old. Tucked coquettishly over one ear was the freshly severed tail of a pig. In one hand he carried a medium-sized bow and an arrow. On his back was a quiverful of arrows. From a sheath hanging about his neck on a thong projected the battered handle of a hunting knife. He was as brown as a berry, and walked softly, with almost a catlike tread. In marked contrast with his sunburned skin were his eyes—blue, deep blue, but keen and sharp as a pair of gimlets. They seemed to bore into all about him in a way that was habitual. As he went along he smelled things, as well, his distended, quivering nostrils carrying to his brain an endless series of messages from the outside world. Also, his hearing was acute, and had been so trained that it operated automatically. Without conscious effort, he heard all the slight sounds in the apparent quiet—heard, and differentiated, and classified these sounds—whether they were of the wind rustling the leaves, of the humming of bees and gnats, of the distant rumble of the sea that drifted to him only in lulls, or of the gopher, just under his foot, shoving a pouchful of earth into the entrance of his hole.

Suddenly he became alertly tense. Sound, sight, and odor had given him a simultaneous warning. His hand went back to the old man, touching him, and the pair stood still. Ahead, at one side of the top of the embankment, arose a crackling sound, and the boy's gaze was fixed on the tops of the agitated bushes. Then a large bear, a grizzly, crashed into view, and likewise stopped abruptly, at sight of the humans. He did not like them, and growled querulously. Slowly the boy fitted the arrow to the bow, and slowly he pulled the bowstring taut. But he never removed his eyes from the bear. The old man peered from under his green leaf at the danger, and stood as quietly as the boy. For a few seconds this mutual scrutinizing went on; then, the bear betraying a growing irritability, the boy, with a movement of his head, indicated that the old man must step aside from the trail and go down the embankment. The boy followed, going backward, still holding the bow taut and ready. They waited till a crashing among the bushes from the opposite side of the embankment told them the bear had gone on. The boy grinned as he led back to the trail.

"A big un, Granser," he chuckled.

The old man shook his head.

"They get thicker every day," he complained in a thin, undependable falsetto. "Who'd have thought I'd live to see the time when a man would be afraid of his life on the way to the Cliff House. When I was a boy, Edwin, men and women and little babies used to come out here from San Francisco by tens of thousands on a nice day. And there weren't any bears then. No, sir. They used to pay money to look at them in cages, they were that rare."

"What is money, Granser?"

Before the old man could answer, the boy recollected and triumphantly shoved his hand into a pouch under his bear-skin and pulled forth a battered and tarnished silver dollar. The old man's eyes glistened, as he held the coin close to them.

"I can't see," he muttered. "You look and see if you can make out the date, Edwin."

The boy laughed.

"You're a great Granser," he cried delightedly, "always making believe them little marks mean something."

The old man manifested an accustomed chagrin as he brought the coin back again close to his own eyes.

"2012," he shrilled, and then fell to cackling grotesquely. "That was the year Morgan the Fifth was appointed President of the United States by the Board of Magnates. It must have been one of the last coins minted, for the Scarlet Death came in 2013. Lord! Lord!—think of it! Sixty years ago, and I am the only person alive to-day that lived in those times. Where did you find it, Edwin?"

The boy, who had been regarding him with the tolerant curiousness one accords to the prattlings of the feeble-minded, answered promptly.

"I got it off of Hoo-Hoo. He found it when we was herdin' goats down near San José last spring. Hoo-Hoo said it was *money*. Ain't you hungry, Granser?"

The ancient caught his staff in a tighter grip and urged along the trail, his old eyes shining greedily.

"I hope Har-Lip's found a crab . . . or two," he mumbled. "They're good eating, crabs, mighty good eating when you've no more teeth and you've got grandsons that love their old grandsire and make a point of catching crabs for him. When I was a boy—"

But Edwin, suddenly stopped by what he saw, was drawing the bowstring on a fitted arrow. He had paused on the brink of a crevasse in the embankment. An ancient culvert had here washed out, and the stream, no longer confined, had cut a passage through the fill. On the opposite side, the end of a rail projected and overhung. It showed rustily through the creeping vines which overran it. Beyond, crouching by a bush, a rabbit looked across at him in trembling hesitancy. Fully fifty feet was the distance, but the arrow flashed true; and the transfixed rabbit, crying out in sudden fright and hurt, struggled painfully away into the brush. The boy himself was a flash of brown skin and flying fur as he bounded down the steep wall of the gap and up the other side. His lean muscles were springs of steel that released into graceful and efficient action. A hundred feet beyond, in a tangle of bushes, he overtook the wounded creature, knocked its head on a convenient tree-trunk, and turned it over to Granser to carry.

"Rabbit is good, very good," the ancient quavered, "but when it comes to a toothsome delicacy I prefer crab. When I was a boy—"

"Why do you say so much that ain't got no sense?" Edwin impatiently interrupted the other's threatened garrulousness.

The boy did not exactly utter these words, but something that remotely resembled them and that was more guttural and explosive and economical of qualifying phrases. His speech showed distant kinship with that of the old man, and the latter's speech was approximately an English that had gone through a bath of corrupt usage.

"What I want to know," Edwin continued, "is why you call crab 'toothsome delicacy'? Crab is crab, ain't it? No one I never heard calls it such funny things."

The old man sighed but did not answer, and they moved on in silence. The surf grew suddenly louder, as they emerged from the forest upon a stretch of sand dunes bordering the sea. A few goats were browsing among the sandy hillocks, and a skin-clad boy, aided by a wolfish-looking dog that was only faintly reminiscent of a collie, was watching them. Mingled with the roar of the surf was a continuous, deep-throated barking or bellowing, which came from a cluster of jagged rocks a hundred yards out from shore. Here huge sea-lions hauled themselves up to lie in the sun or battle with one another. In the immediate foreground arose the smoke of a fire, tended by a third savage-looking boy. Crouched near him were several wolfish dogs similar to the one that guarded the goats.

The old man accelerated his pace, sniffing eagerly as he neared the fire.

"Mussels!" he muttered ecstatically. "Mussels! And ain't that a crab, Hoo-Hoo? Ain't that a crab? My, my, you boys are good to your old grandsire."

Hoo-Hoo, who was apparently of the same age as Edwin, grinned.

"All you want, Granser. I got four."

The old man's palsied eagerness was pitiful. Sitting down in the sand as quickly as his stiff limbs would let him, he poked a large rock-mussel from out of the coals. The heat had forced its shells apart, and the meat, salmon-colored, was thoroughly cooked. Between thumb and forefinger, in trembling haste, he caught the morsel and carried it to his mouth. But it was too hot, and the next moment was violently ejected. The old man spluttered with the pain, and tears ran out of his eyes and down his cheeks.

The boys were true savages, possessing only the cruel humor of the savage. To them the incident was excruciatingly funny, and they burst into loud laughter. Hoo-Hoo danced up and down, while Edwin rolled gleefully on the ground. The boy with the goats came running to join in the fun.

"Set 'em to cool, Edwin, set 'em to cool," the old man besought, in the midst of his grief, making no attempt to wipe away the tears that still flowed from his eyes. "And cool a crab, Edwin, too. You know your grandsire likes crabs."

From the coals arose a great sizzling, which proceeded from the many mussels bursting open their shells and exuding their moisture. They were large shellfish, running from three to six inches in length. The boys raked them out with sticks and placed them on a large piece of driftwood to cool.

"When I was a boy, we did not laugh at our elders; we respected them."

The boys took no notice, and Granser continued to babble an incoherent flow of complaint and censure. But this time he was more careful, and did not burn his mouth. All began to eat, using nothing but their hands and making loud mouth-noises and lip-smackings. The third boy, who was called Hare-Lip, slyly deposited a pinch of sand on a mussel the ancient was carrying to his mouth; and when the grit of it bit into the old fellow's mucous membrane and gums, the laughter was again uproarious. He was unaware that a joke had been played on him, and spluttered and spat until Edwin, relenting, gave him a gourd of fresh water with which to wash out his mouth.

"Where's them crabs, Hoo-Hoo?" Edwin demanded. "Granser's set upon having a snack."

Again Granser's eyes burned with greediness as a large crab was handed to him. It was a shell with legs and all complete, but the meat had long since departed. With shaky fingers and babblings of anticipation, the old man broke off a leg and found it filled with emptiness.

"The crabs, Hoo-Hoo?" he wailed. "The crabs?"

"I was foolin', Granser. They ain't no crabs. I never found one."

The boys were overwhelmed with delight at sight of the tears of senile disappointment that dribbled down the old man's cheeks. Then, unnoticed, Hoo-Hoo replaced the empty shell with a fresh-cooked crab. Already dismembered, from the cracked legs the white meat sent forth a small cloud of savory steam. This attracted the old man's nostrils, and he looked down in amazement. The change of his mood to one of joy was immediate. He snuffled and muttered and mumbled, making almost a croon of delight, as he began to eat. Of this the boys took little notice, for it was an accustomed spectacle. Nor did they notice his occasional exclamations and utterances of phrases which meant nothing to them, as, for instance, when he smacked his lips and champed his gums while muttering: "Mayonnaise! Just think—mayonnaise! And it's sixty years since the last was ever made! Two generations and never a smell of it! Why, in those days it was served in every restaurant with crab."

When he could eat no more, the old man sighed, wiped his hands on his naked legs, and gazed out over the sea. With the content of a full stomach, he waxed reminiscent.

"To think of it! I've seen this beach alive with men, women, and children on a pleasant Sunday. And there weren't any bears to eat them up, either. And right up there on the cliff was a big restaurant where you could get anything you wanted to eat. Four million people lived in San Francisco then. And now, in the whole city and county there aren't forty all told. And out there on the sea were ships and ships always to be seen, going in for the Golden Gate or coming out. And airships in the air—dirigibles and flying machines. They could travel two hundred miles an hour. The mail contracts with the New York and San Francisco Limited demanded that for the minimum. There was a chap, a Frenchman, I forget his name, who succeeded in making three hundred; but the thing was risky, too risky for conservative persons. But he was on the right clew, and he would have managed it if it hadn't been for the Great Plague. When I was a boy, there were men alive who remembered the coming of the first aeroplanes, and now I have lived to see the last of them, and that sixty years ago."

The old man babbled on, unheeded by the boys, who were long accustomed to his garrulousness, and whose vocabularies, besides, lacked the greater portion of the words he used. It was noticeable that in these rambling soliloquies his English seemed to recrudesce into better construction and phraseology. But when he talked directly with the boys it lapsed, largely, into their own uncouth and simpler forms.

"But there weren't many crabs in those days," the old man wandered on. "They were fished out, and they were great delicacies. The open season was only a month long, too. And now crabs are accessible the whole year around. Think of it—catching all the crabs you want, any time you want, in the surf of the Cliff House beach!"

A sudden commotion among the goats brought the boys to their feet. The dogs about the fire rushed to join their snarling fellow who guarded the goats, while the goats themselves stampeded in the direction of their human protectors. A half dozen forms, lean and gray, glided about on the sand hillocks or faced the bristling dogs. Edwin arched an arrow that fell short. But Hare-Lip, with a sling such as David carried into battle against Goliath, hurled a stone through the air that whistled from the speed of its flight. It fell squarely among the wolves and caused them to slink away toward the dark depths of the eucalyptus forest.

The boys laughed and lay down again in the sand, while Granser sighed ponderously. He had eaten too much, and, with hands clasped on his paunch, the fingers interlaced, he resumed his maunderings.

" 'The fleeting systems lapse like foam,' " he mumbled what was evidently a quotation. "That's it—foam, and fleeting. All man's toil upon the planet was just so much foam. He domesticated the serviceable animals, destroyed the hostile ones, and cleared the land of its wild vegetation. And then he passed, and the flood of primordial life rolled back again, sweeping his handiwork away—the weeds and the forest inundated his fields, the beasts of prey swept over his flocks, and now there are wolves on the Cliff House beach." He was appalled by the thought. "Where four million people disported themselves, the wild wolves roam to-day, and the savage progeny of our loins, with prehistoric weapons, defend themselves against the fanged despoilers. Think of it! And all because of the Scarlet Death—"

The adjective had caught Hare-Lip's ear.

"He's always saying that," he said to Edwin. "What is *scarlet?*"

" 'The scarlet of the maples can shake me like the cry of bugles going by,' " the old man quoted.

"It's red," Edwin answered the question. "And you don't know it because you come from the Chauffeur Tribe. They never did know nothing, none of them. *Scarlet* is red—I know that."

"Red is red, ain't it?" Hare-Lip grumbled. "Then what's the good of gettin' cocky and calling it scarlet?"

"Granser, what for do you always say so much what nobody knows?" he asked. "Scarlet ain't anything, but red is red. Why don't you say red, then?"

"Red is not the right word," was the reply. "The plague was scarlet. The whole face and body turned scarlet in an hour's time. Don't I know? Didn't I see enough of it? And I am telling you it was scarlet because—well, because it *was* scarlet. There is no other word for it."

"Red is good enough for me," Hare-Lip muttered obstinately. "My dad calls red red, and he ought to know. He says everybody died of the Red Death."

"Your dad is a common fellow, descended from a common fellow," Granser retorted heatedly. "Don't I know the beginnings of the Chauffeurs? Your grandsire was a chauffeur, a servant, and without education. He worked for other persons. But your grandmother was of good stock, only the children did not take after her. Don't I remember when I first met them, catching fish at Lake Temescal?"

"What is *education?*" Edwin asked.

"Calling red scarlet," Hare-Lip sneered, then returned to the attack on Granser. "My dad told me, an' he got it from his dad afore he croaked, that your wife was a Santa Rosan, an' that she was sure no account. He said she was a *hash-slinger* before the Red Death, though I don't know what a *hash-slinger* is. You can tell me, Edwin."

But Edwin shook his head in token of ignorance.

"It is true, she was a waitress," Granser acknowledged. "But she was a good woman, and your mother was her daughter. Women were very scarce in the days after the Plague. She was the only wife I could find, even if she was a *hash-slinger*, as your father calls it. But it is not nice to talk about our progenitors that way."

"Dad says that the wife of the first Chauffeur was a *lady*—"

"What's a *lady?*" Hoo-Hoo demanded.

"A *lady's* a Chauffeur squaw," was the quick reply of Hare-Lip.

"The first Chauffeur was Bill, a common fellow, as I said before," the old man expounded; "but his wife was a lady, a great lady. Before the Scarlet Death she was the wife of Van Worden. He was President of the Board of Industrial Magnates, and was one of the dozen men who ruled America. He was worth one billion, eight hundred millions of dollars—coins like you have there in your pouch, Edwin. And then came the Scarlet Death, and his wife became the wife of Bill, the first Chauffeur. He used to beat her, too. I have seen it myself."

Hoo-Hoo, lying on his stomach and idly digging his toes in the sand, cried out and investigated, first, his toe-nail, and next, the small hole he had dug. The other two boys joined him, excavating the sand rapidly with their hands till there lay three skeletons exposed. Two were of adults, the third being that of a part-grown child. The old man hudged along on the ground and peered at the find.

"Plague victims," he announced. "That's the way they died everywhere in the last days. This must have been a family, running away from the contagion and perishing here on the Cliff House beach. They—what are you doing, Edwin?"

This question was asked in sudden dismay, as Edwin, using the back of his hunting knife, began to knock out the teeth from the jaws of one of the skulls.

"Going to string 'em," was the response.

The three boys were now hard at it; and quite a knocking and hammering arose, in which Granser babbled on unnoticed.

"You are true savages. Already has begun the custom of wearing human teeth. In another generation you will be perforating your noses and ears and wearing ornaments of bone and shell. I know. The human race is doomed to sink back farther and farther into the primitive night ere again it begins its bloody climb upward to civilization. When we increase and feel the lack of room, we will proceed to kill one another. And then I suppose you will wear human scalp-locks at your waist, as well—as you, Edwin, who are the gentlest of my grandsons, have already begun with that vile pigtail. Throw it away, Edwin, boy; throw it away."

"What a gabble the old geezer makes," Hare-Lip remarked, when, the teeth all extracted, they began an attempt at equal division.

They were very quick and abrupt in their actions, and their speech, in moments of hot discussion over the allotment of the choicer teeth, was truly a gabble. They spoke in monosyllables and short jerky sentences that was more a gibberish than a language. And yet, through it ran hints of grammatical construction, and appeared vestiges of the conjugation of some superior culture. Even the speech of Granser was so corrupt that were it put down literally it would be almost so much nonsense to the reader. This, however, was when he talked with the boys. When he got into the full swing of babbling to himself, it slowly purged itself into pure English. The sentences grew longer and were enunciated with a rhythm and ease that was reminiscent of the lecture platform.

"Tell us about the Red Death, Granser," Hare-Lip demanded, when the teeth affair had been satisfactorily concluded.

"The Scarlet Death," Edwin corrected.

"An' don't work all that funny lingo on us," Hare-Lip went on. "Talk sensible,

Granser, like a Santa Rosan ought to talk. Other Santa Rosans don't talk like you."

II

The old man showed pleasure in being thus called upon. He cleared his throat and began.

"Twenty or thirty years ago my story was in great demand. But in these days nobody seems interested—"

"There you go!" Hare-Lip cried hotly. "Cut out the funny stuff and talk sensible. What's *interested*? You talk like a baby that don't know how."

"Let him alone," Edwin urged, "or he'll get mad and won't talk at all. Skip the funny places. We'll catch on to some of what he tells us."

"Let her go, Granser," Hoo-Hoo encouraged; for the old man was already maundering about the disrespect for elders and the reversion to cruelty of all humans that fell from high culture to primitive conditions.

The tale began.

"There were very many people in the world in those days. San Francisco alone held four millions—"

"What is millions?" Edwin interrupted.

Granser looked at him kindly.

"I know you cannot count beyond ten, so I will tell you. Hold up your two hands. On both of them you have altogether ten fingers and thumbs. Very well. I now take this grain of sand—you hold it, Hoo-Hoo." He dropped the grain of sand into the lad's palm and went on. "Now that grain of sand stands for the ten fingers of Edwin. I add another grain. That's ten more fingers. And I add another, and another, and another, until I have added as many grains as Edwin has fingers and thumbs. That makes what I call one hundred. Remember that word—one hundred. Now I put this pebble in Hare-Lip's hand. It stands for ten grains of sand, or ten tens of fingers, or one hundred fingers. I put in ten pebbles. They stand for a thousand fingers. I take a mussel-shell, and it stands for ten pebbles, or one hundred grains of sand, or one thousand fingers. . . ."

And so on, laboriously, and with much reiteration, he strove to build up in their minds a crude conception of numbers. As the quantities increased, he had the boys holding different magnitudes in each of their hands. For still higher sums, he laid the symbols on the log of driftwood; and for symbols he was hard put, being compelled to use the teeth from the skulls for millions, and the crab-shells for billions. It was here that he stopped, for the boys were showing signs of becoming tired.

"There were four million people in San Francisco—four teeth."

The boys' eyes ranged along from the teeth and from hand to hand, down through the pebbles and sand-grains to Edwin's fingers. And back again they ranged along the ascending series in the effort to grasp such inconceivable numbers.

"That was a lot of folks, Granser," Edwin at last hazarded.

"Like sand on the beach here, like sand on the beach, each grain of sand a man, or woman, or child. Yes, my boy, all those people lived right here in San Francisco. And at one time or another all those people came out on this very beach—more people than there are grains of sand. More—more—more. And San Francisco was a noble city. And across the bay, where we camped last year, even more people lived, clear from Point Richmond, on the level ground and on the hills, all the way around to San Leandro—one great city of seven million people.—Seven teeth . . . there, that's it, seven millions."

Again the boys' eyes ranged up and down from Edwin's fingers to the teeth on the log.

"The world was full of people. The census of 2010 gave eight billions for the whole world—eight crab-shells, yes, eight billions. It was not like to-day. Mankind knew a great deal more about getting food. And the more food there was, the more people there were. In the year 1800, there were one hundred and seventy millions in Europe alone. One hundred years later—a grain of sand, Hoo-Hoo—one hundred years later, at 1900, there were five hundred millions in Europe—five grains of sand, Hoo-Hoo, and this one tooth. This shows how easy was the getting of food, and how men increased. And in the year 2000, there were fifteen hundred millions in Europe. And it was the same all over the rest of the world. Eight crab-shells there, yes, eight billion people were alive on the earth when the Scarlet Death began.

"I was a young man when the Plague came—twenty-seven years old—and I lived on the other side of San Francisco Bay, in Berkeley. You remember those great stone houses, Edwin, when we came down the hills from Contra Costa? That was where I lived, in those stone houses. I was a professor of English literature."

Much of this was over the heads of the boys, but they strove to comprehend dimly this tale of the past.

"What was them stone houses for?" Hare-Lip queried.

"You remember when your dad taught you to swim?" The boy nodded. "Well, in the University of California—that is the name we had for the houses—we taught young men and women how to think, just as I have taught you now, by sand and pebbles and shells, to know how many people lived in those days. There was very much to teach. The young men and women we taught were called students. We had large rooms in which we taught. I talked to them, forty or fifty at a time, just as I am talking to you now. I told them about the books other men had written before their time, and even, sometimes, in their time—"

"Was that all you did?—just talk, talk, talk?" Hoo-Hoo demanded. "Who hunted your meat for you? and milked the goats? and caught the fish?"

"A sensible question, Hoo-Hoo, a sensible question. As I have told you, in those days food-getting was easy. We were very wise. A few men got the food for many men. The other men did other things. As you say, I talked. I talked all the time, and for this food was given me—much food, fine food, beautiful food, food that I have not tasted in sixty years and shall never taste again. I sometimes think the most wonderful achievement of our tremendous civilization was food—its inconceivable abundance, its infinite variety, its marvellous delicacy. O my grandsons, life was life in those days, when we had such wonderful things to eat."

This was beyond the boys, and they let it slip by, words and thoughts, as a mere senile wandering in the narrative.

"Our food-getters were called *freemen*. This was a joke. We of the ruling classes owned all the land, all the machines, everything. These food-getters were our slaves. We took almost all the food they got, and left them a little so that they might eat, and work, and get us more food—"

"I'd have gone into the forest and got food for myself," Hare-Lip announced; "and if any man tried to take it away from me, I'd have killed him."

The old man laughed.

"Did I not tell you that we of the ruling class owned all the land, all the forest, everything? Any food-getter who would not get food for us, him we punished or compelled to starve to death. And very few did that. They preferred to get food for us, and make clothes for us, and prepare and administer to us a thousand—a mussel-shell, Hoo-Hoo—a thousand satisfactions and delights. And I was Professor Smith in those days—Professor James Howard Smith. And my lecture courses were very popular—that is, very many of the young men and women liked to hear me talk about the books other men had written.

"And I was very happy, and I had beautiful things to eat. And my hands were soft, because I did no work with them, and my body was clean all over and dressed in the softest garments—" He surveyed his mangy goat-skin with disgust. "We did not wear such things in those days. Even the slaves had better garments. And we were most clean. We washed our faces and hands often every day. You boys never wash unless you fall into the water or go in swimming."

"Neither do you, Granser," Hoo-Hoo retorted.

"I know, I know. I am a filthy old man. But times have changed. Nobody washes these days, and there are no conveniences. It is sixty years since I have seen a piece of soap. You do not know what soap is, and I shall not tell you, for I am telling the story of the Scarlet Death. You know what sickness is. We called it a disease. Very many of the diseases came from what we called germs. Remember that word—germs. A germ is a very small thing. It is like a woodtick, such as you find on the dogs in the spring of the year when they run in the forest. Only the germ is very small. It is so small that you cannot see it—"

Hoo-Hoo began to laugh.

"You're a queer un, Granser, talking about things you can't see. If you can't see 'em, how do you know they are? That's what I want to know. How do you know anything you can't see?"

"A good question, a very good question, Hoo-Hoo. But we did see—some of them. We had what we called microscopes and ultramicoscopes, and we put them to our eyes and looked through them, so that we saw things larger than they really were, and many things we could not see without the microscopes at all. Our best ultramicroscopes could make a germ look forty thousand times larger. A mussel-shell is a thousand fingers like Edwin's. Take forty mussel-shells, and by as many times larger was the germ when we looked at it through a microscope. And after that, we had other ways, by using what we called moving pictures, of making the forty-thousand-times germ many, many thousand times larger still. And thus we saw all these things which our eyes of themselves could not see. Take a grain of sand. Break it into ten pieces. Take one piece and break it into ten. Break one of those pieces into ten, and one of those into ten, and one of those into ten, and one of those into ten, and do it all day, and maybe, by sunset, you will have a piece as small as one of the germs."

The boys were openly incredulous. Hare-Lip sniffed and sneered and Hoo-Hoo snickered, until Edwin nudged them to be silent.

"The woodtick sucks the blood of the dog, but the germ, being so very small, goes right into the blood of the body, and there it has many children. In those days there would be as many as a billion—a crab-shell, please—as many as that crab-shell in one man's body. We called germs micro-organisms. When a few million, or a billion, of them were in a man, in all the blood of a man, he was sick. These germs were a disease. There were many different kinds of them—more different kinds than there are grains of sand on this beach. We knew only a few of the kinds. The micro-organic world was an invisible world, a world we could not see, and we knew very little about it. Yet we did know something. There was the *bacillus anthracis*; there was the *micrococcus*; there was the *Bacterium termo*, and the *Bacterium lactis*—that's what turns the goat milk sour even to this day, Hare-Lip; and there were *Schizomycetes* without end. And there were many others. . . ."

Here the old man launched into a disquisition on germs and their natures, using words and phrases of such extraordinary length and meaninglessness, that the boys grinned at one another and looked out over the deserted ocean till they forgot the old man was babbling on.

"But the Scarlet Death, Granser," Edwin at last suggested.

Granser recollected himself, and with a start tore himself away from the rostrum of the lecture-hall, where, to another-world audience, he had been expounding the latest theory, sixty years gone, of germs and germ-diseases.

"Yes, yes, Edwin; I had forgotten. Sometimes the memory of the past is very strong upon me, and I forget that I am a dirty old man, clad in goat-skin, wandering with my savage grandsons who are goatherds in the primeval wilderness. 'The fleeting systems lapse like foam,' and so lapsed our glorious, colossal civilization. I am Granser, a tired old man. I belong to the tribe of Santa Rosans. I married into that tribe. My sons and daughters married into the Chauffeurs, the Sacramentos, and the Palo-Altos. You, Hare-Lip, are of the Chauffeurs. You, Edwin, are of the Sacramentos. And you, Hoo-Hoo, are of the Palo-Altos. Your tribe takes its name from a town that was near the seat of another great institution of learning. It was called Stanford University. Yes, I remember now. It is perfectly clear. I was telling you of the Scarlet Death. Where was I in my story?"

"You was telling about germs, the things you can't see but which make men sick," Edwin prompted.

"Yes, that's where I was. A man did not notice at first when only a few of these germs got into his body. But each germ broke in half and became two germs, and they kept doing this very rapidly so that in a short time there were many millions of them in the body. Then the man was sick. He had a disease, and the disease was named after the kind of a germ that was in him. It might be measles, it might be influenza, it might be yellow fever; it might be any of thousands and thousands of kinds of diseases.

"Now this is the strange thing about these germs. There were always new ones coming to live in men's bodies. Long and long and long ago, when there were only a few men in the world, there were few diseases. But as men increased and lived closely together in great cities and civilizations, new diseases arose, new kinds of germs entered their bodies. Thus were countless millions and billions of human beings killed. And the more thickly men packed together, the more terrible were the new diseases that came to be. Long before my time, in the Middle Ages, there was the Black Plague that swept across Europe. It swept across Europe many times. There was tuberculosis, that entered into men wherever they were thickly packed. A hundred years before my time there was the bubonic plague. And in Africa was the sleeping sickness. The bacteriologists fought all these sicknesses and destroyed them, just as you boys fight the wolves away from your goats, or squash the mosquitoes that light on you. The bacteriologists—"

"But, Granser, what is a what-you-call-it?" Edwin interrupted.

"You, Edwin, are a goatherd. Your task is to watch the goats. You know a great deal about goats. A bacteriologist watches germs. That's his task, and he knows a great deal about them. So, as I was saying, the bacteriologists fought with the germs and destroyed them—sometimes. There was leprosy, a horrible disease. A hundred years before I was born, the bacteriologists discovered the germ of leprosy. They knew all about it. They made pictures of it. I have seen those pictures. But they never found a way to kill it. But in 1984, there was the Pantoblast Plague, a disease that broke out in a country called Brazil and that killed millions of people. But the bacteriologists found it out, and found the way to kill it, so that the Pantoblast Plague went no farther. They made what they called a serum, which they put into a man's body and which killed the pantoblast germs without killing the man. And in 1910, there was Pellagra, and also the hookworm. These were easily killed by the bacteriologists. But in 1947 there arose a new disease that had never been seen before. It got into the bodies of babies of only ten months old or less, and it made them unable to move their hands and feet, or to eat, or anything; and the bacteriologists were eleven years in discovering how to kill that particular germ and save the babies.

"In spite of all these diseases, and of all the new ones that continued to arise, there were more and more men in the world. This was because it was easy to get food. The easier it was to get food, the more men there were; the more men there were, the more thickly were they packed together on the earth; and the more thickly they were packed, the more new kinds of germs became diseases. There were warnings. Soldervetzsky, as early as 1929, told the bacteriologists that they had no guaranty against some new disease, a thousand times more deadly than any they knew, arising and killing by the hundreds of millions and even by the billion. You see, the micro-organic world remained a mystery to the end. They knew there was such a world, and that from time to time armies of new germs emerged from it to kill men. And that was all they knew about it. For all they knew, in that invisible micro-organic world there might be as many different kinds of germs as there are grains of sand on this beach. And also, in that same invisible world it might well be that new kinds of germs came to be. It might be there that life originated—the 'abysmal fecundity,' Soldervetzsky called it, applying the words of other men who had written before him. . . ."

It was at this point that Hare-Lip rose to his feet, an expression of huge contempt on his face.

"Granser," he announced, "you make me sick with your gabble. Why don't you tell about the Red Death? If you ain't going to, say so, an' we'll start back for camp."

The old man looked at him and silently began to cry. The weak tears of age rolled down his cheeks, and all the feebleness of his eighty-seven years showed in his grief-stricken countenance.

"Sit down," Edwin counselled soothingly. "Granser's all right. He's just gettin' to the Scarlet Death, ain't you, Granser? He's just goin' to tell us about it right now. Sit down, Hare-Lip. Go ahead, Granser."

III

The old man wiped the tears away on his grimy knuckles and took up the tale in a tremulous, piping voice that soon strengthened as he got the swing of the narrative.

"It was in the summer of 2013 that the Plague came. I was twenty-seven years old, and well do I remember it. Wireless despatches—"

Hare-Lip spat loudly his disgust, and Granser hastened to make amends.

"We talked through the air in those days, thousands and thousands of miles. And the word came of a strange disease that had broken out in New York. There were seventeen millions of people living then in that noblest city of America. Nobody thought anything about the news. It was only a small thing. There had been only a few deaths. It seemed, though, that they had died very quickly, and that one of the first signs of the disease was the turning red of the face and all the body. Within twenty-four hours came the report of the first case in Chicago. And on the same day, it was made public that London, the greatest city in the world, next to Chicago, had been secretly fighting the plague for two weeks and censoring the news despatches—that is, not permitting the word to go forth to the rest of the world that London had the plague.

"It looked serious, but we in California, like everywhere else, were not alarmed. We were sure that the bacteriologists would find a way to overcome this new germ, just as they had overcome other germs in the past. But the trouble was the astonishing quickness with which this germ destroyed human beings, and the fact that it inevitably killed any human body it entered. No one ever recovered. There was the old Asiatic cholera, when you might eat dinner with a well man in the evening, and the next morning, if you got up early enough, you would see him being hauled by your window in the death-cart. But this new plague was quicker than that—much quicker. From the moment of the first signs of it, a man would be dead in an hour. Some lasted for several hours. Many died within ten or fifteen minutes of the appearance of the first signs.

"The heart began to beat faster and the heat of the body to increase. Then came the scarlet rash, spreading like wildfire over the face and body. Most persons never noticed the increase in heat and heart-beat, and the first they knew was when the scarlet rash came out. Usually, they had convulsions at the time of the appearance of the rash. But these convulsions did not last long and were not very severe. If one lived through them, he became perfectly quiet, and only did he feel a numbness swiftly creeping up his body from the feet. The heels became numb first, then the legs, and hips, and when the numbness reached as high as his heart he died. They did not rave or sleep. Their minds always remained cool and calm up to the moment their heart numbed and stopped. And another strange thing was the rapidity of decomposition. No sooner was a person dead than the body seemed to fall to pieces, to fly apart, to melt away even as you looked at it. That was one of the reasons the plague spread so rapidly. All the billions of germs in a corpse were so immediately released.

"And it was because of all this that the bacteriologists had so little chance in fighting the germs. They were killed in their laboratories even as they studied the germ of the Scarlet Death. They were heroes. As fast as they perished, others stepped forth and took their places. It was in London that they first isolated it. The news was telegraphed everywhere. Trask was the name of the man who succeeded in this, but within thirty hours he was dead. Then came the struggle in all the laboratories to find something that would kill the plague germs. All drugs failed. You see, the problem was to get a drug, or serum, that would kill the germs in the body and not kill the body. They tried to fight it with other germs, to put into the body of a sick man germs that were the enemies of the plague germs—"

"And you can't see these germ-things, Granser," Hare-Lip objected, "and here you gabble, gabble, gabble about them as if they was anything, when they're nothing at all. Anything you can't see, ain't, that's what. Fighting things that ain't with things that ain't! They must have been all fools in them days. That's why they croaked. I ain't goin' to believe in such rot, I tell you that."

Granser promptly began to weep, while Edwin hotly took up his defence.

"Look here, Hare-Lip, you believe in lots of things you can't see."

Hare-Lip shook his head.

"You believe in dead men walking about. You never seen one dead man walk about."

"I tell you I seen 'em, last winter, when I was wolf-hunting with Dad."

"Well, you always spit when you cross running water," Edwin challenged.

"That's to keep off bad luck," was Hare-Lip's defence.

"You believe in bad luck?"

"Sure."

"An' you ain't never seen bad luck," Edwin concluded triumphantly. "You're just as bad as Granser and his germs. You believe in what you don't see. Go on, Granser."

Hare-Lip, crushed by this metaphysical defeat, remained silent, and the old man went on. Often and often, though this narrative must not be clogged by the details, was Granser's tale interrupted while the boys squabbled among themselves. Also, among themselves they kept up a constant, low-voiced exchange of explanation and conjecture, as they strove to follow the old man into his unknown and vanished world.

"The Scarlet Death broke out in San Francisco. The first death came on a Monday morning. By Thursday they were dying like flies in Oakland and San Francisco. They died everywhere—in their beds, at their work, walking along the street. It was on Tuesday that I saw my first death—Miss Collbran, one of my students, sitting right there before my eyes, in my lecture-room. I noticed her face while I was talking. It had suddenly turned scarlet. I ceased speaking and could only look at her, for the first fear of the plague was already on all of us and we knew that it had come. The young women screamed and ran out of the room. So did the young men run out, all but two. Miss Collbran's convulsions were very mild and lasted less than a minute. One of the young men fetched her a glass of water. She drank only a little of it, and cried out:

" 'My feet! All sensation has left them.'

"After a minute she said, 'I have no feet. I am unaware that I have any feet. And my knees are cold. I can scarcely feel that I have knees.'

"She lay on the floor, a bundle of notebooks under her head. And we could do nothing. The coldness and the numbness crept up past her hips to her heart, and when it reached her heart she was dead. In fifteen minutes, by the clock—I timed it—she was dead, there, in my own classroom, dead. And she was a very beautiful, strong, healthy young woman. And from the first sign of the plague to her death only fifteen minutes elapsed. That will show you how swift was the Scarlet Death.

"Yet in those few minutes I remained with the dying woman in my classroom, the alarm had spread over the university; and the students, by thousands, all of them, had deserted the lecture-room and laboratories. When I emerged, on my way to make report to the President of the Faculty, I found the university deserted. Across the campus were several stragglers hurrying for their homes. Two of them were running.

"President Hoag, I found in his office, all alone, looking very old and very gray, with a multitude of wrinkles in his face that I had never seen before. At the sight of me, he pulled himself to his feet and tottered away to the inner office, banging the door after him and locking it. You see, he knew I had been exposed, and he was afraid. He shouted to me through the door to go away. I shall never forget my feelings as I walked down the silent corridors and out across that deserted campus. I was not afraid. I had been exposed, and I looked upon myself as already dead. It was not that, but a feeling of awful depression that impressed me. Everything had stopped. It was like the end of the world to me—my world. I had been born within sight and sound of the university. It had been my predestined career. My father had been a professor there before me, and his father before him. For a century and a half had this university, like a splendid machine, been running steadily on. And now, in an instant, it had stopped. It was like seeing the sacred flame die down on some thrice-sacred altar. I was shocked, unutterably shocked.

"When I arrived home, my housekeeper screamed as I entered, and fled away. And when I rang, I found the housemaid had likewise fled. I investigated. In the kitchen I found the cook on the point of departure. But she screamed, too, and in her haste dropped a suitcase of her personal belongings and ran out of the house and across the grounds, still screaming. I can hear her scream to this day. You see, we did not act in this way when ordinary diseases smote us. We were always calm over such things, and sent for the doctors and nurses who knew just what to do. But this was different. It struck so suddenly, and killed so swiftly, and never missed a stroke. When the scarlet rash appeared on a person's face, that person was marked by death. There was never a known case of a recovery.

"I was alone in my big house. As I have told you often before, in those days we could talk with one another over wires or through the air. The telephone bell rang, and I found my brother talking to me. He told me that he was not coming home for fear of catching the plague from me, and that he had taken our two sisters to stop at Professor Bacon's home. He advised me to remain where I was, and wait to find out whether or not I had caught the plague.

"To all of this I agreed, staying in my house and for the first time in my life attempting to cook. And the plague did not come out on me. By means of the telephone I could talk with whomsoever I pleased and get the news. Also, there were the newspapers, and I ordered all of them to be thrown up to my door so that I could know what was happening with the rest of the world.

"New York City and Chicago were in chaos. And what happened with them was happening in all the large cities. A third of the New York police were dead. Their chief was also dead, likewise the mayor. All law and order had ceased. The bodies were lying in the streets unburied. All railroads and vessels carrying food and such things into the great city had ceased running, and mobs of the hungry poor were pillaging the stores and warehouses. Murder and robbery and drunkenness were everywhere. Already the people had fled from the city by millions—at first the rich, in their private motor cars and dirigibles, and then the great mass of the population, on foot, carrying the plague with them, themselves starving and pillaging the farmers and all the towns and villages on the way.

"The man who sent this news, the wireless operator, was alone with his instrument on the top of a lofty building. The people remaining in the city—he estimated them at several hundred thousand—had gone mad from fear and drink, and on all sides of him great fires were raging. He was a hero, that man who staid by his post—an obscure newspaperman, most likely.

"For twenty-four hours, he said, no transatlantic airships had arrived, and no more messages were coming from England. He did state, though, that a message from Berlin—that's in Germany—announced that Hoffmeyer, a bacteriologist of the Metchnikoff School, had discovered the serum for the plague. That was the last word, to this day, that we of America ever received from Europe. If Hoffmeyer discovered the serum, it was too late, or otherwise, long ere this, explorers from Europe would have come looking for us. We can only conclude that what happened in America happened in Europe, and that, at the best, some several score may have survived the Scarlet Death on that whole continent.

"For one day longer the despatches continued to come from New York. Then they, too, ceased. The man who had sent them, perched in his lofty building, had either died of the plague or been consumed in the great conflagrations he had described as raging around him. And what had occurred in New York had been duplicated in all the other cities. It was the same in San Francisco, and Oakland, and Berkeley. By Thursday the people were dying so rapidly that their corpses could not be handled, and dead bodies lay everywhere. Thursday night the panic outrush for the country began. Imagine, my grandsons, people, thicker than the salmon-run you have seen on the Sacramento River, pouring out of the cities by millions, madly over the country, in vain attempt to escape the ubiquitous death. You see, they carried the germs with them. Even the airships of the rich, fleeing for mountain and desert fastnesses, carried the germs.

"Hundreds of these airships escaped to Hawaii, and not only did they bring the plague with them, but they found the plague already there before them. This we learned, by the despatches, until all order in San Francisco vanished, and there were no operators left at their posts to receive or send. It was amazing, astounding, this loss of communication with the world. It was exactly as if the world had ceased, been blotted out. For sixty years that world has no longer existed for me. I know there must be such places as New York, Europe, Asia, and Africa; but not one word has been heard of them—not in sixty years. With the coming of the Scarlet Death the world fell apart, absolutely, irretrievably. Ten thousand years of culture and civilization passed in the twinkling of an eye, 'lapsed like foam.'

"I was telling about the airships of the rich. They carried the plague with them and no matter where they fled, they died. I never encountered but one survivor of any of them—Mungerson. He was afterwards a Santa Rosan, and he married my eldest daughter. He came into the tribe eight years after the plague. He was then nineteen years old, and he was compelled to wait twelve years more before he could marry. You see, there were no unmarried women, and some of the older daughters of the Santa Rosans were already bespoken. So he was forced to wait until my Mary had grown to sixteen years. It was his son, Gimp-Leg, who was killed last year by the mountain lion.

"Mungerson was eleven years old at the time of the plague. His father was one of the Industrial Magnates, a very wealthy, powerful man. It was on his airship, the *Condor*, that they were fleeing, with all the family, for the wilds of British Columbia, which is far to the north of here. But there was some accident, and they were wrecked near Mount Shasta. You have heard of that mountain. It is far to the north. The plague broke out amongst them, and this boy of eleven was the only survivor. For eight years he was alone, wandering over a deserted land and looking vainly for his own kind. And at last, travelling south, he picked up with us, the Santa Rosans.

"But I am ahead of my story. When the great exodus from the cities around San Francisco Bay began, and while the telephones were still working, I talked with my brother. I told him this flight from the cities was insanity, that there were no symptoms of the plague in me, and that the thing for us to do was to isolate ourselves and our relatives in some safe place. We decided on the Chemistry Building, at the university, and we planned to lay in a supply of provisions, and by force of arms to prevent any other persons from forcing their presence upon us after we had retired to our refuge.

"All this being arranged, my brother begged me to stay in my own house for at least twenty-four hours more, on the chance of the plague developing in me. To this I agreed, and he promised to come for me next day. We talked on over the details of the provisioning and the defending of the Chemistry Building until the telephone died. It died in the midst of our conversation. That evening there were no electric lights, and I was alone in my house in the darkness. No more newspapers were being printed, so I had no knowledge of what was taking place outside. I heard sounds of rioting and of pistol shots, and from my windows I could see the glare of the sky of some conflagration in the direction of Oakland. It was a night of terror. I did not sleep a wink. A man—why and how I do not know—was killed on the sidewalk in front of the house. I heard the rapid reports of an automatic pistol, and a few minutes later the wounded wretch crawled up to my door, moaning and crying out for help. Arming myself with two automatics, I went to him. By the light of a match I ascertained that while he was dying of the bullet wounds, at the same time the plague was on him. I fled indoors, whence I heard him moan and cry out for half an hour longer.

"In the morning, my brother came to me. I had gathered into a handbag what things of value I purposed taking, but when I saw his face I knew that he would never accompany me to the Chemistry Building. The plague was on him. He intended shaking my hand, but I went back hurriedly before him.

" 'Look at yourself in the mirror,' I commanded.

"He did so, and at sight of his scarlet face, the color deepening as he looked at it, he sank down nervelessly in a chair.

" 'My God!' he said. 'I've got it. Don't come near me. I am a dead man.'

"Then the convulsions seized him. He was two hours in dying, and he was conscious to the last, complaining about the coldness and loss of sensation in his feet, his calves, his thighs, until at last it was his heart and he was dead.

"That was the way the Scarlet Death slew. I caught up my handbag and fled. The sights in the streets were terrible. One stumbled on bodies everywhere. Some were not yet dead. And even as you looked, you saw men sink down with the death fastened upon them. There were numerous fires burning in Berkeley, while Oakland and San Francisco were apparently being swept by vast conflagrations. The smoke of the burning filled the heavens, so that the midday was as a gloomy twilight, and, in the shifts of wind, sometimes the sun shone through dimly, a dull red orb. Truly, my grandsons, it was like the last days of the end of the world.

"There were numerous stalled motor cars, showing that the gasoline and the engine supplies of the garages had given out. I remember one such car. A man and a woman lay back dead in the seats, and on the pavement near it were two more women and a child. Strange and terrible sights there were on every hand.

People slipped by silently, furtively, like ghosts—white-faced women carrying infants in their arms; fathers leading children by the hand; singly, and in couples, and in families—all fleeing out of the city of death. Some carried supplies of food, others blankets and valuables, and there were many who carried nothing.

"There was a grocery store—a place where food was sold. The man to whom it belonged—I knew him well—a quiet, sober, but stupid and obstinate fellow, was defending it. The windows and doors had been broken in, but he, inside, hiding behind a counter, was discharging his pistol at a number of men on the sidewalk who were breaking in. In the entrance were several bodies—of men, I decided, whom he had killed earlier in the day. Even as I looked on from a distance, I saw one of the robbers break the windows of the adjoining store, a place where shoes were sold, and deliberately set fire to it. I did not go to the groceryman's assistance. The time for such acts had already passed. Civilization was crumbling, and it was each for himself."

IV

"I went away hastily, down a cross-street, and at the first corner I saw another tragedy. Two men of the working class had caught a man and a woman with two children, and were robbing them. I knew the man by sight, though I had never been introduced to him. He was a poet whose verses I had long admired. Yet I did not go to his help, for at the moment I came upon the scene there was a pistol shot, and I saw him sinking to the ground. The woman screamed, and she was felled with a fist-blow by one of the brutes. I cried out threateningly, whereupon they discharged their pistols at me and I ran away around the corner. Here I was blocked by an advancing conflagration. The buildings on both sides were burning, and the street was filled with smoke and flame. From somewhere in that murk came a woman's voice calling shrilly for help. But I did not go to her. A man's heart turned to iron amid such scenes, and one heard all too many appeals for help.

"Returning to the corner, I found the two robbers were gone. The poet and his wife lay dead on the pavement. It was a shocking sight. The two children had vanished—whither I could not tell. And I knew, now, why it was that the fleeing persons I encountered slipped along so furtively and with such white faces. In the midst of our civilization, down in our slums and labor-ghettos, we had bred a race of barbarians, of savages; and now, in the time of our calamity, they turned upon us like the wild beasts they were and destroyed us. And they destroyed themselves as well. They inflamed themselves with strong drink and committed a thousand atrocities, quarreling and killing one another in the general madness. One group of workingmen I saw, of the better sort, who had banded together, and, with their women and children in their midst, the sick and aged in litters and being carried, and with a number of horses pulling a truck-load of provisions, they were fighting their way out of the city. They made a fine spectacle as they came down the street through the drifting smoke, though they nearly shot me when I first appeared in their path. As they went by, one of their leaders shouted out to me in apologetic explanation. He said they were killing the robbers and looters on sight, and that they had thus banded together as the only means by which to escape the prowlers.

"It was here that I saw for the first time what I was soon to see so often. One of the marching men had suddenly shown the unmistakable mark of the plague. Immediately those about him drew away, and he, without a remonstrance, stepped out of his place to let them pass on. A woman, most probably his wife, attempted to follow him. She was leading a little boy by the hand. But the husband commanded her sternly to go on, while others laid hands on her and restrained her from following him. This I saw, and I saw the man also, with his scarlet blaze of face, step into a doorway on the opposite side of the street. I heard the report of his pistol, and saw him sink lifeless to the ground.

"After being turned aside twice again by advancing fires, I succeeded in getting through to the university. On the edge of the campus I came upon a party of university folk who were going in the direction of the Chemistry Building. They were all family men, and their families were with them, including the nurses and the servants.

"Professor Badminton greeted me, and I had difficulty in recognizing him. Somewhere he had gone through flames, and his beard was singed off. About his head was a bloody bandage, and his clothes were filthy. He told me he had been cruelly beaten by prowlers, and that his brother had been killed the previous night, in the defence of their dwelling.

"Midway across the campus, he pointed suddenly to Mrs. Swinton's face. The unmistakable scarlet was there. Immediately all the other women set up a screaming and began to run away from her. Her two children were with a nurse, and these also ran with the women. But her husband, Doctor Swinton, remained with her.

" 'Go on, Smith,' he told me. 'Keep an eye on the children. As for me, I shall stay with my wife. I know she is as already dead, but I can't leave her. Afterwards, if I escape, I shall come to the Chemistry Building, and do you watch for me and let me in.'

"I left him bending over his wife and soothing her last moments, while I ran to overtake the party. We were the last to be admitted to the Chemistry Building. After that, with our automatic rifles we maintained our isolation. By our plans, we had arranged for a company of sixty to be in this refuge. Instead, every one of the number originally planned had added relatives and friends and whole families until there were over four hundred souls. But the Chemistry Building was large, and, standing by itself, was in no danger of being burned by the great fires that raged everywhere in the city.

"A large quantity of provisions had been gathered, and a food committee took charge of it, issuing rations daily to the various families and groups that arranged themselves into messes. A number of committees were appointed, and we developed a very efficient organization. I was on the committee of defence, though for the first day no prowlers came near. We could see them in the distance, however, and by the smoke of their fires knew that several camps of them were occupying the far edge of the campus. Drunkenness was rife, and often we heard them singing ribald songs or insanely shouting. While the world crashed to ruin about them and all the air was filled with the smoke of its burning, these low creatures gave rein to their bestiality and fought and drank and died. And after all, what did it matter? Everybody died anyway, the good and the bad, the efficients and the weaklings, those that loved to live and those that scorned to live. They passed. Everything passed.

"When twenty-four hours had gone by and no signs of the plague were apparent, we congratulated ourselves and set about digging a well. You have seen the great iron pipes which in those days carried water to all the city-dwellers. We feared that the fires in the city would burst the pipes and empty the reservoirs. So we tore up the cement floor of the central court of the Chemistry Building and dug a well. There were many young men, undergraduates, with us, and we worked night and day on the well. And our fears were confirmed. Three hours before we reached water, the pipes went dry.

"A second twenty-four hours passed, and still the plague did not appear among us. We thought we were saved. But we did not know what I afterwards decided to be true, namely, that the period of the incubation of the plague germs in a human's body was a matter of a number of days. It slew so swiftly when once it manifested itself, that we were led to believe that the period of incubation was equally swift. So, when two days had left us unscathed, we were elated with the idea that we were free of the contagion.

"But the third day disillusioned us. I can never forget the night preceding it. I had charge of the night guards from eight to twelve, and from the roof of the building I watched the passing of all man's glorious works. So terrible were the local conflagrations that all the sky was lighted up. One could read the finest print in the red glare. All the world seemed wrapped in flames. San Francisco spouted smoke and fire from a score of vast conflagrations that were like so many active volcanoes. Oakland, San Leandro, Haywards—all were burning; and to the northward, clear to Point Richmond, other fires were at work. It was an awe-inspiring spectacle. Civilization, my grandsons, civilization was passing in a sheet of flame and a breath of death. At ten o'clock that night, the great powder magazines at Point Pinole exploded in rapid succession. So terrific were the concussions that the strong building rocked as in an earthquake, while every pane of glass was broken. It was then that I left the roof and went down the long corridors, from room to room, quieting the alarmed women and telling them what had happened.

"An hour later, at a window on the ground floor, I heard pandemonium break out in the camps of the prowlers. There were cries and screams, and shots from many pistols. As we afterward conjectured, this fight had been precipitated by an attempt on the part of those that were well to drive out those that were sick. At any rate, a number of the plague-stricken prowlers escaped across the campus and drifted against our doors. We warned them back, but they cursed us and discharged a fusillade from their pistols. Professor Merryweather, at one of the windows, was instantly killed, the bullet striking him squarely between the eyes. We opened fire in turn, and all the prowlers fled away with the exception of three. One was a woman. The plague was on them and they were reckless. Like foul fiends, there in the red glare from the skies, with faces blazing, they continued to curse us and fire at us. One of the men I shot with my own hand. After that the other man and the woman, still cursing us, lay down under our windows, where we were compelled to watch them die of the plague.

"The situation was critical. The explosions of the powder magazines had broken all the windows of the Chemistry Building, so that we were exposed to the germs from the corpses. The sanitary committee was called upon to act, and it responded nobly. Two men were required to go out and remove the corpses, and this meant the probable sacrifice of their own lives, for, having performed the task, they were not to be permitted to re-enter the building. One of the professors, who was a bachelor, and one of the undergraduates volunteered. They bade good-bye to us and went forth. They were heroes. They gave up their lives that four hundred others might live. After they had performed their work, they stood for a moment, at a distance, looking at us wistfully. Then they waved their hands in farewell and went away slowly across the campus toward the burning city.

"And yet it was all useless. The next morning the first one of us was smitten with the plague—a little nurse-girl in the family of Professor Stout. It was no time for weak-kneed, sentimental policies. On the chance that she might be the only one, we thrust her forth from the building and commanded her to be gone. She went away slowly across the campus, wringing her hands and crying pitifully. We felt like brutes, but what were we to do? There were four hundred of us, and individuals had to be sacrificed.

"In one of the laboratories three families had domiciled themselves, and that afternoon we found among them no less than four corpses and seven cases of the plague in all its different stages.

"Then it was that the horror began. Leaving the dead lie, we forced the living ones to segregate themselves in another room. The plague began to break out among the rest of us, and as fast as the symptoms appeared, we sent the stricken ones to these segregated rooms. We compelled them to walk there by themselves, so as to avoid laying hands on them. It was heartrending. But still the plague raged among us, and room after room was filled with the dead and dying. And so we who were yet clean retreated to the next floor and to the next, before this sea of the dead, that, room by room and floor by floor, inundated the building.

"The place became a charnel house, and in the middle of the night the survivors fled forth, taking nothing with them except arms and ammunition and a heavy store of tinned foods. We camped on the opposite side of the campus from the prowlers, and, while some stood guard, others of us volunteered to scout into the city in quest of horses, motor cars, carts, and wagons, or anything that would carry our provisions and enable us to emulate the banded workingmen I had seen fighting their way out to the open country.

"I was one of these scouts; and Doctor Hoyle, remembering that his motor car had been left behind in his home garage, told me to look for it. We scouted in pairs, and Dombey, a young undergraduate, accompanied me. We had to cross half a mile of the residence portion of the city to get to Doctor Hoyle's home. Here the buildings stood apart, in the midst of trees and grassy lawns, and here the fires had played freaks, burning whole blocks, skipping blocks and often skipping a single house in a block. And here, too, the prowlers were still at their work. We carried our automatic pistols openly in our hands, and looked desperate enough, forsooth, to keep them from attacking us. But at Doctor Hoyle's house the thing happened. Untouched by fire, even as we came to it the smoke of flames burst forth.

"The miscreant who had set fire to it staggered down the steps and out along the driveway. Sticking out of his coat pockets were bottles of whiskey, and he was very drunk. My first impulse was to shoot him, and I have never ceased regretting that I did not. Staggering and maundering to himself, with bloodshot eyes, and a raw and bleeding slash down one side of his bewhiskered face, he was altogether the most nauseating specimen of degradation and filth I had ever encountered. I did not shoot him, and he leaned against a tree on the lawn to let us go by. It was the most absolute, wanton act. Just as we were opposite him, he suddenly drew a pistol and shot Dombey through the head. The next instant I shot him. But it was too late. Dombey expired without a groan, immediately. I doubt if he even knew what had happened to him.

"Leaving the two corpses, I hurried on past the burning house to the garage, and there found Doctor Hoyle's motor car. The tanks were filled with gasoline, and it was ready for use. And it was in this car that I threaded the streets of the ruined city and came back to the survivors on the campus. The other scouts returned, but none had been so fortunate. Professor Fairmead had found a Shetland pony, but the poor creature, tied in a stable and abandoned for days, was so weak from want of food and water that it could carry no burden at all. Some of the men were for turning it loose, but I insisted that we should lead it along with us, so that, if we got out of food, we would have it to eat.

"There were forty-seven of us when we started, many being women and children. The President of the Faculty, an old man to begin with, and now hopelessly broken by the awful happenings of the past week, rode in the motor car with several young children and the aged mother of Professor Fairmead. Wathope, a young professor of English, who had a grievous bullet-wound in his leg, drove the car. The rest of us walked, Professor Fairmead leading the pony.

"It was what should have been a bright summer day, but the smoke from the burning world filled the sky, through which the sun shone murkily, a dull and lifeless orb, blood-red and ominous. But we had grown accustomed to that blood-red sun. With the smoke it was different. It bit into our nostrils and eyes, and there was not one of us whose eyes were not bloodshot. We directed our course to the southeast through the endless miles of suburban residences, travelling along where the first swells of low hills rose from the flat of the central city. It was by this way, only, that we could expect to gain the country.

"Our progress was painfully slow. The women and children could not walk fast. They did not dream of walking, my grandsons, in the way all people walk to-day. In truth, none of us knew how to walk. It was not until after the plague that I learned really to walk. So it was that the pace of the slowest was the pace of all, for we dared not separate on account of the prowlers. There were not so many now of these human beasts of prey. The plague had already well diminished their numbers, but enough still lived to be a constant menace to us. Many of the beautiful residences were untouched by fire, yet smoking ruins were everywhere. The prowlers, too, seemed to have got over their insensate desire to burn, and it was more rarely that we saw houses freshly on fire.

"Several of us scouted among the private garages in search of motor cars and gasoline. But in this we were unsuccessful. The first great flights from the cities had swept all such utilities away. Calgan, a fine young man, was lost in this work. He was shot by prowlers while crossing a lawn. Yet this was our only casualty, though, once, a drunken brute deliberately opened fire on all of us. Luckily, he fired wildly, and we shot him before he had done any hurt.

"At Fruitvale, still in the heart of the magnificent residence section of the city, the plague again smote us. Professor Fairmead was the victim. Making signs to us that his mother was not to know, he turned aside into the grounds of a beautiful mansion. He sat down forlornly on the steps of the front veranda, and I, having lingered, waved him a last farewell. That night, several miles beyond Fruitvale and still in the city, we made camp. And that night we shifted camp twice to get away from our dead. In the morning there were thirty of us. I shall never forget the President of the Faculty. During the morning's march his wife, who was walking, betrayed the fatal symptoms, and when she drew aside to let us go on, he insisted on leaving the motor car and remaining with her. There was quite a discussion about this, but in the end we gave in. It was just as well, for we knew not which ones of us, if any, might ultimately escape.

"That night, the second of our march, we camped beyond Haywards in the first stretches of country. And in the morning there were eleven of us that lived. Also, during the night, Wathope, the professor with the wounded leg, deserted us in the motor car. He took with him his sister and his mother and most of our tinned provisions. It was that day, in the afternoon, while resting by the wayside, that I saw the last airship I shall ever see. The smoke was much thinner here in the country, and I first sighted the ship drifting and veering helplessly at an elevation of two thousand feet. What had happened I could not conjecture, but even as we looked we saw her bow dip down lower and lower. Then the bulkheads of the various gas-chambers must have burst, for, quite perpendicular, she fell like a plummet to the earth. And from that day to this I have not seen another airship. Often and often, during the next few years, I scanned the sky for them, hoping against hope that somewhere in the world civilization had survived. But it was not to be. What happened with us in California must have happened with everybody everywhere.

"Another day, and at Niles there were three of us. Beyond Niles, in the middle of the highway, we found Wathope. The motor car had broken down, and there, on the rugs which they had spread on the ground, lay the bodies of his sister, his mother, and himself.

"Wearied by the unusual exercise of continual walking, that night I slept heavily. In the morning I was alone in the world. Canfield and Parsons, my last companions, were dead of the plague. Of the four hundred that sought shelter in the Chemistry Building, and of the forty-seven that began the march, I alone remained—I and the Shetland pony. Why this should be so there is no explaining. I did not catch the plague, that is all. I was immune. I was merely the one lucky man in a million—just as every survivor was one in a million, or, rather, in several millions, for the proportion was at least that."

V

"For two days I sheltered in a pleasant grove where there had been no deaths. In those two days, while badly depressed and believing that my turn would come at any moment, nevertheless I rested and recuperated. So did the pony. And on the third day, putting what small store of tinned provisions I possessed on the pony's back, I started on across a very lonely land. Not a live man, woman, or child, did I encounter, though the dead were everywhere. Food, however, was abundant. The land then was not as it is now. It was all cleared of trees and brush, and it was cultivated. The food for millions of mouths was growing, ripening, and going to waste. From the fields and orchards I gathered vegetables, fruits, and berries. Around the deserted farmhouses I got eggs and caught chickens. And frequently I found supplies of tinned provisions in the store-rooms.

"A strange thing was what was taking place with all the domestic animals. Everywhere they were going wild and preying on one another. The chickens and ducks were the first to be destroyed, while the pigs were the first to go wild, followed by the cats. Nor were the dogs long in adapting themselves to the changed conditions. There was a veritable plague of dogs. They devoured the corpses, barked and howled during the nights, and in the daytime slunk about in the distance. As the time went by, I noticed a change in their behavior. At first they were apart from one another, very suspicious and very prone to fight.

But after a not very long while they began to come together and run in packs. The dog, you see, always was a social animal, and this was true before ever he came to be domesticated by man. In the last days of the world before the plague, there were many many very different kinds of dogs—dogs without hair and dogs with warm fur, dogs so small that they would make scarcely a mouthful for other dogs that were as large as mountain lions. Well, all the small dogs, and the weak types, were killed by their fellows. Also, the very large ones were not adapted for the wild life and bred out. As a result, the many different kinds of dogs disappeared, and there remained, running in packs, the medium-sized wolfish dogs that you know to-day."

"But the cats don't run in packs, Granser," Hoo-Hoo objected.

"The cat was never a social animal. As one writer in the nineteenth century said, the cat walks by himself. He always walked by himself, from before the time he was tamed by man, down through the long ages of domestication, to today when once more he is wild.

"The horses also went wild, and all the fine breeds we had degenerated into the small mustang horse you know to-day. The cows likewise went wild, as did the pigeons and the sheep. And that a few of the chickens survived you know yourself. But the wild chicken of to-day is quite a different thing from the chickens we had in those days.

"But I must go on with my story. I travelled through a deserted land. As the time went by I began to yearn more and more for human beings. But I never found one, and I grew lonelier and lonelier. I crossed Livermore Valley and the mountains between it and the great valley of the San Joaquin. You have never seen that valley, but it is very large and it is the home of the wild horse. There are great droves there, thousands and tens of thousands. I revisited it thirty years after, so I know. You think there are lots of wild horses down here in the coast valleys, but they are as nothing compared with those of the San Joaquin. Strange to say, the cows, when they went wild, went back into the lower mountains. Evidently they were better able to protect themselves there.

"In the country districts the ghouls and prowlers had been less in evidence, for I found many villages and towns untouched by fire. But they were filled by the pestilential dead, and I passed by without exploring them. It was near Lathrop that, out of my loneliness, I picked up a pair of collie dogs that were so newly free that they were urgently willing to return to their allegiance to man. These collies accompanied me for many years, and the strains of them are in those very dogs there that you boys have to-day. But in sixty years the collie strain has worked out. These brutes are more like domesticated wolves than anything else."

Hare-Lip rose to his feet, glanced to see that the goats were safe, and looked at the sun's position in the afternoon sky, advertising impatience at the prolixity of the old man's tale. Urged to hurry by Edwin, Granser went on.

"There is little more to tell. With my two dogs and my pony, and riding a horse I had managed to capture, I crossed the San Joaquin and went on to a wonderful valley in the Sierras called Yosemite. In the great hotel there I found a prodigious supply of tinned provisions. The pasture was abundant, as was the game, and the river that ran through the valley was full of trout. I remained there three years in an utter loneliness that none but a man who has once been highly civilized can understand. Then I could stand it no more. I felt that I was going crazy. Like the dog, I was a social animal and I needed my kind. I reasoned that since I had survived the plague, there was a possibility that others had survived. Also, I reasoned that after three years the plague germs must all be gone and the land be clean again.

"With my horse and dogs and pony, I set out. Again I crossed the San Joaquin Valley, the mountains beyond, and came down into Livermore Valley. The change in those three years was amazing. All the land had been splendidly tilled, and now I could scarcely recognize it, such was the sea of rank vegetation that had overrun the agricultural handiwork of man. You see, the wheat, the vegetables, and orchard trees had always been cared for and nursed by man, so that they were soft and tender. The weeds and wild bushes and such things, on the contrary, had always been fought by man, so that they were tough and resistant. As a result, when the hand of man was removed, the wild vegetation smothered and destroyed practically all the domesticated vegetation. The coyotes were greatly increased, and it was at this time that I first encountered wolves, straying in twos and threes and small packs down from the regions where they had always persisted.

"It was at Lake Temescal, not far from the one-time city of Oakland, that I came upon the first live human beings. Oh, my grandsons, how can I describe to you my emotion, when, astride my horse and dropping down the hillside to the lake, I saw the smoke of a campfire rising through the trees. Almost did my heart stop beating. I felt that I was going crazy. Then I heard the cry of a babe—a human babe. And dogs barked, and my dogs answered. I did not know but what I was the one human alive in the whole world. It could not be true that here were others—smoke, and the cry of a babe.

"Emerging on the lake, there, before my eyes, not a hundred yards away, I saw a man, a large man. He was standing on an outjutting rock and fishing. I was overcome. I stopped my horse. I tried to call out but could not. I waved my hand. It seemed to me that the man looked at me, but he did not appear to wave. Then I laid my head on my arms there in the saddle. I was afraid to look again, for I knew it was an hallucination, and I knew that if I looked the man would be gone. And so precious was the hallucination, that I wanted it to persist yet a little while. I knew, too, that as long as I did not look it would persist.

"Thus I remained, until I heard my dogs snarling, and a man's voice. What do you think the voice said? I will tell you. It said: '*Where in hell did you come from?*'

"Those were the words, the exact words. That was what your other grandfather said to me, Hare-Lip, when he greeted me there on the shore of Lake Temescal fifty-seven years ago. And they were the most ineffable words I have ever heard. I opened my eyes, and there he stood before me, a large, dark, hairy man, heavy-jawed, slant-browed, fierce-eyed. How I got off my horse I do not know. But it seemed that the next I knew I was clasping his hand with both of mine and crying. I would have embraced him, but he was ever a narrow-minded, suspicious man, and he drew away from me. Yet did I cling to his hand and cry."

Granser's voice faltered and broke at the recollection, and the weak tears streamed down his cheeks while the boys looked on and giggled.

"Yet did I cry," he continued, "and desire to embrace him, though the Chauffeur was a brute, a perfect brute—the most abhorrent man I have ever known. His name was . . . strange, how I have forgotten his name. Everybody called him Chauffeur—it was the name of his occupation, and it stuck. That is how, to this day, the tribe he founded is called the Chauffeur Tribe.

"He was a violent, unjust man. Why the plague germs spared him I can never understand. It would seem, in spite of our old metaphysical notions about absolute justice, that there is no justice in the universe. Why did he live?—an iniquitous, moral monster, a blot on the face of nature, a cruel, relentless, bestial cheat as well. All he could talk about was motor cars, machinery, gasoline, and garages—and especially, and with huge delight, of his mean pilferings and sordid swindlings of the persons who had employed him in the days before the coming of the plague. And yet he was spared, while hundreds of millions, yea, billions, of better men were destroyed.

"I went on with him to his camp, and there I saw her, Vesta, the one woman. It was glorious and . . . pitiful. There she was, Vesta Van Warden, the young wife of John Van Warden, clad in rags, with marred and scarred and toil-calloused hands, bending over the campfire and doing scullion work—she, Vesta, who had been born to the purple of the greatest baronage of wealth the world has ever known. John Van Warden, her husband, worth one billion, eight hundred millions and President of the Board of Industrial Magnates, had been the ruler of America. Also, sitting on the International Board of Control, he had been one of the seven men who ruled the world. And she herself had come of equally noble stock. Her father, Philip Saxon, had been President of the Board of Industrial Magnates up to the time of his death. This office was in process of becoming hereditary, and had Philip Saxon had a son that son would have succeeded him. But his only child was Vesta, the perfect flower of generations of the highest culture this planet has ever produced. It was not until the engagement between Vesta and Van Warden took place, that Saxon indicated the latter as his successor. It was, I am sure, a political marriage. I have reason to believe that Vesta never really loved her husband in the mad passionate way of which the poets used to sing. It was more like the marriages that obtained among crowned heads in the days before they were displaced by the Magnates.

"And there she was, boiling fish-chowder in a soot-covered pot, her glorious eyes inflamed by the acrid smoke of the open fire. Hers was a sad story. She was the one survivor in a million, as I had been, as the Chauffeur had been. On a crowning eminence of the Alameda Hills, overlooking San Francisco Bay, Van Warden had built a vast summer palace. It was surrounded by a park of a thousand acres. When the plague broke out, Van Warden sent her there. Armed guards patrolled the boundaries of the park, and nothing entered in the way of provisions or even mail matter that was not first fumigated. And yet did the plague enter, killing the guards at their posts, the servants at their tasks, sweeping away the whole army of retainers—or, at least, all of them who did not flee to die elsewhere. So it was that Vesta found herself the sole living person in the palace that had become a charnel house.

"Now the Chauffeur had been one of the servants that ran away. Returning, two months afterward, he discovered Vesta in a little summer pavilion where there had been no deaths and where she had established herself. He was a brute. She was afraid, and she ran away and hid among the trees. That night, on foot, she fled into the mountains—she, whose tender feet and delicate body had never known the bruise of stones nor the scratch of briars. He followed, and that night he caught her. He struck her. Do you understand? He beat her with those terrible fists of his and made her his slave. It was she who had to gather the firewood, build the fires, cook, and do all the degrading camp-labor—she, who had never performed a menial act in her life. These things he compelled her to do, while he, a proper savage, elected to lie around camp and look on. He did nothing, absolutely nothing, except on occasion to hunt meat or catch fish."

"Good for Chauffeur," Hare-Lip commented in an undertone to the other boys. "I remember him before he died. He was a corker. But he did things, and he made things go. You know, Dad married his daughter, an' you ought to see the way he knocked the spots outa Dad. The Chauffeur was a son-of-a-gun. He made us kids stand around. Even when he was croakin', he reached out for me, once, an' laid my head open with that long stick he kept always beside him."

Hare-Lip rubbed his bullet head reminiscently, and the boys returned to the old man, who was maundering ecstatically about Vesta, the squaw of the founder of the Chauffeur Tribe.

"And so I say to you that you cannot understand the awfulness of the situation. The Chauffeur was a servant, understand, a servant. And he cringed, with bowed head, to such as she. She was a lord of life, both by birth and by marriage. The destinies of millions, such as he, she carried in the hollow of her pink-white hand. And, in the days before the plague, the slightest contact with such as he would have been pollution. Oh, I have seen it. Once, I remember, there was Mrs. Goldwin, wife of one of the great magnates. It was on a landing stage, just as she was embarking in her private dirigible, that she dropped her parasol. A servant picked it up and made the mistake of handing it to her—to her, one of the greatest royal ladies of the land! She shrank back, as though he were a leper, and indicated her secretary to receive it. Also, she ordered her secretary to ascertain the creature's name and to see that he was immediately discharged from service. And such a woman was Vesta Van Warden. And her the Chauffeur beat and made his slave.

"—Bill—that was it; Bill, the Chauffeur. That was his name. He was a wretched, primitive man, wholly devoid of the finer instincts and chivalrous promptings of a cultured soul. No, there is no absolute justice, for to him fell that wonder of womanhood, Vesta Van Warden. The grievousness of this you will never understand, my grandsons; for you are yourselves primitive little savages, unaware of aught else but savagery. Why should Vesta not have been mine? I was a man of culture and refinement, a professor in a great university. Even so, in the time before the plague, such was her exalted position, she would not have deigned to know that I existed. Mark, then, the abysmal degradation to which she fell at the hands of the Chauffeur. Nothing less than the destruction of all mankind had made it possible that I should know her, look in her eyes, converse with her, touch her hand—ay, and love her and know that her feelings toward me were very kindly. I have reason to believe that she, even she, would have loved me, there being no other man in the world except the Chauffeur. Why, when it destroyed eight billions of souls, did not the plague destroy just one more man, and that man the Chauffeur?

"Once, when the Chauffeur was away fishing, she begged me to kill him. With tears in her eyes she begged me to kill him. But he was a strong and violent man, and I was afraid. Afterwards, I talked with him. I offered him my horse, my pony, my dogs, all that I possessed, if he would give Vesta to me. And he grinned in my face and shook his head. He was very insulting. He said that in the old days he had been a servant, had been dirt under the feet of men like me and of women like Vesta, and that now he had the greatest lady in the land to be servant to him and cook his food and nurse his brats. 'You had your day before the plague,' he said; 'but this is my day, and a damned good day it is. I wouldn't trade back to the old times for anything.' Such words he spoke, but they are not his words. He was a vulgar, low-minded man, and vile oaths fell continually from his lips.

"Also, he told me that if he caught me making eyes at his woman he'd wring my neck and give her a beating as well. What was I to do? I was afraid. He was a brute. That first night, when I discovered the camp, Vesta and I had great talk about the things of our vanished world. We talked of art, and books, and poetry; and the Chauffeur listened and grinned and sneered. He was bored and angered by our way of speech which he did not comprehend, and finally he spoke up and said: 'And this is Vesta Van Warden, one-time wife of Van Warden the Magnate—a high and stuck-up beauty, who is now my squaw. Eh, Professor Smith, times is changed, times is changed. Here, you, woman, take off my moccasins, and lively about it. I want Professor Smith to see how well I have you trained.'

"I saw her clench her teeth, and the flame of revolt rise in her face. He drew back his gnarled fist to strike, and I was afraid, and sick at heart. I could do nothing to prevail against him. So I got up to go, and not be witness to such indignity. But the Chauffeur laughed and threatened me with a beating if I did not stay and behold. And I sat there, perforce, by the campfire on the shore of Lake Temescal, and saw Vesta, Vesta Van Warden, kneel and remove the moccasins of that grinning, hairy, apelike human brute.

"—Oh, you do not understand, my grandsons. You have never known anything else, and you do not understand.

" 'Halter-broke and bridle-wise,' the Chauffeur gloated, while she performed that dreadful, menial task. 'A trifle balky at times, Professor, a trifle balky; but a clout alongside the jaw makes her as meek and gentle as a lamb.'

"And another time he said: 'We've got to start all over and replenish the earth and multiply. You're handicapped, Professor. You ain't got no wife, and we're up against a regular Garden-of-Eden proposition. But I ain't proud. I'll tell you what, Professor.' He pointed at their little infant, barely a year old. 'There's your wife, though you'll have to wait till she grows up. It's rich, ain't it? We're all equals here, and I'm the biggest toad in the splash. But I ain't stuck up—not I. I do you the honor, Professor Smith, the very great honor of betrothing to you my and Vesta Van Warden's daughter. Ain't it cussed bad that Van Warden ain't here to see?' "

VI

"I lived three weeks of infinite torment there in the Chauffeur's camp. And then, one day, tiring of me, or of what to him was my bad effect on Vesta, he told me that the year before, wandering through the Contra Costa Hills to the Straits of Carquinez, across the Straits he had seen a smoke. This meant that there were still other human beings, and that for three weeks he had kept this inestimably precious information from me. I departed at once, with my dogs and horses, and journeyed across the Contra Costa Hills to the Straits. I saw no smoke on the other side, but at Port Costa discovered a small steel barge on which I was able to embark my animals. Old canvas which I found served me for a sail, and a southerly breeze fanned me across the Straits and up to the ruins of Vallejo. Here, on the outskirts of the city, I found evidences of a recently occupied camp. Many clam-shells showed me why these humans had come to the shores of the Bay. This was the Santa Rosa Tribe, and I followed its track along the old railroad right of way across the salt marshes to Sonoma Valley.

Here, at the old brickyard at Glen Ellen, I came upon the camp. There were eighteen souls all told. Two were old men, one of whom was Jones, a banker. The other was Harrison, a retired pawnbroker, who had taken for wife the matron of the State Hospital for the Insane at Napa. Of all the persons of the city of Napa, and of all the other towns and villages in that rich and populous valley, she had been the only survivor. Next, there were the three young men—Cardiff and Hale, who had been farmers, and Wainwright, a common day-laborer. All three had found wives. To Hale, a crude, illiterate farmer, had fallen Isadore, the greatest prize, next to Vesta, of the women who came through the plague. She was one of the world's most noted singers, and the plague had caught her at San Francisco. She has talked with me for hours at a time, telling me of her adventures, until, at last, rescued by Hale in the Mendocino Forest Reserve, there had remained nothing for her to do but become his wife. But Hale was a good fellow, in spite of his illiteracy. He had a keen sense of justice and right-dealing, and she was far happier with him than was Vesta with the Chauffeur.

"The wives of Cardiff and Wainwright were ordinary women, accustomed to toil with strong constitutions—just the type for the wild new life which they were compelled to live. In addition were two adult idiots from the feeble-minded home at Eldredge, and five or six young children and infants born after the formation of the Santa Rosa Tribe. Also, there was Bertha. She was a good woman, Hare-Lip, in spite of the sneers of your father. Her I took for wife. She was the mother of your father, Edwin, and of yours, Hoo-Hoo. And it was our daughter, Vera, who married your father, Hare-Lip—your father, Sandow, who was the oldest son of Vesta Van Warden and the Chauffeur.

"And so it was that I became the nineteenth member of the Santa Rosa Tribe. There were only two outsiders added after me. One was Mungerson, descended from the Magnates, who wandered alone in the wilds of Northern California for eight years before he came south and joined us. He it was who waited twelve years more before he married my daughter, Mary. The other was Johnson, the man who founded the Utah Tribe. That was where he came from, Utah, a country that lies very far away from here, across the great deserts, to the east. It was not until twenty-seven years after the plague that Johnson reached California. In all that Utah region he reported but three survivors, himself one, and all men. For many years these three men lived and hunted together, until, at last, desperate, fearing that with them the human race would perish utterly from the planet, they headed westward on the possibility of finding women survivors in California. Johnson alone came through the great desert, where his two companions died. He was forty-six years old when he joined us, and he married the fourth daughter of Isadore and Hale, and his eldest son married your aunt, Hare-Lip, who was the third daughter of Vesta and the Chauffeur. Johnson was a strong man, with a will of his own. And it was because of this that he seceded from the Santa Rosans and formed the Utah Tribe at San José. It is a small tribe—there are only nine in it—but, though he is dead, such was his influence and the strength of his breed, that it will grow into a strong tribe and play a leading part in the recivilization of the planet.

"There are only two other tribes that we know of—the Los Angelitos and the Carmelitos. The latter started from one man and woman. He was called Lopez, and he was descended from the ancient Mexicans and was very black. He was a cowherd in the ranges beyond Carmel, and his wife was a maidservant in the great Del Monte Hotel. It was seven years before we first got in touch with the Los Angelitos. They have a good country down there, but it is too warm. I estimate the present population of the world at between three hundred and fifty and four hundred—provided, of course, that there are no scattered little tribes elsewhere in the world. If there be such, we have not heard from them. Since Johnson crossed the desert from Utah, no word nor sign has come from the East or anywhere else. The great world which I knew in my boyhood and early manhood is gone. It has ceased to be. I am the last man who was alive in the days of the plague and who knows the wonders of that far-off time. We, who mastered the planet—its earth, and sea, and sky—and who were as very gods, now live in primitive savagery along the water courses of this California country.

"But we are increasing rapidly—your sister, Hare-Lip, already has four children. We are increasing rapidly and making ready for a new climb toward civilization. In time, pressure of population will compel us to spread out, and a hundred generations from now we may expect our descendants to start across the Sierras, oozing slowly along, generation by generation, over the great continent to the colonization of the East—a new Aryan drift around the world.

"But it will be slow, very slow; we have so far to climb. We fell so hopelessly far. If only one physicist or one chemist had survived! But it was not to be, and we have forgotten everything. The Chauffeur started working in iron. He made the forge which we use to this day. But he was a lazy man, and when he died he took with him all he knew of metals and machinery. What was I to know of such things? I was a classical scholar, not a chemist. The other men who survived were not educated. Only two things did the Chauffeur accomplish—the brewing of strong drink and the growing of tobacco. It was while he was drunk, once, that he killed Vesta. I firmly believe that he killed Vesta in a fit of drunken cruelty though he always maintained that she fell into the lake and was drowned.

"And, my grandsons, let me warn you against the medicine-men. They call themselves *doctors*, travestying what was once a noble profession, but in reality they are medicine-men, devil-devil men, and they make for superstition and darkness. They are cheats and liars. But so debased and degraded are we, that we believe their lies. They, too, will increase in numbers as we increase, and they will strive to rule us. Yet are they liars and charlatans. Look at young Cross-Eyes, posing as a doctor, selling charms against sickness, giving good hunting, exchanging promises of fair weather for good meat and skins, sending the death-stick, performing a thousand abominations. Yet I say to you, that when he says he can do these things, he lies. I, Professor Smith, Professor James Howard Smith, say that he lies. I have told him so to his teeth. Why has he not sent me the death-stick? Because he knows that with me it is without avail. But you, Hare-Lip, so deeply are you sunk in black superstition that did you awake this night and find the death-stick beside you, you would surely die. And you would die, not because of any virtues in the stick, but because you are a savage with the dark and clouded mind of a savage.

"The doctors must be destroyed, and all that was lost must be discovered over again. Wherefore, earnestly, I repeat unto you certain things which you must remember and tell to your children after you. You must tell them that when water is made hot by fire, there resides in it a wonderful thing called steam, which is stronger than ten thousand men and which can do all man's work for him. There are other very useful things. In the lightning flash resides a similarly strong servant of man, which was of old his slave and which some day will be his slave again.

"Quite a different thing is the alphabet. It is what enables me to know the meaning of fine markings, whereas you boys know only rude picture-writing. In that dry cave on Telegraph Hill, where you see me often go when the tribe is down by the sea, I have stored many books. In them is great wisdom. Also, with them, I have placed a key to the alphabet, so that one who knows picture-writing may also know print. Some day men will read again; and then, if no accident has befallen my cave, they will know that Professor James Howard Smith once lived and saved for them the knowledge of the ancients.

"There is another little device that men inevitably will rediscover. It is called gunpowder. It was what enabled us to kill surely and at long distances. Certain things which are found in the ground, when combined in the right proportions, will make this gunpowder. What these things are, I have forgotten, or else I never knew. But I wish I did know. Then would I make powder, and then would I certainly kill Cross-Eyes and rid the land of superstition—"

"After I am man-grown I am going to give Cross-Eyes all the goats, and meat, and skins I can get, so that he'll teach me to be a doctor," Hoo-Hoo asserted. "And when I know, I'll make everybody else sit up and take notice. They'll get down in the dirt to me, you bet."

The old man nodded his head solemnly, and murmured:

"Strange it is to hear the vestiges and remnants of the complicated Aryan speech falling from the lips of a filthy little skin-clad savage. All the world is topsy-turvy. And it has been topsy-turvy ever since the plague."

"You won't make me sit up," Hare-Lip boasted to the would-be medicine-man. "If I paid you for a sending of the death-stick and it didn't work, I'd bust in your head—understand, you Hoo-Hoo, you?"

"I'm going to get Granser to remember this here gunpowder stuff," Edwin said softly, "and then I'll have you all on the run. You, Hare-Lip, will do my fighting for me and get my meat for me, and you, Hoo-Hoo, will send the death-stick for me and make everybody afraid. And if I catch Hare-Lip trying to bust your head, Hoo-Hoo, I'll fix him with that same gunpowder. Granser ain't such a fool as you think, and I'm going to listen to him and some day I'll be boss over the whole bunch of you."

The old man shook his head sadly, and said:

"The gunpowder will come. Nothing can stop it—the same old story over and over. Man will increase, and men will fight. The gunpowder will enable men to kill millions of men, and in this way only, by fire and blood, will a new civilization, in some remote day, be evolved. And of what profit will it be? Just as the old civilization passed, so will the new. It may take fifty thousand years to build, but it will pass. All things pass. Only remain cosmic force and matter, ever in flux, ever acting and reacting and realizing the eternal types—the priest, the soldier, and the king. Out of the mouths of babes comes the wisdom of all the ages. Some will fight, some will rule, some will pray; and all the rest will toil and suffer sore while on their bleeding carcasses is reared again, and yet again, without end, the amazing beauty and surpassing wonder of the civilized state. It were just as well that I destroyed those cave-stored books—whether they remain or perish, all their old truths will be discovered, their old lies lived and handed down. What is the profit—"

Hare-Lip leaped to his feet, giving a quick glance at the pasturing goats and the afternoon sun.

"Gee!" he muttered to Edwin. "The old geezer gets more long-winded every day. Let's pull for camp."

While the other two, aided by the dogs, assembled the goats and started them for the trail through the forest, Edwin stayed by the old man and guided him in the same direction. When they reached the old right of way, Edwin stopped suddenly and looked back. Hare-Lip and Hoo-Hoo and the dogs and the goats passed on. Edwin was looking at a small herd of wild horses which had come down on the hard sand. There were at least twenty of them, young colts and yearlings and mares, led by a beautiful stallion which stood in the foam at the edge of the surf, with arched neck and bright wild eyes, sniffing the salt air from off the sea.

"What is it?" Granser queried.

"Horses," was the answer. "First time I ever seen 'em on the beach. It's the mountain lions getting thicker and thicker and driving 'em down."

The low sun shot red shafts of light, fan-shaped, up from a cloud-tumbled horizon. And close at hand, in the white waste of shore-lashed waters, the sea-lions, bellowing their old primeval chant, hauled up out of the sea on the black rocks and fought and loved.

"Come on, Granser," Edwin prompted.

And old man and boy, skin-clad and barbaric, turned and went along the right of way into the forest in the wake of the goats.

Cordwainer Smith

Cordwainer Smith was the pseudonym of Paul M. A. Linebarger (1913–66), who wrote the first text on psychological warfare and was involved in sensitive government work while a professor of Asiatic politics from 1946 to 1966 in Washington, D.C. His pseudonym was kept a close secret during his lifetime. He went to college with L. Ron Hubbard, the famous pulp SF writer who invented Dianetics (later Scientology), and they published in the same literary magazine. There was apparently some real competitiveness in Linebarger, for he wrote an entire book manuscript (never published) in the late 1940s, at the same time his first SF story was published, on the science of mental health.

His science fiction was nearly all published between 1959 and 1963, and first collected in paperback between 1963 and 1968, then reassembled in 1975 and reissued, at which time serious interest in Smith began to grow. He is now considered a major figure in science fiction. Nearly all of Smith's science fiction takes place in a consistent future history, The Instrumentality of Mankind, comprising many stories (*The Rediscovery of Man* [1993] collects his complete short fiction) and one novel, *Norstrilia* (1975). The series chronicles events in the millennia-long struggle between the human Instrumentality and the Underpeople, intelligent animals biologically transformed into humanlike forms. A devout Christian, Smith built complex levels of religious allegory into his series.

The title of "Drunkboat" is an allusion to Arthur Rimbaud. It is a work that shows Cordwainer Smith's distinctive and unusual voice in science fiction.

DRUNKBOAT

Perhaps it is the saddest, maddest, wildest story in the whole long history of space. It is true that no one else had ever done anything like it before, to travel at such a distance, and at such speeds, and by such means. The hero looked like such an ordinary man—when people looked at him for the first time. The second time, ah! that was different.

And the heroine. Small she was, and ash-blonde, intelligent, perky, and hurt. Hurt—yes, that's the right word. She looked as though she needed comforting or helping, even when she was perfectly all right. Men felt more like men when she was near. Her name was Elizabeth.

Who would have thought that her name would ring loud and clear in the wild vomiting nothing which made up $space_3$?

He took an old, old rocket, of an ancient design. With it he outflew, outfled, outjumped all the machines which had ever existed before. You might almost think that he went so fast that he shocked the great vaults of the sky, so that the ancient poem might have been written for him alone. "All the stars threw down their spears and watered heaven with their tears."

Go he did, so fast, so far that people simply did not believe it at first. They thought it was a joke told by men, a farce spun forth by rumor, a wild story to while away the summer afternoon.

We know his name now.

And our children and their children will know it for always.

Rambo. Artyr Rambo of Earth Four.

But he followed his Elizabeth where no space was. He went where men could not go, had not been, did not dare, would not think.

He did all this of his own free will.

Of course people thought it was a joke at first, and got to making up silly songs about the reported trip.

"Dig me a hole for that reeling feeling . . . !" sang one.

"Push me the call for the umber number . . . !" sang another.

"Where is the ship of the ochre joker . . . ?" sang a third.

Then people everywhere found it was true. Some stood stock still and got gooseflesh. Others turned quickly to everyday things. Space$_3$ had been found, and it had been pierced. Their world would never be the same again. The solid rock had become an open door.

Space itself, so clean, so empty, so tidy, now looked like a million million light-years of tapioca pudding—gummy, mushy, sticky, not fit to breathe, not fit to swim in.

How did it happen?

Everybody took the credit, each in his own different way.

"He came for me," said Elizabeth. "I died and he came for me because the machines were making a mess of my life when they tried to heal my terrible, useless death."

"I went myself," said Rambo. "They tricked me and lied to me and fooled me, but I took the boat and I became the boat and I got there. Nobody made me do it. I was angry, but I went. And I came back, didn't I?"

He too was right, even when he twisted and whined on the green grass of earth, his ship lost in a space so terribly far and strange that it might have been beneath his living hand, or might have been half a galaxy away.

How can anybody tell, with space$_3$?

It was Rambo who got back, looking for his Elizabeth. He loved her. So the trip was his, and the credit his.

But the Lord Crudelta said, many years later, when he spoke in a soft voice and talked confidentially among friends, "The experiment was mine. I designed it, I picked Rambo. I drove the selectors mad, trying to find a man who would meet those specifications. And I had that rocket built to the old, old plans. It was the sort of thing which human beings first used when they jumped out of the air a little bit, leaping like flying fish from one wave to the next and already thinking that they were eagles. If I had used one of the regular planoform ships, it would have disappeared with a sort of reverse gurgle, leaving space milky for a little bit while it faded into nastiness and obliteration. But I did not risk that. I put the rocket on a launching pad. *And the launching pad itself was an interstellar ship!* Since we were using an ancient rocket, we did it up right, with the old, old writing, mysterious letters printed all over the machine. We even had the name of our Organization—I and O and M—for 'the Instrumentality of Mankind' written on it good and sharp.

"How would I know," went on the Lord Crudelta, "that we would succeed more than we wanted to succeed, that Rambo would tear space itself loose from its hinges and leave that ship behind, just because he loved Elizabeth so sharply much, so fiercely much?"

Crudelta sighed.

"I know it and I don't know it. I'm like that ancient man who tried to take a water boat the wrong way around the planet Earth and found a new world instead. Columbus, he was called. And the land, that was Australia or America or something like that. That's what I did. I sent Rambo out in that ancient rocket and he found a way through $space_3$. Now none of us will ever know who might come bulking through the floor or take shape out of the air in front of us."

Crudelta added, almost wistfully: "What's the use of telling the story? Everybody knows it, anyhow. My part in it isn't very glorious. Now the end of it, that's pretty. The bungalow by the waterfall and all the wonderful children that other people gave to them, you could write a poem about that. But the next to the end, how he showed up at the hospital helpless and insane, looking for his own Elizabeth. That was sad and eerie, that was frightening. I'm glad it all came to the happy ending with the bungalow by the waterfall, but it took a crashing long time to get there. And there are parts of it that we will never quite understand, the naked skin against naked space, the eyeballs riding something much faster than light ever was. Do you know what an *aoudad* is? It's an ancient sheep that used to live on Old Earth, and here we are, thousands of years later, with a children's nonsense rhyme about it. The animals are gone but the rhyme remains. It'll be like that with Rambo someday. Everybody will know his name and all about his drunkboat, but they will forget the scientific milestone that he crossed, hunting for Elizabeth in an ancient rocket that couldn't fly from peetle to pootle. . . . Oh, the rhyme? Don't you know that? It's a silly thing. It goes,

> " '*Point your gun at a murky lurky.*
> (Now you're talking ham or turkey!)
> *Shoot a shot at a dying aoudad.*
> (Don't ask the lady why or how, dad!)'

"Don't ask me what 'ham' and 'turkey' are. Probably parts of ancient animals, like beefsteak or sirloin. But the children still say the words. They'll do that with Rambo and his drunken boat some day. They may even tell the story of Elizabeth. But they will never tell the part about how he got to the hospital. That part is too terrible, too real, too sad and wonderful at the end. They found him on the grass. Mind you, naked on the grass, and nobody knew where he had come from!"

They found him naked on the grass and nobody knew where he had come from. They did not even know about the ancient rocket which the Lord Crudelta had sent beyond the end of nowhere with the letters I, O and M written on it. They did not know that this was Rambo, who had gone through $space_3$. The robots noticed him first and brought him in, photographing everything that they did.

They had been programmed that way, to make sure that anything unusual was kept in the records.

Then the nurses found him in an outside room.

They assumed that he was alive, since he was not dead, but they could not prove that he was alive, either.

That heightened the pubzzle.

The doctors were called in. Real doctors, not machines. They were very important men. Citizen Doctor Timofeyev, Citizen Doctor Grosbeck and the director himself, Sir and Doctor Vomact. They took the case.

(Over on the other side of the hospital Elizabeth waited, unconscious, and nobody knew it at all. Elizabeth, for whom he had jumped space, and pierced the stars, but nobody knew it yet!)

The young man could not speak. When they ran eye-prints and fingerprints through the Population Machine, they found that he had been bred on Earth itself, but had been shipped out as a frozen and unborn baby to Earth Four. At tremendous cost, they queried Earth Four with an "instant message," only to discover that the young man who lay before them in the hospital had been lost from an experimental ship on an intergalactic trip.

Lost.

No ship and no sign of ship.

And here he was.

They stood at the edge of space, and did not know what they were looking at. They were doctors and it was their business to repair or rebuild people, not to ship them around. How should such men know about space$_3$ when they did not even know about space$_2$, except for the fact that people got on the planoform ships and made trips through it? They were looking for sickness when their eyes saw engineering. They treated him when he was well.

All he needed was time, to get over the shock of the most tremendous trip ever made by a human being, but the doctors did not know that and they tried to rush his recovery.

When they put clothes on him, he moved from coma to a kind of mechanical spasm and tore the clothing off. Once again stripped, he lay himself roughly on the floor and refused food or speech.

They fed him with needles while the whole energy of space, had they only known it, was radiating out of his body in new forms.

They put him all by himself in a locked room and watched him through the peephole.

He was a nice-looking young man, even though his mind was blank and his body was rigid and unconscious. His hair was very fair and his eyes were light blue but his face showed character—a square chin; a handsome, resolute sullen mouth; old lines in the face which looked as though, when conscious, he must have lived many days or months on the edge of rage.

When they studied him the third day in the hospital, their patient had not changed at all.

He had torn off his pajamas again and lay naked, face down, on the floor.

His body was as immobile and tense as it had been on the day before.

(One year later, this room was going to be a museum with a bronze sign reading, "Here lay Rambo after he left the Old Rocket for space$_3$," but the doctors still had no idea of what they were dealing with.)

His face was turned so sharply to the left that the neck muscles showed. His right arm stuck out straight from the body. The left arm formed an exact right angle from the body, with the left forearm and hand pointing rigidly upward at 90° from the upper arm. The legs were in the grotesque parody of a running position.

Doctor Grosbeck said, "It looks to me like he's swimming. Let's drop him in a tank of water and see if he moves." Grosbeck sometimes went in for drastic solutions to problems.

Timofeyev took his place at the peephole. "Spasm, still," he murmured. "I hope the poor fellow is not feeling pain when his cortical defenses are down. How can a man fight pain if he does not even know what he is experiencing?"

"And you, sir and doctor," said Grosbeck to Vomact, "what do you see?"

Vomact did not need to look. He had come early and had looked long and quietly at the patient through the peephole before the other doctors arrived. Vomact was a wise man, with good insight and rich intuitions. He could guess in an hour more than a machine could diagnose in a year; he was already beginning to understand that this was a sickness which no man had ever had before. Still, there were remedies waiting.

The three doctors tried them.

They tried hypnosis, electrotherapy, massage, subsonics, atropine, surgital, a whole family of the digitalinids, and some quasi-narcotic viruses which had been grown in orbit where they mutated fast. They got the beginning of a response when they tried gas hypnosis combined with an electronically amplied telepath; this showed that something still went on inside the patient's mind. Otherwise the brain might have seemed to be mere fatty tissue, without a nerve in it. The other attempts had shown nothing. The gas showed a faint stirring away from fear and pain. The telepath reported glimpses of unknown skies. (The doctors turned the telepath over to the Space Police promptly, so they could try to code the star patterns which he had seen in a patient's mind, but the patterns did not fit. The telepath, though a keen-witted man, could not remember them in enough detail for them to be scanned against the samples of piloting sheets.)

The doctors went back to their drugs and tried ancient, simple remedies—morphine and caffeine to counteract each other, and a rough massage to make him dream again, so that the telepath could pick it up.

There was no further result that day, or the next.

Meanwhile the Earth authorities were getting restless. They thought, quite rightly, that the hospital had done a good job of proving that the patient had not been on Earth until a few moments before the robots found him on the grass. How had he gotten on the grass?

The airspace of Earth reported no intrusion at all, no vehicle marking a blazing arc of air incandescing against metal, no whisper of the great forces which drove a planoform ship through $space_2$.

(Crudelta, using faster-than-light ships, was creeping slow as a snail back toward Earth, racing his best to see if Rambo had gotten there first.)

On the fifth day, there was the beginning of a breakthrough.

Elizabeth had passed.

This was found out only much later, by a careful check of the hospital records.

The doctors only knew this much: Patients had been moved down the corridor, sheet-covered figures immobile on wheeled beds.

Suddenly the beds stopped rolling.

A nurse screamed.

The heavy steel-and-plastic wall was bending inward. Some slow, silent force was pushing the wall into the corridor itself.

The wall ripped.

A human hand emerged.

One of the quick-witted nurses screamed, "*Push* those beds! *Push* them out of the way."

The nurses and robots obeyed.

The beds rocked like a group of boats crossing a wave when they came to the place where the floor, bonded to the wall, had bent upward to meet the wall as it tore inward. The peace-colored glow of the lights flicked. Robots appeared.

A second human hand came through the wall. Pushing in opposite directions, the hands tore the wall as though it had been wet paper.

The patient from the grass put his head through.

He looked blindly up and down the corridor, his eyes not quite focusing, his skin glowing a strange red-brown from the burns of open space.

"No," he said. Just that one word.

But that "No" was heard. Though the volume was not loud, it carried throughout the hospital. The internal telecommunications system relayed it. Every switch in the place went negative. Frantic nurses and robots, with even the doctors helping them, rushed to turn all the machines back on—the pumps, the ventilators, the artificial kidneys, the brain re-recorders, even the simple air engines which kept the atmosphere clean.

Far overhead an aircraft spun giddily. Its "off" switch, surrounded by triple safeguards, had suddenly been thrown into the negative position. Fortunately the robot-pilot got it going again before crashing into Earth.

The patient did not seem to know that his word had this effect.

(Later the world knew that this was part of the "drunkboat effect." The man himself had developed the capacity for using his neurophysical system as a machine control.)

In the corridor, the machine robot who served as policeman arrived. He wore sterile, padded velvet gloves with a grip of sixty metric tons inside his hands. He approached the patient. The robot had been carefully trained to recognize all kinds of danger from delirious or psychotic humans; later he reported that he had an input of "danger, extreme" on every band of sensation. He had been expecting to seize the prisoner with irreversible firmness and to return him to his bed, but with this kind of danger sizzling in the air, the robot took no chances. His wrist itself contained a hypodermic pistol which operated on compressed argon.

He reached out toward the unknown, naked man who stood in the big torn gap of the wall. The wrist-weapon hissed and a sizeable injection of condamine, the most powerful narcotic in the known universe, spat its way through the skin of Rambo's neck. The patient collapsed.

The robot picked him up gently and tenderly, lifted him through the torn wall, pushed the door open with a kick which broke the lock and put the patient back on his bed. The robot could hear doctors coming, so he used his enormous hands to pat the steel wall back into its proper shape. Work-robots or underpeople could finish the job later, but meanwhile it looked better to have that part of the building set at right angles again.

Doctor Vomact arrived, followed closely by Grosbeck.

"What happened?" he yelled, shaken out of a lifelong calm. The robot pointed at the ripped wall.

"He tore it open. I put it back," said the robot.

The doctors turned to look at the patient. He had crawled off his bed again and was on the floor, but his breathing was light and natural.

"What did you give him?" cried Vomact to the robot.

"Condamine," said the robot, "according to rule 47-B. The drug is not to be mentioned outside the hospital."

"I know that," said Vomact absentmindedly and a little crossly. "You can go along now. Thank you."

"It is not usual to thank robots," said the robot, "but you can read a commendation into my record if you want to."

"Get the blazes out of here!" shouted Vomact at the officious robot.

The robot blinked. "There are no blazes but I have the impression you mean me. I shall leave, with your permission." He jumped with odd gracefulness around the two doctors, fingered the broken doorlock absentmindedly, as though he might have wished to repair it; and then, seeing Vomact glare at him, left the room completely.

A moment later soft muted thuds began. Both doctors listened a moment and then gave up. The robot was out in the corridor, gently patting the steel floor back into shape. He was a tidy robot, probably animated by an amplified chicken-brain, and when he got tidy he became obstinate.

"Two questions, Grosbeck," said the sir and doctor Vomact.

"Your service, sir!"

"Where was the patient standing when he pushed the wall into the corridor, and how did he get the leverage to do it?"

Grosbeck narrowed his eyes in puzzlement. "Now that you mention it, I have no idea of how he did it. In fact, he could not have done it. But he has. And the other question?"

"What do you think of condamine?"

"Dangerous, of course, as always. Addiction can—"

"Can you have addiction with no cortical activity?" interrupted Vomact.

"Of course," said Grosbeck promptly. "Tissue addiction."

"Look for it, then," said Vomact.

Grosbeck knelt beside the patient and felt with his fingertips for the muscle endings. He felt where they knotted themselves into the base of the skull, the tips of the shoulders, the striped area of the back.

When he stood up there was a look of puzzlement on his face. "I never felt a human body like this one before. I am not even sure that it *is* human any longer."

Vomact said nothing. The two doctors confronted one another. Grosbeck fidgeted under the calm stare of the senior man. Finally he blurted out,

"Sir and doctor, I know what we *could* do."

"And that," said Vomact levelly, without the faintest hint of encouragement or of warning, "is what?"

"It wouldn't be the first time that it's been done in a hospital."

"What?" said Vomact, his eyes—those dreaded eyes!—making Grosbeck say what he did not want to say.

Grosbeck flushed. He leaned toward Vomact so as to whisper, even though there was no one standing near them. His words, when they came, had the hasty indecency of a lover's improper suggestion:

"Kill the patient, sir and doctor. Kill him. We have plenty of records of him.

We can get a cadaver out of the basement and make it into a good simulacrum. Who knows what we will turn loose among mankind if we let him get well?"

"Who knows?" said Vomact without tone or quality to his voice. "But citizen and doctor, what is the twelfth duty of a physician?"

" 'Not to take the law into his own hands, keeping healing for the healers and giving to the state or the Instrumentality whatever properly belongs to the state or the Instrumentality.' " Grosbeck sighed as he retracted his own suggestion. "Sir and doctor, I take it back. It wasn't medicine which I was talking about. It was government and politics which were really in my mind."

"And now . . . ?" asked Vomact.

"Heal him, or let him be until he heals himself."

"And which would you do?"

"I'd try to heal him."

"How?" said Vomact.

"Sir and doctor," cried Grosbeck, "do not ride my weaknesses in this case! I know that you like me because I am a bold, confident sort of man. Do not ask me to be myself when we do not even know where this body came from. If I were bold as usual, I would give him typhoid and condamine, stationing telepaths nearby. But this is something new in the history of man. We are people and perhaps he is not a person any more. Perhaps he represents the combination of people with some kind of a new force. How did he get here from the far side of nowhere? How many million times has he been enlarged or reduced? We do not know what he is or what has happened to him. How can we treat a man when we are treating the cold of space, the heat of suns, the frigidity of distance? We know what to do with flesh, but this is not quite flesh any more. Feel him yourself, sir and doctor! You will touch something which nobody has ever touched before."

"I have," Vomact declared, "already felt him. You are right. We will try typhoid and condamine for half a day. Twelve hours from now let us meet each other at this place. I will tell the nurses and the robots what to do in the interim."

They both gave the red-tanned spread-eagled figure on the floor a parting glance. Grosbeck looked at the body with something like distaste mingled with fear; Vomact was expressionless, save for a wry wan smile of pity.

At the door the head nurse awaited them. Grosbeck was surprised at his chief's orders.

"Ma'am and nurse, do you have a weapon-proof vault in this hospital?"

"Yes, sir," she said. "We used to keep our records in it until we telemetered all our records into Computer Orbit. Now it is dirty and empty."

"Clean it out. Run a ventilator tube into it. Who is your military protector?"

"My what?" she cried, in surprise.

"Everyone on Earth has military protection. Where are the forces, the soldiers, who protect this hospital of yours?"

"My sir and doctor!" she called out. "My sir and doctor! I'm an old woman and I have been allowed to work here for three hundred years, but I never thought of that idea before. Why would I need soldiers?"

"Find who they are and ask them to stand by. They are specialists too, with a different kind of art from ours. Let them stand by. They may be needed before this day is out. Give my name as authority to their lieutenant or sergeant. Now here is the medication which I want you to apply to this patient."

Her eyes widened as he went on talking, but she was a disciplined woman and she nodded as she heard him out, point by point. Her eyes looked very sad and weary at the end but she was a trained expert herself and she had enormous respect for the skill and wisdom of the Sir and Doctor Vomact. She also had a warm, feminine pity for the motionless young male figure on the floor, swimming forever on the heavy floor, swimming between archipelagoes of which no man living had ever dreamed before.

Crisis came that night.

The patient had worn handprints into the inner wall of the vault, but he had not escaped.

The soldiers, looking oddly alert with their weapons gleaming in the bright corridor of the hospital, were really very bored, as soldiers always become when they are on duty with no action.

Their lieutenant was keyed up. The wirepoint in his hand buzzed like a dangerous insect. Sir and Doctor Vomact, who knew more about weapons than the soldiers thought he knew, saw that the wirepoint was set to HIGH, with a capacity of paralyzing people five stories up, five stories down or a kilometer sideways. He said nothing. He merely thanked the lieutenant and entered the vault, closely followed by Grosbeck and Timofeyev.

The patient swam here too.

He had changed to an arm-over-arm motion, kicking his legs against the floor. It was as though he had swum on the other floor with the sole purpose of staying afloat, and had now discovered some direction in which to go, albeit very slowly. His motions were deliberate, tense, rigid, and so reduced in time that it seemed as though he hardly moved at all. The ripped pajamas lay on the floor beside him.

Vomact glanced around, wondering what forces the man could have used to make those handprints on the steel wall. He remembered Grosbeck's warning that the patient should die, rather than subject all mankind to new and unthought risks, but though he shared the feeling, he could not condone the recommendation.

Almost irritably, the great doctor thought to himself—where could the man be going?

(To Elizabeth, the truth was, to Elizabeth, now only sixty meters away. Not till much later did people understand what Rambo had been trying to do—crossing sixty mere meters to reach his Elizabeth when he had already jumped an un-count of light-years to return to her. To his own, his dear, his well-beloved who needed him!)

The condamine did not leave its characteristic mark of deep lassitude and glowing skin: perhaps the typhoid was successfully contradicting it. Rambo did seem more lively than before. The name had come through on the regular message system, but it still did not mean anything to the Sir and Doctor Vomact. It would. It would.

Meanwhile the other two doctors, briefed ahead of time, got busy with the apparatus which the robots and the nurses had installed.

Vomact murmured to the others, "I think he's better off. Looser all around. I'll try shouting."

So busy were they that they just nodded.

Vomact screamed at the patient, "Who are you? What are you? Where do you come from?"

The sad blue eyes of the man on the floor glanced at him with a surprisingly quick glance, but there was no other real sign of communication. The limbs kept up their swim against the rough concrete floor of the vault. Two of the bandages which the hospital staff had put on him had worn off again. The right knee, scraped and bruised, deposited a sixty-centimeter trail of blood—some old and black and coagulated, some fresh, new and liquid—on the floor as it moved back and forth.

Vomact stood up and spoke to Grosbeck and Timofeyev. "Now," he said, "let us see what happens when we apply the pain."

The two stepped back without being told to do so.

Timofeyev waved his hand at a small white-enameled orderly-robot who stood in the doorway.

The pain net, a fragile cage of wires, dropped down from the ceiling.

It was Vomact's duty, as senior doctor, to take the greatest risk. The patient was wholly encased by the net of wires, but Vomact dropped to his hands and knees, lifted the net at one corner with his right hand, thrust his own head into it next to the head of the patient. Doctor Vomact's robe trailed on the clean concrete, touching the black old stains of blood left from the patient's "swim" throughout the night.

Now Vomact's mouth was centimeters from the patient's ear.

Said Vomact, "Oh."

The net hummed.

The patient stopped his slow motion, arched his back, looked steadfastly at the doctor.

Doctors Grosbeck and Timofeyev could see Vomact's face go white with the impact of the pain machine, but Vomact kept his voice under control and said evenly and loudly to the patient, "*Who—are—you?*"

The patient said flatly, "Elizabeth."

The answer was foolish but the tone was rational.

Vomact pulled his head out from under the net, shouting again at the patient, "*Who—are—you?*"

The naked man replied, speaking very clearly:

"Chwinkle, chwinkle, little chweeble
I am feeling very feeble!"

Vomact frowned and murmured to the robot, "More pain. Turn it up to pain ultimate."

The body threshed under the net, trying to resume its swim on the concrete.

A loud wild braying cry came from the victim under the net. It sounded like a screamed distortion of the name Elizabeth, echoing out from endless remoteness.

It did not make sense.

Vomact screamed back, "*Who—are—you?*"

With unexpected clarity and resonance, the voice came back to the three doctors from the twisting body under the net of pain:

"I'm the shipped man, the ripped man, the gypped man, the dipped man, the hipped man, the tripped man, the tipped man, the slipped man, the flipped man, the nipped man, the ripped man, the clipped man—aah!" His voice choked off with a cry and he went back to swimming on the floor, despite the intensity of the pain net immediately above him.

The doctor lifted his hand. The pain net stopped buzzing and lifted high into the air.

He felt the patient's pulse. It was quick. He lifted an eyelid. The reactions were much closer to normal.

"Stand back," he said to the others.

"Pain on both of us," he said to the robot.

The net came down on the two of them.

"*Who are you?*" shrieked Vomact, right into the patient's ear, holding the man halfway off the floor and not quite knowing whether the body which tore steel walls might not, somehow, tear both of them apart as they stood.

The man babbled back at him: "I'm the most man, the post man, the host man, the ghost man, the coast man, the boast man, the dosed man, the grossed man, the toast man, the roast man, no! no! no!"

He struggled in Vomact's arms. Grosbeck and Timofeyev stepped forward to rescue their chief when the patient added, very calmly and clearly:

"Your procedure is all right, doctor, whoever you are. More fever, please. More pain, please. Some of that dope to fight the pain. You're pulling me back. I know I am on Earth. Elizabeth is near. For the love of God, get me Elizabeth! But don't rush me. I need days and days to get well."

The rationality was so startling that Grosbeck, without waiting for orders from Vomact, as chief doctor, ordered the pain net lifted.

The patient began babbling again: "I'm the three man, the he man, the tree man, the me man, the three man, the three man. . . ." His voice faded and he slumped unconscious.

Vomact walked out of the vault. He was a little unsteady.

His colleagues took him by the elbows.

He smiled wanly at them: "I wish it were lawful. . . . I could use some of that condamine myself. No wonder the pain nets wake the patients up and even make dead people do twitches! Get me some liquor. My heart is old."

Grosbeck sat him down while Timofeyev ran down the corridor in search of medicinal liquor.

Vomact murmured, "How are we going to find *his* Elizabeth? There must be millions of them. And he's from Earth Four too."

"Sir and doctor, you have worked wonders," said Grosbeck. "To go under the net. To take those chances. To bring him to speech. I will never see anything like it again. It's enough for any one lifetime, to have seen this day."

"But what do we do next?" asked Vomact wearily, almost in confusion.

That particular question needed no answer.

The Lord Crudelta had reached Earth.

His pilot landed the craft and fainted at the controls with sheer exhaustion.

Of the escort cats, who had ridden alongside the space craft in the miniature spaceships, three were dead, one was comatose and the fifth was spitting and raving.

When the port authorities tried to slow the Lord Crudelta down to ascertain his authority, he invoked Top Emergency, took over the command of troops in the name of the Instrumentality, arrested everyone in sight but the troop commander, and requisitioned the troop commander to take him to the hospital. The computers at the port had told him that one Rambo, "sans origine," had arrived mysteriously on the grass of a designated hospital.

Outside the hospital, the Lord Crudelta invoked Top Emergency again, placed all armed men under his own command, ordered a recording monitor to cover all his actions if he should later be channeled into a court-martial, and arrested everyone in sight.

The tramp of heavily armed men, marching in combat order, overtook Timofeyev as he hurried back to Vomact with a drink. The men were jogging along on the double. All of them had live helmets and their wirepoints were buzzing.

Nurses ran forward to drive the intruders out, ran backward when the sting of the stun-rays brushed cruelly over them. The whole hospital was in an uproar.

The Lord Crudelta later admitted that he had made a serious mistake.

The Two Minutes' War broke out immediately.

You have to understand the pattern of the Instrumentality to see how it happened. The Instrumentality was a self-perpetuating body of men with enormous powers and a strict code. Each was a plenum of the low, the middle and the high justice. Each could do anything he found necessary or proper to maintain the Instrumentality and to keep the peace between the worlds. But if he made a mistake or committed a wrong—ah, then, it was suddenly different. Any Lord could put another Lord to death in an emergency, but he was assured of death and disgrace himself if he assumed this responsibility. The only difference between ratification and repudiation came in the fact that Lords who killed in an emergency and were proved wrong were marked down on a very shameful list, while those who killed other Lords rightly (as later examination might prove) were listed on a very honorable list, but still killed.

With three Lords, the situation was different. Three Lords made an emergency court; if they acted together, acted in good faith, and reported to the computers of the Instrumentality, they were exempt from punishment, though not from blame or even reduction to citizen status. Seven Lords, or all the Lords on a given planet at a given moment, were beyond any criticism except that of a dignified reversal of their actions should a later ruling prove them wrong.

This was all the business of the Instrumentality. The Instrumentality had the perpetual slogan: "Watch, but do not govern; stop war, but do not wage it; protect, but do not control; and first, survive!"

The Lord Crudelta had seized the troops—not his troops, but the light regular troops of Manhome Government—because he feared that the greatest danger in the history of man might come from the person whom he himself had sent through $space_3$.

He never expected that the troops would be plucked out from his command—an overriding power reinforced by robotic telepathy and the incomparable communications net, both open and secret, reinforced by thousands of years in trickery, defeat, secrecy, victory, and sheer experience, which the Instrumentality had perfected since it emerged from the Ancient Wars.

Overriding, overridden!

These were the commands which the Instrumentality had used before recorded time began. Sometimes they suspended their antagonists on points of law, sometimes by the deft and deadly insertion of weapons, most often by cutting in on other peoples' mechanical and social controls and doing their will, only to drop the controls as suddenly as they had taken them.

But not Crudelta's hastily called troops.

The war broke out with a change of pace.

Two squads of men were moving into that part of the hospital where Elizabeth lay, waiting the endless returns to the jelly baths which would rebuild her poor ruined body.

The squads changed pace.

The survivors could not account for what happened.

They all admitted to great mental confusion—afterward.

At the time it seemed that they had received a clear, logical command to turn and to defend the women's section by counterattacking their own main battalion right in their rear.

The hospital was a very strong building. Otherwise it would have melted to the ground or shot up in flame.

The leading soldiers suddenly turned around, dropped for cover and blazed their wirepoints at the comrades who followed them. The wirepoints were cued to organic material, though fairly harmless to inorganic. They were powered by the power relays which every soldier wore on his back.

In the first ten seconds of the turnaround, twenty-seven soldiers, two nurses, three patients and one orderly were killed. One hundred and nine other people were wounded in that first exchange of fire.

The troop commander had never seen battle, but he had been well trained. He immediately deployed his reserves around the external exits of the building and sent his favorite squad, commanded by a Sergeant Lansdale whom he trusted well, down into the basement, so that it could rise vertically from the basement into the women's quarters and find out who the enemy was.

As yet, he had no idea that it was his own leading troops turning and fighting their comrades.

He testified later, at the trial, that he personally had no sensations of eerie interference with his own mind. He merely knew that his men had unexpectedly come upon armed resistance from antagonists—identity unknown!—who had weapons identical with theirs. Since the Lord Crudelta had brought them along in case there might be a fight with unspecified antagonists, he felt right in assuming that a Lord of the Instrumentality knew what he was doing. This was the enemy all right.

In less than a minute, the two sides had balanced out. The line of fire had moved right into his own force. The lead men, some of whom were wounded, simply turned around and began defending themselves against the men immediately behind them. It was as though an invisible line, moving rapidly, had parted the two sections of the military force.

The oily black smoke of dissolving bodies began to glut the ventilators.

Patients were screaming, doctors cursing, robots stamping around and nurses trying to call each other.

The war ended when the troop commander saw Sergeant Lansdale, whom he himself had sent upstairs, leading a charge out of the women's quarters—directly at his own commander!

The officer kept his head.

He dropped to the floor and rolled sidewise as the air chittered at him, the emanations of Lansdale's wirepoint killing all the tiny bacteria in the air. On his helmet phone he pushed the manual controls to TOP VOLUME and to NONCOMS ONLY, and he commanded, with a sudden flash of brilliant mother-wit, "Good job, Lansdale!"

Lansdale's voice came back as weak as if it had been off-planet, "We'll keep them out of this section yet, sir!"

The troop commander called back very loudly but calmly, not letting on that he thought his sergeant was psychotic.

"Easy now. Hold on. I'll be with you."

He changed to the other channel and said to his nearby men, "Cease fire. Take cover and wait."

A wild scream came to him from the phones.

It was Lansdale. "Sir! Sir! I'm fighting *you,* sir. I just caught on. It's getting me again. Watch out."

The buzz and burr of the weapons suddenly stopped.

The wild human uproar of the hospital continued.

A tall doctor, with the insignia of high seniority, came gently to the troop commander and said, "You can stand up and take your soldiers out now, young fellow. The fight was a mistake."

"I'm not under your orders," snapped the young officer. "I'm under the Lord Crudelta. He requisitioned this force from the Manhome Government. Who are you?"

"You may salute me, captain," said the doctor, "I am Colonel General Vomact of the Earth Medical Reserve. But you had better not wait for the Lord Crudelta."

"But *where* is he?"

"In my bed," said Vomact.

"Your *bed?*" cried the young officer in complete amazement.

"In bed. Doped to the teeth. I fixed him up. He was excited. Take your men out. We'll treat the wounded on the lawn. You can see the dead in the refrigerators downstairs in a few minutes, except for the ones that went smoky from direct hits."

"But the fight . . . ?"

"A mistake, young man, or else—"

"Or else what?" shouted the young officer, horrified at the utter mess of his own combat experience.

"Or else a weapon no man has ever seen before. Your troops fought each other. Your command was intercepted."

"I could see that," snapped the officer, "as soon as I saw Lansdale coming at me."

"But do you know what took him over?" said Vomact gently, while taking the officer by the arm and beginning to lead him out of the hospital. The captain went willingly, not noticing where he was going, so eagerly did he watch for the other man's words.

"I think I know," said Vomact. "Another man's dreams. Dreams which have learned how to turn themselves into electricity or plastic or stone. Or anything else. Dreams coming to us out of $space_3$."

The young officer nodded dumbly. This was too much. "$Space_3$?" he murmured. It was like being told that the really alien invaders, whom men had been expecting for thirteen thousand years and had never met, were waiting for him on the grass. Until now $space_3$ had been a mathematical idea, a romancer's daydream, but not a fact.

The sir and doctor Vomact did not even ask the young officer. He brushed the young man gently at the nape of the neck and shot him through with tranquilizer. Vomact then led him out to the grass. The young captain stood alone and whistled happily at the stars in the sky. Behind him, his sergeants and corporals were sorting out the survivors and getting treatment for the wounded.

The Two Minutes' War was over.

Rambo had stopped dreaming that his Elizabeth was in danger. He had recognized, even in his deep sick sleep, that the tramping in the corridor was the movement of armed men. His mind had set up defenses to protect Elizabeth. He took over command of the forward troops and set them to stopping the main body. The powers which $space_3$ had worked into him made this easy for him to do, even though he did not know that he was doing it.

"How many dead?" said Vomact to Grosbeck and Timofeyev.

"About two hundred."

"And how many irrecoverable dead?"

"The ones that got turned into smoke. A dozen, maybe fourteen. The other dead can be fixed up, but most of them will have to get new personality prints."

"Do you know what happened?" asked Vomact.

"No, sir and doctor," they both chorused.

"I do. I think I do. No, I *know* I do. It's the wildest story in the history of man. Our patient did it—Rambo. He took over the troops and set them against each other. That Lord of the Instrumentality who came charging in—Crudelta. I've known him for a long long time. He's behind this case. He thought that troops would help, not sensing that troops would invite attack upon themselves. And there is something else."

"Yes?" they said, in unison.

"Rambo's woman—the one he's looking for. She must be here."

"Why?" said Timofeyev.

"Because *he's* here."

"You're assuming that he came here because of his own will, sir and doctor."

Vomact smiled the wise crafty smile of his family; it was almost a trademark of the Vomact house.

"I am assuming all the things which I cannot otherwise prove.

"First, I assume that he came here naked out of space itself, driven by some kind of force of which we cannot even guess.

"Second, I assume he came *here* because he wanted something. A woman named Elizabeth, who must already be here. In a moment we can go inventory all our Elizabeths.

"Third, I assume that the Lord Crudelta knew something about it. He has led troops into the building. He began raving when he saw me. I know hysterical fatigue, as do you, my brothers, so I condamined him for a night's sleep.

"Fourth, let's leave our man alone. There'll be hearings and trials enough, Space knows, when all these events get scrambled out."

Vomact was right.

He usually was.

Trials did follow.

It was lucky that Old Earth no longer permitted newspapers or television news. The population would have been frothed up to riot and terror if they had ever found out what happened at the Old Main Hospital just to the west of Meeya Meefla.

Twenty-one days later, Vomact, Timofeyev and Grosbeck were summoned to the trial of the Lord Crudelta. A full panel of seven Lords of the Instrumentality were there to give Crudelta an ample hearing and, if required, a sudden death. The doctors were present both as doctors for Elizabeth and Rambo and as witnesses for the Investigating Lord.

Elizabeth, fresh up from being dead, was as beautiful as a newborn baby in exquisite, adult feminine form. Rambo could not take his eyes off her, but a look of bewilderment went over his face every time she gave him a friendly, calm remote little smile. (She had been told that she was his girl, and she was prepared to believe it, but she had no memory of him or of anything else more than sixty hours back, when speech had been reinstalled in her mind; and he, for his part, was still thick of speech and subject to strains which the doctors could not quite figure out.)

The Investigating Lord was a man named Starmount.

He asked the panel to rise.

They did so.

He faced the Lord Crudelta with great solemnity. "You are obliged, my Lord Crudelta, to speak quickly and clearly to this court."

"Yes, my Lord," he answered.

"We have the summary power."

"You have the summary power. I recognize it."

"You will tell the truth or else you will lie."

"I shall tell the truth or I will lie."

"You may lie, if you wish, about matters of fact and opinion, but you will in no case lie about human relationships. If you do lie, nevertheless, you will ask that your name be entered in the Roster of Dishonor."

"I understand the panel and the rights of this panel. I will lie if I wish—though I don't think I will need to do so"—and here Crudelta flashed a weary intelligent smile at all of them—"but I will not lie about matters of relationship. If I do, I will ask for dishonor."

"You have yourself been well trained as a Lord of the Instrumentality?"

"I have been so trained and I love the Instrumentality well. In fact, I am myself the Instrumentality, as are you, and as are the honorable Lords beside you. I shall behave well, for as long as I live this afternoon."

"Do you credit him, my Lords?" asked Starmount.

The members of the panel nodded their mitered heads. They had dressed ceremonially for the occasion.

"Do you have a relationship to the woman Elizabeth?"

The members of the trial panel caught their breath as they saw Crudelta turn white: "My Lords!" he cried, and answered no further.

"It is the custom," said Starmount firmly, "that you answer promptly or that you die."

The Lord Crudelta got control of himself. "I am answering. I did not know who she was, except for the fact that Rambo loved her. I sent her to Earth from Earth Four, where I then was. Then I told Rambo that she had been murdered and hung desperately at the edge of death, wanting only his help to return to the green fields of life."

Said Starmount: "Was that the truth?"

"My Lord and Lords, it was a lie."

"Why did you tell it?"

"To induce rage in Rambo and to give him an overriding reason for wanting to come to Earth faster than any man has ever come before."

"A-a-ah! A-a-ah!" Two wild cries came from Rambo, more like the call of an animal than like the sound of a man.

Vomact looked at his patient, felt himself beginning to growl with a deep internal rage. Rambo's powers, generated in the depths of $space_3$, had begun to operate again. Vomact made a sign. The robot behind Rambo had been coded to keep Rambo calm. Though the robot had been enameled to look like a white gleaming hospital orderly, he was actually a police robot of high powers, built up with an electronic cortex based on the frozen midbrain of an old wolf. (A wolf was a rare animal, something like a dog.) The robot touched Rambo, who dropped off to sleep. Doctor Vomact felt the anger in his own mind fade away. He lifted his hand gently; the robot caught the signal and stopped applying the narcoleptic radiation. Rambo slept normally; Elizabeth looked worriedly at the man whom she had been told was her own.

The Lords turned back from the glances at Rambo.

Said Starmount, icily: "And why did you do that?"

"Because I wanted him to travel through space."

"Why?"

"To show it could be done."

"And do you, my Lord Crudelta, affirm that this man has in fact traveled through $space_3$?"

"I do."

"Are you lying?"

"I have the right to lie, but I have no wish to do so. In the name of the Instrumentality itself, I tell you that this is the truth."

The panel members gasped. Now there was no way out. Either the Lord Crudelta was telling the truth, *which meant that all former times had come to an end and that a new age had begun for all the kinds of mankind,* or else he was lying in the face of the most powerful form of affirmation which any of them knew.

Even Starmount himself took a different tone. His teasing, restless, intelligent voice took on a new timbre of kindness.

"You do therefore assert that this man has come back from outside our galaxy with nothing more than his own natural skin to cover him? No instruments? No power?"

"I did not say that," said Crudelta. "Other people have begun to pretend I used such words. I tell you, my Lords, that I planoformed for twelve consecutive Earth days and nights. Some of you may remember where Outpost Baiter Gator is. Well, I had a good Go-captain, and he took me four long jumps beyond there, out into intergalactic space. I left this man there. When I reached Earth, he had been here twelve days, more or less. I have assumed, therefore, that his trip was more or less instantaneous. I was on my way back to Baiter Gator, counting by Earth time, when the doctor here found this man on the grass outside the hospital."

Vomact raised his hand. The Lord Starmount gave him the right to speak. "My sirs and Lords, we did not find this man on the grass. The robots did, and made a record. But even the robots did not see or photograph his arrival."

"We know that," said Starmount angrily, "and we know that we have been told that nothing came to Earth by any means whatever, in that particular quarter hour. Go on, my Lord Crudelta. What relation are you to Rambo?"

"He is my victim."

"Explain yourself!"

"I computered him out. I asked the machines where I would be most apt to find a man with a tremendous lot of rage in him, and was informed that on Earth Four the rage level had been left high because that particular planet had a considerable need for explorers and adventurers, in whom rage was a strong survival trait. When I got to Earth Four, I commanded the authorities to find out which border cases had exceeded the limits of allowable rage. They gave me four men. One was much too large. Two were old. This man was the only candidate for my excitement. I chose him."

"What did you tell him?"

"Tell him? I told him his sweetheart was dead or dying."

"No, no," said Starmount. "Not at the moment of crisis. What did you tell him to make him cooperate in the first place?"

"I told him," said the Lord Crudelta evenly, "that I was myself a Lord of the Instrumentality and that I would kill him myself if he did not obey, and obey promptly."

"And under what custom or law did you act?"

"Reserved material," said the Lord Crudelta promptly. "There are telepaths here who are not a part of the Instrumentality. I beg leave to defer until we have a shielded place."

Several members of the panel nodded and Starmount agreed with them. He changed the line of questioning.

"You forced this man, therefore, to do something which he did not wish to do?"

"That is right," said the Lord Crudelta.

"Why didn't you go yourself, if it is that dangerous?"

"My Lords and honorables, it was the nature of the experiment that the experimenter himself should not be expended in the first try. Artyr Rambo has indeed traveled through $space_3$. I shall follow him myself, in due course." (How the Lord Crudelta did do so is another tale, told about another time.) "If I had gone and if I had been lost, that would have been the end of the $space_3$ trials. At least for our time."

"Tell us the exact circumstances under which you last saw Artyr Rambo before you met after the battle in the Old Main Hospital."

"We had put him in a rocket of the most ancient style. We also wrote writing on the outside of it, just the way the Ancients did when they first ventured into space. Ah, that was a beautiful piece of engineering and archaeology! We copied everything right down to the correct models of fourteen thousand years ago, when the Paroskii and Murkins were racing each other into space. The rocket was white, with a red and white gantry beside it. The letters IOM were on the rocket, not that the words mattered. The rocket has gone into nowhere, but the passenger sits here. It rose on a stool of fire. The stool became a column. Then the landing field disappeared."

"And the landing field," said Starmount quietly, "what was that?"

"A modified planoform ship. We have had ships go milky in space because they faded molecule by molecule. We have had others disappear utterly. The engineers had changed this around. We took out all the machinery needed for circumnavigation, for survival or for comfort. The landing field was to last three or four seconds, no more. Instead, we put in fourteen planoform devices, all operating in tandem, so that the ship would do what other ships do when they planoform—namely, drop one of our familiar dimensions and pick up a new dimension from some unknown category of space—but do it with such force as to get out of what people call $space_2$ and move over into $space_3$."

"And $space_3$, what did you expect of that?"

"I thought that it was universal and instantaneous, in relation to our universe.

That everything was equally distant from everything else. That Rambo, wanting to see his girl again, would move in a thousandth of a second from the empty space beyond Outpost Baiter Gator into the hospital where she was."

"And, my Lord Crudelta, what made you think so?"

"A hunch, my Lord, for which you are welcome to kill me."

Starmount turned to the panel. "I suspect, my Lords, that you are more likely to doom him to long life, great responsibility, immense rewards, and the fatigue of being his own difficult and complicated self."

The miters moved gently and the members of the panel rose.

"You, my Lord Crudelta, will sleep till the trial is finished."

A robot stroked him and he fell asleep.

"Next witness," said the Lord Starmount, "in five minutes."

Vomact tried to keep Rambo from being heard as a witness. He argued fiercely with the Lord Starmount in the intermission. "You Lords have shot up my hospital, abducted two of my patients, and now you are going to torment both Rambo and Elizabeth. Can't you leave them alone? Rambo is in no condition to give coherent answers and Elizabeth may be damaged if she sees him suffer."

The Lord Starmount said to him, "You have your rules, doctor, and we have ours. This trial is being recorded, inch by inch and moment by moment. Nothing is going to be done to Rambo unless we find that he has planet-killing powers. If that is true, of course, we will ask you to take him back to the hospital and to put him to death very pleasantly. But I don't think it will happen. We want his story so that we can judge my colleague Crudelta. Do you think that the Instrumentality would survive if it did not have fierce internal discipline?"

Vomact nodded sadly; he went back to Grosbeck and Timofeyev, murmuring sadly to them, "Rambo's in for it. There's nothing we could do."

The panel reassembled. They put on their judicial miters. The lights of the room darkened and the weird blue light of justice was turned on.

The robot orderly helped Rambo to the witness chair.

"You are obliged," said Starmount, "to speak quickly and clearly to this court."

"You're not Elizabeth," said Rambo.

"I am the Lord Starmount," said the investigating Lord, quickly deciding to dispense with the formalities. "Do you know me?"

"No," said Rambo.

"Do you know where you are?"

"Earth," said Rambo.

"Do you wish to lie or to tell the truth?"

"A lie," said Rambo, "is the only truth which men can share with each other, so I will tell you lies, the way we always do."

"Can you report your trip?"

"No."

"Why not, citizen Rambo?"

"Words won't describe it."

"Do you remember your trip?"

"Do you remember your pulse of two minutes ago?" countered Rambo.

"I am not playing with you," said Starmount. "We think you have been in $space_3$ and we want you to testify about the Lord Crudelta."

"Oh!" said Rambo. "I don't like him. I never did like him."

"Will you nevertheless try to tell us what happened to you?"

"Should I, Elizabeth?" asked Rambo of the girl, who sat in the audience.

She did not stammer. "Yes," she said, in a clear voice which rang through the big room. "Tell them, so that we can find our lives again."

"I will tell you," said Rambo.

"When did you last see the Lord Crudelta?"

"When I was stripped and fitted to the rocket, four jumps out beyond Outpost Baiter Gator. He was on the ground. He waved good-bye to me."

"And then what happened?"

"The rocket rose. It felt very strange, like no craft I had ever been in before. I weighed many, many gravities."

"And then?"

"The engines went on. I was thrown out of space itself."

"What did it seem like?"

"Behind me I left the working ships, the cloth and the food which goes through space. I went down rivers which did not exist. I felt people around me though I could not see them, red people shooting arrows at live bodies."

"*Where* were you?" asked a panel member.

"In the wintertime where there is no summer. In an emptiness like a child's mind. In peninsulas which had torn loose from the land. And I *was* the ship."

"You were what?" asked the same panel member.

"The rocket nose. The cone. The boat. I was drunk. It was drunk. I was the drunkboat myself," said Rambo.

"And where did you go?" resumed Starmount.

"Where crazy lanterns stared with idiot eyes. Where the waves washed back and forth with the dead of all the ages. Where the stars became a pool, and I swam in it. Where blue turns to liquor, stronger than alcohol, wilder than music, fermented with the *red red reds* of love. I saw all the things that men have ever thought they saw, but it was me who really saw them. I've heard phosphorescence singing and tides that seemed like crazy cattle clawing their way out of the ocean, their hooves beating the reefs. You will not believe me, but I found Floridas wilder than this, where the flowers had human skins and eyes like big cats."

"What are you talking about?" asked the Lord Starmount.

"What I found in space$_3$," snapped Artyr Rambo. "Believe it or not. This is what I now remember. Maybe it's a dream, but it's all I have. It was years and years and it was the blink of an eye. I dreamed green nights. I felt places where the whole horizon became one big waterfall. The boat that was me met children and I showed them El Dorado, where the gold men live. The people drowned in space washed gently past me. I was a boat where all the lost spaceships lay drowned and still. Seahorses which were not real ran beside me. The summer month came and hammered down the sun. I went past archipelagoes of stars, where the delirious skies opened up for wanderers. I cried for me. I wept for man. I wanted to be the drunkboat sinking. I sank. I fell. It seemed to me that the grass was a lake, where a sad child, on hands and knees, sailed a toy boat as fragile as a butterfly in spring. I can't forget the pride of unremembered flags, the arrogance of prisons which I suspected, the swimming of the businessmen! Then I was on the grass."

"This may have scientific value," said the Lord Starmount, "but it is not of judicial importance. Do you have any comment on what you did during the battle in the hospital?"

Rambo was quick and looked sane: "What I did, I did not do. What I did not do, I cannot tell. Let me go, because I am tired of you and space, big men and big things. Let me sleep and let me get well."

Starmount lifted his hand for silence.

The panel members stared at him.

Only the few telepaths present knew that they had all said, "*Aye. Let the man go. Let the girl go. Let the doctors go.* But bring back the Lord Crudelta later on. He has many troubles ahead of him, and we wish to add to them."

Between the Instrumentality, the Manhome Government and the authorities at the Old Main Hospital, everyone wished to give Rambo and Elizabeth happiness.

As Rambo got well, much of his Earth Four memory returned. The trip faded from his mind.

When he came to know Elizabeth, he hated the girl.

This was not his girl—his bold, saucy, Elizabeth of the markets and the valleys, of the snowy hills and the long boat rides. This was somebody meek, sweet, sad and hopelessly loving.

Vomact cured that.

He sent Rambo to the Pleasure City of the Herperides, where bold and talkative women pursued him because he was rich and famous.

In a few weeks—a very few indeed—he wanted *his* Elizabeth, this strange shy girl who had been cooked back from the dead while he rode space with his own fragile bones.

"Tell the truth, darling." He spoke to her once gravely and seriously. "The Lord Crudelta did not arrange the accident which killed you?"

"They say he wasn't there," said Elizabeth. "They say it was an actual accident. I don't know. I will never know."

"It doesn't matter now," said Rambo. "Crudelta's off among the stars, looking for trouble and finding it. We have our bungalow, and our waterfall, and each other."

"Yes, my darling," she said, "each other. And no fantastic Floridas for us."

He blinked at this reference to the past, but he said nothing. A man who has been through space$_3$ needs very little in life, outside of *not* going back to space$_3$. Sometimes he dreamed he was the rocket again, the old rocket taking off on an impossible trip. Let other men follow! he thought. Let other men go! I have Elizabeth and I am here.

J. H. Rosny *aîné*

Translated by Damon Knight

J. H. Rosny *aîné* was the pseudonym of the important French (Belgian) writer Joseph-Henri Boëx (1856–1940). He was the author of 107 novels, essays, plays, memoirs, etc., a friend of Alphonse Daudet, and a President of the Académie Goncourt. He wrote a small number of SF works, including prehistoric romances such as *The Giant Cat* (1918; translated 1924) and *The Quest for Fire* (1901; translated 1967), from which the film *Quest for Fire* (1981) was made. Only three of his important SF stories have been translated into English, but he is the most important French SF writer between Jules Verne and the contemporary period. This story has only appeared once before in English, in an early 1960s anthology. So his influence on the evolution of the genre in English has thus far been indirect.

Damon Knight, the well-known SF critic and the translator of this piece, said that while only a few of Rosny's works were science fiction, "those few were precedent-making, germinal works. Rosny, not Verne, is considered the father of French science fiction." Knight goes on to say, "I love this story for its human warmth, and for what it has to tell us, not only about one superman, but about the adolescence of all gifted, 'different' human beings. I admire it for many reasons, but chiefly for the absolute, circumstantial conviction with which it describes an imaginary order of living creatures. Few writers have even attempted this most difficult kind of fictional invention; fewer still have succeeded so brilliantly."

This is both a unique "fourth dimension" story and a superman story, set in a small village in France where the events have no impact on the outside world. It is the earliest story in this anthology, published the same year as Wells's *The Time Machine*, 1895. It is every bit as powerfully imaginative as Wells, and gives evidence of the substantial trend in literature in the 1890s toward the themes and ideas of science fiction in works that later coalesced into the founding documents of the genre in a work by an early Modern writer.

ANOTHER WORLD

I

I was born in Gelderland, where our family holdings had dwindled to a few acres of heath and yellow water. Along the boundary grew pine trees that rustled with a metallic sound. The farmhouse had only a few habitable rooms left and was falling apart stone by stone in the solitude. Ours was an old family of herdsmen, once numerous, now reduced to my parents, my sister and myself.

My fate, dismal enough at the beginning, became the happiest I could imagine: I met the one who understands me; he will teach those things that formerly I alone knew among men. But for many years I suffered and despaired, a prey to doubt and the loneliness of the soul, which nearly ended by eating away my absolute faith.

I came into the world with a unique constitution, and from the very beginning I was the object of wonder. Not that I seemed ill-formed; I was, I am told, more shapely in face and body than is customary in newborn infants. But my color was most unusual, a sort of pale violet—very pale, but quite distinct. By lamplight, especially by the light of oil lamps, this tint grew paler still, turned to a curious whiteness, like that of a lily submerged in water. That, at least, was how I appeared to others (for I saw myself differently, as I saw everything in the world differently). To this first peculiarity others were added which only revealed themselves later.

Though born with a healthy appearance, I developed poorly. I was thin, and I cried incessantly; at the age of eight months, I had never been seen to smile. Soon my life was despaired of. The doctor from Zwartendam declared I was suffering from congenital weakness; he could think of no remedy but a strict regimen. Nonetheless I continued to waste away; the family expected me to disappear altogether from one day to the next. My father, I think, was resigned to it, his pride—the Hollander's pride in regularity and order—little soothed by the grotesque appearance of his child. My mother, on the contrary, loved me all the more for my strangeness, having made up her mind that the color of my skin was pleasing.

So matters stood, when a very simple thing came to my rescue. Since everything concerning me must be out of the ordinary, this event was the cause of scandal and apprehension.

A servant having left us, her place was given to a vigorous girl from Friesland, honest and willing, but inclined to drink. I was placed in her care. Seeing me so feeble, she took it into her head to give me secretly a little beer and water mixed with Schiedam—remedies, according to her, sovereign against all ills.

The curious thing was that I began immediately to regain my strength and from then on showed a remarkable predilection for alcohol. The good girl rejoiced in secret, not without drawing some pleasure from the bafflement of my parents and the doctor. At last, driven into a corner, she revealed the secret. My father flew into a violent passion; the doctor inveighed against superstition and ignorance. Strict orders were given to the servants; I was taken out of the Frieslander's care.

I began to grow thin again, to waste away, until my mother, forgetting everything but her fondness for me, put me back on a diet of beer and Schiedam. I promptly grew strong and lively again. The experiment was conclusive: alcohol was seen to be necessary to my health. My father was humiliated. The doctor got out of the affair by prescribing medicinal wines; and from that time on my health was excellent—but no one hesitated to prophesy a life of drunkenness and debauch for me.

Shortly after this incident, a new oddity grew apparent to the household. My eyes, which had seemed normal at the beginning, grew strangely opaque, took on a horny appearance, like the wing cases of certain beetles. The doctor concluded from this that I was losing my sight, but he confessed that the ailment was absolutely strange to him, of such a nature that he had never had the opportunity to study a like case. Shortly the pupils of my eyes so fused into the irises that it was impossible to tell one from the other. It was remarked, moreover, that I could stare at the sun without showing any discomfort. In truth, I was not blind in the least, and in the end they had to admit that I saw very well.

So I arrived at the age of three. I was then, in the opinion of the neighborhood, a little monster. The violet color of my skin had undergone little change. My eyes were completely opaque. I spoke awkwardly, and with incredible swiftness. I was dextrous with my hands, and well formed for all activities which called for more quickness than strength. It was not denied that I might have been graceful and handsome if my coloring had been normal and my pupils transparent. I showed some intelligence, but with deficiencies which my family did not fully appreciate, since, except for my mother and the Frieslander, they did not care much for me. I was an object of curiosity to strangers, and to my father a continual mortification.

If, moreover, he had clung to any hope of seeing me become like other people, time took ample pains to disabuse him of it. I grew more and more strange, in my tastes, habits and aptitudes. At the age of six I lived almost entirely on alcohol. Only very seldom did I take a few bites of vegetables or fruit. I grew with prodigious swiftness; I became incredibly thin and light. I mean "light" even in its specific sense, which is just the opposite of thinness. Thus, I swam without the slightest difficulty; I floated like a plank of poplar. My head hardly sank deeper than the rest of my body.

I was nimble in proportion to that lightness. I ran like a deer; I easily leaped over ditches and barriers which no man would even have attempted. Quick as a wink, I could be in the crown of a beech tree; or, what caused even more astonishment, I could leap over the roof of our farmhouse. In compensation, the slightest burden was too much for me.

All these things added together were nothing but phenomena indicative of a special nature, which by themselves would have done no more than single me out and make me unwelcome; no one would have classified me outside humanity. No doubt I was a monster, but certainly not to the same degree as those who were born with the ears or horns of animals; a head like a calf's or horse's; fins; no eyes or an extra one; four arms; four legs; or without arms and legs. My skin, in spite of its startling color, was little different from a sun-tanned skin; there was nothing repugnant about my eyes, opaque as they were. My extreme agility was a gift, my need for alcohol might pass for a mere vice, an inheritance of drunkenness; however, the rustics, like our Frieslander servant, viewed it as no more than a confirmation of their ideas about the "strength" of Schiedam, a rather lively demonstration of the excellence of their tastes.

As for the swiftness and volubility of my speech, which made it impossible to follow, this seemed to be confounded with the defects of pronunciation—stammering, lisping, stuttering—common to so many small children. Thus, properly speaking, I had none of the marked characteristics of monstrosity, however extraordinary my general effect might be. The fact was that the most curious aspect of my nature escaped my family's notice, for no one realized that my vision was strangely different from ordinary vision.

If I saw certain things less well than others did, I could see a great many things that no one else could see at all. This difference showed itself especially in relation to colors. All that was termed red, orange, yellow, green, blue or indigo appeared to me as a more or less blackish gray, whereas I could perceive violet, and a series of colors beyond it—colors which were nothing but blackness to normal men. Later I realized that I could distinguish in this way among some fifteen colors as dissimilar as, for instance, yellow and green—with, of course, an infinite range of gradations in between.

In the second place, my eye does not perceive transparency in the ordinary way. I see poorly through glass or water; glass is highly colored for me, water perceptibly so, even at a slight depth. Many crystals said to be clear are more or less opaque, while, on the other hand, a very great number of bodies called opaque do not interfere with my vision. In general, I see through objects much more frequently than you do; and translucence, clouded transparency, occurs so often that I might say it is for my eye the rule of nature, while complete opacity is the exception. In this way I can make out objects through wood, paper, the petals of flowers, magnetized iron, coal, etc. Nevertheless, at variable thicknesses these substances create an obstacle—as a big tree, a meter's depth of water, a thick block of coal or quartz. Gold, platinum and mercury are black and opaque; ice is grayish black. Air and water vapor are transparent and yet tinted, as are certain specimens of steel, certain very pure clays. Clouds do not hinder me from seeing the sun or the stars. On the other hand, I can clearly see these same clouds hanging in the air.

As I have said, this difference between my vision and that of others was very little remarked by those around me. My color perception was thought to be poor, that was all; the infirmity is too common to attract much attention. It had no importance in the small daily acts of my life, for I saw the shapes of objects in the same manner as most people, and perhaps even more accurately. Designating an object by its color, when it was necessary to distinguish it from another of the same shape, troubled me only when the two objects were new. If someone called one waistcoat blue and another red, it made little difference in what colors these waistcoats really appeared to me; blue and red became purely mnemonic terms.

From this you might conclude that there was a system of correspondence between my colors and those of other people, and therefore that it came to the same thing as if I had seen their colors. But, as I have already written, red, green, yellow, blue, etc., *when they are pure*, as the colors of a prism are pure, appear to me as a more or less blackish gray; they are not colors to me at all. In nature, where no color is simple, it is not the same thing. A given substance termed green, for instance, is for me of a certain mixed color;* but another substance called green, which to you is identically the same shade as the first, is not at all the same color to me. You see, therefore, that my range of colors has no correspondence with yours: when I agree to call both brass and gold yellow, it is a little as if you should agree to call both a cornflower and a corn poppy blue.

II

Were this the extent of the difference between my vision and normal vision, certainly it would appear extraordinary enough. Nevertheless, it is but little com-

*And this mixture naturally does not include green, since green, for me, belongs to the realm of darkness.

pared with that which I have yet to tell you. The differently colored world, differently transparent and opaque, the ability to see through clouds, to perceive the stars on the most overcast nights, to see through a wooden wall what is happening in the next room or on the outside of a house—what is all this, compared with the perception of a *living world,* a world of animate Beings, moving around and beside man without man's being aware of them, without his being warned by any sort of immediate contact?

What is all this, compared with the revelation that there exists on this earth another fauna than our fauna, and one without any resemblance to our own in form, or in organization, or in habits, or in manner of growth, birth and death? A fauna which lives beside and in the midst of ours, influences the elements which surround us, and is influenced, vivified, by these elements, without our suspecting its presence. A fauna which, as I have demonstrated, is as unaware of us as we of it, and which has evolved in ignorance of us, as we in ignorance of it. A living world as varied as ours, as puissant as ours—perhaps more so—in its effect on the face of the planet! A kingdom, in short, moving upon the water, in the atmosphere, on the earth, modifying that water, that atmosphere and that earth entirely otherwise than we, but certainly with formidable strength, and in that way acting indirectly upon us and our destiny, as we indirectly act upon it!

Nevertheless, this is what I have seen, what I alone among men and animals still see; this is what I have *studied* ardently for five years, after having spent my childhood and adolescence merely *observing* it.

III

Observing it! As far back as I can remember, I instinctively felt the seductiveness of that creation so foreign to ours. In the beginning, I confounded it with other living things. Seeing that no one took any notice of its presence, that everyone, on the contrary, appeared indifferent to it, I hardly felt the need to point out its peculiarities. At six, I understood perfectly its difference from the plants of the fields, the animals of the farmyard and the stable; but I confused it somewhat with such nonliving phenomena as rays of light, the movement of water, and clouds. That was because these creatures were intangible: when they touched me I felt no sensation of contact. Their shapes, otherwise widely variant, nevertheless had this singularity, that they were so thin, in one of their three dimensions, that they might be compared to drawings, to surfaces, geometric lines that moved. They passed through all organic bodies; on the other hand, they sometimes appeared to be halted, entangled by invisible obstacles.

But I shall describe them later. At present I only wish to draw attention to them, to affirm their variety of contours and lines, their quasi-absence of thickness, their *impalpability,* combined with the autonomy of their movements.

At about my eighth year, I became perfectly sure that they were as distinct from atmospheric phenomena as from the members of our animal kingdom. In the delight this discovery afforded me, I tried to communicate it to others. I never succeeded in doing so. Aside from the fact that my speech was almost entirely incomprehensible, as I have said, the extraordinary nature of my vision rendered it suspect. No one thought of pausing to unravel my gestures and my phrases, any more than to admit that I could see through wooden walls, even though I had given proof of this on many occasions. Between me and the others there was an almost insurmountable barrier.

I fell into discouragement and daydreams; I became a sort of little recluse; I caused uneasiness, and felt it myself, among children of my own age. I was not exactly an underdog, for my swiftness put me beyond the reach of childish tricks and gave me the means of avenging myself easily. At the slightest threat, I was off at a distance—I mocked all pursuit. No matter how many of them there were, children never succeeded in surrounding me, much less in holding me prisoner. It was not worthwhile even to try to seize me by a trick. Weak as I might be at carrying burdens, my leaps were irresistible and freed me at once. I could return at will, overcome my adversary, even more than one, with swift, sure blows. Accordingly I was left in peace. I was looked on as innocent and at the same time a bit magical; but it was a feeble magic, which they scorned.

By degrees I made a life for myself outdoors, wild, meditative, not without its pleasures. Only the affection of my mother humanized me, even though, busy all day long, she found little time for caresses.

IV

I shall try to describe briefly a few scenes from my tenth year, in order to give substance to the explanations which have gone before.

It is morning. A bright glow illumines the kitchen—a pale yellow glow to my parents and the servants, richly various to me. The first breakfast is being served: bread and tea. But I do not take tea. I have been given a glass of Schiedam with a raw egg. My mother is hovering over me tenderly; my father questions me. I try to answer him, I slow down my speech; he understands only a syllable here and there. He shrugs. "He'll never learn to talk!"

My mother looks at me with compassion, convinced that I am a bit simple. The servants and laborers no longer even feel any curiosity about the little violet monster; the Frieslander has long ago gone back to her country. As for my sister, who is two years old, she is playing near me, and I feel a deep affection for her.

Breakfast over, my father goes off to the fields with the laborers; my mother begins to busy herself with her daily tasks. I follow her into the farmyard. The animals come up to her. I watch them with interest; I like them. But, all around, the other Kingdom is in motion, and it attracts me still more; it is the mysterious domain which only I know.

On the brown earth a few shapes are sprawled out; they move, they pause, they palpitate on the surface of the ground. They belong to several species, different in contours, in movement, and above all in the arrangement, design and shadings of the lines which run through them. Taken together, these lines constitute the essential part of their being, and, child though I am, I know it very well. Whereas the mass of their bodies is dull, grayish, the lines are almost always brilliant. They form highly complicated networks, radiating from centers, spreading out until they fade and lose their identity. Their tints and curves are innumerable. These colors vary within a single line, as the form does also, but to a lesser extent. The creature as a whole is distinguished by a rather irregular but very distinct outline; by the radiant centers; by the multicolored lines which intermingle freely. When it moves, the lines tremble, oscillate; the centers contract and dilate, while the outline changes little.

All this I see very well already, though I may be unable to define it; a delightful spell falls over me when I watch the *Moedigen.** One of them, a colossus ten meters long and almost as wide, passes slowly across the farmyard and disappears. This one, with some bands the size of cables, and centers as big as eagles' wings, greatly interests and almost frightens me. I pause for a moment, about to follow it, but then others attract my attention. They are of all sizes: some are no larger than our tiniest insects, while I have seen others more than thirty meters long. They advance on the ground itself, as if attached to solid surfaces. When they meet a material obstacle—a wall, or a house—they cross it by molding themselves to its surface, always without any significant change in their outlines. But when the obstacle is of living or once-living matter, they pass directly through it; thus I have seen them appear thousands of times out of trees and beneath the feet of animals and men. They can pass through water also, but prefer to remain on the surface.

These land *Moedigen* are not the only intangible creatures. There is an aerial population of a marvelous splendor, of an incomparable subtlety, variety and brilliance, beside which the most beautiful birds are dull, slow and heavy. Here again there are internal lines and an outline. But the background is not grayish, it is strangely luminous; it sparkles like sunlight, and the lines stand out from it in trembling veins; the centers palpitate violently. The *Vuren,* as I call them, are of a more irregular form than the land *Moedigen* and commonly propel themselves by means of rhythmic dispositions, intertwinings and untwinings which, in my ignorance, I cannot make out and which baffle my imagination.

Meanwhile I am making my way across a recently mowed meadow; the battle of a *Moedig* with another one has drawn my attention. These battles are frequent, and they excite me tremendously. Sometimes the battles are equal; more often an attack is made by the stronger upon the weaker. (The weaker is not necessarily the smaller.) In the present case, the weaker one, after a short defense, takes to flight, hotly pursued by the aggressor. Despite the swiftness of their motions, I follow them and succeed in keeping them in view until the struggle begins again. They fling themselves on each other—firmly, even rigidly, solid to each other. At the shock, their lines phosphoresce, moving toward the point of contact; their centers grow smaller and paler.

At first the struggle remains more or less equal; the weaker puts forth a more intense energy and even succeeds in gaining a truce from its adversary. It profits by this to flee once more, but is rapidly overtaken, strongly attacked and at last seized—that is to say, held fast in a hollow in the outline of the other. This is exactly what it has been trying to avoid, as it counters the stronger one's buffets with blows that are weaker but swifter. Now I see all its lines shudder, its centers throb desperately; and the lines gradually thin out, grow pale; the centers blur. After a few minutes, it is set free: it withdraws slowly, dull, debilitated. Its antagonist, on the contrary, glows more brightly; its lines are more vivid, its centers clearer and livelier.

This fight has moved me profoundly. I think about it and compare it with

*This is the name which I gave them spontaneously in my childhood and which I have retained, though it corresponds to no quality or form of these creatures.

the fights I sometimes see between *our* animals. I realize confusedly that the *Moedigen*, as a group, do not kill, or rarely kill, that the victor contents itself with *increasing its strength* at the expense of the vanquished.

The morning wears on; it is nearly eight o'clock; the Zwartendam school is about to open. I gain the house in one leap, seize my books, and here I am among my fellows, where no one guesses what profound mysteries palpitate around him, where no one has the least idea of the living things through which all humanity passes and which pass through humanity, leaving no mark of that mutual penetration.

I am a very poor scholar. My writing is nothing but a hasty scrawl, unformed, illegible; my speech remains uncomprehended; my absence of mind is manifest. The master calls out continually, "Karel Ondereet, have you done with watching the flies?"

Alas, my dear master! It is true that I watch the flies in the air, but how much more does my mind accompany the mysterious *Vuren* that pass through the room! And what strange feelings obsess my childish mind, to note everyone's blindness and above all your own, grave shepherd of intellects!

V

The most painful period of my life was that which ran from my twelfth to my eighteenth year.

To begin with, my parents tried to send me to the academy. I knew nothing there but misery and frustration. At the price of exhausting struggles, I succeeded in expressing the most ordinary things in a partially comprehensible manner: slowing my syllables with great effort, I uttered them awkwardly and with the intonations of the deaf. But as soon as I had to do with anything complicated, my speech regained its fatal swiftness; no one could follow me any longer. Therefore I could not register my progress orally. Moreover, my writing was atrocious, my letters piled up one on the other, and in my impatience I forgot whole syllables and words; it was a monstrous hodgepodge. Besides, writing was a torment to me, perhaps even more intolerable than speech—of an asphyxiating slowness, heaviness! If occasionally, by taking much pain and sweating great drops, I succeeded in beginning an exercise, at once I was at the end of my energy and patience; I felt about to faint. Accordingly I preferred the masters' remonstrances, the anger of my father, punishments, privations, scorn, to this horrible labor.

Thus I was almost totally deprived of the means of expression. Already an object of ridicule for my thinness and my strange color, my odd eyes, once more I passed for a kind of idiot. It was necessary for my parents to withdraw me from school and resign themselves to making a peasant of me.

The day my father decided to give up all hope, he said to me with unaccustomed gentleness, "My poor boy, you see I have done my duty—my whole duty. Never reproach me for your fate."

I was strongly moved. I shed warm tears; never had I felt more bitterly my isolation in the midst of men. I dared to embrace my father tenderly; I muttered, "Just the same, it's not true that I'm a halfwit!" And, in fact, I felt myself superior to those who had been my fellow pupils. Some time ago my intelligence had undergone a remarkable development. I read, I understood, I divined; and I had enormous matter for reflection, beyond that of other men, in that universe visible to me alone.

My father could not make out my words, but he softened to my embrace. "Poor boy!" he said.

I looked at him; I was in terrible distress, knowing too well that the gap between us would never be bridged. My mother, through love's intuition, saw in that moment that I was not inferior to the other boys of my age. She gazed at me tenderly, she spoke artless love words that came from the depths of her being. Nonetheless, I was condemned to give up my studies.

Because of my lack of muscular strength, I was given the care of the horses and the cattle. In this I acquitted myself admirably; I needed no dog to guard the herds, in which no colt or stallion was as agile as I.

Thus, from my fourteenth to my seventeenth year I lived the solitary life of the herdsman. It suited me better than any other. Given over to observation and contemplation, together with some reading, my mind never stopped growing. Incessantly I compared the two orders of creation which lay before my eyes; I drew from them ideas about the constitution of the universe; vaguely I sketched out hypotheses and systems. If it be true that in that period my thoughts were not perfectly ordered, did not make a lucid synthesis—for they were adolescent thoughts, uncoordinated, impatient, enthusiastic—nevertheless they were original, and fruitful. That their value may have depended above all upon my unique constitution, I would be the last to deny. But they did not draw all their strength from that source. I think I may say without pride that in subtlety as in logic they notably surpassed those of ordinary young men.

They alone brought consolation to my melancholy half-pariah's life, without companions, without any real communication with the rest of my household, even my adorable mother.

At the age of seventeen, life became definitely unsupportable to me. I was weary of dreaming, weary of vegetating on a desert island of thought. I fell into languor and boredom. I rested immobile for long hours, indifferent to the whole world, inattentive to anything that happened in my family. What mattered it that I knew of more marvelous things than other men, since in any case this knowledge must die with me? What was the mystery of living things to me, or even the duality of the two living systems crossing through each other without awareness of each other? These things might have intoxicated me, filled me with enthusiasm and ardor, if I could have taught them or shared them in any way. But what would you! Vain and sterile, absurd and miserable, they contributed rather to my perpetual psychic quarantine.

Many times I dreamed of setting down, recording, in spite of everything, by dint of continuous effort, some of my observations. But since leaving school I had completely abandoned the pen, and, already so wretched a scribbler, it was all I could do, with the utmost application, to trace the twenty-six letters of the alphabet. If I had still entertained any hope, perhaps I should have persisted. But who would have taken my miserable lucubrations seriously? Where was the reader who would not think me mad? Where the sage who would not show me the door with irony or disdain?

To what end, therefore, should I consecrate myself to that vain task, that exasperating torment, almost comparable to the requirement, for an ordinary man, to grave his thoughts upon tablets of marble with a huge chisel and a

Cyclopean hammer? My penmanship would have had to be stenographic—and yet more: of a superswift stenography! Thus I had no courage at all to write, and at the same time I fervently hoped for I know not what unforeseen event, what happy and singular destiny. It seemed to me that there must exist, in some corner of the earth, impartial minds, lucid, searching, qualified to study me, to understand me, to extract my great secret from me and communicate it to others. But where were these men? What hope had I of ever meeting them?

And I fell once more into a vast melancholy, into the desire for immobility and extinction. During one whole autumn, I despaired of the universe. I languished in a vegetative state, from which I emerged only to give way to long groans, followed by painful rebellions of conscience.

I grew thinner still, thin to a fantastic degree. The villagers called me, ironically, "*den Heyligen Gheest,*" the Holy Ghost. My silhouette was tremulous as that of the young poplars, faint as a shadow; and with all this, I grew to a giant's stature.

Slowly, a project was born. Since my life had been thrown into the discard, since my days were without joy and all was darkness and bitterness to me, why wallow in sloth? Supposing that no mind existed which could respond to my own—at least it would be worth the effort to convince myself of that fact. At least it would be worthwhile to leave this gloomy countryside, to go and search for scientists and philosophers in the great cities. Was I not in myself an object of curiosity? Before calling attention to my extrahuman knowledge, could I not arouse a desire to study my person? Were not the mere physical aspects of my being worthy of analysis—and my sight, and the extreme swiftness of my movements, and the peculiarity of my diet?

The more I thought of it, the more it seemed reasonable to me to hope, and the more my resolution hardened. The day came when it was unshakable, when I confided it to my parents. Neither one nor the other understood much of it, but in the end both gave in to repeated entreaties: I obtained permission to go to Amsterdam, free to return if fortune should not favor me.

One morning, I left.

VI

From Zwartendam to Amsterdam is a matter of a hundred kilometers or thereabouts. I covered that distance easily in two hours, without any other adventure than the extreme surprise of those going and coming to see me run so swiftly, and a few crowds at the edges of the villages and towns I skirted. To make sure of my direction, I spoke two or three times to solitary old people. My sense of orientation, which is excellent, did the rest.

It was about nine o'clock when I reached Amsterdam. I entered the great city resolutely and walked along its beautiful, dreaming canals, where quiet merchant fleets dwell. I did not attract as much attention as I had feared. I walked quickly, among busy people, enduring here and there the gibes of some young street Arabs. Nevertheless, I did not decide to stop. I wandered here and there through the city, until at last I resolved to enter a tavern on one of the quays of the Heerengracht. It was a peaceful spot; the magnificent canal stretched, full of life, between cool rows of trees; and among the *Moedigen* which I saw moving about on its banks it seemed to me that I perceived a new species. After some hesitation, I crossed the sill of the tavern, and addressing myself to the publican as slowly as I could, I begged him to be kind enough to direct me to a hospital.

The landlord looked at me with amazement, suspicion and curiosity; took his huge pipe out of his mouth, put it back in after several attempts, and at last said, "You're from the colonies, I suppose?"

Since it was perfectly useless to contradict him, I answered, "Just so!"

He seemed delighted at his own shrewdness. He asked me another question: "Maybe you come from that part of Borneo where no one has ever been?"

"Exactly right!"

I had spoken too swiftly: his eyes grew round.

"Exactly right," I repeated more slowly.

The landlord smiled with satisfaction. "You can hardly speak Dutch, can you? So, it's a hospital you want. No doubt you're sick?"

"Yes."

Patrons were gathering around. It was whispered already that I was an anthropophagus from Borneo; nevertheless, they looked at me with much more curiosity than aversion. People were running in from the street. I became nervous and uneasy. I kept my composure nonetheless and said, coughing, "I am very sick!"

"Just like the monkeys from that country," said a very fat man benevolently. "The Netherlands kills them!"

"What a funny skin!" added another.

"And how does he see?" asked a third, pointing to my eyes.

The ring moved closer, encircling me with a hundred curious stares, and still newcomers were crowding into the room.

"How tall he is!"

In truth, I was a full head taller than the biggest of them.

"And thin!"

"This anthropophagy doesn't seem to nourish them very well!"

Not all the voices were spiteful. A few sympathetic persons protected me:

"Don't crowd so—he's sick!"

"Come, friend, courage!" said the fat man, remarking my nervousness. "I'll lead you to a hospital myself."

He took me by the arm and set about elbowing the crowd aside, calling, "Way for an invalid!"

Dutch crowds are not very fierce. They let us pass, but they went with us. We walked along the canal, followed by a compact multitude, and people cried out, "It's a cannibal from Borneo!"

At length we reached a hospital. It was the visiting hour. I was taken to an intern, a young man with blue spectacles, who greeted me peevishly. My companion said to him, "He's a savage from the colonies."

"What, a savage!" cried the other.

He took off his spectacles to look at me. Surprise held him motionless for a moment. He asked me brusquely, "Can you see?"

"I see very well."

I had spoken too swiftly.

"It's his accent," said the fat man proudly. "Once more, friend."

I repeated it and made myself understood.

"Those aren't human eyes," murmured the student. "And the color! Is that the color of your race?"

Then I said, with a terrible effort to slow myself down, "I have come to show myself to a scientist."

"Then you're not ill?"

"No."

"And you come from Borneo?"

"No."

"Where are you from, then?"

"From Zwartendam, near Duisburg."

"Why, then, does this man claim you're from Borneo?"

"I didn't want to contradict him."

"And you wish to see a scientist?"

"Yes."

"Why?"

"To be studied."

"So as to earn money?"

"No, for nothing."

"You're not a pauper? A beggar?"

"No!"

"What makes you want to be studied?"

"My constitution—"

But again, in spite of my efforts, I had spoken too swiftly. I had to repeat myself.

"Are you sure you can see me?" he asked, staring at me. "Your eyes are like horn."

"I see very well."

And, moving to left and right, I snatched things up, put them down, threw them in the air and caught them again.

"Extraordinary!" said the young man.

His softened voice, almost friendly, filled me with hope. "See here," he said at last, "I really think Dr. van den Heuvel might be interested in your case. I'll go and inform him. Wait in the next room. And, by the way—I forgot—you're not ill, after all?"

"Not in the least."

"Good. Wait—go in there. The doctor won't be long."

I found myself seated among monsters preserved in alcohol: fetuses, infants with bestial shapes, colossal batrachians, vaguely anthropomorphic saurians.

This is well chosen for my waiting room, I thought. Am I not a candidate for one of these brandy-filled sepulchers?

VII

When Dr. van den Heuvel appeared, emotion overcame me. I had the thrill of the Promised Land—the joy of reaching it, the dread of being banished. The doctor, with his great bald forehead, the analyst's penetrating look, the mouth soft and yet stubborn, examined me in silence. As always, my excessive thinness, my great stature, my horny eyes, my violet color, caused him astonishment.

"You say you wish to be studied?" he asked at length.

I answered forcefully, almost violently, "Yes!"

He smiled with an approving air and asked me the usual question: "Do you see all right, with those eyes?"

"Very well. I can even see through wood, clouds—"

But I had spoken too fast. He glanced at me uneasily. I began again, sweating great drops: "I can even see through wood, clouds—"

"Really! That would be extraordinary. Well, then! What do you see through the door there?" He pointed to a closed door.

"A big library with windows . . . a carved table . . ."

"Really!" he repeated, stunned.

My breast swelled; a deep stillness entered my soul.

The scientist remained silent for a few seconds. Then: "You speak with some difficulty."

"Otherwise I should speak too rapidly! I cannot speak slowly."

"Well, then, speak a little as you do naturally."

Accordingly I told him the story of my entry into Amsterdam. He listened to me with an extreme attention, an air of intelligent observation, which I had never before encountered among my fellows. He understood nothing of what I said, but he showed the keenness of his intellect.

"If I am not mistaken, you speak fifteen to twenty syllables a second, that is to say three or four times more than the human ear can distinguish. Your voice, in addition, is much higher than anything I have ever heard in the way of human voices. Your excessively rapid gestures are well suited to your speech. Your whole constitution is probably more rapid than ours."

"I run," I said, "faster than a greyhound. I write—"

"Ah!" he interrupted. "Let us see your writing."

I scrawled some words on a tablet which he offered me, the first few fairly legible, the rest more and more scrambled, abbreviated.

"Perfect!" he said, and a certain pleasure was mingled with his surprise. "I really think I must congratulate myself on this meeting. Certainly it should be very interesting to study you."

"It is my dearest, my only, desire!"

"And mine, naturally. Science . . ."

He seemed preoccupied, musing. He finished by saying, "If only we could find an easy way of communication."

He walked back and forth, his brows knotted. Suddenly: "What a dolt I am! You must learn shorthand, of course! Hm! . . . Hm!" A cheerful expression spread over his face. "And I've forgotten the phonograph—the perfect confidant! All that's needed is to revolve it more slowly in the reproduction than in the recording. It's agreed: you shall stay with me while you are in Amsterdam!"

The joy of a fulfilled vocation, the delight of ceasing to spend vain and sterile days! Aware of the intelligent personality of the doctor, against this scientific background, I felt a delicious well-being; the melancholy of my spiritual solitude, the sorrow for my lost talents, the pariah's long misery that had weighed me down for so many years, all vanished, evaporated in the sensation of a new life, a real life, a saved destiny!

VIII

Beginning the following day, the doctor made all the necessary arrangements. He wrote to my parents; he sent me to a professor of stenography and obtained some phonographs. As he was quite rich and entirely devoted to science, there was no experiment which he could not undertake, and my vision, my hearing, my musculature, the color of my skin, were submitted to scrupulous investigations, from which he drew more and more enthusiasm, crying, "This verges on the miraculous!"

I very well understood, after the first few days, how important it was to go about things methodically—from the simple to the complex, from the slightly abnormal to the wonderfully abnormal. Thus I had recourse to a little legerdemain, of which I made no secret to the doctor: that is, I revealed my abilities to him only one at a time.

The quickness of my perceptions and movements drew his attention first. He was able to convince himself that the subtlety of my hearing was in proportion to the swiftness of my speech. Graduated trials of the most fugitive sounds, which I imitated with ease, and the words of ten or fifteen persons all talking at once, which I distinguished perfectly, demonstrated this point beyond question. My vision proved no less swift; comparative tests between my ability to resolve the movement of a galloping horse, or an insect in flight, and the same ability of an apparatus for taking instantaneous photographs, proved all in favor of my eye.

As for perceptions of ordinary things, simultaneous movements of a group of people, of children playing, the motion of machines, bits of rubble thrown in the air or little balls tossed into an alley, to be counted in flight—they amazed the doctor's family and friends.

My running in the big garden, my twenty-meter jumps, my instantaneous swiftness to pick up objects or put them back, were admired still more, not by the doctor, but by those around him. And it was an ever renewed pleasure for the wife and children of my host, while walking in the fields, to see me outstrip a horseman at full gallop or follow the flight of any swallow; in truth, there was no thoroughbred but I could give it a start of two-thirds the distance, whatever it might be, nor any bird I could not easily overtake.

As for the doctor, more and more satisfied with the results of his experiments, he described me thus: "A human being, endowed in all his movements with a swiftness incomparably superior, not merely to that of other humans, but also to that of all known animals. This swiftness, found in the most minute constituents of his body as well as in the whole organism, makes him an entity so distinct from the remainder of creation that he merits a special place in the animal kingdom for himself alone. As for the curious structure of his eyes, as well as the skin's violet color, these must be considered simply the earmarks of this special condition."

Tests being made of my muscular system, it proved in no way remarkable, unless for its excessive leanness. Neither did my ears yield any particular information; nor, for that matter, did my skin—except, of course, for its pigmentation. As for my dark hair, a purplish black in color, it was fine as spiderweb, and the doctor made a minute examination of it.

"One would need to dissect you!" he often told me, laughing.

Thus time passed easily. I had quickly learned to write in shorthand, thanks to my intense desire and to the natural aptitude I showed for this method of rapid transcription, into which, by the way, I introduced several new abbreviations. I began to make notes, which my stenographer transcribed; for the rest, we had phonographs built, according to the doctor's special design, which proved perfectly suited to reproduce my voice at a lower speed.

At length my host's confidence in me became complete. During the first few weeks he had not been able to avoid the suspicion—a very natural one—that my peculiar abilities might be accompanied by some mental abnormality, some cerebral derangement. This anxiety once put aside, our relations became perfectly cordial, and I think, as fascinating for one as for the other.

We made analytic tests of my ability to see through a great number of "opaque" substances; and of the dark coloration which water, glass or quartz takes on for me at certain thicknesses. It will be recalled that I can see clearly through wood, leaves, clouds and many other substances; that I can barely make out the bottom of a pool of water half a meter deep; and that a window, though transparent, is less so to me than to the average person and has a rather dark color. A thick piece of glass appears blackish to me. The doctor convinced himself at leisure of all these singularities—astonished above all to see me make out the stars on cloudy nights.

Only then did I begin to tell him that colors too present themselves differently to me. Experience established beyond doubt that red, orange, yellow, green, blue and indigo are perfectly invisible to me, like infrared or ultraviolet to a normal eye. On the other hand, I was able to show that I perceive violet, and beyond violet a range of colors—a spectrum at least double that which extends from the red to the violet.*

This amazed the doctor more than all the rest. His study of it was long and painstaking; it was conducted, besides, with enormous cunning. In this accomplished experimenter's hands, it became the source of subtle discoveries in the order of sciences as they are ranked by humanity; it gave him the key to far-ranging phenomena of magnetism, of chemical affinities, of induction; it guided him toward new conceptions of physiology. To know that a given metal shows a series of unknown tints, variable according to the pressure, the temperature, the electric charge, that the most rarefied gases have distinct colors, even at small depths; to learn of the infinite tonal richness of objects which appear more or less black, whereas they present a more magnificent spectrum in the ultraviolet than that of all known colors; to know, finally, the possible variations in unknown hues of an electric circuit, the bark of a tree, the skin of a man, in a day, an hour, a minute—the use that an ingenious scientist might make of such ideas can readily be imagined.

We worked patiently for a whole year without my mentioning the *Moedigen*. I wished to convince my host absolutely, give him countless proofs of my visual faculties, before daring the supreme confidence. At length, the time came when I felt I could reveal everything.

*Quartz gives me a spectrum of about eight colors: the longest violet and the seven succeeding colors in the ultraviolet. But there remain about eight more colors which are not refracted by quartz, and which are refracted more or less by other substances.

IX

It happened in a mild autumn full of clouds, which rolled across the vault of the sky for a week without shedding a drop of rain. One morning van den Heuvel and I were walking in the garden. The doctor was silent, completely absorbed in his speculations, of which I was the principal subject. At the far end, he began to speak:

"It's a nice thing to dream about, anyhow: to see through clouds, pierce through to the ether, whereas we, blind as we are . . ."

"If the sky were all I saw!" I answered.

"Oh, yes—the whole world, so different . . ."

"Much more different even than I've told you!"

"How's that?" he cried with an avid curiosity. "Have you been hiding something from me?"

"The most important thing!"

He stood facing me, staring at me fixedly, in real distress, in which some element of the mystical seemed to be blended.

"Yes, the most important thing!"

We had come near the house, and I dashed in to ask for a phonograph. The instrument that was brought to me was an advanced model, highly perfected by my friend, and could record a long speech; the servant put it down on the stone table where the doctor and his family took coffee on mild summer evenings. A miracle of exact, fine construction, the device lent itself admirably to recording casual talks. Our dialogue went on, therefore, almost like an ordinary conversation.

"Yes, I've hidden the main thing from you, because I wanted your complete confidence first—and even now, after all the discoveries you've made about my organism, I am afraid you won't find it easy to believe me, at least to begin with."

I stopped to let the machine repeat this sentence. I saw the doctor grow pale, with the pallor of a great scientist in the presence of a new aspect of matter. His hands were trembling.

"I shall believe you!" he said, with a certain solemnity.

"Even if I try to tell you that our order of creation—I mean our animal and vegetable world—isn't the only life on earth, that there is another, as vast, as numerous, as varied, invisible to your eyes?"

He scented occultism and could not refrain from saying, "The world of the fourth state of matter—departed souls, the phantoms of the spiritualists."

"No, no, nothing like that. A world of living creatures, doomed like us to a short life, to organic needs—birth, growth, struggle. A world as weak and ephemeral as ours, a world governed by laws equally rigid, if not identical, a world equally imprisoned by the earth, equally vulnerable to accident, but otherwise completely different from ours, without any influence on ours, as we have no influence on it—except through the changes it makes in our common ground, the earth, or through the parallel changes that we create in the same ground."

I do not know if van den Heuvel believed me, but certainly he was in the grip of strong emotion. "They are fluid, in short?" he asked.

"That's what I don't know how to answer, for their properties are too contradictory to fit into our ideas of matter. The earth is as resistant to them as to us, and the same with most minerals, although they can penetrate a little way into a humus. Also, they are totally impermeable and solid with respect to each other.

But they can pass through plants, animals, organic tissues, although sometimes with a certain difficulty; and we ourselves pass through them the same way. If one of them could be aware of us, we should perhaps seem fluid with respect to them, as they seem fluid with respect to us; but probably he could no more *decide* about it than I can—he would be struck by similar contradictions. There is one peculiarity about their shape: they have hardly any thickness. They are of all sizes. I've known some to reach a hundred meters in length, and others are as tiny as our smallest insects. Some of them feed on earth and air, others on air and on their own kind—without killing as we do, however, because it's enough for the stronger to draw strength from the weaker, and because this strength can be extracted without draining the springs of life."

The doctor said brusquely, "Have you seen them ever since childhood?"

I guessed that he was imagining some more or less recent disorder in my body. "Since childhood," I answered vigorously. "I'll give you all the proofs you like."

"Do you see them now?"

"I see them. There are a great many in the garden."

"Where?"

"On the path, the lawns, on the walls, in the air. For there are terrestrial and aerial ones—and aquatic ones too, but those hardly ever leave the surface of the water."

"Are they numerous everywhere?"

"Yes, and hardly less so in town than in the country, in houses than in the street. Those that like the indoors are smaller, though, no doubt because of the difficulty of getting in and out, even though they find a wooden door no obstacle."

"And iron . . . glass . . . brick?"

"All impermeable to them."

"Will you describe one of them, a fairly large one?"

"I see one near that tree. Its shape is extremely elongated, and rather irregular. It is convex toward the right, concave toward the left, with swellings and hollows: it looks something like an enlarged photograph of a big, fat larva. But its structure is not typical of the Kingdom, because structure varies a great deal from one species (if I may use that word) to another. Its extreme thinness, on the other hand, is a common characteristic: it can hardly be more than a tenth of a millimeter in thickness, whereas it's one hundred and fifty centimeters long and forty centimeters across at its widest.

"What distinguishes this, and the whole Kingdom, above all are the lines that cross it in nearly every direction, ending in networks that fan out between two systems of lines. Each system has a center, a kind of spot that is slightly raised above the mass of the body, or occasionally hollowed out. These centers have no fixed form; sometimes they are almost circular or elliptical, sometimes twisted or helical, sometimes divided by many narrow throats. They are astonishingly mobile, and their size varies from hour to hour. Their borders palpitate strongly, in a sort of transverse undulation. In general, the lines that emerge from them are big, although there are also very fine ones; they diverge, and end in an infinity of delicate traceries which gradually fade away. However, certain lines, much paler than the others, are not produced by the centers; they stay isolated in the system and grow without changing their color. These lines have the faculty of moving within the body, and of varying their curves, while the centers and their connected lines remain stable.

"As for the colors of my *Moedig*, I must forego any attempt to describe them to you; none of them falls within the spectrum perceptible to your eye, and none has a name in your vocabulary. They are extremely brilliant in the networks, weaker in the centers, very much faded in the independent lines, which, however, have a very high brilliance—an ultraviolet metallic effect, so to speak. . . . I have some observations on the habits, the diet and the range of the *Moedigen,* but I don't wish to submit them to you just now."

I fell silent. The doctor listened twice to the words recorded by our faultless interpreter; then for a long time he was silent. Never had I seen him in such a state: his face was rigid, stony, his eyes glassy and cataleptic; a heavy film of sweat covered his temples and dampened his hair. He tried to speak and failed. Trembling, he walked all around the garden; and when he reappeared, his eyes and mouth expressed a violent passion, fervent, religious; he seemed more like the disciple of some new faith than like a peaceful investigator.

At last he muttered, "I'm overwhelmed! Everything you have just said seems terribly lucid—and have I the right to doubt, considering all the wonders you've already shown me?"

"Doubt!" I said warmly. "Doubt as hard as you can! Your experiments will be all the more fruitful for it."

"Ah," he said in a dreaming voice, "it's the pure stuff of wonder, and so magnificently superior to the pointless marvels of fairy tales! My poor human intelligence is so tiny before such knowledge! I feel an enormous enthusiasm. Yet something in me doubts . . ."

"Let's work to dispel your doubt—our efforts will pay for themselves ten times over!"

X

We worked; and it took the doctor only a few weeks to clear up all his uncertainties. Several ingenious experiments, together with the undeniable consistency of all the statements I had made, and two or three lucky discoveries about the *Moedigen*'s influence on atmospheric phenomena, left no question in his mind. When we were joined by the doctor's elder son, a young man of great scientific aptitude, the fruitfulness of our work and the conclusiveness of our findings were again increased.

Thanks to my companions' methodical habits of mind, and their experience in study and classification—qualities which I was absorbing little by little—whatever was uncoordinated or confused in my knowledge of the *Moedigen* rapidly became transformed. Our discoveries multiplied; rigorous experiments gave firm results, in circumstances which in ancient times and even up to the last century would have suggested at most a few trifling diversions.

It is now five years since we began our researches. They are far, very far from completion. Even a preliminary report of our work can hardly appear in the near future. In any case, we have made it a rule to do nothing in haste; our discoveries are too immanent a kind not to be set forth in the most minute detail, with the most sovereign patience and the finest precision. We have no other investigator to forestall, no patent to take out or ambition to satisfy. We stand at a height where vanity and pride fade away. How can there be any comparison between the joys of our work and the wretched lure of human fame? Besides, do not all these things flow from the single accident of my physical organization? What a petty thing it would be, then, for us to boast about them!

No; we live excitedly, always on the verge of wonders, and yet we live in immutable serenity.

I have had an adventure which adds to the interest of my life, and which fills me with infinite joy during my leisure hours. You know how ugly I am; my bizarre appearance is fit only to horrify young women. All the same, I have found a companion who not only can put up with my show of affection, but even takes pleasure in it.

She is a poor girl, hysterical and nervous, whom we met one day in a hospital in Amsterdam. Others find her wretched-looking, plaster-white, hollow-cheeked, with wild eyes. But to me her appearance is pleasant, her company charming. From the very beginning my presence, far from alarming her like all the rest, seemed to please and comfort her. I was touched; I wanted to see her again.

It was quickly discovered that I had a beneficial influence on her health and well-being. On examination, it appeared that I influenced her by animal magnetism: my nearness, and above all the touch of my hands, gave her a really curative gaiety, serenity, and calmness of spirit. In turn, I took pleasure in being near her. Her face seemed lovely to me; her pallor and slenderness were no more than signs of delicacy; for me her eyes, able to perceive the glow of magnets, like those of many hyperesthesiacs, had none at all of the distracted quality that others criticized.

In short, I felt an attraction for her, and she returned it with passion. From that time, I resolved to marry her. I gained my end readily, thanks to the good will of my friends.

This union has been a happy one. My wife's health was re-established, although she remained extremely sensitive and frail. I tasted the joy of being like other men in the essential part of life. But my happiness was crowned six months ago: a child was born to us, and in this child are combined all the faculties of my constitution. Color, vision, hearing, extreme rapidity of movement, diet—he promises to be an exact copy of my physiology.

The doctor watches him grow with delight. A wonderful hope has come to us—that the study of the *Moedig* World, of the Kingdom parallel to our own, this study which demands so much time and patience, will not end when I cease to be. My son will pursue it, undoubtedly, in his turn. Why may he not find collaborators of genius, able to raise it to a new power? Why may he also not give life to seers of the invisible world?

As for myself, may I not look forward to other children, may I not hope that my dear wife may give birth to other sons of my flesh, like unto their father? As I think of it, my heart trembles, I am filled with an infinite beatitude; and I know myself blessed among men.

Gordon Eklund & Gregory Benford

Gregory Benford (1941–) and Gordon Eklund (1945–) were sometime collaborators in the 1970s. At the start, Eklund was "the writer," producing many other stories and novels on his own, and Benford was "the scientist," a full-time physicist who occasionally published science fiction. But by the end of the decade, Benford had become one of the leading younger writers, producing two significant works, *In the Ocean of Night* (1977) and *The Stars in Shroud* (1978) and then the classic *Timescape* (1980), and Eklund, who had published many short stories and nine novels by 1976—*If the Stars Are Gods* (1977) was his tenth—stopped writing for long periods of time after 1979. Of all their works, this one (1975), later developed into the novel of the same title, is the best. It was to a large extent written by Eklund and revised by Benford.

Benford in his later works is the first among the hard SF writers to have mastered and integrated Modernist techniques of characterization and use of metaphor, and some of this may have been assimilated through his early collaboration with Eklund. The tension between the daily work of science and the avocation of writing in Benford's life has led him to write some of the finest science fiction of recent decades. Brian W. Aldiss says: "If he takes the close and narrow view of his characters—an all-too-human view, of illness, work and marital problems—his vision of the universe in which such frail beings exist is one of vast perspectives, rather in the tradition of Stapledon and Clarke."

"If the Stars Are Gods" is an intrusion of the metaphysical into the ordinary world of science fiction. It is very much in the tradition of Clarke, in the mode of *2001: A Space Odyssey.*

IF THE STARS ARE GODS

A dog cannot be a hypocrite, but neither can he be sincere.
—Ludwig Wittgenstein

It was deceptively huge and massive, this alien starship, and somehow seemed as if it belonged almost anywhere else in the universe but here.

Reynolds stepped carefully down the narrow corridor of the ship, still replaying in his mind's eye the approach to the air lock, the act of being swallowed. The ceilings were high, the light poor, the walls made of some dull, burnished metal.

These aspects and others flitted through his mind as he walked. Reynolds was a man who appreciated the fine interlacing pleasures of careful thought, but more than that, thinking so closely of these things kept his mind occupied and drove away the smell. It was an odd thick odor, and something about it upset his careful equilibrium. It clung to him like Pacific fog. Vintage manure, Reynolds had decided the moment he passed through the air lock. Turning, he had glared at Kelly firmly encased inside her suit. He told her about the smell. "Everybody stinks," she had said, evenly, perhaps joking, perhaps not, and pushed him away in the light centrifugal gravity. Away, into a maze of tight passages that would lead him eventually to look the first certified intelligent alien beings straight in the eye. If they happened to have eyes, that is.

It amused him that this privilege should be his. More rightly, the honor should have gone to another, someone younger whose tiny paragraph in the future histories of the human race had not already been enacted. At fifty-eight, Reynolds had long since lived a full and intricate lifetime. Too full, he sometimes thought, for any one man. So then, what about this day now? What about today? It did nothing really, only succeeded in forcing the fullness of his lifetime past the point of all reasonableness into a realm of positive absurdity.

The corridor branched again. He wondered precisely where he was inside the sculpted and twisted skin of the ship. He had tried to memorize everything he saw but there was nothing, absolutely nothing but metal with thin seams, places where he had to stoop or crawl, and the same awful smell. He realized now what it was about the ship that had bothered him the first time he had seen it, through a telescope from the moon. It reminded him, both in size and shape, of a building where he had once lived not so many years ago, during the brief term of his most recent retirement, 1987 and '88, in São Paulo, Brazil: a huge ultramodern lifting apartment complex of a distinctly radical design. There was nothing like it on Earth, the advertising posters had proclaimed; and seeing it, hating it instantly, he had agreed. Now here was something else truly like it, but not on Earth.

The building had certainly not resembled a starship, but then, neither did this thing. At one end was an intricately designed portion, a cylinder with interesting modifications. Then came a long, plain tube and at the end of that something truly absurd: a cone, opening outward away from the rest of the ship and absolutely empty. Absurd, until you realized what it was.

The starship's propulsion source was, literally, hydrogen bombs. The central tube evidently held a vast number of fusion devices. One by one the bombs were released, drifted to the mouth of the cone and were detonated. The cone was a huge shock absorber; the kick from the bomb pushed the ship forward. A Rube Goldberg star drive—

Directly ahead of him, the corridor neatly stopped and split, like the twin prongs of a roasting fork. It jogged his memory: roasting fork, yes, from the days when he still ate meat. Turning left, he followed the proper prong. His directions had been quite clear.

He still felt very ill at ease. Maybe it was the way he was dressed that made everything seem so totally wrong. It didn't seem quite right, walking through an alien maze in his shirtsleeves and plain trousers. Pedestrian.

But the air was breathable, as promised. Did they breathe this particular oxygen-nitrogen balance, too? And like the smell?

Ahead, the corridor parted, branching once more. The odor was horribly powerful at this spot, and he ducked his head low, almost choking, and dashed through a round opening.

This was a big room. Like the corridor, the ceiling was a good seven meters above the floor, but the walls were subdued pastel shades of red, orange and yellow. The colors were mixed on all the walls in random, patternless designs. It was very pretty, Reynolds thought, and not at all strange. Also, standing neatly balanced near the back wall, there were two aliens.

When he saw the creatures, Reynolds stopped and stood tall. Raising his eyes, he stretched to reach the level of their eyes. While he did this, he also reacted. His first reaction was shock. This gave way to the tickling sensation of surprise. Then pleasure and relief. He liked the looks of these two creatures. They were certainly far kinder toward the eyes than what he had expected to find.

Stepping forward, Reynolds stood before both aliens, shifting his gaze from one to the other. Which was the leader? Or were both leaders? Or neither? He decided to wait. But neither alien made a sound or a move. So Reynolds kept waiting.

What had he expected to find? Men? Something like a man, that is, with two arms and two legs and a properly positioned head, with a nose, two eyes and a pair of floppy ears? This was what Kelly had expected him to find—she would be disappointed now—but Reynolds had never believed it for a moment. Kelly thought anything that spoke English had to be a man, but Reynolds was more imaginative. He knew better; he had not expected to find a man, not even a man with four arms and three legs and fourteen fingers or five ears. What he had expected to find was something truly alien. A blob, if worst came to worst, but at best something more like a shark or snake or wolf than a man. As soon as Kelly had told him that the aliens wanted to meet him—"Your man who best knows your star"—he had known this.

Now he said, "I am the man you wished to see. The one who knows the stars."

As he spoke, he carefully shared his gaze with both aliens, still searching for a leader, favoring neither over the other. One—the smaller one—twitched a nostril when Reynolds said, ". . . the stars"; the other remained motionless.

There was one Earth animal that did resemble these creatures, and this was why Reynolds felt happy and relieved. The aliens were sufficiently alien, yes. And they were surely not men. But neither did they resemble blobs or wolves or sharks or snakes. They were giraffes. Nice, kind, friendly, pleasant, smiling, silent giraffes. There were some differences, of course. The aliens' skin was a rainbow collage of pastel purples, greens, reds and yellows, similar in its random design to the colorfully painted walls. Their trunks stood higher off the ground, their necks were stouter than that of a normal giraffe. They did not have tails. Nor hooves. Instead, at the bottom of each of their four legs, they had five blunt short fingers and a single wide thick off-setting thumb.

"My name is Bradley Reynolds," he said. "I know the stars." Despite himself, their continued silence made him nervous. "Is something wrong?" he asked.

The shorter alien bowed its neck toward him. Then, in a shrill high-pitched voice that reminded him of a child, it said, "No." An excited nervous child. "That is no," it said.

"This?" Reynolds lifted his hand, having almost forgotten what was in it. Kelly had ordered him to carry the tape recorder, but now he could truthfully say, "I haven't activated it yet."

"Break it, please," the alien said.

Reynolds did not protest or argue. He let the machine fall to the floor. Then he jumped, landing on the tape recorder with both feet. The light aluminum case split wide open like the hide of a squashed apple. Once more, Reynolds jumped. Then, standing calmly, he kicked the broken bits of glass and metal toward an unoccupied corner of the room. "All right?" he asked.

Now for the first time the second alien moved. Its nostrils twitched daintily, then its legs shifted, lifting and falling. "Welcome," it said, abruptly, stopping all motion. "My name is Jonathon."

"Your name?" asked Reynolds.

"And this is Richard."

"Oh," said Reynolds, not contradicting. He understood now. Having learned the language of man, these creatures had learned his names as well.

"We wish to know your star," Jonathon said respectfully. His voice was a duplicate of the other's. Did the fact that he had not spoken until after the destruction of the tape recorder indicate that he was the leader of the two? Reynolds almost laughed, listening to the words of his own thoughts. Not *he*, he reminded himself: *it*.

"I am willing to tell you whatever you wish to know," Reynolds said.

"You are a . . . priest . . . a reverend of the sun?"

"An astronomer," Reynolds corrected.

"We would like to know everything you know. And then we would like to visit and converse with your star."

"Of course. I will gladly help you in any way I can." Kelly had cautioned him in advance that the aliens were interested in the sun, so none of this came as any surprise to him. But nobody knew what it was in particular that they wanted to know, or why, and Kelly hoped that he might be able to find out. At the moment he could think of only two possible conversational avenues to take; both were questions. He tried the first. "What is it you wish to know? Is our star greatly different from others of its type? If it is, we are unaware of this fact."

"No two stars are the same," the alien said. This was Jonathon again. Its voice began to rise in excitement. "What is it? Do you not wish to speak here? Is our craft an unsatisfactory place?"

"No, this is fine," Reynolds said, wondering if it was wise to continue concealing his puzzlement. "I will tell you what I know. Later, I can bring books."

"No!" The alien did not shout, but from the way its legs quivered and nostrils trembled, Reynolds gathered he had said something very improper indeed.

"I will tell you," he said. "In my own words."

Jonathon stood quietly rigid. "Fine."

Now it was time for Reynolds to ask his second question. He let it fall within the long silence which had followed Jonathon's last statement. "Why do you wish to know about our star?"

"It is the reason why we have come here. On our travels, we have visited many stars. But it is yours we have sought the longest. It is so powerful. And benevolent. A rare combination, as you must know."

"Very rare," Reynolds said, thinking that this wasn't making any sense. But then, why should it? At least he had learned something of the nature of the aliens' mission, and that alone was more than anyone else had managed to learn during the months the aliens had slowly approached the moon, exploding their hydrogen bombs to decelerate.

A sudden burst of confidence surprised Reynolds. He had not felt this sure of himself in years, and just like before, there was no logical reason for his certainty. "Would you be willing to answer some questions for me? About *your* star?"

"Certainly, Bradley Reynolds."

"Can you tell me our name for your star? Its coordinates?"

"No," Jonathon said, dipping its neck. "I cannot." It blinked its right eye in a furious fashion. "Our galaxy is not this one. It is a galaxy too distant for your instruments."

"I see," said Reynolds, because he could not very well call the alien a liar, even if it was. But Jonathon's hesitancy to reveal the location of its homeworld was not unexpected; Reynolds would have acted the same in similar circumstances.

Richard spoke. "May I pay obeisance?"

Jonathon, turning to Richard, spoke in a series of shrill chirping noises. Then Richard replied in kind.

Turning back to Reynolds, Richard again asked, "May I pay obeisance?"

Reynolds could only say, "Yes." Why not?

Richard acted immediately. Its legs abruptly shot out from beneath its trunk at an angle no giraffe could have managed. Richard sat on its belly, legs spread, and its neck came down, the snout gently scraping the floor.

"Thank you," Reynolds said, bowing slightly at the waist. "But there is much we can learn from you, too." He spoke to hide his embarrassment, directing his words at Jonathon while hoping that they might serve to bring Richard back to its feet as well. When this failed to work, Reynolds launched into the speech he had been sent here to deliver. Knowing what he had to say, he ran through the words as hurriedly as possible. "We are a backward people. Compared to you, we are children in the universe. Our travels have carried us no farther than our sister planets, while you have seen stars whose light takes years to reach your home. We realize you have much to teach us, and we approach you as pupils before a grand philosopher. We are gratified at the chance to share our meager knowledge with you and wish only to be granted the privilege of listening to you in return."

"You wish to know deeply of our star?" Jonathon asked.

"Of many things," Reynolds said. "Your spacecraft for instance. It is far beyond our meager knowledge."

Jonathon began to blink its right eye furiously. As it spoke, the speed of the blinking increased. "You wish to know that?"

"Yes, if you are willing to share your knowledge. We, too, would like to visit the stars."

Its eye moved faster than ever now. It said, "Sadly, there is nothing we can tell you of this ship. Unfortunately, we know nothing ourselves."

"Nothing?"

"The ship was a gift."

"You mean that you did not make it yourself. No. But you must have mechanics, individuals capable of repairing the craft in the event of some emergency."

"But that has never happened. I do not think the ship could fail."

"Would you explain?"

"Our race, our world, was once visited by another race of creatures. It was they who presented us with this ship. They had come to us from a distant star in order to make this gift. In return, we have used the ship only to increase the wisdom of our people."

"What can you tell me about this other race?" Reynolds asked.

"Very little, I am afraid. They came from a most ancient star near the true center of the universe."

"And were they like you? Physically?"

"No, more like you. Like people. But—please—may we be excused to converse about that which is essential? Our time is short."

Reynolds nodded, and the moment he did, Jonathon ceased to blink. Reynolds gathered that it had grown tired of lying, which wasn't surprising; Jonathon was a poor liar. Not only were the lies incredible in themselves, but every time it told a lie it blinked like a madman with an ash in his eye.

"If I tell you about our star," Jonathon said, "will you consent to tell of yours in return?" The alien tilted its head forward, long neck swaying gently from side to side. It was plain that Jonathon attached great significance to Reynolds' reply.

So Reynolds said, "Yes, gladly," though he found he could not conceive of any information about the sun which might come as a surprise to these creatures. Still, he had been sent here to discover as much about the aliens as possible without revealing anything important about mankind. This sharing of information about stars seemed a safe enough course to pursue.

"I will begin," Jonathon said, "and you must excuse my impreciseness of expression. My knowledge of your language is limited. I imagine you have a special vocabulary for the subject."

"A technical vocabulary, yes."

The alien said, "Our star is a brother to yours. Or would it be sister? During periods of the most intense communion, his wisdom—or hers?—is faultless. At times he is angry—unlike your star—but these moments are not frequent. Nor do they last for longer than a few fleeting moments. Twice he has prophesied the termination of our civilization during times of great personal anger, but never has he felt it necessary to carry out his prediction. I would say that he is more kind than raging, more gentle than brutal. I believe he loves our people most truly and fully. Among the stars of the universe, his place is not great, but as our home star, we must revere him. And, of course, we do."

"Would you go on?" Reynolds asked.

Jonathon went on. Reynolds listened. The alien spoke of its personal relationship with the star, how the star had helped it during times of individual darkness. Once, the star had assisted it in choosing a proper mate; the choice proved not only perfect but divine. Throughout, Jonathon spoke of the star as a reverent Jewish tribesman might have spoken of the Old Testament God. For the first time, Reynolds regretted having had to dispose of the tape recorder. When he tried to tell Kelly about this conversation, she would never believe a word of it. As it spoke, the alien did not blink, not once, even briefly, for Reynolds watched carefully.

At last the alien was done. It said, "But this is only a beginning. We have so much to share, Bradley Reynolds. Once I am conversant with your technical vocabulary. Communication between separate entities—the great barriers of language . . ."

"I understand," said Reynolds.

"We knew you would. But now—it is your turn. Tell me about your star."

"We call it the sun," Reynolds said. Saying, this, he felt more than mildly foolish—but what else? How could he tell Jonathon what it wished to know when he did not know himself? All he knew about the sun was facts. He knew how hot it was and how old it was and he knew its size and mass and magnitude. He knew about sunspots and solar winds and solar atmosphere. But that was all he knew. Was the sun a benevolent star? Was it constantly enraged? Did all mankind revere it with the proper quantity of love and dedication? "That is its common name. More properly, in an ancient language adopted by science, it is Sol. It lies approximately eight—"

"Oh," said Jonathon. "All of this, yes, we know. But its demeanor. Its attitudes, both normal and abnormal. You play with us, Bradley Reynolds. You joke. We understand your amusement—but, please, we are simple souls and have traveled far. We must know these other things before daring to make our personal approach to the star. Can you tell us in what fashion it has most often affected your individual life? This would help us immensely."

Although his room was totally dark, Reynolds, entering, did not bother with the light. He knew every inch of this room, knew it as well in the dark as the light. For the past four years, he had spent an average of twelve hours a day here. He knew the four walls, the desk, the bed, the bookshelves and the books, knew them more intimately than he had ever known another person. Reaching the cot without once stubbing his toe or tripping over an open book or stumbling across an unfurled map, he sat down and covered his face with his hands, feeling the wrinkles on his forehead like great wide welts. Alone, he played a game with the wrinkles, pretending that each one represented some event or facet of his life. This one here—the big one above his left eyebrow—that was Mars. And this other one—way over here almost by his right ear—that was a girl named Melissa whom he had known back in the 1970s. But he wasn't in the proper mood for the game now. He lowered his hands. He knew the wrinkles for exactly what they really were: age, purely and simply and honestly age. Each one meant nothing without the others. They represented impersonal and unavoidable erosion. On the outside, they reflected the death that was occurring on the inside.

Still, he was happy to be back here in this room. He never realized how important these familiar surroundings were to his state of mind until he was forcefully deprived of them for a length of time. Inside the alien starship, it hadn't been so bad. The time had passed quickly then; he hadn't been allowed to get homesick. It was afterward when it had got bad. With Kelly and the others in her dank, ugly impersonal hole of an office. Those had been the unbearable hours.

But now he was home, and he would not have to leave again until they told him. He had been appointed official emissary to the aliens, though this did not fool him for a moment. He had been given the appointment only because Jonathon had refused to see anyone else. It wasn't because anyone liked him or respected him or thought him competent enough to handle the mission. He was different from them, and that made all the difference. When they were still kids, they had seen his face on the old TV networks every night of the week. Kelly wanted someone like herself to handle the aliens. Someone who knew how to take orders, someone ultimately competent, some computer facsimile of a human being. Like herself. Someone who, when given a job, performed it in the most efficient manner in the least possible time.

Kelly was the director of the moon base. She had come here two years ago, replacing Bill Newton, a contemporary of Reynolds', a friend of his. Kelly was the protégé of some U.S. Senator, some powerful idiot from the Midwest, a leader of the anti-NASA faction in the Congress. Kelly's appointment had been part of a wild attempt to subdue the senator with favors and special attention. It had worked after a fashion. There were still Americans on the moon. Even the Russians had left two years ago.

Leaving the alien starship, he had met Kelly the instant he reached the air lock. He had managed to slip past her and pull on his suit before she could question him. He had known she wouldn't dare try to converse over the radio; too great a chance of being overheard. She would never trust him to say only the right things.

But that little game had done nothing except delay matters a few minutes. The tug had returned to the moon base and then everyone had gone straight to Kelly's office. Then the interrogation had begun. Reynolds had sat near the back of the room while the rest of them flocked around Kelly like pet sheep.

Kelly asked the first question. "What do they want?" He knew her well enough to understand exactly what she meant: What do they want from us in return for what we want from them?

Reynolds told her: They wanted to know about the sun.

"We gathered that much," Kelly said. "But what kind of information do they want? Specifically, what are they after?"

With great difficulty, he tried to explain this too.

Kelly interrupted him quickly. "And what did you tell them?"

"Nothing," he said.

"Why?"

"Because I didn't know what to tell them."

"Didn't you ever happen to think the best thing to tell them might have been whatever it was they wished to hear?"

"I couldn't do that either," he said, "because I didn't know. You tell me: Is the sun benevolent? How does it inspire your daily life? does it constantly rage? I don't know, and you don't know either, and it's not a thing we can risk lying about, because they may very well know themselves. To them, a star is a living entity. It's a god, but more than our gods, because they can see a star and feel its heat and never doubt that it's always there."

"Will they want you back?" she asked.

"I think so. They liked me. Or he liked me. It. I only talked to one of them."

"I thought you told us two."

So he went over the whole story for her once more, from beginning to end, hoping this time she might realize that alien beings are not human beings and should not be expected to respond in familiar ways. When he came to the part about the presence of the two aliens, he said, "Look. There are six men in this room right now besides us. But they are here only for show. The whole time, none of them will say a word or think a thought or decide a point. The other alien was in the room with Jonathon and me the whole time. But if it had not been there, nothing would have been changed. I don't know why it was there and I don't expect I ever will. But neither do I understand why you feel you have to have all these men here with you."

She utterly ignored the point. "Then that is all they are interested in? They're pilgrims and they think the sun is Mecca?"

"More or less," he said, with the emphasis on "less."

"Then they won't want to talk to me—or any of us. You're the one who knows the sun. Is that correct?" She jotted a note on a pad, shaking her elbow briskly.

"That is correct."

"Reynolds," she said, looking up from her pad, "I sure as hell hope you know what you're doing."

He said, "Why?"

She did not bother to attempt to disguise her contempt. Few of them did any more and especially not Kelly. It was her opinion that Reynolds should not be here at all. Put him in a rest home back on Earth, she would say. The other astronauts—they were considerate enough to retire when life got too complicated for them. What makes this one man, Bradley Reynolds, why is he so special? All right—she would admit—ten years, twenty years ago, he was a great brave man struggling to conquer the unknown. When I was sixteen years old, I couldn't walk a dozen feet without tripping over his name or face. But what about now? What is he? I'll tell you what he is: a broken-down, wrinkled relic of an old man. So what if he's an astronomer as well as an astronaut? So what if he's the best possible man for the Lunar observatory? I still say he's more trouble than he's worth. He walks around the moon base like a dog having a dream. Nobody can communicate with him. He hasn't attended a single psychological expansion session since he's been here, and that goes back well before my time. He's a morale problem; nobody can stand the sight of him any more. And, as far as doing his job goes, he does it, yes—but that's all. His heart isn't in it. Look, he didn't even know about the aliens being in orbit until I called him in and told him they wanted to see him.

That last part was not true, of course. Reynolds, like everyone, had known about the aliens, but he did not have to admit that their approach had not overly concerned him. He had not shared the hysteria which had gripped the whole of the Earth when the announcement was made that an alien starship had entered the system. The authorities had known about it for months before ever releasing the news. By the time anything was said publicly, it had been clearly determined that the aliens offered Earth no clear or present danger. But that was about all anyone had learned. Then the starship had gone into orbit around the moon, an action intended to confirm their lack of harmful intent toward Earth, and the entire problem had landed with a thud in Kelly's lap. The aliens said they wanted to meet a man who knew something about the sun, and that had turned out to be Reynolds. Then—and only then—had he had a real reason to become interested in the aliens. That day, for the first time in a half-dozen years, he had actually listened to the daily news broadcasts from Earth. He discovered—and it didn't particularly surprise him—that everyone else had long since got over their initial interest in the aliens. He gathered that war was brewing again. In Africa this time, which was a change in place if not in substance. The aliens were mentioned once, about halfway through the program, but Reynolds could tell they were no longer considered real news. A meeting between a representative of the American moon base and the aliens was being arranged, the newscaster said. It would take place aboard the aliens' ship in orbit around the moon, he added. The name Bradley Reynolds was not mentioned. I wonder if they remember me, he had thought.

"It seems to me that you could get more out of them than some babble about stars being gods," Kelly said, getting up and pacing around the room, one hand on hip. She shook her head in mock disbelief and the brown curls swirled downward, flowing like dark honey in the light gravity.

"Oh, I did," he said casually.

"What?" There was a rustling of interest in the room.

"A few facts about their planet. Some bits of detail I think fit together. It may even explain their theology."

"Explain theology with astronomy?" Kelly said sharply. "There's no mystery to sun worship. It was one of our primitive religions." A man next to her nodded.

"Not quite. Our star is relatively mild-mannered, as Jonathon would say. And our planet has a nice, comfortable orbit, nearly circular."

"Theirs doesn't?"

"No. The planet has a pronounced axial inclination, too, nothing ordinary like Earth's twenty-three degrees. Their world must be tilted at forty degrees or so to give the effects Jonathon mentioned."

"Hot summers?" one of the men he didn't know said, and Reynolds looked up in mild surprise. So the underlings were not just spear-carriers, as he had thought. Well enough.

"Right. The axial tilt causes each hemisphere to alternately slant toward and then away from their star. They have colder winters and hotter summers than we do. But there's something more, as far as I can figure it out. Jonathon says its world 'does not move in the perfect path' and that ours, on the other hand, very nearly does."

"Perfect path?" Kelly said, frowning. "An eight-fold way? The path of enlightenment?"

"More theology," said the man who had spoken.

"Not quite," Reynolds said. "Pythagoras believed the circle was a perfect form, the most beautiful of all figures. I don't see why Jonathon shouldn't."

"Astronomical bodies look like circles. Pythagoras could see the moon," Kelly said.

"And the sun," Reynolds said. "I don't know whether Jonathon's world has a moon or not. But they can see their star, and in profile it's a circle."

"So a circular orbit is a perfect orbit."

"Q.E.D. Jonathon says its planet doesn't have one, though."

"It's an ellipse."

"A very eccentric ellipse. That's my guess, anyway. Jonathon used the terms 'path-summer' and 'pole-summer,' so they do distinguish between the two effects."

"I don't get it," the man said.

"An ellipse alone gives alternate summers and winters, but in both hemispheres at the same time," Kelly said brusquely, her mouth turning slightly downward. "A 'pole-summer' must be the kind Earth has."

"Oh," the man said weakly.

"You left out the 'great-summer,' my dear," Reynolds said with a thin smile.

"What's that?" Kelly said carefully.

"When the 'pole-summer' coincides with the 'path-summer'—which it will, every so often. I wouldn't want to be around when that happens. Evidently neither do the members of Jonathon's race."

"How do they get away?" Kelly said intently.

"Migrate. One hemisphere is having a barely tolerable summer while the other is being fried alive, so they go there. The whole race."

"Nomads," Kelly said. "An entire culture born with a pack on its back," she said distantly. Reynolds raised an eyebrow. It was the first time he had ever heard her say anything that wasn't crisp, efficient and uninteresting.

"I think that's why they're grazing animals, to make it easy—even necessary—to keep on the move. A 'great-summer' wilts all the vegetation; a 'great-winter'—they must have those, too—freezes a continent solid."

"God," Kelly said quietly.

"Jonathon mentioned huge storms, winds that knocked it down, sand that buried it overnight in dunes. The drastic changes in the climate must stir up hurricanes and tornadoes."

"Which they have to migrate through," Kelly said. Reynolds noticed that the room was strangely quiet.

"Jonathon seems to have been born on one of the Treks. They don't have much shelter because of the winds and the winters that erode away the rock. It must be hard to build up any sort of technology in an environment like that. I suppose it's pretty inevitable that they turned out to believe in astrology."

"What?" Kelly said, surprised.

"Of course." Reynolds looked at her, completely deadpan. "What else should I call it? With such a premium on reading the stars correctly, so that they know the precise time of year and when the next 'great-summer' is coming—what else would they believe in? Astrology would be the obvious, unchallengeable religion—because it worked!" Reynolds smiled to himself, imagining a flock of atheist giraffes vainly fighting their way through a sandstorm.

"I see," Kelly said, clearly at a loss. The men stood around them awkwardly, not knowing quite what to say to such a barrage of unlikely ideas. Reynolds felt a surge of joy. Some lost capacity of his youth had returned: to see himself as the center of things, as the only actor onstage who moved of his own volition, spoke his own unscripted lines. *This is the way the world feels when you are winning*, he thought. This was what he had lost, what Mars had taken from him during the long trip back in utter deep silence and loneliness. He had tested himself there and found some inner core, had come to think he did not need people and the fine edge of competition with them. Work and cramped rooms had warped him.

"I think that's why they are technologically retarded, despite their age. They don't really have the feel of machines, they've never gotten used to them. When they needed a starship for their religion, they built the most awkward one imaginable that would work." Reynolds paused, feeling lightheaded. "They live inside that machine, but they don't like it. They stink it up and make it feel like a corral. They mistrusted that tape recorder of mine. They must want to know the stars very badly, to depart so much from their nature just to reach them."

Kelly's lip stiffened and her eyes narrowed. Her face, Reynolds thought, was returning to its usual expression. "This is all very well, Dr. Reynolds," she said, and it was the old Kelly, the one he knew; the Kelly who always came out on top. "But it is speculation. We need facts. Their starship is crude, but it *works*. They must have data and photographs of stars. They know things we don't. There are innumerable details we could only find by making the trip ourselves, and even using their ship, that will take centuries—Houston tells me that bomb-thrower of theirs can't go above one percent of light velocity. I want—"

"I'll try," he said. "But I'm afraid it won't be easy. Whenever I try to approach a subject it does not want to discuss, the alien begins telling me the most fantastic lies."

"Oh?" Kelly said suspiciously, and he was sorry he had mentioned that, because it had taken him another quarter hour of explaining before she had allowed him to escape the confines of her office.

Now he was back home again—in his room. Rolling over, he lay flat on his back in the bed, eyes wide open and staring straight ahead at the emptiness of the darkness. He would have liked to go out and visit the observatory, but Kelly had said he was excused from all duties until the alien situation was resolved. He gathered she meant that as an order. She must have. One thing about Kelly: she seldom said a word unless it was meant as an order.

• • •

They came and woke him up. He had not intended to sleep. His room was still pitch-black, and far away there was a fist pounding furiously upon a door. Getting up, taking his time, he went and let the man inside. Then he turned on the light.

"Hurry and see the director," the man said breathlessly.

"What does she want now?" Reynolds asked.

"How should I know?"

Reynolds shrugged and turned to go. He knew what she wanted anyway. It had to be the aliens; Jonathon was ready to see him again. Well, that was fine, he thought, entering Kelly's office. From the turn of her expression, he saw that he had guessed correctly. And I know exactly what I'm going to tell them, he thought.

Somewhere in his sleep, Reynolds had made an important decision. He had decided he was going to tell Jonathon the truth.

Approaching the alien starship, Reynolds discovered he was no longer so strongly reminded of his old home in São Paulo. Now that he had actually been inside the ship and had met the creatures who resided there, his feelings had changed. This time he was struck by how remarkably this strange twisted chunk of metal resembled what a real starship ought to look like.

The tug banged against the side of the ship. Without having to be told, Reynolds removed his suit and went to the air lock. Kelly jumped out of her seat and dashed after him. She grabbed the camera off the deck and forced it into his hands. She wanted him to photograph the aliens. He had to admit her logic was quite impeccable. If the aliens were as unfearsome as Reynolds claimed, then a clear and honest photograph could only reassure the population of Earth; hysteria was still a worry to many politicians back home. Many people still claimed that a spaceship full of green monsters was up here orbiting the moon only a few hours' flight from New York and Moscow. One click of the camera and this fear would be ended.

Reynolds had told her Jonathon would never permit a photograph to be taken, but Kelly had remained adamant. "Who cares?" he'd asked her.

"Everyone cares," she'd insisted.

"Oh, really? I listened to the news yesterday and the aliens weren't even mentioned. Is that hysteria?"

"That's because of Africa. Wait till the war's over, then listen."

He hadn't argued with her then and he didn't intend to argue with her now. He accepted the camera without a word, her voice burning his ears with last-minute instructions, and plunged ahead.

The smell assaulted him immediately. As he entered the spaceship, the odor seemed to rise up from nowhere and surround him. He made himself push forward. Last time, the odor had been a problem only for a short time. He was sure he could overcome it again this time.

It was cold in the ship. He wore only light pants and a light shirt without underwear, because last time it had been rather warm. Had Jonathon, noticing his discomfort, lowered the ship's temperature accordingly?

He turned the first corner and glanced briefly at the distant ceiling. He called out, "Hello!" but there was only a slight echo. He spoke again and the echo was the same, flat and hard.

Another turn. He was moving much faster than before. The tight passages no longer caused him to pause and think. He simply plunged ahead, trusting his own knowledge. At Kelly's urging he was wearing a radio attached to his belt. He noticed that it was beeping furiously at him. Apparently Kelly had neglected some important last-minute direction. He didn't mind. He already had enough orders to ignore; one less would make little difference.

Here was the place. Pausing in the doorway, he removed the radio, turning it off. Then he placed the camera on the floor beside it, and stepped into the room.

Despite the chill in the air, the room was not otherwise different from before. There were two aliens standing against the farthest wall. Reynolds went straight toward them, holding his hands over his head in greeting. One was taller than the other. Reynolds spoke to it. "Are you Jonathon?"

"Yes," Jonathon said, in its child's piping voice. "And this is Richard."

"May I pay obeisance?" Richard asked eagerly.

Reynolds nodded. "If you wish."

Jonathon waited until Richard had regained its feet, then said, "We wish to discuss your star now."

"All right," Reynolds said. "But there's something I have to tell you first." Saying this, for the first time since he made his decision, he wasn't sure. Was the truth really the best solution in this situation? Kelly wanted him to lie: tell them whatever they wanted to hear, making certain he didn't tell them quite everything. Kelly was afraid the aliens might go sailing off to the sun once they had learned what they had come here to learn. She wanted a chance to get engineers and scientists inside their ship before the aliens left. And wasn't this a real possibility? What if Kelly was right and the aliens went away? Then what would he say?

"You want to tell us that your sun is not a conscious being," Jonathon said. "Am I correct?"

The problem was instantly solved. Reynolds felt no more compulsion to lie. He said, "Yes."

"I am afraid that you are wrong," said Jonathon.

"We live here, don't we? Wouldn't we know? You asked for me because I know our sun, and I do. But there are other men on our homeworld who know far more than I do. But no one has ever discovered the last shred of evidence to support your theory."

"A theory is a guess," Jonathon said. "We do not guess; we know."

"Then," Reynolds said, "explain it to me. Because I don't know." He watched the alien's eyes carefully, waiting for the first indication of a blinking fit.

But Jonathon's gaze remained steady and certain. "Would you like to hear of our journey?" it asked.

"Yes."

"We left our homeworld a great many of your years ago. I cannot tell you exactly when, for reasons I'm certain you can understand, but I will reveal that it was more than a century ago. In that time we have visited nine stars. The ones we would visit were chosen for us beforehand. Our priests—our leaders—determined the stars that were within our reach and also able to help in our quest. You see, we have journeyed here in order to ask certain questions."

"Questions of the stars?"

"Yes, of course. The questions we have are questions only a star may answer."

"And what are they?" Reynolds asked.

"We have discovered the existence of other universes parallel with our own.

Certain creatures—devils and demons—have come from these universes in order to attack and capture our stars. We feel we must—"

"Oh, yes," Reynolds said. "I understand. We've run across several of these creatures recently." And he blinked, matching the twitching of Jonathon's eye. "They are awfully fearsome, aren't they?" When Jonathon stopped, he stopped too. He said, "You don't have to tell me everything. But can you tell me this: these other stars you have visited, have they been able to answer any of your questions?"

"Oh, yes. We have learned much from them. These stars were very great—very different from our own."

"But they weren't able to answer all your questions?"

"If they had, we would not be here now."

"And you believe our star may be able to help you?"

"All may help, but the one we seek is the one that can save us."

"When do you plan to go to the sun?"

"At once," Jonathon said. "As soon as you leave. I am afraid there is little else you can tell us."

"I'd like to ask you to stay," Reynolds said. And he forced himself to go ahead. He knew he could not convince Jonathon without revealing everything, yet, by doing so, he might also be putting an end to all his hopes. Still, he told the alien about Kelly and, more generally, he told it what the attitude of man was toward their visit. He told it what man wished to know from them, and why.

Jonathon seemed amazed. It moved about the floor as Reynolds spoke, its feet clanking dully. Then it stopped and stood, its feet only a few inches apart, a position that impressed Reynolds as one of incredulous amazement. "Your people wish to travel farther into space? You want to visit the stars? But why, Reynolds? Your people do not believe. Why?"

Reynolds smiled. Each time Jonathon said something to him, he felt he knew these people—and how they thought and reacted—a little better than he had before. There was another question he would very much have liked to ask Jonathon. How long have your people possessed the means of visiting the stars? A very long time, he imagined. Perhaps a longer time than the whole life-span of the human race. And why hadn't they gone before now? Reynolds thought he knew: because, until now, they had had no reason for going.

Now Reynolds tried to answer Jonathon's question. If anyone could, it should be he. "We wish to go to the stars because we are a dissatisfied people. Because we do not live a very long time as individuals, we feel we must place an important part of our lives into the human race as a whole. In a sense, we surrender a portion of our individual person in return for a sense of greater immortality. What is an accomplishment for man as a race is also an accomplishment for each individual man. And what are these accomplishments? Basically this: anything a man does that no other man has done before—whether it is good or evil or neither one or both—is considered by us to be a great accomplishment."

And—to add emphasis to the point—he blinked once.

Then, holding his eyes steady, he said, "I want you to teach me to talk to the stars. I want you to stay here around the moon long enough to do that."

Instantly Jonathon said, "No."

There was an added force to the way it said it, an emphasis its voice had not previously possessed. Then Reynolds realized what that was: at the same moment Jonathon had spoken, Richard too had said, "No."

"Then you may be doomed to fail," Reynolds said. "Didn't I tell you? I know our star better than any man available to you. Teach me to talk to the stars and I may be able to help you with this one. Or would you prefer to continue wandering the galaxy forever, failing to find what you seek wherever you go?"

"You are a sensible man, Reynolds. You may be correct. We will ask our home star and see."

"Do that. And if it says yes and I promise to do what you wish, then I must ask you to promise me something in return. I want you to allow a team of our scientists and technicians to enter and inspect your ship. You will answer their questions to the best of your ability. And that means truthfully."

"We always tell the truth," Jonathon said, blinking savagely.

The moon had made one full circuit of the Earth since Reynolds' initial meeting with the aliens, and he was quite satisfied with the progress he had made up to now, especially during the past ten days after Kelly had stopped accompanying him in his daily shuttles to and from the orbiting starship. As a matter of fact, in all that time, he had not had a single face-to-face meeting with her and they had talked on the phone only once. And she wasn't here now either, which was strange, since it was noon and she always ate here with the others.

Reynolds had a table to himself in the cafeteria. The food was poor, but it always was, and he was used to that by now. What did bother him, now that he was thinking about it, was Kelly's absence. Most days he skipped lunch himself. He tried to remember the last time he had come here. It was more than a week ago, he remembered—more than ten days ago. He didn't like the sound of that answer.

Leaning over, he attracted the attention of a girl at an adjoining table. He knew her vaguely. Her father had been an important wheel in NASA when Reynolds was still a star astronaut. He couldn't remember the man's name. His daughter had a tiny cute face and a billowing body about two sizes too big for the head. Also, she had a brain that was much too limited for much of anything. She worked in the administrative section, which meant she slept with most of the men on the base at one time or another.

"Have you seen Kelly?" he asked her.

"Must be in her office."

"No, I mean when was the last time you saw her here?"

"In here? Oh—" The girl thought for a moment. "Doesn't she eat with the other chiefs?"

Kelly never ate with the other chiefs. She always ate in the cafeteria—for morale purposes—and the fact that the girl did not remember having seen her meant that it had been several days at least since Kelly had last put in an appearance. Leaving his lunch where it lay, Reynolds got up, nodded politely at the girl, who stared at him as if he were a freak, and hurried away.

It wasn't a long walk, but he ran. He had no intention of going to see Kelly. He knew that would prove useless. Instead, he was going to see John Sims. At fifty-two, Sims was the second oldest man in the base. Like Reynolds, he was a former astronaut. In 1987, when Reynolds, then a famous man, was living in São Paulo, Sims had commanded the first (and only) truly successful Mars expedition. During those few months, the world had heard his name, but people forgot quickly, and Sims was one of the things they forgot. He had never done more than what he was expected to do; the threat of death had never come near Sims' expedition. Reynolds, on the other hand, had failed. On Mars with him, three men had died. Yet it was he—Reynolds, the failure—who had been the hero, not Sims.

And maybe I'm a hero again, he thought, as he knocked evenly on the door to Sims' office. Maybe down there the world is once more reading about me daily. He hadn't listened to a news broadcast since the night before his first trip to the ship. Had the story been released to the public yet? He couldn't see any reason why it should be suppressed, but that seldom was important. He would ask Sims. Sims would know.

The door opened and Reynolds went inside. Sims was a huge man who wore his black hair in a crewcut. The style had been out of fashion for thirty or forty years; Reynolds doubted there was another crewcut man in the universe. But he could not imagine Sims any other way.

"What's wrong?" Sims asked, guessing accurately the first time. He led Reynolds to a chair and sat him down. The office was big but empty. A local phone sat upon the desk along with a couple of daily status reports. Sims was assistant administrative chief, whatever that meant. Reynolds had never understood the functions of the position, if any. But there was one thing that was clear: Sims knew more about the inner workings of the moon base than any other man. And that included the director as well.

"I want to know about Vonda," Reynolds said. With Sims, everything stood on a first-name basis. Vonda was Vonda Kelly. The name tasted strangely upon Reynolds' lips. "Why isn't she eating at the cafeteria?"

Sims answered unhesitantly. "Because she's afraid to leave her desk."

"It has something to do with the aliens?"

"It does, but I shouldn't tell you what. She doesn't want you to know."

"Tell me. Please." His desperation cleared the smile from Sims' lips. And he had almost added: for old times' sake. He was glad he had controlled himself.

"The main reason is the war," Sims said. "If it starts, she wants to know at once."

"Will it?"

Sims shook his head. "I'm smart but I'm not God. As usual, I imagine everything will work out as long as no one makes a stupid mistake. The worst will be a small local war lasting maybe a month. But how long can you depend upon politicians to act intelligently? It goes against the grain with them."

"But what about the aliens?"

"Well, as I said, that's part of it too." Sims stuck his pipe in his mouth. Reynolds had never seen it lit, never seen him smoking it, but the pipe was invariably there between his teeth. "A group of men are coming here from Washington, arriving tomorrow. They want to talk with your pets. It seems nobody—least of all Vonda—is very happy with your progress."

"I am."

Sims shrugged, as if to say: that is of no significance.

"The aliens will never agree to see them," Reynolds said.

"How are they going to stop them? Withdraw the welcome mat? Turn out the lights? That won't work."

"But that will ruin everything. All my work up until now."

"What work?" Sims got up and walked around his desk until he stood hovering above Reynolds. "As far as anybody can see, you haven't accomplished a damn thing since you went up there. People want results, Bradley, not a lot of noise. All you've given anyone is the noise. This isn't a private game of yours. This is one of the most significant events in the history of the human race. If anyone ought to know that, it's you. Christ." And he wandered back to his chair again, jiggling his pipe.

"What is it they want from me?" Reynolds said. "Look—I got them what they asked for. The aliens have agreed to let a team of scientists study their ship."

"We want more than that now. Among other things, we want an alien to come down and visit Washington. Think of the propaganda value of that, and right now is a time when we damn well need something like that. Here we are, the only country with sense enough to stay on the moon. And being here has finally paid off in a way the politicians can understand. They've given you a month in which to play around—after all, you're a hero and the publicity is good—but how much longer do you expect them to wait? No, they want action and I'm afraid they want it now."

Reynolds was ready to go. He had found out as much as he was apt to find here. And he already knew what he was going to have to do. He would go and find Kelly and tell her she had to keep the men from Earth away from the aliens. If she wouldn't agree, then he would go up and tell the aliens and they would leave for the sun. But what if Kelly wouldn't let him go? He had to consider that. He knew; he would tell her this: If you don't let me see them, if you try to keep me away, they'll know something is wrong and they'll leave without a backward glance. Maybe he could tell her the aliens were telepaths; he doubted she would know any better.

He had the plan all worked out so that it could not fail.

He had his hand on the doorknob when Sims called him back. "There's another thing I better tell you, Bradley."

"All right. What's that?"

"Vonda. She's on your side. She told them to stay away, but it wasn't enough. She's been relieved of duty. A replacement is coming with the others."

"Oh," said Reynolds.

Properly suited, Reynolds sat in the cockpit of the shuttle tug, watching the pilot beside him going through the ritual of a final inspection prior to takeoff. The dead desolate surface of the moon stretched briefly away from where the tug sat, the horizon so near that it almost looked touchable. Reynolds liked the moon. If he had not, he would never have elected to return here to stay. It was the Earth he hated. Better than the moon was space itself, the dark endless void beyond the reach of man's ugly grasping hands. That was where Reynolds was going now. Up. Out. Into the void. He was impatient to leave.

The pilot's voice came to him softly through the suit radio, a low murmur, not loud enough for him to understand what the man was saying. The pilot was talking to himself as he worked, using the rumble of his own voice as a way of patterning his mind so that it would not lose concentration. The pilot was a young man in his middle twenties, probably on loan from the Air Force, a lieutenant or, at most, a junior Air Force captain. He was barely old enough to remember when space had really been a frontier. Mankind had decided to go out, and Reynolds had been one of the men chosen to take the giant steps, but now it was late—the giant steps of twenty years ago were mere tentative contusions in the dust of the centuries—and man was coming back. From where he sat, looking out, Reynolds could see exactly 50 percent of the present American space program: the protruding bubble of the moon base. The other half was the orbiting space lab that circled the Earth itself, a battered relic of the expansive seventies. Well beyond the nearby horizon—maybe a hundred miles away—there had once been another bubble, but it was gone now. The brave men who had lived and worked and struggled and died and survived there—they were all gone too. Where? The Russians still maintained an orbiting space station, so some of their former moon colonists were undoubtedly there, but where were the rest? In Siberia? Working there? Hadn't the Russians decided that Siberia—the old barless prison state of the czars and early Communists—was a more practical frontier than the moon?

And weren't they maybe right? Reynolds did not like to think so, for he had poured his life into this—into the moon and the void beyond. But at times, like now, peering through the artificial window of his suit, seeing the bare bubble of the base clinging to the edge of this dead world like a wart on an old woman's face, starkly vulnerable, he found it hard to see the point of it. He was an old enough man to recall the first time he had ever been moved by the spirit of conquest. As a schoolboy, he remembered the first time men conquered Mount Everest—it was around 1956 or '57—and he had religiously followed the newspaper reports. Afterward, a movie had been made, and watching that film, seeing the shadows of pale mountaineers clinging to the edge of that white god, he had decided that was what he wanted to be. And he had never been taught otherwise; only by the time he was old enough to act, all the mountains had long since been conquered. And he had ended up as an astronomer, able if nothing else to gaze outward at the distant shining peaks of the void, and from there he had been pointed toward space. So he had gone to Mars and become famous, but fame had turned him inward, so that now, without the brilliance of his past, he would have been nobody but another of those anonymous old men who dot the cities of the world, inhabiting identically bleak book-lined rooms, eating daily in bad restaurants, their minds always a billion miles away from the dead shells of their bodies.

"We can go now, Dr. Reynolds," the pilot was saying.

Reynolds grunted in reply, his mind several miles distant from his waiting body. He was thinking that there was something, after all. How could he think in terms of pointlessness and futility when he alone had actually seen them with his own eyes? Creatures, intelligent beings, born far away, light-years from the insignificant world of man? Didn't that in itself prove something? Yes. He was sure that it did. But what?

The tug lifted with a murmur from the surface of the moon. Crouched deeply within his seat, Reynolds thought that it wouldn't be long now.

And they found us, he thought, we did not find them. And when had they gone into space? Late. Very late. At a moment in their history comparable to man a hundred thousand years from now. They had avoided space until a pressing reason had come for venturing out, and then they had gone. He remembered that he had been unable to explain to Jonathon why man wanted to visit the stars when he did not believe in the divinity of the suns. Was there a reason? And, if so, did it make sense?

The journey was not long.

It didn't smell. The air ran clean and sharp and sweet through the corridors, and if there was any odor to it, the odor was one of purity and freshness, almost pine needles or mint. The air was good for his spirits. As soon as Reynolds came aboard the starship, his depression and melancholy were forgotten. Perhaps he was only letting the apparent grimness of the situation get the better of him. It had been too long a time since he'd last had to fight. Jonathon would know what to do. The alien was more than three hundred years old, a product of a civilization and culture that had reached its maturity at a time when man was not yet man, when he was barely a skinny undersized ape, a carrion eater upon the hot plains of Africa.

When Reynolds reached the meeting room, he saw that Jonathon and Richard were not alone this time. The third alien—Reynolds sensed it was someone important—was introduced as Vergnan. No adopted Earth name for it.

"This is ours who best knows the stars," Jonathon said. "It has spoken with yours and hopes it may be able to assist you."

Reynolds had almost forgotten that part. The sudden pressures of the past few hours had driven everything else from his mind. His training. His unsuccessful attempts to speak to the stars. He had failed. Jonathon had been unable to teach him, but he thought that was probably because he simply did not believe.

"Now we shall leave you," Jonathon said.

"But—" said Reynolds.

"We are not permitted to stay."

"But there's something I must tell you."

It was too late. Jonathon and Richard headed for the corridor, walking with surprising gracefulness. Their long necks bobbed, their skinny legs shook, but they still managed to move as swiftly and sleekly as any cat, almost rippling as they went.

Reynolds turned toward Vergnan. Should he tell this one about the visitors from Earth? He did not think so. Vergnan was old, his skin much paler than the others', almost totally hairless. His eyes were wrinkled and one ear was torn.

Vergnan's eyes were closed.

Remembering his lessons, Reynolds too closed his eyes.

And kept them closed. In the dark, time passed more quickly than it seemed, but he was positive that five minutes went by.

Then the alien began to speak. No—he did not speak; he simply sang, his voice trilling with the high searching notes of a well-tuned violin, dashing up and down the scale, a pleasant sound, soothing, cool. Reynolds tried desperately to concentrate upon the song, ignoring the existence of all other sensations, recognizing nothing and no one but Vergnan. Reynolds ignored the taste and smell of the air and the distant throbbing of the ship's machinery. The alien sang deeper and clearer, his voice rising higher and higher, directed now at the stars. Jonathon, too, had sung, but never like this. When Jonathon sang, its voice had dashed away in a frightened search, shifting and darting wildly about, seeking vainly a place to land. Vergnan sang without doubt. It—*he*—was certain. Reynolds sensed the overwhelming maleness of this being, his patriarchal strength and dignity. His voice and song never struggled or wavered. He knew always exactly where he was going.

Had he felt something? Reynolds did not know. If so, then what? No, no, he thought, and concentrated more fully upon the voice, too intently to allow for the logic of thought. Within, he felt strong, alive, renewed, resurrected. *I am a new man. Reynolds is dead. He is another.* These thoughts came to him like the whispering words of another. *Go, Reynolds. Fly. Leave. Fly.*

Then he realized that he was singing too. He could not imitate Vergnan, for his voice was too alien, but he tried and heard his own voice coming frighteningly near, almost fading into and being lost within the constant tones of the other. The two voices suddenly became one—mingling indiscriminately—merging—and that one voice rose higher, floating, then higher again, rising, farther, going farther out—farther and deeper.

Then he felt it. Reynolds. And he knew it for what it was.

The Sun.

More ancient than the whole of the Earth itself. A greater, vaster being, more powerful and knowing. Divinity as a ball of heat and energy.

Reynolds spoke to the stars.

And, knowing this, balking at the concept, he drew back instinctively in fear, his voice faltering, dwindling, collapsing. Reynolds scurried back, seeking the Earth, but, grasping, pulling, Vergnan drew him on. Beyond the shallow exterior light of the sun, he witnessed the totality of that which lay hidden within. The core. The impenetrable darkness within. Fear gripped him once more. He begged to be allowed to flee. Tears streaking his face with the heat of fire, he pleaded. Vergnan benignly drew him on. *Come forward—come—see—know*. Forces coiled to a point.

And he saw.

Could he describe it as evil? Thought was an absurdity. Not thinking, instead sensing and feeling, he experienced the wholeness of this entity—a star—the sun—and saw that it was not evil. He sensed the sheer totality of its opening nothingness. Sensation was absent. Colder than cold, more terrifying than hate, more sordid than fear, blacker than evil. The vast inner whole nothingness of everything that was anything, of all.

I have seen enough. No!

Yes, cried Vergnan, agreeing.

To stay a moment longer would mean never returning again. Vergnan knew this too, and he released Reynolds, allowed him to go.

And still he sang. The song was different from before. Struggling within himself, Reynolds sang too, trying to match his voice to that of the alien. It was easier this time. The two voices merged, mingled, became one.

And then Reynolds awoke.

He was lying on the floor in the starship, the rainbow walls swirling brightly around him.

Vergnan stepped over him. He saw the alien's protruding belly as he passed. He did not look down or back, but continued onward, out the door, gone, as quick and cold as the inner soul of the sun itself. For a brief moment, he hated Vergnan more deeply than he had ever hated anything in his life. Then he sat up, gripping himself, forcing a return to sanity. I am all right now, he insisted. I am back. I am alive. The walls ceased spinning. At his back the floor shed its clinging coat of roughness. The shadows in the corners of his eyes dispersed.

Jonathon entered the room alone. "Now you have been," it said, crossing the room and assuming its usual place beside the wall.

"Yes," said Reynolds, not attempting to stand.

"And now you know why we search. For centuries our star was kind to us, loving, but now it too—like yours—is changed."

"You are looking for a new home?"

"True."

"And?"

"And we find nothing. All are alike. We have seen nine, visiting all. They are nothing."

"Then you leave here too?"

"We must, but first we will approach your star. Not until we have drawn so close that we have seen everything, not until then can we dare admit our failure. This time we thought we had succeeded. When we met you, this is what we thought, for you are unlike your star. We felt that the star could not produce you—or your race—without the presence of benevolence. But it is gone now. We meet only the blackness. We struggle to penetrate to a deeper core. And fail."

"I am not typical of my race," Reynolds said.

"We shall see."

He remained with Jonathon until he felt strong enough to stand. The floor hummed. Feeling it with moist palms, he planted a kiss upon the creased cold metal. A wind swept through the room, carrying a hint of returned life. Jonathon faded, rippled, returned to a sharp outline of crisp reality. Reynolds was suddenly hungry and the oily taste of meat swirled up through his nostrils. The cords in his neck stood out with the strain until, gradually, the tension passed from him.

He left and went to the tug. During the great fall to the silver moon he said not a word, thought not a thought. The trip was long.

Reynolds lay on his back in the dark room, staring upward at the faint shadow of a ceiling, refusing to see.

Hypnosis? Or a more powerful alien equivalent of the same? Wasn't that, as an explanation, more likely than admitting that he had indeed communicated with the sun, discovering a force greater than evil, blacker than black. Or—here was another theory: wasn't it possible that these aliens, because of the conditions on their own world, so thoroughly accepted the consciousness of the stars that they could make him believe as well? Similar things had happened on Earth. Religious miracles, the curing of diseases through faith, men who claimed to have spoken with God. What about flying saucers and little green men and all the other incidents of mass hysteria? Wasn't that the answer here? Hysteria? Hypnosis? Perhaps even a drug of some sort: a drug released into the air. Reynolds had plenty of possible solutions—he could choose one or all—but he decided that he did not really care.

He had gone into this thing knowing exactly what he was doing and now that it had happened he did not regret the experience. He had found a way of fulfilling his required mission while at the same time experiencing something personal that no other man would ever know. Whether he had actually seen the sun was immaterial; the experience, as such, was still his own. Nobody could ever take that away from him.

It was some time after this when he realized that a fist was pounding on the door. He decided he might as well ignore that, because sometimes when you ignored things, they went away. But the knocking did not go away—it only got louder. Finally Reynolds got up. He opened the door.

Kelly glared at his nakedness and said, "Did I wake you?"

"No."

"May I come in?"

"No."

"I've got something to tell you." She forced her way past him, sliding into the room. Then Reynolds saw that she wasn't alone. A big, red-faced beefy man followed, forcing his way into the room too.

Reynolds shut the door, cutting off the corridor light, but the big man went over and turned on the overhead light. "All right," he said, as though it were an order.

"Who the hell are you?" Reynolds said.

"Forget him," Kelly said. "I'll talk."

"Talk," said Reynolds.

"The committee is here. The men from Washington. They arrived an hour ago and I've kept them busy since. You may not believe this, but I'm on your side."

"Sims told me."

"He told me he told you."

"I knew he would. Mind telling me why? He didn't know."

"Because I'm not an idiot," Kelly said. "I've known enough petty bureaucrats in my life. Those things up there are alien beings. You can't send these fools up there to go stomping all over their toes."

Reynolds gathered this would not be over soon. He put on his pants.

"This is George O'Hara," Kelly said. "He's the new director."

"I want to offer my resignation," Reynolds said casually, fixing the snaps of his shirt.

"You have to accompany us to the starship," O'Hara said.

"I want you to," Kelly said. "You owe this to someone. If not me, then the aliens. If you had told me the truth, this might never have happened. If anyone is to blame for this mess, it's you, Reynolds. Why won't you tell me what's been going on up there the last month? It has to be something."

"It is," Reynolds said. "Don't laugh, but I was trying to talk to the sun. I told you that's why the aliens came here. They're taking a cruise of the galaxy, pausing here and there to chat with the stars."

"Don't be frivolous. And, yes, you told me all that."

"I have to be frivolous. Otherwise, it sounds too ridiculous. I made an agreement with them. I wanted to learn to talk to the sun. I told them, since I lived here, I could find out what they wanted to know better than they could. I could tell they were doubtful, but they let me go ahead. In return for my favor, when I was done, whether I succeeded or failed, they would give us what we wanted. A team of men could go and freely examine their ship. They would describe their voyage to us—where they had been, what they had found. They promised cooperation in return for my chat with the sun."

"So, then nothing happened?"

"I didn't say that. I talked with the sun today. And saw it. And now I'm not going to do anything except sit on my hands. You can take it from here."

"What are you talking about?"

He knew he could not answer that. "I failed," he said. "I didn't find out anything they didn't know."

"Well, will you go with us or not? That's all I want to know right now." She was losing her patience, but there was also more than a minor note of pleading in her voice. He knew he ought to feel satisfied hearing that, but he didn't.

"Oh, hell," Reynolds said. "Yes—all right—I will go. But don't ask me why. Just give me an hour to get ready."

"Good man," O'Hara said, beaming happily.

Ignoring him, Reynolds opened his closets and began tossing clothes and other belonging into various boxes and crates.

"What do you think you'll need all that for?" Kelly asked him.

"I don't think I'm coming back," Reynolds said.

"They won't hurt you," she said.

"No. I won't be coming back because I won't be wanting to come back."

"You can't do that," O'Hara said.

"Sure I can," said Reynolds.

It took the base's entire fleet of seven shuttle tugs to ferry the delegation from Washington up to the starship. At that, a good quarter of the group had to be left behind for lack of room. ooReynolds had requested and received permission to call the starship prior to departure, so the aliens were aware of what was coming up to meet them. They had not protested, but Reynolds knew they wouldn't, at least not over the radio. Like almost all mechanical or electronic gadgets, a radio was a fearsome object to them.

Kelly and Reynolds arrived with the first group and entered the air lock. At intervals of a minute or two, the others arrived. When the entire party was clustered in the lock, the last tug holding to the hull in preparation for the return trip, Reynolds signaled that it was time to move out.

"Wait a minute," one of the men called. "We're not all here. Acton and Dodd went back to the tug to get suits."

"Then they'll have to stay there," Reynolds said. "The air is pure here—nobody needs a suit."

"But," said another man, pinching his nose. "This smell. It's awful."

Reynolds smiled. He had barely noticed the odor. Compared to the stench of the first few days, this was nothing today. "The aliens won't talk if you're wearing suits. They have a taboo against artificial communication. The smell gets better as you go farther inside. Until then, hold your nose, breathe through your mouth."

"It's making me almost sick," confided a man at Reynolds' elbow. "You're sure what you say is true, Doctor?"

"Cross my heart," Reynolds said. The two men who had left to fetch the suits returned. Reynolds wasted another minute lecturing them.

"Stop enjoying yourself so much," Kelly whispered when they were at last under way.

Before they reached the first of the tight passages where crawling was necessary, three men had dropped away, dashing back toward the tug. Working from a hasty map given him by the aliens, he was leading the party toward a section of the ship where he had never been before. The walk was less difficult than usual. In most places a man could walk comfortably and the ceilings were high enough to accommodate the aliens themselves. Reynolds ignored the occasional shouted exclamation from the men behind. He steered a silent course toward his destination.

The room, when they reached it, was huge, big as a basketball gymnasium, the ceiling lost in the deep shadows above. Turning, Reynolds counted the aliens present: fifteen . . . twenty . . . thirty . . . forty . . . forty-five . . . forty-six. That had to be about all. He wondered if this was the full crew.

Then he counted his own people: twenty-two. Better than he had expected—only six lost en route, victims of the smell.

He spoke directly to the alien who stood in front of the others. "Greetings," he said. The alien wasn't Vergnan, but it could have been Jonathon.

From behind, he heard, "They're just like giraffes."

"And they even seem intelligent," said another.

"Exceedingly so. Their eyes."

"And friendly too."

"Hello, Reynolds," the alien said. "Are these the ones?"

"Jonathon?" asked Reynolds.

"Yes."

"These are the ones."

"They are your leaders—they wish to question my people?"

"They do."

"May I serve as our spokesman in order to save time?"

"Of course," Reynolds said. He turned and faced his party, looking from face to face, hoping to spot a single glimmer of intelligence, no matter how minute. But he found nothing. "Gentlemen?" he said. "You heard?"

"His name is Jonathon?" said one.

"It is a convenient expression. Do you have a real question?"

"Yes," the man said. He continued speaking to Reynolds. "Where is your homeworld located?"

Jonathon ignored the man's rudeness and promptly named a star.

"Where is that?" the man asked, speaking directly to the alien now.

Reynolds told him it lay some thirty light-years from Earth. As a star, it was very much like the sun, though somewhat larger.

"Exactly how many miles in a light-year?" a man wanted to know.

Reynolds tried to explain. The man claimed he understood, though Reynolds remained skeptical.

It was time for another question.

"Why have you come to our world?"

"Our mission is purely one of exploration and discovery," Jonathon said.

"Have you discovered any other intelligent races besides our own?"

"Yes. Several."

This answer elicited a murmur of surprise from the men. Reynolds wondered who they were, how they had been chosen for this mission. Not what they were, but who. What made them tick. He knew what they were: politicians, NASA bureaucrats, a sprinkling of real scientists. But who?

"Are any of these people aggressive?" asked a man, almost certainly a politician. "Do they pose a threat to you—or—or to us?"

"No," Jonathon said. "None."

Reynolds was barely hearing the questions and answers now. His attention was focused upon Jonathon's eyes. He had stopped blinking now. The last two questions—the ones dealing with intelligent life forms—he had told the truth. Reynolds thought he was beginning to understand. He had underestimated these creatures. Plainly, they had encountered other races during their travels before coming to Earth. They were experienced. Jonathon was lying—yes—but unlike before, he was lying well, only when the truth would not suffice.

"How long do you intend to remain in orbit about our moon?"

"Until the moment you and your friends leave our craft. Then we shall depart."

This set up an immediate clamor among the men. Waving his arms furiously, Reynolds attempted to silence them. The man who had been unfamiliar with the term "light-year" shouted out an invitation for Jonathon to visit Earth.

This did what Reynolds himself could not do. The others fell silent in order to hear Jonathon's reply.

"It is impossible," Jonathon said. "Our established schedule requires us to depart immediately."

"Is it this man's fault?" demanded a voice. "He should have asked you himself long before now."

"No," Jonathon said. "I could not have come—or any of my people—because we were uncertain of your peaceful intentions. Not until we came to know Reynolds well did we fully comprehend the benevolence of your race." The alien blinked rapidly now.

He stopped during the technical questions. The politicians and bureaucrats stepped back to speak among themselves and the scientists came forward. Reynolds was amazed at the intelligence of their questions. To this extent at least, the expedition had not been wholly a farce.

Then the questions were over and all the men came forward to listen to Jonathon's last words.

"We will soon return to our homeworld and when we do we shall tell the leaders of our race of the greatness and glory of the human race. In passing here, we have come to know your star and through it you people who live beneath its soothing rays. I consider your visit here a personal honor to me as an individual. I am sure my brothers share my pride and only regret an inability to utter their gratitude."

Then Jonathon ceased blinking and looked hard at Reynolds. "Will you be going too?"

"No," Reynolds said. "I'd like to talk to you alone if I can."

"Certainly," Jonathon said.

Several of the men in the party protested to Kelly or O'Hara, but there was nothing they could do. One by one they left the chamber to wait in the corridor. Kelly was the last to leave. "Don't be a fool," she cautioned.

"I won't," he said.

When the men had gone, Jonathon took Reynolds away from the central room. It was only a brief walk to the old room where they had always met before. As if practicing a routine, Jonathon promptly marched to the farthest wall and stood there waiting. Reynolds smiled. "Thank you," he said.

"You are welcome."

"For lying to them. I was afraid they would offend you with their stupidity. I thought you would show your contempt by lying badly, offending them in return. I underestimated you. You handled them very well."

"But you have something you wish to ask of me?"

"Yes," Reynolds said. "I want you to take me away with you."

As always, Jonathon remained expressionless. Still, for a long time, it said nothing. Then, "Why do you wish this? We shall never return here."

"I don't care. I told you before: I am not typical of my race. I can never be happy here."

"But are you typical of my race? Would you not be unhappy with us?"

"I don't know. But I'd like to try."

"It is impossible," Jonathon said.

"But—but—why?"

"Because we have neither the time nor the abilities to care for you. Our mission is a most desperate one. Already, during our absence, our homeworld may have gone mad. We must hurry. Our time is growing brief. And you will not be of any help to us. I am sorry, but you know that is true."

"I can talk to the stars."

"No," Jonathon said. "You cannot."

"But I did."

"Vergnan did. Without him, you could not."

"Your answer is final? There's no one else I can ask? The captain?"

"I am the captain."

Reynolds nodded. He had carried his suitcases and crates all this way and now he would have to haul them home again. Home? No, not home. Only the moon. "Could you find out if they left a tug for me?" he asked.

"Yes. One moment."

Jonathon rippled lightly away, disappearing into the corridor. Reynolds turned and looked at the walls. Again, as he stared, the rainbow patterns appeared to shift and dance and swirl of their own volition. Watching this, he felt sad, but his sadness was not that of grief. It was the sadness of emptiness and aloneness. This emptiness had so long been a part of him that he sometimes forgot it was there. He knew it now. He knew, whether consciously aware of it or not, that he had spent the past ten years of his life searching vainly for a way of filling this void. Perhaps even more than that: perhaps his whole life had been nothing more than a search for that one moment of real completion. Only twice had he ever really come close. The first time had been on Mars. When he had lived and watched while the others had died. Then he had not been alone or empty. And the other time had been right here in this very room—with Vergnan. Only twice in his life had he been allowed to approach the edge of true meaning. Twice in fifty-eight long and endless years. Would it ever happen again? When? How?

Jonathon returned, pausing in the doorway. "A pilot is there," it said.

Reynolds went toward the door, ready to leave. "Are you still planning to visit our sun?" he asked.

"Oh, yes. We shall continue trying, searching. We know nothing else. You do not believe—even after what Vergnan showed you—do you, Reynolds?"

"No, I do not believe."

"I understand," Jonathon said. "And I sympathize. All of us—even I—sometimes we have doubts."

Reynolds continued forward into the corridor. Behind, he heard a heavy clipping noise and turned to see Jonathon coming after him. He waited for the alien to join him and then they walked together. In the narrow corridor, there was barely room for both.

Reynolds did not try to talk. As far as he could see, there was nothing left to be said that might possibly be said in so short a time as that which remained. Better to say nothing, he thought, than to say too little.

The air lock was open. Past it, Reynolds glimpsed the squat bulk of the shuttle tug clinging to the creased skin of the starship.

There was nothing left to say. Turning to Jonathon, he said, "Good-bye," and as he said it, for the first time he wondered about what he was going back to. More than likely, he would find himself a hero once again. A celebrity. But that was all right: fame was fleeting; it was bearable. Two hundred forty thousand miles was still a great distance. He would be all right.

As if reading his thoughts, Jonathon asked, "Will you be remaining here or will you return to your homeworld?"

The question surprised Reynolds; it was the first time the alien had ever evidenced a personal interest in him. "I'll stay here. I'm happier."

"And there will be a new director?"

"Yes. How did you know that? But I think I'm going to be famous again. I can get Kelly retained."

"You could have the job yourself," Jonathon said.

"But I don't want it. How do you know all this? About Kelly and so on?"

"I listen to the stars," Jonathon said in its high warbling voice.

"They are alive, aren't they?" Reynolds said suddenly.

"Of course. We are permitted to see them for what they are. You do not. But you are young."

"They are balls of ionized gas. Thermonuclear reactions."

The alien moved, shifting its neck as though a joint lay in the middle of it. Reynolds did not understand the gesture. Nor would he ever. Time had run out at last.

Jonathon said, "When they come to you, they assume a disguise you can see. That is how they spend their time in this universe. Think of them as doorways."

"Through which I cannot pass."

"Yes."

Reynolds smiled, nodded and passed into the lock. It contracted behind him, engulfing the image of his friend. A few moments of drifting silence, then the other end of the lock furled open.

The pilot was a stranger. Ignoring the man, Reynolds dressed, strapped himself down and thought about Jonathon. What was it that it had said? I listen to the stars. Yes, and the stars had told it that Kelly had been fired?

He did not like that part. But the part he liked even less was this: when it said it, Jonathon had not blinked.

(1) It had been telling the truth. (2) It could lie without flicking a lash.

Choose one.

Reynolds did, and the tug fell toward the moon.

George Turner

George Turner (1916–) is the most influential Australian SF writer and critic. From the 1960s onward he was a leading contemporary Australian novelist who also wrote SF criticism. It wasn't until the mid-'70s that he turned to writing science fiction. His first SF novel, *Beloved Son* (1978), published when he was in his early sixties, was recognized as an important debut, and he has gone on to write a number of first-rate SF novels, including *The Sea and Summer* (1987, published as *Drowning Towers* in the U.S.), which won the Arthur C. Clarke Award. *Beloved Son* involves interstellar travel, a post-holocaust civilization in the 21st century, and genetic engineering—this last has remained one of the principal concerns of his fiction, in recent works such as *Brain Child* (1991), *The Destiny Makers* (1993), and *Genetic Soldier* (1994).

Turner's literary execution is contoured by deeply held moral convictions and his life as a contemporary novelist. "I prefer to maintain a low key in my own work," says Turner. "To this end I have concentrated on simple, staple SF ideas, mostly those which have become conventions in the genre, injected without background or discussion into stories on the understanding that readers know all they need to know about such things. My SF method remains the same as for my mainstream novels—set characters in motion in speculative situation and let them work out their destinies with a minimum of auctorial interference."

His future societies have a satisfying complexity, portraying class conflict and economic disparities in a gritty, realistic fashion absent from most American science fiction. While American science fiction generally sees space as simply the new frontier, Turner, the Australian, envisions it as an alien place with a strange and different culture, one with its own moral imperatives and structures—as he envisions the future on Earth as operating under other moral structures different from ours today.

He has written comparatively few short SF stories, less than a dozen to date. This one is about the conflict of values between cultures in the future, and has intriguing resonances with James Tiptree, Jr.'s "Beam Us Home."

I STILL CALL AUSTRALIA HOME

The past is another country; they do things differently there.
—L. P. Hartley

1

The complement of *Starfarer* had no idea, when they started out, of how long they might be gone. They searched the sky, the three hundred of them, men and women, black and brown and white and yellow, and in thirty years landed on forty planets whose life-support parameters appeared—from distant observation—close to those of Earth.

Man, they discovered, might fit his own terrestrial niche perfectly, but those parameters for his existence were tight and inelastic. There were planets where they could have dwelt in sealed environments, venturing out only in special suits, even one planet where they could have existed comfortably through half its year but been burned and suffocated in the other half. They found not one where they could establish a colony of mankind.

In thirty years they achieved nothing but an expectable increase in their numbers and this was a factor in their decision to return home. The ship was becoming crowded and, in the way of crowded tenements, something of a slum.

So they headed for Earth; and, at the end of the thirty-first year, took up a precessing north-south orbit allowing them a leisurely overview, day by day, of the entire planet.

This was wise. They had spent thirty years in space, travelling between solar systems at relativistic speeds, and reckoned that about six hundred local years had passed since they set out. They did not know what manner of world they might find.

They found, with their instruments, that the greenhouse effect had subsided slowly during the centuries, aided by the first wisps of galactic cloud heralding the new ice age, but that the world was still warmer than the interregnal norm. The ozone layer seemed to have healed itself, but the desert areas were still formidably large although the spread of new pasture and forest was heartening.

What they did not see from orbit was the lights of cities by night and this did not greatly surprise them. The world they had left in a desperate search for new habitat had been an ant heap of ungovernable, unsupportable billions whose numbers were destined to shrink drastically if any were to survive at all. The absence of lights suggested that the population problem had solved itself in grim fashion.

They dropped the ship into a lower orbit just outside the atmosphere and brought in the spy cameras.

There were people down there, all kinds of people. The northern hemisphere was home to nomadic tribes, in numbers like migratory nations; the northern temperate zone had become a corn belt, heavily farmed and guarded by soldiers in dispersed forts, with a few towns and many villages; the equatorial jungles were, no doubt, home to hunter-gatherers but their traces were difficult to see; there were signs of urban communities, probably trading centres, around the seacoasts but no evidence of transport networks or lighting by night and no sounds of electronic transmission. Civilisation had regressed, not unexpectedly.

They chose to inspect Australia first because it was separated from the larger landmasses and because the cameras showed small farming communities and a few townlets. It was decided to send down a Contact Officer to inspect and report back.

The ship could not land. It had been built in space and could live only in space; planetary gravity would have warped its huge but light-bodied structure beyond repair. Exploratory smallcraft could have been despatched, but it was reasoned that a crew of obviously powerful supermen might create an untrusting reserve among the inhabitants, even an unhealthy regard for gods or demons from the sky. A single person, powerfully but unobtrusively armed, would a suitable ambassador.

They sent a woman, Nugan Johnson, not because she happened to be Australian but because she was a Contact Officer, and it was her rostered turn for duty.

They chose a point in the south of the continent because it was autumn in the hemisphere, and an average daily temperature of twenty-six C would be bearable, and dropped her by tractor beam on the edge of a banana grove owned by Mrs Flighty Jones, who screamed and fled.

2

Flighty, in the English of her day, meant something like *scatterbrained*. Her name was, in fact, Hallo-Mary (a rough—very rough—descendant of Ave Maria), but she was a creature of fits and starts, so much so that the men at the bottling shed made some fun of her before they were convinced that she had seen *something*, and called the Little Mother of the Bottles.

"There was I, counting banana bunches for squeeging into baby pap, when it goes hissss-bump behind me."

"What went hiss-bump?"

"It did."

"What was it?" Little Mother wondered if the question was unfair to Flighty wits.

"I don't know." Having no words, she took refuge in frustrated tears. She had inherited the orchard but not the self-control proper to a proprietary woman.

In front of the men! Little Mother sighed and tried again. "What did it look like? What shape?"

Flighty tried hard. "Like a bag. With legs. And a glass bowl on top. And it bounced. That's what made the bump. And it made a noise."

"What sort of noise?"

"Just a noise." She thought of something else. "You know the pictures on the library wall? In the holy stories part? The ones where the angels go up? Well, like the angels."

Little Mother knew that the pictures did not represent angels, whatever the congregation were told. Hiding trepidation, she sent the nearest man for Top Mother.

Top Mother came, and listened . . . and said, as though visitations were nothing out of the way, "We will examine the thing that hisses and bumps. The men may come with us in case their strength is needed." That provided at least a bodyguard.

The men were indeed a muscular lot, and also a superstitious lot, but they were expected to show courage when the women claimed protection. They picked up whatever knives and mashing clubs lay to hand and tried to look grim. Man-to-man was a bloodwarming event but man-to-whatisit had queasy overtones. They agreed with Little Mother's warning: "There could be danger."

"There might be greater danger later on if we do *not* investigate. Lead the way, Hallo-Mary." A Top Mother did not use nicknames.

Flighty was now thoroughly terrified and no longer sure that she had seen anything, but Top Mother took her arm and pushed her forward. Perhaps it had gone away; perhaps it had bounced up and up . . .

It had not gone anywhere. It had sat down and pushed back its glass bowl and revealed itself, by its cropped hair, as a man.

"A man," murmured Top Mother, who knew that matriarchy was a historical development and not an evolutionary given. She began to think like the politician which at heart she was. A *man* from—from *outside*—could be a social problem.

The men, who were brought up to revere women but often resented them—except during the free-fathering festivals—grinned and winked at each other and wondered what the old girl would do.

The old girl said, "Lukey! Walk up and observe him."

Lukey started off unwillingly, then noticed that three cows grazed unconcernedly not far from the man in a bag and took heart to cross the patch of pasture at the orchard's edge.

At a long arm's length he stood, leaned forward and sniffed. He was forest bred and able to sort out the man in a bag's scents from the norms about him and, being forest bred, his pheromone sense was better than rudimentary. He came so close that Nugan could have touched him and said, "Just another bloody woman!" The stranger should have been a man, a sex hero!

He called back to Top Mother, "It's only a woman with her hair cut short."

They all crowded forward across the pasture. Females were always peaceable—unless you really scratched their pride.

The hiss Flighty had heard had been the bootjets operating to break the force of a too-fast landing by an ineptly handled tractor beam; the bump had been the reality of a contact that wrenched an ankle. Even the bounce was almost real as she hopped for a moment on one leg. The noise was Nugan's voice through a speaker whose last user had left it tuned to baritone range, a hearty, "Shit! Goddam shit!" before she sat down and became aware of a dumpy figure vanishing among columns of what she remembered vaguely as banana palms. Not much of a start for good PR.

She thought first to strip the boot and bind her ankle, then that she should not be caught minus a boot if the runaway brought unfriendly reinforcements. She did not fear the village primitives; though she carried no identifiable weapons, the thick gloves could spit a variety of deaths through levelled fingers. However, she had never killed a civilised organism and had no wish to do so; her business was to prepare a welcome home.

The scents of the air were strange but pleasant, as the orbital analysis had affirmed; she folded the transparent *fishbowl* back into its neck slot. She became aware of animals nearby. Cows. She recognised them from pictures though she had been wholly city bred in an era of gigantic cities. They took no notice of her. Fascinated and unafraid, she absorbed a landscape of grass and tiny flowers in the grass, trees and shrubs and a few vaguely familiar crawling and hopping insects. The only strangeness was the spaciousness stretching infinitely on all sides, a thing that the lush Ecological Decks of *Starfarer* could not mimic, together with the sky like a distant ceiling with wisps of cloud. Might it rain on her? She scarcely remembered rain.

Time passed. It was swelteringly hot but not as hot as autumn in the greenhouse streets.

They came at last, led by a tall woman in a black dress—rather, a robe cut to enhance dignity though it was trimmed off at the knees. She wore a white headdress like something starched and folded in the way of the old nursing tradition and held together by a brooch. She was old, perhaps in her sixties, but she had presence and the dress suggested status.

She clutched another woman by the arm, urging her forward, and Nugan recognised the clothing, like grey denim jeans, that fled through the palms. Grey Denim Jeans pointed and planted herself firmly in a determined no-further pose. Madam In Black gestured to the escort and spoke a few words.

Nugan became aware of the men and made an appreciative sound unbecoming in a middle-aged matron past child-bearing years. These men wore only G-strings and they were *men*. Not big men but shapely, muscular and very male. *Or am I so accustomed to Starfarer crew that any change rings a festival bell? Nugan, behave!*

The man ordered forward came warily and stopped a safe arm's length from her, sniffing. Nugan examined him. *If I were, even looked, twenty years younger . . .* He spoke suddenly in a resentful, blaming tone. The words were strange (of course they must be) yet hauntingly familiar; she thought that part of the sentence was "dam-dam she!"

She kept quiet. Best to observe and wait. The whole party, led by Madam In Black, came across the pasture. They stopped in front of her, fanning out in silent inspection. The men smelled mildly of sweat, but that was almost a pleasure; after thirty years of propinquity, *Starfarer*'s living quarters stank of sweat.

Madam In Black said something in a voice of authority that seemed part of her. It sounded a little like "Oo're yah?"—interrogative with a clipped note to it; the old front-of-the-mouth Australian vowels had vanished in the gulf of years. It should mean, by association, *Who are you?* but in this age might be a generalised, *Where are you from?*, even, *What are you doing here?*

Nugan played the oldest game in language lesson, tapping her chest and saying, "Nugan. I—Nugan."

Madam In Black nodded and tapped her own breast. "Ay Tup-Ma."

"Tupma?"

"Dit—Tup-Ma, Yah Nuggorn?"

"Nugan."

The woman repeated, "Nugan," with a fair approximation of the old vowels and followed with, "Wurriya arta?"

Nugan made a guess at vowel drift and consonant elision and came up with, *Where are you out of?* meaning, Where do you come from?

They must know, she thought, that something new is in the sky. A ship a kilometre long has been circling for weeks with the sun glittering on it at dawn and twilight. They can't have lost all contact with the past; there must be stories of the bare bones of history . . .

She pointed upwards and said, "From the starship."

The woman nodded as if the statement made perfect sense and said, "Stair-boot."

Nugan found herself fighting sudden tears. *Home, home, HOME has not forgotten us.* Until this moment she had not known what Earth meant to her, swimming in the depths of her shipbound mind. "Yes, stairboot. We say starship."

The woman repeated, hesitantly, "Stairsheep?" She tried again, reaching for the accent, "Starship! I say it right?"

"Yes, you say it *properly*."

The woman repeated, "Prupperly. Ta for that. It is old-speak. I read some of that but not speak—only small bit."

So not everything had been lost. There were those who had rescued and preserved the past. Nugan said, "You are quite good."

Tup-Ma blushed with obvious pleasure. "Now we go." She waved towards the banana grove.

"I can't." A demonstration was needed. Nugan struggled upright, put the injured foot to the ground and tried for a convincing limp. That proved easy; the pain made her gasp and she sat down hard.

"Ah! You bump!"

"Indeed I bump." She unshackled the right boot and broke the seals before fascinated eyes and withdrew a swelling foot.

"We carry."

We meant two husky males with wrists clasped under her, carrying her through the grove to a large wooden shed where more near-naked men worked at vats and tables. They sat on a table and brought cold water *(How do they cool it? Ice? Doubtful.)* and a thick yellow grease which quite miraculously eased the pain somewhat *(A native pharmacopoeia?)* and stout, unbleached bandages to swathe her foot tightly.

She saw that in other parts of the shed the banana flesh was being mashed into long wooden moulds. Then it was fed into glass cylinders whose ends were capped, again with glass, after a pinch of some noisome-looking fungus was added. *(Preservative? Bacteriophage? Why not?)* A preserving industry, featuring glass rather than metal; such details helped to place the culture.

Tup-Ma called, "Lukey!" and the man came forward to be given a long instruction in which the word *Stair-boot* figured often. He nodded and left the shed at a trot.

"Lukey go—goes—to tell Libary. We carry you there."

"Who is Libary?"

The woman thought and finally produced, "Skuller. Old word, I think."

"Scholar? Books? Learning?"

"Yes, yes, books. Scho-lar. Ta." Ta? Of course—thank you. Fancy the child's word persisting.

"You will eat, please?"

Nugan said quickly, "No, thank you. I have this." She dug out a concentrate pack and swallowed one tablet before the uncomprehending Tup-Ma. She dared not risk local food before setting up the test kit, enzymes and once-harmless proteins could change so much. They brought a litter padded like a mattress and laid her on it. Four pleasantly husky men carried it smoothly, waist-high, swinging gently along a broad path towards low hills, one of which was crowned by a surprisingly large building from which smoke plumes issued.

"Tup-Ma goodbyes you."

"Goodbye, Tup-Ma. And ta."

3

It was a stone building, even larger than it had seemed. But that was no real wonder; the medieval stone masons had built cathedrals far more ornate than this squared-off warehouse of a building. It was weathered dirty grey but was probably yellow sandstone, of which there had been quarries in Victoria. Sandstone is easily cut and shaped even with soft iron tools.

There were windows, but the glass seemed not to be of high quality, and a small doorway before which the bearers set down the litter. A thin man of indeterminate middle age stood there, brown eyes examining her from a dark, clean shaven face. He wore a loose shirt, wide-cut, ballooning shorts and sandals, and he smiled brilliantly at her. He was a full-blooded Aborigine.

He said, "Welcome to the Library, Starwoman," with unexceptionable pronunciation though the accent was of the present century.

She sat up. "The language still lives."

He shook his head. "It is a dead language but scholars speak it, as many of yours spoke Latin. Or did that predate your time? There are many uncertainties."

"Yes, Latin was dead. My name is Nugan."

"I am Libary."

"Library?"

"If you would be pedantic, but the people call me Libary. It is both name and title. I preside." His choice of words, hovering between old-fashioned and donnish, made her feel like a child before a tutor, yet he seemed affable.

He gave an order in the modern idiom and the bearers carried her inside. She gathered an impression of stone walls a metre thick, pierced by sequent doors which formed a temperature lock. The moist heat outside was balanced by an equally hot but dry atmosphere inside. She made the connection at once, having a student's reverence for books. The smoke she had seen was given off by a low-temperature furnace stoked to keep the interior air dry and at a reasonably even temperature. This was more than a scholars' library; it was the past, preserved by those who knew its value.

She was carried past open doorways, catching glimpses of bound volumes behind glass, of a room full of hanging maps and once of a white man at a lectern, touching his book with gloved hands.

She was set down on a couch in a rather bare room furnished mainly by a desk of brilliantly polished wood which carried several jars of coloured inks, pens which she thought had split nibs and a pile of thick, greyish paper. *(Unbleached paper? Pollution free? A psychic prohibition from old time?)*

The light came through windows, but there were oil lamps available with shining parabolic reflectors. And smoke marks on the ceiling. Electricity slept still.

The carriers filed out. Libary sat himself behind the desk. "We have much to say to each other."

Nugan marvelled, "You speak so easily. Do you use the old English all the time?"

"There are several hundred scholars in Libary. Most speak the old tongue. We practise continually."

"In order to read the old books?"

"That, yes." He smiled in a fashion frankly conspirational. "Also it allows private discussion in the presence of the uninstructed."

Politics, no doubt—the eternal game that has never slept in all of history. "In front of Tup-Ma, perhaps?"

"A few technical expressions serve to thwart her understanding. But the Tup-Ma is no woman's fool."

"*The* Tup-Ma? I thought it was her name."

"Her title. Literally, Top Mother. As you would have expressed it, Mother Superior."

"A nun!"

Libary shrugged. "She has no cloister and the world is her convent. Call her priest rather than a nun."

"She has authority?"

"She has great authority." He looked suddenly quizzical. "She is very wise. She sent you to me before you should fall into error."

"Error? You mean, like sin?"

"That also, but I speak of social error. It would be easy. Yours was a day of free thinking and irresponsible doing in a world that could not learn discipline for living. This Australian world is a religious matriarchy. It is fragile when ideas can shatter and dangerous when the women make hard decisions."

It sounded like too many dangers to evaluate at once. Patriarchy and equality she could deal with—in theory—but matriarchy was an unknown quantity in history. He had given his warning and waited silently on her response.

She pretended judiciousness. "That is interesting." He waited, smiling faintly. She said, to gain time, "I would like to remove this travel suit. It is hot."

He nodded, stood, turned away.

"Oh, I'm fully dressed under it. You may watch."

He turned back to her and she pressed the release. The suit split at the seams and crumpled round her feet. She stepped out, removed the gloves with their concealed armament and revealed herself in close-cut shirt and trousers and soft slippers. The damaged ankle hurt less than she had feared.

Libary was impressed but not amazed. "One must expect ingenious invention." He felt the crumpled suit fabric. "Fragile."

She took a small knife from her breast pocket and slit the material, which closed up seamlessly behind the blade. Libary said, "Beyond our capability."

"We could demonstrate—"

"No doubt." His interruption was abrupt, uncivil. "There is little we need." He changed direction. "I think Nugan is of Koori derivation."

"Possibly from Noongoon or Nungar or some such. You might know better than I."

His dark face flashed a smile. "I don't soak up old tribal knowledge while the tribes themselves preserve it in their enclaves."

"Enclaves?"

"We value variety of culture." He hesitated, then added, "Under the matriarchal aegis which covers all."

"All the world."

"Most of it."

That raised questions. "You communicate with the whole world? From space we detected no radio, no electronic signals at all."

"Wires on poles and radiating towers, as in the books? Their time has not come yet."

A queer way of phrasing it. "But you hinted at global communication, even global culture."

"The means are simple. Long ago the world was drawn together by trading vessels; so it is today. Ours are very fast; we use catamaran designs of great efficiency, copied from your books. The past does not offer much but there are simple things we take—things we can make and handle by simple means." He indicated the suit. "A self-healing cloth would require art beyond our talent."

"We could show—" But could they? Quantum chemistry was involved and electro-molecular physics and power generation . . . Simple products were not at all simple.

Libary said, "We would not understand your showing. Among your millions of books, few are of use. Most are unintelligible because of the day of simple explanation was already past in your era. We strain to comprehend what you would find plain texts, and we fail. Chemistry, physics—those disciplines of complex numeration and incomprehensible signs and arbitrary terms—are beyond our understanding."

She began to realise that unintegrated piles of precious but mysterious books are not knowledge.

He said, suddenly harsh, "Understanding will come at its own assimilable pace. You can offer us nothing."

"Surely . . . "

"Nothing! You destroyed a world because you could not control your greed for a thing you called progress but which was no more than a snapping up of all that came to hand or to mind. You destroyed yourselves by inability to control your breeding. You did not ever cry *Hold!* for a decade or a century to unravel the noose of a self-strangling culture. You have nothing to teach. You knew little that mattered when sheer existence was at stake."

Nugan sat still, controlling anger. *You don't know how we fought to stem the tides of population and consumption and pollution; how each success brought with it a welter of unforeseen disasters; how impossible it was to coordinate a world riven by colour, nationality, political creed, religious belief and economic strata.*

Because she had been reared to consult intelligence rather than emotion, she stopped thought in mid-tirade. *Oh, you are right. These were the impossible troubles brought by greed and irresponsible use of a finite world. We begged our own downfall. Yet . . .*

"I think," she said, "you speak with the insolence of a lucky survival. You exist only because we did. Tell me how your virtue saved mankind."

Libary bowed his head slightly in apology. "I regret anger and implied contempt." His eyes met hers again. "But I will not pretend humility. We rebuilt the race. In which year did you leave Earth?"

"In twenty-one eighty-nine. Why?"

"In the last decades before the crumbling. How to express it succinctly? Your world was administered by power groups behind national boundaries, few ruling many, pretending to a mystery termed *democracy* but ruling by decree. Do I read the history rightly?"

"Yes." It was a hard admission. "Well, it was beginning to seem so. Oppression sprang from the need to ration food. We fed fifteen billion only by working land and sea until natural fertility cycles were exhausted, and that only at the cost of eliminating other forms of life. We were afraid when the insects began to disappear . . . "

"Rightly. Without insects, nothing flourishes."

"There was also the need to restrict birth, to deny birth to most of the world. When you take away the right to family from those who have nothing else and punish savagely contravention of the population laws . . . " She shrugged hopelessly.

"You remove the ties that bind, the sense of community, the need to consider any but the self. Only brute force remains."

"Yes."

"And fails as it has always failed."

"Yes. What happened after we left?"

Libary said slowly, "At first, riots. Populations rose against despots, or perhaps against those forced by circumstances into despotism. But ignorant masses cannot control a state; bureaucracies collapsed, supply fell into disarray and starvation set in. Pack leaders—not to be called soldiers—fought for arable territory. Then great fools unleashed biological weaponry—I think that meant toxins and bacteria and viruses, whatever such things may have been—and devastated nations with plague and pestilence. There was a time in the northern hemisphere called by a term I read only as Heart of Winter. Has that meaning for you?"

"A time of darkness and cold and starvation?"

"Yes."

"Nuclear winter. They must have stopped the bombing in the nick of time. It could only have been tried by a madman intent on ruling the ruins."

"We do not know his name—their names—even which country. Few records were kept after that time. No machines, perhaps, and no paper."

"And then?"

"Who knows? Cultural darkness covers two centuries. Then history begins again; knowledge is reborn. Some of your great cities saw the darkness falling and sealed their libraries and museums in hermetic vaults. This building houses the contents of the Central Libary of Melbourne; there are others in the world and many yet to be discovered. Knowledge awaits deciphering but there is no hurry. This is, by and large, a happy world."

Sophisticated knowledge was meaningless here. They could not, for instance, create electronic communication until they had a broad base of metallurgy, electrical theory and a suitable mathematics. Text books might as well have been written in cipher.

"And," Libary said, "there were the Ambulant Scholars. They set up farming communities for self support, even in the Dark Age, while they preserved the teachings and even some of the books of their ancestors. They visited each other and established networks around the world. When they set up schools, the new age began."

"Like monks of the earlier Dark Age, fifteen hundred years before."

"So? It has happened before?"

"At least once and with less reason. Tell me about the rise of women to power."

Libary chuckled. "Power? Call it that but it is mostly manipulation. The men don't mind being ruled; they get their own way in most things and women know how to bow with dignity when caught in political error. It is a system of giving and taking wherein women give the decisions and take the blame for their mistakes. The men give them children—under certain rules—and take responsibility for teaching them when maternal rearing is completed."

She made a stab in the dark. "Women established their position by taking control of the birth rate."

"Shrewdly thought, nearly right. They have a mumbo jumbo of herbs and religious observances and fertility periods but in fact it is all contraception, abortion and calculation. Some men believe, more are sceptical, but it results in attractive sexual rituals and occasional carnivals of lust, so nobody minds greatly." He added offhandedly, "Those who cannot restrain their physicality are killed by the women."

That will give Starfarer pause for thought.

"I think," said Libary, "that the idea was conceived by the Ambulant Scholars and preached in religious guise—always a proper approach to basically simple souls who need a creed to cling to. So, you see, the lesson of overpopulation has been learned and put to work."

"This applies across the planet?"

"Not yet, but it will. America is as yet an isolated continent. Our Ambulant Scholars wielded in the end a great deal of respected authority."

"And now call yourselves Librarians?"

His black face split with pleasure. "It is so good to speak with a quick mind."

"Yet a day will come when population will grow again beyond proper maintenance."

"We propose that it shall not. Your machines and factories will arrive in their own good time, but our present interest is in two subjects you never applied usefully to living: psychology and philosophy. Your thinking men and women studied profoundly and made their thoughts public, but who listened? There is a mountain of the works of those thinkers to be sifted and winnowed and applied. Psychology is knowledge of the turbulent self; philosophy is knowledge of the ideals of which that self is capable. Weave these together and there appears a garment of easy discipline wherein the self is fulfilled and the world becomes its temple, not just a heap of values for ravishing. We will solve the problem of population."

Nugan felt, with the uneasiness of someone less than well prepared, that they would. Their *progress* would lie in directions yet unthought of.

"Now," Libary said, "would you please tell me how you came to Earth without a transporting craft?"

"I was dropped by tractor beam."

"A—beam?" She had surprised him at last. "A ray of light that carries a burden?"

"Not light. Monopoles."

"What are those?"

"Do you have magnets? Imagine a magnet with only one end, so that the attraction goes on in a straight line. It is very powerful. Please don't ask how it works because I don't know. It is not in my field."

Libary said moodily, "I would not wish to know. Tell me, rather, what you want here."

Want? Warnings rang in Nugan's head but she could only plough ahead. "After six hundred years we have come home! And Earth is far more beautiful than we remember it to be."

His dark eyebrows rose. "Remember? Are you six hundred years old?"

Explanation would be impossible. She said, despairingly, "Time in heaven is slower than time on Earth. Our thirty years among the stars are six centuries of your time. Please don't ask for explanation. It is not magic; it is just so."

"Magic is unnecessary in a sufficiently wonderful universe. Do you tell me that you do not understand the working of your everyday tools?"

"I don't understand the hundredth part. Knowledge is divided among specialists; nobody knows all of even common things."

Libary considered in silence, then sighed lightly and said, "Leave that and return to the statement that you have come home. This is not your home."

"Not the home we left. It has changed."

"Your home has gone away. For ever."

The finality of his tone must have scattered her wits, she thought later; it roused all the homesickness she had held in check and she said quickly, too quickly, "We can rebuild it."

The black face became still, blank. She would have given years of life to recall the stupid words. He said at last, "After all I have told you of resistance to rapid change you propose to redesign our world!"

She denied without thinking, "No! You misunderstand me!" In her mind she pictured herself facing *Starfarer*'s officers, stumbling out an explanation, seeing disbelief that a trained Contact could be such a yammering fool.

"Do I? Can you mean that your people wish to live as members of our society, in conditions they will see as philosophically unrewarding and physically primitive?"

He knew she could not mean any such thing. She tried, rapidly, "A small piece of land, isolated, perhaps an island, a place where we could live on our own terms. Without contact. You would remain—unspoiled."

Insulting, condescending habit of speech, truthful in its meaning, revealing and irrevocable!

"You will live sequestered? Without travelling for curiosity's sake, without plundering resources for your machines, without prying into our world and arguing with it? In that case, why not stay between the stars?"

Only truth remained. "We left Earth to found new colonies. Old Earth seemed beyond rescue; only new Earths could perpetuate a suffocating race."

"So much we know. The books tell it."

Still she tried: "We found no new Earth. We searched light-years of sky for planets suitable for humans. We found the sky full of planets similar to Earth—but only similar. Man's range of habitable conditions is very narrow. We found planets a few degrees too hot for healthy existence or a few degrees too cool to support a terrestrial ecology, others too seismically young or too aridly old, too deficient in oxygen or too explosively rich in hydrogen, too low in carbon dioxide to support a viable plant life or unbearably foul with methane or lacking an ozone layer. Parent stars, even of G-type, flooded surfaces with overloads of ultraviolet radiation, even gamma radiation, or fluctuated in minute but lethal instabilities. We visited forty worlds in thirty years and found not one where we could live. Now you tell me we are not welcome in our own home!"

"I have told you it is not your home. You come to us out of violence and decay; you are conditioned against serenity. You would be only an eruptive force in a world seeking a middle way. You would debate our beliefs, corrupt our young men by offering toys they do not need, tempt the foolish to extend domination over space and time—and in a few years destroy what has taken six centuries to build."

Anger she could have borne but he was reasonable—as a stone wall is reasonable and unbreachable.

"Search!" he said. "Somewhere in such immensity must be what you seek. You were sent out with a mission to propagate mankind, but in thirty years you betray it."

She burst out, "Can't you understand that we *remember* Earth! After thirty years in a steel box we want to come home."

"I do understand. You accepted the steel box; now you refuse the commitment."

She pleaded, "Surely six hundred people are not too many to harbour? There must be small corners—"

He interrupted, "There are small corners innumerable but not for you. Six hundred, you say, but you forget the books with their descriptions of the starships. You forget that we know of the millions of ova carried in the boxes called cryogenic vaults, of how in a generation you would be an army surging out of its small corner to dominate the culture whose careful virtues mean nothing to you. Go back to your ship, Nugan. Tell your people that time has rolled over them, that their home has vanished."

She sat between desperation and fulmination while he summoned the bearers. Slowly she resumed the travel suit.

From the hilltop she saw a world unrolled around her, stirring memory and calling the heart. It should not be lost for a pedantic Aboriginal's obstinacy.

"I will talk with your women!"

"They may be less restrained than I, Nugan. The Tup-Ma's message said you were to be instructed and sent away. My duty is done."

She surrendered to viciousness. "We'll come in spite of you!"

"Then we will wipe you out as a leprous infection."

She laughed, pointed a gloved finger and a patch of ground glowed red, then white. "Wipe us out?"

He told her, "That will not fight the forces of nature we can unleash against you. Set your colony on a hill and we will surround it with bushfires, a weapon your armoury is not equipped to counter. Set it in a valley and we will show you how a flash flood can be created. Force us at your peril."

All her Contact training vanished in the need to assert. "You have not seen the last of us."

He said equably, "I fear that is true. I fear for you, Nugan, and all of yours."

She tongued the switch at mouth level and the helmet sprang up and over her head, its creases smoothing invisibly out. She had a moment's unease at the thought of the Report Committee on *Starfarer*, then she tongued the microphone switch. "Jack!"

"Here, love. So soon?"

"Yes, so damned soon!" She looked once at the steady figure of Libary, watching and impassive, then gave the standard call for return: "Lift me home, Jack."

Hurtling into the lonely sky, she realised what she had said and began silently to weep.

Alexander Kuprin

Translated by Leland Fetzer

Alexander Kuprin (1879–1938) is the first Russian writer to incorporate the influence of H. G. Wells, in this 1913 story, and to provide a model for later Russian writers such as Evgeny Zamiatin. Kuprin is also clearly influenced by other literature, including various stories of adventure and shipwreck. (Perhaps, also, Poe's *Narrative of Arthur Gordon Pym.*)

Zamiatin said in his enthusiastic essay on H. G. Wells in 1922, "Of course, science fiction could enter the field of fine literature only in the last decades, when truly fantastic potentialities unfolded before science and technology . . . true science fiction clothed in literary form will be found only at the end of the nineteenth century . . . The petrified life of the old, prerevolutionary Russia produced almost no examples of social fantasies or science fiction, as indeed it could not. Perhaps the only representatives of this genre in the recent history of our literature are Kuprin, with his 'The Liquid Sun,' and Bogdanov. . . ."

This is a story that could easily have appeared twenty-five or thirty years later in *Amazing Stories* as a genre story without causing a ripple—and been seen as innovative. It did not, however, appear in English translation until the early 1980s in an academic collection, so it has not been part of the main genre dialogue for decades. It is about the idea of radical transformation of human society through science and technology. Russian and American science fiction share a central fascination with this idea. In the rest of the world, this idea is generally treated ironically, with great suspicion, or as a recipe for disaster.

LIQUID SUNSHINE

I, Henry Dibble, turn to the truthful exposition of certain important and extraordinary events in my life with the greatest concern and absolutely understandable hesitation. Much of what I find essential to put to paper will, without doubt, arouse astonishment, doubt, and even disbelief in the future reader of my account. For this I have long been prepared, and I find such an attitude to my memoirs completely plausible and logical. I must myself admit that even to me those years spent in part in travel and in part on the six-thousand-foot summit of the volcano Cayambe in the South American Republic of Ecuador often seem not to have been actual events in my life, but only a strange and fantastic dream or the ravings of a transient cataclysmic madness.

But the absence of four fingers on my left hand, recurring headaches, and the eye ailment which goes by the common name of night blindness, these incontrovertible phenomena compel me to believe that I was in fact a witness to the most astonishing events in world history. And, finally, it is not madness, not a dream, not a delusion, that punctually three times a year from the firm E. Nideston and Son, 451 Regent Street, I receive 400 pounds sterling. This allowance was generously left to me by my teacher and patron, one of the greatest men in all of human history, who perished in the terrible wreck of the Mexican schooner *Gonzalez.*

I completed studies in the Mathematical Department with special studies in Physics and Chemistry at the Royal University in the year . . . That, too, is yet another persistent reminder of my adventures. In addition to the fact that a pulley or a chain took the fingers of my left hand at the time of the catastrophe, in addition to the damage to my optic nerves, etc., as I fell into the sea I received, not knowing when nor how, a sharp blow on the right upper quarter of my skull. That blow left hardly any external sign but it is strangely reflected in my mind, specifically in my powers of recall. I can remember well words, faces, localities, sounds, and the sequence of events, but I have forgotten forever all numbers and personal names, addresses, telephone numbers, and historical dates; the years, months, and days which marked my personal life have disappeared without a trace, scientific formulae, although I am able to deal with them without difficulty in logical fashion, have fled, and both the names of those I have known and know now have disappeared, and this circumstance is very painful to me. Unfortunately, I did not then maintain a diary, but two or three notebooks which have survived, and a few old letters aid me to a certain degree to orient myself.

Briefly, I completed my studies and received the title Master of Physics two, three, four, or perhaps even five years before the beginning of the twentieth century. Precisely at that time the husband of my elder sister, Maude, a farmer of Norfolk who periodically had loaned me material support and even more important moral support, took ill and died. He firmly believed that I would continue my scientific career at one of the English universities and that in time I would shine as a luminary to cast a ray of glory on his modest family. He was healthy, sanguine, strong as a bull, could drink, write a verse, and box—a lad in the spirit of good old merry England. He died as the result of a stroke one night after consuming one-fourth of a Berkshire mutton roast, which he seasoned with a strong sauce: a bottle of whiskey and two gallons of Scotch light beer.

His predictions and expectations were not fulfilled. I did not join the scientific ranks. Even more, I was not fortunate enough to find the position of a teacher or a tutor in a private or public school; rather, I fell into the vicious, implacable, furious, cold, wearisome world of failure. Oh! who, besides the rare spoiled darlings, has not known and felt on his shoulders this stupid, ridiculous, blind blow of fate? But it abused me for too lengthy a time.

Neither at factories nor at scientific agencies—nowhere could I find a place for myself. Usually I arrived too late: the position was already taken.

In many cases I became convinced that I had fallen into some dark and suspicious conspiracy. Even more often I was paid nothing for two or three months of labor and thrown onto the street like a kitten. One cannot say that I was excessively indecisive, shy, unenterprising, or, on the other hand, sensitive, vain or refractory. No, it was simply that the circumstances of life were against me.

But I was above all an Englishman and I held myself as a gentleman and a representative of the greatest nation in the world. The thought of suicide in this terrible period of my life never came to mind. I fought against the injustice of fate with cold, sober persistence and with the unshakable faith that never, never would an Englishman be a slave. And fate, finally, surrendered in the face of my Anglo-Saxon courage.

I lived then in the most squalid of all the squalid lanes in Bethel Green, in the God-forsaken East End, dwelling behind a chintz curtain in the home of a dock worker, a coal hauler. I paid him four shillings a month for the place, and in addition I helped his wife with the cooking, taught his three oldest children to read and write, and also scrubbed the kitchen and the backstairs. My hosts always cordially invited me to eat with them, but I had decided not to burden their beggar's budget. I dined, rather, in the dark basement and God knows how many cats', dogs', and horses' lives lay on my black conscience. But my landlord, Mr. John Johnson, requited my natural tact with attentiveness: when there was much work on the East End docks and not enough workmen and the wages reached extraordinary heights, he always managed to find a place for me to load heavy cargoes where with no difficulty I could earn eight or ten shillings in a day. It was unfortunate that this handsome, kind, and religious man became intoxicated every Sunday without fail and when he did so he displayed a great inclination toward fisticuffs.

In addition to my duties as cook and occasional work on the docks, I essayed numerous other ridiculous, onerous, and peculiar professions. I helped clip poodles and cut the tails from fox terriers, clerked in a sausage store when its owner was absent, catalogued old libraries, counted the earnings at horse races, at times gave lessons in mathematics, psychology, fencing, theology, and even dancing, copied off the most tedious reports and infantile stories, watched coach horses when the drivers were eating ham and drinking beer; once, in uniform, I spread rugs and raked the sand between acts in a circus, worked as a sandwich man, and even fought as boxer, a middleweight, translated from German to English and vice versa, composed tombstone inscriptions, and what else did I not do! To be candid, thanks to my inexhaustible energy and temperate habits I was never in particular need. I had a stomach like a camel, I weighed 150 pounds without my clothes, had good hands, slept well and was cheerful in temperament. I had so adjusted to poverty and to its unavoidable deprivations, that occasionally I could not only send a little money to my younger sister, Esther, who had been abandoned in Dublin with her two children by her Irish husband, and actor, a drunkard, a liar, a tramp, and a rake—but I also followed the sciences and public life closely, read newspapers and scholarly journals, bought used books, and belonged to rental libraries. I even managed to make two minor inventions: a very cheap device which would warn a railroad engineer in fog or snow of a closed switch ahead, and an unusual, long-lasting welding flame which burned hydrogen. I must say that I did not enjoy the income from these inventions—others did. But I remained true to science, like a knight to his lady, and I never abandoned the belief that the time would come when my beloved would summon me to her chamber with her bright smile.

That smile shone upon me in the most unexpected and commonplace fashion. One foggy autumn morning my landlord, the good Mr. Johnson, went to a neighboring shop for hot water and milk for his children. He returned with a radiant face, the odor of whiskey on his breath, and a newspaper in his hand. He gave me the newspaper, still damp and smelling of ink, and, pointing out an entry marked with a line from the edge of his dirty nail, exclaimed:

"Look, old man. As easy as I can tell anthracite from coke, I know that these lines are for you, lad."

I read, not without interest, the following announcement:

"The solicitors 'E. Nideston and Son,' 451 Regent Street, seek an individual for an equatorial voyage to a location where he must remain for not less than three years engaged in scientific pursuits. Conditions: age, 22 to 30 years, English citizenship, faultless health, discrete, sober and forbearing, must know one, or yet better, two other European languages (French and German), must be a bachelor, and so far as it is possible, free of family and other ties to his native land. Beginning salary: 400 pounds sterling per year. A university education is desirable, and in particular a gentleman knowing theoretical and applied chemistry and physics has an advantage in obtaining the position. Applicants are to call between nine and ten in the morning." I am able to quote this advertisement with such assurance since it is still preserved among my few papers, although I copied it off in haste and has been subject to the action of sea water.

"Nature has given you long legs, son, and good lungs," Johnson said, approvingly pounding my back. "Start up the engine and full steam ahead. No doubt there will be many more young gentlemen there of irreproachable health and honorable character than at Derby. Anne, make him a sandwich with meat and preserves. Perhaps he will have to wait his turn in line for five hours. Well, I wish you luck, my friend. Onward, brave England!"

I arrived barely in time at Regent Street. Silently I thanked nature for my good legs. As he opened the door the porter with indifferent familiarity said: "Your luck, mister. You got the last chance," and promptly fixed on the outside doors the fateful announcement: "The advertised opening is now closed to applicants."

In the darkened, cramped, and rather dirty reception room—such are almost all the reception rooms belonging to the magicians of the City who deal in millions—were about ten men who had come before me. They sat about the walls on dark, time polished, soiled wooden benches, above which, at the height of a sitting man's head, the ancient wallpaper displayed a wide, dirty, band. Good God, what a pitiful collection of hungry, ragged men, driven by need, sick and broken, had gathered here, like a parade of monsters! Involuntarily my heart contracted with pity and wounded self-esteem. Sallow faces, averted, malicious, envious, suspicious glances from under lowered brows, trembling hands, tatters, the smell of poverty, cheap tobacco, and fumes of alcohol long since drunk. Some of these young gentlemen were not yet seventeen years of age while others were past fifty. One after another, like pale shades, they drifted into the office and returned from there looking like drowned men only lately removed from the water. I felt both sickened and ashamed to admit to myself that I was infinitely healthier and stronger than all of them taken together.

Finally my turn came. Someone invisible opened the door from the other side and shouted abruptly and disgustedly in an exasperated voice:

"Number eighteen, and Allah be praised, the last!"

I entered the office, nearly as neglected as the reception room, different only that it was papered in peeling checked paper; it had two side chairs, a couch, and two easy chairs on which sat two middle-aged gentlemen of apparently the same medium height, but the elder of the two, in a long coat was slim, swarthy, and seemingly stern, while the other, dressed in a new jacket with silken lapels, was fair, plump, blue-eyed and sat at his ease one leg placed upon the other.

I gave my name and bowed not deeply, but respectfully. Then, seeing that I was not to be offered a seat, I was at the point of taking a place on the couch.

"Wait," said the swarthy one, "First remove your coat and vest. There is a doctor here who will examine you."

I remembered the clause in the advertisement which referred to irreproachable health, and I silently removed my outer garments. The florid stout man lazily freed himself from his chair and placing his arms around me he pressed his ear to my chest.

"Well, at least we have one with clean linen," he said casually.

He listened to my lungs and heart, tapped my spine and chest with his fingers, sat me down and checked the reflexes of my knees, and finally said lazily:

"As fit as a fiddle. He hasn't eaten too well recently, however. But that is nothing and all that is required is two weeks of good food. To his good fortune, I find no traces of exhaustion from over-indulgences in athletics as is common among our young men. In a word, Mr. Nideston, I present you a gentleman, a fortunate, almost perfect example of the healthy Anglo-Saxon race. May I assume that I am no longer needed?"

"You are free, doctor," said the solicitor. "But can you, may I be assured, visit us tomorrow morning, if I require your professional advice?"

"Oh, Mr. Nideston, I am always at your service."

When we were alone, the solicitor sat opposite me and peered intently into my face. He had little sharp eyes the color of a coffee bean with quite yellow whites. Every now and then when he looked directly at you, it seemed as though diminutive sharp and bright needles issued from those tiny blue pupils.

"Let us talk," he said abruptly. "Your name, origins, and place of birth?"

I answered him in the same expressionless and laconic fashion.

"Education?"

"The Royal University."

"Subject of study?"

"Department of Mathematics, in particular, Physics."

"Foreign languages?"

"I know German comparatively well. I understand when French is not spoken too rapidly, I can put together a few score essential expressions, and I read it without difficulty."

"Relatives and their social position?"

"Is that of any importance to you, Mr. Nideston?"

"To me? Of supreme unimportance. But I act in the interests of a third party."

I described the situations of my two sisters. During my speech he attentively inspected his nails, and then threw two needles at me from his eyes, asking:

"Do you drink? And how much?"

"Sometimes at dinner I drink a half pint of beer."

"A bachelor?"

"Yes, sir."

"Do you have any intention of commiting that blunder? Of marrying?"

"Oh, no."

"Any present love affairs?"

"No, sir."

"How do you support yourself?"

I answered that question briefly and fairly, omitting, for the sake of brevity, five or six of my latest casual professions.

"So," he said, when I had finished, "do you need money?"

"No. My stomach is full and I am adequately clothed. I always find work. So far as it is possible I follow recent developments in science. I am convinced that sooner or later I will find my opportunity."

"Would you like money in advance? A loan?"

"No, that is not my practice. I don't take money from anyone . . . But we're not finished."

"Your principles are commendable. Perhaps we can come to an agreement. Give me your address and I will inform you, and probably very soon, of our decision. Good-bye."

"Excuse me, Mr. Nideston," I responded. "I have answered all your questions, even the most delicate, with complete candor. May I ask you one question?"

"Please."

"What is the purpose of the journey?"

"Oho! Are you concerned about that?"

"We may assume that I am."

"The purpose of the journey is purely scientific."

"That is not an adequate answer."

"Not adequate?" Mr. Nideston abruptly shouted at me, and his coffee eyes poured out sheaves of needles. "Not adequate? Do you have the insolence to assume that the firm of Nideston and Son now in existence for one hundred and fifty years and respected by all of England's commercial establishments would suggest anything dishonorable or which might compromise you? Or that we would undertake any enterprise without possessing reliable guarantees beforehand that it is unconditionally legal?"

"Oh, sir, I have no doubt of that," I responded in confusion.

"Very well, then," he interrupted me and immediately became tranquil, like a stormy sea spread with oil. "But you see, first of all I am bound by the proviso that you not be informed of any substantial details of the journey until you are aboard the steamship out of Southampton . . ."

"Bound where?" I asked suddenly.

"For the time being I cannot tell you. And secondly, the purpose of your journey (if indeed it comes to pass) is not completely clear even to me."

"Strange," said I.

"Passing strange," the solicitor willingly agreed. "But I may also inform you, if you so desire, that it will be fantastic, grandiose, unprecedented, splendid, and audacious to the point of madness!"

Now it was my turn to say "Hmmm," and this I did with a certain restraint.

"Wait," Mr. Nideston exclaimed with sudden fervor. "You are young. I am twenty-five or thirty years older than you. You are not at all astonished by many of the greatest accomplishments of the human mind, but if, when I was your age, someone had predicted that I would work in the evenings by the light of invisible electricity which flowed through wires or that I would converse with an acquaintance at a distance of eighty miles, that I would see moving, laughing human figures on a screen, that I would send telegraph messages without the benefit of wires, and so on, and so on, then I would have waged my honor, my freedom, my career against one pint of bad London beer that I was confronted with a madman."

"You mean the project involves some new invention or a great discovery?"

"If you wish, yes. But I ask you, do not view me with distrust or suspicion. What would you say, for example, if a great genius were to appeal to your young energy, strength, and knowledge, a genius who, we will assume, is engaged with a problem—to create a pleasing, nutritious, economical food out of the elements found in the air? If you were provided the opportunity to labor for the sake of the future organization and adornment of the earth? To dedicate your talents and spiritual energies to the happiness of future generations? What would you say? Here is an example at hand. Look out the window."

Involuntarily I arose under the spell of his compelling, swift gesture and looked through the clouded glass. There, over the streets, hung a black-rust-gray fog, like dirty cotton from heaven to earth. In it only dimly could be perceived the wavering glow from the street lights. It was eleven o'clock in the morning.

"Yes, yes, look," said Mr. Nideston. "Look carefully. Now assume that a gifted, disinterested man is summoning you to a great project to ameliorate and beautify the earth. He tells you that everything that is on the earth depends on the mind, will, and hands of man. He tells you that if God in his righteous anger has turned his face away from man, then man's measureless mind will come to his own aid. This man will tell you that fogs, disease, climatic extremes, winds, volcanic eruptions—they are all subject to the influence and control of the human will—and that finally the earth could become a paradise and its existence extended by several hundred thousand years. What would you say to that man?"

"But what if he who presents me with this radiant dream is wrong? What if I find myself a dumb plaything in the hands of a monomaniac? A capricious madman?"

Mr. Nideston rose, and, presenting me his hand as a sign of farewell, said firmly:

"No. Aboard the steamship in two or three months from now (if we can come to an agreement) I will inform you of the name of that scientist and the meaning of his great task, and you will remove your hat as a mark of your great reverence for the man and his ideas. But I, unfortunately, Mr. Dibble, am a layman. I am only a solicitor—the guardian and representative of others' interests."

After this interview I had almost no doubt that fate, finally, had grown tired of my fixed inspection of her unbending spine and had decided to show me her mysterious face. Therefore, that same evening with the help of my small savings I produced a banquet of extraordinary luxury, which consisted of a roast, a punch, plum pudding and hot chocolate which was enjoyed in addition to myself by the worthy couple, the elder Johnsons, and, I do not remember exactly—six or seven of the younger Johnsons. My left shoulder was quite blue and out of joint from the friendly pounding of my good landlord who sat next to me on my left.

And I was not wrong. The next evening I received a telegram: "Call at noon tomorrow. 451 Regent Street, Nideston."

I arrived punctually at the appointed time. He was not in his office, but a servant who had been forewarned led me to a small room in a restaurant located around the corner at a distance of two hundred paces. Mr. Nideston was there alone. At first he was not that ebullient, and perhaps even poetic, man who had spoken with me so fervently about the future happiness of mankind two days earlier. No, once more he was that dry and laconic solicitor who on the occasion of our first meeting that morning had so commandingly instructed me to remove my outer clothing and had questioned me like a police inspector.

"Good day. Sit down," he said indicating a chair. "It is my lunch hour, a time I have at my disposal. Although my firm is called 'Nideston and Son' I am in fact a bachelor and a lonely man. And so—would you care to dine? To drink?"

I thanked him and asked for tea and toast. Mr. Nideston ate at leisure, sipped an old port and from time to time transfixed me with the bright needles of his eyes. Finally, he wiped his lips, threw down his napkin, and asked:

"Then, you are agreed?"

"To buy a pig in a poke?" I asked in turn.

"No," he said loudly and angrily. "The previous conditions remain in force. Before your departure to the tropics you will receive as much information as I am empowered to give you. If this is not satisfactory, you may, on your part, refuse to sign the contract and I will pay you a recompense for the time which you have employed in fruitless conversations with me."

I observed him carefully. At that moment he was engaged in an effort to crack two nuts, the right hand enveloping the knuckles of the left. The sharp needles of his eyes were concealed behind the curtain of his brows. And suddenly, as though in a moment of illumination, I perceived all the soul of that man—the strange soul of a formalist and a gambler, the narrow specialist and an extraordinarily expansive temperament, the slave of his counting house traditions and at the same time a secret searcher for adventures, a pettifogger, ready for two pennies to put his opponent in prison for a long sentence, and at the same time an eccentric capable of sacrificing the wealth acquired in dozens of years of unbroken labor for the sake of the shadow of a beautiful idea. This thought passed through me like lightning. And Nideston, suddenly, as though we had been united by some invisible current, opened his eyes, with a great effort crushed the nuts into tiny fragments and smiled at me with an open, childlike, almost mischievous smile.

"When all is said and done, you are risking little, my dear Mr. Dibble. Before you leave for the tropics I will give you several commissions on the continent. These commissions will not require from you any particular scientific knowledge, but they will demand great mechanical accuracy, precision, and foresight. You will need no more than about two months, perhaps a week more or less than that. You are to accept in various European locations certain expensive and very fragile optical glasses as well as several extremely delicate and sensitive physical instruments. I entrust to your care, agility, and skills their packing, delivery to the railroad, and sea and rail transport. You must agree that it would mean nothing to a drunken sailor or porter to throw a crate into the hold and smash into fragments a doubly convex lens over which dozens of men have worked for dozens of years . . ."

"An observatory!" I thought joyfully. "Of course, it's an observatory! What happiness! At last I have my elusive fate by the forelock."

I could see that he had guessed my thoughts and his eyes became yet merrier.

"We will not discuss the remuneration for this, your first, task. We will come to agreement on details, of course, as I can see from your expression. But," and then he suddenly laughed heedlessly, like a child, "I want to turn your attention to a very curious fact. Look, through these fingers have passed ten or twenty thousand curious cases, some of them involving very large sums. Several times I have made a fool of myself, and that in spite of all our subtle casuistic precision and diligence. But, imagine that every time that I have rejected all the tricks of my craft and looked a man straight in the eye, as I am now looking at you, I have never gone wrong and never had cause for repentance. And so?"

His eyes were clear, firm, trusting and affectionate. At that second this little swarthy, wrinkled, yellow-faced man indeed took my heart into his hands and conquered it.

"Good," I said. "I believe you. From this time I am at your disposal."

"Oh, why so fast?" Mr. Nideston said genially. "You have plenty of time. We still have time to drink a bottle of claret together." He pulled the cord for the waiter. "But please put your personal affairs in order, and this evening at eight o'clock you will leave with the tide on board the steamship *The Lion and the Magdalene* to which I will in time deliver your itinerary, drafts on various banks, and money for your personal expenses. My dear young man, I drink to your health and your successes. If only," he suddenly exclaimed with unexpected enthusiasm, "if only you knew how I envy you, my dear Mr. Dibble!"

In order to flatter him and in quite an innocent manner, I responded almost sincerely:

"What's detaining you, my dear Mr. Nideston? I swear that in spirit you are as young as I."

The swarthy solicitor lowered his long delicately modeled nose into his claret cup, was silent for a moment and suddenly said with a sigh of feeling:

"Oh, my dear Mr. Dibble! My office, which has existed nearly from the time of the Plantagenets, the honor of my firm, my ancestors, thousands of ties connecting me with my clients, associates, friends, and enemies . . . I couldn't name it all . . . This means you have no doubts?"

"No."

"Well, let us drink a toast and sing 'Rule, Britannia'!"

And we drank a toast and sang—I almost a boy, yesterday a tramp, and that dry man of business, whose influence extended from the gloom of his dirty office to touch the fates of European powers and business magnates—we sang together in the most improbable and unsteady voices in all the world:

> *"Rule, Britannia!*
> *Britannia, rules the waves!*
> *Britons never, never, never will be slaves!"*

A servant entered, and turning politely to Mr. Nideston, he said:

"Excuse me, sir. I listened to your singing with genuine pleasure. I have heard nothing more pleasing even in the Royal Opera, but next to you in the adjoining room is a meeting of lovers of French medieval music. Perhaps I should not refer to them as gentlemen . . . but they all have very discriminating ears."

"You are no doubt correct," the solicitor answered gently. "And therefore I ask you to accept as a keepsake this round yellow object with the likeness of our good king."

Here is a brief list of the cities and the laboratories which I visited after I crossed the Channel. I copy them out in entirety from my notebook: The Pragemow concern in Paris; Repsold in Hamburg; Zeiss, Schott Brothers, and Schlattf in Jena; in Munich the Frauenhof concern and the Wittschneider Optical Institute and also the Mertz laboratory there; Schick in Berlin, and also Bennech and Basserman. And also, not distant in Potsdam, the superb branch of the Pragemow concern which operates in conjunction with the essential and enlightened support of Dr. E. Hartnack.

The itinerary composed by Mr. Nideston was extraordinarily precise and included train schedules and the addresses of inexpensive but comfortable English hotels. He had drawn it up in his own hand. And here, too, one was aware of his strange and unpredictable character. On the corner of one of the pages he had written in pencil in his angular, firm hand: "If Chance and Co. were real Englishmen they would have not abandoned their concern and it would not be necessary for us to obtain lenses and instruments from the French and Germans with names like Schnurbartbindhalter."

I will admit, not in a spirit of boasting, that everywhere I bore myself with the requisite weight and dignity, because many times in critical moments in my ears I heard Mr. Nideston's terrible goat's voice singing, "Britons never, never, never will be slaves."

But, too, I must say that I cannot complain about any lack of attentiveness and courtesy on the part of the learned scientists and famous technicians whom I met. My letters of recommendation signed with large, black, completely illegible flourishes and reinforced below with Mr. Nideston's precise signature served as a magic wand in my hands which opened all doors and all hearts for me. With unremitting and deep-felt concern I watched the manufacture and polishing of convex and curving lenses and the production of the most delicate, complex and beautiful instruments which gleamed with brass and steel, shining with all their screws, tubing, and machined metal. When in one of the most famous workshops of the globe I was shown an almost complete fifty-inch mirror which had required at least two or three years of final polishing—my heart stood still and my breath caught, so overcome was I with delight and awe at the power of the human mind.

But I was also rendered very uneasy by the persistent curiosity of these serious, learned men who in turn attempted to ascertain the mysterious purpose of my patron whose name I did not know. Sometimes subtly and artfully, sometimes crudely and directly, they attempted to extract from me the details and goal of my journey, the addresses of the firms with which I had business, the type and function of our orders to other workshops, etc., etc. But, firstly, I remembered well Mr. Nideston's very serious warnings about indiscretions; secondly, what could I answer even if I wished to? I myself knew nothing and was feeling my way, as though at night in an unknown forest. I was accepting, after verifying drawings and calculations, some kind of strange optical glasses, metal tubing of various sizes, calculators, small-scale propellors, miniaturized cylinders, shutters, heavy glass retorts of a strange form, pressure gauges, hydraulic presses, a host of electrical devices which I had never seen before, several powerful microscopes, three chronometers and two underwater diving suits with helmets. One thing became obvious to me: the strange enterprise which I served had nothing to do with the construction of an observatory, and on the basis of the objects which I was accepting I found it absolutely impossible to guess the purpose which they were to serve. My only concern was to ensure that they were packed with great care and I constantly devised ingenious devices which protected them from vibrations, concussion, and deformation.

I freed myself from impertinent questions by suddenly falling silent, and not saying a word I would look with stony eyes directly at the face of my interrogator. But one time I was compeled to resort to very persuasive eloquence: a fat, insolent Prussian dared to offer me a bribe of two thousand Marks if I would reveal to him the secret of our enterprise. This happened in Berlin in my own room on the fourth floor of my hotel. I succinctly and sternly informed that stout insolent creature that he spoke with an English gentleman. He neighed like a Percheron, slapped me familiarly on the back and exclaimed:

"Oh, come now, my good man, let's forget these jokes. We both understand what they mean. Do you think that I have not offered you enough? But we, like intelligent men of the world, can come to an agreement, I am sure . . ."

His vulgar tone and crude gestures displeased me inordinately. I opened the great window of my room and pointing below at the pavement I said firmly:

"One word more, and you will not find it necessary to employ the elevator to leave this floor. One, two, three . . ."

Pale, cowed, and enraged, he cursed hoarsely in his harsh Berlin accent, and on his way out slammed the door so hard that the floor of my apartment trembled and objects leaped upon the table.

My last visit on the continent was to Amsterdam. There I was to transmit my letters of recommendation to the two owners of two world famous diamond cutting firms, Maas and Daniels, respectively. They were intelligent, polite, dignified, and sceptical Jews. When I visited them in turn, Daniels first of all said to me slyly: "Of course you have a commission also for Mr. Maas." And Maas, as soon as he read the letter addressed to him, said with a query in his voice, "You have no doubt spoken with Mr. Daniels?"

Both of them displayed the greatest reserve and suspicion in their relations with me; they consulted together, sent off simple and coded telegrams, put to me the most subtle and detailed questions about my personal life, and so on. They both visited me on the day of my departure. A kind of Biblical dignity could be perceived in their words and movements.

"Excuse us, young man, and do not consider it a sign of our distrust that we inform you," said the older and more imposing, Daniels, "that on the route Amsterdam–London all steamships are alive with international thieves of the highest skill. It is true that we hold in strictest confidence the execution of your worthy commission, but who can be assured that one or two of these enterprising, intelligent, at times almost brilliant international knights of commerce will not manage to discover our secret? Therefore, we have not considered it excessive to surround you with an invisible but faithful police guard. You, perhaps, will not even notice them. You know that caution is never unwanted. Will you not agree that we and your associates would be much relieved if that which you transport were under reliable, observant, and ceaseless observation during the entire voyage? This is not a matter of a leather cigarette case, but two objects which cost together approximately one million three hundred thousand francs and which are unique in all the world, and perhaps in all the universe."

I, in the most sincere and concerned tone, hastened to assure the worthy diamond cutter of my complete agreement with his wise and farsighted words. Apparently, my trust inclined him even more in my favor, and he asked in a low voice, in which I detected a quaver, an expression of awe:

"Would you like to see them?"

"If that is convenient, then please," I said, barely able to conceal my curiosity and perplexity.

Both the Jews almost simultaneously, with the expression of priests performing a holy ritual, took out of the side pockets of their long frock coats two small boxes—Daniels' was of oak while that of Maas was of red morocco; they carefully unfastened the gold clasps and lifted the lids. Both boxes were lined in white velvet and at first to me they appeared to be empty. It was only when I had bent close over them and looked closely that I saw two round, convex, totally colorless lenses of extraordinary purity and transparency, which would have been almost invisible except for their delicate, round, precise outlines.

"Astonishing workmanship!" I exclaimed, ecstatically. "Undoubtedly the polishing of glass in this manner must have required much expenditure of time."

"Young man!" said Daniels in a startled whisper. "They are not glass, they are two diamonds. The one from my shop weighs thirty and one-half carats and the diamond of Mr. Maas in all weighs seventy-four carats."

I was so stunned that I lost my usual composure.

"Diamonds? Diamonds cut into spheres? But that's a miracle such as I have never seen or heard. Man has never succeeded in producing anything like them!"

"I have already told you that these objects are unique in all the world," the jeweler reminded me solemnly, "but, excuse me, I am somewhat puzzled by your surprise. Did you not know about them? Had you in fact never heard of them?"

"Never in my life. You know that the enterprise which I serve is a closely guarded secret. Not only I, but also Mr. Nideston, are unacquainted with it in detail. I know only that I am collecting parts and equipment in various locations in Europe for some kind of an enormous project, whose purpose and plan I—a scientist by training—as yet understand nothing."

Daniels looked intently at me with his calm capable eyes, light brown in color, and his Biblical face darkened.

"Yes, that is so," he said slowly and thoughtfully after a brief pause. "Apparently you know nothing more than we, but do I perceive, when I look into your eyes, that even if you were informed of the nature of the enterprise, you would not share your information with us?"

"I have given my word, Mr. Daniels," I said as softly as possible.

"Yes, that is so, that is so. Do not think, young man, that you have come to our city of canals and diamonds completely unknown."

The Jew smiled a thin smile.

"We are even aware of the manner in which you suggested an aerial journey out of your window to a certain individual with commercial connections."

"How could anyone have known of that incident except the two of us involved?" I said, astonished. "Apparently, that German swine could not keep his mouth closed."

The Jew's face became enigmatic. He slowly and significantly passed his hand down his long beard.

"You should know that the German said nothing about his humiliation. But we knew about it the next day. We must! We whose guarded fire-proof vaults contain our own and others' valuables sometimes worth hundreds of millions of francs, must maintain our own intelligence. Yes. And three days later Mr. Nideston also knew of your deed."

"That's going too far!" I exclaimed in confusion.

"You have lost nothing, my young Englishman. Rather you have gained. Do you know how Mr. Nideston responded when he heard of the Berlin incident? He said: 'I knew that Mr. Dibble, an excellent young man, would have done nothing else.' For my part I would like to congratulate Mr. Nideston and his patron on the fact that their interests have fallen into such faithful hands. Although . . . Although . . . Although this disrupts certain of our schemes, our plans, and our hopes."

"Yes," confirmed the taciturn Mr. Maas.

"Yes," repeated quietly the Biblical Mr. Daniels, and once more a sad expression passed over his face. "We were given these diamonds in almost the same form in which you now see them, but their surfaces, as they had only recently been removed from the matrix, were crude and rough. We ground them as patiently and lovingly as though they were a commission from an emperor. To express it more accurately; it was impossible to improve on them. But I, an old man, a craftsman and one of the great gem experts of the world, have long been tortured by one cursed question: who could give such a shape to a diamond? Moreover, look at the diamond—here is a lens—not a crack, not a blemish, not a bubble. This prince of diamonds must have been subjected to the greatest heat and pressure. And I," and here Daniels sighed sadly, "and I must admit that I had counted much on your arrival and your candor."

"Forgive me, but I am in no position . . ."

"That's enough, I understand. But we wish you a pleasant journey."

My ship left Amsterdam that evening. The agents who accompanied me were so skilled at their work that I did not know who among the passengers was my guard. But toward midnight when I wished to sleep and retired to my room, to my surprise I found there a bearded, broad-shouldered stranger whom I had never seen on deck. He stretched out, not on the spare bunk, but on the floor near the door where he spread out a coat and an inflatable rubber pillow and covered himself with a robe. Not without repressed anger I informed him that the entire cabin to its full extent including its cubic content of air belonged to me. But he responded calmly and with a good English accent:

"Do not be disturbed, sir. It is my duty to spend this night near you in the position of a faithful watchdog. May I add that here is a letter and a package from Mr. Daniels."

The old Jew had written briefly and affectionately:

Do not deny me a small pleasure: take as a souvenir of our meeting this ring I offer you. It is of no great value, but it will serve as an amulet to guard you from danger at sea. The inscription on it is ancient, and may indeed be in the language of the now extinct Incas.

Daniels

In the packet was a ring with a small flat ruby on whose surface were engraved wondrous signs.

Then my "watchdog" locked the cabin, laid a revolver next to him on the floor and seemingly fell instantly asleep.

"Thank you, my dear Mr. Dibble," Mr. Nideston said to me the next day, shaking my hand firmly. "You have excellently fulfilled all your commissions, which were at times difficult enough, employed your time well, and in addition have borne yourself with dignity. Now you may rest for a week and divert yourself as you wish. Sunday morning we shall dine together and then leave for Southampton and on Monday morning you will be at sea aboard *The Southern Cross*, a splendid steamer. Do not forget, may I remind you, to visit my clerk to receive your two months' salary and expenses, and during the next two days I will examine and re-pack all of your baggage. It is dangerous to trust another's hands, and I doubt if there is anyone in London as skilled as I in the packing of delicate objects."

On Sunday I bade farewell to kind Mr. John Johnson and his numerous family, leaving them to the sound of their best wishes for a happy journey. And on Monday morning Mr. Nideston and I were seated in the luxurious stateroom of the huge liner *The Southern Cross* where we drank coffee in expectation of my departure. A fresh breeze blew over the sea and green waves with white caps dashed against the thick glass of the portholes.

"I must inform you, my dear sir, that you will not be traveling alone," said Mr. Nideston. "A certain Mr. de Mon de Rique will be sailing with you. He is an electrician and mechanic with several years of irreproachable experience behind him and I have only the most favorable reports concerning his abilities. I feel no special affection for the lad, but it may well be in this case the voice of my own erroneous and baseless antipathy—an old man's eccentricity. His father was a Frenchman who took English citizenship and his mother was Irish but he himself has the blood of a Gaelic fighting cock in his veins. He is a dandy, handsome in a common sort of way, much taken with himself and his own appearance, and is fond of women's skirts. It was not I who selected him. I acted only in accordance with the instructions issued to me by Lord Charlesbury, your future director and mentor. De Mon de Rique will arrive in twenty or twenty-five minutes with the morning train from Cardiff and we shall speak with him. At any rate I advise you to establish good relations with him. Whether you like it or not you must live three or four years at his side on God-knows-what desert at the equator on the summit of the extinct volcano Cayambe, where you, white men, will be only five or six, while all the others will be Negroes, Mestizos, Indians and others of their ilk. Are you perhaps frightened at such a prospect? Remember, the choice is yours to make. We could at any moment tear up the contract you signed and return together by the eleven o'clock train to London. And I may assure you that this would in no wise reduce the respect and affection I feel for you."

"No, my dear Mr. Nideston, I see myself already on Cayambe," I said with laughter. "I yearn for regular employment, particularly if it involves science, and when I think of it I lick my chops like a starveling in front of a White Chapel sausage shop. I hope that my work will be interesting enough that I will not become bored and involved in petty concerns and personal differences."

"Oh, my dear sir, you will have much beautiful and lofty labor before you complete your scheme. The time has come to be open with you and I will enlighten you on some matters of which I am informed. Lord Charlesbury has been laboring now nine years on a plan of unheard of dimensions. He has decided at any costs to accomplish the transformation of the sun's rays into a gas and what is more—to compress that gas to an extraordinary degree at terribly low temperatures under colossal pressures into liquid form. If God grants him the power of completing his plan, then his discovery will have enormous consequences . . ."

"Enormous!" I repeated softly, subdued and awed by Mr. Nideston's words.

"That is all I know," said the solicitor. "No, I also know from a personal letter from Lord Charlesbury that he is closer than ever to the successful completion of his work and less than ever has any doubts about the rapid solution of his problem. I must tell you, my dear friend, that Lord Charlesbury is one of the great men of science, one of few touched with genius. In addition, he is a genuine aristocrat both in birth and in spirit, an unselfish and self-denying friend of mankind, a patient and considerate teacher, a charming conversationalist and a faithful friend. He is, moreover, the possessor of such attractive spiritual beauty that all hearts are attracted to him . . . But here is your traveling companion coming up the gang plank now," Mr. Nideston said, breaking off his enthusiastic speech. "Take this envelope. You will find in it your steamship tickets, your exact itinerary and money. You will be at sea for sixteen or seventeen days.

Tomorrow you will be overcome by depression. For such an occasion I have acquired and deposited in your cabin thirty or so books. And in addition, in your baggage you will find a suitcase with a supply of warm clothing and boots. You did not know that you will be required to live in a mountain region with eternal snows. I attempted to select clothing of your size, but I was so afraid of making an error, that I preferred the larger size to the smaller. Also you will find among your things a small box with seasickness remedies. I do not in fact believe in them, but at any rate . . . do you suffer from seasickness?"

"Yes, but not to a particularly painful degree. And anyway, I have a talisman against all dangers at sea."

I showed him the ruby, Daniels' gift. He examined it carefully, shook his head and said thoughtfully:

"Somewhere I have seen such a stone as that, and it seems with the same inscription. But now I see the Frenchman has noticed us and is coming our way. With all my heart, my dear Dibble, I wish you a happy voyage, good spirits and health . . . Greetings, Mr. de Mon de Rique. May I introduce you: Mr. Dibble, Mr. de Mon de Rique, future colleagues and collaborators."

I personally was not particularly impressed by the dandy. He was tall, slender, effete and sleek, with a kind of grace in his movements, an indolent and flexible strength, such as we see in the great cats. He reminded me first of all of a Levantine with his beautiful velvety dark eyes and small gleaming black mustache, which was carefully trimmed over his classic pink mouth. We exchanged a few insignificant and polite phrases. But at that moment a bell rang above us and a whistle sounded, shaking the deck with its full powerful voice—the ship's whistle.

"Well, now, good-bye, gentlemen," said Mr. Nideston. "With all my heart I hope you will become friends. My greetings to Lord Charlesbury. May you have good weather during your crossing. Until we meet again."

He walked briskly down the gang plank, entered a waiting cab, waved affectionately in our direction for the last time, and without looking back disappeared from our sight. I did not know why, but I felt a kind of sadness, as though when that man disappeared I had lost a true and faithful helper and a moral support.

I remember little that was remarkable in our journey. I will say only that those seventeen days seemed as long to me as 170 years, and they were so monotonous and dreary that now from a distance they seem to me to be one endlessly long day.

De Mon de Rique and I met several times a day at dinner in the salon. We had no other close meetings. He was cooly polite with me and I in turn re-paid him with restrained courtesy, but I constantly felt he was not interested in me personally nor indeed in anyone else in the world. But, on the other hand, when our conversation touched upon our special fields, I was overwhelmed by his knowledge, his audacity, and the originality of his hypotheses, and what was important, by his ability to express his ideas in precise and picturesque language.

I tried to read the books which Mr. Nideston had left for me. Most of them were narrowly scientific works which dealt with the theory of light and optic lenses, observations on high and low temperatures, and the description of experiments on the concentration and liquefaction of gases. There were also several books devoted to the description of remarkable expeditions and two or three books about the equatorial countries of South America. But it was difficult to read because a heavy wind blew constantly and the steamship oscillated in long sliding glides. All the passengers gave their due to seasickness except de Mon de Rique, who in spite of his great height and delicate build conducted himself as well as an old sailor.

Finally, we arrived at Colón in the northern part of the isthmus of Panama. When I disembarked my legs were leaden and would not obey my will. According to Mr. Nideston's instructions we were personally to oversee the trans-shipment of our baggage to the train station and its loading into baggage cars. The most delicate and sensitive instruments we took with ourselves into our compartment. The precious polished diamonds were, of course, in my possession, but—it is now painful to admit this—I not only did not even show them to my companion, I never said a word to him about them.

Our journey henceforth was fatiguing and consequently of little interest. We traveled by railroad from Colón to Panama, from Panama we had two days' journey on the ancient quivering steamship *Gonzalez* to the Bay of Guayaquil, then on horseback and rail to Quito. In Quito, in accordance with Mr. Nideston's instruction we sought out the Equator Hotel where we found a party of guides and packers who were expecting us. We spent the night in the hotel and early in the morning, refreshed, we set off for the mountains. What intelligent, good, charming creatures—the mules. With their bells tinkling steadily, shaking their heads decorated with rings and plumes, carefully stepping on the uneven country roads with their long tumbler-shaped hooves, they calmly proceeded along the rim of the abyss over such defiles that involuntarly you closed your eyes and held to the horn of the high saddle.

We reached the snow about five that evening. The road widened and became level. It was obvious that people of a high civilization had labored over it. The sharp turns were always paralleled with a low stone barrier.

At six o'clock when we had passed through a short tunnel, we suddenly saw residences before us: several low white buildings over which proudly rose a white tower which resembled a Byzantine church spire or an observatory. Still higher into the sky rose iron and brick chimneys. A quarter of an hour later we arrived at our destination.

Out of a door belonging to a house larger and more spacious than the rest emerged to meet us a tall thin old man with a long, irreproachably white beard. He said he was Lord Charlesbury and greeted us with unfeigned kindness. It was hard to know his age from his appearance: fifty or seventy-five. His large, slightly protuberant blue eyes, the eyes of a pure Englishman, were as clear as a lad's, shining and penetrating. The clasp of his hand was firm, warm, and open, and his high broad forehead was notable for its delicate and noble lines. And as I admired his slender beautiful face and responded to his handshake it clearly seemed to me that one time long ago I had seen his visage and many times I had heard his name.

"I am infinitely pleased at your arrival," said Lord Charlesbury, climbing up the stairs with us. "Was your journey a pleasant one? And how is the good Mr. Nideston? A remarkable man, is he not? But you can answer all my questions at dinner. Now go refresh yourselves and put yourselves in order. Here is our major-domo, the worthy Sambo," and he indicated a portly old Negro who met us in the foyer. "He will show you to your rooms. We dine punctually at seven, and Sambo will inform you of our remaining schedule."

The worthy Sambo very politely, but without a shadow of servile ingratiation, took us to a small house nearby. Each of us was given three rooms—simple, but at the same time somehow exceptionally comfortable, bright, and cheerful. Our quarters were separated from each other by a stone wall and each had a separate entrance. For some reason I was pleased by this arrangement.

With indescribable pleasure I sank into a huge marble bath (thanks to the rocking of the steamship I had been deprived of this satisfaction, and in the hotels at Colón, Panama and Quito the baths would not have aroused the trust even of my friend John Johnson). But when I luxuriated in the warm water, took a cold shower, shaved, and then dressed with the greatest care I was ridden by the question: why was Lord Charlesbury's face so familiar? And what was it, something almost fabulous, it seemed to me, that I had heard about him? At times in some corner of my consciousness I dimly felt that I could remember something, but then it would disappear, as a light breath disappears from a polished steel surface.

From the window of my study I could see all of this strange settlement with its five or six buildings, a stable, a greenhouse with low sooty equipment sheds, a mass of air hoses, with cars drawn over narrow rails by vigorous sleek mules, with high steam cranes which were smoothly carrying through the air steel containers to be filled with coal and oil shale out of a series of dumps. Here and there workers were active, the majority of them half-naked, although the thermometer attached to the outside of my window showed a temperature below freezing, and who were of all colors: white, yellow, bronze, coffee, and gleaming black.

I observed and thought how a flaming will and colossal wealth had been able to transform the barren summit of the extinct volcano into a veritable outpost of civilization with a manufactory, a workshop, and a laboratory, to transport stone, wood and iron to an altitude of eternal snows, to bring water, to construct buildings and machines, to set into motion precious physical instruments, among which the two lenses alone which I had brought cost 1,300,000 francs, to hire dozens of workers and summon highly paid assistants . . . Once more there arose clearly in my mind the figure of Lord Charlesbury and suddenly—but wait! enlightenment suddenly came to my memory. I recalled very precisely how fifteen years earlier when I was still a green student at my school all the newspapers for months trumpeted various rumors concerning the disappearance of Lord Charlesbury, the English peer, the only scion of an ancient family, a famous scientist and a millionaire. His photograph was printed everywhere as well as conjectures on the causes of this strange event. Some took it as murder; others asserted that he had fallen under the influence of some malevolent hypnotist who for his evil purposes had removed the nobleman from England, leaving no traces; a third opinion held that the nobleman was in the hands of criminals who were holding him in expectation of a great ransom; a fourth opinion, and the most prescient one, asserted that the scientist had secretly undertaken an expedition to the North Pole.

Shortly later it became known that before his disappearance Lord Charlesbury very advantageously had liquidated all his lands, forests, parks, farms, coal and clay pits, castles, pictures, and other collections for cash, guided by a very acute and farsighted financial sense. But no one knew what had happened to this immense sum of money. When he disappeared there also disappeared, no one knew where, the famous Charlesbury diamonds, which were rightly the pride of all of England. No police, no private investigators were able to illuminate this strange affair. Within two months the press and society had forgotten him, diverted by other earthshaking interests. Only the learned journals which had dedicated many pages to the memory of the lost nobleman long continued to recount in great detail and with respectful deference his major scientific accomplishments in the study of light and heat and in particular in the expansion and contraction of gases, thermostatics, thermometrics, and thermodynamics, light refraction, the theory of lenses, and phosphorescence.

Outside resounded the drawn-out doleful sound of a gong. And then almost immediately someone knocked on my door and then entered a little cheerful Negro lad, as active as a monkey, who, bowing to me with a friendly smile, reported:

"Mister, I have been appointed by Lord Charlesbury to be at your service. Would you, sir, please come to dinner?"

On the table in my sitting room was a small, delicate bouquet of flowers in a porcelain vase. I selected a gardenia and inserted it into the lapel of my dinner-jacket. But just at that moment Mr. de Mon de Rique emerged from his door wearing a modest daisy in the buttonhole of his frock coat. I felt a kind of uneasy displeasure sweep over me. And even at that distant time there must have been in me still much shallow juvenile peevishness, because I was very pleased to see that Lord Charlesbury who met us in the salon was not wearing a frock coat but a dinner-jacket as was I.

"Lady Charlesbury will be with us shortly," he said, looking at his watch. "I suggest, gentlemen, that you join me for dinner. During the dinner and afterwards there will be two or three hours of free time to converse about business or whatever. May I add that there is a library, skittles, a billiard room and a smoking room here at your disposal. I ask you to utilize them at your discretion as with everything I possess here. I leave you complete freedom as to breakfast and lunch. And this is true also of dinner. But I know how valuable and fruitful is women's company for young Englishmen and therefore . . ."—he rose and indicated the door through which at that moment entered a slender, young, golden-haired woman escorted by another individual of the female sex, spare and sallow dressed all in black. "And therefore, Lady Charlesbury, I have the honor and the pleasure of introducing to you my future colleagues and, I hope, my friends, Mr. Dibble and Mr. de Mon de Rique."

"Miss Sutton," he said, addressing his wife's faded companion (later I discovered she was a distant relative and companion of Lady Charlesbury), "this is Mr. Dibble and Mr. de Mon de Rique. Please share with them your kindness and attention."

At dinner, which was both simple and refined, Lord Charlesbury revealed himself as a cordial host and a superb conversationalist. He inquired animatedly of political affairs, the latest journalistic and scientific news and the health of one or another public figures. By the way, as strange as it may seem, he appeared to be better informed on these subjects than either of us. In addition, his wine cellar turned out to be above praise.

From time to time I secretly glanced at Lady Charlesbury. She took hardly any part in the conversation, only lifting her dark lashes occasionally in the direction of a speaker. She was much younger, even very much younger, than her husband. Her pale face, untouched by any equatorial tan and distinguished by an unhealthy kind of beauty, was framed by thick golden hair, and she had dark, deep, serious, almost melancholy eyes. And all of her appearance, her attractive, very slim figure in white gauze and delicate white hands with long narrow fingers, was reminiscent of some rare and beautiful, but also perhaps poisonous and exotic flower grown without light in a moist dark conservatory.

But I also noticed that de Mon de Rique, who sat opposite me during the meal, often turned an emotional and meaningful glance from his beautiful eyes on our hostess, a glance which persisted perhaps, a half a second longer than propriety permitted. I found myself disliking him more and more: his soft well-groomed face and hands, his languid sweet eyes, which seemed to conceal something, his confident posture, movements, and tone of voice. In my male opinion he seemed repugnant, but I did not doubt for a moment that he possessed all the marks and attributes of an authentic, life-long, cruel, and indifferent conquerer of women's hearts.

After dinner when everyone had left for the salon and Mr. de Mon de Rique had asked permission to retire to the smoking room, I gave the case with the diamonds to Lord Charlesbury, saying:

"These are from Maas and Daniels in Amsterdam."

"You carried them with you?"

"Yes, sir."

"And you did well. These two stones are more valuable to me than all my laboratory."

He went to his study and returned with an eight-power glass. For a long time he carefully examined the diamonds under an electric lamp, and finally, returning them to the case, he said in a satisfied voice, although not without agitation.

"The polishing is above reproach. They are ideally precise. This evening I will check their curved surfaces with instruments employed to measure lenses. To-morrow morning, Mr. Dibble, we shall fix them into place. Until ten o'clock I shall be occupied with your comrade, Mr. de Mon de Rique, showing him his future laboratory but at ten I ask you to wait for me in your quarters. I shall come for you. Ah, my dear Mr. Dibble, I feel that together we shall advance our project, one of the greatest enterprises ever undertaken by that noble creature, *Homo sapiens.*"

When he said this his eyes burned with a blue light and his hands stroked the lid of the case. And his wife continued to watch him with her deep, dark, fathomless eyes.

The next morning promptly at ten o'clock my doorbell rang and the smartly dressed Negro boy, bowing deeply, admitted Lord Charlesbury.

"You are ready, I'm pleased to see," said my patron in greeting. "I examined the things you brought yesterday and they all seem to be in excellent order. I thank you for your concern and diligence."

"Three-quarters of that honor, if not more, is due to Mr. Nideston, sir."

"Yes, a fine human being and a true friend," the nobleman said with a gracious smile. "But, now, if there is nothing to hinder you, shall we go to the laboratory?"

The laboratory turned out to be a massive round white building, something like a tower, crowned with the dome which had been the first thing to strike my eye when we emerged from the tunnel.

Wearing our coats we passed through a small anteroom lighted by a single electric lamp and then found ourselves in total darkness. But Lord Charlesbury flipped a switch near me and bright light in a moment flooded a huge round room with a regular hemispherical ceiling some forty feet above the floor. In the midst of the room rose something like a small glass room, which resembled those medical isolation rooms which have lately appeared at university clinics in operating rooms which provide the exceptional cleanliness and disinfected air required during long and complicated operations. From that glass chamber which contained strange equipment such as I had never seen before rose three solid copper cylinders. At a height of about twelve feet both of the cylinders split into three pipes of yet larger diameter; those, in turn, were divided into three and the upper ends of these final massive copper pipes touched the concave surface of the dome. A multitude of pressure gauges and levers, curved and straight steel shafts, valves, wiring, and hydraulic presses completed this extraordinary and, for me, absolutely stunning laboratory. Steep circular staircases, iron columns and beams, narrow catwalks with slender hand rails which crossed high above me, hanging electric lamps, a host of thick pendant fiber hoses and long copper pipes—all of this was wound together, fatiguing the eye and giving the impression of a chaos.

Surmising my state of mind, Lord Charlesbury said calmly:

"When a person for the first time sees what is for him a strange mechanism, such as the workings of a watch or a sewing machine, he at first throws up his hands in despair at their complexity. When I, for the first time, saw the disassembled parts of a bicycle, it seemed to me that even the most ingenious mechanic in the world could not assemble them. But a week later I myself put them together and then disassembled them, astonished at the simplicity of its construction. Please, listen to my explanations patiently. If at first you do not understand, do not hesitate to ask me as many questions as you wish. This will give me only pleasure.

"Thus, there are twenty-seven closely placed openings in the roof. And in these openings are inserted cylinders which you see high above you which emerge into the open air through doubly-concave lenses of great power and exceptional clarity. Perhaps you now understand the scheme. We collect the sun's rays in foci and then, thanks to a whole series of mirrors and optic lenses made according to my plans and calculations, we conduct them, at times concentrating them and at other times dispersing them, through a whole system of pipes until the lowest pipes release concentrated sunlight here under the insulated cover into this very narrow and strong cylinder made of vanadium steel in which there is a whole system of pistons equipped with shutters, something like in a camera, which allow absolutely no light to enter when they are closed. Finally to the free end of this major cylinder with its internal closures I attach in a vacuum a vessel in the shape of a retort in the throat of which there are also several valves. When it is necessary I can open these closures and then insert a threaded stopper into the neck of the retort, unfasten the vessel from the end of the cylinder and then I have a superb means of storing compressed solar emanations."

"This means that Hook and Euler and Young . . . ?"

"Yes," Lord Charlesbury interrupted me. "They, and Fresnel, and Cauchy, and Malus, and Huygens and even the great Arago—they were all wrong when they perceived the phenomenon of light as one of the elements of the earth's atmosphere. I will prove this to you in ten minutes in the most striking fashion. Only the wise old Descartes and the genius of geniuses, the divine Newton, were right. The words of Biot and Brewster have only sustained and confirmed my experiments, but this was only much after I began them. Yes! Now it is clear to me and it will be shortly to you also that sunlight is a dense stream of very small resilient bodies, like tiny balls, which with terrible force and energy move through space, transfixing in their course the mass of the earth's atmosphere . . . But we will talk about theory later. Now, to be methodical, I will demonstrate the procedures which you must perform every day. Let us go outside."

We left the laboratory, climbed a circular staircase almost to the roof of the dome and found ourselves on a bright open gallery which circled the entire spherical roof in a spiral and a half.

"You need not struggle to open in turn all the covers which protect the delicate lenses from dust, snow, hail, and birds," said Lord Charlesbury. "All the more so that even a very strong man could not do that. Simply pull this lever toward yourself, and all twenty-seven shutters will turn their fiber rings in identical circular grooves in a counter-clockwise direction, as though they were all being unscrewed. Now the covers are free of pressure. You will now press that foot pedal. Watch!"

Click! And twenty-seven covers, metal surfaces resounding, instantly opened outward revealing glass sparkling in the sunlight.

"Every morning, Mr. Dibble," the scientist went on, "you are to uncover the lenses and carefully wipe them off with a clean chamois. Observe how this is done."

And he, like an experienced workman, rapidly, carefully, almost affectionately wiped all the glasses with a bit of chamois wrapped in cigarette paper which he brought out of his pocket.

"Now, let us go back down," he went on. "I will show you your other responsibilities."

Below in the laboratory he continued his explanations:

"Then you are 'to catch the sun.' To do this, every day at noon check these two chronometers against the sun. By the way, I checked them myself yesterday. The method is, of course, known to you. Note the time. Take the average time of the two chronometers: 10 hours, 31 minutes, 10 seconds. Here are three curving levers: the largest marks the hour, the middle one is for minutes, the smallest for seconds. Note: I turn the large circle until the hand of the indicator shows ten o'clock. Ready. I place the middle lever a little forward to 36 minutes. So. I move the little lever—that is my own favorite—forward to 50 seconds. Now place this plug in the socket. You can hear how the gears are whining and grinding below you. That is a clock device beginning to move which will rotate the entire laboratory and its dome, instruments, lenses and the two of us to follow the movement of the sun. Observe the chronometers and you will see that we are approaching 10:30. Five seconds more. Now. Can you hear how the clock mechanism has changed its sound? Those are the minute gears beginning to turn. A few seconds more . . . Watch! One minute more! Now there's a new sound, which neatly and precisely is marking off the seconds. That's all. The sun has now been captured. But it's not over yet. Because of its bulkiness and quite understandable crudity the clock mechanism cannot be especially accurate. Therefore as often as possible check this dial which indicates its movement. Here are the hours, minutes, and seconds; here is the regulator—forward, back. On the basis of the chronometers which are extraordinarily precise you will be able, as often as it is possible, to correct the revolution of the laboratory to a tenth of a second.

"Now we have caught the sun. But that is not all we must do. The light has to pass through a vacuum, otherwise it would become heated and melt all our equipment. And therefore when it is in our closed vessels from which all the air has been pumped the light is almost as cold as when it was passing through the endless regions of space outside the earth's atmosphere. When you look closely you can see a control button for an electromagnetic coil. In each of the cylinders is a stopper around which is a steel band circled by a wire. I press the control button and the current flows into the wire. All the bands are instantly affected and the stoppers leave their seats. Now I pull a bronze lever which starts a vacuum pump, one line of which is connected to each of the cylinders. The finest dust, microscopic flecks of matter, are removed with the air. Look at the gauge F on which is a red line indicating the pressure limit. Listen through an acoustic tube leading into the pump; the hissing has ceased. The gauge now crosses the red line. Disconnect the electricity by pressing the same control button a second time; the steel bands no longer are activated. The stoppers in response to the attraction of the vacuum close tightly in their conic seats. Now the light is passing through an almost absolute vacuum. But that is not adequate for the precision our work requires. We can transform all our laboratory into a giant vacuum chamber; in time we will be working in underwater diving equipment. Air will flow through the fiber pipes and the waste air systematically removed to the outside. In the meantime the air will be pulled out of the laboratory by powerful pumps. Do you understand? You will be in the position of a diver with the only difference being that you will have a container with compressed gas on your back: in case of an accident, the equipment's malfunction, a leak in the hoses, or anything else, open a small valve on your helmet and you will have enough air to breathe for a quarter of an hour. You must only keep your wits about you and you will leave the laboratory fresh and smiling, like a blooming rose.

"We still must check very carefully the installation of the piping. All of the pipes are firmly joined but at places some triple-unions allow an infinitesimal amount of play, two or three millimeters, and this might prove to be a problem. There are thirteen such points and you must check them about three times a day, working downward. Therefore, let us climb these stairs."

We mounted narrow staircases and unsteady platforms to the very top of the dome. The teacher went ahead with a youthful step while I followed, not without effort, because this was new to me. At the union of the first three pipes he showed me a small cover which he opened with one turn of the hand and lifted back so that it was held precisely vertical by springs. Its reverse side was a rigid, silver, finely polished mirror with various incisions and numbers on its edge. Three parallel gold bands, thin, like telescopic hairs, nearly touching each other, cut the smooth surface of the mirror.

"This is a small well through which we covertly follow the flow of the light. The three bands are reflections from three internal mirrors. Combine them into one. No, you do it yourself. Here you see three minute screws to adjust the positions of the lenses. Here is a very strong magnifying glass. Combine the three light bands into one but in such a manner that the total ray of light falls on zero. It is not difficult to do. You will shortly be able to carry it out in one minute."

In fact, the mechanism was very compliant and three minutes later, barely touching the sensitive screws I combined the light bands into one sharp line which was almost painful to look at, and then I introduced it into a narrow incision at zero. Then I closed the cover and screwed it down. I adjusted the remaining twelve control wells alone without Lord Charlesbury's help. Every time I performed this operation it went more smoothly. But by the time we reached the second level of the laboratory my eyes so ached from the bright light that involuntarily the tears streamed down my face.

"Put on goggles. Here they are," said my chief, handing me a case.

But I could not approach the final cylinder which we were to adjust in its location inside the isolation chamber. My eyes would not accept the glare.

"Take some darker glasses," said Lord Charlesbury. "I have them in ten shades. Today we will attach the lenses which you brought yesterday to the main cylinder and then direct observation will be three times as difficult. Good. That's right. Now I am activating an internal piston. I'm opening the valve of a hydraulic pump. I'm also opening a valve with liquid carbon dioxide. Now the temperature inside the cylinder has reached 150 degrees centigrade and the pressure is equal to 20 atmospheres; the latter is indicated by a gauge, the former by a Witkowski thermometer which I have improved. The following is now underway in the cylinder: light is passing through it in a dense vertical stream of blinding brightness approximately the diameter of a pencil. The valve actuated by an electric current is opening and closing its shutter in one one-thousandth of a second. The valve sends the light on through a small, highly convex lens. From there the stream of light emerges yet denser, narrower, and brighter. There are five such valves and lenses in each cylinder. Under the compression of the last, smallest and most powerful piston, a needle-thin stream of light flows into the vessel, passing through three valves in series.

"That is the basis of my liquid sunlight collector," my teacher said triumphantly. "Now, in order that there can be no doubts at all, we will conduct an experiment. Press control button A. You have just stopped the movement of the valve. Lift that bronze lever. Now you have closed the interior covers of the collecting glasses in the building's dome. Turn the red valve as far as it will go, and lower handle C. The pressure is now released and the supply of carbon dioxide cut off. Now you must close the vessel. This is done by ten turns of that small rounded lever. Everything is now complete, my friend. Notice how I disconnect the receiver vessel from the cylinder. See, I have it in my hands now; it weighs no more than twenty pounds. Its internal shutters are controlled by minute screws on the exterior of the cylinder. I am now opening wide the first and largest shutter. Then the intermediate one. The final shutter I will open only one-half a micron. But, first, go and turn off the electric lights."

I obeyed and the room filled with impenetrable darkness.

"Now watch!" I heard Lord Charlesbury's voice from the other end of the laboratory. "I'm opening it!"

An extraordinary golden light, delicate, radiant, transparent, suddenly flooded the room, softly but clearly outlining its walls, gleaming equipment, and the figure of my teacher himself. And, at the same moment, I felt on my face and hands something like a warm breath of air. This phenomenon lasted not more than a second or a second and a half. Then heavy darkness concealed everything from my eyes.

"Lights, please!" exclaimed Lord Charlesbury and once more I saw him emerging from the door of the glass chamber. His face was pale, but illuminated by joy and pride.

"Those were only the first steps, a schoolboy's trials, the first seeds," he said exultantly. "That was not sunlight condensed into a gas, but only a compressed weightless substance. For months I have compressed sunlight in my containers, but not one of them has become heavier by the weight of a human hair. You saw that marvelous, steady, caressing light. Now do you believe in my project?"

"Yes," I answered heatedly, with profound conviction. "I believe in it and I bow before an invention of great genius."

"But let's go on. Still further on! We will lower the temperature inside the cylinder to minus 275 degrees centigrade, to absolute zero. We will raise the hydraulic pressure to thousands, twenty, thirty thousand times the earth's atmosphere. We will replace our eight-inch light collectors with powerful fifty-inch models. We will melt pounds of diamonds by a technique I have developed and pour them into lenses to the specifications we require and place them in our instruments . . . ! Perhaps I will not live to see the time when men will compress the sun's rays into a liquid form, but I believe and I feel that I will compress them to the density of a gas. I only want to see the hand on an electric scale move even one millimeter to the left—and I will be boundlessly happy.

"But time is passing. Let us lunch and then before dinner we will concern ourselves with the installation of our new diamond lenses. Beginning tomorrow we will work together. For a week you will be with me as an ordinary worker, as a simple, obedient helper. A week from now we will exchange roles. The third week I will give you a helper, to whom in my presence you will teach all the procedures with the instruments. Then I will give you complete freedom. I trust you," he said briskly with a captivating, charming smile and reached out to shake my hand.

I remember very well that evening and dinner with Lord Charlesbury. Lady Charlesbury was in a red silk dress and her red mouth against her pale, slightly weary face glowed like a purple flower, like an incandescent ember. De Mon de Rique, whom I saw at dinner for the first time that day, was alert, handsome, and elegant, as I had never seen him either before or afterwards, while I felt enervated and overwhelmed by the flood of impressions I had received during the day. At first I thought that he had spent the day at his customary, simple labors, mostly observations. But it was not I, but Lady Charlesbury who first drew our attention to the fact that the electrician's left hand was bandaged to above the knuckles. De Mon de Rique modestly recounted how he had scraped his hand as he was climbing down a wall with an insufficiently tightened safety belt. That evening he dominated the conversation, but gently and with tact. He told about his journeys to Abyssinia where he prospected for gold in the mountain valleys on the verge of the Sahara, about lion hunting, the races at Epsom, fox hunting in the north of England, and about Oscar Wilde, then becoming fashionable and with whom he was personally acquainted. He had a surprising and probably too rare conversational trait, which, I will add, I have never noticed in anyone else. When he told a story he was extremely abstracted: he never spoke of himself nor in his own voice. But by some mysterious means his personality, remaining in the background, was illuminated, now in mild, now in heroic half-tones.

Now he was looking at Lady Charlesbury much less frequently than she at him. Only from time to time his caressing and languid eyes passed over her from under his long, lowered lashes. But she hardly took her grave and mysterious eyes away from him. Her gaze followed the movements of his hands and head, his mouth and eyes. Strange! That evening she reminded me of a child's toy: a tin fish or a duck with a bit of iron in its mouth which involuntarily, obediently follows after a magnetized stick which compels it from a distance. Frequently in alarm I observed the expression on my host's face. But he was serenely high-spirited and composed.

After dinner when de Mon de Rique asked permission to smoke, Lady Charlesbury herself offered to play billiards with him. They left while the host and I made our way into his study.

"How about a game of chess," he said. "Do you play?"

"Indifferently, but always with pleasure."

"And do you know what else has happened? Let us have a glass of some lively wine."

He pressed a button.

"What is the occasion?" I asked.

"You already have guessed. Because, it seems to me, I have found in you an assistant, and, if fate wills it, someone to carry on my work."

"Oh, sir!"

"One minute. What drink would you prefer?"

"I'm ashamed to admit that I'm no expert in such matters."

"Very well, in such a case I will name four drinks which I love, and a fifth which I detest. Bordeaux wines, port, Scotch ale, and water. But I cannot bear champagne. And, therefore, let us drink Chateau-la-Rose. My dear Sambo," he commanded the butler who stood near, waiting, "a bottle of Chateau-la-Rose."

Lord Charlesbury, to my surprise, played rather poorly. I quickly checkmated his king. After our first game we abandoned play and once more spoke of my morning's impressions.

"Listen, my dear Dibble," said Lord Charlesbury, laying his little, warm and energetic hand on my knuckles. "You have undoubtedly many times heard that one may obtain an authentic and accurate opinion of a man at first glance. I believe that to be a grave error. Many times I have seen men with the faces of convicts, cheats, or perjurors—and by the way, you will meet your assistant in a few days—and they turned out to be honest, faithful in friendship, and attentive, courteous gentlemen. On the other hand, very rarely, a generous, charming face, adorned with gray hair and the flush of age, and honorable speech conceals, as it becomes clear, such a villain that any London hooligan is by comparison an innocent lamb with a pink ribbon round his neck. Now may I ask you to help me to solve a problem? Mr. de Mon de Rique so far has not been involved in any way in the completion of my scientific work. On his mother's side he is distantly related to me. Mr. Nideston, who has known him from childhood, informed me that de Mon de Rique was in a very difficult position (only not in the material sense). I immediately offered him a position which he accepted with a joy that testified to his precarious situation. I have heard tales about him, but I give no credence to rumors and gossip. He made absolutely no impression upon me when first we met. Perhaps this was because I have never met a person such as he. But for some reason it also seems to me that I have met millions of such men. Today I carefully observed him at work. I believe him to be clever, knowing, ingenious and industrious. In addition, he is cultured and can conduct himself well in any society, as it seems to me, and moreover, he is energetic and intelligent. But in one respect I have my doubts. Tell me frankly, dear Mr. Dibble, your opinion of him."

This unexpected and tactless question agitated and distressed me; to tell the truth I did not expect it at all.

"But, sir, I have none. Indeed, I don't know him as well as you and Mr. Nideston. I saw him for the first time on board the steamship *Southern Cross*, and during our journey we met and talked very rarely. And I must tell you that I suffered from seasickness the entire journey. But from our few meetings and conversations I have obtained approximately the same impression as you, sir:

knowing, ingenious, energetic, eloquent, well-read and . . . a peculiar and perhaps very rare mixture, very cold-hearted but with a fervent imagination."

"You are right, Mr. Dibble, right. Beautifully said. My dear Mr. Sambo, bring another bottle of wine and then you may go. Thank you. I hardly expected any other evaluation from you. But I will return to my difficulty: should I inform him or not of what you witnessed today? Just imagine that a year or two will pass, perhaps less, and our dandy, our Adonis, our admirer of women, will suddenly become bored with his life on this God-forsaken volcano. I think that in such a case he would not come to me for my blessing and approval. Simply one beautiful morning he will pack his things and leave. The fact that I would be left without an assistant and a very valuable assistant at that is of secondary importance, but I cannot assure you that after he has arrived in the Old World he will not turn out to be loose-tongued, perhaps very innocently."

"Are you really concerned about this, sir?"

"I tell you frankly—I fear it very much! I am afraid of the notoriety, the publicity, and the invasion of reporters. I am afraid that some influential but talentless scientific reviewer who will base his attitude on a rejection of all new ideas and audacious conjectures will interpret my scheme to the public as a meaningless fantasy, the ravings of a madman. Finally, I am afraid most of all that some hungry upstart, a greedy failure, a talentless ignoramus will misunderstand my idea, and state, as has happened a thousand times, that it is his, thereby belittling, abusing and sullying something I have brought into the world in anguish and joy. Do you understand me, Mr. Dibble?"

"Completely, sir."

"If this happens, then I and my idea will perish. But what does this little 'I' mean when compared to my idea? I am deeply convinced that on the evening when in one of the huge London halls I order the lights extinguished and blind a selected audience of ten thousand with a stream of sunshine which will make flowers open and cause the birds to sing—that evening I will receive a million pounds for my cause. But, a trifle, an accident, an insignificant mistake, as I said, could destroy in a fateful manner the most selfless and grandiose idea. Therefore, I ask your opinion, should I trust Mr. de Mon de Rique or leave him in false and evasive ignorance? This is a dilemma which I cannot avoid without help. On one hand the possibility of a worldwide scandal and failure, and on the other a sure road for arousing a feeling of anger and revenge in a man thanks to my lack of trust in him. And so, Mr. Dibble?"

I wanted to give him the direct answer: "Tomorrow send this Narcissus with all honors back into the world and you can rest in peace." Now I regret deeply that a foolish sense of delicacy prevented me from giving that advice. Instead of saying this, I took on an air of cool correctness and answered:

"I hope you will not be angry with me, sir, if I decline to pass judgment on such a difficult matter."

Lord Charlesbury looked directly at me, shook his head sadly and said with a mirthless smile:

"Let's finish our wine and visit the billiard room. I would like to smoke a cigar."

In the billiard room we saw the following picture. De Mon de Rique was bent over the billiard table telling some lively tale, while Lady Charlesbury, leaning against the mantelpiece, laughed loudly. This struck me more than if I had seen her weeping. Lord Charlesbury inquired into the cause of the merriment, and when de Mon de Rique repeated his story about a certain vain aristocrat who acquired a tame leopard in a desire to pass himself off as an original and then was compelled to sit three hours in his room with the animal because he was so afraid of it, my patron laughed loud and long, like a child . . .

Everything in the world is inter-related in the strangest manner.

That evening in some inscrutable fashion combined the beginnings, the engagement and the tragic denouement of our lives.

The first two days of my existence at Cayambe I remember very well, but as for the rest, the closer they come to the end, the hazier they become. And therefore, with more reason I turn for help to my notebook. The seawater erased the first and last pages and in part the intervening pages also. But some of it, with difficulty, I can restore. Thus:

December 11. Today I rode on muleback with Lord Charlesbury into Quito to obtain copper wire. It happened that the subject of the material support of our project arose (it was not merely the result of my idle curiosity). Lord Charlesbury, who, it seemed to me, had long given me his full confidence, suddenly turned quickly in his saddle to face me and asked unexpectedly:

"You know Mr. Nideston?"

"Certainly, sir."

"A fine man, is he not so?"

"An excellent man."

"And is it not true, in the world, dry and something of a formalist?"

"Yes, sir. But he is also capable of great enthusiasm and even of high emotion."

"You are observant, Mr. Dibble," my mentor answered. "You should know that for fifteen years he has believed in me and my idea as stubbornly as a Mohammedan believes in his Kaaba. You know he is a London solicitor. He not only does not take any pay for my commissions, but long ago he offered to place his own private fortune at my disposal if I so wished. I am deeply convinced that he is the only eccentric left in old England. Therefore let us be of good cheer."

December 12. Today Lord Charlesbury for the first time showed me the force which drives the timing mechanism which turns the laboratory with the sun. It is obvious, simple, and ingenious. Down the slope of the extinct volcano a dressed basalt block weighing thirty-five tons suspended by a steel cable almost as thick as a man's leg moves on almost vertical rails. This weight puts the mechanism into motion. It functions exactly for eight hours and early in the morning an old blind mule raises this counterweight with the help of another cable and a system of blocks without any great effort.

December 20. Today I sat with Lord Charlesbury after dinner in the hothouse sunk in the heady odor of narcissi, pomegranates and tuberoses. Recently my patron has been very withdrawn and his eyes seemingly have begun to lose their beautiful youthful brightness. I take this to be the result of fatigue because we are working very hard now. I am sure that he has guessed nothing about *it*. He suddenly changed the subject of the conversation, as is his wont:

"Our work is the most selfless and honorable on earth. To think about the happiness of one's children or grandchildren is both natural and egotistical. But you and I are thinking of the lives and happiness of humanity so far in the future that they will not know of us nor of our poets, kings, or conquerers, about our language and religion, about our national borders or even the names of our countries. 'Not for those who are near but those who come later!' Isn't that what our most popular philosopher has said? I am willing to give all my strength to this unselfish and pure service to the distant future."

January 3. I went to Quito today to accept a shipment from London. My relationship with Mr. de Mon de Rique has become cold, almost inimical.

February. Today we completed the work of connecting all our piping with the containers of chilling solutions. A combination of ice and salt gives minus 21 degrees centigrade, dry ice and ether—minus 80 degrees, hydrogen—minus 118 degrees, vaporized dry ice—minus 130 degrees, and it seems that we will be able to reduce the atmospheric pressure indefinitely.

April. My assistant continues to arouse my interest. He is some kind of a Slav. A Russian, or a Pole, and, so it seems, an anarchist. He is intelligent and speaks English well, but it seems he prefers not to speak any language at all, but to remain silent. Here is his appearance: he is tall, thin, slightly round-shouldered; his hair is straight and long and falls onto his face in such a manner that his forehead takes the shape of a trapezoid, the narrow end up; he has a tilted nose with great open hairy, but delicate nostrils. His eyes are clear, gray, and boundlessly impertinent. He hears and understands everything that we say about the happiness of future generations and often smiles with a benevolent but contemptuous smile, which reminds me of the expression on the face of a large old bulldog watching a pack of yelping toy terriers. But his attitude toward my mentor—and this I not only know, but feel to the marrow of my bones—is one of boundless adoration. My colleague's attitude, de Mon de Rique's attitude, is quite different. He often speaks to the teacher about the idea of liquid sunshine with such false enthusiasm that I blush for shame and I fear that the technician is mocking our patron. And he is not interested in him at all as a man, and in the most discourteous manner and in the presence of his wife disparages his position as husband and master of the house, although this is unwise and contrary to common sense, the result of his perverted temperament and, perhaps, out of jealousy.

May. Let us hail the names of three talented Poles—Wrublewski, Olszewski, and Witkowski—and the man who completed their work, Dewar. Today we transformed helium into a liquid, and instantly reducing the pressure, reached a temperature of minus 272 degrees centigrade in our major cylinder and the dial on the electric scales for the first time moved, not one, but *five whole millimeters*. Silently, in solitude, I bow before you, my dear preceptor and teacher.

June 26. Apparently de Mon de Rique has come to believe in liquid sunshine—and now without sickening coyness and forced delight. At least today at dinner he made a remarkable statement. He said that in his opinion liquid sunshine would have a brilliant future as an explosive substance in mines or projectiles.

I objected, it is true, rather violently, in German: "You sound like a Prussian lieutenant."

But Lord Charlesbury responded succinctly and in a conciliatory tone: "Our dreams are not of destruction, but of creation."

June 27. I am writing in great agitation, my hands trembling. I worked late this evening in the laboratory, until two o'clock. It was a matter of urgency to install a cooling unit. As I was returning to my quarters the moon shone brightly. I was wearing warm sealskin boots and my footsteps on the frozen path could not be heard. My route lay in shadow. Reaching my door I stopped when I heard voices.

"Come in, Mary dear, for God's sake, come in for only a minute. What are you always afraid of? And don't you always discover that there's no reason to be afraid?"

And then I saw them both in the bright light of the southern moon. He had his arm around her waist, and her head lay passively on his shoulder. Oh, how beautiful they were at that moment!

"But your friend . . ." Lady Charlesbury said timorously.

"What kind of a friend is he?" de Mon de Rique laughed heedlessly. "He's only a boring and sentimental drudge who goes to bed every night at ten o'clock in order to arise at six. Mary, please come in, I beg you."

And both of them, their arms around each other, went onto the porch illuminated by the blue light of the moon and disappeared in an open door.

June 28. Evening. This morning I went to see Mr. de Mon de Rique, refused his proffered hand, would not sit down on the chair he offered and said quietly:

"I must tell you what I think of you, sir. I believe that you, sir, in a situation where we should work together cheerfully and selflessly for the sake of humanity, are conducting yourself in a most unworthy and shameful manner. Last night at two o'clock I saw you when you entered your quarters."

"Were you spying, you scoundrel?" shouted de Mon de Rique, and his eyes gleamed with a violet light, like a cat at night.

"No, I found myself in an impossible situation. I did not speak out, not because I did not want to cause you pain, but because I did not want to harm another person. But this gives me more reason than ever to tell you to your face that you, sir, are a villain and a sneak."

"You will pay for that with your blood with a weapon in your hands," shouted de Mon de Rique, leaping to his feet.

"No," I answered firmly. "First of all, we have no reason to fight except that I called you a villain, but not in the presence of witnesses, and secondly, because I am engaged in a great work of world-wide importance and I do not want to abandon it thanks to your ridiculous bullet until it is completed. Thirdly, would it not be easiest of all for you to pack your bags, mount the first mule available, leave for Quito, and then by your previous route return to hospitable England? Or did you dishonor someone or steal money there, Mr. Scoundrel?"

He leaped to the table and seized a leather whip which lay there.

"I'll kill you like a dog!" he roared.

But I remembered my old boxing skills. Acting quickly, I feinted with my left hand, and then hit him with my right below his chin. He cried out, spun like a top, and blood rushed out of his nose.

I walked out.

June 29. "Why is it that I haven't seen Mr. de Mon de Rique today?" Lord Charlesbury asked unexpectedly.

"It seems he isn't well," I answered, avoiding his eyes.

We were sitting together on the northern slope of the volcano. It was nine in the evening and the moon had not yet risen. Near us stood two porters and my mysterious helper, Peter. Against the quiet dark blue of the sky the slender electric lines, which we had installed that day, could hardly be seen. And on a great heap of stones rested receiver no. 6, firmly braced by basalt boulders, ready any second to open its shutters.

"Prepare the fuse," ordered Lord Charlesbury. "Roll the spool down the hill, I'm too tired and excited; give me your hand, help me down. This is good. And there is no risk of being blinded. Think on it, my dear Dibble, think on it, my dear boy, now the two of us, in the name of glory and the happiness of future mankind, will light all the world with sunshine concentrated in gaseous form. Ready! Light the fuse."

The fiery snake of the lighted fuse ran up the hill and disappeared over the edge of the deep defile in which we sat. Listening carefully I could hear the instantaneous click of contacts closing and the penetrating roar of motors. According to our calculations gaseous sunshine should issue from the containers next to the explosion sites at a rate of approximately six thousand feet per second. At that moment above our heads there was a flash of blinding sunlight, at which the trees below rustled, clouds turned pink in the sky, distant roofs and the windows of houses in Quito gleamed brightly, and the cocks in the village nearby began crowing.

When the light faded as quickly as it had appeared, my teacher pressed the button on a stop watch, turned his flashlight on it, and said:

"It burned for one minute and eleven seconds. This is a genuine triumph, Mr. Dibble. I assure you that within a year we will be able to fill immense reservoirs with heavy liquid golden sunshine, like mercury, and compel it to provide light, heat and drive all our machinery."

When we returned home that night about midnight we discovered that in our absence Lady Charlesbury and Mr. de Mon de Rique in the daylight hours soon after our departure had seemingly gone for a walk but then on mules saddled beforehand had left for the city of Quito below.

Lord Charlesbury remained true to himself. He said without bitterness, but sadly and in pain:

"Why didn't they say anything to me, why this deceit? Didn't I see that they loved each other? I would not have hindered them."

At this point my notes end, and at that they were so damaged by water that I could restore them only with the greatest difficulty and I cannot guarantee their accuracy. Nor can I in the future guarantee the reliability of my memory. But this is always the case: the closer I draw to the final resolution the more confused my recollections become.

For about twenty-five days we worked steadily in the laboratory filling more and more containers with solar gas. During this period we invented ingenious valves for our solar containers. We equipped each of them with a clock mechanism with a simple face, as on an alarm clock. Adjusting the dials of three cylinders we could obtain light over any given period of time, and lengthen the period of its combustion and its intensity from a dim half-hour of glimmer to an instantaneous explosion—depending on the time set. We worked without inspiration, almost unwillingly, but I must admit that this was the most productive time of my stay on Cayambe. But it all ended abruptly, fantastically, and horribly.

Once, early in August, Lord Charlesbury, even more tired and aged than usual, came to visit me in the laboratory; he said to me calmly and with distaste:

"My dear friend, I feel that my death is not far away, and old convictions are making themselves heard. I want to die and be buried in England. I will leave you some money, these buildings, the equipment, the land and this laboratory. The money, on the basis of what I have spent, should be ample for two or three years. You are younger and more active than I and perhaps you will obtain some results for your labors. Our dear Mr. Nideston would give his support at any time. Please think on it."

This man had become dearer to me than my father, mother, brother, wife or sister. And therefore I answered with deep assurance:

"Dear sir, I would not leave you for one minute."

He embraced me and kissed me on my forehead.

The next day he summoned all the workers and paying them two years in advance said that his work on Cayambe had come to an end and that day they were to leave Cayambe for the valley below.

They left carefree and ungrateful, anticipating the sweet proximity of drunkenness and dissipation in the innumerable taverns which swarmed in the city of Quito. Only my assistant, the silent Slav—an Albanian or a Siberian—tarried near the master. "I will stay with you as long as you or I am alive," he said. But Lord Charlesbury looked at him firmly, almost sternly and said:

"I am leaving for Europe, Mr. Peter."

"Then I will go with you."

"But you know what awaits you there, Mr. Peter."

"I know. A rope. But nonetheless I will not abandon you. I have always laughed in my heart at your sentimental concerns for men in the millions of years to come, but when I came to know you better I also learned that the more insignificant is mankind the more precious is man, and therefore I have stayed with you, like an old, homeless, embittered, hungry, and mangy dog turns to the first hand that sincerely caresses it. And therefore I will stay with you. That is all."

With astonishment and deep feeling I turned my eyes to this man whom I had always thought to be incapable of elevated feelings. But my teacher said to him softly and with authority:

"No, you must leave. Right now. I value your friendship and your tireless labors. But I'm leaving for my native land to die and the possibility that you might suffer would only darken my departure from this world. Be a man, Peter. Take this money, embrace me in farewell, and let us part."

I saw how they embraced and how blunt Peter kissed the hand of Lord Charlesbury several times and then left us, not turning back, almost at a run and disappeared around a nearby building.

I looked at my teacher: covering his face with his hands he was weeping . . .

Three days later we left on the old *Gonzalez* from Guayaquil for Panama. The sea was rough, but we had a following wind and to help out the small engine the captain had sails spread. Lord Charlesbury and I never left our cabins. I was seriously concerned about his condition and there were even times when I feared he was losing his mind. I observed him with helpless pity. I was especially troubled by the manner in which he invariably referred after every two or three phrases to container no. 216 which we had left behind on Cayambe, and every time he referred to it, he would say through tight lips: "Did I forget, how could I forget?" but then his speech would become melancholy and abstracted.

"Do not think," he said, "that a petty personal tragedy forced me to abandon my work and the persistent searches and inspirations which I have patiently worked out during the course of my conscious life. But circumstances jarred my thoughts. Recently I have much altered my ideas and judgments, but only on a different plane than before. If only you knew how difficult it has been to alter my view of life at the age of sixty-five. I have come to believe, or, more correctly, to feel, that the future of mankind is not worth our concern or our selfless work. Mankind, growing more degenerate every day, is becoming flabbier, more decadent, and hard-hearted. Society is falling under the power of the cruelest despotism in the world—capital. Trusts, manipulating the supply of meat, kerosene, and sugar, are creating a generation of fabulous millionaires and next to them millions of hungry unemployed thieves and murderers. And so it will be forever. And my idea of prolonging the sun's life for the earth will become the property of a handful of villains who will control it or employ my liquid sunshine in shells or bombs of unheard of power . . . No, I do not want that . . . Ah, my God! that container! How could I forget! How could I!" and Lord Charlesbury clapped his hands to his head.

"What troubles you, my dear teacher?" I asked.

"You see, kind Henry, . . . I fear that I have made a small but fateful mistake . . ."

But I heard no more. Suddenly in the east flashed an enormous golden flame. In a moment the sky and the sea were all agleam. Then followed a deafening roar and a burning whirlwind threw me to the deck.

I lost consciousness and revived only when I heard my teacher's voice above me.

"What?" asked Lord Charlesbury. "Are you blind?"

"Yes, I can see nothing, except rainbow-colored circles before my eyes. Was it some kind of a catastrophe, Professor? Why did you do it or allow it to happen? Didn't you foresee it?"

But he softly laid his beautiful little white hand on my shoulder and said in a deep and gentle voice (and from that touch and his confident tone I immediately was calmed):

"Don't you believe me? Wait a moment, close your eyes tightly and cover them with the palm of your right hand, and hold it there until I stop talking or until you catch a glimpse of light; then, before you open your eyes, put on these glasses which I am placing in your left hand. They are very dark. Listen to me. It seems that you have come to know me better in a brief time than anyone else close to me. It was only for your sake, my dear friend, that I did not take on my conscience a cruel and pointless experiment which might have brought death to tens of thousands of people. But what difference would the existence of these dissolute blacks, drunken Indians, and degenerate Spaniards have made? If the Republic of Ecuador with its intrigues, mercenary attitudes and revolutions were instantly transformed into a great door to Hell there would be no loss to science, the arts, or history. I am only a little sorry for my intelligent, patient, and affectionate mules. I will tell you candidly that I would have not hesitated for a second to sacrifice you and millions of lives to the triumph of my idea, if only I were convinced of its significance, but as I said only three minutes ago I have become totally disillusioned about the future generations' ability to love, to be happy and to sacrifice themselves. Do you think I could take revenge on a tiny part of humanity for my great philosophical error? But there is one thing for which I cannot forgive myself: that was a purely technical mistake, a mistake which could have been made by any workman. I am like a craftsman who has worked for twenty years with a complicated machine, and on the next day falls into melancholy over his family affairs, forgets his work, ignores the rhythm of his machine so that a belt parts and kills several unthinking workmen. You see, I have been tormented by the idea that thanks to my forgetfulness for the first time in twenty years I neglected to shut down the controls on container no. 216 and left it set at full power. And that realization, like a nightmare, pursued me on board this ship. And I was right. The container exploded and as a result the other storage units also. Once more it was my mistake. Rather than storing such great amounts of liquid sunshine I should have conducted preliminary experiments, it is true at the risk of my life, on the explosive capabilities of compressed light. Now, look in this direction," and he gently but firmly turned my head toward the east. "Remove your hand and then slowly, slowly open your eyes."

At that moment with extraordinary clarity, the way, they say, that occurs in the seconds before death, I saw a smoking red glow to the east, now contracting, now expanding, the steamship's listing deck, waves lashing over the railings, an angry, bloody sea and dark purple clouds in the sky and a beautiful calm face with a gray, silken beard and eyes which shone like mournful stars. A stifling hot wind blew from the shore.

"A fire?" I asked, turning slowly, as though in a dream, to face the south. There, above Cayambe's summit, stood a thick smoky column of fire cut by rapid flashes of lightning.

"No, that is the eruption of our good old volcano. The exploding liquid sunshine has stirred it into life. You must agree that it has enormous power! And to think it was all in vain."

I understood nothing . . . My head was spinning. And then I heard a strange voice near me, both gentle like a mother's voice and commanding like that of a dictator.

"Sit on this bale and do everything faithfully as I tell you. Here is a life belt, put it on and fasten it securely under your arms, but do not restrict your breathing; here is a flask of brandy which you are to place in your left chest pocket along with three bars of chocolate, and here is a waterproof envelope with money and letters. In a moment the *Gonzalez* will be swamped by a terrible wave, such as has rarely been seen since the time of the flood. Lie down on the ship's starboard side. That is so. Place your legs and arms around this railing. Very good. Your head should be behind this steel plate, which will prevent you from becoming deaf from the shock. When you feel the wave hitting the deck, hold your breath for twenty seconds and then throw yourself free, and may God help you! This is all I can wish and advise you. And if you are condemned to die so early and so stupidly . . . I would like to hear you forgive me. I would not say that to any other man, but I know you are an Englishman and a gentleman."

His words, said so calmly and with such dignity, aroused my own sense of self-control. I found enough strength to press his hand and answer calmly:

"You can believe, my dear teacher, that no pleasures in life could replace those happy hours which I spent working with you. I only want to know why you are taking no precautions for yourself?"

I can see him now, holding to a compass box, as the wind blew his clothes and his gray beard, so terrible against the red background of the erupting volcano. That second I noticed with surprise that the unbearably hot shore wind had ceased, but on the contrary a cold, gusty gale blew from the west and our craft nearly lay on its side.

"Oh!" exclaimed Lord Charlesbury indifferently, and waved his arm "I have nothing to lose. I am alone in this world. I have only one tie, that is you, and you I have put into deadly peril from which you have only one chance in a million to escape. I have a fortune, but I do not know what to do with it," and here his voice expressed a melancholy and gentle irony, "except to disperse it to the poor of County Norfolk and thereby increase the number of parasites and supplicants. I have knowledge, but you can see that it too has failed. I have energy but I have no way to employ it now. Oh, no, I will not commit suicide; if I am not condemned to die this night, I will employ the rest of my life in some garden on a bit of land not far from London. But if death comes," he removed his hat and it was strange to see his blowing hair, tossing beard, and kind, melancholy eyes and to hear his voice resounding like an organ, "but if death comes I shall commit my body and my soul to God, may He forgive the errors of my weak human mind."

"Amen," I said.

He turned his back to the wind and lighted a cigar. His dark figure defined sharply against the purple sky was a fantastic, and magnificent, sight. I could smell the odor of his fine Havana cigar.

"Make ready. There is yet only a minute or two. Are you afraid?"

"No . . . But the crew and the other passengers! . . ."

"While you were unconscious I warned them. Now there is not a sober man nor a lifebelt on the ship. I have no fear for you, for you have the talisman on your finger. I had one, too, but I have lost it. Oh, hold on! Henry! . . ."

I turned to the east and froze in horror. Toward our eggshell craft from the east roared an enormous wave as high as the Eiffel tower, black, with a rosy-white, frothing crest. Something crashed, shook . . . and it was as though the whole world fell onto the deck.

I lost consciousness once more and revived only several hours later on a little boat belonging to a fisherman who had rescued me. My damaged left hand was tied in a crude bandage and my head wrapped in rags. A month later, having recovered from my wounds and emotional shock I was on my way back to England.

This history of my strange adventure is complete. I must only add that I live modestly in the quietest part of London, needing nothing, thanks to the generosity of the late Lord Charlesbury. I occupy myself with the sciences and tutoring. Every Sunday Mr. Nideston and I alternate as hosts for dinner. We are bound by close ties of friendship, and our first toast is always to the memory of the great Lord Charlesbury.

H. Dibble

P.S. All the personal names in my tale are not authentic but invented by me for my purposes.

John Crowley

John Crowley (1942–) is the author of the classic fantasy novel *Little, Big* (1981), a monument of the genre and his masterpiece to date, and several SF novels, including the highly regarded *Engine Summer* (1979). He is currently teaching at Yale University and in 1987 embarked on a multi-volume work of the fantastic which began with *Aegypt* and continued with *Love and Sleep* (1994). He is among the most complex and literate of writers to emerge from the contemporary genre. Based upon his recent works, one might usefully consider him a postmodern writer somewhat in the vein of Thomas Pynchon, who sometimes writes in genre. His writing adds substance to critic Brian McHale's contention that contemporary science fiction is the "paraliterary shadow" of postmodernism.

He has written only a dozen or so short stories in the fantastic mode, and of them only a few are genre science fiction. This long piece is his best SF story to date. It was first published in his original collection of four stories, *Novelty* (1989). It is another SF story about time, in the same tradition as Jeschke's "The King and the Dollmaker." The idea that reality is somehow malleable, that a different future, even a different present, might result from some perhaps quite minor change in the past, has become a staple of science fiction since the 1930s. Here it is richly explored.

GREAT WORK OF TIME

I: THE SINGLE EXCURSION OF CASPAR LAST

If what I am to set down is a chronicle, then it must differ from any other chronicle whatever, for it begins, not in one time or place, but everywhere at once—or perhaps *everywhen* is the better word. It might be begun at any point along the infinite, infinitely broken coastline of time.

It might even begin within the forest in the sea: huge trees like American redwoods, with their roots in the black benthos, and their leaves moving slowly in the blue currents overhead. There it might end as well.

It might begin in 1893—or in 1983. Yes: it might be as well to begin with Last, in an American sort of voice (for we are all Americans now, aren't we?). Yes, Last shall be first: pale, fattish Caspar Last, on excursion in the springtime of 1983 to a far, far part of the Empire.

The tropical heat clothed Caspar Last like a suit as he disembarked from the plane. It was nearly as claustrophobic as the hours he had spent in the middle seat of a three-across; economy-class pew between two other cut-rate, one-week-excursion, plane-fare-and-hotel-room holiday-makers in monstrous good spirits. Like them, Caspar had taken the excursion because it was the cheapest possible way to get to and from this equatorial backwater. Unlike them, he hadn't come to soak up sun and molasses-dark rum. He didn't intend to spend all his time at the beach, or even within the twentieth century.

It had come down, in the end, to a matter of money. Caspar Last had never had money, though he certainly hadn't lacked the means to make it; with any application he could have made good money as a consultant to any of a dozen research firms, but that would have required a certain subjection of his time and thought to others, and Caspar was incapable of that. It's often said that genius can live in happy disregard of material circumstances, dress in rags, not notice its nourishment, and serve only its own abstract imperatives. This was Caspar's case, except that he wasn't happy about it: he was bothered, bitter, and rageful at his poverty. Fame he cared nothing for, success was meaningless except when defined as the solution to abstract problems. A great fortune would have been burdensome and useless. All he wanted was a nice bit of change.

He had decided, therefore, to use his "time machine" once only, before it and the principles that animated it were destroyed, for good he hoped. (Caspar always thought of his "time machine" thus, with scare-quotes around it, since it was not really a machine, and Caspar did not believe in time.) He would use it, he decided, to make money. Somehow.

The one brief annihilation of "time" that Caspar intended to allow himself was in no sense a test run. He knew that his "machine" would function as predicted. If he hadn't needed the money, he wouldn't use it at all. As far as he was concerned, the principles once discovered, the task was completed; like a completed jigsaw puzzle, it had no further interest; there was really nothing to do with it except gloat over it briefly and then sweep all the pieces randomly back into the box.

It was a mark of Caspar's odd genius that figuring out a scheme with which to make money out of the past (which was the only "direction" his "machine" would take him) proved almost as hard, given the limitations of his process, as arriving at the process itself.

He had gone through all the standard wish fulfillments and rejected them. He couldn't, armed with today's race results, return to yesterday and hit the daily double. For one thing it would take a couple of thousand in betting money to make it worth it, and Caspar didn't have a couple of thousand. More importantly, Caspar had calculated the results of his present self appearing at any point within the compass of his own biological existence, and those results made him shudder.

Similar difficulties attended any scheme that involved using money to make money. If he returned to 1940 and bought, say, two hundred shares of IBM for next to nothing: in the first place there would be the difficulty of leaving those shares somehow in escrow for his unborn self; there would be the problem of the alteration this growing fortune would have on the linear life he had actually lived; and where was he to acquire the five hundred dollars or whatever was needed in the currency of 1940? The same problem obtained if he wanted to return to 1623 and pick up a First Folio of Shakespeare, or to 1460 and a Gutenberg Bible: the cost of the currency he would need rose in relation to the antiquity, thus the rarity and value, of the object to be bought with it. There was also the problem of walking into a bookseller's and plunking down a First Folio he had just happened to stumble on while cleaning out the attic. In any case, Caspar doubted that anything as large as a book could be successfully transported "through time." He'd be lucky if he could go and return in his clothes.

Outside the airport, Caspar boarded a bus with his fellow excursionists, already hard at work with their cameras and index fingers as they rode through a sweltering lowland out of which concrete-block light industry was struggling to be born. The hotel in the capital was, as he expected, shoddy-American and intermittently refrigerated. He ceased to notice it, forwent the complimentary rum concoction promised with his tour, and after asking that his case be put in the hotel safe—extra charge for that, he noted bitterly—he went immediately to the Hall of Records in the government complex. The collection of old survey maps of the city and environs were more extensive than he had hoped. He spent most of that day among them searching for a blank place on the 1856 map, a place as naked as possible of buildings, brush, water, and that remained thus through the years. He discovered one, visited it by unmuffled taxi, found it suitable. It would save him from the awful inconvenience of "arriving" in the "past" and finding himself inserted into some local's wattle-and-daub wall. Next morning, then, he would be "on his way." If he had believed in time, he would have said that the whole process would take less than a day's time.

Before settling on this present plan, Caspar had toyed with the idea of bringing back from the past something immaterial: some knowledge, some secret that would allow him to make himself rich in his own present. Ships have gone down with millions in bullion: he could learn exactly where. Captain Kidd's treasure. Inca gold. Archaeological rarities buried in China. Leaving aside the obvious physical difficulties of these schemes, he couldn't be sure that their location wouldn't shift in the centuries between his glimpse of them and his "real" life span; and even if he could be certain, no one else would have much reason to believe him, and he didn't have the wherewithal to raise expeditions himself. So all that was out.

He had a more general, theoretical problem to deal with. Of course the very presence of his eidolon in the past would alter, in however inconsequential a way, the succeeding history of the world. The comical paradoxes of shooting one's own grandfather and the like neither amused nor intrigued him, and the chance he took of altering the world he lived in out of all recognition was constantly present to him. Statistically, of course, the chance of this present plan of his altering anything significantly, except his own personal fortunes, was remote to a high power. But his scruples had caused him to reject anything such as, say, discovering the Koh-i-noor diamond before its historical discoverers. No: what he needed to abstract from the past was something immensely trivial, something common, something the past wouldn't miss but that the present held in the highest regard; something that would take the briefest possible time and the least irruption of himself into the past to acquire; something he could reasonably be believed to possess through simple historical chance; and something tiny enough to survive the cross-time "journey" on his person.

It had come to him quite suddenly—all his ideas did, as though handed to him—when he learned that his great-great-grandfather had been a commercial traveler in the tropics, and that in the attic of his mother's house (which Caspar had never had the wherewithal to move out of) some old journals and papers of his still moldered. They were, when he inspected them, completely without interest. But the dates were right.

Caspar had left a wake-up call at the desk for before dawn the next morning.

There was some difficulty about getting his case out of the safe, and more difficulty about getting a substantial breakfast served at that hour (Caspar expected not to eat during his excursion), but he did arrive at his chosen site before the horrendous tropical dawn broke, and after paying the taxi, he had darkness enough left in which to make his preparations and change into his costume. The costume—a linen suit, a shirt, hat, boots—had cost him twenty dollars in rental from a theatrical costumer, and he could only hope it was accurate enough not to cause alarm in 1856. The last item he took from his case was the copper coin, which had cost him quite a bit, as he needed one unworn and of the proper date. He turned it in his fingers for a moment, thinking that if, unthinkably, his calculations were wrong and he didn't survive this journey, it would make an interesting obol for Charon.

Out of the unimaginable chaos of its interminable stochastic fiction, Time thrust only one unforeseen oddity on Caspar Last as he, or somcthing like him, appeared bencath a plantain tree in 1856: he had grown a beard almost down to his waist. It was abominably hot.

The suburbs of the city had of course vanished. The road he stood by was a muddy track down which a cart was being driven by a tiny and close-faced Indian in calico. He followed the cart, and his costume boots were caked with mud when at last he came into the center of town, trying to appear nonchalant and to remember the layout of the city as he had studied it in the maps. He wanted to speak to no one if possible, and he did manage to find the post office without affecting, however minutely, the heterogeneous crowd of blacks, Indians, and Europeans in the filthy streets. Having absolutely no sense of humor and very little imagination other than the most rigidly abstract helped to keep him strictly about his business and not to faint, as another might have, with wonder and astonishment at his translation, the first, last, and only of its kind a man would ever make.

"I would like," he said to the mulatto inside the brass and mahogany cage, "an envelope, please."

"Of course, sir."

"How long will it take for a letter mailed now to arrive locally?"

"Within the city? It would arrive in the afternoon post."

"Very good."

Caspar went to a long, ink-stained table, and with one of the steel pens provided, he addressed the envelope to Georg von Humboldt Last, Esq., Grand Hotel, City, in the approximation of an antique round hand that he had been practicing for weeks. There was a moment's doubt as he tried to figure how to fold up and seal the cumbersome envelope, but he did it, and gave this empty missive to the incurious mulatto. He slipped his precious coin across the marble to him. For the only moment of his adventure, Caspar's heart beat fast as he watched the long, slow brown fingers affix a stamp, cancel and date it with a pen-stroke, and drop it into a brass slot like a hungry mouth behind him.

It only remained to check into the Grand Hotel, explain about his luggage's being on its way up from the port, and sit silent on the hotel terrace, growing faint with heat and hunger and expectation, until the afternoon post.

The one aspect of the process Caspar had never been able to decide about was whether his eidolon's residence in the fiction of the past would consume any "time" in the fiction of the present. It did. When, at evening, with the letter held tight in his hand and pressed to his bosom, Caspar reappeared beardless beneath the plantain tree in the traffic-tormented and smoky suburb, the gaseous red sun was squatting on the horizon in the west, just as it had been in the same place in 1856.

He would have his rum drink after all, he decided.

"Mother," he said, "do you think there might be anything valuable in those papers of your great-grandfather's?"

"What papers, dear? Oh—I remember. I couldn't say. I thought once of donating them to a historical society. How do you mean, valuable?"

"Well, old stamps, for one thing."

"You're free to look, Caspar dear."

Caspar was not surprised (though he supposed the rest of the world was soon to be) that he found, among the faded, water-spotted diaries and papers, an envelope that bore a faint brown address—it had aged nicely in the next-to-no-time it had traveled "forward" with Caspar—and that had in its upper right-hand corner a one-penny magenta stamp, quite undistinguished, issued for a brief time in 1856 by the Crown Colony of British Guiana.

The asking price of the sole known example of this stamp, a "unique," owned by a consortium of wealthy men who preferred to remain anonymous, was a million dollars. Caspar Last had not decided whether it would be more profitable for him to sell the stamp itself, or to approach the owners of the unique, who would certainly pay a large amount to have it destroyed, and thus preserve their unique's uniqueness. It did seem a shame that the only artifact man had ever succeeded in extracting from the nonexistent past should go into the fire, but Caspar didn't really care. His own bonfire—the notes and printouts, the conclusions about the nature and transversability of time and the orthogonal logic by which it was accomplished—would be only a little more painful.

The excursion was over; the only one that remained to him was the brief but, to him, all-important one of his own mortal span. He was looking forward to doing it first class.

II: AN APPOINTMENT IN KHARTOUM

It might be begun very differently, though; and it might now be begun again, in a different time and place, like one of those romances by Stevenson, where different stories only gradually reveal themselves to be parts of a whole . . .

The paradox is acute, so acute that the only possible stance for a chronicler is to ignore it altogether, and carry on. This, the Otherhood's central resignation, required a habit of mind so contrary to ordinary cause-and-effect thinking as to be, literally, unimaginable. It would only have been in the changeless precincts of the Club they had established beyond all frames of reference, when deep in leather armchairs or seated all together around the long table whereon their names were carved, that they dared reflect on it at all.

Take, for a single but not a random instance, the example of Denys Winterset, twenty-three years old, Winchester, Oriel College, younger son of a well-to-do doctor and in 1956 ending a first year as assistant district commissioner of police in Bechuanaland.

He hadn't done strikingly well in his post. Though on the surface he was exactly the sort of man who was chosen, or who chose himself, to serve the

Empire in those years—a respectable second at Oxford, a cricketer more steady than showy, a reserved, sensible, presentable lad with sound principles and few beliefs—still there was an odd strain in him. Too imaginative, perhaps; given to fits of abstraction, even to what his commissioner called "tears, idle tears." Still, he was resourceful and hardworking; he hadn't disgraced himself, and he was now on his way north on the Cape-to-Cairo Railroad, to take a month's holiday in Cairo and England. His anticipation was marred somewhat by a sense that, after a year in the veldt, he would no longer fit into the comfortable old shoe of his childhood home; that he would feel as odd and exiled as he had in Africa. Home had become a dream, in Bechuanaland; if, at home, Bechuanaland became a dream, then he would have no place real at all to be at home in; he would be an exile for good.

The high veldt sped away as he was occupied with these thoughts, the rich farmlands of Southern Rhodesia. In the saloon car a young couple, very evidently on honeymoon, watched expectantly for the first glimpse of the eternal rainbow, visible miles off, that haloed Victoria Falls. Denys watched them and their excitement, feeling old and wise. Americans, doubtless: they had that shy, inoffensive air of all Americans abroad, that wondering quality as of children let out from a dark and oppressive school to play in the sun.

"There!" said the woman as the train took a bend. "Oh, look, how beautiful!"

Even over the train's sound they could hear the sound of the falls now, like distant cannon. The young man looked at his watch and smiled at Denys. "Right on time," he said, and Denys smiled too, amused to be complimented on his railroad's efficiency. The Bulawayo Bridge—longest and highest span on the Cape-to-Cairo line—leapt out over the gorge. "My God, that's something," the young man said. "Cecil Rhodes built this, right?"

"No," Denys said. "He thought of it, but never lived to see it. It would have been far easier to build it a few miles up, but Rhodes pictured the train being washed in the spray of the falls as it passed. And so it was built here."

The noise of the falls was immense now, and weirdly various, a medley of cracks, thumps, and explosions playing over the constant bass roar, which was not so much like a noise at all as it was like an eternal deep-drawn breath. And as the train chugged out across the span, aimed at Cairo thousands of miles away, passing here the place so hard-sought-for a hundred years ago—the place where the Nile had its origin—the spray *did* fall on the train just as Cecil Rhodes had imagined it, flung spindrift hissing on the locomotive, drops speckling the window they looked out of and rainbowing in the white air. The young Americans were still with wonder, and Denys, too, felt a lifting of his heart.

At Khartoum, Denys bid the honeymooners farewell: they were taking the Empire Airways flying boat from here to Gibraltar, and the Atlantic dirigible home. Denys, by now feeling quite proprietary about his Empire's transportation services, assured them that both flights would also certainly be right on time, and would be as comfortable as the sleepers they were leaving, would serve the same excellent meals with the same white napery embossed with the same royal insignia. Denys himself was driven to the Grand Hotel. His Sudan Railways sleeper to Cairo left the next morning.

After a bath in a tiled tub large enough almost to swim in, Denys changed into dinner clothes (which had been carefully laid out for him on the huge bed—for whom had these cavernous rooms been built, a race of Kitcheners?) He reserved a table for one in the grill room and went down to the bar. One thing he *must* do in London, he thought, shooting his cuffs, was to visit his tailor.

Bechuanaland had sweated off his college baby fat, and the tropics seemed to have turned his satin lapels faintly green.

The bar was comfortably filled, before the dinner hour, with men of several sorts and a few women, and with the low various murmur of their talk. Some of the men wore *white* dinner jackets—businessmen and tourists, Denys supposed—and a few even wore shorts with black shoes and stockings, a style Denys found inherently funny, as though a tailor had made a frightful error and cut evening clothes to the pattern of bush clothes. He ordered a whiskey.

Rarely in African kraals or in his bungalow or his whitewashed office did Denys think about his Empire: or if he did, it was in some local, even irritated way, of Imperial trivialities or Imperial red tape, the rain-rusted engines and stacks of tropic-mildewed paperwork that, collectively, Denys and his young associates called the White Man's Burden. It seemed to require a certain remove from the immediacy of Empire before he could perceive it. Only here (beneath the fans' ticking, amid the voices naming places—Kandahar, Durban, Singapore, Penang) did the larger Empire that Denys had never seen but had lived in in thought and feeling since childhood open in his mind. How odd, how far more odd really than admirable or deplorable that the small place which was his childhood, circumscribed and cozy—gray Westminster, chilly Trafalgar Square of the black umbrellas, London of the coal-smoked wallpaper and endless chimney pots—should have opened itself out so ceaselessly and for so long into huge hot places, subcontinents where rain never fell or never stopped, lush with vegetable growth or burdened with seas of sand or stone. Send forth the best ye breed: or at least large numbers of those ye breed. If one thought how odd it was—and if one thought then of what should have been natural empires, enormous spreads of restless real property like America or Russia turning in on themselves, making themselves into what seemed (to Denys, who had never seen them) to be very small places: then it did seem to be Destiny of a kind. Not a Destiny to be proud of, particularly, nor ashamed of either, but one whose compelling inner logic could only be marveled at.

Quite suddenly, and with poignant vividness, Denys saw himself, or rather felt himself once more to be, before his nursery fire, looking into the small glow of it, with animal crackers and cocoa for tea, listening to Nana telling tales of her brother the sergeant, and the Afghan frontier, and the now-dead king he served—listening, and feeling the Empire ranged in widening circles around him: first Harley Street, outside the window, and then Buckingham Palace, where the king lived; and the country then into which the trains went, and then the cold sea, and the Possessions, and the Commonwealth, stretching ever farther outward, worldwide: but always with his small glowing fire and his comfort and wonder at the heart of it.

So, there he is: a young man with the self-possessed air of an older, in evening clothes aged prematurely in places where evening clothes had not been made to go; thinking, if it could be called thinking, of a nursery fire; and about to be spoken to by the man next down the bar. If his feelings could be summed up and spoken, they were that, however odd, there is nothing more real, more pinioned by acts great and small, more clinker-built of time and space and filled brimful of this and that, than is the real world in which his five senses and his memories had their being; and that this was deeply satisfying.

"I beg your pardon," said the man next down the bar.

"Good evening," Denys said.

"My name is Davenant," the man said. He held out a square, blunt-fingered hand, and Denys drew himself up and shook it. "You are, I believe, Denys Winterset?"

"I am," Denys said, searching the smiling face before him and wondering from where he was known to him. It was a big, square, high-fronted head, a little like Bernard Shaw's, with ice-blue eyes of that twinkle; it was crowned far back with a neat hank of white hair, and was crossed above the broad jaw with upright white mustaches.

"You don't mind the intrusion?" the man said. "I wonder if you know whether the grub here is as good as once it was. It's been some time since I last ate a meal in Khartoum."

"The last time I did so was a year ago this week," Denys said. "It was quite good."

"Excellent," said Davenant, looking at Denys as though something about the young man amused him. "In that case, if you have no other engagement, may I ask your company?"

"I have no other engagement," Denys said; in fact he had rather been looking forward to dining alone, but deference to his superiors (of whom this man Davenant was surely in some sense one) was strong in him. "Tell me, though, how you come to know my name."

"Oh, well, there it is," Davenant said. "One has dealings with the Colonial Office. One sees a face, a name is attached to it, one files it but doesn't forget—that sort of thing. Part of one's job."

A civil servant, an inspector of some kind. Denys felt the sinking one feels on running into one's tutor in a wine bar: the evening not well begun. "They may well be crowded for dinner," he said.

"I have reserved a quiet table," said the smiling man, lifting his glass to Denys.

The grub was, in fact, superior. Sir Geoffrey Davenant was an able teller of tales, and he had many to tell. He was, apparently, no such dull thing as an inspector for the Colonial Office, though just what office he did fill Denys couldn't determine. He seemed to have been "attached to" or "had dealings with" or "gone about for" half the establishments of the Empire. He embodied, it seemed to Denys, the entire strange adventure about which Denys had been thinking when Sir Geoffrey had first spoken to him.

"So," Sir Geoffrey said, filling their glasses from a bottle of South African claret—no harm in being patriotic, he'd said, for one bottle—"so, after some months of stumbling about Central Asia and making myself useful one way or another, I was to make my way back to Sadiya. I crossed the Tibetan frontier disguised as a monk—"

"A monk?"

"Yes. Having lost all my gear in Manchuria, I could do the poverty part quite well. I had a roll of rupees, the films, and a compass hidden inside my prayer wheel. Mine didn't whiz around then with the same sanctity as the other fellows', but no matter. After adventures too ordinary to describe—avalanches and so on—I managed to reach the monastery at Rangbok, on the old road up to Everest. Rather near collapse. I was recovering a bit and thinking how to proceed when there was a runner with a telegram. From my superior at Ch'eng-tu. WARN DAVENANT MASSACRE SADIYA, it said. The Old Man then was famously close-mouthed. But this was particularly unhelpful, as it did not say who had massacred whom—or why." He lifted the silver cover of a dish, and found it empty.

"This must have been a good long time ago," Denys said.

"Oh, yes," Davenant said, raising his ice-blue eyes to Denys. "A good long time ago. That was an excellent curry. Nearly as good as at Veeraswamy's, in London—which is, strangely, the best in the world. Shall we have coffee?"

Over this, and brandy and cigars, Sir Geoffrey's stories modulated into reflections. Pleasant as his company was, Denys couldn't overcome a sensation that everything Sir Geoffrey said to him was rehearsed, laid on for his entertainment, or perhaps his enlightenment, and yet with no clue in it as to why he had thus been singled out.

"It amuses me," Sir Geoffrey said, "how constant it is in human nature to think that things might have gone on differently from the way they did. In a man's own life, first of all: how he might have taken this or that very different route, except for this or that accident, this or that slight push—if he'd only known then, and so on. And then in history as well, we ruminate endlessly, if, what if, if only . . . The world seems always somehow malleable to our minds, or to our imaginations anyway."

"Strange you should say so," Denys said. "I was thinking, just before you spoke to me, about how very solid the world seems to me, how very—real. And—if you don't mind my thrusting it into your thoughts—you never did tell me how it is you come to know my name; or why it is you thought good to invite me to that excellent dinner."

"My dear boy," Davenant said, holding up his cigar as though to defend his innocence.

"I can't think it was chance."

"My dear boy," Davenant said in a different tone, "if anything is, that was not. I will explain all. You were on that train of thought. If you will have patience while it trundles by."

Denys said nothing further. He sipped his coffee, feeling a dew of sweat on his forehead.

"History," said Sir Geoffrey. "Yes. Of course the possible worlds we make don't compare to the real one we inhabit—not nearly so well furnished, or tricked out with details. And yet still somehow better. More satisfying. Perhaps the novelist is only a special case of a universal desire to reshape, to 'take this sorry scheme of things entire,' smash it into bits, and 'remold it nearer to the heart's desire'—as old Khayyám says. The egoist is continually doing it with his own life. To dream of doing it with history is no more useful a game, I suppose, but as a game, it shows more sport. There are rules. You can be more objective, if that's an appropriate world." He seemed to grow pensive for a moment. He looked at the end of his cigar. It had gone out, but he didn't relight it.

"Take this Empire," he went on, drawing himself up somewhat to say it. "One doesn't want to be mawkish, but one has served it. Extended it a bit, made it more secure; done one's bit. You and I. Nothing more natural, then, if we have worked for its extension in the future, to imagine its extension in the past. We can put our finger on the occasional bungle, the missed chance, the wrong man in the wrong place, and so on, and we think: if I had only been there, seen to it that the news went through, got the guns there in time, forced the issue at a certain moment—well. But as long as one is dreaming, why stop? A favorite instance of mine is the American civil war. We came very close, you know, to entering that war on the Confederacy's side."

"Did we."

"I think we did. Suppose we had. Suppose we had at first dabbled—sent arms—ignored Northern protests—then got deeper in; suppose the North declared war on us. It seems to me a near certainty that if we had entered the war fully, the South would have won. And I think a British presence would have mitigated the slaughter. There was a point, you know, late in that war, when a new draft call in the North was met with terrible riots. In New York several Negroes were hanged, just to show how little their cause was felt."

Denys had partly lost the thread of this story, unable to imagine himself in it. He thought of the Americans he had met on the train. "Is that so," he said.

"Once having divided the States into two nations, and having helped the South to win, we would have been in place, you see. The fate of the West had not yet been decided. With the North much diminished in power—well, I imagine that by now we, the Empire, would have recouped much of what we lost in 1780."

Denys contemplated this. "Rather stirring," he said mildly. "Rather cold-blooded, too. Wouldn't it have meant condoning slavery? To say nothing of the lives lost. British, I mean."

"Condoning slavery—for a time. I've no doubt the South could have been bullied out of it. Without, perhaps, the awful results that accompanied the Northerners doing it. The eternal resentment. The backlash. The near genocide of the last hundred years. And, in my vision, there would have been a net savings in red men." He smiled. "Whatever might be said against it, the British Empire does not wipe out populations wholesale, as the Americans did in their West. I often wonder if that sin isn't what makes the Americans so gloomy now, so introverted."

Denys nodded. He believed implicitly that his Empire did not wipe out populations wholesale. "Of course," he said, "there's no telling what exactly would have been the result. If we'd interfered as you say."

"No," Sir Geoffrey said. "No doubt whatever result it *did* have would have to be reshaped as well. And the results of that reshaping reshaped, too, the whole thing subtly guided all along its way toward the result desired—after all, if we can imagine how we might want to alter the past we do inherit, so we can imagine that any past might well be liable to the same imagining; that stupidities, blunders, shortsightedness, would occur in any past we might initiate. Oh, yes, it would all have to be reshaped, with each reshaping. . . ."

"The possibilities are endless," Denys said, laughing. "I'm afraid the game's beyond me. I say let the North win—since in any case we can't do the smallest thing about it."

"No," Davenant said, grown sad again, or reflective; he seemed to feel what Denys said deeply. "No, we can't. It's just—just too long ago." With great gravity he relit his cigar. Denys, at the oddness of this response, seeing Sir Geoffrey's eyes veiled, thought: *Perhaps he's mad.* He said, joining the game, "Suppose, though. Suppose Cecil Rhodes hadn't died young, as he did. . . ."

Davenant's eyes caught cold fire again, and his cigar paused in midair. "Hm?" he said with interest.

"I only meant," Denys said, "that your remark about the British not wiping out peoples wholesale was perhaps not tested. If Rhodes had lived to build his empire—hadn't he already named it Rhodesia—I imagine he would have dealt fairly harshly with the natives."

"Very harshly," said Sir Geoffrey.

"Well," Denys said, "I suppose I mean that it's not always evil effects that we inherit from these past accidents."

"Not at all," said Sir Geoffrey. Denys looked away from his regard, which had grown, without losing a certain cool humor, intense. "Do you know, by the way, that remark of George Santayana—the American philosopher—about the British Empire, about young men like yourself? 'Never,' he said, 'never since the Athenians has the world been ruled by such sweet, just, boyish masters.' "

Denys, absurdly, felt himself flush with embarrassment.

"I don't ramble," Sir Geoffrey said. "My trains of thought carry odd goods, but all headed the same way. I want to tell you something, about that historical circumstance, the one you've touched on, whose effects we inherit. Evil or good I will leave you to decide.

"Cecil Rhodes died prematurely, as you say. But not before he had amassed a very great fortune, and laid firm claims to the ground where that fortune would grow far greater. And also not before he had made a will disposing of that fortune."

"I've heard stories," Denys said.

"The stories you have heard are true. Cecil Rhodes, at his death, left his entire fortune, and its increase, to found and continue a secret society which should, by whatever means possible, preserve and extend the British Empire. His entire fortune."

"I have never believed it," Denys said, momentarily feeling untethered, like a balloon: afloat.

"For good reason," Davenant said. "If such a society as I describe were brought into being, its very first task would be to disguise, cast doubt upon, and quite bury its origins. Don't you think that's so? In any case it's true what I say: the society was founded; is secret; continues to exist; is responsible, in some large degree at least, for the Empire we now know, in this year of grace 1956, IV Elizabeth II, the Empire on which the sun does not set."

The veranda where the two men sat was nearly deserted now; the night was loud with tropical noises that Denys had come to think of as silence, but the human noise of the town had nearly ceased.

"You can't know that," Denys said. "If you knew it, if you were privy to it, then you wouldn't say it. Not to me." He almost added: *Therefore you're not in possession of any secret, only a madman's certainty.*

"I *am* privy to it," Davenant said. "I am myself a member. The reason I reveal the secret to you—and you see, here we are, come to you and my odd knowledge of you, at last, as I promised—the reason I reveal it to you is because I wish to ask you to join it. To accept from me an offer of membership."

Denys said nothing. A dark waiter in white crept close, and was waved away by Sir Geoffrey.

"You are quite properly silent," Sir Geoffrey said. "Either I am mad, you think, in which case there is nothing to say; or what I am telling you is true, which likewise leaves you nothing to say. Quite proper. In your place I would be silent also. In your place I was. In any case I have no intention of pressing you for an answer now. I happen to know, by a roundabout sort of means that if I explained to you would certainly convince you I was mad, that you will seriously consider what I've said to you. Later. On your long ride to Cairo: there will be time to think. In London. I ask nothing from you now. Only . . ."

He reached into his waistcoat pocket. Denys watched, fascinated: would he draw out some sign of power, a royal charter, some awesome seal? No: it was a small metal plate, with a strip of brown ribbon affixed to it, like a bit of recording tape. He turned it in his hands thoughtfully. "The difficulty, you see, is that in order to alter history and bring it closer to the heart's desire, it would be necessary to stand outside it altogether. Like Archimedes, who said that if he had a lever long enough, and a place to stand, he could move the world."

He passed the metal plate to Denys, who took it reluctantly.

"A place to stand, you see," Sir Geoffrey said. "A place to stand. I would like you to keep that plate about you, and not misplace it. It's in the nature of a key, though it mayn't look it; and it will let you into a very good London club, though it mayn't look it either, where I would like you to call on me. If, even out of simple curiosity, you would like to hear more of us." He extinguished his cigar. "I am going to describe the rather complicated way in which that key is to be used—I really do apologize for the hugger-mugger, but you will come to understand—and then I am going to bid you good evening. Your train is an early one? I thought so. My own departs at midnight. I possess a veritable Bradshaw's of the world's railroads in this skull. Well. No more. I will just sign this—oh, don't thank me. Dear boy: don't thank me."

When he was gone, Denys sat a long time with his cold cigar in his hand and the night around him. The amounts of wine and brandy he had been given seemed to have evaporated from him into the humid air, leaving him feeling cool, clear, and unreal. When at last he rose to go, he inserted the flimsy plate into his waistcoat pocket; and before he went to bed, to lie a long time awake, he changed it to the waistcoat pocket of the pale suit he would wear next morning.

As Sir Geoffrey suggested he would, he thought on his ride north of all that he had been told, trying to reassemble it in some more reasonable, more everyday fashion: as all day long beside the train the sempiternal Nile—camels, nomads, women washing in the barge canals, the thin line of palms screening the white desert beyond—slipped past. At evening, when at length he lowered the shade of his compartment window on the poignant blue sky pierced with stars, he thought suddenly: But how could he have know he would find me there, at the bar of the Grand, on that night of this year, at that hour of the evening, just as though we had some long-standing agreement to meet there?

If anything is chance, Davenant had said, that was not.

At the airfield at Ismailia there was a surprise: his flight home on the R101, which his father had booked months ago as a special treat for Denys, was to be that grand old airship's last scheduled flight. The oldest airship in the British fleet, commissioned in the year Denys was born, was to be—mothballed? Dry-docked? Deflated? Denys wondered just what one did with a decommissioned airship larger than Westminster Cathedral.

Before dawn it was drawn from its great hangar by a crowd of white-clothed fellahin pulling at its ropes—descendants, Denys thought, of those who had pulled ropes at the Pyramids three thousand years ago, employed now on an object almost as big but lighter than air. It isn't because it is so intensely romantic that great airships must always arrive or depart at dawn or at evening, but only that then the air is cool and most likely to be still: and yet intensely romantic it remains. Denys, standing at the broad, canted windows, watched the ground recede—magically, for there was no sound of engines, no jolt to indicate liftoff, only the waving, cheering fellahin growing smaller. The band on the tarmac played "Land of Hope and Glory." Almost invisible to watchers on the ground—because of its heat-reflective silver dome—the immense ovoid turned delicately in the wind as it arose.

"Well, it's the end of an era," a red-faced man in a checked suit said to Denys.

"In ten years they'll all be gone, these big airships. The propeller chaps will have taken over; and the jet aeroplane, too, I shouldn't wonder."

"I should be sorry to see that," Denys said. "I've loved airships since I was a boy."

"Well, they're just that little bit slower," the red-faced man said sadly. "It's all hurry-up, nowadays. Faster, faster. And for what? I put it to you: for what?"

Now with further gentle pushes of its Rolls-Royce engines, the R101 altered its attitude again; passengers at the lounge windows pointed out the Suez Canal, and the ships passing; Lake Mareotis; Alexandria, like a mirage; British North Africa, as far to the left as one cared to point; and the white-fringed sea. Champagne was being called for, traditional despite the hour, and the red-faced man pressed a glass on Denys.

"The end of an era," he said again, raising his flute of champagne solemnly.

And then the cloudscape beyond the windows shifted, and all Africa had slipped into the south, or into the imaginary, for they had already begun to seem the same thing to Denys. He turned from the windows and decided—the effort to decide it seemed not so great here aloft, amid the potted palms and the wicker, with this pale champagne—that the conversation he had had down in the flat lands far away must have been imaginary as well.

III: THE TALE OF THE PRESIDENT *PRO TEM*

The universe proceeds out of what it has been and into what it will be, inexorably, unstoppably, at the rate of one second per second, one year per year, forever. At right angles to its forward progress lie the past and the future. The future, that is to say, does not lie "ahead" of the present in the stream of time, but at a right angle to it: the future of any present moment can be projected as far as you like outward from it, infinitely in fact, but when the universe has proceeded further, and a new present moment has succeeded this one, the future of this one retreats with it into the what-has-been, forever outdated. It is similar but more complicated with the past.

Now within the great process or procession that the universe makes, there can be no question of "movement," either "forward" or "back." The very idea is contradictory. Any conceivable movement is into the orthogonal futures and pasts that fluoresce from the universe as it is; and from those orthogonal futures and pasts into others, and others, and still others, never returning, always moving at right angles to the stream of time. To the traveler, therefore, who does not ever return from the futures or pasts into which he has gone, it must appear that the times he inhabits grow progressively more remote from the stream of time that generated them, the stream that has since moved on and left his futures behind. Indeed, the longer he remains in the future, the farther off the traveler gets from the moment in actuality whence he started, and the less like actuality the universe he stands in seems to him to be.

It was thoughts of this sort, only inchoate as yet and with the necessary conclusions not yet drawn, that occupied the mind of the President *pro tem* of the Otherhood as he walked the vast length of an iron and glass railway station in the capital city of an aged empire. He stopped to take a cigar case from within the black Norfolk overcoat he wore, and a cigar from the case; this he lit, and with its successive blue clouds hanging lightly about his hat and head, he walked on. There were hominids at work on the glossy engines of the empire's trains that came and went from this terminus; hominids pushing with their long strong arms the carts burdened with the goods and luggage that the trains were to carry; hominids of other sorts, gathered in groups or standing singly at the barricades, clutched their tickets, waiting to depart, some aided by or waited upon by other species—too few creatures, in all, to dispel the extraordinary impression of smoky empty hugeness that the cast-iron arches of the shed made.

The President *pro tem* was certain, or at any rate retained a distinct impression, that at his arrival some days before there were telephones available for citizens to use, in the streets, in public places such as this (he seemed to see an example in his mind, a wooden box whose bright veneer was loosening in the damp climate, a complex instrument within, of enameled steel and heavy celluloid); but if there ever had been, there were none now. Instead he went in at a door above which a yellow globe was alight, a winged foot etched upon it. He chose a telegraph form from a stack of them on a long scarred counter, and with the scratchy pen provided he dashed off a quick note to the Magus in whose apartments he had been staying, telling him that he had returned late from the country and would not be with him till evening.

This missive he handed in at the grille, paying what was asked in large coins; then he went out, up the brass-railed stairs, and into the afternoon, into the quiet and familiar city.

It was the familiarity that had been, from the beginning, the oddest thing. The President *pro tem* was a man who, in the long course of his work for the Otherhood, had become accustomed to stepping out of his London club into a world not quite the same as the world he had left to enter that club. He was used to finding himself in a London—or a Lahore or a Laos—stripped of well-known monuments, with public buildings and private ways unknown to him, and a newspaper (bought with an unfamiliar coin found in his pocket) full of names that should not have been there, or missing events that should have been. But here—where nothing, nothing at all, was as he had known it, no trace remaining of the history he had come from—here where no man should have been able to take steps, where even Caspar Last had thought it not possible to take steps—the President *pro tem* could not help but feel easy: had felt easy from the beginning. He walked up the cobbled streets, his furled umbrella over his shoulder, troubled by nothing but the weird grasp that this unknown dark city had on his heart.

The rain that had somewhat spoiled his day in the country had ceased but had left a pale, still mist over the city, a humid atmosphere that gave to views down avenues a stage-set quality, each receding rank of buildings fainter, more vaguely executed. Trees, too, huge and weeping, still and featureless as though painted on successive scrims. At the great gates, topped with garlanded urns, of a public park, the President *pro tem* looked in toward the piled and sounding waters of a fountain and the dim towers of poplar trees. And as he stood resting on his umbrella, lifting the last of the cigar to his lips, someone passed by him and entered the park.

For a moment the President *pro tem* stood unmoving, thinking what an attractive person (boy? girl?) that had been, and how the smile paid to him in passing seemed to indicate a knowledge of him, a knowledge that gave pleasure or at least amusement; then he dropped his cigar end and passed through the gates through which the figure had gone.

That had *not* been a hominid who had smiled at him. It was not a Magus and surely not one of the draconics either. Why he was sure he could not have said: for the same unsayable reason that he knew this city in this world, this park, these marble urns, these leaf-littered paths. He was sure that the person he had seen belonged to a different species from himself, and different also from the other species who lived in this world.

At the fountain where the paths crossed, he paused, looking this way and that, his heart beating hard and filled absurdly with a sense of loss. The child (had it been a child?) was gone, could not be seen that way, or that way—but then was there again suddenly, down at the end of a yew alley, loitering, not looking his way. Thinking at first to sneak up on her, or him, along the sheltering yews, the President *pro tem* took a sly step that way; then, ashamed, he thought better of it and set off down the path at an even pace, as one would approach a young horse or a tame deer. The one he walked toward took no notice of him, appeared lost in thought, eyes cast down.

Indescribably lovely, the President *pro tem* thought: and yet at the same time negligent and easeful and ordinary. Barefoot, or in light sandals of some kind, light pale clothing that seemed to be part of her, like a bird's dress—and a wristwatch, incongruous, yet not really incongruous at all: someone for whom incongruity was inconceivable. A reverence—almost a holy dread—came over the President *pro tem* as he came closer: as though he had stumbled into a sacred grove. Then the one he walked toward looked up at him, which caused the President *pro tem* to stop still as if a gun had casually been turned on him.

He was known, he understood, to this person. She, or he, stared unembarrassed at the President *pro tem*, with a gaze of the most intense and yet impersonal tenderness, of compassion and amusement and calm interest all mixed; and almost imperceptibly shook her head *no* and smiled again: and the President *pro tem* lowered his eyes, unable to meet that gaze. When he looked up again, the person was gone.

Hesitantly the President *pro tem* walked to the end of the avenue of yews and looked in all directions. No one. A kind of fear flew over him, felt in his breast like the beat of departing wings. He seemed to know, for the first time, what those encounters with gods had been like, when there had been gods; encounters he had puzzled out of the Greek in school.

Anyway he was alone now in the park: he was sure of that. At length he found his way out again into the twilight streets.

By evening he had crossed the city and was climbing the steps of a tall town house, searching in his pockets for the key given him. Beside the varnished door was a small plaque, which said that within were the offices of the Orient Aid Society; but this was not in fact the case. Inside was a tall foyer; a glass-paneled door let him into a hallway wainscoted in dark wood. A pile of gumboots and rubber overshoes in a corner, macs and umbrellas on an ebony tree. Smells of tea, done with, and dinner cooking: a stew, an apple tart, a roast fowl. The tulip-shaped gas lamps along the hall were lit.

He let himself into the library at the hall's end; velvet armchairs regarded the coal fire, and on a drum table a tray of tea things consorted with the books and the papers. The President *pro tem* went to the low shelves that ran beneath the windows and drew out one volume of an old encyclopedia, buckram-bound, with marbled fore-edges and illustrations in brownish photogravure.

The Races. For some reason the major headings and certain other words were in the orthography he knew, but not the closely printed text. His fingers ran down the columns, which were broken into numbered sections headed by the names of species and subspecies. *Hominidae,* with three subspecies. *Draconiidae,* with four: here were etchings of skulls. And lastly *Sylphidae,* with an uncertain number of subspecies. Sylphidae, the Sylphids. Fairies.

"Angels," said a voice behind him. The President *pro tem* turned to see the Magus whose guest he was, recently risen no doubt, in a voluminous dressing gown richly figured. His beard and hair were so long and fine they seemed to float on the currents of air in the room, like filaments of thistledown.

" 'Angels,' is that what you call them?"

"What they would have themselves called," said the Magus. "What name they call themselves, among themselves, no one knows but they."

"I think I met with one this evening."

"Yes."

There was no photogravure to accompany the subsection on Sylphidae in the encyclopedia. "I'm sure I met with one."

"They are gathering, then."

"Not . . . not because of me?"

"Because of you."

"How, though," said the President *pro tem,* feeling again within him the sense of loss, of beating wings departing, "how, how could they have known, how . . ."

The Magus turned away from him to the fire, to the armchairs and the drum table. The President *pro tem* saw that beside one chair a glass of whiskey had been placed, and an ashtray. "Come," said the Magus. "Sit. Continue your tale. It will perhaps become clear to you: perhaps not." He sat then himself, and without looking back at the President *pro tem* he said: "Shall we go on?"

The President *pro tem* knew it was idle to dispute with his host. He did stand unmoving for the space of several heartbeats. Then he took his chair, drew the cigar case from his pocket, and considered where he had left off his tale in the dark of the morning.

"Of course," he said then, "Last knew: he knew, without admitting it to himself, as a good orthogonist must never do, that the world he had returned to from his excursion was not the world he had left. The past he had passed through on his way back was not 'behind' his present at all, but at a right angle to it; the future of that past, which he had to traverse in order to get back again, was not the same road, and 'back' was not where he got. The frame house on Maple Street which, a little sunburned, he reentered on his return was twice removed in reality from the one he had left a week before; the mother he kissed likewise.

"He knew that, for it was predicated by orthogonal logic, and orthogonal logic was in fact what Last had discovered—the transversability of time was only an effect of that discovery. He knew it, and despite his glee over his triumph, he kept his eye open. Sooner or later he would come upon something, something that would betray the fact that this world was not his.

"He could not have guessed it would be me."

The Magus did not look at the President *pro tem* as he was told this story; his pale gray eyes instead wandered from object to object around the great dark library but seemed to see none of them; what, the President *pro tem* wondered, did they see? He had at first supposed the race of Magi to be blind, from this habitual appearance of theirs; he now knew quite well that they were not blind, not blind at all.

"Go on," the Magus said.

"So," said the President *pro tem*, "Last returns from his excursion. A week passes uneventfully. Then one morning he hears his mother call: he has a visitor. Last, pretending annoyance at this interruption of his work (actually he was calculating various forms of compound interest on a half million dollars), comes to the door. There on the step is a figure in tweeds and a bowler hat, leaning on a furled umbrella: me.

" 'Mr. Last,' I said. 'I think we have business.'

"You could see by his expression that he knew I should not have been there, should not have had business with him at all. He really ought to have refused to see me. A good deal of trouble might have been saved if he had. There was no way I could force him, after all. But he didn't refuse; after a goggle-eyed moment he brought me in, up a flight of stairs (Mama waiting anxiously at the bottom), and into his study.

"Geniuses are popularly supposed to live in an atmosphere of the greatest confusion and untidiness, but this wasn't true of Last. The study—it was his bedroom, too—was of a monkish neatness. There was no sign that he worked there, except for a computer terminal, and even it was hidden beneath a cozy that Mama had made for it and Caspar had not dared to spurn.

"He was trembling slightly, poor fellow, and had no idea of the social graces. He only turned to me—his eyeglasses were the kind that oddly diffract the eyes behind and make them unmeetable—and said, 'What do you want?' "

The President *pro tem* caressed the ashtray with the tip of his cigar. He had been offered no tea, and he felt the lack. "We engaged in some preliminary fencing," he continued. "I told him what I had come to acquire. He said he didn't know what I was talking about. I said I thought he did. He laughed and said there must be some mistake. I said, no mistake, Mr. Last. At length he grew silent, and I could see even behind those absurd goggles that he had begun to try to account for me.

"Thinking out the puzzles of orthogonal logic, you see, is not entirely unlike puzzling out moves in chess: theoretically chess can be played by patiently working out the likely consequences of each move, and the consequences of those consequences, and so on; but in fact it is not so played, certainly not by master players. Masters seem to have a more immediate apprehension of possibilities, an almost visceral understanding of the, however rigorously mathematical, logic of the board and pieces, an understanding that they can act on without being able necessarily to explain. Whatever sort of mendacious and feckless fool Caspar Last was in many ways, he was a genius in one or two, and orthogonal logic was one of them.

" 'From when,' he said, 'have you come?'

" 'From not far on,' I answered. He sat then, resigned, stuck in a sort of check impossible to think one's way out of, yet not mated. 'Then,' he said, 'go back the same way you came.'

" 'I cannot,' I said, 'until you explain to me how it is done.'

" 'You know how,' he said, 'if you can come here to ask me.'

" 'Not until you have explained it to me. Now or later.'

" 'I never will,' he said.

" 'You will,' I said. 'You will have done already, before I leave. Otherwise I would not be here now asking. Let us,' I said, and took a seat myself, 'let us assume these preliminaries have been gone through, for they have been of course, and move ahead to the bargaining. My firm are prepared to make you a quite generous offer.'

"That was what convinced him that he must, finally, give up to us the processes he had discovered, which he really had firmly intended to destroy forever: the fact that I had come there to ask for them. Which meant that he had already somehow, somewhen, already yielded them up to us."

The President *pro tem* paused again, and lifted his untouched whiskey. "It was the same argument," he said, "the same incontrovertible argument, that was used to convince me once, too, to do a dreadful thing."

He drank, thoughtfully, or at least (he supposed) appearing thoughtful; more and more often as he grew older it happened that in the midst of an anecdote, a relation, even one of supreme importance, he would begin to forget what it was he was telling; the terrifically improbable events would begin to seem not only improbable but fictitious, without insides, the incidents and characters as false as in any tawdry cinema story, even his own part in them unreal: as though they happened to someone made up—certainly not to him who told them. Often enough he forgot the plot.

"You see," he said, "Last exited from a universe in which travel 'through time' was, apparently, either not possible, or possible only under conditions that would allow such travel to go undetected. That was apparent from the fact that no one, so far as Last knew, up to the time of his own single excursion, had ever detected it going on. No one, from Last's own future that is, had ever come 'back' and disrupted his present, or the past of his present: never ever. Therefore, if his excursion could take place, and he could 'return,' he would have to return to a different universe: a universe where time travel *had* taken place, a universe in which once-upon-a-time a man from 1983 had managed to insert himself into a minor colony of the British Crown one hundred and twenty-seven years earlier. What he couldn't know in advance was whether the universe he 'returned' to was one where time travel was a commonplace, an everyday occurrence, something, anyway, that could deprive his excursion of the value it had; or whether it was one in which one excursion only had taken place, his own. My appearance before him convinced him that it was, or was about to become, common enough: common enough to disturb his own peace and quiet, and alter in unforeseeable ways his comfortable present.

"There was only one solution, or one dash at a solution anyway. I might, myself, be a singularity in Last's new present. It was therefore possible that if he could get rid of me, I would take his process 'away' with me into whatever future I had come out of to get it, and thereupon never be able to find my way again to his present and disturb it or him. Whatever worlds I altered, they would not be his, not his anyway who struck the bargain with me: if each of them also contained a Last, who would suffer or flourish in ways unimaginable to the Last to whom I spoke, then those eidolons would have to make terms for themselves, that's all. The quantum angle obtruded by my coming, and then the one obtruded by my returning, divorced all those Lasts from him for all eternity: that is why, though the angle itself is virtually infinitesimal, it has always to be treated as a right angle.

"Last showed me, on his computer, after our bargain was struck and he was turning over his data and plans to me. I told him I would not probably grasp the theoretical basis of the process, however well I had or would come to manage the practical paradoxes of it, but he liked to show me. He first summoned up x-y coordinates, quite ordinary, and began by showing me how some surprising results were obtained by plotting on such coordinates an imaginary number, specifically the square root of minus one. The only way to describe what happens, he said, is that the plotted figure, one unit high, one unit wide, generates a shadow square of the same measurements 'behind' itself, in space undefined by the coordinates. It was with such tricks that he had begun; the orthogons he obtained had first started him thinking about the generation of inhabitable—if also somehow imaginary—pasts.

"Then he showed me what became of the orthogons so constructed if the upright axis were set in motion. Suppose (he said) that this vertical coordinate were in fact revolving around the axle formed by the other, horizontal coordinate. If it were so revolving, like an aeroplane propeller, we could not apprehend it, edge on as it is to us, so to speak; but what would that motion do to the plots we were making? And of course it was quite simple, given the proper instructions to the computer, to find out. And his orthogons—always remaining at right angles to the original coordinates—began to turn in the prop wash of the whole system's progress at one second per second out of the what-was and into the what-has-never-yet-been; and to generate, when one had come to see them, the paradoxes of orthogonal logic: the cyclonic storm of logic in which all travelers in that medium always stand; the one in which Last and I, I bending over his shoulder hat in hand, he with fat white fingers on his keys and eyeglasses slipping down his nose, stood even as we spoke: a storm as unfeelable as Last's rotating axis was unseeable."

The President *pro tem* tossed his extinguished cigar into the fading fire and crossed his arms upon his breast, weary; weary of the tale.

"I don't yet understand," the other said. "If he had been so adamant, why would he give up his secrets to you?"

"Well," said the President *pro tem*, "there was, also, the matter of money. It came down to that, in the end. We were able to make him a very generous offer, as I said."

"But he didn't need money. He had this stamp."

"Yes. So he did. Yes. We were able to pick up the stamp, too, from him, as part of the bargain. I think we offered him a hundred pounds. Perhaps it was more."

"I thought it was invaluable."

"Well, so did he, of course. And yet he was not really as surprised as one might have expected him to be, when he discovered it was not; when it turned out that the stamp he had gone to such trouble to acquire was in fact rather a common one. I seemed to see it in his face, the expectation of what he was likely to find, as soon as I directed him to look it up in his Scott's, if he didn't believe me. And there it was in Scott's: the one-penny magenta 1856, a nice enough stamp, a stamp many collectors covet, and many also have in their albums. He had begun breathing stertorously, staring down at the page. I'm afraid he was suffering, rather, and I didn't like to observe it.

" 'Come,' I said to him. 'You knew it was possible.' And he did, of course. 'Perhaps it was something you did,' I said. 'Perhaps you bought the last one of a batch, and the postmaster subsequently reordered, a thing he had not before intended to do. Perhaps . . . ' But I could see him think it: there needed to be no such explanation. He needed to have made no error, nor to have influenced the moment's shape in any way by his presence. The very act of his coming and going was sufficient source of unpredictable, stochastic change: this world was not his, and minute changes from his were predicated. But *this* change, this of all possible changes . . .

"His hand had begun to shake, holding the volume of Scott's. I really wanted now to get through the business and be off, but it couldn't be hurried. I knew that, for I'd done it all before. In the end we acquired the stamp. And then destroyed it, of course."

The President *pro tem* remembered: a tiny, momentary fire.

"It's often been observed," he said, "that the cleverest scientists are often the most easily taken in by charlatans. There is a famous instance, famous in some worlds, of a scientist who was brought to believe firmly in ghosts and ectoplasm, because the medium and her manifestations passed all the tests the scientist could devise. The only thing he didn't think to test for was conscious fraud. I suppose it's because the phenomena of nature, or the entities of mathematics, however puzzling and elusive they may be, are not after all bent on fooling the observer; and so a motive that would be evident to the dullest of policemen does not occur to the genius."

"The stamp," said the Magus.

"The stamp, yes. I'm not exactly proud of this part of the story. We were convinced, though, that two *very* small wrongs could go a long way toward making a very great right. And Last, who understood me and the 'firm' I represented to be capable of handling—at least in a practical way—the awful paradoxes of orthogony, did not imagine us to be also skilled, if anything more skilled, at such things as burglary, uttering, fraud, and force. Of such contradictions is Empire made. It was easy enough for us to replace, while Last was off in the tropics, one volume of his Scott's stamp catalog with another printed by ourselves, almost identical to his but containing one difference. It was harder waiting to see, once he had looked up his stamp in our bogus volume, if he would then search out some other source to confirm what he found there. He did not."

The Magus rose slowly from his chair with the articulated dignity, the wasteless lion's motion, of his kind. He tugged the bell pull. He picked up the poker then, and stood with his hand upon the mantel, looking down into the ruby ash of the dying fire. "I would he had," he said.

The dark double doors of the library opened, and the servant entered noiselessly.

"Refresh the gentleman's glass," the Magus said without turning from the fire, "and draw the drapes."

The President *pro tem* thought that no matter how long he lived in this world he would never grow accustomed to the presence of draconics. The servant's dark hand lifted the decanter, poured an exact dram into the glass, and stoppered the bottle again; then his yellow eyes, irises slit like a cat's or a snake's, rose from that task toward the next, the drawing of the drapes. Unlike the eyes of the Magi, these draconic eyes seemed to see and weigh everything—though on a single scale, and from behind a veil of indifference.

Their kind, the President *pro tem* had learned, had been servants for uncounted ages, though the Magus his host had said that once they had been masters, and men and the other hominids their slaves. And they still had, the President *pro tem* observed, that studied reserve which upper servants had in the world from which the President *pro tem* had come, that reserve which says: Very well, I will do your bidding, better than you could do it for yourself; I will maintain the illusion of your superiority to me, as no other creature could.

With a taper he lit at the fire, he lit the lamps along the walls and masked them with glass globes. Then he drew the drapes.

"I'll ring for supper," the Magus said, and the servant stopped at the sound of his voice. "Have it sent in." The servant moved again, crossing the room on narrow naked feet. At the doorway he turned to them, but only to draw the double doors closed together as he left.

For a time the Magus stood regarding the doors the great lizard had closed. Then: "Outside the City," he said, "in the mountains, they have begun to combine. There are more stories every week. In the old forests whence they first emerged, they have begun to collect on appointed days, trying to remember—for they are not really as intelligent as they look—trying to remember what it is they have lost, and to think of gaining it again. In not too long a time we will begin to hear of massacres. Some remote place; a country house; a more than usually careless man; a deed of unfamiliar horridness. And a sign left, the first sign: a writing in blood, or something less obvious. And like a spot symptomatic of a fatal disease, it will begin to spread."

The President *pro tem* drank, then said softly: "We didn't know, you know. We didn't understand that this would be the result." The drawing of the drapes, the lighting of the lamps, had made the old library even more familiar to the President *pro tem:* the dark varnished wood, the old tobacco smoke, the hour between tea and dinner; the draught that whispered at the window's edge, the bitter smell of the coal on the grate; the comfort of this velvet armchair's napless arms, of this whiskey. The President *pro tem* sat grasped by all this, almost unable to think of anything else. "We couldn't know."

"Last knew," the Magus said. "All false, all imaginary, all generated by the wishes and fears of others: all that I am, my head, my heart, my house. Not the world's doing, or time's, but yours." The opacity of his eyes, turned on the President *pro tem,* was fearful. "You have made me; you must unmake me."

"I'll do what I can," the President *pro tem* said. "All that I can."

"For centuries we have studied," the Magus said. "We have spent lifetimes—lifetimes much longer than yours—searching for the flaw in this world, the flaw whose existence we suspected but could not prove. I say 'centuries,' but those centuries have been illusory, have they not? We came, finally, to guess at you, down the defiles of time, working your changes, which we can but suffer.

"We only guessed at you: no more than men or beasts can we Magi remember, once the universe has become different, that it was ever other than it is now. But I think the Sylphids can feel it change: can know when the changes are wrought. Imagine the pain for them."

That was a command: and indeed the President *pro tem* could imagine it, and did. He looked down into his glass.

"That is why they are gathering. They know already of your appearance; they have expected you. The request is theirs to make, not mine: that you put this world out like a light."

He stabbed with the poker at the settling fire, and the coals gave up blue flames for a moment. The mage's eyes caught the light, and then went out.

"I long to die," he said.

IV: CHRONICLES OF THE OTHERHOOD

Once past the door, or what might be considered the door, or what Sir Geoffrey Davenant had told him was a club, Denys Winterset was greeted by the Fellow in Economic History, a gentle, academic-looking man called Platt.

"Not many of the Fellows about, just now," he said. "Most of them fossicking about on one bit of business or another. I'm always here." He smiled, a vague, self-effacing smile. "Be no good out there. But they also serve, eh?"

"Will Sir Geoffrey Davenant be here?" Denys asked him. He followed Platt through what did seem to be a gentlemen's club of the best kind: dark-paneled, smelling richly of leather upholstery and tobacco.

"Davenant, oh, yes," said Platt. "Davenant will be here. All the executive committee will get here, if they can. The President—*pro tem.*" He turned back to look at Denys over his half-glasses. "All our presidents are *pro tem.*" He led on. "There'll be dinner in the executive committee's dining room. After dinner we'll talk. You'll likely have questions." At that Denys almost laughed. He felt made of questions, most of them unputtable in any verbal form.

Platt stopped in the middle of the library. A lone Fellow in a corner by a green-shaded lamp was hidden by the *Times* held up before him. There was a fire burning placidly in the oak-framed fireplace; above it, a large and smoke-dimmed painting: a portrait of a chubby, placid man in a hard collar, thinning blond hair, eyes somehow vacant. Platt, seeing Deny's look, said: "Cecil Rhodes."

Beneath the portrait, carved into the mantelpiece, were words; Denys took a step closer to read them:

To Ruin the Great Work of Time
& Cast the Kingdoms old
Into another mould.

"Marvell," Platt said. "That poem about Cromwell. Don't know who chose it. It's right, though. I look at it often, working here. Now. It's down that corridor, if you want to wash your hands. Would you care for a drink? We have some time to kill. Ah, Davenant."

"Hullo, Denys," said Sir Geoffrey, who had lowered his *Times*. "I'm glad you've come."

"I think we all are," said Platt, taking Denys's elbow in a gentle, almost tender grasp. "Glad you've come."

He had almost not come. If it had been merely an address, a telephone number he'd been given, he might well not have; but the metal card with its brown strip was like a string tied round his finger, making it impossible to forget he had been invited. Don't lose it, Davenant had said. So it lay in his waistcoat pocket; he touched it whenever he reached for matches there; he tried shifting it to other pockets, but wherever it was on his person he felt it. In the end he decided to use it, as much to get rid of its importunity as for any other reason—so he told himself. On a wet afternoon he went to the place Davenant had told him of, the Orient Aid Society, and found it as described, a sooty French-Gothic building, one of those private houses turned to public use, with a discreet brass plaque by the door indicating that within some sort of business is done, one can't imagine what; and inside the double doors, in the vestibule, three telephone boxes, looking identical, the first of which had the nearly invisible slit by the door. His heart for some reason beat slow and hard as he inserted the card within this slot—it was immediately snatched away, like a ticket on the Underground—and entered the box and closed the door behind him.

Though nothing moved, he felt as though he had stepped onto a moving footpath, or onto one of those trick floors in a fun house that slide beneath one's feet. He was going somewhere. The sensation was awful. Beginning to panic, he tried to get out, not knowing whether that might be dangerous, but the door would not open, and its glass could not be seen out of either. It had been transparent from outside but was somehow opaque from within. He shook the door handle fiercely. At that moment the nonmobile motion reversed itself sickeningly, and the door opened. Denys stepped out, not into the vestibule of the Orient Aid Society, but into the foyer of a club. A dim, old-fashioned foyer, with faded Turkey carpet on the stairs, and an aged porter to greet him; a desk, behind which pigeonholes held members' mail; a stand of umbrellas. It was reassuring, almost absurdly so, the "then I woke up" of a silly ghost story. But Denys didn't feel reassured, or exactly awake either.

"Evening, sir."

"Good evening."

"Still raining, sir? Take your things?"

"Thank you."

A member was coming toward him down the long corridor: Platt.

"Sir?"

Denys turned back to the porter. "Your key, sir," the man said, and gave him back the metal plate with the strip of brown ribbon on it.

"Like a lift," Davenant told him as they sipped whiskey in the bar. "Alarming, somewhat, I admit; but imagine using a lift for the first time, not knowing what its function was. Closed inside a box; sensation of movement; the doors open, and you are somewhere else. Might seem odd. Well, this is the same. Only you're not somewhere else: not exactly."

"Hm," Denys said.

"Don't dismiss it, Sir Geoffrey," said Platt. "It *is* mighty odd." He said to Denys: "The paradox is acute: it is. Completely contrary to the usual cause-and-effect thinking we all do, can't stop doing really, no matter how hard we try to adopt other habits of mind. Strictly speaking it is unthinkable: unimaginable. And yet there it is."

"Yes," Davenant said. "To ignore, without ever forgetting, the heart of the matter: that's the trick. I've met monks, Japanese, Tibetan, who know the techniques. They can be learned."

"We speak of the larger paradox," Platt said to Denys. "The door you came in by being only a small instance. The great instance being, of course, the Otherhood's existence at all: we here now sitting and talking of it."

But Denys was not talking of it. He had nothing to say. To be told that in entering the telephone box in the Orient Aid Society he had effectively exited from time and entered a precinct outside it, revolving between the actual and the hypothetical, not quite existent despite the solidity of its parquet floor and the truthful bite of its whiskey; to be told that in these changeless and atemporal halls there gathered a society—"not quite a brotherhood," Davenant said; "that would be mawkish, and untrue of these chaps; we call it an Otherhood"—of men and women who by some means could insert themselves into the stream of the past, and with their foreknowledge alter it, and thus alter the future of that past, the future in which they themselves had their original being; that in effect the world Denys had come from, the world he knew, the year 1956, the whole course of things, the very cast and flavor of his memories, were dependent on the Fellows of this Society, and might change at any moment, though if they did he would know nothing of it; and that he was being asked to join them in their work—he heard the words, spoken to him with a frightening casualness;

he felt his mind fill with the notions, though not able to do anything that might be called thinking about them; and he had nothing to say.

"You can see," Sir Geoffrey said, looking not at Denys but into his whiskey, "why I didn't explain all this to you in Khartoum. The words don't come easily. Here, in the Club, outside all frames of reference, it's possible to explain. To describe, anyway. I suppose if we hadn't a place like this, we should all go mad."

"I wonder," said Platt, "whether we haven't, despite it." He looked at no one. "Gone mad, I mean."

For a moment no one spoke further. The barman glanced at them, to see if their silence required anything of him. Then Platt spoke again. "Of course there are restrictions," he said. "The chap who discovered it was possible to change one's place in time, an American, thought he had proved that it was only possible to displace oneself into the past. In a sense, he was correct. . . ."

"In a sense," Sir Geoffrey said. "Not quite correct. The possibilities are larger than he supposed. Or rather will suppose, all this from your viewpoint is still to happen—which widens the possibilities right there, you see, one man's future being as it were another man's past. (You'll get used to it, dear boy, shall we have another of these?) The past, as it happens, is the only sphere of time we have any interest in; the only sphere in which we can do good. So you see there are natural limits: the time at which this process was made workable is the forward limit; and the rear limit we have made the time of the founding of the Otherhood itself. By Cecil Rhodes's will, in 1893."

"Be pointless, you see, for the Fellows to go back before the Society existed," said Platt. "You can see that."

"One further restriction," said Sir Geoffrey. "A house rule, so to speak. We forbid a man to return to a time he has already visited, at least in the same part of the world. There is the danger—a moment's thought will show you I'm right—of bumping into oneself on a previous, or successive, mission. Unnerving, let me tell you. Unnerving completely. The trick is hard enough to master as it is."

Denys found voice. "Why?" he said. "And why me?"

"Why," said Sir Geoffrey, "is spelled out in our founding charter: to preserve and extend the British Empire in all parts of the world, and to strengthen it against all dangers. Next, to keep peace in the world, insofar as this is compatible with the first; our experience has been that it usually is the same thing. And lastly to keep fellowship among ourselves, this also subject to the first, though any conflict is unimaginable, I should hope, bickering aside."

"The Society was founded to be secret," Platt said. "Rhodes liked that idea—a sort of Jesuits of the Empire. In fact there was no real need for secrecy, not until—well, not until the Society became the Otherhood. This jaunting about in other people's histories would not be understood. So secrecy *is* important. Good thing on the whole that Rhodes insisted on it. And for sure he wouldn't have been displeased at the Society's scope. He wanted the world for England. And more. 'The moon, too,' he used to say. 'I often think of the moon.' "

"Few know of us even now," Sir Geoffrey said. "The Foreign Office, sometimes. The PM. Depending on the nature of H.M. Government at any moment, we explain more, or less. Never the part about time. That is for us alone to know. Though some have guessed a little, over the years. It's not even so much that we wish to act in secret—that was just Rhodes's silly fantasy—but well, it's just damned difficult to explain, don't you see?"

"And the Queen knows of us," Platt said. "Of course."

"I flew back with her, from Africa, that day," Davenant said. "After her father had died. I happened to be among the party. I told her a little then. Didn't want to intrude on her grief, but—it seemed the moment. In the air, over Africa. I explained more later. Plucky girl," he added. "Plucky." He drew his watch out. "And as for the second part of your question—why you?—I shall ask you to reserve that one, for a moment. We'll dine upstairs . . . Good heavens, look at the time."

Platt swallowed his drink hastily. "I remember Lord Cromer's words to us when I was a schoolboy at Leys," he said. " 'Love your country,' he said, 'tell the truth, and don't dawdle.' "

"Words to live by," Sir Geoffrey said, examining the bar chit doubtfully and fumbling for a pen.

The drapes were drawn in the executive dining room; the members of the executive committee were just taking their seats around a long mahogany table, scarred around its edge with what seemed to be initials and dates. The members were of all ages; some sunburned, some pale, some in evening clothes of a cut unfamiliar to Denys; among them were two Indians and a Chinaman. When they were all seated, Denys beside Platt, there were several seats empty. A tall woman with severe gray hair but eyes somehow kind took the head of the table.

"The President *pro tem*," she said as she sat, "is not returned, apparently, from his mission. I'll preside, if there are no objections."

"Oh, balls," said a broad-faced man with the tan of a cinema actor. "Don't give yourself airs, Huntington. Will we really need any presiding?"

"Might be a swearing-in," Huntington said mildly, pressing the bell beside her and not glancing at Denys. "In any case, best to keep up the forms. First order of business—the soup."

It was a mulligatawny, saffrony and various; it was followed by a whiting, and that by a baron of claret-colored beef. Through the clashings of silverware and crystal Denys listened to the table's talk, little enough of which he could understand: only now and then he felt—as though he were coming horribly in two—the import of the Fellows' conversation: that history was malleable, time a fiction; that nothing was necessarily as he supposed it must be. How could they bear that knowledge? How could he?

"Mr. Deng Fa-shen, there," Platt said quietly to him, "is our physicist. Orthogonal physics—as opposed to orthogonal logic—is his invention. What makes this club possible. The mechanics of it. Don't ask me to explain."

Deng Fa-shen was a fine-boned, parchment-colored man with gentle fox's eyes. Denys looked from him to the two Indians in silk. Platt said, as though reading Denys's thought: "The most disagreeable thing about old Rhodes and the Empire of his day was its racialism, of course. Absolutely unworkable, too. Nothing more impossible to sustain than a world order based on some race's supposed inherent superiority." He smiled. "It isn't the only part of Rhodes's scheme that's proved unworkable."

The informal talk began to assemble itself, with small nudges from the woman at the head of the table (who did her presiding with no pomp and few words), around a single date: 1914. Denys knew something of this date, though several of the place names spoken of (the Somme, Jutland, Gallipoli—wherever that was) meant nothing to him. Somehow, in some possible universe, 1914 had changed everything; the Fellows seemed intent on changing 1914, drawing its teeth, teeth that Denys had not known it had—or might still have once had: he felt again the sensation of coming in two, and sipped wine.

"Jutland," a Fellow was saying. "All that's needed is a bit more knowledge, a bit more jump on events. Instead of a foolish stalemate, it could be a solid victory. Then, blockade; war over in six months . . ."

"Who's our man in the Admiralty now? Carteret, isn't it? Can he—"

"Carteret," said the bronze-faced man, "was killed the last time around at Jutland." There was a silence; some of the Fellows seemed to be aware of this, and some taken by surprise. "Shows the foolishness of that kind of thinking," the man said. "Things have simply gone too far by then. That's my opinion."

Other options were put forward. That moment in what the Fellows called the Original Situation was searched for into which a small intrusion might be made, like a surgical incision, the smallest possible intrusion that would have the proper effect; then the succeeding Situation was searched, and the Situation following that, the Fellows feeling with enormous patience and care into the workings of the past and its possibilities, like a blind man weaving. At length a decision seemed to be made, without fuss or a vote taken, about this place Gallipoli, and a Turkish soldier named Mustapha Kemal, who would be apprehended and sequestered in a quick action that took or would take place there; the sun-bronzed man would see, or had seen, to it; and the talk, after a reflective moment, turned again to anecdote and speculation.

Denys listened to the stories, of desert treks and dangerous negotiations, men going into the wilderness of a past catastrophe with a precious load of penicillin or of knowledge, to save one man's life or end another's; to intercept one trivial telegram, get one bit of news through, deflect one column of troops—removing one card from the ever-building possible future of some past moment and seeing the whole of it collapse silently, unknowably, even as another was building, just as fragile but happier: he looked into the faces of the Fellows, knowing that no ruthless stratagem was beyond them, and yet knowing also that they were men of honor, with a great world's peace and benefit in their trust, though the world couldn't know it; and he felt an odd but deep thrill of privilege to be here now, wherever that was—the same sense of privilege that, as a boy, he had expected to feel (and as a man had laughed at himself for expecting to feel) upon being admitted to the ranks of those who—selflessly, though not without reward—had been chosen or had chosen themselves to serve the Empire. "The difference you make makes all the difference," his headmasterish commissioner was fond of telling Denys and his fellows; and it was a joke among them that, in their form-filling, their execution of tedious and sometimes absurd directives, they were following in the footsteps of Gordon and Milner, Warren Hastings and Raffles of Singapore. And yet—Denys perceived it with a kind of inward stillness, as though his heart flowed instead of beating—a difference *could* be made. Had been made. Went on being made, in many times and places, without fuss, without glory, with rewards for others that those others could not recognize or even imagine. He crossed his knife and fork on his plate and sat back slowly.

"This 1914 business has its tricksome aspects," Platt said to him. "Speaking in large terms, not enough can really be done within our time frames. The Situation that issues in war was firmly established well before: in the founding of the German Empire under Prussian leadership. Bismarck. There's the man to get to, or to his financiers, most of whom were Jewish—little did they know, and all that. Even Sedan is too late, and not enough seems to be able to be made, or unmade, out of the Dreyfus affair, though that *does* fall within our provenance. No," he said. "It's all just too long ago. If only . . . Well, no use speculating, is there? Make the best of it, and shorten the war; make it less catastrophic at any rate, a short, sharp shaking-out—above all, win it quickly. We must do the best we can."

He seemed unreconciled.

Denys said: "But I don't understand. I mean, of course I wouldn't expect to understand it as you do, but . . . well, you *did* do all that. I mean we studied 1914 in school—the guns of August and all that, the 1915 peace, the Monaco Conference. What I mean is . . ." He became conscious that the Fellows had turned their attention to him. No one else spoke. "What I mean to say is that *I* know you solved the problem, and how you solved it, in a general way; and I don't see why it remains to be solved. I don't see why you're worried." He laughed in embarrassment, looking around at the faces that looked at him.

"You're right," said Sir Geoffrey, "that you don't understand." He said it smiling, and the others were, if not smiling, patient and not censorious. "The logic of it is orthogonal. I can present you with an even more paradoxical instance. In fact I intend to present you with it; it's the reason you're here."

"The point to remember," the woman called Huntington said (as though to the whole table, but obviously for Denys's instruction), "is that here—in the Club—nothing has yet happened except the Original Situation. All is still to do: all that we have done, all still to do."

"Precisely," said Geoffrey. "All still to do." He took from his waistcoat pocket an eyeglass, polished it with his napkin, and inserted it between cheek and eyebrow. "You had a question, in the bar. You asked *why me*, meaning, I suppose, why is it you should be nominated to this Fellowship, why you and not another."

"Yes," said Denys. He wanted to go on, list what he knew of his inadequacies, but kept silent.

"Let me, before answering your question, ask you this," said Sir Geoffrey. "Supposing that you were chosen by good and sufficient standards—supposing that a list had been gone over carefully, and your name was weighed; supposing that a sort of competitive examination has been passed by you—would you then accept the nomination?"

"I—" said Denys. All eyes were on him, yet they were not somehow expectant; they awaited an answer they knew. Denys seemed to know it, too. He swallowed. "I hope I should," he said.

"Very well," Sir Geoffrey said softly. "Very well." He took a breath. "Then I shall tell you that you have in fact been chosen by good and sufficient standards. Chosen, moreover, for a specific mission, a mission of the greatest importance; a mission on which the very existence of the Otherhood depends. No need to feel flattered; I'm sure you're a brave lad, and all that, but the criteria were not entirely your sterling qualities, whatever they should later turn out to be.

"To explain what I mean, I must further acquaint you with what the oldest, or rather earliest, of the Fellows call the Original Situation.

"You recall our conversation in Khartoum. I told you no lie then; it is the case, in that very pleasant world we talked in, that good year 1956, fourth of a happy reign, on that wide veranda overlooking a world at peace—it is the case, I say, in that world and in most possible worlds like it, that Cecil Rhodes died young, and left the entire immense fortune he had won in the Scramble for the founding of a secret society, a society dedicated to the extension of that Empire which had his entire loyalty. The then Government's extreme confusion over this bequest, their eventual forming of a society—not without some embarrassment and doubt—a society from which this present Otherhood descends; still working toward the same ends, though the British Empire is not now what Rhodes thought it to be, nor the world either in which it has its hegemony—well, one of the Fellows is working up or will work up that story, insofar as it can be told, and it is, as I say, a true one.

"But there is a situation in which it is not true. In that situation which we call Original—the spine of time from which all other possibilities fluoresce—Cecil Rhodes, it appears, changed his mind."

Sir Geoffrey paused to light a cigar. The port was passed him. A cloud of smoke issued from his mouth. "Changed his mind, you see," he said, dispersing the smoke with a wave. "He did not die young, he lived on. His character mellowed, perhaps, as the years fell away; his fortune certainly diminished. It may be that Africa disappointed him, finally; his scheme to take over Tanganyika and join the Cape-to-Cairo with a single All-Red railroad line had ended in failure . . ."

Denys opened his mouth to speak; he had only a week before taken that line. He shut his mouth again.

"Whatever it was," Sir Geoffrey said, "he changed his mind. His last will left his fortune—what was left of it—to his old university, a scholarship fund to allow Americans and others of good character to study in England. No secret society. No Otherhood."

There was a deep silence at the table. No one had altered his casual position, yet there was a stillness of utter attention. Someone poured for Denys, and the liquid rattle of port into his glass was loud.

"Thus the paradox," Sir Geoffrey said. "For it is only the persuasions of the Otherhood that alter this Original Situation. The Otherhood must reach its fingers into the past, once we have learned how to do so; we must send our agents down along the defiles of time and intercept our own grandfather there, at the very moment when he is about to turn away from the work of generating us.

"And persuade him not to, you see; cause him—cause him not to turn away from that work of generation. Yes, cause him not to turn away. And thus ensure our own eventual existence."

Sir Geoffrey pushed back his chair and rose. He turned toward the sideboard, then back again to Denys. "Did I hear you say 'That's madness'?" he asked.

"No," Denys said.

"Oh," Sir Geoffrey said. "I thought you spoke. Or thought I remembered you speaking." He turned again to the sideboard, and returned again to the table with his cigar clenched in his teeth and a small box in his hands. He put this on the table. "You do follow me thus far," he said, his hands on the box and his eyes regarding Denys from under their curling brows.

"Follow you?"

"The man had to die," Sir Geoffrey said. He unlatched the box. "It was his moment. The moment you will find in any biography of him you pick up. Young, or anyway not old; at the height of his triumphs. It would have been downhill for him from there anyway."

"How," Denys asked, and something in his throat intruded on the question; it was a moment before he could complete it: "How did he die?"

"Oh, various ways," Sir Geoffrey said. "In the most useful version, he was shot to death by a young man he'd invited up to his house at Cape Town. Shot twice, in the heart, with a Webley .38-caliber revolver." He took from the box this weapon, and placed it with its handle toward Denys.

"That's madness," Denys said. His hands lay along the arms of his chair, drawing back from the gun. "You can't mean to say you went back and *shot* him, you . . ."

"Not we, dear boy," Sir Geoffrey said. "We, generally, yes; but specifically, not we. You."

"No."

"Oh, you won't be alone—not initially, at least. I can explain why it must be you and not another; I can expound the really quite dreadful paradox of it further, if you think it would help, though it seems to me best if, for now, you simply take our word for it."

Denys felt the corners of his mouth draw down, involuntarily, tightly; his lower lip wanted to tremble. It was a sign he remembered from early childhood: what had usually followed it was a fit of truculent weeping. That could not follow, here, now: and yet he dared not allow himself to speak, for fear he would be unable. For some time, then, no one spoke.

At the head of the table Huntington pushed her empty glass away.

"Mr. Winterset," she said gently. "I wonder if I might put in a word. Sit down, Davenant, will you, just for a moment, and stop looming over us. With your permission, Mr. Winterset—Denys—I should like to describe to you a little more broadly that condition of the world we call the Original Situation."

She regarded Denys with her sad eyes, then closed her fingers together before her. She began to speak, in a low voice which more than once Denys had to lean forward to catch. She told about Rhodes's last sad bad days; she told of Rhodes's chum, the despicable Dr. Jameson, and his infamous raid and the provocations that led to war with the Boers; of the shame of that war, the British defeats and the British atrocities, the brutal intransigence of both sides. She told how in those same years the European powers who confronted each other in Africa were also at work stockpiling arms and building mechanized armies of a size unheard of in the history of the world, to be finally let loose upon one another in August of 1914, unprepared for what was to become of them; armies officered by men who still lived in the previous century, but armed with weapons more dreadful than they could imagine. The machine gun: no one seemed to understand that the machine gun had changed war forever, and though the junior officers and Other Ranks soon learned it, the commanders never did. At the First Battle of the Somme wave after wave of British soldiers were sent against German machine guns, to be mown down like grain. There were a quarter of a million casualties in that battle. And yet the generals went on ordering massed attacks against machine guns for the four long years of the war.

"But they knew," Denys could not help saying. "They did know. Machine guns had been used against massed native armies for years, all over the Empire. In Afghanistan. In the Sudan. Africa. They knew."

"Yes," Huntington said. "They knew. And yet, in the Original Situation, they paid no attention. They went blindly on and made their dreadful mistakes. Why? How could they be so stupid, those generals and statesmen who in the world you knew behaved so wisely and so well? For one reason only: they lacked the help and knowledge of a group of men and women who had seen all those mistakes made, who could act in secret on what they knew, and who had the ear and the confidence of one of the governments—not the least stupid of them, either, mind you. And with all our help it was still a close-run thing."

"Damned close-run," Platt put in. "Still hangs in the balance, in fact."

"Let me go on," Huntington said.

She went on: long hands folded before her, eyes now cast down, she told how at the end a million men, a whole generation, lay dead on the European battlefield, among them men whom Denys might think the modern world could not have been made without. A grotesque tyranny calling itself Socialist had been imposed on a war-weakened Russian empire. Only the intervention of a fully mobilized United States had finally broken the awful deadlock—thereby altering the further history of the world unrecognizably. She told how the vindictive settlement inflicted on a ruined Germany (so unlike the wise dispositions of the Monaco Conference, which had simply reestablished the old pre-Bismarck patchwork of German states and princedoms) had rankled in the German spirit; how a madman had arisen and, almost unbelievably, had ridden a wave of resentment and anti-Jewish hysteria to dictatorship.

"Yes," Denys said. "*That* we didn't escape, did we? I remember that, or almost remember it; it was just before I can remember anything. Anti-Jewish riots all over Germany."

"Yes," said Huntington softly.

"Yes. Terrible. These nice funny Germans, all lederhosen and cuckoo clocks, and suddenly they show a terrible dark side. Thousands of Jews, some of them very highly placed, had to leave Germany. They lost everything. Synagogues attacked, professors fired. Even Einstein, I think, had to leave Germany for a time."

Huntington let him speak. When Denys fell silent, unable to remember more and feeling the eyes of the Fellows on him, Huntington began again. But the things she began to tell of now simply could not have happened, Denys thought; no, they were part of a monstrous, foul dream, atrocities on a scale only a psychopath could conceive, and only the total resources of a strong and perverted science achieve. When Einstein came again into the tale, and the world Huntington described drifted ignorantly and inexorably into an icy and permanent stalemate that could be broken only by the end of civilization, perhaps of life itself, Denys found a loathsome surfeit rising in his throat; he covered his face, he would hear no more.

"So you see," Huntington said, "why we think it possible that the life—nearly over, in any case—of one egotistical, racialist adventurer is worth the chance to alter that situation." She raised her eyes to Denys. "I don't say you need agree. There *is* a sticky moral question, and I don't mean to brush it aside. I only say you see how we might think so."

Denys nodded slowly. He reached out and put his hand on the pistol that had been placed before him. He lifted his eyes and met those of Sir Geoffrey Davenant, which still smiled, though his mouth and his mustaches were grave.

What they were all telling him was that he could help create a better world than the original, which Huntington had described; but that was not how Denys perceived it. What Denys perceived was that reality—reality, the world he had come from, reality sun-shot and whole—was somehow under threat from a disgusting nightmare of death, ignorance, and torture, which could invade and replace it forever unless he acted. He did not think himself capable of interfering with the world to make it better; but to defend the world he knew, the world that with all its shortcomings was life and sustenance and sense and cleanly wakefulness—yes, that he could do. Would do, with all his strength.

Which is why, of course, it was he who had been chosen to do it. He saw that in Davenant's eyes.

And of course, if he refused, he could not then be brought here to be asked. If it was now possible for him to be asked to do this by the Otherhood, then he must have already consented, and done it. That, too, was in Davenant's silence. Denys looked down. His hand was on the Webley; and beside it, carved by a penknife into the surface of the table, almost obscured by later waxings, were the neat initials *D.W.*

"I always remember what Lord Milner said," Platt spoke into his ear. "*Everyone can help.*"

V: THE TEARS OF THE PRESIDENT *PRO TEM*

"I remember," the President *pro tem* of the Otherhood said, "the light: a very clear, very pure, very cool light that seemed somehow potent but reserved, as though it could do terrible blinding things, and give an unbearable heat, if it chose—well, I'm not quite sure what I mean."

There was a midnight fug in the air of the library where the President *pro tem* retold his tale. The Magus to whom he told it did not look at him; his pale gray eyes moved from object to object around the room in the aimless idiot wandering that had at first caused the President *pro tem* to believe him blind.

"The mountain was called Table Mountain—a sort of high mesa. What a place that was then—I think the most beautiful in the Empire, and young then, but not raw; a peninsula simply made to put a city on, and a city being put there, beneath the mountain: and this piercing light.

"Our party put up at the Mount Nelson Hotel, perhaps a little grand for the travelers in electroplating equipment we were pretending to be, but the incognito wasn't really important, it was chiefly to explain the presence of the Last equipment among the luggage.

"A few days were spent in reconnaissance. But you see—this is continually the impossible thing to explain—in a sense those of the party who knew the outcome were only going through the motions of conferring, mapping their victim's movements, choosing a suitable moment and all that: for they knew the story; there was only one way for it to happen, if it was to happen at all. If it was *not* to happen, then no one could predict what was to happen instead; but so long as our party was there, and preparing it, it would evidently have to happen—or would have to have had to have happened."

The President *pro tem* suddenly missed his old friend Davenant, Davenant the witty and deep, who never bumbled over his tenses, never got himself stuck in a sentence such as that one; Davenant lost now with the others in the interstices of imaginary pasthood—or rather about to be lost, in the near future, if the President *pro tem* assented to what was asked of him. "It was rather jolly," he said, "like a game rather, striving to bring about a result that you were sure had already been brought about; an old ritual, if you like, to which not much importance needed to be attached, so long as it was all done correctly . . ."

"I think," said the Magus, "you need not explain these feelings that you then had."

"Sorry," said the President *pro tem*. "The house was called Groote Schuur—

that was the old Dutch name, which he'd revived, for a big granary that had stood on the property; the English had called it the Grange. It was built on the lower slopes of Devil's Peak, with a view up to the mountains, and out to sea as well. He'd only recently seen the need for a house—all his life in Africa he'd more or less pigged it in rented rooms, or stayed in his club or a hotel or even a tent pitched outside town. For a long time he roomed with Dr. Jameson, sleeping on a little truckle bed hardly big enough for his body. But now that he'd become Prime Minister, he felt it was time for something more substantial.

"It seemed to me that it would have been easier to take him out in the bush—the *bundas;* as the Matabele say. Hire a party of natives—wait till all are asleep—ambush. He often went out into the wilds with almost no protection. There was no question of honor involved—I mean, the man had to die, one way or the other, and the more explainably or accidentally the better. But I was quite wrong—I was myself, still young—and had to be put right: the one time that way was tried, the assassination initiated a punitive war against the native populations that lasted for twenty years, which ended only with the virtual extermination of the Matabele and Mashona peoples. Dreadful.

"No, it had to be the house; moreover, it had to be within a very brief span of time—a time when we knew he was there, when we knew where his will was, and *which* will it was—he made eight or nine in his lifetime—and when we knew, also, what assets were in his hands. Business and ownership were fluid things in those days; his partners were quick and subtle men; his sudden death might lose us all that we were intending to acquire by it in the way of a campaign chest, so to speak.

"So it had to be the house, in this week of this year, on this night. In fact orthogonal logic dictated it. Davenant was quite calmly sure of that. After all, that was the night when it had happened: and for sure we ought not to miss it."

That was an attempt at the sort of remark Davenant might make, and the President *pro tem* smiled at the Magus, who remained unmoved. The President *pro tem* thought it impossible that beings as wise as he knew the one before him to be, no matter how grave, could altogether lack any sense of humor. For himself, he had often thought that if he did not find funny the iron laws of orthogony he would go mad; but his jokes apparently amused only himself.

"It was not a question of getting to his house, or into it; he practically kept open house the year round, and his grounds could be walked upon by anyone. The gatekeepers were only instructed to warn walkers about the animals they might come across—he had brought in dozens of species, and he allowed all but the genuinely dangerous to roam at will. Wildebeest. Zebras. Impala. And 'human beings,' as he always called them, roamed at will, too; there were always some about. At dinner he had visitors from all over Africa, and from England and Europe as well; his bedrooms were often full. I think he hated to be alone. All of which provided a fine setting, you see, for a sensational—and insoluble—murder mystery: if only the man could be got alone, and escape made good then through these crowds of hangers-on.

"Our plan depended on a known proclivity of his, or rather two proclivities. The first was a taste he had for the company of a certain sort of a young man. He liked having them around him and could become very attached to them. There was never a breath of scandal in this—well, there was talk, but only talk. His 'angels,' people called them: good-looking, resourceful if not particularly bright, good all-rounders with a rough sense of fun—practical jokes, horseplay—

but completely devoted and ready for anything he might ask them to do. He had a fair crowd of these fellows up at Groote Schuur just then. Harry Curry, his private secretary. Johnny Grimmer, a trooper who was never afraid to give him orders—like a madman's keeper, some people said, scolding him and brushing dust from his shoulders; he never objected. Bob Coryndon, another trooper. They'd all just taken on a butler for themselves, a sergeant in the Inniskillings: good-looking chap, twenty-three years old. Oddly, they had all been just that age when he'd taken an interest in them: twenty-three. Whether that was chance or his conscious choice we didn't know.

"The other proclivity was his quickness in decision-making. And this often involved the young men. The first expedition into Matabeleland had been headed up by a chap he'd met at his club one morning at breakfast just as the column was preparing for departure. Took to the chap instantly: liked his looks, liked his address. Gave him the job on the spot.

"That had worked out very well, of course—his choices often did. The pioneer column had penetrated into the heart of the *bundas*, the flag was flying over a settlement they called Fort Salisbury, and the whole of Matabeleland was in the process of being added to the Empire. Up at Groote Schuur they were kicking around possible names for the new country: Rhodia, perhaps, or Rhodesland, even Cecilia. It was that night that they settled on Rhodesia."

The President *pro tem* felt a moment's shame. There had been, when it came down to it, no doubt in his mind that what they had done had been the right thing to do: and in any case it had all happened a long time ago, more than a century ago in fact. It was not what was done, or that it had been done, only the moment of its doing, that was hard to relate: it was the picture in his mind, of an old man (though he was only forty-eight, he looked far older) sitting in the lamplight reading *The Boy's Own Paper*, as absorbed and as innocent in his absorption as a boy himself; and the vulnerable shine on his balding crown; and the tender and indifferent night: it was all that which raised a lump in the throat of the President *pro tem* and caused him to pause, and roll the tip of his cigar in the ashtray, and clear his throat before continuing.

"And so," he said, "we baited our hook. Rhodes's British South Africa Company was expanding, in the wake of the Fort Salisbury success. He was on the lookout for young men of the right sort. We presented him with one: good-looking lad, public school, cricketer; just twenty-three years old. He was the bait. The mole. The Judas."

And the bait had been taken, of course. The arrangement's having been keyed so nicely to the man's nature, a nature able to be studied from the vantage point of several decades on, it could hardly have failed. That the trick seemed so fragile, even foolish, something itself out of *The Boy's Own Paper* or a story by Henley, only increased the likelihood of its striking just the right note here: the colored fanatic, Rhodes leaving his hotel after luncheon to return to Parliament, the thug stepping out of the black noon shadows with a knife just as Rhodes mounts his carriage steps—then the young man, handily by with a stout walking stick (a gift of his father upon his departure for Africa)—the knife deflected, the would-be assassin slinking off, the great man's gratitude. You must have some reward. Not a bit, sir, anyone would have done the same; just lucky I was nearby. Come to dinner at any rate—my house on the hill—anyone can direct you. Allow me to introduce myself; my name is . . .

No need, sir, everyone knows Cecil Rhodes.

And your name is . . .

The clean hand put frankly forward, the tanned, open, boyish face smiling. My name is Denys Winterset.

"So then you see," the President *pro tem* said, "the road was open. The road up to Groote Schuur. The road that branches, in effect, to lead here: to us here now speaking of it."

"And how many times since then," the Magus said, "has the world branched? How many times has it been bent double, and broken? A thousand times, ten thousand? Each time growing smaller, having to be packed into lesser space, curling into itself like a snail's shell; growing ever weaker as the changes multiply, and more liable to failure of its fabric: how many times?"

The President *pro tem* answered nothing.

"You understand, then," the Magus said to him, "what you will be asked: to find the crossroads that leads this way and to turn the world from it."

"Yes."

"And how will you reply?"

The President *pro tem* had no better answer for this question, and he gave none. He had begun to feel at once heavy as lead and disembodied. He arose from his armchair, with some effort, and crossed the worn Turkish carpet to the tall window.

"You must leave my house now," the Magus said, rising from his chair. "There is much for me to do this night, if this world is to pass out of existence."

"Where shall I go?"

"They will find you. I think in not too long a time." Without looking back he left the room.

The President *pro tem* pushed aside the heavy drape the draconic had drawn. *Where shall I go?* He looked out the window into the square outside, deserted at this late and rainy hour. It was an irregular square, the intersection of three streets, filled with rain-wet cobbles as though with shiny eggs. It was old; it had been the view out these windows for two centuries at the least; there was nothing about it to suggest that it had not been the intersection of three streets for a good many more centuries than that.

And yet it had not been there at all only a few decades earlier, when the President *pro tem* had last walked the city outside the Orient Aid Society. Then the city had been London; it was no more. These three streets, these cobbles, had not been there in 1983; nor in 1893 either. Yet there they were, somewhere early in the twenty-first century; there they had been, too, for time out of mind, familiar no doubt to any dweller in this part of town, familiar for that matter to the President *pro tem* who looked out at them. In each of two lamp-lit cafés on two corners of the square, a man in a soft cap held a glass and looked out into the night, unsurprised, at home.

Someone had broken the rules: there simply was no other explanation.

There had been, of course, no way for anyone, not Deng Fa-shen, not Davenant, not the President *pro tem* himself, to guess what the President *pro tem* might come upon on this, the first expedition the Otherhood was making into the future: not only did the future not exist (Deng Fa-shen was quite clear about that), but, as Davenant reminded him, the Otherhood itself, supposing the continued existence of the Otherhood, would no doubt go busily on changing things in the past far and near—shifting the ground therefore of the future the President *pro tem* was headed for. Deng Fa-shen was satisfied that that future, the ultimate future, sum of all intermediate revisions, was the only one that could be plumbed, if any could; and that was the only one the Otherhood would want to glimpse: to learn how they would do, or would come to have done; to find out, as George V whispered on his death-bed, "How is the Empire."

("Only that isn't what he said," Davenant was fond of telling. "That's what he was, understandably, reported to have said, and what the Queen and the nurses convinced themselves they heard. But he was a bit dazed there at the end, poor good old man. What he said was not 'How is the Empire,' but 'What's at the Empire,' a popular cinema. I happened," he always added gravely, "to have been with him.")

The first question had been how far "forward" the Otherhood should press; those members who thought the whole scheme insane, as Platt did, voted for next Wednesday, and bring back the Derby winners please. Deng Fa-shen was not certain the thrust could be entirely calculated: the imaginary futures of imaginary pasts were not, he thought, likely to be under the control of even the most penetrating orthogonal engineering. Sometime in the first decades of the next century was at length agreed upon, a time just beyond the voyager's own mortal span—for the house rule seemed, no one could say quite why, to apply in both directions—and for as brief a stay as was consistent with learning what was up.

The second question—who was to be the voyager—the President *pro tem* had answered by fiat, assuming an executive privilege he just at that moment claimed to exist, and cutting off further debate. (Why exactly did he insist? I'm not certain why, except that it was not out of a sense of adventure, or of fun or curiosity: whatever of those qualities he may once have had had been much worn away in his rise to the Presidency *pro tem* of the Otherhood. A sense of duty may have been part of it. It may have been to forestall the others, out of a funny sort of premonition. Duty, and premonition: of what, though? Of what?)

"It'll be quite different from any of our imaginings, you know," Davenant said, who for some reason had not vigorously contested the President's decision. "The future of all possible pasts. I envy you, I do. I should rather like to see it for myself."

Quite different from any of our imaginings: very well. The President *pro tem* had braced himself for strangeness. What he had not expected was familiarity. Familiarity—cozy as an old shoe—was certainly different from his imaginings.

And yet what was it he was familiar with? He had stepped out of his club in London and found himself to be, not in the empty corridors of the Orient Aid Society that he knew well, but in private quarters of some kind that he had never seen before. It reminded him, piercingly, of a place he did know, but what place he could not have said: some don's rich but musty rooms, some wealthy and learned bachelor's digs. How had it come to be?

And how had it come to be lit by gas?

One of the pleasant side effects (most of the members thought it pleasant) of the Otherhood's endless efforts in the world had been a general retardation in the rate of material progress: so much of that progress had been, on the one hand, the product of the disastrous wars that it was the Otherhood's chief study to prevent, and on the other hand, American. The British Empire moved more slowly, a great beast without predators, and naturally conservative; it clung to proven techniques and could impose them on the rest of the world by its weight. The telephone, the motor car, the flying boat, the wireless, all were slow to take root in the Empire that the Otherhood shaped. And yet surely, the President *pro tem* thought, electricity was in general use in London in 1893, before which date no member could alter the course of things. And gas lamps lit this place.

Pondering this, the President *pro tem* had entered the somber and apparently little-used dining room and seen the draconic standing in the little butler's pantry: silent as a statue (asleep, the President *pro tem* would later deduce, with lidless eyes only seeming to be open); a polishing-cloth in his claw, and the silver before him; his heavy jaws partly open, and his weight balanced on the thick stub of tail. He wore a baize apron and black sleeve garters to protect his clothes.

Quite different from our imaginings: and yet no conceivable amount of tinkering with the twentieth century, just beyond which the President *pro tem* theoretically stood, could have brought forth this butler, in wing collar and green apron, the soft gaslight ashine on his bald brown head.

So someone had broken the rules. Someone had dared to regress beyond 1893 and meddle in the farther past. That was not, in itself, impossible; Caspar Last had done it on his first and only excursion. It had only been thought impossible for the Otherhood to do it, because it would have taken them "back" before the Otherhood's putative existence, and therefore before the Otherhood could have wrested the techniques of such travel from Last's jealous grip, a power they acquired by already having it—that was what the President *pro tem* had firmly believed.

But it was not, apparently, so. Somewhen in that stretch of years that fell between his entrance into the telephone box of the Club and his exit from it into this familiar and impossible world, someone—many someones, or someone many times—had gone "back" far before Rhodes's death: had gone back far enough to initiate this house, this city, these races who were not men.

A million years? It couldn't have been less. It didn't seem possible it could be less.

And who, then? Deng Fa-shen, the delicate, brilliant Chinaman, who had thoughts and purposes he kept to himself; the only one of them who might have been able to overcome the theoretical limits? Or Platt, who was never satisfied with what was possible within what he called "the damned parameters"?

Or Davenant. Davenant, who was forever quoting Khayyám: *Ah, Love, couldst thou and I with Him conspire To take this sorry scheme of things entire; Would we not smash it into pieces, then Remold it nearer to the heart's desire . . .*

"There is," said the Magus behind him, "one other you have not thought of."

The President *pro tem* let fall the drape and turned from the window. The Magus stood in the doorway, a great ledger in his arms. His eyes did not meet the President *pro tem*'s, and yet seemed to regard him anyway, like the blind eyes of a statue.

One other . . . Yes, the President *pro tem* saw, there *was* one other who might have done this. One other, not so good at the work perhaps as others, as Davenant for example, but who nonetheless would have been, or would come to have been, in a position to take such steps. The President *pro tem* would not have credited himself with the skill, or the nerve, or the dreadnought power. But how else to account for the familiarity, the bottomless *suitability* to him of this world he had never before seen?

"Between the time of your people's decision to plumb our world," said the Magus, "and the time of your standing here within it, you must yourself have brought it into being. I see no likelier explanation."

The President *pro tem* stood still with wonder at the efforts he was apparently to prove capable of making. A million years at least: a million years. How had he known where to begin? Where had he found, would he find, the time?

"Shall I ring," the Magus said, "or will you let yourself out?"

• • •

Deng Fa-shen had always said it, and anyone who traveled in them knew it to be so: the imaginary futures and imaginary pasts of orthogony are imaginary only in the sense that imaginary numbers (which they very much resemble) are imaginary. To a man walking within one, it alone is real, no matter how strange; it is all the others, standing at angles to it, which exist only in imagination. Nightlong the President *pro tem* walked the city, with a measured and unhurried step, but with a constant tremor winding round his rib cage, waiting for what would become of him, and observing the world he had made.

Of course it could not continue to exist. It should not ever have come into existence in the first place; his own sin (if it had been his) had summoned it out of nonbeing, and his repentance must expunge it. The Magus who had taken his confession (which the President *pro tem* had been unable to withhold from him) had drawn that conclusion: it must be put out, like a light. And yet how deeply the President *pro tem* wanted it to last forever; how deeply he believed it *ought* to last forever.

The numinous and inhuman angels, about whom nothing could be said, beings with no ascertainable business among the lesser races and yet beings without whom, the President *pro tem* was sure, this world could not go on functioning. They lived (endless?) lives unimaginable to men, and perhaps to Magi, too, who yet sought continually for knowledge of them: Magi, highest of the hominids, gentle and wise yet inflexible of purpose, living in simplicity and solitude (Were there females? Where? Doing what?) and yet from their shabby studies influencing, perhaps directing, the lives of mere men. The men, such as himself, clever and busy, with their inventions and their politics and their affairs. The lesser hominids, strong, sweet-natured, comic, like placid trolls. The draconics.

It was not simply a world inhabited by intelligent races of different kinds: it was a harder thing to grasp than that. The lives of the races constituted different universes of meaning, different constructions of reality; it was as though four or five different novels, novels of different kinds by different and differently limited writers, were to become interpenetrated and conflated: inside a gigantic Russian thing a stark and violent *policier*, and inside that something Dickensian, full of plot, humors, and eccentricity. Such an interlacing of mutually exclusive universes might be comical, like a sketch in *Punch*; it might be tragic, too. And it might be neither: it might simply be what is, the given against which all airy imaginings must finally be measured: reality.

Near dawn the President *pro tem* stood leaning on a parapet of worked stone that overlooked a streetcar roundabout. A car had just ended its journey there, and the conductor and the motorman descended, squat hominids in great-coats and peaked caps. With their long strong arms they began to swing the car around for its return journey. The President *pro tem* gazed down at this commonplace sight; his nose seemed to know the smell of that car's interior, his bottom to know the feel of its polished seats. But he knew also that yesterday there had not been streetcars in this city. Today they had been here for decades.

No, it was no good, the President *pro tem* knew: the fabric of this world he had made—if it had been he—was fatally weakened with irreality. It was a botched job: as though he were that god of the Gnostics who made the material world, a minor god unversed in putting time together with space. He had not worked well. And how could he have supposed it would be otherwise? What had got into him, that he had dared?

"No," said the angel who stood beside him. "You should not think that it was you."

"If not me," said the President *pro tem,* "then who?"

"Come," said the angel. She (I shall say "she") slipped a small cool hand within his hand. "Let's go over the tracks, and into the trees beyond that gate."

A hard and painful stone had formed in the throat of the President *pro tem.* The angel beside him led him like a daughter, like the daughter of old blind Oedipus. Within the precincts of the park—which apparently had its entrance or its entrances where the angels needed them to be—he was led down an avenue of yew and dim towers of poplar toward the piled and sounding waters of a fountain. They sat together on the fountain's marble lip.

"The Magus told me," the President *pro tem* began, "that you can feel the alterations that we make, back then. Is that true?"

"It's like the snap of a whip infinitely long," the angel said. "The whole length of time snapped and laid out differently: not only the length of time backward to the time of the change, but the length of the future forward. We felt ourselves, come into being, oldest of the Old Races (though the last your changes brought into existence); we saw in that moment the aeons of our past, and we guessed our future, too."

The President *pro tem* took out his pocket handkerchief and pressed it to his face. He must weep, yet no tears came.

"We love this world—this only world—just as you do," she said. "We love it, and we cannot bear to feel it sicken and fail. Better that it not have been than that it die."

"I shall do all I can," said the President *pro tem.* "I shall find who has done this—I suppose I know who it was, if it wasn't me—and dissuade him. Teach him, teach him what I've learned, make him see . . ."

"You don't yet understand," the angel said with careful kindness but at the same time glancing at her wristwatch. "There is no one to tell. There is no one who went beyond the rules."

"There must have been," said the President *pro tem.* "You, your time, it just isn't that far along from ours, from mine! To make this world, this city, these races . . ."

"Not far along in time," said the angel, "but many times removed. You know it to be so: whenever you, your Otherhood, set out across the timelines, your passage generated random variation in the worlds you arrived in. Perhaps you didn't understand how those variations accumulate, here at the sum end of your journeyings."

"But the changes were so minute!" said the President *pro tem.* "Deng Fa-shen explained it. A molecule here and there, no more; the position of a distant star; some trivial thing, the name of a flower or a village. Too few, too small even to notice."

"They increase exponentially with every alteration—and your Otherhood has been busy since you last presided over them. Through the days random changes accumulate, tiny errors silting up like the blown sand that fills the streets of a desert city, that buries it at last."

"But why these changes?" asked the President *pro tem* desperately. "It can't have been chance that a world like this was the sum of those histories, it can't be. A world like *this* . . . "

"Chance, perhaps. Or it may be that as time grows softer the world grows more malleable by wishes. There is no reason to believe this, yet that is what we believe. You—all of you—could not have known that you were bringing this world into being; and yet this is the world you wanted."

She reached out to let the tossed foam of the fountain fall into her hand. The President *pro tem* thought of the bridge over the Zambezi, far away; the tossed foam of the Falls. It was true: this is what they had striven for: a world of perfect hierarchies, of no change forever. God, how they must have longed for it! The loneliness of continual change—no outback, no *bundas* so lonely. He had heard how men can be unsettled for days, for weeks, who have lived through earthquakes and felt the earth to be uncertain: what of his Fellows, who had felt time and space picked apart, never to be rewoven that way again, and not once but a hundred times? What of himself?

"I shall tell you what I see at the end of all your wishings," said the angel softly. "At the far end of the last changed world, after there is nothing left that can change. There is then only a forest, growing in the sea. I say 'forest' and I say 'sea,' though whether they are of the kind I know, or some other sort of thing, I cannot say. The sea is still and the forest is thick; it grows upward from the black bottom, and its topmost branches reach into the sunlight, which penetrates a little into the warm upper waters. That's all. There is nothing else anywhere forever. Your wishes have come true: the Empire is quiet. There is not, nor will there be, change anymore; never will one thing be confused again with another; higher for lower, better for lesser, master for servant. Perpetual Peace."

The President *pro tem* was weeping now, painful sobs drawn up from an interior he had long kept shut and bolted. Tears ran down his cheeks, into the corners of his mouth, under his hard collar. He knew what he must do, but not how to do it.

"The Otherhood cannot be dissuaded from this," the angel said, putting a hand on the wrist of the President *pro tem*. "For all of it, including our sitting here now, all of it—and the forest in the sea—is implicit in the very creation of the Otherhood itself."

"But then . . ."

"Then the Otherhood must be uncreated."

"I can't do that."

"You must."

"No, no, I can't." He had withdrawn from her pellucid gaze, horrified. "I mean it isn't because . . . if it must be done, it must be. But not by me."

"Why?"

"It would be against the rules given me. I don't know what the result would be. I can't imagine. I don't *want* to imagine."

"Rules?"

"The Otherhood came into being," said the President *pro tem*, "when a British adventurer, Cecil Rhodes, was shot and killed by a young man called Denys Winterset."

"Then you must return and stop that killing."

"But you don't see!" said the President *pro tem* in great distress. "The rules given the Otherhood forbid a Fellow from returning to a time and place that he formerly altered by his presence . . ."

"And . . ."

"And I am myself that same Denys Winterset."

The angel regarded the President *pro tem*—the Honorable Denys Winterset, fourteenth President *pro tem* of the Otherhood—and her translucent face registered a sweet surprise, as though the learning of something she had not known gave her pleasure. She laughed, and her laughter was not different from the plashing of the fountain by which they sat. She laughed and laughed, as the old man in his black coat and hat sat silent beside her, bewildered and afraid.

VI: THE BOY DAVID OF HYDE PARK CORNER

There are days when I seem genuinely to remember, and days when I do not remember at all: days when I remember only that sometimes I remember. There are days on which I think I recognize another like myself: someone walking smartly along the Strand or Bond Street, holding the *Times* under one arm and walking a furled umbrella with the other—a sort of military bearing, mustaches white (older than when I seem to have known him, but then so am I, of course), and cheeks permanently tanned by some faraway sun. I do not catch his eye, nor he mine, though I am tempted to stop him, to ask him . . . Later on I wonder—if I can remember to wonder—whether he, too, is making a chronicle, in his evenings, writing up the story: a story that can be told in any direction, starting from anywhen, leading on to a forest in the sea.

I won't look any longer into this chronicle I've compiled. I shall only complete it.

My name is Denys Winterset. I was born in London in 1933; I was the only son of a Harley Street physician, and my earliest memory is of coming upon my father in tears in his surgery: he had just heard the news that the R101 dirigible had crashed on its maiden flight, killing all those aboard.

We lived then above my father's offices, in a little building whose nursery I remember distinctly, though I was taken to the country with the other children of London when I was only six, and that building was knocked down by a bomb in 1940. A falling wall killed my mother; my father was on ambulance duty in the East End and was spared.

He didn't know quite what to do with me, nor I with myself; I have been torn all my life between the drive to discover what others whom I love and admire expect of me, and my discovery that then I don't want to do it, really. After coming down from the University I decided, out of a certain perversity which my father could not sympathize with, to join the Colonial Service. He could not fathom why I would want to fasten myself to an enterprise that everyone save a few antediluvian colonels and letter writers to the *Times* could see was a dead animal. And I couldn't explain. Psychoanalysis later suggested that it was quite simply because no one wanted me to do it. The explanation has since come to seem insufficient to me.

That was a strange late blooming of Empire in the decade after the war, when the Colonial Office took on factitious new life, and thousands of us went out to the Colonies. The Service became larger than it had been in years, swollen with ex-officers too accustomed to military life to do anything else, and with the innocent and the confused, like myself. I ended up a junior member of a transition team in a Central African country I shall not name, helping see to it that as much was given to the new native government as they could be persuaded to accept, in the way of a parliament, a well-disciplined army, a foreign service, a judiciary.

It was not after all very much. Those institutions that the British are sure no civilized nation can do without were, in the minds of many Africans who spoke freely to me, very like those exquisite japanned toffee-boxes from Fortnum & Mason that you used often to come across in native kraals, because the chieftains and shamans loved them so, to keep their juju in. Almost as soon as I arrived, it became evident that the commander in chief of the armed forces was impatient with the pace of things, and felt the need of no special transition to African, i.e., his own, control of the state. The most our Commission were likely to accomplish was to get the British population out without a bloodbath.

Even that would not be easy. We—we young men—were saddled with the duty of explaining to aged planters that there was no one left to defend their estates against confiscation, and that under the new constitution they hadn't a leg to stand on, and that despite how dearly their overseers and house people loved them, they ought to begin seeing what they could pack into a few small trunks. On the other hand, we were to calm the fears of merchants and diamond factors, and tell them that if they all simply dashed for it, they could easily precipitate a closing of the frontiers, with incalculable results.

There came a night when, more than usually certain that not a single Brit under my care would leave the country alive, nor deserved to either, I stood at the bar of the Planters' (just renamed the Republic) Club, drinking gin and Italian (tonic hadn't been reordered in weeks) and listening to the clacking of the fans. A fellow I knew slightly as a regular here saluted me; I nodded and returned to my thoughts. A moment later I found him next to me.

"I wonder," he said, "if I might have your ear for a moment."

The expression, in his mouth, was richly comic, or perhaps it was my exhaustion. He waited for my laughter to subside before speaking. He was called Rossie, and he'd spent a good many years in Africa, doing whatever came to hand. He was one of those Englishmen whom the sun turns not brown but only gray and greasy; his eyes were always watery, the cups of his lids red and painful to look at.

"I am," he said at last, "doing a favor for a chap who would like your help."

"I'll do what I can," I said.

"This is a chap," he said, "who has been too long in this country, and would like to leave it."

"There are many in his situation."

"Not quite."

"What is his name?" I said, taking out a memorandum book. "I'll pass it on to the Commission."

"Just the point," Rossie said. He drew closer to me. At the other end of the bar loud laughter arose from a group consisting of a newly commissioned field marshal—an immense, glossy, nearly blue-black man—and his two colonels, both British, both small and lean. They laughed when the field marshal laughed, though their laugh was not so loud, nor their teeth so large and white.

"He'll want to tell you his name himself," Rossie said. "I've only brought the message. He wants to see you, to talk to you. I said I'd tell you. That's all."

"To tell us . . ."

"Not you, all of you. *You:* you."

I drank. The warm, scented liquor was thick in my throat. "Me?"

"What he asked me to ask you," Rossie said, growing impatient, "was would you come out to his place, and see him. It isn't far. He wanted you, no one else. He said I was to insist. He said you were to come alone. He'll send a boy of his. He said tell no one."

There were many reasons why a man might want to do business with the Commission privately. I could think of none why it should be done with me alone. I agreed, with a shrug. Rossie seemed immediately to put the matter out of his mind, mopped his red face, and ordered drinks for both of us. By the time they were brought we were already discussing the Imperial groundnut scheme, which was to have kept this young republic self-sufficient, but which, it was now evident, would do no such thing.

I too put what had been asked of me out of my mind, with enough success that when on a windless and baking afternoon a native boy shook me awake from a nap, I could not imagine why.

"Who are you? What are you doing in my bungalow?"

He only stared down at me, as though it were he who could not think why I should be there before him. Questions in his own language got no response either. At length he backed out the door, clearly wanting me to follow; and so I did, with the dread one feels on remembering an unpleasant task one has contrived to neglect. I found him outside, standing beside my Land-Rover, ready to get aboard.

"All right," I said. "Very well." I got into the driver's seat. "Point the way."

It was a small spread of tobacco and a few dusty cattle an hour's drive from town, a low bungalow looking beaten in the ocher heat. He gave no greeting as I alighted from the Land-Rover but stood in the shadows of the porch unmoving: as though he had stood so a long time. He went back into the house as I approached, and when I went in, he was standing against the netting of the window, the light behind him. That seemed a conscious choice. He was smiling, I could tell: a strange and eager smile.

"I've waited a long time for you," he said. "I don't mind saying."

"I came as quickly as I could," I said.

"There was no way for me to know, you see," he said, "whether you'd come at all."

"Your boy was quite insistent," I said. "And Mr. Rossie—"

"I meant: to Africa." His voice was light, soft, and dry. "There being so much less reason for it, now. I've wondered often. In fact I don't think a day has passed this year when I haven't wondered." Keeping his back to the sunward windows, he moved to sit on the edge of a creaking wicker sofa. "You'll want a drink," he said.

"No." The place was filled with the detritus of an African bachelor farmer's digs: empty paraffin tins, bottles, tools, hanks of rope and motor parts. He put a hand behind him without looking and put it on the bottle he was no doubt accustomed to find there. "I tried to think reasonably about it," he said, pouring a drink. "As time went on, and things began to sour here, I came to be more and more certain that no lad with any pluck would throw himself away down here. And yet I couldn't know. Whether there might not be some impulse, I don't know, traveling to you from—elsewhere. . . . I even thought of writing to you. Though whether to convince you to come or to dissuade you I'd no idea."

I sat, too. A cool sweat had gathered on my neck and the backs of my hands.

"Then," he said, "when I heard you'd come—well, I was afraid, frankly. I didn't know what to think." He dusted a fly from the rim of his glass, which he had not tasted. "You see," he said, "this was against the rules given me. That I—that I and—that you and I should meet."

Perhaps he's mad, I thought, and even as I thought it I felt intensely the experience called *déjà vu,* an experience I have always hated, hated like the nightmare. I steeled myself to respond coolly and took out my memorandum book and pencil. "I'm afraid you've rather lost me," I said—briskly I hoped. "Perhaps we'd better start with your name."

"Oh," he said, smiling again his mirthless smile, "not the hardest question first, please."

Without having, so far as I knew, the slightest reason for it, I began to feel intensely sorry for this odd dried jerky of a man, whose eyes alone seemed quick and shy. "All right," I said, "nationality, then. You are a British subject."

"Well, yes."

"Proof?" He answered nothing. "Passport?" No. "Army card? Birth certificate? Papers of any kind?" No. "Any connections in Britain? Relatives? Someone who could vouch for you, take you in?"

"No," he said. "None who could. None but you. It will have to be you."

"Now hold hard," I said.

"I don't know why I must," he said, rising suddenly and turning away to the window. "But I must. I must go back. I imagine dying here, being buried here, and my whole soul retreats in horror. I must go back. Even though I fear that, too."

He turned from the window, and in the sharp side light of the late afternoon his face was clearly the face of someone I knew. "Tell me," he said. "Mother and father. Your mother and father. They're alive?"

"No," I said. "Both dead."

"Very well," he said, "very well"; but it did not seem to be very well with him. "I'll tell you my story, then."

"I think you'd best do that."

"It's a long one."

"No matter." I had begun to feel myself transported, like a Sinbad, into somewhere that it were best I listen, and keep my counsel: and yet the first words of this specter's tale made that impossible.

"My name," he said, "is Denys Winterset."

I have come to believe, having had many years in which to think about it, that it must be as he said, that an impulse from somewhere else (he meant: some previous present, some earlier version of these circumstances) must press upon such a life as mine. That I chose the Colonial Service, that I came to Africa—and not just to Africa, but to that country: well, *if anything is chance, that was not*—as I understand Sir Geoffrey Davenant to have once said.

In that long afternoon, there where I perhaps could not have helped arriving eventually, I sat and perspired, listening—though it was for a long time very nearly impossible to hear what was said to me: an appointment in Khartoum some months from now, and some decades past; a club, outside all frames of reference; the Last equipment. It was quite like listening to the unfollowable logic of a madman, as meaningless as the roar of the insects outside. I only began to hear when this aged man, older than my grandfather, told me of something that he—that I—that he and I—had once done in boyhood, something secret, trivial really and yet so shameful that even now I will not write it down; something that only Denys Winterset could know.

"There now," he said, eyes cast down. "There now, you must believe me. You *will* listen. The world has not been as you thought it to be, any more than it was as I thought it to be, when I was as you are now. I shall tell you why: and we will hope that mine is the last story that need be told."

And so it was that I heard how he had gone up the road to Groote Schuur, that evening in 1893 (a young man then of course, only twenty-three), with the Webley revolver in his breast pocket as heavy as his heart, nearly sick with wonder and apprehension. The tropical suit he had been made to wear was monstrously hot, complete with full waistcoat and hard collar; the topee they insisted he use was as weighty as a crown. As he came in sight of the house, he could hear the awesome cries from the lion house, where the cats were evidently being given their dinner.

The big house appeared raw and unfinished to him, the trees yet ungrown and the great masses of scentless flowers—hydrangea, bougainvillaea, canna—that had smothered the place when last he had seen it, some decades later, just beginning to spread.

"Rhodes himself met me at the door—actually he happened to be going out for his afternoon ride—and welcomed me," he said. "I think the most striking thing about Cecil Rhodes, and it hasn't been noticed much, was his utter lack of airs. He was the least self-conscious man I have ever known; he did many things for effect, but he was himself entirely single: as whole as an egg, as the old French used to say.

" 'The house is yours,' he said to me. 'Use it as you like. We don't dress for dinner, as a rule; too many of the guests would be taken short, you see. Now some of the fellows are playing croquet in the Great Hall. Pay them no mind.'

"I remember little of that evening. I wandered the house; the great skins of animals, the heavy beams of teak, the brass chandeliers. I looked into the library, full of the specially transcribed and bound classics that Rhodes had ordered by the yard from Hatchard's: all the authorities that Gibbon had consulted in writing the *Decline and Fall*. All of them: that had been Rhodes's order.

"Dinner was a long and casual affair, entirely male—Rhodes had not even any female servants in the house. There was much toasting and hilarity about the successful march into Matabeleland, and the foundation of a fort, which news had only come that week; but Rhodes seemed quiet at the table's head, even melancholy: many of his closest comrades were gone with the expeditionary column, and he seemed to miss them. I do remember that at one point the conversation turned to America. Rhodes contended—no one disputed him—that if we (he meant the Empire, of course) had not lost America, the peace of the world could have been secured forever. 'Forever,' he said. 'Perpetual Peace.' And his pale opaque eyes were moist.

"How I comported myself at table—how I joined the talk, how I kept up conversations on topics quite unfamiliar to me—none of that do I recall. It helped that I was supposed to have been only recently arrived in Africa: though one of Rhodes's band of merry men looked suspiciously at my sun-browned hands when I said so.

"As soon as I could after dinner, I escaped from the fearsome horseplay that began to develop among those left awake. I pleaded a touch of sun and was shown to my room. I took off the hateful collar and tie (not without difficulty) and lay on the bed otherwise fully clothed, alert and horribly alone. Perhaps you can imagine my thoughts."

"No," I said. "I don't think I can."

"No. Well. No matter. I must have slept at last; it seemed to be after midnight when I opened my eyes and saw Rhodes standing in the doorway, a candlestick in his hand.

" 'Asleep?' he asked softly.

" 'No,' I answered. 'Awake.'

" 'Can't sleep either,' he said. 'Never do, much.' He ventured another step into the room. 'You ought to come out, see the sky,' he said. 'Quite spectacular. As long as you're up.'

"I rose and followed him. He was without his coat and collar; I noticed he wore carpet slippers. One button of his wide braces was undone; I had the urge to button it for him. Pale starlight fell in blocks across the black and white tiles of the hall, and the huge heads of beasts were mobile in the candlelight as we passed. I murmured something about the grandness of his house.

" 'I told my architect,' Rhodes answered. 'I said I wanted the big and simple—the barbaric, if you like.' The candle flame danced before him. 'Simple. The truth is always simple.'

"The chessboard tiles of the hall continued out through the wide doors onto the veranda—the *stoep* as the old Dutch called it. At the frontier of the *stoep* great pillars divided the night into panels filled with clustered stars, thick and near as vine blossoms. From far off came a long cry as of pain: a lion, awake.

"Rhodes leaned on the parapet, looking into the mystery of the sloping lawns beyond the *stoep*. 'That's good news, about the chaps up in Matabeleland,' he said a little wistfully.

" 'Yes.'

" 'Pray God they'll all be safe.'

" 'Yes.'

" '*Zambesia*,' he said after a moment. "What d'you think of that?'

" 'I beg your pardon?'

" 'As a name. For this country we'll be building. *Beyond the Zambesi*, you see.'

" 'It's a fine name.'

"He fell silent a time. A pale, powdery light filled the sky: false dawn. 'They shall say, in London,' he said, ' "Rhodes has taken for the Empire a country larger than Europe, at not a sixpence of cost to us, and we shall have that, and Rhodes shall have six feet by four feet." '

"He said this without bitterness, and turned from the parapet to face me. The Webley was pointed toward him. I had rested my (trembling) right hand on my left forearm, held up before me.

" 'Why, what on earth,' he said.

" 'Look,' I said.

"Drawing his look slowly away from me, he turned again. Out in the lawn, seeming in that illusory light to be but a long leap away, a male lion stood unmoving.

" 'The pistol won't stop him,' I said, 'but it will deflect him. If you will go calmly through the door behind me, I'll follow.'

"Rhodes backed away from the rail, and without haste or panic turned and walked past me into the house. The lion, ochre in the blue night, regarded him with a lion's expression, at once aloof and concerned, and returned his look to me. I thought I smelled him. Then I saw movement in the young trees beyond. I thought for a moment that my lion must be an illusion, or a dream, for he took no notice of these sounds—the crush of a twig, a soft voice—but at length he did turn his eyes from me to them. I could see the dim figure of a gamekeeper in a wide-awake hat, carrying a rifle, and Negroes with nets and poles: they were closing in carefully on the escapee. I stood for a moment longer, still poised to shoot, and then beat my own retreat into the house.

"Lights were being lit down the halls, voices calling: a lion does not appear on the lawn every night. Rhodes stood looking, not out the window, but at me. With deep embarrassment I clumsily pocketed the Webley (*I* knew what it had been given to me for, after all, even if he did not), and only then did I meet Rhodes's eyes.

"I shall never forget their expression, those pale eyes: a kind of exalted wonder, almost a species of adoration.

" 'That's twice now in one day,' he said, 'that you have kept me from harm. You must have been sent, that's all. I really believe you have been sent.'

"I stood before him staring, with a horror dawning in my heart such as, God willing, I shall never feel again. I knew, you see, what it meant that I had let slip the moment: that now I could not go back the way I had come. The world had opened for an instant, and I and my companions had gone down through it to this time and place; and now it had closed over me again, a seamless whole. I had no one and nothing; no Last equipment awaited me at the Mount Nelson Hotel; the Otherhood could not rescue me, for I had canceled it. I was entirely alone.

"Rhodes, of course, knew nothing of this. He crossed the hall to where I stood, with slow steps, almost reverently. He embraced me, a sudden great bear hug. And do you know what he did then?"

"What did he do?"

"He took me by the shoulders and held me at arm's length, and he insisted that I stay there with him. In effect, he offered me a job. For life, if I wanted it."

"What did you do?"

"I took it." He had finished his drink, and poured more. "I took it. You see, I simply had no place else to go."

Afternoon was late in the bungalow where we sat together, day hurried away with this tale. "I think," I said, "I shall have that drink now, if it's no trouble."

He rose and found a glass; he wiped the husk of a bug from it and filled it from his bottle. "It has always astonished me," he said, "how the mind, you know, can construct with lightning speed a reasonable, if quite mistaken, story to account for an essentially unreasonable event: I have had more than one occasion to observe this process.

"I was sure, instantly sure, that a lion which had escaped from Rhodes's lion house had appeared on the lawn at Groote Schuur just at the moment when I tried, but could not bring myself, to murder Cecil Rhodes. I can still see that cat in the pale light of predawn. And yet I cannot know if that is what happened, or if it is only what my mind has substituted for what did happen, which cannot be thought about.

"I am satisfied in my own mind—having had a lifetime to ponder it—that it cannot be possible for one to meet oneself on a trip into the past or future: that is a lie, invented by the Otherhood to forestall its own extinction, which was, however, inevitable.

"But I dream, sometimes, that I am lying on the bed at Groote Schuur, and a man enters—it is not Rhodes, but a man in a black coat and a bowler hat, into whose face I look as into a rotted mirror, who tells me impossible things.

"And I know that in fact there was no lion house at Groote Schuur. Rhodes wanted one, and it was planned, but it was never built."

• • •

In the summer of that year Rhodes—alive, alive-oh—went on expedition up into Pondoland, seeking concessions from an intransigent chief named Sicgau. Denys Winterset—this one, telling me the tale—went with him.

"Rhodes took Sicgau out into a field of mealies where he had had us set up a Maxim gun. Rhodes and the chief stood in the sun for a moment, and then Rhodes gave a signal; we fired the Maxim for a few seconds and mowed down much of the field. The chief stood unmoving for a long moment after the silence returned. Rhodes said to him softly: 'You see, this is what will happen to you and all your warriors if you give us any further trouble.'

"As a stratagem, that seemed to me both sporting and thrifty. It worked, too. But we were later to use the Maxims against men and not mealies. Rhodes knew that the Matabele had finally to be suppressed, or the work of building a white state north of the Zambezi would be hopeless. A way was found to intervene in a quarrel the Matabele were having with the Mashona, and in not too long we were at war with the Matabele. They were terribly, terribly brave; they were, after all, the first eleven in those parts, and they believed with reason that no one could withstand their leaf-bladed spears. I remember how they would come against the Maxims, and be mown down like the mealies, and fall back, and muster for another attack. Your heart sank; you prayed they would go away, but they would not. They came on again, to be cut down again. These puzzled, bewildered faces: I cannot forget them.

"And Christ, such drivel was written in the papers then, about the heroic stand of a few beleaguered South African police against so many battle-crazed natives! The only one who saw the truth was the author of that silly poem—Belloc, was it? You know—'Whatever happens, we have got/The Maxim gun, and they have not.' It was as simple as that. The truth, Rhodes said, is always simple."

He took out a large pocket-handkerchief and mopped his face and his eyes; no doubt it was hot, but it seemed to me that he wept. Tears, idle tears.

"I met Dr. Jameson during the Matabele campaign," he continued. "Leander Starr Jameson. I think I have never met a man—and I have met many wicked and twisted ones—whom I have loathed so completely and so instantly. I had hardly heard of him, of course; he was already dead and unknown in this year as it had occurred in my former past, the only version of these events I knew. Jameson was a great lover of the Maxim; he took several along on the raid he made into the Transvaal in 1896, the raid that would eventually lead to war with the Boers, destroy Rhodes's credit, and begin the end of Empire: so I have come to see it. The fool.

"I took no part in that war, thank God. I went north to help put the railroad through: Cape-to-Cairo." He smiled, seemed almost about to laugh, but did not; only mopped his face again. It was as though I were interrogating him, and he were telling me all this under the threat of the rubber truncheon or the rack. I wanted him to stop, frankly; only I dared say nothing.

"I made up for a lack of engineering expertise by my very uncertain knowledge of where and how, one day, the road would run. The telegraph had already reached Uganda; next stop was Wadi Halfa. The rails would not go through so easily. I became a sort of scout, leading the advance parties, dealing with the chieftains. The Maxim went with me, of course. I learned the weapon well."

Here there came another silence, another inward struggle to continue. I was left to picture what he did not say: *That which I did I should not have done; that which I should have done I did not do.*

"Rhodes gave five thousand pounds to the Liberal party to persuade them not to abandon Egypt: for there his railroad must be hooked to the sea. But then of course came the end of the whole scheme in German Tanganyika: no Cape-to-Cairo road. Germany was growing great in the world; the Germans wanted to have an Empire of their own. It finished Rhodes.

"By that time I was a railroad expert. The nonexistent Uganda Railroad was happy to acquire my services: I had a reputation, among the blacks, you see . . . I think there was a death for every mile of that road as it went through the jungle to the coast: rinderpest, fever, Nanda raids. We would now and then hang a captured Nanda warrior from the telegraph poles, to discourage the others. By the time the rails reached Mombasa, I was an old man; and Cecil Rhodes was dead."

He died of his old heart condition, the condition that had brought him out to Africa in the first place. He couldn't breathe in the awful heat of that summer of 1902, the worst anyone could remember; he wandered from room to room at Groote Schuur, trying to catch his breath. He lay in the darkened drawing room and could not breathe. They took him down to his cottage by the sea, and put ice between the ceiling and the iron roof to cool it; all afternoon the punkahs spooned the air. Then, suddenly, he decided to go to England. April was there: April showers. A cold spring: it seemed that could heal him. So a cabin was fitted out for him aboard a P&O liner, with electric fans and refrigerating pipes and oxygen tanks.

He died on the day he was to sail. He was buried at that place on the Matopos, the place he had chosen himself; buried facing north.

"He wanted the heroes of the Matabele campaign to be buried there with him. I could be one, if I chose; only I think my name would not be found among the register of those who fought. I think my name does not appear at all in history: not in the books of the Uganda Railroad, not in the register of the Mount Nelson Hotel for 1893. I have never had the courage to look."

I could not understand this, though it sent a cold shudder between my shoulder blades. The Original Situation, he explained, could not be returned to; but it could be restored, as those events that the Otherhood brought about were one by one come upon in time, and then not brought about. And as the Original Situation was second by second restored, the whole of his adventure in the past was continually worn away into nonbeing, and a new future replaced his old past ahead of him.

"You must imagine how it has been for me," he said, his voice now a whisper from exertion and grief. "To everyone else it seemed only that time went on—history—the march of events. But to me it has been otherwise. It has been the reverse of the nightmare from which you wake in a sweat of relief to find that the awful disaster has not occurred, the fatal step was not taken: for I have seen the real world gradually replaced by this other, nightmare world, which everyone else assumes is real, until nothing in past or present is as I knew it to be; until I am like the servant in Job: *I only am escaped to tell thee.*"

March 8, 1983

I awoke again this morning from the dream of the forest in the sea: a dream without people or events in it, or anything whatever except the gigantic dendrites, vast masses of pale leaves, and the tideless waters, light and sunshot toward the surface, darkening to impenetrability down below. It seemed there were schools of fish, or flocks of birds, in the leaves, something that faintly disturbed them, now and then; otherwise, stillness.

No matter that orthogonal logic refutes it, I cannot help believing that my present succeeds in time the other presents and futures that have gone into making it. I believe that as I grow older I come to incorporate the experiences I have had as an older man in pasts (and futures) now obsolete: as though in absolute time I continually catch up with myself in the imaginary times that fluoresce from it, gathering dreamlike memories of the lives I have lived therein. Somewhere God (I have come to believe in God; there was simply no existing otherwise) is keeping these universes in a row, and sees to it that they happen in succession, the most recently generated one last—and so felt to be last, no matter where along it I stand.

I remember, being now well past the age that he was then, the Uganda Railroad, the Nanda arrows, all the death.

I remember the shabby library and the coal fire, the encyclopedia in another orthography; the servant at the double doors.

I think that in the end, should I live long enough, I shall remember nothing but the forest in the sea. That is the terminus: complete strangeness that is at the same time utterly changeless; what cannot be becoming all that has ever been.

I took him out myself, in the end, abandoning my commission to do so, for there was no way that he could have crossed the border by himself, without papers, a nonexistent man. And it was just at that moment, as we motored up through the Sudan past Wadi Halfa, that the Anglo-French expeditionary force took Port Said. The Suez incident, that last hopeless spasm of Empire, was taking its inevitable course. Inevitable: I have not used the word before.

When we reached the Canal, the Israelis had already occupied the east bank. The airport at Ismailia was a shambles, the greater part of the Egyptian Air Force shot up, planes scattered in twisted attitudes like dead birds after a storm. We could find no plane to take us. *He* had gone desperately broody, wide-eyed and speechless, useless for anything. I felt as though in a dream where one is somehow saddled with an idiot brother one had not had before.

And yet it was only the confusion and mess that made my task possible at all, I suppose. There were so many semiofficial and unofficial British scurrying or loafing around Port Said when we entered the city that our passage was unremarked. We went through the smoke and dust of that famously squalid port like two ghosts—two ghosts progressing through a ghost city at the retreating edge of a ghost of empire. And the crunch of broken glass continually underfoot.

We went out on an old oiler attached to the retreating invasion fleet, which had been ordered home having accomplished nothing except, I suppose, the end of the British Empire in Africa. He stood on the oiler's boat deck and watched the city grow smaller and said nothing. But once he laughed, his dry, light laugh: it made me think of the noise that Homer says the dead make. I asked the reason.

"I was remembering the last time I went out of Africa," he said. "On a day much like this. Very much like this. This calm weather; this sea. Nothing else the same, though. Nothing else." He turned to me smiling, and toasted me with an imaginary glass. "The end of an era," he said.

March 10

My chronicle seems to be degenerating into a diary.

I note in the *Times* this morning the sale of the single known example of the 1856 magenta British Guiana, for a sum far smaller than was supposed to be its worth. Neither the names of the consortium that sold it nor the names of the buyers were made public. I see in my mind's eye a small, momentary fire.

I see now that there is no reason why this story should come last, no matter my feeling, no matter that in Africa he hoped it would. Indeed there is no reason why it should even fall last in this chronicling, nor why the world, the sad world in which it occurs, should be described as succeeding all others—it does not, any more than it precedes them. For the sake of a narrative only, perhaps; perhaps, like God, we cannot live without narrative.

I used to see him, infrequently, in the years after we both came back from Africa: he didn't die as quickly as we both supposed he would. He used to seek me out, in part to borrow a little money—he was living on the dole and on what he brought out of Africa, which was little enough. I stood him to tea now and then and listened to his stories. He'd appear at our appointed place in a napless British Warm, ill-fitting, as his eyeglasses and National Health false teeth were also. I imagine he was terribly lonely. I know he was.

I remember the last time we met, at a Lyons teashop near the Marble Arch. I'd left the Colonial Service, of course, under a cloud, and taken a position teaching at a crammer's in Holborn until something better came along (nothing ever did; I recently inherited the headmaster's chair at the same school; little has changed there over the decades but the general coloration of the students).

"This curious fancy haunts me," he said to me on that occasion. "I picture the Fellows, all seated around the great table in the executive committee's dining room; only it is rather like Miss Havisham's, you know, in Dickens: the roast beef has long since gone foul, and the silver tarnished, and the draperies rotten; and the Fellows dead in their chairs, or mad, dust on their evening clothes, the port dried up in their glasses. Huntington. Davenant. The President *pro tem*."

He stirred sugar in his tea (he liked it horribly sweet; so, of course, do I). "It's not true, you know, that the Club stood somehow at a nexus of possibilities, amid multiplying realities. If that were so, then what the Fellows did would be trivial or monstrous or both: generating endless new universes just to see if they could get one to their liking. No: it is we, out here, who live in but one of innumerable possible worlds. In there, they were like a man standing at the north pole, whose only view, wherever he looks, is south: they looked out upon a single encompassing reality, which it was their opportunity—no, their duty, as they saw it—to make as happy as possible, as free from the calamities they knew of as they could make it.

"Well, they were limited people, more limited than their means to work good or evil. That which they did they should not have done. And yet what they hoped for us was not despicable. The calamities they saw were real. Anyone who could would try to save us from them: as a mother would pull her child, her foolish child, from the fire. They ought to be forgiven; they ought."

I walked with him up toward Hyde Park Corner. He walked now with agonizing slowness, as I will, too, one day; it was a rainy autumn Sunday, and his pains were severe. At Hyde Park Corner he stopped entirely, and I thought perhaps he could go no farther: but then I saw that he was studying the monument that stands there. He went closer to it, to read what was written on it.

I have myself more than once stopped before this neglected monument. It is a statue of the boy David, a memorial to the Machine Gun Corps, and was put up after the First World War. Some little thought must have gone into deciding how to memorialize that arm which had changed war forever; it seemed to require a religious sentiment, a quote from the Bible, and one was found. Beneath the naked boy are written words from Kings:

Saul has slain his thousands
But David his tens of thousands.

He stood in the rain, in his vast coat, looking down at these words, as though reading them over and over; and the faint rain that clung to his cheeks mingled with his tears:

Saul has slain his thousands
But David his tens of thousands.

I never saw him again after that day, and I did not seek for him: I think it unlikely he could have been found.

AFTERWORD

Much of the impulse and many of the details of the preceding come from the second and third volumes of Jan Morris's enthralling chronicle of the rise and decline of the British Empire, *Pax Britannica* (1968) and *Farewell the Trumpets* (1978). I hope she will forgive the author the liberties he has taken, and accept his gratitude for the many hours she has allowed him to spend dawdling in a world more fantastical than any he could himself invent.

The story of Rhodes's death and many details of his character and conversation are taken from Sarah Gertrude Millin's elegant and neglected biography *Cecil Rhodes* (London, 1933).

The story of Rhodes in Pondoland, along with much else that was suggestive, comes from John Ellis's book *The Social History of the Machine Gun* (1975).

For an introduction to that book, for his convincing analysis of the possibilities and limits of what I have called orthogonal logic, and in general for his infectious enthusiasm for notions, the author's thanks to Bob Chasell (hi, Bob).

Robert Silverberg

Robert Silverberg (1935–) is the author of many SF novels and stories. He has published more than twenty collections of his short fiction. His most famous novels include *Dying Inside* (1972), one of the most impressive SF novels of character, and *Lord Valentine's Castle* (1980), the first of a series of popular fantasy works somewhat in the tradition of Jack Vance.

Silverberg is one of the leading conscious literary craftsmen of the genre in the last forty years. Of particular interest is his anthology *Robert Silverberg's Worlds of Wonder* (1987), which is perhaps the best single discussion, with examples, of the craft of SF writing. It includes an essay on this story that clearly lines out the conscious literary choices involved in the composition of "Sundance."

The range and breadth of Silverberg's vision, as well as his legendary facility, put him in the top rank of SF writers in the contemporary period. If there is a continuum from the pole of sentiment to the pole of artifice, Silverberg's work, when it errs, errs in the direction of artifice. In "Sundance," however, it seems to me Silverberg achieves a fine balance. It is a story of an American Indian in the future on another planet finding himself, and also a formal experiment in technique within genre boundaries.

SUNDANCE

Today you liquidated about 50,000 Eaters in Sector A, and now you are spending an uneasy night. You and Herndon flew east at dawn, with the green-gold sunrise at your backs, and sprayed the neural pellets over a thousand hectares along the Forked River. You flew on into the prairie beyond the river, where the Eaters have already been wiped out, and had lunch sprawled on that thick, soft carpet of grass where the first settlement is expected to rise. Herndon picked some juiceflowers, and you enjoyed half an hour of mild hallucinations. Then, as you headed toward the copter to begin an afternoon of further pellet spraying, he said suddenly, "Tom, how would you feel about this if it turned out that the Eaters weren't just animal pests? That they were *people*, say, with a language and rites and a history and all?"

You thought of how it had been for your own people.

"They aren't," you said.

"Suppose they were. Suppose the Eaters—"

"They aren't. Drop it."

Herndon has this streak of cruelty in him that leads him to ask such questions. He goes for the vulnerabilities; it amuses him. All night now his casual remark has echoed in your mind. Suppose the Eaters . . . supposed the Eaters . . . suppose . . . suppose . . .

You sleep for a while, and dream, and in your dreams you swim through rivers of blood.

Foolishness. A feverish fantasy. You know how important it is to exterminate the Eaters fast, before the settlers get here. They're just animals, and not even harmless animals at that; ecology-wreckers is what they are, devourers of oxygen-liberating plants, and they have to go. A few have been saved for zoological study. The rest must be destroyed. Ritual extirpation of undesirable beings, the old old story. But let's not complicate our job with moral qualms, you tell yourself. Let's not dream of rivers of blood.

The Eaters don't even *have* blood, none that could flow in rivers, anyway. What they have is, well, a kind of lymph that permeates every tissue and transmits nourishment along the interfaces. Waste products go out the same way, osmotically. In terms of process, it's structurally analogous to your own kind of circulatory system, except there's no network of blood vessels hooked to a master pump. The life-stuff just oozes through their bodies as though they were amoebas or sponges or some other low-phylum form. Yet they're definitely high-phylum in nervous system, digestive setup, limb-and-organ template, etc. Odd, you think. The thing about aliens is that they're alien, you tell yourself, not for the first time.

The beauty of their biology for you and your companions is that it lets you exterminate them so neatly.

You fly over the grazing grounds and drop the neural pellets. The Eaters find and ingest them. Within an hour the poison has reached all sectors of the body. Life ceases; a rapid breakdown of cellular matter follows, the Eater literally falling apart molecule by molecule the instant that nutrition is cut off; the lymph-like stuff works like acid; a universal lysis occurs; flesh and even the bones, which are cartilaginous, dissolve. In two hours, a puddle on the ground. In four, nothing at all left. Considering how many millions of Eaters you've scheduled for extermination here, it's sweet of the bodies to be self-disposing. Otherwise what a charnel house this world would become!

Suppose the Eaters . . .

Damn Herndon. You almost feel like getting a memory-editing in the morning. Scrape his stupid speculations out of your head. If you dared. If you dared.

In the morning he does not dare. Memory-editing frightens him; he will try to shake free of his newfound guilt without it. The Eaters, he explains to himself, are mindless herbivores, the unfortunate victims of human expansionism, but not really deserving of passionate defense. Their extermination is not tragic; it's just too bad. If Earthmen are to have this world, the Eaters must relinquish it. There's a difference, he tells himself, between the elimination of the Plains Indians from the American prairie in the nineteenth century and the destruction of the bison on that same prairie. One feels a little wistful about the slaughter of the thundering herds; one regrets the butchering of millions of the noble brown woolly beasts, yes. But one feels outrage, not mere wistful regret, at what was done to the Sioux. There's a difference. Reserve your passions for the proper cause.

He walks from his bubble at the edge of the camp toward the center of things. The flagstone path is moist and glistening. The morning fog has not yet lifted, and every tree is bowed, the long, notched leaves heavy with droplets of water. He pauses, crouching, to observe a spider-analog spinning its asymmetrical web. As he watches, a small amphibian, delicately shaded turquoise, glides as inconspicuously as possible over the mossy ground. Not inconspicuously enough; he gently lifts the little creature and puts it on the back of his hand. The gills flutter in anguish, and the amphibian's sides quiver. Slowly, cunningly, its color changes until it matches the coppery tone of the hand. The camouflage is excellent. He lowers his hand and the amphibian scurries into a puddle. He walks on.

He is forty years old, shorter than most of the other members of the expedition, with wide shoulders, a heavy chest, dark glossy hair, a blunt, spreading nose. He is a biologist. This is his third career, for he has failed as an anthropologist and as a developer of real estate. His name is Tom Two Ribbons. He has been married twice but has had no children. His great-grandfather died of alcoholism; his grandfather was addicted to hallucinogens; his father had compulsively visited cheap memory-editing parlors. Tom Two Ribbons is conscious that he is failing a family tradition, but he has not yet found his own mode of self-destruction.

In the main building he discovers Herndon, Julia, Ellen, Schwartz, Chang, Michaelson, and Nichols. They are eating breakfast; the others are already at work. Ellen rises and comes to him and kisses him. Her short soft yellow hair tickles his cheeks. "I love you," she whispers. She has spent the night in Michaelson's bubble. "I love you," he tells her, and draws a quick vertical line of affection between her small pale breasts. He winks at Michaelson, who nods, touches the tops of two fingers to his lips, and blows them a kiss. We are all good friends here, Tom Two Ribbons thinks.

"Who drops pellets today?" he asks.

"Mike and Chang," says Julia. "Sector C."

Schwartz says, "Eleven more days and we ought to have the whole peninsula clear. Then we can move inland."

"If our pellet supply holds up," Chang points out.

Herndon says, "Did you sleep well, Tom?"

"No," says Tom. He sits down and taps out his breakfast requisition. In the west, the fog is beginning to burn off the mountains. Something throbs in the back of his neck. He has been on this world nine weeks now, and in that time it has undergone its only change of season, shading from dry weather to foggy. The mists will remain for many months. Before the plains parch again, the Eaters will be gone and the settlers will begin to arrive. His food slides down the chute and he seizes it. Ellen sits beside him. She is a little more than half his age; this is her first voyage; she is their keeper of records, but she is also skilled at editing. "You look troubled," Ellen tells him. "Can I help you?"

"No. Thank you."

"I hate it when you get gloomy."

"It's a racial trait," says Tom Two Ribbons.

"I doubt that very much."

"The truth is that maybe my personality reconstruct is wearing thin. The trauma level was so close to the surface. I'm just a walking veneer, you know."

Ellen laughs prettily. She wears only a sprayon half-wrap. Her skin looks damp; she and Michaelson have had a swim at dawn. Tom Two Ribbons is thinking of asking her to marry him, when this job is over. He has not been married since the collapse of the real estate business. The therapist suggested divorce as part of the reconstruct. He sometimes wonders where Terry has gone and whom she lives with now. Ellen says, "You seem pretty stable to me, Tom."

"Thank you," he says. She is young. She does not know.

"If it's just a passing gloom I can edit it out in one quick snip."

"Thank you," he says. "No."

"I forgot. You don't like editing."

"My father—"

"Yes?"

"In fifty years he pared himself down to a thread," Tom Two Ribbons says. "He had his ancestors edited away, his whole heritage, his religion, his wife, his sons, finally his name. Then he sat and smiled all day. Thank you, no editing."

"Where are you working today?" Ellen asks.

"In the compound, running tests."

"Want company? I'm off all morning."

"Thank you, no," he says, too quickly. She looks hurt. He tries to remedy his unintended cruelty by touching her arm lightly and saying, "Maybe this afternoon, all right? I need to commune a while. Yes?"

"Yes," she says, and smiles, and shapes a kiss with her lips.

After breakfast he goes to the compound. It covers a thousand hectares east of the base; they have bordered it with neutral-field projectors at intervals of eighty meters, and this is a sufficient fence to keep the captive population of two hundred Eaters from straying. When all the others have been exterminated, this study group will remain. At the southwest corner of the compound stands a lab bubble from which the experiments are run: metabolic, psychological, physiological, ecological. A stream crosses the compound diagonally. There is a low ridge of grassy hills at its eastern edge. Five distinct corpses of tightly clustered knifeblade trees are separated by patches of dense savanna. Sheltered beneath the grass are the oxygen-plants, almost completely hidden except for the photosynthetic spikes that jut to heights of three or four meters at regular intervals, and for the lemon-colored respiratory bodies, chest high, that make the grassland sweet and dizzying with exhaled gases. Through the fields move the Eaters in a straggling herd, nibbling delicately at the respiratory bodies.

Tom Two Ribbons spies the herd beside the stream and goes toward it. He stumbles over an oxygen-plant hidden in the grass but deftly recovers his balance and, seizing the puckered orifice of the respiratory body, inhales deeply. His despair lifts. He approaches the Eaters. They are spherical, bulky, slow-moving creatures, covered by masses of coarse orange fur. Saucer-like eyes protrude above narrow rubbery lips. Their legs are thin and scaly, like a chicken's, and their arms are short and held close to their bodies. They regard him with bland lack of curiosity. "Good morning, brothers!" is the way he greets them this time, and he wonders why.

I noticed something strange today. Perhaps I simply sniffed too much oxygen in the fields; maybe I was succumbing to a suggestion Herndon planted; or possibly it's the family masochism cropping out. But while I was observing the Eaters in the compound, it seemed to me, for the first time, that they were behaving intelligently, that they were functioning in a ritualized way.

I followed them around for three hours. During that time they uncovered half a dozen outcroppings of oxygen-plants. In each case they went through a stylized pattern of action before starting to munch. They:

Formed a straggly circle around the plants.

Looked toward the sun.

Looked toward their neighbors on left and right around the circle.

Made fuzzy neighing sounds *only* after having done the foregoing.

Looked toward the sun again.

Moved in and ate.

If this wasn't a prayer of thanksgiving, a saying of grace, then what was it? And if they're advanced enough spiritually to say grace, are we not therefore committing genocide here? Do chimpanzees say grace? Christ, we wouldn't even wipe out chimps the way we're cleaning out the Eaters! Of course, chimps don't interfere with human crops, and some kind of coexistence would be possible, whereas Eaters and human agriculturalists simply can't function on the same planet. Nevertheless, there's a moral issue here. The liquidation effort is predicated on the assumption that the intelligence level of the Eaters is about on par with that of oysters, or, at best, sheep. Our consciences stay clear because our poison is quick and painless and because the Eaters thoughtfully dissolve upon dying, sparing us the mess of incinerating millions of corpses. But if they pray—

I won't say anything to the others just yet. I want more evidence—hard, objective. Films, tapes, record cubes. Then we'll see. What if I can show that we're exterminating intelligent beings? My family knows a little about genocide, after all, having been on the receiving end just a few centuries back. I doubt that I could halt what's going on here. But at the very least I could withdraw from the operation. Head back to Earth and stir up public outcries.

I hope I'm imagining this.

I'm not imagining a thing. They gather in circles; they look to the sun; they neigh and pray. They're only balls of jelly on chicken-legs, but they give thanks for their food. Those big round eyes now seem to stare accusingly at me. Our tame herd here knows what's going on: that we have descended from the stars to eradicate their kind, and that they alone will be spared. They have no way of fighting back or even of communicating their displeasure, but they *know*. And hate us. Jesus, we have killed two million of them since we got here, and in a metaphorical sense I'm stained with blood, and what will I do, what can I do?

I must move very carefully, or I'll end up drugged and edited.

I can't let myself seem like a crank, a quack, an agitator. I can't stand up and *denounce!* I have to find allies. Herndon, first. He surely is onto the truth; he's the one who nudged *me* to it, that day we dropped pellets. And I thought he was merely being vicious in his usual way!

I'll talk to him tonight.

He says, "I've been thinking about that suggestion you made. About the Eaters. Perhaps we haven't made sufficiently close psychological studies. I mean, if they really *are* intelligent—"

Herndon blinks. He is a tall man with glossy dark hair, a heavy beard, sharp cheekbones. "Who says they are, Tom?"

"You did. On the far side of the Forked River, you said—"

"It was just a speculative hypothesis. To make conversation."

"No, I think it was more than that. You really believed it."

Herndon looks troubled. "Tom, I don't know what you're trying to start, but don't start it. If I for a moment believed we were killing intelligent creatures, I'd run for an editor so fast I'd start an implosion wave."

"Why did you ask me that thing, then?" Tom Two Ribbons says.

"Idle chatter."

"Amusing yourself by kindling guilts in somebody else? You're a bastard, Herndon. I mean it."

"Well, look, Tom, if I had any idea that you'd get so worked up about a hypothetical suggestion—" Herndon shakes his head. "The Eaters aren't intelligent beings. Obviously. Otherwise we wouldn't be under orders to liquidate them."

"Obviously," says Tom Two Ribbons.

Ellen said, "No, I don't know what Tom's up to. But I'm pretty sure he needs a rest. It's only a year and a half since his personality reconstruct, and he had a pretty bad breakdown back then."

Michaelson consulted a chart. "He's refused three times in a row to make his pellet-dropping run. Claiming he can't take time away from his research. Hell, we can fill in for him, but it's the idea that he's ducking chores that bothers me."

"What kind of research is he doing?" Nichols wanted to know.

"Not biological," said Julia. "He's with the Eaters in the compound all the time, but I don't see him making any tests on them. He just watches them."

"And talks to them," Chang observed.

"And talks, yes," Julia said.

"About what?" Nichols asked.

"Who knows?"

Everyone looked at Ellen. "You're closest to him," Michaelson said. "Can't you bring him out of it?"

"I've got to know what he's in, first," Ellen said. "He isn't saying a thing."

You know that you must be very careful, for they outnumber you, and their concern for your welfare can be deadly. Already they realize you are disturbed, and Ellen has begun to probe for the source of the disturbance. Last night you lay in her arms and she questioned you, obliquely, skillfully, and you knew what she is trying to find out. When the moons appeared she suggested that you and she stroll in the compound, among the sleeping Eaters. You declined, but she sees that you have become involved with the creatures.

You have done probing of your own—subtly, you hope. And you are aware that you can do nothing to save the Eaters. An irrevocable commitment has been made. It is 1876 all over again; these are the bison, these are the Sioux, and they must be destroyed, for the railroad is on its way. If you speak out here, your friends will calm you and pacify you and edit you, for they do not see what you see. If you return to Earth to agitate, you will be mocked and recommended for another reconstruct. You can do nothing. You can do nothing.

You cannot save, but perhaps you can record.

Go out into the prairie. Live with the Eaters; make yourself their friend; learn their ways. Set it down, a full account of their culture, so that at least that much will not be lost. You know the techniques of field anthropology. As was done for your people in the old days, do now for the Eaters.

He finds Michaelson. "Can you spare me for a few weeks?" he asks.

"Spare you, Tom? What do you mean?"

"I've got some field studies to do. I'd like to leave the base and work with Eaters in the wild."

"What's wrong with the ones in the compound?"

"It's the last chance with wild ones, Mike. I've got to go."

"Alone, or with Ellen?"

"Alone."

Michaelson nods slowly. "All right, Tom. Whatever you want. Go. I won't hold you here."

I dance in the prairie under the green-gold sun. About me the Eaters gather. I am stripped; sweat makes my skin glisten; my heart pounds. I talk to them with my feet, and they understand.

They understand.

They have a language of soft sounds. They have a god. They know love and awe and rapture. They have rites. They have names. They have a history. Of all this I am convinced.

I dance on thick grass.

How can I reach them? With my feet, with my hands, with my grunts, with my sweat. They gather by the hundreds, by the thousands, and I dance. I must not stop. They cluster about me and make their sounds. I am a conduit for strange forces. My great-grandfather should see me now! Sitting on his porch in Wyoming, the firewater in his hand, his brain rotting—see me now, old one! See the dance of Tom Two Ribbons! I talk to these strange ones with my feet under a sun that is the wrong color. I dance. I dance.

"Listen to me," I say. "I am your friend, I alone, the only one you can trust. Trust me, talk to me, teach me. Let me preserve your ways, for soon the destruction will come."

I dance, and the sun climbs, and the Eaters murmur.

There is the chief. I dance toward him, back, toward, I bow, I point to the sun, I imagine the being that lives in that ball of flame, I imitate the sounds of these people, I kneel, I rise, I dance. Tom Two Ribbons dances for you.

I summon skills my ancestors forgot. I feel the power flowing in me. As they danced in the days of the bison, I dance now, beyond the Forked River.

I dance, and now the Eaters dance too. Slowly, uncertainly, they move toward me, they shift their weight, lift leg and leg, sway about. "Yes, like that!" I cry. "Dance!"

We dance together as the sun reaches noon height.

Now their eyes are no longer accusing. I see warmth and kinship. I am their brother, their redskinned tribesman, he who dances with them. No longer do they seem clumsy to me. There is a strange ponderous grace in their movements. They dance. They dance. They caper about me. Closer, closer, closer!

We move in holy frenzy.

They sing, now, a blurred hymn of joy. They throw forth their arms, unclench their little claws. In unison they shift weight, left foot forward, right, left, right. Dance, brothers, dance, dance, dance! They press against me. Their flesh quivers; their smell is a sweet one. They gently thrust me across the field, to a part of the meadow where the grass is deep and untrampled. Still dancing, we seek the oxygen-plants, and find clumps of them beneath the grass, and they make their prayer and seize them with their awkward arms, separating the respiratory bodies from the photosynthetic spikes. The plants, in anguish, release floods of oxygen. My mind reels. I laugh and sing. The Eaters are nibbling the lemon-colored perforated globes, nibbling the stalks as well. They thrust their plants at me. It is a religious ceremony, I see. Take from us, eat with us, join with us, this is the body, this is the blood, take, eat, join. I bend forward and put a lemon-colored globe to my lips. I do not bite; I nibble, as they do, my teeth slicing away the skin of the globe. Juice spurts into my mouth while oxygen drenches my nostrils. The Eaters sing hosannas. I should be in full paint for this, paint of my forefathers, feathers too, meeting their religion in the regalia of what should have been mine. Take, eat, join. The juice of the oxygen-plant flows in my veins. I embrace my brothers. I sing, and as my voice leaves my lips it becomes an arch that glistens like new steel, and I pitch my song lower, and the arch turns to tarnished silver. The Eaters crowd close. The scent of their bodies is fiery red to me. Their soft cries are puffs of steam. The sun is very warm; its rays are tiny jagged pings of puckered sound, close to the top of my range of hearing, plink! plink! plink! The thick grass hums to me, deep and rich, and the wind hurls points of flame along the prairie. I devour another oxygen-plant, and then a third. My brothers laugh and shout. They tell me of their gods, the god of warmth, the god of food, the god of pleasure, the god of death, the god of holiness, the god of wrongness, and the others. They recite for me the names of their kings, and I hear their voices as splashes of green mold on the clean sheet of the sky. They instruct me in their holy rites. I must remember this, I tell myself, for when it is gone it will never come again. I continue to dance. They continue to dance. The color of the hills becomes rough and coarse, like abrasive gas. Take, eat, join. Dance. They are so gentle!

I hear the drone of the copter, suddenly.

It hovers far overhead. I am unable to see who flies in it. "No!" I scream. "Not here! Not these people! Listen to me! This is Tom Two Ribbons! Can't you hear me? I'm doing a field study here! You have no right—!"

My voice makes spirals of blue moss edged with red sparks. They drift upward and are scattered by the breeze.

I yell, I shout, I bellow. I dance and shake my fists. From the wings of the copter the jointed arms of the pellet-distributors unfold. The gleaming spigots extend and whirl. The neural pellets rain down into the meadow, each tracing a blazing track that lingers in the sky. The sound of the copter becomes a furry carpet stretching to the horizon, and my shrill voice is lost in it.

The Eaters drift away from me, seeking the pellets, scratching at the roots of the grass to find them. Still dancing, I leap into their midst, striking the pellets from their hands, hurling them into the stream, crushing them to powder. The Eaters growl black needles at me. They turn away and search for more pellets. The copter turns and flies off, leaving a trail of dense oily sound. My brothers are gobbling the pellets eagerly.

There is no way to prevent it.

Joy consumes them and they topple and lie still. Occasionally a limb twitches; then even this stops. They begin to dissolve. Thousands of them melt on the prairie, sinking into shapelessness, losing spherical forms, flattening, ebbing into the ground. The bonds of the molecules will no longer hold. It is the twilight of protoplasm. They perish. They vanish. For hours I walk the prairie. Now I inhale oxygen; now I eat a lemon-colored globe. Sunset begins with the ringing of leaden chimes. Black clouds make brazen trumpet calls in the east and the deepening wind is a swirl of coaly bristles. Silence comes. Night falls. I dance. I am alone.

The copter comes again, and they find you, and you do not resist as they gather you in. You are beyond bitterness. Quietly you explain what you have done and what you have learned, and why it is wrong to exterminate these people. You describe the plant you have eaten and the way it affects your senses, and as you talk of the blessed synesthesia, the texture of the wind and the sound of the clouds and the timbre of the sunlight, they nod and smile and tell you not to worry, that everything will be all right soon, and they touch something cold to your forearm, so cold that it is a whir and a buzz and the deintoxicant sinks into your vein and soon the ecstasy drains away, leaving only the exhaustion and the grief.

He says, "We never learn a thing, do we? We export all our horrors to the stars. Wipe out the Armenians, wipe out the Jews, wipe out the Tasmanians, wipe out the Indians, wipe out everyone who's in the way, and then come here and do the same damned murderous thing. You weren't with me out there. You didn't dance with them. You didn't see what a rich, complex culture the Eaters have. Let me tell you about their tribal structure. It's dense: seven levels of matrimonial relationships, to begin with, and an exogamy factor that requires—"

Softly Ellen says, "Tom, darling, nobody's going to harm the Eaters."

"And the religion," he goes on. "Nine gods, each one an aspect of *the* god. Holiness and wrongness both worshiped. They have hymns, prayers, a theology. And we, the emissaries of the god of wrongness—"

"We're not exterminating them," Michaelson says. "Won't you understand that, Tom? This is all a fantasy of yours. You've been under the influence of drugs, but now we're clearing you out. You'll be clean in a little while. You'll have perspective again."

"A fantasy?" he says bitterly. "A drug dream? I stood out in the prairie and saw you drop pellets. And I watched them die and melt away. I didn't dream that."

"How can we convince you?" Chang asks earnestly. "What will make you believe? Shall we fly over the Eater country with you and show you how many millions there are?"

"But how many millions have been destroyed?" he demands.

They insist that he is wrong. Ellen tells him again that no one has ever desired to harm the Eaters. "This is a scientific expedition, Tom. We're here to *study* them. It's a violation of all we stand for to injure intelligent lifeforms."

"You admit that they're intelligent?"

"Of course. That's never been in doubt."

"Then why drop the pellets?" he asks. "Why slaughter them?"

"None of that has happened, Tom," Ellen says. She takes his hand between her cool palms. "Believe us. Believe us."

He says bitterly, "If you want me to believe you, why don't you do the job properly? Get out the editing machine and go to work on me. You can't simply *talk* me into rejecting the evidence of my own eyes."

"You were under drugs all the time," Michaelson says.

"I've never taken drugs! Except for what I ate in the meadow, when I danced—and that came after I had watched the massacre going on for weeks and weeks. Are you saying that it's a retroactive delusion?"

"No, Tom," Schwartz says. "You've had this delusion all along. It's part of your therapy, your reconstruct. You came here programmed with it."

"Impossible," he says.

Ellen kisses his fevered forehead. "It was done to reconcile you to mankind, you see. You had this terrible resentment of the displacement of your people in the nineteenth century. You were unable to forgive the industrial society for scattering the Sioux, and you were terribly full of hate. Your therapist thought that if you could be made to participate in an imaginary modern extermination, if you could come to see it as a necessary operation, you'd be purged of your resentment and able to take your place in society as—"

He thrusts her away. "Don't talk idiocy! If you knew the first thing about reconstruct therapy, you'd realize that no reputable therapist could be so shallow. There are no one-to-one correlations in reconstructs. No, don't touch me. Keep away. Keep away."

He will not let them persuade him that this is merely a drug-born dream. It is no fantasy, he tells himself, and it is no therapy. He rises. He goes out. They do not follow him. He takes a copter and seeks his brothers.

Again I dance. The sun is much hotter today. The Eaters are more numerous. Today I wear paint, today I wear feathers. My body shines with my sweat. They dance with me, and they have a frenzy in them that I have never seen before. We pound the trampled meadow with our feet. We clutch for the sun with our hands. We sing, we shout, we cry. We will dance until we fall.

This is no fantasy. These people are real, and they are intelligent, and they are doomed. This I know.

We dance. Despite the doom, we dance.

My great-grandfather comes and dances with us. He too is real. His nose is like a hawk's, not blunt like mine, and he wears the big headdress, and his muscles are like cords under his brown skin. He sings, he shouts, he cries.

Others of my family join us.

We eat the oxygen-plants together. We embrace the Eaters. We know, all of us, what it is to be hunted.

The clouds make music and the wind takes on texture and the sun's warmth has color.

We dance. We dance. Our limbs know no weariness.

The sun grows and fills the whole sky, and I see no Eater now, only my own people, my father's fathers across the centuries, thousands of gleaming skins, thousands of hawk's noses, and we eat the plants, and we find sharp sticks and thrust them into our flesh, and the sweet blood flows and dries in the blaze of the sun, and we dance, and we dance, and some of us fall from weariness, and we dance, and the prairie is a sea of bobbing headdresses, an ocean of feathers, and we dance, and my heart makes thunder, and my knees become water, and the sun's fire engulfs me, and I dance, and I fall, and I dance, and I fall, and I fall, and I fall.

Again they find you and bring you back. They give you the cool snout on your arm to take the oxygen-plant drug from your veins, and then they give you something else so you will rest. You rest and you are very calm. Ellen kisses you and you stroke her soft skin, and then the others come in and they talk to you, saying soothing things, but you do not listen, for you are searching for realities. It is not an easy search. It is like falling through many trapdoors, looking for the one room whose floor is not hinged. Everything that has happened on this planet is your therapy, you tell yourself, designed to reconcile an embittered aborigine to the white man's conquest; nothing is really being exterminated here. You reject that and fall through and realize that this must be the therapy of your friends; they carry the weight of accumulated centuries of guilts and have come here to shed that load, and you are here to ease them of their burden, to draw their sins into yourself and give them forgiveness. Again you fall through, and see that the Eaters are mere animals who threaten the ecology and must be removed; the culture you imagined for them is your hallucination, kindled out of old churnings. You try to withdraw your objections to this necessary extermination, but you fall through again and discover that there is no extermination except in your mind, which is troubled and disordered by your obsession with the crime against your ancestors, and you sit up, for you wish to apologize to these friends of yours, these innocent scientists whom you have called murderers. And you fall through.

Frank Herbert

Frank Herbert (1920–1986) is the author of *Dune* (1965), the single most popular SF novel of the century, according to some published polls of readers. In response to that popularity he wrote a number of sequels in the 1970s and 1980s. Herbert was a journalist (he was proud to show a picture of the Army–McCarthy hearings with himself in the front row) and an articulate public speaker. His first major impact came in the 1950s with his impressive novel *The Dragon in the Sea* (1956), which is an intense psychological examination of a small crew enclosed together in a submarine; it forecast an international oil crisis, and Cold War–style submarine oil theft.

Herbert's fiction is often intellectual and discursive, but he was also concerned with dramatic storytelling. He was particularly fascinated by technology and the idea of progress, yet his stories are always grounded in a political and social awareness that made him especially relevant and popular in the 1960s and '70s.

One of his major themes was the evolution of intelligence, artificial or organic. He was influential in the founding of the ecology movement, which he popularized through works such as *Dune,* this story, and *Hellstrom's Hive* (1973). He was the main speaker advertised at the first Earth Day celebration. "Greenslaves" was later expanded into the novel, *The Green Brain* (1966). As opposed to many stories of this type, it has only gained in pertinence since its original publication. It is a stunning ecological parable set in the rain forest of South America.

GREENSLAVES

He looked pretty much like the bastard offspring of a Guarani Indio and some backwoods farmer's daughter, some *sertanista* who had tried to forget her enslavement to the *encomendero* system by "eating the iron"—which is what they call lovemaking through the grill of a consel gate.

The type-look was almost perfect except when he forgot himself while passing through one of the deeper jungle glades.

His skin tended to shade down to green then, fading him into the background of leaves and vines, giving a strange disembodiment to the mud-gray shirt and ragged trousers, the inevitable frayed straw hat and rawhide sandals soled with pieces cut from worn tires.

Such lapses became less and less frequent the farther he got from the Parana headwaters, the *sertao* hinterland of Goyaz where men with his bang-cut black hair and glittering dark eyes were common.

By the time he reached *bandeirantes* country, he had achieved almost perfect control over the chameleon effect.

But now he was out of the jungle growth and into the brown dirt tracks that separated the parceled farms of the resettlement plan. In his own way, he knew he was approaching the *bandeirante* checkpoints, and with an almost human gesture, he fingered the *cedula de gracias al sacar,* the certificate of white blood, tucked safely beneath his shirt. Now and again, when humans were not near, he practiced speaking aloud the name that had been chosen for him—"Antonio Raposo Tavares."

The sound was a bit stridulate, harsh on the edges, but he knew it would pass. It already had. Goyaz Indios were notorious for the strange inflection of their speech. The farm folk who had given him a roof and fed him the previous night had said as much.

When their questions had become pressing, he had squatted on the doorstep and played his flute, the *qena* of the Andes Indian that he carried in a leather purse hung from his shoulder. He had kept the sound to a conventional non-dangerous pitch. The gesture of the flute was a symbol of the region. When a Guarani put flute to nose and began playing, that was a sign words were ended.

The farm folk had shrugged and retired.

Now, he could see red-brown rooftops ahead and the white crystal shimmering of a *bandeirante* tower with its aircars alighting and departing. The scene held an odd hive-look. He stopped, finding himself momentarily overcome by the touch of instincts that he knew he had to master or fail in the ordeal to come.

He united his mental identity then, thinking, *We are greenslaves subservient to the greater whole.* The thought lent him an air of servility that was like a shield against the stares of the humans trudging past all around him. His kind knew many mannerisms and had learned early that servility was a form of concealment.

Presently, he resumed his plodding course toward the town and the tower.

The dirt track gave way to a two-lane paved market road with its footpaths in the ditches on both sides. This, in turn, curved alongside a four-deck commercial transport highway where even the footpaths were paved. And now there were groundcars and aircars in greater number, and he noted that the flow of people on foot was increasing.

Thus far, he had attracted no dangerous attention. The occasional snickering side-glance from natives of the area could be safely ignored, he knew. Probing stares held peril, and he had detected none. The servility shielded him.

The sun was well along toward mid-morning and the day's heat was beginning to press down on the earth, raising a moist hothouse stink from the dirt beside the pathway, mingling the perspiration odors of humanity around him.

And they were around him now, close and pressing, moving slower and slower as they approached the checkpoint bottleneck. Presently, the forward motion stopped. Progress resolved itself into shuffle and stop, shuffle and stop.

This was the critical test now and there was no avoiding it. He waited with something like an Indian's stoic patience. His breathing had grown deeper to compensate for the heat, and he adjusted it to match that of the people around him, suffering the temperature rise for the sake of blending into his surroundings.

Andes Indians didn't breathe deeply here in the lowlands.

Shuffle and stop.

Shuffle and stop.

He could see the checkpoint now.

Fastidious *bandeirantes* in sealed white cloaks with plastic helmets, gloves, and boots stood in a double row within a shaded brick corridor leading into the town. He could see sunlight hot on the street beyond the corridor and people hurrying away there after passing the gantlet.

The sight of that free area beyond the corridor sent an ache of longing through all the parts of him. The suppression warning flashed out instantly on the heels of that instinctive reaching emotion.

No distraction could be permitted now; he was into the hands of the first *bandeirante,* a hulking blond fellow with pink skin and blue eyes.

"Step along now! Lively now!" the fellow said.

A gloved hand propelled him toward two *bandeirantes* standing on the right side of the line.

"Give this one an extra treatment," the blond giant called. "He's from the upcountry by the look of him."

The other two *bandeirantes* had him now, one jamming a breather mask over his face, the other fitting a plastic bag over him. A tube trailed from the bag out to machinery somewhere in the street beyond the corridor.

"Double shot!" one of the *bandeirantes* called.

Fuming blue gas puffed out the bag around him, and he took a sharp, gasping breath through the mask.

Agony!

The gas drove through every multiple linkage of his being with needles of pain.

We must not weaken, he thought.

But it was a deadly pain, killing. The linkages were beginning to weaken.

"Okay on this one," the bag handler called.

The mask was pulled away. The bag was slipped off. Hands propelled him down the corridor toward the sunlight.

"Lively now! Don't hold up the line."

The stink of the poison gas was all around him. It was a new one—a dissembler. They hadn't prepared him for this poison!

Now, he was into the sunlight and turning down a street lined with fruit stalls, merchants bartering with customers or standing fat and watchful behind their displays.

In his extremity, the fruit beckoned to him with the promise of life-saving sanctuary for a few parts of him, but the integrating totality fought off the lure. He shuffled as fast as he dared, dodging past the customers, through the knots of idlers.

"You like to buy some fresh oranges?"

An oily dark hand thrust two oranges toward his face.

"Fresh oranges from the green country. Never been a bug anywhere near these."

He avoided the hand, although the odor of the oranges came near overpowering him.

Now, he was clear of the stalls, around a corner down a narrow side street. Another corner and he saw far away to his left, the lure of greenery in open country, the free area beyond the town.

He turned toward the green, increasing his speed, measuring out the time still available to him. There was still a chance. Poison clung to his clothing, but fresh air was filtering through the fabric—and the thought of victory was like an antidote.

We can make it yet!

The green drew closer and closer—trees and ferns beside a river bank. He heard the running water. There was a bridge thronging with foot traffic from converging streets.

No help for it: he joined the throng, avoided contact as much as possible. The linkages of his legs and back were beginning to go, and he knew the wrong kind of blow could dislodge whole segments. He was over the bridge without disaster. A dirt track led off the path and down toward the river.

He turned toward it, stumbled against one of two men carrying a pig in a net slung between them. Part of the shell on his right upper leg gave way and he could feel it begin to slip down inside his pants.

The man he had hit took two backward steps, almost dropped the end of the burden.

"Careful!" the man shouted.

The man at the other end of the net said: "Damn drunks."

The pig set up a squirming, squealing distraction.

In this moment, he slipped past them onto the dirt track leading down toward the river. He could see the water down there now, boiling with aeration from the barrier filters.

Behind him, one of the pig carriers said: "I don't think he was drunk, Carlos. His skin felt dry and hot. Maybe he was sick."

The track turned around an embankment of raw dirt dark brown with dampness and dipped toward a tunnel through ferns and bushes. The men with the pig could no longer see him, he knew, and he grabbed at his pants where the part of his leg was slipping, scurried into the green tunnel.

Now, he caught sight of his first mutated bee. It was dead, having entered the barrier vibration area here without any protection against that deadliness. The bee was one of the butterfly type with iridescent yellow and orange wings. It lay in the cup of a green leaf at the center of a shaft of sunlight.

He shuffled past, having recorded the bee's shape and color. They had considered the bees as a possible answer, but there were serious drawbacks to this course. A bee could not reason with humans, that was the key fact. And humans had to listen to reason soon, else all life would end.

There came the sound of someone hurrying down the path behind him, heavy footsteps thudding on the earth.

Pursuit . . . ?

He was reduced to a slow shuffling now and soon it would be only crawling progress, he knew. Eyes searched the greenery around him for a place of concealment. A thin break in the fern wall on his left caught his attention. Tiny human footprints led into it—children. He forced his way through the ferns, found himself on a low narrow path along the embankment. Two toy aircars, red and blue, had been abandoned on the path. His staggering foot pressed them into the dirt.

The path led close to a wall of black dirt festooned with creepers, around a sharp turn and onto the lip of a shallow cave. More toys lay in the green gloom at the cave's mouth.

He knelt, crawled over the toys into the blessed dankness, lay there a moment, waiting.

The pounding footsteps hurried past a few feet below.

Voices reached up to him.

"He was headed toward the river. Think he was going to jump in?"

"Who knows? But I think me for sure he was sick."

"Here; down this way. Somebody's been down this way."

The voices grew indistinct, blended with the bubbling sound of the river.

The men were going on down the path. They had missed his hiding place. But why had they pursued him? He had not seriously injured the one by stumbling against him. Surely, they did not suspect.

Slowly, he steeled himself for what had to be done, brought his specialized parts into play and began burrowing into the earth at the end of the cave. Deeper and deeper he burrowed, thrusting the excess dirt behind and out to make it appear the cave had collapsed.

Ten meters in he went before stopping. His store of energy contained just enough reserve for the next stage. He turned on his back, scattering the dead parts of his legs and back, exposing the queen and her guard cluster to the dirt beneath his chitinous spine. Orifices opened at his thighs, exuded the cocoon foam, the soothing green cover that would harden into a protective shell.

This was victory; the essential parts had survived.

Time was the thing now—ten and one half days to gather new energy, go through the metamorphosis and disperse. Soon, there would be thousands of him—each with its carefully mimicked clothing and identification papers and appearance of humanity.

Identical—each of them.

There would be other checkpoints, but not as severe; other barriers, lesser ones.

This human copy had proved a good one. They had learned many things from study of their scattered captives and from the odd crew directed by the red-haired human female they'd trapped in the *sertao.* How strange she was: like a queen and not like a queen. It was so difficult to understand human creatures, even when you permitted them limited freedom . . . almost impossible to reason with them. Their slavery to the planet would have to be proved dramatically, perhaps.

The queen stirred near the cool dirt. They had learned new things this time about escaping notice. All of the subsequent colony clusters would share that knowledge. One of them—at least—would get through to the city by the Amazon "River Sea" where the death-for-all originated. One had to get through.

Senhor Gabriel Martinho, prefect of the Mato Grosso Barrier Compact, paced his study, muttering to himself as he passed the tall, narrow window that admitted the evening sunlight. Occasionally, he paused to glare down at his son, Joao, who sat on a tapir-leather sofa beneath one of the tall bookcases that lined the room.

The elder Martinho was a dark wisp of a man, limb thin, with gray hair and cavernous brown eyes above an eagle nose, slit mouth, and boot-toe chin. He wore old style black clothing as befitted his position, his linen white against the black, and with golden cuffstuds glittering as he waved his arms.

"I am an object of ridicule!" he snarled.

Joao, a younger copy of the father, his hair still black and wavy, absorbed the statement in silence. He wore a *bandeirante*'s white coverall suit sealed into plastic boots at the calf.

"An object of ridicule!" the elder Martinho repeated.

It began to grow dark in the room, the quick tropic darkness hurried by thunderheads piled along the horizon. The waning daylight carried a hazed blue cast. Heat lightning spattered the patch of sky visible through the tall window, sent dazzling electric radiance into the study. Drumming thunder followed. As though that were the signal, the house sensors turned on lights wherever there were humans. Yellow illumination filled the study.

The Prefect stopped in front of his son. "Why does my own son, a *bandeirante*, a jefe of the Irmandades, spout these Carsonite stupidities?"

Joao looked at the floor between his boots. He felt both resentment and shame. To disturb his father this way, that was a hurtful thing, with the elder Martinho's delicate heart. But the old man was so blind!

"Those rabble farmers laughed at me," the elder Martinho said. "I told them we'd increase the green area by ten thousand hectares this month, and they laughed. 'Your own son does not even believe this!' they said. And they told me some of the things you had been saying."

"I am sorry I have caused you distress, Father," Joao said. "The fact that I'm *a bandeirante* . . . " He shrugged. "How else could I have learned the truth about this extermination program?"

His father quivered.

"Joao! Do you sit there and tell me you took a false oath when you formed your Irmandades band?"

"That's not the way it was, Father."

Joao pulled a sprayman's emblem from his breast pocket, fingered it. "I believed it . . . then. We could shape mutated bees to fill every gap in the insect ecology. This I believed. Like the Chinese, I said: 'Only the useful shall live!' But that was several years ago, Father, and since then I have come to realize we don't have a complete understanding of what usefulness means."

"It was a mistake to have you educated in North America," his father said. "That's where you absorbed this Carsonite heresy. It's all well and good for *them* to refuse to join the rest of the world in the Ecological Realignment; they do not have as many million mouths to feed. But my own son!"

Joao spoke defensively: "Out in the red areas you see things, Father. These things are difficult to explain. Plants look healthier out there and the fruit is . . ."

"A purely temporary thing," his father said. "We will shape bees to meet whatever need we find. The destroyers take food from our mouths. It is very simple. They must die and be replaced by creatures which serve a function useful to mankind."

"The birds are dying, Father," Joao said.

"We are saving the birds! We have specimens of every kind in our sanctuaries. We will provide new foods for them to . . ."

"But what happens if our barriers are breached . . . before we can replace the population of natural predators? What happens then?"

The elder Martinho shook a thin finger under his son's nose. "This is nonsense! I will hear no more of it! Do you know what else those *mamaluco* farmers said? They said they have seen *bandeirantes* reinfesting the green areas to prolong their jobs! That is what they said. This, too, is nonsense—but it is a natural consequence of defeatist talk just such as I have heard from you tonight. And every setback we suffer adds strength to such charges!"

"Setbacks, Father?"

"I have said it: setbacks!"

Senhor Prefect Martinho turned, paced to his desk and back. Again, he stopped in front of his son, placed hands on hips. "You refer to the Piratininga, of course?"

"You accuse me, Father?"

"Your Irmandades were on that line."

"Not so much as a flea got through us!"

"Yet, a week ago the Piratininga was green. Now, it is crawling. Crawling!"

"I cannot watch every *bandeirante* in the Mato Grosso," Joao protested. "If they . . ."

"The IEO gives us only six months to clean up," the elder Martinho said. He raised his hands, palms up; his face was flushed. "Six months! Then they throw an embargo around all Brazil—the way they have done with North America." He lowered his hands. "Can you imagine the pressures on me? Can you imagine the things I must listen to about the *bandeirantes* and especially about my own son?"

Joao scratched his chin with the sprayman's emblem. The reference to the International Ecological Organization made him think of Dr. Rhin Kelly, the IEO's lovely field director. His mind pictured her as he had last seen her in the A' Chigua nightclub at Bahia—red-haired, green-eyed . . . so lovely and strange. But she had been missing almost six weeks now—somewhere in the *sertao*—and there were those who said she must be dead.

Joao looked at his father. If only the old man weren't so excitable. "You excite yourself needlessly, Father," he said. "The Piratininga was not a full barrier, just a . . ."

"Excite myself!"

The Prefect's nostrils dilated; he bent toward his son. "Already we have gone past two deadlines. We gained an extension when I announced you and the *bandeirantes* of Diogo Alvarez had cleared the Piratininga. How do I explain now that it is reinfested, that we have the work to do over?"

Joao returned the sprayman's emblem to his pocket. It was obvious he'd not be able to reason with his father this night. Frustration sent a nerve quivering along Joao's jaw. The old man had to be told, though; someone had to tell him. And someone of his father's stature had to get back to the Bureau, shake them up there and make *them* listen.

The Prefect returned to his desk, sat down. He picked up an antique crucifix, one that the great Aleihadinho had carved in ivory. He lifted it, obviously seeking to restore his serenity, but his eyes went wide and glaring. Slowly, he returned the crucifix to its position on the desk, keeping his attention on it.

"Joao," he whispered.

It's his heart! Joao thought.

He leaped to his feet, rushed to his father's side. "Father! What is it?"

The elder Martinho pointed, hand trembling.

Through the spiked crown of thorns, across the agonized ivory face, over the straining muscles of the Christ figure crawled an insect. It was the color of the ivory, faintly reminiscent of a beetle in shape, but with a multi-clawed fringe along its wings and thorax, and with furry edging to its abnormally long antennae.

The elder Martinho reached for a roll of papers to smash the insect, but Joao put out a hand restraining him. "Wait. This is a new one. I've never seen anything like it. Give me a handlight. We must follow it, find where it nests."

Senhor Prefect Martinho muttered under his breath, withdrew a small Permalight from a drawer of the desk, handed the light to his son.

Joao peered at the insect, still not using the light. "How strange it is," he said. "See how it exactly matches the tone of the ivory."

The insect stopped, pointed its antennae toward the two men.

"Things have been seen," Joao said. "There are stories. Something like this was found near one of the barrier villages last month. It was inside the green area, on a path beside a river. Two farmers found it while searching for a sick man." Joao looked at his father. "They are very watchful of sickness in the newly green regions, you know. There have been epidemics . . . and that is another thing."

"There is no relationship," his father snapped. "Without insects to carry disease, we will have less illness."

"Perhaps," Joao said, and his tone said he did not believe it.

Joao returned his attention to the insect. "I do not think our ecologists know all they say they do. And I mistrust our Chinese advisors. They speak in such flowery terms of the benefits from eliminating useless insects, but they will not let us go into their green areas and inspect. Excuses. Always excuses. I think they are having troubles they do not wish us to know."

"That's foolishness," the elder Martinho growled, but his tone said this was not a position he cared to defend. "They are honorable men. Their way of life is closer to our socialism than it is to the decadent capitalism of North America. Your trouble is you see them too much through the eyes of those who educated you."

"I'll wager this insect is one of the spontaneous mutations," Joao said. "It is almost as though they appeared according to some plan. Find me something in which I may capture this creature and take it to the laboratory."

The elder Martinho remained standing by his chair. "Where will you say it was found?"

"Right here," Joao said.

"You will not hesitate to expose me to more ridicule?"

"But Father . . ."

"Can't you hear what they will say? In his own home this insect is found. It is a strange new kind. Perhaps he breeds them there to reinfest the green."

"Now *you* are talking nonsense, father. Mutations are common in a threatened species. And we cannot deny there is threat to insect species—the poisons, the barrier vibrations, the traps. Get me a container, Father. I cannot leave this creature, or I'd get a container myself."

"And you will tell where it was found?"

"I can do nothing else. We must cordon off this area, search it out. This could be . . . an accident . . ."

"Or a deliberate attempt to embarrass me."

Joao took his attention from the insect, studied his father. *That* was a possibility, of course. The Carsonites had friends in many places . . . and some were fanatics who would stoop to any scheme. Still . . .

Decision came to Joao. He returned his attention to the motionless insect. His father had to be told, had to be reasoned with at any cost. Someone whose voice carried authority had to get down to the Capitol and make them listen.

"Our earliest poisons killed off the weak and selected out those insects immune to this threat," Joao said. "Only the immune remained to breed. The poisons we use now . . . some of them do not leave such loopholes and the deadly vibrations at the barriers . . ." He shrugged. "This is a form of beetle, Father. I will show you a thing."

Joao drew a long, thin whistle of shiny metal from his pocket. "There was a time when this called countless beetles to their deaths. I had merely to tune it across their attraction spectrum." He put the whistle to his lips, blew while turning the end of it.

No sound audible to human ears came from the instrument, but the beetle's antennae writhed.

Joao removed the whistle from his mouth.

The antennae stopped writhing.

"It stayed put, you see," Joao said. "And there are indications of malignant intelligence among them. The insects are far from extinction, Father . . . and they are beginning to strike back."

"Malignant intelligence, pah!"

"You must believe me, Father," Joao said. "No one else will listen. They laugh and say we are too long in the jungle. And where is our evidence? And they say such stories could be expected from ignorant farmers but not from *bandeirantes.* You must listen, Father, and believe. It is why I was chosen to come here . . . because you are my father and you might listen to your own son."

"Believe what?" the elder Martinho demanded, and he was the Prefect now, standing erect, glaring coldly at his son.

"In the *sertao* of Goyaz last week," Joao said, "Antonil Lisboa's *bandeirante* lost three men who . . ."

"Accidents."

"They were killed with formic acid and oil of copahu."

"They were careless with their poisons. Men grow careless when they . . ."

"Father! The formic acid was a particularly strong type, but still recognizable as having been . . . or being of a type manufactured by insects. And the men were drenched with it. While the oil of copahu . . ."

"You imply that insects such as this . . ." The Prefect pointed to the motionless creature on the crucifix. ". . . blind creatures such as this . . ."

"They're not blind, Father."

"I did not mean literally blind, but without intelligence," the elder Martinho said. "You cannot be seriously implying that these creatures attacked humans and killed them."

"We have yet to discover precisely how the men were slain," Joao said. "We have only their bodies and the physical evidence at the scene. But there have been other deaths, Father, and men missing and we grow more and more certain that . . ."

He broke off as the beetle crawled off the crucifix onto the desk. Immediately, it darkened to brown, blending with the wood surface.

"Please, Father. Get me a container."

"I will get you a container only if you promise to use discretion in your story of where this creature was found," the Prefect said.

"Father, I . . ."

The beetle leaped off the desk far out into the middle of the room, scuttled to the wall, up the wall, into a crack beside a window.

Joao pressed the switch of the handlight, directed its beam into the hole which had swallowed the strange beetle.

"How long has this hole been here, Father?"

"For years. It was a flaw in the masonry . . . an earthquake, I believe."

Joao turned, crossed to the door in three strides, went through an arched hallway, down a flight of stone steps, through another door and short hall, through a grillwork gate and into the exterior garden. He set the handlight to full intensity, washed its blue glare over the wall beneath the study window.

"Joao, what are you doing?"

"My job, Father," Joao said. He glanced back, saw that the elder Martinho had stopped just outside the gate.

Joao returned his attention to the exterior wall, washed the blue glare of light on the stones beneath the window. He crouched low, running the light along the ground, peering behind each clod, erasing all shadows.

His searching scrutiny passed over the raw earth, turned to the bushes, then the lawn.

Joao heard his father come up behind.

"Do you see it, son?"

"No, Father."

"You should have allowed me to crush it."

From the outer garden that bordered the road and the stone fence, there came a piercing stridulation. It hung on the air in almost tangible waves, making Joao think of the hunting cry of jungle predators. A shiver moved up his spine. He turned toward the driveway where he had parked his airtruck, sent the blue glare of light stabbing there.

He broke off, staring at the lawn. "What is that?"

The ground appeared to be in motion, reaching out toward them like the curling of a wave on a beach. Already, they were cut off from the house. The wave was still some ten paces away, but moving in rapidly.

Joao stood up, clutched his father's arm. He spoke quietly, hoping not to alarm the old man further. "We must get to my truck, Father. We must run across them."

"Them?"

"Those are like the insect we saw inside, father—millions of them. Perhaps they are not beetles, after all. Perhaps they are like army ants. We must make it to the truck. I have equipment and supplies there. We will be safe inside. It is a *bandeirante* truck, Father. You must run with me. I will help you."

They began to run, Joao holding his father's arm, pointing the way with the light.

Let his heart be strong enough, Joao prayed.

They were into the creeping waves of insects then, but the creatures leaped aside, opening a pathway which closed behind the running men.

The white form of the airtruck loomed out of the shadows at the far curve of the driveway about fifteen meters ahead.

"Joao . . . my heart," the elder Martinho gasped.

"You can make it," Joao panted. "Faster!" He almost lifted his father from the ground for the last few paces.

They were at the wide rear door into the truck's lab compartment now. Joao yanked open the door, slapped the light switch, reached for a spray hood and poison gun. He stopped, stared into the yellow-lighted compartment.

Two men sat there—*sertao* Indians by the look of them, with bright glaring eyes and bang-cut black hair beneath straw hats. They looked to be identical twins—even to the mud-gray clothing and sandals, the leather shoulder bags. The beetle-like insects crawled around them, up the walls, over the instruments and vials.

"What the devil?" Joao blurted.

One of the pair held a qena flute. He gestured with it, spoke in a rasping, oddly inflected voice: "Enter. You will not be harmed if you obey."

Joao felt his father sag, caught the old man in his arms. How light he felt! Joao stepped up into the truck, carrying his father. The elder Martinho breathed in short, painful gasps. His face was a pale blue and sweat stood out on his forehead.

"Joao," he whispered. "Pain . . . my chest."

"Medicine, Father," Joao said. "Where is your medicine?"

"House," the old man said.

"It appears to be dying," one of the Indians rasped.

Still holding his father in his arms, Joao, whirled toward the pair, blazed: "I don't know who you are or why you loosed those bugs here, but my father's dying and needs help. Get out of my way!"

"Obey or both die," said the Indian with the flute.

"He needs his medicine and a doctor," Joao pleaded. He didn't like the way the Indian pointed that flute. The motion suggested the instrument was actually a weapon.

"What part has failed?" asked the other Indian. He stared curiously at Joao's father. The old man's breathing had become shallow and rapid.

"It's his heart," Joao said. "I know you farmers don't think he's acted fast enough for . . ."

"Not farmers," said the one with the flute. "Heart?"

"Pump," said the other.

"Pump." The Indian with the flute stood up from the bench at the front of the lab, gestured down. "Put . . . Father here."

The other one got off the bench, stood aside.

In spite of fear for his father, Joao was caught by the strange look of this pair, the fine, scale-like lines in their skin, the glittering brilliance of their eyes.

"Put Father here," repeated the one with the flute, pointing at the bench. "Help can be . . ."

"Attained," said the other one.

"Attained," said the one with the flute.

Joao focused now on the masses of insects around the walls, the waiting quietude in their ranks. They *were* like the one in the study.

The old man's breathing was now very shallow, very rapid.

He's dying, Joao thought in desperation.

"Help can be attained," repeated the one with the flute. "If you obey, we will not harm."

The Indian lifted his flute, pointed it at Joao like a weapon. "Obey."

There was no mistaking the gesture.

Slowly, Joao advanced, deposited his father gently on the bench.

The other Indian bent over the elder Martinho's head, raised an eyelid. There was a professional directness about the gesture. The Indian pushed gently on the dying man's diaphragm, removed the Prefect's belt, loosened his collar. A stubby brown finger was placed against the artery in the old man's neck.

"Very weak," the Indian rasped.

Joao took another, closer look at this Indian, wondering at the sertao backwoodsman who behaved like a doctor.

"We've got to get him to a hospital," Joao said. "And his medicine in . . ."

"Hospital," the Indian agreed.

"Hospital?" asked the one with the flute.

A low, stridulate hissing came from the other Indian.

"Hospital," said the one with the flute.

That stridulate hissing! Joao stared at the Indian beside the Prefect. The sound had been reminiscent of the weird call that had echoed across the lawn.

The one with the flute poked him, said: "You will go into front and maneuver this . . ."

"Vehicle," said the one beside Joao's father.

"Vehicle," said the one with the flute.

"Hospital?" Joao pleaded.

"Hospital," agreed the one with the flute.

Joao looked once more to his father. The other Indian already was strapping the elder Martinho to the bench in preparation for movement. How competent the man appeared in spite of his backwoods look.

"Obey," said the one with the flute.

Joao opened the door into the front compartment, slipped through, feeling the other one follow. A few drops of rain spattered darkly against the curved windshield. Joao squeezed into the operator's seat, noted how the Indian crouched behind him, flute pointed and ready.

A *dart gun of some kind*, Joao guessed.

He punched the ignitor button on the dash, strapped himself in while waiting for the turbines to build up speed. The Indian still crouched behind him, vulnerable now if the airtruck were spun sharply. Joao flicked the communications switch on the lower left corner of the dash, looked into the tiny screen there giving him a view of the lab compartment. The rear doors were open. He closed them by hydraulic remote. His father was securely strapped to the bench now, Joao noted, but the other Indian was equally secured.

The turbines reached their whining peak. Joao switched on the lights, engaged the hydrostatic drive. The truck lifted six inches, angled upward as Joao increased pump displacement. He turned left onto the street, lifted another two meters to increase speed, headed toward the lights of a boulevard.

The Indian spoke beside his ear: "You will turn toward the mountain over there." A hand came forward, pointing to the right.

The Alejandro Clinic is there in the foothills, Joao thought.

He made the indicated turn down the cross street angling toward the boulevard.

Casually, he gave pump displacement another boost, lifted another meter and increased speed once more. In the same motion, he switched on the intercom to the rear compartment, tuned for the spare amplifier and pickup in the compartment beneath the bench where his father lay.

The pickup, capable of making a dropped pin sound like a cannon, gave forth only a distant hissing and rasping. Joao increased amplification. The instrument should have been transmitting the old man's heartbeats now, sending a noticeable drum-thump into the forward cabin.

There was nothing.

Tears blurred Joao's eyes, and he shook his head to clear them.

My father is dead, he thought. *Killed by these crazy backwoodsmen.*

He noted in the dashscreen that the Indian back there had a hand under the elder Martinho's back. The Indian appeared to be massaging the dead man's back, and a rhythmic rasping matched the motion.

Anger filled Joao. He felt like diving the airtruck into an abutment, dying himself to kill these crazy men.

They were approaching the outskirts of the city, and ring-girders circled off to the left giving access to the boulevard. This was an area of small gardens and cottages protected by over-fly canopies.

Joao lifted the airtruck above the canopies, headed toward the boulevard.

To the clinic, yes, he thought. *But it is too late.*

In that instant, he realized there were no heartbeats at all coming from that rear compartment—only that slow, rhythmic grating, a faint susurration and a cicada-like hum up and down scale.

"To the mountains, there," said the Indian behind him.

Again, the hand came forward to point off to the right.

Joao, with that hand close to his eyes and illuminated by the dash, saw the scale-like parts of a finger shift position slightly. In that shift, he recognized the scale-shapes by their claw fringes.

The beetles!

The finger was composed of linked beetles working in unison!

Joao turned, stared into the *Indian's* eyes, seeing now why they glistened so: they were composed of thousands of tiny facets.

"Hospital, there," the creature beside him said, pointing.

Joao turned back to the controls, fighting to keep from losing composure. They were not Indians . . . they weren't even human. They were insects—some kind of hive-cluster shaped and organized to mimic a man.

The implications of this discovery raced through his mind. How did they support their weight? How did they feed and breathe?

How did they speak?

Everything had to be subordinated to the urgency of getting this information and proof of it back to one of the big labs where the facts could be explored.

Even the death of his father could not be considered now. He had to capture one of these things, get out with it.

He reached overhead, flicked on the command transmitter, set its beacon for a homing call. *Let some of my Irmaos be awake and monitoring their sets,* he prayed.

"More to the right," said the creature behind him.

Again, Joao corrected course.

The moon was high overhead now, illuminating a line of *bandeirante* towers off to the left. The first barrier.

They would be out of the green area soon and into the gray—then, beyond that, another barrier and the great red that stretched out in reaching fingers through the Goyaz and the Mato Grosso. Joao could see scattered lights of Resettlement Plan farms ahead, and darkness beyond.

The airtruck was going faster than he wanted, but Joao dared not slow it. They might become suspicious.

"You must go higher," said the creature behind him.

Joao increased pump displacement, raised the nose. He leveled off at three hundred meters.

More *bandeirante* towers loomed ahead, spaced at closer intervals. Joao picked up the barrier signals on his meters, looked back at the *Indian.* The dissembler vibrations seemed not to affect the creature.

Joao looked out his side window and down. No one would challenge him, he knew. This was a *bandeirante* airtruck headed *into* the red zone . . . and with its transmitter sending out a homing call. The men down there would assume he was a bandleader headed out on a contract after a successful bid—and calling his men to him for the job ahead.

He could see the moon-silvered snake of the São Francisco winding off to his left, and the lesser waterways like threads raveled out of the foothills.

I must find the nest—where we're headed, Joao thought. He wondered if he dared turn on his receiver—but if his men started reporting in . . . No. That could make the creatures suspect; they might take violent counter-action.

My men will realize something is wrong when I don't answer, he thought. *They will follow.*

If any of them hear my call.

Hours droned past.

Nothing but moonlighted jungle sped beneath them now, and the moon was low on the horizon, near setting. This was the deep red region where broadcast poisons had been used at first with disastrous results. This was where the wild mutations had originated. It was here that Rhin Kelly had been reported missing.

This was the region being saved for the final assault, using a mobile barrier line when that line could be made short enough.

Joao armed the emergency charge that would separate the front and rear compartments of the truck when he fired it. The stub wings of the front compartment and its emergency rocket motors could get him back into *bandeirante* country.

With the *specimen* sitting behind him safely subdued, Joao hoped.

He looked up through the canopy, scanned the horizon as far as he could. Was that moonlight glistening on a truck far back to the right? He couldn't be sure.

"How much farther?" Joao asked.

"Ahead," the creature rasped.

Now that he was alert for it, Joao heard the modulated stridulation beneath that voice.

"But how long?" Joao asked. "My father . . ."

"Hospital for . . . the father . . . ahead," said the creature.

It would be dawn soon, Joao realized. He could see the first false line of light along the horizon behind. This night had passed so swiftly. Joao wondered if these creatures had injected some time-distorting drug into him without his knowing. He thought not. He was maintaining himself in the necessities of the moment. There was no time for fatigue or boredom when he had to record every landmark half-visible in the night, sense everything there was to sense about these creatures with him.

How did they coordinate all those separate parts?

Dawn came, revealing the plateau of the Mato Grosso. Joao looked out his windows. This region, he knew, stretched across five degrees of latitude and six degrees of longitude. Once, it had been a region of isolated *fazendas* farmed by independent blacks and by *sertanistos* chained to the *encomendero* plantation system. It was hardwood jungles, narrow rivers with banks overgrown by lush trees and ferns, savannahs, and tangled life.

Even in this age it remained primitive, a fact blamed largely on insects and disease. It was one of the last strongholds of *teeming* insect life, if the International Ecological Organization's reports could be believed.

Supplies for the *bandeirantes* making the assault on this insect stronghold would come by way of São Paulo, by air and by transport on the multi-decked highways, then on antique diesel trains to Itapira, on river runners to Bahus and by airtruck to Registo and Leopoldina on the Araguaya.

This area crawled with insects: wire worms in the roots of the savannahs, grubs digging in the moist black earth, hopping beetles, dart-like angita wasps, chalcis flies, chiggers, sphecidae, braconidae, fierce hornets, white termites, hemipteric crawlers, blood roaches, thrips, ants, lice, mosquitoes, mites, moths, exotic butterflies, mantidae—and countless unnatural mutations of them all.

This would be an expensive fight—unless it were stopped . . . because it already had been lost.

I mustn't think that way, Joao told himself. *Out of respect for my father.*

Maps of the IEO showed this region in varied intensities of red. Around the red ran a ring of gray with pink shading where one or two persistent forms of insect life resisted man's poisons, jelly flames, astringents, sonitoxics—the combination of flamant couroq and supersonics that drove insects from their hiding places into waiting death—and all the mechanical traps and lures in the *bandeirante* arsenal.

A grid map would be placed over this area and each thousand-acre square offered for bid to the independent bands to deinfest.

We bandeirantes *are a kind of ultimate predator,* Joao thought. *It's no wonder these creatures mimic us.*

But how good, really, was the mimicry? he asked himself. And how deadly to the predators?

"There," said the creature behind him, and the multipart hand came forward to point toward a black scarp visible ahead in the gray light of morning.

Joao's foot kicked a trigger on the floor releasing a great cloud of orange dye-fog beneath the truck to mark the ground and forest for a mile around under this spot. As he kicked the trigger, Joao began counting down the five-second delay to the firing of the separation charge.

It came in a roaring blast that Joao knew would smear the creature behind him against the rear bulkhead. He sent the stub wings out, fed power to the rocket motors and back hard around. He saw the detached rear compartment settling slowly earthward above the dye cloud, its fall cushioned as the pumps of the hydrostatic drive automatically compensated.

I will come back, Father, Joao thought. *You will be buried among family and friends.*

He locked the controls, twisted in the seat to see what had happened to his captive.

A gasp escaped Joao's lips.

The rear bulkhead crawled with insects clustered around something white and pulsing. The mud-gray shirt and trousers were torn, but insects already were repairing it, spinning out fibers that meshed and sealed on contact. There was a yellow-like extrusion near the pulsing white, and a dark brown skeleton with familiar articulation.

It looked like a human skeleton—but chitinous.

Before his eyes, the thing was reassembling itself, the long, furry antennae burrowing into the structure and interlocking.

The flute-weapon was not visible, and the thing's leather pouch had been thrown into the rear corner, but its eyes were in place in their brown sockets, staring at him. The mouth was re-forming.

The yellow sac contracted, and a voice issued from the half-formed mouth.

"You must listen," it rasped.

Joao gulped, whirled back to the controls, unlocked them and sent the cab into a wild, spinning turn.

A high-pitched rattling buzz sounded behind him. The noise seemed to pick up every bone in his body and shake it. Something crawled on his neck. He slapped at it, felt it squash.

All Joao could think of was escape. He stared frantically out at the earth beneath, seeing a blotch of white in a savannah off to his right and, in the same instant, recognizing another airtruck banking beside him, the insignia of his own Irmandades band bright on its side.

The white blotch in the savannah was resolving itself into a cluster of tents with an IEO orange and green banner flying beside them.

Joao dove for the tents, praying the other airtruck would follow.

Something stung his cheek. They were in his hair—biting, stinging. He stabbed the braking rockets, aimed for open ground about fifty meters from the tent. Insects were all over the inside of the glass now, blocking his vision. Joao said a silent prayer, hauled back on the control arm, felt the cab mush out, touch ground, skidding and slewing across the savannah. He kicked the canopy release before the cab stopped, broke the seal on his safety harness and launched himself up and out to land sprawling in grass.

He rolled through the grass, feeling the insect bites like fire over every exposed part of his body. Hands grabbed him and he felt a jelly hood splash across his face to protect it. A voice he recognized as Thome of his own band said: "This way, Johnny! Run!" They ran.

He heard a spraygun fire: "Whooosh!"

And again.

And again.

Arms lifted him and he felt a leap.

They landed in a heap and a voice said: "Mother of God! Would you look at that!"

Joao clawed the jelly hood from his face, sat up to stare across the savannah. The grass seethed and boiled with insects around the uptilted cab and the airtruck that had landed beside it.

Joao looked around him, counted seven of his Irmaos with Thome, his chief sprayman, in command.

Beyond them clustered five other people, a red-haired woman slightly in front, half turned to look at the savannah and at him. He recognized the woman immediately: Dr. Rhin Kelly of the IEO. When they had met in the A' Chigua nightclub in Bahia, she had seemed exotic and desirable to Joao. Now, she wore a field uniform instead of gown and jewels, and her eyes held no invitation at all.

"I see a certain poetic justice in this . . . traitors," she said.

Joao lifted himself to his feet, took a cloth proffered by one of his men, wiped off the last of the jelly. He felt hands brushing him, clearing dead insects off his coveralls. The pain of his skin was receding under the medicant jelly, and now he found himself dominated by puzzled questioning as he recognized the mood of the IEO personnel.

They were furious and it was directed at him . . . and at his fellow Irmandades.

Joao studied the woman, noting how her green eyes glared at him, the pink flush to her skin.

"Dr. Kelly?" Joao said.

"If it isn't Joao Martinho, jefe of the Irmandades," she said, "the traitor of the Piratininga."

"They are crazy, that is the only thing, I think," said Thome.

"Your pets turned on you, didn't they?" she demanded.

"And wasn't that inevitable?"

"Would you be so kind as to explain," Joao said.

"I don't need to explain," she said. "Let your friends out there explain." She pointed toward the rim of jungle beyond the savannah.

Joao looked where she pointed, saw a line of men in *bandeirante* white standing untouched amidst the leaping, boiling insects in the jungle shadow. He took a pair of binoculars from around the neck of one of his men, focused on the figures. Knowing what to look for made the identification easy.

"Tommy," Joao said.

His chief sprayman, Thome, bent close, rubbing at an insect sting on his swarthy cheek.

In a low voice, Joao explained what the figures at the jungle edge were.

"*Aieeee*," Thome said.

An Irmandade on Joao's left crossed himself.

"What was it we leaped across coming in here?" Joao asked.

"A ditch," Thome said. "It seems to be filled with couroq jelly . . . an insect barrier of some kind."

Joao nodded. He began to have unpleasant suspicions about their position here. He looked at Rhin Kelly. "Dr. Kelly, where are the rest of your people? Surely there are more than five in an IEO field crew."

Her lips compressed, but she remained silent.

"So?" Joao glanced around at the tents, seeing their weathered condition. "And where is your equipment, your trucks and lab huts and jitneys?"

"Funny thing you should ask," she said, but there was uncertainty atop the sneering quality of her voice. "About a kilometer into the trees over there . . ." She nodded to her left. ". . . is a wrecked jungle truck containing most of our . . . equipment, as you call it. The track spools of our truck were eaten away by acid."

"Acid?"

"It smelled like oxalic," said one of her companions, a blond Nordic with a scar beneath his right eye.

"Start from the beginning," Joao said.

"We were cut off here almost six weeks ago," said the blond man. "Something got our radio, our truck—they looked like giant chiggers and they can shoot an acid spray about fifteen meters."

"There's a glass case containing three dead specimens in my lab tent," said Dr. Kelly.

Joao pursued his lips, thinking. "So?"

"I heard part of what you were telling your men there," she said. "Do you expect us to believe that?"

"It is of no importance to me what you believe," Joao said. "How did you get here?"

"We fought our way in here from the truck using *caramuru* cold-fire spray," said the blond man. "We dragged along what supplies we could, dug a trench around our perimeter, poured in the couroq powder, added the jell compound and topped it off with our *copahu* oil . . . and here we sat."

"How many of you?" Joao asked.

"There were fourteen of us," said the man.

Joao rubbed the back of his neck where the insect stings were again beginning to burn. He glanced around at his men, assessing their condition and equipment, counted four spray rifles, saw the men carried spare charge cylinders on slings around their necks.

"The airtruck will take us," he said. "We had better get out of here."

Dr. Kelly looked out to the savannah, said: "I think it has been too late for that since a few seconds after you landed, *bandeirante.* I think in a day or so there'll be a few less traitors around. You're caught in your own trap."

Joao whirled to stare at the airtruck, barked: "Tommy! Vince! Get . . ." He broke off as the airtruck sagged to its left.

"It's only fair to warn you," said Dr. Kelly, "to stay away from the edge of the ditch unless you first spray the opposite side. They can shoot a stream of acid at least fifteen meters . . . and as you can see . . ." She nodded toward the airtruck. ". . . the acid eats metal."

"You're insane," Joao said. "Why didn't you warn us immediately?"

"Warn you?"

Her blond companion said: "Rhin, perhaps we . . ."

"Be quiet, Hogar," she said, and turned back to Joao. "We lost nine men to your playmates." She looked at the small band of Irmandades. "Our lives are little enough to pay now for the extinction of eight of you . . . traitors."

"You *are* insane," Joao said.

"Stop playing innocent, *bandeirante,*" she said. "We have seen your companions out there. We have seen the new playmates you bred . . . and we understand that you were too greedy; now your game has gotten out of hand."

"You've not seen my Irmaos doing these things," Joao said. He looked at Thome. "Tommy, keep an eye on these insane ones." He lifted the spray rifle from one of his men, took the man's spare charges, indicated the other three armed men. "You—come with me."

"Johnny, what do you do?" Thome asked.

"Salvage the supplies from the truck," Joao said. He walked toward the ditch nearest the airtruck, laid down a hard mist of foamal beyond the ditch, beckoned the others to follow and leaped the ditch.

Little more than an hour later, with all of them acid-burned—two seriously—the Irmandades retreated back across the ditch. They had salvaged less than a fourth of the equipment in the truck, and this did not include a transmitter.

"It is evident the little devils went first for the communications equipment," Thome said. "How could they tell?"

Joao said: "I do not want to guess." He broke open a first aid box, began treating his men. One had a cheek and shoulder badly splashed with acid. Another was losing flesh off his back.

Dr. Kelly came up, helped him treat the men, but refused to speak, even to answering the simplest question.

Finally, Joao touched up a spot on his own arm, neutralizing the acid and covering the burn with flesh-tape. He gritted his teeth against the pain, stared at Rhin Kelly. "Where are these chigua you found?"

"Go find them yourself!" she snapped.

"You are a blind, unprincipled megalomaniac," Joao said, speaking in an even voice. "Do not push me too far."

Her face went pale and the green eyes blazed.

Joao grabbed her arm, hauled her roughly toward the tents. "Show me these chigua!"

She jerked free of him, threw back her red hair, stared at him defiantly. Joao faced her, looked her up and down with a calculating slowness.

"Go ahead, do violence to me," she said, "I'm sure I couldn't stop you."

"You act like a woman who wants . . . needs violence," Joao said. "Would you like me to turn you over to my men? They're a little tired of your raving."

Her face flamed. "You would not dare!"

"Don't be so melodramatic," he said, "I wouldn't give you the pleasure."

"You insolent . . . you . . ."

Joao showed her a wolfish grin, said: "Nothing you say will make me turn you over to my men!"

"Johnny."

It was Thome calling.

Joao turned, saw Thome talking to the Nordic IEO man who had volunteered information. What had she called him? Hogar.

Thome beckoned.

Joao crossed to the pair, bent close as Thome signaled secrecy.

"The gentleman here says the female doctor was bitten by an insect that got past their barrier's fumes."

"Two weeks ago," Hogar whispered.

"She has not been the same since," Thome said. "We humor her, jefe, no?"

Joao wet his lips with his tongue. He felt suddenly dizzy and too warm.

"The insect that bit her was similar to the ones that were on you," Hogar said, and his voice sounded apologetic.

They are making fun of me! Joao thought.

"I give the orders here!" he snapped.

"Yes, jefe," Thome said. "But you . . ."

"What difference does it make who gives the orders?"

It was Dr. Kelly close behind him.

Joao turned, glared at her. How hateful she looked . . . in spite of her beauty.

"What's the difference?" she demanded. "We'll all be dead in a few days anyway." She stared out across the savannah. "More of your friends have arrived."

Joao looked to the forest shadow, saw more human-like figures arriving. They appeared familiar and he wondered what it was—something at the edge of his mind, but his head hurt. Then he realized they looked like *sertao* Indians, like the pair who had lured him here. There were at least a hundred of them, apparently identical in every visible respect.

More were arriving by the second.

Each of them carried a qena flute.

There was something about the flutes that Joao felt he should remember.

Another figure came advancing through the *Indians,* a thin man in a black suit, his hair shiny silver in the sunlight.

"Father!" Joao gasped.

I'm sick, he thought. *I must be delirious.*

"That looks like the Prefect," Thome said. "Is it not so, Ramon?"

The Irmandade he addressed said: "If it is not the Prefect, it is his twin. Here, Johnny. Look with the glasses."

Joao took the glasses, focused on the figure advancing toward them through the grass. The glasses felt so heavy. They trembled in his hands and the figure coming toward them was blurred.

"I cannot see!" Joao muttered and he almost dropped the glasses.

A hand steadied him, and he realized he was reeling.

In an instant of clarity, he saw that the line of *Indians* had raised their flutes, pointing at the IEO camp. That buzzing-rasping that had shaken his bones in the airtruck cab filled the universe around him. He saw his companions begin to fall.

In the instant before his world went blank, Joao heard his father's voice calling strongly: "Joao! Do not resist! Put down your weapons!"

The trampled grassy earth of the campsite, Joao saw, was coming up to meet his face.

It cannot be my father, Joao thought. *My father is dead and they've copied him . . . mimicry, nothing more.*

Darkness.

There was a dream of being carried, a dream of tears and shouting, a dream of violent protests and defiance and rejection.

He awoke to yellow-orange light and the figure who could not be his father bending over him, thrusting a hand out, saying: "Then examine my hand if you don't believe!"

But Joao's attention was on the face behind his father. It was a giant face, baleful in the strange light, its eyes brilliant and glaring with pupils within pupils. The face turned, and Joao saw it was no more than two centimeters thick. Again, it turned, and the eyes focused on Joao's feet.

Joao forced himself to look down, began trembling violently as he saw he was half enveloped in a foaming green cocoon, that his skin shared some of the same tone.

"Examine my hand!" ordered the old-man figure beside him.

"He has been dreaming." It was a resonant voice that boomed all around him, seemingly coming from beneath the giant face. "He has been dreaming," the voice repeated. "He is not quite awake."

With an abrupt, violent motion, Joao reached out, clutched the proffered hand.

It felt warm . . . human.

For no reason he could explain, tears came to Joao's eyes.

"Am I dreaming?" he whispered. He shook his head to clear away the tears.

"Joao, my son," said his father's voice.

Joao looked up at the familiar face. It *was* his father and no mistake. "But . . . your heart," Joao said.

"My pump," the old man said. "Look." And he pulled his hand away, turned to display where the back of his black suit had been cut away, its edges held by some gummy substance, and a pulsing surface of oily yellow between those cut edges.

Joao saw the hair-fine scale lines, the multiple shapes, and he recoiled.

So it was a copy, another of their tricks.

The old man turned back to face him. "The old pump failed and they gave me a new one," he said. "It shares my blood and lives off me and it'll give me a few more years. What do you think our bright IEO specialists will say about the *usefulness* of that?"

"Is it really you?" Joao demanded.

"All except the pump," said the old man. "They had to give you and some of the others a whole new blood system because of all the corrosive poison that got into you."

Joao lifted his hands, stared at them.

"They know medical tricks we haven't even dreamed about," the old man said. "I haven't been this excited since I was a boy. I can hardly wait to get back and . . . Joao! What is it?"

Joao was thrusting himself up, glaring at the old man. "We're not human anymore if . . . We're not human!"

"Be still, son!" the old man ordered.

"If this is true," Joao protested, "they're in control." He nodded toward the giant face behind his father. "They'll *rule* us!"

He sank back, gasping. "We'll be their slaves."

"Foolishness," rumbled the drum voice.

Joao looked at the giant face, growing aware of the fluorescent insects above it, seeing that the insects clung to the ceiling of a cave, noting finally a patch of night sky and stars where the fluorescent insects ended.

"What is a slave?" rumbled the voice.

Joao looked beneath the face where the voice originated, saw a white mass about four meters across, a pulsing yellow sac protruding from it, insects crawling over it, into fissures along its surface, back to the ground beneath. The face appeared to be held up from that white mass by a dozen of round stalks, their scaled surfaces betraying their nature.

"Your attention is drawn to our way of answering your threat to us," rumbled the voice, and Joao saw that the sound issued from the pulsing yellow sac. "This is our brain. It is vulnerable, very vulnerable, weak, yet strong . . . just as your brain. Now, tell me what is a slave?"

Joao fought down a shiver of revulsion, said: "I'm a slave now; I'm in bondage to you."

"Not true," rumbled the voice. "A slave is one who must produce wealth for another, and there is only one true wealth in all the universe—living time. Are we slaves because we have given your father more time to live?"

Joao looked up to the giant, glittering eyes, thought he detected amusement there.

"The lives of all those with you have been spared or extended as well," drummed the voice. "That makes us your slaves, does it not?"

"What do you take in return?"

"Ah hah!" the voice fairly barked. "Quid pro quo! You are, indeed, our slaves as well. We are tied to each other by a bond of mutual slavery that cannot be broken—never could be."

"It is very simple once you understand it," Joao's father said.

"Understand what?"

"Some of our kind once lived in greenhouses and their cells remembered the experience," rumbled the voice. "You know about greenhouses, of course?" It turned to look out at the cave mouth where dawn was beginning to touch the world with gray. "That out there, that is a greenhouse, too." Again, it looked down at Joao, the giant eyes glaring. "To sustain life, a greenhouse must achieve a delicate balance—enough of this chemical, enough of that one, another substance available when needed. What is poison one day can be sweet food the next."

"What's all this to do with slavery?" Joao demanded.

"Life has developed over millions of years in this greenhouse we call Earth," the voice rumbled. "Sometimes it developed in the poison excrement of other life . . . and then that poison became necessary to it. Without a substance produced by the wire worm, that savannah grass out there would die . . . in time. Without substances produced by . . . insects, your kind of life would die. Sometimes, just a faint trace of the substance is needed, such as the special copper compound produced by the arachnids. Sometimes, the substance must subtly change each time before it can be used by a life-form at the end of the chain. The more different forms of life there are, the more life the greenhouse can support. This is the lesson of the greenhouse. The successful greenhouse must grow many times many forms of life. The more forms of life it has, the healthier it is."

"You're saying we have to stop killing insects," Joao said. "You're saying we have to let you take over."

"We say you must stop killing yourselves," rumbled the voice. "Already, the Chinese are . . . I believe you would call it: *reinfesting* their land. Perhaps they will be in time, perhaps not. Here, it is not too late. There . . . they were fast and thorough . . . and they may need help."

"You . . . give us no proof," Joao said.

"There will be time for proof, later," said the voice. "Now, join your woman friend outside; let the sun work on your skin and the chlorophyll in your blood, and when you come back, tell me if the sun is your slave."

Jack Vance

John Holbrook Vance (1916–) is one of the premier stylists of science fiction, popular world-wide and influential on other writers for six decades. His book *The Dying Earth* (1950), set in a fantastically distant future, is one of the classics of genre science fiction. It is also one of those genre-stretching works that blur the borders between science fiction and fantasy, in the manner of the *Weird Tales* writers of the 1920s and '30s. He has written award-winning mysteries under his full name, and as Ellery Queen (many of the later novels of Queen were written by SF writers such as Theodore Sturgeon, Avram Davidson, and Vance). He is a huge man, a lover of hot jazz and writing, but also a carpenter by trade who was still, in the 1980s, building and rebuilding his own house.

Vance found his writing voice early and hit his stride in the 1950s. Since then he has produced a continuing stream of exquisite work, much of it brilliant. Critics often praise his intricacies and ironies, his subtle wit, his settings and atmospherics. Yet his characters are usually motivated by common passions, no matter how nicely expressed, and his plots are clever. He is still writing distinctive novels of fantasy and SF and winning genre awards in the mid-'90s. He is most often at his best in the novel form, but this piece is one of his later novellas, pure Vance compressed and distilled.

RUMFUDDLE

I

From *Memoirs and Reflections,* by Alan Robertson:

Often I hear myself declared humanity's preeminent benefactor, though the jocular occasionally raise a claim in favor of the original serpent. After all circumspection I really cannot dispute the judgment. My place in history is secure; my name will persist as if it were printed indelibly across the sky. All of which I find absurd but understandable. For I have given wealth beyond calculation. I have expunged deprivation, famine, overpopulation, territorial constriction: All the first-order causes of contention have vanished. My gifts go freely and carry with them my personal joy, but as a reasonable man (and for lack of other restrictive agency), I feel that I cannot relinquish all control, for when has the human animal ever been celebrated for abnegation and self-discipline?

We now enter an era of plenty and a time of new concerns. The old evils are gone: we must resolutely prohibit a flamboyant and perhaps unnatural set of new vices.

The three girls gulped down breakfast, assembled their homework, and departed noisily for school.

Elizabeth poured coffee for herself and Gilbert. He thought she seemed pensive and moody. Presently she said, "It's so beautiful here. . . . We're very lucky, Gilbert."

"I never forget it."

Elizabeth sipped her coffee and mused a moment, following some vagrant train of thought. She said, "I never liked growing up. I always felt strange—different from the other girls. I really don't know why."

"It's no mystery. Everyone for a fact is different."

"Perhaps . . . But Uncle Peter and Aunt Emma always acted as if I were more different than usual. I remember a hundred little signals. And yet I was such an ordinary little girl . . . Do you remember when you were little?"

"Not very well." Gilbert Duray looked out the window he himself had glazed, across green slopes and down to the placid water his daughters had named the Silver River. The Sounding Sea was thirty miles south; behind the house stood the first trees of the Robber Woods.

Duray considered his past. "Bob owned a ranch in Arizona during the 1870s: one of his fads. The Apaches killed my father and mother. Bob took me to the ranch, and then when I was three he brought me to Alan's house in San Francisco, and that's where I was brought up."

Elizabeth sighed. "Alan must have been wonderful. Uncle Peter was so grim. Aunt Emma never told me anything. Literally, not anything! They never cared the slightest bit for me, one way or the other . . . I wonder why Bob brought the subject up—about the Indians and your mother and father being scalped and all . . . He's such a strange man."

"Was Bob here?"

"He looked in a few minutes yesterday to remind us of his Rumfuddle. I told him I didn't want to leave the girls. He said to bring them along."

"Hah!"

"I told him I didn't want to go to his damn Rumfuddle with or without the girls. In the first place, I don't want to see Uncle Peter, who's sure to be there . . ."

II

From *Memoirs and Reflections:*

I insisted then and I insist now that our dear old Mother Earth, so soiled and toil-worn, never be neglected. Since I pay the piper (in a manner of speaking), I call the tune, and to my secret amusement I am heeded most briskly the world around, in the manner of bellboys, jumping to the command of an irascible old gentleman who is known to be a good tipper. No one dares to defy me. My whims become actualities; my plans progress.

Paris, Vienna, San Francisco, St. Petersburg, Venice, London, Dublin, surely will persist, gradually to become idealized essences of their former selves, as wine in due course becomes the soul of the grape. What of the old vitality? The shouts and curses, the neighborhood quarrels, the raucous music, the vulgarity? Gone, all gone! (But easy of reference at any of the cognates.) Old Earth is to be a gentle, kindly world, rich in treasures and artifacts, a world of old places—old inns, old roads, old forests, old palaces—where folk come to wander and dream, to experience the best of the past without suffering the worst.

Material abundance can now be taken for granted: Our resources are infinite. Metal, timber, soil, rock, water, air: free for anyone's taking. A single commodity remains in finite supply: human toil.

Gilbert Duray, the informally adopted grandson of Alan Robertson, worked on the Urban Removal Program. Six hours a day, four days a week, he guided a trashing machine across deserted Cuperinto, destroying tract houses, service stations, and supermarkets. Knobs and toggles controlled a steel hammer at the end of a hundred-foot boom; with a twitch of the finger, Duray toppled powerpoles, exploded picture windows, smashed siding and stucco, exploded picture windows, smashed siding and stucco, pulverized concrete. A disposal rig crawled fifty feet behind. The detritus was clawed upon a conveyor belt, carried to a twenty-foot orifice, and dumped with a rush and a rumble into the Apathetic Ocean. Aluminum siding, asphalt shingles, corrugated fiber-glass, TV's and barbecues, Swedish Modern furniture, Book-of-the-Month selections, concrete patio-tiles, finally the sidewalk and street itself: all to the bottom of the Apathetic Ocean. Only the trees remained, a strange eclectic forest stretching as far as the eye could reach: liquidambar and Scotch pine; Chinese pistachio, Atlas cedar, and ginkgo; white birch and Norway maple.

At one o'clock Howard Wirtz emerged from the caboose, as they called the small locker room at the rear of the machine. Wirtz had homesteaded a Miocene world; Duray, with a wife and three children, had preferred the milder environment of a contemporary semicognate: the popular Type A world on which man had never evolved.

Duray gave Wirtz the work schedule. "More or less like yesterday—straight out Persimmon to Walden, then right a block and back."

Wirtz, a dour and laconic man, acknowledged the information with a jerk of the head. On his Miocene world he lived alone, in a houseboat on a mountain lake. He harvested wild rice, mushrooms, and berries; he shot geese, groundfowl, deer, young bison, and had once informed Duray that after his five-year work-time he might just retire to his lake and never appear on Earth again, except maybe to buy clothes and ammunition. "Nothing here I want, nothing at all."

Duray had given a derisive snort. "And what will you do with all your time?"

"Hunt, fish, eat, and sleep, maybe sit on the front deck."

"Nothing else?"

"I just might learn to fiddle. Nearest neighbor is fifteen million years away."

"You can't be too careful, I suppose."

Duray descended to the ground and looked over his day's work: a quarter-mile swath of desolation. Duray, who allowed his subconscious few extravagances, nevertheless felt a twinge for the old times, which, for all their disadvantages, at least had been lively. Voices, bicycle bells, the barking of dogs, the slamming of doors, still echoed along Persimmon Avenue. The former inhabitants presumably preferred their new homes. The self-sufficient had taken private worlds; the more gregarious lived in communities on worlds of every description: as early as the Carboniferous, as current as the Type A. A few had even returned to the now-uncrowded cities. An exciting era to live in: a time of flux. Duray, thirty-four years old, remembered no other way of life; the old existence, as exemplified by Persimmon Avenue, seemed antique, cramped, constricted.

He had a word with the operator of the trashing machine; returning to the caboose, Duray paused to look through the orifice across the Apathetic Ocean.

A squall hung black above the southern horizon, toward which a trail of broken lumber drifted, ultimately to wash up on some unknown pre-Cambrian shore. There never would be an inspector sailing forth to protest; the world knew no life other than mollusks and algae, and all the trash of Earth would never fill its submarine gorges. Duray tossed a rock through the gap and watched the alien water splash up and subside. Then he turned away and entered the caboose.

Along the back wall were four doors. The second from the left was marked "G. DURAY." He unlocked the door, pulled it open, and stopped short, staring in astonishment at the blank back wall. He lifted the transparent plastic flap that functioned as an air-seal and brought out the collapsed metal ring that had been the flange surrounding his passway. The inner surface was bare metal; looking through, he saw only the interior of the caboose.

A long minute passed. Duray stood staring at the useless ribbon as if hypnotized, trying to grasp the implications of the situation. To his knowledge no passway had ever failed, unless it had been purposefully closed. Who would play him such a spiteful trick? Certainly not Elizabeth. She detested practical jokes and if anything, like Duray himself, was perhaps a trifle too intense and literal-minded. He jumped down from the caboose and strode off across Cupertino Forest: a sturdy, heavy-shouldered man of about average stature. His features were rough and uncompromising; his brown hair was cut crisply short; his eyes glowed golden-brown and exerted an arresting force. Straight, heavy eyebrows crossed his long, thin nose like the bar of a T; his mouth, compressed against some strong inner urgency, formed a lower horizontal bar. All in all, not a man to be trifled with, or so it would seem.

He trudged through the haunted grove, preoccupied by the strange and inconvenient event that had befallen him. What had happened to the passway? Unless Elizabeth had invited friends out to Home, as they called their world, she was alone, with the three girls at school . . . Duray came out upon Stevens Creek Road. A farmer's pickup truck halted at his signal and took him into San Jose, now little more than a country town.

At the transit center he dropped a coin in the turnstile and entered the lobby. Four portals designated "LOCAL," "CALIFORNIA," "NORTH AMERICA," and "WORLD" opened in the walls, each portal leading to a hub on Utilis.*

Duray passed into the "California" hub, found the "Oakland" portal, returned to the Oakland Transit Center on Earth, passed back through the "Local" portal to the "Oakland" hub on Utilis, and returned to Earth through the "Montclair West" portal to a depot only a quarter mile from Thornhill School,† to which Duray walked.

---

*Utilis: a world cognate to Paleocene Earth, where, by Alan Robertson's decree, all the industries, institutions, warehouses, tanks, dumps, and commercial offices of old Earth were now located. The name Utilis, so it had been remarked, accurately captured the flavor of Alan Robertson's pedantic, quaint, and idealistic personality.

†Alan Robertson had proposed another specialized world, to be known as Tutelar, where the children of all the settled worlds should receive their education in a vast array of pedagogical facilities, To his hurt surprise, he encountered a storm of wrathful opposition from parents. His scheme was termed mechanistic, vast, dehumanizing, repulsive. What better world for schooling than old Earth itself? Here was the source of all tradition; let Earth become Tutelar! So insisted the parents, and Alan Robertson had no choice but to agree.

In the office Duray identified himself to the clerk and requested the presence of his daughter Dolly.

The clerk sent forth a messenger who, after an interval, returned alone. "Dolly Duray isn't at school."

Duray was surprised; Dolly had been in good health and had set off to school as usual. He said, "Either Joan or Ellen will do as well."

The messenger again went forth and again returned. "Neither one is in their classrooms, Mr. Duray. All three of your children are absent."

"I can't understand it," said Duray, now fretful. "All three set off to school this morning."

"Let me ask Miss Haig. I've just come on duty." The clerk spoke into a telephone, listened, then turned back to Duray. "The girls went home at ten o'clock. Mrs. Duray called for them and took them back through the passway."

"Did she give any reason whatever?"

"Miss Haig says no; Mrs. Duray just told her she needed the girls at home."

Duray stifled a sigh of baffled irritation. "Could you take me to their locker? I'll use their passway to get home."

"That's contrary to school regulations, Mr. Duray. You'll understand, I'm sure."

"I can identify myself quite definitely," said Duray. "Mr. Carr knows me well. As a matter of fact, my passway collapsed, and I came here to get home."

"Why don't you speak to Mr. Carr?"

"I'd like to do so."

Duray was conducted into the principal's office, where he explained his predicament. Mr. Carr expressed sympathy and made no difficulty about taking Duray to the children's passway.

They went to a hall at the back of the school and found the locker numbered 382. "Here we are," said Carr. "I'm afraid that you'll find it a tight fit." He unlocked the metal door with his master key and threw it open. Duray looked inside and saw only the black metal at the back of the locker. The passway, like his own, had been closed.

Duray drew back and for a moment could find no words.

Carr spoke in a voice of polite amazement. "How very perplexing! I don't believe I've ever seen anything like it before! Surely the girls wouldn't play such a silly prank!"

"They know better than to touch the passway," Duray said gruffly. "Are you sure that this is the right locker?"

Carr indicated the card on the outside of the locker, where three names had been typed: "DOROTHY DURAY, JOAN DURAY, ELLEN DURAY." "No mistake," said Carr, "and I'm afraid that I can't help you any further. Are you in common residency?"

"It's our private homestead."

Carr nodded with lips judiciously pursed, to suggest that insistence upon so much privacy seemed eccentric. He gave a deprecatory little chuckle. "I suppose if you isolate yourself to such an extent, you more or less must expect a series of emergencies."

"To the contrary," Duray said crisply. "Our life is uneventful, because there's no one to bother us. We love the wild animals, the quiet, the fresh air. We wouldn't have it any differently."

Carr smiled a dry smile. "Mr. Robertson has certainly altered the lives of us all. I understand that he is your grandfather?"

"I was raised in his household. I'm his nephew's foster son. The blood relationship isn't all that close."

III

From *Memoirs and Reflections:*

I early became interested in magnetic fluxes and their control. After taking my degree, I worked exclusively in this field, studying all varieties of magnetic envelopes and developing controls over their formation. For many years my horizons were thus limited, and I lived a placid existence.

Two contemporary developments forced me down from my "ivory castle." First: the fearful overcrowding of the planet and the prospect of worse to come. Cancer already was an affliction of the past; heart diseases were under control; I feared that in another ten years immortality might be a practical reality for many of us, with a consequent augmentation of population pressure.

Secondly, the theoretical work done upon "black holes" and "white holes" suggested that matter compacted in a "black hole" broke through a barrier to spew forth from a "white hole" in another universe. I calculated pressures and considered the self-focusing magnetic sheaths, cones, and whorls with which I was experimenting. Through their innate properties these entities constricted themselves to apexes of a cross section indistinguishable from a geometric point. What if two or more cones (I asked myself) could be arranged in contraposition to produce an equilibrium? In this condition charged particles must be accelerated to near light-speed and at the mutual focus constricted and impinged together. The pressures thus created, though of small scale, would be far in excess of those characteristic of the "black holes": to unknown effect.

I can now report that the mathematics of the multiple focus are a most improbable thicket, and the useful service I enforced upon what I must call a set of absurd contradictions is one of my secrets. I know that thousands of scientists, at home and abroad, are attempting to duplicate my work; they are welcome to the effort. None will succeed. Why do I speak so positively? This is my other secret.

Duray marched back to the Montclair West depot in a state of angry puzzlement. There were four passways to Home, of which two were closed. The third was located in his San Francisco locker: the "front door," so to speak. The last and the original orifice was cased, filed, and indexed in Alan Robertson's vault.

Duray tried to deal with the problem in rational terms. The girls would never tamper with the passways. As for Elizabeth, no more than the girls would she consider such an act. At least Duray could imagine no reason that would so urge or impel her. Elizabeth, like himself, a foster child, was a beautiful, passionate woman, tall, dark-haired, with lustrous dark eyes and a wide mouth that tended to curve in an endearingly crooked grin. She was also responsible, loyal, careful, industrious; she loved her family and Riverview Manor. The theory of erotic intrigue seemed to Duray as incredible as the fact of the closed passways. Though for a fact, Elizabeth was prone to wayward and incomprehensible moods. Suppose Elizabeth had received a visitor who for some sane or insane purpose had forced her to close the passway? . . . Duray shook his head in frustration, like a harassed bull. The matter no doubt had some simple cause. Or on the other hand, Duray reflected, the cause might be complex and intricate. The thought, by some obscure connection, brought before him the image of his nominal foster father, Alan Robertson's nephew, Bob Robertson. Duray gave his head a nod of gloomy asseveration, as if to confirm a fact he long ago should have suspected. He went to the phone booth and called Bob Robertson's apartment in San Francisco. The screen glowed white and an instant later displayed Bob Robertson's alert, clean, and handsome face. "Good afternoon, Gil. Glad you called; I've been anxious to get in touch with you."

Duray became warier than ever. "How so?"

"Nothing serious, or so I hope. I dropped by your locker to leave off some books that I promised Elizabeth, and I noticed through the glass that your passway is closed. Collapsed. Useless."

"Strange," said Duray. "Very strange indeed. I can't understand it. Can you?"

"No . . . not really."

Duray thought he detected a subtlety of intonation. His eyes narrowed in concentration. "The passway at my rig was closed. The passway at the girls' school was closed. Now you tell me that the downtown passway is closed."

Bob Robertson grinned. "That's a pretty broad hint, I would say. Did you and Elizabeth have a row?"

"No."

Bob Robertson rubbed his long aristocratic chin. "A mystery. There's probably some very ordinary explanation."

"Or some very extraordinary explanation."

"True. Nowadays a person can't rule out anything. By the way, tomorrow night is the Rumfuddle, and I expect both you and Elizabeth to be on hand."

"As I recall," said Duray, "I've already declined the invitation." The Rumfuddlers were a group of Bob's cronies. Duray suspected that their activities were not altogether wholesome. "Excuse me; I've got to find an open passway, or Elizabeth and the kids are marooned."

"Try Alan," said Bob. "He'll have the original in his vault."

Duray gave a curt nod. "I don't like to bother him, but that's my last hope."

"Let me know what happens," said Bob Robertson. "And if you're at loose ends, don't forget the Rumfuddle tomorrow night. I mentioned the matter to Elizabeth, and she said she'd be sure to attend."

"Indeed. And when did you consult Elizabeth?"

"A day or so ago. Don't look so damnably gothic, my boy."

"I'm wondering if there's a connection between your invitation and the closed passways. I happen to know that Elizabeth doesn't care for your parties."

Bob Robertson laughed with easy good grace. "Reflect a moment. Two events occur. I invite you and wife Elizabeth to the Rumfuddle. This is event one. Your passways close up, which is event two. By a feat of structured absurdity you equate the two and blame me. Now is that fair?"

"You call it 'structured absurdity,' " said Duray. "I call it instinct."

Bob Robertson laughed again. "You'll have to do better than that. Consult Alan, and if for some reason he can't help you, come to the Rumfuddle. We'll rack our brains and either solve your problem or come up with new and better ones." He gave a cheery nod, and before Duray could roar an angry expostulation, the screen faded.

Duray stood glowering at the screen, convinced that Bob Robertson knew much more about the closed passways than he admitted. Duray went to sit on a bench. . . . If Elizabeth had closed him away from Home, her reasons must have been compelling indeed. But unless she intended to isolate herself permanently from Earth, she would leave at least one passway ajar, and this must be the master orifice in Alan Robertson's vault.

Duray rose to his feet, somewhat heavily, and stood a moment, head bent and shoulders hunched. He gave a surly grunt and returned to the phone booth, where he called a number known to not more than a dozen persons.

The screen glowed white while the person at the other end of the line scrutinized his face. . . . The screen cleared, revealing a round pale face from which pale blue eyes stared forth with a passionless intensity. "Hello, Ernest," said Duray. "Is Alan busy at the moment?"

"I don't think he's doing anything particular—except resting."

Ernest gave the last two words a meaningful emphasis. "I've got some problems," said Duray. "What's the best way to get in touch with him?"

"You'd better come up here. The code is changed. It's MHF now."

"I'll be there in a few minutes."

Back in the "California" hub on Utilis, Duray went into a side chamber lined with private lockers, numbered and variously marked with symbols, names, colored flags, or not marked at all. Duray went to Locker 122, and, ignoring the keyhole, set the code lock to the letters MHF. The door opened; Duray stepped into the locker and through the passway to the High Sierra headquarters of Alan Robertson.

IV

From *Memoirs and Reflections:*

If one basic axiom controls the cosmos, it must be this:

In a situation of infinity every possible condition occurs, not once, but an infinite number of times.

There is no mathematical nor logical limit to the number of dimensions. Our perceptions assure us of three only, but many indications suggest otherwise: parapsychic occurrences of a hundred varieties, the "white holes," the seemingly finite state of our own universe, which, by corollary, asserts the existence of others.

Hence, when I stepped behind the lead slab and first touched the button, I felt confident of success; failure would have surprised me!

But (and here lay my misgivings) what sort of success might I achieve?

Suppose I opened a hole into the interplanetary vacuum?

The chances of this were very good indeed; I surrounded the machine in a strong membrane to prevent the air of Earth from rushing off into the void.

Suppose I discovered a condition totally beyond imagination?

My imagination yielded no safeguards.

I proceeded to press the button.

Duray stepped out into a grotto under damp granite walls. Sunlight poured into the opening from a dark-blue sky. This was Alan Robertson's link to the outside world; like many other persons, he disliked a passway opening directly into his home. A path led fifty yards across bare granite mountainside to the lodge. To the west spread a great vista of diminishing ridges, valleys, and hazy blue air; to the east rose a pair of granite crags, with snow caught in the saddle between. Alan Robertson's lodge was built just below the timberline, beside a small lake fringed with tall dark firs. The lodge was built of rounded granite stones, with a wooden porch across the front; at each end rose a massive chimney.

Duray had visited the lodge on many occasions; as a boy he had scaled both of the crags behind the house, to look wonderingly off across the stillness, which on old Earth had a poignant breathing quality different from the uninhabited solitudes of worlds such as Home.

Ernest came to the door: a middle-aged man with an ingenuous face, small white hands, and soft, damp, mouse-colored hair. Ernest disliked the lodge, the wilderness, and solitude in general; he nevertheless would have suffered tortures before relinquishing his post as subaltern to Alan Robertson. Ernest and Duray were almost antipodal in outlook. Ernest thought Duray brusque, indelicate, a trifle coarse, and probably not disinclined to violence as an argumentative adjunct. Duray considered Ernest, when he thought of him at all, as the kind of man who takes two bites out of a cherry. Ernest had never married; he showed no interest in women, and Duray, as a boy, had often fretted at Ernest's overcautious restrictions.

In particular Ernest resented Duray's free and easy access to Alan Robertson. The power to restrict or admit those countless persons who demanded Alan Robertson's attention was Ernest's most cherished perquisite, and Duray denied him the use of it by simply ignoring Ernest and all his regulations. Ernest had never complained to Alan Robertson for fear of discovering that Duray's influence exceeded his own. A wary truce existed between the two, each conceding the other his privileges.

Ernest performed a polite greeting and admitted Duray into the lodge. Duray looked around the interior, which had not changed during his lifetime: varnished plank floors with red, black, and white Navaho rugs, massive pine furniture with leather cushions, a few shelves of books, a half-dozen pewter mugs on the mantle over the big fireplace—a room almost ostentatiously bare of souvenirs and mementos. Duray turned back to Ernest: "Whereabouts is Alan?"

"On his boat."

"With guests?"

"No," said Ernest, with a faint sniff of disapproval. "He's alone, quite alone."

"How long has he been gone?"

"He just went through an hour ago. I doubt if he's left the dock yet. What is your problem, if I may ask?"

"The passways to my world are closed. All three. There's only one left, in the vault."

Ernest arched his flexible eyebrows. "Who closed them?"

"I don't know. Elizabeth and the girls are alone, so far as I know."

"Extraordinary," said Ernest in a flat metallic voice. "Well, then, come along." He led the way down a hall to a back room. With his hand on the knob, Ernest paused and looked back over his shoulder. "Did you mention the matter to anyone? Robert, for instance?"

"Yes," said Duray curtly, "I did. Why do you ask?"

Ernest hesitated a fraction of a second. "No particular reason. Robert occasionally has a somewhat misplaced sense of humor, he and his Rumfuddlers." He spoke the word with a hiss of distaste.

Duray said nothing of his own suspicions. Ernest opened the door; they entered a large room illuminated by a skylight. The only furnishing was a rug on the varnished floor. Into each wall opened four doors. Ernest went to one of these doors, pulled it open, and made a resigned gesture. "You'll probably find Alan at the dock."

Duray looked into the interior of a rude hut with palm-frond walls, resting on a platform of poles. Through the doorway he saw a path leading under sunlit green foliage toward a strip of white beach. Surf sparkled below a layer of dark-blue ocean and a glimpse of the sky. Duray hesitated, rendered wary by the events of the morning. Anyone and everyone was suspect, even Ernest, who now gave a quiet sniff of contemptuous amusement. Through the foliage Duray glimpsed a spread of sail; he stepped through the passway.

V

From *Memoirs and Reflections:*

Man is a creature whose evolutionary environment has been the open air. His nerves, muscles, and senses have developed across three million years in intimate contiguity with natural earth, crude stone, live wood, wind, and rain. Now this creature is suddenly—on the geologic scale, instantaneously—shifted to an unnatural environment of metal and glass, plastic and plywood, to which his psychic substrata lack all compatibility. The wonder is not that we have so much mental instability but so little. Add to this the weird noises, electrical pleasures, bizarre colors, synthetic foods, abstract entertainments! We should congratulate ourselves on our durability.

I bring this matter up because, with my little device—so simple, so easy, so flexible—I have vastly augmenter the load upon our poor primeval brain, and for a fact many persons find the instant transition from one locale to another unsettling, and even actively unpleasant.

Duray stood on the porch of the cabin, under a vivid green canopy of sunlit foliage. The air was soft and warm and smelled of moist vegetation. He stood listening. The mutter of the surf came to his ears and from a far distance a single birdcall.

Duray stepped down to the ground and followed the path under tall palm trees to a riverbank. A few yards downstream, beside a rough pier of poles and planks, floated a white-and-blue ketch, sails hoisted and distended to a gentle breeze. On the deck stood Alan Robertson, on the point of casting off the mooring lines. Duray hailed him; Alan Robertson turned in surprise and vexation, which vanished when he recognized Duray. "Hello, Gil, glad you're here! For a moment I thought it might be someone to bother me. Jump aboard; you're just in time for a sail."

Duray somberly joined Alan Robertson on the boat. "I'm afraid I am here to bother you."

"Oh?" Alan Robertson raised his eyebrows in instant solicitude. He was a man of no great height, thin, nervously active. Wisps of rumpled white hair fell over his forehead; mild blue eyes inspected Duray with concern, all thoughts of sailing forgotten. "What in the world has happened?"

"I wish I knew. If it were something I could handle myself, I wouldn't bother you."

"Don't worry about me; there's all the time in the world for sailing. Now tell me what's happened."

"I can't get through to Home. All the passways are closed off. Why and how I have no idea. Elizabeth and the girls are out there alone; at least I think they're *out there.*"

Alan Robertson rubbed his chin. "What an odd business! I can certainly understand your agitation. . . . You think Elizabeth closed the passways?"

"It's unreasonable—but there's no one else."

Alan Robertson turned Duray a shrewd, kindly glance. "No little family upsets? Nothing to cause her despair and anguish?"

"Absolutely nothing. I've tried to reason things out, but I draw a blank. I thought that maybe someone—a man had gone through to visit her and decided to take over, but if this were the case, why did she come to the school for the girls? That possibility is out. A secret love affair? Possible but so damn unlikely. Since she wants to keep me off the planet, her only motive could be to protect me or herself or the girls from danger of some sort. Again this means that another person is concerned in the matter. Who? How? Why? I spoke to Bob. He claims to know nothing about the situation, but he wants me to come to his damned Rumfuddle, and he hints very strongly that Elizabeth will be on hand. I can't prove a thing against Bob, but I suspect him. He's always had a taste for odd jokes."

Alan Robertson gave a lugubrious nod. "I won't deny that." He sat down in the cockpit and stared off across the water. "Bob has a complicated sense of humor, but he'd hardly close you away from your world. . . . I hardly think that your family is in actual danger, but of course we can't take chances. The possibility exists that Bob is not responsible, that something uglier is afoot." He jumped to his feet. "Our obvious first step is to use the master orifice in the vault." He looked a shade regretfully toward the ocean. "My little sail can wait. . . . A lovely world this: not fully cognate with Earth—a cousin, so to speak. The fauna and flora are roughly contemporary except for man. The hominids have never developed."

The two men returned up the path, Alan Robertson chatting lightheartedly: "Thousands and thousands of worlds I've visited, and looked into even more, but do you know I've never hit upon a good system of classification. There are exact cognates—of course we're never sure exactly *how* exact they are. These cases are relatively simple but then the problems begin . . . Bah! I don't think about such things anymore. I know that when I keep all the determinates at zero, the cognates appear. Overintellectualizing is the bane of this and every other era. Show me a man who deals only with abstraction, and I'll show you the dead futile end of evolution." Alan Robertson chuckled. "If I could control the machine tightly enough to produce real cognates, our troubles would be over . . . Much confusion, of course. I might step through into the cognate world immediately as a true cognate Alan Robertson steps through into our world, with net effect of zero. An amazing business, really; I never tire of it. . . ."

They returned to the transit room of the mountain lodge. Ernest appeared almost instantly. Duray suspected he had been watching through the passway.

Alan Robertson said briskly, "We'll be busy for an hour or two, Ernest. Gilbert is having difficulties, and we've got to set things straight."

Ernest nodded somewhat grudgingly, or so it seemed to Duray. "The progress report on the Ohio Plan has arrived. Nothing particularly urgent."

"Thank you, Ernest, I'll see to it later. Come along, Gilbert; let's get to the bottom of this affair." They went to door No. 1 and passed through to the Utilis hub. Alan Robertson led the way to a small green door with a three-dial coded lock, which he opened with a flourish. "Very well, in we go." He carefully locked the door behind them, and they walked the length of a short hall. "A shame that I must be so cautious," said Alan Robertson. "You'd be astonished at the outrageous requests otherwise sensible people make of me. I sometimes become exasperated . . . Well, it's understandable, I suppose."

At the end of the hall Alan Robertson worked the locking dials of a red door. "This way, Gilbert; you've been through before." They stepped through a passway into a hall that opened into a circular concrete chamber fifty feet in diameter, located, so Duray knew, deep under the Mad Dog Mountains of the Mojave Desert. Eight halls extended away into the rock; each hall communicated with twelve aisles. The center of the chamber was occupied by a circular desk twenty feet in diameter; here six clerks in white smocks worked at computers and collating machines. In accordance with their instructions they gave Alan Robertson neither recognition nor greeting.

Alan Robertson went up to the desk, at which signal the chief clerk, a solemn young man bald as an egg, came forward. "Good afternoon, sir."

"Good afternoon, Harry. Find me the index for 'Gilbert Duray,' on my personal list."

The clerk bowed smartly. He went to an instrument and ran his fingers over a bank of keys; the instrument ejected a card that Harry handed to Alan Robertson. "There you are, sir."

Alan Robertson showed the card to Duray, who saw the code: "4:8:10/6:13: 29."

"That's your world," said Alan Robertson. "We'll soon learn how the land lies. This way, to Radiant four." He led the way down the hall, turned into the aisle numbered "8," and proceeded to Stack 10. "Shelf six," said Alan Robertson. He checked the card. "Drawer thirteen . . . here we are." He drew forth the drawer and ran his fingers along the tabs. "Item twenty-nine. This should be Home." He brought forth a metal frame four inches square and held it up to his eyes. He frowned in disbelief. "We don't have anything here either." He turned to Duray a glance of dismay. "This is a serious situation!"

"It's no more than I expected," said Duray tonelessly.

"All this demands some careful thought." Alan Robertson clicked his tongue in vexation. "Tst, tst, tst." He examined the identification plaque at the top of the frame. "Four: eight: ten/six: thirteen: twenty-nine," he read. "There seems to be no question of error." He squinted carefully at the numbers, hesitated, then slowly replaced the frame. On second thought he took the frame forth once more. "Come along, Gilbert," said Alan Robertson. "We'll have a cup of coffee and think this matter out."

The two returned to the central chamber, where Alan Robertson gave the empty frame into the custody of Harry the clerk. "Check the records, if you please," said Alan Robertson. "I want to know how many passways were pinched off the master."

Harry manipulated the buttons of his computer. "Three only, Mr. Robertson."

"Three passways and the master—four in all?"

"That's right, sir."

"Thank you, Harry."

VI

From *Memoirs and Reflections:*

I recognized the possibility of many cruel abuses, but the good so outweighed the bad that I thrust aside all thought of secrecy and exclusivity. I consider myself not Alan Robertson but, like Prometheus, an archetype of Man, and my discovery must serve all men.

But caution, caution, caution!

I sorted out my ideas. I myself coveted the amplitude of a private, personal world; such a yearning was not ignoble, I decided. Why should not everyone have the same if he so desired, since the supply was limitless? Think of it! The wealth and beauty of an entire world: mountains and plains, forests and flowers, ocean cliffs and crashing seas, winds and clouds—all beyond value, yet worth no more than a few seconds of effort and a few watts of energy.

I became troubled by a new idea. Would everyone desert old Earth and leave it a vile junk-heap? I found the concepts intolerable. . . . I exchange access to a world for three to six years of remedial toil, depending upon occupancy.

A lounge overlooked the central chamber. Alan Robertson gestured Duray to a seat and drew two mugs of coffee from a dispenser. Settling in a chair, he turned his eyes up to the ceiling. "We must collect our thoughts. The circumstances are somewhat unusual; still, I have lived with unusual circumstances for almost fifty years.

"So then: the situation. We have verified that there are only four passways to Home. These four passways are closed, though we must accept Bob's word in regard to your downtown locker. If this is truly the case, if Elizabeth and the girls are still on Home, you will never see them again."

"Bob is mixed up in this business. I could swear to nothing, but—"

Alan Robertson held up his hand. "I will talk to Bob; this is the obvious first step." He rose to his feet and went to the telephone in the corner of the lounge. Duray joined him. Alan spoke into the screen. "Get me Robert Robertson's apartment in San Francisco."

The screen glowed white. Bob's voice came from the speaker. "Sorry, I'm not at home. I have gone out to my world Fancy, and I cannot be reached. Call back in a week, unless your business is urgent, in which case call back in a month."

"Mmph," said Alan Robertson, returning to his seat. "Bob is sometimes a trifle too flippant. A man with an under-extended intellect . . ." He drummed his fingers on the arm of his chair. "Tomorrow night is his party? What does he call it? A Rumfuddle?"

"Some such nonsense. Why does he want me? I'm a dead dog; I'd rather be home building a fence."

"Perhaps you had better plan to attend the party."

"That means, submit to his extortion."

"Do you want to see your wife and family again?"

"Naturally. But whatever he has in mind won't be for my benefit, or Elizabeth's."

"You're probably right there. I've heard one or two unsavory tales regarding the Rumfuddlers. . . . The fact remains that the passways are closed. All four of them."

Duray's voice became harsh. "Can't you open a new orifice for us?"

Alan Robertson gave his head a sad shake. "I can tune the machine very finely. I can code accurately for the 'Home' class of worlds and as closely as necessary approximate a particular world-state. But at each setting, no matter how fine the tuning, we encounter an infinite number of worlds. In practice, inaccuracies in the machine, backlash, the gross size of electrons, the very difference between one electron and another, make it difficult to tune with absolute precision. So even if we tuned exactly to the 'Home' class, the probability of opening into your particular Home is one of an infinite number: in short, negligible."

Duray stared off across the chamber. "Is it possible that space once entered might tend to open more easily a second time?"

Alan Robertson smiled. "As to that, I can't say. I suspect not, but I really know so little. I see no reason why it should be so."

"If we can open into a world precisely cognate, I can at least learn why the passways are closed."

Alan Robertson sat up in his chair. "Here is a valid point. Perhaps we can accomplish something in this regard." He glanced humorously sidewise at Duray. "On the other hand—consider this situation. We create access into a 'Home' almost exactly cognate to your own—so nearly identical that the difference is not readily apparent. You find there an Elizabeth, a Dolly, a Joan, and an Ellen indistinguishable from your own, and a Gilbert marooned on Earth. You might even convince yourself that this is your very own Home."

"I'd know the difference," said Duray shortly, but Alan Robertson seemed not to hear.

"Think of it! An infinite number of Homes isolated from Earth, an infinite number of Elizabeths, Dollys, Joans, and Ellens marooned, an infinite number of Gilbert Durays trying to regain access . . . The sum effect might be a wholesale reshuffling of families, with everyone more or less good-natured about the situation. I wonder if this could be Bob's idea of a joke to share with his Rumfuddlers."

Duray looked sharply at Alan Robertson, wondering whether the man was serious. "It doesn't sound funny and I wouldn't be very good-natured."

"Of course not," said Alan Robertson hastily. "An afterthought—in rather poor taste, I'm afraid."

"In any event, Bob hinted that Elizabeth would be at the damned Rumfuddle. If that's the case, she must have closed the passways from this side."

"A possibility," Alan Robertson conceded, "but unreasonable. Why should she seal you away from Home?"

"I don't know, but I'd like to find out."

Alan Robertson slapped his hands down upon his shanks and jumped to his feet, only to pause once more. "You're sure you want to look into these cognates? You might see things you wouldn't like."

"So long as I know the truth, I don't care whether I like it or not."

"So be it."

The machine occupied a room behind the balcony. Alan Robertson surveyed the device with pride and affection. "This is the fourth model, and probably optimum; at least I don't see any place for significant improvement. I use a hundred and sixty-seven rods converging upon the center of the reactor sphere. Each rod produces a quotum of energy and is susceptible to several types of adjustment to cope with the very large number of possible states. The number of particles to pack the universe full is on the order of ten raised to the power of sixty; the possible permutations these particles would number two raised to the power of ten raised to the power of sixty. The universe, of course, is built of many different particles, which makes the final number of possible, or let us say, thinkable states a number like two raised to the power of ten raised to the power of sixty, all times *x*, where *x* is the number of particles under consideration. A large, unmanageable number, which we need not consider, because the conditions we deal with—the possible variations of planet Earth—are far fewer."

"Still a very large number," said Duray.

"Indeed yes. But again the sheer unmanageable bulk is swept away by a self-normalizing property of the machine. In what I call floating neutral, the machine reaches the closest cognate—which is to say, that infinite class of perfect cognates. In practice, because of infinitesimal inaccuracies, 'floating neutral' reaches cognates more or less imperfect, perhaps by no more than the shape of a single grain of sand. Still, 'floating neutral' provides a natural base, and by adjusting the controls, we reach cycles at an ever greater departure from base. In practice I search out a good cycle and strike a large number of passways, as many as a hundred thousand. So now to our business." He went to a porthole at the side. "Your code number, what was it now?"

Duray brought forth the card and read the numbers: "Four: eight:ten/six:thirteen:twenty-nine."

"Very good. I give the code to the computer, which searches the files and automatically adjusts the machine. Now then, step over here; the process releases dangerous radiation."

The two stood behind lead slabs. Alan Robertson touched a button; watching through a periscope, Duray saw a spark of purple light and heard a small groaning, gasping sound seeming to come from the air itself.

Alan Robertson stepped forth and walked to the machine. In the delivery tray rested an extensible ring. He picked up the ring and looked through the hole. "This seems to be right." He handed the ring to Duray. "Do you see anything you recognize?"

Duray put the ring to his eye. "That's Home."

"Very good. Do you want me to come with you?"

Duray considered. "The time is now?"

"Yes. This is a time-neutral setting."

"I think I'll go alone."

Alan Robertson nodded. "Whatever you like. Return as soon as you can, so I'll know you're safe."

Duray frowned at him sidewise. "Why shouldn't I be safe? No one is there but my family."

"Not *your* family. The family of a cognate Gilbert Duray. The family may not be absolutely identical. The cognate Duray may not be identical. You can't be sure exactly what you will find—so be careful."

VII

From *Memoirs and Reflections:*

When I think of my machine and my little forays in and out of infinity, and idea keeps recurring to me which is so rather terrible that I close it out of my mind, and I will not even mention it here.

Duray stepped out upon the soil of Home and stood praising the familiar landscape. A vast meadow drenched in sunlight rolled down to wide Silver River. Above the opposite shore rose a line of low bluffs, with copses of trees in the hollows. To the left, the landscape seemed to extend indefinitely and at last become indistinct in the blue haze of distance. To the right, the Robber Woods ended a quarter mile from where Duray stood. On a flat beside the forest, on the bank of a small stream, stood a house of stone and timber: a sight that seemed to Duray the most beautiful one he had ever seen. Polished glass windows sparkled in the sunlight; banks of geraniums glowed green and red. From the chimney rose a wisp of smoke.

The air smelled cool and sweet but seemed—so Duray imagined—to carry a strange tang, different—so he imagined—from the meadow-scent of his own Home. Duray started forward, then halted. The world was his own, yet not his own. If he had been conscious of the fact, would he have recognized the strangeness? Nearby rose an outcrop of weathered gray field-rock: a rounded mossy pad on which he had sat only two days before, contemplating the building of a dock. He walked over and looked down at the stone. Here he had sat; here were the impressions of his heels in the soil; here was the pattern of moss from which he had absently scratched a fragment. Duray bent close. The moss was whole. The man who had sat here, the cognate Duray, had not scratched at the moss. So then: The world was perceptibly different from his own.

Duray was relieved and yet vaguely disturbed. If the world had been the exact simulacrum of his own, he might have been subjected to unmanageable emotions—which still might be the case. He walked toward the house, along the path that led down to the river. He stepped up to the porch. On a deck chair was a book: *Down There: A Study of Satanism,* by J. K. Huysmans. Elizabeth's tastes were eclectic. Duray had not previously seen the book; was it perhaps that Bob Robertson had put through the parcel delivery?

Duray went into the house. Elizabeth stood across the room. She had evidently watched him coming up the path. She said nothing; her face showed no expression.

Duray halted, somewhat at a loss as to how to address this familiar-strange woman. "Good afternoon," he said at last.

Elizabeth allowed a wisp of a smile to show. "Hello, Gilbert."

At least, thought Duray, on cognate worlds the same language was spoken. He studied Elizabeth. Lacking prior knowledge, would he have perceived her to be someone different from his own Elizabeth? Both were beautiful women: tall and slender, with curling black shoulder-length hair, worn without artifice. Their skin was pale, with a dusky undertone; their mouths were wide, passionate, stubborn. Duray knew his Elizabeth to be a woman of explicable moods, and this Elizabeth was doubtless no different—yet somehow a difference existed that Duray could not define, deriving perhaps from the strangeness of her atoms, the stuff of a different universe. He wondered if she sensed the same difference in him.

He asked, "Did you close off the passways?"

Elizabeth nodded, without change of expression.

"Why?"

"I thought it the best thing to do," said Elizabeth in a soft voice.

"That's no answer."

"I suppose not. How did you get here?"

"Alan made an opening."

Elizabeth raised her eyebrows. "I thought that was impossible."

"True. This is a different world to my own. Another Gilbert Duray built this house. I'm not your husband."

Elizabeth's mouth dropped in astonishment. She swayed back a step and put her hand up to her neck: a mannerism Duray could not recall in his own Elizabeth. The sense of strangeness came ever more strongly upon him. He felt an intruder. Elizabeth was watching him with a wide-eyed fascination. She said in a hurried mutter: "I wish you'd leave, go back to your own world; do!"

"If you've closed off all the passways, you'll be isolated," growled Duray. "Marooned, probably forever."

"Whatever I do," said Elizabeth, "it's not your affair."

"It is my affair, if only for the sake of the girls. I won't allow them to live and die alone out here."

"The girls aren't here," said Elizabeth in a flat voice. "They are where neither you nor any other Gilbert Duray will find them. So now go back to your own world, and leave me in whatever peace my soul allows me."

Duray stood glowering at the fiercely beautiful woman. He had never heard his own Elizabeth speak so wildly. He wondered if on his own world another Gilbert Duray similarly confronted his own Elizabeth, and as he analyzed his feelings toward this woman before him, he felt a throb of annoyance. A curious situation. He said in a quiet voice, "Very well. You and my own Elizabeth have decided to isolate yourselves. I can't imagine your reasons."

Elizabeth gave a wild laugh. "They're real enough."

"They may be real now, but ten years from now or forty years from now they may seem unreal. I can't give you access to your own Earth, but if you wish, you can use the—"

Elizabeth turned away and went to look out over the passway to the Earth from which I've just come, and you need never see me again."

Duray spoke to her back. "We've never had secrets between us, you and I—or I mean, Elizabeth and I. Why now? Are you in love with some other man?"

Elizabeth gave a snort of sardonic amusement. "Certainly not . . . I'm disgusted with the entire human race."

"Which presumably includes me."

"It does indeed, and myself as well."

"And you won't tell me why?"

Elizabeth, still looking out the window, wordlessly shook her head.

"Very well," said Duray in a cold voice. "Will you tell me where you've sent the girls? They're mine as much as yours, remember."

"These particular girls aren't yours at all."

"That may be, but the effect is the same."

Elizabeth said tonelessly: "If you want to find your own particular girls, you'd better find your own particular Elizabeth and ask her. I can only speak for myself. . . . To tell you the truth, I don't like being part of a composite person, and

I don't intend to act like one. I'm just me. You're you, a stranger, whom I've never seen before in my life. So I wish you'd leave."

Duray strode from the house, out into the sunlight. He looked once around the wide landscape, then gave his head a surely shake and marched off along the path.

VIII

From *Memoirs and Reflections:*

The past is exposed for our scrutiny; we can wander the epochs like lords through a garden, serene in our purview. We argue with the noble sages, refuting their laborious concepts, should we be so unkind. Remember (at least) two things. First: The more distant from now, the less precise our conjunctures, the less our ability to strike to any given instant. We can break in upon yesterday at a stipulated second; during the Eocene, plus or minus ten years is the limit of our accuracy; as for the Cretaceous or earlier, an impingement with three hundred years of a given date can be considered satisfactory. Secondly: The past we broach is never our own past but at best the past of a cognate world, so that any illumination cast upon historical problems is questionable and perhaps deceptive. We cannot plumb the future; the process involves a negative flow of energy, which is inherently impractical. An instrument constructed of antimatter has been jocularly recommended but would yield no benefit to us. The future, thankfully, remains forever shrouded.

"Aha, you're back!" exclaimed Alan Robertson. "What did you learn?"

Duray described the encounter with Elizabeth. "She makes no excuse for what she's done; she shows hostility, which doesn't seem real, especially since I can't imagine a reason for it."

Alan Robertson had no comment to make.

"The woman isn't my wife, but their motivations must be the same. I can't think of one sensible explanation for conduct so strange, let alone two."

"Elizabeth seemed normal this morning?" asked Alan Robertson.

"I noticed nothing unusual."

Alan Robertson went to the control panel of his machine. He looked over his shoulder at Duray. "What time do you leave for work?"

"About nine."

Alan Robertson set one dial and turned two others until a ball of green light balanced, wavering, precisely halfway along a glass tube. He signaled Duray behind the lead slab and touched the button. From the center of the machine came the impact of 167 colliding nodules of force and the groan of rending dimensional fabric.

Alan Robertson brought forth the new passway. "The time is morning. You'll have to decide for yourself how to handle the situation. You can try to watch without being seen; you can say that you have paperwork to catch up on, that Elizabeth should ignore you and go about her normal routine, while you unobtrusively see what happens."

Duray frowned. "Presumably for each of these worlds there is a Gilbert Duray who finds himself in my fix. Suppose each tries to slip inconspicuously into someone else's world to learn what is happening. Suppose each Elizabeth catches him in the act and furiously accuses the man she believes to be her husband of spying on her—this in itself might be the source of Elizabeth's anger."

"Well, be as discreet as you can. Presumably you'll be several hours, so I'll go back to the boat and putter about. Locker five in my private hub yonder; I'll leave the door open."

Once again Duray stood on the hillside above the river, with the rambling stone house built by still another Gilbert Duray two hundred yards along the slope. From the height of the sun, Duray judged local time to be about nine o'clock—somewhat earlier than necessary. From the chimney of the stone house rose a wisp of smoke; Elizabeth had built a fire in the kitchen fireplace. Duray stood reflecting. This morning in his own house Elizabeth had built no fire. She had been on the point of striking a match and then had decided that the morning was already warm. Duray waited ten minutes, to make sure that the local Gilbert Duray had departed, then set forth toward the house. He paused by the big flat stone to inspect the pattern of moss. The crevice seemed narrower than he remembered, and the moss was dry and discolored. Duray took a deep breath. The air, rich with the odor of grasses and herbs, again seemed to carry an odd, unfamiliar scent. Duray proceeded slowly to the house, uncertain whether, after all, he was engaged in a sensible course of action.

He approached the house. The front door was open. Elizabeth came to look out at him in surprise. "That was a quick day's work!"

Duray said lamely, "The rig is down for repairs. I thought I'd catch up on some paper work. You go ahead with whatever you were doing."

Elizabeth looked at him curiously. "I wasn't doing anything in particular."

He followed Elizabeth into the house. She wore soft black slacks and an old gray jacket; Duray tried to remember what his own Elizabeth had worn, but the garments had been so familiar that he could summon no recollection.

Elizabeth poured coffee into a pair of stoneware mugs, and Duray took a seat at the kitchen table, trying to decide how this Elizabeth differed from his own—if she did. This Elizabeth seemed more subdued and meditative; her mouth might have been a trifle softer. "Why are you looking at me so strangely?" she asked suddenly.

Duray laughed. "I was merely thinking what a beautiful girl you are."

Elizabeth came to sit in his lap and kissed him, and Duray's blood began to flow warm. He restrained himself; this was not his wife; he wanted no complications. And if he yielded to temptations of the moment, might not another Gilbert Duray visiting his own Elizabeth do the same . . . He scowled.

Elizabeth, finding no surge of ardor, went to sit in the chair opposite. For a moment she sipped her coffee in silence. Then she said, "Just as soon as you left, Bob called through."

"Oh?" Duray was at once attentive. "What did he want?"

"That foolish party of his—the Rubble-menders or some such thing. He wants us to come."

"I've already told him no three times."

"I told him no again. His parties are always so peculiar. He said he wanted us to come for a very special reason, but he wouldn't tell me the reason. I told him, 'Thank you but no.' "

Duray looked around the room. "Did he leave any books?"

"No. Why should he leave me books?"

"I wish I knew."

"Gilbert," said Elizabeth, "you're acting rather oddly."

"Yes, I suppose I am." For a fact Duray's mind was whirling. Suppose now he went to the school passway, brought the girls home from school, then closed off all the passways, so that once again he had an Elizabeth and three daughters, more or less his own; then the conditions he had encountered would be satisfied. And another Gilbert Duray, now happily destroying the tract houses of Cupertino, would find himself bereft. . . . Duray recalled the hostile conduct of the previous Elizabeth. The passways in that particular world had certainly not been closed off by an intruding Duray. . . . A startling possibility came to his mind. Suppose a Duray had come to the house and, succumbing to temptation, had closed off all passways except that one communicating with his own world; suppose then that Elizabeth, discovering the imposture, had killed him . . . The theory had a grim plausibility and totally extinguished whatever inclination Duray might have had for making the world his home.

Elizabeth said, "Gilbert, why are you looking at me with that strange expression?"

Duray managed a feeble grin. "I guess I'm just in a bad mood this morning. Don't mind me. I'll go make out my report." He went into the wide cool living room, at once familiar and strange, and brought out the work-records of the other Gilbert Duray. . . . He studied the handwriting: like his own, firm and decisive, but in some indefinable way different—perhaps a trifle more harsh and angular. The three Elizabeths were not identical, nor were the Gilbert Durays.

An hour passed. Elizabeth occupied herself in the kitchen; Duray pretended to write a report.

A bell sounded. "Somebody at the passway," said Elizabeth.

Duray said, "I'll take care of it."

He went to the passage room, stepped through the passway, looked through the peephole—into the large, bland sun-tanned face of Bob Robertson.

Duray opened the door. For a moment he and Bob Robertson confronted each other. Bob Robertson's eyes narrowed. "Why, hello, Gilbert. What are you doing home?"

Duray pointed to the parcel Bob Robertson carried. "What do you have there?"

"Oh, these?" Bob Robertson looked down at the parcel as if he had forgotten it. "Just some books for Elizabeth."

Duray found it hard to control his voice. "You're up to some mischief, you and your Rumfuddlers. Listen, Bob. Keep away from me and Elizabeth. Don't call here, and don't bring around any books. Is this definite enough?"

Bob raised his sun-bleached eyebrows. "Very definite, very explicit. But why the sudden rage? I'm just friendly old Uncle Bob."

"I don't care what you call yourself; stay away from us."

"Just as you like, of course. But do you mind explaining this sudden decree of banishment?"

"The reason is simple enough. We want to be left alone."

Bob made a gesture of mock despair. "All this over a simple invitation to a simple little party, which I'd really like you to come to."

"Don't expect us. We won't be there."

Bob's face suddenly went pink. "You're coming a very high horse over me, my lad, and it's a poor policy. You might just get hauled up with a jerk. Matters aren't all the way you think they are."

"I don't care a rap one way or another," said Duray. "Good-bye." He closed the locker door and backed through the passway. He returned into the living room.

Elizabeth called from the kitchen. "Who was it, dear?"

"Bob Robertson, with some books."

"Books? Why books?"

"I didn't trouble to find out. I told him to stay away. After this, if he's at the passway, don't open it."

Elizabeth looked at him intently. "Gil—you're so strange today! There's something about you that almost scares me."

"Your imagination is working too hard."

"Why should Bob trouble to bring me books? What sort of books? Did you see?"

"Demonology. Black magic. That sort of thing."

"Mmf. Interesting—but not all *that* interesting. . . . I wonder if a world like ours, where no one has ever lived, would have things like goblins and ghosts?"

"I suspect not," said Duray. He looked toward the door. There was nothing more to be accomplished here, and it was time to return to his own Earth. He wondered how to make a graceful departure. And what would occur when the Gilbert Duray now working his rig came home?

Duray said, "Elizabeth, sit down in this chair here."

Elizabeth slowly slid into the chair at the kitchen table and watched him with a puzzled gaze.

"This may come as a shock," he said. "I am Gilbert Duray, but not your personal Gilbert Duray. I'm his cognate."

Elizabeth's eyes widened to lustrous dark pools.

Duray said, "On my own world Bob Robertson caused me and my Elizabeth trouble. I came here to find out what he had done and why and to stop him from doing it again."

Elizabeth asked, "What has he done?"

"I still don't know. He probably won't bother you again. You can tell your personal Gilbert Duray whatever you think best, or even complain to Alan."

"I'm bewildered by all this!"

"No more so than I." He went to the door. "I've got to leave now. Good-bye."

Elizabeth jumped to her feet and came impulsively forward. "Don't say good-bye. It was such a lonesome sound, coming from you. . . . It's like my own Gilbert saying good-bye."

"There's nothing else to do. Certainly I can't follow my inclinations and move in with you. What good are two Gilberts? Who'd get to sit at the head of the table?"

"We could have a round table," said Elizabeth. "Room for six or seven. I like my Gilberts."

"Your Gilberts like their Elizabeths." Duray sighed and said, "I'd better go now."

Elizabeth held out her hand. "Good-bye, cognate Gilbert."

IX

From *Memoirs and Reflections:*

The Oriental world-view differs from our own—specifically my own—in many respects, and I was early confronted with a whole set of dilemmas. I reflected upon Asiatic apathy and its obverse, despotism; warlords and brain-laundries: indifference to disease, filth, and suffering; sacred apes and irresponsible fecundity.

I also took note of my resolve to use my machine in the service of all men.

In the end I decided to make the "mistake" of many before me; I proceeded to impose my own ethical point of view upon the Oriental lifestyle.

Since this was precisely what was expected of me, since I would have been regarded as a fool and a mooncalf had I done otherwise, since the rewards of cooperation far exceeded the gratifications of obduracy and scorn, my programs are a wonderful success, at least to the moment of writing.

Duray walked along the riverbank toward Alan Robertson's boat. A breeze sent twinkling cat's-paws across the water and bellied the sails that Alan Robertson had raised to air; the boat tugged at the mooring lines.

Alan Robertson, wearing white shorts and a white hat with a loose, flapping brim, looked up from the eye he had been splicing at the end of a halyard. "Aha, Gil! You're back. Come aboard and have a bottle of beer."

Duray seated himself in the shade of the sail and drank half the beer at a gulp. "I still don't know what's going on—except that one way or another Bob is responsible. He came while I was there. I told him to clear out. He didn't like it."

Alan Robertson heaved a melancholy sigh. "I realize that Bob has the capacity for mischief."

"I still can't understand how he persuaded Elizabeth to close the passways. He brought out some books, but what effect could they have?"

Alan Robertson was instantly interested. "What were the books?"

"Something about satanism, black magic; I couldn't tell you much else."

"Indeed, indeed!" muttered Alan Robertson. "Is Elizabeth interested in the subject?"

"I don't think so. She's afraid of such things."

"Rightly so. Well, well, that's disturbing." Alan Robertson cleared his throat and made a delicate gesture, as if beseeching Duray to geniality and tolerance. "Still, you mustn't be too irritated with Bob. He's prone to his little mischiefs, but—"

" 'Little mischiefs'!" roared Duray. "Like locking me out of my home and marooning my wife and children? That's going beyond mischief!"

Alan Robertson smiled. "Here, have another beer; cool off a bit. Let's reflect. First, the probabilities. I doubt if Bob has really marooned Elizabeth and the girls or caused Elizabeth to do so."

"Then why are all the passways broken?"

"That's susceptible to explanation. He has access to the vaults; he might have substituted a blank for your master orifice. There's one possibility, at least."

Duray could hardly speak for rage. At last he cried out: "He has no right to do this!"

"Quite right, in the largest sense. I suspect that he only wants to induce you to his Rumfuddle."

"And I don't want to go, expecially when he's trying to put pressure on me."

"You're a stubborn man, Gil. The easy way, of course, would be to relax and look in on the occasion. You might even enjoy yourself."

Duray glared at Alan Robertson. "Are you suggesting that I attend the affair?"

"Well—no. I merely proposed a possible course of action."

Duray drank more beer and glowered out across the river. Alan Robertson said, "In a day or so, when this business is clarified, I think that we—all of us—should go off on a lazy cruise, out there among the islands. Nothing to worry us, no bothers, no upsets. The girls would love such a cruise."

Duray grunted. "I'd like to see them again before I plan any cruises. What goes on at these Rumfuddler events?"

"I've never attended. The members laugh and joke and eat and drink and gossip about the worlds they've visited and show each other movies: that sort of thing. Why don't we look in on last year's party? I'd be interested myself."

Duray hesitated. "What do you have in mind?"

"We'll set the dials to a year-old cognate to Bob's world, Fancy, and see precisely what goes on. What do you say?"

"I suppose it can't do any harm," said Duray grudgingly.

Alan Robertson rose to his feet. "Help me get these sails in."

X

From *Memoirs and Reflections:*

The problems that long have harassed historians have now been resolved. Who were the Cro-Magnons; where did they evolve? Who were the Etruscans? Where were the legendary cities of the proto-Sumerians before they migrated to Mesopotamia? Why the identity between the ideographs of Easter Island and Mohenjo Daro? All these fascinating questions have now been settled and reveal to us the full scope of our early history. We have preserved the library at old Alexandria from the Mohammedans and the Inca codices from the Christians. The Guanches of the Canaries, the Ainu of Hokkaido, the Mandans of Missouri, the blond Kaffirs of Bhutan: All are now known to us. We can chart the development of every language syllable by syllable, from the earliest formulation to the present. We have identified the Hellenic heroes, and I myself have searched the haunted forests of the ancient North and, in their own stone keeps, met face to face those mighty men who generated the Norse myths.

Standing before his machine, Alan Robertson spoke in a voice of humorous self-deprecation. "I'm not as trusting and forthright as I would like to be; in fact I sometimes feel shame for my petty subterfuges, and now I speak in reference to Bob. We all have our small faults, and Bob certainly does not lack his share. His imagination is perhaps his greatest curse: He is easily bored and sometimes tends to overreach himself. So while I deny him nothing, I also make sure that I am in a position to counsel or even remonstrate, if need be. Whenever I open a passway to one of his formulae, I unobstrusively strike a duplicate which I keep in my private file. We will find no difficulty in visiting a cognate to Fancy."

Duray and Alan Robertson stood in the dusk, at the end of a pale white beach. Behind them rose a low basalt cliff. To their right, the ocean reflected the afterglow and a glitter from the waning moon; to the left, palms stood black against the sky. A hundred yards along the beach dozens of fairy lamps had been strung between the trees to illuminate a long table laden with fruit, confections, punch in crystal bowls. Around the table stood several dozen men and women in animated conversation; music and the sounds of gaiety came down the beach to Duray and Alan Robertson.

"We're in good time," said Alan Robertson. He reflected a moment. "No doubt we'd be quite welcome; still, it's probably best to remain inconspicuous. We'll just stroll unobtrusively down the beach, in the shadow of the trees. Be careful not to stumble or fall, and no matter what you see or hear, do nothing! Discretion is essential; we want no awkward confrontations."

Keeping to the shade of the foliage, the two approached the merry group. Fifty yards distant, Alan Robertson held up his hand to signal a halt. "This is as close as we need approach; most of the people you know, or more accurately, their cognates. For instance, there is Royal Hart, and there is James Parham and Elizabeth's aunt, Emma Bathurst, and her uncle Peter and Maude Granger and no end of other folk."

"They all seem very gay."

"Yes, this is an important occasion for them. You and I are surly outsiders who can't understand the fun."

"Is this all they do, eat and drink and talk?"

"I think not," said Alan Robertson. "Notice yonder. Bob seems to be preparing a projection screen. Too bad that we can't move just a bit closer." Alan Robertson peered through the shadows. "But we'd better take no chances; if we were discovered, everyone would be embarrassed."

They watched in silence. Presently Bob Robertson went to the projection equipment and touched a button. The screen became alive with vibrating rings of red and blue. Conversations halted; the group turned toward the screen. Bob Robertson spoke, but his words were inaudible to the two who watched from the darkness. Bob Robertson gestured to the screen, where now appeared the view of a small country town, as if seen from an airplane. Surrounding was flat farm country, a land of wide horizons; Duray assumed the location to be somewhere in the Middle West. The picture changed to show the local high school, with students sitting on the steps. The scene shifted to the football field, on the day of a game—a very important game, to judge from the conduct of the spectators. The local team was introduced; one by one the boys ran out on the field to stand blinking into the autumn sunlight; then they ran off to the pregame huddle.

The game began; Bob Robertson stood by the screen in the capacity of an expert commentator, pointing to one or another of the players, analyzing the play. The game proceeded, to the manifest pleasure of the Rumfuddlers. At half time the bands marched and countermarched, then play resumed. Duray became bored and made fretful comments to Alan Robertson, who only said: "Yes, yes; probably so" and "My word, the agility of that halfback!" and "Have you noticed the precision of the line-play? Very good indeed!" At last the final quarter ended; the victorious team stood under a sign reading:

THE SHOWALTER TORNADOES
CHAMPIONS OF TEXAS
1951

The players came forward to accept trophies; there was a last picture of the team as a whole, standing proud and victorious; then the screen burst out into a red and gold starburst and went blank. The Rumfuddlers rose to their feet and congratulated Bob Robertson, who laughed modestly and went to the table for a goblet of punch.

Duray said disgustedly, "Is this one of Bob's famous parties? Why does he make such a tremendous occasion of the affair? I expected some sort of debauch."

Alan Robertson said, "Yes, from our standpoint at least, the proceedings seem somewhat uninteresting. Well, if your curiosity is satisfied, shall we return?"

"Whenever you like."

Once again in the lounge under the Mad Dog Mountains, Alan Robertson said: "So now and at last we've seen one of Bob's famous Rumfuddles. Are you still determined not to attend the occasion of tomorrow night?"

Duray scowled. "If I have to go to reclaim my family. I'll do so. But I just might lose my temper before the evening is over."

"Bob has gone too far," Alan Robertson declared. "I agree with you there. As for what we saw tonight, I admit to a degree of puzzlement."

"Only a degree? Do you understand it at all?"

Alan Robertson shook his head with a somewhat cryptic smile. "Speculation is pointless. I suppose you'll spend the night with me at the lodge?"

"I might as well," grumbled Duray. "I don't have anywhere else to go."

Alan Robertson clapped him on the back. "Good lad. We'll put some steaks on the fire and turn our problems loose for the night."

XI

From *Memoirs and Reflections:*

When I first put the Mark I machine into operation, I suffered great fears. What did I know of the forces that I might release? . . . With all adjustments at dead neutral, I punched a passway into a cognate Earth. This was simple enough—in fact, almost anticlimactic . . . Little by little I learned to control my wonderful toy; our own world and all its past phases became familiar to me. What of other worlds? I am sure that in due course we will move instantaneously from world to world, from galaxy to galaxy, using a special space-traveling hub on Utilis. At the moment I am candidly afraid to punch through passways at blind random. What if I opened into the interior of a sun? Or into the center of a black hole? Or into an antimatter universe? I would certainly destroy myself and the machine and conceivably Earth itself.

Still, the potentialities are too entrancing to be ignored. With painstaking precautions and a dozen protective devices, I will attempt to find my way to new worlds, and for the first time interstellar travel will be a reality.

Alan Robertson and Duray sat in the bright morning sunlight beside the flinty-blue lake. They had brought their breakfast out to the table and now sat drinking coffee. Alan Robertson made cheerful conversation for the two of them. "These last few years have been easier on me; I've relegated a great deal of responsibility. Ernest and Henry know my policies as well as I do, if not better; and they're never frivolous or inconsistent." Alan Robertson chuckled. "I've worked two miracles: first, my machine, and second, keeping the business as simple as it is. I refuse to keep regular hours; I won't make appointments; I don't keep records;

I pay no taxes; I exert great political and social influence, but only informally; I simply refuse to be bothered with administrative detail, and consequently I find myself able to enjoy life."

"It's a wonder some religious fanatic hasn't assassinated you," said Duray sourly.

"No mystery there! I've given them all their private worlds, with my best regards, and they have no energy left for violence! And as you know, I walk with a very low silhouette. My friends hardly recognize me on the street." Alan Robertson waved his hand. "No doubt you're more concerned with your immediate quandary. Have you come to a decision regarding the Rumfuddle?"

"I don't have any choice," Duray muttered. "I'd prefer to wring Bob's neck. If I could account for Elizabeth's conduct, I'd feel more comfortable. She's not even remotely interested in black magic. Why did Bob bring her books on satanism?"

"Well—the subject is inherently fascinating," Alan Robertson suggested, without conviction. "The name Satan derives from the Hebrew word for 'adversary'; it never applied to a real individual. 'Zeus,' of course, was an Aryan chieftain of about 3500 B.C., while 'Woden' lived somewhat later. He was actually 'Othinn,' a shaman of enormous personal force who did things with his mind that I can't do with the machine. . . . But again I'm rambling."

Duray gave a silent shrug.

"Well, then, you'll be going to the Rumfuddle," said Alan Robertson, "by and large the best course, whatever the consequences."

"I believe that you know more than you're telling me."

Alan Robertson smiled and shook his head. "I've lived with too much uncertainty among my cognate and near-cognate worlds. Nothing is sure; surprises are everywhere. I think the best plan is to fulfill Bob's requirements. Then if Elizabeth is indeed on hand, you can discuss the event with her."

"What of you? Will you be coming?"

"I am of two minds. Would you prefer that I came?"

"Yes," said Duray. "You have more control over Bob than I do."

"Don't exaggerate my influence! He is a strong man, for all his idleness. Confidentially, I'm delighted that he occupies himself with games rather than . . ." Alan Robertson hesitated.

"Rather than what?"

"Than that his imagination should prompt him to less innocent games. Perhaps I have been overingenuous in this connection. We can only wait and see."

XII

From *Memoirs and Reflections:*

If the past is a house of many chambers, then the present is the most recent coat of paint.

At four o'clock Duray and Alan Robertson left the lodge and passed through Utilis to the San Francisco depot. Duray had changed into a somber dark suit; Alan Robertson wore a more informal costume: blue jacket and pale-gray trousers. They went to Bob Robertson's locker, to find a panel with the sign "NOT

HOME! FOR THE RUMFUDDLE GO TO ROGER WAILLE'S LOCKER, RC 3-96, AND PASS THROUGH TO EKSHAYAN!"

The two went on to Locker RC 3-96, where a sign read: "RUMFUDDLERS: PASS! ALL OTHERS: AWAY!"

Duray shrugged contemptuously, and parting the curtain, looked through the passway into a rustic lobby of natural wood, painted in black, red, yellow, blue, and white floral designs. An open door revealed an expanse of open land and water glistening in the afternoon sunlight. Duray and Alan Robertson passed through, crossed the foyer, and looked out upon a vast, slow river flowing from north to south. A rolling plain spread eastward away and over the horizon. The western bank of the river was indistinct in the afternoon glitter. A path led north to a tall house of eccentric architecture. A dozen domes and cupolas stood against the sky; gables and ridges created a hundred unexpected angles. The walls showed a fish-scale texture of hand-hewn shingles; spiral columns supported the second- and third-story entablatures, where wolves and bears, carved in vigorous curves and masses, snarled, fought, howled, and danced. On the side overlooking the river a pergola clothed with vines cast a dappled shade; here sat the Rumfuddlers.

Alan Robertson looked at the house, up and down the river, across the plain. "From the architecture, the vegetation, the height of the sun, the characteristic haze, I assume the river to be either the Don or the Volga, and yonder the steppes. From the absence of habitation, boats, and artifacts, I would guess the time to be early historic—perhaps 2,000 or 3,000 B.C., a colorful era. The inhabitants of the steppes are nomads; Scyths to the east, Celts to the west, and to the north the homeland of the Germanic and Scandinavian tribes; and yonder the mansion of Roger Waille, and very interesting, too, after the extravagant fashion of the Russian baroque. And, my word! I believe I see an ox on the spit! We may even enjoy our little visit!"

"You do as you like," muttered Duray. "I'd just as soon eat at home."

Alan Robertson pursed his lips. "I understand your point of view, of course, but perhaps we should relax a bit. The scene is majestic; the house is delightfully picturesque, the roast beef is undoubtedly delicious; perhaps we should meet the situation on its own terms."

Duray could find no adequate reply and kept his opinions to himself.

"Well, then," said Alan Robertson, "equability is the word. So now let's see what Bob and Roger have up their sleeves." He set off along the path to the house, with Duray sauntering morosely a step or two behind.

Under the pergola a man jumped to his feet and flourished his hand; Duray recognized the tall, spare form of Bob Robertson. "Just in time," Bob called jocosely. "Not to early, not too late. We're glad you could make it."

"Yes, we found we could accept your invitation after all," said Alan Robertson. "Let me see, do I know anyone here? Roger, hello! . . . And William . . . Ah! the lovely Dora Gorski! . . . Cypriano . . ." He looked around the circle of faces, waving to his acquaintances.

Bob clapped Duray on the shoulder. "Really pleased you could come! What'll you drink? The locals distill a liquor out of fermented mare's milk, but I don't recommend it."

"I'm not here to drink," said Duray. "Where's Elizabeth?"

The corners of Bob's wide mouth twitched. "Come now, old man; let's not be grim. This is the Rumfuddle! A time for joy and self-renewal! Go dance about a bit! Cavort! Pour a bottle of champagne over your head! Sport with the girls!"

Duray looked into the blue eyes for a long second. He strained to keep his voice even. "Where is Elizabeth?"

"Somewhere about the place. A charming girl, your Elizabeth! We're delighted to have you both!"

Duray swung away. He walked to the dark and handsome Roger Waille. "Would you be good enough to take me to my wife?"

Waille raised his eyebrows as if puzzled by Duray's tone of voice. "She is primping and gossiping. If necessary I suppose I could pull her away for a moment or two."

Duray began to feel ridiculous, as if he had been locked away from his world, subjected to harrassments and doubts, and made the butt of some obscure joke. "It's necessary," he said. "We're leaving."

"But you've just arrived!"

"I know."

Waille gave a shrug of amused perplexity and turned away toward the house. Duray followed. They went through a tall, narrow doorway into an entry-hall paneled with a beautiful brown-gold wood that Duray automatically identified as chestnut. Four high panes of tawny glass turned to the west filled the room with a smoky half-melancholy light. Oak settees, upholstered in leather, faced each other across a black, brown, and gray rug. Taborets stood at each side of the settees, and each supported an ornate golden candelabra in the form of conventionalized stag's heads. Waille indicated these last. "Striking, aren't they? The Scythians made them for me. I paid them in iron knives. They think I'm a great magician; and for a fact, I am." He reached into the air and plucked forth an orange, which he tossed upon a settee. "Here's Elizabeth now, and the other maenads as well."

Into the chamber came Elizabeth, with three other young women whom Duray vaguely recalled having met before. At the sight of Duray, Elizabeth stopped short. She essayed a smile and said in a light, strained voice, "Hello, Gil. You're here after all." She laughed nervously and, Duray felt, unnaturally. "Yes, of course you're here. I didn't think you'd come."

Duray glanced toward the other women, who stood with Waille, watching half expectantly. Duray said, "I'd like to speak to you alone."

"Excuse us," said Waille. "We'll go on outside."

They departed. Elizabeth looked longingly after them and fidgeted with the buttons of her jacket.

"Where are the children?" Duray demanded curtly.

"Upstairs, getting dressed." She looked down at her own costume, the festival raiment of a Transylvanian peasant girl: a green skirt embroidered with red and blue flowers, a white blouse, a black velvet vest, glossy black boots.

Duray felt his temper slipping; his voice was strained and fretful. "I don't understand anything of this. Why did you close the passways?"

Elizabeth attempted a flippant smile. "I was bored with routine."

"Oh? Why didn't you mention it to me yesterday morning? You didn't need to close the passways."

"Gilbert, please. Let's not discuss it."

Duray stood back, tongue-tied with astonishment. "Very well," he said at last. "We won't discuss it. You go up and get the girls. We're going home."

Elizabeth shook her head. In a neutral voice she said, "It's impossible. There's only one passway open. I don't have it."

"Who does? Bob?"

"I guess so; I'm not really sure."

"How did he get it? There were only four, and all four were closed."

"It's simple enough. He moved the downtown passway from our locker to another and left a blank in its place."

"And who closed off the other three?"

"I did."

"Why?"

"Because Bob told me to. I don't want to talk about it. I'm sick to death of the whole business." And she half whispered: "I don't know what I'm going to do with myself."

"I know what I'm going to do," said Duray. He turned toward the door.

Elizabeth held up her hands and clenched her fists against her breast. "Don't make trouble—please! He'll close our last passway!"

"Is that why you're afraid of him? If so—don't be. Alan wouldn't allow it."

Elizabeth's face began to crumple. She pushed past Duray and walked quickly out upon the terrace. Duray followed, baffled and furious. He looked back and forth across the terrace. Bob was not to be seen. Elizabeth had gone to Alan Robertson; she spoke in a hushed, urgent voice. Duray went to join them. Elizabeth became silent and turned away, avoiding Duray's gaze.

Alan Robertson spoke in a voice of easy geniality. "Isn't this a lovely spot? Look how the setting sun shines on the river!"

Roger Waille came by rolling a cart with ice, goblets, and a dozen bottles. He said: "Of all the places on all the Earths, this is my favorite. I call it Ekshayan, which is the Scythian name for this district."

A woman asked, "Isn't it cold and bleak in the winter?"

"Frightful!" said Waille. "The blizzards howl down from the north; then they stop, and the land is absolutely still. The days are short, and the sun comes up red as a poppy. The wolves slink out of the forests, and at dusk they circle the house. When a full moon shines, they howl like banshees, or maybe the banshees are howling! I sit beside the fireplace, entranced."

"It occurs to me," said Manfred Funk, "that each person, selecting a site for his home, reveals a great deal about himself. Even on old Earth, a man's home was ordinarily a symbolic simulacrum of the man himself; now, with every option available, a person's house is himself."

"This is very true," said Alan Robertson, "and certainly Roger need not fear that he has revealed any discreditable aspects of himself by showing us his rather grotesque home so the lonely steppes of prehistoric Russia."

Roger Waille laughed. "The grotesque house isn't me; I merely felt that it fitted its setting. . . . Here, Duray, you're not drinking. That's chilled vodka; you can mix it or drink it straight in the time-tested manner."

"Nothing for me, thanks."

"Just as you like. Excuse me; I'm wanted elsewhere." Waille moved away, rolling the cart. Elizabeth leaned as if she wanted to follow him, then remained beside Alan Robertson, looking thoughtfully over the river.

Duray spoke to Alan Robertson as if she were not there. "Elizabeth refuses to leave. Bob has hypnotized her."

"That's not true," said Elizabeth softly.

"Somehow, one way or another, he's forced her to stay. She won't tell me why."

"I want the passway back," said Elizabeth. But her voice was muffled and uncertain.

Alan Robertson cleared his throat. "I hardly know what to say. It's a very awkward situation. None of us wants to create a disturbance—"

"There you're wrong," said Duray.

Alan Robertson ignored the remark. "I'll have a word with Bob after the party. In the meantime I don't see why we shouldn't enjoy the company of our friends, and that wonderful roast ox! Who is that turning the spit? I know him from somewhere."

Duray could hardly speak for outrage. "After what he's done to us?"

"He's gone too far, much too far," Alan Robertson agreed. "Still, he's a flamboyant, feckless sort, and I doubt if he understands the full inconvenience he's caused you."

"He understands well enough. He just doesn't care."

"Perhaps so," said Alan Robertson sadly. "I had always hoped—but that's neither here nor there. I still feel that we should act with restraint. It's much easier not to do than to undo."

Elizabeth abruptly crossed the terrace and went to the front door of the tall house, where her three daughters had appeared—Dolly, twelve; Joan, ten; Ellen, eight—all wearing green, white, and black peasant frocks and glossy black boots. Duray thought they made a delightful picture. He followed Elizabeth across the terrace.

"It's Daddy," screamed Ellen, and threw herself in his arms. The other two, not to be outdone, did likewise.

"We thought you weren't coming to the party," cried Dolly. "I'm glad you did, though."

"So'm I."

"So'm I."

"I'm glad I came, too, if only to see you in these pretty costumes. Let's go see Grandpa Alan." He took them across the terrace, and after a moment's hesitation, Elizabeth followed. Duray became aware that everyone had stopped talking to look at him and his family, with, so it seemed, an extraordinary, even avid, curiosity, as if in expectation of some entertaining extravagance of conduct. Duray began to burn with emotion. Once, long ago, while crossing a street in downtown San Francisco, he had been struck by an automobile, suffering a broken leg and a fractured clavicle. Almost as soon as he had been knocked down, pedestrians came pushing to stare down at him, and Duray, looking up in pain and shock, had seen only the ring of white faces and intent eyes, greedy as flies around a puddle of blood. In hysterical fury he had staggered to his feet, striking out into every face within reaching distance, men and women alike. He hated them more than the man who had run him down: the ghouls who had come to enjoy his pain. Had he the miraculous power, he would have crushed them into a screaming bale of detestable flesh and hurled the bundle twenty miles out into the Pacific Ocean . . .

Some faint shadow of this emotion affected him now, but today he would provide them no unnatural pleasure. He turned a single glance of cool contempt around the group, then took his three eager-faced daughters to a bench at the back of the terrace. Elizabeth followed, moving like a mechanical object. She seated herself at the end of the bench and looked off across the river. Duray stared heavily back at the Rumfuddlers, compelling them to shift their gazes to where the ox roasted over a great bed of coals. A young man in a white jacket turned the spit; another basted the meat with a long-handled brush. A pair of Orientals carried out a carving table; another brought a carving set; a fourth wheeled out a cart laden with salads, round crusty loaves, trays of cheese and herrings. A fifth man, dressed as a Transylvanian gypsy, came from the house with a violin. He went to the corner of the terrace and began to play melancholy music of the steppes.

Bob Robertson and Roger Waille inspected the ox, a magnificent sight indeed. Duray attempted a stony detachment, but his nose was under no such strictures; the odor of the roast meat, garlic, and herbs tantalized him unmercifully. Bob Robertson returned to the terrace and held up his hands for attention; the fiddler put down his instrument. "Control your appetites; there'll still be a few minutes, during which we can discuss our next Rumfuddle. Our clever colleague Bernard Ulman recommends a hostelry in the Adirondacks: the Sapphire Lake Lodge. The hotel was built in 1902, to the highest standards of Edwardian comfort. The clientele is derived from the business community of New York. The cuisine is kosher; the management maintains an atmosphere of congenial gentility; the current date is 1930. Bernard has furnished photographs. Roger, if you please."

Waille drew back a curtain to reveal a screen. He manipulated the projection machine, and the hotel was displayed on the screen: a rambling, half-timbered structure overlooking several acres of park and a smooth lake.

"Thank you, Roger. I believe that we also have a photograph of the staff."

On the screen appeared a stiffly posed group of about thirty men and women, all smiling with various degrees of affability. The Rumfuddlers were amused; some among them tittered.

"Bernard gives a very favorable report as to the cuisine, the amenities, and the charm of the general area. Am I right, Bernard?"

"In every detail," declared Bernard Ulman. "The management is attentive and efficient; the clientele is well-established."

"Very good," said Bob Robertson. "Unless someone has a more entertaining idea, we will hold our next Rumfuddle at the Sapphire Lake Lodge. And now I believe that the roast beef should be ready—done to a turn, as the expression goes."

"Quite right," said Roger Waille. "Tom, as always, has done an excellent job at the spit."

The ox was lifted to the table. The carver set to work with a will. Duray went to speak to Alan Robertson, who blinked uneasily at his approach. Duray asked, "Do you understand the reason for these parties? Are you in on the joke?"

Alan Robertson spoke in a precise manner: "I certainly am not 'in on the joke,' as you put it." He hesitated, then said: "The Rumfuddlers will never again intrude upon your life or that of your family. I am sure of this. Bob became overexuberant; he exercised poor judgment, and I intend to have a quiet word with him. In fact, we have already exchanged certain opinions. At the moment your best interests will be served by detachment and unconcern."

Duray spoke with sinister politeness: "You feel, then, that I and my family should bear the brunt of Bob's jokes?"

"This is a harsh view of the situation, but my answer must be Yes."

"I'm not so sure. My relationship with Elizabeth is no longer the same. Bob has done this to me."

"To quote an old apothegm: 'Least said, soonest mended.' "

Duray changed the subject. "When Waille showed the photograph of the hotel staff, I thought some of the faces were familiar. Before I could be quite sure, the picture was gone."

Alan Robertson nodded unhappily. "Let's not develop the subject, Gilbert. Instead—"

"I'm into the situation too far," said Duray. "I want to know the truth."

"Very well, then," said Alan Robertson hollowly, "your instincts are accurate. The management of the Sapphire Lake Lodge, in cognate circumstances, has achieved an unsavory reputation. As you have guessed, they comprise the leadership of the National Socialist party during 1938 or thereabouts. The manager, of course, is Hitler, the desk clerk is Goebbels, the headwaiter is Göring, the bellboys are Himmler and Hess, and so on down the line. They are, of course, not aware of the activities of their cognates of other worlds. The hotel's clientele is for the most part Jewish, which brings a macabre humor to the situation."

"Undeniably," said Duray. "What of that Rumfuddlers party that we looked in on?"

"You refer to the high-school football team? The 1951 Texas champions, as I recall." Alan Robertson grinned. "And well they should be. Bob identified the players for me. Are you interested in the lineup?"

"Very much so."

Alan Robertson drew a sheet of paper from his pocket. "I believe—yes, this is it." He handed the sheet to Duray who saw a schematic lineup:

LE	LT	LG	C	RG	RT	RE
Achilles	Charle- magne	Hercules	Goliath	Samson	Richard the Lion- hearted	Billy the Kid

Q
Machiavelli

LHB
Sir Galahad

RHB
Geronimo

FB
Cuchulain

Duray returned the paper. "You approve of this?"

"I had best put it like this," said Alan Robertson, a trifle uneasily. "One day, chatting with Bob, I remarked that much travail could be spared the human race if the more notorious evildoers were early in their lives shifted to environments which afforded them constructive outlets for their energies. I speculated that having the competence to make such changes, it was perhaps our duty to do so. Bob became interested in the concept and formed his group, the Rumfuddlers, to serve the function I had suggested. In all candor I believe that Bob and his friends have been attracted more by the possibility of entertainment than by altruism, but the effect has been the same."

"The football players aren't evildoers," said Duray. "Sir Galahad, Charlemagne, Samson, Richard the Lion-hearted . . ."

"Exactly true," said Alan Robertson, "and I made this point to Bob. He asserted that all were brawlers and bullyboys, with the possible exception of Sir Galahad; that Charlemagne, for example, had conquered much territory to no particular achievement; that Achilles, a national hero to the Greeks, was a cruel enemy to the Trojans; and so forth. His justifications are somewhat specious perhaps . . . Still, these young men are better employed making touchdowns than breaking heads."

After a pause Duray asked: "How are these matters arranged?"

"I'm not entirely sure. I believe that by one means or another, the desired babies are exchanged with others of similar appearance. The child so obtained is reared in appropriate circumstances."

"The jokes seem elaborate and rather tedious."

"Precisely!" Alan Robertson declared. "Can you think of a better method to keep someone like Bob out of mischief?"

"Certainly," said Duray. "Fear of the consequences." He scowled across the terrace. Bob had stopped to speak to Elizabeth. She and the three girls rose to their feet.

Duray strode across the terrace. "What's going on?"

"Nothing of consequence," said Bob. "Elizabeth and the girls are going to help serve the guests." He glanced toward the serving table, then turned back to Duray. "Would you help with the carving?"

Duray's arm moved of its own volition. His fist caught Bob on the angle of the jaw and sent him reeling back into one of the white-coated Orientals, who carried a tray of food. The two fell into an untidy heap. The Rumfuddlers were shocked and amused and watched with attention.

Bob rose to his feet gracefully enough and gave a hand to the Oriental. Looking toward Duray, Bob shook his head ruefully. Meeting his glance, Duray noted a pale blue glint; then Bob once more became bland and debonair.

Elizabeth spoke in a low despairing voice: "Why couldn't you have done as he asked? It would have all been so simple."

"Elizabeth may well be right," said Alan Robertson.

"Why should she be right?" demanded Duray. "We are his victims! You've allowed him a taste of mischief, and now you can't control him!"

"Not true!" declared Alan Robertson. "I intend to impose rigorous curbs upon the Rumfuddlers, and I will be obeyed."

"The damage is done, so far as I am concerned," said Duray bitterly. "Come along, Elizabeth, we're going Home."

"We can't go Home. Bob has the passway."

Alan Robertson drew a deep sigh and came to a decision. He crossed to where Bob stood with a goblet of wine in one hand, massaging his jaw with the other. Alan Robertson spoke to Bob politely but with authority. Bob was slow in making a reply. Alan Robertson spoke again, sharply. Bob only shrugged. Alan Robertson waited a moment, then returned to Duray, Elizabeth, and the three children.

"The passway is at his San Francisco apartment," said Alan Robertson in a measured voice. "He will give it back to you after the party. He doesn't choose to go for it now."

Bob once more commanded the attention of the Rumfuddlers. "By popular request we replay the record of our last but one Rumfuddle, contrived by one of our most distinguished, diligent, and ingenious Rumfuddlers, Manfred Funk. The locale is the Red Barn, a roadhouse twelve miles west of Urbana, Illinois; the time is the late summer of 1926; the occasion is a Charleston dancing contest. The music is provided by the legendary Wolverines, and you will hear the fabulous cornet of Leon Bismarck Beiderbecke." Bob gave a wry smile, as if the music were not to his personal taste. "This was one of our most rewarding occasions, and here it is again."

The screen showed the interior of a dance-hall, crowded with excited young men and women. At the back of the stage sat the Wolverines, wearing tuxedos; to the front stood the contestants: eight dapper young men and eight pretty girls in short skirts. An announcer stepped forward and spoke to the crowd through a megaphone: "Contestants are numbered one through eight! Please, no encouragement from the audience. The prize is this magnificent trophy and fifty dollars cash; the presentation will be made by last year's winner, Boozy Horman. Remember, on the first number we eliminate four contestants, on the second number, two; and after the third number we select our winter. So then: Bix and the Wolverines and 'Sensation Rag'!"

From the band came music; from the contestants, agitated motion.

Duray asked, "Who are these people?"

Alan Robertson replied in an even voice: "The young men are locals and not important. But notice the girls: No doubt you find them attractive. You are not alone. They are Helen of Troy, Deirdre, Marie Antoinette, Cleopatra, Salome, Lady Godiva, Nefertiti, and Mata Hari."

Duray gave a dour grunt. The music halted; judging applause from the audience, the announcer eliminated Marie Antoinette, Cleopatra, Deirdre, Mata Hari, and their respective partners. The Wolverines played "Fidgety Feet"; the four remaining contestants danced with verve and dedication, but Helen and Nefertiti were eliminated. The Wolverines played "Tiger Rag." Salome and Lady Godiva and their young men performed with amazing zeal. After carefully appraising the volume of applause, the announcer gave his judgment to Lady Godiva and her partner. Large on the screen appeared a close-up view of the two happy faces; in an excess of triumphant joy they hugged and kissed each other. The screen went dim; after the vivacity of the Red Barn the terrace above the Don seemed drab and insipid.

The Rumfuddlers shifted in their seats. Some uttered exclamations to assert their gaiety; others stared out across the vast empty face of the river.

Duray glanced toward Elizabeth; she was gone. Now he saw her circulating among the guests with three other young women, pouring wine from Scythian decanters.

"It makes a pretty picture, does it not?" said a calm voice. Duray turned to find Bob standing behind him; his mouth twisted in an easy half-smile, but his eye glinted pale blue.

Duray turned away. Alan Robertson said, "This is not at all a pleasant situation, Bob, and in fact completely lacks charm."

"Perhaps at future Rumfuddles, when my face feels better, the charm will emerge. . . . Excuse me; I see that I must enliven the meeting." He stepped forward. "We have a final pastiche: oddments and improvisations, vignettes and glimpses, each in its own way entertaining and instructive. Roger, start the mechanism, if you please."

Roger Waille hesitated and glanced sidelong toward Alan Robertson.

"The item number is sixty-two, Roger," said Bob in a calm voice. Roger Waille delayed another instant, then shrugged and went to the projection machine.

"The material is new," said Bob, "hence I will supply a commentary. First we have an episode in the life of Richard Wagner, the dogmatic and occasionally irascible composer. This year is 1843; the place is Dresden. Wagner sets forth on a summer night to attend a new opera, *Der Sanger Krieg*, by an unknown composer. He alights from his carriage before the hall; he enters; he seats himself in his loge. Notice the dignity of his posture, the authority of his gestures! The music begins. Listen!" From the projector came the sound of music. "It is the overture," stated Bob. "But notice Wagner: Why is he stupefied? Why is he overcome with wonder? He listens to the music as if he has never heard it before. And in fact he hasn't; he has only just yesterday set down a few preliminary notes for this particular opus, which he planned to call *Tannhäuser*; today, magically, he hears it in its final form. Wagner will walk home slowly tonight, and perhaps in his abstraction he will kick the dog Schmutzi. . . . Now to a different scene: St. Petersburg in the year 1880 and the stables in back of the Winter Palace. The ivory and gilt carriage rolls forth to convey the czar and the czarina to a reception at the British Embassy. Notice the drivers: stern, well-groomed, intent at their business. Marx's beard is well-trimmed; Lenin's goatee is not so pronounced. A groom comes to watch the carriage roll away. He has a kindly twinkle in his eye, does Stalin." The screen went dim once more, then brightened to show a city street lined with automobile showrooms and used-car lots. "This is one of Shawn Henderson's projects. The four used-car lots are operated by men who in other circumstances were religious notables: prophets and so forth. That alert, keen-featured man in front of Quality Motors, for instance, is Mohammed. Shawn is conducting a careful survey, and at our next Rumfuddle he will report upon his dealings with these four famous figures."

Alan Robertson stepped forward, somewhat diffidently. He cleared his throat. "I don't like to play the part of spoilsport, but I'm afraid I have no choice. There will be no further Rumfuddles. Our original goals have been neglected, and I note far too many episodes of purposeless frivolity and even cruelty. You may wonder at what seems a sudden decision, but I have been considering the matter for several days. The Rumfuddles have taken a turn in an unwholesome direction and conceivably might become a grotesque new vice, which, of course, is far from our original ideal. I'm sure that every sensible person, after a few moments' reflection, will agree that now is the time to stop. Next week you may return to me all passways except those to worlds where you maintain residence."

The Rumfuddlers sat murmuring together. Some turned resentful glances toward Alan Robertson; others served themselves more bread and meat. Bob came over to join Alan and Duray. He spoke in an easy manner. "I must say that your admonitions arrive with all the delicacy of a lightning bolt. I can picture Jehovah smiting the fallen algels in a similar style."

Alan Robertson smiled. "Now, then, Bob, you're talking nonsense. The situations aren't at all similar. Jehovah struck out in fury; I impose my restriction in all goodwill in order that we can once again turn our energies to constructive ends."

Bob threw back his head and laughed. "But the Rumfuddlers have lost the habit of work. We only want to amuse ourselves, and after all, what is so noxious in our activities?"

"The trend is menacing, Bob." Alan Robertson's voice was reasonable. "Unpleasant elements are creeping into your fun, so stealthily that you yourself are unaware of them. For instance, why torment poor Wagner? Surely there was gratuitous cruelty, and only to provide you a few instants of amusement. And since the subject is in the air, I heartily deplore your treatment of Gilbert and Elizabeth. You have brought them both an extraordinary inconvenience, and in Elizabeth's case, actual suffering. Gilbert got something of his own back, and the balance is about even."

"Gilbert is far too impulsive," said Bob. "Self-willed and egocentric, as he always has been."

Alan held up his hand. "There is no need to go further into the subject, Bob. I suggest that you say no more."

"Just as you like, though the matter, considered as practical rehabilitation, isn't irrelevant. We can amply justify the work of the Rumfuddlers."

Duray asked quietly, "Just how do you mean, Bob?"

Alan Robertson made a peremptory sound, but Duray said, "Let him say what he likes and make an end to it. He plans to do so anyway."

There was a moment of silence. Bob looked across the terrace to where the three Orientals were transferring the remains of the beef to a service cart.

"Well?" Alan Robertson asked softly. "Have you made your choice?"

Bob held out his hands in ostensible bewilderment. "I don't understand you! I want only to vindicate myself and the Rumfuddlers. I think we have done splendidly. Today we have allowed Torquemada to roast a dead ox instead of a living heretic; Marquis de Sade has fulfilled his obscure urges by caressing seared flesh with a basting brush, and did you notice the zest with which Ivan the Terrible hacked up the carcass? Nero, who has real talent, played his violin. Attila, Genghis Khan, and Mao Tse-tung efficiently served the guests. Wine was poured by Messalina, Lucrezia Borgia, Delilah, and Gilbert's charming wife, Elizabeth. Only Gilbert failed to demonstrate his rehabilitation, but at least he provided us a touching and memorable picture: Gilles de Rais, Elizabeth Báthory, and their three virgin daughters. It was sufficient. In every case we have shown that rehabilitation is not an empty word."

"Not in every case," said Alan Robertson, "specifically that of your own."

Bob looked at him askance. "I don't follow you."

"No less than Gilbert are you ignorant of your background. I will now reveal the circumstances so that you may understand something of yourself and try to curb the tendencies which have made your cognate an exemplar of cruelty, stealth, and treachery."

Bob laughed: a brittle sound like cracking ice. "I admit to a horrified interest."

"I took you from a forest a thousand miles north of this very spot while I traced the phylogeny of the Norse gods. Your name was Loki. For reasons which are not now important I brought you back to San Francisco, and there you grew to maturity."

"So I am Loki."

"No. You are Bob Robertson, just as this is Gilbert Duray, and here is his wife, Elizabeth. Loki, Gilles de Rais, Elizabeth Báthory: These names applied to human material which has not functioned quite as well. Gilles de Rais, judging from all evidence, suffered from a brain tumor; he fell into his peculiar vices after a long and honorable career. The case of Princess Elizabeth Báthory is less clear, but one might suspect syphilis and consequent cerebral lesions."

"And what of poor Loki?" inquired Bob with exaggerated pathos.

"Loki seemed to suffer from nothing except a case of old-fashioned meanness."

Bob seemed concerned. "So that these qualities apply to me?"

"You are not necessarily identical to your cognate. Still, I advise you to take careful stock of yourself, and so far as I am concerned, you had best regard yourself as on probation."

"Just as you say." Bob looked over Alan Robertson's shoulder. "Excuse me; you've spoiled the party, and everybody is leaving. I want a word with Roger."

Duray moved to stand in his way, but Bob shouldered him aside and strode across the terrace, with Duray glowering at his back.

Elizabeth said in a mournful voice, "I hope we're at the end of all this."

Duray growled. "You should never have listened to him."

"I didn't listen; I read about it in one of Bob's books; I saw your picture; I couldn't—"

Alan Robertson intervened. "Don't harass poor Elizabeth; I consider her both sensible and brave; she did the best she could."

Bob returned. "Everything taken care of," he said cheerfully. "All except one or two details."

"The first of these is the return of the passway. Gilbert and Elizabeth—not to mention Dolly, Joan, and Ellen—are anxious to return to Home."

"They can stay here with you," said Bob. "That's probably the best solution."

"I don't plan to stay here," said Alan Robertson in mild wonder. "We are leaving at once."

"You must change your plans," said Bob. "I have finally become bored with your reproaches. Roger doesn't particularly care to leave his home, but he agrees that now is the time to make a final disposal of the matter."

Alan Robertson frowned in displeasure. "The joke is in very poor taste, Bob."

Roger Waille came from the house, his face somewhat glum. "They're all closed. Only the main gate is open."

Alan Robertson said to Gilbert: "I think that we will leave Bob and Roger to their Rumfuddle fantasies. When he returns to his senses, we'll get your passway. Come along, then, Elizabeth! Girls!"

"Alan," said Bob gently, "you're staying here. Forever. I'm taking over the machine."

Alan Robertson asked mildly: "How do you propose to restrain me? By force?"

"You can stay here alive or dead; take your choice."

"You have weapons, then?"

"I certainly do." Bob displayed a pistol. "There are also the servants. None have brain tumors or syphilis; they're all just plain bad."

Roger said in an awkward voice, "Let's go and get it over."

Alan Robertson's voice took on a harsh edge. "You seriously plan to maroon us here, without food?"

"Consider yourself marooned."

"I'm afraid that I must punish you, Bob, and Roger as well."

Bob laughed gaily. "You yourself are suffering from brain disease—megalomania. You haven't the power to punish anyone."

"I still control the machine, Bob."

"The machine isn't here. So now—"

Alan Robertson turned and looked around the landscape, with a frowning air of expectation. "Let me see. I'd probably come down from the main gate; Gilbert and a group from behind the house. Yes, here we are."

Down the path from the main portal, walking jauntily, came two Alan Robertsons with six men armed with rifles and gas grenades. Simultaneously from behind the house appeared two Gilbert Durays and six more men, similarly armed.

Bob stared in wonder. "Who are these people?"

"Cognates," said Alan, smiling. "I told you I controlled the machine, and so do all my cognates. As soon as Gilbert and I return to our Earth, we must similarly set forth and in our turn do our part on other worlds cognate to this . . . Roger, be good enough to summon your servants. We will take them back to Earth. You and Bob must remain here."

Waille gasped in distress. "Forever?"

"You deserve nothing better," said Alan Robertson. "Bob perhaps deserves worse." He turned to the cognate Alan Robertsons. "What of Gilbert's passway?"

Both replied, "It's in Bob's San Francisco apartment, in a box on the mantelpiece."

"Very good," said Alan Robertson. "We will now depart. Good-bye, Bob. Good-bye, Roger. I am sorry that our association ended on this rather unpleasant basis."

"Wait!" cried Roger. "Take me back with you!"

"Good-bye," said Alan Robertson. "Come along then, Elizabeth. Girls! Run on ahead!"

XIII

Elizabeth and the children had returned to Home; Alan Robertson and Duray sat in the lounge above the machine. "Our first step," said Alan Robertson, "is to dissolve our obligation. There are, of course, an infinite number of Rumfuddles at Ekshayans and an infinite number of Alans and Gilberts. If we visited a single Rumfuddle, we would, by the laws of probability, miss a certain number of the emergency situations. The total number of permutations, assuming that an infinite number of Alans and Gilberts makes a random choice among an infinite number of Ekshayans, is infinity raised to the infinite power. What percentage of this number yields blanks for any given Ekshayan, I haven't calculated. If we visited Ekshayans until we had by our own efforts rescued at least one Gilbert and Alan set, we might be forced to scour fifty or a hundred worlds or more. Or we might achieve our rescue on the first visit. The wisest course, I believe, is for you and I to visit, say, twenty Ekshayans. If each of the Alan and Gilbert sets does the same, then the chances for any particular Alan and Gilbert to be abandoned are one in twenty times nineteen times eighteen times seventeen, et cetera. Even then I think I will arrange that an operator check another five or ten thousand worlds to gather up that one lone chance . . ."

Philip Latham

Philip Latham is the pseudonym of Robert S. Richardson (1902–81), a distinguished astronomer who occasionally wrote articles under his own name, but published fiction between the 1940s and 1960s only under the Latham name. His stories characteristically feature astronomers, and until his later years always focused on science, especially theoretical physics embodied as fact.

From the flamboyant, apocalyptic astronomical fiction of Camille Flammarion in the late 19th century to the works of Fred Hoyle and Gregory Benford, working astronomers and astrophysicists have contributed stories of broad scope and cosmic speculation to the development of science fiction. The word "astronomical" is, after all, a synonym for very large in number or scale. Cosmology and astronomy are primary repositories of images for the SF genre, as was nature for the Romantic poets. And, of course, it is the astronomers who investigate the environments that are the literal settings of much science fiction. But it is also the teasing, ambiguous border between the physical and the metaphysical that astronomical science fiction often confronts, and that gives depth and emotional force to the cold and the distant. As in this story.

THE DIMPLE IN DRACO

There was never any doubt when quitting time came to the Institute for Cosmological Physics, Bill Backus reflected. Promptly at 4:53 P.M. the women all started heading for the powder room, whence shortly thereafter came the sound of water in turbulence. It was one of the zero points in this uneasy world.

For the third time he reached for the telephone and for the third time hesitated. It was 4:57 now. The girl at the switchboard always got sore if you kept her after five o'clock. Oh, well, the hell with her. He needed help. He seized the phone.

"Two-seven, please."

No answer . . . no answer . . . no . . .

"MacCready," came a noncommittal voice.

"Mac, this is Bill."

"Bill! It's so good to hear your voice!"

"Listen, Mac, I've got something down here in the measuring room I think will interest you."

"So's my wife. She's probably mixing it now."

"I'd like your opinion very much. Shouldn't take ten minutes."

One . . . two . . . three . . .

"All right. See you."

A few minutes later MacCready sauntered into the measuring room, hoisted one leg over a corner of the bench that ran along the wall, and applied a match to his pipe. When the tobacco was going to his satisfaction, he folded his arms and gazed expectantly at Bill.

"Here I am. Interest me."

Bill indicated the Toepfer measuring engine beside him.

"Plate's on there. Got it last week with the prime focus spectrograph. Six-hour exposure in the second order blue. I nearly froze. Coldest night in the memory of man—"

"You don't look so good," MacCready remarked.

"Maybe that's because I don't feel so good," Bill said. He rose and began pacing the floor. "Take a look at the plate, will you, and tell me what you think."

"But your feet seem better," MacCready added encouragingly.

"Yeah, they are better. Now will you look at the plate?"

MacCready laid aside his pipe and peered into the eyepiece.

"Nice spectrum," he said. "Real sharp lines."

"But *what* lines?" Bill cried. "I've been working on those lines for three days. Can't identify a single one." He ran his fingers through his black hair. "It's driving me crazy."

"Well, d'you have to get so dramatic about it?" MacCready asked. He gave the focusing screw a touch. "What is this famous object, anyhow?"

"Well, you see, that's what I don't know."

"*You don't know!*" MacCready stared at him. "Do you realize how much it cost the Institute to get this plate? Do you know that we have seventeen applications on file for time at this instrument? Applications from highly qualified individuals with no suspicion of insanity in their background. And then you take our giant eye, as the newspapers are pleased to call it, and bang away at any old—"

"Mac, shut up." Bill lit a cigarette. "I was after NGC 2146, that way-north nebula in Cepheus, I guess it is. This new night assistant was on that evening. Poor guy got all balled up. My fault as much as his. You wouldn't believe it possible, but he got set on the wrong side of the pole. Landed me over in Draco somewhere. I thought the setting looked kind of funny—"

"Couldn't you tell from your star field?"

"Well, I should, but the fields weren't so different. Anyhow—"

"—anyhow you goofed but you got *something*," MacCready finished for him. "By any chance would you have the vaguest notion what it is? Radio source? Interloper? QSG? Haro-Luyten object? Humason-Zwicky star? Have I left out anything?"

"All I know, it's got a spectrum nobody ever saw before."

"Then what are you griping about?" MacCready demanded. "That's *good*. Maybe this object's got the world's biggest red shift. You've probably dredged up some lines buried thousands of angstroms deep in the ultraviolet."

"Nope, won't suit, Mac. Remember the Houston meeting? It was agreed we're living in an exploding universe with a q-zero of 2.5. This thing's way off the beam—much too bright."

"You know what your problem is, Bill?" MacCready was suddenly serious. "You've always got to relate to somebody else. You're afraid to take your results just as they stand."

"But there must be an answer," Bill protested. "What else can it be?"

MacCready shrugged and fell to scrutinizing the plate again.

"Wouldn't surprise me if the answer's staring us right in the face," he said. "Only it's so simple we can't see it."

He moved the plate carriage a bit.

"Now you take these three big lines I see here . . . Why couldn't the one on my left be that HeII line at—what is it?—1640? And the one in the middle—"

"Oh, my gawd, don't you think I've been all through that search list?" Bill said wearily. "None of 'em's any good. I've tried a bunch of hundred-to-one shots. They're no good either. Nothing fits."

"Too bad." MacCready frowned slightly. "Strange . . . these lines are all in absorption, aren't they?"

"Here's my list of wavelengths," Bill said, handing him a sheet of paper. "They're the means of my measures on the machine and some runs with the electronic line-profile comparator. They ought to be pretty good."

"I'm sure they are," MacCready murmured. He shot a sudden glance at Bill. "You sure you set the grating in the right order spectrum?"

"Mac, I *couldn't* make a mistake like that."

"Congratulations."

There was a long silence broken only by an occasional motor starting up in the parking lot, and the steady rumble of traffic from the boulevard nearby. MacCready was the first to speak.

"After you got this plate, did you take another exposure on a familiar object, same spectrograph—same emulsion—same everything?"

"Yes."

"All right?"

"Yes."

"It was?"

"Yes!" Bill shouted. "In France it's *oui*. In Spanish it's *si*. In Russian it's *da*."

MacCready transferred his attention from the plate to Bill's list of wavelengths.

"You know, these three big lines remind me of something," he muttered. "But I'll confess I haven't the faintest notion what it is."

Bill looked completely deflated. He began pacing the room again, clasping and unclasping his hands behind him. MacCready seemed to have forgotten his existence.

Bill tossed away his cigarette.

"Well, thanks for coming down, Mac. I'd gotten to the end of my rope. Thought perhaps you could suggest something."

There was no response. Bill paced the floor for another five minutes.

"Well, I've got to go. We're having company tonight."

"Yeah, you run along," MacCready told him. "Leaving myself in a minute . . . just want to check one thing."

Bill was nearly out the door when MacCready called suddenly, "Bill."

"Yeah?"

"Call my wife, will you? Tell her I'll be a little late."

Bill had to wait forever before he got a break in the traffic at Los Robles. Why did he keep coming this way? he asked himself. There was no answer. You saw an opening—you took a deep breath—uttered a prayer—and if you were lucky you made it.

Turning north toward Hillhurst he saw that the signal at Cordova was going to be red, as usual. The signal was always red at Cordova. In the past five years he must have crossed Cordova going north at least two thousand times. There had been just three times by actual count when he had hit the green light. His confidence in the theory of probability had been badly shaken.

Through the tangle of varicolored lights, leering Santa Clauses, liquor advertisements, and five-pointed stars* of Bethlehem, Bill perceived a huge sign looming ahead, VILLAGE MARKET. *Click!* What was he supposed to do? What was he supposed to—Helen's grocery list, of course. Good old autohypnosis.

Within the Village Market the aisles were abustle with hausfrauen pushing metal carts, their vacant gaze reflecting the trancelike state induced by the sight of merchandise in profusion. Bill took a cart himself and went to work on Helen's grocery list, tracking down the various items by the awkward process of taking them in the order written. Occasionally when it seemed like a good idea he tossed in an extra item or two. How often he had come in for a fifty-nine-cent piece of cheese and departed laden down with a lot of junk he never originally had the slightest intention of buying. But who were we? Mere puppets moving at the bidding of the vast formless things that operate these huge pleasure domes of produce.

Helen wrote her shopping items in a code that might have baffled the best brains in Interpol. This time, however, it had been pretty clear sailing. He now had in the cart the "6 nce rd rpe toms" and the "2 pkes 1mn jlo," and finally had reached the last item, "2 dz Ye Olde Eng Muffs." This sounded almost too easy. On any rational distribution system Olde English Muffins could hardly be anywhere else but in the bread section. He glanced at the Store Guide. Bread? . . . Bread? . . . Section 5. Where was he? Way over in 21 among Frozen Desserts and mouthwash. He deftly changed course and started bearing toward smaller numbers. 2 . . . 3 . . . 4 . . . 6 . . . 7. No 5! Must have missed it. Scan more carefully now . . . 2 . . . 3 . . . 4 . . . 6 . . . 7. Number 5 was absolutely and positively missing.

He looked around for a clerk, but there was none in sight. Neither was there any bread. He explored one aisle after another as fast as traffic permitted. There were shelves and bins loaded with pickles and olives, wieners and knockwurst, yoghurt and horseradish. But no Olde English Muffins. Well, he couldn't spend the evening pushing a metal cart around the Village Market. He picked up a box of Bixmix and headed for Checkers' Row.

The porch lights were already burning when he turned into the driveway. That was bad. It meant that even now company was ominously near. Closing the garage door, he noticed the stars of Auriga rising over the mountains to the north. How odd Capella looked, reddened almost to the color of Mars by the smoke and haze. Auriga had always been his favorite constellation. All the constellations had a background rich in mythological lore—except Auriga. Auriga was known as "the Charioteer." But where were his chariot and horse? Nobody knew. The stars of Auriga were meaningless.

"Well, where have *you* been?" Helen demanded, as he staggered into the kitchen with his load of groceries. She was a small woman whose early blond prettiness was beginning to show signs of wear under the ceaseless battering of suburbia: the Garden Club, the Art League, WAGS,† etc., etc.

"Where do you think?" Bill growled. "Picking up the stuff you forgot."

She started sorting over the groceries. "It shouldn't have taken—*Where's the muffins?*"

---

*Stars do not have points sticking out of them. Stars are spherical.

†Women Against Smog.

"Couldn't find 'em. Got Bixmix instead."

"Why couldn't you find them?"

"Hidden too well, I guess."

"Why, they're right by the bread."

"Couldn't find the bread either."

"Did you ask a clerk?"

"Didn't see any to ask."

"But there's always—"

"It's the truth!" he cried. "What do you want me to do? Lie to you?"

"Oh, do as you like. I don't care." With a resigned air she began putting away the various items. "Now hurry and change your clothes. They'll be here any minute."

He was scarcely halfway up the stairs when she came dashing after him. "Your feet! What's happened to your feet?"

"Don't know." He shrugged. "They just didn't hurt when I got up this morning."

"What did I tell you," Helen told him triumphantly. "You wouldn't go to see Dr. Levine. He's only the best orthopedic specialist in town but of course you know more than he does. If I hadn't made an appointment for you, you'd *never* have gone. Now admit it. Those arch supporters did help, didn't they?"

"If I'd worn those arch supporters one more day I wouldn't be ambulant now."

"But they must have done you *some* good." She regarded him with despair. "If it wasn't the arch supporters, what was it?"

Bill did not answer immediately. He leaned against the railing, gazing thoughtfully at some of Helen's abstract artwork on the opposite wall.

"Last night," he declared solemnly, "my feet were healed."

"Healed?"

He nodded. "What they called a miracle in the old days."

"So it was a miracle and not the arch supporters?"

"Why couldn't I be cured by a miracle?" he demanded angrily. "Other people are. People with their stomach and lungs eaten up by cancer. Suddenly they're all right. They rise from their bed and walk. They've got sworn medical testimony to prove it."

Helen hesitated uncertainly. "But you're not the miracle type."

"What's the matter with me?"

"I always supposed you had to be kind of on the saintly side."

He dismissed her objection with a wave of his hand.

"Merely a technicality." He closed his eyes for a few moments as if in meditation. "I hadn't intended to say anything about it, but for your information, I was healed by an angel who appeared in my room last night."

"So that was what I heard going on in there."

"She appeared over by the filing cabinet," Bill continued. "She was surrounded by a golden halo that illuminated the whole room. I thought I'd forgotten to turn the lights out at first." His voice dropped almost to a whisper. "She was no ordinary angel, either."

"It's so nice you got special attention."

"She had the most beautiful golden red hair." There was a faraway look in his eyes. "Her name was Edna."

"No last name?"

"Naturally I was somewhat startled at the sudden appearance of this apparition. 'What do you want?' I asked, in a voice that trembled.

" 'Have no fear, William,' she replied, approaching the bed. 'I have come to heal you. Not to harm you.'

" 'To heal me?' I whispered.

" 'Move over, William,' she said, 'so that I may touch you.'

"So I shoved over in the bed a little—"

His narrative was interrupted by the flash of headlights and the sound of a car pulling up in the driveway.

"There they are now!" Helen exclaimed. "And here I've been wasting my time talking to you about your feet and this redheaded angel."

Bill slowly mounted the stairs, his lips continuing to move inaudibly. In his room he stood for a while inspecting the place where he had recounted Edna's appearance. From the lower depths came the shriek of feminine voices raised in greeting interspersed with occasional masculine rumbles. Evidently the Nortons had picked up Bernice and Clem on the way over. Clem Tuttle was in advertising and Jim Norton was an agent for Inertia Acres, a real-estate project for the retired. Bernice Tuttle and Dottie Norton were among his favorite wives, but he found it hard to work up much enthusiasm for their husbands. It was while struggling into his shirt that it occurred to him that all the people they saw were friends of Helen's. Outside the office he had no friends.

Bill came downstairs, said hello all around, and made a quick exit to the kitchen to mix the cocktails. He put too much vodka into the martinis and had to drink a couple of glasses to provide more room for the vermouth. Back in the living room he had hoped to strike up a conversation with Bernice or Dottie, but the situation was hopeless. The girls were in ecstasy over Helen's Christmas tree, which was not a Christmas tree at all but a dead limb salvaged from the oak in the back yard. She had adorned its gnarled branches with blue and silver balls, with here and there an aerodynamically inadequate angel in flight. Since the girls were engaged, he was thrown upon the company of Jim and Clem, who were discussing the situation that had developed at Anoakia U., their old alma mater. It appeared that the quality of the faculty and student body had been steadily deteriorating since their departure in '41. Since Bill had never attended Anoakia U., and never had had much use for the place anyhow, he found the conversation less than fascinating. He sipped his cocktail, and moodily contemplated Bernice Tuttle's knees.

As if from a great distance he heard Helen calling him.

"Bill, telephone." He went into the hall, taking his glass with him. As he expected, it was Mac.

"Bill, what's your dispersion on that plate?"

"Hundred and ninety angstroms per millimeter."

"What kind of plate was it?"

"IIa-O, baked. Why?"

"Just checking, was all."

"Say, Mac, I explained to your wife it was my fault about getting home late."

"Well, as a matter of fact, I'm still at the office."

"Still at the office!" Bill went cold sober in an instant. "Mac, what do you know?"

"Nothing I want to talk about yet. But I think I'm gaining on it."

"Give me a ring—" But he had hung up.

Bill's mind was racing. Mac would never have called unless he was on to something big. A "critical" object that might settle the cosmological controversy once and for all. He gulped down the rest of his drink and casually strolled back to the living room. How petty they all were. Jim and Clem were thoroughly in agreement that autonomy was not for Anoakia U. The girls were deploring the Santa Claus situation that had developed at the various department stores around town. That Santa Claus at the Bon Marché, they must have got him from central casting! Did you get a whiff of his breath? And the way he talked to the children! Honestly, you'd have thought he was playing King Lear!

The soggy part of a Hillhurst evening came after dinner, when the guests were swollen with food, and the cocktails only a dull memory. There were two ways to endure the time till departure: (1) the men gathered at one end of the room and talked about their automobiles and their children, while the women went into a huddle at the other end and talked about their clothes and their children; or (2) somebody showed color slides of their trip to Hawaii last summer. One hostess had made a valiant attempt to break the pattern by handing out selected passages from Ovid and Chaucer to be read aloud, but some of the men had balked. But a few bold spirits still fought on. When her guests were comfortably relaxed over their coffee and liqueurs, Helen stepped to the center of the room and clapped her hands.

"Now I'm not going to let you sit around all evening," she informed them. "We're going to play a game called Three Answers. One person, called the Grand Inquisitor, asks the questions. The rest of us give the answers. We make up some sort of story and the Grand Inquisitor, by questioning us, tries to find the key to it."

This announcement was followed by a brief silence.

"Sounds like one of these fun things," Clem grunted, knocking the ashes from his cigar.

Jim raised his hand. "Mrs. Chairman, I would like to nominate my wife for Grand Inquisitor. She can beat any lie detector that was ever invented."

Dottie had a question. "How do we know what answers to give?"

"We answer as a group," Helen said. "The Grand Inquisitor can ask all the questions he likes. But we can only answer in three ways: yes, no, or maybe. I'll explain the details later. Now who'll be Grand Inquisitor?"

"I hereby nominate Bill Backus for G.I.," Clem said.

"Second the motion," Jim said promptly.

"Bill analyzes this deep space stuff all day," Clem said. "Ought to be easy for him.

"I'd *love* to be analyzed by Bill," Dottie cried.

"Well, darling, I guess you're Grand Inquisitor," Helen said. "Now go out in the kitchen and wait there till I call you."

Bill shuffled out to the kitchen, where he began picking at the remains of the turkey. From the front room came snatches of conversation and bursts of stifled laughter, but he was unable to distinguish any words. His mind kept going back to Mac at the office. It was nearly eleven. He had hoped to hear from him by this time if he knew anything exciting. Probably the whole thing had collapsed and Mac was home in bed. He had half a notion to give him a ring when he heard Helen calling him, "All right, you can come now."

Bill strode into the living room trying to assume the grim expression appropriate to a Grand Inquisitor. How to begin this crazy game? Try some questions of a general nature until he got a lead.

"Has Clem landed that brassiere account yet?"

"No," they responded in unison.

"Have Jim and Bernice run off together?"
"No."
"Was it some sort of crime?"
"Yes."
"Was the crime committed in this city?"
"Maybe."
"In this immediate area?"
"Yes."
"Was it a murder?"
"No."
"Something more ghastly?"
"Maybe."

This was tougher than he had anticipated. Why had Helen ever gotten him into this thing? How to proceed? They were gazing at him expectantly . . . gleefully . . .

"Was the person involved a man?"
"No."
"A woman?"
"No."
"An animal, then?"
"No."

No? What on earth . . . ? A suspicion began to dawn. *Was* it something on *Earth?*

"Was the victim a creature from outer space?"
"Yes!"

On the trail at last!

"Was it a creature from Mars?"
"No."
"Was it from Venus?"
"No."
"Mercury?"
"Maybe."

Not what he had expected, but keep on.

"Was it from Jupiter? Saturn? Uranus?"
"No! No! No!"

Well . . . there weren't many planets left. With elaborate casualness he inquired, "Did this creature, by any chance, come from Pluto?"

"Yes!" they shrieked.

At last!

"Is this Plutonian creature at present somewhere within the environs of this city?"

"Maybe."
"So you don't know?"
"Maybe."

Perhaps it would help if he knew more about the creature itself.

"Have you seen this creature?"
"Yes."
"Is it larger than man-size?"
"Yes."
"Is this creature affected adversely by the heat?"
"No."

A flash of inspiration.

"Is it in this house right now?"

"Maybe."

They were hedging now.

"Is it in the basement?"

"No."

"The attic?"

"No."

"The refrigerator?"

"No."

"Under the stairway?"

"Maybe."

Relentlessly he pursued the phantom creature over the house. But despite his best efforts it eluded him. He fancied he detected a hint of scorn . . . even contempt . . . in their eyes. Suddenly he recalled Mac's remark: *The answer may be staring us right in the face. Only it's so simple we can't see it.*

Go back . . . see if he had overlooked anything.

"You said this creature is also an inhabitant of Mercury?"

"Maybe."

"Then it *is* capable of withstanding a high temperature?"

"Yes."

He was groping for the next question when the telephone rang. *Mac!*

"Don't go. Be back in a minute."

It was Mac, all right.

"Well, Bill, I think I've got the answer." He sounded more relaxed. "But I'll be darned if I know what it means."

"Let me have it anyhow."

"Remember those three big lines I said reminded me of something? You naturally assumed they were ultraviolet lines Doppler-shifted into the visible. Only you couldn't identify 'em with anything in the UV. Neither could I. Wasted about two hours convincing myself of the fact."

He took about a three count.

"So, since I was all alone, I decided to play a crazy hunch. Bill, do you know what those lines are?"

"How the hell—"

"They're those three big ionized calcium lines in the infrared."

"*Infrared!*"

"This thing's got a velocity of about 0.6c."

"That wouldn't give so much of a redshift."

"Who said anything about a *red*shift? This is a *violet*shift. Bill, this thing is coming *our way.*"

"Get out!"

"Fact!"

"Mac, you can't screw up the whole universe that easy. Why, it contradicts everything we know. Besides, three lines aren't enough. You could force an agreement . . . a pretty good agreement."

"I'm sorry, Bill, but everything else fits, too. Your line at 3929 is 7699 of potassium . . . 4494 is 8806 of magnesium . . ."

"Mac, what does it *mean?*"

"From the geometry of the situation I would say it means there's a dimple in the expanding universe in the direction of Draco."

It was so long before he spoke again that Bill began to wonder if he'd hung up.

"I'm only giving you an answer, Bill. What it means is *your* problem."

Bill found his guests in various stages of relaxation when he returned to the living room. It was hard to get his mind on Hillhurst again.

"I'm afraid it's getting late," Bernice said. "Clem and I have to be up early tomorrow. We're driving to Carmel, you know."

"Oh, don't go," Helen protested.

"It's been such a lovely evening," Dottie told her. "But really—"

"Now wait a minute," Jim boomed, coming from the bathroom. "We've got to put the Grand Inquisitor straight first."

"Sure do," Clem chuckled. "Bill would toss all night."

Jim shook his head regretfully. "Bill, old boy, I'm afraid the game was rigged."

"Rigged?" He had only been half listening.

"You see," Jim went on, "if the last letter in the last word of a question was a vowel we all answered yes. If it was a consonant we answered no. And if it was a W or Y we answered maybe." He grinned. "Get it?"

It took a while.

"So I could have gone on asking questions forever," Bill said slowly. "And you could have gone on giving me answers forever. And I'd never have known any more than in the beginning."

"Afraid that's about the size of it," Jim said. He crunched out his cigar. "Well, Dottie, go get your costly mink . . ."

Bill accompanied his guests to the door, dutifully went through the ritual of parting, and waved as they went down the driveway.

Back in the living room Helen gazed listlessly at the remains of the hors d'oeuvres and the cigarette trays. "No use cleaning up tonight, I guess." She glanced at Bill standing by the north window. "What's the matter? Aren't you coming to bed?"

"I believe I'll stay down here for a while," he told her.

"I should think you'd be anxious to see your redheaded friend."

"Perhaps I am."

Helen paused at the stairs. "You didn't exactly sparkle tonight, did you?" she remarked. "What was the matter?"

"Tired, I guess."

"Who was it called?"

"MacCready."

"What did he want?"

"Oh . . . nothing."

"Nothing! When he calls after midnight!"

"It was about a dimple in Draco."

"A dimple—"

"Object's headed toward the Earth. Everything else is rushing away. Puts a dimple in the universe out in Draco."

"Headed toward the Earth! Very fast?"

Bill shrugged. "About six-tenths c—hundred thousand miles a second."

"You mean it's going to hit us?"

"Afraid not. You see, it's quite a ways off."

"How far?"

"Oh, hell, I don't know," he said impatiently. "A billion light-years maybe."

"Well, you don't need to be so disagreeable about it. I can ask, can't I?"

"It's like Job asking the Voice out of the Whirlwind how much torque He's got."

Helen stood without speaking for several moments, then turned and went slowly up the stairs. Bill waited until he heard her door close. Then he switched out the lights and drew the curtains away from the window.

Capella was far above the haze now, shining in the stars of Auriga with a golden reddish glow, as bright as the glow of Edna's hair. Suddenly Bill had the most intense sense of identity with Auriga. How lonely he must be up there among all those gods and monsters, the only one without a story. Did the old Charioteer ever ponder the meaning of his stars? If so, what were *his* answers? Or did he bother to ask questions anymore—when the answers had no meaning?

John Wyndham

John Wyndham is the pseudonym of John Beynon Harris (1903–69), an important British genre SF writer of the mid-century. His early career, during which he wrote under a variety of bylines, including John Beynon, John Beynon Harris, Wyndham Parkes, and others, overlapped that of Olaf Stapledon in the 1930s and early '40s; his later career, at which point he changed to the John Wyndham byline, overlapped the advent of Arthur C. Clarke in the late 1940s.

Wyndham and Clarke and Eric Frank Russell, all British SF authors, hit their stride as mature SF writers at about the same time and were major figures in '50s science fiction. "The new Wyndham," said Damon Knight in *In Search of Wonder* (1956), "has turned out to be something remarkably like H. G. Wells—not the wise-old-owl Wells, more interested in sermon than story, but the young Wells, with that astonishing, compelling gift of pure storytelling."

Wyndham is most famous for his disaster novels *Day of the Triffids* (1951) and *The Midwich Cuckoos* (1957), both made into movies. His work ranged from pulp magazine adventure stories and serials in the 1930s to sophisticated and complex works such as this novella. His mature period began in 1950 and continued through 1961, after which he published little.

This story is arguably his best. It is a surprisingly advanced presentation of gender politics. It elicited enthusiastic comments at the time of its first publication in 1956 and shared a special Hugo Award (it was published with two other pieces, by William Golding and Mervyn Peake, in a book, *Sometime, Never,* that won a Hugo). Kingsley Amis, in a discussion of this story in *New Maps of Hell*, says, "The core of the story, occupying one third of its length, is a conversation . . . saying all that can be said for the notion that women would be better off without men and making what seem to me some fairly damaging criticisms of the contemporary female role."

CONSIDER HER WAYS

T*here was nothing but myself.*

I hung in a timeless, spaceless, forceless void that was neither light, nor dark. I had entity, but no form; awareness, but no senses; mind, but no memory. I wondered, is this—this nothingness—my soul? And it seemed that I had wondered that always, and should go on wondering it for ever. . . .

But, somehow, timelessness ceased. I became aware that there was a force: that I was being moved, and that spacelessness had, therefore, ceased, too. There was nothing to show that I moved; I knew simply that I was being drawn. I felt happy because I knew there was something or someone to whom I wanted to be drawn. I had no other wish than to turn like a compass-needle and then fall through the void. . . .

But I was disappointed. No smooth, swift fall followed. Instead, other forces fastened on me. I was pulled this way, and then that. I did not know how I knew it; there was no outside reference, no fixed point, no direction even; yet I could feel that I was tugged hither and thither, as though against the resistance of some inner gyroscope. It was as if one force were in command of me for a time, only to weaken and lose me to a new force. Then I would seem to slide towards some unknown point, until I was arrested, and diverted upon another course. I wafted this way and that, with the sense of awareness continually growing firmer; and I wondered whether rival forces were fighting for me, good and evil, perhaps, or life and death. . . .

The sense of pulling back and forth became more definite until I was almost jerked from one course to another. Then, abruptly, the feeling of struggle finished. I had a sense of travelling faster and faster still, plunging like a wandering meteorite that had been trapped at last. . . .

"All right," said a voice. "Resuscitation was a little retarded, for some reason. Better make a note of that on her card. What's the number? Oh, only her fourth time. Yes, certainly make a note. It's all right. Here she comes!"

It was a woman's voice speaking, with a slightly unfamiliar accent. The surface I was lying on shook under me. I opened my eyes, saw the ceiling moving along above me, and let them close. Presently, another voice, again with an unfamiliar intonation, spoke to me:

"Drink this," she said.

A hand lifted my head, and a cup was pressed against my lips. After I had drunk the stuff I lay back with my eyes closed again. I dozed for a little while, and came out of it feeling stronger. For some minutes I lay looking up at the ceiling and wondering vaguely where I was. I could not recall any ceiling that was painted just this pinkish shade of cream. Then, suddenly, while I was still gazing up at the ceiling, I was shocked, just as if something had hit my mind a sharp blow. I was frighteningly aware that it was not just the pinkish ceiling that was *unfamiliar*—everything was unfamiliar. Where there should have been memories there was just a great gap. I had no idea who I was, or where I was; I could recall nothing of how or why I came to be here. . . . In a rush of panic I tried to sit up, but a hand pressed me back, and presently held the cup to my lips again.

"You're quite all right. Just relax," the same voice told me, reassuringly.

I wanted to ask questions, but somehow I felt immensely weary, and everything was too much trouble. The first rush of panic subsided, leaving me lethargic. I wondered what had happened to me—had I been in an accident, perhaps? Was this the kind of thing that happened when one was badly shocked? I did not know, and now for the moment I did not care: I was being looked after. I felt so drowsy that the questions could wait.

I suppose I dozed, and it may have been for a few minutes, or for an hour. I know only that when I opened my eyes again I felt calmer—more puzzled than alarmed—and I lay for a time without moving. I had recovered enough grasp now to console myself with the thought that if there had been an accident, at least there was no pain.

Presently I gained a little more energy, and, with it, curiosity to know where I was. I rolled my head on the pillow to see more of the surroundings.

A few feet away I saw a contrivance on wheels, something between a bed and a trolley. On it, asleep, with her mouth open, was the most enormous woman I had ever seen. I stared, wondering whether it was some kind of cage over her to take the weight of the covers that gave her the mountainous look, but the movement of her breathing soon showed me that it was not. Then I looked beyond her and saw two more trolleys, both supporting equally enormous women.

I studied the nearest one more closely, and discovered to my surprise that she was quite young—not more than twenty-two, or twenty-three, I guessed. Her face was a little plump, perhaps, but by no means over-fat; indeed, with her fresh, healthy young colouring and her short-cropped gold curls, she was quite pretty. I fell to wondering what curious disorder of the glands could cause such a degree of anomaly at her age.

Ten minutes or so passed, and there was a sound of brisk, business-like footsteps approaching. A voice inquired:

"How are you feeling now?"

I rolled my head to the other side, and found myself looking into a face almost level with my own. For a moment I thought its owner must be a child, then I saw that the features under the white cap were certainly not less than thirty years old. Without waiting for a reply she reached under the bed-clothes and took my pulse. Its rate appeared to satisfy her, for she nodded confidently.

"You'll be all right now, Mother," she told me.

I stared at her, blankly.

"The car's only just outside the door there. Do you think you can walk it?" she went on.

Bemusedly, I asked:

"What car?"

"Why, to take you home, of course," she said, with professional patience. "Come along now." And she pulled away the bedclothes.

I started to move, and looked down. What I saw there held me fixed. I lifted my arm. It was like nothing so much as a plump, white bolster with a ridiculous little hand attached at the end. I stared at it in horror. Then I heard a far-off scream as I fainted. . . .

When I opened my eyes again there was a woman—a normal-sized woman—in white overalls with a stethoscope round her neck, frowning at me in perplexity. The white-capped woman I had taken for a child stood beside her, reaching only a little above her elbow.

"—I don't know, Doctor," she was saying. "She just suddenly screamed and fainted."

"What is it? What's happened to me? I know I'm not like this—I'm not, I'm not," I said, and I could hear my own voice wailing the words.

The doctor went on looking puzzled.

"What does she mean?" she asked.

"I've no idea, Doctor," said the small one. "It was quite sudden, as if she'd had some kind of shock—but I don't know why."

"Well, she's been passed and signed-off, and, anyway, she can't stay here. We need the room," said the doctor. "I'd better give her a sedative."

"But what's happened? Who am I? There's something terribly wrong. I know I'm not like this. P-please t-tell me—" I implored her, and then somehow lost myself in a stammer and a muddle.

The doctor's manner became soothing. She laid a hand gently on my shoulder.

"That's all right, Mother. There's nothing to worry about. Just take things quietly. We'll soon have you back home."

Another white-capped assistant, no taller than the first, hurried up with a syringe, and handed it to the doctor.

"No!" I protested. "I want to know where I am. Who am I? Who are you? What's happened to me?" I tried to slap the syringe out of her hand, but both the small assistants flung themselves on my arm, and held on to it while she pressed in the needle.

It was a sedative, all right. It did not put me out, but it detached me. An odd feeling: I seemed to be floating a few feet outside myself and considering me with an unnatural calmness. I was able, or felt that I was able, to evaluate matters with intelligent clarity. Evidently I was suffering from amnesia. A shock of some kind had caused me to 'lose my memory,' as it is often put. Obviously it was only a very small part of my memory that had gone—just the personal part: who I was, what I was, where I lived—all the mechanism for day-to-day getting along seemed to be intact: I'd not forgotten how to talk, or how to think, and I seemed to have quite a well-stored mind to think with.

On the other hand there was a nagging conviction that everything about me was somehow *wrong*. I *knew*, somehow, that I'd never before seen the place I was in; I *knew*, too, that there was something queer about the presence of the two small nurses; above all, I *knew*, with absolute certainty, that this massive form lying here was not mine. I could not recall what face I ought to see in a mirror, not even whether it would be dark or fair, or old or young, but there was no shadow of doubt in my mind that, whatever it was like, it had never topped such a shape as I had now.

—And there were the other enormous young women, too. Obviously, it could not be a matter of glandular disorder in all of us, or there'd not be this talk of sending me 'home,' wherever that might be. . . .

I was still arguing the situation with myself in, thanks no doubt to the sedative, a most reasonable-seeming manner, though without making any progress at all, when the ceiling above my head began to move again, and I realized I was being wheeled along. Doors opened at the end of the room, and the trolley tilted a little beneath me as we went down a gentle ramp beyond.

At the foot of the ramp, an ambulance-like car, with pink coachwork polished until it gleamed, was waiting with the rear doors open. I observed interestedly that I was playing a part in a routine procedure. A team of eight diminutive attendants carried out the task of transferring me from the trolley to a sprung couch in the ambulance as if it were a kind of drill. Two of them lingered after the rest to tuck in my coverings and place another pillow behind my head. Then they got out, closing the doors behind them, and in a minute or two we started off.

It was at this point—and possibly the sedative helped in this, too—that I began to have an increasing sense of balance and a feeling that I was perceiving the situation. Probably there *had* been an accident, as I had suspected, but obviously my error, and the chief cause of my alarm, proceeded from my assumption that I was a stage further on than I actually was. I had assumed that after an interval I had recovered consciousness in these baffling circumstances, whereas the true state of affairs must clearly be that I had *not* recovered consciousness. I must be still in a suspended state, very likely with concussion, and this was a dream, or hallucination. Presently, I should wake up in conditions that would at least be sensible, if not necessarily familiar.

I wondered now that this consoling and stabilizing thought had not occurred to me before, and decided that it was the alarming sense of detailed reality that had thrown me into panic. It had been astonishingly stupid of me to be taken in to the extent of imagining that I really was a kind of Gulliver among rather over-size Lilliputians. It was quite characteristic of most dreams, too, that I should lack a clear knowledge of my identity, so we did not need to be surprised at that. The thing to do was to take an intelligent interest in all I observed: the whole thing must be chockful of symbolic content which it would be most interesting to work out later.

The discovery quite altered my attitude and I looked about me with a new attention. It struck me as odd right away that here was so much circumstantial detail, and all of it in focus—there was none of that sense of foreground in sharp relief against a muzzy, or even non-existent, background that one usually meets in a dream. Everything was presented with a most convincing, three-dimensional solidity. My own sensations, too, seemed perfectly valid. The injection, in particular, had been quite acutely authentic. The illusion of reality fascinated me into taking mental notes with some care.

The interior of the van, or ambulance, or whatever it was, was finished in the same shell-pink as the outside—except for the roof, which was powder-blue with a scatter of small silver stars. Against the front partition were mounted several cupboards, with plated handles. My couch, or stretcher, lay along the left side: on the other were two fixed seats, rather small, and upholstered in a semi-glazed material to match the colour of the rest. Two long windows on each side left little solid wall. Each of them was provided with curtains of a fine net, gathered back now in pink braid loops, and had a roller blind furled above it. Simply by turning my head on the pillow I was able to observe the passing scenery—though somewhat jerkily, for either the springing of the vehicle scarcely matched its appointments, or the road surface was bad: whichever the cause, I was glad my own couch was independently and quite comfortably sprung.

The external view did not offer a great deal of variety save in its hues. Our way was lined by buildings standing back behind some twenty yards of tidy lawn. Each block was three storeys high, about fifty yards long, and had a tiled roof of somewhat low pitch, suggesting a vaguely Italian influence. Structurally the blocks appeared identical, but each was differently coloured, with contrasting window-frames and doors, and carefully considered, uniform curtains. I could see no one behind the windows; indeed there appeared to be no one about at all except here and there a woman in overalls mowing a lawn, or tending one of the inset flowerbeds.

Further back from the road, perhaps two hundred yards away, stood larger, taller, more utilitarian-looking blocks, some of them with high, factory-type chimneys. I thought they might actually be factories of some kind, but at the distance, and because I had no more than fugitive views of them between the foreground blocks, I could not be sure.

The road itself seldom ran straight for more than a hundred yards at a stretch, and its windings made one wonder whether the buildings had not been more concerned to follow a contour line than a direction. There was little other traffic, and what there was consisted of lorries, large or small, mostly large. They were painted in one primary colour or another, with only a five-fold combination of letters and figures on their sides for further identification. In design they might have been any lorries anywhere.

We continued this uneventful progress at a modest pace for some twenty minutes, until we came to a stretch where the road was under repair. The car slowed, and the workers moved to one side, out of our way. As we crawled forward over the broken surface I was able to get a good look at them. They were all women or girls dressed in denim-like trousers, sleeveless singlets and working boots. All had their hair cut quite short, and a few wore hats. They were tall and broad-shouldered, bronzed and healthy-looking. The biceps of their arms were like a man's, and the hafts of their picks and shovels rested in the hard, strong hands of manual toilers.

They watched with concern as the car edged its way on to the rough patch, but when it drew level with them they transferred their attention, and jostled and craned to look inside at me.

They smiled widely, showing strong white teeth in their browned faces. All of them raised their right hands, making some sign to me, still smiling. Their good-will was so evident that I smiled back. They walked along, keeping pace with the crawling car, looking at me expectantly while their smiles faded into puzzlement. They were saying something but I could not hear the words. Some of them insistently repeated the sign. Their disappointed look made it clear that I was expected to respond with more than a smile. The only way that occurred to me was to raise my own right hand in imitation of their gesture. It was at least a qualified success; their faces brightened though a rather puzzled look remained. Then the car lurched on to the made-up road again and their still somewhat troubled faces slid back as we speeded up to our former sedate pace. More dream symbols, of course—but certainly not one of the stock symbols from the book. What on earth, I wondered, could a party of friendly Amazons, equipped with navvying implements instead of bows, stand for in my subconscious? Something frustrated, I imagined. A suppressed desire to dominate? I did not seem to be getting much further along that line when we passed the last of the variegated but nevertheless monotonous blocks, and ran into open country.

The flower beds had shown me already that it was spring, and now I was able to look on healthy pastures, and neat arable fields already touched with green; there was a haze-like green smoke along the trim hedges, and some of the trees in the tidily placed spinneys were in young leaf. The sun was shining with a bright benignity upon the most precise countryside I had ever seen; only the cattle dotted about the fields introduced a slight disorder into the careful dispositions. The farmhouses themselves were part of the pattern; hollow squares of neat buildings with an acre or so of vegetable garden on one side, an orchard on another, and a rickyard on a third. There was a suggestion of a doll's landscape about it—Grandma Moses, but tidied up and rationalized. I could see no random cottages, casually sited sheds, or unplanned outgrowths from the farm buildings. And what, I asked myself, should we conclude from this rather pathological exhibition of tidiness? That I was a more uncertain person than I had supposed, one who was subconsciously yearning for simplicity and security? Well, well. . . .

An open lorry which must have been travelling ahead of us turned off down a lane bordered by beautifully laid hedges, towards one of the farms. There were half a dozen young women in it, holding implements of some kind; Amazons, again. One of them, looking back, drew the attention of the rest to us. They raised their hands in the same sign that the others had made, and then waved cheerfully. I waved back.

Rather bewildering, I thought: Amazons for domination and this landscape for passive security: the two did not seem to tie up very well.

We trundled on, at our unambitious pace of twenty miles an hour or so, for what I guessed to be three-quarters of an hour, with the prospect changing very little. The country undulated gently and appeared to continue like that to the foot of a line of low blue hills many miles away. The tidy farmhouses went by with almost the regularity of milestones, though with something like twice the frequency. Occasionally there were working-parties in the fields; more rarely, one saw individuals busy about the farms, and others hoeing with tractors, but they were all too far off for me to make out any details. Presently, however, came a change.

Off to the left of the road, stretching back at right angles to it for more than a mile, appeared a row of trees. At first I thought it just a wood, but then I noticed that the trunks were evenly spaced, and the trees themselves topped and pruned until they gave more the impression of a high fence.

The end of it came to within twenty feet of the road, where it turned, and we ran along beside it for almost half a mile until the car slowed, turned to the left, and stopped in front of a pair of tall gates. There were a couple of toots on the horn.

The gates were ornamental, and possibly of wrought iron under their pink paint. The archway that they barred was stucco-covered, and painted the same colour.

Why, I inquired of myself, this prevalence of pink, which I regard as a namby-pamby colour, anyway? Flesh-colour? Symbolic of an ardency for the flesh which I had insufficiently gratified? I scarcely thought so. Not pink. Surely a burning red. . . . I don't think I know anyone who can be really ardent in a pink way. . . .

While we waited, a feeling that there was something wrong with the gatehouse grew upon me. The structure was a single-storey building, standing against the left, inner side of the archway, and coloured to match it. The woodwork was pale blue, and there were white net curtains at the windows. The door opened, and a middle-aged woman in a white blouse-and-trouser suit came out. She was bare-headed, with a few grey locks in her short, dark hair. Seeing me, she raised her hand in the same sign the Amazons had used, though perfunctorily, and walked over to open the gates. It was only as she pushed them back to admit us that I suddenly saw how small she was—certainly not over four feet tall. And that explained what was wrong with the gatehouse: it was built entirely to her scale. . .

I went on staring at her and her little house as we passed. Well, what about that? Mythology is rich in gnomes and 'little people', and they are fairly pervasive of dreams, too. Somebody, I was sure, must have decided that they are a standard symbol of something, but for the moment I could not recall what it was. Would it be repressed philo-progenitiveness, or was that too unsubtle? I stowed that away, too, for later contemplation and brought my attention back to the surroundings.

We were on our way, unhurriedly, along something more like a drive than a road, with surroundings that suggested a compromise between a public garden and a municipal housing estate. There were wide lawns of an unblemished velvet green, set here and there with flower beds, delicate groups of silver birch, and occasional larger, single trees. Among them stood pink, three-storey blocks, dotted about, seemingly to no particular plan.

A couple of the Amazon-types in singlets and trousers of a faded rust-red were engaged in planting-out a bed close beside the drive, and we had to pause while they dragged their handcart full of tulips onto the grass to let us pass. They gave me the usual salute and amiable grin as we went by.

A moment later I had a feeling that something had gone wrong with my sight, but as we passed one block we came in sight of another. It was white instead of pink, but otherwise exactly similar to the rest—except that it was scaled down by at least one-third. . . .

I blinked at it and stared hard, but it continued to seem just the same size.

A little further on, a grotesquely huge woman in pink draperies was walking slowly and heavily across a lawn. She was accompanied by three of the small, white-suited women looking, in contrast, like children, or very animated dolls: one was involuntarily reminded of tugs fussing round a liner.

I began to feel swamped: the proliferation and combination of symbols was getting well out of my class.

The car forked to the right, and presently we drew up before a flight of steps leading to one of the pink buildings—a normal-sized building, but still not free from oddity, for the steps were divided by a central balustrade; those to the left of it were normal, those to right, smaller and more numerous.

Three toots on the horn announced our arrival. In about ten seconds half a dozen small women appeared in the doorway and came running down the right-hand side of the steps. A door slammed as the driver got out and went to meet them. When she came into my range of view I saw that she was one of the little ones, too, but not in white as the rest were; she wore a shining pink suit like a livery that exactly matched the car.

They had a word together before they came round to open the door behind me, then a voice said brightly:

"Welcome, Mother Orchis. Welcome home."

The couch or stretcher slid back on runners, and between them they lowered it to the ground. One young woman whose blouse was badged with a pink St. Andrew's cross on the left breast leaned over me. She inquired considerately:

"Do you think you can walk, Mother?"

It did not seem the moment to inquire into the form of address. I was obviously the only possible target for the question.

"Walk?" I repeated. "Of course I can walk." And I sat up, with about eight hands assisting me.

'Of course' had been an overstatement. I realized that by the time I had been heaved to my feet. Even with all the help that was going on around me it was an exertion which brought on heavy breathing. I looked down at the monstrous form that billowed under my pink draperies, with a sick revulsion and a feeling that, whatever this particular mass of symbolism disguised, it was likely to prove a distasteful revelation later on. I tried a step. 'Walk' was scarcely the word for my progress. It felt like, and must have looked like, a slow series of forward surges. The women, at little more than my elbow height, fluttered about me like a flock of anxious hens. Once started, I was determined to go on, and I progressed with a kind of wave-motion, first across a few yards of gravel, and then, with ponderous deliberation, up the left-hand side of the steps.

There was a perceptible sense of relief and triumph all round as I reached the summit. We paused there a few moments for me to regain my breath, then we moved on into the building. A corridor led straight ahead, with three or four closed doors on each side; at the end it branched right and left. We took the left arm, and, at the end of it, I came face to face, for the first time since the hallucination had set in, with a mirror.

It took every volt of my resolution not to panic again at what I saw in it. The first few seconds of my stare were spent in fighting down a leaping hysteria.

In front of me stood an outrageous travesty, an elephantine female form, looking the more huge for its pink swathings. Mercifully, they covered everything but the head and hands, but these exposures were themselves another kind of shock, for the hands, though soft and dimpled and looking utterly out of proportion, were not uncomely, and the head and face were those of a girl.

She was pretty, too. She could not have been more than twenty-one, if that. Her curling fair hair was touched with auburn lights, and cut in a kind of bob. The complexion of her face was pink and cream, her mouth was gentle, and red without any artifice. She looked back at me, and at the little women anxiously clustering round me, from a pair of blue-green eyes beneath lightly arched brows. And this delicate face, this little Fragonard, was set upon that monstrous body: no less outrageously might a blossom of freesia sprout from a turnip.

When I moved my lips, hers moved; when I bent my arm, hers bent; and yet, once I got the better of that threatening panic, she ceased to be a reflection. She was nothing like me, so she must be a stranger whom I was observing, though in a most bewildering way. My panic and revulsion gave way to sadness, an aching pity for her. I could weep for the shame of it. I did. I watched the tears brim on her lower lids; mistily, I saw them overflow.

One of the little women beside me caught hold of my hand.

"Mother Orchis, dear, what's the matter?" she asked, full of concern.

I could not tell her: I had no clear idea myself. The image in the mirror shook her head, with tears running down her cheeks. Small hands patted me here and there; small, soothing voices encouraged me onward. The next door was opened for me and, amid concerned fussing, I was led into the room beyond.

We entered a place that struck me as a cross between a boudoir and a ward. The boudoir impression was sustained by a great deal of pink—in the carpet, coverlets, cushions, lampshades, and filmy window curtains; the ward motif, by an array of six divans, or couches, one of which was unoccupied.

It was a large enough room for six couches, separated by a chest, a chair and table for each, to be arranged on each side without an effect of crowding, and the open space in the middle was still big enough to contain several expansive easy chairs and a central table bearing an intricate flower-arrangement. A not displeasing scent faintly pervaded the place, and from somewhere came the subdued sound of a string quartette in a sentimental mood. Five of the bed-couches were already mountainously occupied. Two of my attendant party detached themselves and hurried ahead to turn back the pink satin cover on the sixth.

Faces from all the five other beds were turned towards me. Three of them smiling in welcome, the other two were less committal.

"Hallo, Orchis," one of them greeted me in a friendly tone. Then, with a touch of concern, she added: "What's the matter, dear? Did you have a bad time?"

I looked at her. She had a kindly, plumply pretty face, framed by light brown hair as she lay back against a cushion. The face looked about twenty-three or twenty-four years old. The rest of her was a huge mound of pink satin. I couldn't make any reply, but I did my best to return her smile as we passed.

Our convoy hove-to by the empty bed. After some preparation and positioning I was helped into it by all hands, and a cushion was arranged behind my head.

The exertion of my journey from the car had been considerable, and I was thankful to relax. While two of the little women pulled up the coverlet and arranged it over me, another produced a handkerchief and dabbed gently at my cheeks. She encouraged me:

"There you are, dear. Safely home again now. You'll be quite all right when you've rested a bit. Just try to sleep for a little."

"What's the matter with her?" inquired a forthright voice from one of the other beds. "Did she make a mess of it?"

The little woman with the handkerchief—she was the one who wore the St. Andrew's cross and appeared to be in charge of the operation—turned her head sharply.

"There's no need for that tone, Mother Hazel. Of course Mother Orchis had four beautiful babies—didn't you, dear?" she added to me. "She's just a bit tired after the journey, that's all."

"H'mph," said the girl addressed, in an unaccommodating tone, but she made no further comment.

A degree of fussing continued. Presently the small woman handed me a glass of something that looked like water, but had unsuspected strength. I spluttered a little at the first taste, but quickly felt the better for it. After a little more tidying and ordering, my retinue departed, leaving me propped against my cushion, with the eyes of the five other monstrous women dwelling upon me speculatively.

An awkward silence was broken by the girl who had greeted me as I came in. "Where did they send you for your holiday, Orchis?"

"Holiday?" I asked blankly.

She and the rest stared at me in astonishment.

"I don't know what you're talking about," I told them.

They went on staring, stupidly, stolidly.

"It can't have been much of a holiday," observed one, obviously puzzled. "I'll not forget my last one. They sent me to the sea, and gave me a little car so that I could get about everywhere. Everybody was lovely to us, and there were only six Mothers there, including me. Did you go by the sea, or in the mountains?"

They were determined to be inquisitive, and one would have to make some answer sooner or later. I chose what seemed the simplest way out for the moment.

"I can't remember," I said. "I can't remember a thing. I seem to have lost my memory altogether."

That was not very sympathetically received, either.

"Oh," said the one who had been addressed as Hazel, with a degree of satisfaction. "I thought there was something. And I suppose you can't even remember for certain whether your babies were Grade One this time, Orchis?"

"Don't be stupid, Hazel," one of the others told her. "Of course they were Grade One. If they'd not been, Orchis wouldn't be back here now—she'd have been re-rated as a Class Two Mother, and sent to Whitewich." In a more kindly tone she asked me: "When did it happen, Orchis?"

"I—I don't know," I said. "I can't remember anything before this morning at the hospital. It's all gone entirely."

"Hospital!" repeated Hazel, scornfully.

"She must mean the Centre," said the other. "But do you mean to say you can't even remember *us*, Orchis?"

"No," I admitted, shaking my head. "I'm sorry, but everything before I came round in the Hosp—in the Centre—is all blank."

"That's queer," Hazel said, in an unsympathetic tone. "Do they know?"

One of the others took my part.

"Of course they're bound to know. I expect they don't think that remembering or not has anything to do with having Grade One babies. And why should it, anyway? But look, Orchis—"

"Why not let her rest for a bit," another cut in. "I don't suppose she's feeling too good after the Centre, and the journey, and getting in here. I never do myself. Don't take any notice of them, Orchis, dear. You just go to sleep for a bit. You'll probably find it's all quite all right when you wake up."

I accepted her suggestion gratefully. The whole thing was far too bewildering to cope with at the moment; moreover, I did feel exhausted. I thanked her for her advice, and lay back on my pillow. In so far as the closing of one's eyes can be made ostentatious, I made it so. What was more surprising was that, if one can be said to sleep within an hallucination or a dream, I slept. . . .

In the moment of waking, before opening my eyes, I had a flash of hope that I should find the illusion had spent itself. Unfortunately, it had not. A hand was shaking my shoulder gently, and the first thing that I saw was the face of the little women's leader, close to mine.

In the way of nurses she said:

"There, Mother Orchis, dear. You'll be feeling a lot better after that nice sleep, won't you?"

Beyond her, two more of the small women were carrying a long-legged bed-tray towards me. They set it down so that it bridged me and was convenient to reach. I stared at the load on it. It was, with no exception, the most enormous and nourishing meal I had ever seen put before one person. The first sight of it revolted me—but then I became aware of a schism within, for it did not revolt the physical form that I occupied: that, in fact, had a watering mouth, and was eager to begin. An inner part of me marvelled in a kind of semidetachment while the rest consumed two or three fish, a whole chicken, some slices of meat, a pile of vegetables, fruit hidden under mounds of stiff cream, and more than a quart of milk, without any sense of surfeit. Occasional glances showed me that the other 'Mothers' were dealing just as thoroughly with the contents of their similar trays.

I caught one or two curious looks from them, but they were too seriously occupied to take up their inquisition again at the moment. I wondered how to fend them off later, and it occurred to me that if only I had a book or a magazine I might be able to bury myself effectively, if not very politely, in it.

When the attendants returned, I asked the badged one if she could let me have something to read. The effect of such a simple request was astonishing: the two who were removing my tray all but dropped it. The one beside me gaped for an amazed moment before she collected her wits. She looked at me, first with suspicion and then with concern.

"Not feeling quite yourself yet, dear?" she suggested.

"But I am," I protested. "I'm quite all right now."

The look of concern persisted, however.

"If I were you I'd try to sleep again," she advised.

"But I don't want to. I'd just like to read quietly," I objected.

She patted my shoulder, a little uncertainly.

"I'm afraid you've had an exhausting time, Mother. Never mind, I'm sure it'll pass quite soon."

I felt impatient. "What's wrong with wanting to read?"

I demanded.

She smiled a smug, professional-nurse smile.

"There, there, dear. Just you try to rest a little more. Why, bless me, what on earth would a Mother want with knowing how to read?"

With that she tidied my coverlet, and bustled away, leaving me to the wide-eyed stares of my five companions. Hazel gave a kind of contemptuous snigger; otherwise there was no audible comment for several minutes.

I had reached a stage where the persistence of the hallucination was beginning to wear away my detachment. I could feel that under a little more pressure I should be losing my confidence and starting to doubt its unreality. I did not at all care for its calm continuity: inconsequent exaggerations and jumps, foolish perspectives, indeed, any of the usual dream characteristics would have been reassuring; but, instead, it continued to present obvious nonsense, with an alarming air of conviction and consequence. Effects, for instance, were unmistakably following causes. I began to have an uncomfortable feeling that were one to dig deep enough one might begin to find logical causes for the absurdities, too. The integration was far too good for mental comfort—even the fact that I had enjoyed my meal as if I were fully awake, and was consciously feeling the better for it, encouraged the disturbing quality of reality.

"Read!" Hazel said suddenly, with a scornful laugh. "And write, too, I suppose?"

"Well, why not?" I retorted.

They all gazed at me more attentively than ever, and then exchanged meaningful glances among themselves. Two of them smiled at each other. I demanded irritably: "What on earth's wrong with that? Am I supposed not to be able to read or write, or something?"

One said kindly, soothingly:

"Orchis, dear. Don't you think it would be better if you were to ask to see the doctor? Just for a check-up?"

"No," I told her flatly. "There's nothing wrong with me. I'm just trying to understand. I simply ask for a book, and you all look at me as if I were mad. Why?"

After an awkward pause the same one said humouringly, and almost in the words of the little attendant:

"Orchis, dear, do try to pull yourself together. What sort of good would reading and writing be to a Mother? How could they help her to have better babies?"

"There are other things in life besides having babies," I said, shortly.

If they had been surprised before, they were thunderstruck now. Even Hazel seemed bereft of suitable comment. Their idiotic astonishment exasperated me and made me suddenly sick of the whole nonsensical business. Temporarily, I *did* forget to be the detached observer of a dream.

"Damn it," I broke out. "What is all this rubbish? Orchis! Mother Orchis!—for God's sake! Where am I? Is this some kind of lunatic asylum?"

I stared at them, angrily, loathing the sight of them, wondering if they were all in some spiteful complicity against me. Somehow I was quite convinced in my own mind that whoever, or whatever, I was, I was not a mother. I said so, forcibly, and then, to my annoyance, burst into tears.

For lack of anything else to use, I dabbed at my eyes with my sleeve. When I could see clearly again I found that four of them were looking at me with kindly concern. Hazel, however, was not.

"I said there was something queer about her," she told the others, triumphantly. "She's mad, that's what it is."

The one who had been most kindly disposed before, tried again:

"But, Orchis, *of course* you are a Mother. You're a Class One Mother—with three births registered. Twelve fine Grade One babies, dear. You *can't* have forgotten that!"

For some reason I wept again. I had a feeling that something was trying to break through the blankness in my mind; but I did not know what it was, only that it made me feel intensely miserable.

"Oh, this is cruel, cruel! Why can't I stop it? Why won't it go away and leave me?" I pleaded. "There's a horrible cruel mockery here—but I don't understand it. What's wrong with me? I'm not obsessional—I'm not—I—oh, can't somebody help me . . . ?"

I kept my eyes tight shut for a time, willing with all my mind that the whole hallucination should fade and disappear.

But it did not. When I looked again they were still there, their silly, pretty faces gaping stupidly at me across the revolting mounds of pink satin.

"I'm going to get out of this," I said.

It was a tremendous effort to raise myself to a sitting position. I was aware of the rest watching me, wide-eyed, while I made it. I struggled to get my feet round and over the side of the bed, but they were all tangled in the satin coverlet and I could not reach to free them. It was the true, desperate frustration of a dream. I heard my voice pleading: "Help me! Oh, Donald, darling, please help me. . . ."

And suddenly, as if the word "Donald" had released a spring, something seemed to click in my head. The shutter in my mind opened, not entirely, but enough to let me know who I was. I understood, suddenly, where the cruelty had lain.

I looked at the others again. They were still staring half-bewildered, half-alarmed. I gave up the attempt to move, and lay back on my pillows again.

"You can't fool me anymore," I told them. "I know who I am, now."

"But, Mother Orchis—" one began.

"Stop that," I snapped at her. I seemed to have swung suddenly out of self-pity into a kind of masochistic callousness. "I am *not* a mother," I said harshly. "I am just a woman who, for a short time, had a husband, and who hoped—but only hoped—that she would have babies by him."

A pause followed that; a rather odd pause, where there should have been at least a murmur. What I had said did not seem to have registered. The faces showed no understanding; they were as uncomprehending as dolls.

Presently, the most friendly one seemed to feel an obligation to break the silence. With a little vertical crease between her brows: "What," she inquired tentatively, "what is a husband?"

I looked hard from one face to another. There was no trace of guile in any of them; nothing but puzzled speculation such as one sometimes sees in a child's eyes. I felt close to hysteria for a moment; then I took a grip on myself. Very well, then, since the hallucination would not leave me alone, I would play it at its own game, and see what came of that. I began to explain with a kind of dead-pan, simple-word seriousness:

"A husband is a man whom a woman takes . . ."

Evidently, from their expressions I was not very enlightening. However, they let me go on for three or four sentences without interruption. Then, when I paused for breath, the kindly one chipped in with a point which she evidently felt needed clearing up:

"But what," she asked, in evident perplexity, "what is a man?"

A cool silence hung over the room after my exposition. I had an impression I had been sent to Coventry, or semi-Coventry, by them, but I did not bother to test it. I was too much occupied trying to force the door of my memory further open, and finding that beyond a certain point it would not budge.

I knew now that I was Jane. I had been Jane Summers, and had become Jane Waterleigh when I had married Donald.

I was—had been—twenty-four when we were married: just twenty-five when Donald was killed, six months later. And there it stopped. It seemed like yesterday, but I couldn't tell. . . .

Before that, everything was perfectly clear. My parents and friends, my home, my schools, my training, my job, as Dr. Summers, at the Wraychester Hospital. I could remember my first sight of Donald when they brought him in one evening with a broken leg—and all that followed. . . .

I could remember now the face that I ought to see in a looking-glass—and it was certainly nothing like that I had seen in the corridor outside—it should be more oval, with a complexion looking faintly sun-tanned; with a smaller, neater mouth; surrounded by chestnut hair that curled naturally; with brown eyes rather wide apart and perhaps a little grave as a rule.

I knew, too, how the rest of me should look—slender, long-legged, with small, firm breasts—a nice body but one that I had simply taken for granted until Donald gave me pride in it by loving it. . . .

I looked down at the repulsive mound of pink satin, and shuddered. A sense of outrage came welling up. I longed for Donald to comfort and pet me and love me and tell me it would be all right; that I wasn't as I was seeing myself at all, and that it *really* was a dream. At the same time I was stricken with horror at the thought that he should ever see me gross and obese like this. And then I remembered that Donald would never see me again at all—never anymore—and I was wretched and miserable, and the tears trickled down my cheeks again.

The five others just went on looking at me, wide-eyed and wondering. Half an hour passed, still in silence, then the door opened to admit a whole troop of the little women, all in white suits. I saw Hazel look at me, and then at the leader. She seemed about to speak, and then to change her mind. The little women split up, two to a couch. Standing one on each side, they stripped away the coverlet, rolled up their sleeves, and set to work at massage.

At first it was not unpleasant, and quite soothing. One lay back and relaxed. Presently, however, I liked it less: soon I found it offensive.

"Stop that!" I told the one on the right, sharply.

She paused, smiled at me amiably, though a trifle uncertainly, and then continued.

"I said stop it," I told her, pushing her away.

Her eyes met mine. They were troubled and hurt, although a professional smile still curved her mouth.

"I mean it," I added, curtly.

She continued to hesitate, and glanced across at her partner on the farther side of the bed.

"You, too," I told the other. "That'll do."

She did not even pause in her rhythm. The one on the right plucked a decision and returned. She restarted just what I had stopped. I reached out and pushed her, harder this time. There must have been a lot more muscle in that bolster of an arm than one would have supposed. The shove carried her half across the room, and she tripped and fell.

All movement in the room suddenly ceased. Everybody stared, first at her, and then at me. The pause was brief. They all set to work again. I pushed away the girl on the left, too, though more gently. The other one picked herself up. She was crying and she looked frightened, but she set her jaw doggedly and started to come back.

"You keep away from me, you little horrors," I told them threateningly.

That checked them. They stood off, and looked miserably at each other. The one with the badge of seniority fussed up.

"What's the trouble, Mother Orchis?" she inquired.

I told her. She looked puzzled.

"But that's quite right," she expostulated.

"Not for me. I don't like it, and I won't have it," I replied.

She stood awkwardly, at a loss.

Hazel's voice came from the other side of the room:

"Orchis is off her head. She's been telling us the most disgusting things. She's quite mad."

The little woman turned to regard her, and then looked inquiringly at one of the others. When the girl confirmed with a nod and an expression of distaste she turned back to me, giving me a searching inspection.

"You two go and report," she told my dicomfited masseuses.

They were both crying now, and they went wretchedly down the room together. The one in charge gave me another long, thoughtful look, and then followed them.

A few minutes later all the rest had packed up and gone. The six of us were alone again. It was Hazel who broke the ensuing silence.

"That was a bitchy piece of work. The poor little devils were only doing their job," she observed.

"If that's their job, I don't like it," I told her.

"So you just get them a beating, poor things. But I suppose that's the lost memory again. You wouldn't remember that a Servitor who upsets a Mother is beaten, would you?" she added sarcastically.

"Beaten?" I repeated, uneasily.

"Yes, beaten," she mimicked. "But you don't care what becomes of them, do you? I don't know what's happened to you while you were away, but whatever it was it seems to have produced a thoroughly nasty result. I never did care for you, Orchis, though the others thought I was wrong. Well, now we all know."

None of the rest offered any comment. The feeling that they shared her opinion was strong, but luckily I was spared confirmation by the opening of the door.

The senior attendant re-entered with half a dozen small myrmidons, but this time the group was dominated by a handsome woman of about thirty. Her appearance gave me immense relief. She was neither little, nor Amazonian, nor was she huge. Her present company made her look a little over-tall, perhaps, but I judged her at about five foot ten; a normal, pleasant-featured young woman with brown hair, cut somewhat short, and a pleated black skirt showing beneath white overalls. The senior attendant was almost trotting to keep up with her longer steps, and was saying something about delusions and 'only from the Centre today, Doctor.'

The woman stopped beside my couch while the smaller women huddled together, looking at me with some misgiving. She thrust a thermometer into my mouth and held my wrist. Satisfied on both these counts, she inquired:

"Headache? Any other aches or pains?"

"No," I told her.

She regarded me carefully. I looked back at her.

"What—?" she began.

"She's mad," Hazel put in from the other side of the room. "She says she's lost her memory and doesn't know us."

"She's been talking about horrid, disgusting things," added one of the others.

"She's got delusions. She thinks she can read and write," Hazel supplemented.

The doctor smiled at that.

"Do you?" she asked me.

"I don't see why not—but it should be easy enough to prove," I replied, brusquely.

She looked startled, a little taken aback, then she recovered her tolerant half-smile.

"All right," she said, humouring me.

She pulled a small notepad out of her pocket and offered it to me, with a pencil. The pencil felt a little odd in my hand; the fingers did not fall into place readily on it, nevertheless I wrote:

I'M ONLY TOO WELL AWARE THAT I HAVE DELUSIONS—AND THAT YOU ARE PART OF THEM.

Hazel tittered as I handed the pad back.

The doctor's jaw did not actually drop, but her smile came right off. She looked at me very hard indeed. The rest of the room, seeing her expression, went quiet, as though I had performed some startling feat of magic. The doctor turned towards Hazel.

"What sort of things has she been telling you?" she inquired.

Hazel hesitated, then she blurted out:

"Horrible things. She's been talking about two human sexes—just as if we were like the animals. It was disgusting!"

The doctor considered a moment, then she told the senior attendant:

"Better get her along to the sick bay. I'll examine her there."

As she walked off there was a rush of little women to fetch a low trolley from the corner to the side of my couch. A dozen hands assisted me on to it, and then wheeled me briskly away.

"Now," said the doctor grimly, "let's get down to it. Who told you all this stuff about two human sexes? I want her name."

We were alone in a small room with a gold-dotted pink wallpaper. The attendants, after transferring me from the trolley to a couch again, had taken themselves off. The doctor was sitting with a pad on her knee and a pencil at the ready. Her manner was that of an unbluffable inquisitor.

I was not feeling tactful. I told her not to be a fool.

She looked staggered, flushed with anger for a moment, and then took a hold on herself. She went on:

"After you left the Clinic you had your holiday, of course. Now, where did they send you?"

"I don't know," I replied. "All I can tell you is what I told the others—that this hallucination, or delusion, or whatever it is, started in that hospital place you call the Centre."

With resolute patience she said:

"Look here, Orchis. You were perfectly normal when you left here six weeks ago. You went to the Clinic and had your babies in the ordinary way. *But* between then and now somebody has been filling your head with all this rubbish—and teaching you to read and write, as well. Now you are going to tell me who that somebody was. I warn you you won't get away with this loss of memory nonsense with me. If you are able to remember this nauseating stuff you told the others, then you're able to remember where you got it from."

"Oh, for heaven's sake, talk sense," I told her. She flushed again.

"I can find out from the Clinic where they sent you, and I can find out from the Rest Home who were your chief associates while you were there, but I don't want to waste time following up all your contacts, so I'm asking you to save trouble by telling me now. You might just as well. We don't want to have to make you talk," she concluded, ominously.

I shook my head.

"You're on the wrong track. As far as I am concerned this whole hallucination, including my connection with this Orchis, began somehow at the Centre—how it happened I can't tell you, and what happened to her before that just isn't there to be remembered."

She frowned, obviously disturbed.

"What hallucination?" she inquired, carefully.

"Why this fantastic set-up—and you, too." I waved my hand to include it all. "This revolting great body, all those little women, everything. Obviously it is all some projection of the subconscious—and the state of my subconscious is worrying me, for it's certainly no wish-fulfillment."

She went on staring at me, more worried now.

"Who on earth has been telling you about the subconscious and wish-fulfillments?" she asked uncertainly.

"I don't see why, even in an hallucination, I am expected to be an illiterate moron," I replied.

"But a Mother doesn't know anything about such things. She doesn't need to."

"Listen," I said. "I've told you, as I've told those poor grotesques in the other room, that I am not a Mother. What I am is just an unfortunate M.B. who is having some kind of nightmare."

"M.B.?" she inquired, vaguely.

"Bachelor of Medicine. I practise medicine," I told her.

She went on looking at me curiously. Her eyes wandered over my mountainous form, uncertainly.

"You are claiming to be a doctor?" she said, in an odd voice.

"Colloquially—yes," I agreed.

There was indignation mixed with bewilderment as she protested:

"But this is sheer nonsense! You were brought up and developed to be a Mother. You are a Mother. Just look at you!"

"Yes," I said, bitterly. "Just look at me!"

There was a pause.

"It seems to me," I suggested at last, "that, hallucination or not, we shan't get much further simply by going on accusing each other of talking nonsense. Suppose you explain to me what this place is, and who you think I am. It might jog my memory."

She countered that. "Suppose," she said, "that first you tell me what you can remember. It would give me more idea of what is puzzling you."

"Very well," I agreed, and launched upon a potted history of myself as far as I could recollect it—up to the time, that is to say, when Donald's aircraft crashed.

It was foolish of me to fall for that one. Of course, she had no intention of telling me anything. When she had listened to all I had to say, she went away, leaving me impotently furious.

I waited until the place quietened down. The music had been switched off. An attendant had looked in to inquire, with an air of polishing off the day's duties, whether there was anything I wanted, and presently there was nothing to be heard. I let a margin of half an hour elapse, and then struggled to get up—taking it by very easy stages this time. The greatest part of the effort was to get on to my feet from a sitting position, but I managed it at the cost of heavy breathing. Presently I crossed to the door, and found it unfastened. I held it a little open, listening. There was no sound of movement in the corridor, so I pulled it wide open, and set out to discover what I could about the place for myself. All the doors of the rooms were shut. Putting my ear close to them I could hear regular, heavy breathing behind some, but there were no other sounds in the stillness. I kept on, turning several corners, until I recognized the front door ahead of me. I tried the latch, and found that it was neither barred nor bolted. I paused again, listening for some moments, and then pulled it open and stepped outside.

The park-like garden stretched out before me, sharp-shadowed in the moonlight. Through the trees to the right was a glint of water, to the left was a house similar to the one behind me, with not a light showing in any of its windows.

I wondered what to do. Trapped in this huge carcase, all but helpless in it, there was very little I could do, but I decided to go on and at least find out what I could while I had the chance. I went forward to the edge of the steps that I had earlier climbed from the ambulance, and started down them cautiously, holding on to the balustrade.

"Mother," said a sharp, incisive voice behind me. "What are you doing?"

I turned and saw one of the little women, her white suit gleaming in the moonlight. She was alone. I made no reply, but took another step down. I could have wept at the outrage of the heavy, ungainly body, and the caution it imposed on me.

"Come back. Come back at once," she told me.

I took no notice. She came pattering down after me and laid hold of my draperies.

"Mother," she said again, "you must come back. You'll catch cold out here."

I started to take another step, and she pulled at the draperies to hold me back. I leant forward against the pull. There was a sharp tearing sound as the material gave. I swung round and lost my balance. The last thing I saw was the rest of the flight of steps coming up to meet me. . . .

As I opened my eyes a voice said:

"That's better, but it was very naughty of you, Mother Orchis, And lucky it wasn't a lot worse. Such a silly thing to do. I'm ashamed of you—really, I am."

My head was aching, and I was exasperated to find that the whole stupid business was still going on; altogether I was in no mood for reproachful drip. I told her to go to hell. Her small face goggled at me for a moment, and then became icily prim. She applied a piece of lint and plaster to the left side of my forehead, in silence, and then departed, stiffly.

Reluctantly, I had to admit to myself that she was perfectly right. What on earth had I been expecting to do—what on earth *could* I do, encumbered by this horrible mass of flesh? A great surge of loathing for it and a feeling of helpless frustration brought me to the verge of tears again. I longed for my own nice, slim body that pleased me and did what I asked of it. I remembered how Donald had once pointed to a young tree swaying in the wind, and introduced it to me as my twin sister. And only a day or two ago . . .

Then, suddenly, I made a discovery which brought me struggling to sit up. The blank part of my mind had filled up. I could remember everything. . . . The effort made my head throb, so I relaxed and lay back once more, recalling it all, right up to the point where the needle was withdrawn and someone swabbed my arm. . . .

But what had happened after that? Dreams and hallucinations I had expected . . . but not the sharp-focused, detailed sense of reality . . . not this state which was like a nightmare made solid. . . .

What, what in heaven's name, had they done to me . . . ?

I must have fallen asleep again soon, for when I opened my eyes again there was daylight outside, and a covey of little women had arrived to attend to my toilet.

They spread their sheets dexterously and rolled me this way and that with expert technique as they cleaned me up. I suffered their industry patiently, feeling the fresher for it, and glad to discover that the headache had all but gone.

When we were almost at the end of our ablutions there came a peremptory knock, and without invitation two figures, dressed in black uniforms with silver buttons, entered. They were the Amazon type, tall, broad, well set-up, and handsome. The little women dropped everything and fled with squeaks of dismay into the far corner of the room where they cowered in a huddle.

The two gave me the familiar salute. With an odd mixture of decision and deference one of them inquired:

"You are Orchis—Mother Orchis?"

"That's what they're calling me," I admitted.

The girl hesitated, then in a tone rather more pleading than ordering she said: "I have orders for your arrest, Mother. You will please come with us."

An excited, incredulous twittering broke out among the little women in the corner. The uniformed girl quelled them with a look.

"Get the Mother dressed and make her ready," she commanded.

The little women came out of their corner hesitantly, directing nervous, propitiatory smiles towards the pair. The second one told them briskly, though not altogether unkindly:

"Come along now. Jump to it."

They jumped.

I was almost swathed in my pink draperies again when the doctor strode in. She frowned at the two in uniform.

"What's all this? What are you doing here?" she demanded.

The leader of the two explained.

"Arrest!" exclaimed the doctor. "Arrest a Mother! I never heard such nonsense. What's the charge?"

The uniformed girl said, a little sheepishly:

"She is accused of Reactionism."

The doctor simply stared at her.

"A Reactionist Mother! What'll you people think of next? Go on, get out, both of you."

The young woman protested:

"We have our orders, Doctor."

"Rubbish. There's no authority. Have you ever heard of a Mother being arrested?"

"No, Doctor."

"Well, you aren't going to make a precedent now. Go on."

The uniformed girl hesitated unhappily, then an idea occurred to her.

"If you would let me have a signed refusal to surrender the Mother . . . ?" she suggested helpfully.

When the two had departed, quite satisfied with their piece of paper, the doctor looked at the little women gloomily.

"You can't help tattling, you Servitors, can you? Anything you happen to hear goes through the lot of you like a fire in a cornfield, and makes trouble all round. Well, if I hear anymore of this I shall know where it comes from." She turned to me. "And you, Mother Orchis, will in future please restrict yourself to yes-and-no in the hearing of these nattering little pests. I'll see you again shortly. We want to ask you some questions," she added, as she went out, leaving a subdued, industrious silence behind her.

She returned just as the tray which had held my gargantuan breakfast was being removed, and not alone. The four women who accompanied her and looked as normal as herself were followed by a number of little women lugging in chairs which they arranged beside my couch. When they had departed, the five women, all in white overalls, sat down and regarded me as if I were an exhibit. One appeared to be much the same age as the first doctor, two nearer fifty, and one sixty, or more.

"Now, Mother Orchis," said the doctor, with an air of opening the proceedings, "it is quite clear that something highly unusual has taken place. Naturally we are interested to understand just what and, if possible, why. You don't need to worry about those police this morning—it was quite improper of them to come here at all. This is simply an inquiry—a scientific inquiry—to establish what has happened."

"You can't want to understand more than I do," I replied. I looked at them, at the room about me, and finally at my massive prone figure. "I am aware that all this must be an hallucination, but what is troubling me most is that I have always supposed that any hallucination must be deficient in at least one dimension—must lack reality to some of the senses. But this does not. I have all my senses, and can use them. Nothing is insubstantial: I am trapped in flesh that is, very palpably too, too solid. The only striking deficiency, so far as I can see, is reason—even symbolic reason."

The four other women stared at me in astonishment. The doctor gave them a sort of now-perhaps-you'll-believe-me glance, and then turned to me again.

"We'll start with a few questions," she said.

"Before you begin," I put in, "I have something to add to what I told you last night. It has come back to me."

"Perhaps the knock when you fell," she suggested, looking at my piece of plaster. "What were you trying to do?"

I ignored that. "I think I'd better tell you the missing part—it might help—a bit, anyway."

"Very well," she agreed. "You told me you were—er—married, and that your—er—husband was killed soon afterwards." She glanced at the others; their blankness of expression was somehow studious. "It was the part after that that was missing," she added.

"Yes," I said. "He was a test-pilot," I explained to them. "It happened six months after we were married—only one month before his contract was due to expire.

"After that, an aunt took me away for some weeks. I don't suppose I'll ever remember that part very well—I—I wasn't noticing anything very much. . . .

"But then I remember waking up one morning and suddenly seeing things differently, and telling myself that I couldn't go on like that. I knew I must have some work, something that would keep me busy.

"Dr. Hellyer, who is in charge of the Wraychester Hospital, where I was working before I married, told me he would be glad to have me with them again. I went back, and worked very hard, so that I did not have much time to think. That would be about eight months ago, now.

"Then one day Dr. Hellyer spoke about a drug that a friend of his had succeeded in synthesizing. I don't think he was really asking for volunteers, but I offered to try it out. From what he said it sounded as if the drug might have some quite important properties. It struck me as a chance to do something useful. Sooner or later, someone would try it, and as I didn't have any ties and didn't care very much what happened, anyway, I thought I might as well be the one to try it."

The spokeswoman doctor interrupted to ask:

"What was this drug?"

"It's called chuinjuatin," I told her. "Do you know it?"

She shook her head. One of the others put in:

"I've heard the name. What is it?"

"It's a narcotic," I told her. "The original form is in the leaves of a tree that grows chiefly in the South of Venezuela. The tribe of Indians who live there discovered it somehow, like others did quinine, and mescaline. And in much the same way they use it for orgies. Some of them sit and chew the leaves—they have to chew about six ounces of them—and gradually they go into a zombie-like, trance state. It lasts three or four days during which they are quite helpless and incapable of doing the simplest thing for themselves, so that other members of the tribe are appointed to look after them as if they were children, and to guard them.

"It's necessary to guard them because the Indian belief is that chuinjuatin liberates the spirit from the body, setting it free to wander anywhere in space and time, and the guardian's most important job is to see that no other wandering spirit shall slip into the body while the true owner is away. When the subjects recover they claim to have had wonderful mystical experiences. There seem to be no physical ill-effects, and no craving results from it. The mystical experiences, though, are said to be intense, and clearly remembered.

"Dr. Hellyer's friend had tested his synthesized chuinjuatin on a number of laboratory animals and worked out the dosage, and tolerances, and that kind of thing, but what he could not tell, of course, was what validity, if any, the reports of the mystical experiences had. Presumably they were the product of the drug's influence on the nervous system—but whether that effect produced a sensation of pleasure, ecstasy, awe, fear, horror, or any of a dozen more, it was impossible to tell without a human guinea-pig. So that was what I volunteered for."

I stopped. I looked at their serious, puzzled faces, at the billow of pink satin in front of me. . . .

"In fact," I added, "it appears to have produced a combination of the absurd, the incomprehensible, and the grotesque."

They were earnest women, these, not to be sidetracked. They were there to disprove an anomaly—if they could.

"I *see*," said the spokeswoman with an air of preserving reasonableness, rather than meaning anything. She glanced down at a paper on which she had made a note from time to time.

"Now, can you give us the time and date at which this experiment took place?"

I could, and did, and after that the questions went on and on and on. . . .

The least satisfactory part of it from my point of view was that even though my answers caused them to grow more uncertain of themselves as we went on, they did at least get them; whereas when I put a question it was usually evaded, or answered perfunctorily, as an unimportant digression.

They went on steadily, and only broke off when my next meal arrived. Then they went away, leaving me thankfully in peace—but little the wiser. I half-expected them to return, but when they did not I fell into a doze from which I was awakened by the incursion of a cluster of the little women once more. They brought a trolley with them, and in a short time were wheeling me out of the building on it—but not by the way I had arrived. This time we went down a ramp where another, or the same, pink ambulance waited at the bottom. When they had me safely loaded aboard three of them climbed in, too, to keep me company. They were chattering as they did so, and they kept it up inconsequentially, and almost incomprehensibly, for the whole hour and a half of the journey that ensued.

The countryside differed little from that I had already seen. Once we were outside the gates there were the same tidy fields and standardized farms. The occasional built-up areas were not extensive and consisted of the same types of blocks close by, and we ran on the same, not very good, road surfaces. There were groups of the Amazon types, and, more rarely, individuals, to be seen at work in the fields; the sparse traffic was lorries, large or small, and occasional buses, but with never a private car to be seen. My illusion, I reflected, was remarkably consistent in its details. Not a single group of Amazons, for instance, failed to raise its right hands in friendly, respectful greeting to the pink car.

Once, we crossed a cutting. Looking down from the bridge I thought at first that we were over the dried bed of a canal, but then I noticed a post leaning at a crazy angle among the grass and weeds: most of its attachments had fallen off, but there were enough left to identify it as a railway signal.

We passed through one concentration of identical blocks which was in size, though in no other way, quite a town, and then, two or three miles further on, ran through an ornamental gateway into a kind of park.

In one way it was not unlike the estate we had left, for everything was meticulously tended; the lawns like velvet, the flower beds vivid with spring blossoms, but it differed essentially in that the buildings were not blocks. They were houses, quite small for the most part, and varied in style, often no larger than roomy cottages. The place had a subduing effect on my small companions; for the first time they left off chattering, and gazed about them with obvious awe.

The driver stopped once to inquire the way of an overalled Amazon who was striding along with a hod on her shoulder. She directed us, and gave me a cheerful, respectful grin through the window, and presently we drew up again in front of a neat little two-storey Regency-style house.

This time there was no trolley. The little women, assisted by the driver, fussed over helping me out, and then half-supported me into the house, in a kind of buttressing formation.

Inside, I was manœuvred with some difficulty through a door on the left, and found myself in a beautiful room, elegantly decorated and furnished in the period-style of the house. A white-haired woman in a purple silk dress was sitting in a wing-chair beside a wood fire. Both her face and her hands told of considerable age, but she looked at me from keen, lively eyes.

"Welcome, my dear," she said, in a voice which had no trace of the quaver I half-expected.

Her glance went to a chair. Then she looked at me again, and thought better of it.

"I expect you'd be more comfortable on the couch," she suggested.

I regarded the couch—a genuine Georgian piece, I thought—doubtfully.

"Will it stand it?" I wondered.

"Oh, I think so," she said, but not too certainly.

The retinue deposited me there carefully, and stood by, with anxious expressions. When it was clear that, though it creaked, it was probably going to hold, the old lady shooed them away, and rang a little silver bell. A diminutive figure, a perfect parlourmaid three foot ten in height, entered.

"The brown sherry, please, Mildred," instructed the old lady. "You'll take sherry, my dear?" she added to me.

"Y-yes—yes, thank you," I said, faintly. After a pause I added: "You will excuse me, Mrs.—er—Miss—?"

"Oh, I should have introduced myself. My name is Laura—not Miss, or Mrs., just Laura. You, I know, are Orchis—Mother Orchis."

"So they tell me," I owned, distastefully.

We studied one another. For the first time since the hallucination had set in I saw sympathy, even pity, in someone else's eyes. I looked round the room again, noticing the perfection of details.

"This is—I'm not mad, am I?" I asked.

She shook her head slowly, but before she could reply the miniature parlourmaid returned, bearing a cut-glass decanter and glasses on a silver tray. As she poured out a glass for each of us I saw the old lady glance from her to me and back again, as though comparing us. There was a curious, uninterpretable expression on her face. I made an effort.

"Shouldn't it be madeira?" I suggested.

She looked surprised, and then smiled, and nodded appreciatively.

"I think you have accomplished the purpose of this visit in one sentence," she said.

The parlourmaid left, and we raised our glasses. The old lady sipped at hers and then placed it on an occasional table beside her.

"Nevertheless," she went on, "we had better go into it a little more. Did they tell you why they have sent you to me, my dear?"

"No." I shook my head.

"It is because I am a historian," she informed me. "Access to history is a privilege. It is not granted to many of us nowadays—and then somewhat reluctantly. Fortunately, a feeling that no branches of knowledge should be allowed to perish entirely still exists—though some of them are pursued at the cost of a certain political suspicion." She smiled deprecatingly, and then went on. "So when confirmation is required it is necessary to appeal to a specialist. Did they give you any report on their diagnosis?"

I shook my head again.

"I thought not. So like the profession, isn't it? Well, I'll tell you what they told me on the telephone from the Mother's Home, and we shall have a better idea of what we are about. I was informed that you have been interviewed by several doctors whom you have interested, puzzled—and, I suspect, distressed—very much, poor things. None of them has more than a minimum smattering of history, you see. Well, briefly, two of them are of the opinion that you are suffering from delusions of a schizophrenic nature: and three are inclined to think you are a genuine case of projected perception. It is an extremely rare condition. There are not more than three reliably documented cases, and one that is more debatable, they tell me; but of those confirmed two are associated with the drug chuinjuatin, and the third with a drug of very similar properties.

"Now, the majority of three found your answers coherent for the most part, and felt that they were authentically circumstantial. That is to say that nothing you told them conflicted directly with what they know, but, since they know so little outside their professional field, they found a great deal of the rest both hard to believe and impossible to check. Therefore, I, with my better means of checking, have been asked for my opinion."

She paused, and looked me over thoughtfully.

"I rather think," she added, "that this is going to be one of the most curiously interesting things that has happened to me in my quite long life—your glass is empty, my dear."

"Projected perception," I repeated wonderingly, as I held out my glass. "Now, if *that* were possible—"

"Oh, there's no doubt about the *possibility*. Those three cases I mentioned are fully authenticated."

"It might be that—almost," I admitted. "At least, in some ways it might be—but not in others. There *is* this nightmare quality. You seem perfectly normal to me, but look at me, myself—and at your little maid! There's certainly an element of delusion. I *seem* to be here, like this, and talking to you—but it can't really be so, so where am I?"

"I can understand, better than most, I think, how unreal this must seem to you. In fact, I have spent so much of my time in books that it sometimes seems unreal to me—as if I did not quite belong anywhere. Now, tell me, my dear, when were you born?"

I told her. She thought for a moment.

"H'm," she said. "George the Sixth—but you'd not remember the second big war?"

"No," I agreed.

"But you might remember the coronation of the next monarch? Whose was that?"

"Elizabeth—Elizabeth the Second. My mother took me to see the procession," I told her.

"Do you remember anything about it?"

"Not a lot really—except that it rained, nearly all day," I admitted.

We went on like that for a little while, then she smiled, reassuringly.

"Well, I don't think we need anymore to establish our point. I've heard about that coronation before—at secondhand. It must have been a wonderful scene in the Abbey." She mused a moment, and gave a little sigh. "You've been very patient with me, my dear. It is only fair that you should have your turn—but I'm afraid you must prepare yourself for some shocks."

"I think I must be inured after my last thirty-six hours—or what has appeared to be thirty-six hours," I told her.

"I doubt it," she said, looking at me seriously.

"Tell me," I asked her. "Please, explain it all—if you can."

"Your glass, my dear. Then I'll get the crux of it over." She poured for each of us, then she asked:

"What strikes you as the oddest feature of your experience, so far?"

I considered. "There's so much—"

"Might it not be that you have not seen a single man?" she suggested.

I thought back. I remembered the wondering tone of one of the Mothers asking: "What is a man?"

"That's certainly one of them," I agreed. "Where are they?"

She shook her head, watching me steadily.

"There aren't any, my dear. Not anymore. None at all."

I simply went on staring at her. Her expression was perfectly serious and sympathetic. There was no trace of guile there or deception while I struggled with the idea. At last I managed:

"But—but that's impossible! There must be some somewhere. . . . You couldn't—I mean, how—? I mean . . ." My expostulation trailed off in confusion.

She shook her head.

"I know it must seem impossible to you, Jane—may I call you Jane? But it is so. I am an old woman now, nearly eighty, and in all my long life I have never seen a man—save in old pictures and photographs. Drink your sherry, my dear. It will do you good." She paused. "I'm afraid this upsets you."

I obeyed, too bewildered for further comment at the moment, protesting inwardly, yet not altogether disbelieving, for certainly I had not seen one man, nor sign of any. She went on quietly, giving me time to collect my wits:

"I can understand a little how you must feel. I haven't had to learn all my history entirely from books, you see. When I was a girl, sixteen or seventeen, I used to listen a lot to my grandmother. She was as old then as I am now, but her memory of her youth was still very good. I was able almost to see the places she talked about—but they were part of such a different world that it was difficult for me to understand how she felt. When she spoke about the young man she had been engaged to, tears would roll down her cheeks, even then—not just for him, of course, but for the whole world that she had known as a girl. I was sorry for her, although I could not really understand how she felt—How should I? But now that I am old, too, and have read so much, I am perhaps a little nearer to understanding her feelings, I think." She looked at me curiously. "And you, my dear. Perhaps you, too, were engaged to be married?"

"I was married—for a little time," I told her.

She contemplated that for some seconds, then:

"It must be a very strange experience to be owned," she remarked, reflectively.

"Owned?" I exclaimed, in astonishment.

"Ruled by a husband," she explained, sympathetically.

I stared at her.

"But it—it wasn't like that—it wasn't like that at all," I protested. "It was—" But there I broke off, with tears too close. To steer her away I asked:

"But what happened? What on earth happened to the men?"

"They all died," she told me. "They fell sick. Nobody could do anything for them, so they died. In little more than a year they were all gone—all but a very few."

"But surely—surely everything would collapse?"

"Oh, yes. Very largely it did. It was very bad. There was a dreadful lot of starvation. The industrial parts were the worst hit, of course. In the more backward countries and in rural areas women were able to turn to the land and till it to keep themselves and their children alive, but almost all the large organizations broke down entirely. Transport ceased very soon: petrol ran out, and no coal was being mined. It was quite a dreadful state of affairs because, although there were a great many women, and they had outnumbered the men, in fact, they had only really been important as consumers and spenders of money. So when the crisis came it turned out that scarcely any of them knew how to do any of the important things because they had nearly all been owned by men, and had to lead their lives as pets and parasites."

I started to protest, but her frail hand waved me aside.

"It wasn't their *fault*—not entirely," she explained. "They were caught up in a process, and everything conspired against their escape. It was a long process, going right back to the eleventh century, in Southern France. The Romantic conception started there as an elegant and amusing fashion for the leisured classes. Gradually, as time went on, it permeated through most levels of society, but it was not until the latter part of the nineteenth century that its commercial possibilities were intelligently perceived, and not until the twentieth that it was really exploited.

"At the beginning of the twentieth century women were starting to have their chance to lead useful, creative, interesting lives. But that did not suit commerce: it needed them much more as mass-consumers than as producers—except on the most routine levels. So Romance was adopted and developed as a weapon against their further progress and to promote consumption, and it was used intensively.

"Women must never for a moment be allowed to forget their sex, and compete as equals. Everything had to have a 'feminine angle' which must be different from the masculine angle, and be dinned in without ceasing. It would have been unpopular for manufacturers actually to issue an order 'back to the kitchen,' but there were other ways. A profession without a difference, called 'housewife,' could be invented. The kitchen could be glorified and made more expensive; it could be made to seem desirable, and it could be shown that the way to realize this heart's desire was through marriage. So the presses turned out, by the hundred thousand a week, journals which concentrated the attention of women ceaselessly and relentlessly upon selling themselves to some man in order that they might achieve some small, uneconomic unit of a home upon which money could be spent.

"Whole trades adopted the romantic approach and the glamour was spread thicker and thicker in the articles, the write-ups, and most of all in the advertisements. Romance found a place in everything that women might buy, from underclothes to motor-bicycles, from 'health' foods to kitchen stoves, from deodorants to foreign travel, until soon they were too bemused to be amused anymore.

"The air was filled with frustrated moanings. Women maundered in front of microphones yearning only to 'surrender,' and 'give themselves,' to adore and to be adored. The cinema most of all maintained the propaganda, persuading the main and important part of their audience, which was female, that nothing in life was worth achieving but dewy-eyed passivity in the strong arms of Romance. The pressure became such that the majority of young women spent all their leisure time dreaming of Romance, and the means of securing it. They were brought to a state of honestly believing that to be owned by some man and set down in a little brick box to buy all the things that the manufacturers wanted them to buy would be the highest form of bliss that life could offer."

"But—" I began to protest again. The old lady was now well launched, however, and swept on without a check.

"All this could not help distorting society, of course. The divorce-rate went up. Real life simply could not come near to providing the degree of romantic glamour which was being represented as every girl's proper inheritance. There was probably, in the aggregate, more disappointment, disillusion, and dissatisfaction among women than there had ever been before. Yet, with this ridiculous and ornamented ideal grained-in by unceasing propaganda, what could a conscientious idealist do but take steps to break up the short-weight marriage she had made, and seek elsewhere for the ideal which was hers, she understood, by right?

"It was a wretched state of affairs brought about by deliberately promoted dissatisfactions; a kind of rat-race with, somewhere safely out of reach, the glamourized romantic ideal always luring. Perhaps an exceptional few almost attained it, but, for all except those very few, it was a cruel, tantalizing sham on which they spent themselves, and of course their money, in vain."

This time I did get in my protest.

"But it wasn't like that. Some of what you say may be true—but that's all the superficial part. It didn't feel a bit like the way you put it. I was in it. I *know*."

She shook her head reprovingly.

"There is such a thing as being too close to make a proper evaluation. At a distance we are able to see more clearly. We can perceive it for what it was—a gross and heartless exploitation of the weaker-willed majority. Some women of education and resolution were able to withstand it, of course, but at a cost. There must always be a painful price for resisting majority pressure—even they could not always altogether escape the feeling that they might be wrong, and that the rat-racers were having the better time of it.

"You see, the great hopes for the emancipation of women with which the century had started had been outflanked. Purchasing-power had passed into the hands of the ill-educated and highly suggestible. The desire for Romance is essentially a selfish wish, and when it is encouraged to dominate every other it breaks down all corporate loyalties. The individual woman thus separated from, and yet at the same time thrust into competition with, all other women was almost defenceless; she became the prey of organized suggestion. When it was represented to her that the lack of certain goods or amenities would be fatal to Romance she became alarmed and, thus, eminently exploitable. She could only believe what she was told, and spent a great deal of time worrying about whether she was doing all the right things to encourage Romance. Thus, she became, in a new, a subtler way, more exploited, more dependent, and less creative than she had ever been before."

"Well," I said, "this is the most curiously unrecognizable account of my world that I have ever heard—it's like something copied, but with all the proportions wrong. And as for 'less creative'—well, perhaps families were smaller, but women still went on having babies. The population was still increasing."

The old lady's eyes dwelt on me a moment.

"You are undoubtedly a thought-child of your time, in some ways," she observed. "What makes you think there is anything creative about having babies? Would you call a plant-pot creative because seeds grow in it? It is a mechanical operation—and, like most mechanical operations, is most easily performed by the least intelligent. Now, bringing up a child, educating, helping her to become a person, that *is* creative. But unfortunately, in the time we are speaking of, women had, in the main, been successfully conditioned into bringing up their daughters to be unintelligent consumers, like themselves."

"But," I said helplessly, "I *know* the time. It's my time. This is all distorted."

"The perspective of history must be truer," she told me again, unimpressed, and went on: "But if what happened *had* to happen, then it chose a fortunate time to happen. A hundred years earlier, even fifty years earlier, it would very likely have meant extinction. Fifty years later might easily have been too late—it might have come upon a world in which all women were profitably restricted to domesticity and consumership. Luckily, however, in the middle of the century women were still entering the professions, and by far the greatest number of professional women was to be found in medicine—which is to say that they were only really numerous in, and skilled in, the very profession which immediately became of vital importance if we were to survive at all.

"I have no medical knowledge, so I cannot give you any details of the steps they took. All I can tell you is that there was intensive research on lines which will probably be more obvious to you than they are to me.

"A species, even our species, has great will to survive, and the doctors saw to it that the will had the means of expression. Through all the hunger, and the chaos, and the other privations, babies somehow continued to be born. That had to be. Reconstruction could wait: the priority was the new generation that would help in the reconstruction, and then inherit it. So babies were born: the girl babies lived, the boy babies died. That was distressing, and wasteful, too, and so, presently, only girl babies were born—again, the means by which that could be achieved will be easier for you to understand than for me.

"It is, they tell me, not nearly so remarkable as it would appear at first sight. The locust, it seems, will continue to produce female locusts without male, or any other kind of assistance; the aphis, too, is able to go on breeding alone and in seclusion, certainly for eight generations, perhaps more. So it would be a poor thing if we, with all our knowledge and powers of research to assist us, should find ourselves inferior to the locust and the aphis in this respect, would it not?"

She paused, looking at me somewhat quizzically for my response. Perhaps she expected amazed—or possibly shocked—disbelief. If so, I disappointed her: technical achievements have ceased to arouse simple wonder since atomic physics showed how barriers fall before the pressure of a good brainsteam. One can take it that most things are possible: whether they are desirable, or worth doing, is a different matter—and one that seemed to me particularly pertinent to her question. I asked her:

"And what is it that you have achieved?"

"Survival," she said, simply.

"Materially," I agreed. "I suppose you have. But when it has cost all the rest, when love, art, poetry, excitement, and physical joy have all been sacrificed to mere continued existence, what is left but a soulless waste? What reason is there any longer for survival?"

"As to the reason, I don't know—except that survival is a desire common to all species. I am quite sure that the reason for that desire was no clearer in the twentieth century than it is now. But, for the rest, why should you assume that they are gone. Did not Sappho write poetry? And your assumption that the possession of a soul depends upon a duality of sexes surprises me: it has so often been held that the two are in some sort of conflict, has it not?"

"As a historian who must have studied men, women, and motives you should have taken my meaning better," I told her.

She shook her head, with reproof. "You are so much the conditioned product of your age, my dear. They told you, on all levels, from the works of Freud to that of the most nugatory magazines for women, that it was sex, civilized into romantic love, that made the world go round—and you believed them. But the world continues to go round for others, too—for the insects, the fish, the birds, the animals—and how much do you suppose they know of romantic love, even in their brief mating-seasons? They hoodwinked you, my dear. Between them they channelled your interests and ambitions along courses that were socially convenient, economically profitable, and almost harmless."

I shook my head.

"I just don't believe it. Oh, yes, you know something of my world—from the outside. But you don't understand it, or feel it."

"That's your conditioning, my dear," she told me, calmly.

Her repeated assumption irritated me. I asked:

"Suppose I were to believe what you say, what is it, then, that *does* make the world go round?"

"That's simple, my dear. It is the will to power. We have that as babies; we have it still in old age. It occurs in men and women alike. It is more fundamental, and more desirable, than sex; I tell you, you were misled—exploited, sublimated for economic convenience.

"After the disease had struck, women ceased, for the first time in history, to be an exploited class. Without male rulers to confuse and divert them they began to perceive that all true power resides in the female principle. The male had served only one brief useful purpose; for the rest of his life he was a painful and costly parasite.

"As they became aware of power, the doctors grasped it. In twenty years they were in full control. With them were the few women engineers, architects, lawyers, administrators, some teachers, and so on, but it was the doctors who held the keys of life and death. The future was in their hands and, as things began gradually to revive, they, together with the other professions, remained the dominant class and became known as the Doctorate. It assumed authority; it made the laws; it enforced them.

"There was opposition, of course. Neither the memory of the old days, nor the effect of twenty years of lawlessness, could be wiped out at once, but the doctors had the whip-hand—any woman who wanted a child had to come to them, and they saw to it that she was satisfactorily settled in a community. The roving gangs dwindled away, and gradually order was restored.

"Later on, they faced better organized opposition. There was a party which contended that the disease which had struck down the men had run its course, and the balance could, and should, be restored—they were known as Reactionists, and they became an embarrassment.

"Most of the Council of the Doctorate still had clear memories of a system which used every weakness of women, and had been no more than a more civilized culmination of their exploitation through the ages. They remembered how they themselves had only grudgingly been allowed to qualify for their careers. They were now in command: they felt no obligation to surrender their power and authority, and eventually, no doubt, their freedom to a creature whom they had proved to be biologically, and in all other ways, expendable. They refused unanimously to take a step that would lead to corporate suicide, and the Reactionists were proscribed as a subversive criminal organization.

"That, however, was just a palliative. It quickly became clear that they were attacking a symptom and neglecting the cause. The Council was driven to realize that it had an unbalanced society at its hands—a society that was capable of continuity, but was in structure, you might say, little more than the residue of a vanished form. It could not continue in that truncated shape and, as long as it tried to, disaffection would increase. Therefore, if power were to become stable, a new form suitable to the circumstances must be found.

"In deciding the shape it should take, the natural tendencies of the little-educated and uneducated woman were carefully considered—such qualities as her feeling for hierarchical principles and her disposition to respect artificial distinctions. You will no doubt recollect that in your own time any fool of a woman whose husband was ennobled or honoured at once acquired increased respect and envy from other women though she remained the same fool; and also, that any gathering or society of unoccupied women would soon become obsessionally enmeshed in the creation and preservation of social distinctions. Allied to this is the high value they usually place upon a feeling of security. Important, too, is the capacity for devoted self-sacrifice, and slavery to conscience within the canons of any local convention. We are naturally very biddable creatures. Most of us are happiest when we are being orthodox, however odd our customs may appear to an outsider; the difficulty in handling us lies chiefly in establishing the required standards of orthodoxy.

"Obviously, the broad outline of a system which was going to stand any chance of success would have to provide scope for these and other characteristic traits. It must be a scheme where the interplay of forces would preserve equilibrium and respect for authority. The details of such an organization, however, were less easy to determine.

"An extensive study of social forms and orders was undertaken, but for several years every plan put forward was rejected as in some way unsuitable. The architecture of that finally chosen was said, though I do not know with how much truth, to have been inspired by the Bible—a book at that time still unprohibited, and the source of much unrest. I am told that it ran something like: 'Go to the ant, thou sluggard; consider her ways.'

"The Council appears to have felt that this advice, suitably modified, could be expected to lead to a state of affairs which would provide most of the requisite characteristics.

"A four-class system was chosen as the basis, and strong differentiations were gradually introduced. These, now that they have become well established, greatly help to ensure stability: there is scope for ambition within one's class, but none for passing from one class to another. Thus, we have the Doctorate—the educated ruling-classes, fifty percent of whom are actually of the medical profession. The Mothers, whose title is self-explanatory. The Servitors, who are numerous and, for psychological reasons, small. The Workers, who are physically and muscularly strong, to do the heavier work. All the three lower classes respect the authority of the Doctorate. Both the employed classes revere the Mothers. The Servitors consider themselves more favoured in their tasks than the Workers; and the Workers tend to regard the puniness of the Servitors with a semi-affectionate contempt.

"So you see a balance has been struck, and though it works somewhat crudely as yet, no doubt it will improve. It seems likely, for instance, that it would be advantageous to introduce sub-divisions into the Servitor class before long, and the police are thought by some to be put at a disadvantage by having no more than a little education to distinguish them from the ordinary Worker . . ."

She went on explaining with increasing detail while the enormity of the whole process gradually grew upon me.

"Ants!" I broke in, suddenly. "The ant-nest! You've taken *that* for your model?"

She looked surprised, either at my tone, or the fact that what she was saying had taken so long to register.

"And why not?" she asked. "Surely it is one of the most enduring social patterns that nature has evolved—though of course some adaptation—"

"You're—are you telling me that only the Mothers have children?" I demanded.

"Oh, members of the Doctorate do, too, when they wish," she assured me.

"But—but."

"The Council decides the ratios," she went on to explain. "The doctors at the clinic examine the babies and allocate them suitably to the different classes. After that, of course, it is just a matter of seeing to their specialized feeding, glandular control, and proper training."

"But," I objected wildly, "what's it *for*? Where's the sense in it? What's the good of being alive, like that?"

"Well, what *is* the sense in being alive? You tell me," she suggested.

"But we're *meant* to love and be loved, to have babies we love by people we love."

"There's your conditioning again; glorifying and romanticizing primitive animalism. Surely you consider that we are superior to the animals?"

"Of course I do, but—"

"Love, you say, but what can you know of the love there can be between mother and daughter when there are no men to introduce jealousy? Do you know of any purer sentiment than the love of a girl for her little sisters?"

"But you don't understand," I protested again. "How should you understand a love that colours the whole world? How it centers in your heart and reaches out from there to pervade your whole being, how it can affect everything you are, everything you touch, everything you hear . . . It can hurt dreadfully, I know, oh, I know, but it can run like sunlight in your veins . . . It can make you a garden out of a slum; brocade out of rags; music out of speaking voice. It can show you a whole universe in someone else's eyes. Oh, you don't understand . . . you don't know . . . you can't. . . . Oh, Donald, darling, how can I show her what she's never even guessed at . . . ?"

There was an uncertain pause, but presently she said:

"Naturally, in your form of society it was necessary for you to be given such a conditioned reaction, but you can scarcely expect us to surrender our freedom, to connive at our own re-subjection by calling our oppressors into existence again."

"Oh, you *won't* understand. It was only the more stupid men and women who were continually at war with one another. Lots of us were complementary. We were pairs who formed units."

She smiled. "My dear, either you are surprisingly ill-informed on your own period, or else the stupidity you speak of was astonishingly dominant. Neither as myself, nor as a historian, can I consider that we should be justified in resurrecting such a state of affairs. A primitive stage of our development has now given way to a civilized era. Woman, who is the vessel of life, had the misfortune to find man necessary for a time, but now she does so no longer. Are you suggesting that such a useless and dangerous encumbrance ought to be preserved, out of sheer sentimentality? I will admit that we have lost some minor conveniences—you will have noticed, I expect, that we are less inventive mechanically, and tend to copy the patterns we have inherited; but that troubles us very little; our interests lie not in the inorganic, but in the organic and the sentient. Perhaps men could show us how to travel twice as fast, or how to fly to the moon, or how to kill more people more quickly; but it does not seem to us that such kinds of knowledge would be good payment for re-enslaving ourselves. No, our kind of world suits us better—all of us except a few Reactionists. You have seen our Servitors. They are a little timid in manner, perhaps, but are they oppressed, or sad? Don't they chatter among themselves as brightly and perkily as sparrows? And the Workers—those you called the Amazons—don't they look strong, healthy, and cheerful?"

"But you're robbing them all—robbing them of their birthright."

"You mustn't give me cant, my dear. Did not your social system conspire to rob a woman of her 'birthright' unless she married? You not only let her know it, but socially you rubbed it in: here, our Servitors and Workers do not know it, and they are not worried by a sense of inadequacy. Motherhood is the function of the Mothers, and understood as such."

I shook my head. "Nevertheless, they are being robbed.

A woman has a right to love—"

For once she was a little impatient as she cut me short.

"You keep repeating to me the propaganda of your age. The love you talk about, my dear, existed in your little sheltered part of the world by polite and profitable convention. You were scarcely ever allowed to see its other face, unglamourized by Romance. You were never openly bought and sold, like livestock; you never had to sell yourself to the first comer in order to live; you did not happen to be one of the women who through the centuries screamed in agony and suffered and died under invaders in a sacked city—nor were you ever flung into a pit of fire to be saved from them; *you* were never compelled to suttee upon you dead husband's pyre; *you* did not have to spend your whole life imprisoned in a harem; *you* were never part of the cargo of a slave-ship; *you* never retained your own life only at the pleasure of your lord and master. . . .

"That is the other side—the age-long side. There is going to be no more of such things. They are finished at last. Dare you suggest that we should call them back, to suffer them all again?"

"But most of these things had already gone," I protested. "The world was getting better."

"Was it?" she said. "I wonder if the women of Berlin thought so when it fell? Was it, indeed?—or was it on the edge of a new barbarism?"

"But if you can only get rid of evil by throwing out the good, too, what is there left?"

"There is a great deal. Man was only a means to an end. We needed him in order to have babies. The rest of his vitality accounted for all the misery in the world. We are a great deal better off without him."

"So you really consider that you've improved on nature?"

"Tcha!" she said, impatient with my tone. "Civilization *is* improvement on nature. Would you want to live in a cave and have most of your babies die in infancy?"

"There are some things, some fundamental things—" I began, but she checked me, holding up her hand for silence.

Outside, the long shadows had crept across the lawns. In the evening quiet I could hear a choir of women's voices singing some little distance away. We listened for some minutes until the song was finished.

"Beautiful!" said the old lady. "Could angels themselves sing more sweetly? They sound happy enough, don't they? Our own lovely children—two of my granddaughters are there among them. They are happy, and they've reason to be happy: they're not growing up into a world where they must gamble on the goodwill of some man to keep them; they'll never need to be servile before a lord and master; they'll never stand in danger of rape and butchery, either. Listen to them!"

Another song had started and came lilting lightly to us out of the dusk.

"Why are you crying?" the old lady asked me as it ended.

"I know it's stupid—I don't really believe any of this is what it seems to be—so I suppose I'm crying for all you would have lost if it were true," I told her. "There should be lovers out there under the trees; they should be listening hand in hand to that song while they watch the moon rise. But there are no lovers now, there won't be any more. . . ." I looked back at her.

"Did you ever read the lines: 'Full many a flower is born to blush unseen, and waste its sweetness on the desert air'? Can't you feel the forlornness of this world you've made? Do you *really* not understand?" I asked.

"I know you've only seen a little of us, but do *you* not begin to understand what it can be like when women are no longer forced to fight one another for the favours of men?" she countered.

We talked on while the dusk gave way to darkness and the lights of other houses started to twinkle through the trees. Her reading had been wide. It had given her even an affection for some periods of the past, but her approval of her own era was unshaken. She felt no aridity in it. Always it was my 'conditioning' which prevented me from seeing that the golden age of woman had begun at last.

"You cling to too many myths," she told me. "You speak of a full life, and your instance is some unfortunate woman hugging her chains in a suburban villa. Full life, fiddlesticks! But it was convenient for the traders that she could be made to think so. A truly full life would be an exceedingly short one, in any form of society."

And so on. . . .

At length, the little parlourmaid reappeared to say that my attendants were ready to leave when it should be convenient. But there was one thing I very much wanted to know before I left. I put the question to the old lady.

"Please tell me. How did it—how could it—happen?"

"Simply by accident, my dear—though it was the kind of accident that was entirely the product of its time. A piece of research which showed unexpected, secondary results, that's all."

"But how?"

"Rather curiously—almost irrelevantly, you might say. Did you ever hear of a man called Perrigan?"

"Perrigan?" I repeated. "I don't think so; it's an uncommon name."

"It became very commonly known indeed," she assured me. "Doctor Perrigan was a biologist, and his concern was the extermination of rats—particularly the brown rat, which used to do a great deal of expensive damage.

"His approach to the problem was to find a disease which would attack them fatally. In order to produce it he took as his basis a virus infection often fatal to rabbits—or, rather, a group of virus infections that were highly selective, and also unstable since they were highly liable to mutation. Indeed, there was so much variation in the strains that when infection of rabbits in Australia was tried, it was only at the sixth attempt that it was successful; all the earlier strains died out as the rabbits developed immunity. It was tried in other places, too, though with indifferent success until a still more effective strain was started in France, and ran through the rabbit population of Europe.

"Well, taking some of these viruses as a basis, Perrigan induced new mutations by irradiation and other means, and succeeded in producing a variant that would attack rats. That was not enough, however, and he continued his work until he had a strain that had enough of its ancestral selectivity to attack only the brown rat, and with great virulence.

"In that way he settled the question of a long-standing pest, for there are no brown rats now. But something went amiss. It is still an open question whether the successful virus mutated again, or whether one of his earlier experimental viruses was accidentally liberated by escaped 'carrier' rats, but that's academic. The important thing is that somehow a strain capable of attacking human beings got loose, and that it was already widely disseminated before it was traced—also, that once it was free, it spread with devastating speed; too fast for any effective steps to be taken to check it.

"The majority of women were found to be immune; and of the ten percent or so whom it attacked over eight percent recovered. Among men, however, there was almost no immunity, and the few recoveries were only partial. A few men were preserved by the most elaborate precautions, but they could not be kept confined forever, and in the end the virus, which had a remarkable capacity for dormancy, got them, too."

Inevitably several questions of professional interest occurred to me, but for an answer she shook her head.

"I'm afraid I can't help you there. Possibly the medical people will be willing to explain," she said, but her expression was doubtful.

I maneuvered myself into a sitting position on the side of the couch.

"I see," I said. "Just an accident—yes, I suppose one could scarcely think of it happening any other way."

"Unless," she remarked, "unless one were to look upon it as divine intervention."

"Isn't that a little impious?"

"I was thinking of the Death of the Firstborn," she said, reflectively.

There did not seem to be an immediate answer to that. Instead, I asked:

"Can you honestly tell me that you never have the feeling that you are living in a dreary kind of nightmare?"

"Never," she said. "There was a nightmare—but it's over now. Listen!"

The voices of the choir, reinforced now by an orchestra, reached us distantly out of the darkened garden. No, they were not dreary: they even sounded almost exultant—but then, poor things, how were they to understand . . . ?

My attendants arrived and helped me to my feet. I thanked the old lady for her patience with me and her kindness. But she shook her head.

"My dear, it is I who am indebted to you. In a short time I have learnt more about the conditioning of women in a mixed society than all my books have been able to show me in the rest of my long life. I hope, my dear, that the doctors will find some way of enabling you to forget it and live happily here with us."

At the door I paused and turned, still helpfully shored up by my attendants.

"Laura," I said, using her name for the first time, "so many of your arguments are right—yet, over all, you're, oh, so *wrong*. Did you never read of lovers? Did you never, as a girl, sigh for a Romeo who would say: 'It is the east, and Laura is the sun!'?"

"I think not. Though I have read the play. A pretty, idealized tale—I wonder how much heartbreak it has given to how many would-be Juliets? But I would set a question against yours, my dear Jane. Did you ever see Goya's cycle of pictures called 'The Horrors of War'?"

The pink car did not return me to the 'Home'. Our destination turned out to be a more austere and hospital-like building where I was fussed into bed in a room alone. In the morning, after my massive breakfast, three new doctors visited me. Their manner was more social than professional, and we chatted amiably for half an hour. They had evidently been fully informed on my conversation with the old lady, and they were not averse to answering my questions. Indeed, they found some amusement in many of them, though I found none, for there was nothing consolingly vague in what they told me—it all sounded too disturbingly practicable, once the technique had been worked out. At the end of that time, however, their mood changed. One of them, with an air of getting down to business, said:

"You will understand that you present us with a problem. Your fellow Mothers, of course, are scarcely susceptible to Reactionist disaffection—though you have in quite a short time managed to disgust and bewilder them considerably—but on others less stable your influence might be more serious. It is not just a matter of what you may say; your difference from the rest is implicit in your whole attitude. You cannot help that, and, frankly, we do not see how you, as a woman of education, could possibly adapt yourself to the placid, unthinking acceptance that is expected of a Mother. You would quickly feel frustrated beyond endurance. Furthermore, it is clear that the conditioning you have had under your system prevents you from feeling any goodwill towards ours."

I took that straight; simply as a judgment without bias. Moreover, I could not dispute it. The prospect of spending the rest of my life in pink, scented, soft-musicked illiteracy, interrupted, one gathered, only by the production of quadruplet daughters at regular intervals, would certainly have me violently unhinged in a very short time.

"And so—what?" I asked. "Can you reduce this great carcass to normal shape and size?"

She shook her head. "I imagine not—though I don't know that it has ever been attempted. But even if it were possible, you would be just as much of a misfit in the Doctorate—and far more of a liability as a Reactionist influence."

I could understand that, too.

"What, then?" I inquired.

She hesitated, then she said gently:

"The only practicable proposal we can make is that you should agree to a hypnotic treatment which will remove your memory."

As the meaning of that came home to me I had to fight off a rush of panic. After all, I told myself, they were being reasonable with me. I must do my best to respond sensibly. Nevertheless, some minutes must have passed before I answered, unsteadily.

"You are asking me to commit suicide. My mind is my memories: they are me. If I lose them I shall die, just as surely as if you were to kill my—this body."

They did not dispute that. How could they?

There is just one thing that makes my life worth living—knowing that you loved me, my sweet, sweet Donald. It is only in my memory that you live now. If you ever leave there you will die again—and forever.

"No!" I told them. "No! No!"

At intervals during the day small Servitors staggered in under the weight of my meals. In between their visits I had only my thoughts to occupy me, and they were not good company.

"Frankly," one of the doctors had put it to me, not unsympathetically, "we can see no alternative. For years after it happened the annual figures of mental breakdowns were our greatest worry. Even though the women then could keep themselves fully occupied with the tremendous amount of work that had to be done, so many of them could not adjust. And we can't even offer you work."

I knew that it was a fair warning she was giving me—and I knew that, unless the hallucination which seemed to grow more real all the time could soon be induced to dissolve, I was trapped.

During the long day and the following night I tried my hardest to get back to the objectivity I had managed earlier, but I failed. The whole dialectic was too strong for me now; my senses too consciously aware of my surroundings; the air of consequence and coherence too convincingly persistent. . . .

When they had let me have twenty-four hours to think it over, the same trio visited me again.

"I think," I told them, "that I understand better now. What you are offering me is painless oblivion, in place of a breakdown followed by oblivion—and you see no other choice."

"We don't," admitted the spokeswoman, and the other two nodded. "But, of course, for the hypnosis we shall need your co-operation."

"I realize that," I told her, "and I also see now that in the circumstances it would be obstinately futile to withhold it. So I—I—yes, I'm willing to give it—but on one condition."

They looked at me questioningly.

"It is this," I explained, "that you will try one other course first. I want you to give me an injection of chuinjuatin. I want it in precisely the same strength as I had it before—I can tell you the dose.

"You see, whether this is an intense hallucination, or whether it is some kind of projection which makes it seem very similar, it must have something to do with that drug. I'm sure it must—nothing remotely like this has ever happened to me before. So, I thought that if I could repeat the condition—or, would you say, believe myself to be repeating the condition?—there may be just a chance . . . I don't know. It may be simply silly . . . but even if nothing comes of it, it can't make things worse in any way now, can it? So, if you will let me try it . . . ?"

The three of them considered for some moments.

"I can see no reason why not . . ." said one.

The spokeswoman nodded.

"I shouldn't think there'll be any difficulty with authorization in the circumstances," she agreed. "If you want to try, well, it's fair to let you, but—I'd not count on it too much. . . ."

In the afternoon half a dozen small servitors arrived, bustling around, making me and the room ready, with anxious industry. Presently there came one more, scarcely tall enough to see over the trolley of bottles, trays, and phials which she pushed to my bedside.

The three doctors entered together. One of the little Servitors began rolling up my sleeve. The doctor who had done most of the talking looked at me, kindly, but seriously.

"This is a sheer gamble, you know that?" she said.

"I know. But it's my only chance. I'm willing to take it."

She nodded, picked up the syringe, and charged it while the little servitor swabbed my monstrous arm. She approached the bedside, and hesitated.

"Go on," I told her. "What is there for me here, anyway?"

She nodded, and pressed in the needle. . . .

Now, I have written the foregoing for a purpose. I shall deposit it with my bank, where it will remain unread unless it should be needed.

I have spoken of it to no one. The report on the effect of chuinjuatin—the one that I made to Dr Hellyer where I described my sensation as simply one of floating in space—was false. The foregoing was my true experience.

I concealed it because after I came around, when I found that I was back in my own body in my normal world, the experience haunted me as vividly as if it had been actuality. The details were too sharp, too vivid, for me to get them out of my mind. It overhung me all the time, like a threat. It would not leave me alone. . . .

I did not dare to tell Dr. Hellyer how it worried me—he would have put me under treatment. If my other friends did not take it seriously enough to recommend treatment, too, then they would have laughed over it, and amused themselves at my expense interpreting the symbolism. So I kept it to myself.

As I went over parts of it again and again in detail, I grew angry with myself for not asking the old lady for more facts, things like dates, and details that could be verified. If, for instance, the thing should, by her account, have started two or three years ago, then the whole sense of threat would fall to pieces: it would all be discredited. But it had not occurred to me to ask that crucial question. . . . And then, as I went on thinking about it, I remembered that there was one, just one, piece of information that I could check, and I made inquiries. I wish now that I had not, but I felt forced to. . . .

So I have discovered that:

There *is* a Dr. Perrigan, he *is* a biologist, he does work with rabbits and rats. . . .

He is quite well known in his field. He has published papers on pest-control in a number of journals. It is no secret that he is evolving new strains of myxomatosis to attack rats; indeed, he has already developed a group of them and calls them mucosimorbus, though he has not yet succeeded in making them either stable or selective enough for general use. . . .

But I had never heard of this man or his work until his name was mentioned by the old lady in my 'hallucination.' . . .

I have given a great deal of thought to this whole matter. What sort of experience is it that I have recorded above? If it should be a kind of pre-vision of an inevitable, predestined future, then nothing anyone could do would change it. But this does not seem to me to make sense: it is what has happened, and is happening now, that determines the future. Therefore, there must be a great number of *possible* futures, each a possible consequence of what is being done now. It seems to me that under chuinjuatin I saw *one* of those futures. . . .

It was, I think, a warning of what *may* happen—unless it is prevented. . . .

The whole idea is so repulsive and misconceived, it amounts to such a monstrous aberration of the normal course, that failure to heed the warning would be neglect of duty to one's kind.

I shall, therefore, on my own responsibility and without taking any other person into my confidence, do my best to ensure that such a state as I have described *cannot* come about.

Should it happen that any other person is unjustly accused of doing, or of assisting me to do, what I intend to do, this document must stand in his defence. That is why I have written it.

It is my own unaided decision that Dr. Perrigan must not be permitted to continue his work.

(Signed) JANE WATERLEIGH.

The solicitor stared at the signature for some moments; then he nodded.

"And so," he said, "she then took her car and drove over to Perrigan's—with this tragic result.

"From the little I do know of her, I'd say that she probably did her best to persuade him to give up his work—though she can scarcely have expected any success with that. It is difficult to imagine a man who would be willing to give up the work of years on account of what must sound to him like a sort of gypsy's warning. So, clearly, she went prepared to fall back on direct action, if necessary. It looks as if the police are quite right when they suppose her to have shot him deliberately; but not so right when they suppose that she burnt the place down to hide evidence of the crime. The statement makes it pretty obvious that her main intention in doing that was to wipe out Perrigan's work."

He shook his head. "Poor girl! There's a clear conviction of duty in her last page or two: the sort of simplified clarity that drives martyrs on, regardless of consequences. She has never denied that she did it. What she wouldn't tell the police is *why* she did it."

He paused again, before he added: "Anyway, thank goodness for this document. It ought at least to save her life. I should be very surprised indeed if a plea of insanity could fail, backed up by this." He tapped the pile of manuscript with his finger. "It's a lucky thing she put off her intention of taking it to her bank."

Dr. Hellyer's face was lined and worried.

"I blame myself most bitterly for the whole thing," he said. "I never ought to have let her try the damned drug in the first place, but I thought she was over the shock of her husband's death. She was trying to keep her time fully occupied, and she was anxious to volunteer. You've met her enough to know how purposeful she can be. She saw it as a chance to contribute something to medical knowledge—which it was, of course. But I ought to have been more careful, and I ought to have seen afterwards that there was something wrong. The real responsibility for this thing runs right back to me."

"H'm," said the solicitor. "Putting that forward as a main line of defence isn't going to do you a lot of good professionally, you know, Hellyer."

"Possibly not. I can look after that when we come to it. The point is that I hold a responsibility for her as a member of my staff, if for no other reason. It can't be denied that, if I had refused her offer to take part in the experiment, this would not have happened. Therefore it seems to me that we ought to be able to argue a state of temporary insanity; that the balance of her mind was disturbed by the effects of the drug which I administered. And if we can get that as a verdict it will result in detention at a mental hospital for observation and treatment—perhaps quite a short spell of treatment."

"I can't say. We can certainly put it up to counsel and see what he thinks of it."

"It's valid, too," Hellyer persisted. "People like Jane don't do murder if they are in their right minds, not unless they're really in a corner, then they do it more cleverly. Certainly they don't murder perfect strangers. Clearly, the drug caused an hallucination sufficiently vivid to confuse her to a point where she was unable to make a proper distinction between the actual and the hypothetical. She got into a state where she believed the mirage was real, and acted accordingly."

"Yes. Yes, I suppose one might put it that way," agreed the solicitor. He looked down again at the pile of paper before him. "The whole account is, of course, unreasonable," he said, "and yet it is pervaded throughout with such an air of reasonableness. I wonder . . ." He paused pensively, and went on: "This expendability of the male, Hellyer. She doesn't seem to find it so much incredible, as undesirable. That seems odd in itself to a layman who takes the natural order for granted, but would you, as a medical scientist, say it was—well, not impossible, in theory?"

Dr. Hellyer frowned.

"That's very much the kind of question one wants more notice of. It would be very rash to proclaim it *impossible*. Considering it purely as an abstract problem, I can see two or three lines of approach. . . . Of course, if an utterly improbable situation were to arise calling for intensive research—research, that is, on the sort of scale they tackled the atom—well, who can tell . . . ?" He shrugged.

The solicitor nodded again.

"That's just what I was getting at," he observed. "Basically it is only just such a little way off the beam; quite near enough to possibility to be faintly disturbing. Mind you, as far as the defense is concerned, her air of thorough conviction, taken in conjunction with the near-plausibility of the thing, will probably help. But as far as I am concerned it is just that nearness that is enough to make me a trifle uneasy."

The doctor looked at him rather sharply.

"Oh, come! Really now! A hard-boiled solicitor, too! Don't tell me you're going in for fantasy-building. Anyway, if you are, you'll have to conjure up another one. If Jane, poor girl, has settled one thing, it is that there's no future in this particular fantasy. Perrigan's finished with, and all his work's gone up in smoke."

"H'm," said the solicitor again. "All the same, it would be more satisfactory if we knew of some way other than this"—he tapped the pile of papers—"some other way in which she is likely to have acquired a knowledge of Perrigan and his work. There is, as far as one knows, *no* other way in which he can have come into her orbit at all—unless, perhaps, she takes an interest in veterinary subjects?"

"She doesn't. I'm sure of that," Hellyer told him, shaking his head.

"Well, that, then, remains one slightly disturbing aspect. And there is another. You'll think it foolish of me, I'm sure—and no doubt time will prove you right to do so—but I have to admit I'd be feeling easier in my mind if Jane had been just a bit more thorough in her inquiries before she went into action."

"Meaning—?" asked Dr. Hellyer, looking puzzled.

"Only that she does not seem to have found out that there is a son. But there is, you see. He appears to have taken quite a close interest in his father's work, and is determined that it shan't be wasted. In fact he has already announced that he will do his best to carry it on with the very few specimens that were saved from the fire. . . .

"Laudably filial, no doubt. All the same it does disturb me a little to find that he, also, happens to be D.Sc., a biochemist; and that, very naturally, his name, too, is Perrigan. . . ."

Eddy C. Bertin

Eddy C. Bertin (1944–) lives in Flanders and is a leading Belgian SF and horror writer. He has published over 500 stories, over fifty in English, some Lovecraftian horror, some science fiction. He started writing at age thirteen, in Dutch, and published twenty-five books for adults between 1970 and 1986 in the Netherlands; he then switched to writing for children and young adults, and has published sixteen more books since 1986. He has in the past published poetry, translations, and 140 issues of his own *SF Guide* over eighteen years. He has written an SF future history trilogy that has not been published in English.

Most European countries have at least a few long-time science fiction writers, who have been producing fiction for decades. They are not always highly regarded internationally, but they have kept the international SF movement alive for its own sake for decades, in spite of the waves of literary fashion. Often they travel to meet other SF people at their own expense in other countries, and publish small press magazines to keep their own culture informed. Bertin is a distinguished representative of these men from the 1960s and the present. This story is a small jewel of a mood piece.

SOMETHING ENDING

"You don't exist," was the first thing the ugly little fat man said to me as I entered the pub. He was seated on a barstool which was much too tall for someone his size, and his short stubby legs in their wrinkled trousers dangled freely without even touching the floor. He could hardly be called an attractive specimen of homo sapiens. His face looked like a sponge, with flabby cheeks and slobbering thin lips. His deep-sunken eyes were blurred by the amount of strong drinks he had had, and in these he showed an amazing appetite for variations, as indicated by the outstanding series of different empty glasses in front of him, and which he refused to let be taken away. The barman was eyeing him with open hostility and annoyance.

He looked me over once more, nodded, satisfied at his own reflection in the mirror, and repeated with more intonation: "No, you really don't exist." Satisfied with the approval of his mirror-image, he ordered another drink. There was no other place vacant, so I took the stool beside him, and since he made no gesture of buying me a drink, I ordered my own.

"You seem very certain of that," I said. Not that I cared very much what any fat drunk muttered to me, but I hate just sitting and drinking. I had been obliged to spent the evening in town, with no friends I cared to see, and no movie worth going to, either. In fact I had been preparing myself for a quiet evening at home with a good novel or maybe a rock-show on the tube, and a couple of good

Napoleon brandies, when Vodier had called me on the phone, asking if I were at home that evening. This had immediately resulted in my stating that I had to rush off to an urgent press-conference in a couple of minutes, and wouldn't be home till the next day. Vodier was a nice chap, but he had the irritating habit of hanging around till the early hours of the next morning, and his conversational habits were limited to one single subject: himself. Since I knew Vodier was liable to drive over anyway, just in the vague hope that my conference had been cancelled at the last instant, there was only one thing to do: get out as fast as possible. Which I had done.

Maybe this weirdo would bring some amusement in an otherwise dreary evening, and since there seemed to be no free female companionship available in this pub, I might as well make the best of it. Ghent is a nice city to live in, but it hasn't much to offer as nightlife, compared to Brussels or Antwerp, and I didn't feel like driving another couple of miles to find another more interesting café.

The stranger shook his head pityingly, murmuring: "Poor, poor chap, so utterly convinced that he really exists, that he has real life, and what is he in fact? Phut. Nothing. Zero. A hole. A vacuum."

"Can't say I ever thought about myself that way," I said grinning. "Maybe my reasoning is a bit confused, but I feel my hands here, flesh and bone, and here a head on top of my body. *Cogito ergo sum*, I think therefore I am. More, I FEEL that I am. Seems quite logical to me."

"Bloody nonsense," he said angrily. "You only BELIEVE that you exist; there's quite a difference between believing and being. You have no real proof of your existence. You're just a dummy; you may as well believe me. Knowing the truth about oneself always makes one happier, or so I've been told."

I laughed. The funny chap had his voice remarkably under control, but he clearly was completely stoned. You don't meet them often that way and still able to talk.

"All right, I don't exist," I grinned. "So what next?What makes you so goddamn sure anyway? If I don't exist, then why are you speaking to me?"

He looked me over with what surely must be the special look he reserved for people asking insane questions. "I am speaking to you because I want to," he said. "Because nothing exists except me and what I want. You are here because of me, you exist because I want you to exist here and now. I would have thought that was very simple to see, don't you? Oh, go to hell! One can't talk with someone of your kind. You understand nothing, accept nothing, bah."

He rose and dropped himself from his high seat of judgment. He threw some money at the barman and walked away, without saying as much as good night.

I concentrated on my drink and had two more, still thinking with amusement of the words of the funny madman. Then I drove home, got out and walked straight in the arms of a grinning Vodier, who had brought a crate of beer with him and kept me up till four o'clock in the morning.

The second time I ran into the funny-talking fat stranger was at quite a different place, at a charity ball of all things. It was one of those dry and hot evenings, which reassures you in advance that it will be raining like hell before the evening is done. The heat was unbearable in the dancing hall, and the fridge of the bar had chosen that exact evening to break down, so they had no ice cubes for the warm drinks. I decided to get a breath of fresh air on the terrace. And just guess who was standing there, his small hands on his back, staring up at the night stars? Yes, you got it right the first time. Mister You-don't-exist himself.

He looked over his shoulder as he heard my footsteps approaching and smiled amicably. He seemed sober this time.

"Hello, Mister Dummy," he said as a manner of greeting. "Made your mind up yet about whether or not you exist?"

"One day or other you're gonna get punched in the mouth if you speak to anyone like that," I said. For a moment I considered whether I should turn around and just walk away. After all he was no more than a bizarre but harmless weirdo. Still something about the fat little man intrigued me, and I decided to stay around for a couple of minutes. But he had already turned away from me and contemplated the night sky. He spoke again, this time more to himself, as if it were totally unimportant whether I listened or not.

"Nice shining stars up there," he said. "Specially the great sparkling one over there. You know, if I could stand up high enough and stretch my arms, I could just pick them right out of the sky. That specific star as well as all the other fake ones. It might convince you that I'm not crazy. And maybe then I would find out what's on the other side of that sky."

I shrugged. "Then why don't you just do that?"

He grinned. "It doesn't work," he said. "I tried it a couple of times, but they're faster than me. As soon as I stand on my toes, they just raise the sky a bit higher, out of my reach."

"So?" I asked. "First I don't exist. Now the sky is a curtain where you can pick the fake stars from. You do hold some pretty cranky ideas."

"Cranky?" He seemed shocked. "Wasn't it Shakespeare who said that the world's a stage? Or was that someone else? Not that it matters that much who said it, he or she surely had some idea about the truth of existence. But why am I bothering with you? One can't talk sense into an empty head. You're nothing, go away, shoo!"

"So, I am nothing. Well, just feel this hand. Feel the flesh, the muscles, the bones. That seems real enough to me. And you do hear me, don't you? So I can speak, too."

He smiled, all sympathy. "You got me all wrong, Mister. I am not talking about your material body. Of course that exists, just as this terrace and these stars exist for the time being. A window dummy exists, which doesn't means that he IS. The ego, the mind, the 'I' which you call 'me,' that doesn't exist. The material body you have, the streets over there, they are for real, too, but only temporary. They're make-believes, stage settings, just as the whole neighborhood. As soon as I'll be gone, they and you will stop existing. It's all here, because I am here. There must be air for me to breathe, there must be a terrace since I can't be standing here floating in empty air, and since I feel like talking to someone, you are here. If I decided to go to China now, this Europe would cease to exist the moment I left it. It would no longer be needed, since I would have left it."

This was just too much, and my laughing exploded in his face. It wasn't very polite, I admit, and it even might have been dangerous. You never know with a crazy; he didn't look aggressive, but you never know. But then, I was bigger than he, and I was certain that I could handle him if he tried to attack me. But he didn't.

"That's a good one," I said after I had stopped laughing. "Well, let me tell you that I know very well what I've been doing those last weeks, and I don't recall you being with me then or being in the neighborhood where I was."

"Artificial memories," he shrugged. "They're very good at them. They just put them inside your head so that you would be able to play your part as true-to-life as possible."

"They did, huh? And the rest of the world, all those other countries? I suppose they don't exist now since you aren't there?"

"Quite right," he said as if stating an indisputable fact. "They're just illusions, make-believes created to convince me that the world does exist. Tell me, were you ever really there? In China or Australia, in India or in Hungary?"

"Well no," I said. "I haven't been there. I wouldn't know why I should go there. But there are photographs, films, libraries . . ."

"Nonsense, it's all fake. You know only that small part of the world or even of this country in which you are, here and now. All the rest you know only by hearsay. I tell you, there is no world, no other countries, not even a real sky. It's just a stage curtain. Humanity, as such, is a dream. The only reality is my own being, and the stage they erect wherever I go. And of course all the dummies like yourself who only come into existence whenever I am near. People like you, and taxi drivers, and barkeepers, and cops, and traveling salesmen and housewives . . . people . . ."

I gasped at him. He couldn't mean that, could he? If he did . . . well, I had met quite some weirdos in my life, but this one was really too much. He was ready for the men in the white suits to come and drag him away.

"The truth hurts, doesn't it?" he asked innocently. "But don't worry about it, Mister. After a while, you'll get used to being a third-rate character in the play I'm performing."

With these words, he turned and disappeared into the crowd inside.

During the following months, somehow or other, my thoughts often returned to the crazy little fellow. Strange how some crazies manage to sound too utterly convincing and logical, even while they're talking absolute nonsense. Like when he spoke of those other faraway countries which only existed on films and photographs or just because others tell us they do exist. But, then, in the little man's mind, all those others were no more than animated showroom dummies themselves, so it hardly mattered. Must be quite a frightening stage in his own mind, I thought, a world-wide theater in which performs one fat little ugly performer.

History tends to repeat itself, as they say, and so does this story, because when I met the stranger the third time, he was stone-drunk again. It was in another bar this time, one which had chairs small enough for him to sit on with his feet on the ground, which was as well, since I doubt if he would have managed his balance otherwise. I sat down in front of him, his eyes seemed more hidden below the ridges of fat than before, and he had to look three times before recognizing me.

"Oh, yes, it's you again," he said. "My own Mister Nothing. They must think quite a lot of your character for giving you three stage acts. Have a drink with me, since you're here anyway."

He seemed preoccupied and moody. We had a drink and then another one, but he didn't brighten. He did talk, however.

"I'm scared," he said in an appropriate stage whisper. "You see, I've started doubting my own existence. Suppose, just suppose that I, too, don't really exist?

What if I am no more than one of the dummies, a walking-talking-singing-drinking doll with a set of false memories? What sense would the world have then if it wasn't made for me? What if it is made and kept in existence for someone else? I couldn't bear that thought. If I was sure, I would have to hunt and kill that man or woman. But who knows? Maybe I would then cease to exist completely, as well as the rest of the world."

"That would be some problem indeed," I agreed.

"And it's not that fantastic at all," he continued. "I know, I have always known that I exist. But how can I prove it to myself? There is only one way to go about it: catch them! CATCH THEM AT IT! But how? I've tried everything possible so far. I went somewhere and suddenly changed direction. I bought a ticket to Africa and to London. But they're so fast, by the time the plane got there, they had built Africa and peopled it, complete with animals and tourists, just like in the traveler's catalogues. And when I got to London, they had already gotten it ready, except for part of the Tower, but they had their explanation ready: the Tower was being repaired just then. Everything turns out to be exactly as in the movies and pictures. They're good all right! It's almost as if they know in advance what I intend to do, or else they're just too damned fast and good at stage-building. They're smart, and they know I'm trying to catch them."

"THEY," I said. "You're always rambling about THEM. Who or what are THEY?"

"Isn't that clear yet? The builders, the owners of the stage, of course. They who hide themselves behind the sky-curtain, they who have built this world-theater and put me here in their play. You see, I think this is something like those intelligence tests they're always supposed to be doing with rats and mice and guinea pigs. They put them in a maze, and the food is at the other end of the maze. The guinea pig has to find its way through the corridors of the maze or it'll starve to death. Since the guinea pig has no gun to burn itself a straight way through the maze, it has to search, but at regular intervals they change the corridors of the maze, so the guinea pig has to adapt all the time in order to get to the food and survive. See, that's what I think I am. A rat in a maze, and they control the corridors. But I am more than a rat, I know they're THERE, and I intend to find out about them. I'm gonna burn myself through that maze in a straight line!"

"But why . . . would THEY go to all that trouble?"

"I don't know, but I have several ideas," he whispered. "Maybe all of this is just THAT: an experiment with a lower animal. A kind of reaction test. Maybe they just want to know how I'll work it all out, how fast I react to stimulations. And maybe . . . they're afraid of me. It isn't that silly, there must be a very logical reason for my being that all-important to them, to go to all that work and trouble. Maybe this is some kind of prison they've put me in, and they've taken some memories out of my mind, so I can't remember who I am or why I'm here. Maybe it's some kind of mental symbiosis: maybe they only exist because I exist, and MY being is their only reason for being. Maybe I'm a psychotic god, a lonely god, who has built a neurotic wall around himself and is now trying to get sane again. Maybe I even created THEM myself, so they could put me in their own play! As a snake eating its own tail. Maybe I am the one and only center of the universe, and therefore they—as my creations—are afraid of me."

He took a sip of his drink, and wiped his mouth with his sleeve. The drink was getting to him, his speech was becoming less clear every minute.

"But it'll be over soon now," he whispered. "I'm not that stupid, you see. I said I would burn my way through at them in a straight line, and that's what I'm gonna do. I've found the way to get them, the bastards!"

He ordered new drinks and bent lower so that I had trouble understanding his words. "I'm going to them damn stars," he whispered. "Sounds like nut talk, doesn't it? I don't look like a scientist or a spaceman, but I'm going anyway. Right through those fake stars, and then let them try to make a universe for me. I've been thinking about it for some time. I can't make a spaceship, but if I'm that important, then there must be other ways for me to get out of their maze. I've built a ship. Well, no, not exactly what you could call a spaceship. It's no more than just a hollow sphere with a chair in it. I can seal it airtight from the inside, and I'm taking oxygen tanks, food and drink. Probably I won't even need any of that, if the powers I've tapped inside my mind work out as I intend them to. Because I'm going to do it with my mind and nothing else."

He patted his head, grinning. "Yeah, ol' man, inside my head, there it is. Inside my brain, all the power I need to get at them. I've been reading up on such things as telekinesis, the transportation of matter by mental powers. Enough to lift the sphere and myself up to that damn sky, and burn through it. If there is only one really existing mind, which is mine, then that mind must possess those powers. I'm getting out of here tonight. You're the only one who knows now, and you're just another dummy, after all. Now once I'm through their sky-curtain let them try to keep up the illusion. Let them try to create real space, real stars, out there!"

"It's crazy." I said. "You need a real spaceship for that, engines, computers, technicians. It's an absurd idea!"

"Course it is," he agreed. "That's why it's genius. They'll never think of it before I get there and see for myself! You don't think I'm doing this without some preparations, do you? I've been testing my mental powers for weeks now, lifting tables, opening doors without touching them. Then other things, more heavy. Then giving them speed, always more speed! Oh, yes, I'm certain it'll work as I planned it. I just . . . FEEL it. I set my starting date for next month, so of course I'll be taking off tonight! I'll catch them all right when they're totally unprepared for me. But I thought I'd have a couple of drinks first, to test my courage. It may turn out to be a long trip if they try to create the universe when I'm coming, and I'm pretty sure they'll try. Even if I manage to drive my speed up towards the speed of light, it's still more than five light-years to the closest star, Alpha Centauri. But I may encounter them sooner than that."

When I left him, he was still drinking and muttering to himself how he'd finally get them, the bastards.

About eleven o'clock, I saw his sphere rising from the center of the city where I knew he lived. It was just a small, dark ball, which rose hesitatingly above the buildings, but then suddenly picked up speed, floating faster and faster towards the skies. It looked like a toy balloon, getting smaller and smaller, but it moved in one straight line up. He was going to burn his way through all right, just as he had said he would. He had left earlier than he had said, but I had expected that, too.

I waited till he had left the atmosphere, calculating the orbit he would follow to get away from earth and then the trajectory he would be following in the years to come, beyond the outer planets and into the void beyond, towards Alpha Centauri. I had already set the apparatus, and the projections of the outer planets and the stars would pass off satisfactorily on his eyes. There would be no errors. I still had time enough to catch up with him before he reached his destination. After all, I would have to be on the meeting committee.

"Boy, do your best," I thought. "You've wasted thirty-seven years down here: you should already be in the second-stage for a long time. Why doesn't your mind work faster, better?"

It wasn't my fault, nor my symbiont-wife's; our genes matched perfectly. Our getting a retarded child was just one of those things, it happens sometimes.

But now he HAD to succeed. He had left the nursery now, and was speeding towards the kindergarten. By then he would have figured it all out, he would have to! If he didn't he would be considered a total failure. I would be allowed no more children, and he . . . he would be erased from existence. The committee didn't lose its time with the unfit for the universe. They will be waiting for him, when he gets there, at Alpha Centauri, and I will be among them, unable to help him. He'll have to make it on his own, my son. And, though retarded, he hasn't been doing too badly after all. It was fortunate that they had at least let me work on the nursery years.

He has made a few errors and misjudgments, of course. What infant doesn't? He had drawn the wrong conclusion also when he had said that the world doesn't exist. When I do something, I do it well. There IS a real world. Now I'm beginning to tear it down.

Roger Zelazny

Roger Zelazny (1937–95) was among the leading SF writers to emerge in the 1960s. His body of work in that decade was enormously influential, particularly his twelve novellas, of which this is one. With the way paved by the impact of his early stories, his first novel, *This Immortal* (1966) shared the Hugo Award with Frank Herbert's *Dune*. Zelazny became one of the most popular and respected writers of that decade, with five more novels and a collection of novellas by 1970.

At the beginning of the 1970s he launched what was to become his most popular series of books with *Nine Princes in Amber* (1970). With the enormous popularity and financial success of the Amber books, Zelazny lost interest in experimentation with the novel form and limited his most intense aesthetic efforts to occasional short stories and novellas for most of the following twenty-five years. Novels such as *Doorways in the Sand* (1976), *Eye of Cat* (1982), and *A Night in the Lonesome October* (1993) stand out as exceptions. This novella, one of the works upon which his initial fame rests, is a powerful fusion of technology, psychology, and myths of godlike power.

HE WHO SHAPES

I

Lovely as it was, with the blood and all, Render could sense that it was about to end.

Therefore, each microsecond would be better off as a minute, he decided—and perhaps the temperature should be increased . . . Somewhere, just at the periphery of everything, the darkness halted its constriction.

Something, like a crescendo of subliminal thunders, was arrested at one raging note. That note was a distillate of shame and pain and fear.

The Forum was stifling.

Caesar cowered outside the frantic circle. His forearm covered his eyes but it could not stop the seeing, not this time.

The senators had no faces and their garments were spattered with blood. All their voices were like the cries of birds. With an inhuman frenzy they plunged their daggers into the fallen figure.

All, that is, but Render.

The pool of blood in which he stood continued to widen. His arm seemed to be rising and falling with a mechanical regularity and his throat might have been shaping birdcries, but he was simultaneously apart from and a part of the scene.

For he was Render, the Shaper.

Crouched, anguished and envious, Caesar wailed his protests.

"You have slain him! You have murdered Marcus Antonius—a blameless, useless fellow!"

Render turned to him and the dagger in his hand was quite enormous and quite gory.

"Aye," said he.

The blade moved from side to side. Caesar, fascinated by the sharpened steel, swayed to the same rhythm.

"Why?" he cried. "Why?"

"Because," answered Render, "he was a far nobler Roman than yourself."

"You lie! It is not so!"

Render shrugged and returned to the stabbing.

"It is not true!" screamed Caesar. "Not true!"

Render turned to him again and waved the dagger. Puppetlike, Caesar mimicked the pendulum of the blade.

"Not true?" smiled Render. "And who are you to question an assassination such as this? You are no one! You detract from the dignity of this occasion! Begone!"

Jerkily, the pink-faced man rose to his feet, his hair half-wispy, half-wetplastered, a disarray of cotton. He turned, moved away; and as he walked, he looked back over his shoulder.

He had moved far from the circle of assassins, but the scene did not diminish in size. It retained an electric clarity. It made him feel even further removed, ever more alone and apart.

Render rounded a previously unnoticed corner and stood before him, a blind beggar.

Caesar grasped the front of his garment.

"Have you an ill omen for me this day?"

"Beware!" jeered Render.

"Yes! Yes!" cried Caesar. " 'Beware!' That is good! Beware what?"

"The ides—"

"Yes? The ides—?"

"—of Octember."

He released the garment.

"What is that you say? What is Octember?"

"A month."

"You lie! There is no month of Octember!"

"And that is the date noble Caesar need fear—the non-existent time, the never-to-be-calendared occasion."

Render vanished around another sudden corner.

"Wait! Come back!"

Render laughed, and the Forum laughed with him. The birdcries became a chorus of inhuman jeers.

"You mock me!" wept Caesar.

The Forum was an oven, and the perspiration formed like a glassy mask over Caesar's narrow forehead, sharp nose and chinless jaw.

"I want to be assassinated too!" he sobbed. "It isn't fair!"

And Render tore the Forum and the senators and the grinning corpse of Antony to pieces and stuffed them into a black sack—with the unseen movement of a single finger—and last of all went Caesar.

• • •

Charles Render sat before the ninety white buttons and the two red ones, not really looking at any of them. His right arm moved, in its soundless sling, across the lap-level surface of the console—pushing some of the buttons, skipping over others, moving on, retracing its path to press the next in the order of the Recall Series.

Sensations throttled, emotions reduced to nothing, Representative Erikson knew the oblivion of the womb.

There was a soft click.

Render's hand had glided to the end of the bottom row of buttons. An act of conscious intent—will, if you like—was required to push the red button.

Render freed his arm and lifted off his crown of Medusa-hair leads and microminiature circuitry. He slid from behind his desk-couch and raised the hood. He walked to the window and transpared it, fingering forth a cigarette.

One minute in the ro-womb, he decided. *No more. This is a crucial one . . . Hope it doesn't snow till later—those clouds look mean. . . .*

It was smooth yellow trellises and high towers, glassy and gray, all smouldering into evening under a shale-colored sky; the city was squared volcanic islands, glowing in the end-of-day light, rumbling deep down under the earth; it was fat, incessant rivers of traffic, rushing.

Render turned away from the window and approached the great egg that lay beside his desk, smooth and glittering. It threw back a reflection that smashed all aquilinity from his nose, turned his eyes to gray saucers, transformed his hair into a light-streaked skyline; his reddish necktie became the wide tongue of a ghoul.

He smiled, reached across the desk. He pressed the second red button.

With a sigh, the egg lost its dazzling opacity and a horizontal crack appeared about its middle. Through the now-transparent shell, Render could see Erikson grimacing, squeezing his eyes tight, fighting against a return to consciousness and the thing it would contain. The upper half of the egg rose vertical to the base, exposing him knobby and pink on half-shell. When his eyes opened he did not look at Render. He rose to his feet and began dressing. Render used this time to check the ro-womb.

He leaned back across his desk and pressed the buttons: temperature control, full range, *check;* exotic sounds—he raised the earphone—*check,* on bells, on buzzes, on violin notes and whistles, on squeals and moans, on traffic noises and the sound of surf; *check,* on the feedback circuit—holding the patient's own voice, trapped earlier in analysis; *check,* on the sound blanket, the moisture spray, the odor banks; *check,* on the couch agitator and the colored lights, the taste stimulants . . .

Render closed the egg and shut off its power. He pushed the unit into the closet, palmed shut the door. The tapes had registered a valid sequence.

"Sit down," he directed Erikson.

The man did so, fidgeting with his collar.

"You have full recall," said Render, "so there is no need for me to summarize what occurred. Nothing can be hidden from me. I was there."

Erikson nodded.

"The significance of the episode should be apparent to you."

Erikson nodded again, finally finding his voice. "But was it valid?" he asked. "I mean, you constructed the dream and you controlled it, all the way. I didn't really *dream* it—in the way I would normally dream. Your ability to make things happen stacks the deck for whatever you're going to say—doesn't it?"

Render shook his head slowly, flicked an ash into the southern hemisphere of his globe-made-ashtray, and met Erikson's eyes.

"It is true that I supplied the format and modified the forms. You, however, filled them with an emotional significance, promoted them to the status of symbols corresponding to your problem. If the dream was not a valid analogue it would not have provoked the reactions it did. It would have been devoid of the anxiety-patterns which were registered on the tapes.

"You have been in analysis for many months now," he continued, "and everything I have learned thus far serves to convince me that your fears of assassination are without any basis in fact."

Erikson glared.

"Then why the hell do I have them?"

"Because," said Render, "you would like very much to be the subject of an assassination."

Erikson smiled then, his composure beginning to return.

"I assure you, doctor, I have never contemplated suicide, nor have I any desire to stop living."

He produced a cigar and applied a flame to it. His hand shook.

"When you came to me this summer," said Render, "you stated that you were in fear of an attempt on your life. You were quite vague as to why anyone should want to kill you—"

"My position! You can't be a Representative as long as I have and make no enemies!"

"Yet," replied Render, "it appears that you have managed it. When you permitted me to discuss this with your detectives I was informed that they could unearth nothing to indicate that your fears might have any real foundation. Nothing."

"They haven't looked far enough—or in the right places. They'll turn up something."

"I'm afraid not."

"Why?"

"Because, I repeat, your feelings are without any objective basis.—Be honest with me. Have you any information whatsoever indicating that someone hates you enough to want to kill you?"

"I receive many threatening letters . . ."

"As do all Representatives—and all of those directed to you during the past year have been investigated and found to be the work of cranks. Can you offer me *one* piece of evidence to substantiate your claims?"

Erikson studied the tip of his cigar.

"I came to you on the advice of a colleague," he said, "came to you to have you poke around inside my mind to find me something of that sort, to give my detectives something to work with.—Someone I've injured severely perhaps—or some damaging piece of legislation I've dealt with. . . ."

"—And I found nothing," said Render, "nothing, that is, but the cause of your discontent. Now, of course, you are afraid to hear it, and you are attempting to divert me from explaining my diagnosis—"

"I am not!"

"Then listen. You can comment afterward if you want, but you've poked and dawdled around here for months, unwilling to accept what I presented to you in a dozen different forms. Now I am going to tell you outright what it is, and you can do what you want about it."

"Fine."

"First," he said, "you would like very much to have an enemy or enemies—"

"Ridiculous!"

"—Because it is the only alternative to having friends—"

"I have lots of friends!"

"—Because nobody wants to be completely ignored, to be an object for whom no one has really strong feelings. Hatred and love are the ultimate forms of human regard. Lacking one, and unable to achieve it, you sought the other. You wanted it so badly that you succeeded in convincing yourself it existed. But there is always a psychic pricetag on these things. Answering a genuine emotional need with a body of desire-surrogates does not produce real satisfaction, but anxiety, discomfort—because in these matters the psyche should be an open system. You did not seek outside yourself for human regard. You were closed off. You created that which you needed from the stuff of your own being. You are a man very much in need of strong relationships with other people."

"Manure!"

"Take it or leave it," said Render. "I suggest you take it."

"I've been paying you half a year to help find out who wants to kill me. Now you sit there and tell me I made the whole thing up to satisfy a desire to have someone hate me."

"Hate you, or love you. That's right."

"It's absurd! I meet so many people that I carry a pocket recorder and a lapel-camera, just so I can recall them all. . . ."

"Meeting quantities of people is hardly what I was speaking of.—Tell me, *did* that dream sequence have a strong meaning for you?"

Erikson was silent for several tickings of the huge wall-clock.

"Yes," he finally conceded, "it did. But your interpretation of the matter is still absurd. Granting though, just for the sake of argument, that what you say is correct—what would I do to get out of this bind?"

Render leaned back in his chair.

"Rechannel the energies that went into producing the thing. Meet some people as yourself, Joe Erikson, rather than Representative Erikson. Take up something you can do with other people—something non-political, and perhaps somewhat competitive—and make some real friends or enemies, preferably the former. I've encouraged you to do this all along."

"Then tell me something else."

"Gladly."

"Assuming you *are* right, why is it that I am neither liked nor hated, and never have been? I have a responsible position in the Legislature. I meet people all the time. Why am I so neutral a—thing?"

Highly familiar now with Erikson's career, Render had to push aside his true thoughts on the matter, as they were of no operational value. He wanted to cite him Dante's observations concerning the trimmers—those souls who, denied heaven for their lack of virtue, were also denied entrance to hell for a lack of significant vices—in short, the ones who trimmed their sails to move them with every wind of the times, who lacked direction, who were not really concerned toward which ports they were pushed. Such was Erikson's long and colorless career of migrant loyalties, of political reversals.

Render said:

"More and more people find themselves in such circumstances these days. It is due largely to the increasing complexity of society and the depersonalization of the individual into a sociometric unit. Even the act of cathecting toward other persons has grown more forced as a result. There are so many of us these days."

Erikson nodded, and Render smiled inwardly.

Sometimes the gruff line, and then the lecture . . .

"I've got the feeling you could be right," said Erikson. "Sometimes I *do* feel like what you just described—a unit, something depersonalized. . . ."

Render glanced at the clock.

"What you choose to do about it from here is, of course, your own decision to make. I think you'd be wasting your time to remain in analysis any longer. We are now both aware of the cause of your complaint. I can't take you by the hand and show you how to lead your life. I can indicate, I can commiserate—but no more deep probing. Make an appointment as soon as you feel a need to discuss your activities and relate them to my diagnosis."

"I will," nodded Erikson, "and—damn that dream! It got to me. You can make them seem as vivid as waking life—more vivid. . . . It may be a long while before I can forget it."

"I hope so."

"Okay, doctor." He rose to his feet, extended a hand. "I'll probably be back in a couple weeks. I'll give this socializing a fair try." He grinned at the word he normally frowned upon. "In fact, I'll start now. May I buy you a drink around the corner, downstairs?"

Render met the moist palm which seemed as weary of the performance as a lead actor in too successful a play. He felt almost sorry as he said, "Thank you, but I have an engagement."

Render helped him on with his coat then, handed him his hat and saw him to the door.

"Well, good night."

"Good night."

As the door closed soundlessly behind him, Render recrossed the dark Astrakhan to his mahogany fortress and flipped his cigarette into the southern hemisphere of a globe ashtray. He leaned back in his chair, hands behind his head, eyes closed.

"Of course it was more real than life," he informed no one in particular, "I shaped it."

Smiling, he reviewed the dream sequence step by step, wishing some of his former instructors could have witnessed it. It had been well-constructed and powerfully executed, as well as being precisely appropriate for the case at hand. But then, he was Render, the Shaper—one of the two hundred or so special analysts whose own psychic makeup permitted them to enter into neurotic patterns without carrying away more than an esthetic gratification from the mimesis of aberrance—a Sane Hatter.

Render stirred his recollections. He had been analyzed himself, analyzed and passed upon as a granite-willed, ultra-stable outsider—tough enough to weather the basilisk gaze of a fixation, walk unscathed amidst the chimarae of perversions, force dark Mother Medusa to close her eyes before the caduceus of his art. His own analysis had not been difficult. Nine years before (it seemed much longer) he had suffered a willing injection of novocain into the most painful area of his spirit. It was after the auto wreck, after the death of Ruth, and of Miranda, their daughter, that he had begun to feel detached. Perhaps he did not want to recover certain empathies; perhaps his own world was now based upon a certain rigidity of feeling. If this was true, he was wise enough in the ways of the mind to realize it, and perhaps he had decided that such a world had its own compensations.

His son Peter was now ten years old. He was attending a school of quality, and he penned his father a letter every week. The letters were becoming progressively literate, showing signs of a precociousness of which Render could not but approve. He would take the boy with him to Europe in the summer.

As for Jill—Jill DeVille (what a luscious, ridiculous name!—he loved her for it)—she was growing if anything, more interesting to him. (He wondered if this was an indication of early middle age.) He was vastly taken by her unmusical nasal voice, her sudden interest in architecture, her concern with the unremovable mole on the right side of her otherwise well-designed nose. He should really call her immediately and go in search of a new restaurant. For some reason though, he did not feel like it.

It had been several weeks since he had visited his club, The Partridge and Scalpel, and he felt a strong desire to eat from an oaken table, alone, in the split-level dining room with the three fireplaces, beneath the artificial torches and the boars' heads like gin ads. So he pushed his perforated membership card into the phone-slot on his desk and there were two buzzes behind the voice-screen.

"Hello, Partridge and Scalpel," said the voice. "May I help you?"

"Charles Render," he said. "I'd like a table in about half an hour."

"How many will there be?"

"Just me."

"Very good, sir. Half an hour, then.—That's 'Render'?—R-e-n-d-er-?"

"Right."

"Thank you."

He broke the connection and rose from his desk. Outside, the day had vanished.

The monoliths and the towers gave forth their own light now. A soft snow, like sugar, was sifting down through the shadows and transforming itself into beads on the windowpane.

Render shrugged into his overcoat, turned off the lights, locked the inner office. There was a note on Mrs. Hedges' blotter.

Miss DeVille called, it said.

He crumpled the note and tossed it into the waste-chute. He would call her tomorrow and say he had been working until late on his lecture.

He switched off the final light, clapped his hat onto his head and passed through the outer door, locking it as he went. The drop took him to the sub-subcellar where his auto was parked.

It was chilly in the sub-sub, and his footsteps seemed loud on the concrete as he passed among the parked vehicles. Beneath the glare of the naked lights, his S-7 Spinner was a sleek gray cocoon from which it seemed turbulent wings might at any moment emerge. The double row of antennae which fanned forward from the slope of its hood added to this feeling. Render thumbed open the door.

He touched the ignition and there was the sound of a lone bee awakening in a great hive. The door swung soundlessly shut as he raised the steering wheel and locked it into place. He spun up the spiral ramp and came to a rolling stop before the big overhead.

As the door rattled upward he lighted his destination screen and turned the knob that shifted the broadcast map.—Left to right, top to bottom, section by section he shifted it, until he located the portion of Carnegie Avenue he desired. He punched out its coordinates and lowered the wheel. The car switched over to monitor and moved out onto the highway marginal. Render lit a cigarette.

Pushing his seat back into the centerspace, he left all the windows transparent. It was pleasant to half-recline and watch the oncoming cars drift past him like swarms of fireflies. He pushed his hat back on his head and stared upward.

He could remember a time when he had loved snow, when it had reminded him of novels by Thomas Mann and music by Scandinavian composers. In his mind now, though, there was another element from which it could never be wholly dissociated. He could visualize so clearly the eddies of milk-white coldness that swirled about his old manual-steer auto, flowing into its fire-charred interior to rewhiten that which had been blackened; so clearly—as though he had walked toward it across a chalky lakebottom—it, the sunken wreck, and he, the diver—unable to open his mouth to speak, for fear of drowning; and he knew, whenever he looked upon falling snow, that somewhere skulls were whitening. But nine years had washed away much of the pain, and he also knew that the night was lovely.

He was sped along the wide, wide roads, shot across high bridges, their surfaces slick and gleaming beneath his lights, was woven through frantic cloverleafs and plunged into a tunnel whose dimly glowing walls blurred by him like a mirage. Finally, he switched the windows to opaque and closed his eyes.

He could not remember whether he had dozed for a moment or not, which meant he probably had. He felt the car slowing, and he moved the seat forward and turned on the windows again. Almost simultaneously, the cut-off buzzer sounded. He raised the steering wheel and pulled into the parking dome, stepped out onto the ramp and left the car to the parking unit, receiving his ticket from that box-headed robot which took its solemn revenge on mankind by sticking forth a cardboard tongue at everyone it served.

As always, the noises were as subdued as the lighting. The place seemed to absorb sound and convert it into warmth, to lull the tongue with aromas strong enough to be tasted, to hypnotize the ear with the vivid crackle of the triple hearths. Render was pleased to see that his favorite table, in the corner off the right of the smaller fireplace, had been held for him. He knew the menu from memory, but he studied it with zeal as he sipped a Manhattan and worked up an order to match his appetite. Shaping sessions always left him ravenously hungry.

"Doctor Render . . . ?"

"Yes?" He looked up.

"Doctor Shallot would like to speak with you," said the waiter.

"I don't know anyone named Shallot," he said. "Are you sure he doesn't want Bender? He's a surgeon from Metro who sometimes eats here. . . ."

The waiter shook his head.

"No, sir—'Render'. See here?" He extended a three-by-five card on which Render's full name was typed in capital letters. "Doctor Shallot has dined here nearly every night for the past two weeks," he explained, "and on each occasion has asked to be notified if you came in."

"Hm?" mused Render. "That's odd. Why didn't he just call me at my office?"

The waiter smiled and made a vague gesture.

"Well, tell him to come on over," he said, gulping his Manhattan, "and bring me another of these."

"Unfortunately, Doctor Shallot is blind," explained the waiter. "It would be easier if you—"

"All right, sure." Render stood up, relinquishing his favorite table with a strong premonition that he would not be returning to it that evening.

"Lead on."

They threaded their way among the diners, heading up to the next level. A familiar face said "hello" from a table set back against the wall, and Render nodded a greeting to a former seminar pupil whose name was Jurgens or Jirkans or something like that.

He moved on, into the smaller dining room wherein only two tables were occupied. No, three. There was one set in the corner at the far end of the darkened bar, partly masked by an ancient suit of armor. The waiter was heading him in that direction.

They stopped before the table and Render stared down into the darkened glasses that had tilted upward as they approached. Doctor Shallot was a woman, somewhere in the vicinity of her early thirties. Her low bronze bangs did not fully conceal the spot of silver which she wore on her forehead like a caste-mark. Render inhaled, and her head jerked slightly as the tip of his cigarette flared. She appeared to be staring straight up into his eyes. It was an uncomfortable feeling, even knowing that all she could distinguish of him was that which her minute photoelectric cell transmitted to her visual cortex over the hair-fine wire implants attached to that oscillator convertor: in short, the glow of his cigarette.

"Doctor Shallot, this is Doctor Render," the waiter was saying.

"Good evening," said Render.

"Good evening," she said. "My name is Eileen and I've wanted very badly to meet you." He thought he detected a slight quaver in her voice. "Will you join me for dinner?"

"My pleasure," he acknowledged, and the waiter drew out the chair.

Render sat down, noting that the woman across from him already had a drink. He reminded the waiter of his second Manhattan.

"Have you ordered yet?" he inquired.

"No."

". . . And two menus—" he started to say, then bit his tongue.

"Only one," she smiled.

"Make it none," he amended, and recited the menu.

They ordered. Then:

"Do you always do that?"

"What?"

"Carry menus in your head."

"Only a few," he said, "for awkward occasions. What was it you wanted to see—talk to me about?"

"You're a neuroparticipant therapist," she stated, "a Shaper."

"And you are—?"

"—a resident in psychiatry at State Psych. I have a year remaining."

"You knew Sam Riscomb then."

"Yes, he helped me get my appointment. He was my adviser."

"He was a very good friend of mine. We studied together at Menninger."

She nodded.

"I'd often heard him speak of you—that's one of the reasons I wanted to meet you. He's responsible for encouraging me to go ahead with my plans, despite my handicap."

Render stared at her. She was wearing a dark green dress which appeared to be made of velvet. About three inches to the left of the bodice was a pin which might have been gold. It displayed a red stone which the outline of a goblet was cast. Or was it really two profiles that were outlined, staring through the stone at one another? It seemed vaguely familiar to him, but he could not place it at the moment. It glittered expensively in the dim light.

Render accepted his drink from the waiter.

"I want to become a neuroparticipant therapist," she told him.

And if she had possessed vision Render would have thought she was staring at him, hoping for some response in his expression. He could not quite calculate what she wanted him to say.

"I commend your choice," he said, "and I respect your ambition." He tried to put his smile into his voice. "It is not an easy thing, of course, not all of the requirements being academic ones."

"I know," she said. "But then, I have been blind since birth and it was not an easy thing to come this far."

"Since birth?" he repeated. "I thought you might have lost your sight recently. You did your undergrad work then, and went on through med school without eyes . . . That's—rather impressive."

"Thank you," she said, "but it isn't. Not really. I heard about the first neuroparticipants—Bartelmetz and the rest—when I was a child, and I decided then that I wanted to be one. My life ever since has been governed by that desire."

"What did you do in the labs?" he inquired. "—Not being able to see a specimen, look through a microscope . . . ? Or all that reading?"

"I hired people to read my assignments to me. I taped everything. The school understood that I wanted to go into psychiatry and they permitted a special arrangement for labs. I've been guided through the dissection of cadavers by lab assistants, and I've had everything described to me. I can tell things by touch . . . and I have a memory like yours with the menu," she smiled. " 'The quality of psychoparticipation phenomena can only be gauged by the therapist himself, at that moment outside of time and space as we normally know it, when he stands in the midst of a world erected from the stuff of another man's dreams, recognizes there the non-Euclidian architecture of aberrance, and then takes his patient by the hand and tours the landscape . . . If he can lead him back to the common earth, then his judgments were sound, his actions valid.' "

"From *Why No Psychometrics in This Place,*" reflected Render.

"—by Charles Render, M.D."

"Our dinner is already moving in this direction," he noted, picking up his drink as the speed-cooked meal was pushed toward them in the kitchen-buoy.

"That's one of the reasons I wanted to meet you," she continued, raising her glass as the dishes rattled before her. "I want you to help me become a Shaper."

Her shaded eyes, as vacant as a statue's, sought him again.

"Yours is a completely unique situation," he commented. "There has never been a congenitally blind neuroparticipant—for obvious reasons. I'd have to consider all the aspects of the situation before I could advise you. Let's eat now, though. I'm starved."

"All right. But my blindness does not mean that I have never seen."

He did not ask her what she meant by that, because prime ribs were standing in front of him now and there was a bottle of Chambertin at his elbow. He did pause long enough to notice though, as she raised her left hand from beneath the table, that she wore no rings.

"I wonder if it's still snowing," he commented as they drank their coffee. "It was coming down pretty hard when I pulled into the dome."

"I hope so," she said, "even though it diffuses the light and I can't 'see' anything at all through it. I like to feel it falling about me and blowing against my face."

"How do you get about?"

"My dog, Sigmund—I gave him the night off," she smiled, "—he can guide me anywhere. He's a mutie Shepherd."

"Oh?" Render grew curious. "Can he talk much?"

She nodded.

"That operation wasn't as successful on him as on some of them, though. He has a vocabulary of about four hundred words, but I think it causes him pain to speak. He's quite intelligent. You'll have to meet him sometime."

Render began speculating immediately. He had spoken with such animals at recent medical conferences, and had been startled by their combination of reasoning ability and their devotion to their handlers. Much chromosome tinkering, followed by delicate embryo-surgery, was required to give a dog a brain capacity greater than a chimpanzee's. Several followup operations were necessary to produce vocal abilities. Most such experiments ended in failure, and the dozen or so puppies a year on which they succeeded were valued in the neighborhood of a hundred thousand dollars each. He realized then, as he lit a cigarette and held the light for a moment, that the stone in Miss Shallot's medallion was a genuine ruby. He began to suspect that her admission to a medical school might, in addition to her academic record, have been based upon a sizeable endowment to the college of her choice. Perhaps he was being unfair though, he chided himself.

"Yes," he said, "we might do a paper on canine neuroses. Does he ever refer to his father as 'that son of a female Shepherd'?"

"He never met his father," she said, quite soberly. "He was raised apart from other dogs. His attitude could hardly be typical. I don't think you'll ever learn the functional psychology of the dog from a mutie."

"I imagine you're right," he dismissed it. "More coffee?"

"No, thanks."

Deciding it was time to continue the discussion, he said, "So you want to be a Shaper. . . ."

"Yes."

"I hate to be the one to destroy anybody's high ambitions," he told her. "Like poison, I hate it. Unless they have no foundation at all in reality. Then I can be ruthless. So—honestly, frankly, and in all sincerity, I do not see how it could ever be managed. Perhaps you're a fine psychiatrist—but in my opinion, it is a physical and mental impossibility for you ever to become a neuroparticipant. As for my reasons—"

"Wait," she said. "Not here, please. Humor me. I'm tired of this stuffy place—take me somewhere else to talk. I think I might be able to convince you there *is* a way."

"Why not?" he shrugged. "I have plenty of time. Sure—you call it. Where?"

"Blindspin?"

He suppressed an unwilling chuckle at the expression, but she laughed aloud.

"Fine," he said, "but I'm still thirsty."

A bottle of champagne was tallied and he signed the check despite her protests. It arrived in a colorful "Drink While You Drive" basket, and they stood then, and she was tall, but he was taller.

Blindspin.

A single name of a multitude of practices centered about the auto-driven auto. Flashing across the country in the sure hands of an invisible chauffeur, windows all opaque, night dark, sky high, tires assailing the road below like four phantom buzzsaws—and starting from scratch and ending in the same place, and never knowing where you are going or where you have been—it is possible, for a moment, to kindle some feeling of individuality in the coldest brainpan, to produce a momentary awareness of self by virtue of an apartness from all but a sense of motion. This is because movement through darkness is the ultimate abstraction of life itself—at least that's what one of the Vital Comedians said, and everybody in the place laughed.

Actually, now, the phenomenon known as blindspin first became prevalent (as might be suspected) among certain younger members of the community, when monitored highways deprived them of the means to exercise their automobiles in some of the more individualistic ways which had come to be frowned upon by the National Traffic Control Authority. Something had to be done.

It was.

The first, disastrous reaction involved the simple engineering feat of disconnecting the broadcast control unit after one had entered onto a monitored highway. This resulted in the car's vanishing from the ken of the monitor and passing back into the control of its occupants. Jealous as a deity, a monitor will not tolerate that which denies its programmed omniscience: it will thunder and lightning in the Highway Control Station nearest the point of last contact, sending winged seraphs in search of that which has slipped from sight.

Often, however, this was too late in happening, for the roads are many and well-paved. Escape from detection was, at first, relatively easy to achieve.

Other vehicles, though, necessarily behave as if a rebel has no actual existence. Its presence cannot be allowed for.

Boxed-in on a heavily traveled section of roadway, the offender is subject to immediate annihilation in the event of any overall speedup or shift in traffic pattern which involves movement through his theoretically vacant position. This, in the early days of monitor-controls, caused a rapid series of collisions. Monitoring devices later became far more sophisticated, and mechanized cutoffs reduced the collision incidence subsequent to such an action. The quality of the pulpefactions and contusions which did occur, however, remained unaltered.

The next reaction was based on a thing which had been overlooked because it was obvious. The monitors took people where they wanted to go only because people told them they wanted to go there. A person pressing a random series of coordinates, without reference to any map, would either be left with a stalled automobile and a "RECHECK YOUR COORDINATES" light, or would suddenly be whisked away in any direction. The latter possesses a certain romantic appeal in that it offers speed, unexpected sights, and free hands. Also, it is perfectly legal; and it is possible to navigate all over two continents in this manner, if one is possessed of sufficient wherewithal and gluteal stamina.

As is the case in all such matters, the practice diffused upwards through the age brackets. School teachers who only drove on Sundays fell into disrepute as selling points for used autos. Such is the way a world ends, said the entertainer.

End or no, the car designed to move on monitored highways is a mobile efficiency unit, complete with latrine, cupboard, refrigerator compartment and gaming table. It also sleeps two with ease and four with some crowding. On occasion, three can be a real crowd.

Render drove out of the dome and into the marginal aisle. He halted the car.

"Want to jab some coordinates?" he asked.

"You do it. My fingers know too many."

Render punched random buttons. The Spinner moved onto the highway. Render asked speed of the vehicle then, and it moved into the high-acceleration lane.

The Spinner's lights burnt holes in the darkness. The city backed away fast; it was a smouldering bonfire on both sides of the road, stirred by sudden gusts of wind, hidden by white swirlings, obscured by the steady fall of gray ash. Render knew his speed was only about sixty percent of what it would have been on a clear, dry night.

He did not blank the windows, but leaned back and stared out through them. Eileen "looked" ahead into what light there was. Neither of them said anything for ten or fifteen minutes.

The city shrank to sub-city as they sped on. After a time, short sections of open road began to appear.

"Tell me what it looks like outside," she said.

"Why didn't you ask me to describe your dinner, or the suit of armor beside our table?"

"Because I tasted one and felt the other. This is different."

"There is snow falling outside. Take it away and what you have left is black."

"What else?"

"There is slush on the road. When it starts to freeze, traffic will drop to a crawl unless we outrun this storm. The slush looks like an old, dark syrup, just starting to get sugary on top."

"Anything else?"

"That's it, lady."

"Is it snowing harder or less hard than when we left the club?"

"Harder, I should say."

"Would you pour me a drink?" she asked him.

"Certainly."

They turned their seats inward and Render raised the table. He fetched two glasses from the cupboard.

"Your health," said Render, after he had poured.

"Here's looking at you."

Render downed his drink. She sipped hers. He waited for her next comment.

He knew that two cannot play at the Socratic game, and he expected more questions before she said what she wanted to say.

She said: "What is the most beautiful thing you have ever seen?"

Yes, he decided, he had guessed correctly.

He replied without hesitation: "The sinking of Atlantis."

"I was serious."

"So was I."

"Would you care to elaborate?"

"I sank Atlantis," he said, "personally.

"It was about three years ago. And God! it was lovely! It was all ivory towers and golden minarets and silver balconies. There were bridges of opal, and crimson pendants, and a milk-white river flowing between lemon-colored banks. There were jade steeples, and trees as old as the world tickling the bellies of clouds, and ships in the great sea-harbor of Xanadu, as delicately constructed as musical instruments, all swaying with the tides. The twelve princes of the realm held court in the dozen-pillared Colliseum of the Zodiac, to listen to a Greek tenor saxophonist play at sunset.

"The Greek, of course, was a patient of mine—paranoiac. The etiology of the thing is rather complicated, but that's what I wandered into inside his mind. I gave him free rein for a while, and in the end I had to split Atlantis in half and sink it full fathom five. He's playing again and you've doubtless heard his sounds, if you like such sounds at all. He's good. I still see him periodically, but he is no longer the last descendent of the greatest minstrel of Atlantis. He's just a fine, late twentieth-century saxman.

"Sometimes though, as I look back on the apocalypse I worked within his vision of grandeur, I experience a fleeting sense of lost beauty—because, for a single moment, his abnormally intense feelings were my feelings, and he felt that his dream was the most beautiful thing in the world."

He refilled their glasses.

"That wasn't exactly what I meant," she said.

"I know."

"I meant something real."

"It was more real than real, I assure you."

"I don't doubt it, but . . ."

"—But I destroyed the foundation you were laying for your argument. Okay, I apologize. I'll hand it back to you. Here's something that could be real:

"We are moving along the edge of a great bowl of sand," he said. "Into it, the snow is gently drifting. In the spring the snow will melt, the waters will run down into the earth, or be evaporated away by the heat of the sun. Then only the sand will remain. Nothing grows in the sand, except for an occasional cactus. Nothing lives here but snakes, a few birds, insects, burrowing things, and a wandering coyote or two. In the afternoon these things will look for shade. Any place where there's an old fence post or a rock or a skull or a cactus to block out the sun, there you will witness life cowering before the elements. But the colors are beyond belief, and the elements are more lovely, almost, than the things they destroy."

"There is no such place near here," she said.

"If I say it, then there is. Isn't there? I've seen it."

"Yes . . . you're right."

"And it doesn't matter if it's a painting by a woman named O'Keefe, or something right outside our window, does it? If I've seen it?"

"I acknowledge the truth of the diagnosis," she said. "Do you want to speak it for me?"

"No, go ahead."

He refilled the small glasses once more.

"The damage is in my eyes," she told him, "not my brain."

He lit her cigarette.

"I can see with other eyes if I can enter other brains."

He lit his own cigarette.

"Neuroparticipation is based upon the fact that two nervous systems can share the same impulses, the same fantasies. . . ."

"*Controlled* fantasies."

"I could perform therapy and at the same time experience genuine visual impressions."

"No," said Render.

"You don't know what it's like to be cut off from a whole area of stimuli! To know that a Mongoloid idiot can experience something you can never know—and that he cannot appreciate it because, like you, he was condemned before birth in a court of biological happenstance, in a place where there is no justice—only fortuity, pure and simple."

"The universe did not invent justice. Man did. Unfortunately, man must reside in the universe."

"I'm not asking the universe to help me—I'm asking you."

"I'm sorry," said Render.

"Why won't you help me?"

"At this moment you are demonstrating my main reason."

"Which is . . . ?"

"Emotion. This thing means far too much to you. When the therapist is in-phase with a patient he is narcoelectrically removed from most of his own bodily sensations. This is necessary—because his mind must be completely absorbed by the task at hand. It is also necessary that his emotions undergo a similar suspension. This, of course, is impossible in the one sense that a person always emotes to some degree. But the therapist's emotions are sublimated into a generalized feeling of exhilaration—or, as in my own case, into an artistic reverie. With you, however, the 'seeing' would be too much. You would be in constant danger of losing control of the dream."

"I disagree with you."

"Of course you do. But the fact remains that you would be dealing, and dealing constantly, with the abnormal. The power of a neurosis is unimaginable to ninety-nine point et cetera percent of the population, because we can never adequately judge the intensity of our own—let alone those of others, when we only see them from the outside. That is why no neuroparticipant will ever undertake to treat a full-blown psychotic. The few pioneers in that area are all themselves in therapy today. It would be like diving into a maelstrom. If the therapist loses the upper hand in an intense session, he becomes the Shaped rather than the Shaper. The synapses respond like a fission reaction when nervous impulses are artificially augmented. The transference effect is almost instantaneous.

"I did an awful lot of skiing five years ago. This is because I was a claustrophobe. I had to run and it took me six months to beat the thing—all because of one tiny lapse that occurred in a measureless fraction of an instant. I had to refer the patient to another therapist. And this was only a minor repercussion.—

If you were to go gaga over the scenery, girl, you could wind up in a rest home for life."

She finished her drink and Render refilled the glass. The night raced by. They had left the city far behind them, and the road was open and clear. The darkness eased more and more of itself between the falling flakes. The Spinner picked up speed.

"All right," she admitted, "maybe you're right. Still, though, I think you can help me."

"How?" he asked.

"Accustom me to seeing, so that the images will lose their novelty, the emotions wear off. Accept me as a patient and rid me of my sight-anxiety. Then what you have said so far will cease to apply. I will be able to undertake the training then, and give my full attention to therapy. I'll be able to sublimate the sight-pleasure into something else."

Render wondered.

Perhaps it could be done. It would be a difficult undertaking, though.

It might also make therapeutic history.

No one was really qualified to try it, because no one had ever tried it before.

But Eileen Shallot was a rarity—no, a unique item—for it was likely she was the only person in the world who combined the necessary technical background with the unique problem.

He drained his glass, refilled it, refilled hers.

He was still considering the problem as the "RECOORDINATE" light came on and the car pulled into a cutoff and stood there. He switched off the buzzer and sat there for a long while, thinking.

It was not often that other persons heard him acknowledge his feelings regarding his skill. His colleagues considered him modest. Offhand, though, it might be noted that he was aware that the day a better neuroparticipant began practicing would be the day that a troubled homo sapien was to be treated by something but immeasurably less than angels.

Two drinks remained. Then he tossed the emptied bottle into the backbin.

"You know something?" he finally said.

"What?"

"It might be worth a try."

He swiveled about then and leaned forward to recoordinate, but she was there first. As he pressed the buttons and the S-7 swung around, she kissed him. Below her dark glasses her cheeks were moist.

II

The suicide bothered him more than it should have, and Mrs. Lambert had called the day before to cancel her appointment. So Render decided to spend the morning being pensive. Accordingly, he entered the office wearing a cigar and a frown.

"Did you see . . . ?" asked Mrs. Hedges.

"Yes." He pitched his coat onto the table that stood in the far corner of the room. He crossed to the window, stared down. "Yes," he repeated, "I was driving by with my windows clear. They were still cleaning up when I passed."

"Did you know him?"

"I don't even know the name yet. How could I?"

"Priss Tully just called me—she's a receptionist for that engineering outfit up on the eighty-sixth. She says it was James Irizarry, and ad designer who had offices down the hall from them—That's a long way to fall. He must have been unconscious when he hit, huh? He bounced off the building. If you open the window and lean out you can see—off to the left there—where . . ."

"Never mind, Bennie. —Your friend have any idea why he did it?"

"Not really. His secretary came running up the hall, screaming. Seems she went in his office to see him about some drawings, just as he was getting up over the sill. There was a note on his board. 'I've had everything I wanted,' it said. 'Why wait around?' Sort of funny, huh? I don't mean *funny*. . . . "

"Yeah. —Know anything about his personal affairs?"

"Married. Coupla kids. Good professional rep. Lots of business. Sober as anybody. —He could afford an office in this building."

"Good Lord!" Render turned. "Have you got a case file there or something?"

"You know," she shrugged her thick shoulders, "I've got friends all over this hive. We always talk when things go slow. Prissy's my sister-in-law, anyhow—"

"You mean that if I dived through this window right now, my current biography would make the rounds in the next five minutes?"

"Probably," she twisted her bright lips into a smile, "give or take a couple. But don't do it today, huh? —You know, it would be kind of anticlimactic, and it wouldn't get the same coverage as a solus.

"Anyhow," she continued, "you're a mind-mixer. You wouldn't do it."

"You're betting against statistics," he observed. "The medical profession, along with attorneys, manages about three times as many as most other work areas."

"Hey!" She looked worried. "Go 'way from my window!

"I'd have to go to work for Dr. Hanson then," she added, "and he's a slob."

He moved to her desk.

"I never know when to take you seriously," she decided.

"I appreciate your concern," he nodded, "indeed I do. As a matter of fact, I have never been statistic-prone—I should have repercussed out of the neuropy game four years ago."

"You'd be a headline, though," she mused. "All those reporters asking me about you . . . Hey, why do they do it, huh?"

"Who?"

"Anybody."

"How should I know, Bennie? I'm only a humble psyche-stirrer. If I could pinpoint a general underlying cause—and then maybe figure a way to anticipate the thing—why, it might even be better than my jumping, for newscopy. But I can't do it, because there is no single, simple reason—I don't think."

"Oh."

"About thirty-five years ago it was the ninth leading cause of death in the United States. Now it's number six for North and South America. I think it's seventh in Europe."

"And nobody will ever really know why Irizarry jumped?"

Render swung a chair backward and seated himself. He knocked an ash into her petite and gleaming tray. She emptied it into the waste-chute, hastily, and coughed a significant cough.

"Oh, one can always speculate," he said, "and one in my profession will. The first thing to consider would be the personality traits which might predispose a man to periods of depression. People who keep their emotions under rigid control, people who are conscientious and rather compulsively concerned with small matters . . ." He knocked another fleck of ash into her tray and watched as she reached out to dump it, then quickly drew her hand back again. He grinned an evil grin. "In short," he finished, "some of the characteristics of people in professions which require individual, rather than group performance—medicine, law, the arts."

She regarded him speculatively.

"Don't worry though," he chuckled, "I'm pleased as hell with life."

"You're kind of down in the mouth this morning."

"Pete called me. He broke his ankle yesterday in gym class. They ought to supervise those things more closely. I'm thinking of changing his school."

"Again?"

"Maybe. I'll see. The headmaster is going to call me this afternoon. I don't like to keep shuffling him, but I do want him to finish school in one piece."

"A kid can't grow up without an accident or two. It's—statistics."

"Statistics aren't the same thing as destiny, Bennie. Everybody makes his own."

"Statistics or destiny?"

"Both, I guess."

"I think that if something's going to happen, it's going to happen."

"I don't. I happen to think that the human will, backed by a sane mind can exercise some measure of control over events. If I didn't think so, I wouldn't be in the racket I'm in."

"The world's a machine—you know—cause, effect. Statistics do imply the prob—"

"The human mind is not a machine, and I do not know cause and effect. Nobody does."

"You have a degree in chemistry, as I recall. You're a scientist, Doc."

"So I'm a Trotskyite deviationist," he smiled, stretching, "and you were once a ballet teacher." He got to his feet and picked up his coat.

"By the way, Miss DeVille called, left a message. She said: 'How about St. Moritz?' "

"Too ritzy," he decided aloud. "It's going to be Davos."

Because the suicide bothered him more than it should have, Render closed the door to his office and turned off the windows and turned on the phonograph. He put on the desk light only.

How has the quality of human life been changed, he wrote, *since the beginnings of the industrial revolution?*

He picked up the paper and reread the sentence. It was the topic he had been asked to discuss that coming Saturday. As was typical in such cases he did not know what to say because he had too much to say, and only an hour to say it in.

He got up and began to pace the office, now filled with Beethoven's Eighth Symphony.

"The power to hurt," he said, snapping on a lapel microphone and activating his recorder, "has evolved in a direct relationship to technological advancement." His imaginary audience grew quiet. He smiled. "Man's potential for working simple mayhem has been multiplied by mass-production; his capacity for injuring the psyche through personal contacts has expanded in an exact ratio to improved communication facilities. But these are all matters of common knowledge, and are not the things I wish to consider tonight. Rather, I should like to discuss what I choose to call autopsychomimesis—the self-generated anxiety complexes which on first scrutiny appear quite similar to classic patterns, but which actually represent radical dispersions of psychic energy. They are peculiar to our times. . . ."

He paused to dispose of his cigar and formulate his next words.

"Autopsychomimesis," he thought aloud, "a self-perpetuated imitation complex—almost an attention-getting affair. —A jazzman, for example, who acted hopped-up half the time, even though he had never used an addictive narcotic and only dimly remembered anyone who had—because all the stimulants and tranquilizers of today are quite benign. Like Quixote, he aspired after a legend when his music alone should have been sufficient outlet for his tensions.

"Or my Korean War Orphan, alive today by virtue of the Red Cross and UNICEF and foster parents whom he never met. He wanted a family so badly that he made one up. And what then? —He hated his imaginary father and he loved his imaginary mother quite dearly—for he was a highly intelligent boy, and he too longed after the half-true complexes of tradition. Why?

"Today, everyone is sophisticated enough to understand the time-honored patterns of psychic disturbance. Today, many of the reasons for those disturbances have been removed—not as radically as my now-adult war orphan's, but with as remarkable an effect. We are living in a neurotic past. —Again, why? Because our present times are geared to physical health, security, and well-being. We have abolished hunger, though the backwoods orphan would still rather receive a package of food concentrates from a human being who cares for him than to obtain a warm meal from an automat unit in the middle of the jungle.

"Physical welfare is now every man's right in excess. The reaction to this has occurred in the area of mental health. Thanks to technology, the reasons for many of the old social problems have passed, and along with them went many of the reasons for psychic distress. But between the black of yesterday and the white of tomorrow is the great gray of today, filled with nostalgia and fear of the future, which cannot be expressed on a purely material plane, is now being represented by a willful seeking after historical anxiety-modes. . . ."

The phone-box buzzed briefly. Render did not hear it over the Eighth.

"We are afraid of what we do not know," he continued, "and tomorrow is a very great unknown. My own specialized area of psychiatry did not even exist thirty years ago. Science is capable of advancing itself so rapidly now that there is a genuine public uneasiness—I might even say 'distress'—as to the logical outcome: the total mechanization of everything in the world. . . ."

He passed near the desk as the phone buzzed again. He switched off his microphone and softened the Eighth.

"Hello?"

"Saint Moritz," she said.

"Davos," he replied firmly.

"Charlie, you are most exasperating!"

"Jill, dear—so are you."

"Shall we discuss it tonight?"

"There is nothing to discuss!"

"You'll pick me up at five, though?"

He hesitated, then:

"Yes, at five. How come the screen is blank?"

"I've had my hair fixed. I'm going to surprise you again."

He suppressed an idiot chuckle, said, "Pleasantly, I hope. Okay, see you then," waited for her "good-bye," and broke the connection.

He transpared the windows, turned off the light on his desk, and looked outside.

Gray again overhead, and many slow flakes of snow—wandering, not being blown about much—moving downward and then losing themselves in the tumult. . . .

He also saw, when he opened the window and leaned out, the place off to the left where Irizarry had left his next-to-last mark on the world.

He closed the window and listened to the rest of the symphony. It had been a week since he had gone blindspinning with Eileen. Her appointment was for one o'clock.

He remembered her fingertips brushing over his face, like leaves, or the bodies of insects, learning his appearance in the ancient manner of the blind. The memory was not altogether pleasant. He wondered why.

Far below, a patch of hosed pavement was blank once again; under a thin, fresh shroud of white, it was slippery as glass. A building custodian hurried outside and spread salt on it, before someone slipped and hurt themself.

Sigmund was the myth of Fenris come alive. After Render had instructed Mrs. Hedges, "Show them in," the door had begun to open, was suddenly pushed wider, and a pair of smoky yellow eyes stared in at him. The eyes were set in a strangely misshapen dog-skull.

Sigmund's was not a low canine brow, slanting up slightly from the muzzle; it was a high, shaggy cranium making the eyes appear even more deep-set than they actually were. Render shivered slightly at the size and aspect of that head. The muties he had seen had all been puppies. Sigmund was full-grown, and his gray-black fur had a tendency to bristle, which made him appear somewhat larger than a normal specimen of the breed.

He stared in at Render in a very un-doglike way and made a growling noise which sounded too much like, "Hello, doctor," to have been an accident.

Render nodded and stood.

"Hello, Sigmund," he said. "Come in."

The dog turned his head, sniffing the air of the room—as though deciding whether or not to trust his ward within its confines. Then he returned his stare to Render, dipped his head in an affirmative, and shouldered the door open. Perhaps the entire encounter had taken only one disconcerting second.

Eileen followed him, holding lightly to the double-leashed harness. The dog padded soundlessly across the thick rug—head low, as though he were stalking something. His eyes never left Render's.

"So this is Sigmund . . . ? How are you, Eileen?"

"Fine. —Yes, he wanted very badly to come along, and *I* wanted you to meet him."

Render led her to a chair and seated her. She unsnapped the double guide from the dog's harness and placed it on the floor. Sigmund sat down beside it and continued to stare at Render.

"How is everything at State Psych?"

"Same as always.—May I bum a cigarette, Doctor? I forgot mine."

He placed it between her fingers, furnished a light. She was wearing a dark blue suit and her glasses were flame blue. The silver spot on her forehead reflected the glow of his lighter; she continued to stare at that point in space after he had withdrawn his hand. Her shoulder-length hair appeared a trifle lighter than it had seemed on the night they met; today it was like a fresh-minted copper coin.

Render seated himself on the corner of his desk, drawing up his world-ashtray with his toe.

"You told me before that being blind did not mean that you had never seen. I didn't ask you to explain it then. But I'd like to ask you now."

"I had a neuroparticipation session with Dr. Riscomb," she told him, "before he had his accident. He wanted to accommodate my mind to visual impressions. Unfortunately, there was never a second session."

"I see. What did you do in that session?"

She crossed her ankles and Render noted they were well-turned.

"Colors, mostly. The experience was quite overwhelming."

"How well do you remember them? How long ago was it?"

"About six months ago—and I shall never forget them. I have even dreamed in color patterns since then."

"How often?"

"Several times a week."

"What sort of associations do they carry?"

"Nothing special. They just come into my mind along with other stimuli now—in a pretty haphazard way."

"How?"

"Well, for instance, when you ask me a question it's a sort of yellowish-orangish pattern that I 'see.' Your greeting was a kind of silvery thing. Now that you're just sitting there listening to me, saying nothing, I associate you with a deep, almost violet, blue."

Sigmund shifted his gaze to the desk and stared at the side panel.

Can he hear the recorder spinning inside? wondered Render. *And if he can, can he guess what it is and what it's doing?*

If so, the dog would doubtless tell Eileen—not that she was unaware of what was now an accepted practice—and she might not like being reminded that he considered her case as therapy, rather than a mere mechanical adaptation process. If he thought it would do any good (he smiled inwardly at the notion), he would talk to the dog in private about it.

Inwardly, he shrugged.

"I'll construct a rather elementary fantasy world then," he said finally, "and introduce you to some basic forms today."

She smiled; and Render looked down at the myth who crouched by her side, its tongue a piece of beefsteak hanging over a picket fence.

Is he smiling too?

"Thank you," she said.

Sigmund wagged his tail.

"Well then," Render disposed of his cigarette near Madagascar, "I'll fetch out the 'egg' now and test it. In the meantime," he pressed an unobtrusive button, "perhaps some music would prove relaxing."

She started to reply, but a Wagnerian overture snuffed out the words. Render jammed the button again, and there was a moment of silence during which he said, "Heh heh. Thought Respighi was next."

It took two more pushes for him to locate some Roman pines.

"You could have left him on," she observed. "I'm quite fond of Wagner."

"No thanks," he said, opening the closet, "I'd keep stepping in all those piles of leitmotifs."

The great egg drifted out into the office, soundless as a cloud. Render heard a soft growl behind as he drew it toward the desk. He turned quickly.

Like the shadow of a bird, Sigmund had gotten to his feet, crossed the room, and was already circling the machine and sniffing at it—tail taut, ears flat, teeth bared.

"Easy, Sig," said Render. "It's an Omnichannel Neural T & R Unit. It won't bite or anything like that. It's just a machine, like a car, or a teevee, or a dishwasher. That's what we're going to use today to show Eileen what some things look like."

"Don't like it," rumbled the dog.

"Why?"

Sigmund had no reply, so he stalked back to Eileen and laid his head in her lap.

"Don't like it," he repeated, looking up at her.

"Why?"

"No words," he decided. "We go home now?"

"No," she answered him. "You're going to curl up in the corner and take a nap, and I'm going to curl up in that machine and do the same thing—sort of."

"No good," he said, tail drooping.

"Go on now," she pushed him, "lie down and behave yourself."

He acquiesced, but he whined when Render blanked the windows and touched the button which transformed his desk into the operator's seat.

He whined once more—when the egg, connected now to an outlet, broke in the middle and the top slid back and up, revealing the interior.

Render seated himself. His chair became a contour couch and moved in halfway beneath the console. He sat upright and it moved back again, becoming a chair. He touched a part of the desk and half the ceiling disengaged itself, reshaped itself, and lowered to hover overhead like a huge bell. He stood and moved around to the side of the ro-womb. Respighi spoke of pines and such, and Render disengaged an earphone from beneath the egg and leaned back across his desk. Blocking one ear with his shoulder and pressing the microphone to the other, he played upon the buttons with his free hand. Leagues of surf drowned the tone poem; miles of traffic overrode it; a great clanging bell sent fracture lines running through it; and the feedback said: ". . . Now that you are just sitting there listening to me, saying nothing, I associate you with a deep, almost violet, blue. . . ."

He switched to the face mask and monitored, *one* cinnamon, *two*—leaf mold, *three*—deep reptilian musk . . . and down through thirst, and the tastes of honey and vinegar and salt, and back on up through lilacs and wet concrete, a before-the-storm whiff of ozone, and all the basic olfactory and gustatory cues for morning, afternoon, and evening in the town.

The couch floated normally in its pool of mercury, magnetically stabilized by the walls of the egg. He set the tapes.

The ro-womb was in perfect condition.

"Okay," said Render, turning, "everything checks."

She was just placing her glasses atop her folded garments. She had undressed while Render was testing the machine. He was perturbed by her narrow waist, her large, dark-pointed breasts, her long legs. She was too well-formed for a woman her height, he decided.

He realized though, as he stared at her, that his main annoyance was, of course, the fact that she was his patient.

"Ready here," she said, and he moved to her side.

He took her elbow and guided her to the machine. Her fingers explored its interior. As he helped her enter the unit, he saw that her eyes were a vivid seagreen. Of this, too, he disapproved.

"Comfortable?"

"Yes."

"Okay then, we're set. I'm going to close it now. Sweet dreams."

The upper shell dropped slowly. Closed, it grew opaque, then dazzling. Render was staring down at his own distorted reflection.

He moved back in the direction of his desk.

Sigmund was on his feet, blocking the way.

Render reached down to pat his head, but the dog jerked it aside.

"Take me, with," he growled.

"I'm afraid that can't be done, old fellow," said Render. "Besides, we're not really going anywhere. We'll just be dozing, right here, in this room."

The dog did not seem mollified.

"Why?"

Render sighed. An argument with a dog was about the most ludicrous thing he could imagine when sober.

"Sig," he said, "I'm trying to help her learn what things look like. You doubtless do a fine job guiding her around in this world which she cannot see—but she needs to know what it looks like now, and I'm going to show her."

"Then she, will not, need me."

"Of course she will." Render almost laughed. The pathetic thing was here bound so closely to the absurd thing that he could not help it. "I can't restore her sight," he explained. "I'm just going to transfer her some sight-abstractions—sort of lend her my eyes for a short time. Savvy?"

"No," said the dog. "Take mine."

Render turned off the music.

The whole mutie-master relationship might be worth six volumes, he decided, *in German.*

He pointed to the far corner.

"Lie down, over there, like Eileen told you. This isn't going to take long, and when it's all over you're going to leave the same way you came—you leading. Okay?"

Sigmund did not answer, but he turned and moved off to the corner, tail drooping again.

Render seated himself and lowered the hood, the operator's modified version of the ro-womb. He was alone before the ninety white buttons and the two red ones. The world ended in the blackness beyond the console. He loosened his necktie and unbuttoned his collar.

He removed the helmet from its receptacle and checked its leads. Donning it then, he swung the half-mask up over his lower face and dropped the darksheet down to meet with it. He rested his right arm in the sling, and with a single tapping gesture, he eliminated his patient's consciousness.

A Shaper does not press white buttons consciously. He wills conditions. Then deeply implanted muscular reflexes exert an almost imperceptible pressure against the sensitive arm-sling, which glides into the proper position and encourages an extended finger to move forward. A button is pressed. The sling moves on.

Render felt a tingling at the base of his skull; he smelled fresh-cut grass.

Suddenly he was moving up the great gray alley between the worlds.

After what seemed a long time, Render felt that he was footed on a strange Earth. He could see nothing; it was only a sense of presence that informed him he had arrived. It was the darkest of all the dark nights he had ever known.

He willed that the darkness disperse. Nothing happened.

A part of his mind came awake again, a part he had not realized was sleeping; he recalled whose world he had entered.

He listened for her presence. He heard fear and anticipation.

He willed color. First, red . . .

He felt a correspondence. Then there was an echo.

Everything became red; he inhabited the center of an infinite ruby.

Orange. Yellow. . . .

He was caught in a piece of amber.

Green now, and he added the exhalations of a sultry sea. Blue, and the coolness of evening.

He stretched his mind then, producing all the colors at once. They came in great swirling plumes.

Then he tore them apart and forced a form upon them.

An incandescent rainbow arced across the black sky.

He fought for browns and grays below him. Self-luminescent, they appeared—in shimmering, shifting patches.

Somewhere, a sense of awe. There was no trace of hysteria though, so he continued with the Shaping.

He managed a horizon, and the blackness drained away beyond it. The sky grew faintly blue, and he ventured a herd of dark clouds. There was resistance to his efforts at creating distance and depth, so he reinforced the tableau with a very faint sound of surf. A transference from an auditory concept of distance came slowly then, as he pushed the clouds about. Quickly, he threw up a high forest to offset a rising wave of acrophobia.

The panic vanished.

Render focused his attention on tall trees—oaks and pines, poplars and sycamores. He hurled them about like spears, in ragged arrays of greens and browns and yellows, unrolled a thick mat of morning-moist grass, dropped a series of gray boulders and greenish logs at irregular intervals, and tangled and twined the branches overhead, casting a uniform shade throughout the glen.

The effect was staggering. It seemed as if the entire world was shaken with a sob, then silent.

Through the stillness he felt her presence. He had decided it would be best to lay the groundwork quickly, to set up a tangible headquarters, to prepare a field for operations. He could backtrack later, he could repair and amend the results of the trauma in the sessions yet to come; but this much, at least, was necessary for a beginning.

With a start, he realized that the silence was not a withdrawal. Eileen had made herself immanent in the trees and the grass, the stones and the bushes; she was personalizing their forms, relating them to tactile sensations, sounds, temperatures, aromas.

With a soft breeze, he stirred the branches of the trees. Just beyond the bounds of seeing he worked out the splashing sounds of a brook.

There was a feeling of joy. He shared it.

She was bearing it extremely well, so he decided to extend the scope of the exercise. He let his mind wander among the trees, experiencing a momentary doubling of vision, during which time he saw an enormous hand riding in an aluminum carriage toward a circle of white.

He was beside the brook now and he was seeking her, carefully.

He drifted with the water. He had not yet taken on a form. The splashes became a gurgling as he pushed the brook through shallow places and over rocks. At his insistence, the waters became more articulate.

"Where are you?" asked the brook.

Here! Here!

Here!

. . . *and here!* replied the trees, the bushes, the stones, the grass.

"Choose one," said the brook, as it widened, rounded a mass of rock, then bent its way down a slope, heading toward a blue pool.

I cannot, was the answer from the wind.

"You must." The brook widened and poured into the pool, swirled about the surface, then stilled itself and reflected branches and dark clouds. "Now!"

Very well, echoed the wood, *in a moment.*

The mist rose above the lake and drifted to the bank of the pool.

"Now," tinkled the mist.

Here, then . . .

She had chosen a small willow. It swayed in the wind; it trailed its branches in the water.

"Eileen Shallot," he said, "regard the lake."

The breezes shifted; the willow bent.

It was not difficult for him to recall her face, her body. The tree spun as though rootless. Eileen stood in the midst of a quiet explosion of leaves; she stared, frightened, into the deep blue mirror of Render's mind, the lake.

She covered her face with her hands, but it could not stop the seeing.

"Behold yourself," said Render.

She lowered her hands and peered downward. Then she turned in every direction, slowly; she studied herself. Finally:

"I feel I am quite lovely," she said. "Do I feel so because you want me to, or is it true?"

She looked all about as she spoke, seeking the Shaper.

"It is true," said Render, from everywhere.

"Thank you."

There was a swirl of white and she was wearing a belted garment of damask. The light in the distance brightened almost imperceptibly. A faint touch of pink began at the base of the lowest cloudbank.

"What is happening there?" she asked, facing that direction.

"I am going to show you a sunrise," said Render, "and I shall probably botch it a bit—but then, it's my first professional sunrise under these circumstances."

"Where are *you?*" she asked.

"Everywhere," he replied.

"Please take on a form so that I can see you."

"All right."

"Your natural form."

He willed that he be beside her on the bank, and he was.

Startled by a metallic flash, he looked downward. The world receded for an instant, then grew stable once again. He laughed, and the laugh froze as he thought of something.

He was wearing the suit of armor which had stood beside their table in the Partridge and Scalpel on the night they met.

She reached out and touched it.

"The suit of armor by our table," she acknowledged, running her fingertips over the plates and the junctures. "I associated it with you that night."

". . . And you stuffed me into it just now," he commented. "You're a strong-willed woman."

The armor vanished and he was wearing his gray-brown suit and looseknit bloodclot necktie and a professional expression.

"Behold the real me," he smiled faintly. "Now, to the sunset. I'm going to use all the colors. Watch!"

They seated themselves on the green park bench which had appeared behind them, and Render pointed in the direction he had decided upon as east.

Slowly, the sun worked through its morning attitudes. For the first time in this particular world it shone down like a god, and reflected off the lake, and broke the clouds, and set the landscape to smouldering beneath the mist that arose from the moist wood.

Watching, watching intently, staring directly into the ascending bonfire, Eileen did not move for a long while, nor speak. Render could sense her fascination.

She was staring at the source of all light; it reflected back from the gleaming coin on her brow, like a single drop of blood.

Render said, "That is the sun, and those are clouds," and he clapped his hands and the clouds covered the sun and there was a soft rumble overhead, "and that is thunder," he finished.

The rain fell then, shattering the lake and tickling their faces, making sharp striking sounds on the leaves, then soft tapping sounds, dripping down from the branches overhead, soaking their garments and plastering their hair, running down their necks and falling into their eyes, turning patches of brown earth to mud.

A splash of lightning covered the sky, and a second later there was another peal of thunder.

". . . And this is a summer storm," he lectured. "You see how the rain affects the foliage and ourselves. What you just saw in the sky before the thunderclap was lightning."

". . . Too much," she said. "Let up on it for a moment, please."

The rain stopped instantly and the sun broke through the clouds.

"I have the damndest desire for a cigarette," she said, "but I left mine in another world."

As she said it one appeared, already lighted, between her fingers.

"It's going to taste rather flat," said Render strangely. He watched her for a moment, then:

"I didn't give you that cigarette," he noted. "You picked it from my mind."

The smoke laddered and spiraled upward, was swept away.

". . . Which means that, for the second time today, I have underestimated the pull of that vacuum in your mind—in the place where sight ought to be. You are assimilating these new impressions very rapidly. You're even going to the extent of groping after new ones. Be careful. Try to contain that impulse."

"It's like a hunger," she said.

"Perhaps we had best conclude this session now."

Their clothing was dry again. A bird began to sing.

"No, wait! Please! I'll be careful. I want to see more things."

"There is always the next visit," said Render. "But I suppose we can manage one more. Is there something you want very badly to see?"

"Yes. Winter. Snow."

"Okay," smiled the Shaper, "then wrap yourself in that fur-piece. . . ."

The afternoon slipped by rapidly after the departure of his patient. Render was in a good mood. He felt emptied and filled again. He had come through the first trial without suffering any repercussions. He decided that he was going to succeed. His satisfaction was greater than his fear. It was with a sense of exhilaration that he returned to working on his speech.

". . . And what is the power to hurt?" he inquired of the microphone.

"We live by pleasure and we live by pain," he answered himself. "Either can frustrate and either can encourage. But while pleasure and pain are rooted in biology, they are conditioned by society: thus are values to be derived. Because of the enormous masses of humanity, hectically changing positions in space every day throughout the cities of the world, there has come into necessary being a series of totally inhuman controls upon these movements. Every day they nibble their way into new areas—driving our cars, flying our planes, interviewing us, diagnosing our diseases—and I cannot even venture a moral judgment upon these intrusions. They have become necessary. Ultimately, they may prove salutary.

"The point I wish to make, however, is that we are often unaware of our own values. We cannot honestly tell what a thing means to us until it is removed from our life-situation. If an object of value ceases to exist, then the psychic energies which were bound up in it are released. We seek after new objects of value in which to invest this—mana, if you like, or libido, if you don't. And no one thing which has vanished during the past three or four or five decades was, in itself, massively significant; and no new thing which came into being during that time is massively malicious toward the people it has replaced or the people it in some manner controls. A society, though, is made up of many things, and when these things are changed too rapidly the results are unpredictable. An intense study of mental illness is often quite revealing as to the nature of the stresses in the society where the illness was made. If anxiety-patterns fall into special groups and classes, then something of the discontent of society can be learned from them. Karl Jung pointed out that when consciousness is repeatedly frustrated in a quest for values, it will turn its search to the unconscious; failing there, it will proceed to quarry its way into the hypothetical collective unconscious. He noted, in the postwar analyses of ex-Nazis, that the longer they searched for something to erect from the ruins of their lives—having lived through a period of classical iconoclasm, and then seen their new ideals topple as well—the longer they searched, the further back they seemed to reach into the collective unconscious of their people. Their dreams themselves came to take on patterns out of the Teutonic mythos.

"This, in a much less dramatic sense, is happening today. There are historical periods when the group tendency for the mind to turn in upon itself, to turn back, is greater than at other times. We are living in such a period of Quixotism, in the original sense of the term. This is because the power to hurt, in our time, is the power to ignore, to baffle—and it is no longer the exclusive property of human beings—"

A buzz interrupted him then. He switched off the recorder, touched the phone-box.

"Charles Render speaking," he told it.

"This is Paul Charter," lisped the box. "I am headmaster at Dilling."

"Yes?"

The picture cleared. Render saw a man whose eyes were set close together beneath a high forehead. The forehead was heavily creased; the mouth twitched as it spoke.

"Well, I want to apologize again for what happened. It was a faulty piece of equipment that caused—"

"Can't you afford proper facilities? Your fees are high enough."

"It was a *new* piece of equipment. It was a factory defect—"

"Wasn't there anybody in charge of the class?"

"Yes, but—"

"Why didn't he inspect the equipment? Why wasn't he on hand to prevent the fall?"

"He *was* on hand, but it happened too fast for him to do anything. As for inspecting the equipment for factory defects, that isn't his job. Look, I'm very sorry. I'm quite fond of your boy. I can assure you nothing like this will ever happen again."

"You're right, there. But that's because I'm picking him up tomorrow morning and enrolling him in a school that exercises proper safety precautions."

Render ended the conversation with a flick of his finger. After several minutes had passed he stood and crossed the room to his small wall safe, which was partly masked, though not concealed, by a shelf of books. It took only a moment for him to open it and withdraw a jewel box containing a cheap necklace and a framed photograph of a man resembling himself, though somewhat younger, and a woman whose upswept hair was dark and whose chin was small, and two youngsters between them—the girl holding the baby in her arms and forcing her bright bored smile on ahead. Render always stared for only a few seconds on such occasions, fondling the necklace, and then he shut the box and locked it away again for many months.

Whump! Whump! went the bass. *Tchg-tchg-tchga-tchg,* the gourds.

The gelatins splayed reds, greens, blues, and godawful yellows about the amazing metal dancers.

HUMAN? asked the marquee.

ROBOTS? (immediately below).

COME SEE FOR YOURSELF! (across the bottom, cryptically).

So they did.

Render and Jill were sitting at a microscopic table, thankfully set back against a wall, beneath charcoal caricatures of personalities largely unknown (there being so many personalities among the subcultures of a city of fourteen million people). Nose crinkled with pleasure, Jill stared at the present focal point of this particular subculture, occasionally raising her shoulders to ear level to add emphasis to a silent laugh or a small squeal, because the performers were just *too* human—the way the ebon robot ran his fingers along the silver robot's forearm as they parted and passed. . . .

Render alternated his attention between Jill and the dancers and a wicked-looking decoction that resembled nothing so much as a small bucket of whiskey sours strewn with seaweed (through which the Kraken might at any moment arise to drag some hapless ship down to its doom).

"Charlie, I think they're really people!"

Render disentangled his gaze from her hair and bouncing earrings.

He studied the dancers down on the floor, somewhat below the table area, surrounded by music.

There *could* be humans within those metal shells. If so, their dance was a thing of extreme skill. Though the manufacture of sufficiently light alloys was no problem, it would be some trick for a dancer to cavort so freely—and for so long a period of time, and with such effortless-seeming ease—within a head-to-toe suit of armor, without so much as a grate or a click or a clank.

Soundless . . .

They glided like two gulls; the larger, the color of polished anthracite, and the other, like a moonbeam falling through a window upon a silk-wrapped manikin.

Even when they touched there was no sound—or if there was, it was wholly masked by the rhythms of the band.

Whump-whump! Tchga-tchg!

Render took another drink.

Slowly, it turned into an apache-dance. Render checked his watch. Too long for normal entertainers, he decided. They must be robots. As he looked up again the black robot hurled the silver robot perhaps ten feet and turned his back on her.

There was no sound of striking metal.

Wonder what a setup like that costs? he mused.

"Charlie! There was no sound! How do they do that?"

"I've no idea," said Render.

The gelatins were yellow again, then red, then blue, then green.

"You'd think it would damage their mechanisms, wouldn't you?"

The white robot crawled back and the other swiveled his wrist around and around, a lighted cigarette between the fingers. There was laughter as he pressed it mechanically to his lipless faceless face. The silver robot confronted him. He turned away again, dropped the cigarette, ground it out slowly, soundlessly, then suddenly turned back to his partner. Would he throw her again? No . . .

Slowly then, like the great-legged birds of the East, they recommenced their movement, slowly, and with many turnings away.

Something deep within Render was amused, but he was too far gone to ask it what was funny. So he went looking for the Kraken in the bottom of the glass instead.

Jill was clutching his biceps then, drawing his attention back to the floor.

As the spotlight tortured the spectrum, the black robot raised the silver one high above his head, slowly, slowly, and then commenced spinning with her in that position—arms outstretched, back arched, legs scissored—very slowly, at first. Then faster.

Suddenly they were whirling with an unbelievable speed, and the gelatins rotated faster and faster.

Render shook his head to clear it.

They were moving so rapidly that they *had* to fall—human or robot. But they didn't. They were a mandala. They were a gray form uniformity. Render looked down.

Then slowing, and slower, slower. Stopped.

The music stopped.

Blackness followed. Applause filled it.

When the lights came on again the two robots were standing statue-like, facing the audience. Very, very slowly, they bowed.

The applause increased.

Then they turned and were gone.

The music came on and the light was clear again. A babble of voices arose. Render slew the Kraken.

"What d'you think of that?" she asked him.

Render made his face serious and said: "Am I a man dreaming I am a robot, or a robot dreaming I am a man?" He grinned, then added: "I don't know."

She punched his shoulder gaily at that and he observed that she was drunk.

"I am not," she protested. "Not much, anyhow. Not as much as you."

"Still, I think you ought to see a doctor about it. Like me. Like now. Let's get out of here and go for a drive."

"Not yet, Charlie. I want to see them once more, huh? Please?"

"If I have another drink I won't be able to see that far."

"Then order a cup of coffee."

"Yaagh!"

"Then order a beer."

"I'll suffer without."

There were people on the dance floor now, but Render's feet felt like lead.

He lit a cigarette.

"So you had a dog talk to you today?"

"Yes. Something very disconcerting about that. . . ."

"Was she pretty?"

"It was a boy dog. And boy, was he ugly!"

"Silly. I mean his mistress."

"You know I never discuss cases, Jill."

"You told me about her being blind and about the dog. All I want to know is if she's pretty."

"Well . . . Yes and no." He bumped her under the table and gestured vaguely. "Well, you know . . ."

"Same thing all the way around," she told the waiter who had appeared suddenly out of an adjacent pool of darkness, nodded, and vanished as abruptly.

"There go my good intentions," sighed Render. "See how you like being examined by a drunken sot, that's all I can say."

"You'll sober up fast, you always do. Hippocratics and all that."

He sniffed, glanced at his watch.

"I have to be in Connecticut tomorrow. Pulling Pete out of that damned school. . . ."

She sighed, already tired of the subject.

"I think you worry too much about him. Any kid can bust an ankle. It's part of growing up. I broke my wrist when I was seven. It was an accident. It's not the school's fault, those things sometimes happen."

"Like hell," said Render, accepting his dark drink from the dark tray the dark man carried. "If they can't do a good job, I'll find someone who can."

She shrugged.

"You're the boss. All I know is what I read in the papers.

"—And you're still set on Davos, even though you know you meet a better class of people at Saint Moritz?" she added.

"We're going there to ski, remember? I like the runs better at Davos."

"I can't score any tonight, can I?"

He squeezed her hand.

"You always score with me, honey."

And they drank their drinks and smoked their cigarettes and held their hands until the people left the dance floor and filed back to their microscopic tables, and the gelatins spun round and round, tinting clouds of smoke from hell to sunrise and back again, and the bass went *whump!*

Tchga-tchga!

"Oh, Charlie! Here they come again!"

The sky was clear as crystal. The roads were clean. The snow had stopped.

Jill's breathing was the breathing of a sleeper. The S-7 raced across the bridges of the city. If Render sat very still he could convince himself that only his body was drunk; but whenever he moved his head the universe began to dance about him. As it did so, he imagined himself within a dream, and Shaper of it all.

For one instant this was true. He turned the big clock in the sky backward, smiling as he dozed. Another instant and he was awake again, and unsmiling.

The universe had taken revenge for his presumption. For one reknown moment with the helplessness which he had loved beyond helping, it had charged him the price of the lake-bottom vision once again; and as he had moved once more toward the wreck at the bottom of the world—like a swimmer, as unable to speak—he heard, from somewhere high over the Earth, and filtered down to him through the waters above the Earth, the howl of the Fenris Wolf as it prepared to devour the moon; and as this occurred, he knew that the sound was as like to the trump of a judgment as the lady by his side was unlike the moon. Every bit. In all ways. And he was afraid.

III

". . . The plain, the direct, and the blunt. This is Winchester Cathedral," said the guidebook. "With its floor-to-ceiling shafts, like so many huge tree trunks, it achieves a ruthless control over its spaces: the ceilings are flat; each bay, separated by those shafts, is itself a thing of certainty and stability. It seems, indeed, to reflect something of the spirit of William the Conqueror. Its disdain of mere elaboration and its passionate dedication to the love of another world would make it seem, too, an appropriate setting for some tale out of Mallory. . . ."

"Observe the scalloped capitals," said the guide. "In their primitive fluting they anticipated what was later to become a common motif. . . ."

"Faugh!" said Render—softly though, because he was in a group inside a church.

"Shh!" said Jill (Fotlock—that was her real last name) DeVille.

But Render was impressed as well as distressed.

Hating Jill's hobby, though, had become so much of a reflex with him that he would sooner have taken his rest seated beneath an oriental device which dripped water onto his head than to admit he occasionally enjoyed walking through the arcades and the galleries, the passages and the tunnels, and getting all out of breath climbing up the high twisty stairways of towers.

So he ran his eyes over everything, burned everything down by shutting them, then built the place up again out of the still smouldering ashes of memory, all so that at a later date he would be able to repeat the performance, offering the vision to his one patient who could see only in this manner. This building he disliked less than most. Yes, he would take it back to her.

The camera in his mind photographing the surroundings, Render walked with the others, overcoat over his arm, his fingers anxious to reach after a cigarette. He kept busy ignoring his guide, realizing this to be the nadir of all forms of human protest. As he walked through Winchester he thought of his last two sessions with Eileen Shallot. He recalled his almost unwilling Adam-attitude as he had named all the animals passing before them, led of course by the *one* she had wanted to see, colored fearsome by his own unease. He had felt pleasantly bucolic after boning up on an old Botany text and then proceeding to Shape and name the flowers of the fields.

So far they had stayed out of the cities, far away from the machines. Her emotions were still too powerful at the sight of the simple, carefully introduced objects to risk plunging her into so complicated and chaotic a wilderness yet; he would build her city slowly.

Something passed rapidly, high above the cathedral, uttering a sonic boom. Render took Jill's hand in his for a moment and smiled as she looked up at him. Knowing she verged upon beauty, Jill normally took great pains to achieve it. But today her hair was simply drawn back and knotted behind her head, and her lips and her eyes were pale; and her exposed ears were tiny and white and somewhat pointed.

"Observe the scalloped capitals," he whispered. "In their primitive fluting they anticipated what was later to become a common motif."

"Faugh!" said she.

"Shh!" said a sunburned little woman nearby, whose face seemed to crack and fall back together again as she pursed and unpursed her lips.

Later as they strolled back toward their hotel, Render said, "Okay on Winchester?"

"Okay on Winchester."

"Happy?"

"Happy."

"Good, then we can leave this afternoon."

"All right."

"For Switzerland. . . ."

She stopped and toyed with a button on his coat.

"Couldn't we just spend a day or two looking at some old chateaux first? After all, they're just across the channel, and you could be sampling all the local wines while I looked . . ."

"Okay," he said.

She looked up—a trifle surprised.

"What? No argument?" she smiled. "Where is your fighting spirit?—to let me push you around like this?"

She took his arm then and they walked on as he said, "Yesterday, while we were galloping about in the innards of that old castle, I heard a weak moan, and then a voice cried out, 'For the love of God, Montresor!' I think it was my fighting spirit, because I'm certain it was my voice. I've given up *der Geist der stets verneint. Pax vobiscum!* Let us be gone to France. *Alors!*"

"Dear Rendy, it'll only be another day or two. . . ."

"Amen," he said, "though my skis that were waxed are already waning."

So they did that, and on the morn of the third day, when she spoke to him of castles in Spain, he reflected aloud that while psychologists drink and only grow angry, psychiatrists have been known to drink, grow angry, and break things. Construing this as a veiled threat aimed at the Wedgewoods she had collected, she acquiesced to his desire to go skiing.

Free! Render almost screamed it.

His heart was pounding inside his head. He leaned hard. He cut to the left. The wind strapped at his face; a shower of ice crystals, like bullets of emery, fled by him, scraped against his cheek.

He was moving. Aye—the world had ended as Weissflujoch, and Dorftali led down and away from this portal.

His feet were two gleaming rivers which raced across the stark, curving plains; they could not be frozen in their course. Downward. He flowed. Away from all the rooms of the world. Away from the stifling lack of intensity, from the day's hundred spoon-fed welfares, from the killing pace of the forced amusements that hacked at the Hydra, leisure; away.

And as he fled down the run he felt a strong desire to look back over his shoulder, as though to see whether the world he had left behind and above had set one fearsome embodiment of itself, like a shadow, to trail along after him, hunt him down and drag him back to a warm and well-lit coffin in the sky, there to be laid to rest with a spike of aluminum driven through his will and a garland of alternating currents smothering his spirit.

"I hate you," he breathed between clenched teeth, and the wind carried the words back; and he laughed then, for he always analyzed his emotions, as a matter of reflex; and he added, "Exit Orestes, mad, pursued by the Furies. . . ."

After a time the slope leveled out and he reached the bottom of the run and had to stop.

He smoked one cigarette then and rode back up to the top so that he could come down it again for nontherapeutic reasons.

That night he sat before a fire in the big lodge, feeling its warmth soaking into his tired muscles. Jill massaged his shoulders as he played Rorschach with the flames, and he came upon a blazing goblet which was snatched away from him in the same instant by the sound of his name being spoken somewhere across the Hall of the Nine Hearths.

"Charles Render!" said the voice (only it sounded more like "Sharlz Runder"), and his head instantly jerked in that direction, but his eyes danced with too many afterimages for him to isolate the source of the calling.

"Maurice?" he queried after a moment. "Bartelmetz?"

"Aye," came the reply, and then Render saw the familiar grizzled visage, set neckless and balding above the red and blue shag sweater that was stretched mercilessly about the wine-keg rotundity of the man who now picked his way in their direction, deftly avoiding the strewn crutches and the stacked skis and the people who, like Jill and Render, disdained sitting in chairs.

Render stood, stretching, and shook hands as he came upon them.

"You've put on more weight," Render observed. "That's unhealthy."

"Nonsense, it's all muscle. How have you been, and what are you up to these days?" He looked down at Jill and she smiled back at him.

"This is Miss DeVille," said Render.

"Jill," she acknowledged.

He bowed slightly, finally releasing Render's aching hand.

". . . And this is Professor Maurice Bartelmetz of Vienna," finished Render, "a benighted disciple of all forms of dialectical pessimism, and a very distinguished pioneer in neuroparticipation—although you'd never guess it to look at him. I had the good fortune to be his pupil for over a year."

Bartelmetz nodded and agreed with him, taking in the Schnapsflasche Render brought forth from a small plastic bag, and accepting the collapsible cup which he filled to the brim.

"Ah, you are a good doctor still," he sighed. "You have diagnosed the case in an instant and you make the proper prescription. Nozdrovia!"

"Seven years in a gulp," Render acknowledged, refilling their glasses.

"Then we shall make time more malleable by sipping it."

They seated themselves on the floor, and the fire roared up through the great brick chimney as the logs burned themselves back to branches, to twigs, to thin sticks, ring by yearly ring.

Render replenished the fire.

"I read your last book," said Bartelmetz finally, casually, "about four years ago."

Render reckoned that to be correct.

"Are you doing any research work these days?"

Render poked lazily at the fire.

"Yes," he answered, "sort of."

He glanced at Jill, who was dozing with her cheek against the arm of the huge leather chair that held his emergency bag, the planes of her face all crimson and flickering shadow.

"I've hit upon a rather unusual subject and started with a piece of jobbery I eventually intend to write about."

"Unusual? In what way?"

"Blind from birth, for one thing."

"You're using the ONT&R?"

"Yes. She's going to be a Shaper."

"Verfluchter!—Are you aware of the possible repercussions?"

"Of course."

"You've heard of unlucky Pierre?"

"No."

"Good, then it was successfully hushed. Pierre was a philosophy student at the University of Paris, and was doing a dissertation on the evolution of consciousness. This past summer he decided it would be necessary for him to explore the mind of an ape, for purposes of comparing a moins-nausee mind with his own, I suppose. At any rate, he obtained illegal access to an ONT&R and to the mind of our hairy cousin. It was never ascertained how far along he got in exposing the animal to the stimulibank, but it is to be assumed that such items as would not be immediately trans-subjective between man and ape—traffic sounds and *so weiter*—were what frightened the creature. Pierre is still residing in a padded cell, and all his responses are those of a frightened ape.

"So, while he did not complete his own dissertation," he finished, "he may provide significant material for someone else's."

Render shook his head.

"Quite a story," he said softly, "but I have nothing that dramatic to contend with. I've found an exceedingly stable individual—a psychiatrist, in fact—one who's already spent time in ordinary analysis. She wants to go into neuroparticipation—but the fear of a sight-trauma was what was keeping her out. I've been gradually exposing her to a full range of visual phenomena. When I've finished she should be completely accommodated to sight, so that she can give her full attention to therapy and not be blinded by vision, so to speak. We've already had four sessions."

"And?"

". . . And it's working fine."

"You are certain about it?"

"Yes, as certain as anyone can be in these matters."

"Mm-hm," said Bartelmetz. "Tell me, do you find her excessively strong-willed? By that I mean, say, perhaps an obsessive-compulsive pattern concerning anything to which she's been introduced so far?"

"No."

"Has she ever succeeded in taking over control of the fantasy?"

"No!"

"You lie," he said simply.

Render found a cigarette. After lighting it, he smiled.

"Old father, old artificer," he conceded, "age has not withered your perceptiveness. I may trick me, but never you.—Yes, as a matter of fact, she *is* very difficult to keep under control. She is not satisfied just to see. She wants to Shape things for herself already. It's quite understandable—both to her and to me—but conscious apprehension and emotional acceptance never do seem to get together on things. She has become dominant on several occasions, but I've succeeded in resuming control almost immediately. After all, I *am* master of the bank."

"Hm," mused Bartelmetz. "Are you familiar with a Buddhist text—*Shankara's Catechism?*"

"I'm afraid not."

"Then I lecture you on it now. It posits—obviously not for therapeutic purposes—a true ego and a false ego. The true ego is that part of man which is immortal and shall proceed on to nirvana: the soul, if you like. Very good. Well, the false ego, on the other hand, is the normal mind, bound round with the illusions—the consciousness of you and me and everyone we have ever known professionally. Good?—Good. Now, the stuff this false ego is made up of they call skandhas. These include the feelings, the perceptions, the aptitudes, consciousness itself, and even the physical form. Very unscientific. Yes. Now they are not the same thing as neuroses, or one of Mr. Ibsen's life-lies, or an hallucination—no, even though they are all wrong, being parts of a false thing to begin with. Each of the five skandhas is a part of the eccentricity that we call identity—then on top come the neuroses and all the other messes which follow after and keep us in business. Okay?—Okay. I give you this lecture because I need a dramatic term for what I will say, because I wish to say something dramatic. View the skandhas as lying at the bottom of the pond; the neuroses, they are ripples on the top of the water; the 'true ego,' if there is one, is buried deep beneath the sand at the bottom. So. The ripples fill up the-the—*zwischenwelt*—between the object and the subject. The skandhas are a part of the subject, basic, unique, the stuff of his being.—So far, you are with me?"

"With many reservations."

"Good. Now I have defined my term somewhat, I will use it. You are fooling around with skandhas, not simple neuroses. You are attempting to adjust this woman's overall conception of herself and of the world. You are using the ONT&R to do it. It is the same thing as fooling with a psychotic or an ape. All may seem to go well, but—at any moment, it is possible you may do something, show her some sight, or some way of seeing which will break in upon her selfhood, break a skandha—and pouf!—it will be like breaking through the bottom of the pond. A whirlpool will result, pulling you—where? I do not want you for a patient, young man, young artificer, so I counsel you not to proceed with this experiment. The ONT&R should not be used in such a manner."

Render flipped his cigarette into the fire and counted on his fingers:

"One," he said, "you are making a mystical mountain out of a pebble. All I am doing is adjusting her consciousness to accept an additional area of perception. Much of it is simple transference work from the other senses—Two, her emotions were quite intense initially because it *did* involve a trauma—but we've passed that stage already. Now it is only a novelty to her. Soon it will be a commonplace—Three, Eileen is a psychiatrist herself; she is educated in these matters and deeply aware of the delicate nature of what we are doing—Four, her sense of identity and her desires, or her skandhas, or whatever you want to call them, are as firm as the Rock of Gibraltar. Do you realize the intense application required for a blind person to obtain the education she has obtained? It took a will of ten-point steel and the emotional control of an ascetic as well—"

"—And if something that strong should break, in a timeless moment of anxiety," smiled Bartelmetz sadly, "may the shades of Sigmund Freud and Karl Jung walk by your side in the valley of darkness.

"—And five," he added suddenly, staring into Render's eyes. "Five," he ticked it off on one finger. "Is she pretty?"

Render looked back into the fire.

"Very clever," sighed Bartelmetz. "I cannot tell whether you are blushing or not, with the rosy glow of the flames upon your face. I fear that you are, though, which would mean that you are aware that you yourself could be the source of the inciting stimulus. I shall burn a candle tonight before a portrait of Adler and pray that he give you the strength to compete successfully in your duel with your patient."

Render looked at Jill, who was still sleeping. He reached out and brushed a lock of her hair back into place.

"Still," said Bartelmetz, "if you do proceed and all goes well, I shall look forward with great interest to the reading of your work. Did I ever tell you that I have treated several Buddhists and never found a 'true ego'?"

Both men laughed.

Like me but not like me, that one on a leash, smelling of fear, small, gray, and unseeing. *Rrowl* and he'll choke on his collar. His head is empty as the oven till. She pushes the button and it makes dinner. Make talk and they never understand, but they are like me. One day I will kill one—why . . . ? Turn here.

"Three steps. Up. Glass doors. Handle to right."

Why? Ahead, drop-shaft. Gardens under, down. Smells nice, there. Grass, wet dirt, trees, and clean air. I see. Birds are recorded though. I see all. I.

"Dropshaft. Four steps."

Down Yes. Want to make loud noises in throat, feel silly. Clean, smooth, many of trees. God . . . She likes sitting on bench chewing leaves smelling smooth air. Can't see them like me. Maybe now, some . . . ? No.

Can't Bad Sigmund me on grass, trees, here. Must hold it. Pity. Best place . . .

"Watch for steps."

Ahead. To right, to left, to right, to left, trees and grass now. Sigmund sees. Walking . . . Doctor with machine gives her his eyes. *Rrowl* and he will not choke. No fearsmell.

Dig deep hole in ground, bury eyes. God is blind. Sigmund to see. Her eyes now filled, and he is afraid of teeth. Will make her to see and take her high up in the sky to see, away. Leave me here, leave Sigmund with none to see, alone. I will dig a deep hole in the ground . . .

It was after ten in the morning when Jill awoke. She did not have to turn her head to know that Render was already gone. He never slept late. She rubbed her eyes, stretched, turned onto her side and raised herself on her elbow. She squinted at the clock on the bedside table, simultaneously reaching for a cigarette and her lighter.

As she inhaled, she realized there was no ashtray. Doubtless Render had moved it to the dresser because he did not approve of smoking in bed. With a sigh that ended in a snort she slid out of the bed and drew on her wrap before the ash grew too long.

She hated getting up, but once she did she would permit the day to begin and continue on without lapse through its orderly progression of events.

"Damn him," she smiled. She had wanted her breakfast in bed, but it was too late now.

Between thoughts as to what she would wear, she observed an alien pair of skis standing in the corner. A sheet of paper was impaled on one. She approached it.

"Join me?" asked the scrawl.

She shook her head in an emphatic negative and felt somewhat sad. She had been on skis twice in her life and she was afraid of them. She felt that she should really try again, after his being a reasonably good sport about the chateaux, but she could not even bear the memory of the unseemly downward rushing—which, on two occasions, had promptly deposited her in a snowbank—without wincing and feeling once again the vertigo that had seized her during the attempts.

So she showered and dressed and went downstairs for breakfast.

All nine fires were already roaring as she passed the big hall and looked inside. Some red-faced skiers were holding their hands up before the blaze of the central hearth. It was not crowded though. The racks held only a few pairs of dripping boots, bright caps hung on pegs, moist skis stood upright in their place beside the door. A few people were seated in the chairs set further back toward the center of the hall, reading papers, smoking, or talking quietly. She saw no one she knew, so she moved on toward the dining room.

As she passed the registration desk the old man who worked there called out her name. She approached him and smiled.

"Letter," he explained, turning to a rack. "Here it is," he announced, handing it to her. "Looks important."

It had been forwarded three times, she noted. It was a bulky brown envelope, and the return address was that of her attorney.

"Thank you."

She moved off to a seat beside the big window that looked out upon a snow garden, a skating rink, and a distant winding trail dotted with figures carrying skis over their shoulders. She squinted against the brightness as she tore open the envelope.

Yes, it was final. Her attorney's note was accompanied by a copy of the divorce decree. She had only recently decided to end her legal relationship to Mr. Fotlock, whose name she had stopped using five years earlier, when they had separated. Now that she had the thing, she wasn't sure exactly what she was going to do with it. It would be a hell of a surprise for dear Rendy, though, she decided. She would have to find a reasonably innocent way of getting the information to him. She withdrew her compact and practiced a "Well?" expression. Well, there would be time for that later, she mused. Not too much later, though. . . . Her thirtieth birthday, like a huge black cloud, filled an April but four months distant. Well . . . She touched her quizzical lips with color, dusted more powder over her mole, and locked the expression within her compact for future use.

In the dining room she saw Doctor Bartelmetz, seated before an enormous mound of scrambled eggs, great chains of dark sausages, several heaps of yellow toast, and a half-emptied flask of orange juice. A pot of coffee steamed on the warmer at his elbow. He leaned slightly forward as he ate, wielding his fork like a windmill blade.

"Good morning," she said.

He looked up.

"Miss DeVille—Jill . . . Good morning." He nodded at the chair across from him. "Join me, please."

She did so, and when the waiter approached she nodded and said, "I'll have the same thing, only about ninety percent less."

She turned back to Bartelmetz.

"Have you seen Charles today?"

"Alas, I have not," he gestured, open-handed, "and I wanted to continue our discussion while his mind was still in the early stages of wakefulness and somewhat malleable. Unfortunately," he took a sip of coffee, "he who sleeps well enters the day somewhere in the middle of its second act."

"Myself, I usually come in around intermission and ask someone for a synopsis," she explained. "So why not continue the discussion with me?—I'm always malleable, and my skandhas are in good shape."

Their eyes met, and he took a bite of toast.

"Aye," he said, at length, "I had guessed as much. Well—good. What do you know of Render's work?"

She adjusted herself in the chair.

"Mm. He being a special specialist in a highly specialized area, I find it difficult to appreciate the few things he does say about it. I'd like to be able to look inside other people's minds sometimes—to see what they're thinking about *me*, of course—but I don't think I could stand staying there very long. Especially," she gave a mock-shudder, "the mind of somebody with—problems. I'm afraid I'd be too sympathetic or too frightened or something. Then, according to what I've read—pow!—like sympathetic magic, it would be my problem.

"Charles never has problems though," she continued, "at least, none that he speaks to me about. Lately I've been wondering, though. That blind girl and her talking dog seem to be too much with him."

"Talking dog?"

"Yes, her seeing-eye dog is one of those surgical mutants."

"How interesting. . . . Have you ever met her?"

"Never."

"So," he mused.

"Sometimes a therapist encounters a patient whose problems are so akin to his own that the sessions become extremely mordant," he noted. "It has always been the case with me when I treat a fellow-psychiatrist. Perhaps Charles sees in this situation a parallel to something which has been troubling him personally. I did not administer his personal analysis. I do not know all the ways of his mind, even though he was a pupil of mine for a long while. He was always self-contained, somewhat reticent; he could be quite authoritative on occasion, however.—What are some of the other things which occupy his attention these days?"

"His son Peter is a constant concern. He's changed the boy's school five times in five years."

Her breakfast arrived. She adjusted her napkin and drew her chair closer to the table.

"And he has been reading case histories of suicides recently, and talking about them, and talking about them, and talking about them."

"To what end?"

She shrugged and began eating.

"He never mentioned why," she said, looking up again. "Maybe he's writing something. . . ."

Bartelmetz finished his eggs and poured more coffee.

"Are you afraid of this patient of his?" he inquired.

"No . . . Yes," she responded, "I am."

"Why?"

"I am afraid of sympathetic magic," she said, flushing slightly.

"Many things could fall under that heading."

"Many indeed," she acknowledged. And, after a moment, "We are united in our concern for his welfare and in agreement as to what represents the threat. So, may I ask a favor?"

"You may."

"Talk to him again," she said. "Persuade him to drop the case."

He folded his napkin.

"I intend to do that after dinner," he stated, "because I believe in the ritualistic value of rescue-motions. They shall be made."

Dear Father-image,

Yes, the school is fine, my ankle is getting that way, and my classmates are a congenial lot. No, I am not short on cash, undernourished, or having difficulty fitting into the new curriculum. Okay?

The building I will not describe, as you have already seen the macabre thing. The grounds I cannot describe, as they are currently residing beneath cold white sheets. Brr! I trust yourself to be enjoying the arts wint'rish. I do not share your enthusiasm for summer's opposite, except within picture frames or as an emblem on ice-cream bars.

The ankle inhibits my mobility and my roommate has gone home for the weekend—both of which are really blessings (saith Pangloss), for I now have the opportunity to catch up on some reading. I will do so forthwith.
Prodigally,
Peter

Render reached down to pat the huge head. It accepted the gesture stoically, then turned its gaze up to the Austrian whom Render had asked for a light, as if to say, "Must I endure this indignity?" The man laughed at the expression, snapping shut the engraved lighter on which Render noted the middle initial to be a small 'v.'

"Thank you," he said, and to the dog: "What is your name?"

"Bismark," it growled.

Render smiled.

"You remind me of another of your kind," he told the dog. "One Sigmund, by name, a companion and guide to a blind friend of mine, in America."

"My Bismark is a hunter," said the young man. "There is no quarry that can outthink him, neither the deer nor the big cats."

The dog's ears pricked forward and he stared up at Render with proud, blazing eyes.

"We have hunted in Africa and the northern and southwestern parts of America. Central America, too. He never loses the trail. He never gives up. He is a beautiful brute, and his teeth could have been made in Solingen."

"You are indeed fortunate to have such a hunting companion."

"I hunt," growled the dog. "I follow . . . Sometimes, I have, the kill . . ."

"You would not know of the one called Sigmund then, or the woman he guides—Miss Eileen Shallot?" asked Render.

The man shook his head.

"No, Bismark came to me from Massachusetts, but I was never to the Center personally. I am not acquainted with other mutie handlers."

"I see. Well, thank you for the light. Good afternoon."

"Good afternoon . . ."

"Good, after, noon . . ."

Render strolled on up the narrow street, hands in his pockets. He had excused himself and not said where he was going. This was because he had had no destination in mind. Bartelmetz' second essay at counseling had almost led him to say things he would later regret. It was easier to take a walk than to continue the conversation.

On a sudden impulse he entered a small shop and bought a cuckoo clock which had caught his eye. He felt certain that Bartelmetz would accept the gift in the proper spirit. He smiled and walked on. *And what was that letter to Jill which the desk clerk had made a special trip to their table to deliver at dinnertime?* he wondered. It had been forwarded three times, and its return address was that of a law firm. Jill had not even opened it, but had smiled, overtipped the old man, and tucked it into her purse. He would have to hint subtly as to its contents. His curiosity so aroused, she would be sure to tell him out of pity.

The icy pillars of the sky suddenly seemed to sway before him as a cold wind leaped down out of the north. Render hunched his shoulders and drew his head further below his collar. Clutching the cuckoo clock, he hurried back up the street.

• • •

That night the serpent which holds its tail in its mouth belched, the Fenris Wolf made a pass at the moon, the little clock said "cuckoo" and tomorrow came on like Manolete's last bull, shaking the gate of horn with the bellowed promise to tread a river of lions to sand.

Render promised himself he would lay off the gooey fondue.

Later, much later, when they skipped through the skies in a kite-shaped cruiser, Render looked down upon the darkened Earth dreaming its cities full of stars, looked up at the sky where they were all reflected, looked about him at the tape-screens watching all the people who blinked into them, and at the coffee, tea, and mixed drink dispensers who sent their fluids forth to explore the insides of the people they required to push their buttons, then looked across at Jill, whom the old buildings had compelled to walk among their walls—because he knew she felt he should be looking at her then—felt his seat's demand that he convert it into a couch, did so, and slept.

IV

Her office was full of flowers, and she liked exotic perfumes. Sometimes she burned incense.

She liked soaking in overheated pools, walking through falling snow, listening to too much music, played perhaps too loudly, drinking five or six varieties of liqueurs (usually reeking of anise, sometimes touched with wormwood) every evening. Her hands were soft and lightly freckled. Her fingers were long and tapered. She wore no rings.

Her fingers traced and retraced the floral swellings on the side of her chair as she spoke into the recording unit.

". . . Patient's chief complaints on admission were nervousness, insomnia, stomach pains, and a period of depression. Patient has had a record of previous admissions for short periods of time. He had been in this hospital in 1995 for a manic depressive psychosis, depressed type, and he returned here again, 2-3-96. He was in another hospital, 9-20-97. Physical examination revealed a BP of 170/100. He was normally developed and well-nourished on the date of examination, 12-11-98. On this date patient complained of chronic backache, and there was noted some moderate symptoms of alcohol withdrawal. Physical examination further revealed no pathology except that the patient's tendon reflexes were exaggerated but equal. These symptoms were the result of alcohol withdrawal. Upon admission he was shown to be not psychotic, neither delusional nor hallucinated. He was well-oriented as to place, time, and person. His psychological condition was evaluated and he was found to be somewhat grandiose and expansive and more than a little hostile. He was considered a potential troublemaker. Because of his experience as a cook, he was assigned to work in the kitchen. His general condition then showed definite improvement. He is less tense and is cooperative. Diagnosis: Manic depressive reaction (external precipitating stress unknown). The degree of psychiatric impairment is mild. He is considered competent. To be continued on therapy and hospitalization."

She turned off the recorder then and laughed. The sound frightened her. Laughter is a social phenomenon and she was alone. She played back the recording then, chewing on the corner of her handkerchief while the soft, clipped words were returned to her. She ceased to hear them after the first dozen or so.

When the recorder stopped talking she turned it off. She was alone. She was very alone. She was so damned alone that the little pool of brightness which occurred when she stroked her forehead and faced the window—that little pool of brightness suddenly became the most important thing in the world. She wanted it to be immense. She wanted it to be an ocean of light. Or else she wanted to grow so small herself that the effect would be the same: she wanted to drown in it.

It had been three weeks, yesterday . . .

Too long, she decided, *I should have waited. No! Impossible! But what if he goes as Riscomb went? No! He won't. He would not. Nothing can hurt him. Never. He is all strength and armor. But—but we should have waited till next month to start. Three weeks . . . Sight withdrawal—that's what it is. Are the memories fading? Are they weaker? (What does a tree look like? Or a cloud—I can't remember! What is red? What is green? God! It's hysterical! I'm watching and I can't stop it!—Take a pill! A pill!*

Her shoulders began to shake. She did not take a pill though, but bit down harder on the handkerchief until her sharp teeth tore through its fabric.

"Beware," she recited a personal beatitude, "those who hunger and thirst after justice, for we *will* be satisfied.

"And beware the meek," she continued, "for we shall attempt to inherit the Earth.

"And beware . . ."

There was a brief buzz from the phone-box. She put away her handkerchief, composed her face, turned the unit on.

"Hello . . . ?"

"Eileen, I'm back. How've you been?"

"Good, quite well in fact. How was your vacation?"

"Oh, I can't complain. I had it coming for a long time. I guess I deserve it. Listen, I brought some things back to show you—like Winchester Cathedral. You want to come in this week? I can make it any evening."

Tonight. No. I want it too badly. It will set me back if he sees . . .

"How about tomorrow night?" she asked. "Or the one after?"

"Tomorrow will be fine," he said. "Meet you at the P & S, around seven?"

"Yes, that would be pleasant. Same table?"

"Why not?—I'll reserve it."

"All right. I'll see you then."

"Good-bye."

The connection was broken.

Suddenly, then, at that moment, colors swirled again through her head; and she saw trees—oaks and pines, poplars and sycamores—great, and green and brown, and iron-colored; and she saw wads of fleecy clouds, dipped in paintpots, swabbing a pastel sky; and a burning sun, and a small willow tree, and a lake of a deep, almost violet, blue. She folded her torn handkerchief and put it away.

She pushed a button beside her desk and music filled the office: Scriabin. Then she pushed another button and replayed the tape she had dictated, half-listening to each.

Pierre sniffed suspiciously at the food. The attendant moved away from the tray and stepped out into the hall, locking the door behind him. The enormous salad waited on the floor. Pierre approached cautiously, snatched a handful of lettuce, gulped it.

He was afraid.

If only the steel would stop crashing and crashing against steel, somewhere in that dark night . . . If only . . .

Sigmund rose to his feet, yawned, stretched. His hind legs trailed out behind him for a moment, then he snapped to attention and shook himself. She would be coming home soon. Wagging his tail slowly, he glanced up at the human-level clock with the raised numerals, verified his feelings, then crossed the apartment to the teevee. He rose onto his hind legs, rested one paw against the table and used the other to turn on the set.

It was nearly time for the weather report and the roads would be icy.

"I have driven through countrywide graveyards," wrote Render, "vast forests of stone that spread further every day.

"Why does man so zealously guard his dead? Is it because this is the monumentally democratic way of immortalization, the ultimate affirmation of the power to hurt—that is to say, life—and the desire that it continue on forever? Unamuno has suggested that this is the case. If it is, then a greater percentage of the population actively sought immortality last year than ever before in history. . . ."

Tch-tchg, tchga-tchg!

"Do you think they're really people?"

"Naw, they're too good."

The evening was starglint and soda over ice. Render wound the S-7 into the cold sub-subcellar, found his parking place, nosed into it.

There was a damp chill that emerged from the concrete to gnaw like rats' teeth at their flesh. Render guided her toward the lift, their breath preceding them in dissolving clouds.

"A bit of a chill in the air," he noted.

She nodded, biting her lip.

Inside the lift, he sighed, unwound his scarf, lit a cigarette.

"Give me one, please," she requested, smelling the tobacco.

He did.

They rose slowly, and Render leaned against the wall, puffing a mixture of smoke and crystallized moisture.

"I met another mutie shep," he recalled, "in Switzerland. Big as Sigmund. A hunter though, and as Prussian as they come," he grinned.

"Sigmund likes to hunt, too," she observed. "Twice every year we go up to the North Woods and I turn him loose. He's gone for days at a time, and he's always quite happy when he returns. Never says what he's done, but he's never hungry. Back when I got him I guessed that he would need vacations from humanity to stay stable. I think I was right."

The lift stopped, the door opened and they walked out into the hall, Render guiding her again.

Inside his office, he poked at the thermostat and warm air sighed through the room. He hung their coats in the inner office and brought the great egg out from its nest behind the wall. He connected it to an outlet and moved to convert his desk into a control panel.

"How long do you think it will take?" she asked, running her fingertips over the smooth, cold curves of the egg. "The whole thing, I mean. The entire adaptation to seeing."

He wondered.

"I have no idea," he said, "no idea whatsoever, yet. We got off to a good start, but there's still a lot of work to be done. I think I'll be able to make a good guess in another three months."

She nodded wistfully, moved to his desk, explored the controls with finger strokes like ten feathers.

"Careful you don't push any of those."

"I won't. How long do you think it will take me to learn to operate one?"

"Three months to learn it. Six, to actually become proficient enough to use it on anyone, and an additional six under close supervision before you can be trusted on your own.—About a year altogether."

"Uh-huh." She chose a chair.

Render touched the seasons to life, and the phases of day and night, the breath of the country, the city, the elements that raced naked through the skies, and all the dozens of dancing cues he used to build worlds. He smashed the clock of time and tasted the seven or so ages of man.

"Okay," he turned, "everything is ready."

It came quickly, and with a minimum of suggestion on Render's part. One moment there was grayness. Then a dead-white fog. Then it broke itself apart, as though a quick wind had risen, although he neither heard nor felt a wind.

He stood beside the willow tree beside the lake, and she stood half-hidden among the branches and the lattices of shadow. The sun was slanting its way into evening.

"We have come back," she said, stepping out, leaves in her hair. "For a time I was afraid it had never happened, but I see it all again, and I remember now."

"Good," he said. "Behold yourself." And she looked into the lake.

"I have not changed," she said. "I haven't changed. . . ."

"No."

"But you have," she continued, looking up at him. "You are taller, and there is something different. . . ."

"No," he answered.

"I am mistaken," she said quickly. "I don't understand everything I see yet.

"I will, though."

"Of course."

"What are we going to do?"

"Watch," he instructed her.

Along a flat, no-colored river of road she just then noticed beyond the trees came the car. It came from the farthest quarter of the sky, skipping over the mountains, buzzing down the hills, circling through the glades, and splashing them with the colors of its voice—the gray and the silver of synchronized potency—and the lake shivered from its sounds, and the car stopped a hundred feet away, masked by the shrubberies; and it waited. It was the S-7.

"Come with me," he said, taking her hand. "We're going for a ride."

They walked among the trees and rounded the final cluster of bushes. She touched the sleek cocoon, its antennae, its tires, its windows—and the windows transpared as she did so. She stared through them at the inside of the car, and she nodded.

"It is your Spinner."

"Yes." He held the door for her. "Get in. We'll return to the club. The time is now. The memories are fresh, and they should be reasonably pleasant, or neutral."

"Pleasant," she said, getting in.

He closed the door, then circled the car and entered. She watched as he punched imaginary coordinates. The car leaped ahead and he kept a steady stream of trees flowing by them. He could feel the rising tension, so he did not vary the scenery. She swiveled her seat and studied the interior of the car.

"Yes," she finally said, "I can perceive what everything is."

She stared out the window again. She looked at the rushing trees. Render stared out and looked upon rushing anxiety patterns. He opaqued the windows.

"Good," she said, "thank you. Suddenly it was too much to see—all of it, moving past like a . . ."

"Of course," said Render, maintaining the sensations of forward motion. "I'd anticipated that. You're getting tougher, though."

After a moment, "Relax," he said, "relax now," and somewhere a button was pushed, and she relaxed, and they drove on, and on and on, and finally the car began to slow, and Render said, "Just for one nice, slow glimpse now, look out your window."

She did.

He drew upon every stimulus in the bank which could promote sensations of pleasure and relaxation, and he dropped the city around the car, and the windows became transparent, and she looked out upon the profiles of towers and a block of monolithic apartments, and then she saw three rapid cafeterias, an entertainment palace, a drugstore, a medical center of yellow brick with an aluminum Caduceus set above its archway, and a glassed-in high school, now emptied of its pupils, a fifty-pump gas station, another drugstore, and many more cars, parked or roaring by them, and people, people moving in and out of the doorways and walking before the buildings and getting into the cars and getting out of the cars; and it was summer, and the light of late afternoon filtered down upon the colors of the city and the colors of the garments the people wore as they moved along the boulevard, as they loafed upon the terraces, as they crossed the balconies, leaned on balustrades and windowsills, emerged from a corner kiosk, entered one, stood talking to one another; a woman walking a poodle rounded a corner; rockets went to and fro in the high sky.

The world fell apart then and Render caught the pieces.

He maintained an absolute blackness, blanketing every sensation but that of their movement forward.

After a time a dim light occurred, and they were still seated in the Spinner, windows blanked again, and the air as they breathed it became a soothing unguent.

"Lord," she said, "the world is so filled. Did I really see all of that?"

"I wasn't going to do that tonight, but you wanted me to. You seemed ready."

"Yes," she said, and the windows became transparent again. She turned away quickly.

"It's gone," he said. "I only wanted to give you a glimpse."

She looked, and it was dark outside now, and they were crossing over a high bridge. They were moving slowly. There was no other traffic. Below them were the Flats, where an occasional smelter flared like a tiny, drowsing volcano, spitting showers of orange sparks skyward; and there were many stars: they glistened on the breathing water that went beneath the bridge; they silhouetted by pinprick the skyline that hovered dimly below its surface. The slanting struts of the bridge marched steadily by.

"You have done it," she said, "and I thank you." Then: "Who are you, really?" (He must have wanted her to ask that.)

"I am Render," he laughed. And they wound their way through a dark, now-vacant city, coming at last to their club and entering the great parking dome.

Inside, he scrutinized all her feelings, ready to banish the world at a moment's notice. He did not feel he would have to, though.

They left the car, moved ahead. They passed into the club, which he had decided would not be crowded tonight. They were shown to their table at the foot of the bar in the small room with the suit of armor, and they sat down and ordered the same meal over again.

"No," he said, looking down, "it belongs over there."

The suit of armor appeared once again beside the table, and he was once again inside his gray suit and black tie and silver tie clasp shaped like a tree limb.

They laughed.

"I'm just not the type to wear a tin suit, so I wish you'd stop seeing me that way."

"I'm sorry," she smiled. "I don't know how I did that, or why."

"I do, and I decline the nomination. Also, I caution you once again. You are conscious of the fact that this is all an illusion. I had to do it that way for you to get the full benefit of the thing. For most of my patients though, it is the real item while they are experiencing it. It makes a counter-trauma or a symbolic sequence even more powerful. You are aware of the parameters of the game, however, and whether you want it or not this gives you a different sort of control over it than I normally have to deal with. Please be careful."

"I'm sorry. I didn't mean to."

"I know. Here comes the meal we just had."

"Ugh! It looks dreadful! Did we eat all that stuff?"

"Yes," he chuckled. "That's a knife, that's a fork, that's a spoon. That's roast beef, and those are mashed potatoes, those are peas, that's butter . . ."

"Goodness! I don't feel so well."

". . . And those are the salads, and those are the salad dressings. This is a brook trout—mm! These are French fried potatoes. This is a bottle of wine. Hmm—let's see—Romanee-Conti, since I'm not paying for it—and a bottle of Yquem for the trou—Hey!"

The room was wavering.

He bared the table, he banished the restaurant. They were back in the glade. Through the transparent fabric of the world he watched a hand moving along a panel. Buttons were being pushed. The world grew substantial again. Their emptied table was set beside the lake now, and it was still nighttime and summer, and the tablecloth was very white under the glow of the giant moon that hung overhead.

"That was stupid of me," he said. "Awfully stupid. I should have introduced them one at a time. The actual sight of basic, oral stimuli can be very distressing to a person seeing them for the first time. I got so wrapped up in the Shaping that I forgot the patient, which is just dandy! I apologize."

"I'm okay now. Really I am."

He summoned a cool breeze from the lake.

". . . And that is the moon," he added lamely.

She nodded, and she was wearing a tiny moon in the center of her forehead; it glowed like the one above them, and her hair and dress were all of silver.

The bottle of Romanee-Conti stood on the table, and two glasses.

"Where did that come from?"

She shrugged. He poured out a glassful.

"It may taste kind of flat," he said.

"It doesn't. Here—" She passed it to him.

As he sipped it he realized it had a taste—a *fruite* such as might be quashed from the grapes grown in the Isles of the Blest, a smooth, muscular *charnu*, and a *capiteux* centrifuged from the fumes of a field of burning poppies. With a start, he knew that his hand must be traversing the route of the perceptions, symphonizing the sensual cues of a transference and a counter-transference which had come upon him all unaware, there beside the lake.

"So it does," he noted, "and now it is time we returned."

"So soon? I haven't seen the cathedral yet. . . ."

"So soon."

He willed the world to end, and it did.

"It is cold out there," she said as she dressed, "and dark."

"I know. I'll mix us something to drink while I clear the unit."

"Fine."

He glanced at the tapes and shook his head. He crossed to his bar cabinet.

"It's not exactly Romanee-Conti," he observed, reaching for a bottle.

"So what? I don't mind."

Neither did he, at that moment. So he cleared the unit, they drank their drinks, he helped her into her coat and they left.

As they rode the lift down to the sub-sub he willed the world to end again, but it didn't.

Dad,

I hobbled from school to taxi and taxi to spaceport, for the local Air Force Exhibit—Outward, it was called. (Okay; I exaggerated the hobble. It got me extra attention though.) The whole bit was aimed at seducing young manhood into a five-year hitch, as I saw it. But it worked. I wanna join up. I wanna go Out There. Think they'll take me when I'm old enuf? I mean take me Out—not some crummy desk job. Think so?

I do.

There was this damn lite colonel ('scuse the French) who saw this kid lurching around and pressing his nose 'gainst the big windowpanes, and he decided to give him the subliminal sell. Great! He pushed me through the gallery and showed me all the pitchers of AF triumphs, from Moonbase to Marsport. He lectured me on the Great Traditions of the Service, and marched me into a flic room where the Corps had good clean fun on tape, wrestling one another in null-G "where it's all skill and no brawn," and making tinted water sculpture-work way in the middle of the air and doing dismounted drill on the skin of a cruiser. Oh joy!

Seriously though, I'd like to be there when they hit the Outer Five—and On Out. Not because of the bogus balonus in the throwaways, and suchlike crud, but because I think someone of sensibility should be along to chronicle the thing in the proper way. You know, raw frontier observer. Francis Parkman. Mary Austin, like that. So I decided I'm going.

The AF boy with the chicken stuff on his shoulders wasn't in the least way patronizing, gods be praised. We stood on the balcony and watched ships lift off and he told me to go forth and study real hard and I might be riding them someday. I did not bother to tell him that I'm hardly intellectually deficient and that I'll have my B.A. before I'm old enough to do anything with it, even join his Corps. I just watched the ships lift off and said, "Ten years from now I'll be looking down, not up." Then he told me how hard his own training had been, so I did not ask howcum he got stuck with a lousy dirt-side assignment like this one. Glad I didn't, now I think on it. He looked more like one of their ads than one of their real people. Hope I never look like an ad.

Thank you for the monies and the warm sox and Mozart's String Quintets, which I'm hearing right now. I wanna put in my bid for Luna instead of Europe next summer. Maybe . . . ? Possibly . . . ? Contingently . . . ? Huh?—If I can smash that new test you're designing for me . . . ? Anyhow, please think about it.

Your son,
Pete

"Hello. State Psychiatric Institute."

"I'd like to make an appointment for an examination."

"Just a moment. I'll connect you with the Appointment Desk."

"Hello. Appointment Desk."

"I'd like to make an appointment for an examination."

"Just a moment . . . What sort of examination."

"I want to see Doctor Shallot, Eileen Shallot. As soon as possible."

"Just a moment. I'll have to check her schedule . . . Could you make it at two o'clock next Tuesday?"

"That would be just fine."

"What is the name, please?"

"DeVille. Jill DeVille.

"All right, Miss DeVille. That's two o'clock, Tuesday."

"Thank you."

The man walked beside the highway. Cars passed along the highway. The cars in the high-acceleration lane blurred by.

Traffic was light.

It was 10:30 in the morning, and cold.

The man's fur-lined collar was turned up, his hands were in his pockets, and he leaned into the wind. Beyond the fence, the road was clean and dry.

The morning sun was buried in clouds. In the dirty light, the man could see the tree a quarter mile ahead.

His pace did not change. His eyes did not leave the tree. The small stones clicked and crunched beneath his shoes.

When he reached the tree he took off his jacket and folded it neatly.

He placed it upon the ground and climbed the tree.

As he moved out onto the limb which extended over the fence, he looked to see that no traffic was approaching. Then he seized the branch with both hands, lowered himself, hung a moment, and dropped onto the highway.

It was a hundred yards wide, the eastbound half of the highway.

He glanced west, saw there was still no traffic coming his way, then began to walk toward the center island. He knew he would never reach it. At this time of day the cars were moving at approximately one hundred sixty miles an hour in the high-acceleration lane. He walked on.

A car passed behind him. He did not look back. If the windows were opaqued, as was usually the case, then the occupants were unaware he had crossed their path. They would hear of it later and examine the front end of their vehicle for possible sign of such an encounter.

A car passed in front of him. Its windows were clear. A glimpse of two faces, their mouths made into O's, was presented to him, then torn from his sight. His own face remained without expression. His pace did not change. Two more cars rushed by, windows darkened. He had crossed perhaps twenty yards of highway.

Twenty-five . . .

Something in the wind, or beneath his feet, told him it was coming. He did not look.

Something in the corner of his eye assured him it was coming. His gait did not alter.

Cecil Green had the windows transpared because he liked it that way. His left hand was inside her blouse and her skirt was piled up on her lap, and his right hand was resting on the lever which would lower the seats. Then she pulled away, making a noise down inside her throat.

His head snapped to the left.

He saw the walking man

He saw the profile which never turned to face him fully. He saw that the man's gait did not alter.

Then he did not see the man.

There was a slight jar, and the windshield began cleaning itself. Cecil Green raced on.

He opaqued the windows.

"How . . . ?" he asked after she was in his arms again, and sobbing.

"The monitor didn't pick him up. . . ."

"He must not have touched the fence. . . ."

"He must have been out of his mind!"

"Still, he could have picked an easier way."

It could have been any face. . . . Mine?

Frightened, Cecil lowered the seats.

Charles Render was writing the "Necropolis" chapter for *The Missing Link Is Man*, which was to be his first book in over four years. Since his return he had set aside every Tuesday and Thursday afternoon to work on it, isolating himself in his office, filling pages with a chaotic longhand.

"There are many varieties of death, as opposed to dying . . ." he was writing, just as the intercom buzzed briefly, then long, then briefly again.

"Yes?" he asked it, pushing down on the switch.

"You have a visitor," and there was a short intake of breath between "a" and "visitor."

He slipped a small aerosol into his side pocket, then rose and crossed the office.

He opened the door and looked out.

"Doctor . . . Help . . ."

Render took three steps, then dropped to one knee.

"What's the matter?"

"Come—she is . . . sick," he growled.

"Sick? How? What's wrong?"

"Don't know. You come."

Render stared into the unhuman eyes.

"What kind of sick?" he insisted.

"Don't know," repeated the dog. "Won't talk. Sits. I . . . feel, she is sick."

"How did you get here?"

"Drove. Know the co, or, din, ates. . . . Left car, outside."

"I'll call her right now." Render turned.

"No good. Won't answer."

He was right.

Render returned to his inner office for his coat and medkit. He glanced out the window and saw where her car was parked, far below, just inside the entrance to the marginal, where the monitor had released it into manual control. If no one assumed that control a car was automatically parked in neutral. The other vehicles were passed around it.

So simple even a dog can drive one, he reflected. *Better get downstairs before a cruiser comes along. It's probably reported itself stopped there already. Maybe not, though. Might still have a few minutes grace.*

He glanced at the huge clock.

"Okay, Sig," he called out. "Let's go."

They took the lift to the ground floor, left by way of the front entrance and hurried to the car.

Its engine was still idling.

Render opened the passengerside door and Sigmund leaped in. He squeezed by him into the driver's seat then, but the dog was already pushing the primary coordinates and the address tabs with his paw.

Looks like I'm in the wrong seat.

He lit a cigarette as the car swept ahead into a U-underpass. It emerged on the opposite marginal, sat poised a moment, then joined the traffic flow. The dog directed the car into the high-acceleration lane.

"Oh," said the dog, "oh."

Render felt like patting his head at that moment, but he looked at him, saw that his teeth were bared, and decided against it.

"When did she start acting peculiar?" he asked.

"Came home from work. Did not eat. Would not answer me when I talked. Just sits."

"Has she ever been like this before?"

"No."

What could have precipitated it?—But maybe she just had a bad day. After all, he's only a dog—sort of.—No. He'd know. But what, then?

"How was she yesterday—and when she left home this morning?"

"Like always."

Render tried calling her again. There was still no answer.

"You did, it," said the dog.

"What do you mean?"

"Eyes. Seeing. You. Machine. Bad."

"No," said Render, and his hand rested on the unit of stun-spray in his pocket.

"Yes," said the dog, turning to him again. "You will, make her well . . . ?"

"Of course," said Render.

Sigmund stared ahead again.

Render felt physically exhilarated and mentally sluggish. He sought the confusion factor. He had had these feelings about the case since that first session. There was something very unsettling about Eileen Shallot; a combination of high intelligence and helplessness, of determination and vulnerability, of sensitivity and bitterness.

Do I find that especially attractive?—No. It's just the counter-transference, damn it!

"You smell afraid," said the dog.

"Then color me afraid," said Render, "and turn the page."

They slowed for a series of turns, picked up speed again, slowed again, picked up speed again. Finally, they were traveling along a narrow section of roadway through a semi-residential area of town. The car turned up a side street, proceeded about half a mile further, clicked softly beneath its dashboard, and turned into the parking lot behind a high brick apartment building. The click must have been a special servomech which took over from the point where the monitor released it, because the car crawled across the lot, headed into its transparent parking stall, then stopped. Render turned off the ignition.

Sigmund had already opened the door on his side. Render followed him into the building, and they rode the elevator to the fiftieth floor. The dog dashed on ahead up the hallway, pressed his nose against a plate set low in a doorframe and waited. After a moment, the door swung several inches inward. He pushed it open with his shoulder and entered. Render followed, closing the door behind him.

The apartment was large, its walls pretty much unadorned, its color combinations unnerving. A great library of tapes filled one corner: a monstrous combination-broadcaster stood beside it. There was a wide bowlegged table set in front of the window, and a low couch along the right-hand wall; there was a closed door beside the couch; an archway to the left apparently led to other rooms. Eileen sat in an overstuffed chair in the far corner by the window. Sigmund stood beside the chair.

Render crossed the room and extracted a cigarette from his case. Snapping open his lighter, he held the flame until her head turned in that direction.

"Cigarette?" he asked.

"Charles?"

"Right."

"Yes, thank you. I will."

She held out her hand, accepted the cigarette, put it to her lips.

"Thanks—What are you doing here?"

"Social call. I happened to be in the neighborhood."

"I didn't hear a buzz or a knock."

"You must have been dozing. Sig let me in."

"Yes, I must have." She stretched. "What time is it?"

"It's close to four-thirty."

"I've been home over two hours then. . . . Must have been very tired. . . ."

"How do you feel now?"

"Fine," she declared. "Care for a cup of coffee?"

"Don't mind if I do."

"A steak to go with it?"

"No, thanks."

"Barcardi in the coffee?"

"Sounds good."

"Excuse me, then. It'll only take a moment."

She went through the door beside the sofa and Render caught a glimpse of a large, shiny, automatic kitchen.

"Well?" he whispered to the dog.

Sigmund shook his head.

"Not same."

Render shook his head.

He deposited his coat on the sofa, folding it carefully about the medkit. He sat beside it and thought.

Did I throw too big a chunk of seeing at once? Is she suffering from depressive side-effects—say, memory repressions, nervous fatigue? Did I upset her sensory-adaptation syndrome somehow? Why have I been proceeding so rapidly anyway? There's no real hurry. Am I so damned eager to write the thing up?—Or am I doing it because she wants me to? Could she be that strong, consciously or unconsciously? Or am I that vulnerable—somehow?

She called him to the kitchen to carry out the tray. He set it on the table and seated himself across from her.

"Good coffee," he said, burning his lips on the cup.

"Smart machine," she stated, facing his voice.

Sigmund stretched out on the carpet next to the table, lowered his head between his forepaws, sighed and closed his eyes.

"I've been wondering," said Render, "whether or not there were any after effects to that last session—like increased synesthesiac experiences, or dreams involving forms, or hallucinations or . . ."

"Yes," she said flatly, "dreams."

"What kind?"

"That last session. I've dreamed it over, and over."

"Beginning to end?"

"No, there's no special order to the events. We're riding through the city, or over the bridge, or sitting at the table, or walking toward the car—just flashes, like that. Vivid ones."

"What sort of feelings accompany these—flashes?"

"I don't know, they're all mixed up."

"What are your feelings now, as you recall them?"

"The same, all mixed up."

"Are you afraid?"

"N-no. I don't think so."

"Do you want to take a vacation from the thing? Do you feel we've been proceeding too rapidly?"

"No. That's not it at all. It's—well, it's like learning to swim. When you finally learn how, why then you swim and you swim and you swim until you're all exhausted. Then you just lie there gasping in air and remembering what it was like, while your friends all hover and chew you out for overexerting yourself—and it's a good feeling, even though you do take a chill and there are pins and needles inside all your muscles. At least, that's the way I do things. I felt that way after the first session and after this last one. First Times are always very special times. . . . The pins and the needles are gone, though, and I've caught my breath again. Lord, I don't want to stop now! I feel fine."

"Do you usually take a nap in the afternoon?"

The ten red nails of her fingers moved across the tabletop as she stretched.

". . . Tired," she smiled, swallowing a yawn. "Half the staff's on vacation or sick leave and I've been beating my brains out all week. I was about ready to fall on my face when I left work. I feel all right now that I've rested, though."

She picked up her coffee cup with both hands, took a large swallow.

"Uh-huh," he said. "Good. I was a bit worried about you. I'm glad to see there was no reason."

She laughed.

"Worried? You've read Dr. Riscomb's notes on my analysis—and on the ONT&R trial—and you think I'm the sort to worry about? Ha! I have an operationally beneficent neurosis concerning my adequacy as a human being. It focuses my energies, coordinates my efforts toward achievement. It enhances my sense of identity. . . ."

"You do have on hell of a memory," he noted "That's almost verbatim."

"Of course."

"You had Sigmund worried today, too."

"Sig? How?"

The dog stirred uneasily, opened one eye.

"Yes," he growled, glaring up at Render. "He needs, a ride, home."

"Have you been driving the car again?"

"Yes."

"After I told you not to?"

"Yes."

"Why?"

"I was a, fraid. You would, not, answer me, when I talked."

"I was *very* tired—and if you ever take the car again, I'm going to have the door fixed so you can't come and go as you please."

"Sorry."

"There's nothing wrong with me."

"I, see."

"You are *never* to do it again."

"Sorry." His eye never left Render; it was like a burning lens.

Render looked away.

"Don't be too hard on the poor fellow," he said. "After all, he thought you were ill and he went for the doctor. Suppose he'd been right? You'd owe him thanks, not a scolding."

Unmollified, Sigmund glared a moment longer and closed his eye.

"He has to be told when he does wrong," she finished.

"I suppose," he said, drinking his coffee. "No harm done, anyhow. Since I'm here, let's talk shop. I'm writing something and I'd like an opinion."

"Great. Give me a footnote?"

"Two or three.—In your opinion, do the general underlying motivations that lead to suicide differ in different periods of history or in different cultures?"

"My well-considered opinion is no, they don't," she said. "Frustrations can lead to depressions or frenzies; and if these are severe enough, they can lead to self-destruction. You ask me about motivations and I think they stay pretty much the same. I feel this is a cross-cultural, cross-temporal aspect of the human condition. I don't think it could be changed without changing the basic nature of man."

"Okay. Check. Now, what of the inciting element?" he asked. "Let man be a constant, his environment is still a variable. If he is placed in an overprotective life-situation, do you feel it would take more or less to depress him—or stimulate him to frenzy—than it would take in a not so protective environment?"

"Hm. Being case-oriented, I'd say it would depend on the man. But I see what you're driving at: a mass predisposition to jump out windows at the drop of a hat—the window even opening itself for you, because you asked it to—the revolt of the bored masses. I don't like the notion. I hope it's wrong."

"So do I, but I was thinking of symbolic suicides too—functional disorders that occur for pretty flimsy reasons."

"Aha! Your lecture last month: autopsychomimesis. I have the tape. Well-told, but I can't agree."

"Neither can I, now. I'm rewriting that whole section—'Thanatos in Cloud-cuckooland,' I'm calling it. It's really the death-instinct moved nearer the surface."

"If I get you a scalpel and a cadaver, will you cut out the death-instinct and let me touch it?"

"Couldn't," he put the grin into his voice, "it would be all used up in a cadaver. Find me a volunteer though, and he'll prove my case by volunteering."

"Your logic is unassailable," she smiled. "Get us some more coffee, okay?"

Render went to the kitchen, spiked and filled the cups, drank a glass of water and returned to the living room. Eileen had not moved; neither had Sigmund.

"What do you do when you're not busy being a Shaper?" she asked him.

"The same things most people do—eat, drink, sleep, talk, visit friends and not-friends, visit places, read . . ."

"Are you a forgiving man?"

"Sometimes. Why?"

"Then forgive me. I argued with a woman today, a woman named De Ville."

"What about?"

"You—and she accused me of such things it were better my mother had not born me. Are you going to marry her?"

"No, marriage is like alchemy. It served an important purpose once, but I hardly feel it's here to stay."

"Good."

"What did you say to her?"

"I gave her a clinic referral card that said, 'Diagnosis:
Bitch. Prescription: Drug therapy and a tight gag.' "

"Oh," said Render, showing interest.

"She tore it up and threw it in my face."

"I wonder why?"

She shrugged, smiled, made a gridwork on the tablecloth.

" 'Fathers and elders, I ponder,' " sighed Render, " 'what is hell?' "

" 'I maintain it is the suffering of being unable to love,' " she finished. "Was Dostoevsky right?"

"I doubt it. I'd put him into group therapy myself. That'd be *real* hell for him—with all those people acting like his characters and enjoying it so."

Render put down his cup and pushed his chair away from the table.

"I suppose you must be going now?"

"I really should," said Render.

"And I can't interest you in food?"

"No."

She stood.

"Okay, I'll get my coat."

"I could drive back myself and just set the car to return."

"No! I'm frightened by the notion of empty cars driving around the city. I'd feel the thing was haunted for the next two and a half weeks.

"Besides," she said, passing through the archway, "you promised me Winchester Cathedral."

"You want to do it today?"

"If you can be persuaded."

As Render stood deciding, Sigmund rose to his feet. He stood directly before him and stared upward into his eyes. He opened his mouth and closed it, several times, but no sounds emerged. Then he turned away and left the room.

"No," Eileen's voice came back, "you will stay here until I return."

Render picked up his coat and put it on, stuffing the medkit into the far pocket.

As they walked up the hall toward the elevator Render thought he heard a very faint and very distant howling sound.

In this place, of all places, Render knew he was the master of all things.

He was at home on those alien worlds, without time, those worlds where flowers copulate and the stars do battle in the heavens, falling at last to the ground, bleeding, like so many split and shattered chalices, and the seas part to reveal stairways leading down, and arms emerge from caverns, waving torches that flame like liquid faces—a midwinter night's nightmare, summer go a-begging, Render knew—for he had visited those worlds on a professional basis for the better part of a decade. With the crooking of a finger he could isolate the sorcerers, bring them to trial for treason against the realm—aye, and he could execute them, could appoint their successors.

Fortunately, this trip was only a courtesy call. . . .

He moved forward through the glade, seeking her.

He could feel her awakening presence all about him.

He pushed through the branches, stood beside the lake. It was cold, blue, and bottomless, the lake, reflecting that slender willow which had become the station of her arrival.

"Eileen!"

The willow swayed toward him, swayed away.

"Eileen! Come forth!"

Leaves fell, floated upon the lake, disturbed its mirror-like placidity, distorted the reflections.

"Eileen?"

All the leaves yellowed at once then, dropped down into the water. The tree ceased its swaying. There was a strange sound in the darkening sky, like the humming of high wires on a cold day.

Suddenly there was a double file of moons passing through the heavens.

Render selected one, reached up and pressed it. The others vanished as he did so, and the world brightened; the humming went out of the air.

He circled the lake to gain a subjective respite from the rejection-action and his counter to it. He moved up along an aisle of pines toward the place where he wanted the cathedral to occur. Birds sang now in the trees. The wind came softly by him. He felt her presence quite strongly.

"Here, Eileen. Here."

She walked beside him then, green silk, hair of bronze, eyes of molten emerald;

she wore an emerald in her forehead. She walked in green slippers over the pine needles, saying: "What happened?"

"You were afraid."

"Why?"

"Perhaps you fear the cathedral. Are you a witch?" he smiled.

"Yes, but it's my day off."

He laughed, and he took her arm, and they rounded an island of foliage, and there was the cathedral reconstructed on a grassy rise, pushing its way above them and above the trees, climbing into the middle air, breathing out organ notes, reflecting a stray ray of sunlight from a plane of glass.

"Hold tight to the world," he said. "Here comes the guided tour."

They moved forward and entered.

" '. . . With its floor-to-ceiling shafts, like so many huge tree trunks, it achieves a ruthless control over its spaces,' " he said. "—Got that from the guidebook. This is the north transept. . . ."

" 'Greensleeves.' " she said, "the organ is playing 'Greensleeves.' "

"So it is. You can't blame me for that though.—Observe the scalloped capitals—"

"I want to go nearer to the music."

"Very well. This way then."

Render felt that something was wrong. He could not put his finger on it.

Everything retained its solidity. . . .

Something passed rapidly then, high above the cathedral, uttering a sonic boom. Render smiled at that, remembering now; it was like a slip of the tongue: for a moment he had confused Eileen with Jill—yes, that was what had happened.

Why, then . . .

A burst of white was the altar. He had never seen it before, anywhere. All the walls were dark and cold about them. Candles flickered in corners and high niches. The organ chorded thunder under invisible hands.

Render knew that something was wrong.

He turned to Eileen Shallot, whose hat was a green cone towering up into the darkness, trailing wisps of green veiling. Her throat was in shadow, but . . .

"That necklace—Where?"

"I don't know," she smiled.

The goblet she held radiated a rosy light. It was reflected from her emerald. It washed him like a draft of cool air.

"Drink?" she asked.

"Stand still," he ordered.

He willed the walls to fall down. They swam in shadow.

"Stand still!" he repeated urgently. "Don't do anything. Try not even to think.

"—Fall down!" he cried. And the walls were blasted in all directions and the roof was flung over the top of the world, and they stood amid ruins lighted by a single taper. The night was black as pitch.

"Why did you do that?" she asked, still holding the goblet out toward him.

"Don't think. Don't think anything," he said. "Relax. You are very tired. As that candle flickers and wanes so does your consciousness. You can barely keep awake. You can hardly stay on your feet. Your eyes are closing. There is nothing to see here anyway."

He willed the candle to go out. It continued to burn.

"I'm not tired. Please have a drink."

He heard organ music through the night. A different tune, one he did not recognize at first.

"I need your cooperation."

"All right. Anything."

"Look! The moon!" he pointed

She looked upward and the moon appeared from behind an inky cloud.

". . . And another, and another."

Moons, like strung pearls, proceeded across the blackness.

"The last one will be red," he stated.

It was.

He reached out then with his right index finger, slid his arm sideways along his field of vision, then tried to touch the red moon.

His arm ached, it burned. He could not move it.

"Wake up!" he screamed.

The red moon vanished, and the white ones.

"Please take a drink."

He dashed the goblet from her hand and turned away. When he turned back she was still holding it before him.

"A drink?"

He turned and fled into the night.

It was like running through a waist-high snowdrift. It was wrong. He was compounding the error by running—he was minimizing his strength, maximizing hers. It was sapping his energies, draining him.

He stood still in the midst of the blackness.

"The world around me moves," he said. "I am its center."

"Please have a drink." she said, and he was standing in the glade beside their table set beside the lake. The lake was black and the moon was silver, and high, and out of his reach. A single candle flickered on the table, making her hair as silver as her dress. She wore the moon on her brow. A bottle of Romanee-Conti stood on the white cloth beside a wide-brimmed wine glass. It was filled to overflowing, that glass, and rosy beads clung to its lip. He was very thirsty, and she was lovelier than anyone he had ever seen before, and her necklace sparkled, and the breeze came cool off the lake, and there was something—something he should remember. . . .

He took a step toward her and his armor clinked lightly as he moved. He reached toward the glass and his right arm stiffened with pain and fell back to his side.

"You are wounded!"

Slowly, he turned his head. The blood flowed from the open wound in his biceps and ran down his arm and dripped from his fingertips. His armor had been breached. He forced himself to look away.

"Drink this, love. It will heal you."

She stood.

Bruce Sterling

Bruce Sterling (1954–   ) is a journalist and SF writer who was the chief polemicist behind the launch of "cyberpunk" science fiction in the 1980s. Sterling's pseudonymous presentation (as Vincent Omniveritas) of the Movement, in his small press fanzine, *Cheap Truth,* and elsewhere, particularly in *Mirrorshades: the Cyberpunk Anthology,* invigorated science fiction in the 1980s. Sterling, William Gibson, Lewis Shiner, and John Shirley, the four central figures of the Movement, positioned themselves as radical reformers of hard science fiction, and attracted many followers and imitators. Sterling and Gibson, at least, became public figures far outside science fiction.

Now Sterling is a major voice of his generation, a successful revolutionary. His picture has been on the cover of *Wired.* His stories, from pure fantasy to hard science fiction, are collected in *Crystal Express* (1989) and *Globalhead: Stories* (1994). He has also published a novel in collaboration with William Gibson, *The Difference Engine* (1990).

Sterling, whose career in SF began in the mid-70s, began the major phase of his writing with his stories of the Shaper/Mech series in the early 1980s. Sterling's first novel, *Involution Ocean* (1977), was billed as "A Harlan Ellison Discovery," and is a work heavily influenced by the 1960s New Wave writers, particularly J. G. Ballard. His second novel, *The Artificial Kid* (1980), first showed serious interest in technological speculation. It escaped general notice in the early 1980s that Sterling had begun a series of stories rich in scientific speculation and technological detail set in a future solar system swarming with humanity and aliens. The first of these is "Swarm."

Then came *Schismatrix* (1985), the culmination of his "swarm" stories of the early 80s, one of the best SF novels of the decade. *Schismatrix* is in the tradition of van Vogtian SF adventure, artfully written to a literary standard far above the general run of hard science fiction, but definitely genre science fiction. The stories and the novel have recently been republished together as *Schismatrix Plus* (1996).

"Swarm" is thematically in the man versus machine tradition of SF stories of biological versus technological progress, one of the great intellectual and social conflicts of our century.

SWARM

"I will miss your conversation during the rest of the voyage," the alien said.

Captain-Doctor Simon Afriel folded his jeweled hands over his gold-embroidered waistcoat. "I regret it also, ensign," he said in the alien's own hissing language. "Our talks together have been very useful to me. I would have paid to learn so much, but you gave it freely."

"But that was only information," the alien said. He shrouded his bead-bright eyes behind thick nictitating membranes. "We Investors deal in energy, and precious metals. To prize and pursue mere knowledge is an immature racial trait." The alien lifted the long ribbed frill behind his pinhole-sized ears.

"No doubt you are right," Afriel said, despising him. "We humans are as children to other races, however; so a certain immaturity seems natural to us." Afriel pulled off his sunglasses to rub the bridge of his nose. The starship cabin was drenched in searing blue light, heavily ultraviolet. It was the light the Investors preferred, and they were not about to change it for one human passenger.

"You have not done badly," the alien said magnanimously. "You are the kind of race we like to do business with: young, eager, plastic, ready for a wide variety of goods and experiences. We would have contacted you much earlier, but your technology was still too feeble to afford us a profit."

"Things are different now," Afriel said. "We'll make you rich."

"Indeed," the Investor said. The frill behind his scaly head flickered rapidly, a sign of amusement. "Within two hundred years you will be wealthy enough to buy from us the secret of our starflight. Or perhaps your Mechanist faction will discover the secret through research."

Afriel was annoyed. As a member of Reshaped faction, he did not appreciate the reference to the rival Mechanists. "Don't put too much stock in mere technical expertise," he said. "Consider the aptitude for languages we Shapers have. It makes our faction a much better trading partner. To a Mechanist, all Investors look alike."

The alien hesitated. Afriel smiled. He had appealed to the alien's personal ambition with his last statement, and the hint had been taken. That was where the Mechanists always erred. They tried to treat all Investors consistently, using the same programmed routines each time. They lacked imagination.

Something would have to be done about the Mechanists, Afriel thought. Something more permanent than the small but deadly confrontations between isolated ships in the Asteroid Belt and the ice-rich Rings of Saturn. Both factions maneuvered constantly, looking for a decisive stroke, bribing away each other's best talent, practicing ambush, assassination, and industrial espionage.

Captain-Doctor Simon Afriel was a past master of these pursuits. That was why the Reshaped faction had paid the millions of kilowatts necessary to buy his passage. Afriel held doctorates in biochemistry and alien linguistics, and a master's degree in magnetic weapons engineering. He was thirty-eight years old and had been Reshaped according to the state of the art at the time of his conception. His hormonal balance had been altered slightly to compensate for long periods spent in free-fall. He had no appendix. The structure of his heart had been redesigned for greater efficiency, and his large intestine had been altered to produce the vitamins normally made by intestinal bacteria. Genetic engineering and rigorous training in childhood had given him an intelligence quotient of one hundred and eighty. He was not the brightest of the agents of the Ring Council, but he was one of the most mentally stable and the best trusted.

"It seems a shame," the alien said, "that a human of your accomplishments should have to rot for two years in this miserable, profitless outpost."

"The years won't be wasted," Afriel said.

"But why have you chosen to study the Swarm? They can teach you nothing, since they cannot speak. They have no wish to trade, having no tools or technology. They are the only spacefaring race that is essentially without intelligence."

"That alone should make them worthy of study."

"Do you seek to imitate them, then? You would make monsters of yourselves." Again the ensign hesitated. "Perhaps you could do it. It would be bad for business, however."

There came a fluting burst of alien music over the ship's speakers, then a screeching fragment of Investor language. Most of it was too high-pitched for Afriel's ears to follow.

The alien stood, his jeweled skirt brushing the tips of his clawed birdlike feet. "The Swarm's symbiote has arrived," he said.

"Thank you," Afriel said. When the ensign opened the cabin door, Afriel could smell the Swarm's representative; the creature's warm yeasty scent had spread rapidly through the starship's recycled air.

Afriel quickly checked his appearance in a pocket mirror. He touched powder to his face and straightened the round velvet hat on his shoulder-length reddish-blond hair. His earlobes glittered with red impact-rubies, thick as his thumbs' ends, mined from the Asteroid Belt. His knee-length coat and waistcoat were of gold brocade; the shirt beneath was of dazzling fineness, woven with red-gold thread. He had dressed to impress the Investors, who expected and appreciated a prosperous look from their customers. How could he impress this new alien? Smell, perhaps. He freshened his perfume.

Beside the starship's secondary airlock, the Swarm's symbiote was chittering rapidly at the ship's commander. The commander was an old and sleepy Investor, twice the size of most of her crewmen. Her massive head was encrusted in a jeweled helmet. From within the helmet her clouded eyes glittered like cameras.

The symbiote lifted on its six posterior legs and gestured feebly with its four clawed forelimbs. The ship's artificial gravity, a third again as strong as Earth's, seemed to bother it. Its rudimentary eyes, dangling on stalks, were shut tight against the glare. It must be used to darkness, Afriel thought.

The commander answered the creature in its own language. Afriel grimaced, for he had hoped that the creature spoke Investor. Now he would have to learn another language, a language designed for a being without a tongue.

After another brief interchange the commander turned to Afriel. "The symbiote is not pleased with your arrival," she told Afriel in the Investor language. "There has apparently been some disturbance here involving humans, in the recent past. However, I have prevailed upon it to admit you to the Nest. The episode has been recorded. Payment for my diplomatic services will be arranged with your faction when I return to your native star system."

"I thank Your Authority," Afriel said. "Please convey to the symbiote my best personal wishes, and the harmlessness and humility of my intentions—" He broke off short as the symbiote lunged toward him, biting him savagely in the calf of his left leg. Afriel jerked free and leaped backward in the heavy artificial gravity, going into a defensive position. The symbiote had ripped away a long shred of his pants leg; it now crouched quietly, eating it.

"It will convey your scent and composition to its nestmates," said the commander. "This is necessary. Otherwise you would be classed as an invader, and the Swarm's warrior caste would kill you at once."

Afriel relaxed quickly and pressed his hand against the puncture wound to stop the bleeding. He hoped that none of the Investors had noticed his reflexive action. It would not mesh well with his story of being a harmless researcher.

"We will reopen the airlock soon," the commander said phlegmatically, leaning back on her thick reptilian tail. The symbiote continued to munch the shred of cloth. Afriel studied the creature's neckless segmented head. It had a mouth and nostrils; it had bulbous atrophied eyes on stalks; there were hinged slats that might be radio receivers, and two parallel ridges of clumped wriggling antennae, sprouting among three chitinous plates. Their function was unknown to him.

The airlock door opened. A rush of dense, smoky aroma entered the departure cabin. It seemed to bother the half-dozen Investors, who left rapidly. "We will return in six hundred and twelve of your days, as by our agreement," the commander said.

"I thank Your Authority," Afriel said.

"Good luck," the commander said in English. Afriel smiled.

The symbiote, with a sinuous wriggle of its segmented body, crept into the airlock. Afriel followed it. The airlock door shut behind them. The creature said nothing to him but continued munching loudly. The second door opened, and the symbiote sprang through it, into a wide, round stone tunnel. It disappeared at once into the gloom.

Afriel put his sunglasses into a pocket of his jacket and pulled out a pair of infrared goggles. He strapped them to his head and stepped out of the airlock. The artificial gravity vanished, replaced by the almost imperceptible gravity of the Swarm's asteroid nest. Afriel smiled, comfortable for the first time in weeks. Most of his adult life had been spent in free-fall, in the Shapers' colonies in the Rings of Saturn.

Squatting in a dark cavity in the side of the tunnel was a disk-headed furred animal the size of an elephant. It was clearly visible in the infrared of its own body heat. Afriel could hear it breathing. It waited patiently until Afriel had launched himself past it, deeper into the tunnel. Then it took its place in the end of the tunnel, puffing itself up with air until its swollen head securely plugged the exit into space. Its multiple legs sank firmly into sockets in the walls.

The Investors' ship had left. Afriel remained here, inside one of the millions of planetoids that circled the giant star Betelgeuse in a girdling ring with almost five times the mass of Jupiter. As a source of potential wealth it dwarfed the entire solar system, and it belonged, more or less, to the Swarm. At least, no other race had challenged them for it within the memory of the Investors.

Afriel peered up the corridor. It seemed deserted, and without other bodies to cast infrared heat, he could not see very far. Kicking against the wall, he floated hesitantly down the corridor.

He heard a human voice. "Dr. Afriel!"

"Dr. Mirny!" he called out. "This way!"

He first saw a pair of young symbiotes scuttling toward him, the tips of their clawed feet barely touching the walls. Behind them came a woman wearing goggles like his own. She was young, and attractive in the trim, anonymous way of the genetically reshaped.

She screeched something at the symbiotes in their own language, and they halted, waiting. She coasted forward, and Afriel caught her arm, expertly stopping their momentum.

"You didn't bring any luggage?" she said anxiously.

He shook his head. "We got your warning before I was sent out. I have only the clothes I'm wearing and a few items in my pockets."

She looked at him critically. "Is that what people are wearing in the Rings these days? Things have changed more than I thought."

Afriel glanced at his brocaded coat and laughed. "It's a matter of policy. The Investors are always readier to talk to a human who looks ready to do business on a large scale. All the Shapers' representatives dress like this these days. We've stolen a jump on the Mechanists; they still dress in those coveralls."

He hesitated, not wanting to offend her. Galina Mirny's intelligence was rated at almost two hundred. Men and women that bright were sometimes flighty and unstable, likely to retreat into private fantasy worlds or become enmeshed in strange and impenetrable webs of plotting and rationalization. High intelligence was the strategy the Shapers had chosen in the struggle for cultural dominance, and they were obliged to stick to it, despite its occasional disadvantages. They had tried breeding the Superbright—those with quotients over two hundred—but so many had defected from the Shapers' colonies that the faction had stopped producing them.

"You wonder about my own clothing," Mirny said.

"It certainly has the appeal of novelty," Afriel said with a smile.

"It was woven from the fibers of a pupa's cocoon," she said. "My original wardrobe was eaten by a scavenger symbiote during the troubles last year. I usually go nude, but I didn't want to offend you by too great a show of intimacy."

Afriel shrugged. "I often go nude myself, I never had much use for clothes except for pockets. I have a few tools on my person, but most are of little importance. We're Shapers, our tools are here." He tapped his head. "If you can show me a safe place to put my clothes . . ."

She shook her head. It was impossible to see her eyes for the goggles, which made her expression hard to read. "You've made your first mistake, Doctor. There are no places of our own here. It was the same mistake the Mechanist agents made, the same one that almost killed me as well. There is no concept of privacy or property here. This is the Nest. If you seize any part of it for yourself—to store equipment, to sleep in, whatever—then you become an intruder, an enemy. The two Mechanists—a man and a woman—tried to secure an empty chamber for their computer lab. Warriors broke down their door and devoured them. Scavengers ate their equipment, glass, metal, and all."

Afriel smiled coldly. "It must have cost them a fortune to ship all that material here."

Mirny shrugged. "They're wealthier than we are. Their machines, their mining. They meant to kill me, I think. Surreptitiously, so the warriors wouldn't be upset by a show of violence. They had a computer that was learning the language of the springtails faster than I could."

"But you survived," Afriel pointed out. "And your tapes and reports—especially the early ones, when you still had most of your equipment—were of tremendous interest. The Council is behind you all the way. You've become quite a celebrity in the Rings, during your absence."

"Yes, I expected as much," she said.

Afriel was nonplused. "If I found any deficiency in them," he said carefully, "it was in my own field, alien linguistics." He waved vaguely at the two symbiotes who accompanied her. "I assume you've made great progress in communicating with the symbiotes, since they seem to do all the talking for the Nest."

She looked at him with an unreadable expression and shrugged. "There are at least fifteen different kinds of symbiotes here. Those that accompany me are called the springtails, and they speak only for themselves. They are savages, Doctor, who received attention from the Investors only because they can still talk. They were a spacefaring race once, but they've forgotten it. They discovered the Nest and they were absorbed, they became parasites." She tapped one of them on the head. "I tamed these two because I learned to steal and beg food better than they can. They stay with me now and protect me from the larger ones. They are jealous, you know. They have only been with the Nest for perhaps ten thousand years and are still uncertain of their position. They still think, and wonder sometimes. After ten thousand years there is still a little of that left to them."

"Savages," Afriel said. "I can well believe that. One of them bit me while I was still aboard the starship. He left a lot to be desired as an ambassador."

"Yes, I warned him you were coming," said Mirny. "He didn't much like the idea, but I was able to bribe him with food. . . . I hope he didn't hurt you badly."

"A scratch," Afriel said. "I assume there's no chance of infection."

"I doubt it very much. Unless you brought your own bacteria with you."

"Hardly likely," Afriel said, offended. "I have no bacteria. And I wouldn't have brought microorganisms to an alien culture anyway."

Mirny looked away. "I thought you might have some of the special genetically altered ones. . . . I think we can go now. The springtail will have spread your scent by mouth-touching in the subsidiary chamber, ahead of us. It will be spread throughout the Nest in a few hours. Once it reaches the Queen, it will spread very quickly."

She jammed her feet against the hard shell of one of the young springtails and launched herself down the hall. Afriel followed her. The air was warm and he was beginning to sweat under his elaborate clothing, but his antiseptic sweat was odorless.

They exited into a vast chamber dug from the living rock. It was arched and oblong, eighty meters long and about twenty in diameter. It swarmed with members of the Nest.

There were hundreds of them. Most of them were workers, eight-legged and furred, the size of Great Danes. Here and there were members of the warrior caste, horse-sized furry monsters with heavy fanged heads the size and shape of overstuffed chairs.

A few meters away, two workers were carrying a member of the sensor caste, a being whose immense flattened head was attached to an atrophied body that was mostly lungs. The sensor had great platelike eyes, and its furred chitin sprouted long coiled antennae that twitched feebly as the workers bore it along. The workers clung to the hollowed rock of the chamber walls with hooked and suckered feet.

A paddle-limbed monster with a hairless, faceless head came sculling past them, through the warm reeking air. The front of its head was a nightmare of sharp grinding jaws and blunt armored acid spouts. "A tunneler," Mirny said. "It can take us deeper into the Nest—come with me." She launched herself toward it and took a handhold on its furry, segmented back. Afriel followed her, joined by the two immature springtails, who clung to the thing's hide with their forelimbs. Afriel shuddered at the warm, greasy feel of its rank, damp fur. It continued to scull through the air, its eight fringed paddle feet catching the air like wings.

"There must be thousands of them," Afriel said.

"I said a hundred thousand in my last report, but that was before I had fully explored the Nest. Even now there are long stretches I haven't seen. They must number close to a quarter of a million. This asteroid is about the size of the Mechanists' biggest base—Ceres. It still has rich veins of carbonaceous material. It's far from mined out."

Afriel closed his eyes. If he was to lose his goggles, he would have to feel his way, blind, through these teeming, twitching, wriggling thousands. "The population's still expanding, then?"

"Definitely," she said. "In fact, the colony will launch a mating swarm soon. There are three dozen male and female alates in the chambers near the Queen. Once they're launched, they'll mate and start new Nests. I'll take you to see them presently." She hesitated. "We're entering one of the fungal gardens now."

One of the young springtails quietly shifted position. Grabbing the tunneler's fur with its forelimbs, it began to gnaw on the cuff of Afriel's pants. Afriel kicked it soundly, and it jerked back, retracting its eyestalks.

When he looked up again, he saw that had entered a second chamber, much larger than the first. The walls around, overhead, and below were buried under an explosive profusion of fungus. The most common types were swollen barrel-like domes, multibranched massed thickets, and spaghetti-like tangled extrusions that moved very slightly in the faint and odorous breeze. Some of the barrels were surrounded by dim mists of exhaled spores.

"You see those caked-up piles beneath the fungus, its growth medium?" Mirny said.

"Yes."

"I'm not sure whether it is a plant form or just some kind of complex biochemical sludge," she said. "The point is that it grows in sunlight, on the outside of the asteroid. A food source that grows in naked space! Imagine what that would be worth, back in the Rings."

"There aren't words for its value," Afriel said.

"It's inedible by itself," she said. "I tried to eat a very small piece of it once. It was like trying to eat plastic."

"Have you eaten well, generally speaking?"

"Yes. Our biochemistry is quite similar to the Swarm's. The fungus itself is perfectly edible. The regurgitate is more nourishing, though. Internal fermentation in the worker hindgut adds to its nutritional value."

Afriel stared. "You grow used to it," Mirny said. "Later I'll teach you how to solicit food from the workers. It's a simple matter of reflex tapping—it's not controlled by pheromones, like most of their behavior." She brushed a long lock of clumped and dirty hair from the side of her face. "I hope the pheromonal samples I sent back were worth the cost of transportation."

"Oh, yes," said Afriel. "The chemistry of them was fascinating. We managed to synthesize most of the compounds. I was part of the research team myself." He hesitated. How far did he dare trust her? She had not been told about the experiment he and his superiors had planned. As far as Mirny knew, he was a simple, peaceful researcher, like herself. The Shapers' scientific community was suspicious of the minority involved in military work and espionage.

As an investment in the future, the Shapers had sent researchers of each of the nineteen alien races described to them by the Investors. This had cost the Shaper economy many gigawatts of precious energy and tons of rare metals and isotopes. In most cases, only two or three researchers could be sent; in seven cases, only one. For the Swarm, Galina Mirny had been chosen. She had gone peacefully, trusting in her intelligence and her good intentions to keep her alive and sane. Those who had sent her had not known whether her findings would be of any use or importance. They had only known that it was imperative that she be sent, even alone, even ill-equipped, before some other faction sent their own people and possibly discovered some technique or fact of overwhelming importance. And Dr. Mirny had indeed discovered such a situation. It had made her mission into a matter of Ring security. That was why Afriel had come.

"You synthesized the compounds?" she said. "Why?"

Afriel smiled disarmingly. "Just to prove to ourselves that we could do it, perhaps."

She shook her head. "No mind-games, Dr. Afriel, please. I came this far partly to escape from such things. Tell me the truth."

Afriel stared at her, regretting that the goggles meant he could not meet her eyes. "Very well," he said. "You should know, then, that I have been ordered by the Ring Council to carry out an experiment that may endanger both our lives."

Mirny was silent for a moment. "You're from Security, then?"

"My rank is captain."

"I knew it. . . . I knew it when those two Mechanists arrived. They were so polite, and so suspicious—I think they would have killed me at once if they hadn't hoped to bribe or torture some secret out of me. They scared the life out of me, Captain Afriel. . . . You scare me, too."

"We live in a frightening world, Doctor. It's a matter of faction security."

"Everything's a matter of faction security with your lot," she said. "I shouldn't take you any farther, or show you anything more. This Nest, these creatures—they're not *intelligent*, Captain. They can't think, they can't learn. They're innocent, primordially innocent. They have no knowledge of good and evil. They have no knowledge of *anything*. The last thing they need is to become pawns in a power struggle within some other race, light-years away."

The tunneler had turned into an exit from the fungal chambers and was paddling slowly along in the warm darkness. A group of creatures like gray, flattened basketballs floated by from the opposite direction. One of them settled on Afriel's sleeve, clinging with frail whiplike tentacles. Afriel brushed it gently away, and it broke loose, emitting a stream of foul reddish droplets.

"Naturally I agree with you in principle, Doctor," Afriel said smoothly. "But consider these Mechanists. Some of their extreme factions are already more than half machine. Do you expect humanitarian motives from them? They're cold, Doctor—cold and soulless creatures who can cut a living man or woman to bits and never feel their pain. Most of the other factions hate us. They call us racist supermen. Would you rather that one of these cults do what we must do, and use the results against us?"

"This is double-talk." She looked away. All around them workers laden down with fungus, their jaws full and guts stuffed with it, were spreading out into the Nest, scuttling alongside them or disappearing into branch tunnels departing in every direction, including straight up and straight down. Afriel saw a creature much like a worker, but with only six legs, scuttle past in the opposite direction, overhead. It was a parasite mimic. How long, he wondered, did it take a creature to evolve to look like that?

"It's no wonder that we've had so many defectors, back in the Rings," she said sadly. "If humanity is so stupid as to work itself into a corner like you describe, then it's better to have nothing to do with them. Better to live alone. Better not to help the madness spread."

"That kind of talk will only get us killed," Afriel said. "We owe an allegiance to the faction that produced us."

"Tell me truly, Captain," she said. "Haven't you ever felt the urge to leave everything—everyone—all your duties and constraints, and just go somewhere to think it all out? Your whole world, and your part in it? We're trained so hard, from childhood, and so much is demanded from us. Don't you think it's made us lose sight of our goals, somehow?"

"We live in space," Afriel said flatly. "Space is an unnatural environment, and it takes an unnatural effort from unnatural people to prosper there. Our minds are our tools, and philosophy has to come second. Naturally I've felt those urges you mention. They're just another threat to guard against. I believe in an ordered society. Technology has unleashed tremendous forces that are ripping society apart. Some one faction must arise from the struggle and integrate things. We Shapers have the wisdom and restraint to do it humanely. That's why I do the work I do." He hesitated. "I don't expect to see our day of triumph. I expect to die in some brush-fire conflict, or through assassination. It's enough that I can foresee that day."

"But the arrogance of it, Captain!" she said suddenly. "The arrogance of your little life and its little sacrifice! Consider the Swarm, if you really want your humane and perfect order. Here it is! Where it's always warm and dark, and it smells good, and food is easy to get, and everything is endlessly and perfectly recycled. The only resources that are ever lost are the bodies of the mating swarms, and a little air. A Nest like this one could last unchanged for hundreds of thousands of years. Hundreds . . . of thousands . . . of years. Who, or what, will remember us and our stupid faction in even a thousand years?"

Afriel shook his head. "That's not a valid comparison. There is no such long view for us. In another thousand years we'll be machines, or gods." He felt the top of his head; his velvet cap was gone. No doubt something was eating it by now.

The tunneler took them deeper into the asteroid's honeycombed free-fall maze. They saw the pupal chambers, where pallid larvae twitched in swaddled silk; the main fungal gardens; the graveyard pits, where winged workers beat ceaselessly at the soupy air, feverishly hot from the heat of decomposition. Corrosive black fungus ate the bodies of the dead into coarse black powder, carried off by blackened workers themselves three-quarters dead.

Later they left the tunneler and floated on by themselves. The woman moved with the ease of long habit; Afriel followed her, colliding bruisingly with squeaking workers. There were thousands of them, clinging to ceiling, walls, and floor, clustering and scurrying at every conceivable angle.

Later still they visited the chamber of the winged princes and princesses, an echoing round vault where creatures forty meters long hung crooked-legged in midair. Their bodies were segmented and metallic, with organic rocket nozzles on their thoraxes, where wings might have been. Folded along their sleek backs were radar antennae on long sweeping booms. They looked more like interplanetary probes under construction than anything biological. Workers fed them ceaselessly. Their bulging spiracled abdomens were full of compressed oxygen.

Mirny begged a large chunk of fungus from a passing worker, deftly tapping its antennae and provoking a reflex action. She handed most of the fungus to the two springtails, who devoured it greedily and looked expectantly for more.

Afriel tucked his legs into a free-fall lotus position and began chewing with determination on the leathery fungus. It was tough, but tasted good, like smoked meat—a delicacy he had tasted only once. The smell of smoke meant disaster in a Shaper's colony.

Mirny maintained a stony silence. "Food's no problem," Afriel said. "Where do we sleep?"

She shrugged. "Anywhere . . . there are unused niches and tunnels here and there. I suppose you'll want to see the Queen's chamber next."

"By all means."

"I'll have to get more fungus. The warriors are on guard there and have to be bribed with food."

She gathered an armful of fungus from another worker in the endless stream, and they moved on. Afriel, already totally lost, was further confused in the maze of chambers and tunnels. At last they exited into an immense lightless cavern, bright with infrared heat from the Queen's monstrous body. It was the colony's central factory. The fact that it was made of warm and pulpy flesh did not conceal its essentially industrial nature. Tons of predigested fungal pap went into the slick blind jaws at one end. The rounded billows of soft flesh digested and processed it, squirming, sucking, and undulating, with loud machine-like churnings and gurglings. Out of the other end came an endless conveyor-like blobbed stream of eggs, each one packed in a thick hormonal paste of lubrication. The workers avidly licked the eggs clean and bore them off to nurseries. Each egg was the size of a man's torso.

The process went on and on. There was no day or night here in the lightless center of the asteroid. There was no remnant of a diurnal rhythm in the genes of these creatures. The flow of production was as constant and even as the working of an automated mine.

"This is why I'm here," Afriel murmured in awe. "Just look at this, Doctor. The Mechanists have cybernetic mining machinery that is generations ahead of ours. But here—in the bowels of this nameless little world—is a genetic technology that feeds itself, maintains itself, runs itself, efficiently, endlessly, mindlessly. It's the perfect organic tool. The faction that could use these tireless workers could make itself an industrial titan. And our knowledge of biochemistry is unsurpassed. We Shapers are just the ones to do it."

"How do you propose to do that?" Mirny asked with open skepticism. "You would have to ship a fertilized queen all the way to the solar system. We could scarcely afford that, even if the Investors would let us, which they wouldn't."

"I don't need an entire Nest," Afriel said patiently. "I only need the genetic information from one egg. Our laboratories back in the Rings could clone endless numbers of workers."

"But the workers are useless without the Nest's pheromones. They need chemical cues to trigger their behavior modes."

"Exactly," Afriel said. "As it so happens, I possess those pheromones, synthesized and concentrated. What I must do now is test them. I must prove that I can use them to make the workers do what I choose. Once I've proven it's possible, I'm authorized to smuggle the genetic information necessary back to the Rings. The Investors won't approve. There are, of course, moral questions involved, and the Investors are not genetically advanced. But we can win their approval back with the profits we make. Best of all, we can beat the Mechanists at their own game."

"You've carried the pheromones here?" Mirny said. "Didn't the Investors suspect something when they found them?"

"Now it's you who has made an error," Afriel said calmly. "You assume that the Investors are infallible. You are wrong. A race without curiosity will never explore every possibility, the way we Shapers did." Afriel pulled up his pants cuff and extended his right leg. "Consider this varicose vein along my shin. Circulatory problems of this sort are common among those who spend a lot of time in free-fall. This vein, however, has been blocked artificially and treated to reduce osmosis. Within the vein are ten separate colonies of genetically altered bacteria, each one specially bred to produce a different Swarm pheromone."

He smiled. "The Investors searched me very thoroughly, including X-rays. But the vein appears normal to X-rays, and the bacteria are trapped within compartments in the vein. They are indetectable. I have a small medical kit on my person. It includes a syringe. We can use it to extract the pheromones and test them. When the tests are finished—and I feel sure they will be successful, in fact I've staked my career on it—we can empty the vein and all its compartments. The bacteria will die on contact with air. We can refill the vein with the yolk from a developing embryo. The cells may survive during the trip back, but even if they die, they can't rot inside my body. They'll never come in contact with any agent of decay. Back in the Rings, we can learn to activate and suppress different genes to produce the different castes, just as is done in nature. We'll have millions of workers, armies of warriors if need be, perhaps even organic rocketships, grown from altered alates. If this works, who do you think will remember me then, eh? Me and my arrogant little life and little sacrifice?"

She stared at him; even the bulky goggles could not hide her new respect and even fear. "You really mean to do it, then."

"I made the sacrifice of my time and energy. I expect results, Doctor."

"But it's kidnapping. You're talking about breeding a slave race."

Afriel shrugged, with contempt. "You're juggling words, Doctor. I'll cause this colony no harm. I may steal some of its workers' labor while they obey my own chemical orders, but that tiny theft won't be missed. I admit to the murder of one egg, but that is no more a crime than a human abortion. Can the theft of one strand of genetic material be called 'kidnapping'? I think not. As for the scandalous idea of a slave race—I reject it out of hand. These creatures are genetic robots. They will no more be slaves than are laser drills or cargo tankers. At the very worst, they will be our domestic animals."

Mirny considered the issue. It did not take her long. "It's true. It's not as if a common worker will be staring at the stars, pining for its freedom. They're just brainless neuters."

"Exactly, Doctor."

"They simply work. Whether they work for us or the Swarm makes no difference to them."

"I see that you've seized on the beauty of the idea."

"And if it worked," Mirny said, "if it worked, our faction would profit astronomically."

Afriel smiled genuinely, unaware of the chilling sarcasm of his expression. "And the personal profit, Doctor . . . the valuable expertise of the first to exploit the technique." He spoke gently, quietly. "Ever see a nitrogen snowfall on Titan? I think a habitat of one's own there—larger, much larger than anything possible before. . . . A genuine city, Galina, a place where a man can scrap the rules and discipline that madden him. . . ."

"Now it's you who are talking defection, Captain-Doctor."

Afriel was silent for a moment, then smiled with an effort. "Now you've ruined my perfect reverie," he said. "Besides, what I was describing was the well-earned retirement of a wealthy man, not some self-indulgent hermitage. . . . There's a clear difference." He hesitated. "In any case, may I conclude that you're with me in this project?"

She laughed and touched his arm. There was something uncanny about the small sound of her laugh, drowned by a great organic rumble from the Queen's monstrous intestines. . . . "Do you expect me to resist your arguments for two long years? Better that I give in now and save us friction."

"Yes."

"After all, you won't do any harm to the Nest. They'll never know anything has happened. And if their genetic line is successfully reproduced back home, there'll never be any reason for humanity to bother them again."

"True enough," said Afriel, though in the back of his mind he instantly thought of the fabulous wealth of Betelgeuse's asteroid system. A day would come, inevitably, when humanity would move to the stars en masse, in earnest. It would be well to know the ins and outs of every race that might become a rival.

"I'll help you as best I can," she said. There was a moment's silence. "Have you seen enough of this area?"

"Yes." They left the Queen's chamber.

"I didn't think I'd like you at first," she said candidly. "I think I like you better now. You seem to have a sense of humor that most Security people lack."

"It's not a sense of humor," Afriel said sadly. "It's a sense of irony disguised as one."

There were no days in the unending stream of hours that followed. There were only ragged periods of sleep, apart at first, later together, as they held each other in free-fall. The sexual feel of skin and body became an anchor to their common humanity, a divided, frayed humanity so many light-years away that the concept no longer had any meaning. Life in the warm and swarming tunnels was the here and now; the two of them were like germs in a bloodstream, moving ceaselessly with the pulsing ebb and flow. Hours stretched into months, and time itself grew meaningless.

The pheromonal tests were complex, but not impossibly difficult. The first of the ten pheromones was a simple grouping stimulus, causing large numbers of workers to gather as the chemical was spread from palp to palp. The workers then waited for further instructions; if none were forthcoming, they dispersed. To work effectively, the pheromones had to be given in a mix, or series, like computer commands; number one, grouping, for instance, together with the third pheromone, a transferral order, which caused the workers to empty any given chamber and move its effects to another. The ninth pheromone had the best industrial possibilities; it was a building order, causing the workers to gather tunnelers and dredgers and set them to work. Others were annoying; the tenth pheromone provoked grooming behavior, and the workers' furry palps stripped off the remaining rags of Afriel's clothing. The eighth pheromone sent the workers off to harvest material on the asteroid's surface, and in their eagerness to observe its effects the two explorers were almost trapped and swept off into space.

The two of them no longer feared the warrior caste. They knew that a dose of the sixth pheromone would send them scurrying off to defend the eggs, just as it sent the workers to tend them. Mirny and Afriel took advantage of this and secured their own chambers, dug by chemically hijacked workers and defended by a hijacked airlock guardian. They had their own fungal gardens to refresh the air, stocked with the fungus they liked best, and digested by a worker they kept drugged for their own food use. From constant stuffing and lack of exercise the worker had swollen up into its replete form and hung from one wall like a monstrous grape.

Afriel was tired. He had been without sleep recently for a long time; how long, he didn't know. His body rhythms had not adjusted as well as Mirny's, and he was prone to fits of depression and irritability that he had to repress with an effort. "The Investors will be back sometime," he said. "Sometime soon."

Mirny was indifferent. "The Investors," she said, and followed the remark with something in the language of the springtails, which he didn't catch. Despite his linguistic training, Afriel had never caught up with her in her use of the springtails' grating jargon. His training was almost a liability; the springtail language had decayed so much that it was a pidgin tongue, without rules or regularity. He knew enough to give them simple orders, and with his partial control of the warriors he had the power to back it up. The springtails were afraid of him, and the two juveniles that Mirny had tamed had developed into fat, overgrown tyrants that freely terrorized their elders. Afriel had been too busy to seriously study the springtails or the other symbiotes. There were too many practical matters at hand.

"If they come too soon, I won't be able to finish my latest study," she said in English.

Afriel pulled off his infrared goggles and knotted them tightly around his neck. "There's a limit, Galina," he said, yawning. "You can only memorize so much data without equipment. We'll just have to wait quietly until we can get back. I hope the Investors aren't shocked when they see me. I lost a fortune with those clothes."

"It's been so dull since the mating swarm was launched. If it weren't for the new growth in the alates' chamber, I'd be bored to death." She pushed greasy hair from her face with both hands. "Are you going to sleep?"

"Yes, if I can."

"You won't come with me? I keep telling you that this new growth is important. I think it's a new caste. It's definitely not an alate. It has eyes like an alate, but it's clinging to the wall."

"It's probably not a Swarm member at all, then," he said tiredly, humoring her. "It's probably a parasite, an alate mimic. Go on and see it, if you want to. I'll be here waiting for you."

He heard her leave. Without his infrareds on, the darkness was still not quite total; there was a very faint luminosity from the steaming, growing fungus in the chamber beyond. The stuffed worker replete moved slightly on the wall, rustling and gurgling. He fell asleep.

When he awoke, Mirny had not yet returned. He was not alarmed. First, he visited the original airlock tunnel, where the Investors had first left him. It was irrational—the Investors always fulfilled their contracts—but he feared that they would arrive someday, become impatient, and leave without him. The Investors would have to wait, of course. Mirny could keep them occupied in the short time it would take him to hurry to the nursery and rob a developing egg of its living cells. It was best that the egg be as fresh as possible.

Later he ate. He was munching fungus in one of the anterior chambers when Mirny's two tamed springtails found him. "What do you want?" he asked in their language.

"Food-giver no good," the larger one screeched, waving its forelegs in brainless agitation. "Not work, not sleep."

"Not move," the second one said. It added hopefully, "Eat it now?"

Afriel gave them some of his food. They ate it, seemingly more out of habit than real appetite, which alarmed him. "Take me to her," he told them.

The two springtails scurried off; he followed them easily, adroitly dodging and weaving through the crowds of workers. They led him several miles through the network, to the alates' chamber. There they stopped, confused. "Gone," the large one said.

The chamber was empty. Afriel had never seen it empty before, and it was very unusual for the Swarm to waste so much space. He felt dread. "Follow the food-giver," he said. "Follow the smell."

The springtails snuffled without much enthusiasm along one wall; they knew he had no food and were reluctant to do anything without an immediate reward. At last one of them picked up the scent, or pretended to, and followed it up across the ceiling and into the mouth of a tunnel.

It was hard for Afriel to see much in the abandoned chamber; there was not enough infrared heat. He leaped upward after the springtail.

He heard the roar of a warrior and the springtail's choked-off screech. It came flying from the tunnel's mouth, a spray of clotted fluid bursting from its ruptured head. It tumbled end over end until it hit the far wall with a flaccid crunch. It was already dead.

The second springtail fled at once, screeching with grief and terror. Afriel landed on the lip of the tunnel, sinking into a crouch as his legs soaked up momentum. He could smell the acrid stench of the warrior's anger, a pheromone so thick that even a human could scent it. Dozens of other warriors would group here within minutes, or seconds. Behind the enraged warrior he could hear workers and tunnelers shifting and cementing rock.

He might be able to control one enraged warrior, but never two, or twenty. He launched himself from the chamber wall and out an exit.

He searched for the other springtail—he felt sure he could recognize it, since it was so much bigger than the others—but he could not find it. With its keen sense of smell, it could easily avoid him if it wanted to.

Mirny did not return. Uncountable hours passed. He slept again. He returned to the alates' chamber; there were warriors on guard there, warriors that were not interested in food and brandished their immense serrated fangs when he approached. They looked ready to rip him apart; the faint reek of aggressive pheromones hung about the place like a fog. He did not see any symbiotes of any kind on the warriors' bodies. There was one species, a thing like a huge tick, that clung only to warriors, but even the ticks were gone.

He returned to his chambers to wait and think. Mirny's body was not in the garbage pits. Of course, it was possible that something else might have eaten her. Should he extract the remaining pheromone from the spaces in his vein and try to break into the alates' chamber? He suspected that Mirny, or whatever was left of her, was somewhere in the tunnel where the springtail had been killed. He had never explored that tunnel himself. There were thousands of tunnels he had never explored.

He felt paralyzed by indecision and fear. If he was quiet, if he did nothing, the Investors might arrive at any moment. He could tell the Ring Council anything he wanted about Mirny's death; if he had the genetics with him, no one would quibble. He did not love her; he respected her, but not enough to give up his life, or his faction's investment. He had not thought of the Ring Council in a long time, and the thought sobered him. He would have to explain his decision. . . .

He was still in a brown study when he heard a whoosh of air as his living airlock deflated itself. Three warriors had come for him. There was no reek of anger about them. They moved slowly and carefully. He knew better than to try to resist. One of them seized him gently in its massive jaws and carried him off.

It took him to the alates' chamber and into the guarded tunnel. A new, large chamber had been excavated at the end of the tunnel. It was filled almost to bursting by a black-splattered white mass of flesh. In the center of the soft speckled mass were a mouth and two damp, shining eyes, on stalks. Long tendrils like conduits dangled, writhing, from a clumped ridge above the eyes. The tendrils ended in pink, fleshy pluglike clumps.

One of the tendrils had been thrust through Mirny's skull. Her body hung in midair, limp as wax. Her eyes were open, but blind.

Another tendril was plugged into the braincase of a mutated worker. The worker still had the pallid tinge of a larva; it was shrunken and deformed, and its mouth had the wrinkled look of a human mouth. There was a blob like a tongue in the mouth, and white ridges like human teeth. It had no eyes.

It spoke with Mirny's voice. "Captain-Doctor Afriel . . ."

"Galina . . ."

"I have no such name. You may address me as Swarm."

Afriel vomited. The central mass was an immense head. Its brain almost filled the room.

It waited politely until Afriel had finished.

"I find myself awakened again," Swarm said dreamily. "I am pleased to see that there is no major emergency to concern me. Instead it is a threat that has become almost routine." It hesitated delicately. Mirny's body moved slightly in midair; her breathing was inhumanly regular. The eyes opened and closed. "Another young race."

"What are you?"

"I am the Swarm. That is, I am one of its castes. I am a tool, an adaptation; my specialty is intelligence. I am not often needed. It is good to be needed again."

"Have you been here all along? Why didn't you greet us? We'd have dealt with you. We meant no harm."

The wet mouth on the end of the plug made laughing sounds. "Like yourself, I enjoy irony," it said. "It is a pretty trap you have found yourself in, Captain-Doctor. You meant to make the Swarm work for you and your race. You meant to breed us and study us and use us. It is an excellent plan, but one we hit upon long before your race evolved."

Stung by panic, Afriel's mind raced frantically. "You're an intelligent being," he said. "There's no reason to do us any harm. Let us talk together. We can help you."

"Yes," Swarm agreed. "You will be helpful. Your companion's memories tell me that this is one of those uncomfortable periods when galactic intelligence is rife. Intelligence is a great bother. It makes all kinds of trouble for us."

"What do you mean?"

"You are a young race and lay great stock by your own cleverness," Swarm said. "As usual, you fail to see that intelligence is not a survival trait."

Afriel wiped sweat from his face. "We've done well," he said. "We came to you, and peacefully. You didn't come to us."

"I refer to exactly that," Swarm said urbanely. "This urge to expand, to explore, to develop, is just what will make you extinct. You naively suppose that you can continue to feed your curiosity indefinitely. It is an old story, pursued by countless races before you. Within a thousand years—perhaps a little longer—your species will vanish."

"You intend to destroy us, then? I warn you it will not be an easy task—"

"Again you miss the point. Knowledge is power! Do you suppose that fragile little form of yours—your primitive legs, your ludicrous arms and hands, your tiny, scarcely wrinkled brain—can *contain* all that power? Certainly not! Already your race is flying to pieces under the impact of your own expertise. The original human form is becoming obsolete. Your own genes have been altered, and you, Captain-Doctor, are a crude experiment. In a hundred years you will be a relic. In a thousand years you will not even be a memory. Your race will go the same way as a thousand others."

"And what way is that?"

"I do not know." The thing on the end of the Swarm's arm made a chuckling sound. "They have passed beyond my ken. They have all discovered something, learned something, that has caused them to transcend my understanding. It may be that they even transcend *being.* At any rate, I cannot sense their presence anywhere. They seem to do nothing, they seem to interfere in nothing; for all intents and purposes, they seem to be dead. Vanished. They may have become gods, or ghosts. In either case, I have no wish to join them."

"So then—so then you have—"

"Intelligence is very much a two-edged sword, Captain-Doctor. It is useful only up to a point. It interferes with the business of living. Life, and intelligence, do not mix very well. They are not at all closely related, as you childishly assume."

"But you, then—you are a rational being—"

"I am a tool, as I said." The mutated device on the end of its arm made a sighing noise. "When you began your pheromonal experiments, the chemical imbalance became apparent to the Queen. It triggered certain genetic patterns within her body, and I was reborn. Chemical sabotage is a problem that can best be dealt with by intelligence. I am a brain replete, you see, specially designed to be far more intelligent than any young race. Within three days I was fully self-conscious. Within five days I had deciphered these markings on my body. They are the genetically encoded history of my race . . . within five days and two hours I recognized the problem at hand and knew what to do. I am now doing it. I am six days old."

"What is it you intend to do?"

"Your race is a very vigorous one. I expect it to be here, competing with us, within five hundred years. Perhaps much sooner. It will be necessary to make a thorough study of such a rival. I invite you to join our community on a permanent basis."

"What do you mean?"

"I invite you to become a symbiote. I have here a male and a female, whose genes are altered and therefore without defects. You make a perfect breeding pair. It will save me a great deal of trouble with cloning."

"You think I'll betray my race and deliver a slave species into your hands?"

"Your choice is simple, Captain-Doctor. Remain an intelligent, living being, or become a mindless puppet, like your partner. I have taken over all the functions of her nervous system; I can do the same to you."

"I can kill myself."

"That might be troublesome, because it would make me resort to developing a cloning technology. Technology, though I am capable of it, is painful to me. I am a genetic artifact; there are fail-safes within me that prevent me from taking over the Nest for my own uses. That would mean falling into the same trap of progress as other intelligent races. For similar reasons, my life span is limited. I will live for only a thousand years, until your race's brief flurry of energy is over and peace resumes once more."

"Only a thousand years?" Afriel laughed bitterly. "What then? You kill off my descendants, I assume, having no further use for them."

"No. We have not killed any of the fifteen other races we have taken for defensive study. It has not been necessary. Consider that small scavenger floating by your head, Captain-Doctor, that is feeding on your vomit. Five hundred million years ago its ancestors made the galaxy tremble. When they attacked us, we unleashed their own kind upon them. Of course, we altered our side, so that they were smarter, tougher, and, naturally, totally loyal to us. Our Nests were the only world they knew, and they fought with a valor and inventiveness we never could have matched. . . . Should your race arrive to exploit us, we will naturally do the same."

"We humans are different."

"Of course."

"A thousand years here won't change us. You will die and our descendants will take over this Nest. We'll be running things, despite you, in a few generations. The darkness won't make any difference."

"Certainly not. You don't need eyes here. You don't need anything."

"You'll allow me to stay alive? To teach them anything I want?"

"Certainly, Captain-Doctor. We are doing you a favor, in all truth. In a thousand years your descendants here will be the only remnants of the human race. We are generous with our immortality; we will take it upon ourselves to preserve you."

"You're wrong, Swarm. You're wrong about intelligence, and you're wrong about everything else. Maybe other races would crumble into parasitism, but we humans are different."

"Certainly. You'll do it, then?"

"Yes. I accept your challenge. And I will defeat you."

"Splendid. When the Investors return here, the springtails will say that they have killed you, and will tell them to never return. They will not return. The humans should be the next to arrive."

"If I don't defeat you, they will."

"Perhaps." Again it sighed. "I'm glad I don't have to absorb you. I would have missed your conversation."

Nancy Kress

Nancy Kress (1948–) entered science fiction in the early 1980s but flowered by the early 90s. Kress's early novels were genre fantasy, but her short fiction, which gained her initial recognition, was SF, collected in *Trinity and Other Stories* (1985). Her most ambitious work, in which it became clear that she was determined to develop both character and science in her fiction, began with the novel *An Alien Light* (1988), and then *Brain Rose* (1990). Meanwhile, she continued to write an impressive body of short fiction, much of it collected in *The Aliens of Earth* (1993). With the publication of her Beggars novels (*Beggars in Spain* [1993], *Beggars and Choosers* [1994], and *Beggars Ride* [1996]), and in the technothriller *Oaths and Miracles* (1996), she showed the full strength of her powers.

Kress, as much as any SF writer today, is an heir to the tradition of H. G. Wells. Nowhere in her work is this more evident than in "Beggars in Spain" and the novels that have grown out of it. With this story, she began her magnum opus. In this story she deals with human and social evolution, with class and economic issues, and with ordinary characters, as Wells did in "A Story of the Days to Come."

BEGGARS IN SPAIN

With energy and sleepless vigilance go forward and give us victories.
—Abraham Lincoln, to Maj. Gen. Joseph Hooker, 1863

I

They sat stiffly on his antique Eames chairs, two people who didn't want to be here, or one person who didn't want to and one who resented the other's reluctance. Dr. Ong had seen this before. Within two minutes he was sure: the woman was the silently furious resister. She would lose. The man would pay for it later, in little ways, for a long time.

"I presume you've performed the necessary credit checks already," Roger Camden said pleasantly. "So let's get right on to details, shall we, Doctor?"

"Certainly," Ong said. "Why don't we start by your telling me all the genetic modifications you're interested in for the baby."

The woman shifted suddenly on her chair. She was in her late twenties—clearly a second wife—but already had a faded look, as if keeping up with Roger Camden was wearing her out. Ong could easily believe that. Mrs. Camden's hair was brown, her eyes were brown, her skin had a brown tinge that might have been pretty if her cheeks had had any color. She wore a brown coat, neither fashionable nor cheap, and shoes that looked vaguely orthopedic. Ong glanced at his records for her name: Elizabeth. He would bet people forgot it often.

Next to her, Roger Camden radiated nervous vitality, a man in late middle-age whose bullet-shaped head did not match his careful haircut and Italian-silk business suit. Ong did not need to consult his file to recall anything about Camden. A caricature of the bullet-shaped head had been the leading graphic of yesterday's on-line edition of the *Wall Street Journal*: Camden had led a major coup in cross-border data-atoll investment. Ong was not sure what cross-border data-atoll investment was.

"A girl," Elizabeth Camden said. Ong hadn't expected her to speak first. Her voice was another surprise: upper-class British. "Blond. Green eyes. Tall. Slender."

Ong smiled. "Appearance factors are the easiest to achieve, as I'm sure you already know. But all we can do about 'slenderness' is give her a genetic disposition in that direction. How you feed the child will naturally—"

"Yes, yes," Roger Camden said, "that's obvious. Now: intelligence. *High* intelligence. And a sense of daring."

"I'm sorry, Mr. Camden—personality factors are not yet understood well enough to allow genet—"

"Just testing," Camden said, with a smile that Ong thought was probably supposed to be lighthearted.

Elizabeth Camden said, "Musical ability."

"Again, Mrs. Camden, a disposition to be musical is all we can guarantee."

"Good enough," Camden said. "The full array of corrections for any potential gene-linked health problem, of course."

"Of course," Dr. Ong said. Neither client spoke. So far theirs was a fairly modest list, given Camden's money; most clients had to be argued out of contradictory genetic tendencies, alteration overload, or unrealistic expectations. Ong waited. Tension prickled in the room like heat.

"And," Camden said, "no need to sleep."

Elizabeth Camden jerked her head sideways to look out the window.

Ong picked a paper magnet off his desk. He made his voice pleasant. "May I ask how you learned whether that genetic-modification program exists?"

Camden grinned. "You're not denying it exists. I give you full credit for that, Doctor."

Ong held onto his temper. "May I ask how you learned whether the program exists?"

Camden reached into an inner pocket of his suit. The silk crinkled and pulled; body and suit came from different social classes. Camden was, Ong remembered, a Yagaiist, a personal friend of Kenzo Yagai himself. Camden handed Ong hard copy: program specifications.

"Don't bother hunting down the security leak in your data banks, Doctor—you won't find it. But if it's any consolation, neither will anybody else. Now." He leaned suddenly forward. His tone changed. "I know that you've created twenty children so far who don't need to sleep at all. That so far nineteen are healthy, intelligent, and psychologically normal. In fact, better than normal—they're all unusually precocious. The oldest is already four years old and can read in two languages. I know you're thinking of offering this genetic modification on the open market in a few years. All I want is a chance to buy it for my daughter *now*. At whatever price you name."

Ong stood. "I can't possibly discuss this with you unilaterally, Mr. Camden. Neither the theft of our data—"

"Which wasn't a theft—your system developed a spontaneous bubble regurgitation into a public gate, have a hell of a time proving otherwise—"

"—*nor* the offer to purchase this particular genetic modification lies in my sole area of authority. Both have to be discussed with the Institute's board of directors."

"By all means, by all means. When can I talk to them, too?"

"You?"

Camden, still seated, looked at him. It occurred to Ong that there were few men who could look so confident eighteen inches below eye level. "Certainly. I'd like the chance to present my offer to whoever has the actual authority to accept it. That's only good business."

"This isn't solely a business transaction, Mr. Camden."

"It isn't solely pure scientific research, either," Camden retorted. "You're a for-profit corporation here. *With* certain tax breaks available only to firms meeting certain fair-practice laws."

For a minute Ong couldn't think what Camden meant. "Fair-practice laws . . ."

". . . are designed to protect minorities who are suppliers. I know, it hasn't ever been tested in the case of customers, except for redlining in Y-energy installations. But it could be tested, Dr. Ong. Minorities are entitled to the same product offerings as nonminorities. I know the Institute would not welcome a court case, Doctor. None of your twenty genetic beta-test families is either black or Jewish."

"A court . . . but you're not black *or* Jewish!"

"I'm a different minority. Polish-American. The name was Kaminisky." Camden finally stood. And smiled warmly. "Look, it is preposterous. You know that, and I know that, and we both know what a grand time journalists would have with it anyway. And you know that I don't want to sue you with a preposterous case, just to use the threat of premature and adverse publicity to get what I want. I don't want to make threats at all, believe me I don't. I just want this marvelous advancement you've come up with for my daughter." His face changed, to an expression Ong wouldn't have believed possible on those particular features: wistfulness. "Doctor—do you know how much more I could have accomplished if I hadn't had to *sleep* all my life?"

Elizabeth Camden said harshly, "You hardly sleep now."

Camden looked down at her as if he had forgotten she was there. "Well, no, my dear, not now. But when I was young . . . college, I might have been able to finish college and still support . . . well. None of that matters now. What matters, Doctor, is that you and I and your board come to an agreement."

"Mr. Camden, please leave my office now."

"You mean before you lose your temper at my presumptuousness? You wouldn't be the first. I'll expect to have a meeting set up by the end of next week, whenever and wherever you say, of course. Just let my personal secretary, Diane Clavers, know the details. Anytime that's best for you."

Ong did not accompany them to the door. Pressure throbbed behind his temples. In the doorway Elizabeth Camden turned. "What happened to the twentieth one?"

"What?"

"The twentieth baby. My husband said nineteen of them are healthy and normal. What happened to the twentieth?"

The pressure grew stronger, hotter. Ong knew that he should not answer; that Camden probably already knew the answer even if his wife didn't; that he, Ong, was going to answer anyway; that he would regret the lack of self-control, bitterly, later.

"The twentieth baby is dead. His parents turned out to be unstable. They separated during the pregnancy, and his mother could not bear the twenty-four-hour crying of a baby who never sleeps."

Elizabeth Camden's eyes widened. "She killed it?"

"By mistake," Camden said shortly. "Shook the little thing too hard." He frowned at Ong. "Nurses, doctor. In shifts. You should have picked only parents wealthy enough to afford nurses in shifts."

"That's horrible!" Mrs. Camden burst out, and Ong could not tell if she meant the child's death, the lack of nurses, or the Institute's carelessness. Ong closed his eyes.

When they had gone, he took ten milligrams of cyclobenzaprine-III. For his back—it was solely for his back. The old injury hurting again. Afterward he stood for a long time at the window, still holding the paper magnet, feeling the pressure recede from his temples, feeling himself calm down. Below him Lake Michigan lapped peacefully at the shore; the police had driven away the homeless in another raid just last night, and they hadn't yet had time to return. Only their debris remained, thrown into the bushes of the lakeshore park: tattered blankets, newspapers, plastic bags like pathetic trampled standards. It was illegal to sleep in the park, illegal to enter it without a resident's permit, illegal to be homeless and without a residence. As Ong watched, uniformed park attendants began methodically spearing newspapers and shoving them into clean self-propelled receptacles.

Ong picked up the phone to call the president of Biotech Institute's board of directors.

Four men and three women sat around the polished mahogany table of the conference room. *Doctor, lawyer, Indian chief,* thought Susan Melling, looking from Ong to Sullivan to Camden. She smiled. Ong caught the smile and looked frosty. Pompous ass. Judy Sullivan, the Institute lawyer, turned to speak in a low voice to Camden's lawyer, a thin, nervous man with the look of being owned. The owner, Roger Camden, the Indian chief himself, was the happiest-looking person in the room. The lethal little man—what did it take to become that rich, starting from nothing? She, Susan, would certainly never know—radiated excitement. He beamed, he glowed, so unlike the usual parents-to-be that Susan was intrigued. Usually the prospective daddies and mommies—especially the daddies—sat there looking as if they were at a corporate merger. Camden looked as if he were at a birthday party.

Which, of course, he was. Susan grinned at him and was pleased when he grinned back. Wolfish, but with a sort of delight that could only be called innocent—what would he be like in bed? Ong frowned majestically and rose to speak.

"Ladies and gentlemen, I think we're ready to start. Perhaps introductions are in order. Mr. Roger Camden, Mrs. Camden are, of course, our clients. Mr. John Jaworski, Mr. Camden's lawyer. Mr. Camden, this is Judith Sullivan, the Institute's head of legal; Samuel Krenshaw, representing Institute director Dr. Brad Marsteiner, who unfortunately couldn't be here today; and Dr. Susan Melling, who developed the genetic modification affecting sleep. A few legal points of interest to both parties—"

"Forget the contracts for a minute," Camden interrupted. "Let's talk about the sleep thing. I'd like to ask a few questions."

Susan said, "What would you like to know?" Camden's eyes were very blue in his blunt-featured face; he wasn't what she had expected. Mrs. Camden, who apparently lacked both a first name and a lawyer, since Jaworski had been introduced as her husband's but not hers, looked either sullen or scared; it was difficult to tell which.

Ong said sourly, "Then perhaps we should start with a short presentation by Dr. Melling."

Susan would have preferred a Q&A, to see what Camden would ask. But she had annoyed Ong enough for one session. Obediently she rose.

"Let me start with a brief description of sleep. Researchers have known for a long time that there are actually three kinds of sleep. One is 'slow-wave sleep,' characterized on an EEG by delta waves. One is 'rapid-eye-movement sleep' or REM sleep, which is much lighter sleep and contains most dreaming. Together, these two make up 'core sleep.' The third type of sleep is 'optional sleep,' so-called because people seem to get along without it with no ill effects, and some short sleepers don't do it at all, sleeping naturally only three or four hours a night."

"That's me," Camden said. "I trained myself into it. Couldn't everybody do that?"

Apparently they were going to have a Q&A after all. "No. The actual sleep mechanism has some flexibility, but not the same amount for every person. The raphe nuclei on the brain stem—"

Ong said, "I don't think we need that level of detail, Susan. Let's stick to basics."

Camden said, "The raphe nuclei regulate the balance among neurotransmitters and peptides that lead to a pressure to sleep, don't they?"

Susan couldn't help it; she grinned. Camden, the laser-sharp ruthless financier, sat trying to look solemn, a third-grader waiting to have his homework praised. Ong looked sour. Mrs. Camden looked away, out the window.

"Yes, that's correct, Mr. Camden. You've done your research."

Camden said, "This is my *daughter*," and Susan caught her breath. When was the last time she had heard that note of reverence in anyone's voice? But no one in the room seemed to notice.

"Well, then," Susan said, "you already know that the reason people sleep is because a pressure to sleep builds up in the brain. Over the last twenty years, research has determined that's the *only* reason. Neither slow-wave sleep nor REM sleep serves functions that can't be carried on while the body and brain are awake. A lot goes on during sleep, but it can go awake just as well, if other hormonal adjustments are made.

"Sleep once served an important evolutionary function. Once Clem Pre-mammal was done filling his stomach and squirting his sperm around, sleep kept him immobile and away from predators. Sleep was an aid to survival. But now it's a leftover mechanism, like the appendix. It switches on every night, but the need is gone. So we turn off the switch at its source, in the genes."

Ong winced. He hated it when she oversimplified like that. Or maybe it was the lightheartedness he hated. If Marsteiner were making this presentation, there'd be no Clem Pre-mammal.

Camden said, "What about the need to dream?"

"Not necessary. A leftover bombardment of the cortex to keep it on semialert in case a predator attacked during sleep. Wakefulness does that better."

"Why not have wakefulness instead, then? From the start of the evolution?"

He was testing her. Susan gave him a full, lavish smile, enjoying his brass. "I told you. Safety from predators. But when a modern predator attacks—say, a cross-border data-atoll investor—it's safer to be awake."

Camden shot at her, "What about the high percentage of REM sleep in fetuses and babies?"

"Still an evolutionary hangover. Cerebrum develops perfectly well without it."

"What about neural repair during slow-wave sleep?"

"That does go on. But it can go on during wakefulness, if the DNA is programmed to do so. No loss of neural efficiency, as far as we know."

"What about the release of human growth enzyme in such large concentrations during slow-wave sleep?"

Susan looked at him admiringly. "Goes on without the sleep. Genetic adjustments tie it to other changes in the pineal gland."

"What about the—"

"The *side effects?*" Mrs. Camden said. Her mouth turned down. "What about the bloody side effects?"

Susan turned to Elizabeth Camden. She had forgotten she was there. The younger woman stared at Susan, mouth still turned down at the corners.

"I'm glad you asked that, Mrs. Camden. Because there *are* side effects." Susan paused; she was enjoying herself. "Compared to their age mates, the nonsleep children—who have *not* had IQ genetic manipulation—are more intelligent, better at problem-solving, and more joyous."

Camden took out a cigarette. The archaic, filthy habit surprised Susan. Then she saw that it was deliberate: Roger Camden drawing attention to an ostentatious display to draw attention away from what he was feeling. His cigarette lighter was gold, monogrammed, innocently gaudy.

"Let me explain," Susan said. "REM sleep bombards the cerebral cortex with random neural firings from the brainstem; dreaming occurs because the poor besieged cortex tries so hard to make sense of the activated images and memories. It spends a lot of energy doing that. Without that energy expenditure, nonsleep cerebrums save the wear and tear and do better at coordinating real-life input. Thus—greater intelligence and problem-solving.

"Also, doctors have known for sixty years that antidepressants, which lift the mood of depressed patients, also suppress REM sleep entirely. What they have proved in the last ten years is that the reverse is equally true: suppress REM sleep and people don't *get* depressed. The nonsleep kids are cheerful, outgoing . . . *joyous.* There's no other word for it."

"At what cost?" Mrs. Camden said. She held her neck rigid, but the corners of her jaw worked.

"No cost. No negative side effects at all."

"So far," Mrs. Camden shot back.

Susan shrugged. "So far."

"They're only four years old! At the most!"

Ong and Krenshaw were studying her closely. Susan saw the moment the

Camden woman realized it; she sank back into her chair, drawing her fur coat around her, her face blank.

Camden did not look at his wife. He blew a cloud of cigarette smoke. "Everything has costs, Dr. Melling."

She liked the way he said her name. "Ordinarily, yes. Especially in genetic modification. But we honestly have not been able to find any here, despite looking." She smiled directly into Camden's eyes. "Is it too much to believe that just once the universe has given us something wholly good, wholly a step forward, wholly beneficial? Without hidden penalties?"

"Not the universe. The intelligence of people like you," Camden said, surprising Susan more than anything that had gone before. His eyes held hers. She felt her chest tighten.

"I think," Dr. Ong said dryly, "that the philosophy of the universe may be beyond our concerns here. Mr. Camden, if you have no further medical questions, perhaps we can return to the legal points Ms. Sullivan and Mr. Jaworski have raised. Thank you, Dr. Melling."

Susan nodded. She didn't look again at Camden. But she knew what he said, how he looked, that he was there.

The house was about what she had expected, a huge mock Tudor on Lake Michigan north of Chicago. The land heavily wooded between the gate and the house, open between the house and the surging water. Patches of snow dotted the dormant grass. Biotech had been working with the Camdens for four months, but this was the first time Susan had driven to their home.

As she walked toward the house, another car drove up behind her. No, a truck, continuing around the curved driveway to a service entry at the side of the house. One man rang the service bell; a second began to unload a plastic-wrapped playpen from the back of the truck. White, with pink and yellow bunnies. Susan briefly closed her eyes.

Camden opened the door himself. She could see the effort not to look worried. "You didn't have to drive out, Susan—I'd have come into the city."

"No, I didn't want you to do that, Roger. Mrs. Camden is here?"

"In the living room." Camden led her into a large room with a stone fireplace. English country-house furniture; prints of dogs or boats, all hung eighteen inches too high: Elizabeth Camden must have done the decorating. She did not rise from her wing chair as Susan entered.

"Let me be concise and fast," Susan said. "I don't want to make this any more drawn out for you than I have to. We have all the amniocentesis, ultrasound, and Langston test results. The fetus is fine, developing normally for two weeks, no problems with the implant on the uterus wall. But a complication has developed."

"What?" Camden said. He took out a cigarette, looked at his wife, put it back unlit.

Susan said quietly, "Mrs. Camden, by sheer chance both your ovaries released eggs last month. We removed one for the gene surgery. By more sheer chance the second fertilized and implanted. You're carrying two fetuses."

Elizabeth Camden grew still. "Twins?"

"No," Susan said. Then she realized what she had said. "I mean, yes. They're twins, but nonidentical. Only one has been genetically altered. The other will be no more similar to her than any two siblings. It's a so-called 'normal' baby. And I know you didn't want a so-called normal baby."

Camden said, "No. I didn't."

Elizabeth Camden said, "I did."

Camden shot her a fierce look that Susan couldn't read. He took out the cigarette again, lit it. His face was in profile to Susan, thinking intently; she doubted he knew the cigarette was there or that he was lighting it. "Is the baby being affected by the other one's being there?"

"No," Susan said. "No, of course not. They're just . . . coexisting."

"Can you abort it?"

"Not without risk of aborting both of them. Removing the unaltered fetus might cause changes in the uterus lining that could lead to a spontaneous miscarriage of the other." She drew a deep breath. "There's that option, of course. We can start the whole process over again. But, as I told you at the time, you were very lucky to have the in vitro fertilization take on only the second try. Some couples take eight or ten tries. If we started all over, the process could be a lengthy one."

Camden said, "Is the presence of this second fetus harming my daughter? Taking away nutrients or anything? Or will it change anything for her later on in the pregnancy?"

"No. Except that there is a chance of premature birth. Two fetuses take up a lot more room in the womb, and if it gets too crowded birth can be premature. But the—"

"How premature? Enough to threaten survival?"

"Most probably not."

Camden went on smoking. A man appeared at the door. "Sir, London calling. James Kendall for Mr. Yagai."

"I'll take it." Camden rose. Susan watched him study his wife's face. When he spoke, it was to her. "All right, Elizabeth. All right." He left the room.

For a long moment the two women sat in silence. Susan was aware of disappointment; this was not the Camden she had expected to see. She became aware of Elizabeth Camden watching her with amusement.

"Oh, yes, Doctor. He's like that."

Susan said nothing.

"Completely overbearing. But not this time." She laughed softly, with excitement. "Two. Do you . . . do you know what sex the other one is?"

"Both fetuses are female."

"I wanted a girl, you know. And now I'll have one."

"Then you'll go ahead with the pregnancy."

"Oh, yes. Thank you for coming, Doctor."

She was dismissed. No one saw her out. But as she was getting into her car, Camden rushed out of the house, coatless. "Susan! I wanted to thank you. For coming all the way out here to tell us yourself."

"You already thanked me."

"Yes. Well. You're sure the second fetus is no threat to my daughter?"

Susan said deliberately, "Nor is the genetically altered fetus a threat to the naturally conceived one."

He smiled. His voice was low and wistful. "And you think that should matter to me just as much. But it doesn't. And why should I fake what I feel? Especially to you?"

Susan opened her car door. She wasn't ready for this, or she had changed her mind, or something. But then Camden leaned over to close the door, and his manner held no trace of flirtatiousness, no smarmy ingratiation. "I better order a second playpen."

"Yes."

"And a second car seat."

"Yes."

"But not a second night-shift nurse."

"That's up to you."

"And you." Abruptly he leaned over and kissed her, a kiss so polite and respectful that Susan was shocked. Neither lust nor conquest would have shocked her; this did. Camden didn't give her a chance to react; he closed the car door and turned back toward the house. Susan drove toward the gate, her hands shaky on the wheel until amusement replaced shock: it *had* been a deliberately distant, respectful kiss, an engineered enigma. And nothing else could have guaranteed so well that there would have to be another.

She wondered what the Camdens would name their daughters.

Dr. Ong strode the hospital corridor, which had been dimmed to half-light. From the nurse's station in Maternity a nurse stepped forward as if to stop him—it was the middle of the night, long past visiting hours—got a good look at his face, and faded back into her station. Around a corner was the viewing glass to the nursery. To Ong's annoyance, Susan Melling stood pressed against the glass. To his further annoyance, she was crying.

Ong realized that he had never liked the woman. Maybe not any women. Even those with superior minds could not seem to refrain from being made damn fools by their emotions.

"Look," Susan said, laughing a little, swiping at her face. "Doctor—*look*."

Behind the glass Roger Camden, gowned and masked, was holding up a baby in a white undershirt and pink blanket. Camden's blue eyes—theatrically blue; a man really should not have such garish eyes—glowed. The baby had a head covered with blond fuzz, wide eyes, pink skin. Camden's eyes above the mask said that no other child had ever had these attributes.

Ong said, "An uncomplicated birth?"

"Yes," Susan Melling sobbed. "Perfectly straightforward. Elizabeth is fine. She's asleep. Isn't she beautiful? He has the most adventurous spirit I've ever known." She wiped her nose on her sleeve; Ong realized that she was drunk. "Did I ever tell you that I was engaged once? Fifteen years ago, in med school? I broke it off because he grew to seem so ordinary, so boring. Oh, God, I shouldn't be telling you all this I'm sorry I'm sorry."

Ong moved away from her. Behind the glass Roger Camden laid the baby in a small wheeled crib. The nameplate said BABY GIRL CAMDEN #1. 5.9 POUNDS. A night nurse watched indulgently.

Ong did not wait to see Camden emerge from the nursery or to hear Susan Melling say to him whatever she was going to say. Ong went to have the OB paged. Melling's report was not, under the circumstances, to be trusted. A perfect, unprecedented chance to record every detail of gene alteration with a nonaltered control, and Melling was more interested in her own sloppy emotions. Ong would obviously have to do the report himself, after talking to the OB. He was hungry for every detail. And not just about the pink-cheeked baby in Camden's arms. He wanted to know everything about the birth of the child in the other glass-sided crib: BABY GIRL CAMDEN #2 5.1 POUNDS. The dark-haired baby with the mottled red features, lying scrunched down in her pink blanket, asleep.

II

Leisha's earliest memory was of flowing lines that were not there. She knew they were not there because when she reached out her fist to touch them, her fist was empty. Later she realized that the flowing lines were light: sunshine slanting in bars between curtains in her room, between the wooden blinds in the dining room, between the crisscross lattices in the conservatory. The day she realized the golden flow was light she laughed out loud with the sheer joy of discovery, and Daddy turned from putting flowers in pots and smiled at her.

The whole house was full of light. Light bounded off the lake, streamed across the high white ceilings, puddled on the shining wooden floors. She and Alice moved continually through light, and sometimes Leisha would stop and tip back her head and let it flow over her face. She could feel it, like water.

The best light, of course, was in the conservatory. That's where Daddy liked to be when he was home from making money. Daddy potted plants and watered trees, humming, and Leisha and Alice ran between the wooden tables of flowers with their wonderful earthy smells, running from the dark side of the conservatory where the big purple flowers grew to the sunshine side with sprays of yellow flowers, running back and forth, in and out of the light. "Growth," Daddy said to her. "Flowers all fulfilling their promise. Alice, be careful! You almost knocked over that orchid." Alice, obedient, would stop running for a while. Daddy never told Leisha to stop running.

After a while the light would go away. Alice and Leisha would have their baths, and then Alice would get quiet, or cranky. She wouldn't play nice with Leisha, even when Leisha let her choose the game or even have all the best dolls. Then Nanny would take Alice to "bed," and Leisha would talk with Daddy some more until Daddy said he had to work in his study with the papers that made money. Leisha always felt a moment of regret that he had to go do that, but the moment never lasted very long, because Mamselle would arrive and start Leisha's lessons, which she liked. Learning things was so interesting! She could already sing twenty songs and write all the letters in the alphabet and count to fifty. And by the time lessons were done, the light had come back, and it was time for breakfast.

Breakfast was the only time Leisha didn't like. Daddy had gone to the office, and Leisha and Alice had breakfast with Mommy in the big dining room. Mommy sat in a red robe, which Leisha liked, and she didn't smell funny or talk funny the way she would later in the day, but, still, breakfast wasn't fun. Mommy always started with the Question.

"Alice, sweetheart, how did you sleep?"

"Fine, Mommy."

"Did you have any nice dreams?"

For a long time Alice said no. Then one day she said, "I dreamed about a horse. I was riding him." Mommy clapped her hands and kissed Alice and gave her an extra sticky bun. After that Alice always had a dream to tell Mommy.

Once Leisha said, "I had a dream, too. I dreamed light was coming in the window and it wrapped all around me like a blanket and then it kissed me on my eyes."

Mommy put down her coffee cup so hard that coffee sloshed out of it. "Don't lie to me, Leisha. You did not have a dream."

"Yes, I did," Leisha said.

"Only children who sleep can have dreams. Don't lie to me. You did not have a dream."

"Yes, I did! I did!" Leisha shouted. She could see it, almost: the light streaming in the window and wrapping around her like a golden blanket.

"I will not tolerate a child who is a liar. Do you hear me, Leisha—I won't tolerate it!"

"You're a liar!" Leisha shouted, knowing the words weren't true, hating herself because they weren't true but hating Mommy more, and that was wrong, too, and there sat Alice stiff and frozen with her eyes wide. Alice was scared and it was Leisha's fault.

Mommy called sharply, "Nanny! Nanny! Take Leisha to her room at once. She can't sit with civilized people if she can't refrain from telling lies."

Leisha started to cry. Nanny carried her out of the room. Leisha hadn't even had her breakfast. But she didn't care about that; all she could see while she cried was Alice's eyes, scared like that, reflecting broken bits of light.

But Leisha didn't cry long. Nanny read her a story and then played Data Jump with her, and then Alice came up and Nanny drove them both into Chicago to the zoo, where there were wonderful animals to see, animals Leisha could not have dreamed—nor Alice *either*. And by the time they came back Mommy had gone to her room, and Leisha knew that she would stay there with the glasses of funny-smelling stuff the rest of the day, and Leisha would not have to see her.

But that night she went to her mother's room.

"I have to go to the bathroom," she told Mamselle. Mamselle said, "Do you need any help?" maybe because Alice still needed help in the bathroom. But Leisha didn't, and she thanked Mamselle. Then she sat on the toilet for a minute even though nothing came, so that what she had told Mamselle wouldn't be a lie.

Leisha tiptoed down the hall. She went first into Alice's room. A little light in a wall socket burned near the "crib." There was no crib in Leisha's room. Leisha looked at her sister through the bars. Alice lay on her side with her eyes closed. The lids of the eyes fluttered quickly, like curtains blowing in the wind. Alice's chin and neck looked loose.

Leisha closed the door very carefully and went to her parents' room.

They didn't "sleep" in a crib but in a huge enormous "bed," with enough room between them for more people. Mommy's eyelids weren't fluttering; she lay on her back making a hrrr-hrrr sound through her nose. The funny smell was strong on her. Leisha backed away and tiptoed over to Daddy. He looked like Alice, except that his neck and chin looked even looser, folds of skin collapsed like the tent that had fallen down in the backyard. It scared Leisha to see him like that. Then Daddy's eyes flew open so suddenly that Leisha screamed.

Daddy rolled out of bed and picked her up, looking quickly at Mommy. But she didn't move. Daddy was wearing only his underpants. He carried Leisha out into the hall, where Mamselle came rushing up saying, "Oh, sir. I'm sorry, she just said she was going to the bathroom—"

"It's all right," Daddy said. "I'll take her with me."

"No!" Leisha screamed, because Daddy was only in his underpants and his neck had looked all funny and the room smelled bad because of Mommy. But Daddy carried her into the conservatory, set her down on a bench, wrapped himself in a piece of green plastic that was supposed to cover up plants, and sat down next to her.

"Now, what happened, Leisha? What were you doing?"

Leisha didn't answer.

"You were looking at people sleeping, weren't you?" Daddy said, and because his voice was softer Leisha mumbled, "Yes." She immediately felt better; it felt good not to lie.

"You were looking at people sleeping because you don't sleep and you were curious, weren't you? Like Curious George in your book?"

"Yes," Leisha said. "I thought you said you made money in your study all night!"

Daddy smiled. "Not all night. Some of it. But then I sleep, although not very much." He took Leisha on his lap. "I don't need much sleep, so I get a lot more done at night than most people. Different people need different amounts of sleep. And a few, a very few, are like you. You don't need any."

"Why not?"

"Because you're special. Better than other people. Before you were born, I had some doctors help make you that way."

"Why?"

"So you could do anything you want to and make manifest your own individuality."

Leisha twisted in his arms to stare at him; the words meant nothing. Daddy reached over and touched a single flower growing on a tall potted tree. The flower had thick white petals like the cream he put in coffee, and the center was a light pink.

"See, Leisha—this tree made this flower. Because it *can*. Only this tree can make this kind of wonderful flower. That plant hanging up there can't, and those can't either. Only this tree. Therefore the most important thing in the world for this tree to do is grow this flower. The flower is the tree's individuality—that means just *it*, and nothing else—made manifest. Nothing else matters."

"I don't understand, Daddy."

"You will. Someday."

"But I want to understand *now*," Leisha said, and Daddy laughed with pure delight and hugged her. The hug felt good, but Leisha still wanted to understand.

"When you make money, is that your indiv . . . that thing?"

"Yes," Daddy said happily.

"Then nobody else can make money? Like only that tree can make that flower?"

"Nobody else can make it just the ways I do."

"What do you do with the money?"

"I buy things for you. This house, your dresses, Mamselle to teach you, the car to ride in."

"What does the tree do with the flower?"

"Glories in it," Daddy said, which made no sense. "Excellence is what counts, Leisha. Excellence supported by individual effort. And that's *all* that counts."

"I'm cold, Daddy."

"Then I better bring you back to Mamselle."

Leisha didn't move. She touched the flower with one finger. "I want to sleep, Daddy."

"No, you don't, sweetheart. Sleep is just lost time, wasted life. It's a little death."

"Alice sleeps."

"Alice isn't like you."

"Alice isn't special?"

"No. You are."

"Why didn't you make Alice special, too?"

"Alice made herself. I didn't have a chance to make her special."

The whole thing was too hard. Leisha stopped stroking the flower and slipped off Daddy's lap. He smiled at her. "My little questioner. When you grow up, you'll find your own excellence, and it will be a new order, a specialness the world hasn't ever seen before. You might even be like Kenzo Yagai. He made the Yagai generator that powers the world."

"Daddy, you look funny wrapped in the flower plastic." Leisha laughed. Daddy did, too. But then she said, "When I grow up, I'll make my specialness find a way to make Alice special, too," and Daddy stopped laughing.

He took her back to Mamselle, who taught her to write her name, which was so exciting she forgot about the puzzling talk with Daddy. There were six letters, all different, and together they were *her name*. Leisha wrote it over and over, laughing, and Mamselle laughed, too. But later, in the morning, Leisha thought again about the talk with Daddy. She thought of it often, turning the unfamiliar words over in and over in her mind like small hard stones, but the part she thought about most wasn't a word. It was the frown on Daddy's face when she told him she would use her specialness to make Alice special, too.

Every week Dr. Melling came to see Leisha and Alice, sometimes alone, sometimes with other people. Leisha and Alice both liked Dr. Melling, who laughed a lot and whose eyes were bright and warm. Often Daddy was there, too. Dr. Melling played games with them, first with Alice and Leisha separately and then together. She took their pictures and weighed them. She made them lie down on a table and stuck little metal things to their temples, which sounded scary but wasn't because there were so many machines to watch, all making interesting noises, while you were lying there. Dr. Melling was as good at answering questions as Daddy. Once Leisha said, "Is Dr. Melling a special person? Like Kenzo Yagai?" And Daddy laughed and glanced at Dr. Melling and said, "Oh, yes, indeed."

When Leisha was five, she and Alice started school. Daddy's driver took them every day into Chicago. They were in different rooms, which disappointed Leisha. The kids in Leisha's room were all older. But from the first day she adored school, with its fascinating science equipment and electronic drawers full of math puzzlers and other children to find countries on the map with. In half a year she had been moved to yet a different room, where the kids were still older, but they were nonetheless nice to her. Leisha started to learn Japanese. She loved drawing the beautiful characters on thick white paper. "The Sauley School was a good choice," Daddy said.

But Alice didn't like the Sauley School. She wanted to go to school on the same yellow bus as cook's daughter. She cried and threw her paints on the floor at the Sauley School. Then Mommy came out of her room—Leisha hadn't seen her for a few weeks, although she knew Alice had—and threw some candlesticks from the mantelpiece on the floor. The candlesticks, which were china, broke. Leisha ran to pick up the pieces while Mommy and Daddy screamed at each other in the hall by the big staircase.

"She's my daughter, too. And I say she can go!"

"You don't have the right to say anything about it! A weepy drunk, the most rotten role model possible for both of them . . . and I thought I was getting a fine English aristocrat."

"You got what you paid for. Nothing! Not that you ever needed anything from me or anybody else."

"Stop it!" Leisha cried. "Stop it!" and there was silence in the hall. Leisha cut her fingers on the china; blood streamed onto the rug. Daddy rushed in and picked her up. "Stop it," Leisha sobbed, and didn't understand when Daddy said quietly, "*You* stop it, Leisha. Nothing *they* do should touch you at all. You have to be at least that strong."

Leisha buried her head in Daddy's shoulder. Alice transferred to Carl Sandburg Elementary School, riding there on the yellow school bus with cook's daughter.

A few weeks later Daddy told them that Mommy was going away for a few weeks to a hospital, to stop drinking so much. When Mommy came out, he said, she was going to live somewhere else for a while. She and Daddy were not happy. Leisha and Alice would stay with Daddy, and they would visit Mommy sometimes. He told them this very carefully, finding the right words for truth. Truth was very important, Leisha already knew. Truth was being true to your self, your specialness. Your individuality. An individual respected facts, and so always told the truth.

Mommy, Daddy did not say but Leisha knew, did not respect facts.

"I don't want Mommy to go away," Alice said. She started to cry. Leisha thought Daddy would pick Alice up, but he didn't. He just stood there looking at them both.

Leisha put her arms around Alice. "It's all right, Alice. It's all right! We'll make it all right! I'll play with you all the time we're not in school so you don't miss Mommy."

Alice clung to Leisha. Leisha turned her head so she didn't have to see Daddy's face.

III

Kenzo Yagai was coming to the United States to lecture. The title of his talk, which he would give in New York, Los Angeles, Chicago, and Washington, with a repeat in Washington as a special address to Congress, was "The Further Political Implications of Inexpensive Power." Leisha Camden, eleven years old, was going to have a private introduction after the Chicago talk, arranged by her father.

She had studied the theory of cold fusion at school, and her Global Studies teacher had traced the changes in the world resulting from Yagai's patented, low-cost applications of what had, until him, been unworkable theory. The rising prosperity of the Third World, the last death throes of the old communist systems, the decline of the oil states, the renewed economic power of the United States. Her study group had written a news script, filmed with the school's professional-quality equipment, about how a 1985 American family lived with expensive energy costs and a belief in tax-supported help, while a 2019 family lived with cheap energy and a belief in the contract as the basis of civilization. Parts of her own research puzzled Leisha.

"Japan thinks Kenzo Yagai was a traitor to his own country," she said to Daddy at supper.

"No," Camden said. "*Some* Japanese think that. Watch out for generalizations, Leisha. Yagai patented and marketed Y-energy first in the United States because here there were at least the dying embers of individual enterprise. Because of his invention, our entire country has slowly swung back toward an individual meritocracy, and Japan has slowly been forced to follow."

"Your father held that belief all along," Susan said. "Eat your peas, Leisha." Leisha ate her peas. Susan and Daddy had only been married less than a year; it still felt a little strange to have her there. But nice. Daddy said Susan was a valuable addition to their household: intelligent, motivated, and cheerful. Like Leisha herself.

"Remember, Leisha," Camden said. "A man's worth to society and to himself doesn't rest on what he thinks other people should do or be or feel, but on himself. On what he can actually do, and do well. People trade what they do well, and everyone benefits. The basic tool of civilization is the contract. Contracts are voluntary and mutually beneficial. As opposed to coercion, which is wrong."

"The strong have no right to take anything from the weak by force," Susan said. "Alice, eat your peas, too, honey."

"Nor the weak to take anything by force from the strong," Camden said. "That's the basis of what you'll hear Kenzo Yagai discuss tonight, Leisha."

Alice said, "I don't like peas."

Camden said, "Your body does. They're good for you."

Alice smiled. Leisha felt her heart lift; Alice didn't smile much at dinner anymore. "My body doesn't have a contract with the peas."

Camden said, a little impatiently, "Yes, it does. Your body benefits from them. Now eat."

Alice's smile vanished. Leisha looked down at her plate. Suddenly she saw a way out. "No, Daddy, look—Alice's body benefits, but the peas don't. It's not a mutually beneficial consideration—so there's no contract. Alice is right!"

Camden let out a shout of laughter. To Susan he said, "Eleven years old . . . *eleven*." Even Alice smiled, and Leisha waved her spoon triumphantly, light glinting off the bowl and dancing silver on the opposite wall.

But, even so, Alice did not want to go hear Kenzo Yagai. She was going to sleep over at her friend Julie's house; they were going to curl their hair together. More surprisingly, Susan wasn't coming, either. She and Daddy looked at each other a little funny at the front door, Leisha thought, but Leisha was too excited to think about this. She was going to hear *Kenzo Yagai*.

Yagai was a small man, dark and slim. Leisha liked his accent. She liked, too, something about him that took her awhile to name. "Daddy," she whispered in the half-darkness of the auditorium, "he's a joyful man."

Daddy hugged her in the darkness.

Yagai spoke about spirituality and economics. "A man's spirituality—which is only his dignity as a man—rests on his own efforts. Dignity and worth are not automatically conferred by aristocratic birth—we have only to look at history to see that. Dignity and worth are not automatically conferred by inherited wealth—a great heir may be a thief, a wastrel, cruel, an exploiter, a person who leaves the world much poorer than he found it. Nor are dignity and worth automatically conferred by existence itself—a mass murderer exists, but is of negative worth to his society and possess no dignity in his lust to kill.

"No, the only dignity, the only spirituality, rests on what a man can achieve with his own efforts. To rob a man of the chance to achieve, and to trade what he achieves with others, is to rob him of his spiritual dignity as a man. This is why communism has failed in our time. *All* coercion—all force to take from a man his own efforts to achieve—causes spiritual damage and weakens a society. Conscription, theft, fraud, violence, welfare, lack of legislative representation—*all* rob a man of his chance to choose, to achieve on his own, to trade the results of his achievement with others. Coercion is a cheat. It produces nothing new. Only freedom—the freedom to achieve, the freedom to trade freely the results of achievement—creates the environment proper to the dignity and spirituality of man."

Leisha applauded so hard her hands hurt. Going backstage with Daddy, she thought she could hardly breathe. Kenzo Yagai!

But backstage was more crowded than she had expected. There were cameras everywhere. Daddy said, "Mr. Yagai, may I present my daughter Leisha," and the cameras moved in close and fast—on *her*. A Japanese man whispered something in Kenzo Yagai's ear, and he looked more closely at Leisha. "Ah, yes."

"Look over here, Leisha," someone called, and she did. A robot camera zoomed so close to her face that Leisha stepped back, startled. Daddy spoke very sharply to someone, then to someone else. The cameras didn't move. A woman suddenly knelt in front of Leisha and thrust a microphone at her. "What does it feel like to never sleep, Leisha?"

"What?"

Someone laughed. The laugh was not kind. "Breeding geniuses . . ."

Leisha felt a hand on her shoulder. Kenzo Yagai gripped her very firmly, pulled her away from the cameras. Immediately, as if by magic, a line of Japanese men formed behind Yagai, parting only to let Daddy through. Behind the line, the three of them moved into a dressing room, and Kenzo Yagai shut the door.

"You must not let them bother you, Leisha," he said in his wonderful accent. "Not ever. There is an old Oriental proverb: 'The dogs bark, but the caravan moves on.' You must never let your individual caravan be slowed by the barking of rude or envious dogs."

"I won't," Leisha breathed, not sure yet what the words really meant, knowing there was time later to sort them out, to talk about them with Daddy. For now she was dazzled by Kenzo Yagai, the actual man himself, who was changing the world without force, without guns, with trading his special individual efforts. "We study your philosophy at my school, Mr. Yagai."

Kenzo Yagai looked at Daddy. Daddy said, "A private school. But Leisha's sister also studies it, although cursorily, in the public system. Slowly, Kenzo, but it comes. It comes." Leisha noticed that he did not say why Alice was not here tonight with them.

Back home, Leisha sat in her room for hours, thinking over everything that had happened. When Alice came home from Julie's the next morning, Leisha rushed toward her. But Alice seemed angry about something.

"Alice—what is it?"

"Don't you think I have enough to put up with at school already?" Alice shouted. "Everybody knows, but at least when you stayed quiet it didn't matter too much. They'd stopped teasing me. Why did you have to do it?"

"Do what?" Leisha said, bewildered.

Alice threw something at her: a hard-copy morning paper, on newsprint flimsier than the Camden system used. The paper dropped open at Leisha's feet.

She stared at her own picture, three columns wide, with Kenzo Yagai. The headline said, YAGAI AND THE FUTURE: ROOM FOR THE REST OF US? Y-ENERGY INVENTOR CONFERS WITH "SLEEP-FREE" DAUGHTER OF MEGA-FINANCIER ROGER CAMDEN.

Alice kicked the paper. "It was on TV last night, too—on *TV*. I work hard not to look stuck-up or creepy, and you go and do this! Now Julie probably won't even invite me to her slumber party next week." She rushed up the broad curving stairs toward her room.

Leisha looked down at the paper. She heard Kenzo Yagai's voice in her head: "The dogs bark, but the caravan moves on." She looked at the empty stairs. Aloud she said, "Alice—your hair looks really pretty curled like that."

IV

"I want to meet the rest of them," Leisha said. "Why have you kept them from me this long?"

"I haven't kept them from you at all," Camden said. "Not offering is not the same as denial. Why shouldn't you be the one to do the asking? You're the one who now wants it."

Leisha looked at him. She was fifteen, in her last year at the Sauley School. "Why didn't you offer?"

"Why should I?"

"I don't know," Leisha said. "But you gave me everything else."

"Including the freedom to ask for what you want."

Leisha looked for the contradiction and found it. "Most things that you provided for my education I didn't ask for, because I didn't know enough to ask and you, as the adult, did. But you've never offered the opportunity for me to meet any of the other sleepless mutants—"

"Don't use that word," Camden said sharply.

"—so either you must think it was not essential to my education or else you had another motive for not wanting me to meet them."

"Wrong," Camden said. "There's a third possibility. That I think meeting them is essential to your education, that I do not want you to, but this issue provided a chance to further the education of your self-initiative by waiting for *you* to ask."

"All right," Leisha said, a little defiantly; there seemed to be a lot of defiance between them lately, for no good reason. She squared her shoulders. Her new breasts thrust forward. "I'm asking. How many of the Sleepless are there, who are they, and where are they?"

Camden said, "If you're using that term—'the Sleepless'—you've already; done some reading on your own. So you probably know that there are 1,082 of you so far in the United States, a few more in foreign countries, most of them in major metropolitan areas. Seventy-nine are in Chicago, most of them still small children. Only nineteen anywhere are older than you."

Leisha didn't deny reading any of this. Camden leaned forward in his study chair to peer at her. Leisha wondered if he needed glasses. His hair was completely gray now, sparse and stiff, like lonely broomstraws. The *Wall Street Journal* listed him among the hundred richest men in America; *Women's Wear Daily* pointed out that he was the only billionaire in the country who did not move in the society of international parties, charity balls, and personal jets. Camden's jet ferried him to business meetings around the world, to the chairmanship of the Yagai Economics Institute, and to very little else. Over the years he had grown richer, more reclusive, and more cerebral. Leisha felt a rush of her old affection.

She threw herself sideways into a leather chair, her long slim legs dangling over the arm. Absently she scratched a mosquito bite on her thigh. "Well, then, I'd like to meet Richard Keller." He lived in Chicago and was the beta-test Sleepless closest to her own age. He was seventeen.

"Why ask me? Why not just go?"

Leisha thought there was a note of impatience in his voice. He liked her to explore things first, then report on them to him later. Both parts were important.

Leisha laughed. "You know what, Daddy? You're predictable."

Camden laughed, too. In the middle of the laugh Susan came in.

"He certainly is not. Roger, what about that meeting in Buenos Aires Thursday? Is it on or off?" When he didn't answer, her voice grew shriller. "Roger? I'm talking to you!"

Leisha averted her eyes. Two years ago Susan had finally left genetic research to run Camden's house and schedule; before that she had tried hard to do both. Since she had left Biotech, it seemed to Leisha, Susan had changed. Her voice was tighter. She was more insistent that cook and the gardener follow her directions exactly, without deviation. Her blond braids had become stiff sculptured waves of platinum.

"It's on," Roger said.

"Well, thanks for at least answering. Am I going?"

"If you like."

"I like."

Susan left the room. Leisha rose and stretched. Her long legs rose on tiptoe. It felt good to reach, to stretch, to feel sunlight from the wide windows wash over her face. She smiled at her father and found him watching her with an unexpected expression.

"Leisha—"

"What?"

"See Keller. But be careful."

"Of what?"

But Camden wouldn't answer.

The voice on the phone had been noncommittal. "Leisha Camden? Yes, I know who you are. Three o'clock on Thursday?" The house was modest, a thirty-year-old Colonial on a quiet suburban street where small children on bicycles could be watched from the front window. Few roofs had more than one Y-energy cell. The trees, huge old sugar maples, were beautiful.

"Come in," Richard Keller said.

He was no taller than she, stocky, with a bad case of acne. Probably no genetic alterations except sleep, Leisha guessed. He had thick dark hair, a low forehead, and bushy black brows. Before he closed the door Leisha saw him stare at her car and driver, parked in the driveway next to a rusty ten-speed bike.

"I can't drive yet," she said. "I'm still fifteen."

"It's easy to learn," Keller said. "So, you want to tell me why you're here?"

Leisha liked his directness. "To meet some other Sleepless."

"You mean you never have? Not any of us?"

"You mean the rest of you know each other?" She hadn't expected that.

"Come to my room, Leisha."

She followed him to the back of the house. No one else seemed to be home. His room was large and airy, filled with computers and filing cabinets. A rowing machine sat in one corner. It looked like a shabbier version of the room of any bright classmate at the Sauley School, except there was more space without a bed. She walked over to the computer screen.

"Hey—you working on Boesc equations?"

"On an application of them."

"To what?"

"Fish migration patterns."

Leisha smiled. "Yeah—that would work. I never thought of that."

Keller seemed not to know what to do with her smile. He looked at the wall, then at her chin. "You interested in Gaea patterns? In the environment?"

"Well, no," Leisha confessed. "Not particularly. I'm going to study politics at Harvard. Prelaw. But of course we had Gaea patterns at school."

Keller's gaze finally came unstuck from her face. He ran a hand through his dark hair. "Sit down, if you want."

Leisha sat, looking appreciatively at the wall posters, shifting green on blue, like ocean currents. "I like those. Did you program them yourself?"

"You're not at all what I pictured," Keller said.

"How did you picture me?"

He didn't hesitate. "Stuck-up. Superior. Shallow, despite your IQ."

She was more hurt than she had expected to be.

Keller blurted, "You're the only one of the Sleepless who's really rich. But you already know that."

"No, I don't. I've never checked."

He took the chair beside her, stretching his stocky legs straight in front of him, in a slouch that had nothing to do with relaxation. "It makes sense, really. Rich people don't have their children genetically modified to be superior—they think any offspring of theirs is already superior. By their values. And poor people can't afford it. We Sleepless are upper-middle class, no more. Children of professors, scientists, people who value brains and time."

"My father values brains and time," Leisha said. "He's the biggest supporter of Kenzo Yagai."

"Oh, Leisha, do you think I don't already know that? Are you flashing me or what?"

Leisha said with great deliberateness, "I'm *talking* to you." But the next minute she could feel the hurt break through on her face.

"I'm sorry," Keller muttered. He shot off his chair and paced to the computer, back. "I *am* sorry. But I don't . . . I don't understand what you're doing here."

"I'm lonely," Leisha said, astonished at herself. She looked up at him. "It's true. I'm lonely. I am. I have friends and Daddy and Alice—but no one really knows, really understands—what? I don't know what I'm saying."

Keller smiled. The smile changed his whole face, opened up its dark planes to the light. "I do. Oh, do I. What do you do when they say, 'I had such a dream last night!'?"

"Yes!" Leisha said. "But that's even really minor—it's when *I* say, 'I'll look that up for you tonight,' and they get that funny look on their face that means 'She'll do it while I'm asleep.' "

"But that's even really minor," Keller said. "It's when you're playing basketball in the gym after supper and then you go to the diner for food and then you say, 'Let's have a walk by the lake,' and they say, 'I'm really tired. I'm going home to bed now.' "

"But that's really minor," Leisha said, jumping up. "It's when you really are absorbed by the movie and then you get the point and it's so goddamn beautiful you leap up and say, 'Yes! Yes!' and Susan says, 'Leisha, really—you'd think nobody but you ever enjoyed anything before.' "

"Who's Susan?" Keller said.

The mood was broken. But not really; Leisha could say "my stepmother" without much discomfort over what Susan had promised to be and what she had become. Keller stood inches from her, smiling that joyous smile, understanding, and suddenly relief washed over Leisha so strong that she walked straight into him and put her arms around his neck, tightening them only when she felt his startled jerk. She started to sob—she, Leisha, who never cried.

"Hey," Richard said. "Hey."

"Brilliant," Leisha said, laughing. "Brilliant remark."

She could feel his embarrassed smile. "Wanta see my fish migration curves instead?"

"No," Leisha sobbed, and he went on holding her, patting her back awkwardly, telling her without words that she was home.

Camden waited up for her, although it was past midnight. He had been smoking heavily. Through the blue air he said quietly,

"Did you have a good time, Leisha?"

"Yes."

"I'm glad," he said, and put out his last cigarette and climbed the stairs—slowly, stiffly; he was nearly seventy now—to bed.

They went everywhere together for nearly a year: swimming, dancing, to the museums, the theater, the library. Richard introduced her to the others, a group of twelve kids between fourteen and nineteen, all of them intelligent and eager. All Sleepless.

Leisha learned.

Tony's parents, like her own, had divorced. But Tony, fourteen, lived with his mother, who had not particularly wanted a Sleepless child, while his father, who had, acquired a red hovercar and a young girlfriend who designed ergonomic chairs in Paris. Tony was not allowed to tell anyone—relatives, schoolmates—that he was Sleepless. "They'll think you're a freak," his mother said, eyes averted from her son's face. The one time Tony disobeyed her and told a friend that he never slept, his mother beat him. Then she moved the family to a new neighborhood. He was nine years old.

Jeanine, almost as long-legged and slim as Leisha, was training for the Olympics in ice skating. She practiced twelve hours a day, hours no Sleeper still in high school could ever have. So far the newspapers had not picked up the story. Jeanine was afraid that if they did they would somehow not let her compete.

Jack, like Leisha, would start college in September. Unlike Leisha, he had already started his career. The practice of law had to wait for law school; the practice of investment required only money. Jack didn't have much, but his precise financial analyses parlayed $600 saved from summer jobs to $3,000 through stock-market investing, then to $10,000, and then he had enough to qualify for information-fund speculation. Jack was fifteen, not old enough to make legal investments; the transactions were all in the name of Kevin Baker, the oldest of the Sleepless, who lived in Austin. Jack told Leisha, "When I hit eighty-four percent profit over two consecutive quarters, the data analysts logged onto me. They were just sniffing. Well, that's their job, even when the overall amounts are actually small. It's the patterns they care about. If they take the trouble to cross-reference data banks and come up with the fact that Kevin is a Sleepless, will they try to stop us from investing somehow?"

"That's paranoid," Leisha said.

"No, it's not," Jeanine said. "Leisha, you don't *know*."

"You mean because I've been protected by my father's money and caring," Leisha said. No one grimaced; all of them confronted ideas openly, without shadowy allusions. Without dreams.

"Yes," Jeanine said. "Your father sounds terrific. And he raised you to think that achievement should not be fettered—Jesus Christ, he's a Yagaiist. Well, good. We're glad for you." She said it without sarcasm. Leisha nodded. "But the world isn't always like that. They hate us."

"That's too strong," Carol said. "Not hate."

"Well, maybe," Jeanine said. "But they're different from us. We're better, and they naturally resent that."

"I don't see what's natural about it," Tony said. "Why shouldn't it be just as natural to admire what's better? We do. Does any one of us resent Kenzo Yagai for his genius? Or Nelson Wade, the physicist? Or Catherine Raduski?"

"We don't resent them because we *are* better," Richard said. "Q.E.D."

"What we should do is have our own society," Tony said. "Why should we allow their regulations to restrict our natural, honest achievements? Why should Jeanine be barred from skating against them and Jack from investing on their same terms just because we're Sleepless? Some of them are brighter than others of them. Some have greater persistence. Well, we have greater concentration, more biochemical stability, and more time. All men are not created equal."

"Be fair, Tony—no one has been barred from anything yet," Jeanine said.

"But we will be."

"*Wait*." Leisha said. She was deeply troubled by the conversation. "I mean, yes, in many ways we're better. But you quoted out of context, Tony. The Declaration of Independence doesn't say all men are created equal in ability. It's talking about rights and power—it means that all are created equal *under the law*. We have no more right to a separate society or to being free of society's restrictions than anyone else does. There's no other way to freely trade one's efforts, unless the same contractual rules apply to all."

"Spoken like a true Yagaiist," Richard said, squeezing her hand.

"That's enough intellectual discussion for me," Carol said, laughing. "We've been at this for hours. We're at the beach, for Chrissake. Who wants to swim with me?"

"I do," Jeanine said. "Come on, Jack."

All of them rose, brushing sand off their suits, discarding sunglasses. Richard pulled Leisha to her feet. But just before they ran into the water, Tony put his skinny hand on her arm. "One more question, Leisha. Just to think about. If we achieve better than most other people, and we trade with the Sleepers when it's mutually beneficial, making no distinction there between the strong and the weak—what obligation do we have to those so weak they don't have anything to trade with us? We're already going to give more than we get—do we have to do it when we get nothing at all? Do we have to take care of their deformed and handicapped and sick and lazy and shiftless with the products of our work?"

"Do the Sleepers have to?" Leisha countered.

"Kenzo Yagai would say no. He's a Sleeper."

"He would say they would receive the benefits of contractual trade even if they aren't direct parties to the contract. The whole world is better fed and healthier because of Y-energy."

"Come on," Jeanine yelled. "Leisha, they're dunking me. Jack, you stop that. Leisha, help me!"

Leisha laughed. Just before she grabbed for Jeanine, she caught the look on Richard's face, on Tony's: Richard frankly lustful, Tony angry. At her. But why? What had she done, except argue in favor of dignity and trade?

Then Jack threw water on her, and Carol pushed Jack into the warm spray, and Richard was there with his arms around her, laughing.

When she got the water out of her eyes, Tony was gone.

Midnight. "Okay," Carol said. "Who's first?"

The six teenagers in the bramble clearing looked at each other. A Y-lamp, kept on low for atmosphere, cast weird shadows across their faces and over their bare legs. Around the clearing Roger Camden's trees stood thick and dark, a wall between them and the closest of the estate's outbuildings. It was very hot. August air hung heavy, sullen. They had voted against bringing an air-conditioned Y-field because this was a return to the primitive, the dangerous; let it be primitive.

Six pairs of eyes stared at the glass in Carol's hand.

"Come *on*," she said. "Who wants to drink up?" Her voice was jaunty, theatrically hard. "It was difficult enough to get this."

"How *did* you get it?" said Richard, the group member—except for Tony—with the least influential family contacts, the least money. "In a drinkable form like that?"

"My cousin Brian is a pharmaceutical supplier to the Biotech Institute. He's curious." Nods around the circle; except for Leisha, they were Sleepless precisely because they had relatives somehow connected to Biotech. And everyone was curious. The glass held interleukin-1, an immune-system booster, one of many substances that as a side effect induced the brain to swift and deep sleep.

Leisha stared at the glass. A warm feeling crept through her lower belly, not unlike the feeling when she and Richard made love.

Tony said, "Give it to me!"

Carol did. "Remember—you only need a little sip."

Tony raised the glass to his mouth, stopped, looked at them over the rim with his fierce eyes. He drank.

Carol took back the glass. They all watched Tony. Within a minute he lay on the rough ground; within two, his eyes closed in sleep.

It wasn't like seeing parents sleep, siblings, friends. It was Tony. They looked away, didn't meet each other's eyes. Leisha felt the warmth between her legs tug and tingle, faintly obscene.

When it was her turn, she drank slowly, then passed the glass to Jeanine. Her head turned heavy, as if it were being stuffed with damp rags. The trees at the edge of the clearing blurred. The portable lamp blurred, too—it wasn't bright and clean anymore but squishy, blobby; if she touched it, it would smear. Then darkness swooped over her brain, taking it away: *taking away her mind.* "Daddy!" She tried to call, to clutch for him, but then the darkness obliterated her.

Afterward they all had headaches. Dragging themselves back through the woods in the thin morning light was torture, compounded by an odd shame. They didn't touch each other. Leisha walked as far away from Richard as she could. It was a whole day before the throbbing left the base of her skull or the nausea her stomach.

There had not even been any dreams.

"I want you to come with me tonight," Leisha said, for the tenth or twelfth time. "We both leave for college in just two days; this is the last chance. I really want you to meet Richard."

Alice lay on her stomach across her bed. Her hair, brown and lusterless, fell around her face. She wore an expensive yellow jump suit, silk by Ann Patterson, which rucked up in wrinkles around her knees.

"Why? What do you care if I meet Richard or not?"

"Because you're my sister," Leisha said. She knew better than to say "my twin." Nothing got Alice angry faster.

"I don't want to." The next moment Alice's face changed. "Oh, I'm sorry, Leisha—I didn't mean to sound so snotty. But . . . but I don't want to."

"It won't be all of them. Just Richard. And just for an hour or so. Then you can come back here and pack for Northwestern."

"I'm not going to Northwestern."

Leisha stared at her.

Alice said, "I'm pregnant."

Leisha sat on the bed. Alice rolled onto her back, brushed the hair out of her eyes, and laughed. Leisha's ears closed against the sound. "Look at you," Alice said. "You'd think it was *you* who was pregnant. But you never would be, would you, Leisha? Not until it was the proper time. Not you."

"How?" Leisha said. "We both had our caps put in . . ."

"I had the cap removed," Alice said.

"You wanted to get pregnant?"

"Damn flash I did. And there's not a thing Daddy can do about it. Except, of course, cut off all credit completely, but I don't think he'll do that, do you?" She laughed again. "Even to me?"

"But, Alice . . . why? Not just to anger Daddy."

"No," Alice said. "Although you would think of that, wouldn't you? Because I want something to love. Something of my *own.* Something that has nothing to do with this house."

Leisha thought of her and Alice running through the conservatory, years ago, her and Alice darting in and out of the sunlight. "It hasn't been so bad growing up in this house."

"Leisha, you're stupid. I don't know how anyone so smart can be so stupid. Get out of my room! Get out!"

"But, Alice . . . *a baby* . . ."

"Get out!" Alice shrieked. "Go to Harvard. Go be successful. Just get out!"

Leisha jerked off the bed. "Gladly! You're irrational, Alice. You don't think ahead; you don't plan a *baby* . . . " But she could never sustain anger. It dribbled away, leaving her mind empty. She looked at Alice, who suddenly put out her arms. Leisha went into them.

"You're the baby," Alice said wonderingly. "You *are*. You're so . . . I don't know what. You're a baby."

Leisha said nothing. Alice's arms felt warm, felt whole, felt like two children running in and out of sunlight. "I'll help you, Alice. If Daddy won't."

Alice abruptly pushed her away. "I don't need your help."

Alice stood. Leisha rubbed her empty arms, fingertips scraping across opposite elbows. Alice kicked the empty, open truck in which she was supposed to pack for Northwestern and then abruptly smiled, a smile that made Leisha look away. She braced herself for more abuse. But what Alice said, very softly, was, "Have a good time at Harvard."

V

She loved it.

From the first sight of Massachusetts Hall, older than the United States by a half century, Leisha felt something that had been missing in Chicago: Age. Roots. Tradition. She touched the bricks of Widener Library, the glass cases in the Peabody Museum, as if they were the grail. She had never been particularly sensitive to myth or drama; the anguish of Juliet seemed to her artificial, that of Willy Loman merely wasteful. Only King Arthur, struggling to create a better social order, had interested her. But now, walking under the huge autumn trees, she suddenly caught a glimpse of a force that could span generations, fortunes left to endow learning and achievement the benefactors would never see, individual effort spanning and shaping centuries to come. She stopped and looked at the sky through the leaves, at the buildings solid with purpose. At such moments she thought of Camden, bending the will of an entire genetic-research institute to create her in the image he wanted.

Within a month she had forgotten all such mega-musings.

The workload was incredible, even for her. The Sauley School had encouraged individual exploration at her own pace; Harvard knew what it wanted from her, at its pace. In the last twenty years, under the academic leadership of a man who in his youth had watched Japanese economic domination with dismay, Harvard had become the controversial leader of a return to hard-edged learning of facts, theories, applications, problem solving, intellectual efficiency. The school accepted one out of every two hundred applications from around the world. The daughter of England's prime minister had flunked out her first year and been sent home.

Leisha had a single room in a new dormitory, the dorm because she had spent so many years isolated in Chicago and was hungry for people, the single so she would not disturb anyone else when she worked all night. Her second day, a boy from down the hall sauntered in and perched on the edge of her desk.

"So you're Leisha Camden."

"Yes."

"Sixteen years old."

"Almost seventeen."

"Going to outperform us all, I understand, without even trying."

Leisha's smile faded. The boy stared at her from under lowered downy brows.

He was smiling, his eyes sharp. From Richard and Tony and the others, Leisha had learned to recognize the anger that presented itself as contempt.

"Yes," Leisha said coolly. "I am."

"Are you sure? With your pretty little-girl hair and your mutant little-girl brain?"

"Oh, leave her alone, Hannaway," said another voice. A tall blond boy, so thin his ribs looked like ripples in brown sand, stood in jeans and bare feet, drying his wet hair. "Don't you ever get tired of walking around being an asshole?"

"Do you?" Hannaway said. He heaved himself off the desk and started toward the door. The blond moved out of his way. Leisha moved into it.

"The reason I'm going to do better than you," she said evenly, "is because I have certain advantages you don't. Including sleeplessness. And then after I 'outperform' you I'll be glad to help you study for your tests so that you can pass, too."

The blond, drying his ears, laughed. But Hannaway stood still, and into his eyes came an expression that made Leisha back away. He pushed past her and stormed out.

"Nice going, Camden," the blond said. "He deserved that."

"But I meant it," Leisha said. "I will help him study."

The blond lowered his towel and stared. "You did, didn't you? You meant it."

"Yes! Why does everybody keep questioning that?"

"Well," the boy said, "*I* don't. You can help me if I get into trouble." Suddenly he smiled. "But I won't."

"Why not?"

"Because I'm just as good at anything as you are, Leisha Camden."

She studied him. "You're not one of us. Not Sleepless."

"Don't have to be. I know what I can do. Do, be, create, trade."

She said, delighted, "You're a Yagaiist!"

"Of course." He held out his hand. "Stewart Sutter. How about a fishburger in the Yard?"

"Great," Leisha said. They walked out together, talking excitedly.

When people stared at her she tried not to notice. She was here. At Harvard. With space ahead of her, time to learn, and with people like Stewart Sutter who accepted and challenged her.

All the hours he was awake.

She became totally absorbed in her classwork. Roger Camden drove up once, walking the campus with her, listening, smiling. He was more at home than Leisha would have expected: he knew Stewart Sutter's father, Kate Addams's grandfather. They talked about Harvard, business, Harvard, the Yagai Economics Institute, Harvard. "How's Alice?" Leisha asked once, but Camden said that he didn't know; she had moved out and did not want to see him. He made her an allowance through his attorney. While he said this, his face remained serene.

Leisha went to the Homecoming Ball with Stewart, who was also majoring in prelaw but was two years ahead of Leisha. She took a weekend trip to Paris with Kate Addams and two other girlfriends, taking the Concorde III. She had a fight with Stewart over whether the metaphor of superconductivity could apply to Yagaiism, a stupid fight they both knew was stupid but had anyway, and afterward they became lovers. After the fumbling sexual explorations with Richard, Stewart was deft, experienced, smiling faintly as he taught her how to have an orgasm both by herself and with him. Leisha was dazzled.

"It's so *joyful*," she said, and Stewart looked at her with a tenderness she knew was part disturbance but didn't know why.

At midsemester she had the highest grades in the freshman class. She got every answer right on every single question on her midterms. She and Stewart went out for a beer to celebrate, and when they came back Leisha's room had been destroyed. The computer was smashed, the data banks wiped, hard copies and books smoldering in a metal wastebasket. Her clothes were ripped to pieces, her desk and bureau hacked apart. The only thing untouched, pristine, was the bed.

Stewart said, "There's no way this could have been done in silence. Everyone on the floor—hell, on the floor *below*—had to know. Someone will talk to the police." No one did. Leisha sat on the edge of the bed, dazed, and looked at the remnants of her homecoming gown. The next day Dave Hannaway gave her a long, wide smile.

Camden flew east again, taut with rage. He rented her an apartment in Cambridge with E-lock security and a bodyguard named Toshio. After he left Leisha fired the bodyguard but kept the apartment. It gave her and Stewart more privacy, which they used to endlessly discuss the situation. It was Leisha who argued that it was an aberration, an immaturity.

"There have always been haters, Stewart. Hate Jews, hate blacks, hate immigrants, hate Yagaiists who have more initiative and dignity than you do. I'm just the latest object of hatred. It's not new, it's not remarkable. It doesn't mean any basic kind of schism between the Sleepless and Sleepers."

Stewart sat up in bed and reached for the sandwiches on the night stand. "Doesn't it? Leisha, you're a different kind of person entirely. More evolutionarily fit, not only to survive but to prevail. Those other 'objects of hatred' you cite except Yagaiists—they were all powerless in their societies. They occupied *inferior* positions. You, on the other hand—all three Sleepless in Harvard Law are on the *Law Review*. All of them. Kevin Baker, your oldest, has already founded a successful bio-interface software firm and is making money, a lot of it. Every Sleepless is making superb grades, none have psychological problems, all are healthy—and most of you aren't even adults yet. How much hatred do you think you're going to encounter once you hit the big-stakes world of finance and business and scarce endowed chairs and national politics?"

"Give me a sandwich," Leisha said. "Here's my evidence you're wrong: you yourself. Kenzo Yagai. Kate Addams. Professor Lane. My father. Every Sleeper who inhabits the world of fair trade, mutually beneficial contracts. And that's most of you, or at least most of you who are worth considering. You believe that competition among the most capable leads to the most beneficial trades for everyone, strong and weak. Sleepless are making real and concrete contributions to society, in a lot of fields. That has to outweigh the discomfort we cause. We're *valuable* to you. You know that."

Stewart brushed crumbs off the sheets. "Yes. I do. Yagaiists do."

"Yagaiists run the business and financial and academic worlds. Or they will. In a meritocracy, they *should*. You underestimate the majority of people, Stew. Ethics aren't confined to the ones out front."

"I hope you're right," Stewart said. "Because, you know, I'm in love with you."

Leisha put down her sandwich.

"Joy," Stewart mumbled into her breasts. "You are joy."

When Leisha went home for Thanksgiving, she told Richard about Stewart. He listened tight-lipped.

"A Sleeper."

"A *person*," Leisha said. "A good, intelligent, achieving person."

"Do you know what your good intelligent achieving Sleepers have done, Leisha? Jeanine has been barred from Olympic skating. 'Genetic alteration, analogous to steroid abuse to create an unsportsmanlike advantage.' Chris Devereaux's left Stanford. They trashed his laboratory, destroyed two years' work in memory-formation proteins. Kevin Baker's software company is fighting a nasty advertising campaign, all underground, of course, about kids using software designed by 'nonhuman minds.' Corruption, mental slavery, satanic influences: the whole bag of witch-hunt tricks. Wake up, Leisha!"

They both heard his words. Moments dragged by. Richard stood like a boxer, forward on the balls of his feet, teeth clenched. Finally he said, very quietly, "Do you love him?"

"Yes," Leisha said. "I'm sorry."

"Your choice," Richard said coldly. "What do you do while he's asleep? Watch?"

"You make it sound like a perversion!"

Richard said nothing. Leisha drew a deep breath. She spoke rapidly but calmly, a controlled rush: "While Stewart is asleep I work. The same as you do. Richard—don't do this. I didn't mean to hurt you. And I don't want to lose the group. I believe the Sleepers are the same species as we are—are you going to punish me for that? Are you going to *add* to the hatred? Are you going to tell me that I can't belong to a wider world that includes all honest, worthwhile people whether they sleep or not? Are you going to tell me that the most important division is by genetics and not by economic spirituality? Are you going to force me into an artificial choice, 'us' or 'them'?"

Richard picked up a bracelet. Leisha recognized it: she had given it to him in the summer. His voice was quiet. "No. It's not a choice." He played with the gold links a minute, then looked up at her. "Not yet."

By spring break, Camden walked more slowly. He took medicine for his blood pressure, his heart. He and Susan, he told Leisha, were getting a divorce. "She changed, Leisha, after I married her. You saw that. She was independent and productive and happy, and then after a few years she stopped all that and became a shrew. A whining shrew." He shook his head in genuine bewilderment. "You saw the change."

Leisha had. A memory came to her: Susan leading her and Alice in "games" that were actually controlled cerebral-performance tests. Susan's braids dancing around her sparkling eyes. Alice had loved Susan, then, as much as Leisha had.

"Dad, I want Alice's address."

"I told you up at Harvard, I don't have it," Camden said. He shifted in his chair, the impatient gesture of a body that never expected to wear out. In January Kenzo Yagai had died of pancreatic cancer; Camden had taken the news hard. "I make her allowance through an attorney. By her choice."

"Then I want the address of the attorney."

The attorney, however, refused to tell Leisha where Alice was. "She doesn't want to be found, Ms. Camden. She wanted a complete break."

"Not from me," Leisha said.

"Yes," the attorney said, and something flickered behind his eyes, something she had last seen in Dave Hannaway's face.

She flew to Austin before returning to Boston, making her a day late for classes. Kevin Baker saw her instantly, canceling a meeting with IBM. She told him what she needed, and he set his best datanet people on it, without telling them why. Within two hours she had Alice's address from the attorney's electronic files. It was the first time, she realized, that she had ever turned to one of the Sleepless for help, and it had been given instantly. Without trade.

Alice was in Pennsylvania. The next weekend Leisha rented a hovercar and driver—she had learned to drive, but only groundcars as yet—and went to High Ridge, in the Appalachian Mountains.

It was an isolated hamlet, twenty-five miles from the nearest hospital. Alice lived with a man named Ed, a silent carpenter twenty years older than she, in a cabin in the woods. The cabin had water and electricity but no news net. In the early spring light the earth was raw and bare, slashed with icy gullies. Alice and Ed apparently worked at nothing. Alice was eight months pregnant.

"I didn't want you here," she said to Leisha. "So why are you?"

"Because you're my sister."

"God, look at you. Is that what they're wearing at Harvard? Boots like that? When did you become fashionable, Leisha? You were always too busy being intellectual to care."

"What's this all about, Alice? Why here? What are you doing?"

"Living," Alice said. "Away from dear Daddy, away from Chicago, away from drunken broken Susan—did you know she drinks? Just like Mom. He does that to people. But not to me. I got out. I wonder if you ever will."

"Got out? To *this*?"

"I'm happy," Alice said angrily. "Isn't that what it's supposed to be about? Isn't that the aim of your great Kenzo Yagai—happiness through individual effort?"

Leisha thought of saying that Alice was making no efforts that she could see. She didn't say it. A chicken ran through the yard of the cabin. Behind, the Appalachian Mountains rose in layers of blue haze. Leisha thought what this place must have been like in winter: cut off from the world where people strived toward goals, learned, changed.

"I'm glad you're happy, Alice."

"Are you?"

"Yes."

"Then I'm glad, too," Alice said, almost defiantly. The next moment she abruptly hugged Leisha, fiercely, the huge hard mound of her belly crushed between them. Alice's hair smelled sweet, like fresh grass in sunlight.

"I'll come see you again, Alice."

"Don't," Alice said.

VI

SLEEPLESS MUTIE BEGS FOR REVERSAL OF GENE TAMPERING, screamed the headline in the Food Mart. "PLEASE LET ME SLEEP LIKE REAL PEOPLE!" CHILD PLEADS.

Leisha typed in her credit number and pressed the news kiosk for a printout, although ordinarily she ignored the electronic tabloids. The headline went on circling the kiosk. A Food Mart employee stopped stacking boxes on shelves and watched her. Bruce, Leisha's bodyguard, watched the employee.

She was twenty-two, in her final year at Harvard Law, editor of the *Law Review*, ranked first in her class. The next three were Jonathan Cocchiara, Len Carter, and Martha Wentz. All Sleepless.

In her apartment she skimmed the printout. Then she accessed the Groupnet run from Austin. The files had more news stories about the child, with comments from other Sleepless, but before she could call them up Kevin Baker came online himself, on voice.

"Leisha. I'm glad you called. I was going to call you."

"What's the situation with this Stella Bevington, Kev? Has anybody checked it out?"

"Randy Davies. He's from Chicago, but I don't think you've met him; he's still in high school. He's in Park Ridge; Stella's in Skokie. Her parents wouldn't talk to him—were pretty abusive, in fact—but he got to see Stella face-to-face anyway. It doesn't look like an abuse case, just the usual stupidity: parents wanted a genius child, scrimped and saved, and now they can't handle that she *is* one. They scream at her to sleep, get emotionally abusive when she contradicts them, but so far no violence."

"Is the emotional abuse actionable?"

"I don't think we want to move on it yet. Two of us will keep in close touch with Stella—she does have a modem, and she hasn't told her parents about the net—and Randy will drive out weekly."

Leisha bit her lip. "A tabloid shitpiece said she's seven years old."

"Yes."

"Maybe she shouldn't be left there. I'm an Illinois resident, I can file an abuse grievance from here if Candy's got too much in her briefcase. . . ." *Seven years old.*

"No. Let it sit awhile. Stella will probably be all right. You know that."

She did. Nearly all of the Sleepless stayed "all right," no matter how much opposition came from the stupid segment of society. And it was only the stupid segment, Leisha argued—a small if vocal minority. Most people could, and would, adjust to the growing presence of the Sleepless, when it became clear that that presence included not only growing power but growing benefits to the country as a whole.

Kevin Baker, now twenty-six, had made a fortune in microchips so revolutionary that artificial intelligence, once a debated dream, was yearly closer to reality. Carolyn Rizzolo had won the Pulitzer Prize in drama for her play *Morning Light*. She was twenty-four. Jeremy Robinson had done significant work in superconductivity applications while still a graduate student at Stanford. William Thaine, *Law Review* editor when Leisha first came to Harvard, was now in private practice. He had never lost a case. He was twenty-six, and the cases were becoming important. His clients valued his ability more than his age.

But not everyone reacted that way.

Kevin Baker and Richard Keller had started the datanet that bound the Sleepless into a tight group, constantly aware of each other's personal fights. Leisha Camden financed the legal battles, the educational costs of Sleepless whose parents were unable to meet them, the support of children in emotionally bad situations. Rhonda Lavelier got herself licensed as a foster mother in California, and whenever possible the Group maneuvered to have small Sleepless who were removed from their homes assigned to Rhonda. The Group now had three ABA lawyers; within the next year they would gain four more, licensed to practice in five different states.

The one time they had not been able to remove an abused Sleepless child legally, they kidnapped him.

Timmy DeMarzo, four years old. Leisha had been opposed to the action. She had argued the case morally and pragmatically—to her they were the same thing—thus: if they believed in their society, in its fundamental laws and in their ability to belong to it as free-trading productive individuals, they must remain bound by the society's contractual laws. The Sleepless were, for the most part, Yagaiists. They should already know this. And if the FBI caught them, the courts and press would crucify them.

They were not caught.

Timmy DeMarzo—not even old enough to call for help on the datanet; they had learned of the situation through the automatic police-record scan Kevin maintained through his company—was stolen from his own backyard in Wichita. He had lived the last year in an isolated trailer in North Dakota; no place was too isolated for a modem. He was cared for by a legally irreproachable foster mother who had lived there all her life. The foster mother was second cousin to a Sleepless, a broad cheerful woman with a much better brain than her appearance indicated. She was a Yagaiist. No record of the child's existence appeared in any data bank: not the IRS's, not any school's, not even the local grocery store's computerized checkout slips. Food specifically for the child was shipped in monthly on a truck owned by a Sleepless in State College, Pennsylvania. Ten of the Group knew about the kidnapping, out of the total 3,428 born in the United States. Of that total, 2,691 were part of the Group via the net. Another 701 were as yet too young to use a modem. Only 36 Sleepless, for whatever reason, were not part of the Group.

The kidnapping had been arranged by Tony Indivino.

"It's Tony I wanted to talk to you about," Kevin said to Leisha. "He's started again. This time he means it. He's buying land."

She folded the tabloid very small and laid it carefully on the table. "Where?"

"Allegheny Mountains. In southern New York State. A lot of land. He's putting in the roads now. In the spring, the first buildings."

"Jennifer Sharifi still financing it?" She was the American-born daughter of an Arab prince who had wanted a Sleepless child. The prince was dead, and Jennifer, dark-eyed and multilingual, was richer than Leisha would one day be.

"Yes. He's starting to get a following, Leisha."

"I know."

"Call him."

"I will. Keep me informed about Stella."

She worked until midnight at the *Law Review*, then until four A.M. preparing her classes. From four to five she handled legal matters for the Group. At five A.M. she called Tony, still in Chicago. He had finished high school, done one semester at Northwestern, and at Christmas vacation he had finally exploded at his mother for forcing him to live as a Sleeper. The explosion, it seemed to Leisha, had never ended.

"Tony? Leisha."

"The answer is yes, yes, no, and go to hell."

Leisha gritted her teeth. "Fine. Now tell me the questions."

"Are you really serious about the Sleepless withdrawing into their own self-sufficient society? Is Jennifer Sharifi willing to finance a project the size of building a small city? Don't you think that's a cheat of all that can be accomplished by patient integration of the Group into the mainstream? And what about the contradictions of living in an armed restricted city and still trading with the Outside?"

"I would never tell *you* to go to hell."

"Hooray for you," Tony said. After a moment he added, "I'm sorry. That sounds like one of *them.*"

"It's wrong for us, Tony."

"Thanks for not saying I couldn't pull it off."

She wondered if he could. "We're not a separate species, Tony."

"Tell that to the Sleepers."

"You exaggerate. There are haters out there, there are *always* haters, but to give up . . ."

"We're not giving up. Whatever we create can be freely traded: software, hardware, novels, information, theories, legal counsel. We can travel in and out. But we'll have a safe place to return *to.* Without the leeches who think we owe them blood because we're better than they are."

"It isn't a matter of owing."

"Really?" Tony said. "Let's have this out, Leisha. All the way. You're a Yagaiist—what do you believe in?"

"Tony . . ."

"*Do it,*" Tony said, and in his voice she heard the fourteen-year-old Richard had introduced her to. Simultaneously, she saw her father's face: not as he was now, since the bypass, but as he had been when she was a little girl, holding her on his lap to explain that she was special.

"I believe in voluntary trade that is mutually beneficial. That spiritual dignity comes from supporting one's life through one's own efforts, and trading the results of those efforts in mutual cooperation throughout the society. That the symbol of this is the contract. And that we need each other for the fullest, most beneficial trade."

"Fine," Tony bit off. "Now what about the beggars in Spain?"

"The what?"

"You walk down a street in a poor country like Spain and you see a beggar. Do you give him a dollar?"

"Probably."

"Why? He's trading nothing with you. He has nothing to trade."

"I know. Out of kindness. Compassion."

"You see six beggars. Do you give them all a dollar?"

"Probably," Leisha said.

"You would. You see a hundred beggars and you haven't got Leisha Camden's money—do you give them each a dollar?"

"No."

"Why not?"

Leisha reached for patience. Few people could make her want to cut off a comm link; Tony was one of them. "Too draining on my own resources. My life has first claim on the resources I earn."

"All right. Now consider this. At Biotech Institute—where you and I began, dear pseudo sister—Dr. Melling has just yesterday—"

"*Who?*"

"Dr. Susan Melling. Oh, God, I completely forgot—she used to be married to your father!"

"I lost track of her," Leisha said. "I didn't realize she'd gone back to research. Alice once said . . . never mind. What's going on at Biotech?"

"Two crucial items, just released. Carla Dutcher has had first-month fetal genetic analysis. Sleeplessness is a dominant gene. The next generation of the Group won't sleep, either."

"We all knew that," Leisha said. Carla Dutcher was the world's first pregnant Sleepless. Her husband was a Sleeper. "The whole world expected that."

"But the press will have a windfall with it anyway. Just watch. 'Muties Breed!' 'New Race Set to Dominate Next Generation of Children!' "

Leisha didn't deny it. "And the second item?"

"It's sad, Leisha. We've just had our first death."

Her stomach tightened. "Who?"

"Bernie Kuhn. Seattle." She didn't know him. "A car accident. It looks pretty straightforward—he lost control on a steep curve when his brakes failed. He had only been driving a few months. He was seventeen. But the significance here is that his parents have donated his brain and body to Biotech, in conjunction with the pathology department at the Chicago Medical School. They're going to take him apart to get the first good look at what prolonged sleeplessness does to the body and brain."

"They should," Leisha said. "That poor kid. But what are you so afraid they'll find?"

"I don't know. I'm not a doctor. But whatever it is, if the haters can use it against us, they will."

"You're paranoid, Tony."

"Impossible. The Sleepless have personalities calmer and more reality-oriented than the norm. Don't you read the literature?"

"Tony—"

"What if you walk down that street in Spain and a hundred beggars each want a dollar and you say no and they have nothing to trade you, but they're so rotten with anger about what you have that they knock you down and grab it and then beat you out of sheer envy and despair?"

Leisha didn't answer.

"Are you going to say that's not a human scenario, Leisha? That it never happens?"

"It happens," Leisha said evenly. "But not all that often."

"Bullshit. Read more history. Read more *newspapers*. But the point is: what do you owe the beggars then? What does a good Yagaiist who believes in mutually beneficial contracts do with people who have nothing to trade and can only take?"

"You're not—"

"*What*, Leisha? In the most objective terms you can manage, what do we owe the grasping and nonproductive needy?"

"What I said originally. Kindness. Compassion."

"Even if they don't trade it back? Why?"

"Because . . ." She stopped.

"Why? Why do law-abiding and productive human beings owe anything to those who neither produce very much nor abide by laws? What philosophical or economic or spiritual justification is there for owing them anything? Be as honest as I know you are."

Leisha put her head between her knees. The question gaped beneath her, but she didn't try to evade it. "I don't know. I just know we do."

"*Why?*"

She didn't answer. After a moment Tony did. The intellectual challenge was gone from his voice. He said, almost tenderly, "Come down in the spring and see the site for Sanctuary. The buildings will be going up then."

"No," Leisha said.

"I'd like you to."

"No. Armed retreat is not the way."

Tony said, "The beggars are getting nastier, Leisha. As the Sleepless grow richer. And I don't mean in money."

"Tony—" she said, and stopped. She couldn't think what to say.

"Don't walk too many streets armed with just the memory of Kenzo Yagai."

In March, a bitterly cold March of winds whipping down the Charles River, Richard Keller came to Cambridge. Leisha had not seen him for four years. He didn't send her word on the Groupnet that he was coming. She hurried up the walk to her townhouse, muffled to the eyes in a red wool scarf against the snowy cold, and he stood there blocking the doorway. Behind Leisha, her bodyguard tensed.

"Richard! Bruce, it's all right; this is an old friend."

"Hello, Leisha."

He was heavier, sturdier looking, with a breadth of shoulder she didn't recognize. But the face was Richard's, older but unchanged: dark low brows, unruly dark hair. He had grown a beard.

"You look beautiful," he said.

She handed him a cup of coffee. "Are you here on business?" From the Groupnet she knew that he had finished his master's and had done outstanding work in marine biology in the Caribbean but had left that a year ago and disappeared from the net.

"No. Pleasure." He smiled suddenly, the old smile that opened up his dark face. "I almost forgot about that for a long time. Contentment, yes, we're all good at the contentment that comes from sustained work, but pleasure? Whim? Caprice? When was the last time you did something silly, Leisha?"

She smiled. "I ate cotton candy in the shower."

"Really? Why?"

"To see if it would dissolve in gooey pink patterns."

"Did it?"

"Yes. Lovely ones."

"And that was your last silly thing? When was it?"

"Last summer," Leisha said, and laughed.

"Well, mine is sooner than that. It's now. I'm in Boston for no other reason than the spontaneous pleasure of seeing you."

Leisha stopped laughing. "That's an intense tone for a spontaneous pleasure, Richard."

"Yup," he said, intensely. She laughed again. He didn't.

"I've been in India, Leisha. And China and Africa. Thinking, mostly. Watching. First I traveled like a Sleeper, attracting no attention. Then I set out to meet the Sleepless in India and China. There are a few, you know, whose parents were willing to come here for the operation. They pretty much are accepted and left alone. I tried to figure out why desperately poor countries—by our standards, anyway; over there Y-energy is mostly available only in big cities—don't have any trouble accepting the superiority of Sleepless, whereas Americans, with more prosperity than any time in history, build in resentment more and more."

Leisha said, "Did you figure it out?"

"No. But I figured out something else, watching all those communes and villages and kampongs. We are too individualistic."

Disappointment swept Leisha. She saw her father's face: *Excellence is what counts, Leisha. Excellence supported by individual effort. . . .* She reached for Richard's cup. "More coffee?"

He caught her wrist and looked up into her face. "Don't misunderstand me, Leisha. I'm not talking about work. We are too much individuals in the rest of our lives. Too emotionally rational. Too much alone. Isolation kills more than the free flow of ideas. It kills joy."

He didn't let go of her wrist. She looked down into his eyes, into depths she hadn't seen before: it was the feeling of looking into a mine shaft, both giddy and frightening, knowing that at the bottom might be gold or darkness. Or both.

Richard said softly, "Stewart?"

"Over long ago. An undergraduate thing." Her voice didn't sound like her own.

"Kevin?"

"No, never—we're just friends."

"I wasn't sure. Anyone?"

"No."

He let go of her wrist. Leisha peered at him timidly. He suddenly laughed. "Joy, Leisha." An echo sounded in her mind, but she couldn't place it and then it was gone and she laughed, too, a laugh airy and frothy as pink cotton candy in summer.

"Come home, Leisha. He's had another heart attack."

Susan Melling's voice on the phone was tired. Leisha said, "How bad?"

"The doctors aren't sure. Or say they're not sure. He wants to see you. Can you leave your studies?"

It was May, the last push toward her finals. The *Law Review* proofs were behind schedule. Richard had started a new business, marine consulting to Boston fishermen plagued with sudden inexplicable shifts in ocean currents, and was working twenty hours a day. "I'll come," Leisha said.

Chicago was colder than Boston. The trees were half budded. On Lake Michigan, filling the huge east windows of her father's house, whitecaps tossed up cold spray. Leisha saw that Susan was living in the house: her brushes on Camden's dresser, her journals on the credenza in the foyer.

"Leisha," Camden said. He looked old. Gray skin, sunken cheeks, the fretful and bewildered look of men who accepted potency like air, indivisible from their lives. In the corner of the room, on a small eighteenth-century slipper chair, sat a short, stocky woman with brown braids.

"*Alice.*"

"Hello, Leisha."

"*Alice*. I've looked for you. . . ." The wrong thing to say. Leisha had looked but not very hard, deterred by the knowledge that Alice had not wanted to be found. "How are you?"

"I'm fine," Alice said. She seemed remote, gentle, unlike the angry Alice of six years ago in the raw Pennsylvania hills. Camden moved painfully on the bed. He looked at Leisha with eyes that, she saw, were undimmed in their blue brightness.

"I asked Alice to come. And Susan. Susan came a while ago. I'm dying, Leisha."

No one contradicted him. Leisha, knowing his respect for facts, remained silent. Love hurt her chest.

"John Jaworski has my will. None of you can break it. But I wanted to tell you myself what's in it. The last few years I've been selling, liquidating. Most of my holdings are accessible now. I've left a tenth to Alice, a tenth to Susan, a tenth to Elizabeth, and the rest to you, Leisha, because you're the only one with the individual ability to use the money to its full potential for achievement."

Leisha looked wildly at Alice, who gazed back with her strange remote calm. "Elizabeth? My . . . mother? Is alive?"

"Yes," Camden said.

"You told me she was dead! Years and years ago."

"Yes. I thought it was better for you that way. She didn't like what you were, was jealous of what you could become. And she had nothing to give you. She would only have caused you emotional harm."

Beggars in Spain . . .

"That was wrong, Dad. You were *wrong*. She's my *mother . . .*" She couldn't finish the sentence.

Camden didn't flinch. "I don't think I was. But you're an adult now. You can see her if you wish."

He went on looking at her from his bright, sunken eyes, while around Leisha the air heaved and snapped. Her father had lied to her. Susan watched her closely, a small smile on her lips. Was she glad to see Camden fall in his daughter's estimation? Had she all along been that jealous of their relationship, of Leisha . . .

She was thinking like Tony.

The thought steadied her a little. But she went on staring at Camden, who went on staring implacably back, unbudged, a man positive even on his deathbed that he was right.

Alice's hand was on her elbow, Alice's voice so soft that no one but Leisha could hear. "He's done now, Leisha. And after a while you'll be all right."

Alice had left her son in California with her husband of two years, Beck Watrous, a building contractor she had met while waitressing in a resort on the Artificial Islands. Beck had adopted Jordan, Alice's son.

"Before Beck there was a real bad time," Alice said in her remote voice. "You know, when I was carrying Jordan I actually used to dream that he would be Sleepless? Like you. Every night I'd dream that, and every morning I'd wake up and have morning sickness with a baby that was only going to be a stupid nothing like me. I stayed with Ed—in Pennsylvania, remember? You came to see me there once—for two more years. When he beat me, I was glad. I wished Daddy could see. At least Ed was touching me."

Leisha made a sound in her throat.

"I finally left because I was afraid for Jordan. I went to California, did nothing but eat for a year. I got up to a hundred and ninety pounds." Alice was, Leisha estimated, five-foot-four. "Then I came home to see Mother."

"You didn't tell me," Leisha said. "You knew she was alive and you didn't tell me."

"She's in a drying-out tank half the time," Alice said, with brutal simplicity. "She wouldn't see you if you wanted to. But she saw me, and she fell slobbering all over me as her 'real' daughter, and she threw up on my dress. And I backed away from her and looked at the dress and knew it *should* be thrown up on, it was so ugly. Deliberately ugly. She started screaming how Dad had ruined her life, ruined mine, all for *you*. And do you know what I did?"

"What?" Leisha said. Her voice was shaky.

"I flew home, burned all my clothes, got a job, started college, lost fifty pounds, and put Jordan in play therapy."

The sisters sat silent. Beyond the window the lake was dark, unlit by moon or stars. It was Leisha who suddenly shook, and Alice who patted her shoulder.

"Tell me . . ." Leisha couldn't think what she wanted to be told, except that she wanted to hear Alice's voice in the gloom, Alice's voice as it was now, gentle and remote, without damage anymore from the damaging fact of Leisha's existence. Her very existence as damage. ". . . tell me about Jordan. He's five now? What's he like?"

Alice turned her head to look levelly into Leisha's eyes. "He's a happy, ordinary little boy. Completely ordinary."

Camden died a week later. After the funeral, Leisha tried to see her mother at the Brookfield Drug and Alcohol Abuse Center. Elizabeth Camden, she was told, saw no one except her only child, Alice Camden Watrous.

Susan Melling, dressed in black, drove Leisha to the airport. Susan talked deftly, determinedly, about Leisha's studies, about Harvard, about the *Review*. Leisha answered in monosyllables, but Susan persisted, asking questions, quietly insisting on answers: When would Leisha take her bar exams? Where was she interviewing for jobs? Gradually Leisha began to lose the numbness she had felt since her father's casket was lowered into the ground. She realized that Susan's persistent questioning was a kindness.

"He sacrificed a lot of people," Leisha said suddenly.

"Not me," Susan said. She pulled the car into the airport parking lot. "Only for a while there, when I gave up my work to do his. Roger didn't respect sacrifice much."

"Was he wrong?" Leisha said. The question came out with a kind of desperation she hadn't intended.

Susan smiled sadly. "No. He wasn't wrong. I should never have left my research. It took me a long time to come back to myself after that."

He does that to people, Leisha heard inside her head. Susan? Or Alice? She couldn't, for once, remember clearly. She saw her father in the old conservatory, potting and repotting the dramatic exotic flowers he had loved.

She was tired. It was muscle fatigue from stress, she knew; twenty minutes of rest would restore her. Her eyes burned from unaccustomed tears. She leaned her head back against the car seat and closed them.

Susan pulled the car into the airport parking lot and turned off the ignition. "There's something I want to tell you, Leisha."

Leisha opened her eyes. "About the will?"

Susan smiled tightly. "No. You really don't have any problems with how he divided the estate, do you? It seems to you reasonable. But that's not it. The research team from Biotech and Chicago Medical has finished its analysis of Bernie Kuhn's brain."

Leisha turned to face Susan. She was startled by the complexity of Susan's expression. Determination, and satisfaction, and anger, and something else Leisha could not name.

Susan said, "We're going to publish next week, in the *New England Journal of Medicine*. Security has been unbelievably restricted—no leaks to the popular press. But I want to tell you now, myself, what we found. So you'll be prepared."

"Go on," Leisha said. Her chest felt tight.

"Do you remember when you and the other Sleepless kids took interleukin-1 to see what sleep was like? When you were sixteen?"

"How did you know about that?"

"You kids were watched a lot more closely than you think. Remember the headache you got?"

"Yes." She and Richard and Tony and Carol and Jeanine . . . after her rejection by the Olympic Committee, Jeanine had never skated again. She was a kindergarten teacher in Butte, Montana.

"Interleukin-1 is what I want to talk about. At least, partly. It's one of a whole group of substances that boost the immune system. They stimulate the production of antibodies, the activity of white blood cells, and a host of other immunoenhancements. Normal people have surges of IL-1 released during the slow-wave phases of sleep. That means that they—we—are getting boosts to the immune system during sleep. One of the questions we researchers asked ourselves twenty-eight years ago was: will Sleepless kids who don't get those surges of IL-1 get sick more often?"

"I've never been sick," Leisha said.

"Yes, you have. Chicken pox and three minor colds by the end of your fourth year," Susan said precisely. "But in general you were all a very healthy lot. So we researchers were left with the alternative theory of sleep-driven immunoenhancement: that the burst of immune activity existed as a counterpart to a greater vulnerability of the body in sleep to disease, probably in some way connected to the fluctuations in body temperature during REM sleep. In other words, sleep *caused* the immune vulnerability that endogenous pyrogens like IL-1 counteract. Sleep was the problem; immune-system enhancements were the solution. Without sleep, there would be no problem. Are you following this?"

"Yes."

"Of course you are. Stupid question." Susan brushed her hair off her face. It was going gray at the temples. There was a tiny brown age spot beneath her right ear.

"Over the years we collected thousands—maybe hundreds of thousands—of Single Photon Emission Tomography scans of you and the other kids' brains, plus endless EEGs, samples of cerebrospinal fluid, and all the rest of it. But we couldn't really see inside your brains, really know what's going on in there. Until Bernie Kuhn hit that embankment."

"Susan," Leisha said, "give it to me straight. Without more buildup."

"You're not going to age."

"What?"

"Oh, cosmetically, yes. Gray hair, wrinkles, sags. But the absence of sleep peptides and all the rest of it affects the immune and tissue-restoration systems in ways we don't understand. Bernie Kuhn had a perfect liver. Perfect lungs, perfect heart, perfect lymph nodes, perfect pancreas, perfect medulla oblongata. Not just healthy or young—*perfect*. There's a tissue-regeneration enhancement that clearly derives from the operation of the immune system but is radically different from anything we ever suspected. Organs show no wear and tear—not even the minimal amount expected in a seventeen-year-old. They just repair themselves, perfectly, on and on . . . and on."

"For how long?" Leisha whispered.

"Who the hell knows? Bernie Kuhn was young—maybe there's some compensatory mechanism that cuts in at some point and you'll all just collapse, like an entire fucking gallery of Dorian Grays. But I don't think so. Neither do I think it can go on forever; no tissue regeneration can do that. But a long, long time."

Leisha stared at the blurred reflections in the car windshield. She saw her father's face against the blue satin of his casket, banked with white roses. His heart, unregenerated, had given out.

Susan said, "The future is all speculative at this point. We know that the peptide structures that build up the pressure to sleep in normal people resemble the components of bacterial cell walls. Maybe there's a connection between sleep and pathogen receptivity. We don't know. But ignorance never stopped the tabloids. I wanted to prepare you because you're going to get called supermen, *Homo perfectus*, who all knows what. Immortal."

The two women sat in silence. Finally Leisha said, "I'm going to tell the others. On our datanet. Don't worry about the security. Kevin Baker designed Groupnet; nobody knows anything we don't want them to."

"You're that well organized already?"

"Yes."

Susan's mouth worked. She looked away from Leisha. "We better go in. You'll miss your flight."

"Susan . . ."

"What?"

"Thank you."

"You're welcome," Susan said, and in her voice Leisha heard the thing she had seen before in Susan's expression and not been able to name: it was longing.

Tissue regeneration. A long, long time, sang the blood in Leisha's ears on the flight to Boston. *Tissue regeneration.* And, eventually: *immortal.* No, not that, she told herself severely. Not that. The blood didn't listen.

"You sure smile a lot," said the man next to her in first class, a business traveler who had not recognized Leisha. "You coming from a big party in Chicago?"

"No. From a funeral."

The man looked shocked, then disgusted. Leisha looked out the window at the ground far below. Rivers like microcircuits, fields like neat index cards. And on the horizon fluffy white clouds like masses of exotic flowers, blooms in a conservatory filled with light.

The letter was no thicker than any hard-copy mail, but hard-copy mail addressed by hand to either of them was so rare that Richard was nervous. "It might be explosive." Leisha looked at the letter on their hall credenza. MS. LIESHA CAMDEN. Block letters, misspelled.

"It looks like a child's writing," she said.

Richard stood with head lowered, legs braced apart. But his expression was only weary. "Perhaps deliberately like a child's. You'd be more open to a child's writing, they might have figured."

" 'They'? Richard, are we getting that paranoid?"

He didn't flinch from the question. "Yes. For the time being."

A week earlier the *New England Journal of Medicine* had published Susan's careful, sober article. An hour later the broadcast and datanet news had exploded in speculation, drama, outrage, and fear. Leisha and Richard, along with all the Sleepless on the Groupnet, had tracked and charted each of four components, looking for a dominant reaction: speculation ("The Sleepless may live for centuries, and this might lead to the following events . . ."); drama ("If a Sleepless marries only Sleepers, he may have lifetime enough for a dozen brides—and several dozen children, a bewildering blended family . . ."); outrage ("Tampering with the law of nature has only brought among us unnatural so-called people who will live with the unfair advantage of time: time to accumulate more kin, more power, more property than the rest of us could ever know . . ."); and fear ("How soon before the Superrace takes over?").

"They're all fear, of one kind or another," Carolyn Rizzolo finally said, and the Groupnet stopped their differentiated tracking.

Leisha was taking the final exams of her last year of law school. Each day comments followed her to the campus, along the corridors, and in the classroom; each day she forgot them in the grueling exam sessions, all students reduced to the same status of petitioner to the great university. Afterward, temporarily drained, she walked silently back home to Richard and the Groupnet, aware of the looks of people on the street, aware of her bodyguard, Bruce, striding between her and them.

"It will calm down," Leisha said. Richard didn't answer.

The town of Salt Springs, Texas, passed a local ordinance that no Sleepless could obtain a liquor license, on the grounds that civil rights statutes were built on the "all men were created equal" clause of the Declaration of Independence and Sleepless clearly were not covered. There were no Sleepless within a hundred miles of Salt Springs, and no one had applied for a new liquor license there for the past ten years, but the story was picked up by United Press and by Datanet News, and within twenty-four hours heated editorials appeared, on both sides of the issue, across the nation.

More local ordinances appeared. In Pollux, Pennsylvania, the Sleepless could be denied apartment rental on the grounds that their prolonged wakefulness would increase both wear and tear on the landlord's property and utility bills. In Cranston Estates, California, Sleepless were barred from operating twenty-four-hour businesses: "unfair competition." Iroquois County, New York, barred them from serving on county juries, arguing that a jury containing Sleepless, with their skewed idea of time, did not constitute "a jury of one's peers."

"All those statutes will be thrown out in superior courts," Leisha said. "But, God, the waste of money and docket time to do it!" A part of her mind noticed that her tone as she said this was Roger Camden's.

The state of Georgia, in which some sex acts between consenting adults were still a crime, made sex between a Sleepless and a Sleeper a third-degree felony, classing it with bestiality.

Kevin Baker had designed software that scanned the newsnets at high speed, flagged all stories involving discrimination or attacks on Sleepless, and categorized them by type. The files were available on Groupnet. Leisha read through them, then called Kevin. "Can't you create a parallel program to flag defenses of us? We're getting a skewed picture."

"You're right," Kevin said, a little startled. "I didn't think of it."

"Think of it," Leisha said, grimly. Richard, watching her, said nothing.

She was most upset by the stories about Sleepless children. Shunned at school, verbal abuse by siblings, attacks by neighborhood bullies, confused resentment from parents who had wanted an exceptional child but had not bargained on one who might live centuries. The school board of Cold River, Iowa, voted to bar Sleepless children from conventional classrooms because their rapid learning "created feelings of inadequacy in others, interfering with their education." The board made funds available for Sleepless to have tutors at home. There were no volunteers among the teaching staff. Leisha started spending as much time on Groupnet with the kids, talking to them all night long, as she did studying for her bar exams, scheduled for July.

Stella Bevington stopped using her modem.

Kevin's second program catalogued editorials urging fairness toward Sleepless. The school board of Denver set aside funds for a program in which gifted children, including the Sleepless, could use their talents and build teamwork through tutoring even younger children. Rive Beau, Louisiana, elected Sleepless Danielle du Cherncy to the city council, although Danielle was twenty-two and technically too young to qualify. The prestigious medical research firm of Halley-Hall gave much publicity to their hiring of Christopher Amren, a Sleepless with a Ph.D. in cellular physics.

Dora Clarq, a Sleepless in Dallas, opened a letter addressed to her, and a plastic explosive blew off her arm.

Leisha and Richard stared at the envelope on the hall credenza. The paper was thick, cream-colored, but not expensive: the kind of paper made of bulky newsprint dyed the shade of vellum. There was no return address. Richard called Liz Bishop, a Sleepless who was majoring in criminal justice in Michigan. He had never spoken with her before—neither had Leisha—but she came on Groupnet immediately and told them how to open it, or she could fly up and do it if they preferred. Richard and Leisha followed her directions for remote detonation in the basement of the townhouse. Nothing blew up. When the letter was open, they took it out and read it:

Dear Ms. Camden,

You been pretty good to me and I'm sorry to do this but I quit. They are making it pretty hot for me at the union not officially but you know how it is. If I was you I wouldn't go to the union for another bodyguard I'd try to find one privately. But be careful. Again I'm sorry but I have to live too.

Bruce

"I don't know whether to laugh or cry," Leisha said. "The two of us getting all this equipment, spending hours on this set-up so an explosive won't detonate . . ."

"It's not as if I at least had a whole lot else to do," Richard said. Since the wave of anti-Sleepless sentiment, all but two of his marine-consultant clients, vulnerable to the marketplace and thus to public opinion, had canceled their accounts.

Groupnet, still up on Leisha's terminal, shrilled in emergency override. Leisha got there first. It was Tony.

"Leisha. I'll need your legal help, if you'll give it. They're trying to fight me on Sanctuary. Please fly down here."

Sanctuary was raw brown gashes in the late-spring earth. It was situated in the Allegheny Mountains of southern New York State, old hills rounded by age and covered with pine and hickory. A superb road led from the closest town, Belmont, to Sanctuary. Low, maintenance-free buildings, whose design was plain but graceful, stood in various stages of completion. Jennifer Sharifi, looking strained, met Leisha and Richard. "Tony wants to talk to you, but first he asked me to show you both around."

"What's wrong?" Leisha asked quietly. She had never met Jennifer before, but no Sleepless looked like that—pinched, spent, *weary*—unless the stress level was enormous.

Jennifer didn't try to evade the question. "Later. First look at Sanctuary. Tony respects your opinion enormously, Leisha; he wants you to see everything."

The dormitories each held fifty, with communal rooms for cooking, dining, relaxing, and bathing, and a warren of separate offices and studios and labs for work. "We're calling them 'dorms' anyway, despite the etymology," Jennifer said, trying to smile. Leisha glanced at Richard. The smile was a failure.

She was impressed, despite herself, with the completeness of Tony's plans for lives that would be both communal and intensely private. There was a gym, a small hospital—"By the end of next year, we'll have eighteen AMA-certified doctors, you know, and four are thinking of coming here"—a day-care facility, a school, an intensive-crop farm. "Most of our food will come in from the outside, of course. So will most people's jobs, although they'll do as much of them as possible from here, over datanets. We're not cutting ourselves off from the world—only creating a safe place from which to trade with it." Leisha didn't answer.

Apart from the power facilities, self-supported Y-energy, she was most impressed with the human planning. Tony had Sleepless interested from virtually every field they would need both to care for themselves and to deal with the outside world. "Lawyers and accountants come first," Jennifer said. "That's our first line of defense in safeguarding ourselves. Tony recognizes that most modern battles for power are fought in the courtroom and boardroom."

But not all. Last, Jennifer showed them the plans for physical defense. She explained them with a mixture of defiance and pride: every effort had been made to stop attackers without hurting them. Electronic surveillance completely circled the 150 square miles Jennifer had purchased—some *counties* were smaller than that, Leisha thought, dazed. When breached, a force field a half-mile within the E-gate activated, delivering electric shocks to anyone on foot—"But only on the *outside* of the field. We don't want any of our kids hurt." Unmanned penetration by vehicles or robots was identified by a system that located all moving metal above a certain mass within Sanctuary. Any moving metal that did not carry a special signaling device designed by Donna Pospula, a Sleepless who had patented important electronic components, was suspect.

"Of course, we're not set up for an air attack or an outright army assault," Jennifer said. "But we don't expect that. Only the haters in self-motivated hate." Her voice sagged.

Leisha touched the hard copy of the security plans with one finger. They troubled her. "If we can't integrate ourselves into the world . . . free trade should imply free movement."

"Yeah. Well," Jennifer said, such an uncharacteristic Sleepless remark—both cynical and inarticulate—that Leisha looked up. "I have something to tell you, Leisha."

"What?"

"Tony isn't here."

"Where is he?"

"In Allegheny County Jail. It's true we're having zoning battles about Sanctuary—zoning! In this isolated spot. But this is something else, something that just happened this morning. Tony's been arrested for the kidnapping of Timmy DeMarzo."

The room wavered. "FBI?"

"Yes."

"How . . . how did they find out?"

"Some agent eventually cracked the case. They didn't tell us how. Tony needs a lawyer, Leisha. Dana Monteiro has already agreed, but Tony wants you."

"Jennifer—I don't even take the bar exams until July."

"He says he'll wait. Dana will act as his lawyer in the meantime. Will you pass the bar?"

"Of course. But I already have a job lined up with Morehouse, Kennedy & Anderson in New York—" She stopped. Richard was looking at her hard, Jennifer gazing down at the floor. Leisha said quietly, "What will he plead?"

"Guilty," Jennifer said. "With—what is it called legally?—extenuating circumstances."

Leisha nodded. She had been afraid Tony would want to plead not guilty: more lies, subterfuge, ugly politics. Her mind ran swiftly over extenuating circumstances, precedents, tests to precedents. . . . They could use *Clements v. Voy* . . .

"Dana is at the jail now," Jennifer said. "Will you drive in with me?"

"Yes."

In Belmont, the county seat, they were not allowed to see Tony. Dana Monteiro, as his attorney, could go in and out freely. Leisha, not officially an attorney at all, could go nowhere. This was told them by a man in the D.A.'s office whose face stayed immobile while he spoke to them and who spat on the ground behind their shoes when they turned to leave, even though this left him with a smear of spittle on his courthouse floor.

Richard and Leisha drove their rental car to the airport for the flight back to Boston. On the way Richard told Leisha he was leaving her. He was moving to Sanctuary, now, even before it was functional, to help with the planning and building.

She stayed most of the time in her townhouse, studying ferociously for the bar exams or checking on the Sleepless children through Groupnet. She had not hired another bodyguard to replace Bruce, which made her reluctant to go outside very much; the reluctance in turn made her angry with herself. Once or twice a day she scanned Kevin's electronic news clippings.

There were signs of hope. The *New York Times* ran an editorial, widely reprinted on the electronic news services:

PROSPERITY AND HATRED: A LOGIC CURVE WE'D RATHER NOT SEE

The United States has never been a country that much values calm, logic, rationality. We have, as a people, tended to label these things "cold." We have, as a people, tended to admire feeling and action: we exalt in our stories and our memorials; not the creation of the Constitution but its defense at Iwo Jima; not the intellectual achievements of a Stephen Hawking but the heroic passion of a Charles Lindbergh; not the inventors of the monorails and computers that unite us but the composers of the angry songs of rebellion that divide us.

A peculiar aspect of this phenomenon is that it grows stronger in times of prosperity. The better off our citizenry, the greater their contempt for the calm reasoning that got them there, and the more passionate their indulgence in emotion. Consider, in the last century, the gaudy excesses of the Roaring Twenties and the antiestablishment contempt of the sixties. Consider, in our own century, the unprecedented prosperity brought about by Y-energy—and then consider that Kenzo Yagai, except to his followers, was seen as a greedy and bloodless logician, while our national adulation goes to neonihilist writer Stephen Castelli, to "feelie" actress Brenda Foss, and to daredevil gravity-well diver Jim Morse Luter.

But most of all, as you ponder this phenomenon in your Y-energy houses, consider the current outpouring of irrational feeling directed at the "Sleepless" since the publication of the joint findings of the Biotech Institute and the Chicago Medical School concerning Sleepless tissue regeneration.

Most of the Sleepless are intelligent. Most of them are calm, if you define that much-maligned word to mean directing one's energies into solving problems rather than to emoting about them. (Even Pulitzer Prize winner Carolyn Rizzolo gave us a stunning play of ideas, not of passions run amok.) All of them show a natural bent toward achievement, a bent given a decided boost by the one-third more time in their days to achieve in. Their achievements lie, for the most part, in logical fields rather than emotional ones: Computers. Law. Finance. Physics. Medical research. They are rational, orderly, calm, intelligent, cheerful, young, and possibly very long-lived.

And, in our United States of unprecedented prosperity, increasingly hated.

Does the hatred that we have seen flower so fully over the last few months really grow, as many claim, from the "unfair advantage" the Sleepless have over the rest of us in securing jobs, promotions, money, success? Is it really envy over the Sleepless' good fortune? Or does it come from something more pernicious, rooted in our tradition of shoot-from-the-hip American action: hatred of the logical, the calm, the considered? Hatred in fact of the superior mind?

If so, perhaps we should think deeply about the founders of this country: Jefferson, Washington, Paine, Adams—inhabitants of the Age of Reason, all. These men created our orderly and balanced system of laws precisely to protect the property and achievements created by the individual efforts of balanced and rational minds. The Sleepless may be our severest internal test yet of our own sober belief in law and order. No, the Sleepless were not "created equal," but our attitudes toward them should be examined with a care equal to our soberest jurisprudence. We may not like what we learn about our own motives, but our credibility as a people may depend on the rationality and intelligence of the examination.

Both have been in short supply in the public reaction to last month's research findings.

Law is not theater. Before we write laws reflecting gaudy and dramatic feelings, we must be very sure we understand the difference.

Leisha hugged herself, gazing in delight at the screen, smiling. She called the *New York Times:* who had written the editorial? The receptionist, cordial when she answered the phone, grew brusque. The *Times* was not releasing that information, "prior to internal investigation."

It could not dampen her mood. She whirled around the apartment, after days of sitting at her desk or screen. Delight demanded physical action. She washed dishes, picked up books. There were gaps in the furniture patterns where Richard had taken pieces that belonged to him; a little quieter now, she moved the furniture to close the gaps.

Susan Melling called to tell her about the *Times* editorial; they talked warmly for a few minutes. When Susan hung up, the phone rang again.

"Leisha? Your voice still sounds the same. This is Stewart Sutter."

"Stewart." She had not seen him for years. Their romance had lasted two years and then dissolved, not from any painful issue so much as from the press of both their studies. Standing by the comm terminal, hearing his voice, Leisha suddenly felt again his hands on her breasts in the cramped dormitory bed: all those years before she had found a good use for a bed. The phantom hands became Richard's hands, and a sudden pain pierced her.

"Listen," Stewart said. "I'm calling because there's some information I think you should know. You take your bar exams next week, right? And then you have a tentative job with Morehouse, Kennedy & Anderson."

"How do you know all that, Stewart?"

"Men's-room gossip. Well, not as bad as that. But the New York legal community—that part of it, anyway—is smaller than you think. And you're a pretty visible figure."

"Yes," Leisha said neutrally.

"Nobody has the slightest doubt you'll be called to the bar. But there is some doubt about the job with Morehouse, Kennedy. You've got two senior partners, Alan Morehouse and Seth Brown, who have changed their minds since this . . . flap. 'Adverse publicity for the firm,' 'turning law into a circus,' blah blah blah. You know the drill. But you've also got two powerful champions, Ann Carlyle and Michael Kennedy, the old man himself. He's quite a mind. Anyway, I wanted you to know all this so you can recognize exactly what the situation is and know whom to count on in the in-fighting."

"Thank you," Leisha said. "Stew . . . why do you care if I get it or not? Why should it matter to you?"

There was a silence on the other end of the phone. Then Stewart said, very low, "We're not all noodleheads out here, Leisha. Justice does still matter to some of us. So does achievement."

Light rose in her, a bubble of buoyant light.

Stewart said, "You have a lot of support here for that stupid zoning fight over Sanctuary, too. You might not realize that, but you do. What the parks commission crowd is trying to pull is . . . but they're just being used as fronts. You know that. Anyway, when it gets as far as the courts, you'll have all the help you need."

"Sanctuary isn't my doing. At all."

"No? Well, I meant the plural you."

"Thank you. I mean that. How are you doing?"

"Fine. I'm a daddy now."

"Really! Boy or girl?"

"Girl. A beautiful little bitch, drives me crazy. I'd like you to meet my wife sometime, Leisha."

"I'd like that," Leisha said.

She spent the rest of the night studying for her bar exams. The bubble stayed with her. She recognized exactly what it was: joy.

It was going to be all right. The contract, unwritten, between her and her society—Kenzo Yagai's society, Roger Camden's society—would hold. With dissent and strife and, yes, some hatred: she suddenly thought of Tony's beggars in Spain, furious at the strong because they themselves were not. Yes. But it would hold.

She believed that.

She did.

VII

Leisha took her bar exams in July. They did not seem hard to her. Afterward three classmates, two men and a woman, made a fakely casual point of talking to Leisha until she had climbed safely into a taxi whose driver obviously did not recognize her, or stop signs. The three were all Sleepers. A pair of undergraduates, clean-shaven blond men with the long faces and pointless arrogance of rich stupidity, eyed Leisha and sneered. Leisha's female classmate sneered back.

Leisha had a flight to Chicago the next morning. Alice was going to join her there. They had to clean out the big house on the lake, dispose of Roger's personal property, put the house on the market. Leisha had had no time to do it earlier.

She remembered her father in the conservatory, wearing an ancient flat-topped hat he had picked up somewhere, potting orchids and jasmine and passion flowers.

When the doorbell rang she was startled: she almost never had visitors. Eagerly, she turned on the outside camera—maybe it was Jonathan or Martha, back in Boston to surprise her, to celebrate—why hadn't she thought before about some sort of celebration?

Richard stood gazing up at the camera. He had been crying.

She tore open the door. Richard made no move to come in. Leisha saw that what the camera had registered as grief was actually something else: tears of rage.

"Tony's dead."

Leisha put out her hand, blindly. Richard did not take it.

"They killed him in prison. Not the authorities—the other prisoners. In the recreation yard. Murderers, rapists, looters, scum of the earth—and they thought they had the right to kill *him* because he was different."

Now Richard did grab her arm, so hard that something, some bone, shifted beneath the flesh and pressed on a nerve. "Not just different—*better.* Because he was better, because we all are, we goddamn just don't stand up and shout it out of some misplaced feeling for *their* feelings . . . God!"

Leisha pulled her arm free and rubbed it, numb, staring at Richard's contorted face.

"They beat him to death with a lead pipe. No one even knows how they got a lead pipe. They beat him on the back of the head and they rolled him over and—"

"Don't!" Leisha said. It came out a whimper.

Richard looked at her. Despite his shouting, his violent grip on her arm, Leisha had the confused impression that this was the first time he had actually seen her. She went on rubbing her arm, staring at him in terror.

He said quietly, "I've come to take you to Sanctuary, Leisha. Dan Walcott and Vernon Bulriss are in the car outside. The three of us will carry you out, if necessary. But you're coming. You see that, don't you? You're not safe here, with your high profile and your spectacular looks—you're a natural target if anyone is. Do we have to force you? Or do you finally see for yourself that we have no choice—the bastards have left us no choice—except Sanctuary?"

Leisha closed her eyes. Tony, at fourteen, at the beach. Tony, his eyes ferocious and alight, the first to reach out his hand for the glass of Interleukin-1. Beggars in Spain.

"I'll come."

• • •

She had never known such anger. It scared her, coming in bouts throughout the long night, receding but always returning again. Richard held her in his arms, sitting with their backs against the wall of her library, and his holding made no difference at all. In the living room Dan and Vernon talked in low voices.

Sometimes the anger erupted in shouting, and Leisha heard herself and thought, *I don't know you*. Sometimes it became crying, sometimes talking about Tony, about all of them. Not the shouting nor the crying nor the talking, eased her at all.

Planning did, a little. In a cold dry voice she didn't recognize, Leisha told Richard about the trip to close the house in Chicago. She had to go; Alice was already there. If Richard and Dan and Vernon put Leisha on the plane, and Alice met her at the other end with union bodyguards, she should be safe enough. Then she would change her return ticket from Boston to Belmont and drive with Richard to Sanctuary.

"People are already arriving," Richard said. "Jennifer Sharifi is organizing it, greasing the Sleeper suppliers with so much money they can't resist. What about this townhouse here, Leisha? Your furniture and terminal and clothes?"

Leisha looked around her familiar office. Law books lined the walls, red and green and brown, although most of the same information was on-line. A coffee cup rested on a printout on the desk. Beside it was the receipt she had requested from the taxi driver this afternoon, a giddy souvenir of the day she had passed her bar exams; she had thought of having it framed. Above the desk was a holographic portrait of Kenzo Yagai.

"Let it rot," Leisha said.

Richard's arm tightened around her.

"I've never seen you like this," Alice said, subdued. "It's more than just clearing out the house, isn't it?"

"Let's get on with it," Leisha said. She yanked a suit from her father's closet. "Do you want any of this stuff for your husband?"

"It wouldn't fit."

"The hats?"

"No," Alice said. "Leisha—what is it?"

"Let's just *do* it!" She yanked all the clothes from Camden's closet, piled them on the floor, scrawled FOR VOLUNTEER AGENCY on a piece of paper, and dropped it on top of the pile. Silently, Alice started adding clothes from the dresser, which already bore a taped paper scrawled ESTATE AUCTION.

The curtains were already down throughout the house; Alice had done that yesterday. She had also rolled up the rugs. Sunset glared redly on the bare wooden floors.

"What about your old room?" Leisha said. "What do you want there?"

"I've already tagged it," Alice said. "A mover will come Thursday."

"Fine. What else?"

"The conservatory. Sanderson has been watering everything, but he didn't really know what needed how much, so some of the plants are—"

"Fire Sanderson," Leisha said curtly. "The exotics can die. Or have them sent to a hospital, if you'd rather. Just watch out for the ones that are poisonous. Come on, let's do the library."

Alice sat slowly on a rolled-up rug in the middle of Camden's bedroom. She had cut her hair; Leisha thought it looked ugly, jagged brown spikes around her broad face. She had also gained more weight. She was starting to look like their mother.

Alice said, "Do you remember the night I told you I was pregnant? Just before you left for Harvard?"

"Let's do the library."

"Do you?" Alice said. "For God's sake, can't you just once listen to someone else, Leisha? Do you have to be so much like Daddy every single minute?"

"I'm not like Daddy!"

"The hell you're not. You're exactly what he made you. But that's not the point. Do you remember that night?"

Leisha walked over the rug and out the door. Alice simply sat. After a minute Leisha walked back in. "I remember."

"You were near tears," Alice said implacably. Her voice was quiet. "I don't even remember exactly why. Maybe because I wasn't going to college after all. But I put my arms around you, and for the first time in years—years, Leisha—I felt you really were my sister. Despite all of it—the roaming the halls all night and the show-off arguments with Daddy and the special school and the artificially long legs and golden hair—all that crap. You seemed to need me to hold you. You seemed to need me. You seemed to *need*."

"What are you saying?" Leisha demanded. "That you can only be close to someone if they're in trouble and need you? That you can only be a sister if I was in some kind of pain, open sores running? Is that the bond between you Sleepers? 'Protect me while I'm unconscious, I'm just as crippled as you are'?"

"No," Alice said. "I'm saying that *you* could be a sister only if you were in some kind of pain."

Leisha stared at her. "You're stupid, Alice."

Alice said calmly, "I know that. Compared to you, I am. I know that."

Leisha jerked her head angrily. She felt ashamed of what she had just said, and yet it was true, and they both knew it was true, and anger still lay in her like a dark void, formless and hot. It was the formless part that was the worst. Without shape, there could be no action; without action, the anger went on burning her, choking her.

Alice said, "When I was twelve, Susan gave me a dress for our birthday. You were away somewhere, on one of those overnight field trips your fancy progressive school did all the time. The dress was silk, pale blue, with antique lace—very beautiful. I was thrilled, not only because it was beautiful but because Susan had gotten it for me and gotten software for you. The dress was mine. Was, I thought, *me*." In the gathering gloom Leisha could barely make out her broad, plain features. "The first time I wore it a boy said, 'Stole your sister's dress, Alice? Snitched it while she was *sleeping?*' Then he laughed like crazy, the way they always did.

"I threw the dress away. I didn't even explain to Susan, although I think she would have understood. Whatever was yours was yours, and whatever wasn't yours was yours, too. That's the way Daddy set it up. The way he hard-wired it into our genes."

"You, too?" Leisha said. "You're no different from the other envious beggars?"

Alice stood up from the rug. She did it slowly, leisurely, brushing dust off the back of her wrinkled skirt, smoothing the print fabric. Then she walked over and hit Leisha in the mouth.

"Now do you see me as real?" Alice asked quietly.

Leisha put her hand to her mouth. She felt blood. The phone rang, Camden's unlisted personal line. Alice walked over, picked it up, listened, and held it calmly out to Leisha. "It's for you."

Numb, Leisha took it.

"Leisha? This is Kevin. Listen; something's happened. Stella Bevington called me, on the phone, not Groupnet; I think her parents took away her modem. I picked up the phone and she screamed, 'This is Stella! They're hitting me, he's drunk—' and then the line went dead. Randy's gone to Sanctuary—hell, they've *all* gone. You're closest to her; she's still in Skokie. You better get there fast. Have you got bodyguards you trust?"

"Yes," Leisha said, although she hadn't. The anger—finally—took form. "I can handle it."

"I don't know how you'll get her out of there," Kevin said. "They'll recognize you, they know she called somebody, they might even have knocked her out . . ."

"I'll handle it," Leisha said.

"Handle what?" Alice said.

Leisha faced her. Even though she knew she shouldn't, she said, "What your people do. To one of ours. A seven-year-old kid who's getting beaten up by her parents because she's Sleepless—because she's *better* than you are—" She ran down the stairs and out to the rental car she had driven from the airport.

Alice ran right down with her. "Not your car, Leisha. They can trace a rental car just like that. My car."

Leisha screamed. "If you think you're—"

Alice yanked open the door of her battered Toyota, a model so old the Y-energy cones weren't even concealed but hung like drooping jowls on either side. She shoved Leisha into the passenger seat, slammed the door, and rammed herself behind the wheel. Her hands were steady. "Where?"

Blackness swooped over Leisha. She put her head down, as far between her knees as the cramped Toyota would allow. Two—no, three—days since she had eaten. Since the night before the bar exams. The faintness receded, swept over her again as soon as she raised her head.

She told Alice the address in Skokie.

"Stay way in the back," Alice said. "And there's a scarf in the glove compartment—put it on. Low, to hide as much of your face as possible."

Alice had stopped the car along Highway 42. Leisha said. "This isn't—"

"It's a union quick-guard place. We have to look like we have some protection, Leisha. We don't need to tell him anything. I'll hurry."

She was out in three minutes with a huge man in a cheap dark suit. He squeezed into the front seat beside Alice and said nothing at all. Alice did not introduce him.

The house was small, a little shabby, with lights on downstairs, none upstairs. The first stars shone in the north, away from Chicago. Alice said to the guard, "Get out of the car and stand here by the car door—no, more in the light—and don't do anything unless I'm attacked in some way." The man nodded. Alice started up the walk. Leisha scrambled out of the backseat and caught her sister two-thirds of the way to the plastic front door.

"Alice, what the hell are you doing? *I* have to—"

"Keep your voice down," Alice said, glancing at the guard. "Leisha, *think*. You'll be recognized. Here, near Chicago, with a Sleepless daughter—these people have looked at your picture in magazines for years. They've watched long-range holovids of you. They know you. They know you're going to be a lawyer. Me they've never seen. I'm nobody."

"Alice—"

"For Chrissake, get back in the car!" Alice hissed, and pounded on the front door.

Leisha drew off the walk, into the shadow of a willow tree. A man opened the door. His face was completely blank.

Alice said, "Child Protection Agency. We got a call from a little girl, this number. Let me in."

"There's no little girl here."

"This is an emergency, priority one," Alice said. "Child Protection Act 186. Let me in!"

The man, still blank-faced, glanced at the huge figure by the car. "You got a search warrant?"

"I don't need one in a priority-one child emergency. If you don't let me in, you're going to have legal snarls like you never bargained for."

Leisha clamped her lips together. No one would believe that; it was legal gobbledygook. . . . Her lip throbbed where Alice had hit her.

The man stood aside to let Alice enter.

The guard started forward. Leisha hesitated, then let him. He entered with Alice.

Leisha waited, alone, in the dark.

In three minutes they were out, the guard carrying a child. Alice's broad face gleamed pale in the porch light. Leisha sprang forward, opened the car door, and helped the guard ease the child inside. The guard was frowning, a slow puzzled frown shot with wariness.

Alice said, "Here. This is an extra hundred dollars. To get back to the city by yourself."

"Hey . . ." the guard said, but he took the money. He stood looking after them as Alice pulled away.

"He'll go straight to the police," Leisha said despairingly. "He has to, or risk his union membership."

"I know," Alice said. "But by that time we'll be out of the car."

"*Where?*"

"At the hospital," Alice said.

"Alice, we can't—" Leisha didn't finish. She turned to the backseat. "Stella? Are you conscious?"

"Yes," said the small voice.

Leisha groped until her fingers found the rear-seat illuminator. Stella lay stretched out on the backseat, her face distorted with pain. She cradled her left arm in her right. A single bruise colored her face, above the left eye.

"You're Leisha Camden," the child said, and started to cry.

"Her arm's broken," Alice said.

"Honey, can you . . ." Leisha's throat felt thick; she had trouble getting the words out ". . . can you hold on till we get you to a doctor?"

"Yes," Stella said. "Just don't take me back there!"

"We won't," Leisha said. "Ever." She glanced at Alice and saw Tony's face.

Alice said, "There's a community hospital about ten miles south of here."

"How do you know that?"

"I was there once. Drug overdose," Alice said briefly. She drove hunched over the wheel, with the face of someone thinking furiously. Leisha thought, too, trying to see a way around the legal charge of kidnapping. They probably couldn't say the child came willingly: Stella would undoubtedly cooperate, but at her age and in her condition she was probably *non sui juris*, her word would have no legal weight. . . .

"Alice, we can't even get her into the hospital without insurance information. Verifiable on-line."

"Listen," Alice said, not to Leisha but over her shoulder, toward the backseat. "Here's what we're going to do, Stella. I'm going to tell them you're my daughter and you fell off a big rock you were climbing while we stopped for a snack at a roadside picnic area. We're driving from California to Philadelphia to see your grandmother. Your name is Jordan Watrous and you're five years old. Got that, honey?"

"I'm seven," Stella said. "Almost eight."

"You're a very large five. Your birthday is March twenty-third. Can you do this, Stella?"

"Yes," the little girl said. Her voice was stronger.

Leisha stared at Alice. "Can *you* do this?"

"Of course I can," Alice said. "I'm Roger Camden's daughter."

Alice half carried, half supported Stella into the emergency room of the small community hospital. Leisha watched from the car: the short stocky woman, the child's thin body with the twisted arm. Then she drove Alice's car to the farthest corner of the parking lot, under the dubious cover of a skimpy maple, and locked it. She tied the scarf more securely around her face.

Alice's license plate number, and her name, would be in every police and rental-car databank by now. The medical banks were slower; often they uploaded from local precincts only once a day, resenting the governmental interference in what was still, despite a half century of battle, a private-sector enterprise. Alice and Stella would probably be all right in the hospital. Probably. But Alice could not rent another car.

Leisha could.

But the data file that would flash to rental agencies on Alice Camden Watrous might or might not include that she was Leisha Camden's twin.

Leisha looked at the rows of cars in the lot. A flashy luxury Chrysler, an Ikeda van, a row of middle-class Toyotas and Mercedes, a vintage '99 Cadillac—she could imagine the owner's face if that were missing—ten or twelve cheap run-abouts, a hovercar with the uniformed driver asleep at the wheel. And a battered farm truck.

Leisha walked over to the truck. A man sat at the wheel, smoking. She thought of her father.

"Hello," Leisha said.

The man rolled down his window but didn't answer. He had greasy brown hair.

"See that hovercar over there?" Leisha said. She made her voice sound young, high. The man glanced at it indifferently; from this angle you couldn't see that the driver was asleep. "That's my bodyguard. He thinks I'm in the hospital, the way my father told me to, getting this lip looked at." She could feel her mouth swollen from Alice's blow.

"So?"

Leisha stamped her foot. "So I don't want to be inside. He's a shit and so's Daddy. I want *out*. I'll give you four thousand bank credits for your truck. Cash."

The man's eyes widened. He tossed away his cigarette, looked again at the hovercar. The driver's shoulders were broad, and the car was within easy screaming distance.

"All nice and legal," Leisha said, and tried to smirk. Her knees felt watery.

"Let me see the cash."

Leisha backed away from the truck, to where he could not reach her. She took the money from her arm clip. She was used to carrying a lot of cash; there had always been Bruce, or someone like Bruce. There had always been safety.

"Get out of the truck on the other side," Leisha said, "and lock the door behind you. Leave the keys on the seat, where I can see them from here. Then I'll put the money on the roof where you can see it."

The man laughed, a sound like gravel pouring. "Regular little Dabney Engh, aren't you? Is that what they teach you society debs at your fancy schools?"

Leisha had no idea who Dabney Engh was. She waited, watching the man try to think of a way to cheat her, and tried to hide her contempt. She thought of Tony.

"All right," he said, and slid out of the truck.

"Lock the door!"

He grinned, opened the door again, locked it. Leisha put the money on the roof, yanked open the driver's door, clambered in, locked the door, and powered up the window. The man laughed. She put the key into the ignition, started the truck, and drove toward the street. Her hands trembled.

She drove slowly around the block twice. When she came back, the man was gone, and the driver of the hovercar was still asleep. She had wondered if the man would wake him, out of sheer malice, but he had not. She parked the truck and waited.

An hour and a half later Alice and a nurse wheeled Stella out of the emergency entrance. Leisha leaped out of the truck and yelled, "Coming, Alice!" waving both her arms. It was too dark to see Alice's expression; Leisha could only hope that Alice showed no dismay at the battered truck, that she had not told the nurse to expect a red car.

Alice said, "This is Julie Bergadon, a friend that I called while you were setting Jordan's arm." The nurse nodded, uninterested. The two women helped Stella into the high truck cab; there was no backseat. Stella had a cast on her arm and looked drugged.

"How?" Alice said as they drove off.

Leisha didn't answer. She was watching a police hovercar land at the other end of the parking lot. Two officers got out and strode purposefully toward Alice's locked car under the skimpy maple.

"My God," Alice said. For the first time she sounded frightened.

"They won't trace us," Leisha said. "Not to this truck. Count on it."

"Leisha." Alice's voice spiked with fear. "Stella's *asleep*."

Leisha glanced at the child, slumped against Alice's shoulder. "No, she's not. She's unconscious from painkillers."

"Is that all right? Normal? For . . . her?"

"We can black out. We can even experience substance-induced sleep." Tony and she and Richard and Jeanine in the midnight woods. . . . "Didn't you know that, Alice?"

"No."

"We don't know very much about each other, do we?"

They drove south in silence. Finally Alice said, "Where are we going to take her, Leisha?"

"I don't know. Any one of the Sleepless would be the first place the police would check—"

"You can't risk it. Not the way things are," Alice said. She sounded weary. "But all my friends are in California. I don't think we could drive this rust bucket that far before getting stopped."

"It wouldn't make it anyway."

"What should we do?"

"Let me think."

At an expressway exit stood a pay phone. It wouldn't be data shielded, as Groupnet was. Would Kevin's open line be tapped? Probably.

There was no doubt the Sanctuary line would be.

Sanctuary. All of them going there or already there, Kevin had said. Holed up, trying to pull the worn Allegheny Mountains around them like a safe little den. Except for the children like Stella, who could not.

Where? With whom?

Leisha closed her eyes. The Sleepless were out; the police would find Stella within hours. Susan Melling? But she had been Alice's all-too-visible stepmother and was cobeneficiary of Camden's will; they would question her almost immediately. It couldn't be anyone traceable to Alice. It could only be a Sleeper that Leisha knew, and trusted, and why should anyone at all fit that description? Why should she risk so much on anyone who did? She stood a long time in the dark phone kiosk. Then she walked to the truck. Alice was asleep, her head thrown back against the seat. A tiny line of drool ran down her chin. Her face was white and drained in the bad light from the kiosk. Leisha walked back to the phone.

"Stewart? Stewart Sutter?"

"Yes?"

"This is Leisha Camden. Something has happened." She told the story tersely, in bald sentences. Stewart did not interrupt.

"Leisha—" Stewart said, and stopped.

"I need help, Stewart." *"I'll help you, Alice." "I don't need your help."* A wind whistled over the dark field beside the kiosk, and Leisha shivered. She heard in the wind the thin keen of a beggar. In the wind, in her own voice.

"All right," Stewart said, "this is what we'll do. I have a cousin in Ripley, New York, just over the state line from Pennsylvania on the route you'll be driving east. It has to be in New York; I'm licensed in New York. Take the little girl there. I'll call my cousin and tell her you're coming. She's an elderly woman, was quite an activist in her youth; her name is Janet Patterson. The town is—"

"What makes you so sure she'll get involved? She could go to jail. And so could you."

"She's been in jail so many times you wouldn't believe it. Political protests going all the way back to Vietnam. But no one's going to jail. I'm now your attorney of record, I'm privileged. I'm going to get Stella declared a ward of the state. That shouldn't be too hard with the hospital records you established in Skokie. Then she can be transferred to a foster home in New York; I know just the place, people who are fair and kind. Then Alice—"

"She's resident in Illinois. You can't—"

"Yes, I can. Since those research findings about the Sleepless life span have come out, legislators have been railroaded by stupid constituents scared or jealous or just plain angry. The result is a body of so-called 'law' riddled with contradictions, absurdities, and loopholes. None of it will stand in the long run—or at least I hope not—but in the meantime it can all be exploited. I can use it to create the most goddamn convoluted case for Stella that anybody ever saw, and in the meantime she won't be returned home. But that won't work for Alice—she'll need an attorney licensed in Illinois."

"We have one," Leisha said. "Candace Holt."

"No, not a Sleepless. Trust me on this, Leisha. I'll find somebody good. There's a man in—are you crying?"

"No," Leisha said, crying.

"Ah, God," Stewart said. "Bastards. I'm sorry all this happened, Leisha."

"Don't be," Leisha said.

When she had directions to Stewart's cousin, she walked back to the truck. Alice was still asleep, Stella still unconscious. Leisha closed the truck door as quietly as possible. The engine balked and roared, but Alice didn't wake. There was a crowd of people with them in the narrow and darkened cab: Stewart Sutter, Tony Indivino, Susan Melling, Kenzo Yagai, Roger Camden.

To Stewart Sutter she said, You called to inform me about the situation at Morehouse, Kennedy. You are risking your career and your cousin for Stella. And you stand to gain nothing. Like Susan telling me in advance about Bernie Kuhn's brain. Susan, who lost her life to Daddy's dream and regained it by her own strength. A contract without consideration for each side is not a contract: every first-year student knows that.

To Kenzo Yagai she said, Trade isn't always linear. You missed that. If Stewart gives me something, and I give Stella something, and ten years from now Stella is a different person because of that and gives something to someone else as yet unknown—it's an ecology. An *ecology* of trade, yes, each niche needed, even if they're not contractually bound. Does a horse need a fish? *Yes.*

To Tony she said, Yes, there are beggars in Spain who trade nothing, give nothing, do nothing. But there are *more* than beggars in Spain. Withdraw from the beggars, you withdraw from the whole damn country. And you withdraw from the possibility of the ecology of help. That's what Alice wanted, all those years ago in her bedroom. Pregnant, scared, angry, jealous, she wanted to help *me,* and I wouldn't let her because I didn't need it. But I do now. And she did then. Beggars need to help as well as be helped.

And, finally, there was only Daddy left. She could *see* him, bright-eyed, holding thick-leaved exotic flowers in his strong hands. To Camden she said, You were wrong. Alice *is* special. Oh, Daddy—the specialness of Alice! You were *wrong.*

As soon as she thought this, lightness filled her. Not the buoyant bubble of joy, not the hard clarity of examination, but something else: sunshine, soft through the conservatory glass, where two children ran in and out. She suddenly felt light herself, not buoyant but translucent, a medium for the sunshine to pass clear through, on its way to somewhere else.

She drove the sleeping woman and the wounded child through the night, east, toward the state line.

William Gibson

William Gibson (1948–) is the avatar of cyberpunk, whose novel *Neuromancer* (1984) took the SF field by storm and made him one of the big names of science fiction. He occupies a central position in that decade as J. G. Ballard did in the 1960s, as a nexus of controversy and attention. One can readily see why postmodern writers such as Kathy Acker and publications from *The Village Voice* to *Vogue* have picked up the banner of cyberpunk. *Neuromancer,* and the stories collected in *Burning Chrome* (1986), are the pure essence of the Movement. With his cohort Bruce Sterling, Gibson remains the spokesman for the attitudes and images of cyberpunk, although they have declared the Movement dead. Yet the imagery and the name as a marketing term survive as a major influence on the science fiction of the 1990s.

Gibson's immense popularity among SF readers is rooted in his ability to intuit and portray intimate connections of mind and technology in a plausible fashion. This was especially powerful in a decade where many SF readers for the first time were using home computers and connecting directly by modem to the computers of others through vast networks, and playing sophisticated video games with characters with whom they might identify on the screen—as in the films *Tron* (1982) and *Bladerunner* (1982), the twin sources whose imagery has perhaps overwhelmed Gibson's works as the prime influence on later cyberpunk fictions.

The conventional setting of cyberpunk fiction is a future world dominated by computer technology, massive cartels and cyberspace, an artificial universe created through the link up of tens of millions of machines. This is the world of "Johnny Mnemonic." It is in this story that William Gibson introduced the word "cyberspace" into the English language and invented a new setting, as well as a metaphor that has aided in the transformation of communications technology by giving a name to the place you metaphorically inhabit when you are connected to a network of personal and other computers.

JOHNNY MNEMONIC

I put the shotgun in an Adidas bag and padded it out with four pairs of tennis socks, not my style at all, but that was what I was aiming for: If they think you're crude, go technical; if they think you're technical, go crude. I'm a very technical boy. So I decided to get as crude as possible. These days, though, you have to be pretty technical before you can even aspire to crudeness. I'd had to turn both those twelve-gauge shells from brass stock, on a lathe, and then load them myself; I'd had to dig up an old microfiche with instructions for hand-loading cartridges; I'd had to build a lever-action press to seat the primers—all very tricky. But I knew they'd work.

The meet was set for the Drome at 2300, but I rode the tube three stops past the closest platform and walked back. Immaculate procedure.

I checked myself out in the chrome-siding of a coffee kiosk, your basic sharp-faced Caucasoid with a ruff of stiff, dark hair. The girls at Under the Knife were big on Sony Mao, and it was getting harder to keep them from adding the chic suggestion of epicanthic folds. It probably wouldn't fool Ralfi Face, but it might get me next to his table.

The Drome is a single narrow space with a bar down one side and tables along the other, thick with pimps and handlers and an arcane array of dealers. The Magnetic Dog Sisters were on the door that night, and I didn't relish trying to get out past them if things didn't work out. They were two meters tall and thin as greyhounds. One was black and the other white, but aside from that they were as nearly identical as cosmetic surgery could make them. They'd been lovers for years and were bad news in a tussle. I was never quite sure which one had originally been male.

Ralfi was sitting at his usual table. Owing me a lot of money. I had hundreds of megabytes stashed in my head on an idiot/savant basis, information I had no conscious access to. Ralfi had left it there. He hadn't, however, come back for it. Only Ralfi could retrieve the data, with a code phrase of his own invention. I'm not cheap to begin with, but my overtime on storage is astronomical. And Ralfi had been very scarce.

Then I'd heard that Ralfi Face wanted to put out a contract on me. So I'd arranged to meet him in the Drome, but I'd arranged it as Edward Bax, clandestine importer, late of Rio and Peking.

The Drome stank of biz, a metallic tang of nervous tension. Muscle-boys scattered through the crowd were flexing stock parts of one another and trying on thin, cold grins, some of them so lost under superstructures of muscle graft that their outlines weren't really human.

Pardon me. Pardon me, friends. Just Eddie Bax here, Fast Eddie the Importer, with his professionally nondescript gym bag, and please ignore this slit, just wide enough to admit his right hand.

Ralfi wasn't alone. Eighty kilos of blond California beef perched alertly in the chair next to his, martial arts written all over him.

Fast Eddie Bax was in the chair opposite them before the beef's hands were off the table. "You black belt?" I asked eagerly. He nodded, blue eyes running an automatic scanning pattern between my eyes and my hands. "Me, too," I said. "Got mine here in the bag." And I shoved my hand through the slit and thumbed the safety off. Click. "Double twelve-gauge with the triggers wired together."

"That's a gun," Ralfi said, putting a plump, restraining hand on his boy's taut blue nylon chest. "Johnny has an antique firearm in his bag." So much for Edward Bax.

I guess he'd always been Ralfi Something or Other, but he owed his acquired surname to a singular vanity. Built something like an overripe pear, he'd worn the once-famous face of Christian White for twenty years—Christian White of the Aryan Reggae Band, Sony Mao to his generation, and final champion of race rock. I'm a whiz at trivia.

Christian White: classic pop face with a singer's high-definition muscles, chiseled cheekbones. Angelic in one light, handsomely depraved in another. But Ralfi's eyes lived behind that face, and they were small and cold and black.

"Please," he said, "let's work this out like businessmen." His voice was marked by a horrible prehensile sincerity, and the corners of his beautiful Christian White mouth were always wet. "Lewis here," nodding in the beefboy's direction, "is a meatball." Lewis took this impassively, looking like something built from a kit. "You aren't a meatball, Johnny."

"Sure I am, Ralfi, a nice meatball chock-full of implants where you can store your dirty laundry while you go off shopping for people to kill me. From my end of this bag, Ralfi, it looks like you've got some explaining to do."

"It's this last batch of product, Johnny." He sighed deeply. "In my role as broker—"

"Fence," I corrected.

"As broker, I'm usually very careful as to sources."

"You buy only from those who steal the best. Got it."

He sighed again. "I try," he said wearily, "not to buy from fools. This time, I'm afraid, I've done that." Third sigh was the cue for Lewis to trigger the neural disruptor they'd taped under my side of the table.

I put everything I had into curling the index finger of my right hand, but I no longer seemed to be connected to it. I could feel the metal of the gun and the foam-padded tape I'd wrapped around the stubby grip, but my hands were cool wax, distant and inert. I was hoping Lewis was a true meatball, thick enough to go for the gym bag and snag my rigid trigger finger, but he wasn't.

"We've been very worried about you, Johnny. Very worried. You see, that's Yakuza property you have there. A fool took it from them. Johnny. A dead fool."

Lewis giggled.

It all made sense then, an ugly kind of sense, like bags of wet sand settling around my head. Killing wasn't Ralfi's style. Lewis wasn't even Ralfi's style. But he'd got himself stuck between the Sons of the Neon Chrysanthemum and something that belonged to them—or, more likely, something of theirs that belonged to someone else. Ralfi, of course, could use the code phrase to throw me into idiot savant, and I'd spill their hot program without remembering a single quarter tone. For a fence like Ralfi, that would ordinarily have been enough. But not for the Yakuza. The Yakuza would know about Squids, for one thing, and they wouldn't want to worry about one lifting those dim and permanent traces of their program out of my head. I didn't know very much about Squids, but I'd heard stories, and I made it a point never to repeat them to my clients. No, the Yakuza wouldn't like that; it looked too much like evidence. They hadn't got where they were by leaving evidence around. Or alive.

Lewis was grinning. I think he was visualizing a point just behind my forehead and imagining how he could get there the hard way.

"Hey," said a low voice, feminine, from somewhere behind my right shoulder, "you cowboys sure aren't having too lively a time."

"Pack it, bitch," Lewis said, his tanned face very still. Ralfi looked blank.

"Lighten up. You want to buy some good freebase?" She pulled up a chair and quickly sat before either of them could stop her. She was barely inside my fixed field of vision, a thin girl with mirrored glasses, her dark hair cut in a rough shag. She wore black leather, open over a T-shirt slashed diagonally with stripes of red and black. "Eight thou a gram weight."

Lewis snorted his exasperation and tried to slap her out of the chair. Somehow he didn't quite connect, and her hand came up and seemed to brush his wrist as it passed. Bright blood sprayed the table. He was clutching his wrist white-knuckle tight, blood trickling from between his fingers.

But hadn't her hand been empty?

He was going to need a tendon stapler. He stood up carefully, without bothering to push his chair back. The chair toppled backward, and he stepped out of my line of sight without a word.

"He better get a medic to look at that," she said. "That's a nasty cut."

"You have no idea," said Ralfi, suddenly sounding very tired, "the depths of shit you have just gotten yourself into."

"No kidding? Mystery. I get real excited by mysteries. Like why your friend here's so quiet. Frozen, like. Or what this thing here is for," and she held up the little control unit that she'd somehow taken from Lewis. Ralfi looked ill.

"You, ah, want maybe a quarter-million to give me that and take a walk?" A fat hand came up to stroke his pale, lean face nervously.

"What I want," she said, snapping her fingers so that the unit spun and glittered, "is work. A job. Your boy hurt his wrist. But a quarter'll do for a retainer."

Ralfi let his breath out explosively and began to laugh, exposing teeth that hadn't been kept up to the Christian White standard. Then she turned the disruptor off.

"Two million," I said.

"My kind of man," she said, and laughed. "What's in the bag?"

"A shotgun."

"Crude." It might have been a compliment.

Ralfi said nothing at all.

"Name's Millions. Molly Millions. You want to get out of here, boss? People are starting to stare." She stood up. She was wearing leather jeans the color of dried blood.

And I saw for the first time that the mirrored lenses were surgical inlays, the silver rising smoothly from her high cheekbones, sealing her eyes in their sockets. I saw my new face twinned there.

"I'm Johnny," I said. "We're taking Mr. Face with us."

He was outside, waiting. Looking like your standard tourist tech, in plastic zoris and a silly Hawaiian shirt printed with blowups of his firm's most popular microprocessor; a mild little guy, the kind most likely to wind up drunk on sake in a bar that puts out miniature rice crackers with seaweed garnish. He looked like the kind who sings the corporate anthem and cries, who shake hands endlessly with the bartender. And the pimps and the dealers would leave him alone, pegging him as innately conservative. Not up for much, and careful with his credit when he was.

The way I figured it later, they must have amputated part of his left thumb, somewhere behind the first joint, replacing it with a prosthetic tip, and cored the stump, fitting it with a spool and socket molded from one of the Ono-Sendai diamond analogs. Then they'd carefully wound the spool with three meters of monomolecular filament.

Molly got into some kind of exchange with the Magnetic Dog Sisters, giving me a chance to usher Ralfi through the door with the gym bag pressed lightly against the base of his spine. She seemed to know them. I heard the black one laugh.

I glanced up, out of some passing reflex, maybe because I've never got used to it, to the soaring arcs of light and the shadows of the geodesics above them. Maybe that saved me.

Ralfi kept walking, but I don't think he was trying to escape. I think he'd already given up. Probably he already had an idea of what we were up against.

I looked back down in time to see him explode.

Playback on full recall shows Ralfi stepping forward as the little tech sidles out of nowhere, smiling. Just a suggestion of a bow, and his left thumb falls off. It's a conjuring trick. The thumb hangs suspended. Mirrors? Wires? And Ralfi stops, his back to us, dark crescents of sweat under the armpits of his pale summer suit. He knows. He must have known. And then the joke-shop thumb-tip, heavy as lead, arcs out in a lightning yo-yo trick, and the invisible thread connecting it to the killer's hand passes laterally through Ralfi's skull, just above his eyebrows, whips up, and descends, slicing the pear-shaped torso diagonally from shoulder to rib cage. Cuts so fine that no blood flows until synapses misfire and the first tremors surrender the body to gravity.

Ralfi tumbled apart in a pink cloud of fluids, the three mismatched sections rolling forward onto the tiled pavement. In total silence.

I brought the gym bag up, and my hand convulsed. The recoil nearly broke my wrist.

It must have been raining; ribbons of water cascaded from a ruptured geodesic and spattered on the tile behind us. We crouched in the narrow gap between a surgical boutique and an antique shop. She'd just edged one mirrored eye around the corner to report a single Volks module in front of the Drome, red lights flashing. They were sweeping Ralfi up. Asking questions.

I was covered in scorched white fluff. The tennis socks. The gym bag was a ragged plastic cuff around my wrist. "I don't see how the hell I missed him."

" 'Cause he's fast, so fast." She hugged her knees and rocked back and forth on her bootheels. "His nervous system's jacked up. He's factory custom." She grinned and gave a little squeal of delight. "I'm gonna get that boy. Tonight. He's the best, number one, top dollar, state of the art."

"What you're going to get, for this boy's two million, is my ass out of here. Your boyfriend back there was mostly grown in a vat in Chiba City. He's a Yakuza assassin."

"Chiba. Yeah. See, Molly's been Chiba, too." And she showed me her hands, fingers slightly spread. Her fingers were slender, tapered, very white against the polished burgundy nails. Ten blades snicked straight out from their recesses beneath her nails, each one a narrow, double-edged scalpel in pale blue steel.

I'd never spent much time in Nighttown. Nobody there had anything to pay me to remember, and most of them had a lot they paid regularly to forget. Generations of sharpshooters had chipped away at the neon until the maintenance crews gave up. Even at noon the arcs were soot-black against faintest pearl.

Where do you go when the world's wealthiest criminal order is feeling for you with calm, distant fingers? Where do you hide from the Yakuza, so powerful that it owns comsats and at least three shuttles? The Yakuza is a true multinational, like ITT and Ono-Sendai. Fifty years before I was born the Yakuza had already absorbed the Triads, the Mafia, the Union Corse.

Molly had an answer: You hide in the Pit, in the lowest circle, where any outside influence generates swift, concentric ripples of raw menace. You hide in Nighttown. Better yet, you hide *above* Nighttown, because the Pit's inverted, and the bottom of its bowl touches the sky, the sky that Nighttown never sees, sweating under its own firmament of acrylic resin, up where the Lo Teks crouch in the dark like gargoyles, black-market cigarettes dangling from their lips.

She had another answer, too.

"So you're locked up good and tight, Johnny-san? No way to get that program without the password?" She led me into the shadows that waited beyond the bright tube platform. The concrete walls were overlaid with graffiti, years of them twisting into a single metascrawl of rage and frustration.

"The stored data are fed in through a modified series of microsurgical contraautism prostheses." I reeled off a numb version of my standard sales pitch. "Client's code is stored in a special chip; barring Squids, which we in the trade don't like to talk about, there's no way to recover your phrase. Can't drug it out, cut it out, torture it. I don't *know* it, never did."

"Squids? Crawly things with arms?" We emerged into a deserted street market. Shadowy figures watched us from across a makeshift square littered with fish heads and rotting fruit.

"Superconducting quantum interference detectors. Used them in the war to find submarines, suss out enemy cyber sytems."

"Yeah? Navy stuff? From the war? Squid'll read that chip of yours?" She'd stopped walking, and I felt her eyes on me behind those twin mirrors.

"Even the primitive models could measure a magnetic field a billionth the strength of geomagnetic force; it's like pulling a whisper out of a cheering stadium."

"Cops can do that already, with parabolic microphones and lasers."

"But your data's still secure." Pride in profession. "No government'll let their cops have Squids, not even the security heavies. Too much chance of interdepartmental funnies; they're too likely to watergate you."

"Navy stuff," she said, and her grin gleamed in the shadows. "Navy stuff. I got a friend down here who was in the navy, name's Jones. I think you'd better meet him. He's a junkie, though. So we'll have to take him something."

"A junkie?"

"A dolphin."

He was more than a dolphin, but from another dolphin's point of view he might have seemed like something less. I watched him swirling sluggishly in his galvanized tank. Water slopped over the side, wetting my shoes. He was surplus from the last war. A cyborg.

He rose out of the water, showing us the crusted plates along his sides, a kind of visual pun, his grace nearly lost under articulated armor, clumsy and prehistoric. Twin deformities on either side of his skull had been engineered to house sensor units. Silver lesions gleamed on exposed sections of his gray-white hide.

Molly whistled. Jones thrashed his tail, and more water cascaded down the side of the tank.

"What is this place?" I peered at vague shapes in the dark, rusting chain link and things under tarps. Above the tank hung a clumsy wooden framework, crossed and recrossed by rows of dusty Christmas lights.

"Funland. Zoo and carnival rides. 'Talk with the War Whale.' All that. Some whale Jones is. . . ."

Jones reared again and fixed me with a sad and ancient eye.

"How's he talk?" Suddenly I was anxious to go.

"That's the catch. Say 'hi,' Jones."

And all the bulbs lit simultaneously. They were flashing red, white, and blue.

```
RWBRWBRWB
RWBRWBRWB
RWBRWBRWB
RWBRWBRWB
RWBRWBRWB
```

"Good with symbols, see, but the code's restricted. In the navy they had him wired into an audiovisual display." She drew the narrow package from a jacket pocket. "Pure shit, Jones. Want it?" He froze in the water and started to sink. I felt a strange panic, remembering that he wasn't a fish, that he could drown. "We want the key to Johnny's bank, Jones. We want it fast."

The lights flickered, died.

"Go for it, Jones!"

```
    B
BBBBBBBBB
    B
    B
    B
```

Blue bulbs, cruciform.

Darkness.

"Pure! It's *clean*. Come on, Jones."

```
WWWWWWWWW
WWWWWWWWW
WWWWWWWWW
WWWWWWWWW
WWWWWWWWW
```

White sodium glare washed her features, stark monochrome, shadows cleaving from her cheekbones.

```
R   RRRRR
R   R
RRRRRRRRR
    R   R
RRRRR   R
```

The arms of the red swastika were twisted in her silver glasses. "Give it to him," I said. "We've got it."

Ralfi Face. No imagination.

Jones heaved half his armored bulk over the edge of his tank, and I thought the metal would give way. Molly stabbed him overhand with the Syrette, driving the needle between two plates. Propellant hissed. Patterns of light exploded, spasming across the frame and then fading to black.

We left him drifting, rolling languorously in the dark water. Maybe he was dreaming of his war in the Pacific, of the cyber mines he'd swept, nosing gently into their circuitry with the Squid he'd used to pick Ralfi's pathetic password from the chip buried in my head.

"I can see them slipping up when he was demobbed, letting him out of the navy with that gear intact, but how does a cybernetic dolphin get wired to smack?"

"The war," she said. "They all were. Navy did it. How else you get 'em working for you?"

"I'm not sure this profiles as good business," the pirate said, angling for better money. "Target specs on a comsat that isn't in the book—"

"Waste my time and you won't profile at all," said Molly, leaning across his scarred plastic desk to prod him with her forefinger.

"So maybe you want to buy your microwaves somewhere else?" He was a tough kid, behind his Mao-job. A Nighttowner by birth, probably.

Her hand blurred down the front of his jacket, completely severing a lapel without even rumpling the fabric.

"So we got a deal or not?"

"Deal," he said, staring at his ruined lapel with what he must have hoped was only polite interest. "Deal."

While I checked the two recorders we'd bought, she extracted the slip of paper I'd given her from the zippered wrist pocket of her jacket. She unfolded it and read silently, moving her lips. She shrugged. "This is it?"

"Shoot," I said, punching the RECORD studs of the two decks simultaneously.

"Christian White," she recited, "and his Aryan Reggae Band."

Faithful Ralfi, a fan to his dying day.

Transition to idiot-savant mode is always less abrupt than I expect it to be. The pirate broadcaster's front was a failing travel agency in a pastel cube that boasted a desk, three chairs, and a faded poster of a Swiss orbital spa. A pair of toy birds with blown-glass bodies and tin legs were sipping monotonously from a Styrofoam cup of water on a ledge beside Molly's shoulder. As I phased into mode, they accelerated gradually until their Day-Glo-feathered crowns became solid arcs of color. The LEDs that told seconds on the plastic wall clock had become meaningless pulsing grids, and Molly and the Mao-faced boy grew hazy, their arms blurring occasionally in insect-quick ghosts of gesture. And then it all faded to cool gray static and an endless tone poem in an artificial language.

I sat and sang dead Ralfi's stolen program for three hours.

The mall runs forty kilometers from end to end, a ragged overlap of Fuller domes roofing what was once a suburban artery. If they turn off the arcs on a clear day, a gray approximation of sunlight filters through layers of acrylic, a view like the prison sketches of Giovanni Piranesi. The three southernmost kilometers roof Nighttown. Nighttown pays no taxes, no utilities. The neon arcs are dead, and the geodesics have been smoked black by decades of cooking fires. In the nearly total darkness of a Nighttown noon, who notices a few dozen mad children lost in the rafters?

We'd been climbing for two hours, up concrete stairs and steel ladders with perforated rungs, past abandoned gantries and dust-covered tools. We'd started in what looked like a disused maintenance yard, stacked with triangular roofing segments. Everything there had been covered with that same uniform layer of spraybomb graffiti: gang names, initials, dates back to the turn of the century. The graffiti followed us up, gradually thinning until a single name was repeated at intervals. LO TEK. In dripping black capitals.

"Who's Lo Tek?"

"Not us, boss." She climbed a shivering aluminum ladder and vanished through a hole in a sheet of corrugated plastic. " 'Low technique, low technology.' " The plastic muffled her voice. I followed her up, nursing my aching wrist. "Lo Teks, they'd think that shotgun trick of yours was effete."

An hour later I dragged myself up through another hole, this one sawed crookedly in a sagging sheet of plywood, and met my first Lo Tek.

" 'S okay," Molly said, her hand brushing my shoulder. "It's just Dog. Hey, Dog."

In the narrow beam of her taped flash, he regarded us with one eye and slowly extruded a thick length of grayish tongue, licking huge canines. I wondered how they wrote off tooth-bud transplants from Dobermans as low technology. Immunosuppressives don't exactly grow on trees.

"Moll." Dental augmentation impeded his speech. A string of saliva dangled from his twisted lower lip. "Heard ya comin'. Long time." He might have been fifteen, but the fangs and a bright mosaic of scars combined with the gaping socket to present a mask of total bestiality. It had taken time and a certain kind of creativity to assemble that face, and his posture told me he enjoyed living behind it. He wore a pair of decaying jeans, black with grime and shiny along the creases. His chest and feet were bare. He did something with his mouth that approximated a grin. "Bein' followed, you."

Far off, down in Nighttown, a water vendor cried his trade.

"Strings jumping, Dog?" She swung her flash to the side, and I saw thin cords tied to eyebolts, cords that ran to the edge and vanished.

"Kill the fuckin' light!"

She snapped it off.

"How come the one who's followin' you's got no light?"

"Doesn't need it. That one's bad news, Dog. Your sentries give him a tumble, they'll come home in easy-to-carry sections."

"This a *friend* friend, Moll?" He sounded uneasy. I heard his feet shift on the worn plywood.

"No. But he's mine. And this one," slapping my shoulder, "he's a friend. Got that?"

"Sure," he said, without much enthusiasm, padding to the platform's edge, where the eyebolts were. He began to pluck out some kind of message on the taut cords.

Nighttown spread beneath us like a toy village for rats; tiny windows showed candlelight, with only a few harsh, bright squares lit by battery lanterns and carbide lamps. I imagined the old men at their endless games of dominoes, under warm, fat drops of water that fell from wet wash hung out on poles between the plywood shanties. Then I tried to imagine him climbing patiently up through the darkness in his zoris and ugly tourist shirt, bland and unhurried. How was he tracking us?

"Good," said Molly. "He smells us."

"Smoke?" Dog dragged a crumpled pack from his pocket and pried out a flattened cigarette. I squinted at the trademark while he lit it for me with a kitchen match. Yiheyuan filters. Beijing Cigarette Factory. I decided that the Lo Teks were black marketeers. Dog and Molly went back to their argument, which seemed to revolve around Molly's desire to use some particular piece of Lo Tek real estate.

"I've done you a lot of favors, man. I want that floor. And I want the music."

"You're not Lo Tek. . . ."

This must have been going on for the better part of a twisted kilometer, Dog leading us along swaying catwalks and up rope ladders. The Lo Teks leech their webs and huddling places to the city's fabric with thick gobs of epoxy and sleep above the abyss in mesh hammocks. Their country is so attenuated that in places it consists of little more than holds for hands and feet, sawed into geodesic struts.

The Killing Floor, she called it. Scrambling after her, my new Eddie Bax shoes slipping on worn metal and damp plywood, I wondered how it could be any more lethal than the rest of the territory. At the same time I sensed that Dog's protests were ritual and that she already expected to get whatever it was she wanted.

Somewhere beneath us, Jones would be circling his tank, feeling the first twinges of junk sickness. The police would be boring the Drome regulars with questions about Ralfi. What did he do? Who was he with before he stepped outside? And the Yakuza would be settling its ghostly bulk over the city's data banks, probing for faint images of me reflected in numbered accounts, securities transactions, bills for utilities. We're an information economy. They teach you that in school. What they don't tell you is that it's impossible to move, to live, to operate at any level without leaving traces, bits, seemingly meaningless fragments of personal information. Fragments that can be retrieved, amplified . . .

But by now the pirate would have shuttled our message into line for blackbox transmission to the Yakuza comsat. A simple message: Call off the dogs or we wideband your program.

The program. I had no idea what it contained. I still don't. I only sing the song, with zero comprehension. It was probably research data, the Yakuza being given to advanced forms of industrial espionage. A genteel business, stealing from Ono-Sendai as a matter of course and politely holding their data for ransom, threatening to blunt the conglomerate's research edge by making the product public.

But why couldn't any number play? Wouldn't they be happier with something to sell back to Ono-Sendai, happier than they'd be with one dead Johnny from Memory Lane?

Their program was on its way to an address in Sydney, to a place that held letters for clients and didn't ask questions once you'd paid a small retainer. Fourth-class surface mail. I'd erased most of the other copy and recorded our message in the resulting gap, leaving just enough of the program to identify it as the real thing.

My wrist hurt. I wanted to stop, to lie down, to sleep. I knew that I'd lose my grip and fall soon, knew that the sharp black shoes I'd bought for my evening as Eddie Bax would lose their purchase and carry me down to Nighttown. But he rose in my mind like a cheap religious hologram, glowing, the enlarged chip on his Hawaiian shirt looming like a reconnaissance shot of some doomed urban nucleus.

So I followed Dog and Molly through Lo Tek heaven, jury-rigged and jerry-built from scraps that even Nighttown didn't want.

The Killing Floor was eight meters on a side. A giant had threaded steel cable back and forth through a junkyard and drawn it all taut. It creaked when it moved, and it moved constantly, swaying and bucking as the gathering Lo Teks arranged themselves on the shelf of plywood surrounding it. The wood was silver with age, polished with long use and deeply etched with initials, threats, declarations of passion. This was suspended from a separate set of cables, which lost themselves in darkness beyond the raw white glare of the two ancient floods suspended above the Floor.

A girl with teeth like Dog's hit the Floor on all fours. Her breasts were tattooed with indigo spirals. Then she was across the Floor, laughing, grappling with a boy who was drinking dark liquid from a liter flask.

Lo Tek fashion ran to scars and tattoos. And teeth. The electricity they were tapping to light the Killing Floor seemed to be an exception to their overall aesthetic, made in the name of . . . ritual, sport, art? I didn't know, but I could see that the Floor was something special. It had the look of having been assembled over generations.

I held the useless shotgun under my jacket. Its hardness and heft were comforting, even though I had no more shells. And it came to me that I had no idea at all of what was really happening, or of what was supposed to happen. And that was the nature of my game, because I'd spent most of my life as a blind receptacle to be filled with other people's knowledge and then drained, spouting synthetic languages I'd never understand. A very technical boy. Sure.

And then I noticed just how quiet the Lo Teks had become.

He was there, at the edge of the light, taking in the Killing Floor and the gallery of silent Lo Teks with a tourist's calm. And as our eyes met for the first time with mutual recognition, a memory clicked into place for me, of Paris, and the long Mercedes electrics gliding through the rain to Notre Dame; mobile greenhouses, Japanese faces behind the glass, and a hundred Nikons rising in blind phototropism, flowers of steel and crystal. Behind his eyes, as they found me, those same shutters whirring.

I looked for Molly Millions, but she was gone.

The Lo Teks parted to let him step up onto the bench. He bowed, smiling, and stepped smoothly out of his sandals, leaving them side by side, perfectly aligned, and then he stepped down onto the Killing Floor. He came for me, across that shifting trampoline of scrap, as easily as any tourist padding across synthetic pile in any featureless hotel.

Molly hit the Floor, moving.

The Floor screamed.

It was miked and amplified, with pickups riding the four fat coil springs at the corners and contact mikes taped at random to rusting machine fragments. Somewhere the Lo Teks had an amp and a synthesizer, and now I made out the shapes of speakers overhead, above the cruel white floods.

A drumbeat began, electronic, like an amplified heart, steady as a metronome.

She'd removed her leather jacket and boots; her T-shirt was sleeveless, faint telltales of Chiba City circuitry traced along her thin arms. Her leather jeans gleamed under the floods. She began to dance.

She flexed her knees, white feet tensed on a flattened gas tank, and the Killing Floor began to heave in response. The sound it made was like a world ending, like the wires that hold heaven snapping and coiling across the sky.

He rode with it, for a few heartbeats, and then he moved, judging the movement of the Floor perfectly, like a man stepping from one flat stone to another in an ornamental garden.

He pulled the tip from his thumb with the grace of a man at ease with social gesture and flung it at her. Under the floods, the filament was a refracting thread of rainbow. She threw herself flat and rolled, jackknifing up as the molecule whipped past, steel claws snapping into the light in what must have been an automatic rictus of defense.

The drum pulse quickened, and she bounced with it, her dark hair wild around the blank silver lenses, her mouth thin, lips taut with concentration. The Killing Floor boomed and roared, and the Lo Teks were screaming their excitement.

He retracted the filament to a whirling meter-wide circle of ghostly polychrome and spun it in front of him, thumbless hand held level with his sternum. A shield.

And Molly seemed to let something go, something inside, and that was the real start of her mad-dog dance. She jumped, twisting, lunging sideways, landing with both feet on an alloy engine block wire directly to one of the coil springs. I cupped my hands over my ears and knelt in a vertigo of sound, thinking Floor and benches were on their way down, down to Nighttown, and I saw us tearing through the shanties, the wet wash, exploding on the tiles like rotten fruit. But the cables held, and the Killing Floor rose and fell like a crazy metal sea. And Molly danced on it.

And at the end, just before he made his final cast with the filament, I saw something in his face, an expression that didn't seem to belong there. It wasn't fear and it wasn't anger. I think it was disbelief, stunned incomprehension mingled with pure aesthetic revulsion at what he was seeing, hearing—at what was happening to him. He retracted the whirling filament, the ghost disk shrinking to the size of a dinner plate as he whipped his arm above his head and brought it down, the thumbtip curving out for Molly like a live thing.

The Floor carried her down, the molecule passing just above her head; the Floor whiplashed, lifting him into the path of the taut molecule. It should have passed harmlessly over his head and been withdrawn into its diamond-hard socket. It took his hand off just behind the wrist. There was a gap in the Floor in front of him, and he went through it like a diver, with a strange deliberate grace, a defeated kamikaze on his way down to Nighttown. Partly, I think, he took that dive to buy himself a few seconds of the dignity of silence. She'd killed him with culture shock.

The Lo Teks roared, but someone shut the amplifier off, and Molly rode the Killing Floor into silence, hanging on now, her face white and blank, until the pitching slowed and there was only a faint pinging of tortured metal and the grating of rust on rust.

We searched the Floor for the severed hand, but we never found it. All we found was a graceful curve in one piece of rusted steel, where the molecule went through. Its edge was bright as new chrome.

We never learned whether the Yakuza had accepted our terms, or even whether they got our message. As far as I know, their program is still waiting for Eddie Bax on a shelf in the backroom of a gift shop on the third level of Sydney Central-5. Probably they sold the original back to Ono-Sendai months ago. But maybe they did get the pirate's broadcast, because nobody's come looking for me yet, and it's been nearly a year. If they do come, they'll have a long climb up through the dark, past Dog's sentries, and I don't look much like Eddie Bax these days. I let Molly take care of that, with a local anesthetic. And my new teeth have almost grown in.

I decided to stay up here. When I looked out across the Killing Floor, before he came, I saw how hollow I was. And I knew I was sick of being a bucket. So now I climb down and visit Jones, almost every night.

We're partners now, Jones and I, and Molly Millions, too. Molly handles our business in the Drome. Jones is still in Funland, but he has a bigger tank, with fresh seawater trucked in once a week. And he has his junk, when he needs it. He still talks to the kids with his frame of lights, but he talks to me on a new display unit in a shed that I rent there, a better unit than the one he used in the navy.

And we're all making good money, better money than I made before, because Jones's Squid can read the traces of anything that anyone ever stored in me, and he gives it to me on the display unit in languages I can understand. So we're learning a lot about all my former clients. And one day I'll have a surgeon dig all the silicon out of my amygdalae, and I'll live with my own memories and nobody else's, the way other people do. But not for a while.

In the meantime it's really okay up here, way up in the dark, smoking a Chinese filtertip and listening to the condensation that drips from the geodesics. Real quiet up here—unless a pair of Lo Teks decide to dance on the Killing Floor.

It's educational, too. With Jones to help me figure things out, I'm getting to be the most technical boy in town.

Harlan Ellison

Harlan Ellison (1934–) is the author of nearly a thousand short stories, essays, screenplays, and novels. Starting out as a teenager writing science fiction, by his early twenties he was widely published. His fame grew, and in the 1960s Ellison flowered into one of the leading, and cutting-edge, writers of *speculative fiction*—the term in fashion in the 1960s for science fiction with literary ambition and without central dependence on science. He won many awards in that decade and the next, and edited two hugely influential anthologies of original fiction, *Dangerous Visions* and *Again, Dangerous Visions*—and collected stories for a third, *The Last Dangerous Visions,* that remains to date, legendary and unpublished. *The Essential Ellison: a Thirty-five Year Retrospective* (1987) is a generous sampling of his short fiction.

Ellison is a powerful public figure in the SF field. In recent years he has cut back on his convention appearances, but in the 1990s he has his own show on The Sci-Fi Channel on cable television. He is a man of boundless energy and ambition, passionate, outspoken, peripatetic. In the words of Pogo artist Walt Kelly, he never retreats, though sometimes he advances backwards.

This story is one of the award-winning works upon which his literary reputation was built in the 1960s. It is perhaps reminiscent of Kurt Vonnegut, Jr.'s "Harrison Bergeron," and certainly grows out of the whole tradition of revolt against social and political repression in literature. Its central character is the cocky young rebel artist whom Ellison represented to SF in the 1960s, Harlan the Harlequin.

"REPENT, HARLEQUIN!" SAID THE TICKTOCKMAN

There are always those who ask, what is it all about? For those who need to ask, for those who need points sharply made, who need to know "where it's at," this:

The mass of men serve the state thus, not as men mainly, but as machines, with their bodies. They are the standing army, and the militia, jailors, constables, posse comitatus, etc. In most cases there is no free exercise whatever of the judgment or of the moral sense; but they put themselves on a level with wood and earth and stones; and wooden men can perhaps be manufactured that will serve the purposes as well. Such command no more respect than men of straw or a lump of dirt. They have the same sort of worth only as horses and dogs. Yet such as these even are commonly esteemed good citizens. Others—as most legislators, politicians, lawyers, ministers, and office-holders—serve the state chiefly with their heads; and, as they rarely make any moral distinctions, they are as likely to serve the Devil, without intending it, as God. A very few, as heroes, patriots, martyrs, reformers in the great sense, and men, serve the state with their consciences also, and so necessarily resist it for the most part; and they are commonly treated as enemies by it.

—Henry David Thoreau,
"Civil Disobedience"

That is the heart of it. Now begin in the middle, and later learn the beginning; the end will take care of itself.

But because it was the very world it was, the very world they had allowed it to *become*, for months his activities did not come to the alarmed attention of The Ones Who Keep the Machine Functioning Smoothly, the ones who poured the very best butter over the cams and mainsprings of the culture. Not until it had become obvious that somehow, someway, he had become a notoriety, a celebrity, perhaps even a hero for (what Officialdom inescapably tagged) "an emotionally disturbed segment of the populace," did they turn it over to the Ticktockman and his legal machinery. But by then, because it was the very world it was, and they had no way to predict he would happen—possibly a strain of disease long-defunct, now, suddenly, reborn in a system where immunity had been forgotten, had lapsed—he had been allowed to become too real. Now he had form and substance.

He had become a *personality*, something they had filtered out of the system many decades ago. But there it was, and there *he* was, a very definitely imposing personality. In certain circles—middle-class circles—it was thought disgusting. Vulgar ostentation. Anarchistic. Shameful. In others, there was only sniggering, those strata where thought is subjugated to form and ritual, niceties, proprieties. But down below, ah, down below, where the people always needed their saints and sinners, their bread and circuses, their heroes and villains, he was considered a Bolivar; a Napoleon; a Robin Hood; a Dick Bong (Ace of Aces), a Jesus; a Jomo Kenyatta.

And at the top—where, like socially attuned Shipwreck Kellys, even tremor and vibration threatens to dislodge the wealthy, powerful, and titled from their flagpoles—he was considered a menace; a heretic; a rebel; a disgrace; a peril. He was known down the line, to the very heartmeat core, but the important reactions were high above and far below. At the very top, at the very bottom.

So his file was turned over, along with his time-card and his cardioplate, to the office of the Ticktockman.

The Ticktockman: very much over six feet tall, often silent, a soft purring man when things went timewise. The Ticktockman.

Even in the cubicles of the hierarchy, where fear was generated, seldom suffered, he was called the Ticktockman. But no one called him that to his mask.

You don't call a man a hated name, not when that man, behind his mask, is capable of revoking the minutes, the hours, the days and nights, the years of your life. He was called the Master Timekeeper to his mask. It was safer that way.

"This is *what* he is," said the Ticktockman with genuine softness, "but not *who* he is? This time-card I'm holding in my left hand has a name on it, but it is the name of *what* he is, not *who* he is. This cardioplate here in my right hand is also named, but not whom named, merely what named. Before I can exercise proper revocation, I have to know who this what is."

To his staff, all the ferrets, all the loggers, all the finks, all the commex, even the mineez, he said, "Who is this Harlequin?"

He was not purring smoothly. Timewise, it was jangle.

However, it *was* the longest speech they had ever heard him utter at one time, the staff, the ferrets, the loggers, the finks, the commex, but not the mineez, who usually weren't around to know, in any case. But even they scurried to find out.

Who is the Harlequin?

High above the third level of the city, he crouched on the humming aluminum-frame platform of the air-boat (foof! air-boat, indeed! swizzleskid is what it was, with a tow-rack jerry-rigged) and stared down at the neat Mondrian arrangement of the buildings.

Somewhere nearby, he could hear the metronomic left-right-left of the 2:47 P.M. shift, entering the Timkin roller-bearing plant in their sneakers. A minute later, precisely, he heard the softer right-left-right of the 5:00 A.M. formation, going home.

An elfish grin spread across his tanned features, and his dimples appeared for a moment. Then, scratching at his thatch of auburn hair, he shrugged within his motley, as though girding himself for what came next, and threw the joystick forward, and bent into the wind as the air-boat dropped. He skimmed over a slidewalk, purposely dropping a few feet to crease the tassels of the ladies of fashion, and—inserting thumbs in large ears—he stuck out his tongue, rolled his eyes and went wugga-wugga-wugga. It was a minor diversion. One pedestrian skittered and tumbled, sending parcels everywhichway, another wet herself, a third keeled slantwise and the walk was stopped automatically by the servitors till she could be resuscitated. It was a minor diversion.

Then he swirled away on a vagrant breeze, and was gone. Hi-ho.

As he rounded the cornice of the Time-Motion Study Building, he saw the shift, just boarding the slidewalk. With practiced motion and an absolute conservation of movement, they sidestepped up onto the slowstrip and (in a chorus line reminiscent of a Busby Berkeley film of the antediluvian 1930s) advanced across the strips ostrich-walking till they were lined up on the expresstrip.

Once more, in anticipation, the elfin grin spread, and there was a tooth missing back there on the left side. He dipped, skimmed, and swooped over them; and then, scrunching about on the air-boat, he released the holding pins that fastened shut the ends of the homemade pouring troughs that kept his cargo from dumping prematurely. And as he pulled the trough-pins, the air-boat slid over the factory workers and one hundred and fifty thousand dollars' worth of jelly beans cascaded down on the expresstrip.

Jelly beans! Millions and billions of purples and yellows and greens and licorice and grape and raspberry and mint and round and smooth and crunchy outside and soft-mealy inside and sugary and bouncing jouncing tumbling clittering clattering skittering fell on the heads and shoulders and hard-hats and carapaces of the Timkin workers, tinkling on the slidewalk and bouncing away and rolling about underfoot and filling the sky on their way down with all the colors of joy and childhood and holidays, coming down in a steady rain, a solid wash, a torrent of color and sweetness out of the sky from above, and entering a universe of sanity and metronomic order with quite-mad coocoo newness. Jelly beans!

The shift workers howled and laughed and were pelted, and broke ranks, and the jelly beans managed to work their way into the mechanism of the slidewalks after which there was a hideous scraping as the sound of a million fingernails rasped down a quarter of a million blackboards, followed by a coughing and a sputtering, and then the slidewalks all stopped and everyone was dumped thisawayandthataway in a jackstraw tumble, and still laughing and popping little jelly bean eggs of childish color into their mouths. It was a holiday, and a jollity, an absolute insanity, a giggle. But . . .

The shift was delayed seven minutes.

They did not get home for seven minutes.

The master schedule was thrown off by seven minutes.

Quotas were delayed by inoperative slidewalks for seven minutes.

He had tapped the first domino in the line, and one after another, like chik chik chik, the others had fallen.

The System had been seven minutes' worth of disrupted. It was a tiny matter, one hardly worthy of note, but in a society where the single driving force was order and unity and promptness and clocklike precision and attention to the clock, reverence of the gods of the passage of time, it was a disaster of major importance.

So he was ordered to appear before the Ticktockman. It was broadcast across every channel of the communications web. He was ordered to be *there* at 7:00 P.M. dammit on time. And they waited, and they waited, but he didn't show up till almost ten-thirty, at which time he merely sang a little song about moonlight in a place no one had ever heard of, called Vermont, and vanished again. But they had all been waiting since seven, and it wrecked *hell* with their schedules. So the question remained: Who is the Harlequin?

But the *unasked* question (more important of the two) was: how did we get *into* this position, where a laughing, irresponsible japer of jabberwocky and jive could disrupt our entire economic and cultural life with a hundred and fifty thousand dollars' worth of jelly beans . . .

Jelly for God's sake beans! This is madness! Where did he get the money to buy a hundred and fifty thousand dollars' worth of jelly beans? (They knew it would have cost that much, because they had a team of Situation Analysts pulled off another assignment, and rushed to the slidewalk scene to sweep up and count the candies, and produce findings, which disrupted *their* schedules and threw their entire branch at least a day behind.) Jelly beans! Jelly . . . *beans?* Now wait a second—a second accounted for—no one has manufactured jelly beans for over a hundred years. Where did he get jelly beans?

That's another good question. More than likely it will never be answered to your complete satisfaction. But then, how many questions ever are?

The middle you know. Here is the beginning. How it starts:

A desk pad. Day for day, and turn each day, 9:00—open the mail. 9:45—appointment with planning commission board. 10:30—discuss installation pro gress charts with J.L. 11:45—pray for rain. 12:00—lunch. *And so it goes.*

"I'm sorry, Miss Grant, but the time for interviews was set at 2:30, and it's almost five now. I'm sorry you're late, but those are the rules. You'll have to wait till next year to submit application for this college again." *And so it goes.*

The 10:10 local stops at Cresthaven, Galesville, Tonawanda Junction, Selby and Farnhurst, but not at Indiana City, Lucasville and Colton, except on Sunday. The 10:35 express stops at Galesville, Selby and Indiana City, except on Sundays & Holidays, at which time it stops at . . . *And so it goes.*

"I couldn't wait, Fred. I had to be at Pierre Cartain's by 3:00, and you said you'd meet me under the clock in the terminal at 2:45, and you weren't there, so I had to go on. You're always late, Fred. If you'd been there, we could have sewed it up together, but as it was, well I took the order alone . . ." *And so it goes.*

Dear Mr. and Mrs. Atterley: in reference to your son Gerold's constant tardiness, I am afraid we will have to suspend him from school unless some more reliable method can be instituted guaranteeing he will arrive at his classes on time. Granted he is an exemplary student, and his marks are high, his constant flouting of the schedules of this school makes it impractical to maintain him in a system where the other children seem capable of getting where they are supposed to be on time. *And so it goes.*

YOU CANNOT VOTE UNLESS YOU APPEAR AT 8:45 A.M.

"I don't care if the script is *good*, I need it Thursday!"

CHECK-OUT TIME IS 2:00 P.M.

"You got here late. The job's taken. Sorry."

YOUR SALARY HAS BEEN DOCKED FOR TWENTY MINUTES TIME LOST.

"God, what time is it, I've gotta run!"

And so it goes. And so it goes. And so it goes. And so it goes goes goes goes goes tick tock tick tock tick tock and one day we no longer let time serve us, we serve time and we are slaves of the schedule, worshippers of the sun's passing, bound into a life predicted on restrictions because the system will not function if we don't keep the schedule tight.

Until it becomes more than a minor inconvenience to be late. It becomes a sin. Then a crime. Then a crime punishable by this:

EFFECTIVE 15 JULY 2389, 12:00:00 midnight, the office of the Master Timekeeper will require all citizens to submit their time-cards and cardioplates for processing. In accordance with Statute 555-7-SGH-999 governing the revocation of time per capita, all cardioplates will be keyed to the individual holder and—

What they had done was devise a method of curtailing the amount of life a person could have. If he was ten minutes late, he lost ten minutes of his life. An hour was proportionately worth more revocation. If someone was consistently tardy, he might find himself, on a Sunday night, receiving a communique from the Master Timekeeper that his time had run out, and he would be "turned off" at high noon on Monday, please straighten your affairs, sir.

And so, by this simple scientific expedient (utilizing a scientific process held dearly secret by the Ticktockman's office) the System was maintained. It was the only expedient thing to do. It was, after all, patriotic. The schedules had to be met. After all, there *was* a war on!

But wasn't there always?

"Now that is really disgusting," the Harlequin said, when pretty Alice showed him the wanted poster. "Disgusting and *highly* improbable. After all, this isn't the days of desperadoes. A *wanted* poster!"

"You know," Alice noted, "you speak with a great deal of inflection."

"I'm sorry," said the Harlequin, humbly.

"No need to be sorry. You're always saying, 'I'm sorry.' You have such massive guilt, Everett, it's really very sad."

"I'm sorry," he repeated, then pursed his lips so the dimples appeared momentarily. He hadn't wanted to say that at all. "I have to go out again. I have to *do* something."

Alice slammed her coffee-bulb down on the counter. "Oh for God's *sake*,

Everett, can't you stay home just *one* night! Must you always be out in that ghastly clown suit, running around *annoying* people?"

"I'm—" He stopped, and clapped the jester's hat onto his auburn thatch with a tiny tingling of bells. He rose, rinsed out his coffee-bulb at the tap, and put it into the drier for a moment. "I have to go."

She didn't answer. The faxbox was purring, and she pulled a sheet out, read it, threw it toward him on the counter. "It's about you. Of course. You're ridiculous."

He read it quickly. It said the Ticktockman was trying to locate him. He didn't care, he was going out to be late again. At the door, dredging for an exit line, he hurled back petulantly, "Well, *you* speak with inflection, *too!*"

Alice rolled her pretty eyes heavenward. "You're ridiculous." The Harlequin stalked out, slamming the door, which sighed shut softly, and locked itself.

There was a gentle knock, and Alice got up with an exhalation of exasperated breath, and opened the door. He stood there. "I'll be back about ten-thirty, okay?"

She pulled a rueful face. "Why do you tell me that? Why? You *know* you'll be late! You *know* it! You're *always* late, so why do you tell me these dumb things?" She closed the door.

On the other side, the Harlequin nodded to himself. *She's right. She's always right. I'll be late. I'm always late. Why do I tell her these dumb things?*

He shrugged again, and went off to be late once more.

He had fired off the firecracker rockets that said: I will attend the 115th annual International Medical Association Invocation at 8:00 P.M. precisely. I do hope you will all be able to join me.

The words had burned in the sky, and of course the authorities were there, lying in wait for him. They assumed, naturally, that he would be late. He arrived twenty minutes early, while they were setting up the spiderwebs to trap and hold him, and blowing a large bullhorn, he frightened and unnerved them so, their own moisturized encirclement webs sucked closed, and they were hauled up, kicking and shrieking, high above the amphitheater's floor. The Harlequin laughed and laughed, and apologized profusely. The physicians, gathered in solemn conclave, roared with laughter, and accepted the Harlequin's apologies with exaggerated bowing and posturing, and a merry time was had by all, who thought the Harlequin was a regular foofaraw in fancy pants; all, that is, but the authorities, who had been sent out by the office of the Ticktockman, who hung there like so much dockside cargo, hauled up above the floor of the amphitheater in a most unseemly fashion.

(In another part of the same city where the Harlequin carried on his "activities," totally unrelated in every way to what concerns here, save that it illustrates the Ticktockman's power and import, a man named Marshall Delahanty received his turn-off notice from the Ticktockman's office. His wife received the notification from the grey-suited minee who delivered it, with the traditional "look of sorrow" plastered hideously across his face. She knew what it was, even without unsealing it. It was a billet-doux of immediate recognition to everyone these days. She gasped, and held it as though it were a glass slide tinged with botulism, and prayed it was not for her. Let it be for Marsh, she thought, brutally, realistically, or one of the kids, but not for me, please dear God, not for me. And then she opened it, and it *was* for Marsh, and she was at one and the same time horrified and relieved. The next trooper in the line had caught the bullet. "Marshall," she screamed, "Marshall! Termination, Marshall ohmigod, Marshall, whattl we do, whattl we do, Marshall omigodmarshall . . ." and in their home that night was the sound of tearing paper and fear, and the stink of madness went up the flue and there was nothing, absolutely nothing they could do about it.)

(But Marshall Delahanty tried to run. And early the next day, when turn-off time came, he was deep in the forest two hundred miles away, and the office of the Ticktockman blanked his cardioplate, and Marshall Delahanty keeled over, running, and his heart stopped, and the blood dried up on its way to his brain, and he was dead that's all. One light went out on his sector map in the office of the Master Timekeeper, while notification was entered for fax reproduction, and Georgette Delahanty's name was entered on the dole roles till she could remarry. Which is the end of the footnote, and all the point that need be made, except don't laugh, because that is what would happen to the Harlequin if ever the Ticktockman found out his real name. It isn't funny.)

The shopping level of the city was thronged with the Thursday-colors of the buyers. Women in canary yellow chitons and men in pseudo-Tyrolean outfits that were jade and leather and fit very tightly, save for the balloon pants.

When the Harlequin appeared on the still-being-constructed shell of new Efficiency Shopping Center, his bullhorn to his elfishly laughing lips, everyone pointed and stared, and he berated them:

"Why let them order you about? Why let them tell you to hurry and scurry like ants or maggots? Take your time! Saunter a while! Enjoy the sunshine, enjoy the breeze, let life carry you at your own pace! Don't be slaves of time, it's a helluva way to die, slowly, by degrees . . . down with the Ticktockman!"

Who's the nut? most of the shoppers wanted to know. Who's the nut oh wow I'm gonna be late. I gotta run . . .

And the construction gang on the Shopping Center received an urgent order from the office of the Master Timekeeper that the dangerous criminal known as the Harlequin was atop their spire, and their aid was urgently needed in apprehending him. The work crew said no, they would lose time on their construction schedule, but the Ticktockman managed to pull the proper threads of governmental webbing, and they were told to cease work and catch that nitwit up there on the spire with the bullhorn. So a dozen and more burly workers began climbing into their construction platforms, releasing the a-grav plates, and rising toward the Harlequin.

After the debacle (in which, through the Harlequin's attention to personal safety, no one was seriously injured), the workers tried to reassemble, and assault him again, but it was too late. He had vanished. It had attracted quite a crowd, however, and the shopping cycle was thrown off by hours, simply hours. The purchasing needs of the system were therefore falling behind, and so measures were taken to accelerate the cycle for the rest of the day, but it got bogged down and speeded up and they sold too many float-valves and not nearly enough wegglers, which meant that the popli ratio was off, which made it necessary to rush cases and cases of spoiling Smash-O to stores that usually needed a case only every three or four hours. The shipments were bollixed, the trans-shipments were misrouted, and in the end, even the swizzleskid industries felt it.

"Don't come back till you have him!" the Ticktockman said, very quietly, very sincerely, extremely dangerously.

They used dogs. They used probes. They used cardioplate crossoffs. They used teepers. They used bribery. They used stiktytes. They used intimidation. They used torment. They used torture. They used finks. They used cops. They used search&seizure. They used fallaron. They used betterment incentive. They used fingerprints. They used Bertillon. They used cunning. They used guile. They used treachery. They used Raoul Mitgong, but he didn't help much. They used applied physics. They used techniques of criminology.

And what the hell: they caught him.

After all, his name was Everett C. Marm, and he wasn't much to begin with, except a man who had no sense of time.

"Repent, Harlequin!" said the Ticktockman.

"Get stuffed!" the Harlequin replied, sneering.

"You've been late a total of sixty-three years, five months, three weeks, two days, twelve hours, forty-one minutes, fifty-nine seconds, point oh three six one one one microseconds. You've used up everything you can, and more. I'm going to turn you off."

"Scare someone else. I'd rather be dead than live in a dumb world with a bogeyman like you."

"It's my job."

"You're full of it. You're a tyrant. You have no right to order people around and kill them if they show up late."

"You can't adjust. You can't fit in."

"Unstrap me, and I'll fit my fist into your mouth."

"You're a non-conformist."

"That didn't used to be a felony."

"It is now. Live in the world around you."

"I hate it. It's a terrible world."

"Not everyone thinks so. Most people enjoy order."

"I don't, and most of the people I know don't."

"That's not true. How do you think we caught you?"

"I'm not interested."

"A girl named pretty Alice told us who you were."

"That's a lie."

"It's true. You unnerve her. She wants to belong, she wants to conform, I'm going to turn you off."

"Then do it already, and stop arguing with me."

"I'm not going to turn you off."

"You're an idiot!"

"Repent, Harlequin!" said the Ticktockman.

"Get stuffed."

So they sent him to Coventry. And in Coventry they worked him over. It was just like what they did to Winston Smith in *1984*, which was a book none of them knew about, but the techniques are really quite ancient, and so they did it to Everett C. Marm, and one day quite a long time later, the Harlequin appeared on the communications web, appearing elfish and dimpled and bright-eyed, and not at all brainwashed, and he said he had been wrong, that it was a good, a very good thing indeed, to belong, and be right on time hip-ho and away we go, and everyone stared up at him on the public screens that covered an entire city block, and they said to themselves, well, you see, he was just a nut after all, and if that's the way the system is run, then let's do it that way, because it doesn't pay to fight city hall, or in this case, the Ticktockman. So Everett C. Marm was destroyed, which was a loss, because of what Thoreau said earlier, but you can't make an omelet without breaking a few eggs, and in every revolution, a few die who shouldn't, but they have to, because that's the way it happens, and if you make only a little change, then it seems to be worthwhile. Or, to make the point lucidly:

"Uh, excuse me, sir, I, uh, don't know how to uh, to uh, tell you this, but you were three minutes late. The schedule is a little, uh, bit off."

He grinned sheepishly.

"That's ridiculous!" murmured the Ticktockman behind his mask. "Check your watch." And then he went into his office, going mrmee, mrmee, mrmee, mrmee.

1967
25th Convention
New York

Chad Oliver

Chad Oliver (1928–93) was the man who brought the science of anthropology into the arena of sciences used in science fiction. In his novel *Shadows in the Sun* (1954) and in the stories collected in *Another Kind* (1955) and *The Edge of Forever* (1971), Oliver introduced and popularized the concepts of his discipline. "Our field's most fascinating and comprehensive collection of anthropological science fiction," said Damon Knight in 1956, and praised him for his "ability to touch the human heart of the problem."

Until the 1950s, when Oliver entered the field and experienced his most productive decade as a writer of SF, there was a great deal of prejudice against the "soft" or life sciences, especially against the areas of psychology, the social sciences, and economics. They were second class sciences because they were not mathematically predictive, not reliable, therefore not real knowledge, so the argument went. Real science fiction, before Oliver, could use them only by making them into predictive sciences in the future (see, for instance, Katherine MacLean's "The Snowball Effect" [1952]). Oliver's easy, pleasant exposition of anthropological ideas and attitudes in his fiction throughout the 1950s paved the way for later writers such as Ursula K. Le Guin and Michael Bishop to write sophisticated anthropological science fiction in the following decades. Oliver himself continued to write novels in and out of the SF genre in the 1960s,'70s, and '80s while a professor of anthropology at the University of Texas in Austin, but no notable short fiction.

Oliver tends to focus on motivations and values, rather than violence or action, in his fiction. "I was strongly influenced by writers outside the science fiction field, notably Hemingway and Steinbeck," he said. As in this story, he usually rewards a connection to the natural world.

BLOOD'S A ROVER

Clay lies still, but blood's a rover;
Breath's a ware that will not keep.
Up, lad: when the journey's over
There'll be time enough to sleep.
—*A. E. Housman*

I

Night sifted through the city like flakes of soft black snow drifting down from the stars. It whispered along the tree-lined canyons between the clean shafts of white buildings and pressed darkly against windows filled with warm light.

Conan Lang watched the illumination in his office increase subtly in adjusting to the growing darkness outside and then looked again at the directive he held in his hand.

It still read the same way.

"Another day, another world," he said aloud. And then, paraphrasing: "The worlds are too much with us—"

Conan Lang fired up his pipe and puffed carefully on it to get it going properly. Then he concentrated on blowing neat cloudy smoke rings that wobbled across the room and impaled themselves on the nose of the three-dimensional portrait of the President. It wasn't that he had anything against President Austin, he assured himself. It was simply that Austin represented that nebulous being, Authority, and at the moment it happened that Authority was singularly unwelcome in the office of Conan Lang.

He looked back at the directive. The wording was friendly and informal enough, but the meaning was clear:

Headquarters, Gal. Administration.
Office of Admiral Nelson White,
Commander, Process Planning Division.
15 April, 2701. Confidential.

One Agent Conan Lang
Applied Process Corps
G.A. Department Seven
Conan:

We got another directive from the Buzzard yesterday. Seems that the powers that be have decided that a change in Sirius Ten is in order—a shift from Four to Five. You're it. Make a prelim check and report to me at your convenience. Cheer up—maybe you'll get another bag of medals out of it.

Nelson.

Conan Lang left the directive on his desk and got to his feet. He walked over to the window and looked out at the lights sprinkled over the city. There weren't many. Most people were long ago home in the country, sitting around the living room, playing with the kids. He puffed slowly on his pipe.

Another bag of medals. Nelson wasn't kidding anybody—wasn't even trying to, really. He knew how Conan felt because he felt the same way. They all did, sooner or later. It was fascinating at first, even fun, this tampering with the lives of other people. But the novelty wore off in a hurry—shriveled like flesh in acid under a million eyes of hate, a million talks with your soul at three in the morning, a million shattered lives. Sure, it was necessary. You could always tell yourself that; that was the charm, the magic word that was supposed to make everything fine and dandy. Necessary—but for *you*, not for them. Or perhaps for them too, in the long run.

Conan Lang returned to his desk and flipped on the intercom. "I want out," he said. "The Administration Library, Division of Extraterrestrial Anthropology. I'd like to speak to Bailey if he's there."

He had to wait thirty seconds.

"Bailey here," the intercom said.

"This is Lang. What've you got on Sirius Ten?"

"Just like that, huh? Hang on a second."

There was a short silence. Conan Lang smoked his pipe slowly and smiled as he visualized Bailey punching enough buttons to control a space fleet.

"Let's see," Bailey's voice came through the speaker. "We've got a good bit. There's McAllister's *Kinship Systems of Sirius Ten*; Jenkins'—that's B. J. Jenkins, the one who worked with Holden—*Sirius Ten Social Organization*; Bartheim's *Economic Life of Sirius Ten*; Robert Patterson's *Basic Personality Types of the Sirius Group*; *Preliminary and Supplementary Ethnological Surveys of the Galactic Advance Fleet*—the works."

Conan Lang sighed. "O.K.," he said. "Shoot them out to my place, will you?"

"Check—be there before you are. One thing more, Cone."

"Yes?"

"Been reading a splendid eight-volume historical novel of the Twentieth Century. Hot stuff, I'll tell you. You want me to send it along in case you run out of reading material?"

"Very funny. See you around."

"So long."

Conan Lang switched off the intercom and destroyed the directive. He tapped out his pipe in the waster and left the office, locking the door behind him. The empty hallway was sterile and impersonal. It seemed dead at night, somehow, and it was difficult to believe that living, breathing human beings walked through it all day long. It was like a tunnel to nowhere. He had the odd feeling that there was nothing around it at all, just space and less than space—no building, no air, no city. Just a white antiseptic tunnel to nowhere.

He shook off the feeling and caught the lift to the roof. The cool night air was crisp and clean and there was a whisper of a breeze out of the north. A half moon hung in the night, framed by stars. He looked up at it and wondered how Johnny was getting along up there, and whether perhaps Johnny was even then looking down on Earth.

Conan Lang climbed into his bullet and set the controls. The little ship rose vertically on her copter blades for two thousand feet, hovered a moment over the silent city, and then flashed off on her jets into the west.

Conan Lang sat back in his cushioned seat, looking at the stars, trying not to think, letting the ship carry him home.

Conan Lang relaxed in his armchair, his eyes closed, an icy bourbon and soda in his hand. The books he had requested—neat, white, uniform microfilm blow-ups from the Administration Library—were stacked neatly on the floor by his side, waiting. Waiting, he thought, sipping his drink. They were always waiting. No matter how much a man knew, there was always more—waiting.

The room closed in around him. He could feel it—warm, friendly, personal. It was a good room. It was a room filled with life, his life and Kit's. It was almost as if he could see the room better with his eyes closed, for then he saw the past as well as the present. There was the silver and black tapestry on the wall, given to him by old Maharani so long ago, on a world so far away that the very light given off by its sun when he was there had yet to reach the Earth as the twinkle of a star in the night sky. There were his books, there were Kit's paintings. There was the smudge—the current one—on the carpet where Rob had tracked dirt into the house before supper.

He opened his eyes and looked at his wife.

"I must be getting old, Kit," he said. "Right at the moment, it all looks pretty pointless."

Kit raised her eyebrows and said nothing.

"We tear around over the galaxy like a bunch of kids playing Spacemen and Pirates," he said, downing his drink. "Push here, pull there, shove here, reverse there. It's like some kind of half-wit game where one side doesn't even know it's playing, or on which side of the field. Sometimes—"

"Want another drink?" Kit asked softly.

"Yes. Kit—"

"I know," she said, touching his shoulder with her hand. "Go ahead and talk; you'll feel better. We go through this every time there's a new one, remember? I know you don't really mean things the way you say them, and I know why you say them that way anyhow." She kissed him lightly on the forehead and her lips were cool and patient. "I understand."

Conan Lang watched her leave the room with his empty glass. "Yes," he whispered to himself. "Yes, I guess you do."

It *was* necessary, of course. Terribly, urgently necessary. But it got to you sometimes. All those people out there, living their lives, laughing and crying, raising children. It hurt you to think about them. And it wasn't necessary for them, not for him, not for Kit. Or was it? You couldn't tell; there was always a chance. But if only they could just forget it all, just live, there was so much to enjoy—

Kit handed him a fresh bourbon and soda, icy and with just a trace of lemon in it the way he liked it, and then curled up again on the couch, smiling at him.

"I'm sorry, angel," he said. "You must get pretty sick of hearing the same sad song over and over again."

"Not when you sing it, Cone."

"It's just that sometimes I chuck my mind out the nearest window and wonder why—"

There was a thump and a bang from the rear of the house. Conan Lang tasted his drink. That meant Rob was home. He listened, waiting. There was the hollow crack—that was the bat going into the corner. There was the heavy thud—that was the fielder's glove.

"That's why," Kit said.

Conan Lang nodded and picked up the first book off the floor.

Three days later, Conan Lang went up the white steps, presented his credentials, and walked into the Buzzard's Cage. The place made him nervous. Irritated with himself, he paused deliberately and lit his pipe before going on. The Cage seemed cold, inhuman. And the Buzzard—

He shouldn't feel that way, he told himself, again offering his identification before entering the lift to the Nest. Intellectually, he understood cybernetics; there was nothing supernatural about it. The Cage was just a machine, for all its powers, even if the Buzzard did sometimes seem more—or perhaps less—than a man. Still, the place gave him the creeps. A vast thinking machine, filling a huge building, a brain beside which his own was as nothing. Of course, men had built it. Men made guns, too, but the knowledge was scant comfort when you looked into a metallic muzzle and someone pulled the trigger.

"Lang," he said to himself, "you're headed for the giggle ward."

He smiled then, knowing it wasn't so. Imagination was a prime requisite for his job, and he just had more than his share. It got in the way sometimes, but it was a part of him and that was that.

Conan Lang waded through a battery of attendants and security personnel and finally reached the Nest. He opened the door and stepped into the small, dark room. There, behind the desk where he always was, perched the Buzzard.

"Hello, Dr. Gottleib," said Conan Lang.

The man behind the desk eyed him silently. His name was Fritz Gottleib, but he had been tagged the Buzzard long ago. No one used the name to his face, and it was impossible to tell whether or not the name amused him. He spoke but seldom, and his appearance, even after you got used to it, was startling. Fritz Gottleib was squat and completely bald. He always dressed in black and his heavy eyebrows were like horizontal splashes of ink against the whiteness of his face. The Buzzard analogy, thought Conan Lang, was more than understandable; it was inevitable. The man sat high in his tower, in his Nest of controls, brooding over a machine that perhaps he alone fully understood. Alone. He always seemed alone, no matter how many people surrounded him. His was a life apart, a life whose vital force pulsed in the shifting lights of the tubes of a great machine.

"Dr. Lang," he acknowledged, unmoving, his voice sibilant, almost a hiss.

Conan Lang puffed on his pipe and dropped into the chair across from Gottleib. He had dealt with the Buzzard before and most of the shock had worn off. You could get used to anything, he supposed. Man was a very adaptable animal.

"The smoke doesn't bother you, I hope?"

Gottleib did not comment. He simply stared at him, his dark eyes unblinking. Like looking at a piece of meat, thought Conan Lang.

"Well," he said, trying again, "I guess you know what I'm here for."

"You waste words," Fritz Gottleib hissed.

"I hadn't realized they were in short supply," Lang replied, smiling. The Buzzard was irritating, but he could see the justice in the man's remark. It *was* curious the number of useless things that were said all the time—useless, at any rate, from a purely communicative point of view. It would have been sheerly incredible for Gottleib—who after all had been checking his results in the computer—*not* to have known the nature of his mission.

"O.K.," said Lang, "what's the verdict?"

Fritz Gottleib fingered a square card in his surprisingly long-fingered hands, seeming to hover over it like a bird of prey.

"It checks out," he said sibilantly, his voice low and hard to hear. "Your plan will achieve the desired transfer in Sirius Ten, and the transfer integrates positively with the Plan."

"Anything else? Anything I should know?"

"We should all know many more things than we do, Dr. Lang."

"Um-m-m. But that was all the machine said with respect to my proposed plan of operations?"

"That was all."

Conan Lang sat back, watching Gottleib. A strange man. But he commanded respect.

"I'd like to get hold of that baby sometime," he said easily. "I've got a question or two of my own."

"Sometimes it is best not to know the answers to one's questions, Dr. Lang."

"No. But I'd like to have a shot at it all the same. Don't tell the security boys I said that; they'd string me up by the toes."

"Perhaps one day, Dr. Lang. When you are old like me."

Conan Lang stood up, cupping his pipe in his hand. "I guess that's all," he said.

"Yes," said Fritz Gottleib.

"See you around."

No answer. Cold shadows seemed to fill the room.

Conan Lang turned and left the way he had come. Behind him, drilling into his back, he could feel the eyes of Fritz Gottleib following him, cold and deep like the frozen waters of an arctic sea.

The ship stood on Earth but she was not of Earth. She was poised, a mighty lance of silver, a creature of the deeps. She waited, impatient, while Conan Lang slowly walked across the vast duralloy tarmac of Space One, Admiral White at his side. The sun was bright in a clean blue sky. It touched the ship with lambent flame and warmed Conan Lang's shoulders under his uniform. A slight puff of breeze rustled across the spaceport, pushing along a stray scrap of white paper ahead of it.

"Here we go again," said Conan Lang.

"That's what you get for being good," the admiral said with a smile. "You get good enough and you'll get my job—which ought to be a grim enough prospect even for you. If you're smart, you'll botch this job six ways from Sunday and then we'll have to give you a rest."

"Yeah—play a little joke, strictly for laughs, and give 'em an atom bomb or two to stick on the ends of their hatchets. Or take 'em back to the caves. There are plenty of delicious possibilities."

The two men walked on, toward the silver ship.

"Everything's set, I suppose?" asked Conan Lang.

"Yep. Your staff is already on board and the stuff is loaded."

"Any further instructions?"

"No—you know your business or you wouldn't be going. Just try to make it as quick as you can, Cone. They're getting warm over at Research on that integration-acceleration principle for correlating data—it's going to be big and I'll want you around when it breaks."

Conan Lang grinned. "What happens if I just up and disappear one day, Nels? Does the galaxy moan and lie down and quit?"

"Search me," said Admiral Nelson White. "But don't take any more risks than you absolutely have to. Don't get the idea that you're indispensable, either. It's just that it's tiresome to break in new men."

"I'll try to stay alive if you're positive that's what you want."

They approached the ship. Kit and Rob were waiting. The admiral touched his cap and moved on, leaving Conan Lang alone with his family. Kit was lovely—she always was, Conan Lang thought. He couldn't imagine a life without her.

"Bye, darlin'," he whispered, taking her in his arms. "One of these days I'm coming back and I'm never going to leave you again."

"This is till then," Kit said softly and kissed him for keeps.

Much later, Conan Lang released her and shook hands with his son.

"So long, old-timer," he said.

"Hurry back, Dad," Rob said, trying not to cry.

Conan Lang turned and joined Admiral White at the star cruiser. He did not look back.

"Good luck, Cone," the admiral said, patting him on the back. "I'll keep the medals warm and a light in the cabin window."

"OK, Nels," said Conan Lang.

He swung aboard the great ship and stepped into the lift. There was a muted hum of machinery as the car whispered up through the pneumatic tube, up into the hollowness of the ship. Already it seemed to Conan Lang that he had left Earth far behind him. The endless loneliness of the star trails rode up with him in the humming lift.

The ship rested, quiescent, on Earth. Ahead of her, calling to her, the stars flamed coldly in an infinite sea of night.

II

Conan Lang walked down the long white corridor to the afterhold, his footsteps muffled and almost inaudible in the murmur of the atomics. It *would* be a long white corridor, he thought to himself. Wherever man went, there went the long white corridors—offices, hospitals, command posts. It was almost as if he had spent half a lifetime walking through long white corridors, and now here was yet another one—cold and antiseptic, hanging in space eight light-years from Earth.

"Halt."

"Lang here," he told the Fleetman. "Kindly point that thing the other way."

"Identification, please."

Lang sighed and handed it over. The man should know him by now; after all, the ship was on his mission, and he was hardly a subversive character. Still, orders were orders—a principle that covered a multitude of sins. And they couldn't afford to take chances, not *any* chances.

"All right, sir," the Fleetman said, returning the identification. "Sorry to bother you."

"Forget it," said Conan Lang. "Keep your eyes peeled for space pirates."

The guard smiled. "Who'd want to steal space, sir?" he asked. "It's free and I reckon there's enough to go around."

"Your inning," acknowledged Conan Lang, moving into the afterhold. The kid was already there.

"Hello, sir," said Andrew Irvin.

"Hi, Andy—and cut the 'sir,' what do you say? You make me feel like I should be extinct or embalmed or something."

The kid smiled almost shyly. Conan Lang had half expected to find him there in the hold; Andy was always poking around, asking questions, trying to learn. His quick brown eyes and alert carriage reminded Conan of a young hunting dog, frisking through the brush, perpetually on the verge of flushing the grandfather of all jack rabbits.

"It doesn't seem possible, does it?" asked the kid.

Conan Lang raised his eyebrows.

"All this, I mean," Andy Irvin said, gesturing at the neat brown sacks stacked row upon row in the brightly lighted hold. "To think that a couple of sacks of that stuff can remold a planet, change the lives of millions of people—"

"It's not just the sacks, Andy. It took man a good many hundreds of thousands of years to learn what to *do* with those sacks."

"Yes, sir," the kid said, hanging on every word.

"No 'sir,' remember? I'm not giving you a lecture, and you don't have to look attentive. I'm sure that elementary anthropology isn't *too* dumbfounding to a guy who took honors at the Academy."

"Well—"

"Never mind." Conan Lang eyed him speculatively. The kid reminded him, almost too much, of someone else—a kid named Conan Lang who had started out on a great adventure himself too many years ago. "I . . . um-m-m . . . guess you know you're going to work with me on Ten."

Andy looked like Conan had just handed him a harem on a silver platter. "No, sir," he said. "I didn't know. Thank you, sir."

"The name is Conan."

"Yes, sir."

"Hellfire," said Conan Lang. How did you go about telling a kid that you were happy to have someone around with stars in his eyes again? Without sounding like a fool? The answer was simple—you didn't.

"I can't wait," Andy said. "To really *do* something at last—it's a great feeling. I hope I'll do OK."

"It won't be long now, Andy. Twenty-four hours from now you and I go to work. The buggy ride is about over."

The two men fell silent then, looking at the neat brown rows of sacks, feeling the star ship tremble slightly under them with the thunder of her great atomics.

It was night on Sirius Ten—a hot, humid night with a single moon hanging like frozen fire in the darkness. A small patrol craft from the cruiser floated motionless in the night sky, her batteries pouring down a protective screen around the newly cleared field. Conan Lang wiped the sweat from his forehead and washed his hands off in the clean river water that gurgled through the trench at his feet.

"That about does it, Andy," he said wearily. "Toss 'em a Four signal."

Andy Irvin turned the rheostat on his small control board to Four and flipped the switch. They waited, listening to the faint murmur of the night breeze off the river. There was no change, nothing that they could see, but they could almost feel the intense radiation pounding into the field from the patrol ship, seeping into the ground, accelerating by thousands of times the growth factor in the seeds.

"That's got it," said Conan Lang. "Give 'em release."

Andy shot the patrol craft the release signal and shut off his control board. The little ship seemed to hover uncertainly. There was a humming sound and a spot of intense white light in the sky. That was all. The ship was gone and they were alone.

"It's been a long night, kid," yawned Conan Lang. "We'd better get some sack time—we're liable to need it before morning."

"You go ahead," Andy Irvin said. "I'm not sleepy; the sunrise here ought to be something."

"Yeah," said Conan Lang. "The sunrise ought to be something."

He walked across the field and entered a structure that closely resembled a native hut in appearance but was actually quite, quite different. Too tired even to undress, he piled into bed with his clothes on and rested quietly in the darkness.

The strange, haunting, familiar-with-a-difference sounds of an alien world whispered around the hut on the soft, moist breeze from the sluggish river. Far away, an animal screamed hoarsely in the clogging brush. Conan Lang kept his eyes closed and tried not to think, but his mind ignored him. It went right on working, asking questions, demanding answers, bringing up into the light many memories that were good and some that were better forgotten.

"Kit," he said, very softly.

Tired as he was, he knew there would be no sleep for him that night.

The sunrise was a glory. The blue-white inferno of Sirius hung in the treetops across the field and then climbed into the morning sky, her white dwarf companion a smaller sun by her side. The low cumulus clouds were edged with flame—fiery red, pale blue, cool green. The fresh morning winds washed the field with air and already the young plants were out of the ground, thirsty for the sun. The chuckling water in the trenches sparkled in the light.

With the morning, the natives came.

"They're all around us," Conan Lang said quietly.

"I can't see them," whispered Andy Irvin, looking at the brush.

"They're there."

"Do you . . . expect trouble, sir?"

"Not yet, assuming we've got this deal figured right. They're more afraid of us than we are of them."

"What if we *don't* have it figured right?"

Conan Lang smiled. "Three guesses," he said.

The kid managed a wry grin. He was taking it well, Lang thought. He remembered how he'd felt the first time. It didn't really hit you until that first day, and then it upped and kicked you in the teeth. Quite suddenly, it was all a very different proposition from the manuals and the viewers and the classrooms of the Academy. *Just you, all alone,* the alien breeze sighed in your ear. *You're all alone in the middle of nowhere,* the wind whispered through the trees. *Our eyes are watching you, our world is pressing you back, waiting. What do you know of us really? What good is your knowledge now?*

"What next?" Andy asked.

"Just tend the field, kid. And try to act like a ghost. You're an ancestor of those people watching us from the brush, remember. If we've got this figured wrong—if those survey reports were haywire somewhere, or if someone's been through here who didn't belong—you should have a little warning at least. They don't use blowguns or anything—just spears, and they'd prefer a hatchet. If there's trouble, you hightail it back to the hut *at once* and man the projector. That's all."

"I'm not so sure I care to be an ancestor," Andy Irvin muttered, picking up his hoe. "Not yet, anyhow." He moved off along a water trench, checking on the plants.

Conan Lang picked up his own hoe and set to work. He could feel the natives watching him, wondering, whispering to themselves. But he was careful not to look around him. He kept his head down and dug at the plants with his hoe, clearing the water channels. The plants were growing with astonishing rapidity, thanks to the dose of radiation. They should be mature in a week. And then—

The sun blazed down on his treated skin and the sweat rolled off his body in tiny rivulets. The field was strangely silent around him; there was only the gurgle of the water and the soft sigh of the humid breeze. His hoe chopped and slushed at the mud and his back was tired from bending over so long. It was too still, unnaturally still.

Behind that brush, back in the trees—a thousand eyes.

He did not look around. Step by step, he moved down the trench, under the hellish sun, working with his hoe.

• • •

The fire-burned days and the still, hushed nights alternated rapidly. On the morning of the third day, Andy Irvin found what they had been waiting for.

In the far corner of the field, placed on a rude wood platform about four feet high, there were three objects. There was a five-foot-square bark mat, neatly woven. There was a small animal that closely resembled a terrestrial pig, face down, its throat neatly slashed. And there was a child. It was a female baby, evidently not over a week old. It had been strangled to death.

"It's . . . different . . . when you see it for yourself," Andy said quietly, visibly shaken.

"You'll get used to it," said Conan Lang, his voice purposely flat and matter-of-fact. "Get the pig and the mat—and stop looking like a prohibitionist who just found a jug of joy water in the freezer. This is old stuff to ancestors."

"Old stuff," repeated Andy without conviction.

They carried the contents of the platform back to their hut and Conan Lang wrapped the body of the child in a cloth.

"We'll bury her tonight after dark," he said. "The pig we eat. It won't do any harm to sit on the mat where they can see us while we're eating it, either."

"Well," Andy muttered. "Glad to see you're not going to eat the baby, too."

"You never can tell," smiled Conan Lang. "We anthropologists are all crazy, or hadn't you heard?"

"I've heard," agreed Andy Irvin, getting his nerves under control again. "Where's the hot sauce?"

Conan Lang stepped back outside and picked up his hoe. The blazing double sun had already produced shimmering heat waves that danced like live things in the still air over the green field. The kid was going to be all right. He'd known it all along, of course—but you could never be *sure* of a man until you worked with him under field conditions. And a misfit, an unstable personality, was anything but a joke on an alien planet where unknowable forces hung in the balance.

"Let's see if I've got this thing figured straight," Andy said, puffing away on one of Conan's pipes. "The natives are afraid of us, and still they feel that they must make us an offering because we, as their supposed ancestors, control their lives. So they pick a system of dumb barter rather than sending out the usual contact man to ferret out kinship connections."

"You're OK so far," Conan Lang said. "I guess you've studied about the dumb barter systems used on Earth in the old days; it was used whenever trade took place between groups of markedly unequal strength, such as the African pygmies and trading vessels from the west. There's a fear factor involved."

"Yes, sir."

"Forget the 'sir.' I didn't mean to lecture. I think I'll start calling you Junior."

"Sorry. The bark mat is a unit in a reciprocal trade system and the pig is a sacred animal—I get that part of it. But the baby—that's terrible, Conan. After all, we caused that death in a way—"

"Afraid not," Conan Lang corrected him. "These people practice infanticide; it's part of their religion. If the preliminary reports were correct—and they've checked out so far—they kill all the female children born on the last three days of alternate months. There's an economic reason, too—not enough food to go around, and that's a pretty effective method of birth control. The baby would have been killed regardless—we had nothing to do with it."

"Still—"

"I know. But maybe she was the lucky one after all."

"I don't quite follow you there."

"Skip it—you'll find out soon enough."

"What are you going to leave them tonight?"

"Not sure yet," Conan Lang said. "We'll have to integrate with their value system, of course. We brought some mats, and I guess a good steel knife won't hurt things any. We'll worry about that later. Come on, farmer—back to work."

Andy Irvin picked up his hoe and followed Conan Lang into the field. The clear water bubbled softly as it flowed through the trenches. The growing plants sent their roots thirstily into the ground and the fresh green shoots stretched up like tentacles into the humid air of Sirius Ten.

That night, under the great yellow moon that swam far away and lonesome among the stars, they placed exchange gifts of their own on the platform. Next morning, the invisible traders had replaced them with four mats and another dead pig.

"No babies, anyhow," Andy Irvin said, puffing industriously on one of Conan's pipes. They had decided that cigarettes, as an unfamiliar cultural trait to the natives, were out. Now, with Andy taking with unholy enthusiasm to pipe smoking, Conan Lang was threatened with a shortage of tobacco. He watched the smoke from the kid's pipe with something less than ecstasy.

"We can have smoked ham," he observed.

"It was your idea," Andy grinned.

"Call me 'sir.' "

Andy laughed, relaxed now, and picked up the pig. Conan gathered up the somewhat cumbersome mats and followed him back into the hut. The hot, close sun was already burning his shoulders. The plants were green and healthy-looking, and the air was a trifle fresher in the growing field.

"Now what?" Andy asked, standing outside the hut and letting the faint breeze cool him off as best it could.

"I figure we're about ready for an overt contact," Conan Lang said. "Everything has checked out beautifully so far, and the natives don't seem to be suspicious or hostile. We might as well get the ball rolling."

"The green branch, isn't it?"

"That's right."

They still did not get a glimpse of the natives throughout the steaming day, and that night they placed a single mat on the platform. On top of the mat they put a slim branch of green leaves, twisted around back on itself and tied loosely to form a circle. The green branch was by no means a universal symbol of peace, but, in this particular form, it chanced to be so on Sirius Ten. Conan Lang smiled a little. Man had found many curious things among the stars, and most of them were of just this unsensational but very useful sort.

By dawn, the mat and the circle branch were gone and the natives had left them nothing in return.

"Today's the day," Conan Lang said, rubbing the sleep out of his eyes. "They'll either give us the works or accept our offer. Nothing to do now but wait."

They picked up their hoes and went back into the field. Waiting can be the most difficult of all things, and the long, hot morning passed without incident. The two men ate their lunch in silence, thankful for the odorless injection that kept the swarming insects away from them. Late in the afternoon when the long blue shadows of evening were already touching the green plants and the clean, flowing water, the natives came.

There were five of them and they appeared to be unarmed. One man walked slightly in advance of the others, a circular branch of green leaves in his hand. Conan Lang waited for them, with Andy standing by at his side. It was moments like this, he thought, that made you suddenly realize that you were all alone and a long, long way from friends. The natives came on steadily. Conan felt a surge of admiration for the young man who led them. From his point of view, he was walking into a situation filled with the terror of the supernatural, which was a very real part of his life. His steps did not falter. He would, Conan supposed, be the eldest son of the most powerful chief.

The natives stopped when they were three paces away. Their leader extended the circular green branch. "We would serve you, fathers from the mountains," the native said in his own tongue.

Conan Lang stepped forward and received the branch. "We are brothers," he replied in the same language, "and we would be your friends."

The native smiled, his teeth very white. "I am Ren," he said. "I am your brother."

Conan Lang kept his face expressionless, but deep within him a dark regret and sadness coursed like ice through his veins.

It had begun again.

III

For many days, Conan Lang listened to the Oripesh natives preparing for the feast. Their small village, only a quarter of a mile from the field, was alive with excitement. The women prepared great piles of the staple ricefruit and broiled river fish in great green leaves on hot coals. The men chanted and danced interminably, cleansing the village by ritual for the coming visitation, while the children, forgotten for once, played on the banks of the river. On the appointed day, Conan Lang walked into the village with Andy Irvin at his side.

It was a crude village, necessarily so because of its transient nature. But it was not dirty. The natives watched the two men with awe, but they did not seem unfriendly. The supernatural was for them always just on the other side of the hill, hidden in the night, and now it was among them, in the open. That was all. And what, after all, thought Conan Lang, could have seemed more supernatural to them than a silver ship that dropped out of the stars? What was supernatural depended on one's point of view—and on how much one happened to know about what was *natural*.

The box he carried was heavy, and it took both arms to handle it. He watched Andy puffing at his side and smiled.

"Stick with it, kid," he said, walking steadily through the watching natives. "You may earn your pay yet."

Andy muttered something under his breath and blinked to get the sweat out of his eyes.

When they reached the clearing in the center of the village, they stopped and put their boxes down. Ren, the eldest son of the chief Ra Renne, approached them at once and offered them a drink from a large wooden bowl. Conan drank and passed the container on to Andy, who grinned broadly and took a long swallow of the warm fluid. It was sweet, although not too sweet, and it burned pleasantly on the way down. It was, Conan decided instantly, a great improvement over some native fermented horrors he had been subjected to in times past.

The natives gathered around them in a great circle. There must have been nearly five hundred of them—far more than the small village could accommodate for any length of time.

"We're celebrities," Conan Lang whispered out of the side of his mouth as he waited to be presented ceremonially to the chiefs.

"You want my autograph?" hissed Andy, his face just a trifle flushed from the drink he had taken. "I make a real fine X."

The feast followed a pattern familiar to Conan Lang. They were presented ceremonially to the tribe, having identified themselves as ancestors of four generations ago, thus making themselves kin to virtually all the tribe with their complicated lineage system, and also making refutation impossible since no one remembered that far back. They were seated with the chiefs, and ate the ritual feast rapidly. The food was good, and Conan Lang was interested in getting a good taste of the ricefruit plant, which was the basic food staple of the Oripesh.

After the eating came the drinking, and after the drinking the dancing. The Oripesh were not a musical people, and they had no drums. The men and the women danced apart from one another, each one doing an individual dance—which he owned, just as the men from Earth owned material property—to his own rhythm pattern. Conan Lang and Andy Irvin contented themselves with watching, not trusting themselves to improvise an authentic dance. They were aware that their conduct was at variance with the somewhat impulsive conduct usually attributed to ancestors in native folklore, but that was a chance they had to take. Conan was very conscious of one old chief who watched him closely with narrowed eyes.

Conan ignored him, enjoying the dancers. The Oripesh seemed to be a happy people, although short on material wealth. Conan Lang almost envied them as they danced—envied them for their simple lives and envied them their ability to enjoy it, an ability that civilized man had left by the wayside in his climb up the ladder. Climb—or descent? Conan Lang sometimes wondered.

Ren came over, his color high with the excitement of the dance. Great fires were burning now, and Conan noticed with surprise that it was night.

"That is Loe," Ren said, pointing. "My *am-ren,* my bride-to-be." His voice was filled with pride.

Conan Lang followed his gesture and saw the girl. Her name was a native word roughly translatable as *fawn,* and she was well named. Loe was a slim, very shy girl of really striking beauty. She danced with diffidence, looking into Ren's eyes. The two were obviously, almost painfully, in love—love being a part of the culture of the Oripesh. It was difficult to realize, sometimes, even after years of personal experience, that there were whole worlds of basically humanoid peoples where the very concept of romantic love did not exist. Conan Lang smiled. Loe was, if anything, a trifle *too* beautiful for his taste. Dancing there, with the yellow moon in her hair, moving gracefully with the leaping shadows from the crackling fires, she was ethereal, a fantasy, like a painting of a woman from another, unattainable century.

"We would give gifts to the chiefs," Conan Lang said finally. "Your Loe—she is very beautiful."

Ren smiled, quickly grateful, and summoned the chiefs. Conan Lang rose to greet them, signaling to Andy to break open the boxes. The chiefs watched intently. Conan Lang did not speak. He waited until Andy had opened both boxes and then pointed to them.

"They are yours, my brothers," he said.

The natives pressed forward. A chief picked the first object out of the box and stared at it in disbelief. The shadows flickered eerily and the night wind sighed through the village. He held the object up to the light and there was a gasp of astonishment.

The object was a ricefruit—a ricefruit the likes of which had never before been seen on Sirius Ten. It was round, fully a foot in diameter, and of a lush, ripe consistency. It made the potato-sized ricefruits of the Oripesh seem puny by comparison.

It was then that Conan Lang exploded his bombshell.

"We have come back to show you, our brothers, how to grow the great ricefruit," he said. "You can grow them over and over again, *in the same field*. You will never have to move your village again."

The natives stared at him in wonder, moving back a little in fear.

"It cannot be done," a chief whispered. "The ricefruit devours the land—every year we must move or perish."

"That is over now," Conan Lang said. "We have come to show you the way."

The dancing had stopped. The natives waited, nervous, suddenly uncertain. The yellow moon watched through the trees. As though someone had flipped a switch, sound disappeared. There was silence. The great ricefruit was magic. They looked at the two men as though seeing them for the first time. This was not the way of the past, not the way of the ancestors. This was something completely *new* and they found themselves lost, without precedent for action. Ren alone smiled at them, and even he had fear in his eyes.

Conan Lang waited tensely. He must make no move; this was the crisis point. Andy stood at his side, very still, hardly breathing.

A native walked solemnly into the silence, carrying a young pig under his arm. Conan Lang watched him narrowly. The man was obviously a shaman, a witch doctor, and his trembling body and too-bright eyes were all too clear an indication of why he had been chosen for his role in the society.

With a swiftness of motion that was numbing, the shaman slit the pig's throat with a stone knife. At once he cut the body open. The blood stained his body with crimson. His long, thin hands poked into the entrails. He looked up, his eyes wild.

"They are not ancestors," he screamed, his voice high like an hysterical woman's. "They have come to do us evil!"

The very air was taut with tension.

"No," Conan Lang said loudly, keeping his voice clear and confident. "The *barath-tui*, the shaman, has been bewitched by sorcerers! Take care that you do not offend our ancestors!"

Conan Lang stood very still, fighting to keep the alarm off his face. He and Andy were helpless here, and he knew it. They were without weapons of any sort—the native loincloth being a poor place to conceal firearms. There was nothing they could do—they had miscalculated, moved too swiftly, and now they were paying the price.

"We are your brothers," he said into the ominous silence. "We are your fathers and your father's fathers. There are others who watch."

The flames leaped and danced in the stillness. An old man stepped forward. It was the chief that Conan had noticed watching him before.

"You say you are our brothers who have taken the long journey," the old chief said. "That is good. We would see you walk through the fire."

The wind sighed in the trees. Without a moment's hesitation, Conan Lang turned and walked swiftly toward the flames that crackled and hissed in the great stone fire pits.

There was nothing else in all the world except the flickering tongues of orange flame that licked nearer and nearer to his face. He saw the red, pulsing coals waiting beneath the twisted black branches in the fire and he closed his eyes. The heat singed his eyebrows and he could feel his hair shrivel and start to burn.

Conan Lang kept moving, and moved fast. He twisted a rigid clamp on his mind and refused to feel pain. He wrenched his mind out of his body, thinking as he had been trained to think, until it was as if his mind floated a thing apart, free in the air, looking down upon the body of Conan Lang walking through hell.

He knew that one of the attributes of the Oripesh ancestor gods was that they could walk through flame without injury—a fairly common myth pattern. He had known it before he left Earth. He should have been prepared, he knew that. But man was not perfect, which would have been a dangerous flaw had it not been his most valuable characteristic.

He saw that his legs were black and blistered and he smelled the suffocating smell of burning flesh. The smoke was in his head, in his lungs, everywhere, choking him. Some of the pain was coming through—

He was out. He felt Andy's hands beating out the rivulets of flame that clung to his body and he forced the clean, pure air of night into his sick lungs. The pain, the pain—

"Stick with it, Cone," Andy whispered in his ear. "Stick with it."

Conan Lang managed to open his eyes and stared blankly into a hot-red haze. The haze cleared and he was faintly surprised to find that he could still see. The natives were awestruck with fear—they had angered their gods and death was in the air. Conan Lang knew that the shaman who had denounced him would quite probably be dead of fear before the night was over—if he did not die before then of some less subtle malady. He had endangered the tribe without reason, and he would pay with his life.

Conan Lang kept his face expressionless. Inside, he was on fire. Water, he had to have water, cold water—

Ren came to him, his eyes filled with pain. "I am sorry, my brother," he whispered. "For my people, I am sorry."

"It is all right, Ren," Conan Lang heard his voice say steadily. "I am, of course, unharmed."

Conan Lang touched Andy's arm and moved across to the chiefs. He felt Andy standing behind him, ready to catch him, just in case. He could feel nothing in his feet—quite suddenly, he was convinced that he was standing on the charred stumps of his legs and he fought to keep from looking down to make sure he still had feet.

"You have doubted your brothers who have come far to help their people," he said quietly, looking directly into the eyes of the old chief who had sent him into the flames. "We are disappointed in our people—there are sorcerers at work among you, and they must be destroyed. We leave you now. If you anger your brothers again, the Oripesh shall cease to be."

He did not wait for an answer but turned and started away from the clearing, back through the village. Andy was at his side. Conan Lang set his teeth and moved at a steady pace. He must have no help until they were beyond the village; the natives must not suspect—

He walked on. The great yellow moon was high in the night sky, and there was the face of Loe with stars in her hair. The moon shuddered and burst into flame and he heard himself laughing. He bit his lips until the blood came and kept going, into the darkness, into nothing. The pain clawed at his body.

They were through the village. Something snapped in Conan Lang—the steel clamp that had carried him through a nightmare parted with a clean *ping*. There was emptiness, space. Conan Lang collapsed. He felt Andy's arm around him, holding him up.

"You'll have to carry me, kid," he whispered. "I can't walk at all."

Andy Irvin picked him up in his arms and set out through the night.

"It should have been me," he said in bitter self-reproach. "It should have been me."

Conan Lang closed his eyes and, at last, nothing mattered anymore, and there was only darkness.

A week later, Conan Lang stood in the dawn of Sirius Ten, watching the great double sun lift above the horizon and chase the shadows from the green field that they had carved out of the wilderness. He was still a very sick man, but Andy had pulled him through as best he could and now the star cruiser was coming in to pick him up and leave a replacement with the kid.

The fresh leaves of the ricefruit plants were shoulder high and the water in the irrigation trenches chuckled cleanly, waiting for the full fury of the sun. The tenuous, almost hesitant breeze crawled through the still air.

Conan Lang watched the green plants silently. The words of the dead *barathtui*, the shaman, echoed in his brain. *They are not ancestors*, the man had screamed. *They have come to do us evil!*

They have come to do us evil. . . .

How could he have known—with only a pig and a stone knife? A crazy shaman working the discredited magic of divination—and he had been *right*. Coincidence? Yes, of course. There was no other way to look at it, no other *sane* way. Conan Lang smiled weakly. He remembered reading about the Snake Dance of the Hopi, long ago back on Earth. The Snake Dance had been a rain-making ceremonial, and invariably when the very early anthropologists had attended the dance they had gotten drenched on the way home. It was only coincidence and good timing, of course, but it was difficult to tell yourself that when the rain began to pour.

"Here she comes," said Andy Irvin.

There was a splitting whistle and then a soft hum as a small patrol ship settled down toward the field on her anti-gravs. She hung there in the dawn like a little silver fish seen through the glassite walls of a great aquarium, and Conan Lang could sense what he could not see—the massive bulk of the sleek star cruiser waiting out in space.

The patrol ship came down out of the sky and hovered a few feet off the ground. A man swung down out of the outlift and waved. Conan Lang recognized him as Julio Medina, who had been lifted out of another sector of Sirius Ten to come in and replace him with Andy. The ricefruit was green and fresh in the field and it hurt Conan to leave his job unfinished. There wasn't a great deal to do now until the check, of course, and Julio was a very competent and experienced man, but there was still so much that could go wrong, so much that you could never anticipate—

And he didn't want anything to happen to the kid.

"So long, Cone," Andy said, his voice very quiet. "And—thanks. I won't forget what you did."

Conan Lang leaned on Andy's arm and moved toward the ship. "I'll be back, Andy," he said, trying to keep the weight off his feet. "Hold the fort—I know it'll be in good hands."

Conan Lang shook hands with Julio and then Julio and Andy helped him into the outlift. He had time for a brief wave and a final glimpse of the green field under the fiery sun, and then he was inside the patrol ship. They had somehow rigged up a bunk for him in the cramped quarters, and he collapsed into it gratefully.

"Home, James," he whispered, trying not to think about what would happen if they could not save his legs.

Conan Lang closed his eyes and lay very still, feeling the ship pulse and surge as it carried him out into the dark sea from which he had come.

IV

The doctors saved his legs, but years were to pass before Conan Lang again set foot upon Earth. Space was vast and star cruisers comparatively few. In addition, star ships were fabulously expensive to operate—it was out of the question for a ship on a mission to make the long run from Sirius to Sol for the sake of one man. Conan Lang became the prize patient of the ship medics and he stayed with the star cruiser as it operated in the Sirius area.

A star cruiser on operations was never dull and there were books to read and reports to write. Conan Lang curbed his impatience and made the best of the situation. The local treatments applied by Andy had been effective enough so that the ship medics were able to regenerate his burned tissue, and it was only a question of time before he would be strong again.

The star cruiser worked efficiently and effectively in support of Administration units in the Sirius area, sliding through the blackness of space like some leviathan of the deep, and Conan Lang rested and made himself as useful as he could. He often went up into the control room and stood watching the visiplate that looked out upon the great emptiness of space. Somewhere, on a far shore of that mighty sea, was a tiny planet called Earth. There, the air was cool and fresh under the pines and the beauty of the world, once you got away from it and could see it in perspective, was fantastic. There were Rob and Kit, friendship and tears and laughter.

There was home.

While his body healed, Conan Lang lived on the star cruiser. There was plenty of time to think. Even for a race with a life span of almost two hundred years, the days and the weeks and the months can seem interminable. He asked himself all the old questions, examined all the old answers. Here he was, on a star ship light-years from home, his body burned, waiting to go back to Sirius Ten to change the life of a planet. What thin shreds of chance, what strange webs of history, had put him there? When you added up the life of Conan Lang, of all the Conan Langs, what did you get? Where was Earth going, that pebble that hurled its puny challenge at the infinite?

Sometimes, it was all hard to believe.

It had all started, he supposed, with cybernetics. Of course, cybernetics itself was but the logical outgrowth of a long cultural and technological trend. For centuries, man's ally, the machine, had helped him physically in his adjustment to his environment. What more natural than that it should one day help him mentally as well? There was really nothing sinister about thinking machines, except to a certain breed of perpetually gloomy poets who were unable to realize that values were never destroyed but were simply molded into new patterns in the evolution of culture. No, thinking machines were fine and comforting—for a while.

But with the dawn of space travel, man's comfortable, complacent progress toward a vague somewhere was suddenly knocked into a cocked hat. Man's horizons exploded to the rims of the universe with the perfection of the star drive—he was no longer living *on* a world but *in* an inhabited universe. His bickerings and absurdities and wars were seen as the petty things they were—and man in a few tremendous years emerged at last from adolescence.

Science gave to men a life span of nearly two hundred active years and gave him the key to forever. But there was a catch, a fearful catch. Man, who had had all he could do to survive the conflicts of local groups of his own species, was suddenly faced with the staggering prospect of living in an inhabited *universe.* He had known, of course, about the millions and millions of stars, about the infinity of planets, about the distant galaxies that swam like island universes through the dark seas of space. But he had known about them as figures on a page, as photographs, as dots of unwinking light in a telescope. They had been curiosities, a stimulus to the imagination. Now they were vital parts of his life, factors to be reckoned with in the struggle for existence. In the universe were incredible numbers of integers to be equated in the problem of survival—*and the mind of man could not even learn them all, much less form intelligent conclusions about future actions.*

And so, inevitably, man turned again to the machine. But this time there was a difference. The machine was the only instrument capable of handling the data—and man, in a million years, could not even check its most elementary conclusions. Man fed in the facts, the machine reached the conclusions, and man acted upon them—not through choice, but simply because he had no other guide he could trust.

Men operated the machines—but the machines operated men.

The science of cybernetics expanded by leaps and bounds. Men made machines to develop new machines. The great mechanical brains grew so complex that only a few men could even pretend to understand them. Looking at them, it was virtually impossible to believe that they had been born in the minds of men.

The machines did not interfere in the everyday routine of living—man would never submit to that, and in problems which he could understand he was still the best judge of his own happiness. It was in the larger problems, the problems of man's destiny in the universe in which he found himself, that the great brains were beyond value. For the machines could integrate trends, patterns, and complexes of the known worlds and go on from there to extrapolate into the unknown. The machines could, in very general terms, predict the outcome of any given set of circumstances. They could, in a very real sense, see into the future. They could see where Earth was headed.

And Earth was headed for disaster.

The machines were infallible. They dealt not with short-term probabilities, but with long-range certainties. And they stated flatly that, given the equation of the known universe, Earth would be destroyed in a matter of centuries. There was only one thing to do—man must change the equation.

It was difficult for man, so recently Earthbound, to really *think* and *act* in terms of an inhabited universe. But the machines showed conclusively that in as yet inaccessible galaxies life had evolved that was physically and mentally hostile to that of Earth. A collision of the two life-forms would come about within a thousand years, and a life-and-death struggle was inevitable. The facts were all too plain—Earth would lose and the human race would be exterminated.

Unless the equation could be changed.

It was a question of preparing the galaxy for combat. The struggle would be a long one, and factors of reserves, replacements, different cultural approaches to common problems, planets in varying stages of development, would be important. It was like a cosmic chess game, with worlds aligning themselves on a monstrous board. In battles of galactic dimensions, the outcome would be determined by centuries of preparation before contact was even made; it was not a romantic question of heroic spaceships and iron-jawed men of action, but rather one of the cultural, psychological, technological, and individual patterns which each side could bring to bear—patterns which were the outgrowths of millennia of slow evolution and development.

Earth was ready, or would be by the time contact came. But the rest of the galaxy—or at any rate as much of it as they had managed to explore—was not, and would not be. The human race was found somewhere on most of the star systems within the galaxy, but not one of them was as far advanced as were the men from Earth. That was why Earth had never been contacted from space—indeed, it was the only possible explanation, at least in retrospect. And the other galaxies, with their totally alien and forever nonunderstandable principles, were not interested in undeveloped cultures.

The problem thus became one of accelerating the cultural evolution of Earth's sister planets by means of diffusion, in order to build them up into an effective totality to combat the coming challenge. And it had to be done in such a manner that the natives of the planets were completely unaware that they were not the masters of their own destiny, since such a concept produced cultural stagnation and introduced corrupting elements into the planetary configurations. It had often been argued that Earth herself was in such a position, being controlled by the machines, but such was not the case—their choice had been a rational one, and they could abandon the machines at any time at their own risk.

Or so, at any rate, argued the thinkers of Earth.

The long months lengthened into years and, inactive though he was, Conan Lang spent his time well. It was good to have a chance to relax and think things through; it was good for the soul to stop midway in life and take stock. Almost, it was possible to make sense out of things, and the frantic rush to nowhere lost some of its shrieking senselessness.

Conan Lang smiled without humor. That was all very well for him, but what about the natives whose lives they were uprooting? Of course, they were human beings, too, and stood to lose as much as anyone in the long run—but they did not understand the problem, *could* not understand it. The plain truth was that they were being used—used for their own benefit as well as that of others, but used nonetheless.

It was true that primitive life was no bed of roses—it was not as if, Conan Lang assured himself, the men from Earth were slithering, serpent-like, into an idyllic Garden of Eden. All they were doing was accelerating the normal rate of change for a given planet. But this caused far-reaching changes in the culture as it existed—it threw some people to the dogs and elevated others to commanding positions. This was perhaps no more than was done by life itself, and possibly with better reason, but you couldn't tell yourself that when you had to face the eyes of a man who had gone from ruler to slave because of what you had done.

The real difficulty was that you couldn't *see* the threat. It was there all right—a menace besides which all the conflicts of the human race were as nothing. But it had always been difficult for men to work before the last possible moment, to prepare rather than just sit back and hope for the best. That man was working now as he had never worked before, in the face of an unseen threat from out of the stars, even to save his own existence, was a monument to his hard-won maturity. It would have been so easy, so pleasant, just to take it easy and enjoy a safe and comfortable life—and beyond question it would have meant the end of the human race.

Of one thing, Conan Lang was sure—whenever man stopped trying, stopped working and dreaming and reaching for impossible heights, whenever he settled back in complacency, on that day he shrunk to atrophied insignificance.

Sirius Ten had been a relatively easy project because of the planet-wide nature of its culture. Sirius Ten had only one huge land mass, and one great sea. The natives all shared basically the same life pattern, built around the cultivation of dry ricefruit, and the teams of the Applied Process Corps were faced with only one major problem rather than hundreds of them as was more often the case. It was true that certain peoples who lived on the shores of the sea, together with one island group, had a variant culture based on fishing, but these were insignificant numerically and could for practical purposes be ignored.

The dry ricefruit was grown by a cutting and burning method, under which a field gave a good yield only once before the land was exhausted and the people had to move on. Under these conditions, individual ownership of land never developed, and there were no inequalities of wealth to speak of. The joint families worked different fields every year, and since there was no market for a surplus there was no effort made to cultivate more land than was really needed.

The Oripesh natives of Sirius Ten had a well-developed cult of ancestor worship, thinking of their dead as always watching over them and guiding their steps. Since whatever the ancestors did automatically had the sanction of tradition behind it, it was through them that the Corps had decided to work—it being simply a question of palming off Corps Agents as ancestors come back from their dwelling place in the mountains to help their people. With careful preparations and experienced men, this had not proved overly difficult—but there were always miscalculations, accidents. Men were not like chemicals, and they did not always react as they were supposed to react. There was always an individual variable to be considered. That was why if a Corps Agent lived long enough to retire you knew both that he knew his stuff and that he had had more than his share of plain old-fashioned luck.

Sirius Ten had to be shifted from Stage Four to Stage Five. This was a staggering change in economics, social structure, and technology—one that had taken men on Earth many centuries to accomplish. The men of the Applied Process Corps had to do it in a matter of a few years. And so they set out, armed with a variety of ricefruit that grew well in marshy land and a sound knowledge of irrigation.

With such a lever they could move a world.

It was three years to the day when Conan Lang returned to Sirius Ten. The patrol ship came in on her anti-gravs and he waited eagerly for the outlift shaft to open. His heart was pounding in his chest and his lips were dry—it was almost like coming home again.

He swung his newly strong body into the outlift and came out of it in the green field he had planted so long ago. He took a deep breath of the familiar humid air and grinned broadly at the hot, burning sun over his head. It *was* good to be back—back at a place like so many other places he had known, places that were as close to a home as any he could ever have without Kit. The breeze whispered softly through the green ricefruit and he waved at Julio who came running across the field to meet him. These were, he knew, his kind of people—and he had missed Andy all these years.

"Hey there, Julio!" he laughed, shaking Medina's hand. "How goes it?"

"Pretty good, Conan," Julio said quietly. "Pretty good."

"The kid—how's the kid?"

"Andy is dead," said Julio Medina.

Conan Lang stood stock-still while an iron fist smacked into his stomach with cold, monotonous precision. Andy dead. It could not be, *could not be*. There had been no word, nothing. He clenched his fists. It couldn't be true.

But it was. He knew that with ice cold certainty.

"It just happened the other day, Conan," Julio said. "He was a fine boy."

Conan Lang couldn't speak. *The whole planet*, his mind tortured him. *The whole stinking planet isn't worth Andy's life.*

"It was an accident," Julio said, his voice carefully matter-of-fact. "Warfare has sprung up between the rival villages like we figured. Andy was out after information and he got between them—he was hit by mistake with a spear. He never had a chance, but he managed to walk away and get back here before he died. The Oripesh don't suspect that he wasn't a god and could die just like anyone else. He saved the rest of us by coming back here—that's something."

"Yeah," Conan Lang said bitterly, "that's something."

"I buried him here in the field," Julio Medina went on. "I thought he'd like that. He . . . said good-bye to you, Conan."

It had been a long time since Conan Lang had had tears in his eyes. He turned without a word and walked away, across the green field and into the hut where he could be alone.

V

From that time on, by unspoken mutual consent, the two men never again mentioned the kid's name. They gave him the best possible write-up in their reports, and that was all that they could ever do for Andy Irvin.

"I think we've about done it here, Conan," Julio told him. "I'd like to have you make your own check and see if you come up with the same stuff I did. There's a lull in the raiding right now—the natives are worried because that spear hit an ancestor by mistake and they're pretty well occupied with rituals designed to make us feel better about the whole thing. You shouldn't have any trouble, and that ought to about wind things up."

Conan Lang nodded. "It'll be good to get home again, eh Julio?"

"Yes, you know that—and for you it should be for keeps."

Conan Lang raised his eyebrows.

"It's no secret that you're due to be kicked upstairs," Julio said. "I rather think this is your last field job."

"Well, it's a nice theory anyhow."

"You remember all us old men out here in the stars, the slave labor of the Process Corps. Bring us all home, Conan, and we'll sit around in the shade and drink cold wine and fish and tell lies to each other."

"Consider it done," said Conan Lang. "And I'll give you all some more medals."

"I've got medals."

"Can't have too many medals, Julio. They're good for what ails you."

"They're not good for what ails *me*," said Julio Medina.

Conan Lang smiled and fired up his pipe. *The kid*, his mind whispered. *The kid liked that pipe.* He thrust the thought from his mind. A man had to take death in his stride out here, he told himself. Even when it was a kid who reminded you of yourself a million years ago—

A million years ago.

"I'll start in tomorrow," Conan Lang said, puffing on his pipe. "Do you know Ren, Julio?"

"The chief's son? Yes."

"How did he come out?"

"Not well, Conan. He lost his woman, Loe, to one of the men we made wealthy; he has not been the same since."

"We're great people, Julio."

"Yes."

Conan Lang was silent then and the two men stood together in the warm evening air, watching the great double sun float slowly down below the horizon as the long black shadows came marching up from the far edge of the world.

Next morning, Conan Lang was off with the dawn on his final check. He pretty well knew what he would find—Julio Medina was an experienced hand and his information was reliable. But it was always a shock when you saw it for yourself. You never got used to it. To think that such a tiny, seemingly insignificant thing could change a planet beyond recognition. A ricefruit—

It was already hot when he passed the native fields. Their ricefruit plants were tall and healthy, and their irrigation channels well constructed. He shook his head and walked on to the native village.

Where the open, crude, friendly village had stood there was a great log wall. In front of the wall was a series of deep and ugly-looking moats. Behind the wall, he could see the tops of sturdy wooden buildings, a far cry from the huts of only a few short years ago. Conan Lang made no attempt at concealment but walked openly up to the moats and crossed them on a log bridge. He stopped outside the closed gate.

"You will remember me who walked through the flames," he said loudly in the Oripesh tongue. "You will open the gate for your brother as he would visit you."

For a moment nothing happened, and then the gate swung open. Conan Lang entered the village.

The native guard eyed him with suspicion, but he kept his distance. Conan Lang noticed that he had a bow by the log wall. There was nothing like constant warfare for the production of new weapons, he reflected. Civilization was bringing its blessings to the Oripesh with leaps and bounds.

Conan Lang walked through the village unmolested, taking rapid mental notes. He saw storehouses for ricefruit and observed slaves being marched off to work in the fields. The houses in the village were strong and comfortable, but there was a tense air in the village, a feeling of strain. Conan Lang approached a native and stopped him.

"Brother," he said, "I would see your chiefs. Where are they?"

The native looked at him warily. "The Oripesh have no chiefs," he said. "Our king is in council."

Conan Lang nodded, a sick feeling inside him. "It is well," he said. "Ren—I would see him."

The native jerked his thumb contemptuously toward the back of the village. "He is there," he said. "Outside."

Conan Lang moved through the village, watching, missing nothing. He went all the way through and came out through the back wall. There, the old-style native huts baked in squalor under the blazing sun. There was no log wall around them, although they were inside the moat system. A pig rooted around for garbage between the huts.

"Slums," Conan Lang said to himself.

He walked among the huts, ignoring the fearful, suspicious eyes of the natives. He found Ren preparing to go out into the fields. The chief's son was thin. He looked tired and his eyes were dull. He saw Conan and said nothing.

"Hello, Ren," said Conan Lang.

The native just looked at him.

Conan Lang tried to think of something to say. He knew what had happened—the chiefs and their sons had been so busy with ritual work for the tribe that they had lagged behind in the cultivation of the new ricefruit. They had stuck to the old ways too long and their people had passed them by.

"I can help you, my brother," Conan Lang said softly. "It is not too late."

Ren said nothing.

"I will help you with a field of your own," said Conan Lang. "Will you let me help you?"

The native looked at him and there was naked hate in his eyes. "You said you were my friend," he said. Without another word, he turned and left. He did not look back.

Conan Lang wiped the sweat from his forehead and went on with his work.

The sensitive part of his mind retreated back into a dark, insulated corner and he let his training take over. He moved along, asking questions, watching, taking mental notes.

A little thing, he thought.

A new kind of plant.

A week later, Conan Lang had completed his check. He sat by the evening cook fire with Julio, smoking his pipe, watching the shadows in the field.

"Well, we did a good job," he said. "It's awful."

"It would have come without us," Julio reminded him. "It does no good to brood about it. It is tough, sometimes, but it is a small price to pay for survival."

"Yes," said Conan Lang. "Sure."

"Your results check out with mine?"

"Mostly. It's the same old story, Julio."

Conan Lang puffed slowly on his pipe, reconstructing what had happened. The new ricefruit had made it valuable for a family to hang on to one piece of land that could be used over and over again. But only a limited amount of the land could be used, because of natural factors like the presence or absence of available water. The families that had not taken the plunge right away were virtually excluded, and the society was divided into the landed and the landless. The landless gradually had to move farther and farther from the main village to find land upon which to grow the older type of ricefruit—sometimes their fields were so far away that they could not make the round trip in a single day. And they could not get too far away and start over, because of the tribal warfare that had broken out between villages now that valuable stores of ricefruit were there for the taking. The old joint family co-operation broke down, and slaves became economically feasible.

Now that the village need not be periodically moved, it too became valuable and so was strongly fortified for defense. One old chief, grown powerful with fields of the staple ricefruit, set himself up as a king and the other chiefs went to work in his fields.

Of course, Sirius Ten was still in transition. While the old patterns were being destroyed, new ones, less obvious to the untrained eye, were taking their place. Disintegration and reintegration marched hand in hand, but it would be tough on the natives for a while. Process Corps techniques had speeded up the action almost beyond belief, but from here on in the Oripesh were on their own. They would go on and on in their individual development—although no two peoples ever went through exactly the same stages at the same time, it was possible to predict a general planet-wide trend. The Oripesh would one day learn to write, since they already had a crude pictographic system for ritual use. When the contact finally came from the hostile stars in the future, what histories would they have written? Who would they remember, what would they forget? Would there be any twisted legend or myth left that recalled the long-ago time when the gods had come out of the mountains to change the lives of their people?

That was the way to look at it. Conan Lang tapped out his pipe on a rock. Just look at it like a problem, a textbook example. Forget about the people, the individuals you could not help, the lives you had made and the lives you had destroyed. Turn off that part of your mind and think in terms of the long-range good.

Or try to.

"We're all through here, Julio," Conan Lang said. "We can head for home now."

"Yes," said Julio Medina. "It has been a long time."

The two men sat silently in the darkness, each thinking his own thoughts, watching the yellow moon sail through silver stars.

After the patrol ship had been signaled, there was nothing to do but wait until their pickup could be coordinated with the time schedules of the other Corps men and the operational schedule of the star cruiser. Conan Lang busied himself with his reports while Julio sprawled in the shade and devised intricate and impossible card games with a battered deck that was old enough to be in itself of anthropological interest.

Conan Lang was playing a game, too. He played it with his mind and he was a somewhat unwilling participant. His mind had played the game before and he was tired of it, but there was nothing he could do about it. There wasn't any button that would turn his mind off, and while it was on it played games.

It was engaged in putting two and two together.

This was not in itself uncommon, although it was not as widespread as some people fondly imagined it to be. But Conan Lang played the game where others did not even see one, much less a set of twos with a relationship between them. There is nothing so hard to see as what is termed obvious after the fact. Conan Lang's mind had played with the obvious all his life; it would not let well enough alone. He didn't like it, there were times when he would have preferred to junk it all and go fishing without a thought in his head, but he was stuck with it. When his mind wanted to play the game, it played and that was that.

While he waited for the patrol ship, his mind was playing with a set of factors. There was the history of Earth, taken as a vast overall sequence. There were thinking machines, atomic power, and the field techniques of the Process Corps. There was the fact that Earth had no record of ever having been contacted by another world—they had always done the contacting themselves. There was the new principle that Admiral White had spoken to him about, the integration-acceleration factor for correlating data. There was the incredible, explosive energy of man that had hurled him light-years into space. There was his defiant heart that could tackle the prodigious job of reshaping a galaxy when the chips were down.

Conan Lang put two and two together, and he did not get four. He got five.

He didn't know the answers yet, but he knew enough to formulate the right questions. From past experience, he knew that that was the toughest part of the game. Incorrect answers were usually the products of off-center questions. Once you had the right question, the rest was a matter of time.

The patrol ship came for them finally, and Conan Lang and Julio Medina walked across the soil of Sirius Ten for the last time. They crossed the field where the green plants grew, and neither tried to say what was in his heart. Three had come and only two could leave. Andy Irvin had lived and worked and dreamed only to fall on an alien planet light-years away from earth that could have been his. He was part of the price that was exacted for survival—and he was also a kid with stars in his eyes who had gotten a rotten, senseless break.

After the patrol ship had gone, the green leaves of the ricefruit plants stretched hungrily up toward the flaming sun. The clean water chuckled along the irrigation trenches, feeding the roots in the field. Softly, as though sad with all the memories it carried, the lonesome breeze whispered through the empty hut that had housed the men from Earth.

VI

Through the trackless depths of interstellar space the star cruiser rode on the power from her atomics. The hum that filled the ship was a good sound, and she seemed to quiver with pride and impatience. It did make a difference which way you were going in space, and the ship was going home.

Conan Lang paced through the long white corridors and walked around the afterhold where the brown sacks of ricefruit had been. He read in the library and joked with the medics who had salvaged his burned body. And, always ahead of him, swimming in the great emptiness of space, were the faces of Kit and of his son, waiting for him, calling him home again.

Rob must have grown a lot, he thought. Soon, he wouldn't be a boy any longer—he would be a man, taking his place in the world. Conan remembered his son's voice from a thousand quiet talks in the cool air of evening, his quick, eager eyes—

Like Andy's.

"Dad, when I grow up can I be like you? Can I be an Agent and ride on the ships to other worlds and have a uniform and everything?"

What could you tell your son now that you had lived so long and were supposed to know so much? That life in the Process Corps filled a man with things that were perhaps better unknown? That the star trails were cold and lonely? That there were easier, more comfortable lives? All that was true; all the men who rode the ships knew it. But they knew, too, that for them this was the only life worth living.

The time passed slowly. Conan Lang was impatient to see his family again, anxious to get home. But his mind gave him no rest. There were things he had to know, things he *would* know before he went home to stay.

Conan Lang had the right questions now. He had the right questions, and he knew where the answers were hidden.

Fritz Gottleib.

The star cruiser had hardly touched Earth again at Space One before Conan Lang was outside on the duralloy tarmac. Since the movements of the star ships were at all times top-secret matters, there was no one at the port to greet him and for once Conan was glad to have a few extra hours to himself. Admiral White wouldn't expect him to check in until tomorrow anyway, and before he saw Kit he wanted to get things straight once and for all.

The friendly sun of Earth warmed him gently as he hurried across the tarmac and the air felt cool and fresh. He helped himself to an official bullet, rose into the blue sky, and jetted eastward over the city. His brain was seething and he felt cold sweat in the palms of his hands. What was it that Gottleib had said to him on that long-ago day?

"Sometimes it is best not to know the answers to one's questions, Dr. Lang."

Well, he was going to know the answers anyhow. All of them. He landed the bullet in the space adjoining the cybernetics building and hurried inside, flashing his identification as he went. He stopped at a switchboard and showed his priority credentials.

"Call the Nest, please," he told the operator. "Tell Dr. Gottleib that Conan Lang is down here and would like to see him."

The operator nodded and spoke into the intercom. There was a moment's delay, and then he took his earphones off and smiled at Conan Lang.

"Go right on up, Dr. Lang," the operator said. "Dr. Gottleib is expecting you."

Conan Lang controlled his astonishment and went up the lift and down the long white corridors. *Expecting* him? But that was impossible. No one even knew the star cruiser was coming back, much less that he was coming here to the Nest. Impossible—

All around him in the great building he felt the gigantic mechanical brain with its millions of circuits and flashing tubes. The brain crowded him, pressed him down until he felt tiny and insignificant. It hummed and buzzed through the great shielded walls.

Laughing at him.

Conan Lang pushed past the attendants and security men and opened the door of the Nest. He moved into the small, dark room and paused to allow his eyes to become accustomed to the dim light. The room was silent. Gradually, the shadow behind the desk took form and he found himself looking into the arctic eyes of Fritz Gottleib.

"Dr. Lang," he hissed softly. "Welcome to the Buzzard's Nest."

The man had not changed; he was timeless, eternal. He was still dressed in black and it might have been minutes ago instead of years when Conan Lang had last seen him. His black eyebrows slashed across his white face and his long-fingered hands were bent slightly like claws upon his desk.

"How did you know I was coming here?" Now that he was face-to-face with Gottleib, Conan Lang felt suddenly uncertain, unsure of himself.

"I know many things, Dr. Lang," Fritz Gottleib said sibilantly. "Had I cared to, I could have told you ten years ago the exact date, within a day or so, upon which we would have this meeting. I could even have told you what you would say when you came through the door, and what you are going to say five minutes from now."

Conan Lang just stared at him, feeling like an absurd little child who had presumed to wrestle a gorilla. His mind recoiled from the strange man before him and he knew at last that he knew nothing.

"I do not waste words, Dr. Lang," Gottleib said, his eyes cold and unmoving in his head. "You will remember that when we last met you said you wanted to ask some questions of the machine. Do you remember what I said, Dr. Lang?"

Conan Lang thought back across the years. *"Perhaps one day, Dr. Lang,"* Gottleib had said. *"When you are old like me."*

"Yes," said Conan Lang. "Yes, I remember."

"You were not ready then," Dr. Gottleib said, his white face ghostly in the dim light. "You could not even have framed the right questions, at least not all of them."

Conan Lang was silent. How much *did* Gottleib know? Was there anything he *didn't* know?

"You are old enough now," said Fritz Gottleib.

He turned a switch and the surface of his desk glowed with dull red light. His face, reflected in the flamelike glow, was unearthly. His cold eyes looked out of hell. He rose to his feet, seeming to loom larger than life, filling the room. Moving without a sound, he left the room, and the door clicked shut behind him.

Conan Lang was alone in the red room. His heart hammered in his throat and his lips were dry. He clenched his fists and swallowed hard. Alone—

Alone with the great machine.

Conan Lang steadied himself. Purposefully, he made himself go through the prosaic, regular motions of lighting up his pipe. The tobacco was healthily full-bodied and fragrant and it helped to relax him. He smoked slowly, taking his time.

The red glow from the desk filled the room with the color of unreality. Crimson shadows seemed to crouch in the corners with an impossible life of their own. But was anything impossible, here? Conan Lang felt the pulse of the great machine around him and wondered.

Trying to shake off a persistent feeling of dreamlike unreality, Conan Lang moved around and sat down behind Gottleib's desk. The red panel was a maze of switches which were used to integrate it with technical panels in other sections of the building. In the center of the panel was a keyboard on an open circuit to the machine and set into the desk was a clear square like a very fine telescreen. Conan Lang noticed that there was nothing on Gottleib's desk that was not directly connected with the machine—no curios, no pictures, no paperweights, not a single one of the many odds and ends most men picked up for their desks during a long lifetime. The whole room was frightening in its very impersonality, as though every human emotion had been beaten out of it long ago and the room had been insulated against its return.

The machines never slept and the circuits were open. Conan Lang had only to ask and any question that could be answered would be answered. The red glow in the room reminded him of the fire and he shuddered a little in spite of himself. Had that really been over three years ago? How much had he learned in those three years when he had seen the Oripesh change before his eyes and had had time for once to really think his life through? How much did he still have to learn?

Conan Lang took a long pull on his pipe and set the desk panel for manual type questioning and visual screen reception. He hesitated a moment, almost afraid of the machine at his disposal. He didn't *want* to know, he suddenly realized. It wasn't like that. It was rather that he *had* to know.

Framing his words carefully, Conan Lang typed out the question that had been haunting him for years:

IS THE EARTH ITSELF THE SUBJECT OF PROCESS MANIPULATION?

He waited nervously, sure of the answer, but fearful of it nevertheless. There was a faint, all but inaudible, hum from the machine and Conan Lang could almost feel the circuits closing in the great walls around him. The air was filled with tension. There was a brief click and one word etched itself blackly on the clear screen:

YES.

Conan Lang leaned forward, sure of himself now, and typed out another question:

HOW LONG HAS THE EARTH BEEN MANIPULATED AND HAS THIS CONTROL BEEN FOR GOOD OR EVIL?

The machine hummed and answered at once:

THE EARTH HAS BEEN GUIDED SINCE EARTH YEAR NINETEEN HUNDRED A.D. *THE SECOND PART OF YOUR QUESTION IS MEANINGLESS.*

Conan Lang hesitated, staggered in spite of himself by the information he was getting. Then he typed rapidly:

WITH REFERENCE TO GOOD, EQUATE SURVIVAL OF THE HUMAN RACE.

The screen clouded, cleared, and the words formed:

THE CONTROL HAS BEEN FOR GOOD.

Conan Lang's breathing was shallow now. He typed tensely:

HAS THIS CONTROL COME FROM WITHIN THIS GALAXY? IF SO, WHERE? IS THERE USUALLY AN AGENT OTHER THAN EARTH'S IN CHARGE OF THIS MACHINE?

The hum of the machine filled the bloodred room and the screen framed the answers:

THE CONTROL HAS COME FROM WITHIN THE GALAXY. THE SOURCE IS A WORLD KNOWN AS RERMA, CIRCLING A STAR ON THE EDGE OF THE GALAXY WHICH IS UNKNOWN TO EARTH. THE MAN KNOWN AS GOTTLEIB IS A RERMAN AGENT.

Conan Lang's pipe had been forgotten and gone out. He put it down and licked his dry lips. So far so good. But the one prime, all-important question had not yet been asked. He asked it:

IF THE PLAN IS FOLLOWED, WHAT WILL BE THE FINAL OUTCOME WITH RESPECT TO RERMA AND THE EARTH?

The machine hummed again in the red glow and the answer came swiftly, with a glorious, mute tragedy untold between its naked lines:

RERMA WILL BE DESTROYED. THE EARTH WILL SURVIVE IF THE PLAN IS CAREFULLY FOLLOWED.

Conan Lang felt tears in his eyes and he was unashamed. With time forgotten now, he leaned forward, asking questions, reading replies, as the terrible, wonderful story unfolded.

Far out on the edge of the galaxy, the ancient planet of Rerma circled her yellow sun. Life had evolved early on Rerma—had evolved early and developed fast. While the other humanoid peoples of the galaxy were living in caves, the Rerma were building a great civilization. When Earth forged its first metal sword, the Rerma split the atom.

Rerma was a world of science—true science. Science had eliminated war and turned the planet into a paradise. Literature and the arts flourished hand in hand with scientific progress, and scientists worked surrounded by cool gardens in which graceful fountains splashed and chuckled in the sun. Every man was free to develop himself as an individual and no man bent his head to any other man.

The Rerma were the human race in full flower.

But the Rerma were few, and they were not a warlike people. It was not that they would not fight in an emergency, but simply that they could not possibly win an extended encounter. Their minds didn't work that way. The Rerma had evolved to a point where they were too specialized, too well-adjusted to their environment.

And their environment changed.

It was only a question of time until the Rerma asked the right questions of their thinking machines and came up with the knowledge that their world, situated on the edge of the galaxy, was directly in the path of a coming cultural collision between two star systems. The Rerma fed in the data over and over again, and each time the great machines came up with the same answer.

Rerma would be destroyed.

It was too late for the equation to be changed with respect to Rerma—she had gone too far and was unfortunately located. But for the rest of the human race, scattered on the far-flung worlds that marched along the star trails, there was a chance. There was time for the equation to be changed for them—if only someone could be found to change it! For the Rerma had the knowledge, but they had neither the manpower nor the driving, defiant spirit to do the job themselves. They were capable of making heroic decisions and sticking by them, but the task of remolding a star system was not for them. That was a job for a young race, a proud and unconquerable race. That was a job for the men of Earth.

The ships of the Rerma found Earth in the earth year 1900. They knew that in order for their plan to succeed the Rerma must stand and fight on that distant day when galaxies collided, for their power was not negligible despite their lack of know-how for a long-range combat. They must stand and fight and be destroyed—the plan, the equation, was that finely balanced. Earth was the only other planet they found that was sufficiently advanced to work with, and it was imperative that Earth should not know that she was being manipulated. She must not suspect that her plans were not her own, for a young race with its pride wounded is a dubious ally and an ineffective fighting mechanism.

The Rerma set to work—willing even to die for a future they had already lived. The scientists of Rerma came secretly to Earth, and behind them, light-years away, their crystal fountains still sparkled sadly in the sun.

Rerma would be destroyed—but humanity would not die.

Conan Lang sat alone in the red room, talking to a machine. It was all clear enough, even obvious, once you knew the facts. Either there were no advanced races in the galaxy, which would account for Earth having no record of any contact—or else the Earth *had* been contacted secretly, been manipulated by the very techniques that she herself was later to use on undeveloped worlds.

He looked back on history. Such profound and important changes as the Neolithic food revolution and the steam engine had been produced by Earth alone, making her the most advanced planet in the galaxy except for the Rerma. Earth had a tradition of technological skill behind her, and she was young and pliable. The Rerma came—and the so-called world wars had followed. Why? Not to avenge the honor of insulted royalty, not because of fanatics, not because of conflicting creeds—but in a very real sense to save the world. The world wars had been fought to produce atomic power.

After 1900, the development of Earth had snowballed in a fantastic manner. The atom was liberated and man flashed upward to other planets of the solar system. Just as Conan Lang himself had worked through the ancestor gods of the Oripesh to bring about sweeping changes on Sirius Ten, the Rerma had worked through one of the gods of the Earthmen—the machine.

Cybernetics.

Man swept out to the stars, and the great thinking machines inevitably confronted them with the menace from beyond that drew nearer with each passing year. Young and proud, the men of Earth accepted the most astounding challenge ever hurled—they set out to reshape a galaxy to give their children and their children's children a chance for life.

And always, behind the scenes, beneath the headlines, were the ancient Rerma. They subtly directed and hinted and helped. With a selflessness unmatched in the universe, these representatives of a human race that had matured too far prepared Earth for galactic leadership—and themselves for death on the edge of the galaxy. They had unified Earth and pushed and prodded her along the road to survival.

When the Rerma could have fled and purchased extra time for themselves, they chose instead—these peace-loving people—to fight for another chance for man.

Conan Lang looked up, startled, to find the black figure of Fritz Gottleib standing by his side. He looked old, very old, in the bloodred light and Conan Lang looked at him with new understanding. Gottleib's impatience with others and the vast, empty loneliness in those strange eyes—all that was meaningful now. What a life that man had led on Earth, Conan Lang thought with wonder. Alone, wanting friendship and understanding—and having always to discourage close personal contacts, having always to fight his lonely battle alone in a sterile little room, knowing that the very men he had dedicated his life to help laughed behind his back and compared him to a bird of prey.

"I've been a fool, sir," Conan Lang said, getting to his feet. "We've all been fools."

Fritz Gottleib sat down again behind his desk and turned the machine off. The red glow vanished and they were left in the semidarkness.

"Not fools, Dr. Lang," he said. "It was necessary for you to feel as you did. The feelings of one old man—what are they worth in this game we are playing? We must set our sights high, Dr. Lang."

Conan Lang waited in the shadows, thinking, watching the man who sat across from him as though seeing him for the first time. His mind was still groping, trying to assimilate all he had learned. It was a lot to swallow in a few short hours, even when you were prepared for it beforehand by guesswork and conjecture. There were still questions, of course, many questions. He knew that he still had much to learn.

"Why me?" Conan Lang asked finally. "Why have I been told all this? Am I the only one who knows?"

Fritz Gottleib shook his head, his face ghost-white in the darkened room. "There are others who know," he said sibilantly. "Your superior officer, Nelson White, has known for years of course. You were told because you have been selected to take over his command when he retires. If you are willing, you will work very closely with him here on Earth for the next five years, and then you will be in charge."

"Will I . . . leave Earth again?"

"Not for a long time, Dr. Lang. The integration-acceleration principle will keep you busy—we are in effect lifting Earth another stage and the results will be far-reaching. But you will be home, Dr. Lang—home with your family and your people.

"That is all, Dr. Lang," Gottleib hissed.

Conan Lang hesitated. "I'll do my level best," he said finally. "Good-bye, sir . . . I'll see you again."

Conan Lang put out his hand to the man he had called the Buzzard and Gottleib shook it with a firm, powerful grip.

"Good-bye, Conan," Fritz Gottleib said softly.

Conan Lang turned and walked from the dark room, leaving the man from Rerma sitting alone in the shadows of the Nest.

The little bullet rose vertically on her copter blades through the evening sky, hovered a moment in the cool air under the frosty stars, and then flashed off on her jets into the west. Conan Lang set the controls and leaned back in the seat, at peace with himself at last. There *was* meaning to it all, there was a purpose—and Andy and all the others like him on the far trails had not sacrificed their lives for nothing.

Conan Lang breathed the clean air of Earth and smiled happily. Ahead of him, waiting for him, were Kit and Rob, and he would never have to leave them again. He opened the lateral ports and let the wind hurl itself at his face.

Richard A. Lupoff

Richard A. Lupoff (1935–   ) is an editor, critic, historian of popular culture, and writer—the author of twenty SF and fantasy novels and more than a hundred short stories. The extraordinary scope of his career encompasses novels and stories in every sub-genre of science fiction and fantasy, as well as a series of mystery novels. Notable works include *Sword of the Demon* (1977), a fantastic novel based on Japanese mythology; *Space War Blues* (1978), his experimental SF novel of race war in space, of which "Sail the Tide of Mourning" became a segment; and *Lovecraft's Book* (1985), a fiction adventure featuring H. P. Lovecraft, detective. Indeed, one of the hallmarks of his career is that no two Lupoff works are alike. The result is, as *The Encyclopedia of Science Fiction* says, "it is at times difficult, in spite of his clear and abundant intelligence, to identify a unique Richard A. Lupoff voice."

This story has resonances with the work of Cordwainer Smith, interesting echoes that give some evidence of the inner conversations among texts that are the very nature of a literary genre. The link between mysteries of the psyche and space travel is an enduring one in genre science fiction.

SAIL THE TIDE OF MOURNING

Nurundere, captain, ordered his lighter to be hauled from the storage deck of *Djanggawul* and fitted for use of Jiritzu. Sky heroes bent their efforts, sweat glistening on black skin, dirt of labor staining white duck trousers and grip-soled shoes.

Much thought was given to their work and the reasons for it although little was said of the matter. The people of Yurakosi were not given greatly to speech: a taciturnity, self-containment, was part of the heritage of their race, from the days of their desert isolation in the heartland of Australia, O'Earth.

They alone of the scattered children of Sol carried the gene that let them sail the membrane ships. They alone carried in their skin the pigment that filtered out the deadly radiation of the tracks between the stars, that permitted them to clamber up masts and through rigging as had their ancestors on the pacific waters of O'Earth centuries before, while spacemen of other breeds clumped and heaved about in their massive vacuum armor.

The brilliant light of the multiple star Yirrkalla wheeled overhead; *Djanggawul* had completed her great tack and pointed her figureheaded prow toward home, toward Yurakosi, bearing the melancholy tale of her voyage to N'Jaja and N'Ala and the death of a passenger, Ham Tamdje of N'Jaja, at the hands of the sky hero Jiritzu.

Djanggawul bore yet the scars of the attempt by surner meat to seize control of the membrane ship and force from her crew the secret of their ability to live unsuited in space. At N'Ala she had shuttled the surviving surners to the orbiting Port Corley, along with the bodies of those killed in the mutiny.

And now, passing the great tack at Yirrkalla, *Djanggawul* heeled beneath the titanic solar wind that would fill all sails that bellied out from the rows of masts on her three flat decks. With each moment the ship gained momentum. Under the careful piloting of her first officer Uraroju she would sail to Yurakosi on this momentum and on the force of the interstellar winds she encountered on her great arcing course. There would be no need to start her auxiliary engines, to annihilate any of the precious rod of collapsed matter that hung suspended through the long axis of *Djanggawul*, where it provided the artificial gravity for the ship.

Sky heroes swarmed the storage deck of the ship, readying Nurundere's lighter for Jiritzu. They fitted the tiny ship with food concentrate, tested her recyclers, tried her hinged mast fittings, and clamped the masts to the hull of the lighter in anticipation of her catapulting from the deck of *Djanggawul.*

When the lighter was fully prepared, the sky hero Baime went to *Djanggawul*'s bridge to inform Nurundere and Uraroju. Others in the work party hauled the lighter from its place in the storage deck, refixed the now vacant moorings that had held the lighter, and worked the tiny ship through a great cargo hatch onto the main deck of *Djanggawul.*

High above the deck Jiritzu stood balanced lightly on a spar near the top of a mainmast. He was dressed like any sky hero of the crew of *Djanggawul*, in white trousers and canvas shoes, black knitted cap and turtleneck sweater, the costume declared by Yurakosi tradition to have been the costume of the sky heroes' ancestors on O'Earth.

A tiny radio had been implanted behind one ear, and strapped to his thigh was a close-air generator. The oxygen-rich mixture that it slowly emitted clung to Jiritzu, providing him with the air he needed for breath, insulating him from the extreme temperatures of space, providing an invisible pressure suit that protected him from the vacuum all around.

He watched the cargo hatch roll slowly back onto the deck beneath him, the one of *Djanggawul*'s three identical outer decks most easily accessible from the lighter's storage place, and watched his fellow sky heroes haul the lighter onto the deck. He kept his radio turned off, and by tacit agreement no man or woman of *Djanggawul*'s crew, not even Jiritzu's kunapi half Dua, approached the mast he had climbed or made any sign of knowing of his presence.

Nurundere himself strode from the bridge of his ship to inspect the lighter, now standing empty on the deck. Jiritzu could tell him easily, not merely by his distinctive cap of white with its wide black band, but by his pale skin, the protective pigmentation of the Yurakosi almost totally faded now, whited out by the passing years and long exposure to the radiation of the naked stars.

Soon Nurundere would have to return to Yurakosi himself, give himself over to the life of a ground squirmer, crawl with the small children and the old men and women of Yurakosi, the only inhabitants of the planet whose able sons and daughters were desperately needed to sail the membrane ships between the stars.

Not so Jiritzu.

Again and again his mind flashed to the terrible scene inside the passenger tank of *Djanggawul*, the moments when the surner meat, the passengers whose payments financed the flights of the membrane ships and filled the coffers of the sky heroes' home planet, had shown firearms—an act unknown on the peaceful, neutral ships—and had briefly imprisoned much of the crew.

Again Jiritzu relived the horror of finding his betrothed, Miralaidj, daughter of Wuluwaid and Bunbulama, dead at the hand of Ham Tamdje.

Again Jiritzu relived the pleasure, the terrible pleasure of killing Ham Tamdje himself, with his bare hands. At the thought he felt sweat burst from his face and hands. His legs, where a bullet fired by Ham Tamdje had torn the flesh, throbbed with pain.

He closed his eyes tightly, turned his face from the deck below him to the blackness above, reopened his eyes.

Above him gleamed the constellation Yirrkalla, beneath which *Djanggawul* had made her great tack. The colored stars formed the facial features of the Rainbow Serpent: the pale, yellow-green eyes, the angry white nostrils, the bloodred venomous fangs. And beyond Yirrkalla, fading, fading across the immensity of the heavens, the body of the Rainbow Serpent himself, writhing and curving across the void that separated galaxies.

A drop of sweat fell from Jiritzu's forehead, rolled to the edge of one eye where it stung like a tiny insect, then rolled on, enlarged by a tear.

He looked downward, saw that the work on the deck was completed, the lighter ready for his use. With heavy heart he lowered himself slowly to the deck of *Djanggawul,* avoiding the acrobatic tumbles that had been his great joy since his earliest days on the membrane ships.

He walked slowly across the deck of the great ship, halted before the captain's lighter. A party of sky heroes had assembled at the lighter. Jiritzu examined their faces, found in them a mixture of sadness at the loss of a friend and fellow and resignation at what they knew would follow.

Nurundere was there himself. The captain of *Djanggawul* opened his arms, facing directly toward Jiritzu. He moved his lips in speech, but Jiritzu left his implanted radio turned off. The meaning of Nurundere was clear without words.

Jiritzu came to his captain. They embraced. Jiritzu felt the strong arms of the older man clasp about his shoulders. Then he was released, stepped back.

Beside Nurundere stood Uraroju, first officer of *Djanggawul.* Some junior officer, then, had been left upon the bridge. Uraroju was a younger person than Nurundere, her protective pigmentation still strong, barely beginning to white out; she would have many years before her as a sky hero, would surely become captain of *Djanggawul* with Nurundere's retirement to Yurakosi.

They embraced, Jiritzu for a moment closing his eyes, permitting himself to pretend that Uraroju was his own mother, that he was visiting his old people in their town of Kaitjouga on Yurakosi. The warmth of Uraroju, the feel of her womanhood, comforted Jiritzu. Then they released each other, and he turned to other men and women he would never again see, men and women who must return to Yurakosi with the tale of the tragic things that had transpired between Port Upatoi and Yirrkalla on the outward leg of their sail, and with the tale of the end of Jiritzu.

Watilun he embraced, Watilun the machinist and hero of the battle against the mutineers.

Baime he embraced, a common sailor, Jiritzu's messmate.

Kutjara he embraced, Kutjara with whom he had often swarmed the lines of *Djanggawul.*

Only Dua, kunapi half to Jiritzu of the aranda, spoke in their parting embrace. Radios mute, Dua spoke in the moments when his close-air envelope and that of Jiritzu were merged, when common speech could be carried without electronic aid.

"Bidjiwara is not here," Dua said. None but Jiritzu could hear this. "The loss of her aranda half Miralaidj is too great for little Bidjiwara to bear. The loss of yourself, Jiritzu, is too great for Bidjiwara. She remains below, weeping alone.

"I too have wept for you, my aranda half, but I could not remain below. I could not forego our parting time."

He kissed Jiritzu on the cheek, his lips brushing the *maraiin*, the swirling scarifications born by all kunapi and aranda, whose meaning he, Dua alone of all Jiritzu's shipmates, understood.

Jiritzu clasped both Dua's hands in his own, saying nothing. Then he turned away and went to inspect the lighter given him by Nurundere. He found all in order, climbed upon the deck of the tiny membrane craft, signaled to the sky heroes on *Djanggawul*'s deck.

Watilun himself operated the catapult.

Jiritzu found himself cast from *Djanggawul*, forward and upward from her deck, the distance between the great membrane ship and tiny lighter growing with each moment. He sighed only once, then turned to the task of sailing his new ship.

Above him lay the writhing length of the Rainbow Serpent. By conference with Nurundere and Uraroju over many days it had been settled that Jiritzu would not return with *Djanggawul* to Yurakosi. His act in killing Ham Tamdje was understood. There was no question of trial, no accusation, or even suggestion of crime.

But the tradition of the sky-hero peoples held sacred any passenger on the membrane ships.

Death of meat, membrane-ship passengers, ground squirmers traveling between the stars in the tanks of sky-hero craft instead of sealed in the bellies of massive conventional spacecraft, was almost unknown. There was the half-legendary story of Elyun El-Kumarbis, traveler from the pan-semite empire of O'Earth sailing aboard *Makarata* to Al-ghoul Phi, who had passed as a sky hero and died of space radiation, his body later launched into deep space at his dying request.

And there was the new tragedy of Ham Tamdje and his killer Jiritzu, who could never again be permitted to ride the membrane ships as a sky hero.

Beneath Jiritzu and the lighter, *Djanggawul* dwindled, her great membrane ships bellied out with starwinds, her golden skin reflecting the multicolored lights of the Yirrkalla constellation.

And above Jiritzu, Yirrkalla itself, the serpent face, leering and glowing its brightness.

He erected the masts of the lighter, fixed their bases on the three equilaterally mounted decks of the lighter, climbed each mast in turn, rotating gimbaled spars into position and locking them perpendicular to the masts. The sails, the fine, almost monomolecular membranes that would catch the starwinds and carry the lighter onward, he left furled for the time being.

From the top of a mast he pushed himself gently, parallel with the deck of the lighter. He floated softly to the deck, landing with bent knees to absorb the light impact of his lean frame on the lighter's deck.

He opened the hatch and crawled into the cramped interior of the lighter to check the instruments and supplies he knew were there—the compact rations, the lighter's multiradiational telescope that he would bring with him to the deck and mount for use, the lighter's miniature guidance computer.

Instead, before even switching on the cabin light, he saw two brief reflections of the colored illumination of Yirrkalla—what he knew must be two eyes.

He flicked on his implanted radio and demanded to know the identity of the stowaway.

"Don't be angry, Jiritzu," her voice quivered, "I had to come along."

"Bidjiwara!" he cried.

She launched herself across the cabin, crossing it in an easy, gliding trajectory. She caught his hand in her two, brought it to her face, pressed his palm to the *maraiin,* the graceful scarifications on her cheek.

"Don't be angry with me," she repeated.

He felt himself slump to the deck of the cabin, sitting with his back to the bulkhead, the hatchway leading to the outer deck overhead, light pouring in. He shook himself, turned to look into the face of Bidjiwara, young Bidjiwara, she who was barely entering womanhood, whose voyage on *Djanggawul* was her first as a sky hero, her first offplanet, her first away from Yurakosi.

"Angry? Angry?" Jiritzu repeated stupidly. "No, Bidjiwara, my—my dear Bidjiwara." He brought his face close to hers, felt as she cupped his cheeks in the palms of her hands.

He shook his head. "I couldn't be angry with you. But do you understand? Do you know where this little ship is bound?"

Suddenly he pulled away from her grasp, sprang back to the deck of the lighter, sighted back in the direction of *Djanggawul.* Could he see her as a distant speck? Was that the great membrane ship—or a faint, remote star?

His radio was still on. He stood on the lighter's deck, shouted after *Djanggawul* and her crew. "Dua! Nurundere! Uraroju!"

There was no answer, only a faint, random crackling in his skull, the signals of cosmic radio emanations broadcast by colliding clouds of interstellar gas.

He dropped back through the hatch, into the cabin of the lighter.

He reached for Bidjiwara, took her extended hand, drew her with him back onto the deck of the lighter.

"You know why I am here," he said, half in question, half assertion.

She nodded, spoke softly a word in confirmation.

Still, he said, "I will die. I am here to die."

She made no answer, stood with her face to his sweater, her hands resting lightly against his shoulders. He looked down at her, saw how thin her body was, the contours of womanhood but barely emergent from the skinny, sticklike figure of the boisterous child his dead Miralaidj had loved as a little sister.

Jiritzu felt tears in his eyes.

"I could not go back to Yurakosi," he said. "I am a young man, my skin still fine and black, protecting me from the poison of the stars. I could not become a squirmer, alone in a world of children and ancients.

"I would have thrown myself with all my strength from the top of *Djanggawul*'s highest mast. I would have escaped the ship, fallen forever through space like the corpse of El-Kumarbis.

"Nurundere said no." Jiritzu stopped, looked down at Bidjiwara, at her glossy, midnight hair spilling from beneath her knitted cap, her black, rounded forehead. For a moment he bent and pressed his cheek against the top of her head, then raised his eyes again to the Rainbow Serpent and spoke.

"Nurundere gave me his own ship, his captain's lighter. 'Take the lighter, Jiritzu,' he said. 'I can unload at Port Bralku with the others, by shuttle. I need no glorious captain's barge. Sail on forever,' Nurundere said, 'a better fate than the one awaiting me.'

"You understand, Bidjiwara? I mean to sail the Rainbow Serpent, the tide that flows between the galaxies. I will sail as long as the rations aboard last. I will die on this little ship, my soul will return to the Dreamtime, my body will continue onward, borne by the Rainbow Serpent.

"I will never become a ground crawler. I will never return to Yurakosi. No world will know my tread—ever."

Bidjiwara turned her face, raising her eyes from Jiritzu's ribbed sweater to look directly into his eyes.

"Very well, Jiritzu. I will sail the Rainbow Serpent with you. Where else was there for me to go?"

Jiritzu laughed bitterly. "You are a child. You should have remained aboard *Djanggawul.* You had many years before you as a sky hero. Look at your skin," he said, raising her hand to hold it before them both. No power lights were burning on the little ship, but the colors of Yirrkalla glowed white, green-yellow, bloodred.

"Black, Bidjiwara, black with the precious shield that only our people claim."

"And your own?" she responded.

"My own pigment—yes, I too would have had many more years to play at sky hero. But I killed Ham Tamdje. I broke the sacred trust. I could sail the great membrane ships no longer."

He dropped her hand and walked a few paces away. He stood, his back half-turned to her, and his words were carried to her by the tiny radios implanted in both their skulls.

"And Miralaidj," he almost whispered, "Miralaidj—in the Dreamtime. And her father Wuluwaid in the Dreamtime. No."

He turned and looked upward through naked spars to the glowing stars of Yirrkalla and the Rainbow Serpent. "We should set to work rigging sails," he said.

"I *will* stay with you then," she said. "You will not send me away, send me back."

"Dua knew you were hidden?"

She nodded yes.

"My closest friend, my half, kunapi to my aranda. Dua told me a lie."

"I begged him, Jiritzu."

For a moment he almost glared at her, anger filling his face. "Why do you wish to die?"

She shook her head. "I wish to be with you."

"You will die with me."

"I will return to the Dreamtime with you."

"You believe the old stories."

She shrugged. "We should set to work rigging sails." And scurried away, flung open lockers, drew out furled sheets of nearly monomolecular membrane, scampered up a mast and began fixing the sail to spars.

Jiritzu stood on the deck, watching. Then he crossed to another of the lighter's three equilateral decks and followed the example of Bidjiwara.

He worked until he had completed the rigging of the masts of the deck, then crossed again, to the third of the lighter's decks, opened a locker, drew membrane and clambered to the top of a mast. There he clung, knees gripping the vertical shaft, arms flung over the topmost spar, rigging the sail.

He completed the work, looked across to the farthermost mast, near the stern of the lighter. The Rainbow Serpent drew a gleaming polychromatic backdrop. The mast was silhouetted against the Serpent, and standing on the highest spar, one hand outstretched clinging to the mast, the other arm and leg extended parallel to the spar, was Bidjiwara.

Her envelope of close air shimmered with refraction of the colors of Yirrkalla. Jiritzu clung to the rigging where he had worked, struck still and silent by the beauty of the child. He wondered why she did not see him, then gradually realized, aided by the misty sidereal light of the region, that she stood with her back to him, her face raised to the great tide that flowed between the galaxies, her mind wholly unconcerned with her surroundings and unaware of his presence.

Jiritzu lowered himself silently through the spars and rigging of the lighter, through a hatchway and into the tiny cabin of the lighter. There he prepared a light meal and set it aside, lay down to rest and waited for the return of Bidjiwara.

He may have dozed and seen into the Dreamtime, for he saw the figures of Miralaidj and her father Wuluwaid floating in a vague jumble of shapes and slow, wavering movement. He opened his eyes and saw Bidjiwara lower herself through the hatchway into the cabin, white rope-soled shoes first, white duck trousers clinging close to her long skinny legs and narrow hips, then her black ribbed sweater.

"Our ship has no name," she said.

He pondered for a moment, shrugged, said, "Does it need one?"

"It would be—somehow I think we would be more with our people," Bidjiwara replied.

"Well, if you wish. What shall we make her name?"

"You have no choice?"

"None."

"We will truly sail on the great tide? On the Rainbow Serpent?"

"We are already."

"Then I would call our ship after the sacred fish. Let it bear us to the Dreamtime."

"*Baramundi.*"

"Yes."

"As you wish."

She came and sat by him, her hands folded in her lap. She sat silently.

"Food is ready," he said.

She looked at the tiny table that served in the lighter as work space, desk, and dining table. Jiritzu saw her smile, wondered at the mixture in her face of little child and wise woman. She looked somehow as he thought the Great Mother must look, if only he believed in the Great Mother.

Bidjiwara crossed the small distance and brought two thin slices of hot biscuit. She held them both to Jiritzu. He took one, pressed the other back upon her.

Silently they ate the biscuit.

Afterward she said, "Jiritzu, is there more to do now?"

He said, "We should check our position." He undogged the ship's telescope and carried it to the deck of *Baramundi.*

Bidjiwara helped him to mount it on the gimbaled base that stood waiting for it. Jiritzu sighted on the brightest star in Yirrkalla for reference—it was a gleaming crimson star that marked the end of a fang in the serpent face, that Yurakosi tradition called Blood of Hero.

On the barrel of the telescope where control squares were mounted he tapped all of the radiational senors into life, to cycle through filters and permit the eyepiece to observe the Rainbow Serpent by turns under optical, radio, x-ray, gamma radiation.

He put his eye to the eyepiece and watched the Serpent as it seemed to move with life, its regions responding to the cycling sensitivity of the telescope.

He drew away and Bidjiwara put her eye to the telescope, standing transfixed for minutes until at last she too drew away and turned to Jiritzu.

"The Serpent truly lives," she said. "Is it—a real creature?"

Jiritzu shook his head. "The tides of the galaxies draw each other. The Serpent is a flow of matter. Stars, dust, gas. To ride with it would mean a journey of billions of years to reach the next of its kind. To sail the starwinds that fill the Rainbow Serpent, we will reach marvelous speed. As long as we can sail our craft, we can tack from wind to wind.

"And once we have gone to the Dreamtime, *Baramundi* will float on, on the tide, along the Rainbow Serpent. Someday she may beach on some distant shore."

He looked at Bidjiwara, smiled, repeated his statement.

Bidjiwara replied, "And if she does not?"

"Then she may be destroyed in some way, or simply—drift forever. Forever."

Jiritzu saw the girl stretch and yawn. She crossed the cabin and drew him down alongside the bulkhead, nestled up to him and went to sleep.

He lay with her in his arms, wondering at her trust, watching the play of sidereal light that reflected through the hatchway and illuminated her face dimly.

He extended one finger and gently, gently traced the *maraiin* on her cheek, wondering at its meaning. He pressed his face to her head again, pulled away her knitted cap and let her hair tumble loose, feeling its softness with his own face, smelling the odor of her hair.

He too slept.

They awoke together, stirring and stretching and looked into each other's face and laughed. They used the lighter's sanitary gear and nibbled a little breakfast and went on deck. Together they checked *Baramundi*'s rigging, took sightings with her multiradiational telescope, and fed information into her little computer.

The computer offered course settings in tiny, glowing display lights and Jiritzu and Bidjiwara reset *Baramundi*'s sails.

They sat on deck, bathed in the perpetual twilight of the Rainbow Serpent's softly glowing colors.

They spoke of their childhoods on Yurakosi, of their old people, their skins whited out by years of sailing the membrane ships, retired to the home planet to raise the children while all the race's vigorous adults crewed the great ships, sailed between the stars carrying freight and occasional passengers sealed inside their hulls, laughing at the clumsy craft and clumsy crews of all others than the aranda and the kunapi.

They climbed through the rigging of *Baramundi*, shinnying up masts lightly, balancing on spars, occasionally falling—or leaping—from the ship's heights, to drop gently, gently back onto her deck.

They ate and drank the smallest amounts they could of the lighter's provisions, tacitly stretching the supplies as far as they could be stretched, carefully recycling to add still more to the time they could continue.

They lay on *Baramundi*'s deck sometimes, when the rest time they had agreed upon came, Bidjiwara nestling against the taller Jiritzu, falling asleep as untroubledly as a young child, Jiritzu wondering over and over at this girl who had come to die with him, who asked few questions, who lived each hour as if it were the beginning of a long and joyous life rather than the final act of a tragedy.

Jiritzu felt very old.

He was nearly twenty by the ancient, arbitrary scale of age carried to the star worlds from O'Earth, the scale of the seasons and the years in old Arnhem Land in the great desert of their ancestral home. Six years older than Bidjiwara, he had traveled the star routes for five, had sailed the membrane ships across tens of billions of miles in that time.

And Bidjiwara asked little of him. They were more playmates than—than anything else, he thought.

"Tell me of El-Kumarbis," she said one day, perched high on a spar above *Baramundi*'s deck.

"You know all about him," Jiritzu replied.

"Where is he now?"

Jiritzu shrugged, exasperated. "Somewhere beyond Al-ghoul, no one knows where. He was buried in space."

"What if we find his body?" Bidjiwara shivered.

"Impossible."

"Why?"

"In infinite space? What chance that two objects moving at random will collide?"

"No?"

He shook his head.

"Could the computer find him?"

He shrugged. "If we knew exactly when he was buried, and where, and his trajectory and speed and momentum . . . No, it's still impossible."

"Dinnertime," she said. "You wait here, I'll fix it."

She came back with the customary biscuits and a jar filled with dark fluid. Jiritzu took the jar, held it high against the ambient light—they seldom used any of *Baramundi*'s power lights.

"Wine," Bidjiwara said.

He looked amazed.

"I found a few capsules in the ship's supplies. You just put one in some water."

They ate and drank. The wine was warm, its flavor soft. They sprawled on the deck of *Baramundi* after the biscuits were gone, passing the jar back and forth, slowly drinking the wine.

When it was gone Bidjiwara nestled against Jiritzu; for once, instead of sleeping she lay looking into his face, holding her hands to the sides of his head.

She said his name softly, then flicked off her radio and pressed her lips close to his neck so their air envelopes were one, the sound carried directly from her lips to his ear, and whispered his name again.

"Bidjiwara," he said, "you never answered why you came on board *Baramundi*."

"To be with you, Jiritzu," she said.

"Yes, but why? Why come to die with me?"

"Tall Jiritzu," she said, "strong Jiritzu. You saw me aboard *Djanggawul*, you were kind to me but as you are kind to children. Men never know, only women know love."

He laughed, not cruelly. "You're only—"

"A woman," she said.

"And you want—?"

Now she laughed at him. "You man, you mighty man. You don't understand that all men are the children of women."

She drew away from him, slid her black ribbed sweater over her head and dropped it to the deck. He put his hands onto her naked back, trembling, then slowly slid them around her, touching her little, half-developed breasts, fondling her soft nipples with his hands.

She buried her forehead in the side of his neck, whispered against his throat, "For this, Jiritzu, I came aboard *Baramundi* for this."

He ran his thumbs down her breastbone, to her navel, to her white duck trousers, and peeled them down, and took her.

And the next day they were nearly out of biscuit and they went on half rations to make their supplies last longer.

They played children's games, shouting and chasing each other up and down the lighter's masts.

They leaped and sailed from the decks, past the membrane sails, into the emptiness, then hung for a moment and fell back, gently, to *Baramundi*.

Jiritzu leaped too hard, too high, and feared that he had broken from the ship. He looked up—down—into the coils of the Rainbow Serpent. He felt himself revolving slowly, helplessly hanging in the emptiness, alone and unshielded except by the close air his generator made and the protection of the pigment he carried in his skin.

He thought to cry for help, then held back. If he was afloat, Bidjiwara could not help him. He turned slowly, facing toward *Baramundi*, her membranes bellied with stellar wind, her deck reflecting the lights of the Serpent; he could not see Bidjiwara.

He turned slowly, facing toward the Rainbow Serpent, feeling as if he could fall forever into its colored bands, its long coils stretching no lesser distance than the span between galaxies.

He turned slowly, revolving on the axis of his own body, feeling no motion himself but watching the stars and the Serpent and *Baramundi* the sacred fish revolve slowly around him, wheeling, wheeling, when his out-flung arm struck an object as hard and cold as the ultimate ice of a deadstar world.

He recoiled, spun involuntarily, stared.

It was—yes.

He looked back toward *Baramundi*, revolved using his own limbs as counterweights, placed himself between the corpse and the lighter, and pressed gently with the soles of his rope-soled shoes against the hard, frigid corpse.

Slowly he drifted back toward *Baramundi*—and, wheeling again as he drifted, saw the corpse drifting away, upward or downward into the lights of the Rainbow Serpent.

As he approached *Baramundi* he pondered whether or not to tell Bidjiwara of his find. Finally he told her—the incredible happenstance had occurred.

Later they crept to the farthermost deck for their loving, then back into the tiny cabin to sleep.

And soon *Baramundi*'s supplies were exhausted, and still Jiritzu and Bidjiwara continued. Their water remained, and a few of the capsules. They had wine from time to time. They gave less effort to running the ship, ceased to play in the rigging, ceased to leap.

The wound in Jiritzu's leg resumed its throbbing intermittently. He would rub it, or Bidjiwara would rub it for him, and the pain would ease.

They made love, it seemed, with increasing frequency. The sensations of their couplings seemed to increase as lack of nourishment drew their bodies ever tighter, ever more acutely into awareness of each other.

They lay together most of the time, seldom dressing fully.

They drank water only, their wine capsules exhausted.

They slept increasingly.

In *Baramundi*'s cabin Jiritzu fed telescopic data into the lighter's computer, read the responses displayed on its little illuminated screen. After the acclimatization of his eyes to none but sidereal light, even the miniature display lights were dazzling: his eyes pulsed with after-images for minutes following the exercise.

It was difficult to climb from the cabin back onto the deck.

Bidjiwara waited for him there, barefoot, sitting on the deck with her wrists clasped around her knees, wearing only her white trousers and black knitted cap. She smiled a welcome to him, asked a question wordlessly.

"Here," he said with a shrug. "Here is where we are. As we have been. Riding the Rainbow Serpent. Riding the tide. Sailing the starwinds."

He felt dizzy for a moment, reached out with one hand to steady himself against the telescope mount, then sank to a squat beside Bidjiwara.

She put her arms around him and he lay on the deck, his head in her lap. He looked up into her face. She was Bidjiwara the lovely child, Miralaidj her aranda half, she was Jiritzu's own mother on Yurakosi, the Great Mother.

He opened and closed his eyes, unable to tell which woman this was.

He reached and traced the *maraiin* on her cheek.

She nodded, began speaking softly, telling him the meaning of the scarifications.

When she had finished he took her hand, held it against his chest, and slowly told her the meaning of his own *maraiin*. He spoke with closed eyes, opened them when he felt a drop of wetness, saw her weeping softly, drew her face down to his own to kiss.

She lay down beside him and they embraced gently, then both slept.

After that they paid less attention to *Baramundi*'s needs. Jiritzu and Bidjiwara grew weaker. They slept more, confined their activity to occasional short walks on *Baramundi*'s decks. Both of them grew thinner, lighter. Their growing weakness seemed almost to be offset by the decreasing demands of the ship's artificial gravity.

They lay on deck for hours, watching the glow of the Rainbow Serpent. They were far beyond the Serpent's head now, the stars of Yirrkalla clustered now into a meaningless sparkler jumble far, far astern of *Baramundi*.

Jiritzu was awake, had taken a sparse sip of their little remaining water, left Bidjiwara to doze where she lay, her hair a mourning wreath circling her emaciated features. Jiritzu made his way unsteadily to the prow of *Baramundi*, bracing himself against masts and small stanchions as he walked.

He sighted through the ship's telescope, enjoying in a faint, detached manner the endless, kaleidoscopic changes of the Rainbow Serpent's multiradiational forms. At length he turned away from the scope and looked back toward Bidjiwara. He could not tell if she was breathing. He could not tell for a certainty who she was.

He returned to the telescope, tapped its power squares to cause it to superimpose its multiple images rather than run them in sequence. He gazed, rapt, at the Serpent for a time, then swung the scope overhead, sweeping back and forth across the sky above *Baramundi*.

He settled on a black speck that floated silhouetted against the glow of the Serpent. For a while he watched it grow larger.

He turned from the telescope back to the deck of the lighter. Bidjiwara had wakened and risen; she was walking slowly, slowly toward him.

In the glow of the Rainbow Serpent her emaciation was transformed to a fine perception that etched every line, every muscle beneath her skin. She wore sweater and trousers; Jiritzu could see her high breasts, the ribbed sweater conforming to their sharp grace, her nipples standing as points of reference for the beauty of her torso.

Her white trousers managed to retain their fit despite her starvation; Jiritzu discerned the lines of her thighs, the pubic swell over her crotch.

Her face, always thin, seemed all vertical planes now, forehead and temple, nostril and cheek. The ridges of her brows, the lines of her mouth were as if drawn on her face.

Her eyes seemed to have gained an intense brightness.

As she crossed the deck to Jiritzu she gained in strength and steadiness.

She held her hands toward him, smiling, and he felt his own strength returning to him. He took the steps needed to come to her, reached and took her two hands, clasped them in his. They embraced, calling each other's name.

The dark figure of Elyun El-Kumarbis dropped onto the deck of *Baramundi*. He strode to Jiritzu and Bidjiwara.

"Lovers!" he said. "Sky heroes!"

They turned to him, arms still around each other. Each extended a hand to him, felt his: cold, cold.

"All my years," the O'Earther said, "I wanted no thing but to sail a membrane ship. To be a sky hero."

"Yes," Jiritzu said, "you are known to all sky heroes, Elyun El-Kumarbis. Your fame spans the galaxy."

"And where do you sail, sky heroes?"

"We sail the tide, we sail the Rainbow Serpent."

"Aboard your ship?"

"*Baramundi* has brought us this far, but no farther. It is fit now for us to return to the Dreamtime."

Elyun El-Kumarbis nodded. "May I—may I greet you as brother and sister sky heroes?" he asked.

"Yes," answered Jiritzu.

"Yes," answered Bidjiwara.

Elyun El-Kumarbis kissed them each on the cheek, on the *maraiin* scarifications of each. And his kiss was cold, cold.

Full of strength Jiritzu and Bidjiwara sprang to the spars of *Baramundi*'s highest mast, scrambled up lines to the topmost spar of the lighter.

They looked back at Elyun El-Kumarbis, who stood wondering beside the ship's telescope.

They took each other's hands, dropped into place on the topmost spar, and together sprang with the full strength of their sky heroes' legs, toughened and muscled by years of training in the rigging of membrane ships.

They flew up from the spar, up from *Baramundi* the sacred fish, and, looking back, saw the fish flip his tail once in farewell.

They peered ahead of themselves, into the Rainbow Serpent, saw it writhe toward the far galaxies, heard its hissing voice urging, welcoming them.

They laughed loudly, loudly, feeling strength, warmth, and joy. They plunged on and on, skimming the tide of the Rainbow Serpent, feeling the strength of the aranda, of all Yurakosi, of all sky heroes, mighty in their blood.

They threw their arms around each other, laughing for joy, and sped to the Rainbow Serpent, to the galaxies beyond the galaxies, to the Dreamtime forever.